MASTER INDEX

GRADES Pre-K–8

SPOTLIGHT on MUSIC

SERIES AUTHORS

Judy Bond

René Boyer

Margaret Campbelle-Holman

Emily Crocker

Marilyn C. Davidson

Robert de Frece

Virginia Ebinger

Mary Goetze

Betsy M. Henderson

John Jacobson

Michael Jothen

Chris Judah-Lauder

Carol King

Vincent P. Lawrence

Ellen McCullough-Brabson

Janet McMillion

Nancy L.T. Miller

Ivy Rawlins

Susan Snyder

Gilberto D. Soto

Kodály Contributing Consultant

Sr. Lorna Zemke

Mc Graw Hill Macmillan/McGraw-Hill

INTRODUCTION

The *Master Index* of *Spotlight on Music* provides convenient access to music, art, literature, themes, and activities from Grades Pre-K–8. Using the Index, you will be able to locate materials to suit all of your students' needs, interests, and teaching requirements.

The *Master Index* allows you to select songs, listening selections, art, literature, and activities:

- by subject
- by theme
- by concept or skill
- by specific pitch and rhythm patterns
- for curriculum integration
- for programs and assemblies
- for multicultural instruction

The Index will assist you in locating materials from across the grade levels to reinforce and enrich learning.

A

The McGraw·Hill Companies

 Macmillan/McGraw-Hill

Published by Macmillan/McGraw-Hill, of McGraw-Hill Education, a division of The McGraw-Hill Companies, Inc., Two Penn Plaza, New York, New York 10121

Printed in the United States of America
ISBN: 978-0-02-296754-3
MHID: 0-02-296754-0

2 3 4 5 6 7 8 9 WDQ 14 13 12 11 10

Table of Contents

▶ **Alphabetical Index of Songs and Speech Pieces** 1
   by Title 1
   by Grade Level 17

▶ **Alphabetical Index of Listening Selections** 35
   by Composer 35
   by Title 41

▶ **Alphabetical Index of Literature** 51
   Poetry 51
   Stories 52

▶ **Thematic Index** 55
   Adventures *Taking a chance on meeting new people, going new places, and having different experiences helps us grow and learn* 55

   Adventures and Challenges *Meeting challenges with courage and initiative enriches our lives* 55

   American Heritage *We take pride in our country and its traditions. See Classified Index: Multicultural Materials; Patriotic Music* 56

   Animals, Farm, and Pets *Animals can be our good friends and valued helpers* 56

   Animals, Wild *Life in the jungle, forest, and desert can be full of adventure* 57

   Change *People experience many changes in their lives* 58

   Communication *We get to know ourselves and others by sharing, listening, learning, and understanding* 58

   Cooperation *There are many ways to work together and help others* 58

   Diversity *We can celebrate ways we are alike and ways we are different. See also Classified Index: Multicultural Materials* 59

   Dreams and Hopes *Dreams and hopes can come true.* 61

   Ecology and the Environment *We share responsibility for understanding and protecting the world around us* 62

   Expressing Viewpoints and Feelings *Sharing thoughts, feelings, and opinions opens the door to understanding* 63

   Expressing Yourself *Sharing thoughts and feelings opens the door to understanding* ... 64

   Family and Friends *There are many ways to care about the important people in our lives* 64

   Favorite Things *Each person has special things that he or she enjoys* 65

   Freedom and Justice *Throughout history people around the world have worked to achieve freedom for themselves and others* 65

   Friendship and Family Life *There are many ways to care about the important people in our lives* 66

Table of Contents (continued)

Fun *Humor and surprise bring special delight* 67

Games and Play *Games and play help us enjoy life* 70

Growing Up *As we grow, we are able to do many new things* 71

Healthy Living *Good habits, food, and exercise keep our bodies strong and healthy.* 71

Heroes and Leaders *We learn important lessons and develop values from people
we admire* 72

History *Throughout time people have met many challenges and made
valuable contributions* 72

Imagination and Fantasy *Our imaginations can take us to new places and help us
develop our creative spirits.* 73

Individuality *We are each special in our own way* 73

Memories *Our memories help us link our past and present, and shape our future* 74

Nature *We enjoy the beauty of our world* 74

Neighborhood and School *Visiting familiar places and people brings special joy* 77

Personal Growth *Developing our strengths and learning about our weaknesses
is a lifelong challenge* 77

Pretending *Our imaginations can take us to new places* 78

Resourcefulness and Problem Solving *Trying hard and looking at problems
in new ways help us find answers.* 78

Seasons, Weather, Night and Day *Learning about the ways of nature helps us
understand our world* 79

Stories and Tales *People have always enjoyed sharing stories* 79

Traditions *Traditions enrich special celebrations as well as our daily lives.*
See Classified Index: Folk and Traditional Music; Holiday and Seasonal Music;
Multicultural Materials; Patriotic Music 81

Travel *Trips to places old and new can bring adventure.* 81

Water *Watery places are a special world of wonder* 82

Wishes *Hopes and dreams for ourselves, our loved ones, and our world can
come true at unexpected times* 82

Work *Music can help us work together* 82

▶ **Classified Index of Songs, Selected Concepts, Skills, and Activities**. 85

Action Songs. *See also* Movement 85

Biographies 86

Broadway for Kids. *See also* Performance 89

Canons. *See* Form and Genre, Canon 90

Careers. *See also* Biographies 90

Character Development 90

Table of Contents (continued)

Choreography 90

Cumulative Songs 92

Curriculum Connection 92

Descant 102

Fine Art Reproductions and Architecture 103

Folk and Traditional Music 104

Form and Genre 113

From the Top. *See also* Careers; Music News, Instrument Spotlights 120

Game Songs 120

Global Voices. *See also* Multicultural Materials 122

History and Culture. *See also* Biographies 122

Holiday and Seasonal Music. *See also* Patriotic Music 126

Instrumental/Vocal Ensembles 128

Instruments, Playing. *See also* Music Skills; Ostinatos; Playalongs 129

Limited Tone Songs 130

Listening Maps 133

Lullabies 135

Minor/Modal Songs 135

Movement. *See also* Game Songs 136

Multicultural Materials 139

    Africa (Sub-Saharan) 139

    African American 140

    Asia: Central and South 141

    Asia: East and Southeast 141

    Asian American 142

    Australia and Pacific Islands 142

    Canada 143

    Caribbean 143

    Central and South America (including Mexico) 143

    Europe 145

    European American 151

    Hispanic American 158

    Jewish/Israeli 158

    Middle East and North Africa 158

    Native American (North and South America) 158

Music News. *See also* Careers; From the Top, Instrument Spotlights 159

Music Skills 159

Non-English Language Songs 160

Orff. *See* Instruments, Playing; Playalongs, Orff accompaniments 163

Ostinatos. *See also* Creative Activities; Playalongs; Texture body percussion 163

Part Songs. *See also* Form and Genre, Canon; Partner Songs 163

Table of Contents (continued)

Patriotic Music. *See also* Holiday and Seasonal Music 164

Pentatonic Songs. *See* Limited Tone Songs 165

Performance. *See also* Broadway for Kids; Spotlight on Performance 165

Playalongs. *See also* Instruments, Playing 165

Reaching All Learners (Universal Access) 167
    English Language Learners 167
    Gifted and Talented 168
    Inclusion 169

Recorded Interviews 170

Signing 171

Solo/Group Songs 171

SoundCheck. *See also* Recorded Interviews 172

Style 172

Technology 174
    DVD *Resource Library* 174
    Global Voices DVD 174
    Grade-Level DVD 174
    MiDisaurus CD-ROM 174
    music.mmhschool.com 174
    Orchestral Instruments CD-ROM 175
    Spotlight on MIDI 175
    Web Tips 176
    World Instruments CD-ROM 176

Tone Color. *See also* Instruments, Identifying; Instruments, Playing; SoundCheck 177

Vocal Development 177

▶ **Pitch and Rhythm Index** **179**
Pitch 179
Rhythm 190

▶ **Index of Songs for Recorder** **201**

▶ **Index of Curriculum Links and Activities** **203**

▶ **Index of Reading and Language Arts Skills** **211**

▶ **Thematic Correlations to Reading** **215**
Macmillan/McGraw-Hill Reading ©2005 215
Harcourt Trophies ©2003 245
Houghton Mifflin Reading ©2005 275
Scholastic Literacy Place ©2004 303
Scott Foresman Reading ©2004 327

▶ **Alphabetical Index of Interactive Listening Maps** **351**

Multicultural Songs

CM Festival of Caribbean Music
WM Festival of World Music
FC-Int ¡Fiesta de canciones! Intermediate
FC-Pri ¡Fiesta de canciones! Primary

A be ce, **Gr. 1,** T213 **CD9:33**
A la nanita nana (A Little Lullaby), **Gr. 4,** 230 **CD11:28**
A la nanita nana, FC-Int 45
A la puerta del cielo (At the Gates of Heaven), **Gr. 4,** 12 **CD1:12**
A la rueda de San Miguel (To the Wheel of San Miguel), **Gr. 2,** 60 **CD3:27**
A la rueda rueda ('Round and 'Round), **Gr. 1,** T240 **CD11:6**
A Tisket A Tasket, **Gr. 1,** T107 **CD4:31**
A Zing-A Za, **Gr. 5,** 338 **CD20:12**
Ach, du lieber Augustin (The More We Get Together), **Gr. 2,** 35 **CD2:12**
Achshav (Now), **Gr. 4,** 112 **CD6:18**
Acka Backa, **Gr. 1,** T256 **CD12:2**
Addams Family Theme, The, **Gr. 3,** 307 **CD14:1; Gr. 8,** 142 **CD7:1**
¡Adivina lo que es! (Guess What It Is!), **Gr. 1,** T170 **CD7:30**
Adongko Dongko a Gakit (Philippine Kulintang Wedding Processional), WM 112
Aeyaya balano sakkad (Come, Children), **Gr. 5,** 402 **CD23:26**
Agahu, **Gr. 5,** 72 **CD5:2**
Al lado de mi cabaña (Beside My Cottage), **Gr. 6,** 141 **CD8:6**
Alison's Camel, **Gr. K,** T201 **CD11:21**
All Around the Buttercup, **Gr. 2,** 210 **CD11:1**
All Night, All Day, **Gr. 1,** T232 **CD10:24**
All Through the Night, **Gr. 4,** 277 **CD15:26**
All Work Together, **Gr. K,** T12 **CD1:1**
All Ye Who Music Love, **Gr. 6,** 336 **CD18:7**
Allá en el rancho grande (My Ranch), **Gr. 5,** 66 **CD4:17**
Alleluia, **Gr. 6,** 186 **CD10:13;** (Heleluyan), **Gr. 6,** 188 **CD10:17**
Alligator Dance (Tekanionton'néha'), **Gr. 5,** 223 **CD12:27**
Allundé, Alluia, **Gr. 4,** 34 **CD2:20**
Alphabet Song, **Gr. K,** T54 **CD3:6**
Amazing Grace, **Gr. 5,** 19 **CD1:23**
Ame fure (Rain), **Gr. 4,** 26 **CD2:9**
Amen, **Gr. 3,** 376 **CD18:1**
America, **Pre-K,** 47; **Gr. K,** T303 **CD16:14; Gr. 1,** T326 **CD15:15; Gr. 2,** 338 **CD17:2; Gr. 4,** 354 **CD20:10; Gr. 6,** 388 **CD21:1**
America, My Homeland, **Gr. 4,** 358 **CD20:17**
America, the Beautiful, **Gr. 3,** 354 **CD16:13; Gr. 5,** 388 **CD23:1**
Angelina, CM 13
Angelina, **Gr. 6,** 8 **CD1:10**

Angels We Have Heard on High (Les anges dans nos campagnes), **Gr. 6,** 406 **CD22:7**
Ani Purim (Purim), **Gr. 2,** 372 **CD19:15**
Animal Fair, **Gr. 2,** 214 **CD11:8**
Animal Song, **Gr. 1,** T288 **CD13:25**
Animales (Animals), **Gr. K,** T192 **CD11:6**
Animals (Animales), **Gr. K,** T192 **CD 11:6**
Another Busy Day, **Gr. 1,** T41 **CD2:1**
Ants Go Marching, The, **Gr. 1,** T22 **CD1:15**
Apple Picker's Reel, **Gr. 2,** 343 **CD17:15**
Apples and Bananas, **Pre-K,** 34; **Gr. 1,** T151 **CD7:1**
Aquaqua, **Gr. 5,** 258 **CD15:11**
Are You Sleeping? (Frère Jacques), **Gr. 4,** 260 **CD14:1**
Arirang, **Gr. 5,** 50 **CD3:13**
Arirang, WM 51
Army Is Marching, An (Singabahambayo) (unison), **Gr. 5,** 56 **CD4:1;** (parts), **Gr. 5,** 76 **CD4:1**
A-Rovin', **Gr. 6,** 319 **CD17:25**
Arre, mi burrito (Gid'yup, Little Burro), **Gr. 1,** T257 **CD12:5**
Arroyito serrano (Mountain Stream), **Gr. 4,** 340 **CD19:15**
Artichokes, **Gr. 2,** 314 **CD16:8**
As I Roll My Ball (En roulant ma boule), **Gr. 3,** 100 **CD4:26**
Aserejé, FC-Int 62
At the Gates of Heaven (A la puerta del cielo), **Gr. 4,** 12 **CD1:12**
At the Hop, **Gr. 4,** 306 **CD17:16**
Atlantic City, **Gr. 7,** 248 **CD11:5**
Atole, The (El atole), **Gr. 3,** 396 **CD19:12**
Australia's on the Wallaby, **Gr. 2,** 106 **CD6:3**
Autumn Leaves Are Falling, **Gr. 1,** T330 **CD15:30**
Autumn Leaves, **Gr. 1,** T331 **CD15:27**
Away for Rio, **Gr. 2,** 170 **CD8:29**
Ay, Jalisco, Never Fail Her (¡Ay, Jalisco no te rajes!), **Gr. 5,** 188 **CD 10:22**
¡Ay, Jalisco no te rajes! (Ay, Jalisco, Never Fail Her), **Gr. 5,** 188 **CD10:22**
Babe, The (El rorro), **Gr. 1,** T356 **CD17:21**
Baby Beluga, **Gr. 2,** 26 **CD2:3**
Baby Nodja, **Gr. 2,** 154 **CD8:10**
Babylon's Fallin', **Gr. 5,** 243 **CD13: 22**
Backwater Blues, **Gr. 5,** 175 **CD10:8**
Bahay Kubo (My Nipa Hut), **Gr. 2,** 382 **CD19:36**
Baila esta cumbia, FC-Int 49
Baile del pescadito, FC-Pri 7
Ballad of the Bedbugs and the Beetles, The, **Gr. 3,** 206 **CD9:18**
Ballad of the Underground Railroad, The, (complete song) **Gr. 5,** 154 **CD8:11;** (refrain) **Gr. 5,** 145 **CD8:11**
Bamboo Flute, **Gr. 4,** 134 **CD7:11**
Bamboo, **Gr. 4,** 218 **CD11:8**
Ban Dal (Half Moon), **Gr. 2,** 219 **CD11:15**
Banyan Tree, **Gr. 2,** 321 **CD16:22**
Barbry Ellen, **Gr. 6,** 208 **CD11:9**

Alphabetical Index of Songs and Speech Pieces (continued)

Bashana Haba'ah (In the Year to Come), **Gr. 6**, 360 **CD19:19**

Bate, bate (Stir, Stir), **Gr. 2**, 242 **CD12:15**

Battle Hymn of the Republic (refrain only), **Gr. K**, T331 **CD18:26**; (entire) **Gr. 5**, 391 **CD23:5**

Be Yours, **Gr. 7**, 189 **CD8:7**

Bear Hunt, **Gr. 1**, T126 **CD5:29**

Bear Went Over the Mountain, The, **Gr. K**, T204 **CD11:25**; **Gr. 1**, T115 **CD5:5**

Beautiful Gardener, The (La bella hortelana), **Gr. 2**, 208 **CD10:23**

Beauty and the Beast, **Gr. 5**, 124 **CD7:5**

Bee, Bee, Bumblebee, **Gr. 1**, T250 **CD11:24**

Bei Fang Chre (North Wind Blows), **Gr. 2**, 367 **CD19:1**

Bell Doth Toll, The, **Gr. 4**, 276 **CD15:22**

Bell Horses, **Gr. K**, T262 **CD14:33**

Bella bimba (Pretty Girl), **Gr. 3**, 172 **CD8:4**

Belle qui tiens ma vie (My Love, You Hold My Life), **Gr. 6**, 99 **CD6:4**

Beryoza (The Birch Tree), **Gr. 4**, 286 **CD16:25**

Beside My Cottage (Al lado de mi cabaña), **Gr. 6**, 141 **CD8:6**

Best Friends, **Gr. 1**, T222 **CD10:13**

Best That I Can Be!, The, **Gr. K**, T48 **CD2:27**

Bickle, Bockle, **Pre-K**, 17; **Gr. K**, T187 **CD10:27**

Big and Small, **Gr. 1**, T201 **CD9:13**; (speech piece), **Gr. 1**, T200 **CD9:16**

Big Beautiful Planet, **Gr. 2**, 376 **CD19:24**

Big Big World, **Gr. 5**, 438 **CD25:28**

Big Bunch, a Little Bunch, **Gr. 4**, 267 **CD14:24**

Big Yellow Taxi, **Gr. 5**, E **Spotlight CD7**

Billy, **Gr. 3**, 7 **CD1:4**

Bim Bom, **Gr. 3**, 218 **CD10:5**

Bingo, **Gr. K**, T64 **CD3:21**

Birch Tree, The (Beryoza), **Gr. 4**, 286 **CD16:25**

Blow, Ye Winds, Blow, **Gr. 3**, 192 **CD9:1**

Blue Suede Shoes, **Gr. 6**, 236 **CD12:25**

Bluebells, **Gr. 1**, T209 **CD9:24**

Bluebirds (Nikosi), **Gr. 2**, 230 **CD12:2**

Bo Hai Huan Ten, WM 113

Bobby Shafto, **Gr. K**, T265 **CD15:4**

Bohm (Spring Has Come!), **Gr. 3**, 392 **CD19:2**

Bohm Dong Sahn, Gohd Dong Sahn (Spring Valley, Flower Valley), **Gr. K**, T337 **CD19:6**

Boll Weevil, **Gr. 3**, 171 **CD8:1**

Bonjour, mes amis (Hello, My Friends), **Gr. 1**, T18 **CD1:8**

Boo!, **Gr. 3**, 362 **CD17:5**

Boogie Woogie Ghost, The, **Gr. 4**, 368 **CD21:6**

Bop 'til You Drop, **Gr. 6**, 87 **CD5:17**

Boris, the Singing Bear, **Gr. 1**, T312 **CD15:5**

Bounce High, Bounce Low, **Gr. K**, T131 **CD7:22**

Bow, Wow, Wow, **Gr. 2**, 264 **CD14:4**

Bows, **Gr. 5**, 305 **CD18:14**

Brinca la tablita (Hop, Hop!), **Gr. 1**, T71 **CD3:1**

Brotherhood of Man, **Gr. 8**, 248 **CD10:4**

Brush Your Teeth, **Gr. 1**, T66 **CD2:36**; (speech piece) **Gr. 1**, T66 **CD2:39**

Buckeye Jim, **Gr. 4**, 136 **CD7:15**

Buffalo Dance Entrance Song, **Gr. 3**, 325 **CD15:4**

Built My Lady a Fine Brick House, **Gr. 4**, 252 **CD13:9**

Bulbes ('Taters), **Gr. 6**, 280 **CD15:40**

Burn Little Candles, **Pre-K**, 85

Bus, The, **Pre-K**, 55; **Gr. K**, T137 **CD8:1**

But the Critter Got Away (speech piece), **Gr. 1**, T89 **CD3:29**

Butterfly (Farfallina), **Gr. 4**, 244 **CD12:16**

Butterfly Come Play with Me, **Gr. 3**, 112 **CD5:14**

Butterfly, Flutter By, **Gr. 1**, T333 **CD15:33**

Button, You Must Wander, **Gr. 2**, 176 **CD9:2**

Bu-Vah (Sleep), **Gr. 4**, 18 **CD1:27**

By the Singing Water, **Gr. 5**, 270 **CD16:26**

Bye 'n Bye, **Pre-K**, 77; **Gr. K**, T67 **CD3:24**

Caballito blanco (Little White Pony), **Gr. 4**, 278 **CD15:30**

Caissons Go Rolling Along, The, **Gr. 5**, 37 **CD2:21**

Cake, Cake, Cake! (Uga, Uga, Uga), **Gr. 1**, T313 **CD15:8**

Camelot, **Gr. 6**, 310 **CD17:8**

Caminito de la escuela, FC-Pri 35

Canción de Amapola, FC-Pri 39

Canción de la cafetera, FC-Pri 54

Canción del pie, FC-Pri 73

Candle on the Water, **Gr. 2**, 296 **CD15:7**

Canon, **Gr. 6**, 256 **CD14:1**

Cantaré, cantarás, FC-Int 53

Cape Cod Chantey, **Gr. 6**, 258 **CD14:7**

Captain Jinks, **Gr. 6**, 266 **CD14:29**

Caranguejo (The Crab), **Gr. 2**, 306 **CD15:27**

Caribbean Amphibian, **Gr. 1**, T294 **CD13:38**

Carnival Is Coming, The (De allacito carnavalito), **Gr. 5**, 269 **CD16:22**

Carol from an Irish Cabin, **Gr. 6**, 408 **CD22:12**

Casa de chocolate, FC-Int 15

Castle on a Cloud, **Gr. 7**, 82 **CD4:1**

Cat and Dog, **Gr. 3**, 259 **CD11:47**

Cat and Rat (Pusa't daga), **Gr. 1**, T289 **CD13:28**

Cat, Cat! (Mos', Mos'!), **Gr. 1**, T53 **CD2:16**

Categories, **Gr. 1**, T146 **CD6:25**

Ɔbɔɔ Asi Me Nsa, **Gr. K**, T159 **CD9:14**

Cedar Swamp, **Gr. 4**, 50 **CD3:13**

Chag Asif (Harvest Time), **Gr. 3**, 360 **CD17:1**

Chairs to Mend, **Gr. 4**, 272 **CD15:7**

Chan mali chan, **Gr. 3**, 10 **CD1:10**

Chang (Elephant), **Gr. 1**, T199 **CD9:9**

Chang (Elephant), WM 3

Change Is Good, **Gr. 5**, 84 **CD5:13**

Change the World, **Gr. 5**, 314 **CD19:14**

Charleston, **Gr. 6**, 112 **CD6:28**

Charlie over the Ocean, **Gr. 1**, T75 **CD3:10**

Charlie, **Gr. 3**, 208 **CD9:21**

Charlotte Town, **Gr. 6**, 261 **CD14:17**

Chase the Squirrel, **Gr. 1**, T88 **CD3:26**

Check It Out! (It's About Respect), **Gr. 2**, 10 **CD1:14**

Cheers, **Gr. 7**, 34 **CD2:1**

Cherry Blossoms (Sakura), **Gr. 6**, 14 **CD1:19**

Chiapanecas (Ladies of Chiapas), **Gr. 2**, 128 **CD7:8**

Chichipapa (The Sparrows' Singing School), **Gr. 2**, 22 **CD1:33**

Chicka-hanka, **Gr. 4**, 138 **CD7:18**

Chicka-ma, Chicka-ma, Craney Crow, **Gr. 3**, 263 **CD11:54**

Chicken on the Fence Post, **Gr. 3**, 265 **CD12:1**

Chickery Chick, **Gr. 1**, T292 **CD13:35**

Children's Festival (Tết Trung), **Gr. 4**, 366 **CD21:1**

Chinese Fishing Song (Wang Ü Ger), **Gr. 3**, 190 **CD 8:32**

Alphabetical Index of Songs and Speech Pieces (continued)

Chinese Lion Dance (Chinese Folk Music), WM 112
Chinese New Year Song (Gong xi fa cai), **Gr. 3**, 384 **CD18:19**
Chiribim, **Gr. 6**, 57 **CD3:24**
Chirimbolo Game, The (El juego chirimbolo) **Gr. 1**, T103 **CD4:24**
Chirp, Chirp, Chirp (Chíu, chíu, chíu), **Gr. 2**, 302 **CD15:16**
Chirri Bim, **Gr. 2**, 70 **CD4:14**
Chíu, chíu, chíu (Chirp, Chirp, Chirp), **Gr. 2**, 302 **CD15:16;** **Gr. 6**, 172 **CD9:16**
Choo, Choo, Ch'Boogie, **Gr. 6**, 180 **CD10:4**
Chopsticks (Juhtgarak), **Gr. K**, T108 **CD6:16**
Chorus of Villagers from The Bartered Bride, **Gr. 5**, 275 **CD17:7**
Christmas Candies, The (La colación), **Gr. 1**, T357 **CD17:25**
Christmas Eve (Nochebuena), **Gr. K**, T323 **CD18:5**
Chumbara, **Gr. 4**, 172 **CD8:24**
Chuvt Cvp, WM 23
Cidade Maravilhosa (Wonderful City), **Gr. 5**, 432 **CD25:15**
Cielito Lindo, **Gr. 3**, 166 **CD7:28**
Cindy, **Gr. 5**, 265 **CD16:10**
Circle 'Round the Zero, **Gr. 3**, 267 **CD12:7**
Circle of Friends, **Gr. 5**, 196 **CD11:14**
Circle of Life, **Gr. 7**, 40 **CD2:3**
Circle of Song, **Gr. 4**, 330 **CD18:26**
City Blues, **Gr. 5**, 278 **CD17:19**
City Life (with "I Love the Mountains"), **Gr. 3**, 341 **CD16:10**
Clap Your Hands, **Gr. 1**, T247 **CD11:20**
Cliffs of Doneen, The, **Gr. 5**, 46 **CD3:8**
Clock, The (La cloche), **Gr. 3**, 67 **CD3:21**
Clocks, **Gr. 3**, 266 **CD12:4**
Coasts of High Barbary, The, **Gr. 6**, 329 **CD18:1**
Cobbler, Cobbler, Mend My Shoe, **Gr. K**, T169 **CD10:6**
Cobbler, The (El zapatero), **Gr. 2**, 138 **CD7:24**
Coffee Break, **Gr. 8**, 241 **CD10:2**
Colorful Dragon Boat, **Gr. K**, T328 **CD18:19**
Colors of the Wind, **Gr. 3**, 84 **CD4:5**
Columbus Sailed with Three Ships, **Gr. 2**, 344 **CD17:18**
Come All You People (Uyai Mose), **Gr. 7**, 66 **CD3:7**
Come and Sing Together, **Gr. 6**, 281 **CD16:1**
Come Back, My Little Chicks, **Gr. 1**, T134 **CD 6:11**
Come, Children (Aeyaya balano sakkad), **Gr. 5**, 402 **CD23:26**
Come, Firefly (Hotaru Koi), **Gr. 6**, 255 **CD13:45**
Come, Pick the Moon (Dal taro kacha), **Gr. 2**, 98 **CD5:20**
Comedy Tonight, **Gr. 6**, 204 **CD11:3**
Company Way, The, **Gr. 8**, 244 **CD10:3**
Conga, **Gr. 6**, 34 **CD2:9**
Consider Yourself, **Gr. 3**, 335 **CD16:1**
Cookies, **Gr. 1**, T277 **CD13:4**
Coral, **Gr. 3**, 249 **CD11:21**
Corner Grocery Store, **Gr. 2**, 311 **CD16:1**
Cornfields, The (Los maizales), **Gr. 5**, 268 **CD16:17**
Cornstalk Fiddle and a Shoestring Bow, **Gr. 3**, 284 **CD13:13**
Cotton-Eye Joe, **Gr. 4**, 52, 53 **CD3:16**
Countermelody for Cotton Eye Joe, **Gr. 4**, 53 **CD3:19**
Counting Song, **Gr. K**, T92 **CD5:19; Gr. 1**, T195 **CD9:1**
Cowboy, The (El Charro), **Gr. 6**, 278 **CD15:33**
Crab, The (Caranguejo), **Gr. 2**, 306 **CD15:27**
Crawdad Song, **Gr. 3**, 107 **CD5:5**

Crescent Moon (Yüe liang wan wan), **Gr. 6**, 26 **CD1:34**
Cripple Creek, **Gr. 6**, 372 **CD20:1**
Cuando salí de Cuba (I Went Away from Cuba), **Gr. 5**, 168 **CD9:22**
Cuckoo, Where Are You?, **Gr. 2**, 244 **CD12:22**
Cumberland Gap, **Gr. 3**, 99 **CD4:23**
Cumbia del sol (Cumbia of the Sun), **Gr. 5**, 16 **CD1:19**
Cumbia of the Sun (Cumbia del sol), **Gr. 5**, 16 **CD1:19**
Cum-ma-la Be-stay, **Gr. 6**, 370 **CD19:26**
Cut the Cake, **Gr. 1**, T232 **CD10:27**
Da pacem Domine (Give Us Peace), **Gr. 5**, 261 **CD15:22**
Daisy Chain, **Gr. 2**, 255 **CD13:15**
Dal taro kacha (Come, Pick the Moon), **Gr. 2**, 98 **CD5:20**
¡Dale, dale, dale!, **Gr. 3**, 378 **CD18:7**
Damsel Fly Song (Ushkana), **Gr. K**, T75 **CD4:15**
Dance, Dance, Dance!, **Gr. 2**, 5 **CD1:1**
Dance for the Nations, **Gr. 5**, 206 **CD11:26**
Dance Myself to Sleep, **Gr. 1**, T314 **CD15:12**
Dance of Orpheus (Samba de Orfeu), **Gr. 6**, 190 **CD 10:20**
Dance Together, **Gr. 2**, 264 **CD14:1**
Dancing in the Street, **Gr. 6**, 84 **CD5:14**
Dandansoy, **Gr. 6**, 356 **CD19:9**
Day-O, CM 3
Days of the Week, **Gr. K**, T81 **CD5:2**
De allacito carnavalito (The Carnival Is Coming), **Gr. 5**, 269 **CD16:22**
De aquel cerro (On the Darkened Hillside), **Gr. 3**, 32 **CD2:3**
De colores (Many Colors) (unison), **Gr. 5**, 88 **CD5:22;** (2-part), **Gr. 5**, 98 **CD5:22**
Death of the Robin, **Gr. 3**, 275 **CD12:33**
December Nights, December Lights, **Gr. 4**, 372 **CD21:15**
Deck the Hall, **Gr. 3**, 374 **CD17:25**
Derby Ram, The, **Gr. 4**, 259 **CD13:30**
Dere Geliyor (River Overflowing), **Gr. 6**, 232 **CD12:18**
Derry Ding Dong Dason, **Gr. 6**, 249 **CD13:19**
Deta, Deta (The Moon), **Gr. 5**, 246 **CD14:4**
Deta, Deta (The Moon), WM 27
Di por qué, FC-Int 32
Diana (Play the Bugle), **Gr. 1**, T334 **CD16:1**
Dide, **Gr. 3**, 279 **CD12:45**
Didn't It Rain, **Gr. 6**, 345 **CD18:22**
Digga Digga Dog, **Gr. 3**, 164 **CD7:25**
Dima, **Gr. 4**, 265 **CD14:16**
Dinah, **Gr. 3**, 150 **CD7:8**
Ding Dong Diggy Diggy Dong, **Gr. 3**, 269 **CD12:16**
Diou Shou Juan'er (Hide a Handkerchief!), **Gr. 1**, T212 **CD9:29**
Diwali Song, **Gr. 6**, 396 **CD21:22**
Diwali Song, WM 67
Do Lord, **Gr. 6**, 260 **CD14:14**
Do Not Wake My Little Son (No despiertes a mi niño), **Gr. 5**, 217 **CD12:14**
Do-Re-Mi, **Gr. 2 C Spotlight CD4**
Doctor Jazz, **Gr. 6**, 378 **CD20:11**
Doggie, Doggie, **Gr. 2**, 59 **CD3:23**
Doing the Latest Rag, **Gr. 6**, 314 **CD17:16**
Doing the Weekly Walk, **Gr. K**, T78 **CD4:21**
Dok Djampa (The White Jasmine Flower), **Gr. 4**, 392 **CD22:20**
Don't Laugh at Me, **Gr. 7**, 93 **CD4:10**

Don't Let the Music Stop, **Gr. 4,** 334 **CD19:1**

Dona Nobis Pacem, **Gr. 6,** 335 **CD18:6**

Doney Gal, **Gr. 6,** 115 **CD6:32**

Donkey, Donkey, **Gr. 2,** 256 **CD13:18**

Do-Re-Mi, **Gr. 2,** C **SpotlightCD 7**

Double This, **Gr. 1,** T95 **CD4:4**

Dove That Flew Away, The (La paloma se fue), **Gr. 5,** 259 **CD15:15**

Doves, The (El palomo y la paloma), **Gr. 2,** 381 **CD19:32**

Down at the Station, **Pre-K,** 54

Down at the Twist and Shout, **Gr. 4,** 308 **CD17:19**

Down by the Bay, **Gr. 1,** T48 **CD2:9**

Down by the Riverside, **Gr. 6,** 22 **CD1:30**

Down the Hill, **Gr. 1,** T281 **CD13:5**

Draw a Bucket of Water, **Gr. 3,** 222 **CD10:11**

Dreamers, **Gr. 5,** 430 **CD25:12**

Dreidel Spin (S'vivon Sov), **Gr. 1,** T348 **CD16:33; Gr. 4,** 374 **CD21:18**

Drum, The (El tambor), **Gr. K,** T129 **CD7:18; Gr. 6,** 222 **CD11:28**

Dry Bones, **Gr. 5,** 406 **CD24:5**

Ducks, The (Itik Besenda Gurau), **Gr. 2,** 100 **CD5:25**

Duérmete mi niño (Go to Sleep, My Baby), **Gr. 1,** T61 **CD2:28**

Dumplin's, **Gr. 2,** 172 **CD8:32**

Ēinīnī (Little Birds Sleep), **Gr. 5,** 340 **CD20:16**

E nānā kākou i nā manu (Look at the Birds in the Sky), **Gr. 4,** 338 **CD19:11**

Eagle, **Gr. 4,** 337 **CD19:5**

Early in the Morning at Eight O'Clock, **Gr. 4,** 59 **CD4:1**

Earth Child, **Gr. 6,** 426 **CD23:14**

Earth is Our Mother, The, **Gr. 7,** 220 **CD10:6**

Eating Lizards, **Gr. 2,** 250 **CD12:42**

Eency Weency Spider (La pequeñita araña), **Gr. K,** T9 **Spotlight CD13**

Eency Weency Spider, **Gr. K,** T8 **Spotlight CD10**

Egy üveg alma (One Jar of Apples), **Gr. 3,** 22 **CD1:27**

Eh Soom Boo Kawaya (Nigerian Boat Song), **Gr. 3,** 58 **CD3:11**

Eight Bells, **Gr. 4,** 281 **CD16:6**

Eight Days of Hanukkah, The, **Gr. 3,** 370 **CD17:19**

Eka Muda (Red Mule), **Gr. 5,** 28 **CD2:9**

El arroyo que murmura (The Murmuring Brook), **Gr. 3,** 318 **CD14:21**

El atole (The Atole), **Gr. 3,** 396 **CD19:12**

El barquito (The Tiny Boat), **Gr. 4,** 214 **CD11:1**

El burrito enfermo (The Sick Little Donkey), **Gr. 2,** 180 **CD9:11**

El charro (The Cowboy), **Gr. 6,** 278 **CD15:33**

El chorrito, FC-Pri 22

El coquí (The Frog), **Gr. 4,** 178 **CD9:2**

El florón (The Flower), **Gr. 1,** T117 **CD5:11; Gr. 3,** 46 **CD2:22**

El jarabe (Mexican Hat Dance), **Gr. 5,** 396 **CD23:13**

El juego chirimbolo (The Chirimbolo Game), **Gr. 1,** T103 **CD4:24**

El manisero (Peanut Vendor), **Gr. 4,** 106 **CD6:10**

El nacimiento (The Nativity), **Gr. K,** T322 **CD18:1**

El nido (The Nest), **Gr. 3,** 214 **CD9:29**

El palomo y la paloma (The Doves), **Gr. 2,** 380 **CD19:32**

El picaflor (The Hummingbird), **Gr. K,** T141 **CD8:10**

El quelite (The Village), **Gr. 4,** 362 **CD20:23**

El rorro (The Babe), **Gr. 1,** T356 **CD17:21**

El tambor (The Drum), **Gr. K,** T129 **CD7:18; Gr. 6,** 222 **CD11:28**

El tecolote (The Owlet), **Gr. 6,** 392 **CD 21:13**

El tren (The Train), **Gr. 2,** 326 **CD16:36**

El vito, **Gr. 5,** 210 **CD12:5**

El zapatero (The Cobbler), **Gr. 2,** 138 **CD7:24**

Elephant (Chang), **Gr. 1,** T199 **CD9:9**

Elephant, The (Yanai), **Gr. 2,** 305 **CD15:23**

Elijah Rock, **Gr. 6,** 52 **CD3:15**

En la feria de San Juan (In the Market of San Juan), **Gr. 2,** 226 **CD11:27**

En la Pulga de San José, FC-Pri 61

En nuestra Tierra tan linda (On Our Beautiful Planet Earth), **Gr. 2,** 114 **CD6:15**

En roulant ma boule (As I Roll My Ball), **Gr. 3,** 100 **CD4:26**

Engine, Engine Number Nine, **Pre-K,** 57; **Gr. 2,** 13 **CD1:17**

Enter, Holy Pilgrims (Entren santos peregrinos), **Gr. 4,** 379 **CD21:26**

Entren santos peregrinos (Enter, Holy Pilgrims), **Gr. 4,** 379 **CD 21:26**

Erie Canal, **Gr. 5,** 132 **CD7:22**

Ésta sí que es Nochebuena (This Is Christmas Eve), **Gr. 2,** 361 **CD18:21**

Estrella brillante (Shining Star), **Gr. 5,** 373 **CD22:17**

Ev'ry Time I Feel the Spirit, **Gr. 6,** C **Spotlight CD4**

Ev'rybody Loves Saturday Night (Mɔ-fia mo-ni), **Gr. 5,** 277 **CD17:15**

Evergreen, Everblue, **Gr. 3,** 330 **CD15:23**

Every Day I Have the Blues, **Gr. 5,** 179 **CD10:15**

Every Mornin' When I Wake Up, **Gr. 6,** 275 **CD15:30**

Everybody Has Music Inside, **Gr. 2,** 164 **CD8:22**

Everybody Oughta Know, **Gr. 1,** T361 **CD18:4**

Everybody Rejoice, **Gr. 5,** 226 **CD13:7**

Everything Grows, **Gr. 2,** 204 **CD10:17**

Fall (Ga Eul), **Gr. 5,** 401 **CD23:22**

Farfallina (Butterfly), **Gr. 4,** 244 **CD12:16**

Farmer in the Dell, The, **Gr. K,** T100 **CD6:5**

Feel Good, **Gr. 5,** 358 **CD21:20**

Fehér liliomszál (Little Water Lily), **Gr. K,** T139 **CD8:5**

Feliz Navidad (Merry Christmas), **Gr. 5,** 420 **CD25:1**

Fiesta en América, FC-Int 28

Fifty Nifty United States, **Gr. 5,** 392 **CD23:9**

Finnish Forest, The (Suomen Salossa), **Gr. 6,** 422 **CD23:5**

First of January (Uno de enero), **Gr. 3,** 210 **CD9:24**

Five Fat Turkeys, **Pre-K,** 84; **Gr. K,** T309 **CD16:31**

Flip, Flop and Fly, **Gr. 3,** 336 **CD16:4**

Flower, The (El florón) **Gr. 1,** T117 **CD5:11; Gr. 3,** 46 **CD2:22**

Follow Me, **Gr. K,** T133 **CD7:26**

Follow the Drinkin' Gourd, **Gr. 5,** 142 **CD8:7**

Follow Your Dream, **Gr. 4,** 234 **CD12:5; Gr. 7,** 207 **CD9:3**

Food Song, The, **Gr. 2,** 318 **CD16:19**

Fortune Favors the Brave, **Gr. 6,** 316 **CD17:20**

Fotografía, FC-Int 24

Four White Horses, **Gr. 2,** 301 **CD15:13**

Freedom Is a Constant Struggle, **Gr. 7,** 211 **CD9:9**

Frère Jacques (Are You Sleeping?), **Gr. 4,** 260 **CD14:1**

Frog in the Meadow, **Gr. 3**, 243 **CD11:4**
Frog Went A-Courtin', **Gr. 4**, 46 **CD3:7**
Frog, The (El coquí), **Gr. 4**, 178 **CD9:2**
Frog's Song (Kaeru no Uta), **Gr. 1**, T112 **CD5:1**
Frogs (I Chih ha Ma), **Gr. 2**, 186 **CD9:22**
Frosty Weather, **Gr. 3**, 250 **CD11:24**
Frosty, the Snowman, **Gr. 3**, 366 **CD17:12**
Full Moon Song (Pleeng loy krathong), **Gr. 6**, 398 **CD21:26**
Fun wa ni alaafia (Send Us Your Peace), **Gr. 5**, 248 **CD14:9**
Fung Yang Song, **Gr. 5**, 58 **CD4:8**
Fung Yang Song, WM 61
Funiculi, Funicula, **Gr. 5**, 62 **CD4:13**
Ga Eul (Fall), **Gr. 5**, 401 **CD23:22**
Garden Hoedown, The, **Pre-K**, 37; **Gr. K**, T290 **CD16:11**
Garden Song, **Gr. 2**, 236 **CD12:11**
Gee, Mom, I Want to Go Home, **Gr. 6**, 148 **CD8:18**
Gentle River Runs, A, **Gr. 5**, 342 **CD20:21**
George Washington, **Gr. 1**, T368 **CD18:22**
Ghost Ship, The, **Gr. 6**, 323 **CD17:29**
Gi'Me Elbow Room, **Gr. 3**, 88 **CD 4:12**
Gid'yup, Little Burro (Arre, mi burrito), **Gr. 1**, T257 **CD12:5**
Gilly, Gilly, Gilly Good Morning, **Gr. 1**, T12 **CD1:1**
Girl from San Juan, The (La sanjuanerita), **Gr. 4**, 100 **CD6:1**
Girl I Left Behind Me, The, **Gr. 4**, 249 **CD12:35**
Girl with a Shiny Ribbon, A (Och Jungfrun Hon Går I Ringen), **Gr. 5**, 190 **CD11:1**
Git Along, Little Dogies, **Gr. 6**, 284 **CD16:11**
Git on Board, **Gr. K**, T145 **CD8:18**
Give a Little Love, **Gr. 7**, 128 **CD5:11**
Give Me Your Hand (Simi Yadech), **Gr. K**, T168 **CD10:2**
Give Us Peace (Da pacem Domine), **Gr. 5**, 261 **CD15:22**
Gloria, **Gr. 7**, 222 **CD10:11**
Go A Tin (Lantern Song), **Gr. 1**, T363 **CD18:9**
Go Tell It on the Mountain, **Gr. 3**, 377 **CD18:4**
Go to Sleep, My Baby (Duérmete mi niño), **Gr. 1**, T61 **CD2:28**
Go, Go, Go, **Gr. K**, T276 **CD15:45**
God Bless America, **Gr. 5**, 4 **CD1:1**
God Bless the U.S.A., **Gr. 7**, 136 **CD5:17**
Gogo, **Gr. K**, T188 **CD11:1**
Goin' Home, **Gr. 5**, 108 **CD6:17**
Goin' to the Zoo, **Gr. 1**, T192 **CD8:29**
Going Over the Sea, **Gr. 2**, 216 **CD11:1**
Going Round (Hashewie), **Gr. 2**, 362 **CD18:25**
Golden Ring Around the Susan Girl, **Gr. 3**, 264 **CD11:57**
Gong xi fa cai (Chinese New Year Song), **Gr. 3**, 384 **CD18:19**
Gonna Build a Mountain, **Gr. 6**, 4 **CD1:1**
Goober Peas, **Gr. 6**, 269 **CD15:2**
Good Day Song, **Pre-K**, 44; **Gr. K**, T50 **CD2:30**
Good Mornin', Blues, **Gr. 5**, 177 **CD10:12**
Good News, **Gr. 6**, 242 **CD12:29**
Good Night, Sleep Tight, **Gr. 2**, 76 **CD4:21**
Goodbye Brother, **Gr. 4**, 273 **CD15:11**
Goodbye, My Riley O, **Gr. 4**, 257 **CD13:24**
Grandma's Feather Bed, **Gr. 4**, E **Spotlight CD7**
Granny (speech piece), **Gr. 1**, T104 **CD4:28**
Grasshoppers Three, **Gr. 1**, T284 **CD13:19**
Great Big House, **Gr. 3**, 14 **CD1:18**
Great Big Sea, A, **Gr. 5**, 334 **CD20:9**

Great Outdoors, The, **Gr. 2**, 290 **CD14:49**
Greatest Show on Earth, The, **Gr. 3**, 308 **CD14:4**
Green Eggs and Ham, **Gr. 2**, 284 **CD14:41**
Green Grass Grows All Around, The, **Gr. 1**, T148 **CD6:28**
Green Gravel, **Gr. 4**, 247 **CD12:29**
Greenland Whale Fishery, The, **Gr. 6**, 212 **CD11:15**
Grizzly Bear, **Gr. K**, T252 **CD14:17**
Guantanamera, **Gr. 5**, 215 **CD12:10**
Guess What It Is! (¡Adivina lo que es!), **Gr. 1**, T170 **CD7:30**
Guitar Man, The, **Gr. 6**, 138 **CD8:1**
Hae Wa Be (Sun and Rain), **Gr. 6**, 273 **CD15:17**
Haere Ra (Now Is the Hour), **Gr. 5**, 151 **CD9:3**
Hag Shavuot (Festival of First Fruits), WM 33
Haji Firuz, **Gr. 6**, 421 **CD23:1**
Haji Firuz, WM 113
Hakuna Matata, **Gr. 2**, 292 **CD15:1**
Hakyo Jong (School Bells), **Gr. 1**, T302 **CD14:7**
Hala lala layya, **Gr. 4**, 222 **CD11:16**
Half Moon (Ban Dal), **Gr. 2**, 219 **CD11:15**
Hallelujah, Get on Board, **Gr. 5**, 345 **CD21:1**
Halloween, **Gr. 1**, T340 **CD16:16**
Haneirot Halalu (These Lights), **Gr. 5**, 414 **CD24:21**
Hang on Sloopy, **Gr. 7**, 30 **CD1:15**
Hanukkah Chag Yafeh (Hanukkah Joyous Holiday), **Gr. 1**, T350 **CD17:1**
Hanukkah Is Here, **Gr. K**, T314 **CD17:6**
Hanukkah Joyous Holiday (Hanukkah Chag Yafeh), **Gr. 1**, T350 **CD17:1**
Happiest Street in the World, The, **Gr. 1**, T304 **CD14:15**
Happiness, **Gr. 4**, 124 **CD6:31**; (speech piece), **Gr. 1**, T254 **CD11:37**
Happy Birthday, **Gr. K**, T347 **CD19:24**
Happy Birthday, Happy Birthday, **Gr. K**, T273 **CD15:42**
Happy Talk, **Gr. 4**, 84 **CD5:8**
Happy Wanderer, The, **Gr. 3**, 18 **CD1:24**
Harvest Time (Chag Asif), **Gr. 3**, 360 **CD17:1**
Harvest, **Gr. 2**, 342 **CD17:12**
Hashewie (Going Round), **Gr. 2**, 362 **CD18:25**
Hasta mañana, FC-Int 11
Hava Nagila, **Gr. 5**, 54 **CD3:23**
Hava Nashira (Sing Alleluia), **Gr. 6**, 67 **CD4:14**
Have You Not Seen My Daughters? (Neviděli jste tu mé panenky), **Gr. 6**, 228 **CD12:10**
He's Got the Whole World in His Hands, **Gr. 2**, 116 **CD6:22**
Head and Shoulders, Baby, **Gr. 1**, T40 **CD1:39**
Head and Shoulders, **Gr. K**, T238 **CD13:21**
Heart, **Gr. 6**, 166 **CD9:9**
Heave-Ho, Me Laddies, **Gr. 4**, 258 **CD13:27**
Heigh Ho, Here We Go, **Gr. 2**, 252 **CD13:5**
Heleluyan (Alleluia), **Gr. 6**, 188 **CD10:17**
Hello (Jambo), **Gr. 1**, T230 **CD10:20**
Hello Song, **Gr. K**, T2 **Spotlight CD1**
Hello!, **Gr. 3**, 283 **CD13:10**
Hello, Hello There, **Gr. 2**, 126 **CD7:4**
Hello, My Friends (Bonjour, mes amis), **Gr. 1**, T18 **CD1:8**
Hello, There!, **Gr. 1**, T230 **CD10:17**
Henry Ford, **Gr. 7**, 244 **CD11:3**
Here Comes a Bluebird, **Gr. 2**, 263 **CD13:51**
Here Comes Sally, **Gr. 2**, 220 **CD11:19**
Here Is the Beehive, **Gr. K**, T258 **CD14:26**

Alphabetical Index of Songs and Speech Pieces (continued)

Here We Come A-Wassailing, **Gr. 1,** T355 **CD17:18**

Here We Sit, **Gr. 1,** T251 **CD11:27**

Hero, **Gr. 5,** 312 **CD19:11**

Herring, The, **Gr. 3,** 316 **CD14:17**

Hey, Children, Who's in Town? (speech piece), **Gr. 1,** T14 **CD1:4**

Hey, Hey, Look at Me, **Gr. 2,** 245 **CD12:26**

Hey, Look Me Over, **Gr. 4,** 114 **CD6:22**

Hey, Motswala, **Gr. 3,** 34 **CD2:8**

Hi! My Name is Joe! (speech piece), **Gr. 1,** T220 **CD10:10**

Hide a Handkerchief! (Diou Shou Juan'er), **Gr. 1,** T212 **CD9:29**

Hill an' Gully, **Gr. 5,** 250 **CD14:16**

Himmel und Erde (Music Alone Shall Live), **Gr. 4,** 280 **CD16:1**

Hine Ma Tov (How Good It Is), **Gr. 4,** 66 **CD4:13**

Hitori, **Gr. 4,** 345 **CD19:27**

Hoe Ana Te Vaka (Paddle the Canoe), WM 41

Hojas de té (Tea Leaves) (speech piece), **Gr. 4,** 256 **CD13:20**

Hokey Pokey, **Pre-K,** 4; **Gr. K,** T68 **CD4:1**

Hold My Mule, **Gr. 4,** 248 **CD12:32**

Holi Song, WM 112

Holly and the Ivy, The, **Gr. 5,** 418 **CD24:28**

Home on the Range, **Gr. 5,** D **Spotlight CD4**

Hong Tsai Me Me (Rainbow Sister), WM 57

Honorable Bear (Kuma San), **Gr. 3,** 244 **CD11:7**

Hoo, Hoo!, **Gr. 1,** T55 **CD2:21**

Hop Up and Jump Up, **Gr. 4,** 271 **CD15:4**

Hop! Chirp! Moo! Oh, Happy Springtime Day!, **Gr. 1,** T372 **CD18:29**

Hop, Hop! (Brinca la tablita), **Gr. 1,** T71 **CD3:1**

Hop, Hop, Hop, **Gr. K,** T197 **CD11:15**

Hop, Old Squirrel, **Gr. 2,** 258 **CD13:30**

Horton Hears a Who!, **Gr. 2,** 279 **CD14:44**

Horton Hears a Who! Two, **Gr. 2,** 280 **CD14:45**

Hot Cross Buns, **Gr. 2,** 258 **CD13:27**

Hot Dog, **Gr. K,** T69 **CD4:4**

Hotaru Koi (Come, Firefly), **Gr. 6,** 255 **CD13:45**

Hours, The (Las horas), **Gr. K,** T70 **CD4:7**

How Brightly Shines the Morning Star (Wie schön leuchtet der Morgenstern), **Gr. 5,** 370 **CD22:12**

How Can I Keep from Singing?, **Gr. 5,** 287 **CD18:5**

How Does Your Garden Grow?, **Gr. 1,** T144 **CD6:22**

How Good It Is (Hine Ma Tov), **Gr. 4,** 66 **CD4:13**

How Long the Train Been Gone?, **Gr. 4,** 264 **CD14:13**

How to Succeed, **Gr. 8,** 237 **CD10:1**

How Wonderful It Is (Qué bonito es), **Gr. K,** T234 **CD13:13**

Hoy tengo que decirte papá, FC-Int 57

Huainito, **Gr. 6,** 351 **CD19:1**

Hullaballoo Balay, **Gr. 6,** 10 **CD1:13**

Hummingbird, The (El picaflor), **Gr. K,** T141 **CD8:10**

Hunt the Cows, **Gr. 1,** T236 **CD10:35**

Hush, Little Baby, **Pre-K,** 24

I Am But a Small Voice, **Gr. 5,** 323 **CD19:30**

I Am Poor (Pauper sum ego), **Gr. 6,** 254 **CD13:38**

I Am Slowly Going Crazy, **Gr. 1,** T127 **CD5:30**

I Bought Me a Cat, **Gr. 2,** 14 **CD1:21**

I Can't Spell Hippopotamus, **Gr. K,** T199 **CD11:18**

I Chih ha Ma (Frogs), **Gr. 2,** 186 **CD9:22**

I Got a Letter, **Gr. 6,** 270 **CD15:6**

I Got Rhythm, **Gr. 5,** 187 **CD10:19**

I Got Shoes , **Gr. K,** T33 **CD2:1**

I Have a Car, **Gr. 3,** 252 **CD11:28**

I Have, I Have, I Have (Tengo, Tengo, Tengo), **Gr. K,** T212 **CD12:12**

I Hear America Singing, **Gr. 5,** 327 **CD20:2**

I Hear the Windmill (J'entends le moulin), **Gr. 3,** 135 **CD6:18**

I Heard a Mockingbird, **Gr. 4,** 150 **CD7:31**

I Know an Old Lady, **Gr. K,** T26 **CD1:22**

I Like Spinach, **Pre-K,** 35; **Gr. 1,** T163 **CD7:19**

I Lost the Farmer's Dairy Key, **Gr. 3,** 273 **CD12:26**

I Love a Piano, **Gr. 6,** 130 **CD7:15**

I Love My Country, **Gr. 1,** T328 **CD15:21**

I Made a Valentine, **Gr. K,** T333 **CD18:32**

I Planted Watermelons (Ja posejah lubenice), **Gr. 2,** 316 **CD16:11**

I Saw the Light, **Gr. 5,** 252 **CD14:22**

I Saw Three Ships, **Gr. 2,** 359 **CD18:15**

I See, **Gr. 2,** 266 **CD14:33**

I Think I'm Gonna Like It Here, **Gr. 4,** 299 **CD17:3**

I Walk in Beauty, **Gr. 3,** 329 **CD15:19**

I Wanna Be a Friend of Yours, **Pre-K,** 16; **Gr. 1,** T84 **CD3:23**

I Want to Be Ready, **Gr. 6,** 12 **CD1:16**

I Went Away from Cuba (Cuando salí de Cuba), **Gr. 5,** 168 **CD9:22**

I Will Be Your Friend, **Gr. 4,** 388 **CD22:11**

I Will Sing Hello, **Gr. K,** T156 **CD9:10**

I'll Rise When the Rooster Crows, **Gr. 4,** 36 **CD2:24**

I'm a Believer, **Gr. 3,** 312 **CD14:10**

I'm Going to Georgia, **Gr. 6,** 244 **CD12:35**

I'm Gonna Sing, **Gr. 2,** 9 **CD1:11**

I'm Gonna Sit at the Welcome Table, **Gr. 6,** 416 **CD22:24**

I'm on My Way, **Gr. 3,** 382 **CD18:16**

I's the B'y, **Gr. 3,** 13 **CD1:15**

I've a Pair of Fishes, **Gr. 1,** T124 **CD5:23**

I've Been Working on the Railroad, **Gr. 3,** C **Spotlight CD4**

I've Got a Robe, **Gr. 7,** 162 **CD7:12**

If All the World Were Paper, **Gr. 1,** T296 **CD13:41**

If I Had a Hammer, **Gr. 6,** 174 **CD9:20**

If You're Happy, **Gr. K,** T6 **Spotlight CD7**

Ifetayo (Love Brings Happiness), **Gr. K,** T325 **CD18:10**

In and Out, **Gr. 2,** 245 **CD12:29**

In Bahia Town (Na Bahia Tem), **Gr. K,** T163 **CD9:22; Gr. 1,** T297 **CD13:44**

In Good Old Colony Times, **Gr. 3,** 326 **CD15:8**

In My Little Motor Boat, **Gr. 1,** T159 **CD7:13**

In That Great Git'n Up Mornin', **Gr. 5,** 10 **CD1:11**

In the Market of San Juan (En la feria de San Juan), **Gr. 2,** 226 **CD11:27**

In the Window, **Gr. 2,** 352 **CD17:35**

In the Year to Come (Bashana Haba'ah), **Gr. 6,** 360 **CD19:17**

Instrument Game, **Gr. K,** T36 **CD2:8**

Interjections, **Gr. 3,** 303 **CD13:26**

Interplanet Janet, **Gr. 3,** 298 **CD13:25**

Iowa Stubborn, **Gr. 5,** 293 **CD18:10**

Is That Mister Reilly?, **Gr. 5,** 282 **CD17:28**

Island in the Sun, CM 33

Alphabetical Index of Songs and Speech Pieces (continued)

It Don't Mean a Thing, **Gr. 6**, 164 **CD9:5**
It Rained a Mist, **Gr. 4**, 262 **CD14:9**
It's a Small World, **Gr. 2**, 298 **CD15:10**
It's Possible, **Gr. 2**, 281 **CD14:40**
It's Raining (Que llueva), **Gr. 3**, 274 **CD12:29**
It's Raining! It's Pouring!, **Gr. 2**, 233 **CD12:6**
It's So Good to See You, **Gr. K**, T86 **CD5:9**
It's So Nice on the Ice, **Gr. 1**, T346 **CD16:27**
It's Such a Good Feeling, **Gr. K**, T282 **CD15:49**
It's the Hard-Knock Life, **Gr. 4**, 293 **CD17:1**
It's Time to Get Ready for Christmas, **Gr. 3**, 372 **CD17:22**
It's You I Like, **Gr. K**, T280 **CD15:48**
Itik Besenda Gurau (The Ducks), **Gr. 2**, 100 **CD5:25**
J'entends le moulin (I Hear the Windmill), **Gr. 3**, 135 **CD6:18**
Já do lesa nepojedu (To the Woods I Will Not Go), **Gr. 6**, 227 **CD12:6**
Ja posejah lubenice (I Planted Watermelons), **Gr. 2**, 316 **CD16:11**
Jack Was Ev'ry Bit a Sailor, **Gr. 6**, 170 **CD9:13**
Jack, Be Nimble, **Gr. K**, T88 **CD5:12**
Jack-in-the-Box, **Gr. K**, T250 **CD14:14**
Jack-o'-Lantern, **Gr. K**, T307 **CD16:25**
Jamaica Farewell, CM 17
Jamaica Farewell, **Gr. 3**, 156 **CD7:17**
Jambo (Hello), **Gr. 1**, T230 **CD10:20**
Jasmine Flower, **Gr. 3**, 146 **CD7:1**
Jede, jede poštovský panáček (Riding, Riding, Is Mr. Postman), **Gr. 6**, 226 **CD12:2**
Jig Jog, Jig Jog, **Gr. K**, T260 **CD14:30**
Jikel' emaweni (Throw It in the Slope), **Gr. 6**, 70 **CD4:22**
Jim Along, Josie, **Gr. 2**, 194 **CD10:4**
Jingle at the Window, **Gr. 3**, 268 **CD12:13**
Jingle Bells, **Pre-K**, 86; **Gr. 1**, T354 **CD17:15**
Jingle-Bell Rock, **Gr. 5**, 424 **CD25:5**
Jó ashílá (Traveling Together), **Gr. 5**, 224 **CD13:2**
Joban Miners' Song (Joban tanko bushi), **Gr. 6**, 142 **CD8:10**
Joban Tanko Bushi (Joban Miners' Song), **Gr. 6**, 142 **CD8:10**
John Henry, **Gr. 5**, 146 **CD8:16**
John Jacob Jingleheimer Schmidt, **Gr. 3**, 68 **CD3:25**
John Kanaka, **Gr. 5**, 249 **CD14:13**
John the Rabbit, **Gr. 1**, T74 **CD3:7**
Johnny Works with One Hammer, **Gr. 1**, T96 **CD4:7**
Johnny's Flea, **Gr. 1**, T158 **CD7:10**
Johnson Boys, **Gr. 4**, 233 **CD12:2**
Jolly Old Saint Nicholas, **Gr. 1**, T353 **CD17:8**; **Gr. 4**, 382 **CD21:33**
Jordan's Angels, **Gr. 6**, 365 **CD19:22**
Joshua Fit the Battle of Jericho, **Gr. 5**, 126 **CD7:9**
Journey, A (speech piece), **Gr. 4**, 14 **CD1:17**
Joy to the World, **Gr. 4**, 383 **CD22:1**
Joy, **Gr. 2**, 46 **CD3:1**
Joyful, Joyful, **Gr. 5**, 105 **CD6:13**
Joyful, Joyful, We Adore Thee, **Gr. 5**, 103 **CD6:10**
Juan Pírulero, **Gr. 2**, 270 **CD14:27**
Juanito, FC-Pri 15
Jugaremos en el bosque (We'll Be Playing in the Forest), **Gr. 2**, 188 **CD9:26**
Juhtgarak (Chopsticks), **Gr. K**, T108 **CD6:16**
Jump, Jim Joe, **Gr. 1**, T89 **CD3:32**

Just Give Me the Beat (speech piece), **Gr. 5**, 9 **CD1:8**
Just Keep Goin' On, **Gr. 7**, 18 **CD1:10**
Just Like Me, **Gr. K**, T242 **CD14:1**
Just Like the Sun, **Gr. 3**, 394 **CD19:9**
Just One Planet, **Gr. 4**, 164 **CD8:12**
Kaeru no Uta (Frog's Song), **Gr. 1**, T112 **CD5:1**
Kaeru No Uta (Frog's Song), WM 9
Kakokolo, **Gr. 6**, 262 **CD14:20**
Kalinka (Little Snowball Bush), **Gr. 3**, 224 **CD10:14**
Kangaroo, The, **Gr. K**, T197 **CD11:11**
Kari (Wild Geese), **Gr. 1**, T261 **CD12:20**
Karşi Bar (Turkish Dance), WM 112
Katyusha, **Gr. 4**, 188 **CD9:15**
Kettle Valley Line, The, **Gr. 4**, 348 **CD20:1**
King's Land, **Gr. 2**, 257 **CD13:21**
Kingston Market, CM 9
Kite Song, The (Tako No Uta), **Gr. 1**, T370 **CD18:25**
Knock the Cymbals, **Gr. 2**, 265 **CD14:10**
Kobuta, **Gr. 1**, T168 **CD7:25**
Kojo No Tsuki (Moon at the Ruined Castle), **Gr. 5**, 149 **CD8:20**
Kokoleoko, **Gr. 6**, 279 **CD15:37**
Korobushka, **Gr. 4**, 285 **CD16:21**
Korobushka, WM 47
Kreely Kranky, **Gr. 3**, 258 **CD11:44**
Kum Ba Yah, **Gr. K**, T327 **CD18:16**
Kum Bachur (The Rooster), **Gr. 3**, 75 **CD3:31**
Kuma San (Honorable Bear), **Gr. 3**, 244 **CD11:7**
Kye Kye Kule, **Gr. 7**, 225 **CD10:13**
L'inverno è già passato (Winter is Over), **Gr. 4**, 390 **CD22:15**
La Bamba, **Gr. 3**, 236 **CD10:27**; **Gr. 6**, 381 **CD20:15**
La bella hortelana (The Beautiful Gardener), **Gr. 2**, 208 **CD10:23**
La carcacha, FC-Int 7
La cloche (The Clock), **Gr. 3**, 67 **CD3:21**
La colación (Christmas Candies), **Gr. 1**, T357 **CD17:25**
La Gallina Turuleca, FC-Pri 27
La mar (The Sea), **Gr. 3**, 110 **CD5:9**
La marcha de las letras, FC-Pri 57
La otra España (The Other Spain), **Gr. 4**, 62 **CD4:5**
La pájara pinta (The Speckled Bird), **Gr. 6**, 268 **CD14:32**
La paloma se fue (The Dove That Flew Away), **Gr. 5**, 259 **CD15:15**
La patita, FC-Pri 64
La pequeñita araña (Eency Weency Spider), **Gr. K**, T9 **Spotlight CD13**
La ranita cri (The Little Frog Croaks), **Gr. 1**, T27 **CD1:23**
La risa de las vocales, FC-Pri 50
La sanjuanerita (The Girl from San Juan), **Gr. 4**, 100 **CD6:1**
La víbora de la mar (The Serpent from the Sea), **Gr. 5**, 440 **CD26:1**
La Yunsita, **Gr. 4**, 350 **CD20:5**
Ladies of Chiapas (Chiapanecas), **Gr. 2**, 128 **CD7:8**
Lady, Lady, **Gr. K**, T184 **CD10:24**
Ladybug's Picnic, **Gr. 1**, T290 **CD13:32**
Land of a Thousand Dances, **Gr. 7**, 12 **CD1:6**
Land of the Silver Birch, **Gr. 2**, 88 **CD5:5**
Lantern Song (Go A Tin), **Gr. 1**, T363 **CD18:9**
Las horas (The Hours), **Gr. K**, T70 **CD4:7**

Las mañanitas (The Morning Song), **Gr. 4**, 194 **CD9:24**

Lavender's Blue, **Gr. 1**, T174 **CD8:4**

Lead Man Holler, **Gr. 7**, 148 **CD6:8**

Lean Man Holler, CM 21

Lean on Me, **Gr. 6**, 150 **CD8:22**

Leatherwing Bat, **Gr. 2**, 304 **CD15:20**

Leila, **Gr. 6**, 376 **CD20:6**

Lek Kansaing (Hiding the Towel), WM 15

Lemonade, **Gr. 2**, 19 **CD1:25**

Les Anges dans nos Campagnes (Angels We Have Heard on High), **Gr. 6**, 406 **CD22:7**

Let It Roll, **Gr. 6**, 124 **CD7:8**

Let Music Surround You, **Gr. 6**, 285 **CD16:14**

Let Us Chase the Squirrel, **Gr. 3**, 248 **CD11:18**

Let's Go Dancing, **Gr. 3**, 196 **CD9:7**

Let's Go Driving, **Gr. 1**, T52 **CD2:12**

Let's Go Fly a Kite, **Gr. 2**, 134 **CD7:19**

Let's Go to the Sea (Vamos a la mar), **Gr. 3**, 256 **CD11:37**

Let's Think of Something to Do, **Gr. K**, T270 **CD15:40**

Li'l 'Liza Jane, **Gr. 4**, 20 **CD2:1**

Library Song, **Gr. 1**, T42 **CD2:4**

Lift Every Voice and Sing, **Gr. 5**, 86 **CD5:18**

Lift Up Your Voices, **Gr. 5**, 319 **CD19:20**

Light One Candle, **Gr. 5**, 416 **CD24:25**

Light the Candles, **Gr. 1**, T351 **CD17:5**

Like a Mighty Stream, **Gr. 5**, 320 **CD19:26**

Limbo Rock, **Gr. 3**, 232 **CD10:24**

Lion Sleeps Tonight, The, **Gr. 5**, 172 **CD10:1**; **Gr. 7**, 214 **CD9:16**

Listen How It Goes (Oye como va), **Gr. 5**, 69 **CD4:22**

Listen to the Music, **Gr. 6**, 63 **CD4:6**

Little Bear Song (Ucha Tirvarch), **Gr. 3**, 53 **CD3:4**

Little Bird (Pajarillo barranqueño), **Gr. 3**, 358 **CD16:25**

Little Birds Sleep (Ēinīnī), **Gr. 5**, 340 **CD20:16**

Little Black Bug, **Gr. 1**, T166 **CD7:22**

Little Blue Truck, **Gr. K**, T136 **CD7:30**

Little Boy of the Sheep, **Gr. 3**, 188 **CD8:29**

Little Chickens (Los Pollitos), **Pre-K**, 67; **Gr. K**, T288 **CD16:4**

Little Coffee Mill (Molinillo de café) (speech piece), **Gr. 4**, 250 **CD13:1**

Little David Play on Your Harp, **Gr. 4**, 323 **CD18:14**

Little Ducky Duddle, **Pre-K**, 65; **Gr. K**, T289 **CD16:8**

Little Frog Croaks, The (La ranita cri), **Gr. 1**, T27 **CD1:23**

Little Hawk (Sansa kroma), **Gr. 4**, 166 **CD8:15**

Little Heron (Na belo), **Gr. 2**, 322 **CD16:25**

Little Lullaby, A (A la nanita nana), **Gr. 4**, 230 **CD11:28**

Little Red Caboose, **Gr. 1**, T97 **CD4:10**

Little Robin Red Breast, **Gr. 1**, T208 **CD9:21**

Little Sally Walker, **Gr. 3**, 105 **CD5:2**

Little Sally Water, **Gr. 2**, 249 **CD12:39**

Little Sir Echo, **Gr. K**, T103 **CD6:9**

Little Snowball Bush (Kalinka), **Gr. 3**, 224 **CD10:14**

Little Spotted Puppy, **Gr. K**, T147 **CD8:21**

Little Tommy Tinker, **Gr. 3**, 277 **CD12:39**

Little Water Lily (Fehér liliomszál), **Gr. K**, T139 **CD8:5**

Little White Duck, **Gr. K**, T208 **CD12:5**

Little White Pony (Caballito blanco), **Gr. 4**, 278 **CD15:30**

Loch Lomond, **Gr. 5**, 138 **CD8:4**

Loco-Motion, The, **Gr. 4**, 312 **CD17:25**

London Bridge, **Gr. K**, T99 **CD5:25**

Lonesome Dove, **Gr. 6**, 249 **CD13:16**

Long-Legged Sailor, **Gr. 4**, 243 **CD12:12**

Looby Loo, **Pre-K**, 6; **Gr. 1**, T262 **CD12:24**

Look at the Birds in the Sky (E nānā kākou i nā manu), **Gr. 4**, 338 **CD19:11**

Look High, Look Low, **Gr. 3**, 338 **CD16:7**

Look Who's Here!, **Gr. K**, T84 **CD5:6**

Looking for Shelter (Para pedir Posada), **Gr. 4**, 376 **CD21:22**

Loose Tooth (speech piece), **Gr. 2**, 28 **CD2:6**

Lord Bless Africa (N'kosi sikelel' i Afrika), **Gr. 6**, 339 **CD18:11**

Los cochinitos, FC-Pri 11

Los maizales (The Cornfields), **Gr. 5**, 268 **CD16:17**

Los mariachis (Mexican folk song), **Gr. 7**, 90 **CD4:9**

Los pollitos (Little Chickens), **Pre-K**, 67; **Gr. K**, T288 **CD16:4**

Lots o' Fish in Bonavist' Harbor, **Gr. 5**, 263 **CD16:4**

Love Brings Happiness (Ifetayo), **Gr. K**, T325 **CD18:10**

Love Grows One by One, **Gr. 1**, T202 **CD9:17**

Love Is the Magic Word, **Gr. 1**, T366 **CD18:19**

Love Somebody, **Gr. 4**, 94 **CD5:22**

Lucy Locket, **Gr. 1**, T253 **CD11:34**

Lukey's Boat, **Gr. 3**, 114 **CD5:17**

Lullaby of Broadway, **Gr. 6**, 182 **CD10:7**

Lumber Camp Song, The, **Gr. 6**, 136 **CD7:28**

Ma'oz Tsur (Rock of Ages), **Gr. 6**, 405 **CD22:2**

Macnamara's Band, **Gr. 4**, 88 **CD5:14**

Mail Myself to You, **Gr. 1**, T366 **CD18:16**

Maliit Na Gagamba (Little Spider), WM 5

Mama Don't 'Low, **Gr. 6**, 126 **CD7:11**

Mama Paquita, **Gr. 2**, 92 **CD5:13**

Mama Will Provide, **Gr. 6**, 296 **CD16:22**

Mama, Bake the Johnnycake, **Gr. K**, T318 **CD17:16**

Mamá, FC-Int 75

Mamacita, ¿Dónde Está Santa Claus?, FC-Int 41

Mango Walk, **Gr. 5**, 90 **CD5:27**

Many Colors (De colores) (unison), **Gr. 5**, 88 **CD5:22**; (2-part), **Gr. 5**, 98 **CD5:22**

Marco Polo (speech piece), **Gr. 1**, T90 **CD3:35**

Mardi Gras Mambo, **Gr. 7**, 88 **CD4:8**

María Blanca, **Gr. K**, T99 **CD6:1**

Marken er mejet (Out in the Meadow), **Gr. 4**, 365 **CD20:28**

Martin Luther King, **Gr. 1**, T360 **CD18:1**; **Gr. 2**, 364 **CD18:29**; (speech piece), **Gr. K**, T326 **CD18:13**

Marvelous Toy, The, **Gr. 3**, 182 **CD8:19**

Mary Ann, **Gr. 5**, 166 **CD9:19**

Mary Had a Baby, **Gr. 2**, 360 **CD18:18**

Mary Wore a Red Dress, **Pre-K**, 15

Mary's Coal Black Lamb, **Gr. 1**, T286 **CD13:22**

Matarile, **Gr. 2**, 261 **CD13:43**

May Day Carol, **Gr. 3**, 393 **CD19:6**

Mayim, Mayim (Water, Water), **Gr. 6**, 102 **CD6:9**

Mbombela (The Train Comes), **Gr. K**, T152 **CD9:4**

Me gase boho (Orange Tree), **Gr. 2**, 317 **CD16:15**

Me Stone, **Gr. 2**, 48 **CD3:5**

Mein Hut (My Hat), **Gr. 2**, 142 **CD7:32**

Mele Kalikimaka (Merry Christmas), **Gr. 6**, 410 **CD22:16**

Merecumbé, **Gr. 6**, 276 **CD15:26**

Merrily, We Roll Along, **Gr. K**, T110 **CD6:21**

Merry Christmas (Feliz Navidad), **Gr. 5**, 420 **CD25:1**

Merry Christmas (Mele Kalikimaka), **Gr. 6**, 410 **CD21:16**

Merry-Go-Round, **Gr. 2**, 267 **CD14:16**

Merry-Go-Round, The, **Gr. K**, T224 **CD13:3**

Mexican Hat Dance (El jarabe), **Gr. 5**, 396 **CD23:13**

México lindo y, FC-Int 20

Mi caballo blanco (My White Horse), **Gr. 6**, 60 **CD4:1**

Mi chacra (My Farm), **Gr. K**, T207 **CD12:1**

Mi cuerpo (My Body), **Pre-K**, 5; **Gr. 1**, T32 **CD1:28**

Mi gallo (My Rooster), **Gr. 5**, 272 **CD16:30**

Mi tierra, FC-Int 36

Mighty River (speech piece), **Gr. 4**, 217 **CD11:5**

Mil juguetes y un amigo, FC-Pri 68

Mill Song, The, **Gr. 2**, 52 **CD3:12**

Minuteman Minute Song, The, **Gr. 3**, 322 **CD14:28**

Miss Mary Mack, **Gr. 1**, T15 **CD1:5**

Mister Bamboo Bug (Wavvuuvuumira), **Gr. K**, T165 **CD9:27**

Mister Rabbit, Mister Rabbit, **Gr. 2**, 150 **CD8:6**

Mister Sun, **Pre-K**, 45; **Gr. K**, T343 **CD19:19**

Mizuguruma (Water Wheel), **Gr. 1**, T260 **CD12:16**

Modern Dragon, A (speech piece), **Gr. 4**, 98 **CD5:27**

Mɔ-fia mo-ni (Ev'rybody Loves Saturday Night), **Gr. 5**, 277 **CD17:15**

Molinillo de café (Little Coffee Mill) (speech piece), **Gr. 4**, 250 **CD13:1**

Monkey, Monkey, **Gr. K**, T215 **CD12:17**

Monté sur un éléphant (Riding on an Elephant), **Gr. K**, T217 **CD12:20**

Moon and Me, **Gr. 3**, 220 **CD10:8**

Moon at the Ruined Castle (Kojo No Tsuki), **Gr. 5**, 149 **CD8:20**

Moon, The (Deta, Deta), **Gr. 5**, 246 **CD14:4**

More We Get Together, The (Ach, du lieber Augustin), **Gr. 2**, 35 **CD2:12**

Morning Bells, **Gr. 3**, 270 **CD12:19**

Morning Has Broken, **Gr. 4**, 22 **CD2:4**

Morning Song, The (Las mañanitas), **Gr. 4**, 194 **CD9:24**

Mos', Mos'! (Cat, Cat!), **Gr. 1**, T53 **CD2:16**

'Most Done Ling'rin' Here, **Gr. 4**, 65 **CD4:10**

Mother, Mother, **Gr. 2**, 254 **CD13:9**

Mothers (Nampaya omame), **Gr. K**, T128 **CD7:14**

Mountain Music, **Gr. 6**, 20 **CD1:27**

Mountain Stream (Arroyito serrano), **Gr. 4**, 340 **CD19:15**

Mouse in the Rice Sack (Zui Zui Zukkorbashi), **Gr. 1**, T98 **CD4:13**

Mouse, Mousie, **Gr. 2**, 254 **CD13:12**

Movin' Right Along, **Gr. 3**, 124 **CD6:1**

Mr. Frog, **Gr. 2**, 257 **CD13:24**

Mr. Scott Joplin's Ragtime Rag!, **Gr. 6**, 110 **CD6:25**

Mrs. Murphy's Chowder, **Gr. 3**, 390 **CD18:31**

Muffin Man, The, **Gr. K**, T105 **CD6:12**

Mulberry Bush, The, **Gr. K**, T112 **CD6:27**

Murmuring Brook, The (El arroyo que murmura), **Gr. 3**, 318 **CD14:21**

Music Alone Shall Live (Himmel und Erde), **Gr. 4**, 280 **CD16:1**

Music of the World A-Turnin', **Gr. 3**, 44 **CD2:19**

Must Be Santa, **Gr. K**, T316 **CD17:12**

My Body (Mi cuerpo), **Pre-K**, 5; **Gr. 1**, T32 **CD1:28**

My Dreidel, **Gr. 2**, 353 **CD18:1**

My Farm (Mi chacra), **Gr. K**, T207 **CD12:1**

My Friend Tom, **Gr. 3**, 364 **CD17:9**

My Government Claim (unison), **Gr. 5**, 95 **CD6:5**; (3-part), **Gr. 5**, 110 **CD6:20**

My Grandfather, **Gr. K**, T23 **CD1:16**

My Hat (Mein Hut), **Gr. 2**, 142 **CD7:32**

My Home's in Montana, **Gr. 4**, 274 **CD15:14**

My Horses Ain't Hungry, **Gr. 3**, 278 **CD12:42**

My Love, You Hold My Life (Belle qui tiens ma vie), **Gr. 6**, 99 **CD6:4**

My Mama's Calling Me, **Pre-K**, 25; **Gr. 1**, T54 **CD2:18**

My Mom, **Gr. 1**, T372 **CD18:32**

My Nipa Hut (Bahay Kubo), **Gr. 2**, 382 **CD19:36**

My Oak Tree, **Gr. K**, T236 **CD13:18**

My Ranch (Allá en el rancho grande), **Gr. 5**, 66 **CD4:17**

My Rooster (Mi gallo), **Gr. 5**, 272 **CD16:30**

My Thumbs Are Starting to Wiggle, **Gr. K**, T35 **CD2:5**

My Town, My World, **Gr. 4**, 6 **CD1:4**

My White Horse (Mi caballo blanco), **Gr. 6**, 60 **CD4:1**

N.Y.C., **Gr. 4**, 302 **CD17:4**

N'kosi sikelel' i Afrika (Lord Bless Africa), **Gr. 6**, 339 **CD18:11**

Na Bahia Tem (In Bahia Town), **Gr. K**, T163 **CD9:22**; **Gr. 1**, T297 **CD13:44**

Na belo (Little Heron), **Gr. 2**, 322 **CD16:25**

Nabe, Nabe, Soku, Nuke (Stewpot, Stewpot, Bottomless Pot), WM 17

Nabe, Nabe, Soku, Nuke (Stewpot, Stewpot, Bottomless Pot), **Gr. 2**, 259 **CD13:33**

Name Game, **Gr. K**, T57 **CD3:10**

Nampaya omame (Mothers), **Gr. K**, T128 **CD7:14**

Nani Wale Na Hala (The Swaying Pandanus Trees), **Gr. 5**, 276 **CD17:11**

Nanticoke Women's Honoring Song (O Hal' lwe), **Gr. 6**, 428 **CD23:18**

Naranja dulce (Sweet Orange), **Gr. 1**, T303 **CD14:11**

Nativity, The (El nacimiento), **Gr. K**, T322 **CD18:1**

Naughty Kitty Cat, **Gr. 1**, T171 **CD7:34**

Navidad campesina, FC-Pri 46

Nest, The (El nido), **Gr. 3**, 214 **CD9:29**

Never Sleep Late Anymore, **Gr. 6**, 274 **CD15:23**

Neviděli jste tu mé panenky (Have You Not Seen My Daughters?), **Gr. 6**, 228 **CD12:10**

New Ashmolean Marching Society and Students Conservatory Band, The, **Gr. 6**, 308 **CD17:5**

New Day, The, **Gr. 4**, 316 **CD18:4**

New Year's Song (Suk San Wan Pi Mai), **Gr. 5**, 437 **CD25:24**

Ngam sang duan (Shining Moon), **Gr. 5**, 376 **CD22:23**

Nia, **Gr. 4**, 384 **CD22:4**

Niam Es, WM 69

Nigerian Boat Song (Eh Soom Boo Kawaya), **Gr. 3**, 58 **CD3:11**

Night Herding Song, **Gr. 4**, 110 **CD6:15**

Night of Stars/Silent Night , **Gr. 6**, 412 **CD22:19**

Night Song, **Gr. 3**, 186 **CD8:26**

Night That Goldman Spoke, The, **Gr. 7**, 246 **CD11:4**

Nikosi (Bluebirds), **Gr. 2**, 230 **CD12:2**

Nim Yog Xyoo Nuav (In This Year), WM 59

No despiertes a mi niño (Do Not Wake My Little Son), **Gr. 5**, 217 **CD12:14**

No One Like You, **Gr. 1**, T300 **CD14:4**

Noble Duke of York, The, **Gr. K**, T232 **CD13:10**

Nochebuena (Christmas Eve), **Gr. K,** T323 **CD18:5**
North Wind Blows (Bei Fang Chre), **Gr. 2,** 367 **CD19:1**
North Winds Blow, **Gr. K,** T305 **CD16:18**
Nottamun Town, **Gr. 5,** 405 **CD24:2**
Now (Achshav), **Gr. 4,** 112 **CD6:18**
Now Is the Hour (Haere Ra), **Gr. 5,** 151 **CD9:3**
Now We Are Going to Sing (Y ahora vamos a cantar), **Gr. K,** T340 **CD19:14**
O Christmas Tree! (O Tannenbaum!), **Gr. K,** T320 **CD17:26**
O Hal' Iwe (Nanticoke Women's Honoring Song), **Gr. 6,** 428 **CD23:18**
O Hanukkah (Oy Chanuke), **Gr. 3,** 368 **CD17:15**
O Mama Bakudala, **Gr. 3,** 328 **CD15:15**
O Tannenbaum! (O Christmas Tree!), **Gr. K,** T320 **CD17:25**
O, Desayo, **Gr. 6,** 50 **CD3:10**
O, I'm Gonna Sing, **Gr. 5,** 245 **CD14:1**
O, La Le!, **Gr. 6,** 6 **CD1:5**
O, the Train's Off the Track, **Gr. 3,** 176 **CD8:12**
Oats, Peas, Beans, and Barley Grow, **Pre-K,** 36; **Gr. K,** T287 **CD16:1**
Och Jungfrun Hon Går I Ringen (A Girl with a Shiny Ribbon), **Gr. 5,** 190 **CD11:1**
Octopus's Garden, **Gr. 4,** 30 **CD2:14**
Ogguere, **Gr. 4,** 327 **CD18:21**
Oh, A-Hunting We Will Go, **Gr. K,** T62 **CD3:18**
Oh, Come Sing a Song, **Gr. 7,** 65 **CD3:1**
Oh, How Lovely Is the Evening, **Gr. 6,** 252 **CD13:31**
Oh, Mama, Oh (Yo, Mamana, Yo), **Gr. 1,** T307 **CD14:21**
Oh, Shope, Shope (Shope, Shope), **Gr. 5,** 220 **CD12:20**
Oh, Susanna, **Gr. 3,** 153 **CD7:11**
Oh, the Thinks You Can Think!, **Gr. 2,** 276 **CD14:43**
Oh, Won't You Sit Down?, **Gr. 4,** 70 **CD4:18**
Old Abram Brown, **Gr. 4,** 32 **CD2:17**
Old Ark's A-Moverin', **Gr. 4,** 130 **CD7:5**
Old Aunt Dinah, **Gr. 4,** 245 **CD12:23**
Old Barn Dance, The, **Gr. 6,** 94 **CD5:25**
Old Blue, **Gr. 2,** 213 **CD11:5**
Old Carrion Crow, **Gr. 4,** 192 **CD9:21**
Old Dan Tucker, **Gr. 5,** 253 **CD14:25**
Old Gray Cat, The, **Pre-K,** 64; **Gr. K,** T43 **CD2:20**
Old House, **Gr. 4,** 282 **CD16:9**
Old Jim John, **Gr. 6,** 253 **CD13:34**
Old Joe Clark, **Gr. 4,** 74 **CD4:23**
Old King Glory, **Gr. 1,** T217 **CD10:4**
Old MacDonald Had a Farm, **Gr. K,** T211 **CD12:9**
Old Mister Rabbit, **Gr. 3,** 254 **CD11:31**
Old Mister Woodpecker, **Gr. K,** T172 **CD10:10**
Old Paint, **Gr. 4,** 275 **CD15:18**
Old Roger, **Gr. 3,** 280 **CD12:49**
Old Turkey Buzzard, **Gr. 5,** 264 **CD16:7**
Old Woman and the Pig, **Gr. 2,** 130 **CD7:12**
Ole La'u Papa e, **Gr. 6,** 91 **CD5:20**
Oleanna, **Gr. 3,** 144 **CD6:30**
Oliver Cromwell, **Gr. 4,** 269 **CD14:31**
Oliver Twist, **Gr. 2,** 268 **CD14:20**
Oma Rapeti (Run Rabbit), **Gr. 2,** 108 **CD6:6**
On a Clear Day, **Gr. 6,** 206 **CD11:6**
On Our Beautiful Planet Earth (En nuestra Tierra tan linda), **Gr. 2,** 114 **CD6:15**
On the Darkened Hillside (De aquel cerro), **Gr. 3,** 32 **CD2:3**

On the Sunny Side of the Street, **Gr. 5,** 361 **CD21:24**
On This Night, **Gr. K,** T315 **CD17:9**
On Top of Spaghetti, **Gr. 2,** 312 **CD16:5**
Once Upon a Christmastime, **Gr. 4,** 380 **CD21:30**
One Dime Blues, **Gr. 6,** 178 **CD10:1**
One Finger, One Thumb, **Gr. K,** T38 **CD2:12**
One Jar of Apples (Egy üveg alma), **Gr. 3,** 23 **CD1:27**
One Little Elephant, **Gr. 1,** T194 **CD8:32**
One More River, **Gr. 3,** 216 **CD10:2**
One of Those Songs, **Gr. 6,** 54 **CD3:19**
One Potato, Two Potato, **Gr. 3,** 267 **CD12:10**
One Small Voice, **Gr. 3,** F **Spotlight CD7**
One, Two, and Three (Uno, dos y tres), **Gr. 5,** 364 **CD22:1**
One, Two, Three, Four, Five, **Gr. 1,** T265 **CD12:28**
One, Two, Three, Four, **Gr. 1,** T123 **CD5:20**
One, Two, Tie My Shoe, **Gr. K,** T151 **CD9:1**
One-Eyed Ford, **Gr. 7,** 200 **CD8:18**
Open the Window, Noah, **Gr. 3,** 324 **CD15:1**
Orange Blossom Special, **Gr. 6,** 33 **CD2:6**
Orange Tree (Me gase boho), **Gr. 2,** 317 **CD16:15**
Orchestra Song, **Gr. 5,** 332 **CD20:6**
Orff Instruments (speech piece), **Gr. 2,** 183 **CD9:18**
Oro, My Bodeen, **Gr. 4,** 279 **CD15:34**
Other Spain, The (La otra España), **Gr. 4,** 62 **CD4:5**
Our Goodman, **Gr. 6,** 245 **CD13:1**
Our World, **Gr. 5,** 381 **CD22:31**
Out from the Wilderness, **Gr. 3,** 388 **CD18:28**
Out in the Meadow (Marken er mejet), **Gr. 4,** 364 **CD20:28**
Over in the Meadow, **Gr. 1,** T78 **CD3:17**
Over My Head, **Gr. 3,** 286 **CD13:17**
Over the Rainbow, **Gr. 4,** 126 **CD7:1**
Over the River and Through the Wood, **Gr. 4,** 370 **CD21:9**
Over the Sea to Skye, **Gr. 4,** 344 **CD19:24**
Owl and the Cuckoo, The, **Gr. 4,** 337 **CD19:8**
Owlet, The (El tecolote), **Gr. 6,** 392 **CD21:13**
Oy Chanuke (O Hanukkah), **Gr. 3,** 368 **CD17:15**
Oye como va (Listen How It Goes), **Gr. 5,** 69 **CD4:22**
Page's Train, **Gr. 4,** 246 **CD12:26**
Pairs or Pears, **Gr. 2,** 265 **CD14:7**
Pajarillo barranqueño (Little Bird), **Gr. 3,** 358 **CD16:25**
Pajaritos a volar, FC-Pri 31
Para dormir a un elefante, FC-Pri 19
Para pedir posada (Looking for Shelter), **Gr. 4,** 376 **CD21:22**
Parrot from Verapaz, A (Un lorito de Verapaz), **Gr. 5,** 349 **CD21:6**
Part of Your World, **Gr. 2,** 294 **CD15:4**
Pat on the Back, A, **Gr. 2,** 74 **CD4:18**
Pat Pat Patty Pat, **Gr. 1,** T308 **CD14:25**
Pat Works on the Railway, **Gr. 4,** 86 **CD5:11**
Pat-a-Pan, **Gr. 3,** 375 **CD17:28**
Path to the Moon, The, **Gr. 5,** 368 **CD22:9**
Patito color de café, FC-Pri 43
Patriotic Medley, **Gr. 1,** T8 **Spotlight CD4; Gr. 2,** H **Spotlight CD10; Gr. 3,** H **Spotlight CD10; Gr. 4,** G **Spotlight CD10; Gr. 5,** H **Spotlight CD10; Gr. 6,** H **Spotlight CD11**
Pauper sum ego (I Am Poor), **Gr. 6,** 254 **CD13:38**
Paw Paw Patch, The, **Gr. 3,** 195 **CD9:4**
Pay Me My Money Down, **Gr. 3,** 149 **CD7:5**

Peace and Quiet, **Gr. K,** T278 **CD15:14**
Peace in this House, **Gr. 7,** 152 **CD6:15**
Peace Round, **Gr. 4,** 16 **CD1:22**
Peanut Butter, **Gr. 1,** T218 **CD10:7**
Peanut Vendor (El manisero), **Gr. 4,** 106 **C 6:10**
Peasant's Dancing Day, **Gr. 4,** 132 **CD7:8**
Pease Porridge Hot, **Gr. 1,** T255 **CD11:38**
Perfect Winter Day, A, **Gr. 6,** 400 **CD21:28**
Peter Cottontail, **Gr. K,** T338 **CD19:10**
Pick a Bale of Cotton, **Gr. 6,** 254 **CD13:42**
Pick a Pumpkin, **Gr. 2,** 347 **CD17:25**
Pick-a-Little/Goodnight Ladies, **Gr. 5,** 299 **CD18:12**
Pimpón, **Gr. K,** T22 **CD1:12**
Piñón Pirulín, **Gr. 1,** T311 **CD15:1**
Pitty Patty Polt, **Gr. 1,** T180 **CD8:15**
Pizza, Pizza, Daddy-O, **Gr. 2,** 62 **CD4:1**
Place in the Choir, A, **Gr. 2,** 308 **CD15:32**
Plainsies, Clapsies, **Gr. 2,** 248 **CD12:33**
Planting Seeds, **Gr. K,** T284 **CD15:50**
Plate Passing (Sara Watashi), **Gr. 1,** T67 **CD2:40**
Play the Bugle (Diana), **Gr. 1,** T334 **CD16:1**
Please, Mr. Postman, **Gr. 4,** 44 **CD3:4**
Pleeng loy krathong (Full Moon Song), **Gr. 6,** 398 **CD21:26**
Plenty Fishes in the Sea, **Pre-K,** 27; **Gr. 1,** T310 **CD14:28**
Polly Wolly Doodle, **Gr. 3,** 132 **CD6:15**
Pop! Goes the Weasel, **Gr. 5,** 94 **CD6:2**
Popping Corn, **Gr. K,** T161 **CD9:18**
Powama, **Gr. 7,** 63 **CD2:19**
Power of the Dream, The, **Gr. 5,** 44 **CD3:5**
Preamble, The, **Gr. 3,** 293 **CD13:23**
Presidents, **Gr. K,** T330 **CD18:23**
Pretty Girl (Bella bimba), **Gr. 3,** 172 **C 8:4**
Propel, Propel, Propel, **Gr. K,** T275 **CD15:44**
Puddle Hopping, **Gr. 1,** T60 **CD2:25**
Puff, the Magic Dragon, **Gr. 2,** 54 **CD3:17**
Pumpkin Song, **Gr. 1,** T342 **CD16:19**
Punchinella, **Gr. 1,** T216 **CD10:1**
Pung Noy Loy Kratong (Full Moon Float), WM 55
Purim (Ani Purim), **Gr. 2,** 372 **CD19:15**
Pusa't daga (Cat and Rat), **Gr. 1,** T289 **CD13:28**
Push Boat Song, **Gr. 4,** 266 **CD14:20**
Put on a Costume, **Gr. 1,** T336 **CD16:7**
Put Your Finger in the Air, **Gr. K,** T230 **CD13:7**
Quaker, Quaker, **Gr. 1,** T100 **CD4:17**
Qué bonita bandera (What a Beautiful Flag), **Gr. 5,** 442 **CD26:5**
Qué bonito es (How Wonderful It Is), **Gr. K,** T234 **CD13:13**
Que llueva (It's Raining), **Gr. 3,** 274 **CD12:29**
¿Quién es ese pajarito? (Who Is That Little Bird?), **Gr. 4,** 284 **CD16:17**
Raccoon Dance Song, **Gr. 3,** 87 **CD4:8**
Rage and Roar, **Gr. 6,** 48 **CD3:7**
Ragtime Epilogue and Finale, **Gr. 7,** 250 **CD11:6**
Ragtime, **Gr. 7,** 237 **CD11:1**
Rain (Ame fure), **Gr. 4,** 26 **CD2:9**
Rain Is Falling Down, **Gr. 3,** 242 **CD11:1**
Rain, Rain, Go Away, **Pre-K,** 76; **Gr. 1,** T259 **CD12:13**
Rainbow Connection, The, **Gr. 3,** 310 **CD14:7**
Rainbow Song, The, **Gr. K,** T61 **CD3:15**
Rattlesnake, **Gr. 1,** T185 **CD8:21; Gr. 3,** 72 **CD3:28**

Raza de mil colores, FC-Int 3
Reach, **Gr. 5,** 14 **CD1:16**
Recycle Rap, **Gr. 3,** 332 **CD15:27**
Red Iron Ore, **Gr. 6,** 134 **CD7:25**
Red Mule (Eka Muda), **Gr. 5,** 28 **CD2:9**
Red Rover, **Gr. 2,** 249 **CD12:36**
Respect (two versions), **Gr. 7,** 5 **CD1:2**
Riddle, A (Una adivinanza), **Gr. 1,** T138 **CD6:15**
Riddle Song, **Gr. 2,** 251 **CD12:45**
Ride Like the Wind, **Gr. 5,** 130 **CD7:17**
Ride on the Wind, **Gr. 6,** 326 **CD17:33**
Ride the Train, **Gr. K,** T144 **CD8:15**
Ridin' of a Goat, Leadin' of a Sheep, **Gr. 4,** 251 **CD13:5**
Riding in the Buggy, **Gr. 3,** 131 **CD6:12**
Riding on an Elephant (Monté sur un éléphant), **Gr. K,** T217 **CD12:20**
Riding, Riding, Is Mr. Postman (Jede, jede poštovský panáček), **Gr. 6,** 226 **CD12:2**
Rig a Jig Jig, **Gr. 1,** T116 **CD5:8**
Ring Around the Rosy, **Gr. K,** T246 **CD14:8**
Riqui Ran (Sawing Song), **Gr. 2,** 21 **CD1:29**
Rise Up Singin', **Gr. 3,** 138 **CD6:22**
Rise Up, O Flame, **Gr. 4,** 283 **CD16:12**
Rise Up, Shepherd, and Follow, **Gr. 5,** 422 **CD25:4**
Rise, Sally, Rise, **Pre-K,** 14; **Gr. 1,** T162 **CD7:16**
Risseldy, Rosseldy, **Gr. 6,** 264 **CD14:25**
River Come Down, **Gr. 8,** 10 **CD1:6**
River Come Down, CM 29
River of My People, **Gr. 6,** 176 **CD9:23**
River Overflowing (Dere Geliyor), **Gr. 6,** 232 **CD12:18**
Rock and Roll Is Here to Stay, **Gr. 5,** 316 **CD19:17**
Rock Around the Clock, **Gr. 6,** 234 **CD12:22**
Rock Island, **Gr. 5,** 291 **CD18:9**
Rock of Ages (Ma'oz Tsur), **Gr. 6,** 405 **CD22:2**
Rocky Top, **Gr. 5,** 352 **CD21:11**
Roll de Ole Chariot Along, **Gr. 6,** 243 **CD12:32**
Roll on, Columbia, **Gr. 4,** 182 **CD9:8**
Rooster, The (Kum Bachur), **Gr. 3,** 75 **CD3:31**
Round and Round, **Gr. 6,** 104 **CD6:13**
'Round and 'Round (A la rueda rueda), **Gr. 1,** T240 **CD11:6**
Round Dance (Tsiothwatasè:tha), **Gr. 6,** 109 **CD6:21**
'Round the Corner, Sally, **Gr. 5,** 251 **CD14:19**
Rover, **Gr. 2,** 260 **CD13:37**
Row, Row, Row Your Boat, **Gr. 4,** 268 **CD14:28**
Row, Row, Row, **Gr. K,** T274 **CD15:43**
Rudolph, the Red-Nosed Reindeer, **Gr. 1,** T354 **CD17:12**
Run, Rabbit (Oma Rapeti), **Gr. 2,** 108 **CD6:6**
Sail Away, Ladies, **Gr. 4,** 54 **CD3:20**
Sailor Went to Sea, Sea, Sea, A, **Pre-K,** 56; **Gr. 1,** T38 **CD1:36**
Sailor, Sailor on the Sea, **Gr. 2,** 262 **CD13:47**
Saint Lucia (Sankta Lucia), **Gr. 5,** 413 **CD24:15**
Sakura (Cherry Blossoms), **Gr. 6,** 14 **CD1:19**
Sakura (Cherry Blossoms), WM 35
Salamanca Market, **Gr. 6,** 247 **CD13:7**
Sally Go 'Round the Sun, **Gr. 2,** 268 **CD14:23**
Samba de Orfeu (Dance of Orpheus), **Gr. 6,** 190 **CD10:20**
Samiotissa, **Gr. 5,** 284 **CD18:1**
Sammy Sackett, **Gr. 2,** 146 **CD8:2**
San Lun Tsa (Three-Wheeled Taxi), WM 45

Alphabetical Index of Songs and Speech Pieces

San Serení, **Gr. 2**, 323 **CD16:29**

Sandpiper, The ('Ulili E), **Gr. 4**, 396 **CD22:28**

Sandy McNab, **Gr. 4**, 142 **CD7:23**

Sankta Lucia (Saint Lucia), **Gr. 5**, 413 **CD24:15**

Sansa kroma (Little Hawk), **Gr. 4**, 166 **CD8:15**

Santa Clara Corn Grinding Song, **Gr. K**, T164 **CD9:26**

Santa Marta, **Gr. 5**, 398 **CD23:18**

Sara Watashi (Plate Passing), **Gr. 1**, T67 **CD2:40**

Sarasponda, **Gr. 4**, 210 **CD10:15**

Sarika Kaio (Myna Birds), WM 11

Sasara Ang Bulaklak (The Flower Fades), WM 13

Saw, Saw Lumberjack (Serra, serra serrador), **Gr. 1**, T131, T133 **CD6:7**

Sawing Song (Riqui Ran), **Gr. 2**, 21 **CD1:29**

Say Your Name, **Gr. 2**, 243 **CD12:19**

School Bells (Hakyo Jong), **Gr. 1**, T302 **CD14:7**

Scotland's Burning, **Gr. 3**, 257 **CD11:41**

Scraping Up Sand, **Gr. 6**, 248 **CD13:13**

Sea Shell, **Gr. 4**, 245 **CD12:20**

Sea, The (La mar), **Gr. 3**, 110 **CD5:9**

Season of Hope, The, **Gr. 5**, 410 **CD24:12**

See the Pony Galloping, **Gr. K**, T44 **CD2:23**

See the Rabbit Running, **Gr. 3**, 255 **CD11:34**

Seeds and Seasons, **Gr. 2**, 206 **CD10:20**

Seeds, **Gr. 1**, T120 **CD5:16**

Seesaw, **Gr. 1**, T242 **CD11:11**

Seesaw, Margery Daw, **Gr. K**, T264 **CD15:1**

Send Us Your Peace (Fun wa ni alaafia), **Gr. 5**, 248 **CD14:9**

Serpent from the Sea, The (La víbora de la mar), **Gr. 5**, 440 **CD26:1**

Serra, serra serrador (Saw, Saw Lumberjack), **Gr. 1**, T131, T133 **CD6:7**

Sesame Street, **Gr. 1**, T298 **CD14:1**

Seussical Mega-Mix, **Gr. 2**, 287 **CD14:48**

Seven Evenings (Tanabata), **Gr. 3**, 62 **CD3:15**

Seventy-Six Trombones, **Gr. 5**, 296 **CD18:11**

Shabat Shalom, **Gr. 4**, 170 **CD8:20**

Shady Grove, **Gr. 6**, 286 **CD16:17**

Shake My Sillies Out, **Gr. K**, T175 **CD10:13**

Shake the Papaya Down, **Gr. 2**, 90 **CD5:9**

Shalom Chaveyrim (Shalom, My Friends), **Gr. 3**, 141 **CD6:25**

Shalom, My Friends (Shalom Chaveyrim), **Gr. 3**, 141 **CD6:25**

She'll Be Comin' 'Round the Mountain, **Gr. 2**, 33 **CD2:9**

Sheep in the Meadow (speech piece), **Gr. 2**, 8 **CD1:7**

Sheep Shearing, **Pre-K**, 26; **Gr. 2**, 102 **CD5:29**

Shenandoah, **Gr. 4**, D **Spotlight CD4**

Shepherd, Shepherd, **Gr. 3**, 56 **CD 3:8**

Shiau Ya (Little Duck), WM 7

Shibolet Basadeh (Wheat in the Field), **Gr. 6**, 424 **CD23:10**

Shining Moon (Ngam sang duan), **Gr. 5**, 376 **CD22:23**

Shining Star (Estrella brillante), **Gr. 5**, 373 **CD22:17**

Ship Ahoy, **Gr. 3**, 314 **CD14:14**

Ship in Distress, The, **Gr. 6**, 211 **CD11:12**

Shoes of John, **Gr. 6**, 246 **CD13:4**

Shoheen Sho, **Gr. 2**, 140 **CD7:28**

Shoo Fly Pie and Apple Pan Dowdy, **Gr. 3**, 227 **CD10:19**

Shoo, Fly, **Gr. 2**, 222 **CD11:22**

Shoo, Turkey, **Gr. 1**, T76 **CD3:14**

Shope Shope (Oh, Shope, Shope), **Gr. 5**, 220 **CD12:20**

Shrimp Boats, **Gr. 2**, 179 **CD9:7**

Sick Little Donkey, The (El burrito enfermo), **Gr. 2**, 180 **CD9:11**

Side Show, The, **Gr. 5**, 283 **CD17:31**

Simi Yadech (Give Me Your Hand), **Gr. K**, T168 **CD10:2**

Simon Says, **Gr. 3**, 4 **CD1:1**

Simple Gifts, **Gr. 5**, 136 **CD8:1**

Simple Simon (speech piece), **Gr. 1**, T175 **CD8:8**

Sing a Little Song, **Gr. K**, T179 **CD10:18**

Sing a Song of Sixpence, **Gr. K**, T111 **CD6:24**

Sing after Me, **Gr. 1**, T34 **CD1:32**

Sing Alleluia (Hava Nashira), **Gr. 6**, 67 **CD4:14**

Sing Alleluia, Allelu, **Gr. 4**, 220 **CD11:11**

Sing Hosanna, **Gr. 6**, 362 **CD19:20**

Sing! Sing! Sing!, **Gr. 2**, 196 **CD10:7**

Sing, America Sing!, **Gr. 5**, 6 **CD1:5**

Sing, Sing, Sing, **Gr. 5**, 30 **CD2:13**

Singabahambayo (An Army Is Marching) (unison), **Gr. 5**, 56 **CD4:1**; (parts), **Gr. 5**, 76 **CD4:1**

Sitsiritsit, **Gr. 4**, 102 **CD6:5**

Sittin' Down to Eat, **Gr. 1**, T182 **CD8:18**

Six Little Ducks, **Gr. 1**, T64 **CD2:33**

Sixteen Tons, **Gr. 7**, 151 **CD6:12**

Skating, **Gr. 2**, 350 **CD17:32**

Skin and Bones, **Gr. 1**, T340 **CD16:13**

Skinnamarink, **Gr. 2**, 368 **CD19:5**

Skip to My Lou, **Gr. 1**, T102 **CD4:20**

Sky Dances, **Gr. 4**, 206 **CD10:8**

Slap That Bass, **Gr. 6**, 146 **CD8:15**

Sleep (Bu-Vah), **Gr. 4**, 18 **CD1:27**

Sleep, Bonnie Bairnie, **Gr. 1**, T26 **CD1:20**

Smilin', **Gr. 8**, 80 **CD4:9**

Smoke Goes Up the Chimney, **Gr. 3**, 272 **CD12:23**

Snail With the Mail, **Gr. 1**, T275 **CD13:3**

Snail, Snail, **Gr. 1**, T252 **CD11:31**

Snowman, The, **Gr. K**, T313 **CD17:3**

Somebody Come and Play, **Gr. 1**, T92 **CD4:1**

Somebody's Knockin' at Your Door, **Gr. 5**, 254 **CD14:28**

Something For Me, Something For You, **Gr. 4**, 4 **CD1:1**

Something Funny Outside, **Gr. 1**, T338 **CD16:10**

Sometimes I Feel Like a Motherless Child, **Gr. 6**, 271 **CD15:9**

Somos el barco (We Are the Boat), **Gr. 4**, 10 **CD1:8**

Song of Peace, **Gr. 5**, 257 **CD15:8**

Song of Thanksgiving, **Gr. 4**, 371 **CD21:12**

Sorida, **Gr. 2**, 96 **CD5:17**

Sound the Trumpet, **Gr. 5**, 279 **CD17:22**

Soup, Soup, **Gr. 1**, T358 **CD17:30**

Southern Nights, **Gr. 5**, 310 **CD19:8**

Soy así, FC-Int 66

Sparrows' Singing School, The (Chichipapa), **Gr. 2**, 22 **CD1:33**

Speckled Bird, The (La pájara pinta), **Gr. 6**, 268 **CD14:32**

Speedy Delivery, **Gr. K**, T279 **CD15:47**

Spiders, **Gr. 3**, 282 **CD13:5**

Spring, **Gr. 1**, T273 **CD13:2**

Spring Has Come! (Bohm), **Gr. 3**, 392 **CD19:2**

Spring Valley, Flower Valley (Bohm Dong Sahn, Gohd Dong Sahn), **Gr. K**, T337 **CD19:6**

St. Patrick's Day, **Gr. 5**, 434 **CD25:20**

Stamping Land, **Pre-K**, 46; **Gr. K**, T24 **CD 1:19**

Star Canon, **Gr. 5**, 367 **CD22:6**

Star Light, Star Bright, **Gr. 1**, T258 **CD12:9**

Stars and Stripes Forever, The, **Gr. 6**, 390 **CD21:9**

Star-Spangled Banner, The, **Gr. 4**, 356 **CD20:14; Gr. 5**, 386 **CD22:35; Gr. 6**, 386 **CD20:21; Gr. 7**, 194 **CD8:12**

Step in Time, **Gr. 2**, 6 **CD1:4**

Step into the Spotlight, **Gr. 1**, T7 **Spotlight CD1; Gr. 2**, A **Spotlight CD1; Gr. 3**, A **Spotlight CD1; Gr. 4**, A **Spotlight CD1; Gr. 5**, A **Spotlight CD1; Gr. 6**, A **Spotlight CD1**

Stevedore's Song, **Gr. 3**, 127 **CD6:4**

Stewpot, Stewpot, Bottomless Pot (Nabe, Nabe, Soku, Nuke), **Gr. 2**, 259 **CD13:33**

Stir, Stir (Bate, bate), **Gr. 2**, 242 **CD12:15**

Strawberry Roan, **Gr. 2**, 66 **CD4:5**

Streets of Laredo, **Gr. 5**, 260 **CD15:19**

Success, **Gr. 7**, 241 **CD11:2**

Sugar in the Gourd, **Gr. 6**, 251 **CD13:27**

Suk San Wan Pi Mai (New Year's Song), **Gr. 5**, 437 **CD25:24**

Suk San Wan Pi Mai (New Year's Song), WM 43

Suliram, **Gr. 6**, 59 **CD3:28**

Sun and Rain (Hae Wa Be), **Gr. 6**, 273 **CD15:17**

Sun Don't Set in the Mornin', **Gr. 3**, 48, 60 **CD2:27**

Suomen Salossa (The Finnish Forest), **Gr. 6**, 422 **CD23:5**

Surfin' U.S.A., **Gr. 5**, 306 **CD19:1**

Susanita tiene un ratón, FC-Pri 3

S'vivon Sov (Dreidel Spin), **Gr. 1**, T348 **CD16:33; Gr. 4**, 374 **CD21:18**

Swapping Song, **Gr. 4**, 253 **CD13:12**

Swaying Pandanus Trees, The (Nani Wale Na Hala), **Gr. 5**, 276 **CD17:11**

Sweep, Sweep Away, **Gr. 3**, 276 **CD12:36**

Sweet and Low, **Gr. 6**, 184 **CD10:10**

Sweet Music, **Gr. 5**, 319 **CD19:23**

Sweet Orange (Naranja dulce), **Gr. 1**, T303 **CD14:11**

Sweet Potatoes, **Gr. 3**, 16 **CD1:21**

Sweetly Sings the Donkey, **Gr. K**, T244 **CD14:4**

Swing, The, **Gr. 4**, 320 **CD18:11**

Tai Yau Tsai (Herding the Cows), WM 37

Tain't What You Do, **Gr. 6**, 18 **CD 1:24**

Tak for Maden (Thanks for Food), **Gr. 1**, T343 **CD16:22**

Take Me Out to the Ball Game, **Gr. 2**, 56 **CD3:20**

Take Time in Life, **Gr. 4**, 156 **CD8:4**

Tako No Uta (The Kite Song), **Gr. 1**, T370 **CD18:25**

Tanabata (Seven Evenings), **Gr. 3**, 62 **CD3:15**

Tang Tang Juen (Round, Round, Turn), WM 19

Taps, **Gr. 3**, 281 **CD13:2**

'Taters (Bulbes), **Gr. 6**, 280 **CD15:40**

Tea Leaves (Hojas de té) (speech piece), **Gr. 4**, 256 **CD13:20**

Teddy Bear, **Pre-K**, 66

Tekanionton'néha' (Alligator Dance), **Gr. 5**, 223 **CD12:27**

Ten in a Bed, **Gr. K**, T256 **CD14:23**

Ten Little Frogs, **Gr. K**, T240 **CD13:24**

Tengo, Tengo, Tengo (I Have, I Have, I Have), **Gr. K**, T212 **CD12:12**

Tết Trung (Children's Festival), **Gr. 4**, 366 **CD21:1**

Tết Trung (Children's Festival), WM 53

Thank You, **Gr. 2**, 349 **CD17:29**

Thanks for Food (Tak for Maden), **Gr. 1**, T343 **CD16:22**

That Great Come and Get It Day, **Gr. 6**, 306 **CD17:1**

The Birch Tree (Beryoza), **Gr. 4**, 286 **CD16:25**

There Are Many Flags in Many Lands, **Gr. 1**, T328 **CD15:24; Gr. 2**, 341 **CD17:9**

There Was a Blue Flower, **Gr. 6**, 221 **CD11:24**

There Was a Jolly Miller, **Gr. 6**, 250 **CD13:24**

There's a Hole in the Bucket, **Gr. 2**, 132 **CD7:15**

There's a Hole in the Middle of the Sea, **Gr. 1**, T178 **CD8:12**

There's a Little Wheel A-Turnin' in My Heart, **Gr. 3**, 129, 137 **CD6:9**

There's a Song in Me, (melody) **Gr. 5**, 164 **CD 9:14**; (2-part) **Gr. 5**, 183 **CD9:14**

There's No Hidin' Place, **Gr. 5**, 266 **CD16:14**

These Lights (Haneirot Halalu), **Gr. 5**, 414 **CD24:21**

They Call the Wind Maria, **Gr. 6**, 312 **CD17:12**

They Were Tall, **Gr. K**, T52 **CD3:3**

Things I'm Thankful For, **Gr. K**, T308 **CD16:28**

This a Way and That a Way, **Gr. 3**, 386 **CD18:24**

This Is America, **Gr. 3**, 356 **CD16:19**

This is Christmas Eve (Ésta sí que es Nochebuena), **Gr. 2**, 361 **CD18:21**

This Is Halloween, **Gr. 2**, 346 **CD17:21**

This Is My City, **Gr. K**, T120 **CD7:4**

This Is My Country, **Gr. 2**, 87 **CD5:2**

This Is What I Can Do, **Gr. K**, T123 **CD7:8**

This Land Is Your Land, **Gr. 4**, 146 **CD7:28**

This Little Light of Mine, **Pre-K**, 7; **Gr. 1**, T238 **CD11:2; Gr. 2**, F **Spotlight CD7**

This Old Man, **Gr. 1**, T306 **CD14:18**

This Pretty Planet, **Gr. 6**, 194 **CD10:25**

This Train, **Gr. 4**, 343 **CD19:20**

Three is a Magic Number, **Gr. 3**, 296 **CD13:24**

Three Little Birds, **Gr. 3**, 204 **CD9:15**

Three Little Kittens, **Gr. K**, T148 **CD8:24**

Three Little Muffins (speech piece), **Gr. K**, T127 **CD7:11**

Three Little Penguins (speech piece), **Gr. 2**, 112 **CD6:12**

Throw It in the Slope (Jikel' emaweni), **Gr. 6**, 70 **CD4:22**

Throw It Out the Window, **Gr. 3**, 94 **CD4:19**

Tiki Tiki Tiki Room, The, **Gr. 2**, 324 **CD16:33**

Tim McCoy, FC-Int 79

Time for Love, A, **Gr. 1**, T347 **CD16:30**

Time to Sing, **Gr. K**, T16 **CD1:4**

Times They Are A-Changin', The, **Gr. 5**, 204 **CD11:23**

Tina singu, **Gr. 6**, 36 **CD2:13**

Tinga Layo, **Gr. 2**, 50 **CD3:8**

Tinker, Tailor, **Gr. 1**, T130 **CD6:4**

Tiny Boat, The (El barquito), **Gr. 4**, 214 **CD11:1**

Tititorea (Maori Stick Game), WM 31

Tititorea, **Gr. 3**, 174 **CD8:8**

To the Wheel of San Miguel (A la rueda de San Miguel), **Gr. 2**, 60 **CD3:27**

To the Woods I Will Not Go (Já do lesa nepojedu), **Gr. 6**, 227 **CD12:6**

Tomorrow, **Gr. 4**, 295 **CD17:2**

Toodala, **Gr. K**, T39 **CD2:15**

Touch Your Shoulders, **Gr. K**, T254 **CD14:20**

Town Hall Halloween Ball, **Gr. K**, T306 **CD16:21**

Train Comes, The (Mbombela), **Gr. K**, T152 **CD9:4**

Train Is A-Coming, **Gr. 4**, 270 **CD15:1**

Train, The (El tren), **Gr. 2**, 326 **CD16:36**

Trampin', **Gr. 3**, 287 **CD13:20**

Alphabetical Index of Songs and Speech Pieces (continued)

Traveling Together (Jó ashílá), **Gr. 5,** 224 **CD13:2**
Treasure Chests, **Gr. 3,** 90 **CD4:15**
Tree of Peace (speech piece), **Gr. K,** T320 **CD17:22**
Triple Play, **Gr. 5,** 355 **CD21:15**
Troika, **Gr. 6,** 230 **CD12:15**
Trout, The, **Gr. 6,** 342 **CD18:17**
Tsing Chun U Chü (Youth Dance Song), **Gr. 6,** 272 **CD15:13**
Tsing Chun U Chü (Youth Dance Song), WM 113
Tsiothwatasè:tha (Round Dance), **Gr. 6,** 109 **CD6:21**
Tugboat, **Gr. K,** T95 **CD5:22**
Tum Balalaika, **Gr. 6,** 68 **CD4:18**
Tumbai, **Gr. 5,** 194 **CD11:8**
Turn the Glasses Over, **Gr. 3,** 260 **CD11:50**
Turn the World Around, **Gr. 5,** 208 **CD12:1**
Twenty-four Robbers, **Gr. 1,** T173 **CD8:1**
Twinkle, Twinkle, Little Star, **Pre-K,** 76; **Gr. K,** T90 **CD5:16**
Twist and Shout, **Gr. 4,** 314 **CD18:1; Gr. 7,** 160 **CD7:7**
Two, Four, Six, Eight, **Gr. 1,** T246 **CD11:17**
Tzena, Tzena, **Gr. 5,** 171 **CD9:26**
Ua txiab (The Village), **Gr. 6,** 394 **CD21:18**
Ua Txiab, WM 49
Ucha Tirvarch (Little Bear Song), **Gr. 3,** 53 **CD3:4**
Uga Uga Uga (Cake, Cake, Cake!), **Gr. 1,** T313 **CD15:8**
Ujamaa, **Gr. 3,** 380 **CD18:11**
Ujima, **Gr. 5,** 427 **CD25:9**
`Ulili E (The Sandpiper), **Gr. 4,** 396 **CD22:28**
Un lorito de Verapaz (A Parrot from Verapaz), **Gr. 5,** 349 **CD21:6**
Un, dos, tres, FC-Int 70
Una adivinanza (A Riddle), **Gr. 1,** T138 **CD6:15**
Uncle Jessie, **Gr. 3,** 327 **CD15:11**
Uncle Pen, **Gr. 5,** 24 **CD2:2**
Uno de enero (First of January), **Gr. 3,** 210 **CD9:24**
Uno, dos y tres (One, Two, and Three), **Gr. 5,** 364 **CD22:1**
Up on the Housetop, **Gr. 2,** 356 **CD18:9**
Ushkana (Damselfly Song), **Gr. K,** T75 **CD4:15**
Üsküdar, **Gr. 5,** 128 **CD7:13**
Üsküdar, WM 65
Uyai Mose (Come All You People), **Gr. 7,** 66 **CD3:7**
Vamos a contar, FC-Int 83
Vamos a jugar, FC-Pri 77
Vamos a la mar (Let's Go to the Sea), **Gr. 3,** 256 **CD11:37**
Vem Kan Segla (Who Can Sail?), **Gr. 6,** 419 **CD22:28**
Village, The (El quelite), **Gr. 4,** 362 **CD20:23**
Village, The (Ua txiab), **Gr. 6,** 394 **CD21:18**
Viva la musica, **Gr. 4,** 174 **CD8:28**
Viva Valentine!, **Gr. 1,** T364 **CD18:13**
Vive l'amour, **Gr. 5,** 262 **CD16:1**
Wabash Cannonball, The, **Gr. 6,** 30 **CD2:2**
Wachet auf (Waken Now), **Gr. 6,** 259 **CD14:10**
Wait and See, **Gr. K,** T334 **CD19:1**
Waiting for Life, **Gr. 6,** 292 **CD16:21**
Wake Me, Shake Me, **Gr. 1,** T198 **CD9:6**
Wake Up Canon, **Gr. 4,** 326 **CD18:18**
Wake Up the Sun, **Gr. 2,** 124 **CD7:1**
Waken Now (Wachet auf), **Gr. 6,** 259 **CD14:10**
Walk by the River, **Gr. 6,** 74 **CD5:2**
Walk in the Parlor, **Gr. 4,** 226 **CD11:21**
Walk to School, **Gr. K,** T18 **CD1:8**

Walking in the Air, **Gr. 4,** 317 **CD18:7**
Wang Ü Ger (Chinese Fishing Song), **Gr. 3,** 190 **CD8:32**
Wang Ü Ger (Chinese Fishing Song), WM 29
Water Come a Me Eye, **Gr. 4,** 90 **CD5:17**
Water Is Wide, The, **Gr. 6,** 46 **CD3:4**
Water Wheels, The (Mizuguruma), **Gr. 1,** T260 **CD12:16**
Water, Water (Mayim, Mayim), **Gr. 6,** 102 **CD6:9**
Wavvuuvuumira (Mister Bamboo Bug), **Gr. K,** T165 **CD9:27**
Way Down South (speech piece) **Gr. 3,** 8 **CD1:7**
'Way Down Yonder in the Brickyard, **Gr. 5,** 255 **CD15:1**
Wayfaring Stranger, **Gr. 6,** 283 **CD16:8**
We All Sing with the Same Voice, **Gr. 1,** T156 **CD7:7**
We Are Here, **Gr. 4,** 394 **CD22:24**
We Are Playing in the Forest, **Gr. K,** T248 **CD14:11**
We Are the Boat (Somos el barco), **Gr. 4,** 10 **CD1:8**
We Are the Children of Tomorrow, **Gr. 5,** 114 **CD6:24**
We Go Together, **Gr. 7,** 158 **CD7:4**
We Got the Beat, **Gr. 4,** 310 **CD17:22**
We Remember, **Gr. 4,** 360 **CD20:20**
We Shall Overcome, **Gr. 4,** 387 **CD22:8; Gr. 7,** 212 **CD9:12**
We Want to Sing, **Gr. 5,** 235 **CD13:17**
We'll Be Playing in the Forest (Jugaremos en el bosque), **Gr. 2,** 188 **CD9:26**
We Wish You a Merry Christmas, **Gr. 2,** 358 **CD18:12**
We're Sailing Down the River, **Gr. 2,** 166 **CD8:25**
Wéané, **Gr. 3,** 184 **CD8:22**
Wee Falorie Man, The, **Gr. 2,** 375 **CD19:21**
Welcome Is the Month of May, **Gr. 2,** 378 **CD19:28**
Wells Fargo Wagon, The, **Gr. 5,** 303 **CD18:13**
What a Beautiful Flag (Qué bonita bandera), **Gr. 5,** 442 **CD26:5**
What a Wonderful World, **Gr. 2,** 84 **CD4:31**
What Can One Little Person Do?, **Gr. 4,** 204 **CD10:5**
What Did Delaware?, **Gr. 2,** 190 **CD9:32**
What the World Needs Now, **Gr. 5,** 230 **CD13:12**
What You Gonna Call Your Pretty Little Baby?, **Gr. K,** T319 **CD17:19**
What's Your Name?, **Gr. 1,** T125 **CD5:26**
Wheat in the Field (Shibolet Basadeh), **Gr. 6,** 424 **CD23:10**
When I First Came to This Land, **Gr. 3,** 28 **CD1:32**
When I Sing, **Gr. 6,** 44 **CD3:1**
When I Was Young, **Gr. 4,** 187 **CD9:12**
When Johnny Comes Marching Home, **Gr. 5,** 34 **CD2:18**
When the Flag Goes By, **Gr. 1,** T327 **CD15:18**
When the Saints Go Marching In, **Gr. 5,** 256 **CD15:5**
When You Send a Valentine, **Gr. K,** T332 **CD18:29**
Where Is John?, **Gr. 5,** 274 **CD17:1**
White Jasmine Flower, The (Dok Djampa), **Gr. 4,** 392 **CD22:20**
Who Can Sail? (Vem Kan Segla), **Gr. 6,** 419 **CD22:28**
Who Chopped the Cherry Tree Down?, **Gr. 2,** 371 **CD19:12**
Who Has the Penny?, **Gr. 2,** 252 **CD13:2**
Who Is That Little Bird? (¿Quién es ese pajarito?), **Gr. 4,** 284 **CD 16:17**
Who's Got the Fishpole?, **Gr. 4,** 261 **CD14:5**
Who's That Tapping at the Window?, **Gr. 2,** 261 **CD13:40**
Who's That Yonder? **Gr. 3,** 245 **CD11:11**

Why We Tell the Story, **Gr. 6,** 303 **CD16:23**

Wie schön leuchtet der Morgenstern (How Brightly Shines the Morning Star), **Gr. 5,** 370 **CD22:12**

Wild Geese (Kari), **Gr. 1,** T260 **CD12:20**

Willoughby Wallaby Woo, **Gr. K,** T241 **CD13:27**

Willowbee, **Gr. 2,** 69 **CD4:11**

Willum, **Gr. 1,** T19 **CD1:12**

Wind Beneath My Wings, The, **Gr. 6,** E **Spotlight CD8**

Wind Blew East, The, **Pre-K,** 74; **Gr. 1,** T234 **CD10:31**

Wind Blow, **Gr. 1,** T187 **CD8:24**

Winter ade (G Major), **Gr. 6,** 132 **CD7:18;** (G Minor), **Gr. 6,** 133 **CD7:22**

Winter is Over (L'inverno è già passato), **Gr. 4,** 390 **CD22:15**

Winter Wonderland, **Gr. 5,** 408 **CD24:8**

Woke Up This Morning, **Gr. 3,** 180 **CD8:16**

Won't You Be My Neighbor?, **Gr. K,** T268 **CD15:39**

Wonderful City (Cidade Maravilhosa), **Gr. 5,** 432 **CD25:15**

Wondering, **Gr. 6,** 282 **CD16:5**

Woodchuck, **Gr. 3,** 246 **CD11:14**

Woodpecker, The (speech piece), **Gr. 4,** 48 **CD3:10**

Words of Wisdom, **Gr. 5,** 244 **CD13:25**

Worms, **Gr. K,** T286 **CD15:53**

Y ahora vamos a cantar (Now We Are Going to Sing), **Gr. K,** T340 **CD19:14**

Yakety Yak, **Gr. 5,** 308 **CD19:5**

Yanai (The Elephant), **Gr. 2,** 305 **CD15:23**

Yankee Doodle, **Pre-K,** 87; **Gr. 2,** 340 **CD17:6; Gr. 4,** 154 **CD8:1**

Yankee Doodle Boy, **Gr. 3,** 357 **CD16:22**

Year With Frog and Toad, A, **Gr. 1,** T270 **CD13:1;** (Reprise), **Gr. 1,** T283 **CD13:6**

Yellow Bird, CM 25

Yellow Bird, **Gr. 6,** 154 **CD8:27**

Yellow Submarine, **Gr. 3,** 320 **CD14:25**

Yerakina, **Gr. 6,** 216 **CD11:19**

Yo, Mamana, Yo (Oh, Mama, Oh), **Gr. 1,** T307 **CD14:21**

You Are My Sunshine, **Gr. 2,** 369 **CD19:8**

You Sing for Me, **Gr. 6,** 106 **CD6:17**

You'll Sing a Song and I'll Sing a Song, **Gr. 2,** 156 **CD8:13**

You're a Grand Old Flag, **Gr. K,** T4 **Spotlight CD4; Gr. 3,** 355 **CD16:16**

You're Never Fully Dressed Without a Smile, **Gr. 4,** 304 **CD17:5**

You've Got a Friend in Me, **Gr. 2,** 44 **CD2:24**

Youth Dance Song (Tsing Chun U Chü), **Gr. 6,** 272 **CD15:13**

Yüe lìang wan wan (Crescent Moon), **Gr. 6,** 26 **CD1:34**

Zudio, **Gr. 7,** 164 **CD7:15**

Zui Zui Zukkorbashi (Mouse in the Rice Sack), **Gr. 1,** T98 **CD4:13**

Zum gali gali, **Gr. 4,** 255 **CD13:16**

Alphabetical Index of Songs and Speech Pieces by Grade Level

Pre-K

A
America (My Country 'Tis of Thee), 47, **Track 30**
Apples and Bananas, 34, **Track 19**

B
Bickle, Bockle, 17, **Track 13**
Burn Little Candles, 85, **Track 48**
Bus, The, 55, **Track 32**
Bye 'n' Bye, 77, **Track 46**

D
Down at the Station, 54, **Track 31**

E
Engine, Engine Number Nine, 57, **Track 35**

F
Five Fat Turkeys, 84, **Track 47**

G
Garden Hoedown, The, 37, **Track 25**
Good Day Song, 44, **Track 26**

H
Hokey Pokey, The, 4, **Track 1**
Hush, Little Baby, 24, **Track 14**

I
I Like Spinach, 35, **Track 23**
I Wanna Be a Friend of Yours, 16, **Track 12**

J
Jingle Bells, 86, **Track 49**

L
Little Chickens (Los pollitos), 67, **Track 40**
Little Ducky Duddle, 65, **Track 38**
Looby Loo, 6, **Track 5**
Los pollitos (Little Chickens), 67, **Track 40**

M
Mary Wore a Red Dress, 15, **Track 11**
Mi cuerpo (My Body), 5, **Track 3**
Mister Sun, 45, **Track 27**
My Body (Mi cuerpo), 5, **Track 3**
My Mama's Calling Me, 25, **Track 15**

O
Oats, Peas, Beans, and Barley Grow, 36, **Track 24**
Old Gray Cat, The, 64, **Track 37**

P
Plenty Fishes in the Sea, 27, **Track 18**

R
Rain, Rain, Go Away, 76, **Track 45**
Rise, Sally, Rise, 14, **Track 10**

S
Sailor Went to Sea, Sea, Sea, A, 56, **Track 33**
Sheep Shearing, 26, **Track 17**
Stamping Land, 46, **Track 29**

T
Teddy Bear, 66, **Track 39**
This Little Light of Mine, 7, **Track 6**
Twinkle, Twinkle, Little Star, 76, **Track 44**

W
Wind Blew East, The, 74, **Track 43**

Y
Yankee Doodle, 87, **Track 51**

Grade K

A
Alison's Camel, T201 **CD 11:21**
All Work Together, T12 **CD1:1**
Alphabet Song, T54 **CD 3:6**
America, T303 **CD 16:14**
Animales (Animals), T192 **CD 11:6**
Animals (Animales), T192 **CD 11:6**

B
Battle Hymn of the Republic (refrain only), T331 **CD 18:26**
Bear Went Over the Mountain, The, T204 **CD 11:25**
Bell Horses, T262 **CD 14:33**
Best That I Can Be!, The, T48 **CD 2:27**
Bickle, Bockle, T187 **CD 10:27**
Bingo, T64 **CD 3:21**
Bobby Shafto, T265 **CD 15:4**
Bohm Dong Sahn, Gohd Dong Sahn (Spring Valley, Flower Valley), T337 **CD 19:6**
Bounce High, Bounce Low, T131 **CD 7:22**
Bus, The, T137 **CD 8:1**
Bye 'n' Bye, T67 **CD 3:24**

C
Chopsticks (Juhtgarak), T108 **CD 6:16**
Christmas Eve (Nochebuena), T323 **CD 18:5**
Cobbler, Cobbler, Mend My Shoe, T169 **CD 10:6**
Colorful Dragon Boat, T328 **CD 18:19**
Counting Song, T92 **CD 5:19**

Alphabetical Index of Songs and Speech Pieces (continued)

D

Damselfly Song (Ushkana), T75 **CD 4:15**
Days of the Week, T81 **CD 5:2**
Doing the Weekly Walk, T78 **CD 4:21**
Drum, The (El tambor), T129 **CD 7:18**

E

Eency Weency Spider, T8 **Spotlight CD 10**
Eency Weency Spider (La pequeñita araña), T9
  Spotlight CD 13
El nacimiento (The Nativity), T322 **CD 18:1**
El picaflor (The Hummingbird), T141 **CD 8:10**
El tambor (The Drum), T129 **CD 7:18**

F

Farmer in the Dell, The, T100 **CD 6:5**
Fehér liliomszál (Little Water Lily), T139 **CD 8:5**
Five Fat Turkeys, T309 **CD 16:31**
Follow Me, T133 **CD 7:26**

G

Garden Hoedown, The, T290 **CD 16:11**
Git on Board, T145 **CD 8:18**
Give Me Your Hand (Simi Yadech), T168 **CD 10:2**
Go, Go, Go, T276 **CD 15:45**
Gogo, T188 **CD 11:1**
Good Day Song, T50 **CD 2:30**
Grizzly Bear, T252 **CD 14:17**

H

Hanukkah Is Here, T314 **CD 17:6**
Happy Birthday, T347 **CD 19:24**
Happy Birthday, Happy Birthday, T273 **CD 15:42**
Head and Shoulders, T238 **CD 13:21**
Hello Song, T2 **Spotlight CD 1**
Here Is the Beehive, T258 **CD 14:26**
Hokey Pokey, T68 **CD 4:1**
Hop, Hop, Hop, T197 **CD 11:15**
Hot Dog, T69 **CD 4:4**
Hours, The (Las horas), T70 **CD 4:7**
How Wonderful It Is (Qué bonito es), T234 **CD 13:13**
Hummingbird, The (El picaflor), T141 **CD 8:10**

I

I Can't Spell Hippopotamus, T199 **CD 11:18**
I Got Shoes, T33 **CD 2:1**
I Have, I Have, I Have (Tengo, Tengo, Tengo), T212
  CD 12:12
I Know an Old Lady, T26 **CD 1:22**
I Made a Valentine, T333 **CD 18:32**
I Will Sing Hello, T156 **CD 9:10**
If You're Happy, T6 **Spotlight CD 7**
Ifetayo (Love Brings Happiness), T325 **CD 18:10**
In Bahia Town (Na Bahia Tem), T163 **CD 9:22**
Instrument Game, T36 **CD 2:8**
It's So Good to See You, T86 **CD 5:9**
It's Such a Good Feeling, T282 **CD 15:49**
It's You I Like, T280 **CD 15:48**

J

Jack, Be Nimble, T88 **CD 5:12**
Jack-in-the-Box, T250 **CD 14:14**
Jack-o'-Lantern, T307 **CD 16:25**
Jig Jog, Jig Jog, T260 **CD 14:30**
Juhtgarak (Chopsticks), T108 **CD 6:16**
Just Like Me, T242 **CD 14:1**

K

Kangaroo, The, T197 **CD 11:11**
Kum Ba Yah, T327 **CD 18:16**

L

La pequeñita araña (Eency Weency Spider), T9
  Spotlight CD 13
Lady, Lady, T184 **CD 10:24**
Las horas (The Hours), T70 **CD 4:7**
Let's Think of Something to Do, T270 **CD 15:40**
Little Blue Truck, T136 **CD 7:30**
Little Chickens (Los Pollitos), T288 **CD 16:4**
Little Ducky Duddle, T289 **CD 16:8**
Little Sir Echo, T103 **CD 6:9**
Little Spotted Puppy, T147 **CD 8:21**
Little Water Lily (Fehér liliomszál), T139 **CD 8:5**
Little White Duck, T208 **CD 12:5**
London Bridge, T99 **CD 5:25**
Look Who's Here!, T84 **CD 5:6**
Los pollitos (Little Chickens), T288 **CD 16:4**
Love Brings Happiness (Ifetayo), T325 **CD 18:10**

M

Mama, Bake the Johnnycake, T318 **CD 17:16**
María Blanca, T99 **CD 6:1**
Martin Luther King (speech piece), T326 **CD 18:13**
Mbombela (The Train Comes), T152 **CD 9:4**
Merrily, We Roll Along, T110 **CD 6:21**
Merry-Go-Round, The, T224 **CD 13:3**
Mi chacra (My Farm), T207 **CD 12:1**
Mister Bamboo Bug (Wavvuuvuumira), T165 **CD 9:27**
Mister Sun, T343 **CD 19:19**
Monkey, Monkey, T215 **CD 12:17**
Monté sur un éléphant (Riding on an Elephant), T217
  CD 12:20
Mothers (Nampaya omame), T128 **CD 7:14**
Muffin Man, The, T105 **CD 6:12**
Mulberry Bush, The, T112 **CD 6:27**
Must Be Santa, T316 **CD 17:12**
My Farm (Mi chacra), T207 **CD 12:1**
My Grandfather, T23 **CD 1:16**
My Oak Tree, T236 **CD 13:18**
My Thumbs Are Starting to Wiggle, T35 **CD 2:5**

N

Na Bahia Tem (In Bahia Town), T163 **CD 9:22**
Name Game, T57 **CD 3:10**
Nampaya omame (Mothers), T128 **CD 7:14**
Nativity, The (El nacimiento), T322 **CD 18:1**
Noble Duke of York, The, T232 **CD 13:10**

Alphabetical Index of Songs and Speech Pieces (continued)

Nochebuena (Christmas Eve), T323 **CD 18:5**
North Winds Blow, T305 **CD 16:18**
Now We Are Going to Sing (Y ahora vamos a cantar), T340
   CD 19:14

O

O Christmas Tree! (O Tannenbaum!), T320 **CD 17:26**
O Tannenbaum! (O Christmas Tree!), T320 **CD 17:26**
Oats, Peas, Beans, and Barley Grow, T287 **CD 16:1**
Ɔbɔɔ Asi Me Nsa, T159 **CD 9:14**
Oh, A-Hunting We Will Go, T62 **CD 3:18**
Old Gray Cat, The, T43 **CD 2:20**
Old MacDonald Had a Farm, T211 **CD 12:9**
Old Mister Woodpecker, T172 **CD 10:10**
On This Night, T315 **CD 17:9**
One Finger, One Thumb, T38 **CD 2:12**
One, Two, Tie My Shoe, T151 **CD 9:1**

P

Peace and Quiet, T278 **CD 15:46**
Peter Cottontail, T338 **CD 19:10**
Pimpón, T22 **CD 1:12**
Planting Seeds, T284 **CD 15:50**
Popping Corn, T161 **CD 9:18**
Presidents, T330 **CD 18:23**
Propel, Propel, Propel, T275 **CD 15:44**
Put Your Finger in the Air, T230 **CD 13:7**

Q

Qué bonito es (How Wonderful It Is), T234 **CD 13:13**

R

Rainbow Song, The, T61 **CD 3:15**
Ride the Train, T144 **CD 8:15**
Riding on an Elephant (Monté sur un éléphant), T217
   CD 12:20
Ring Around the Rosy, T246 **CD 14:8**
Row, Row, Row, T274 **CD 15:43**

S

Santa Clara Corn Grinding Song, T164 **CD 9:26**
See the Pony Galloping, T44 **CD 2:23**
Seesaw, Margery Daw, T264 **CD 15:1**
Shake My Sillies Out, T175 **CD 10:13**
Simi Yadech (Give Me Your Hand), T168 **CD 10:2**
Sing a Little Song, T179 **CD 10:18**
Sing a Song of Sixpence, T111 **CD 6:24**
Snowman, The, T313 **CD 17:3**
Speedy Delivery, T279 **CD 15:47**
Spring Valley, Flower Valley (Bohm Dong Sahn, Gohd Dong
   Sahn), T337 **CD 19:6**
Stamping Land, T24 **CD 1:19**
Sweetly Sings the Donkey, T244 **CD 14:4**

T

Ten in a Bed, T256 **CD 14:23**
Ten Little Frogs, T240 **CD 13:24**
Tengo, Tengo, Tengo (I Have, I Have, I Have), T212
   CD 12:12

They Were Tall, T52 **CD 3:3**
Things I'm Thankful For, T308 **CD 16:28**
This Is My City, T120 **CD 7:4**
This Is What I Can Do, T123 **CD 7:8**
Three Little Kittens, T148 **CD 8:24**
Three Little Muffins (speech piece), T127 **CD 7:11**
Time to Sing, T16 **CD 1:4**
Toodala, T39 **CD 2:15**
Touch Your Shoulders, T254 **CD 14:20**
Town Hall Halloween Ball, T306 **CD 16:21**
Train Comes, The (Mbombela), T152 **CD 9:4**
Tree of Peace (speech piece), T320 **CD 17:22**
Tugboat, T95 **CD 5:22**
Twinkle, Twinkle, Little Star, T90 **CD 5:16**

U

Ushkana (Damselfly Song), T75 **CD 4:15**

W

Wait and See, T334 **CD 19:1**
Walk to School, T18 **CD 1:8**
Wavvuuvuumira (Mister Bamboo Bug), T165 **CD 9:27**
We Are Playing in the Forest, T248 **CD 14:11**
What You Gonna Call Your Pretty Little Baby?, T319
   CD 17:19
When You Send a Valentine, T332 **CD 18:29**
Willoughby Wallaby Woo, T241 **CD 13:27**
Won't You Be My Neighbor?, T268 **CD 15:39**
Worms, T286 **CD 15:53**

Y

Y ahora vamos a cantar (Now We Are Going to Sing), T340
   CD 19:14
You're a Grand Old Flag, T4 **Spotlight CD 4**

Grade 1

A

¡Adivina lo que es! (Guess What It Is!), T170 **CD 7:30**
A be ce, T213 **CD 9:33**
A la rueda rueda ('Round and 'Round), T240 **CD 11:6**
A Tisket A Tasket, T107 **CD 4:31**
Acka Backa, T256 **CD 12:2**
All Night, All Day, T232 **CD 10:25**
America, T326 **CD 15:15**
Animal Song, The, T288 **CD 13:25**
Another Busy Day, T41 **CD 2:1**
Ants Go Marching, The, T22 **CD 1:15**
Apples and Bananas, T151 **CD 7:1**
Arre, mi burrito (Gid'yup, Little Burro), T257 **CD 12:5**
Autumn Leaves Are Falling, T330 **CD 15:30**
Autumn Leaves, T331 **CD 15:27**

B

Babe, The (El rorro), T356 **CD 17:21**
Bear Hunt, T126 **CD 5:29**
Bear Went Over the Mountain, The, T115 **CD 5:5**
Bee, Bee, Bumblebee, T250 **CD 11:24**

Grade-Level Index of Songs and Speech Pieces

Best Friends, T222 **CD 10:13**
Big and Small (speech piece), T200 **CD 9:16**
Big and Small (song), T201 **CD 9:13**
Bluebells, T209 **CD 9:24**
Bonjour, mes amis (Hello, My Friends), T18 **CD 1:8**
Boris, the Singing Bear, T312 **CD 15:5**
Brinca la tablita (Hop, Hop!), T71 **CD 3:1**
Brush Your Teeth, T66 **CD 2:36**
Brush Your Teeth (speech piece), T66 **CD 2:39**
But the Critter Got Away (speech piece), T89 **CD 3:29**
Butterfly, Flutter By, T333 **CD 15:33**

C

Cake, Cake, Cake! (Uga, Uga, Uga), T313 **CD 15:8**
Caribbean Amphibian, T294 **CD 13:38**
Cat and Rat (Pusa't daga), T289 **CD 13:28**
Cat, Cat! (Mos', Mos'!), T53 **CD 2:16**
Categories, T146 **CD 6:25**
Chang (Elephant), T199 **CD 9:9**
Charlie over the Ocean, T75 **CD 3:10**
Chase the Squirrel, T88 **CD 3:26**
Chickery Chick, T292 **CD 13:35**
Chirimbolo Game, The (El juego chirimbolo), T103 **CD 4:24**
Christmas Candies, The (La colación), T357 **CD 17:25**
Clap Your Hands, T247 **CD 11:20**
Come Back, My Little Chicks, T134 **CD 6:11**
Cookies, T277 **CD 13:4**
Counting Song, T195 **CD 9:1**
Cut the Cake, T232 **CD 10:27**

D

Dance Myself to Sleep, T314 **CD 15:12**
Diana (Play the Bugle), T334 **CD 16:1**
Diou Shou Juan'er (Hide a Handkerchief!), T212 **CD 9:29**
Double This, T95 **CD 4:4**
Down by the Bay, T48 **CD 2:9**
Down the Hill, T281 **CD 13:5**
Dreidel Spin (S'vivon Sov), T348 **CD 16:33**
Duérmete mi niño (Go to Sleep, My Baby), T61 **CD 2:28**

E

El florón (The Flower), T117 **CD 5:11**
El juego chirimbolo (The Chirimbolo Game), T103 **CD 4:24**
El rorro (The Babe), T356 **CD 17:21**
Elephant (Chang), T199 **CD 9:9**
Everybody Oughta Know, T361 **CD 18:4**

F

Flower, The (El florón) T117 **CD 5:11**
Frog's Song (Kaeru no Uta), T112 **CD 5:1**

G

George Washington, T368 **CD 18:22**
Gid'yup, Little Burro (Arre, mi burrito), T257 **CD 12:5**
Gilly, Gilly, Gilly Good Morning, T12 **CD 1:1**
Go A Tin (Lantern Song), T363 **CD 18:9**
Go to Sleep, My Baby (Duérmete mi niño), T61 **CD 2:28**
Goin' to the Zoo, T192 **CD 8:29**
Granny (speech piece), T104 **CD 4:28**

Grasshoppers Three, T284 **CD 13:19**
Green Grass Grows All Around, The, T148 **CD 6:28**
Guess What It Is! (¡Adivina lo que es!), T170 **CD 7:30**

H

Hakyo Jong (School Bell), T302 **CD 14:7**
Halloween, T340 **CD 16:16**
Hanukkah Chag Yafeh (Hanukkah Joyous Holiday), T350 **CD 17:1**
Hanukkah Joyous Holiday (Hanukkah Chag Yafeh), T350 **CD 17:1**
Happiest Street in the World, The, T304 **CD 14:15**
Happiness (speech piece), T254 **CD 11:37**
Head and Shoulders, Baby, T40 **CD 1:39**
Hello (Jambo), T230 **CD 10:20**
Hello, My Friends (Bonjour, mes amis), T18 **CD 1:8**
Hello, There!, T230 **CD 10:17**
Here We Come A-Wassailing, T355 **CD 17:18**
Here We Sit, T251 **CD 11:27**
Hey, Children, Who's in Town? (speech piece), T14 **CD 1:4**
Hi! My Name is Joe! (speech piece), T220 **CD 10:10**
Hide a Handkerchief! (Diou Shou Juan'er), T212 **CD 9:29**
Hoo, Hoo!, T55 **CD 2:21**
Hop! Chirp! Moo! Oh, Happy Springtime Day!, T372 **CD 18:29**
Hop, Hop! (Brinca la tablita), T71 **CD 3:1**
How Does Your Garden Grow?, T144 **CD 6:22**
Hunt the Cows, T236 **CD 10:35**

I

I Am Slowly Going Crazy, T127 **CD 5:30**
I Like Spinach, T163 **CD 7:19**
I Love My Country, T328 **CD 15:21**
I Wanna Be a Friend of Yours, T84 **CD 3:23**
I've a Pair of Fishes, T124 **CD 5:23**
If All the World Were Paper, T296 **CD 13:41**
In Bahia Town (Na Bahia Tem), T297 **CD 13:44**
In My Little Motor Boat, T159 **CD 7:13**
It's So Nice on the Ice, T346 **CD 16:27**

J

Jambo (Hello), T230 **CD 10:20**
Jingle Bells, T354 **CD 17:15**
John the Rabbit, T74 **CD 3:7**
Johnny Works with One Hammer, T96 **CD 4:7**
Johnny's Flea, T158 **CD 7:10**
Jolly Old Saint Nicholas, T353 **CD 17:8**
Jump, Jim Joe, T89 **CD 3:32**

K

Kaeru no Uta (Frog's Song), T112 **CD 5:1**
Kari (Wild Geese), T261 **CD 12:20**
Kite Song, The (Tako No Uta), T370 **CD 18:25**
Kobuta (Piglet), T168 **CD 7:25**

L

La colación (Christmas Candies), T357 **CD 17:25**
La ranita cri (The Little Frog Croaks), T27 **CD 1:23**

Alphabetical Index of Songs and Speech Pieces (continued)

Ladybug's Picnic, T290 **CD 13:32**
Lantern Song (Go A Tin), T363 **CD 18:9**
Lavender's Blue, T174 **CD 8:4**
Let's Go Driving, T52 **CD 2:12**
Library Song, T42 **CD 2:4**
Light the Candles, T351 **CD 17:5**
Little Black Bug, T166 **CD 7:22**
Little Frog Croaks, The (La ranita cri), T27 **CD 1:23**
Little Red Caboose, T97 **CD 4:10**
Little Robin Red Breast, T208 **CD 9:21**
Looby Loo, T262 **CD 12:24**
Love Grows, T202 **CD 9:17**
Love Is the Magic Word, T366 **CD 18:19**
Lucy Locket, T253 **CD 11:34**

M

Mail Myself to You, T366 **CD 18:16**
Marco Polo (speech piece), T90 **CD 3:35**
Martin Luther King, T360 **CD 18:1**
Mary's Coal Black Lamb, T286 **CD 13:22**
Mi cuerpo (My Body), T32 **CD 1:28**
Miss Mary Mack, T15 **CD 1:5**
Mizuguruma (Water Wheel), T260 **CD 12:16**
Mos', Mos'! (Cat, Cat!), T53 **CD 2:16**
Mouse in the Rice Sack (Zui Zui Zukkorbashi), T98 **CD 4:13**
My Body (Mi cuerpo), T32 **CD 1:28**
My Mama's Calling Me, T54 **CD 2:18**
My Mom, T372 **CD 18:32**

N

Na Bahia Tem (In Bahia Town), T297 **CD 13:44**
Naranja dulce (Sweet Orange), T303 **CD 14:11**
Naughty Kitty Cat, T171 **CD 7:34**
No One Like You, T300 **CD 14:4**

O

Oh, Mama, Oh (Yo, Mamana, Yo), T307 **CD 14:21**
Old King Glory, T217 **CD 10:4**
One Little Elephant, T194 **CD 8:32**
One, Two, Three, Four, Five, T265 **CD 12:28**
One, Two, Three, Four, T123 **CD 5:20**
Over in the Meadow, T78 **CD 3:17**

P

Pat Pat Patty Pat, T308 **CD 14:25**
Patriotic Medley, T8 **Spotlight CD 4**
Peanut Butter, T218 **CD 10:7**
Pease Porridge Hot, T255 **CD 11:38**
Piglet (Kobuta), T168 **CD 7:25**
Piñón Pirulín, T311 **CD 15:1**
Pitty Patty Polt, T180 **CD 8:15**
Plate Passing (Sara Watashi), T67 **CD 2:40**
Play the Bugle (Diana), T334 **CD 16:1**
Plenty Fishes in the Sea, T310 **CD 14:28**
Puddle Hopping, T60 **CD 2:25**
Pumpkin Song, T342 **CD 16:19**
Punchinella, T216 **CD 10:1**
Pusa't daga (Cat and Rat), T289 **CD 13:28**
Put on a Costume, T336 **CD 16:7**

Q

Quaker, Quaker, T100 **CD 4:17**

R

Rain, Rain, Go Away, T259 **CD 12:13**
Rattlesnake, T185 **CD 8:21**
Riddle, A (Una adivinanza), T138 **CD 6:15**
Rig a Jig Jig, T116 **CD 5:8**
Rise, Sally, Rise, T162 **CD 7:16**
'Round and 'Round (A la rueda rueda), T240 **CD 11:6**
Rudolph, the Red-Nosed Reindeer, T354 **CD 17:12**

S

Sailor Went to Sea, Sea, Sea, A, T38 **CD 1:36**
Sara Watashi (Plate Passing), T67 **CD 2:40**
Saw, Saw Lumberjack (Serra, serra serrador), T131, T133 **CD 6:7**
School Bells (Hakyo Jong), T302 **CD 14:7**
Seeds, T120 **CD 5:16**
Seesaw, T242 **CD 11:11**
Serra, serra serrador (Saw, Saw Lumberjack), T131, T133 **CD 6:7**
Sesame Street, T298 **CD 14:1**
Shoo, Turkey, T76 **CD 3:14**
Simple Simon (speech piece), T175 **CD 8:8**
Sing after Me, T34 **CD 1:32**
Sittin' Down to Eat, T182 **CD 8:18**
Six Little Ducks, T64 **CD 2:33**
Skin and Bones, T340 **CD 16:13**
Skip to My Lou, T102 **CD 4:20**
Sleep, Bonnie Bairnie, T26 **CD 1:20**
Snail With the Mail, T275 **CD 13:3**
Snail, Snail, T252 **CD 11:31**
Somebody Come and Play, T92 **CD 4:1**
Something Funny Outside, T338 **CD 16:10**
Soup, Soup, T358 **CD 17:30**
Spring, T273 **CD 13:2**
Star Light, Star Bright, T258 **CD 12:9**
Step into the Spotlight, T7 **Spotlight CD 1**
S'vivon Sov (Dreidel Spin), T348 **CD 16:33**
Sweet Orange (Naranja dulce), T303 **CD 14:11**

T

Tak for Maden (Thanks for Food), T343 **CD 16:22**
Tako No Uta (The Kite Song), T370 **CD 18:25**
Thanks for Food (Tak for Maden), T343 **CD 16:22**
There Are Many Flags in Many Lands, T328 **CD 15:24**
There's a Hole in the Middle of the Sea, T178 **CD 8:12**
This Little Light of Mine, T238 **CD 11:2**
This Old Man, T306 **CD 14:18**
Time for Love, A, T347 **CD 16:30**
Tinker, Tailor, T130 **CD 6:4**
Twenty-four Robbers, T173 **CD 8:1**
Two, Four, Six, Eight, T246 **CD 11:17**

U

Uga Uga Uga (Cake, Cake, Cake!), T313 **CD 15:8**
Una adivinanza (A Riddle), T138 **CD 6:15**

Alphabetical Index of Songs and Speech Pieces (continued)

V

Viva Valentine!, T364 **CD 18:13**

W

Wake Me, Shake Me, T198 **CD 9:6**
Water Wheel (Mizuguruma), T260 **CD 12:16**
We All Sing with the Same Voice, T156 **CD 7:7**
What's Your Name?, T125 **CD 5:26**
When the Flag Goes By, T327 **CD 15:18**
Wild Geese (Kari), T260 **CD 12:20**
Willum, T19 **CD 1:12**
Wind Blew East, The, T234 **CD 10:31**
Wind Blow, T187 **CD 8:24**

Y

Year With Frog and Toad, A, T270 **CD 13:1**
Year With Frog and Toad (Reprise), A, T283 **CD 13:6**
Yo, Mamana, Yo (Oh, Mama, Oh), T307 **CD 14:21**

Z

Zui Zui Zukkorbashi (Mouse in the Rice Sack), T98 **CD 4:13**

Grade 2

A

A la rueda de San Miguel (To the Wheel of San Miguel), 60 **CD 3:27**
Ach, du lieber Augustin (The More We Get Together), 35 **CD 2:12**
All Around the Buttercup, 210 **CD 11:1**
America, 338 **CD 17:2**
Ani Purim (Purim), 372 **CD 19:15**
Animal Fair, 214 **CD 11:8**
Apple Picker's Reel, 343 **CD 17:15**
Artichokes, 314 **CD 16:8**
Australia's on the Wallaby, 106 **CD 6:3**
Away for Rio, 170 **CD 8:29**

B

Baby Beluga, 26 **CD 2:3**
Baby Nodja, 154 **CD 8:10**
Bahay Kubo (My Nipa Hut), 382 **CD 19:36**
Ban Dal (Half Moon), 219 **CD 11:15**
Banyan Tree, 321 **CD 16:22**
Bate, bate (Stir, Stir), 242 **CD 12:15**
Beautiful Gardener, The (La bella hortelana), 208 **CD 10:23**
Bei Fang Chre (North Wind Blows), 367 **CD 19:1**
Big Beautiful Planet, 376 **CD 19:24**
Bluebirds (Nikosi), 230 **CD 12:2**
Bow, Wow, Wow, 264 **CD 14:4**
Button, You Must Wander, 176 **CD 9:2**

C

Candle on the Water, 296 **CD 15:7**
Caranguejo (The Crab), 306 **CD 15:27**
Check It Out! (It's About Respect), 10 **CD 1:14**
Chiapanecas (Ladies of Chiapas), 128 **CD 7:8**
Chichipapa (The Sparrows' Singing School), 22 **CD 1:33**
Chirp, Chirp, Chirp (Chíu, chíu, chíu), 302 **CD 15:16**
Chirri Bim, 70 **CD 4:14**
Chíu, chíu, chíu (Chirp, Chirp, Chirp), 302 **CD 15:16**
Cobbler, The (El zapatero), 138 **CD 7:24**
Columbus Sailed with Three Ships, 344 **CD 17:18**
Come, Pick the Moon (Dal taro kacha), 98 **CD 5:20**
Corner Grocery Store, 311 **CD 16:1**
Crab, The (Caranguejo), 306 **CD 15:27**
Cuckoo, Where Are You?, 244 **CD 12:22**

D

Daisy Chain, 255 **CD 13:15**
Dal taro kacha (Come, Pick the Moon), 98 **CD 5:20**
Dance, Dance, Dance!, 5 **CD 1:1**
Dance Together, 264 **CD 14:1**
Do-Re-Mi, C **Spotlight CD 4**
Doggie, Doggie, 59 **CD 3:23**
Donkey, Donkey, 256 **CD 13:18**
Doves, The (El palomo y la paloma), 381 **CD 19:32**
Ducks, The (Itik Besenda Gurau), 100 **CD 5:25**
Dumplin's, 172 **CD 8:32**

E

Eating Lizards, 250 **CD 12:42**
El burrito enfermo (The Sick Little Donkey), 180 **CD 9:11**
El palomo y la paloma (The Doves), 380 **CD 19:32**
El tren (The Train), 326 **CD 16:36**
El zapatero (The Cobbler), 138 **CD 7:24**
Elephant, The (Yanai), 305 **CD 15:23**
En la feria de San Juan (In the Market of San Juan), 226 **CD 11:27**
En nuestra Tierra tan linda (On Our Beautiful Planet Earth), 114 **CD 6:15**
Engine, Engine Number Nine, 13 **CD 1:17**
Ésta sí que es Nochebuena (This Is Christmas Eve), 361 **CD 18:21**
Everybody Has Music Inside, 164 **CD 8:22**
Everything Grows, 204 **CD 10:17**

F

Food Song, The, 318 **CD 16:19**
Four White Horses, 301 **CD 15:13**
Frogs (I Chih Ching Wa), 186 **CD 9:22**

G

Garden Song, 236 **CD 12:11**
Going Over the Sea, 216 **CD 11:11**
Going Round (Hashewie), 362 **CD 18:25**
Good Night, Sleep Tight, 76 **CD 4:21**
Great Outdoors, The, 290 **CD 14:49**
Green Eggs and Ham, 284 **CD 14:41**

H

Hakuna Matata, 292 **CD 15:1**
Half Moon (Ban Dal), 219 **CD 11:15**
Harvest, 342 **CD 17:12**
Hashewie (Going Round), 362 **CD 18:25**
He's Got the Whole World in His Hands, 116 **CD 6:22**
Heigh Ho, Here We Go, 252 **CD 13:5**

Hello, Hello There, 126 **CD 7:4**
Here Comes a Bluebird, 263 **CD 13:51**
Here Comes Sally, 220 **CD 11:19**
Hey, Hey, Look at Me, 245 **CD 12:26**
Hop, Old Squirrel, 258 **CD 13:30**
Horton Hears a Who!, 279 **CD 14:44**
Horton Hears a Who! Two, 280 **CD 14:45**
Hot Cross Buns, 258 **CD 13:27**

I

I Bought Me a Cat, 14 **CD 1:21**
I Chih Ching Wa (Frogs), 186 **CD 9:22**
I Planted Watermelons (Ja posejah lubenice), 316 **CD 16:11**
I Saw Three Ships, 359 **CD 18:15**
I See, 266 **CD 14:33**
I'm Gonna Sing, 9 **CD 1:11**
In and Out, 245 **CD 12:29**
In the Market of San Juan (En la feria de San Juan), 226 **CD 11:27**
In the Window, 352 **CD 17:35**
Itik Besenda Gurau (The Ducks), 100 **CD 5:25**
It's a Small World, 298 **CD 15:10**
It's Possible, 281 **CD 14:40**
It's Raining! It's Pouring!, 233 **CD 12:6**

J

Ja posejah lubenice (I Planted Watermelons), 316 **CD 16:11**
Jim Along, Josie, 194 **CD 10:4**
Joy, 46 **CD 3:1**
Juan Pírulero, 270 **CD 14:27**
Jugaremos en el bosque (We'll Be Playing in the Forest), 188 **CD 9:26**

K

King's Land, 257 **CD 13:21**
Knock the Cymbals, 265 **CD 14:10**

L

La bella hortelana (The Beautiful Gardener), 208 **CD 10:23**
Ladies of Chiapas (Chiapanecas), 128 **CD 7:8**
Land of the Silver Birch, 88 **CD 5:5**
Leatherwing Bat, 304 **CD 15:20**
Lemonade, 19 **CD 1:25**
Let's Go Fly a Kite, 134 **CD 7:19**
Little Heron (Na belo), 322 **CD 16:25**
Little Sally Water, 249 **CD 12:39**
Loose Tooth (speech piece), 28 **CD 2:6**

M

Mama Paquita, 92 **CD 5:13**
Martin Luther King, 364 **CD 18:29**
Mary Had a Baby, 360 **CD 18:18**
Matarile, 261 **CD 13:43**
Me gase boho (Orange Tree), 317 **CD 16:15**
Me Stone, 48 **CD 3:5**
Mein Hut (My Hat), 142 **CD 7:32**
Merry-Go-Round, 267 **CD 14:16**
Mill Song, The, 52 **CD 3:12**
Mister Rabbit, Mister Rabbit, 150 **CD 8:6**

More We Get Together, The (Ach, du lieber Augustin), 35 **CD 2:12**
Mother, Mother, 254 **CD 13:9**
Mouse, Mousie, 254 **CD 13:12**
Mr. Frog, 257 **CD 13:24**
My Dreidel, 353 **CD 18:1**
My Hat (Mein Hut), 142 **CD 7:32**
My Nipa Hut (Bahay Kubo), 382 **CD 19:36**

N

Na belo (Little Heron), 322 **CD 16:25**
Nabe, Nabe, Soku, Nuke (Stewpot, Stewpot, Bottomless Pot), 259 **CD 13:33**
Nikosi (Bluebirds), 230 **CD 12:2**
North Wind Blows (Bei Fang Chre), 367 **CD 19:1**

O

Oh, the Thinks You Can Think!, 276 **CD 14:43**
Old Blue, 213 **CD 11:5**
Old Woman and the Pig, 130 **CD 7:12**
Oliver Twist, 268 **CD 14:20**
Oma Rapeti (Run Rabbit), 108 **CD 6:6**
On Our Beautiful Planet Earth (En nuestra Tierra tan linda), 114 **CD 6:15**
On Top of Spaghetti, 312 **CD 16:5**
Orange Tree (Me gase boho), 317 **CD 16:15**
Orff Instruments (speech piece), 183 **CD 9:18**

P

Pairs or Pears, 265 **CD 14:7**
Part of Your World, 294 **CD 15:4**
Pat on the Back, A, 74 **CD 4:18**
Patriotic Medley, H **Spotlight CD 10**
Pick a Pumpkin, 347 **CD 17:25**
Pizza, Pizza, Daddy-O, 62 **CD 4:1**
Place in the Choir, A, 308 **CD 15:32**
Plainsies, Clapsies, 248 **CD 12:33**
Puff, the Magic Dragon, 54 **CD 3:17**
Purim (Ani Purim), 372 **CD 19:15**

R

Red Rover, 249 **CD 12:36**
Riddle Song, 251 **CD 12:45**
Riqui Ran (Sawing Song), 21 **CD 1:29**
Rover, 260 **CD 13:37**
Run, Rabbit (Oma Rapeti), 108 **CD 6:6**

S

Sailor, Sailor on the Sea, 262 **CD 13:47**
Sally Go 'Round the Sun, 268 **CD 14:23**
Sammy Sackett, 146 **CD 8:2**
San Sereni, 323 **CD 16:29**
Sawing Song (Riqui Ran), 21 **CD 1:29**
Say Your Name, 243 **CD 12:19**
Seeds and Seasons, 206 **CD 10:20**
Seussical Mega-Mix, 247 **CD 14:48**
Shake the Papaya Down, 90 **CD 5:9**
She'll Be Comin' 'Round the Mountain, 33 **CD 2:9**
Sheep in the Meadow (speech piece), 8 **CD 1:7**

Alphabetical Index of Songs and Speech Pieces (continued)

Sheep Shearing, 102 **CD 5:29**
Shoheen Sho, 140 **CD 7:28**
Shoo, Fly, 222 **CD 11:22**
Shrimp Boats, 179 **CD 9:7**
Sick Little Donkey, The (El burrito enfermo), 180 **CD 9:11**
Sing! Sing! Sing!, 196 **CD 10:7**
Skating, 350 **CD 17:32**
Skinnamarink, 368 **CD 19:5**
Sorida, 96 **CD 5:17**
Sparrows' Singing School, The (Chichipapa), 22 **CD 1:33**
Step in Time, 6 **CD 1:4**
Step Into the Spotlight, A **Spotlight CD 1**
Stewpot, Stewpot, Bottomless Pot (Nabe, Nabe, Soku, Nuke), 259 **CD 13:33**
Stir, Stir (Bate, bate), 242 **CD 12:15**
Strawberry Roan, 66 **CD 4:5**

T

Take Me Out to the Ball Game, 56 **CD 3:20**
Thank You, 349 **CD 17:29**
There Are Many Flags in Many Lands, 341 **CD 17:9**
There's a Hole in the Bucket, 132 **CD 7:15**
This Is Halloween, 346 **CD 17:21**
This Is My Country, 87 **CD 5:2**
This Is Christmas Eve (Ésta sí que es Nochebuena), 361 **CD 18:21**
This Little Light of Mine, F **Spotlight CD 7**
Three Little Penguins (speech piece), 112 **CD 6:12**
Tiki Tiki Tiki Room, The, 324 **CD 16:33**
Tinga Layo, 50 **CD 3:8**
To the Wheel of San Miguel (A la rueda de San Miguel), 60 **CD 3:27**
Train, The (El tren), 326 **CD 16:36**

U

Up on the Housetop, 356 **CD 18:9**

W

Wake Up the Sun, 124 **CD 7:1**
We'll Be Playing in the Forest (Jugaremos en el bosque), 188 **CD 9:26**
We Wish You a Merry Christmas, 358 **CD 18:12**
We're Sailing Down the River, 166 **CD 8:25**
Wee Falorie Man, The, 375 **CD 19:21**
Welcome Is the Month of May, 378 **CD 19:28**
What a Wonderful World, 84 **CD 4:31**
What Did Delaware?, 190 **CD 9:32**
Who Chopped the Cherry Tree Down?, 371 **CD 19:12**
Who Has the Penny?, 252 **CD 13:2**
Who's That Tapping at the Window?, 261 **CD 13:40**
Willowbee, 69 **CD 4:11**

Y

Yanai (The Elephant), 305 **CD 15:23**
Yankee Doodle, 340 **CD 17:6**
You Are My Sunshine, 369 **CD 19:8**
You'll Sing a Song and I'll Sing a Song, 156 **CD 8:13**
You've Got a Friend in Me, 44 **CD 2:24**

Grade 3

A
Addams Family Theme, The, 307 **CD 14:1**
Amen, 376 **CD 18:1**
America, the Beautiful, 354 **CD 16:13**
As I Roll My Ball (En roulant ma boule), 100 **CD 4:26**
Atole, The (El atole), 396 **CD 19:12**

B
Ballad of the Bedbugs and the Beetles, The, 206 **CD 9:18**
Bella bimba (Pretty Girl), 172 **CD 8:4**
Billy, 7 **CD 1:4**
Bim Bom, 218 **CD 10:5**
Blow, Ye Winds, Blow, 192 **CD 9:1**
Bohm (Spring Has Come!), 392 **CD 19:2**
Boll Weevil, 171 **CD 8:1**
Boo!, 362 **CD 17:5**
Buffalo Dance Entrance Song, 325 **CD 15:4**
Butterfly Come Play with Me, 112 **CD 5:14**

C
Cat and Dog, 259 **CD 11:47**
Chag Asif (Harvest Time), 360 **CD 17:1**
Chan mali chan, 10 **CD 1:10**
Charlie, 208 **CD 9:21**
Chicka-ma, Chicka-ma, Craney Crow, 263 **CD 11:54**
Chicken on the Fence Post, 265 **CD 12:1**
Chinese Fishing Song (Wang Ü Ger), 190 **CD 8:32**
Chinese New Year Song (Gong xi fa cai), 384 **CD 18:19**
Cielito Lindo, 166 **CD 7:28**
Circle 'Round the Zero, 267 **CD 12:7**
City Life (with "I Love the Mountains"), 341 **CD 16:10**
Clock, The (La cloche), 67 **CD 3:21**
Clocks, 266 **CD 12:4**
Colors of the Wind, 84 **CD 4:5**
Consider Yourself, 335 **CD 16:1**
Coral, 249 **CD 11:21**
Cornstalk Fiddle and a Shoestring Bow, 284 **CD 13:13**
Crawdad Song, 107 **CD 5:5**
Cumberland Gap, 99 **CD 4:23**

D
¡Dale, dale, dale!, 378 **CD 18:7**
De aquel cerro (On the Darkened Hillside), 32 **CD 2:3**
Death of the Robin, 275 **CD 12:33**
Deck the Hall, 374 **CD 17:25**
Dide, 279 **CD 12:45**
Digga Digga Dog, 164 **CD 7:25**
Dinah, 150 **CD 7:8**
Ding Dong Diggy Diggy Dong, 269 **CD 12:16**
Draw a Bucket of Water, 222 **CD 10:11**

E
Egy üveg alma (One Jar of Apples), 22 **CD 1:27**
Eh Soom Boo Kawaya (Nigerian Boat Song), 58 **CD 3:11**
Eight Days of Hanukkah, The, 370 **CD 17:19**
El arroyo que murmura (The Murmuring Brook), 318 **CD 14:21**

Alphabetical Index of Songs and Speech Pieces (continued)

El atole (The Atole), 396 **CD 19:12**
El florón (The Flower), 46 **CD 2:22**
El nido (The Nest), 214 **CD 9:29**
En roulant ma boule (As I Roll My Ball), 100 **CD 4:26**
Evergreen, Everblue, 330 **CD 15:23**

F

First of January (Uno de enero), 210 **CD 9:24**
Flip, Flop and Fly, 336 **CD 16:4**
Flower, The (El florón), 46 **CD 2:22**
Frog in the Meadow, 243 **CD 11:4**
Frosty, the Snowman, 366 **CD 17:12**
Frosty Weather, 250 **CD 11:24**

G

Gi'Me Elbow Room, 88 **CD 4:12**
Go Tell It on the Mountain, 377 **CD 18:4**
Golden Ring Around the Susan Girl, 264 **CD 11:57**
Gong xi fa cai (Chinese New Year Song), 384 **CD 18:19**
Great Big House, 14 **CD 1:18**
Greatest Show on Earth, The, 308 **CD 14:4**

H

Happy Wanderer, The, 18 **CD 1:24**
Harvest Time (Chag Asif), 360 **CD 17:1**
Hello!, 283 **CD 13:10**
Herring, The, 316 **CD 14:17**
Hey, Motswala, 34 **CD 2:8**
Honorable Bear (Kuma San), 244 **CD 11:7**

I

I Have a Car, 252 **CD 11:28**
I Hear the Windmill (J'entends le moulin), 135 **CD 6:18**
I Lost the Farmer's Dairy Key, 273 **CD 12:26**
I Walk in Beauty, 329 **CD 15:19**
I'm a Believer, 312 **CD 14:10**
I'm on My Way, 382 **CD 18:16**
I've Been Working on the Railroad, C **Spotlight CD 4**
In Good Old Colony Times, 326 **CD 15:8**
Interjections, 303 **CD 13:26**
Interplanet Janet, 298 **CD 13:25**
I's the B'y, 13 **CD 1:15**
It's Time to Get Ready for Christmas, 372 **CD 17:22**
It's Raining (Que llueva), 274 **CD 12:29**

J

J'entends le moulin (I Hear the Windmill), 135 **CD 6:18**
Jamaica Farewell, 156 **CD 7:17**
Jasmine Flower, 146 **CD 7:1**
Jingle at the Window, 268 **CD 12:13**
John Jacob Jingleheimer Schmidt, 68 **CD 3:25**
Just Like the Sun, 394 **CD 19:9**

K

Kalinka (Little Snowball Bush), 224 **CD 10:14**
Kreely Kranky, 258 **CD 11:44**
Kum Bachur (The Rooster), 75 **CD 3:31**
Kuma San (Honorable Bear), 244 **CD 11:7**

L

La bamba, 236 **CD 10:27**
La cloche (The Clock), 67 **CD 3:21**
La mar (The Sea), 110 **CD 5:9**
Let Us Chase the Squirrel, 248 **CD 11:18**
Let's Go Dancing, 196 **CD 9:7**
Let's Go to the Sea (Vamos a la mar), 256 **CD 11:37**
Limbo Rock, 232 **CD 10:24**
Little Bear Song (Ucha Tirvarch), 53 **CD 3:4**
Little Bird (Pajarillo barranqueño), 358 **CD 16:25**
Little Boy of the Sheep, 188 **CD 8:29**
Little Sally Walker, 105 **CD 5:2**
Little Snowball Bush (Kalinka), 224 **CD 10:14**
Little Tommy Tinker, 277 **CD 12:39**
Look High, Look Low, 338 **CD 16:7**
Lukey's Boat, 114 **CD 5:17**

M

Marvelous Toy, The, 182 **CD 8:19**
May Day Carol, 393 **CD 19:6**
Minuteman Minute Song, The, 322 **CD 14:28**
Moon and Me, 220 **CD 10:8**
Morning Bells, 270 **CD 12:19**
Movin' Right Along, 124 **CD 6:1**
Mrs. Murphy's Chowder, 390 **CD 18:31**
Murmuring Brook, The (El arroyo que murmura), 318 **CD 14:21**
Music of the World A-Turnin', 44 **CD 2:19**
My Friend Tom, 364 **CD 17:9**
My Horses Ain't Hungry, 278 **CD 12:42**

N

Nest, The (El nido), 214 **CD 9:29**
Nigerian Boat Song (Eh Soom Boo Kawaya), 58 **CD 3:11**
Night Song, 186 **CD 8:26**

O

O Hanukkah (Oy Chanuke), 368 **CD 17:15**
O Mama Bakudala, 328 **CD 15:15**
O, the Train's Off the Track, 176 **CD 8:12**
Oh, Susanna, 153 **CD 7:11**
Old Mister Rabbit, 254 **CD 11:31**
Old Roger, 280 **CD 12:49**
Oleanna, 144 **CD 6:30**
On the Darkened Hillside (De aquel cerro), 32 **CD 2:3**
One Jar of Apples (Egy üveg alma), 22 **CD 1:27**
One More River, 216 **CD 10:2**
One Potato, Two Potato, 267 **CD 12:10**
One Small Voice, F **Spotlight CD 7**
Open the Window, Noah, 324 **CD 15:1**
Out from the Wilderness, 388 **CD 18:28**
Over My Head, 286 **CD 13:17**
Oy Chanuke (O Hanukkah), 368 **CD 17:15**

P

Pajarillo barranqueño (Little Bird), 358 **CD 16:25**
Pat-a-Pan, 375 **CD 17:28**
Patriotic Medley, H **Spotlight CD 10**
Paw Paw Patch, The, 195 **CD 9:4**

Pay Me My Money Down, 149 **CD 7:5**
Polly Wolly Doodle, 132 **CD 6:15**
Preamble, The, 293 **CD 13:23**
Pretty Girl (Bella bimba), 172 **CD 8:4**

Q

Que llueva (It's Raining), 274 **CD 12:29**

R

Raccoon Dance Song, 87 **CD 4:8**
Rain Is Falling Down, 242 **CD 11:1**
Rainbow Connection, The, 310 **CD 14:7**
Rattlesnake, 72 **CD 3:28**
Recycle Rap, 332 **CD 15:27**
Riding in the Buggy, 131 **CD 6:12**
Rise Up Singin', 138 **CD 6:22**
Rooster, The (Kum Bachur), 75 **CD 3:31**

S

Scotland's Burning, 257 **CD 11:41**
Sea, The (La mar), 110 **CD 5:9**
See the Rabbit Running, 255 **CD 11:34**
Seven Evenings (Tanabata), 62 **CD 3:15**
Shalom Chaveyrim (Shalom, My Friends), 141 **CD 6:25**
Shalom, My Friends (Shalom Chaveyrim), 141 **CD 6:25**
Shepherd, Shepherd, 56 **CD 3:8**
Ship Ahoy, 314 **CD 14:14**
Shoo Fly Pie and Apple Pan Dowdy, 227 **CD 10:19**
Simon Says, 4 **CD 1:1**
Smoke Goes Up the Chimney, 272 **CD 12:23**
Spiders, 282 **CD 13:5**
Spring Has Come! (Bohm), 392 **CD 19:2**
Step into the Spotlight, A **Spotlight CD 1**
Stevedore's Song, 127 **CD 6:4**
Sun Don't Set in the Mornin', 48, 60 **CD 2:27**
Sweep, Sweep Away, 276 **CD 12:36**
Sweet Potatoes, 16 **CD 1:21**

T

Tanabata (Seven Evenings), 62 **CD 3:15**
Taps, 281 **CD 13:2**
There's a Little Wheel A-Turnin' in My Heart, 129, 137 **CD 6:9**
This a Way and That a Way, 386 **CD 18:24**
This Is America, 356 **CD 16:19**
Three is a Magic Number, 296 **CD 13:24**
Three Little Birds, 204 **CD 9:15**
Throw It Out the Window, 94 **CD 4:19**
Tititorea, 174 **CD 8:8**
Trampin', 287 **CD 13:20**
Treasure Chests, 90 **CD 4:15**
Turn the Glasses Over, 260 **CD 11:50**

U

Ucha Tirvarch (Little Bear Song), 53 **CD 3:4**
Ujamaa, 380 **CD 18:11**
Uncle Jessie, 327 **CD 15:11**
Uno de enero (First of January), 210 **CD 9:24**

V

Vamos a la mar (Let's Go to the Sea), 256 **CD 11:37**

W

Wang Ü Ger (Chinese Fishing Song), 190 **CD 8:32**
Way Down South (speech piece) 8 **CD 1:7**
Wéané, 184 **CD 8:22**
When I First Came to This Land, 28 **CD 1:32**
Who's That Yonder? 245 **CD 11:11**
Woke Up This Morning, 180 **CD 8:16**
Woodchuck, 246 **CD 11:14**

Y

Yankee Doodle Boy, 357 **CD 16:22**
Yellow Submarine, 320 **CD 14:25**
You're a Grand Old Flag, 355 **CD 16:16**

Grade 4

A

A la nanita nana (A Little Lullaby), 230 **CD 11:28**
A la puerta del cielo (At the Gates of Heaven), 12 **CD 1:12**
Achshav (Now), 112 **CD 6:18**
All Through the Night, 277 **CD 15:26**
Allundé, Alluia, 34 **CD 2:20**
Ame fure (Rain), 26 **CD 2:9**
America, 354 **CD 20:10**
America, My Homeland, 358 **CD 20:17**
Are You Sleeping? (Frère Jacques), 260 **CD 14:1**
Arroyito serrano (Mountain Stream), 340 **CD 19:15**
At the Gates of Heaven (A la puerta del cielo), 12 **CD 1:12**
At the Hop, 306 **CD 17:16**

B

Bamboo Flute, 134 **CD 7:11**
Bamboo, 218 **CD 11:8**
Bell Doth Toll, The, 276 **CD 15:22**
Beryoza (The Birch Tree), 286 **CD 16:25**
Big Bunch, a Little Bunch, 267 **CD 14:24**
Birch Tree, The (Beryoza), 286 **CD 16:25**
Boogie Woogie Ghost, The, 368 **CD 21:6**
Buckeye Jim, 136 **CD 7:15**
Built My Lady a Fine Brick House, 252 **CD 13:9**
Butterfly (Farfallina), 244 **CD 12:16**
Bu-Vah (Sleep), 18 **CD 1:27**

C

Caballito blanco (Little White Pony), 278 **CD 15:30**
Cedar Swamp, 50 **CD 3:13**
Chairs to Mend, 272 **CD 15:7**
Chicka-hanka, 138 **CD 7:18**
Children's Festival (Tết Trung), 366 **CD 21:1**
Chumbara, 172 **CD 8:24**
Circle of Song, 330 **CD 18:26**
Cotton-Eye Joe, 52, 53 **CD 3:16**
Countermelody for Cotton-Eye Joe, 53 **CD 3:19**

Alphabetical Index of Songs and Speech Pieces (continued)

D

December Nights, December Lights, 372 **CD 21:15**
Derby Ram, The, 259 **CD 13:30**
Dima, 265 **CD 14:16**
Dok Djampa (The White Jasmine Flower), 392 **CD 22:20**
Don't Let the Music Stop, 334 **CD 19:1**
Down at the Twist and Shout, 308 **CD 17:19**
Dreidel Spin (S'vivon Sov), 374 **CD 21:18**

E

E nānā kākou i nā manu (Look at the Birds in the Sky), 338 **CD 19:11**
Eagle, 337 **CD 19:5**
Early in the Morning at Eight O'Clock, 59 **CD 4:1**
Eight Bells, 281 **CD 16:6**
El barquito (The Tiny Boat), 214 **CD 11:1**
El coquí (The Frog), 178 **CD 9:2**
El manisero (Peanut Vendor), 106 **CD 6:10**
El quelite (The Village), 362 **CD 20:23**
Enter, Holy Pilgrims (Entren santos peregrinos), 379 **CD 21:26**
Entren santos peregrinos (Enter, Holy Pilgrims), 379 **CD 21:26**

F

Farfallina (Butterfly), 244 **CD 12:16**
Follow Your Dream, 234 **CD 12:5**
Frère Jacques (Are You Sleeping?), 260 **CD 14:1**
Frog, The (El coquí), 178 **CD 9:2**
Frog Went A-Courtin', 46 **CD 3:7**

G

Girl from San Juan, The (La sanjuanerita), 100 **CD 6:1**
Girl I Left Behind Me, The, 249 **CD 12:35**
Goodbye Brother, 273 **CD 15:11**
Goodbye, My Riley O, 257 **CD 13:24**
Grandma's Feather Bed, E **Spotlight CD 7**
Green Gravel, 247 **CD 12:29**

H

Hala lala layya, 222 **CD 11:16**
Happiness, 124 **CD 6:31**
Happy Talk, 84 **CD 5:8**
Heave-Ho, Me Laddies, 258 **CD 13:27**
Hey, Look Me Over, 114 **CD 6:22**
Himmel und Erde (Music Alone Shall Live), 280 **CD 16:1**
Hine Ma Tov (How Good It Is), 66 **CD 4:13**
Hitori, 345 **CD 19:27**
Hojas de té (Tea Leaves) (speech piece), 256 **CD 13:20**
Hold My Mule, 248 **CD 12:32**
Hop Up and Jump Up, 271 **CD 15:4**
How Good It Is (Hine Ma Tov), 66 **CD 4:13**
How Long the Train Been Gone?, 264 **CD 14:13**

I

I Heard a Mockingbird, 150 **CD 7:31**
I Think I'm Gonna Like It Here, 299 **CD 17:3**
I Will Be Your Friend, 388 **CD 22:11**
I'll Rise When the Rooster Crows, 36 **CD 2:24**
It Rained a Mist, 262 **CD 14:9**
It's the Hard-Knock Life, 293 **CD 17:1**

J

Johnson Boys, 233 **CD 12:2**
Jolly Old St. Nicholas, 382 **CD 21:33**
Journey, A (speech piece), 14 **CD 1:17**
Joy to the World, 383 **CD 22:1**
Just One Planet, 164 **CD 8:12**

K

Katyusha, 188 **CD 9:15**
Kettle Valley Line, The, 348 **CD 20:1**
Korobushka, 285 **CD 16:21**

L

L'inverno è già passato (Winter is Over), 390 **CD 22:15**
La otra España (The Other Spain), 62 **CD 4:5**
La sanjuanerita (The Girl from San Juan), 100 **CD 6:1**
La Yunsita, 350 **CD 20:5**
Las mañanitas (The Morning Song), 194 **CD 9:24**
Li'l 'Liza Jane, 20 **CD 2:1**
Little Coffee Mill (Molinillo de café) (speech piece), 250 **CD 13:1**
Little David Play on Your Harp, 323 **CD 18:14**
Little Hawk (Sansa kroma), 166 **CD 8:15**
Little Lullaby, A (A la nanita nana), 230 **CD 11:28**
Little Mountain Stream (Arroyito serrano), 340 **CD 19:15**
Little White Pony (Caballito blanco), 278 **CD 15:30**
Loco-Motion, The, 312 **CD 17:25**
Long-Legged Sailor, 243 **CD 12:12**
Look at the Birds in the Sky (E nānā kākou i nā manu), 338 **CD 19:11**
Looking for Shelter (Para pedir Posada), 376 **CD 21:22**
Love Somebody, 94 **CD 5:22**

M

Macnamara's Band, 88 **CD 5:14**
Marken er mejet (Out in the Meadow), 365 **CD 20:28**
Mighty River (speech piece), 217 **CD 11:5**
Modern Dragon, A (speech piece), 98 **CD 5:27**
Molinillo de café (Little Coffee Mill) (speech piece), 250 **CD 13:1**
Morning Has Broken, 22 **CD 2:4**
Morning Song, The (Las mañanitas), 194 **CD 9:24**
'Most Done Ling'rin' Here, 65 **CD 4:10**
Music Alone Shall Live (Himmel und Erde), 280 **CD 16:1**
My Home's in Montana, 274 **CD 15:14**
My Town, My World, 6 **CD 1:4**

N

N.Y.C., 302 **CD 17:4**
New Day, The, 316 **CD 18:4**
Nia, 384 **CD 22:4**
Night Herding Song, 110 **CD 6:15**
Now (Achshav), 112 **CD 6:18**

O

Octopus's Garden, 30 **CD 2:14**
Ogguere, 327 **CD 18:21**
Oh, Won't You Sit Down?, 70 **CD 4:18**
Old Abram Brown, 32 **CD 2:17**
Old Ark's A-Moverin', 130 **CD 7:5**
Old Aunt Dinah, 245 **CD 12:23**
Old Carrion Crow, 192 **CD 9:21**
Old House, 282 **CD 16:9**
Old Joe Clark, 74 **CD 4:23**
Old Paint, 275 **CD 15:18**
Oliver Cromwell, 269 **CD 14:31**
Once Upon a Christmastime, 380 **CD 21:30**
Oro, My Bodeen, 279 **CD 15:34**
Other Spain, The (La otra España), 62 **CD 4:5**
Out in the Meadow (Marken er mejet), 364 **CD 20:28**
Over the Rainbow, 126 **CD 7:1**
Over the River and Through the Wood, 370 **CD 21:9**
Over the Sea to Skye, 344 **CD 19:24**
Owl and the Cuckoo, The, 337 **CD 19:8**

P

Page's Train, 246 **CD 12:26**
Para pedir posada (Looking for Shelter), 377 **CD 21:22**
Pat Works on the Railway, 86 **CD 5:11**
Patriotic Medley, H **Spotlight CD 10**
Peace Round, 16 **CD 1:22**
Peanut Vendor (El manisero), 106 **CD 6:10**
Peasant's Dancing Day, 132 **CD 7:8**
Please, Mr. Postman, 44 **CD 3:4**
Purpose (Nia), 384 **CD 22:4**
Push Boat Song, 266 **CD 14:20**

Q

¿Quién es ese pajarito? (Who Is That Little Bird?), 284 **CD 16:17**

R

Rain (Ame fure), 26 **CD 2:9**
Ridin' of a Goat, Leadin' of a Sheep, 251 **CD 13:5**
Rise Up, O Flame, 283 **CD 16:12**
Roll on, Columbia, 182 **CD 9:8**
Row, Row, Row Your Boat, 268 **CD 14:28**

S

S'vivon Sov (Dreidel Spin), 374 **CD 21:18**
Sail Away, Ladies, 54 **CD 3:20**
Sandpiper, The ('Ulili E), 396 **CD 22:28**
Sandy McNab, 142 **CD 7:23**
Sansa kroma (Little Hawk), 166 **CD 8:15**
Sarasponda, 210 **CD 10:15**
Sea Shell, 245 **CD 12:20**
Shabat Shalom, 170 **CD 8:20**
Shenandoah, D **Spotlight CD 4**
Sing Alleluia, Allelu, 220 **CD 11:11**
Sitsiritsit, 102 **CD 6:5**
Sky Dances, 206 **CD 10:8**
Sleep (Bu-Vah), 18 **CD 1:27**

Something For Me, Something For You, 4 **CD 1:1**
Somos el barco (We Are the Boat), 10 **CD 1:8**
Song of Thanksgiving, 371 **CD 21:12**
Star-Spangled Banner, The, 356 **CD 20:14**
Step into the Spotlight, A **Spotlight CD 1**
Swapping Song, 253 **CD 13:12**
Swing, The, 320 **CD 18:11**

T

Take Time in Life, 156 **CD 8:4**
Tea Leaves (Hojas de té) (speech piece), 256 **CD 13:20**
Tết Trung (Children's Festival), 366 **CD 21:1**
This Land Is Your Land, 146 **CD 7:28**
This Train, 343 **CD 19:20**
Tiny Boat, The (El barquito), 214 **CD 11:1**
Tomorrow, 295 **CD 17:2**
Train Is A-Coming, 270 **CD 15:1**
Twist and Shout, 314 **CD 18:1**

U

`Ulili E (The Sandpiper), 396 **CD 22:28**

V

Village, The (El quelite), 362 **CD 20:23**
Viva la musica, 174 **CD 8:28**

W

Wake Up Canon, 326 **CD 18:18**
Walk in the Parlor, 226 **CD 11:21**
Walking in the Air, 317 **CD 18:7**
Water Come a Me Eye, 90 **CD 5:17**
We Are Here, 394 **CD 22:24**
We Are the Boat (Somos el barco), 10 **CD 1:8**
We Got the Beat, 310 **CD 17:22**
We Remember, 360 **CD 20:20**
We Shall Overcome, 387 **CD 22:8**
What Can One Little Person Do?, 204 **CD 10:5**
When I Was Young, 187 **CD 9:12**
White Jasmine Flower, The (Dok Djampa), 392 **CD 22:20**
Who Is That Little Bird? (¿Quién es ese pajarito?), 284 **CD 16:17**
Who's Got the Fishpole?, 261 **CD 14:5**
Winter is Over (L'inverno è già passato), 390 **CD 22:15**
Woodpecker, The (speech piece), 48 **CD 3:10**

Y

Yankee Doodle, 154 **CD 8:1**
You're Never Fully Dressed Without a Smile, 304 **CD 17:5**

Z

Zum gali gali, 255 **CD 13:16**

Grade 5

A

A Zing-A Za, 338 **CD 20:12**
Aeyaya balano sakkad (Come, Children), 402 **CD 23:26**

Grade-Level Index of Songs and Speech Pieces

Agahu, 72 **CD 5:2**

Allá en el rancho grande (My Ranch), 66 **CD 4:17**

Alligator Dance (Tekanionton'néha'), 223 **CD 12:27**

Amazing Grace, 19 **CD 1:23**

America, the Beautiful, 388 **CD 23:1**

Aquaqua, 258 **CD 15:11**

Arirang, 50 **CD 3:13**

Army Is Marching, An (Singabahambayo) (parts), 76 **CD 4:1**

Army Is Marching, An (Singabahambayo) (unison), 56 **CD 4:1**

¡Ay, Jalisco no te rajes! (Ay, Jalisco, Never Fail Her), 188 **CD 10:22**

Ay, Jalisco, Never Fail Her (¡Ay, Jalisco no te rajes!), 188 **CD 10:22**

B

Babylon's Fallin', 243 **CD 13:22**

Backwater Blues, 175 **CD 10:8**

Ballad of the Underground Railroad, The, (complete song), 154 **CD 8:11**

Ballad of the Underground Railroad, The, (refrain) 145 **CD 8:11**

Battle Hymn of the Republic, 391 **CD 23:5**

Beauty and the Beast, 124 **CD 7:5**

Big Big World, 438 **CD 25:28**

Big Yellow Taxi, E **Spotlight CD 7**

Bows, 305 **CD 18:14**

By the Singing Water, 270 **CD 16:26**

C

Caissons Go Rolling Along, The, 37 **CD 2:21**

Carnival Is Coming, The (De allacito carnavalito), 269 **CD 16:22**

Change Is Good, 84 **CD 5:13**

Change the World, 314 **CD 19:14**

Chorus of Villagers from *The Bartered Bride*, 275 **CD 17:7**

Cidade Maravilhosa (Wonderful City), 432 **CD 25:15**

Cindy, 265 **CD 16:10**

Circle of Friends, 196 **CD 11:14**

City Blues, 278 **CD 17:19**

Cliffs of Doneen, The, 46 **CD 3:8**

Come, Children (Aeyaya balano sakkad), 402 **CD 23:26**

Cornfields, The (Los maizales), 268 **CD 16:17**

Cuando salí de Cuba (I Went Away from Cuba), 168 **CD 9:22**

Cumbia del sol (Cumbia of the Sun), 16 **CD 1:19**

Cumbia of the Sun (Cumbia del sol), 16 **CD 1:19**

D

Da pacem Domine (Give Us Peace), 261 **CD 15:22**

Dance for the Nations, 206 **CD 11:26**

De allacito carnavalito (The Carnival Is Coming), 269 **CD 16:22**

De colores (Many Colors) (2-part), 98 **CD 5:22**

De colores (Many Colors) (unison), 88 **CD 5:22**

Deta, Deta (The Moon), 246 **CD 14:4**

Do Not Wake My Little Son (No despiertes a mi niño), 217 **CD 12:14**

Dove That Flew Away, The (La paloma se fue), 259 **CD 15:15**

Dreamers, 430 **CD 25:12**

Dry Bones, 406 **CD 24:5**

E

Ēinīnī (Little Birds Sleep), 340 **CD 20:16**

Eka Muda (Red Mule), 28 **CD 2:9**

El jarabe (Mexican Hat Dance), 396 **CD 23:13**

El vito, 210 **CD 12:5**

Erie Canal, 132 **CD 7:22**

Estrella brillante (Shining Star), 373 **CD 22:17**

Ev'rybody Loves Saturday Night (Mɔfia moni), 277 **CD 17:15**

Every Day I Have the Blues, 179 **CD 10:15**

Everybody Rejoice, 226 **CD 13:7**

F

Fall (Ga Eul), 401 **CD 23:22**

Feel Good, 358 **CD 21:20**

Feliz Navidad (Merry Christmas), 420 **CD 25:1**

Fifty Nifty United States, 392 **CD 23:9**

Follow the Drinkin' Gourd, 142 **CD 8:7**

Fun wa ni alaafia (Send Us Your Peace), 248 **CD 14:9**

Fung Yang Song, 58 **CD 4:8**

Funiculi, Funicula, 62 **CD 4:13**

G

Ga Eul (Fall), 401 **CD 23:22**

Gentle River Runs, A, 342 **CD 20:21**

Girl with a Shiny Ribbon, A (Och Jungfrun Hon Går I Ringen), 190 **CD 11:1**

Give Us Peace (Da pacem Domine), 261 **CD 15:22**

God Bless America, 4 **CD 1:1**

Goin' Home, 108 **CD 6:17**

Good Mornin', Blues, 177 **CD 10:12**

Great Big Sea, A, 334 **CD 20:9**

Guantanamera, 215 **CD 12:10**

H

Haere Ra (Now Is the Hour), 151 **CD 9:3**

Hallelujah, Get on Board, 345 **CD 21:1**

Haneirot Halalu (These Lights), 414 **CD 24:21**

Hava Nagila, 54 **CD 3:23**

Hero, 312 **CD 19:11**

Hill an' Gully, 250 **CD 14:16**

Holly and the Ivy, The, 418 **CD 24:28**

Home on the Range, D **Spotlight CD 4**

How Brightly Shines the Morning Star (Wie schön leuchtet der Morgenstern), 370 **CD 22:12**

How Can I Keep from Singing?, 287 **CD 18:5**

I

I Am But a Small Voice, 323 **CD 19:30**

I Got Rhythm, 187 **CD 10:19**

I Hear America Singing, 327 **CD 20:2**

I Saw the Light, 252 **CD 14:22**

I Went Away from Cuba (Cuando salí de Cuba), 168 **CD 9:22**

Alphabetical Index of Songs and Speech Pieces (continued)

In That Great Git'n Up Mornin', 10 **CD 1:11**
Iowa Stubborn, 293 **CD 18:10**
Is That Mister Reilly?, 282 **CD 17:28**

J

Jingle-Bell Rock, 424 **CD 25:5**
John Henry, 146 **CD 8:16**
John Kanaka, 249 **CD 14:13**
Jó ashílá (Traveling Together), 224 **CD 13:2**
Joshua Fit the Battle of Jericho, 126 **CD 7:9**
Joyful, Joyful, 105 **CD 6:13**
Joyful, Joyful, We Adore Thee, 103 **CD 6:10**
Just Give Me the Beat (speech piece), 9 **CD 1:8**

K

Kojo No Tsuki (Moon at the Ruined Castle), 149 **CD 8:20**

L

La paloma se fue (The Dove That Flew Away),
 259 **CD 15:15**
La víbora de la mar (The Serpent from the Sea),
 440 **CD 26:1**
Lift Every Voice and Sing, 86 **CD 5:18**
Lift Up Your Voices, 319 **CD 19:20**
Light One Candle, 416 **CD 24:25**
Like a Mighty Stream, 320 **CD 19:26**
Lion Sleeps Tonight, The, 172 **CD 10:1**
Listen How It Goes (Oye como va), 69 **CD 4:22**
Little Birds Sleep (Ēinīnī), 340 **CD 20:16**
Loch Lomond, 138 **CD 8:4**
Los maizales (The Cornfields), 268 **CD 16:17**
Lots o' Fish in Bonavist' Harbor, 263 **CD 16:4**

M

Mango Walk, 90 **CD 5:27**
Many Colors (De colores) (2-part), 98 **CD 5:22**
Many Colors (De colores) (unison), 88 **CD 5:22**
Mary Ann, 166 **CD 9:19**
Merry Christmas (Feliz Navidad), 420 **CD 25:1**
Mexican Hat Dance (El jarabe), 396 **CD 23:13**
Mi gallo (My Rooster), 272 **CD 16:30**
Mɔfia moni (Ev'rybody Loves Saturday Night),
 277 **CD 17:15**
Moon, The (Deta, Deta), 246 **CD 14:4**
Moon at the Ruined Castle (Kojo No Tsuki), 149 **CD 8:20**
My Government Claim (3-part), 110 **CD 6:20**
My Government Claim (unison), 95 **CD 6:5**
My Ranch (Allá en el rancho grande), 66 **CD 4:17**
My Rooster (Mi gallo), 272 **CD 16:30**

N

Nani Wale Na Hala (The Swaying Pandanus Trees),
 276 **CD 17:11**
New Year's Song (Suk San Wan Pi Mai), 437 **CD 25:24**
Ngam sang duan (Shining Moon), 376 **CD 22:23**
No despiertes a mi niño (Do Not Wake My Little Son),
 217 **CD 12:14**
Nottamun Town, 405 **CD 24:2**
Now Is the Hour (Haere Ra), 151 **CD 9:3**

O

O, I'm Gonna Sing, 245 **CD 14:1**
Och Jungfrun Hon Går I Ringen (A Girl with a Shiny Ribbon),
 190 **CD 11:1**
Oh, Shope, Shope (Shope, Shope), 220 **CD 12:20**
Old Dan Tucker, 253 **CD 14:25**
Old Turkey Buzzard, 264 **CD 16:7**
One, Two, and Three (Uno, dos y tres), 364 **CD 22:1**
On the Sunny Side of the Street, 361 **CD 21:24**
Orchestra Song, 332 **CD 20:6**
Our World, 381 **CD 22:31**
Oye como va (Listen How It Goes), 69 **CD 4:22**

P

Parrot from Verapaz, A (Un lorito de Verapaz), 349 **CD 21:6**
Path to the Moon, The, 368 **CD 22:9**
Patriotic Medley, H **Spotlight CD 10**
Pick-a-Little/Goodnight Ladies, 299 **CD 18:12**
Pop! Goes the Weasel, 94 **CD 6:2**
Power of the Dream, The, 44 **CD 3:5**

Q

Qué bonita bandera (What a Beautiful Flag), 442 **CD 26:5**

R

Reach, 14 **CD 1:16**
Red Mule (Eka Muda), 28 **CD 2:9**
Ride Like the Wind, 130 **CD 7:17**
Rise Up, Shepherd, and Follow, 422 **CD 25:4**
Rock and Roll Is Here to Stay, 316 **CD 19:17**
Rock Island, 291 **CD 18:9**
Rocky Top, 352 **CD 21:11**
'Round the Corner, Sally, 251 **CD 14:19**

S

St. Patrick's Day, 434 **CD 25:20**
Samiotissa, 284 **CD 18:1**
Saint Lucia (Sankta Lucia), 413 **CD 24:15**
Sankta Lucia (Saint Lucia), 413 **CD 24:15**
Santa Marta, 398 **CD 23:18**
Season of Hope, The, 410 **CD 24:12**
Serpent from the Sea, The (La víbora de la mar), 440 **CD 26:1**
Send Us Your Peace (Fun wa ni alaafia), 248 **CD 14:9**
Seventy-Six Trombones, 296 **CD 18:11**
Shining Moon (Ngam sang duan), 376 **CD 22:23**
Shining Star (Estrella brillante), 373 **CD 22:17**
Shope Shope (Oh, Shope, Shope), 220 **CD 12:20**
Side Show, The, 283 **CD 17:31**
Simple Gifts, 136 **CD 8:1**
Sing, America Sing!, 6 **CD 1:5**
Sing, Sing, Sing, 30 **CD 2:13**
Singabahambayo (An Army Is Marching) (parts), 76 **CD 4:1**
Singabahambayo (An Army Is Marching) (unison),
 56 **CD 4:1**
Somebody's Knockin' at Your Door, 254 **CD 14:28**
Song of Peace, 257 **CD 15:8**
Sound the Trumpet, 279 **CD 17:22**
Southern Nights, 310 **CD 19:8**
Star Canon, 367 **CD 22:6**
Star-Spangled Banner, The, 386 **CD 22:35**

Step into the Spotlight, A **Spotlight CD 1**
Streets of Laredo, 260 **CD 15:19**
Suk San Wan Pi Mai (New Year's Song), 437 **CD 25:24**
Surfin' U.S.A., 306 **CD 19:1**
Swaying Pandanus Trees, The (Nani Wale Na Hala), 276 **CD 17:11**
Sweet Music, 319 **CD 19:23**

T

Tekanionton'néha' (Alligator Dance), 223 **12:27**
These Lights (Haneirot Halalu), 414 **CD 24:21**
There's a Song in Me, (2-part) 183 **CD 9:14**
There's a Song in Me, (melody) 164 **CD 9:14**
There's No Hidin' Place, 266 **CD 16:14**
Times They Are A-Changin', The, 204 **CD 11:23**
Traveling Together (Jó ashílá), 224 **CD 13:2**
Triple Play, 355 **CD 21:15**
Tumbai, 194 **CD 11:8**
Turn the World Around, 208 **CD 12:1**
Tzena, Tzena, 171 **CD 9:26**

U

Ujima, 427 **CD 25:9**
Un lorito de Verapaz (A Parrot from Verapaz), 349 **CD 21:6**
Uncle Pen, 24 **CD 2:2**
Uno, dos y tres (One, Two, and Three), 364 **CD 22:1**
Üsküdar, 128 **CD 7:13**

V

Vive l'amour, 262 **CD 16:1**

W

'Way Down Yonder in the Brickyard, 255 **CD 15:1**
We Are the Children of Tomorrow, 114 **CD 6:24**
We Want to Sing, 235 **CD 13:17**
Wells Fargo Wagon, The, 303 **CD 18:13**
What a Beautiful Flag (Qué bonita bandera), 442 **CD 26:5**
What the World Needs Now, 230 **CD 13:12**
When Johnny Comes Marching Home, 34 **CD 2:18**
When the Saints Go Marching In, 256 **CD 15:5**
Where Is John?, 274 **CD 17:1**
Wie schön leuchtet der Morgenstern (How Brightly Shines the Morning Star), 370 **CD 22:12**
Winter Wonderland, 408 **CD 24:8**
Wonderful City (Cidade Maravilhosa), 432 **CD 25:15**
Words of Wisdom, 244 **CD 13:25**

Y

Yakety Yak, 308 **CD 19:5**

Grade 6

A

Al lado de mi cabaña (Beside My Cottage), 141 **CD 8:6**
All Ye Who Music Love, 336 **CD 18:7**
Alleluia, 186 **CD 10:13**
Alleluia (Heleluyan), 188 **CD 10:17**
America, 388 **CD 21:1**
Angelina, 8 **CD 1:10**
Angels We Have Heard on High (Les anges dans nos campagnes), 406 **CD 22:7**
A-Rovin', 319 **CD 17:25**

B

Barbry Ellen, 208 **CD 11:9**
Bashana Haba'ah (In the Year to Come), 360 **CD 19:19**
Belle qui tiens ma vie (My Love, You Hold My Life), 99 **CD 6:4**
Beside My Cottage (Al lado de mi cabaña), 141 **CD 8:6**
Blue Suede Shoes, 236 **CD 12:25**
Bop 'til You Drop, 87 **CD 5:17**
Bulbes ('Taters), 280 **CD 15:40**

C

Camelot, 310 **CD 17:8**
Canon, 256 **CD 14:1**
Cape Cod Chantey, 258 **CD 14:7**
Captain Jinks, 266 **CD 14:29**
Carol from an Irish Cabin, 408 **CD 22:12**
Charleston, 112 **CD 6:28**
Charlotte Town, 261 **CD 14:17**
Cherry Blossoms (Sakura), 14 **CD 1:19**
Chiribim, 57 **CD 3:24**
Choo, Choo, Ch'Boogie, 180 **CD 10:4**
Chiu, chiu, chiu, 172 **CD 9:16**
Coasts of High Barbary, The, 329 **CD 18:1**
Come and Sing Together, 281 **CD 16:1**
Come, Firefly (Hotaru Koi), 255 **CD 13:45**
Comedy Tonight, 204 **CD 11:3**
Conga, 34 **CD 2:9**
Cowboy, The (El Charro), 278 **CD 15:33**
Crescent Moon (Yüe líang wan wan), 26 **CD 1:34**
Cripple Creek, 372 **CD 20:1**
Cum-ma-la Be-stay, **370 CD 19:26**

D

Dance of Orpheus (Samba de Orfeu), 190 **CD 10:20**
Dancing in the Street, 84 **CD 5:14**
Dandansoy, 356 **CD 19:9**
Dere Geliyor (River Overflowing), 232 **CD 12:18**
Derry Ding Dong Dason, 249 **CD 13:19**
Didn't It Rain, 345 **CD 18:22**
Diwali Song, 396 **CD 21:22**
Do Lord, 260 **CD 14:14**
Doctor Jazz, 378 **CD 20:11**
Doing the Latest Rag, 314 **CD 17:16**
Dona Nobis Pacem, 335 **CD 18:6**
Doney Gal, 115 **CD 6:32**
Down by the Riverside, 22 **CD 1:30**
Drum, The (El tambor), 222 **CD 11:28**

E

Earth Child, 426 **CD 23:14**
El charro (The Cowboy), 278 **CD 15:33**
El tambor (The Drum), 222 **CD 11:28**
El tecolote (The Owlet), 392 **CD 21:13**
Elijah Rock, 52 **CD 3:15**

Alphabetical Index of Songs and Speech Pieces (continued)

Ev'ry Time I Feel the Spirit, C **Spotlight CD 4**
Every Mornin' When I Wake Up, 275 **CD 15:30**

F

Finnish Forest, The (Suomen Salossa), 422 **CD 23:5**
Fortune Favors the Brave, 316 **CD 17:20**
Full Moon Song (Pleeng loy krathong), 399 **CD 21:26**

G

Gee, Mom, I Want to Go Home, 148 **CD 8:18**
Ghost Ship, The, 323 **CD 17:29**
Git Along, Little Dogies, 284 **CD 16:11**
Gonna Build a Mountain, 4 **CD 1:1**
Goober Peas, 269 **CD 15:2**
Good News, 242 **CD 12:29**
Greenland Whale Fishery, The, 212 **CD 11:15**
Guitar Man, The, 138 **CD 8:1**

H

Haji Firuz, 421 **CD 23:1**
Hava Nashira (Sing Alleluia), 67 **CD 4:14**
Have You Not Seen My Daughters? (Neviděli jste tu mé panenky?), 228 **CD 12:10**
Heart, 166 **CD 9:9**
Hae Wa Be (Sun and Rain), 273 **CD 15:17**
Heleluyan (Alleluia), 188 **CD 10:17**
Hotaru Koi (Come, Firefly), 255 **CD 13:45**
Huainito, 351 **CD 19:1**
Hullaballoo Balay, 10 **CD 1:13**

I

I Am Poor (Pauper sum ego), 254 **CD 13:38**
I Got a Letter, 270 **CD 15:6**
I Love a Piano, 130 **CD 7:15**
I Want to Be Ready, 12 **CD 1:16**
I'm Going to Georgia, 244 **CD 12:35**
I'm Gonna Sit at the Welcome Table, 416 **CD 22:24**
If I Had a Hammer, 174 **CD 9:20**
In the Year to Come (Bashana Haba'ah), 360 **CD 19:17**
It Don't Mean a Thing, 164 **CD 9:5**

J

Já do lesa nepojedu (To the Woods I Will Not Go), 227 **CD 12:6**
Jack Was Ev'ry Bit a Sailor, 170 **CD 9:13**
Jede, jede poštovský panáček (Riding, Riding, Is Mr. Postman), 226 **CD 12:2**
Jikel' emaweni (Throw It in the Slope), 70 **CD 4:22**
Joban Miners' Song (Joban Tanko Bushi), 142 **CD 8:10**
Joban Tanko Bushi (Joban Miners' Song), 142 **CD 8:10**
Jordan's Angels, 365 **CD 19:22**

K

Kakokolo, 262 **CD 14:20**
Kokoleoko, 279 **CD 15:37**

L

La Bamba, 381 **CD 20:15**
La pájara pinta (The Speckled Bird), 268 **CD 14:32**

Lean on Me, 150 **CD 8:22**
Leila, 376 **CD 20:6**
Les anges dans nos campagnes (Angels We Have Heard on High), 406 **CD 22:7**
Let It Roll, 124 **CD 7:8**
Let Music Surround You, 285 **CD 16:14**
Listen to the Music, 63 **CD 4:6**
Lonesome Dove, 249 **CD 13:16**
Lord Bless Africa (N'kosi sikelel' i Afrika), 339 **CD 18:11**
Lullaby of Broadway, 182 **CD 10:7**
Lumber Camp Song, The, 136 **CD 7:28**

M

Ma'oz Tsur (Rock of Ages), 405 **CD 22:2**
Mama Don't 'Low, 126 **CD 7:11**
Mama Will Provide, 296 **CD 16:22**
Mayim, Mayim (Water, Water), 102 **CD 6:9**
Mele Kalikimaka (Merry Christmas), 410 **CD 22:16**
Merecumbé, 276 **CD 15:26**
Merry Christmas (Mele Kalikimaka), 410 **CD 22:16**
Mi caballo blanco (My White Horse), 60 **CD 4:1**
Mountain Music, 20 **CD 1:27**
Mr. Scott Joplin's Ragtime Rag!, 110 **CD 6:25**
My Love, You Hold My Life (Belle qui tiens ma vie), 99 **CD 6:4**
My White Horse (Mi caballo blanco), 60 **CD 4:1**

N

Nanticoke Women's Honoring Song (O Hal' lwe), 428 **CD 23:18**
Neviděli jste tu mé panenky? (Have You Not Seen My Daughters?), 228 **CD 12:10**
Night of Stars/Silent Night, 412 **CD 22:19**
Never Sleep Late Anymore, 274 **CD 15:23**
New Ashmolean Marching Society and Students Conservatory Band, The, 308 **CD 17:5**
N'kosi sikelel' i Afrika (Lord Bless Africa), 339 **CD 18:11**

O

O, Desayo, 50 **CD 3:10**
O Hal' lwe (Nanticoke Women's Honoring Song), 428 **CD 23:18**
O, La Le!, 6 **CD 1:5**
Oh, How Lovely Is the Evening, 252 **CD 13:31**
Old Barn Dance, The, 94 **CD 5:25**
Old Jim John, 253 **CD 13:34**
Ole La'u Papa e, 91 **CD 5:20**
On a Clear Day, 206 **CD 11:6**
One Dime Blues, 178 **CD 10:1**
One of Those Songs, 54 **CD 3:19**
Orange Blossom Special, 33 **CD 2:6**
Our Goodman, 245 **CD 13:1**
Owlet, The (El tecolote), 392 **CD 21:13**

P

Patriotic Medley, H **Spotlight CD 11**
Pauper sum ego (I Am Poor), 254 **CD 13:38**
Perfect Winter Day, A, 400 **CD 21:28**
Pick a Bale of Cotton, 254 **CD 13:42**
Pleeng loy krathong (Full Moon Song), 399 **CD 21:26**

Alphabetical Index of Songs and Speech Pieces (continued)

R

Rage and Roar, 48 **CD 3:7**
Red Iron Ore, 134 **CD 7:25**
Ride on the Wind, 326 **CD 17:33**
Riding, Riding, Is Mr. Postman (Jede, jede poštovský
 panáček), 226 **CD 12:2**
Risseldy, Rosseldy, 264 **CD 14:25**
River of My People, 176 **CD 9:23**
River Overflowing (Dere Geliyor), 232 **CD 12:18**
Rock Around the Clock, 234 **CD 12:22**
Rock of Ages (Ma'oz Tsur), 405 **CD 22:2**
Roll de Ole Chariot Along, 243 **CD 12:32**
Round and Round, 104 **CD 6:13**
Round Dance (Tsiothwatasè:tha), 109 **CD 6:21**

S

Sakura (Cherry Blossoms), 14 **CD 1:19**
Salamanca Market, 247 **CD 13:7**
Samba de Orfeu (Dance of Orpheus), 190 **CD 10:20**
Scraping Up Sand, 248 **CD 13:13**
Shady Grove, 286 **CD 16:17**
Shibolet Basadeh (Wheat in the Field), 424 **CD 23:10**
Ship in Distress, The, 211 **CD 11:12**
Shoes of John, 246 **CD 13:4**
Sing Alleluia (Hava Nashira), 67 **CD 4:14**
Sing Hosanna, 362 **CD 19:20**
Slap That Bass, 146 **CD 8:15**
Sometimes I Feel Like a Motherless Child, 271 **CD 15:9**
Speckled Bird, The (La pájara pinta), 268 **CD 14:32**
Stars and Stripes Forever, The, 390 **CD 21:9**
Star-Spangled Banner, The, 386 **CD 20:21**
Step into the Spotlight, A **Spotlight CD 1**
Sugar in the Gourd, 251 **CD 13:27**
Suliram, 59 **CD 3:28**
Sun and Rain (Hae Wa Be), 273 **CD 15:17**
Suomen Salossa (The Finnish Forest), 422 **CD 23:5**
Sweet and Low, 184 **CD 10:10**

T

Tain't What You Do, 18 **CD 1:24**
'Taters (Bulbes), 280 **CD 15:40**
That Great Come and Get It Day, 306 **CD 17:1**
There Was a Blue Flower, 221 **CD 11:24**
There Was a Jolly Miller, 250 **CD 13:24**

They Call the Wind Maria, 312 **CD 17:12**
This Pretty Planet, 194 **CD 10:25**
Throw It Down the Slope (Jikel' emaweni), 70 **CD 4:22**
Tina singu, 36 **CD 2:13**
To the Woods I Will Not Go (Já do lesa nepojedu),
 227 **CD 12:6**
Troika, 230 **CD 12:15**
Trout, The, 342 **CD 18:17**
Tsing Chun U Chü (Youth Dance Song), 272 **CD 15:13**
Tsiothwatasè:tha (Round Dance), 109 **CD 6:21**
Tum Balalaika, 68 **CD 4:18**

U

Ua txiab (The Village), 394 **CD 21:18**

V

Vem Kan Segla (Who Can Sail?), 419 **CD 22:28**
Village, The (Ua txiab), 394 **CD 21:18**

W

Wabash Cannonball, The, 30 **CD 2:2**
Wachet auf (Waken Now), 259 **CD 14:10**
Waiting for Life, 292 **CD 16:21**
Waken Now (Wachet auf), 259 **CD 14:10**
Walk by the River, 74 **CD 5:2**
Water Is Wide, The, 46 **CD 3:4**
Water, Water (Mayim, Mayim), 102 **CD 6:9**
Wayfaring Stranger, 283 **CD 16:8**
Wheat in the Field (Shibolet Basadeh), 424 **CD 23:10**
When I Sing, 44 **CD 3:1**
Who Can Sail? (Vem Kan Segla), 419 **CD 22:28**
Why We Tell the Story, 303 **CD 16:23**
Wind Beneath My wings, The, E **Spotlight CD 8**
Winter ade (G Major), 132 **CD 7:18**
Winter ade (G Minor), 133 **CD 7:22**
Wondering, 282 **CD 16:5**

Y

Yellow Bird, 154 **CD 8:27**
Yerakina, 216 **CD 11:19**
You Sing for Me, 106 **CD 6:17**
Youth Dance Song (Tsing Chun U Chü), 272 **CD 15:13**
Yüe líang wan wan (Crescent Moon), 26 **CD 1:34**

Grade-Level Index of
Songs and Speech Pieces

By Composer

Adams: *Short Ride in a Fast Machine*, **Gr. 5**, 125

Anderson (arr.): Old MacDonald Had a Farm, **Gr. 2**, 133

ILM Anderson: *Waltzing Cat*, **Gr. K**, T223

Appell and Mann: Let's Twist Again, **Gr. 7**, 11

ILM Arban: *Carnival of Venice, The*, **Gr. 6**, 40

Arbeau: Belle qui tiens ma vie (My Love, You Have My Heart), **Gr. 6**, 100

Arlen and Harburg: Over the Rainbow from *The Wizard of Oz*, **Gr. K**, T60

ILM Bach: Badinerie from Suite for Orchestra No. 2 in B Minor, **Gr. 4**, 61; **Gr. 5**, 41

Bach: *Brandenburg Concerto No. 5*, Third Movement, **Gr. 6**, 128

Bach: Concerto for Violin and Oboe BWV 1060, Adagio (excerpt), **Gr. 2**, 127

Bach: Gavotte from Suite No. 5 for Cello, **Gr. 2**, 41

ILM Bach: Gigue from Suite for Orchestra No. 3, **Gr. 2**, 269

ILM Bach: Gigue from Suite No. 1 for Cello, **Gr. 3**, 178

Bach: Have pity, Lord on me from *St. Matthew Passion*, **Gr. 7**, 232

Bach: *Jesu, Joy of Man's Desiring*, **Gr. 3**, 41

Bach: Musette from *Notebook for Anna Magdalena Bach*, **Gr. 4**, 261

Bach: Partita No. 2 in D Minor, **Gr. 8**, 95

Bach: Toccata and Fugue in D Minor, **Gr. 7**, 108

Bach: Wie schön leuchtet der Morgenstern (How Brightly Shines the Morning Star) from *Cantata No. 1*, BWV 1, **Gr. 5**, 371

Bagley: *National Emblem*, **Gr. 7**, 76

Barney: Tsidii-Bird, **Gr. 6**, 429

Barnwell (arr.): Everybody Oughta Know (African American song), **Gr. 1**, T361

Bart: Consider Yourself from *Oliver!*, **Gr. 3**, 334

ILM Bart: Food, Glorious Food from *Oliver!*, **Gr. 2**, 310

Bartók Grasshopper's Wedding, **Gr. 1**, T245

Bartók: *Concerto for Orchestra*, Second Movement (Game of Pairs) (excerpt), **Gr. 6**, 41

Bartók: Dance No. 2 from *Six Dances in Bulgarian Rhythm* from *Mikrokosmos*, Volume 6, No. 149, **Gr. 5**, 221

Bartók: *Music for Strings, Percussion and Celesta* (excerpt), **Gr. 5**, 201

Bartók: String Quartet No. 2, Op. 17, Allegro molto caprizzioso, **Gr. 2**, 121

Beach: *Gavotte Fantastique* Op. 54, No. 2, **Gr. 2**, 26

ILM Beach: Hummingbird, A, **Gr. K**, T140

Beethoven: Concerto for Piano, Violin, and Cello in C Major, Op. 56 ("Triple Concerto") Third Movement (excerpt), **Gr. 5**, 121

Beethoven: *King Stephen* (Overture), **Gr. 5**, 255

ILM Beethoven: Rondo a capriccio Op. 129 ("Rage Over a Lost Penny") (excerpt), **Gr. 2**, 225

ILM Beethoven: Symphony No. 5 in C Minor, Third and Fourth Movements, **Gr. 8**, 115

Beethoven: Symphony No. 6 ("Pastoral") (excerpts), **Gr. 8**, 20

ILM Beethoven: Symphony No. 7 in A Major, Second Movement (excerpt), **Gr. 4**, 242

Beethoven: Symphony No. 7, Second Movement, **Gr. 7**, 118

ILM Beethoven: Symphony No. 8, Second Movement (excerpt), **Gr. K**, T235

ILM Beethoven: Symphony No. 9 ("Choral"), Fourth Movement (excerpt), **Gr. 7**, 156

Beethoven: Symphony No. 9 in D Minor ("Choral"), Fourth Movement (excerpt), **Gr. 5**, 102

Belafonte, Burgie, and Attaway: Day-O (excerpt) **Gr. 4**, 72

Bellini: Sound the Trumpet from *I Puritani*, **Gr. 5**, 279

Benjamin, Jamaican Rumba, **Gr. 5**, 92

Benson: Boogie Back to Texas, **Gr. 8**, 52

Berlin: Give Me Your Tired, Your Poor from *Miss Liberty*, **Gr. 5**, 42

Berlin: God Bless America (excerpt), **Gr. 5**, 5

Berlioz: *Benevenuto Cellini* (Overture) (excerpt), **Gr. 6**, 121

Bernstein: Rondo for Lifey, **Gr. 2**, 81

Bizet: Ball, The, from *Children's Games*, **Gr. K**, T133

ILM Bizet: Carillon from *L'Arlésienne Suite No. 1*, **Gr. 4**, 244; **Gr. 7**, 123

ILM Bizet: March from *Children's Games*, **Gr. 1**, T31

Bizet: Merry-Go-Round from *Children's Games*, **Gr. 2**, 266

Bizet: Prelude to Act I from *Carmen*, **Gr. 4**, 250

Bizet: Trumpet and Drum from *Children's Games*, **Gr. 1**, T231

Blake: Walking in the Air, **Gr. 4**, 319

Bloomer Deussen: *Pegasus Suite*, First Movement (excerpt), **Gr. 5**, 41

Bolcom: Machine from Symphony No. 5, **Gr. 8**, 51

Borodin: Polovtsian Dances from *Prince Igor* (excerpt), **Gr. 3**, 81

Bottesini: Concerto No. 2 for Double Bass, First Movement (excerpt), **Gr. 5**, 161

Boulanger: Cortège, **Gr. 6**, 253

Boyce and Hart: Monkees, The (Theme from), **Gr. 8**, 110

Bozza: Sonatine for Brass Quintet, First Movement (excerpt), **Gr. 3**, 121

Bradshaw, Bruce, Feyne, Johnson, and Plater: Jersey Bounce, **Gr. 5**, 363

Brahms: Concerto for Piano No. 2, Third Movement, **Gr. 2**, 41

ILM Bremer: Early Light, **Gr. 6**, 201

Britten: Hunt the Squirrel from *Suite on English Folk Tunes*, **Gr. 1**, T136

Britten: Playful Pizzicato from *Simple Symphony*, **Gr. 3**, 263

Britten: Theme and Percussion Variation from *Young Person's Guide to the Orchestra*, **Gr. 5**, 229

Britten: Tragic Story, A, **Gr. 4**, 190

ILM Britten: *Young Person's Guide to the Orchestra* (excerpt), **Gr. 2**, 229

Bunnell: Horse with No Name, A, **Gr. 8**, 161

Burch: Ałchíní Yázhí, **Gr. 5**, 225

Burgie: Jamaica Farewell, **Gr. 4**, 73

Cage: *Sonata X*, **Gr. 6**, 32

ILM Caillet: Variations on the Theme "Pop! Goes the Weasel," **Gr. 5**, 96

Calderon: La otra España (The Other Spain), **Gr. 4,** 64

Carpenter: Down at the Twist and Shout, **Gr. 7,** 96

Cash: I Walk the Line, **Gr. 6,** 97

Cassado: Requiebros, **Gr. 6,** 80

Castilla, Espinoza, Leguizamón, and Moreno: Medley Polleritas, **Gr. 3,** 111

ILM Chaminade: Sérénade Op. 29, **Gr. 2,** 262

Chaminade: Trio for Piano, Violin, and Cello, Op. 11, Third Movement (Presto Leggiero) , **Gr. 5,** 121

Chang: *Moonlight Masquerade for Violin and Piano,* **Gr. 7,** 127

Chávez: Symphony No. 2 ("Sinfonía india") (excerpt), **Gr. 2,** 61

Chenier: Bon Chien, **Gr. 2,** 178

Chopin: Étude in C Sharp Minor, Op. 10, No. 4, **Gr. 5,** 80

ILM Chopin: Étude Op. 25, No. 11 ("The Winter Wind"), **Gr. 2,** 136

Chulamani: Champa Muang Lao, **Gr. 5,** 436

Clapton and Jennings: Tears in Heaven (choral arrangement), **Gr. 7,** 140

Clarke: Prince of Denmark's March, **Gr. 2,** 81

ILM Clayton-Thomas: Spinning Wheel, **Gr. 4,** 211

ILM Coleman and Mohi: Pukaea (excerpt), **Gr. 2,** 109

ILM Coltrane: Locomotion, **Gr. 6,** 157

Cooder and Toure: Gomni (excerpt), **Gr. 4,** 209

Copland (arr.): I Bought Me a Cat (excerpt), **Gr. 2,** 14

Copland: *Appalachian Spring* (excerpt), **Gr. 2,** 378

Copland: Cat and the Mouse, The, **Gr. 2,** 80

ILM Copland: Circus Music from *The Red Pony Suite,* **Gr. 3,** 285

Copland: Promise of Living, The, from *The Tender Land,* **Gr. 6,** 77

Copland: Variations on "Simple Gifts" from *Appalachian Spring,* **Gr. 5,** 152 **ILM**

Corelli: Concerto Grosso No. 9 in F Major, Gavotta (Allegro), **Gr. 1,** T175

Corelli: Gigue from *Sonata for Violin and Continuo* (excerpt), **Pre-K,** 14

Corrette: La choisy, **Gr. 2,** 177

Creston: Concertino for Marimba Op. 21, First Movement ("Vigorous"), **Gr. 4,** 120

Cypress: Sweet Sound, **Gr. 8,** 233

Daniel: La vida es un carnival (Life Is a Carnival), **Gr. 4,** 228

Davids: Singing Woods, The, **Gr. 7,** 201

Davies, Gordon, and Tognetti: Into the Fog from *Master and Commander* (excerpt), **Gr. 3,** 201

Debussy: *Danse Profane,* **Gr. 3,** 200

Debussy: Gardens in the Rain from *Estampes,* **Gr. K,** T337

Denver: Stonehaven Sunset, **Gr. 7,** 221

Desmond: Take Five (excerpt), **Gr. 4,** 41; (entire) **Gr. 5,** 213

Dickow: *Entrance Fanfare,* **Gr. 2,** 86

Diop: Sing Lo-Lo from *Afrika Wassa,* **Gr. 4,** 385

Domino: When I'm Walking (Let Me Walk), **Gr. 8,** 70

Dubinsky: Son de Camaguey, **Gr. 8,** 51

Dukas: Sorcerer's Apprentice, The (excerpt), **Gr. 4,** 116

ILM Dun: Night Fight from *Crouching Tiger, Hidden Dragon,* **Gr. 6,** 28

Dun: Water Cadenza from *Water Passion After St. Matthew,* **Gr. 7,** 233

Dvořák: Symphony No. 9 ("From the New World"), Largo (excerpt), **Gr. 3,** 81

ILM Dvořák: Symphony No. 9 in E Minor, Op. 95 ("From the New World"), Largo (excerpt), **Gr. 5,** 106

Dvořák: Waltz in A Major, Op. 54, No. 1, **Gr. K,** T109

Dvorin: Funny Road, The, **Gr. 3,** 40

ILM Elgar: Faeries and Giants from *Wand of Youth Suite No. 1,* **Gr. K,** T52

Elgar: Fountain Dance from *Wand of Youth Suite No. 2,* **Gr. 1,** T233

ILM Elgar: *Pomp and Circumstance March No. 1,* Trio, **Gr. 7,** 50

Elgar: Tame Bear from *Wand of Youth Suite No. 2,* **Gr. K,** T203

Elgar: Wagon Passes, The, from *Nursery Suite,* **Gr. 1,** T242

Ellington: East St. Louis Toodle-Oo, **Gr. 4,** 232

ILM Ellington: It Don't Mean a Thing, **Gr. 6,** 165

Ellington: Rumpus in Richmond, **Gr. 8,** 32

ILM Ellmenreich: Spinning Song, **Gr. 3,** 128

ILM Enya et al: Only Time, **Gr. 7,** 142

Eto: Lion, **Gr. 6,** 16

Evans: In the Good Old Summertime, **Gr. K,** T343

Farka Toure: Jangali Famata, **Gr. 4,** 209

Farrell and Russell: Hang on Sloopy (The McCoys), **Gr. 7,** 29; (The Ohio State Glee Club and Marching Band), **Gr. 7,** 32

Fauré: Mi-a-ou from *Dolly Suite,* **Gr. K,** T149

Fillmore: Lassus Trombone, **Gr. 2,** 191

Fleischman: Grasshoppers from *Joyful Noise: Poems for Two Voices,* **Gr. 1,** T244

Fleischman: Mayflies (poem), **Gr. K,** T76

Frazier et al: Papa-oom-mow-mow, **Gr. 7,** 177

Frazier: Alley-Oop, **Gr. 8,** 64

Galindo: Sones de mariachi, **Gr. 2,** 380

Gardens in the Rain from *Estampes* by C. Debussy, **Gr. K,** T337

ILM Garland: In the Mood, **Gr. 4,** 143

ILM Gershwin: Fascinating Rhythm from *Lady Be Good,* **Gr. 5,** 186

ILM Gershwin: Summertime from *Porgy and Bess,* **Gr. 1,** T375; **Gr. 4,** 160; **Gr. 6,** 120

ILM Gershwin: Walking the Dog from *Shall We Dance,* **Gr. 1,** T169

Gervaise: Bransle de Champaigne, **Gr. 3,** 96

Gibson: Wide Open Spaces, **Gr. 7,** 208

Gil: Refavela, **Gr. 4,** 209

Gilbert and Sullivan: Modern Major General, A, from *The Pirates of Penzance,* **Gr. 6,** 56

Gill: Dance for Piccolo, Oboe, Bassoon, and Side Drum, **Gr. 5,** 218

Gilmore: When Johnny Comes Marching Home, **Gr. 7,** 168

Ginastera: Concerto for Harp, Op. 25, Third Movement (excerpt), **Gr. 6,** 81

ILM Ginastera: Los trabajadores agricolas (The Farmers) from *Estancia,* **Gr. 6,** 116

Glass: Dance No. 4 (excerpt), **Gr. 4,** 144

ILM Glière: Russian Sailor's Dance from *The Red Poppy,* **Gr. 4,** 266

Gluck: Ballet Music from *Iphigénie en Aulide,* **Gr. 2,** 25

Goldman: Children's March, **Gr. K,** T113

Gonna Build a Mountain from *Stop the World—I Want to Get Off* by A. Newley and L. Bricusse, **Gr. 6,** 5

ILM Gould: *American Salute,* **Gr. 3,** 193; **Gr. 5,** 36; **Gr. 7,** 170

Gounod: *Funeral March of a Marionette* (excerpt), **Pre-K,** 57; **Gr. 1,** T337

Grainger: Country Gardens, **Gr. 2,** 16

Grainger: Shepherd's Hey, **Gr. 6,** 201

ILM Grieg: Anitra's Dance from *Peer Gynt Suite No. 1,* Op. 46, **Gr. 5,** 193

ILM Grieg: In the Hall of the Mountain King from *Peer Gynt Suite No. 1,* Op. 46, **Gr. 2,** 346

Grieg: Morning Mood from *Peer Gynt Suite No. 1,* Op. 46, **Gr. 3,** 251

Grieg: *Norwegian Dance,* Op. 35, No. 2, **Gr. 3,** 145

Grieg: Solveig's Song from *Peer Gynt Suite No. 2,* Op. 55, **Gr. 5,** 192

Grieg: Symphonic Dances Op. 64, No. 4 (excerpt), **Gr. 2,** 105

ILM Grofé: On the Trail from *Grand Canyon Suite,* **Gr. 8,** 112

Guastavino: Arroyito serrano, **Gr. 4,** 341

ILM Guem: Le Serpent (excerpt), **Gr. 1,** T359

Guiliani: Allegro, **Gr. 2,** 200

ILM Guthrie: Car Song, **Gr. K,** T135

Gutiérrez: Somos Boricuas (We Are Puerto Rican), **Gr. 2,** 138

Haack and Nelson: Motorcycle Ride, **Gr. 2,** 192

Hadar and Dor: Erev Shel Shoshanim, **Gr. 4,** 68

Handel: Bourrée from *Music for the Royal Fireworks,* **Gr. 1,** T263

Handel: Concerto for Harp, Op. 4, No. 6, First Movement (excerpt), **Gr. 6,** 81

Handel: Concerto Grosso, Op. 6, No. 11, First Movement, **Gr. 6,** 247

Handel: Concerto in B Minor, Second Movement (Andante ma non troppo), **Gr. 3,** 120

ILM Handel: Hallelujah Chorus from *Messiah,* **Gr. 5,** 419; **Gr. 7,** 110

Handel: Hornpipe from *Water Music Suite* (excerpt), **Gr. 3,** 26

Handel: Minuet II from *Music for the Royal Fireworks,* **Pre-K,** 87

Hanson: Children's Dance from *Merry Mount,* **Gr. 2,** 246

Hardesty: Conducting Mirror, **Gr. 8,** 220

Hardesty: Marvin's Music's Midnight Music Sale Jingle, **Gr. 8,** 223

Harris: Emergency, **Gr. 7,** 174

ILM Hatfield: La lluvia, **Gr. 2,** 232

Have pity, Lord, on me from *St. Matthew Passion,* **Gr. 7,** 232

Haydn: Concerto for Cello in C Major, Third Movement, **Gr. 8,** 171

Haydn: Rondo all'Ongarese (Trio for Piano, Violin, and Cello No. 39, Finale), **Gr. 7,** 115

Haydn: Sonata for Piano No. 48 in C, First Movement, **Gr. 8,** 122

ILM Haydn: String Quartet Op. 76, No. 2 in D Minor, Andante (excerpt), **Gr. 1,** T129

Haydn: String Quartet Op. 33, No. 3 ("The Bird"), Fourth Movement, **Gr. 1,** T251

Haydn: String Quartet Op. 76, No. 2 in D Minor, Andante o piu tosto allegretto (excerpt), **Gr. 2,** 121

Haydn: Symphony No. 101 in D Major ("Clock"), **Gr. 8,** 128

ILM Haydn: Symphony No. 35, Fourth Movement (excerpt), **Gr. 5,** 247

Haydn: Symphony No. 45 ("Farewell"), First Movement, **Gr. 8,** 124

Haydn: Symphony No. 73 ("La Chasse") ("The Hunt"), Fourth Movement, **Gr. 4,** 263

ILM Haydn: Trio for Piano, Violin and Cello No. 39, Finale ("Gypsy Rondo"), **Gr. 3,** 155; (Rondo all'Ongarese), **Gr. 7,** 115

Herbert: March of the Toys from *Babes in Toyland,* **Gr. K,** T317

Higdon: *Autumn Music,* First Movement (excerpt), **Gr. 4,** 121

Hindemith: Turandot from *Symphonic Metamorphosis on Themes of Carl Maria von Weber* (excerpt), **Gr. 4,** 81

Hirsh: Seven Jumps from *Dance Music for Children,* **Gr. K,** T80

ILM Hogan (arr.): Wade in the Water (African American spiritual), **Gr. 5,** 144

Holst: First Suite in E-Flat for Military Band, **Gr. 8,** 51

Holst: Jupiter, the Bringer of Jollity, **Gr. 8,** 40

ILM Holst: Mars from *The Planets,* **Gr. 6,** 196

Horton et al: We Shall Overcome (Howard University Gospel Choir), **Gr. 7,** 213

Howard and Weston: Shrimp Boats (excerpt), **Gr. 2,** 178

Howe and Steffe: Battle Hymn of the Republic, **Gr. 5,** 390; **Gr. 6,** 389

Huling: *Night of the Mockingbird,* **Gr. 4,** 153

Humperdinck: Brother, Come and Dance With Me from *Hansel and Gretel,* **Gr. K,** T180 **ILM**

Humperdinck: Children's Chorus from *Hansel and Gretel,* **Gr. 4,** 280

Huseynli and Mutallibov: Cip cip cüclrim, **Gr. 3,** 215

ILM Ibert: Concertino da Camera, First Movement, **Gr. 7,** 161

Ibert: Concerto for Flute, First Movement (excerpt), **Gr. 2,** 120

Ibert: Little White Donkey, The, **Gr. K,** T245

ILM Ibert: Parade from *Divertissement* from *Un Chapeau de paille d'Italie,* **Gr. K,** T183

Ives: Side Show, The, **Gr. 5,** 283

Ives: *Washington's Birthday,* **Gr. 2,** 370 **ILM**

Jackson and Jones: Old Time Rock and Roll, **Gr. 7,** 98

James and James: Hen wlad fy nhadau (The Land of My Fathers), **Gr. 2,** 141

Jenkins: Kwanzaa Time, **Gr. K,** T324

Jenkins: Pole, Pole, **Gr. K,** T215

Jobim: One Note Samba, **Gr. 4,** 92

John and Rice: Circle of Life from *The Lion King* (choral arrangement and The King's Singers), **Gr. 7,** 84

John and Rice: Hakuna Matata from *The Lion King,* **Gr. K,** T222

Johnson Reagon (arr.): So Glad I'm Here, **Gr. 2,** 47

Johnson: Lift Every Voice and Sing (gospel version), **Gr. 5,** 87; (arr. by Carter) **Gr. 5,** 117

ILM Joplin: Entertainer, The (piano version), **Gr. 7,** 22; (orchestra version), **Gr. 7,** 23

Jothen: School Band Rondo, **Gr. 7,** 36

Judah-Lauder: It's Only Monday, **Gr. 8,** 14

Judah-Lauder: Park Rap 1, **Gr. 7,** 70; Park Rap 2, **Gr. 7,** 72

ILM Kabalevsky: Galop from *The Comedians,* **Gr. 4,** 254

Kabalevsky: Pantomime from *The Comedians,* **Gr. 1,** T256

Kaecher, Tullio and Danko: Change Is Good, **Gr. 5,** 85

Kale: Milan (Meeting of the Two Rivers) (excerpt), **Gr. 4,** 208 **ILM**

Kaneko: Bird Island, **Gr. 8,** 56

ILM Kay: Sleight of Feet from *Cakewalk Suite,* **Gr. 1,** T239

Keetman: Berceuse, **Gr. 2,** 184

ILM Keetman: Flute and Drum from *Gunild Keetman Collection,* **Gr. 1,** T235

Kenner: Land of a Thousand Dances (Wilson Pickett version), **Gr. 7,** 10; (Garage Band version), **Gr. 7,** 14

ILM Khachaturian: Galop from *Masquerade Suite,* **Gr. 1,** T259

ILM Kibble and Kibble: My Friend, **Gr. 4,** 389

ILM Kidjo et al: Afirika, **Gr. 7,** 226

King: You've Got a Friend, **Gr. 6,** 418

Kleinsinger: Tubby the Tuba, **Gr. 1,** T80

ILM Knopfler: Bug, The, **Gr. 8,** 88

Knowles et al, Happy Face, **Gr. 7,** 134

Koutev: Polegnala e Todora, **Gr. K,** T163

ILM Kozak: Assembly Required, **Gr. 2,** 36

Kretzmer and Schönberg: Empty Chairs at Empty Tables from *Les Misérables,* **Gr. 8,** 197

Kuo-Huang and Campbell: Shi wu (Lion Dance), **Gr. K,** T329

Kyekyoung: Ban Dal, **Gr. 4,** 184

Lang Zaimont: December: Sleighride from *Calendar Collection,* **Gr. 1,** T128

Larsen: Get a Car/Polka Dot from *Dreaming Blue,* **Gr. 6,** 221

ILM Larsen: Gloria from *Mass for the Earth,* **Gr. 7,** 222

Larsen: Symphony: Water Music, Movements 3 and 4, **Gr. 8,** 155

Larsen: There Was a Blue Flower from *Dreaming Blue,* **Gr. 6,** 218

ILM Larson: Seasons of Love from *Rent* (choral arrangement), **Gr. 7,** 86

Larsson: Concertino for Trombone, Third Movement (Allegro Giocoso), **Gr. 7,** 155

ILM Lasso: Echo Song, **Gr. K,** T103

Le: Azouke Legba, **Gr. 5,** 426

Lecuona: Tabu, **Gr. 2,** 20

Ledbetter: Good Mornin', Blues, **Gr. 5,** 176

Ligeti: Big Turtle–Fanfare from *The South China Sea,* **Gr. 4,** 201

Ling Tam (arr.): Magnificent Horses, **Gr. 7,** 104

Liszt: *Nightingale, The,* **Gr. 6,** 160 ILM

Lobos: Flor de huevo, **Gr. 3,** 359

Lorenzo Fernândez: Batuque, **Gr. 3,** 265; **Gr. 7,** 202

Lowry and Warner: How Can I Keep From Singing?, **Gr. 5,** 287

Lully: Marche, **Gr. 8,** 167 ILM

Luting: Evening Party, **Gr. 2,** 99

Lutoslawski: *Dance Preludes for Clarinet and Piano, No. 3,* **Gr. 2,** 161

Mahler: Symphony No. 1 ("Titan"), Third Movement (excerpt), **Gr. 5,** 161

Makeba and Ragovoy: Pata Pata, **Gr. 3,** 35 ILM

Makeba: Pata Pata (excerpt), **Gr. 2,** 94

Manilow: One Voice, **Gr. 5,** 326

Maraire: Mai Nozipo, **Gr. 1,** T211; **Gr. 7,** 228

Marcello: Concerto in C Minor, Second Movement (Adagio), **Gr. 5,** 120

Marx: *Dance for Clarinet and Piano,* **Gr. 6,** 189

Maurice: Sigh of the Soul for Alyscamp (Fourth Movement) from *Tableaux de Provence,* **Gr. 3,** 80

Mayuzumi: Concerto for Xylophone and Orchestra, **Gr. 8,** 41

McBeth: Daniel in the Lion's Den (excerpt), **Gr. 3,** 161

McCartney: We All Stand Together (excerpt), **Gr. K,** T153

McCarty: Sonata for Bass Trombone, First Movement (Andantino), **Gr. 5,** 160

McFerrin: Simple Pleasures, **Gr. 8,** 191

McGrath and Rex: Elbows off the Table, **Gr. K,** T106

Melendez: Good Morning America, **Gr. 8,** 181

ILM Mellencamp: Peaceful World, **Gr. 7,** 154

Mendelssohn Hensel: Schwanenlied, **Gr. 7,** 124

Meyer: Speed the Plow Medley, **Gr. 6,** 149

Milhaud: Larenjeiras from *Saudades do Brasil,* **Gr. K,** T56

Miller: String of Pearls, A, **Gr. 3,** 12

Milne: Happiness (speech piece), **Gr. 1,** T254

ILM Miloslavskiy: Clock at Night, A, **Gr. 3,** 66

ILM Monahan, Stafford, Hotchkiss, Colin, and Underwood: Drops of Jupiter (Tell Me), **Gr. 8,** 103

Monk: Panda Chant II, **Gr. 6,** 263

Monroe: Blue Moon of Kentucky, **Gr. 5,** 23

Monteverdi and Schwartz: Arianna, **Gr. 7,** 94

ILM Montsalvatge: Allegretto, **Gr. 6,** 193

Moss: People in Your Neighborhood, The (sung verses), **Gr. K,** T122; (instrumental verses), **Gr. K,** T171

Mozart: Concerto for Piano No. 1, Allegro, **Gr. 8,** 179

ILM Mozart: *Eine kleine Nachtmusik* (Serenade No. 13 in G, K. 525), Romance (Andante), **Gr. K,** T176; Minuet, **Gr. 3,** 168

ILM Mozart: *Exsulate, jubilate,* Third Movement, **Gr. 6,** 187

Mozart: *Magic Flute, The* (Overture), **Gr. 4,** 252

ILM Mozart: Papagena! Papagena! Papagena! from *The Magic Flute,* **Gr. 2,** 152

ILM Mozart: Piano Sonata No. 11 in A Major, Third Movement (Rondo alla turca), **Gr. 7,** 116

ILM Mozart: Serenade No. 10 in B Flat Major, K.361 ("Gran Partita"), Theme and Variations (excerpt), **Gr. 4,** 235

ILM Mozart: Symphony No. 40 in G Minor, First Movement, **Gr. 8,** 218

Mozart: Una donna a quindici anni from *Così fan tutte,* **Gr. 8,** 187

ILM Mussorgsky: Ballet of the Unhatched Chicks from *Pictures at an Exhibition,* **Gr. 3,** 76

ILM Mussorgsky: Bydlo from *Pictures at an Exhibition,* **Gr. 1,** T152

ILM Mussorgsky: Tuileries from *Pictures at an Exhibition,* **Gr. 1,** T249

N'Dour and Faye: New Africa, **Gr. 4,** 209

ILM Nakai: December Snow, **Gr. K,** T313

Newley and Bricusse: Gonna Build a Mountain from *Stop the World—I Want to Get Off,* **Gr. 6,** 5

Newman: You've Got a Friend in Me, **Gr. 2,** 44

Newton (words): Amazing Grace, 4 versions (traditional American melody), **Gr. 5,** 21

Nielsen: Quintet, Op. 43, Menuet (excerpt), **Gr. 4,** 121

ILM Offenbach: Barcarolle (Belle nuit) from *Tales of Hoffman,* **Gr. 6,** 265

Offenbach: Doll Song, The, from *Tales of Hoffman,* **Gr. K,** T179

Oliver: Have to Have a Habitat, **Gr. 3,** 331

Orbison and Nelson: Blue Bayou, **Gr. 8,** 71

Ortega: ¡El pueblo unido jamás será vencido!, **Gr. 8,** 90

Pace: Glad About It, **Gr. 8,** 63

Pachelbel: Canon in D, **Gr. 4,** 17; (transposed to C Major), **Gr. 8,** 67

Palmer: Colors, **Gr. K,** T58

Perez y Soto: La cigarra (The Cicada), **Gr. 6,** 268

Perkins: Blue Suede Shoes, **Gr. 7,** 8

Perren and Ferakis: I Will Survive, **Gr. 8,** 208

Pixinguinha: Oito Batutas, **Gr. 4,** 128

ILM Ponce: Música indígena from *Instantaneas Mexicanas,* **Gr. 8,** 126

Porter: Anything Goes, **Gr. 8,** 186

Poulenc: Sonata for Flute and Piano, Third Movement, **Gr. 4,** 200

ILM Praetorius: Courante from *Terpsichore,* **Gr. 8,** 130

ILM Praetorius: La canarie from *Dances from Terpsichore*, **Gr. 4,** 176

ILM Praetorius: Volta from *Dances from Terpsichore*, **Gr. 3,** 121

ILM Prima: Sing, Sing, Sing (with a Swing), **Gr. 5,** 32

ILM Prokofiev: *March for Military Band*, Op. 99, **Gr. 8,** 37

Prokofiev: March from *Love for Three Oranges* (excerpt), **Gr. 3,** 201

Prokofiev: *Peter and the Wolf* (excerpt), **Gr. 2,** 160

Prokofiev: *Peter and the Wolf* (Introduction), **Gr. 1,** T140

ILM Prokofiev: Sonata for Piano No. 2 in D Minor, Vivace (excerpt), **Gr. 4,** 181

ILM Prokofiev: Symphony No. 1 in D Major, Op. 25 ("Classical"), Third Movement (Gavotte), **Gr. 1,** T92

ILM Prokofiev: Troika from *Lieutenant Kijé Suite* (excerpt), **Gr. 3,** 225

Puccini and Larson: Death Scene Themes (from *La Bohème* and *Rent*), **Gr. 7,** 182

Puccini and Larson: Signature Themes (from *La Bohème* and *Rent*), **Gr. 7,** 180

Puccini: Humming Chorus from *Madama Butterfly*, **Gr. 6,** 257

ILM Puccini: Nessun dorma from *Turandot*, **Gr. 5,** 64

ILM Puente: Oye como va, **Gr. 5,** 69

Purcell: Canon, **Gr. 8,** 4

Purcell: Entrada from *The Indian Queen*, **Gr. 7,** 113

ILM Purcell: Minuet from *Abdelazar*, **Gr. 2,** 145

Purcell: Rondeau from *Abdelazar*, **Gr. 6,** 121

Rameau: Contredanse from *Les Indes galantes* (excerpt), **Gr. 4,** 97

ILM Ramzy: Belhadawa walla belshaawa, **Gr. 6,** 35

Ravel: *Boléro* (excerpt), **Gr. 4,** 41

ILM Ravel: Laideronette, Empress of the Pagodas from *Mother Goose Suite*, **Gr. 1,** T237

Redding: Respect (two versions), **Gr. 7,** 5

Reed: *Festival Prelude, A,* **Gr. 8,** 65

Reich: *Clapping Music,* **Gr. 7,** 130

Revueltas: *Sensemayá* (excerpt), **Gr. 3,** 161

ILM Rimsky-Korsakov: *Flight of the Bumblebee, The,* **Gr. K,** T259; **Gr. 2,** 40

ILM Rimsky-Korsakov: Scheherazade (excerpt), **Gr. 4,** 161

Rodgers and Hammerstein: Carousel Waltz, The, from *Carousel,* **Gr. 7,** 69

ILM Rodgers and Hammerstein: My Favorite Things from *The Sound of Music,* **Gr. 3,** 313

Rodgers and Hammerstein: So Long, Farewell from *The Sound of Music,* **Gr. K,** T189

Rodgers: Guadalcanal March from *Victory at Sea,* **Gr. 4,** 108

ILM Rodrigo: Adagio from *Concierto de Aranjuez* (excerpt), **Gr. 4,** 13

ILM Rodrigo: Concierto de Aranjuez, First Movement (excerpt), **Gr. 3,** 41

ILM Rodríguez: La cumparsita, **Gr. 6,** 113

Roland: Five-Step Waltz, **Gr. 6,** 287

Rose: Chants du Burgam, **Gr. 3,** 381

Rose: Holiday for Strings, **Gr. 3,** 229

Rossini: *Barber of Seville, The* (Overture), **Gr. 6,** 152; (King Singers, arr.), **Gr. 6,** 153

ILM Rossini: Largo al factotum from *Il Barbiere di Siviglia,* **Gr. 2,** 217

ILM Rossini: *William Tell* (Overture) (excerpt), **Gr. 3,** 64

Roussel: Birth and Dance of the Mayfly, The, from *The Spider's Feast,* **Gr. K,** T76

ILM Rzewski: People United Will Never Be Defeated!, The, **Gr. 8,** 93

Saint-Denis: Shimmering Air, **Gr. K,** T139 **ILM**

Saint-Saëns: Cuckoo in the Heart of the Woods from *The Carnival of the Animals,* **Gr. 2,** 253

ILM Saint-Saëns: *Danse Macabre ,* **Gr. 3,** 363

ILM Saint-Saëns: Elephant, The, from *The Carnival of the Animals,* **Gr. 1,** T204

ILM Saint-Saëns: Finale from *The Carnival of the Animals,* **Gr. K,** T195

Saint-Saëns: Kangaroos from *The Carnival of the Animals,* **Gr. K,** T196

Saint-Saëns: *Morceau de Concert,* First Movement, **Gr. 8,** 59

Saint-Saëns: Royal March of the Lions, The, from *The Carnival of the Animals,* **Gr. 1,** T25

Saint-Saëns: Sonata for Piano and Bassoon, First Movement, **Gr. 8,** 19

Saint-Saëns: Tortoises from *The Carnival of the Animals* (excerpt), **Pre-K,** 64

Sanchez: Listening for Walking and Galloping/Skipping, **Gr. K,** T41

ILM Sandström: Concerto for Trombone ("Motorbike Concerto"), Fifth Movement, **Gr. 2,** 193

Sarasate: *Carmen Fantasy for Violin and Piano,* Op. 25, **Gr. 5,** 200

Saroyan and Bagdasarian: Come On-A My House, **Gr. 7,** 138

Savage: Firecracker, **Gr. 8,** 182

Scarlatti: Sonata in C Major, Longo 104, **Gr. K,** T89

Scarlatti: Sonata in G Minor ("The Cat's Fugue"), **Pre-K,** 5

Schafer: Miniwanka (or The Moments of Water) (excerpt), **Gr. 4,** 28

Schein: Allemande Tripla from *Suite No. 4 in D Minor,* **Pre-K,** 46

Schickele: What Did You Do Today at Jeffrey's House?, **Gr. 4,** 80

Schubert: Das Wandern from *Die schöne Müllerin,* **Gr. 6,** 251

Schubert: Quintet for Piano and Strings in A Major ("Trout"), Second Movement, **Gr. 6,** 344

Schubert: Quintet, Op. 114 ("Trout") (excerpt), **Gr. 8,** 189

Schumann: Child Falling Asleep from *Scenes from Childhood,* Op. 15, **Gr. 2,** 77

Schumann: Happy Farmer, The, from *Album for the Young,* **Gr. K,** T209

ILM Scruggs: Foggy Mountain Breakdown, **Gr. 6,** 140

Shannon: Too-ra-loo-ra-loo-ral (That's an Irish Lullaby), **Gr. K,** T335

Sherman: Step in Time from *Mary Poppins,* **Gr. K,** T159

ILM Shostakovich: Dance from *Ballet Suite No. 1,* **Gr. K,** T167

Shostakovich: Sonata for Cello and Piano, Op. 40, Second Movement, **Gr. 4,** 40

Shostakovich: Symphony No. 5, First Movement (excerpt), **Gr. 6,** 161

ILM Sibelius: *Finlandia,* Op. 26, No. 7, **Gr. 5,** 257

Siegmeister: Round-up from *Western Suite,* **Gr. 2,** 67

Smetana: Chorus of Villagers from *The Bartered Bride,* **Gr. 5,** 274

Smetana: From Bohemia's Forests and Meadows from *Má Vlast,* **Gr. 6,** 229

ILM Smetana: Moldau, The, from *Má Vlast (My Country),* **Gr. 5,** 271; (entire), **Gr. 7,** 219

Smith, Key (words), and Hogan (arr.): Star-Spangled Banner, The, **Gr. 5,** 86

Smith: Backwater Blues, **Gr. 5,** 174

Alphabetical Index of Listening Selections (continued)

Smith: Freedom, **Gr. 7,** 195

Smith: Just Keep Goin' On, **Gr. 7,** 16

Solo Pueblo: Macoklis Mango, **Gr. 8,** 46

ILM Sondheim: No One Is Alone from *Into the Woods*, **Gr. 8,** 86

Sousa: El Capitán, **Gr. 8,** 6

Sousa: Liberty Bell, The, **Gr. 5,** 395

ILM Sousa: Semper Fidelis, **Gr. 3,** 281; **Gr. 6,** 391

ILM Sousa: Stars and Stripes Forever, The, **Gr. 4,** 355; **Gr. 7,** 197

ILM Sousa: Washington Post, The, **Gr. 2,** 339

ILM Sowande: Akinla from *African Suite*, **Gr. 2,** 97

Spottswood: Seven Principles of Kwanzaa, **Gr. 6,** 415

Stamitz: Concerto No. 3 in B Flat, First Movement (Allegro Moderato), **Gr. 5,** 40

Stomp: Encore, **Gr. 8,** 13

Stowers: Railroad Blues, **Gr. 2,** 327

Strauss: Csárdás from *Ritter Pásmán*, **Gr. K,** T28

Strauss: Im Krapfenwaldl (In Krapfen Woods) Op. 336 **Gr. 2,** 244

Strauss: Moulinet (Polka) Op. 57, **Gr. 2,** 53

Strauss: Radetzky March, **Gr. K,** T177

Strauss: *Till Eulenspiegel's Merry Pranks*, **Gr. 5,** 81

Stravinsky: Ballerina's Dance from *Petrushka* (excerpt), **Gr. 6,** 161

ILM Stravinsky: Galop from *Suite No. 2 for Small Orchestra*, **Gr. 7,** 126

Stravinsky: Infernal Dance of King Kashchei from *The Firebird Suite* (excerpt), **Gr. 4,** 191

ILM Stravinsky: Introduction from *The Rite of Spring*, **Gr. 6,** 423

ILM Stravinsky: Pulcinella Suite (excerpt), **Gr. 4,** 201

Stravinsky: *Rite of Spring, The,* (excerpt), **Gr. 2,** 201

Stravinsky: Spring Round Dances from *The Rite of Spring*, **Gr. 7,** 232

Tailleferre: Tug of War from *Outdoor Games*, **Gr. K,** T339

Taubman: Hashkivenu, **Gr. 7,** 190

Taylor: C-A-G, **Gr. 1,** T241 ILM

Taylor: Jump in the Line, **Gr. 7,** 199

Tchaikovsky: *1812 Overture*, **Gr. 8,** 72

Tchaikovsky: Chinese Dance from *The Nutcracker Suite*, **Gr. 2,** 354

Tchaikovsky: Dance of the Mirlitons from *The Nutcracker*, **Gr. 4,** 173 ILM

Tchaikovsky: Dance of the Sugar Plum Fairy from *The Nutcracker Suite* (excerpt), **Gr. 2,** 354 ILM

Tchaikovsky: March from *The Nutcracker Suite* (excerpt), **Gr. 2,** 354

Tchaikovsky: Overture from *The Nutcracker Suite* (excerpt), **Gr. 2,** 354

Tchaikovsky: Symphony No. 4, First Movement (excerpt) and Second Movement (excerpt), **Gr. 6,** 41

Tchaikovsky: Symphony No. 4, Fourth Movement, **Gr. 4,** 287

Tchaikovsky: Symphony No. 5, Second Movement (excerpt), **Gr. 5,** 81

Tchaikovsky: Symphony No. 6 ("Pathetique"), Second Movement, **Gr. 5,** 281

ILM Tchaikovsky: Trepak from *The Nutcracker*, **Gr. 6,** 408

ILM Tchaikovsky: Waltz of the Flowers from *The Nutcracker Suite* (excerpt), **Gr. 1,** T353; **Gr. 2,** 354

Tchaikovsky: Waltz of the Snowflakes from *The Nutcracker* (excerpt), **Gr. K,** T311

Tcherepnin: Sonatina for Three Timpani and Piano, First

Movement (excerpt), **Gr. 4,** 81

Telemann: Galop of Sancho's Donkey from *Don Quixote*, **Gr. 3,** 271

ILM Thile: Ode to a Butterfly, **Gr. 5,** 25

ILM Thomson: Cattle from *The Plow That Broke the Plains*, **Gr. 4,** 274

ILM Thomson: Walking Song from *Acadian Songs and Dances* (from the movie *Louisiana Story*), **Gr. K,** T20

Traugh and Connelly: Dinosaurs Dancing, **Gr. K,** T72

ILM Travis: Sixteen Tons (Tennessee Ernie Ford), **Gr. 7,** 150

Troup: Route 66, **Gr. 7,** 191

Unobsky and Scott: Gift, The, **Gr. 7,** 205

Ureña: Este son, **Gr. 6,** 393

Van Eyck: Al Hebben de Princen haren, **Gr. 4,** 225

Vaughan Williams: Bright Is the Ring of Words, **Gr. 7,** 78

ILM Vaughan Williams: March Past of the Kitchen Utensils from *The Wasps*, **Gr. 3,** 247

ILM Vaughan Williams: Seventeen Come Sunday from *English Folk Song Suite*, **Gr. 7,** 102

Vaughan Williams: Vagabond, The, **Gr. 7,** 78

ILM Verdi: Anvil Chorus from *Il Trovatore*, **Gr. 5,** 148

ILM Verdi: Va Pensiero from *Nabucco*, **Gr. 6,** 169

Vila: Batuque na cozinha (Samba kitchen band), **Gr. 2,** 307

Vila: Canta, Canta, Minha Gente, **Gr. 8,** 45

Villa-Lobos: Let's Run Across the Hill, **Gr. 5,** 268

ILM Villa-Lobos: Little Train of the Caipira, The, from *Bachianas Brasileiras No. 2*, **Gr. K,** T142

Villarreal and Ortiz: Chango Guango, **Gr. 2,** 60

ILM Vivaldi: Concerto for Two Trumpets, Allegro, **Gr. 2,** 73

ILM Vivaldi: Fall (Allegro) from *The Four Seasons* (Concerto No. 3 in F Major) (excerpt), **Gr. K,** T305

ILM Vivaldi: Spring (Allegro) from *The Four Seasons* (Concerto No. 1 in E Major), **Gr. 4,** 391; (excerpt) **Gr. 7,** 112

Vivaldi: Summer (Allegro Non Molto) from *The Four Seasons* (Concerto No. 2 in G Minor) (excerpt), **Gr. 4,** 161

ILM Vivaldi: Winter (Allegro non molto) from *The Four Seasons* (Concerto No. 4 in F Minor), **Gr. 6,** 403

Wagner: Prelude to Act II from *Siegfried* (excerpt), **Gr. 2,** 58

ILM Waldteufel: Skaters' Waltz, The (excerpt), **Gr. 1,** T345

Walton: Leggiero (Hopscotch) from *Music for Children*, **Gr. 5,** 281

Walton: Violin Concerto, First Movement (Andante Tranquillo), **Gr. 7,** 52

Ward and Richardson: America, **Gr. 8,** 31

Warren (arr.): Joyful, Joyful from *Sister Act 2* (excerpt), **Gr. 5,** 104

Watson, et al.: The Golden Age of Xylophone (excerpt), **Gr. 5,** 201

ILM Weiss and Thiele: What a Wonderful World (entire), **Gr. 2,** 84; (choral arrangement), **Gr. 8,** 8; (Louis Armstrong version), **Gr. 8,** 9

Wettlin-Larsen: Lakota Flute Song, **Gr. 6,** 429

Wieniawski: Scherzo and Tarantella, **Gr. 2,** 160

Wilder: Effie Goes Folk Dancing, **Gr. 2,** 168

ILM Williams: Augie's Great Municipal Band from *Star Wars Episode 1: The Phantom Menace* (excerpt), **Gr. 4,** 56

ILM Williams: *Liberty Fanfare* (excerpt), **Gr. 7,** 187

Williams: We're Looking Good, **Gr. 2,** 149

Williams, J.: John Williams Montage 1, **Gr. 8,** 134

Williams, J.: John Williams Montage 2, **Gr. 8,** 136

Willson: Rock Island from *The Music Man*, **Gr. 8,** 74

ILM Willson: Seventy-Six Trombones from *The Music Man,* **Gr. 8,** 76

Willson: Wells Fargo Wagon, The, from *The Music Man,* **Gr. 8,** 78

Winter and Pokrovsky Singers: Kurski Funk, **Gr. 8,** 153

Winter Consort and Pokrovsky Singers: Down in Belgorod, **Gr. 8,** 153

Winter: Antarctica, **Gr. 2,** 110

Winter: Buffalo Prairie from *Prayer for the Wild Things,* **Gr. K,** T219

ILM Winter: Ocean Child, **Gr. 7,** 218

Work: Big Bunch of Roses, **Gr. 4,** 267

Worsley: Batik, **Gr. 2,** 201

ILM Worsley: Promenade from *Golden Goose,* **Gr. 1,** T177

ILM Yanjun: Moon Mirrored in a Pool, The, **Gr. K,** T115

York: Faire, **Gr. 8,** 215

ILM York: Skeleton, **Gr. 8,** 215

ILM York: Sunburst, **Gr. 7,** 216

York: Walking, **Gr. 8,** 214

Ysaÿe: Sonata for Violin No. 4, First Movement, **Gr. 8,** 156

Yupanqui: Duerme Negrito, **Gr. 3,** 108

Zador: Farm, The, from *Children's Symphony,* **Gr. 2,** 211

By Title

1812 Overture by P. I. Tchaikovsky, **Gr. 8,** 72

Acitrón (Mexican stone-passing song), **Gr. 6,** 93

ILM Adagio from *Concierto de Aranjuez* (excerpt) by J. Rodrigo, **Gr. 4,** 13

ILM Adukbe (Adenkum traditional), **Gr. 8,** 177

ILM Afirika by A. Kidjo et al, **Gr. 7,** 226

ILM Afoxé, **Gr. 8,** 34

Afrakakraba (Ghanaian game song), **Gr. 3,** 102

African Postal Workers, **Gr. 7,** 147

Agahu (dance-drumming piece from Ghana), **Gr. 5,** 73

Aideu (Yoruban folk song), **Gr. 7,** 223

Ake Tonu (Maori song), **Gr. 5,** 150

ILM Akinla from *African Suite* by F. Sowande, **Gr. 2,** 97

Al Hebben de Princen haren by J. Van Eyck, **Gr. 4,** 225

Ałchíní Yázhí by S. Burch, **Gr. 5,** 225

All Through the Night (Welsh folk song), **Gr. 4,** 277

ILM Allegretto by X. Montsalvatge, **Gr. 6,** 193

Allegro by M. Guiliani, **Gr. 2,** 200

Allemande Tripla from *Suite No. 4 in D Minor* by J. H. Schein, **Pre-K,** 46

Alley-Oop by D. Frazier, **Gr. 8,** 64

Amazing Grace, 4 versions (traditional American melody) words by J. Newton, **Gr. 5,** 21;

ILM (violin and bagpipe version), **Gr. 7,** 144

America by S. Ward and A. Richardson, **Gr. 8,** 31

ILM *American Salute* by M. Gould, **Gr. 3,** 193; **Gr. 5,** 36; **Gr. 7,** 170

ILM Anitra's Dance from *Peer Gynt Suite No. 1,* Op. 46 by E. Grieg, **Gr. 5,** 193

Antarctica by P. Winter, **Gr. 2,** 110

Antiphonal Singing Song (Chinese folk song), **Gr. 6,** 65

ILM Anvil Chorus from *Il Trovatore* by G. Verdi, **Gr. 5,** 148

Anything Goes by C. Porter, **Gr. 8,** 186

Appalachian Spring (excerpt) by A. Copland, **Gr. 2,** 378

Arianna by C. Monteverdi and P. Schwartz, **Gr. 7,** 94

Arirang (Korean folk song), **Gr. 5,** 53

Arroyito serrano by C. Guastavino, **Gr. 4,** 341

Assembly Memories (montage), **Gr. 7,** 42

ILM Assembly Required by G. Kozak, **Gr. 2,** 36

Athabascan Song (traditional Athabascan beat-chant song), **Gr. 5,** 26

ILM Augie's Great Municipal Band from *Star Wars Episode 1: The Phantom Menace* (excerpt) by J. Williams, **Gr. 4,** 56

Autumn Music, First Movement (excerpt) by J. Higdon, **Gr. 4,** 121

Azouke Legba by V. Le, **Gr. 5,** 426

Bach/Stravinsky Medley (montage), **Gr. 7,** 232

Background Music (montage), **Gr. 8,** 26

Backwater Blues by B. Smith, **Gr. 5,** 174

ILM Badinerie from Suite for Orchestra No. 2 in B Minor by J. S. Bach, **Gr. 4,** 61; **Gr. 5,** 41

Ball, The, from *Children's Games* by G. Bizet, **Gr. K,** T133

Ballerina's Dance from *Petrushka* (excerpt) by I. Stravinsky, **Gr. 6,** 161

Ballet Music from *Iphigénie en Aulide* by C. Gluck, **Gr. 2,** 25

ILM Ballet of the Unhatched Chicks from *Pictures at an Exhibition* by M. Mussorgsky, **Gr. 3,** 76

Ban Dal by Yoon Kyekyoung, **Gr. 4,** 184

Barber of Seville, The (Overture) by G. Rossini, **Gr. 6,** 152; (arr. by The King Singers), **Gr. 6,** 153

ILM Barcarolle (Belle nuit) from *Tales of Hoffman* by J. Offenbach, **Gr. 6,** 265

Batik by L. Worsley, **Gr. 2,** 201

Battle Hymn of the Republic by J. W. Howe and W. Steffe, **Gr. 5,** 390; **Gr. 6,** 389

ILM Batucada Brasileira (Brazilian folk song), **Gr. 5,** 433

ILM Batuque by O. Lorenzo Fernândez, **Gr. 3,** 265; **Gr. 7,** 202

Batuque na cozinha (Samba kitchen band) by M. Vila, **Gr. 2,** 307

Bear Dance (Haliwa-Saponi dance song), **Gr. 1,** T103

Beatles Medley (montage), **Gr. 8,** 149

ILM Belhadawa walla belshaawa by H. Ramzy, **Gr. 6,** 35

Belle qui tiens ma vie (My Love, You Have My Heart) by T. Arbeau, **Gr. 6,** 100

Benevenuto Cellini (Overture) (excerpt) by H. Berlioz, **Gr. 6,** 121

Berceuse by G. Keetman, **Gr. 2,** 184

Bri Bax! (Azerbaijani folk song), **Gr. 5,** 233

Big Bunch of Roses by J. W. Work III, **Gr. 4,** 267

Big Turtle–Fanfare from *The South China Sea* by G. Ligeti, **Gr. 4,** 201

ILM Bird Island by R. Kaneko, **Gr. 8,** 56

Birth and Dance of the Mayfly, The, from *The Spider's Feast* by A. Roussel, **Gr. K,** T76

Blue Bayou by R. Orbison and J. Nelson, **Gr. 8,** 71

ILM Blue Little Flower, **Gr. 8,** 82

Blue Moon of Kentucky by B. Monroe, **Gr. 5,** 23

Blue Suede Shoes by C. Perkins, **Gr. 7,** 8

ILM Bo Hai Huan Ten (Chinese folk music), **Gr. 7,** 56

Boléro (excerpt) by M. Ravel, **Gr. 4,** 41

Bon Chien by C. Chenier, **Gr. 2,** 178

Boogie Back to Texas by R. Benson, **Gr. 8,** 52

Born to Be with You (bluegrass song), **Gr. 3,** 387

Alphabetical Index of Listening Selections

Alphabetical Index of Listening Selections (continued)

Bourrée from *Music for the Royal Fireworks* by G. F. Handel, **Gr. 1,** T263

ILM Brafferton Village/Walsh's Hornpipe (Irish folk music), **Gr. 3,** 391

Brandenburg Concerto No. 5, Third Movement by J. S. Bach, **Gr. 6,** 128

Bransle de Champaigne by C. Gervaise, **Gr. 3,** 96

Bright Is the Ring of Words by R. Vaughan Williams, **Gr. 7,** 78

Brooklyn Jugs by Brooklyn Jugs, **Gr. 4,** 77

ILM Brother, Come and Dance With Me from *Hansel and Gretel* by E. Humperdinck, **Gr. K,** T180

Buffalo Prairie from *Prayer for the Wild Things* by P. Winter, **Gr. K,** T219

ILM Bug, The, by M. Knopfler, **Gr. 8,** 88

Bulgarian Folk Melody (traditional Bulgarian), **Gr. 5,** 219

Bu-Vah (Hopi lullaby), **Gr. 4,** 19

ILM Bydlo from *Pictures at an Exhibition* by M. Mussorgsky, **Gr. 1,** T152

ILM C-A-G by B. Taylor, **Gr. 1,** T241

Canon by H. Purcell, **Gr. 8,** 4

Canon in D by J. Pachelbel, **Gr. 4,** 17; (transposed to C Major), **Gr. 8,** 67

Canta, Canta, Minha Gente by M. da Vila, **Gr. 8,** 45

ILM Car Song by W. Guthrie, **Gr. K,** T135

ILM Carillon from *L'Arlésienne Suite No. 1,* by G. Bizet, **Gr. 4,** 244; **Gr. 7,** 123

Carmen Fantasy for Violin and Piano, Op. 25 by P. de Sarasate, **Gr. 5,** 200

Carnavalito (Bolivian folk dance), **Gr. 2,** 251

ILM *Carnival of Venice, The,* by J. B. Arban, **Gr. 6,** 40

Carousel Waltz, The, from *Carousel* by R. Rodgers and O. Hammerstein II, **Gr. 7,** 69

Cat and the Mouse, The, by A. Copland, **Gr. 2,** 80

Cattle from *The Plow That Broke the Plains* by V. Thomson, **Gr. 4,** 274 **ILM**

Celebration Medley (montage), **Gr. 7,** 185

Celebration Mosaic (montage), **Gr. 8,** 69

Chamber Ensembles (montage), **Gr. 5,** 228

Champa Muang Lao by U. Chulamani, **Gr. 5,** 436

Change Is Good by E. Kaecher, J. Tullio, and R. Danko, **Gr. 5,** 85

Chango Guango by T. Villarreal and J. Ortiz, **Gr. 2,** 60 **ILM**

Chants du Burgam by D. Rose, **Gr. 3,** 381

Cherkassiya (Israeli folk dance), **Gr. 2,** 373

Chicken Dance, The (traditional), **Gr. 7,** 60

Child Falling Asleep from *Scenes from Childhood,* Op. 15 by R. Schumann, **Gr. 2,** 77

Children's Chorus from *Hansel and Gretel* by E. Humperdinck, **Gr. 4,** 280

Children's Dance from *Merry Mount* by H. Hanson, **Gr. 2,** 246

ILM Children's March by E. Goldman, **Gr. K,** T113

Chinese Dance from *The Nutcracker Suite* by P. Tchaikovsky, **Gr. 2,** 354

Chinese Lion Dance (Chinese folk music), **Gr. 1,** T363

Chorus of Villagers from *The Bartered Bride* by B. Smetana, **Gr. 5,** 274

Cip cip cücələrim by G. Huseynli and T. Mutallibov, **Gr. 3,** 215

Circle of Life from *The Lion King* (choral arrangement and The King's Singers) by E. John and T. Rice, **Gr. 7,** 84

ILM Circus Music from *The Red Pony Suite* by A. Copland, **Gr. 3,** 285

Clapping Music by S. Reich, **Gr. 7,** 130

ILM Clock at Night, A, by S. Miloslavskiy, **Gr. 3,** 66

Clog (oldtime music), **Gr. 2,** 68

Colors by H. Palmer, **Gr. K,** T58

Come On-A My House by W. Saroyan and R. Bagdasarian, **Gr. 7,** 138

Common Step (traditional), **Gr. 8,** 39

ILM Concertino da Camera, First Movement by J. Ibert, **Gr. 7,** 161

Concertino for Marimba Op. 21, First Movement ("Vigorous") by P. Creston, **Gr. 4,** 120

Concertino for Trombone, Third Movement (Allegro Giocoso) by L. Larsson, **Gr. 7,** 155

Concerto for Cello in C Major, Third Movement by F. J. Haydn, **Gr. 8,** 171

Concerto for Flute, First Movement (excerpt) by J. Ibert, **Gr. 2,** 120

Concerto for Harp, Op. 25, Third Movement (excerpt) by A. Ginastera, **Gr. 6,** 81

Concerto for Harp, Op. 4, No. 6, First Movement (excerpt) by G. F. Handel, **Gr. 6,** 81

Concerto for Orchestra, Second Movement (Game of Pairs) (excerpt) by B. Bartók, **Gr. 6,** 41

Concerto for Piano No. 1, Allegro by W. A. Mozart, **Gr. 8,** 179

Concerto for Piano No. 2, Third Movement by J. Brahms, **Gr. 2,** 41

Concerto for Piano, Violin, and Cello in C Major, Op. 56 ("Triple Concerto") Third Movement (excerpt) by L. van Beethoven, **Gr. 5,** 121

ILM Concerto for Trombone ("Motorbike Concerto"), Fifth Movement by J. Sandström, **Gr. 2,** 193

ILM Concerto for Two Trumpets, Allegro by A. Vivaldi, **Gr. 2,** 73

Concerto for Violin and Oboe BWV 1060, Adagio (excerpt) by J. S. Bach, **Gr. 2,** 127

Concerto for Xylophone and Orchestra by T. Mayuzumi, **Gr. 8,** 41

Concerto Grosso No. 9 in F Major, Gavotta (Allegro) by A. Corelli, **Gr. 1,** T175

Concerto Grosso, Op. 6, No. 11, First Movement by G. F. Handel, **Gr. 6,** 247

Concerto in B Minor, Second Movement (Andante ma non troppo) by G. F. Handel, **Gr. 3,** 120

Concerto in C Minor, Second Movement (Adagio) by A. Marcello, **Gr. 5,** 120

Concerto No. 2 for Double Bass, First Movement (excerpt) by G. Bottesini, **Gr. 5,** 161

Concerto No. 3 in B Flat, First Movement (Allegro Moderato) by C. Stamitz, **Gr. 5,** 40

ILM Concierto de Aranjuez, First Movement (excerpt) by J. Rodrigo, **Gr. 3,** 41

Conducting Mirror by B. Hardesty, **Gr. 8,** 220

Consider Yourself from *Oliver!* by L. Bart, **Gr. 3,** 334

Contredanse from *Les Indes galantes* (excerpt) by J. P. Rameau, **Gr. 4,** 97

Cortège by L. Boulanger, **Gr. 6,** 253

Country Gardens by P. Grainger, **Gr. 2,** 16

ILM Courante from *Terpsichore* by M. Praetorius, **Gr. 8,** 130

Coyote and the Bluebirds, The (traditional Hopi story), **Gr. 2,** 231

ILM Crazy Songs by M. Kopelent, **Gr. 6,** 65

Cripple Creek (American folk song), **Gr. 6,** 375

Csárdás from *Ritter Pásmán* by J. Strauss, Jr., **Gr. K,** T28

Cuckoo in the Heart of the Woods from *The Carnival of the Animals* by C. Saint-Saëns, **Gr. 2,** 253

Dance for Clarinet and Piano by A. Marx, **Gr. 6,** 189

Dance for Piccolo, Oboe, Bassoon, and Side Drum by R. Gill, **Gr. 5,** 218

ILM Dance from *Ballet Suite No. 1* by D. Shostakovich, **Gr. K,** T167

Dance No. 2 from *Six Dances in Bulgarian Rhythm* from *Mikrokosmos,* Volume 6, No. 149 by B. Bartók, **Gr. 5,** 221

Dance No. 4 (excerpt) by P. Glass, **Gr. 4,** 144

ILM Dance of the Mirlitons from *The Nutcracker* by P. Tchaikovsky, **Gr. 4,** 173

ILM Dance of the Sugar Plum Fairy from *The Nutcracker Suite* (excerpt) by P. Tchaikovsky, **Gr. 2,** 354

Dance Preludes for Clarinet and Piano, No. 3 by W. Lutoslawski, **Gr. 2,** 161

Daniel in the Lion's Den (excerpt) by F. McBeth, **Gr. 3,** 161

ILM *Danse Macabre* by C. Saint-Saëns, **Gr. 3,** 363

Danse Profane by C. Debussy, **Gr. 3,** 200

Das Wandern from *Die schöne Müllerin* by F. Schubert, **Gr. 6,** 251

Day-O (excerpt) by H. Belafonte, I. Burgie, and W. Attaway, **Gr. 4,** 72

Death Scene Themes (from *La Bohème* and *Rent*) by G. Puccini and J. Larson, **Gr. 7,** 182

Debka Kurdit (Yemeni folk dance), **Gr. 4,** 236

ILM December Snow by R. C. Nakai, **Gr. K,** T313

December: Sleighride from *Calendar Collection* by J. Lang Zaimont, **Gr. 1,** T128

Dinosaurs Dancing by S. Traugh and L. Connelly, **Gr. K,** T72

Djurdjevka kolo (Yugoslavian folk song), **Gr. 6,** 105

Doll Song, The, from *Tales of Hoffman* by J. Offenbach, **Gr. K,** T179

Down at the Twist and Shout by M. C. Carpenter, **Gr. 7,** 96

Down by the Riverside (African American spiritual), **Gr. 3,** 382

Down in Belgorod by the P. Winter Consort and the D. Pokrovsky Singers, **Gr. 8,** 153

Dragon Dance (Chinese folk music), **Gr. 2,** 366

ILM Drops of Jupiter (Tell Me) by P. Monahan, J. Stafford, R. Hotchkiss, C. Colin, and S. Underwood, **Gr. 8,** 103

Duerme Negrito by A. Yupanqui, **Gr. 3,** 108

ILM Early Light by C. Bremer, **Gr. 6,** 201

Earth is Our Mother, The (Libana), **Gr. 7,** 220

East St. Louis Toodle-Oo by D. Ellington, **Gr. 4,** 232

ILM Echo Song by O. di Lasso, **Gr. K,** T103

Effie Goes Folk Dancing by A. Wilder, **Gr. 2,** 168

ILM *Eine kleine Nachtmusik* (Serenade No. 13 in G, K. 525) by W. A. Mozart, Romance (Andante), **Gr. K,** T176; Minuet, **Gr. 3,** 168

Eka Muda (Comanche hand-game song), **Gr. 5,** 27

El Capitán by J. P. Sousa, **Gr. 8,** 6

El cóndor pasa (Andean folk song), **Gr. 7,** 69

El jarabe tapatío (Mexican folk dance), **Gr. 7,** 58

¡El pueblo unido jamás será vencido! by S. Ortega, **Gr. 8,** 90

El tecolote (excerpt) (Mexican folk song), **Gr. 4,** 363

El vaquerito (Mexican folk song) (excerpt), **Gr. 1,** T335

Elbows off the Table by B. McGrath and K. Rex, **Gr. K,** T106

ILM Elephant, The, from *The Carnival of the Animals* by C. Saint-Saëns, **Gr. 1,** T204

ILM Elijah Rock (African American spiritual), **Gr. 6,** 52

Emergency by E. M. Harris, **Gr. 7,** 174

Emotions Through Music (montage), **Gr. 8,** 178

Empty Chairs at Empty Tables from *Les Misérables* by H. Kretzmer and C.-M. Schönberg, **Gr. 8,** 197

Encore by Stomp, **Gr. 8,** 13

Entertainer, The by S. Joplin (piano version), **Gr. 7,** 22;

ILM (orchestra version), **Gr. 7,** 23

Entrada from *The Indian Queen* by H. Purcell, **Gr. 7,** 113

Entrance Fanfare by R. Dickow, **Gr. 2,** 86

Erev Shel Shoshanim by J. Hadar and M. Dor, **Gr. 4,** 68

Este son by J. C. Ureña, **Gr. 6,** 393

Étude in C Sharp Minor, Op. 10, No. 4 by F. Chopin, **Gr. 5,** 80

ILM Étude Op. 25, No. 11 ("The Winter Wind") by F. Chopin, **Gr. 2,** 136

Evening Party by H. Luting, **Gr. 2,** 99

Everybody Oughta Know (African American song) arr. by Y. M. Barnwell, **Gr. 1,** T361

ILM *Exsultate, jubilate,* Third Movement by W.A. Mozart, **Gr. 6,** 187

ILM Faeries and Giants from *Wand of Youth Suite No. 1* by E. Elgar, **Gr. K,** T52

Faire by A. York, **Gr. 8,** 215

ILM Fall (Allegro) from *The Four Seasons* (Concerto No. 3 in F Major) (excerpt) by A. Vivaldi, **Gr. K,** T305

Famous TV Show Themes (montage), **Gr. 8,** 140

Fancy Dance Song (intertribal song), **Gr. 5,** 444

Farm, The, from *Children's Symphony* by E. Zador, **Gr. 2,** 211

ILM Fascinating Rhythm from *Lady Be Good* by G. and I. Gershwin, **Gr. 5,** 186

Festival Dance (Peruvian folk melody), **Pre-K,** 74; **Gr. 4,** 140

Festival Prelude, A, by A. Reed, **Gr. 8,** 65

ILM Finale from *The Carnival of the Animals* by C. Saint-Saëns, **Gr. K,** T195

ILM *Finlandia,* Op. 26, No. 7 by J. Sibelius, **Gr. 5,** 257

Firecracker by M. Savage, **Gr. 8,** 182

First Suite in E-Flat for Military Band by G. Holst, **Gr. 8,** 51

Five-Step Waltz by E. Roland, **Gr. 6,** 287

ILM *Flight of the Bumblebee, The,* by N. Rimsky-Korsakov, **Gr. K,** T259; **Gr. 2,** 40

Flor de huevo by Los Lobos, **Gr. 3,** 359

ILM Flute and Drum from *Gunild Keetman Collection* by G. Keetman, **Gr. 1,** T235

ILM Foggy Mountain Breakdown by E. Scruggs, **Gr. 6,** 140

ILM Food, Glorious Food from *Oliver!* by L. Bart, **Gr. 2,** 310

Fountain Dance from *Wand of Youth Suite No. 2* by E. Elgar, **Gr. 1,** T233

Freedom by M. W. Smith, **Gr. 7,** 195

From Bohemia's Forests and Meadows from *Má Vlast* by B. Smetana, **Gr. 6,** 229

Funeral March of a Marionette (excerpt) by C. Gounod, **Pre-K,** 57; **Gr. 1,** T337

Funny Road, The, by D. Dvorin, **Gr. 3,** 40

ILM Galop from *Masquerade Suite* by A. Khachaturian, **Gr. 1,** T259

ILM Galop from *Suite No. 2 for Small Orchestra* by I. Stravinsky, **Gr. 7,** 126

ILM Galop from *The Comedians* by D. Kabalevsky, **Gr. 4,** 254

Alphabetical Index of Listening Selections (continued)

Galop of Sancho's Donkey from *Don Quixote* by G. P. Telemann, **Gr. 3,** 271

Gardens in the Rain from *Estampes* by C. Debussy, **Gr. K,** T337

Gavotte Fantastique Op. 54, No. 2 by A. Beach, **Gr. 2,** 26

Gavotte from Suite No. 5 for Cello by J. S. Bach, **Gr. 2,** 41

Gêndhing KÊMBANG MARA (excerpt) (Balinese gamelan music), **Gr. 7,** 101

Get a Car/Polka Dot from *Dreaming Blue* by L. Larsen, **Gr. 6,** 221

Get on Board, Children (African American freedom song), **Gr. 5,** 347

Gift, The, by M. Unobsky and A. Scott, **Gr. 7,** 205

Gigue from *Sonata for Violin and Continuo* (excerpt) by A. Corelli, **Pre-K,** 14

ILM Gigue from Suite for Orchestra No. 3 by J. S. Bach, **Gr. 2,** 269

ILM Gigue from Suite No. 1 for Cello by J. S. Bach, **Gr. 3,** 178

Give Me Your Tired, Your Poor from *Miss Liberty* by I. Berlin, **Gr. 5,** 42

Glad About It by Joe Pace and the Colorado Mass Choir, **Gr. 8,** 63

ILM Gloria from *Mass for the Earth* by L. Larsen, **Gr. 7,** 222

God Bless America (excerpt) by I. Berlin, **Gr. 5,** 5

Gold Ring, The (traditional Irish jig), **Gr. 3,** 160

Golden Age of Xylophone, The (excerpt) by Watson, et al., **Gr. 5,** 201

Gomni (excerpt) by R. Cooder and A. F. Toure, **Gr. 4,** 209

Gonna Build a Mountain from *Stop the World—I Want to Get Off* by A. Newley and L. Bricusse, **Gr. 6,** 5

Goober Peas (Civil War marching song), **Gr. 6,** 269

Good Mornin', Blues by H. Ledbetter, **Gr. 5,** 176

Good Morning America by T. Melendez, **Gr. 8,** 181

Grand Entry (powwow), **Gr. K,** T344

Grasshopper's Wedding by B. Bartók, **Gr. 1,** T245

Grasshoppers from *Joyful Noise: Poems for Two Voices* by P. Fleischman, **Gr. 1,** T244

Guadalcanal March from *Victory at Sea* by R. Rodgers, **Gr. 4,** 108

Guadalquivir (Andean dance song), **Gr. 3,** 30

Hakuna Matata from *The Lion King* by E. John and T. Rice, **Gr. K,** T222

Hallelujah Chorus from *Messiah* by G. F. Handel, **Gr. 5,** 419; **Gr. 7,** 110 ILM

Halloween Montage, **Gr. 5,** 404

Hang on Sloopy by W. Farrell and B. Russell (The McCoys), **Gr. 7,** 29; (The Ohio State Glee Club and Marching Band), **Gr. 7,** 32

Happiness (speech piece) by A. A. Milne, **Gr. 1,** T254

Happy Face by B. Knowles et al, **Gr. 7,** 134

Happy Farmer, The, from *Album for the Young* by R. Schumann, **Gr. K,** T209

Hashkivenu by C. Taubman, **Gr. 7,** 190

Hashual (Israeli folk dance), **Gr. 6,** 404

Have pity, Lord, on me from *St. Matthew Passion* by J. S. Bach, **Gr. 7,** 232

Have to Have a Habitat by B. Oliver, **Gr. 3,** 331

Haydn Montage, **Gr. 8,** 123

He's Got the Whole World in His Hands (traditional spiritual), **Gr. 2,** 116

Hen wlad fy nhadau (The Land of My Fathers) by E. James and J. James, **Gr. 2,** 141

Her kommer vennen min (Norwegian folk song), **Gr. 3,** 142

Heritage Festival Music (montage), **Gr. 7,** 55

Hoedown (American folk song), **Gr. 6,** 116

Holiday for Strings by D. Rose, **Gr. 3,** 229

Hornpipe from *Water Music Suite* (excerpt) by G. F. Handel, **Gr. 3,** 26

Horse with No Name, A, by D. Bunnell, **Gr. 8,** 161

How Can I Keep From Singing? by Rev. R. Lowry and A. Warner, **Gr. 5,** 287

Humming Chorus from *Madama Butterfly* by G. Puccini, **Gr. 6,** 257

ILM Hummingbird, A, by A. Beach, **Gr. K,** T140

Hunt the Squirrel from *Suite on English Folk Tunes* by B. Britten, **Gr. 1,** T136

Hush, Little Baby (American folk song), **Gr. 4,** 9

I Bought Me a Cat (excerpt) arr. by A. Copland, **Gr. 2,** 14

I Got Shoes (African American spiritual), **Gr. K,** T33

I Walk the Line by J. Cash, **Gr. 6,** 97

I Will Survive by F. Perren and D. Ferakis, **Gr. 8,** 208

Im Krapfenwaldl (In Krapfen Woods) Op. 336 by J. Strauss, Jr. **Gr. 2,** 244

In the Good Old Summertime by G. Evans, **Gr. K,** T343

ILM In the Hall of the Mountain King from *Peer Gynt Suite No. 1,* Op. 46 by E. Grieg, **Gr. 2,** 346

ILM In the Mood by J. Garland, **Gr. 4,** 143

Individual Career Mosaic (montage), **Gr. 8,** 190

Infernal Dance of King Kashchei from *The Firebird Suite* (excerpt) by I. Stravinsky, **Gr. 4,** 191

Into the Fog from *Master and Commander* (excerpt) by I. Davies, C. Gordon, and R. Tognetti, **Gr. 3,** 201

ILM Introduction from *The Rite of Spring* by I. Stravinsky, **Gr. 6,** 423

ILM It Don't Mean a Thing by D. Ellington, **Gr. 6,** 165

It's Only Monday by C. Judah-Lauder, **Gr. 8,** 14

Jamaica Farewell by I. Burgie, **Gr. 4,** 73

Jamaican Rumba by A. Benjamin, **Gr. 5,** 92

Jangali Famata by A. Farka Toure, **Gr. 4,** 209

Jersey Bounce by M. Bradshaw, R. Bruce, B. Feyne, E. Johnson, and B. Plater, **Gr. 5,** 363

Jesu, Joy of Man's Desiring by J. S. Bach, **Gr. 3,** 41

Jó Ashílá (Navajo song), **Gr. 5,** 224

John Williams Montage 1, **Gr. 8,** 134

John Williams Montage 2, **Gr. 8,** 136

Joshua Fit the Battle of Jericho (African American spiritual), **Gr. 5,** 127

Joyful, Joyful from *Sister Act 2* (excerpt) arr. by M. Warren, **Gr. 5,** 104

Juan Pirulero (Mexican children's song), **Gr. 1,** T153

Jump in the Line by J. T. Taylor, **Gr. 7,** 199

Jupiter, the Bringer of Jollity by G. Holst, **Gr. 8,** 40

Just Keep Goin' On by D. Smith, **Gr. 7,** 16

Kangaroos from *The Carnival of the Animals* by C. Saint-Saëns, **Gr. K,** T196

Kia Ora (Maori greeting song), **Gr. 2,** 65

King Stephen (Overture) by L. van Beethoven, **Gr. 5,** 255

Kokiriko (traditional Japanese folk song), **Gr. 6,** 145

Kurski Funk by P. Winter and the D. Pokrovsky Singers, **Gr. 8,** 153

Kwanzaa Time by E. Jenkins, **Gr. K,** T324

La camilla (Hispanic fiesta dance song), **Gr. 1,** T196

Alphabetical Index of Listening Selections (continued)

ILM La canarie from *Dances from Terpsichore* by M. Praetorius, **Gr. 4,** 176

La choisy by M. Corrette, **Gr. 2,** 177

La cigarra (The Cicada) by R. Perez y Soto, **Gr. 6,** 268

ILM La cumparsita by G. M. Rodríguez, **Gr. 6,** 113

ILM La lluvia by S. Hatfield, **Gr. 2,** 232

La otra España (The Other Spain) by J. C. Calderon, **Gr. 4,** 64

La raspa (Mexican folk dance), **Gr. 3,** 211

La vida es un carnival (Life Is a Carnival) by V. Daniel, **Gr. 4,** 228

ILM Laideronette, Empress of the Pagodas from *Mother Goose Suite* by M. Ravel, **Gr. 1,** T237

Lakota Flute Song by G. Wettlin-Larsen, **Gr. 6,** 429

Land of a Thousand Dances by C. Kenner (Wilson Pickett version), **Gr. 7,** 10; (Garage Band version), **Gr. 7,** 14

Larenjeiras from *Saudades do Brasil* by D. Milhaud, **Gr. K,** T56

ILM Largo al factotum from *Il Barbiere di Siviglia* by G. Rossini, **Gr. 2,** 217

Las mañanitas (Mexican song), **Gr. 4,** 197

Lassus Trombone by H. Fillmore, **Gr. 2,** 191

ILM Le Serpent (excerpt) by Guem, **Gr. 1,** T359

Leggiero (Hopscotch) from *Music for Children* by Sir W. Walton, **Gr. 5,** 281

Les saluts (French Canadian folk dance), **Gr. 3,** 92

Let's Run Across the Hill by H. Villa-Lobos, **Gr. 5,** 268

Let's Twist Again by D. Appell and K. Mann, **Gr. 7,** 11

Liberty Bell, The, by J. P. Sousa, **Gr. 5,** 395

ILM *Liberty Fanfare* (excerpt) by J. Williams, **Gr. 7,** 187

Lift Every Voice and Sing by J. R. and J. W. Johnson (gospel version), **Gr. 5,** 87; (arr. by R. Carter), **Gr. 5,** 117

Lion by L. Eto, **Gr. 6,** 16

Listening for Walking and Galloping/Skipping by M. Sanchez, **Gr. K,** T41

Little David, Play on Your Harp (African American spiritual), **Gr. 2,** 9

ILM Little Train of the Caipira, The, from *Bachianas Brasileiras No. 2* by H. Villa-Lobos, **Gr. K,** T142

Little White Donkey, The, by J. Ibert, **Gr. K,** T245

ILM Locomotion by J. Coltrane, **Gr. 6,** 157

ILM Los mariachis (Mexican folk song), **Gr. 3,** 397; **Gr. 7,** 90

ILM Los trabajadores agricolas (The Farmers) from *Estancia* by A. Ginastera, **Gr. 6,** 116

Machine from Symphony No. 5 by W. Bolcom, **Gr. 8,** 51

Macoklis Mango by Un Solo Pueblo, **Gr. 8,** 46

Maggie in the Wood (traditional Irish song), **Gr. 5,** 49

Magic Flute, The (Overture) by W. A. Mozart, **Gr. 4,** 252

Magnificent Horses arr. by Jing Ling Tam, **Gr. 7,** 104

Mai Nozipo by D. Maraire, **Gr. 1,** T211; **Gr. 7,** 228

Major Bowes' Original Amateur Hour (excerpts), **Gr. 8,** 108

Mama eu quero (I Want My Mama) (Brazilian carnival song), **Gr. 2,** 92

ILM *March for Military Band,* Op. 99 by S. Prokofiev, **Gr. 8,** 37

ILM March from *Children's Games* by G. Bizet, **Gr. 1,** T31

March from *Love for Three Oranges* (excerpt) by S. Prokofiev, **Gr. 3,** 201

March from *The Nutcracker Suite* (excerpt) by P. Tchaikovsky, **Gr. 2,** 354

March of the Toys from *Babes in Toyland* by V. Herbert, **Gr. K,** T317

ILM March Past of the Kitchen Utensils from *The Wasps* by R. Vaughan Williams, **Gr. 3,** 247

ILM Marche by J.-B. Lully, **Gr. 8,** 167

ILM Mars from *The Planets* by G. Holst, **Gr. 6,** 196

Marvin's Music's Midnight Music Sale Jingle by B. Hardesty, **Gr. 8,** 223

Mayflies (poem) by P. Fleischman, **Gr. K,** T76

Medley Polleritas by M. J. Castilla, J. Espinoza, G. Leguizamón, and R. S. Moreno, **Gr. 3,** 111

Merry-Go-Round from *Children's Games* by G. Bizet, **Gr. 2,** 266

Mi-a-ou from *Dolly Suite* by G. Fauré, **Gr. K,** T149

ILM Milan (Meeting of the Two Rivers) (excerpt) by K. Kale, **Gr. 4,** 208

Miniwanka (or The Moments of Water) (excerpt) by R. M. Schafer, **Gr. 4,** 28

ILM Minuet from *Abdelazar* by H. Purcell, **Gr. 2,** 145

Minuet II from *Music for the Royal Fireworks* by G. F. Handel, **Pre-K,** 87

Mississippi Mud (American folk song), **Gr. 6,** 65

Modern Major General, A, from *The Pirates of Penzance,* by W. S. Gilbert and A. Sullivan, **Gr. 6,** 56

ILM Moldau, The, from *Má Vlast (My Country)* by B. Smetana, **Gr. 5,** 271; (entire), **Gr. 7,** 219

Monkees, The (Theme from) by T. Boyce and B. Hart, **Gr. 8,** 110

Mood Music (montage), **Gr. 7,** 133

ILM Moon Mirrored in a Pool, The, by H. Yanjun, **Gr. K,** T115

Moonlight Masquerade for Violin and Piano by S. Chang, **Gr. 7,** 127

Morceau de Concert, First Movement by C. Saint-Saëns, **Gr. 8,** 59

Morning Has Broken (traditional Gaelic melody), **Gr. 4,** 23

Morning Mood from *Peer Gynt Suite No. 1,* Op. 46 by E. Grieg, **Gr. 3,** 251

Motorcycle Ride by B. Haack and E. Nelson, **Gr. 2,** 192

Moulinet (Polka) Op. 57 by J. Strauss, **Gr. 2,** 53

Musette from *Notebook for Anna Magdalena Bach* by J. S. Bach, **Gr. 4,** 261

Music for Strings, Percussion and Celesta (excerpt) by B. Bartók, **Gr. 5,** 201

Music from Bali (gamelan ensemble), **Gr. 1,** T143

Music of the Generations (montage), **Gr. 7,** 3

ILM Música indígena from *Instantaneas Mexicanas* by M. M. Ponce, **Gr. 8,** 126

Muss i denn (German March) (excerpt), **Pre-K,** 35

Mwiji Mwena (traditional African spiritual), **Gr. 2,** 235

ILM My Favorite Things from *The Sound of Music* by R. Rodgers and O. Hammerstein II, **Gr. 3,** 313

ILM My Friend by M. Kibble and J. Kibble, **Gr. 4,** 389

Nach Nach Nach (Punjabi song), **Gr. 6,** 224

National Emblem by E. E. Bagley, **Gr. 7,** 76

Nature Sounds (montage), **Gr. 8,** 18

Nead na lachan sa mhúta (Irish folk song), **Gr. 5,** 48

ILM Nessun dorma from *Turandot* by G. Puccini, **Gr. 5,** 64

New Africa by Y. N'Dour and H. Faye, **Gr. 4,** 209

New Orleans Jazz Funeral (excerpts), **Gr. 7,** 143

Ngikhumbula (Swazi song), **Gr. 5,** 195

ILM Night Fight from *Crouching Tiger, Hidden Dragon* by Tan Dun, **Gr. 6,** 28

Alphabetical Index of Listening Selections (continued)

Night of the Mockingbird by J. Huling, **Gr. 4**, 153

ILM *Nightingale, The,* by F. Liszt, **Gr. 6**, 160

ILM Nigun Atik (Israeli folk dance), **Gr. 3**, 47

ILM No One Is Alone from *Into the Woods* by S. Sondheim, **Gr. 8**, 86

ILM Nokken Danser (Norwegian folk melody), **Pre-K**, 26; **Gr. 4**, 168

Norwegian Dance, Op. 35, No. 2 by E. Grieg, **Gr. 3**, 145

ILM Ocean Child by P. Winter, **Gr. 7**, 218

Och Jungfrun Hon Går I Ringen (Swedish dance song), **Gr. 5**, 191

ILM Ode to a Butterfly by C. Thile, **Gr. 5**, 25

Ogguere (Afro-Cuban lullaby), **Gr. 4**, 329

Oito Batutas by Pixinguinha, **Gr. 4**, 128

Old MacDonald Had a Farm, arr. by L. Anderson, **Gr. 2**, 133

Old Time Rock and Roll by G. Jackson and T. Jones, **Gr. 7**, 98

ILM On the Trail from *Grand Canyon Suite* by F. Grofé, **Gr. 8**, 112

One Note Samba by A. C. Jobim, **Gr. 4**, 92

One Voice by B. Manilow, **Gr. 5**, 326

ILM Only Time by Enya et al., **Gr. 7**, 142

Over the Rainbow from *The Wizard of Oz* by H. Arlen and E. Y. Harburg, **Gr. K**, T60

Overture from *La forza del destino* by G. Verdi, **Gr. 3**, 201

Overture from *The Nutcracker Suite* (excerpt) by P. Tchaikovsky, **Gr. 2**, 354

ILM Oye como va by T. Puente, **Gr. 5**, 69

ILM Packington's Pound (anonymous), **Gr. 2**, 200

Panda Chant II by M. Monk, **Gr. 6**, 263

Pantomime from *The Comedians* by D. Kabalevsky, **Gr. 1**, T256

Papagena! Papagena! Papagena! from *The Magic Flute* by W. A. Mozart, **Gr. 2**, 152 **ILM**

Papa-oom-mow-mow by A. Frazier et al, **Gr. 7**, 177

Parade from *Divertissement* by J. Ibert, **Gr. K**, T183 **ILM**

Parade in the Parlor (North Carolina folk melody), **Gr. 4**, 229

Park Rap 1 by C. Judah-Lauder, **Gr. 7**, 70

Park Rap 2 by C. Judah-Lauder, **Gr. 7**, 72

Partita No. 2 in D Minor by J. S. Bach, **Gr. 8**, 95

Pat Works on the Railway (Orff version), **Gr. 1**, T144

Pata Pata (excerpt) by M. Makeba, **Gr. 2**, 94; (entire) by M. Makeba and J. Ragovoy, **Gr. 3**, 35 **ILM**

Peaceful World by J. Mellencamp, **Gr. 7**, 154 **ILM**

Pegasus Suite, First Movement (excerpt) by N. Bloomer Deussen, **Gr. 5**, 41

People in Your Neighborhood, The, by J. Moss (sung verses), **Gr. K**, T122; (instrumental verses), **Gr. K**, T171

ILM People United Will Never Be Defeated!, The, by F. Rzewski, **Gr. 8**, 93

Performance Mosaic (montage), **Gr. 8**, 185

Performances (montage), **Gr. 8**, 23

Peter and the Wolf (excerpt) by S. Prokofiev, **Gr. 2**, 160

Peter and the Wolf (Introduction) by S. Prokofiev, **Gr. 1**, T140

Pezinho (Brazilian cantiga), **Gr. 3**, 230

Pitch Review Warm-Up, **Gr. 7**, 47

Playful Pizzicato from *Simple Symphony* by B. Britten, **Gr. 3**, 263

Po Atarau (Maori song), **Gr. 5**, 150

Pole, Pole by E. Jenkins, **Gr. K**, T215

Polegnala e Todora by P. Koutev, **Gr. K**, T163

Polovtsian Dances from *Prince Igor* (excerpt) by A. Borodin, **Gr. 3**, 81

ILM *Pomp and Circumstance March No. 1,* Trio by E. Elgar, **Gr. 7**, 50

Pop! Goes the Weasel (expanded dance version) (English ring game), **Gr. 5**, 112

Porushka-Paranya (Russian folk song), **Gr. 4**, 208

Poun to, Poun to (Where Is It? Where Is It?) (Greek and Cypriot song), **Gr. 2**, 175

Prairie Dog Song (Kiowa children's song), **Gr. K**, T220

Prelude to Act I from *Carmen* by G. Bizet, **Gr. 4**, 250

Prelude to Act II from *Siegfried* (excerpt) by R. Wagner, **Gr. 2**, 58

Prince of Denmark's March by J. Clarke, **Gr. 2**, 81

Processional Medley (montage), **Gr. 7**, 75

ILM Promenade from *Golden Goose* by L. Worsley, **Gr. 1**, T177

Promise of Living, The, from *The Tender Land* by A. Copland, **Gr. 6**, 77

ILM Pukaea (excerpt) by J. Coleman and H. Mohi, **Gr. 2**, 109

ILM Pulcinella Suite (excerpt) by I. Stravinsky, **Gr. 4**, 201

Qua Cầu Gió Bay (Vietnamese folk song), **Gr. 4**, 367

Quintet for Piano and Strings in A Major ("Trout"), Second Movement by F. Schubert, **Gr. 6**, 344

Quintet, Op. 114 ("Trout") (excerpt) by F. Schubert, **Gr. 8**, 189

Quintet, Op. 43, Menuet (excerpt) by C. Nielsen, **Gr. 4**, 121

ILM Radetzky March by J. Strauss, Sr., **Gr. K**, T177

ILM Raga Malika (Indian classical music), **Gr. 5**, 402

Railroad Blues by F. Stowers, **Gr. 2**, 327

Red River Valley (traditional American cowboy song), **Gr. 6**, 96

Reel á bouche (French Canadian song), **Gr. 6**, 56

Refavela by G. Gil, **Gr. 4**, 209

Repicados sobre Madera (excerpt) (Uruguayan candombe), **Gr. 4**, 93

Requiebros by G. Cassado, **Gr. 6**, 80

Respect (two versions) by O. Redding, **Gr. 7**, 5

Rhythm Review Warm-Up, **Gr. 7**, 44

Rite of Spring, The, (excerpt) by I. Stravinsky, **Gr. 2**, 201

Rock Island from *The Music Man* by M. Willson, **Gr. 8**, 74

Romantic Period Music (montage), **Gr. 8**, 119

Rondeau from *Abdelazar* by H. Purcell, **Gr. 6**, 121

ILM Rondo "alla turca" from Piano Sonata No. 11 in A Major, Third Movement by W. A. Mozart, **Gr. 7**, 116

ILM Rondo a capriccio Op. 129 ("Rage Over a Lost Penny") (excerpt) by L. van Beethoven, **Gr. 2**, 225

Rondo all'Ongarese (Trio for Piano, Violin, and Cello No. 39, Finale) by F. J. Haydn, **Gr. 7**, 115

Rondo for Lifey by L. Bernstein, **Gr. 2**, 81

Round-up from *Western Suite* by E. Siegmeister, **Gr. 2**, 67

Route 66 by B. Troup, **Gr. 7**, 191

Royal March of the Lions, The, from *The Carnival of the Animals* by C. Saint-Saëns, **Gr. 1**, T25

Rumpus in Richmond by D. Ellington, **Gr. 8**, 32

ILM Russian Sailor's Dance from *The Red Poppy* by R. Glière, **Gr. 4**, 266

Såg du nøko? (Norwegian folk song), **Gr. 2**, 104

ILM Sail Away (mountain dance), **Gr. 4**, 55

Salsa in the Parlor (North Carolina folk melody), **Gr. 4**, 229

Sambalelê (Brazilian children's song), **Gr. 1**, T205

Santoki (Mountain Rabbit) (Korean singing game), **Gr. 1**, T187

ILM Scheherazade (excerpt) by N. Rimsky-Korsakov, **Gr. 4,** 161

Scherzo and Tarantella by H. Wieniawski, **Gr. 2,** 160

School Band Rondo by M. Jothen, **Gr. 7,** 36

School Ensembles (montage), **Gr. 8,** 2

Schwanenlied by F. Mendelssohn Hensel, **Gr. 7,** 124

ILM Seasons of Love from *Rent* (choral arrangement) by J. Larson, **Gr. 7,** 86

Sellinger's Round (English Renaissance dance), **Gr. 6,** 98

ILM Semper Fidelis by J. P. Sousa, **Gr. 3,** 281; **Gr. 6,** 391

Seneca Stomp Dance, **Gr. K,** T345

Sensemayá (excerpt) by S. Revueltas, **Gr. 3,** 161

ILM Serenade No. 10 in B Flat Major, K.361 ("Gran Partita"), Theme and Variations (excerpt) by W. A. Mozart, **Gr. 4,** 235

Sérénade Op. 29 by C. Chaminade, **Gr. 2,** 262

Seven Jumps from *Dance Music for Children* by N. Hirsh, **Gr. K,** T80

Seven Principles of Kwanzaa, The, by S. Spottswood, **Gr. 6,** 415

ILM Seventeen Come Sunday from *English Folk Song Suite* by R. Vaughan Williams , **Gr. 7,** 102

ILM Seventy-Six Trombones from *The Music Man* by M. Willson, **Gr. 8,** 76

ILM Shady Grove (traditional), **Gr. 8,** 59

Shepherd's Hey by P. Grainger, **Gr. 6,** 201

Shí Naashá (Navajo folk song), **Gr. 1,** T72

Shi wu (Lion Dance) by H. Kuo-Huang and P. Campbell, **Gr. K,** T329

ILM Shimmering Air by R. Saint-Denis, **Gr. K,** T139

Short Ride in a Fast Machine by J. Adams, **Gr. 5,** 125

Shrimp Boats (excerpt) by P. Howard and P. Weston, **Gr. 2,** 178

Side Show, The by C. Ives, **Gr. 5,** 283

Sigh of the Soul for Alyscamp (Fourth Movement) from *Tableaux de Provence* by P. Maurice, **Gr. 3,** 80

Signature Themes (from *La Bohème* and *Rent*) by G. Puccini and J. Larson, **Gr. 7,** 180

Simple Pleasures by B. McFerrin, **Gr. 8,** 191

Sing Lo-Lo from *Afrika Wassa* by V. Diop, **Gr. 4,** 385

ILM Sing, Sing, Sing (with a Swing) by L. Prima, **Gr. 5,** 32

ILM Singing on the Fisherboats at Dusk (Chinese folk song), **Gr. 1,** T129

Singing Woods, The, by B. M. Davids, **Gr. 7,** 201

ILM Sixteen Tons (Tennessee Ernie Ford) by M. Travis, **Gr. 7,** 150

ILM Skaters' Waltz, The (excerpt) by E. Waldteufel, **Gr. 1,** T345

ILM Skeleton by A. York, **Gr. 8,** 215

ILM Sleight of Feet from *Cakewalk Suite* by H. Kay, **Gr. 1,** T239

So Glad I'm Here arr. by B. Johnson Reagon, **Gr. 2,** 47

ILM So Long, Farewell from *The Sound of Music* by R. Rodgers and O. Hammerstein II, **Gr. K,** T189

Solveig's Song from *Peer Gynt Suite No. 2*, Op. 55 by E. Grieg, **Gr. 5,** 192

Sometimes I Feel Like a Motherless Child (African American spiritual), **Gr. 6,** 271

Somos Boricuas (We Are Puerto Rican) by J. Gutiérrez, **Gr. 2,** 138

Son de Camaguey by L. Dubinsky, **Gr. 8,** 51

Son de la negra (Mexican folk music), **Gr. 5,** 397

Sonata for Bass Trombone, First Movement (Andantino) by P. McCarty, **Gr. 5,** 160

Sonata for Cello and Piano, Op. 40, Second Movement by D. Shostakovich, **Gr. 4,** 40

Sonata for Flute and Piano, Third Movement by F. Poulenc, **Gr. 4,** 200

Sonata for Piano and Bassoon, First Movement by C. Saint-Saëns, **Gr. 8,** 19

ILM Sonata for Piano No. 2 in D Minor, Vivace (excerpt) by S. Prokofiev, **Gr. 4,** 181

Sonata for Piano No. 48 in C, First Movement by F. J. Haydn, **Gr. 8,** 122

Sonata for Violin No. 4, First Movement by E. Ysaÿe, **Gr. 8,** 156

Sonata in C Major, Longo 104 by D. Scarlatti, **Gr. K,** T89

Sonata in G Minor ("The Cat's Fugue") by D. Scarlatti, **Pre-K,** 5

Sonata X by J. Cage, **Gr. 6,** 32

Sonatina for Three Timpani and Piano, First Movement (excerpt) by A. Tcherepnin, **Gr. 4,** 81

Sonatine for Brass Quintet, First Movement (excerpt) by E. Bozza, **Gr. 3,** 121

Sones de mariachi by B. Galindo, **Gr. 2,** 380

Song of a Seashore (traditional Inuit), **Gr. 7,** 176

Sorcerer's Apprentice, The (excerpt) by P. Dukas, **Gr. 4,** 116

Sound the Trumpet from *I Puritani* by V. Bellini, **Gr. 5,** 279

Speed the Plow Medley by E. Meyer, **Gr. 6,** 149

ILM Spinning Song by A. Ellmenreich, **Gr. 3,** 128

ILM Spinning Wheel by D. Clayton-Thomas, **Gr. 4,** 211

ILM Spring (Allegro) from *The Four Seasons* (Concerto No. 1 in E Major) by A. Vivaldi, **Gr. 4,** 391; (excerpt) **Gr. 7,** 112

Spring Round Dances from *The Rite of Spring* by I. Stravinsky, **Gr. 7,** 232

Spirit Medley Rondo (montage), **Gr. 7,** 45

St. Patrick's Day (Irish folk music), **Gr. 2,** 374

ILM Stars and Stripes Forever, The, by J. P. Sousa, **Gr. 4,** 355; **Gr. 7,** 197

Star-Spangled Banner, The, music attributed to J. Smith, words by F. S. Key, arr. by M. Hogan, **Gr. 5,** 86

Steel Drums Jam (excerpt), **Gr. 2,** 90

Step in Time from *Mary Poppins* by R. and R. Sherman, **Gr. K,** T159

Stonehaven Sunset by J. Denver, **Gr. 7,** 221

Strawberry Roan (excerpt) (cowboy song), **Gr. 2,** 66

String Instruments in the Orchestra (montage), **Gr. 7,** 48

ILM String of Pearls, A, by G. Miller, **Gr. 3,** 12

ILM String Quartet Op. 76, No. 2 in D Minor, Andante (excerpt) by F. J. Haydn, **Gr. 1,** T129

String Quartet No. 2, Op. 17, Allegro molto caprizzioso by B. Bartók, **Gr. 2,** 121

String Quartet Op. 33, No. 3 ("The Bird"), Fourth Movement by F. J. Haydn, **Gr. 1,** T251

String Quartet Op. 76, No. 2 in D Minor, Andante o piu tosto allegretto (excerpt) by F. J. Haydn, **Gr. 2,** 121

Strings in the Media (montage), **Gr. 7,** 49

Summer (Allegro Non Molto) from *The Four Seasons* (Concerto No. 2 in G Minor) (excerpt) by A. Vivaldi, **Gr. 4,** 161

ILM Summertime from *Porgy and Bess* by G. and I. Gershwin, **Gr. 1,** T375, **Gr. 4,** 160; **Gr. 6,** 120

ILM Sunburst by A. York, **Gr. 7,** 216

Sweet Sound by E. Cypress, **Gr. 8,** 233

Alphabetical Index of Listening Selections (continued)

Symphonic Dances Op. 64, No. 4 (excerpt) by E. Grieg, **Gr. 2,** 105

Symphony No. 1 ("Titan"), Third Movement (excerpt) by G. Mahler, **Gr. 5,** 161

ILM Symphony No. 1 in D Major, Op. 25 ("Classical"), Third Movement (Gavotte) by S. Prokofiev, **Gr. 1,** T92

Symphony No. 2 ("Sinfonía india") (excerpt) by C. Chávez, **Gr. 2,** 61

Symphony No. 4, First Movement (excerpt) and Second Movement (excerpt) by P. Tchaikovsky, **Gr. 6,** 41

Symphony No. 4, Fourth Movement by P. Tchaikovsky, **Gr. 4,** 287

ILM Symphony No. 5 in C Minor, Third and Fourth Movements by L. van Beethoven, **Gr. 8,** 115

Symphony No. 5, First Movement (excerpt) by D. Shostakovich, **Gr. 6,** 161

Symphony No. 5, Second Movement (excerpt) by P. Tchaikovsky, **Gr. 5,** 81

Symphony No. 6 ("Pastoral") (excerpts) by L. van Beethoven, **Gr. 8,** 20

Symphony No. 6 ("Pathetique"), Second Movement by P. Tchaikovsky, **Gr. 5,** 281

Symphony No. 7 in A Major, Second Movement (excerpt) by L. van Beethoven, **Gr. 4,** 242

ILM Symphony No. 7, Second Movement by L. van Beethoven, **Gr. 7,** 118

ILM Symphony No. 8, Second Movement (excerpt) by L. van Beethoven, **Gr. K,** T235

Symphony No. 9 ("Choral"), Fourth Movement (excerpt) by L. van Beethoven, **Gr. 7,** 156

Symphony No. 9 ("From the New World"), Largo (excerpt) by A. Dvořák, **Gr. 3,** 81

Symphony No. 9 in D Minor ("Choral"), Fourth Movement (excerpt) by L. van Beethoven, **Gr. 5,** 102 **ILM**

Symphony No. 9 in E Minor, Op. 95 ("From the New World"), Largo (excerpt) by A. Dvořák, **Gr. 5,** 106 **ILM**

Symphony No. 35, Fourth Movement (excerpt) by F. J. Haydn, **Gr. 5,** 247 **ILM**

Symphony No. 40 in G Minor, First Movement by W. A. Mozart, **Gr. 8,** 218 **ILM**

Symphony No. 45 ("Farewell"), First Movement by F. J. Haydn, **Gr. 8,** 124

Symphony No. 73 ("La Chasse") ("The Hunt"), Fourth Movement by F. J. Haydn, **Gr. 4,** 263

Symphony No. 101 in D Major ("Clock") by F. J. Haydn, **Gr. 8,** 128

Symphony: Water Music, Movements 3 and 4 by L. Larsen, **Gr. 8,** 155

Tabu by M. Lecuona, **Gr. 2,** 20

Take Five by P. Desmond (excerpt), **Gr. 4,** 41; (entire) **Gr. 5,** 213

Talent Show Audition Pieces (montage), **Gr. 8,** 24

Tame Bear from *Wand of Youth Suite No. 2* by E. Elgar, **Gr. K,** T203

Taos Round Dance (traditional), **Gr. 2,** 155

Taps (traditional), **Gr. 7,** 144

Tears in Heaven (choral arrangement) by E. Clapton and W. Jennings, **Gr. 7,** 140

Tehahontanekenhnêha' (Rabbit Dance story), **Gr. 3,** 50; (Rabbit Dance song), **Gr. 3,** 51

Tekanionton'néha' (Mohawk social song and dance), **Gr. 5,** 222

Theme and Percussion Variation from *Young Person's Guide to the Orchestra* by B. Britten, **Gr. 5,** 229

There Was a Blue Flower from *Dreaming Blue* by L. Larsen, **Gr. 6,** 218

This Train (African American spiritual), **Gr. 4,** 343

ILM Three Little Birds by B. Marley, **Gr. 8,** 84

Thula Sizwe (South African freedom song), **Gr. 6,** 73

Ti Ayat (Filipino folk song), **Gr. 6,** 359

Till Eulenspiegel's Merry Pranks by R. Strauss, **Gr. 5,** 81

Tinikling (national dance of the Philippines), **Gr. 4,** 105

Toccata and Fugue in D Minor by J. S. Bach, **Gr. 7,** 108

Too-ra-loo-ra-loo-ral (That's an Irish Lullaby) by J. Shannon, **Gr. K,** T335

Tortoises from *The Carnival of the Animals* (excerpt) by C. Saint-Saëns, **Pre-K,** 64

Tragic Story, A, by B. Britten, **Gr. 4,** 190

ILM Trepak from *The Nutcracker* by P. Tchaikovsky, **Gr. 6,** 408

ILM Trio for Piano, Violin and Cello No. 39, Finale ("Gypsy Rondo") by F. J. Haydn, **Gr. 3,** 155; **Gr. 7,** 115

ILM Trio for Piano, Violin, and Cello, Op. 11, Third Movement (Presto Leggiero) by C. Chaminade, **Gr. 5,** 121

ILM Troika from *Lieutenant Kijé Suite* (excerpt) by S. Prokofiev, **Gr. 3,** 225

Trumpet and Drum from *Children's Games* by G. Bizet, **Gr. 1,** T231

ILM Tshotsholoza (South African folk song), **Gr. 1,** T76

Tsidii-Bird by G. Barney, **Gr. 6,** 429

Tubby the Tuba by K. Kleinsinger, **Gr. 1,** T80

Tue Tue (Ghanaian song), **Gr. 2,** 234

Tug of War from *Outdoor Games* by G. Tailleferre, **Gr. K,** T339

ILM Tuileries from *Pictures at an Exhibition* by M. Mussorgsky, **Gr. 1,** T249

Tulloch Castle/Flowers of Red Hill (traditional Celtic songs), **Gr. 6,** 200

Turandot from *Symphonic Metamorphosis on Themes of Carl Maria von Weber* (excerpt) by P. Hindemith, **Gr. 4,** 81

Turkey in the Straw (American folk song), **Gr. 2,** 348

Tutira Mai Nga Iwi (Maori folk song), **Gr. K,** T17

Twee emmertjes (traditional spinning song), **Gr. 4,** 212

Two in a Boat (American folk song), **Gr. 3,** 316

Tzakonikos (Greek circle dance), **Gr. 6,** 215

Una donna a quindici anni from *Così fan tutte* by W. A. Mozart, **Gr. 8,** 187

Uncle Jessie (African American folk song), **Gr. 3,** 327

Ushkana (Native American folk song), **Gr. 1,** T44

ILM Va Pensiero from *Nabucco* by G. Verdi, **Gr. 6,** 169

Vagabond, The, by R. Vaughan Williams, **Gr. 7,** 78

ILM Variations on "Simple Gifts" from *Appalachian Spring* by A. Copland, **Gr. 5,** 152

ILM Variations on the Theme "Pop! Goes the Weasel" by L. Caillet, **Gr. 5,** 96

Vhaya Kadhimba (Zimbabwean children's song), **Gr. 1,** T24

Vinqo (Zulu song), **Gr. 4,** 24

Violin Concerto, First Movement (Andante Tranquillo) by W. Walton, **Gr. 7,** 52

Vocal Expressions (montage), **Gr. 5,** 165

Alphabetical Index of Listening Selections (continued)

ILM Volta from *Dances from Terpsichore* by M. Praetorius, **Gr. 3,** 121

ILM Wade in the Water (African American spiritual) arr. by M. Hogan, **Gr. 5,** 144

Wagon Passes, The, from *Nursery Suite* by E. Elgar, **Gr. 1,** T242

Walking by A. York, **Gr. 8,** 214

Walking in the Air by H. Blake, **Gr. 4,** 319

ILM Walking Song from *Acadian Songs and Dances* (from the movie *Louisiana Story*) by V. Thomson, **Gr. K,** T20

ILM Walking the Dog from *Shall We Dance* by G. Gershwin, **Gr. 1,** T169

Waltz in A Major, Op. 54, No. 1 by A. Dvořák, **Gr. K,** T109

Waltz in the Parlor (North Carolina folk melody), **Gr. 4,** 229

ILM Waltz of the Flowers from *The Nutcracker Suite* (excerpt) by P. Tchaikovsky, **Gr. 1,** T353; **Gr. 2,** 354

Waltz of the Snowflakes from *The Nutcracker* (excerpt) by P. Tchaikovsky, **Gr. K,** T311

ILM Waltzing Cat by L. Anderson, **Gr. K,** T223

ILM Washington Post, The by J. P. Sousa, **Gr. 2,** 339

ILM *Washington's Birthday* by C. Ives, **Gr. 2,** 370

Water Cadenza from *Water Passion After St. Matthew* by Tan Dun, **Gr. 7,** 233

We All Stand Together (excerpt) by P. McCartney, **Gr. K,** T153

We Shall Overcome (Howard University Gospel Choir) by Z. Horton et al, **Gr. 7,** 213

We're Looking Good by J. Williams, **Gr. 2,** 149

Wells Fargo Wagon, The, from *The Music Man* by M. Willson, **Gr. 8,** 78

ILM What a Wonderful World by G. D. Weiss and B. Thiele (entire), **Gr. 2,** 84; (choral arrangement), **Gr. 8,** 8; (Louis Armstrong version), **Gr. 8,** 9

What Did You Do Today at Jeffrey's House? by P. Schickele, **Gr. 4,** 80

When I'm Walking (Let Me Walk) by A. Domino, Jr., **Gr. 8,** 70

When Johnny Comes Marching Home by P. S. Gilmore, **Gr. 7,** 168

Whup! Jamboree (English sea chantey), **Gr. 6,** 318

Wide Open Spaces by S. Gibson, **Gr. 7,** 208

Wie schön leuchtet der Morgenstern (How Brightly Shines the Morning Star) from *Cantata No. 1,* BWV 1 by J. S. Bach, **Gr. 5,** 371

ILM *William Tell* (Overture) (excerpt) by G. Rossini, **Gr. 3,** 64

ILM Winter (Allegro non molto) from *The Four Seasons* (Concerto No. 4 in F Minor) by A. Vivaldi, **Gr. 6,** 403

Year-Naming Race, The (Chinese folk tale), **Gr. 3,** 385

Yongnam Nongak (Korean agricultural music), **Gr. 5,** 70

You've Got a Friend by C. King, **Gr. 6,** 418

You've Got a Friend in Me by R. Newman, **Gr. 2,** 44

ILM *Young Person's Guide to the Orchestra* (excerpt) by B. Britten, **Gr. 2,** 229

Youth Ensembles (montage), **Gr. 8,** 28

Global Voices

Acitrón (Mexican stone-passing song), **Gr. 6,** 93

Afrakakabra (Ghanaian Game Song), **Gr. 3,** 102

Ake Tonu (Maori song), **Gr. 5,** 150

Ban Dal by Yoon Kyekyoung, **Gr. 4,** 184

Bəri Bax! (Azerbaijani folk song), **Gr. 5,** 233

Cip cip cücəlǝrim by G. Huseynli and T. Mutallibov, **Gr. 3,** 215

Her kommer vennen min (Norwegian folk song), **Gr. 3,** 142

Juan Pirulero (Mexican children's song), **Gr. 1,** T153

Kia Ora (Maori greeting song), **Gr. 2,** 65

Kokiriko (traditional Japanese folk song), **Gr. 6,** 145

Nach Nach Nach (Punjabi song), **Gr. 6,** 224

Nead na lachan sa mhúta (Irish folk song), **Gr. 5,** 48

Ngikhumbula (Swazi song), **Gr. 5,** 195

Pezinho (Brazilian cantiga), **Gr. 3,** 230

Poun to, Poun to (Where Is It? Where Is It?) (Greek and Cypriot song), **Gr. 2,** 175

Såg du nøko? (Norwegian folk song), **Gr. 2,** 104

Sambalelê (Brazilian children's song), **Gr. 1,** T205

Santoki (Mountain Rabbit) (Korean singing game), **Gr. 1,** T187

Thula Sizwe (South African freedom song), **Gr. 6,** 73

Tinikling (national dance of the Philippines), **Gr. 4,** 105

Tue Tue (Ghanaian song), **Gr. 2,** 234

Twee emmertjes (traditional spinning song), **Gr. 4,** 212

Vhaya Kadhimba (Zimbabwean children's song), **Gr. 1,** T24

Vinqo (Zulu song), **Gr. 4,** 24

Interviews

Ban Dal by Yoon Kyekyoung, **Gr. 4,** 184

Bremer, Lous (From the Top), **Gr. 5,** 160

Brown, Randall (From the Top), **Gr. 3,** 80

Brown, Rebecca (From the Top), **Gr. 2,** 200

Conway, Eoghan (From the Top), **Gr. 3,** 160

Cope, Todd (From the Top), **Gr. 5,** 40

Fortenberry, Jewel "Tre," (From the Top), **Gr. 5,** 80

Garcia, Bianca (From the Top), **Gr. 2,** 120

Gorton, Heidi (From the Top), **Gr. 3,** 200

Jantsch, Carol (From the Top), **Gr. 2,** 40

Jenkins, Ella, **Gr. 2,** 157

Kissin, Evgeny, **Gr. 2,** 224

Kozak, Greg, **Gr. 2,** 36

Ladzekpo, Kobla, **Gr. 5,** 72

MacMorran, William (From the Top), **Gr. 6,** 200

Marchioni, Toni (From the Top), **Gr. 5,** 120

Marx, Aaron, **Gr. 6,** 189

McDonald, Jerry Thundercloud, **Gr. 3,** 52

Muckey, Matthew (From the Top), **Gr. 6,** 40

Ochieng, Trevor (From the Top), **Gr. 2,** 160

Partk, Ariana and Rexton (From the Top), **Gr. 3,** 40

Premo, Evan (From the Top), **Gr. 6,** 120

Ritterling, Soojin Kim, **Gr. 5,** 51

Talens, Deanna (From the Top), **Gr. 6,** 80

Tan, Lucy (From the Top), **Gr. 6,** 160

Tinikling (national dance of the Philippines), **Gr. 4,** 105

Twee emmertjes (traditional spinning song), **Gr. 4,** 212

Urioste, Elena (From the Top), **Gr. 5,** 200

Vante, Barbara (From the Top), **Gr. 3,** 120

Vinqo (Zulu song), **Gr. 4,** 24

Yu, Vincent (From the Top), **Gr. 2,** 80

Poetry

An Apple a Day, **Gr. 1**, T152
Animal Rhythms, **Gr. K**, T56
Apple Tree by K. Forrai, **Gr. 3**, 24
Autumn Fires by R. L. Stevenson, **Gr. 7**, 26
Big and Small by E. McCullough-Brabson, **Gr. 1**, T200
Bliss by E. Farjeon, **Gr. 2**, 212
Borinquen by I. Freire de Matos, **Gr. 5**, 443
Bound No'th Blues by L. Hughes, **Gr. 5**, 181
Bow-Wow, **Gr. 1**, T81
Buffalo Dusk by C. Sandburg, **Gr. K**, T219
Bullfrogs, Bullfrogs on Parade by J. Prelutsky, **Gr. K**, T183
Call of the Wild, The, by R. Service, **Gr. 1**, T139
Christmas Tree by M. Livingston, **Gr. 1**, T352
City by L. Hughes, **Gr. K**, T134
City Music by T. Mitton, **Gr. 3**, 74
City Traffic by B. Franco, **Gr. 2**, 328
Clouds, **Gr. 1**, T330
Cobbler, The, by E. Chaffee, **Gr. K**, T169
Colores de caracol by E. Galarza, **Gr. 5**, 101
Concord Hymn, by R. W. Emerson, **Gr. 7**, 66
Corre el rio (haiku) by P. Vasquez, **Gr. 4**, 183
Cow, The, by R. Stevenson, **Gr. 1**, T236
Damsel Fly and the Mayfly, The, by H. Hamilton, **Gr. K**, T74
Daydreams on a Subway Train by Patricia M. Fagan, **Gr. 8**, 85
Deedle, Deedle Dumpling, **Gr. K**, T87
Do You Want My Little Frog? adapted by H. Copeland, **Gr. 2**, 187
Dragonfly by D. Violin, **Gr. 1**, T44
Dream Dust by L. Hughes, **Gr. 4**, 235
Dreidel Song by E. Rosenzweig, **Gr. 1**, T349
Ears, Far and Near by M. Campbelle-Holman and S. Snyder, **Gr. 1**, T16
Earth Folk by W. de la Mare, **Gr. 7**, 174
Echo by W. de la Mare, **Gr. K**, T104
Elephant Carries a Great Big Trunk, The, **Gr. 2**, 169
Excuse Us, Animals in the Zoo by A. Wynne, **Gr. K**, T195
Field of Joys by M. Morand, **Gr. 1**, T224
Finis by Sir H. Newbolt, **Gr. 2**, 76
Five Little Pumpkins, **Gr. 1**, T337
Flag Goes By, The, by H. Holcomb Bennett, **Gr. 7**, 45
Follow the Leader by K. Fraser, **Gr. K**, T132
From My Window by Deanna Bailey, **Gr. 8**, 19
Furry Bear by A. A. Milne, **Gr. K**, T205
Giant's Shoes, The, by E. Fallis, **Gr. K**, T32
Girls and Boys, Come Out to Play (excerpt) (traditional), **Gr. K**, T98
Grasshoppers by P. Fleischman, **Gr. 1**, T244
Gus: The Theatre Cat by T.S. Eliot, **Gr. 8**, 195
Haiku (Butterfly) by M. Frall, **Gr. 1**, T332
Hairy Dog, The, by H. Asquith, **Gr. 2**, 58
Halloween by I. Crichton Smith, **Gr. 1**, T338

Happiness by A.A. Milne, **Gr. 1**, T254
Happy Thoughts by R. L. Stevenson, **Gr. 2**, 195
Heartbeat of Democracy by V. Brasier, **Gr. 5**, 389
Here Comes the Band by W. Cole, **Gr. 1**, T80
Hickory, Dickory, Dock (traditional), **Gr. K**, T49
Hinges by A. Fisher, **Gr. K**, T23
Hippopotamus, The, by J. Prelutsky, **Gr. K**, T199
Hope by E. Dickinson, **Gr. 3**, 166
Hopping Frog by C. Rossetti, **Gr. 1**, T113
Horses of the Sea, The, by C. Rossetti, **Gr. 1**, T179
Hullabaloo, **Gr. 3**, 234
Humming Birds by B. Sage, **Gr. K**, T140
I Am a Little Tugboat by C. Huffman, **Gr. K**, T95
I Asked a Little Child by Anonymous, **Gr. 6**, 218
I Had a Little Hen, **Gr. 1**, T136
I Have a Friend, **Gr. 1**, T225
I Heard a Bird Sing by O. Herford, **Gr. 2**, 271
I Know Not Why by Morris Rosenfeld, **Gr. 8**, 179
I Like by M. Hoberman, **Gr. 1**, T110
I Wandered Lonely as a Cloud by William Wordsworth, **Gr. 7**, 125; **Gr. 8**, 19
I Woke Up in the Morning by S. Dunn, **Gr. 3**, 262
I'd Like to Be a Lighthouse by R. Field, **Gr. 1**, T238
I'm Getting Sick of Peanut Butter by K. Nesbitt, **Gr. 1**, T219
Ice by D. Aldis, **Gr. 1**, T346
If Things Grew Down by R. Hoeft, **Gr. K**, T293
In the Barnyard by D. Aldis, **Gr. K**, T207
Inward Morning, The, **Gr. 4**, 23
It Dropped So Low by E. Dickinson, **Gr. 7**, 20
It Fell in the City by E. Merriam, **Gr. K**, T312
Jack-in-the-box by L. Birkenshaw-Fleming, **Gr. K**, T251
Jolly Old St. Nicholas (traditional American), **Gr. 4**, 382
Jump or Jiggle by E. Beyer, **Gr. 1**, T316
Jump or Jiggle by E. Beyer, **Gr. K**, T193
Just Give Me the Beat (speech piece) by R. Boyer-Alexander, **Gr. 5**, 9
Kangaroo, The, by E. Coatsworth, **Gr. K**, T196
Kwanzaa Is... by C. McClester, **Gr. 6**, 414
Life by S. DeShetler, **Gr. 5**, 205
Limericks, **Gr. 4**, 84
Lincoln by M.C. Livingston, **Gr. 3**, 389
Little Seeds (excerpt) by E. H. Minarik, **Gr. 2**, 207
Locust, The, **Gr. 1**, T285
Long Gone by J. Prelutsky, **Gr. K**, T72
Look at the Sky (traditional Korean), **Gr. 5**, 71
Loose Tooth (speech piece), **Gr. 2**, 28
Mayflies (excerpt) by P. Fleischman, **Gr. K**, T76
Me I Am! by J. Prelutsky, **Gr. K**, T346
Merry-Go-Round by R. Field, **Gr. K**, T225
Mighty River (speech piece) by W. Brecht, **Gr. 4**, 217
Minor Bird, A, by R. Frost, **Gr. 6**, 156
Modern Dragon, A (speech piece), by R. B. Bennett, **Gr. 4**, 98
Moon Boat by C. Pomerantz, **Gr. 2**, 218
Music by E. Farjeon, **Gr. K**, T157

Alphabetical Index of Literature (continued)

Music by M. O'Neill, **Gr. 5,** 122
My Feet by L. Jacobs, **Gr. 1,** T264
My Kite by B. Brown and B. Brown, **Gr. 1,** T371
My Legs and I by L. Jacobs, **Gr. K,** T19
My Valentine by M. Parsons, **Gr. 1,** T364
Naming Things by A. Davidson, **Gr. 1,** T221
Neat Feet (excerpt) by B. Schmidt, **Gr. K,** T30
New Colossus, The (excerpt) by E. Lazarus, **Gr. 5,** 42
New Colossus, The, by E. Lazarus, **Gr. 7,** 187
Night by S. Teasdale, **Gr. 3,** 162
Night Comes by B. de Regniers, **Gr. 1,** T233
O Wind by C. Rossetti, **Gr. 1,** T235
Ode to Joy, by Frederich Schiller, **Gr. 7,** 157
Old Mother Goose, **Gr. 1,** T181
Oliphaunt by J. R. R. Tolkien, **Gr. K,** T216
On Hearing a Symphony of Beethoven by Edna St. Vincent Millay, **Gr. 8,** 226
One Song, America, Before I Go (excerpt) by W. Whitman, **Gr. 4,** 147
Only My Opinion by M. Shannon, **Gr. K,** T29
Opposite of Two, The, by R. Wilbur, **Gr. 2,** 45
Oranges and Lemons, **Gr. 1,** T150
Orff Instruments (speech piece) by J. Graham and D. Otto, **Gr. 2,** 183
Our Washing Machine by P. Hubbel, **Gr. 3,** 262
Ourchestra by S. Silverstein, **Gr. K,** T171
Ourchestra by Shel Silverstein, **Gr. 8,** 35
Piggy by W. Cole, **Gr. 2,** 315
Piñata Song, **Gr. 1,** T153
Poets to Come by W. Whitman, **Gr. 7,** 231
Popalong hopcorn! by J. Nicholls, **Gr. K,** T160
Rabbit, The, by M. Stelmach, **Gr. 1,** T186
Rain (haiku) by M. A. Mohanraj, **Gr. 4,** 27
Rain Poem, **Gr. 1,** T31
Rain Sizes by J. Ciardi, **Gr. 1,** T33
Ring Around the Rosy (Mother Goose), **Gr. K,** T247
River, The, by C. Zolotow, **Gr. K,** T342
Running Song (excerpt) by M. Ridlon, **Gr. K,** T98
School Is Over by K. Greenaway, **Gr. K,** T85
Shapes by S. Silverstein, **Gr. K,** T37
Sheep in the Meadow (speech piece), **Gr. 2,** 8
Sidewalks by P. Hubbell, **Gr. K,** T98
Sing Ho! For the Life of a Bear! by A. A. Milne, **Gr. 1,** T114
Sing of America by H. Wilburr, **Gr. 4,** 359
Singing-Time by R. Fyleman, **Gr. K,** T15
Sitting in the Sand by K. Kuskin, **Gr. 1,** T374
Snail's Dream, **Gr. 4,** 209
Snail's Pace by A. Fisher, **Gr. K,** T29
Snow Toward Evening by M. Cane, **Gr. K,** T311
Somebody Has To by S. Silverstein, **Gr. 1,** T258
Something About Me, **Gr. K,** T13
Something Told the Wild Geese by R. Field, **Gr. 1,** T261
Songs for the People by F. E. Watkins Harper, **Gr. 6,** 62
Sounds of Africa, The, by Wandile, **Gr. 5,** 74
Sounds of Swing by T. Igus, **Gr. 5,** 32
Spanish Days of the Week, **Gr. 1,** T108
Spell of the Moon (excerpt) by L. Norris, **Gr. K,** T116
Spinning Song by C. Shields, **Gr. K,** T67

Sun Is First to Rise, The, by E. Coatsworth, **Gr. 2,** 383
Swing, The, by R. Stevenson, **Gr. 1,** T109
Table Manners by G. Burgess, **Gr. K,** T107
Tailor, Tailor, **Gr. 1,** T132
Taking Off by M. Green, **Gr. K,** T136
There Was a Young Lady by E. Lear, **Gr. 7,** 83
There Was an Old Lady by D. Lee, **Gr. 3,** 344
Thoughts of a Rattlesnake by K. Sexton, **Gr. 1,** T185
Three Little Penguins (speech piece), **Gr. 2,** 112
To a Friend Who Sent Me Some Roses by John Keats, **Gr. 8,** 115
Together by P. Engle, **Gr. 2,** 34
Trains at Night by F. M. Post, **Gr. 4,** 246
Travel by E. St. Vincent Millay, **Gr. K,** T144
Umoja! by M. Evans, **Gr. K,** T325
Una de dola, **Gr. 3,** 359
Unfolding Bud by N. Koriyama, **Gr. 6,** 209
Untitled haiku by Matsuo Basho, **Gr. 8,** 57
Up the Hill by W. Smith, **Gr. 1,** T45
Up the Tree and Down Again by A. Seear, **Gr. 1,** T65
Way Down South (speech piece), **Gr. 3,** 8
Wheels, Wheels, Wheels by N. Carlstrom, **Gr. 1,** T106
Whispers by M. C. Livingston, **Gr. 4,** 95
White Sheep, **Gr. 1,** T235
Who Has Seen the Wind? by C.G. Rossetti, **Gr. 2,** 137
Who's Afraid of the Big Bad Wolf?, **Gr. 1,** T137
Wings, by A. Fisher, **Gr. 1,** T250
Woodpecker, The (speech piece), by E. M. Roberts, **Gr. 4,** 48
Woodpecker, The, by E. Roberts, **Gr. K,** T172

Stories

Anansi (Ashanti folk tale) (listening), **Gr. 3,** 104
Coyote and the Bluebirds by K. B. Judson (recorded), **Gr. 2,** 231
Drumming Spider, The (West African folk tale), collected by H. East, **Gr. 2,** 333
Fox, the Hen, and the Drum, The (Indian fable), **Gr. K,** T295
Gebeta Board, The (Ethiopian folk tale), **Gr. 3,** 346
Isabel and the Troll (Spanish folk tale), **Gr. 3,** 349
Legend of George Washington and the Cherry Tree, The, **Gr. 1,** T369
Pile of Stuff, A, by H. Fujita, **Gr. 1,** T188
Rabbit in the Moon, The, Japanese folk tale, **Gr. 1,** T318
Romper, Stomper, and Boo by J. Anderson, **Gr. 1,** T36
Señor Coyote (Mexican folk tale), **Gr. 2,** 330
Snake and the Frog, The, **Gr. K,** T298
Tehahontanekenhnêha' (Rabbit Dance story) (listening), **Gr. 3,** 50
Why the Beatle Has a Gold Coat (Brazilian folk tale), **Gr. 1,** T321
Year-Naming Race, The (Chinese folk tale) (listening), **Gr. 3,** 385

Quote

We Are All Really the Same, by Vivienne, **Gr. 5,** 77

Alphabetical Index of Literature (continued)

Nursery Rhymes

Bell Horses, **Pre-K,** 19
Chook, Chook, Chook, **Pre-K,** 61
Hey, Diddle, Diddle, **Pre-K,** 78, 80, 100
Hickory, Dickory, Dock, **Pre-K,** 44, 71, 100
Humpty Dumpty, **Pre-K,** 31, 100
Jack and Jill, **Pre-K,** 41
Little Miss Muffet, **Pre-K,** 41
Mulberry Bush, The, **Pre-K,** 8, 102
1, 2, Buckle My Shoe, **Pre-K,** 10

Pizza Pie, **Pre-K,** 38
Polly, Put the Kettle, **Pre-K,** On 102
Pop! Goes the Weasel, **Pre-K,** 29
Ring Around the Rosy, **Pre-K,** 103
Sally Go 'Round the Sun, **Pre-K,** 45, 81, 103
This Is My Cat, **Pre-K,** 51
Teddy Bear, **Pre-K,** 66, 71
To Market, To Market, **Pre-K,** 50
Wee Willie Winkie, **Pre-K,** 20

Alphabetical Index
of Literature

Adventures. *Taking a chance on meeting new people, going new places, and having different experiences helps us grow and learn.*

Animal Fair, **Gr. 2,** 214
Arre, mi burrito (Gid'yup, Little Burro), **Gr. 1,** T257
Away for Rio, **Gr. 2,** 170
Bear Hunt (poem), **Gr. 1,** T126
Call of the Wild, The (excerpt) by R. W. Service (poem),
   Gr. 1, T139
Columbus Sailed with Three Ships, **Gr. 2,** 344
Coronation of Emperor Napoleon I Bonaparte and Empress
   Josephine, The (detail) by J. L. David (fine art), **Gr. 1,** T176
Goin' to the Zoo, **Gr. 1,** T192
Going Over the Sea, **Gr. 2,** 216
Great Outdoors, The, **Gr. 2,** 290
Hello, Hello There, **Gr. 2,** 126
Hoo, Hoo!, **Gr. 1,** T55
Hunt the Squirrel from *Suite on English Folk Tunes*
   by B. Britten (listening), **Gr. 1,** T136
I Am a Little Tugboat by C. Huffman (poem), **Gr. K,** T95
In My Little Motor Boat, **Gr. 1,** T159
Jig, Jog, Jig, Jog, **Gr. K,** T260
Leatherwing Bat, **Gr. 2,** 304
Let's Go Driving, **Gr. 1,** T52
Library Song, **Gr. 1,** T42
Merry-Go-Round by R. Field (poem), **Gr. K,** T223
Merry-Go-Round, The, **Gr. K,** T225
Music from Bali (gamelan ensemble) (listening), **Gr. 1,** T142
Na Bahia Tem (In Bahia Town), **Gr. K,** T163
Over the Rainbow from *The Wizard of Oz* by H. Arlen and
   E. Y. Harburg (listening), **Gr. K,** T60
Part of Your World, **Gr. 2,** 294
Peter and the Wolf (Introduction and excerpt) by S. Prokofiev
   (listening), **Gr. 1,** T140
Peter Cottontail, **Gr. K,** T338
Promenade from *Golden Goose* by L. Worsley (listening),
   Gr. 1, T177
Puff, the Magic Dragon, **Gr. 2,** 54
Romper, Stomper, and Boo (traditional story), **Gr. 1,** T36
Singing on the Fisherboats at Dusk (Chinese folk song)
   (listening), **Gr. 1,** T129
Skating in Central Park by A. Tait (fine art), **Gr. K,** T310
Spanish Days of the Week by Anonymous (poem),
   Gr. 1, T108
Strawberry Roan (excerpt) (cowboy song) (song and
   listening), **Gr. 2,** 66
Take Me Out to the Ball Game, **Gr. 2,** 56
Tugboat, **Gr. K,** T95
Wagon Passes, The, from *Nursery Suite* by E. Elgar (listening),
   Gr. 1, T243
We Are Playing in the Forest, **Gr. K,** T248
Wheels, Wheels, Wheels by N. White Carlstrom (poem),
   Gr. 1, T106
Yankee Doodle, **Gr. 2,** 340

Adventures and Challenges. *Meeting challenges with courage and initiative enriches our lives.*

1812 Overture by P. I. Tchaikovsky (listening), **Gr. 8,** 72
Blue Bayou by R. Orbison and J. Nelson (listening), **Gr. 8,** 71
Bug, The, by M. Knopfler (listening), **Gr. 8,** 88
Caissons Go Rolling Along, The, **Gr. 5,** 37
Canta, Canta, Minha Gente by M. da Vila (listening), **Gr. 8,** 45
Change the World, **Gr. 5,** 314
Choo, Choo, Ch'Boogie, **Gr. 6,** 180
Common Step (military traditional) (listening), **Gr. 8,** 39
Daydreams on a Subway Train by P. M. Fagan (poem),
   Gr. 8, 84
Dreamers, **Gr. 5,** 430
¡El pueblo unido jamás será vencido! by S. Ortega (listening),
   Gr. 8, 90
Fortune Favors the Brave, **Gr. 6,** 316
Fugitives Arriving at Levi Coffin's Indiana Farm by C. Webber
   (fine art), **Gr. 5,** 11
Galop of Sancho's Donkey, The, from *Don Quixote*
   by G. P. Telemann (listening), **Gr. 3,** 271
Gebeta Board, The (Ethiopian folk tale), **Gr. 3,** 346
Gee, Mom, I Want to Go Home, **Gr. 6,** 148
Gonna Build a Mountain from *Stop the World—I Want to*
   Get Off by A. Newley and L. Bricusse (song), **Gr. 6,** 4,
   (listening), **Gr. 6,** 5
Good Morning America by T. Melendez (listening),
   Gr. 8, 181
Goodbye, My Riley O, **Gr. 4,** 257
Greenland Whale Fishery, The, **Gr. 6,** 212
Guadalcanal March from *Victory at Sea* by R. Rodgers
   (listening), **Gr. 4,** 108
Heart, **Gr. 6,** 166
Heave-Ho, Me Laddies, **Gr. 4,** 258
Hero, **Gr. 5,** 312
Hey, Look Me Over, **Gr. 4,** 114
I Will Survive by F. Perren and D. Ferakis (listening),
   Gr. 8, 208
I'm Gonna Sit at the Welcome Table, **Gr. 6,** 416
Into the Fog from *Master and Commander* (excerpt)
   by I. Davies, C. Gordon, and R. Tognetti (listening),
   Gr. 3, 271
It's the Hard-Knock Life, **Gr. 4,** 293
Johnson Boys, **Gr. 4,** 233
Kettle Valley Line, The, **Gr. 4,** 348
La otra España (The Other Spain) by J. C. Calderon (song),
   Gr. 4, 62, (listening), **Gr. 4,** 64
Light One Candle, **Gr. 5,** 416
Lumber Camp Song, The, **Gr. 6,** 136
Ma'oz Tsur (Rock of Ages), **Gr. 6,** 405
March for Military Band, Op. 99 by S. Prokofiev (listening),
   Gr. 8, 37

Night Fight from *Crouching Tiger, Hidden Dragon* by Tan Dun (listening), **Gr. 6,** 28

No One Is Alone from *Into the Woods* by S. Sondheim (listening), **Gr. 8,** 86

Oh, Won't You Sit Down?, **Gr. 4,** 70

Old Ark's A-Moverin', **Gr. 4,** 130

One Dime Blues, **Gr. 6,** 178

Over the Sea to Skye, **Gr. 4,** 344

People United Will Never Be Defeated!, The, by F. Rzewski (listening), **Gr. 8,** 93

Power of the Dream, **Gr. 5,** 44

Red Iron Ore, **Gr. 6,** 134

Ride Like the Wind, **Gr. 5,** 130

River Come Down, **Gr. 8,** 10

River of My People, **Gr. 6,** 176

Scotland's Burning, **Gr. 3,** 257

Ship in Distress, The, **Gr. 6,** 211

Short Ride in a Fast Machine by J. Adams (listening), **Gr. 5,** 125

Smilin', **Gr. 8,** 80

Sorcerer's Apprentice, The (excerpt) by P. Dukas (listening), **Gr. 4,** 116

Sound the Trumpet from *I Puritani* by V. Bellini (song), **Gr. 5,** 279, (listening), **Gr. 5,** 279

Surfin' U.S.A., **Gr. 5,** 306

Tain't What You Do, **Gr. 6,** 18

There Was a Blue Flower from *Dreaming Blue* by L. Larsen (song), **Gr. 6,** 219, (listening), **Gr. 6,** 218

Va Pensiero from *Nabucco* by G. Verdi (listening), **Gr. 6,** 169

We Shall Overcome, **Gr. 4,** 387

What Can One Little Person Do?, **Gr. 4,** 204

William Tell (Overture) (excerpt) by G. Rossini, **Gr. 3,** 64

American Heritage. *We take pride in our country and its traditions.* See Classified Index: Multicultural Materials; Patriotic Music

Animals, Farm, and Pets. *Animals can be our good friends and valued helpers.*

Alison's Camel, **Gr. K,** T201

Animal Rhythms (poem), **Gr. K,** T56

Animal Song, **Gr. 1,** T288

Ants Go Marching, The, **Gr. 1,** T22

Arre, mi burrito (Gid'yup, Little Burro), **Gr. 1,** T257

Big and Small, **Gr. 1,** T200

Bingo, **Gr. K,** T64

Bliss by E. Farjeon (poem), **Gr. 2,** 212

Bon Chien by C. Chenier (listening), **Gr. 2,** 178

Boris, the Singing Bear, **Gr. 1,** T312

Bow, Wow, Wow, **Gr. 2,** 264

Bow-Wow by Mother Goose (poem), **Gr. 1,** T81

Boy and His Dog, A by N. Rockwell (fine art), **Gr. 2,** 212

Bullfrogs, Bullfrogs on Parade by J. Prelutsky (poem), **Gr. K,** T183

But the Critter Got Away (speech piece), **Gr. 1,** T88; (poem), **Gr. 1,** T89

Butterfly, Flutter By, **Gr. 1,** T333

Caribbean Amphibian, **Gr. 1,** T294

Cat and Rat (Pusa't daga), **Gr. 1,** T289

Cat and the Mouse, The, by A. Copland (listening), **Gr. 2,** 80

Chase the Squirrel, **Gr. 1,** T88

Chickery Chick, **Gr. 1,** T292

Come Back, My Little Chicks, **Gr. 1,** T134

Counting Song, **Gr. K,** T92

Cow, The, by R. L. Stevenson (poem), **Gr. 1,** T236

Do You Want My Little Frog? by H. Copeland (poem), **Gr. 2,** 187

Doggie, Doggie, **Gr. 2,** 59

Donkey, Donkey, **Gr. 2,** 256

Dragonfly by D. M. Violin (poem), **Gr. 1,** T44

El burrito enfermo (The Sick Little Donkey), **Gr. 2,** 180

Farm, The, from *Children's Symphony* by E. Zador (listening), **Gr. 2,** 211

Five Fat Turkeys, **Gr. K,** T309

Four White Horses, **Gr. 2,** 300

Fox, the Hen, and the Drum, The (Indian fable), **Gr. K,** T294

Goin' to the Zoo, **Gr. 1,** T192

Good Day Song, **Gr. K,** T50

Granny (traditional poem), **Gr. 1,** T104

Grasshopper's Wedding by B. Bartók (listening), **Gr. 1,** T245

Grasshoppers from *Joyful Noise: Poems for Two Voices* by P. Fleischman (poem) (listening), **Gr. 1,** T244

Grasshoppers Three, **Gr. 1,** T284

Haiku (Butterflies), **Gr. 1,** T332

Hairy Dog, The, by H. Asquith (poem), **Gr. 2,** 58

Happy Farmer, The, from *Album for the Young* by R. Schumann (listening), **Gr. K,** T209

Hickory, Dickory, Dock (poem), **Gr. K,** T49

Hop! Chirp! Moo! Oh, Happy Springtime Day!, **Gr. 1,** T372

Hopping Frog by C. Rossetti (poem), **Gr. 1,** T113

Horses of the Sea, The, by C. Rossetti (poem), **Gr. 1,** T179

Hot Dog, **Gr. K,** T69

Hunt the Cows, **Gr. 1,** T236

Hunt the Squirrel from *Suite on English Folk Tunes* by B. Britten (listening), **Gr. 1,** T136

I Bought Me a Cat (excerpt) arr. by A. Copland (song and listening), **Gr. 2,** 14

I Had a Little Hen (nursery rhyme), **Gr. 1,** T136

I've a Pair of Fishes, **Gr. 1,** T124

In the Barnyard by D. Aldis (poem), **Gr. K,** T207

Itik Besenda Gurau (The Ducks), **Gr. 2,** 100

Johnny's Flea, **Gr. 1,** T158

Jump or Jiggle by E. Beyer (poem), **Gr. 1,** T316

Kaeru no Uta, **Gr. 1,** T112

La ranita cri (The Little Frog Croaks), **Gr. 1,** T27

Ladybugs' Picnic, **Gr. 1,** T290

Little Black Bug, **Gr. 1,** T166

Little Robin Red Breast (English rhyme) (song), **Gr. 1,** T208; (rhythmic pattern), **Gr. 1,** T207

Little Spotted Puppy, **Gr. K,** T146

Little White Donkey, The, by J. Ibert (listening), **Gr. K,** T245

Locust, The (Zuñi poem), **Gr. 1,** T285

Los pollitos (Little Chickens), **Gr. K,** T288

Mary's Coal Black Lamb, **Gr. 1,** T286

Mi chacra (My Farm), **Gr. K,** T207

Mos', Mos'! (Cat, Cat!), **Gr. 1,** T53

Naughty Kitty Cat, **Gr. 1,** T171

Old Blue, **Gr. 2,** 213

Old Gray Cat, The, **Gr. K,** T43

Old MacDonald Had a Farm, **Gr. K,** T207

Old MacDonald Had a Farm arr. by L. Anderson (listening), **Gr. 2,** 133

Old Woman and the Pig, **Gr. 2,** 130

One Little Elephant, **Gr. 1,** T194

Over in the Meadow, **Gr. 1,** T78

Piggy by W. Cole (poem), **Gr. 2,** 315

Pusa't daga (Cat and Rat), **Gr. 1,** T289

Rabbit, The, by M. Stelmach (poem), **Gr. 1,** T186

Rattlesnake, **Gr. 1,** T185

Romper, Stomper, and Boo (traditional story), **Gr. 1,** T36

Rover, **Gr. 2,** 260

Santa Clara Corn Grinding Song, **Gr. K,** T164

See the Pony Galloping, **Gr. K,** T44

Sheep in the Meadow (speech piece), **Gr. 2,** 8

Sheep Shearing, **Gr. 2,** 102

Simple Simon, **Gr. 1,** T175

Sing Ho! For the Life of a Bear! by A. A. Milne (poem), **Gr. 1,** T114

Sittin' Down to Eat, **Gr. 1,** T182

Six Little Ducks, **Gr. 1,** T64

Snail With the Mail, **Gr. 1,** T274

Snail, Snail, **Gr. 1,** T252

String Quartet in C, Op. 33, No. 3 ("The Bird"), Fourth Movement by F. J. Haydn (listening), **Gr. 1,** T251

Sweetly Sings the Donkey, **Gr. K,** T244

Tengo, Tengo, Tengo (I Have, I Have, I Have), **Gr. K,** T212

Thoughts of a Rattlesnake by K. Sexton (poem), **Gr. 1,** T185

Three Little Kittens, **Gr. K,** T146

Tinga Layo, **Gr. 2,** 50

Two Mandarin Ducks by A. Hiroshige (fine art), **Gr. 2,** 101

Up the Hill by W. J. Smith (poem), **Gr. 1,** T45

Walking the Dog from Shall We Dance by G. Gershwin (listening), **Gr. 1,** T169

Waltzing Cat by L. Anderson (listening), **Gr. K,** T223

White Sheep by Anonymous (poem), **Gr. 1,** T234

Year With Frog and Toad, A, **Gr. 1,** T270

Year With Frog and Toad, A (reprise), **Gr. 1,** T283

Animals, Wild. *Life in the jungle, forest, and desert can be full of adventure.*

Animal Fair, **Gr. 2,** 214

Animales (Animals), **Gr. K,** T192

Australia's on the Wallaby, **Gr. 2,** 106

Baby Beluga, **Gr. 2,** 26

Bear Dance (Haliwa-Saponi dance song) (listening), **Gr. 1,** T103

Bear Hunt (poem), **Gr. 1,** T126

Bear Went Over the Mountain, The, **Gr. K,** T204, **Gr. 1,** T115

Birth and Dance of the Mayfly, The, from The Spider's Feast by A. Roussel (listening), **Gr. K,** T76

Bison by J. J. Audubon (fine art), **Gr. K,** T218

Buffalo Dusk by C. Sandburg (poem), **Gr. K,** T219

Buffalo Prairie from Prayer for the Wild Things by P. Winter (listening), **Gr. K,** T219

Caranguejo (The Crab), **Gr. 2,** 306

Chang (Elephant), **Gr. 1,** T199

Chichipapa (The Sparrows' Singing School), **Gr. 2,** 22, 31

Coyote and the Bluebirds (traditional Hopi story) (listening), **Gr. 2,** 231

Cuckoo in the Heart of the Woods from The Carnival of the Animals by C. Saint-Saëns (listening), **Gr. 2,** 253

Cuckoo, Where Are You?, **Gr. 2,** 244

Drumming Spider, The (West African folktale), **Gr. 2,** 333

Eating Lizards, **Gr. 2,** 250

Egyptian Hippo (fine art), **Gr. K,** T198

El palomo y la paloma (The Doves), **Gr. 2,** 380

El picaflor (The Hummingbird), **Gr. K,** T141

Elephant Carries a Great Big Trunk, The, by Anonymous (poem), **Gr. 2,** 169

Elephant, The, from The Carnival of the Animals by C. Saint-Saëns (listening), **Gr. 1,** T204

Excuse Us, Animals in the Zoo by A. Wynne (poem), **Gr. K,** T195

Finale from The Carnival of the Animals by C. Saint-Saëns (listening), **Gr. K,** T195

Furry Bear by A. A. Milne (poem), **Gr. K,** T205

Grizzly Bear, **Gr. K,** T252

Here Comes a Bluebird, **Gr. 2,** 263

Hippopotamus, The, by J. Prelutsky (poem), **Gr. K,** T199

Hop, Old Squirrel, **Gr. 2,** 258

Humming Birds by B. Sage (poem), **Gr. K,** T140

Hummingbird, A, by A. Beach (listening), **Gr. K,** T140

I Chih ha Ma (Frogs), **Gr. 2,** 186

I Heard a Bird Sing by O. Herford (poem), **Gr. 2,** 271

Jugaremos en el bosque (We'll Be Playing in the Forest), **Gr. 2,** 188

Kangaroo, The, **Gr. K,** T196

Kangaroo, The, by E. Coatsworth (poem), **Gr. K,** T196

Kangaroos from The Carnival of the Animals by C. Saint-Saëns (listening), **Gr. K,** T196

Kari (Wild Geese), **Gr. 1,** T101

La pequeñita araña (Eency Weency Spider), **Gr. K,** T9

Le Serpent (excerpt) by Guem (listening), **Gr. 1,** T359

Leatherwing Bat, **Gr. 2,** 304

Little White Duck, **Gr. K,** T208

Magpie, The, by C. Monet (fine art), **Gr. 2,** 271

Mayflies by P. Fleischman (poem), **Gr. K,** T76

Mister Rabbit, Mister Rabbit, **Gr. 2,** 150

Mizuguruma (The Water Wheel), **Gr. 1,** T260

Monkey, Monkey (speech piece), **Gr. K,** T215

Monté sur un éléphant (Riding on an Elephant), **Gr. K,** T218

Mouse, Mousie, **Gr. 2,** 254

Mr. Frog, **Gr. 2,** 257

Na belo (Little Heron), **Gr. 2,** 322

Oh, A-Hunting We Will Go, **Gr. K,** T62

Old Mister Woodpecker, **Gr. K,** T172

Oliphaunt by J. R. R. Tolkien (poem), **Gr. K,** T216

Oma Rapeti (Run, Rabbit), **Gr. 2,** 108

Peaceable Kingdom, The by E. Hicks (fine art), **Gr. 1,** T25

Peter Cottontail, **Gr. K,** T338

Place in the Choir, A, **Gr. 2,** 308

Pole, Pole by E. Jenkins (listening), **Gr. K,** T215

Prairie Dog Song (Kiowa children's song), **Gr. K,** T220

Royal March of the Lions, The, from The Carnival of the Animals by C. Saint-Saëns (listening), **Gr. 1,** T25

Santoki (Mountain Rabbit) (Korean singing game) (listening), **Gr. 1,** T187

Señor Coyote (Mexican folktale), **Gr. 2,** 330

Thematic Index

Thematic Index (continued)

Snail's Pace by A. Fisher (poem), **Gr. K,** T29

Snake and the Frog, The (story), **Gr. K,** T297

Something Told the Wild Geese by R. Field (poem), **Gr. 1,** T261

Tame Bear from *Wand of Youth Suite No. 2* by E. Elgar (listening), **Gr. K,** T203

Three Little Penguins (speech piece), **Gr. 2,** 112

Tiki Tiki Tiki Room, The, **Gr. 2,** 324

Turkey in the Straw (American folk song) (listening), **Gr. 2,** 348

Ushkana (Damselfly Song), **Gr. K,** T75

Wavvuuvuumira (Mister Bamboo Bug), **Gr. K,** T165

Who's Afraid of the Big Bad Wolf? (nursery rhyme), **Gr. 1,** T137

Woodpecker, The, by E. Roberts (poem), **Gr. K,** T173

Worms, **Gr. K,** T286

Yanai (The Elephant), **Gr. 2,** 305

Young Hare by A. Dürer (fine art), **Gr. 2,** 151

Change. *People experience many changes in their lives.*

America, My Homeland, **Gr. 4,** 358

A-Rovin', **Gr. 6,** 319

Ballad of the Unhatched Chicks from *Pictures at an Exhibition* by M. Mussorgsky (listening), **Gr. 3,** 76

Canta, Canta, Minha Gente by M. da Vila (listening), **Gr. 8,** 45

¡El pueblo unido jamás será vencido! by S. Ortega (listening), **Gr. 8,** 90

'Most Done Ling'rin Here, **Gr. 4,** 65

Communication. *We get to know ourselves and others by sharing, listening, learning, and understanding.*

Daydreams on a Subway Train by P. M. Fagan (poem), **Gr. 8,** 84

Death of the Robin, **Gr. 3,** 275

Down by the Riverside, **Gr. 6,** 22

Git Along, Little Dogies, **Gr. 6,** 284

Goodbye Brother, **Gr. 4,** 273

Guitar Man, The, **Gr. 3,** 138

Happy Talk, **Gr. 4,** 84

Hello!, **Gr. 3,** 283

Horse with No Name, A, by D. Bunnell (listening), **Gr. 8,** 161

I Think I'm Gonna Like It Here, **Gr. 4,** 299

I Want to Be Ready, **Gr. 6,** 12

I Will Survive by F. Perren and D. Ferakis (listening), **Gr. 8,** 208

I'm a Believer, **Gr. 3,** 312

I'm Gonna Sit at the Welcome Table, **Gr. 6,** 416

Jamaica Farewell by I. Burgie (listening), **Gr. 4,** 73

Just One Planet, **Gr. 4,** 164

Music of the World A-Turnin', **Gr. 3,** 44

O, The Train's Off the Track, **Gr. 3,** 176

Old Aunt Dinah, **Gr. 4,** 245

Old Paint, **Gr. 4,** 275

People United Will Never Be Defeated!, The, by F. Rzewski (listening), **Gr. 8,** 93

Please, Mr. Postman, **Gr. 4,** 44

Sail Away (mountain dance) (listening), **Gr. 4,** 55

Sail Away, Ladies, **Gr. 4,** 54

Sigh of the Soul for Alyscamp (Fourth Movement) from *Tableaux de Provence* by P. Maurice (listening), **Gr. 3,** 80

Sing of America, **Gr. 4,** 359

Something for Me, Something for You, **Gr. 4,** 4

Swapping Song, **Gr. 4,** 253

Three Is a Magic Number, **Gr. 3,** 94

Three Little Birds, **Gr. 3,** 204

Water Come a Me Eye, **Gr. 4,** 90

Water Is Wide, The, **Gr. 6,** 46

Way Down South by Anonymous (poem), **Gr. 3,** 8

We Shall Overcome, **Gr. 4,** 387

Whispers by M. Cohn Livingston (poem), **Gr. 4,** 95

Cooperation. *There are many ways to work together and help others.*

Ach, du lieber Augustin (The More We Get Together), **Gr. 2,** 35

All Work Together, **Gr. K,** T12

Allundé Alluia, **Gr. 4,** 34

Alphabet Song, The, **Gr. K,** T54

Angelina, **Gr. 6,** 8

Azouke Legba by V. Le (listening), **Gr. 5,** 426

Best That I Can Be!, The, **Gr. K,** T48

Brotherhood of Man, **Gr. 8,** 248

Carol by K. Grahame (poem), **Gr. 6,** 407

Cedar Swamp, **Gr. 4,** 50

Check It Out! (It's About Respect), **Gr. 2,** 10

Chicka Hanka, **Gr. 4,** 138

Child with a Dove by P. Picasso (fine art), **Gr. 4,** 8

Chíu, chíu, chíu (Chirp, Chirp, Chirp), **Gr. 2,** 302

Circle of Friends, **Gr. 5,** 196

Circle of Song, **Gr. 4,** 330

Clapping Music by S. Reich (listening), **Gr. 7,** 130

Come and Sing Together, **Gr. 6,** 281

Cotton-Eye Joe (song), **Gr. 4,** 52, (countermelody), **Gr. 4,** 53

Crawdad Song, **Gr. 3,** 107

Da pacem Domine (Give Us Peace), **Gr. 5,** 261

Dancing in the Street, **Gr. 6,** 84

Day-O by H. Belafonte, I. Burgie, and W. Attaway (listening), **Gr. 4,** 72

Down by the Riverside, **Gr. 6,** 22

Drumming Spider, The (West African folktale), **Gr. 2,** 333

Eh Soom Boo Kawaya (Nigerian boat song), **Gr. 3,** 58

El rorro (The Babe), **Gr. 1,** T356

¡El pueblo unido jamás será vencido! by S. Ortega (listening), **Gr. 8,** 90

El zapatero (The Cobbler), **Gr. 2,** 138

Flor de huevo by Los Lobos (listening), **Gr. 3,** 359

Fun wa ni alaafia (Send Us Your Peace), **Gr. 5,** 248

Gebeta Board, The (Ethiopian folk tale), **Gr. 3,** 346

Gentle River Runs, A, **Gr. 5,** 342

Gi'Me Elbow Room, **Gr. 3,** 88

Give a Little Love, **Gr. 7,** 128

Harvesters, The, by P. Brueghel (fine art), **Gr. 4,** 365

Hashkivenu by C. Taubman (listening), **Gr. 7,** 190

Heigh Ho, Here We Go, **Gr. 2,** 252

Hold My Mule, **Gr. 4,** 248

Thematic Index (continued)

How Does Your Garden Grow?, **Gr. 1**, T144

I Am but a Small Voice, **Gr. 5**, 323

I Hear America Singing, **Gr. 5**, 327

I Like by M. A. Hoberman (poem), **Gr. 1**, T110

I Will Be Your Friend, **Gr. 4**, 388

I'm Gonna Sit at the Welcome Table, **Gr. 6**, 416

It's a Small World, **Gr. 2**, 298

Just One Planet, **Gr. 4**, 164

Kwanzaa stamp by S. Saint James (art), **Gr. 5**, 429

La Yunsita, **Gr. 4**, 350

Lean on Me, **Gr. 6**, 150

Let Music Surround You, **Gr. 6**, 285

Life by S. DeShetler (poem), **Gr. 5**, 205

Listen to the Music, **Gr. 6**, 63

London Bridge, **Gr. K**, T99

Lucy Locket, **Gr. 1**, T253

Lumber Camp Song, The, **Gr. 6**, 136

Macnamara's Band, **Gr. 4**, 88

Making Music at a Harpsichord by F. Renaldi (fine art),
  Gr. K, T89

March from *Children's Games* by G. Bizet (listening),
  Gr. 1, T31

Martin Luther King, **Gr. 2**, 364

Mi caballo blanco (My White Horse), **Gr. 6**, 60

Miss Mary Mack, **Gr. 1**, T15

Monkees, The (Theme from) by T. Boyce and B. Hart
  (listening), **Gr. 8**, 110

'Most Done Ling'rin Here, **Gr. 4**, 65

Mouse, Mousie, **Gr. 2**, 254

Mulberry Bush, The, **Gr. K**, T112

Música indígena from *Instantaneas Mexicanas*
  by M. M. Ponce (listening), **Gr. 8**, 126

My Friend by M. Kibble and J. Kibble (listening), **Gr. 4**, 389

My Town, My World, **Gr. 4**, 6

No One Is Alone from *Into the Woods* by S. Sondheim
  (listening), **Gr. 8**, 86

Oh, Won't You Sit Down?, **Gr. 4**, 70

Old House, **Gr. 4**, 282

On This Night, **Gr. K**, T315

One, Two, Tie My Shoe, **Gr. K**, T150

Ourchestra by S. Silverstein (poem), **Gr. 8**, 34

Pat Works on the Railway, **Gr. 4**, 86

Peace and Quiet, **Gr. K**, T278

Peace in this House, **Gr. 7**, 152

Peace Round, **Gr. 4**, 16

Peaceable Kingdom, The by E. Hicks (fine art), **Gr. 1**, T25

Peaceful World by J. Mellencamp (listening), **Gr. 7**, 154

People United Will Never Be Defeated!, The, by F. Rzewski
  (listening), **Gr. 8**, 93

Peter Cottontail, **Gr. K**, T338

Pimpón, **Gr. K**, T22

Please, Mr. Postman, **Gr. 4**, 44

Rage and Roar, **Gr. 6**, 48

Rudolph, the Red-Nosed Reindeer, **Gr. 1**, T354

Sail Away (mountain dance) (listening), **Gr. 4**, 55

Sail Away, Ladies, **Gr. 4**, 54

School Ensembles (montage) (listening), **Gr. 8**, 2

Serra, serra serrador (Saw, Saw Lumberjack), **Gr. 1**, T133

Shake the Papaya Down, **Gr. 2**, 90

Shalom Chaveyrim (Shalom, My Friends), **Gr. 3**, 141

Something for Me, Something for You, **Gr. 4**, 4

Somos el barco (We are the Boat), **Gr. 4**, 10

Song of Peace by R. Riviere (fine art), **Gr. 7**, 155

Song of Peace, **Gr. 5**, 257

Step in Time, **Gr. 2**, 6

Tejedoras by J. Coché Mendoza (fine art), **Gr. 4**, 101

Tekanionton'néha' (Mohawk social song and dance) (song),
  Gr. 5, 223, (listening), **Gr. 5**, 222

There's a Hole in the Bucket, **Gr. 2**, 132

Time to Sing, **Gr. K**, T16

Together by P. Engle (poem), **Gr. 2**, 34

Treasure Chests, **Gr. 3**, 90

Tshotsholoza (South African folk song) (listening), **Gr. 1**, T76

Tutira Mai Nga Iwi (Maori folk song) (listening), **Gr. K**, T17

Ucha Tirvarch (Little Bear Song), **Gr. 3**, 53

Ujima (Collective Work and Responsibility), **Gr. 5**, 427

Umoja! by M. Evans (poem), **Gr. K**, T325

Walk by the River (unison), **Gr. 6**, 74, (parts), **Gr. 6**, 76

Wang Ü Ger (Chinese fishing song), **Gr. 3**, 190

We All Sing With the Same Voice, **Gr. 1**, T156

We All Stand Together (excerpt) by P. McCartney (listening),
  Gr. K, T153

We Are the Children of Tomorrow, **Gr. 5**, 114

We Shall Overcome by Z. Horton et al (song), **Gr. 7**, 212,
  (Howard University Gospel Choir) (listening), **Gr. 7**, 213

We Shall Overcome, **Gr. 4**, 387

We Want to Sing, **Gr. 5**, 235

What Can One Little Person Do?, **Gr. 4**, 204

What the World Needs Now, **Gr. 5**, 230

Yerakina, **Gr. 6**, 216

You Sing for Me, **Gr. 6**, 106

Zum gali gali, **Gr. 4**, 255

Diversity. *We can celebrate ways we are alike and ways we are different.* See also Classified Index: Multicultural Materials

A la rueda rueda ('Round and 'Round), **Gr. 1**, T240

Ach, du lieber Augustin (The More We Get Together),
  Gr. 2, 35

Afirika by A. Kidjo et al (listening), **Gr. 7**, 226

Afoxé (listening), **Gr. 8**, 34

African Postal Workers (listening), **Gr. 7**, 147

Aideu (Yoruban folk song), (listening), **Gr. 7**, 223

Ake Tonu (Maori song) (listening), **Gr. 5**, 150

Allundé Alluia, **Gr. 4**, 34

America, **Gr. 1**, T326; **Gr. 2**, 338

America, the Beautiful, **Gr. 5**, 388

Arre, mi burrito (Gid'yup, Little Burro), **Gr. 1**, T257

Batuque by O. Lorenzo Fernândez (listening), **Gr. 7**, 202

Beaded Hair by D. N. Rose (fine art), **Gr. 3**, 381

B'ri Bax! (Azerbaijani folk song) (listening), **Gr. 5**, 233

Blue Little Flower (listening), **Gr. 8**, 82

Bo Hai Huan Ten (Chinese folk music) (listening), **Gr. 7**, 56

Bonjour, mes amis (Hello, My Friends), **Gr. 1**, T18

Brotherhood of Man, **Gr. 8**, 248

Bydlo from *Pictures at an Exhibition* by M. Mussorgsky
  (listening), **Gr. 1**, T152

Carnavalito (Bolivian folk dance) (listening), **Gr. 2**, 251

Thematic Index

Thematic Index (continued)

Celebration Medley (montage) (listening), **Gr. 7,** 185

Check It Out! (It's About Respect), **Gr. 2,** 10

Cherkassiya (Israeli folk dance) (listening), **Gr. 2,** 373

Chinese Lion Dance (Chinese folk music) (listening),
Gr. 1, T363

Clog (oldtime music) (listening), **Gr. 2,** 68

Colors of the Wind, **Gr. 3,** 84

Counting Song, **Gr. 1,** T195

Damdama Sahib Temple (architecture), **Gr. 6,** 225

Dance for Clarinet and Piano by A. Marx (listening), **Gr. 6,** 189

Dance for the Nations, **Gr. 5,** 206

Daydreams on a Subway Train by P. M. Fagan (poem),
Gr. 8, 84

De colores (Many Colors) (unison), **Gr. 5,** 88, (parts),
Gr. 5, 98

Didn't It Rain, **Gr. 6,** 345

Don't Laugh at Me, **Gr. 7,** 93

Down in Belgorod by the P. Winter Consort and the
D. Pokrovsky Singers (listening), **Gr. 8,** 153

Dragon Dance (Chinese folk music) (listening), **Gr. 2,** 366

Duérmete mi niño (Go to Sleep, My Baby), **Gr. 1,** T61

Eight Day of Hanukkah!, The, **Gr. 3,** 370

El atole (The Atole), **Gr. 3,** 396

El cóndor pasa (Andean folk song) (listening), **Gr. 7,** 69

El jarabe tapatío (Mexican folk dance) (listening), **Gr. 7,** 58

El juego chirimbolo (The Chirimbolo Game), **Gr. 1,** T103

El nacimiento (The Nativity), **Gr. K,** T388

El Tambor (The Drum), 2 **Gr. 6,** 22

El vaquerito (excerpt) (Mexican folk song) (listening),
Gr. 1, T335

Erev Shel Shoshanim by J. Hadar and M. Dor (listening),
Gr. 4, 68

Fifty Nifty United States, **Gr. 5,** 392

Food Song, The, **Gr. 2,** 318

From My Window by D. Bailey (poem), **Gr. 8,** 19

Galop from Masquerade Suite by A. Khachaturian (listening),
Gr. 1, T259

Gêndhing KÊMBANG MARA (excerpt) (Balinese gamelan
music) (listening), **Gr. 7,** 101

Gift, The, by M. Unobsky and A. Scott (listening), **Gr. 7,** 205

Go A Tin (Lantern Song), **Gr. 1,** T363

Gong xi fa cai (Chinese New Year song), **Gr. 3,** 384

Guadalquivir (Andean dance song) (listening), **Gr. 3,** 30

Haiku (Butterflies), **Gr. 1,** T332

Hakyo jong (School Bells), **Gr. 1,** T302

Hanukkah Is Here, **Gr. K,** T314

Hashkivenu by C. Taubman (listening), **Gr. 7,** 190

Heleluyan (Alleluia), **Gr. 6,** 188

Heritage Festival Music (montage) (listening), **Gr. 7,** 55

I Got Shoes (African American spiritual) (song and listening),
Gr. K, T33

I Hear America Singing, **Gr. 5,** 327

I'm Gonna Sit at the Welcome Table, **Gr. 6,** 416

Imbenge Baskets (art), **Gr. 5,** 75

It's a Small World, **Gr. 2,** 298

Jambo (Hello), **Gr. 1,** T230

Japanese country house (architecture), **Gr. 6,** 145

Jewish Musicians in Jerusalem by V. Mnev (fine art), **Gr. 6,** 425

Juhtgarak (Chopsticks), **Gr. K,** T108

Just One Planet, **Gr. 4,** 164

Kaeru no Uta, **Gr. 1,** T112

Kia Ora (Maori greeting song) (listening), **Gr. 2,** 65

Kobuta (listening), **Gr. 1,** T168

Kokiriko (traditional Japanese folk song) (listening),
Gr. 6, 145

Kum Ba Yah, **Gr. K,** T327

Kwanzaa is… by C. McClester (poem), **Gr. 6,** 414

Kwanzaa Time by E. Jenkins (listening), **Gr. K,** T324

Kye Kye Kule, **Gr. 7,** 225

La camilla (Hispanic fiesta dance song) (listening),
Gr. 1, T196

Lincoln Gives the Gettysburg Address by Anonymous (fine art),
Gr. 7, 173

Locust, The (Zuñi poem), **Gr. 1,** T285

Los mariachis (Mexican folk song) (listening), **Gr. 7,** 90

Los trabajadores agricolas (The Farmers) from Estancia
by A. Ginastera (listening), **Gr. 6,** 116

Macoklis Mango by Un Solo Pueblo (listening), **Gr. 8,** 46

Magnificent Horses arr. by Jing Ling Tam (listening),
Gr. 7, 104

Mai Nozipo by D. Maraire (listening), **Gr. 1,** T211,
Gr. 7, 228

Martin Luther King, **Gr. 1,** T360, **Gr. 2,** 364

Miniwanka (or The Moments of Water) by R. M. Schafer
(listening), **Gr. 4,** 28

Miss Mary Mack, **Gr. 1,** T15

Mizuguruma (The Water Wheel), **Gr. 1,** T260

Monkees, The (Theme from) by T. Boyce and B. Hart
(listening), **Gr. 8,** 110

Music from Bali (gamelan ensemble) (listening),
Gr. 1, T142

Music of the World A-Turnin', **Gr. 3,** 44

N'kosi sikelel' iAfrika (Lord Bless Africa), **Gr. 6,** 339

Na Bahia Tem (In Bahia Town), **Gr. 1,** T297

Nach Nach Nach (Punjabi song) (listening), **Gr. 6,** 224

Nead na lachan sa mhúta (Irish folk song) (listening),
Gr. 5, 48

Ngikhumbula (Swazi song) (listening), **Gr. 5,** 195

O Hanukkah, **Gr. 3,** 368

O-Bon Festival by K. Eitaku (fine art), **Gr. K,** T31

Oh, Come Sing a Song, **Gr. 7,** 65

Old Ark's A-Moverin', **Gr. 4,** 130

One-Eyed Ford, **Gr. 7,** 200

People United Will Never Be Defeated!, The, by F. Rzewski
(listening), **Gr. 8,** 93

Piano Sonata No. 11 in A Major, Third Movement (Rondo
alla turca) by W. A. Mozart (listening), **Gr. 7,** 116

Piñon, Pirulín, **Gr. 1,** T311

Place in the Choir, A, **Gr. 2,** 308

Plenty Fishes in the Sea, **Gr. 1,** T310

Powama, **Gr. 7,** 63

Punchinella, **Gr. 1,** T216

Pusa't daga (Cat and Rat), **Gr. 1,** T289

Quaker, Quaker, **Gr. 1,** T100

Rondo "alla turca" from Piano Sonata No. 11 in A Major,
Third Movement by W. A. Mozart (listening), **Gr. 7,** 116

Såg du nøko? (Norwegian folk song) (listening), **Gr. 2,** 104

Samba de Orfeu (Dance of Orpheus), **Gr. 6,** 190

Thematic Index (continued)

Sambalelê (Brazilian children's song) (listening), **Gr. 1,** T205, T211

Santoki (Mountain Rabbit) (Korean singing game) (listening), **Gr. 1,** T187

Sellinger's Round (English Renaissance dance) (listening), **Gr. 6,** 98

Señor Coyote (Mexican folktale), **Gr. 2,** 330

Seven Principles of Kwanzaa, The, by S. Spottswood (listening), **Gr. 6,** 415

Shapes by S. Silverstein (poem), **Gr. K,** T37

Shí Naashá (Navajo folk song) (listening), **Gr. 1,** T72

Sing, America Sing!, **Gr. 5,** 6

Singing on the Fisherboats at Dusk (Chinese folk song) (listening), **Gr. 1,** T129

Song of Peace, **Gr. 5,** 257

Soup, Soup!, **Gr. 1,** T358

Spanish Days of the Week by Anonymous (poem), **Gr. 1,** T108

St. Patrick's Day (Irish folk music) (listening), **Gr. 2,** 374

Tak for Maden (Thanks for Food), **Gr. 1,** T343

Tako No Uta (The Kite Song), **Gr. 1,** T370

Taos Round Dance (traditional) (listening), **Gr. 2,** 155

There Are Many Flags in Many Lands, **Gr. 1,** T329 **Gr. 2,** 341

Tinikling (national dance of the Philippines) (listening), **Gr. 4,** 105

Treasure Chests, **Gr. 3,** 90

Tree of Peace (speech piece), **Gr. K,** T321

Tshotsholoza (South African folk song) (listening), **Gr. 1,** T76

Tsidii-Bird by G. Barney (listening), **Gr. 6,** 429

Tsiothwatasè:tha (Round Dance), **Gr. 6,** 109

Tue Tue (Ghanaian children's song) (listening), **Gr. 2,** 234

Tulloch Castle/Flowers of Red Hill (listening), **Gr. 6,** 200

Turkish Carpet (art), **Gr. 5,** 135

Turn the World Around, **Gr. 5,** 208

Uga, Uga, Uga (Cake, Cake, Cake), **Gr. 1,** T313

Ujamaa, **Gr. 3,** 380

Uyai Mose (Come All You People), **Gr. 7,** 66

Vhaya Kadhimba (Zimbabwean children's song) (listening), **Gr. 1,** T24; (game), **Gr. 1,** T23

We Shall Overcome, **Gr. 4,** 387

Well of Toledo, The by D. Rivera (fine art), **Gr. 1,** T197

What a Wonderful World by G. D. Weiss and B. Thiele (song and listening), **Gr. 2,** 84

Yo, Mamana, Yo (Oh, Mama), **Gr. 1,** T307

Zui Zui Zukkorbashi (song), **Gr. 1,** T98, (game) **Gr. 1,** T99

Dreams and Hopes. *Dreams and hopes can come true.*

A la nanita nana (A Little Lullaby), **Gr. 4,** 230

A la puerta del cielo (At the Gates of Heaven), **Gr. 4,** 12

Allundé Alluia, **Gr. 4,** 34

Amazing Grace (violin and bagpipe version) by J. Newton (listening), **Gr. 7,** 144

Amazing Grace, 4 versions (traditional American melody) words by J. Newton (listening), **Gr. 5,** 21

Amazing Grace, **Gr. 5,** 19

America, the Beautiful, **Gr. 5,** 388

Be Yours, **Gr. 7,** 189

Bu-Vah (Hopi Lullaby) (song), **Gr. 4,** 18, (listening), **Gr. 4,** 19

Canta, Canta, Minha Gente by M. da Vila (listening), **Gr. 8,** 45

Change the World, **Gr. 5,** 314

Cielito lindo (Mexican folk song), **Gr. 3,** 166

Circle of Song, **Gr. 4,** 330

Daniel Boone Leading Settlers Through the Cumberland Gap by G. C. Bingham (fine art), **Gr. 3,** 98

Daybreak in Alabama (excerpt) by L. Hughes (poem), **Gr. 6,** 162

Daydreams on a Subway Train by P. M. Fagan (poem), **Gr. 8,** 84

Do Lord, **Gr. 6,** 260

Don't Let the Music Stop, **Gr. 4,** 334

El florón (The Flower), **Gr. 3,** 46

¡El pueblo unido jamás será vencido! by S. Ortega (listening), **Gr. 8,** 90

Elijah Rock (African American spiritual) (song and listening), **Gr. 6,** 52

Este son by J. C. Ureña (listening), **Gr. 6,** 393

Everybody Rejoice, **Gr. 5,** 226

Finlandia, Op. 26, No. 7 by J. Sibelius (listening), **Gr. 5,** 257

Follow Your Dream, **Gr. 4,** 234; **Gr. 7,** 207

Frog Went A-Courtin', **Gr. 4,** 46

Gentle River Runs, A, **Gr. 5,** 342

Give Me Your Tired, Your Poor from *Miss Liberty* by I. Berlin (listening), **Gr. 5,** 42

Gonna Build a Mountain from *Stop the World—I Want to Get Off* by A. Newley and L. Bricusse (song), **Gr. 6,** 4, (listening), **Gr. 6,** 5

Good Morning America by T. Melendez (listening), **Gr. 8,** 181

Happy Talk, **Gr. 4,** 84

Hashkivenu by C. Taubman (listening), **Gr. 7,** 190

Heart, **Gr. 6,** 166

Hine Ma Tov (How Good It Is), **Gr. 4,** 66

Hope by E. Dickinson (poem), **Gr. 3,** 166

Horse with No Name, A, by D. Bunnell (listening), **Gr. 8,** 161

How to Succeed, **Gr. 8,** 237

Hush, Little Baby (American folk song) (listening), **Gr. 4,** 9

I Am But a Small Voice, **Gr. 5,** 323

I Saw the Light, **Gr. 5,** 252

I Want to Be Ready, **Gr. 6,** 12

I Will Survive by F. Perren and D. Ferakis (listening), **Gr. 8,** 208

I'm a Believer, **Gr. 3,** 312

I'm Gonna Sit at the Welcome Table, **Gr. 6,** 416

I'm On My Way, **Gr. 3,** 382

If I Had a Hammer, **Gr. 6,** 174

Just One Planet, **Gr. 4,** 164

La otra España (The Other Spain) by J. C. Calderon (song), **Gr. 4,** 62, (listening), **Gr. 4,** 64

Lift Every Voice and Sing by J. W. and J. R. Johnson (song), **Gr. 5,** 86, (gospel version) (listening), **Gr. 5,** 87,

Lift Every Voice and Sing by J. W. and J. R. Johnson, arr. by J. W. Johnson (listening), **Gr. 5,** 117

Like a Mighty Stream, **Gr. 5,** 320

Thematic Index (continued)

Lincoln Gives the Gettysburg Address by Anonymous (fine art), **Gr. 7,** 173

Major Bowes' Original Amateur Hour (excerpts) (listening), **Gr. 8,** 108

Marvelous Toy, The, **Gr. 3,** 182

Moon and Me, **Gr. 3,** 220

'Most Done Ling'rin Here, **Gr. 4,** 65

Never Sleep Late Anymore, **Gr. 6,** 274

New Colossus, The, by E. Lazarus (poem) **Gr. 7,** 187

New Colossus, The, (excerpt) by E. Lazarus (poem), **Gr. 5,** 42

Oleanna, **Gr. 3,** 144

On a Clear Day, **Gr. 6,** 206

Over the Rainbow, **Gr. 4,** 126

Peace in this House, **Gr. 7,** 152

People United Will Never Be Defeated!, The, by F. Rzewski (listening), **Gr. 8,** 93

Please, Mr. Postman, **Gr. 4,** 44

Power of the Dream, The, **Gr. 5,** 44

Rainbow Connection, The, **Gr. 3,** 310

Reach, **Gr. 5,** 14

Ride on the Wind, **Gr. 6,** 326

Rise Up, O Flame, **Gr. 4,** 283

Sail Away (mountain dance) (listening), **Gr. 4,** 55

Sail Away, Ladies, **Gr. 4,** 54

Season of Hope, The, **Gr. 5,** 410

Shabat Shalom, **Gr. 4,** 170

Shady Grove (traditional) (listening), **Gr. 8,** 59

Song of Peace by R. Riviere (fine art), **Gr. 7,** 155

Songs for the People (excerpt) by F. E. Watkins Harper (poem), **Gr. 6,** 62

Star-Spangled Banner, The, music attributed to J. Smith, words by F. S. Key, arr. by M. Hogan (song), **Gr. 5,** 386, (listening), **Gr. 5,** 86

Success, **Gr. 7,** 241

Suliram, **Gr. 6,** 58

Sun Don't Set in the Mornin', **Gr. 3,** 48, 60

Sweet and Low, **Gr. 6,** 184

Symphony No. 9 in D Minor ("Choral") Fourth Movement (excerpt) by L. van Beethoven (listening), **Gr. 5,** 102

That Great Come and Get It Day, **Gr. 6,** 306

There Was a Blue Flower from *Dreaming Blue* by L. Larsen (song), **Gr. 6,** 219, (listening), **Gr. 6,** 218

Tomorrow, **Gr. 4,** 295

Trampin', **Gr. 3,** 287

Wabash Cannonball, The, **Gr. 6,** 30

Waiting for Life, **Gr. 6,** 292

Water Is Wide, The, **Gr. 6,** 46

We Shall Overcome, **Gr. 4,** 387

We Want to Sing, **Gr. 5,** 235

Wells Fargo Wagon, The, from *The Music Man* by M. Willson (listening), **Gr. 8,** 78

Wide Open Spaces by S. Gibson (listening), **Gr. 7,** 208

Ecology and the Environment. *We share responsibility for understanding and protecting the world around us.*

Ame fure (Rain), **Gr. 4,** 26

Antarctica by P. Winter (listening), **Gr. 2,** 110

Australia's on the Wallaby, **Gr. 2,** 106

Barcas de Pesca by G. Wells-Hess (fine art), **Gr. 5,** 167

Big Beautiful Planet, **Gr. 2,** 376

Big Big World, **Gr. 5,** 438

Bye 'n' Bye, **Gr. K,** T67

City by L. Hughes (poem), **Gr. K,** T134

Colors of the Wind, **Gr. 3,** 84

Crawdad Song, **Gr. 3,** 107

Dal taro kacha (Come, Pick the Moon), **Gr. 2,** 98

De aquel cerro (On the Darkened Hillside), **Gr. 3,** 32

Earth is Our Mother, The (Líbana) (song and listening), **Gr. 7,** 220

Echo by W. de la Mare (poem), **Gr. K,** T104

En nuestra Tierra tan linda (On Our Beautiful Planet Earth), **Gr. 2,** 114

Evergreen, Everblue, **Gr. 3,** 330

Everything Grows, **Gr. 2,** 204

Garden Song, **Gr. 2,** 236

Great Outdoors, The, **Gr. 2,** 290

Have to Have a Habitat by B. Oliver (listening), **Gr. 3,** 331

Here Is the Beehive, **Gr. K,** T258

I Am But a Small Voice, **Gr. 5,** 323

I Wandered Lonely as a Cloud by W. Wordsworth (poem), **Gr. 7,** 125

It Fell in the City by E. Merriam (poem), **Gr. K,** T312

Jack-o'-Lantern, **Gr. K,** T307

Just Like the Sun, **Gr. 3,** 394

La bella hortelana (The Beautiful Gardener), **Gr. 2,** 208

La lluvia by S. Hatfield (listening), **Gr. 2,** 232

Land of the Silver Birch, **Gr. 2,** 88

Little Seeds (except) by E. Holmelund Minarik (poem), **Gr. 2,** 207

Little Sir Echo, **Gr. K,** T103

Mi chacra (My Farm), **Gr. K,** T207

Miniwanka (or The Moments of Water) by R. M. Schafer (listening), **Gr. 4,** 28

Morning Has Broken (traditional Gaelic melody) (song), **Gr. 4,** 22, (listening), **Gr. 4,** 23

Oh Mama Bakdala (Xhosa folk song), **Gr. 3,** 328

Oma Rapeti (Run, Rabbit), **Gr. 2,** 108

Our World, **Gr. 5,** 381

Rain (haiku), **Gr. 4,** 27

Rainbow Song, The, **Gr. K,** T61

Recycle Rap, **Gr. 3,** 332

Seeds and Seasons, **Gr. 2,** 206

Sidewalks by P. Hubbell (poem), **Gr. K,** T98

Star Canon, **Gr. 5,** 367

Starry Night, The, by V. van Gogh (fine art), **Gr. K,** T66

Stonehaven Sunset by J. Denver (listening), **Gr. 7,** 221

Thank You, **Gr. 2,** 349

This Land Is Your Land, **Gr. 4,** 146

Twinkle, Twinkle, Little Star, **Gr. K,** T90

Wake Up the Sun, **Gr. 2,** 124

Water Lilies by C. Monet (fine art), **Gr. K,** T138

Watermill in Christiania, A, by L. Gurlitt (fine art), **Gr. 4,** 169

We Are Here, **Gr. 4,** 394

Who Has Seen the Wind? by C. G. Rossetti (poem), **Gr. 2,** 137

Woodpecker, The, by E. Madox Roberts (poem), **Gr. 4,** 48

Expressing Viewpoints and Feelings.
Sharing thoughts, feelings, and opinions opens the door to understanding.

Aeyaya balano sakkad (Come, Children), **Gr. 5,** 402

Amazing Grace (violin and bagpipe version) by J. Newton (listening), **Gr. 7,** 144

Angelina, **Gr. 6,** 8

Be Yours, **Gr. 7,** 189

Beatles Medley (montage) (listening), **Gr. 8,** 149

Belle qui tiens ma vie (My Love, You Have My Heart) by T. Arbeau (song), **Gr. 6,** 99, (listening), **Gr. 6,** 100

Blue Bayou by R. Orbison and J. Nelson (listening), **Gr. 8,** 71

Bound No'th Blues by L. Hughes (poem), **Gr. 5,** 181

Bug, The, by M. Knopfler, **Gr. 8,** 88

Castle on a Cloud, **Gr. 7,** 82

Change Is Good by E. Kaecher, J. Tullio, R. Danko (song), **Gr. 5,** 84, (listening), **Gr. 5,** 85

Cheers, **Gr. 7,** 34

Concerto for Piano No. 1, Allegro by W. A. Mozart (listening), **Gr. 8,** 179

Cripple Creek (American folk song) (song), **Gr. 6,** 372, (listening), **Gr. 6,** 375

Daydreams on a Subway Train by P. M. Fagan (poem), **Gr. 8,** 84

De allacito carnavalito (The Carnival Is Coming), **Gr. 5,** 269

Don't Laugh at Me, **Gr. 7,** 93

¡El pueblo unido jamás será vencido! by S. Ortega (listening), **Gr. 8,** 90

Emotions Through Music (montage) (listening), **Gr. 8,** 178

Empty Chairs at Empty Tables from *Les Misérables* by H. Kretzmer and C.-M. Schönberg (listening), **Gr. 8,** 197

Every Day I Have the Blues, **Gr. 5,** 179

Everybody Rejoice, **Gr. 5,** 226

Feel Good, **Gr. 5,** 358

Feliz Navidad (Merry Christmas), **Gr. 5,** 420

Flag Goes By, The, by H. Holcomb Bennett (poem), **Gr. 7,** 45

Freedom by M. W. Smith (listening), **Gr. 7,** 195

From My Window by D. Bailey (poem), **Gr. 8,** 19

Gee, Mom, I Want to Go Home, **Gr. 6,** 148

Glad About It by Joe Pace and the Colorado Mass Choir, **Gr. 8,** 63

God Bless America by I. Berlin (song), **Gr. 5,** 4, (excerpt) (listening), **Gr. 5,** 5

Good Mornin', Blues by H. Ledbetter (song), **Gr. 5,** 177, (listening), **Gr. 5,** 176

Good Morning America by T. Melendez (listening), **Gr. 8,** 181

Guitar Man, The, **Gr. 6,** 138

Heart, **Gr. 6,** 166

Horse with No Name, A, by D. Bunnell (listening), **Gr. 8,** 161

How Can I Keep from Singing? by Rev. R. Lowry and A. Warner (song and listening), **Gr. 5,** 287

Huainito, **Gr. 6,** 351

I Am But a Small Voice, **Gr. 5,** 323

I Got Rhythm, **Gr. 5,** 187

I Hear America Singing, **Gr. 5,** 327

I Know Not Why by M. Rosenfeld (poem), **Gr. 8,** 179

I Walk the Line by J. Cash (listening), **Gr. 6,** 97

I Wandered Lonely as a Cloud by W. Wordsworth (poem), **Gr. 8,** 18

I Will Survive by F. Perren and D. Ferakis (listening), **Gr. 8,** 208

I'm Gonna Sit at the Welcome Table, **Gr. 6,** 416

Iowa Stubborn, **Gr. 5,** 293

It Dropped So Low by E. Dickinson (poem), **Gr. 7,** 20

Joban Tanko Bushi (Joban Miners' Song), **Gr. 6,** 142

Kurski Funk by P. Winter and the D. Pokrovsky Singers (listening), **Gr. 8,** 153

Lean on Me, **Gr. 6,** 150

Leila, **Gr. 6,** 376

Let It Roll, **Gr. 6,** 124

Life by S. DeShetler (poem), **Gr. 5,** 205

Lift Up Your Voices, **Gr. 5,** 319

Lincoln Gives the Gettysburg Address by Anonymous (fine art), **Gr. 7,** 173

Listen to the Music, **Gr. 6,** 63

Machine from Symphony No. 5 by W. Bolcom (listening), **Gr. 8,** 51

Mi caballo blanco (My White Horse), **Gr. 6,** 60

Mɔ-fia mo-ni (Ev'rybody Loves Saturday Night), **Gr. 5,** 277

Monkees, The (Theme from) by T. Boyce and B. Hart (listening), **Gr. 8,** 110

Mood Music (montage) (listening), **Gr. 7,** 133

Music by M. O'Neill (poem), **Gr. 5,** 122

My Government Claim (unison), **Gr. 5,** 95, (parts), **Gr. 5,** 110

New Colossus, The, by E. Lazarus (poem), **Gr. 7,** 187

New Orleans Jazz Funeral (excerpts) (listening), **Gr. 7,** 143

No One Is Alone from *Into the Woods* by S. Sondheim (listening), **Gr. 8,** 86

O, I'm Gonna Sing, **Gr. 5,** 245

On Hearing a Symphony of Beethoven by E. S. V. Millay (poem), **Gr. 8,** 226

One Dime Blues, **Gr. 6,** 178

Only Time by Enya at al (listening), **Gr. 7,** 142

People United Will Never Be Defeated!, The, by F. Rzewski (listening), **Gr. 8,** 93

Pomp and Circumstance March No. 1, Trio by E. Elgar (listening), **Gr. 7,** 50

Rocky Top, **Gr. 5,** 352

Schwanenlied by F. Mendelssohn Hensel (listening), **Gr. 7,** 124

Semper Fidelis by J. P. Sousa (listening), **Gr. 6,** 391

Seventeen Come Sunday from *English Folk Song Suite* by R. Vaughan Williams (listening), **Gr. 7,** 102

Shady Grove, **Gr. 6,** 286

Simple Gifts, **Gr. 5,** 136

Sing Hosanna, **Gr. 6,** 362

Sixteen Tons by M. Travis (song), **Gr. 7,** 151, (Tennessee Ernie Ford) (listening), **Gr. 7,** 150

Smilin' by A. Mayo, W. Luther, C. Lindsey, and M. Green, **Gr. 8,** 80

Sometimes I Feel Like a Motherless Child (African American spiritual) (song and listening), **Gr. 6,** 271

Son de Camaguey by L. Dubinsky (listening), **Gr. 8,** 51

Song of Peace, **Gr. 5,** 257

Symphony No. 45 ("Farewell"), First Movement by F. J. Haydn (listening), **Gr. 8,** 124

Thematic Index (continued)

Symphony No. 9 ("Choral"), Fourth Movement (excerpt) by L. van Beethoven (listening), **Gr. 7,** 156

Taps (traditional) (listening), **Gr. 7,** 144

There's a Song In Me (unison) **Gr. 5,** 164, (parts), **Gr. 5,** 183

Three Little Birds (traditional) (listening), **Gr. 8,** 84

To a Friend Who Sent Me Some Roses by J. Keats (poem), 115

Tsiothwatasè:tha (Round Dance), **Gr. 6,** 109

Tum Balalaika, **Gr. 6,** 68

Untitled (Engraving of St. Stephen's Cathedral, Vienna, 1825) (architecture), **Gr. 8,** 121

Vocal Expressions (montage) (listening), **Gr. 5,** 165

Water Is Wide, The, **Gr. 6,** 46

We Return Thanks (Iroquois prayer), **Gr. 6,** 108

We Want to Sing, **Gr. 5,** 235

What a Wonderful World (choral arrangement) by G. D. Weiss and B. Thiele (listening), **Gr. 8,** 8

What a Wonderful World by G. D. Weiss and B. Thiele (Louis Armstrong version) (listening), **Gr. 8,** 9

When I'm Walking (Let Me Walk) by A. Domino, Jr. (listening), **Gr. 8,** 70

You Sing for Me, **Gr. 6,** 106

You've Got a Friend by C. King (listening), **Gr. 6,** 418

Expressing Yourself. *Sharing thoughts and feelings opens the door to understanding.*

America, **Gr. K,** T303

America, My Homeland, **Gr. 4,** 358

Artichokes, **Gr. 2,** 314

Bagpipe Player by Giambologna (fine art), **Gr. 4,** 176

Battle Hymn of the Republic, **Gr. K,** T331

Best Friends, **Gr. 1,** T222

Born to Be with You (bluegrass song) (listening), **Gr. 3,** 387

Caballito blanco (Little White Pony), **Gr. 4,** 278

Chíu, chíu, chíu (Chirp, Chirp, Chirp), **Gr. 2,** 302

Day-O by H. Belafonte, I. Burgie, and W. Attaway (listening), **Gr. 4,** 72

El nido (The Nest), **Gr. 3,** 214

Everybody Has Music Inside, **Gr. 2,** 164

Flip, Flop, and Fly!, **Gr. 3,** 336

Food, Glorious Food from *Oliver!* by L. Bart (listening), **Gr. 2,** 310

Go Tell It on the Mountain, **Gr. 3,** 377

Green Eggs and Ham, **Gr. 2,** 284

Happiness by A. A. Milne (poem) (listening), **Gr. 1,** T254

Happiness, **Gr. 4,** 124

Happy Wanderer, The, **Gr. 3,** 18

Himmel und Erde (Music Alone Shall Live), **Gr. 4,** 280

I Love My Country, **Gr. 1,** T328

I Will Sing Hello, **Gr. K,** T156

I'll Rise When the Rooster Crows, **Gr. 4,** 36

I'm Gonna Sing, **Gr. 2,** 9

If You're Happy, **Gr. K,** T6

It's Such a Good Feeling, **Gr. K,** T282

It's You I Like, **Gr. K,** T280

Jamaica Farewell, **Gr. 3,** 156

Joy, **Gr. 2,** 46

Korobushka, **Gr. 4,** 285

Love Grows, **Gr. 1,** T202

Love Is the Magic Word, **Gr. 1,** T366

Love Somebody, **Gr. 4,** 94

Mail Myself to You, **Gr. 1,** T366

Making Music at a Harpsichord by F. Renaldi (fine art), **Gr. K,** T89

My Favorite Things from *The Sound of Music* by R. Rodgers and O. Hammerstein II (listening), **Gr. 3,** 313

My Home's in Montana, **Gr. 4,** 274

My Mom, **Gr. 1,** T372

My Valentine by M. C. Parsons (poem), **Gr. 1,** T364

Naranja dulce, **Gr. 1,** T303

Night Comes… by B. Schenk de Regniers (poem), **Gr. 1,** T233

Old Paint, **Gr. 4,** 275

One Finger, One Thumb, **Gr. K,** T46

Ourchestra by S. Silverstein (poem), **Gr. K,** T171

Over My Head, **Gr. 3,** 286

Part of Your World, **Gr. 2,** 294

Pat Works on the Railway, **Gr. 4,** 86

Place in the Choir, A, **Gr. 2,** 308

¿Quién es ese pajarito? (Who Is That Little Bird?), **Gr. 4,** 284

Riding in the Buggy, **Gr. 3,** 131

Rise Up Singin', **Gr. 3,** 138

School of Ballet by E. Degas (fine art), **Gr. K,** T166

Sing After Me, **Gr. 1,** T34

Sing Alleluia, Allelu, **Gr. 4,** 220

Skating, **Gr. 2,** 350

Skinnamarink, **Gr. 2,** 368

So Glad I'm Here arr. by B. Johnson Reagon (listening), **Gr. 2,** 47

Spinning Song by C. Shields (poem), **Gr. K,** T67

Thank You, **Gr. 2,** 349

There's a Little Wheel A-Turnin' in My Heart, **Gr. 3,** 129, 137

This a Way and That a Way, **Gr. 3,** 386

This is My Country, **Gr. 2,** 87

Three Little Birds, **Gr. 3,** 204

Three Musicians by Anonymous (fine art), **Gr. 4,** 175

Tisket A Tasket, A, **Gr. 1,** T107

Two Musicians by A. Dürer (fine art), **Gr. 4,** 177

Viva Valentine!, **Gr. 1,** T365

Walk by the River (song), **Gr. 3,** 74, (harmony parts), **Gr. 3,** 76

We Remember, **Gr. 4,** 360

What a Wonderful World by G. D. Weiss and B. Thiele (song and listening), **Gr. 2,** 84

When the Flag Goes By, **Gr. 1,** T327

When You Send a Valentine, **Gr. K,** T332

Whoop and a Holler on Independence Day, A, by J. W. Scott (fine art), **Gr. K,** T302

Wings by A. Fisher (poem), **Gr. 1,** T250

Woke Up This Morning, **Gr. 3,** 180

You Are My Sunshine, **Gr. 2,** 369

Family and Friends. *There are many ways to care about the important people in our lives.*

Another Busy Day (speech piece), **Gr. 1,** T41

Best Friends, **Gr. 1,** T222

Bickle, Bockle, **Gr. K,** T187

Candle on the Water, **Gr. 2,** 296

Chinese Dance from *The Nutcracker Suite* by P. Tchaikovsky (listening), **Gr. 2,** 354

Thematic Index (continued)

Daisy Chain, **Gr. 2,** 255

Dal taro kacha (Come, Pick the Moon), **Gr. 2,** 98

Duérmete mi niño (Go to Sleep, My Baby), **Gr. 1,** T61

El rorro (The Babe), **Gr. 1,** T356

Field of Joys by M. Morand (poem), **Gr. 1,** T224

Gilly, Gilly, Gilly Good Morning, **Gr. 1,** T12

Go, Go, Go, **Gr. K,** T276

Hakuna Matata, **Gr. 2,** 292

Hanukkah Chag Yafeh (Hanukkah Joyous Holiday), **Gr. 1,** T350

Happiest Street in the World, The, **Gr. 1,** T304

Happy Birthday, Happy Birthday, **Gr. K,** T273

Hello Song, **Gr. K,** T2

Hello, Hello There, **Gr. 2,** 126

Horton Hears a Who!, **Gr. 2,** 279

How Does Your Garden Grow?, **Gr. 1,** T144

I Have a Friend by Anonymous (poem), **Gr. 1,** T225

I Wanna Be a Friend of Yours, **Gr. 1,** T84

Ifetayo (Love Brings Happiness), **Gr. K,** T325

It's So Good to See You, **Gr. K,** T86

It's You I Like, **Gr. K,** T280

Jambo (Hello), **Gr. 1,** T230

Just Like Me, **Gr. K,** T242

Light the Candles, **Gr. 1,** T351

Look Who's Here!, **Gr. K,** T84

Mama eu quero (I Want My Mama) (Brazilian carnival song), **Gr. 2,** 92

Mary Had a Baby, **Gr. 2,** 360

Mbombela (The Train Comes), **Gr. K,** T152

Mother and Child by M. Cassatt (fine art), **Gr. 2,** 185

My Grandfather, **Gr. K,** T23

My Mom, **Gr. 1,** T372

Nampaya omame (Mothers), **Gr. K,** T128

O Tannenbaum! (Oh, Christmas Tree!), **Gr. K,** T320

Opposite of Two, The, by R. Wilbur (poem), **Gr. 2,** 45

Pat on the Back, A, **Gr. 2,** 74

Quaker, Quaker, **Gr. 1,** T100

Rig a Jig Jig, **Gr. 1,** T116

Shoheen Sho, **Gr. 2,** 140

Simi Yadech (Give Me Your Hand), **Gr. K,** T168

Somebody Come and Play, **Gr. 1,** T92

Spanish Days of the Week by Anonymous (poem), **Gr. 1,** T108

They Were Tall, **Gr. K,** T53

Time for Love, A, **Gr. 1,** T347

Wake Me, Shake Me, **Gr. 1,** 198

Walk to School, **Gr. K,** T18

What You Gonna Call Your Pretty Little Baby?, **Gr. K,** T319

What's Your Name?, **Gr. 1,** T125

Willum, **Gr. 1,** T19

Y ahora vamos a cantar (Now We Are Going to Sing), **Gr. K,** T340

Yo, Mamana, Yo (Oh, Mama, Oh), **Gr. 1,** T307

You'll Sing a Song and I'll Sing a Song, **Gr. 2,** 156

You've Got a Friend in Me by R. Newman (song and listening), **Gr. 2,** 44

Favorite Things. *Each person has special things that he or she enjoys.*

Bell Horses, **Gr. K,** T262

Butterfly, Flutter By, **Gr. 1,** T333

Christmas Tree by M. Cohn Livingston (poem), **Gr. 1,** T352

Clouds by Anonymous (poem), **Gr. 1,** T331

Cookies, **Gr. 1,** T278

Cow, The, by R. L. Stevenson (poem), **Gr. 1,** T236

Cut the Cake, **Gr. 1,** T232

December: Sleighride from Calendar Collection by J. Lang Zaimont (listening), **Gr. 1,** T128

Down the Hill, **Gr. 1,** T281

El colación (The Christmas Candies), **Gr. 1,** T357

El tambor (The Drum), **Gr. K,** T129

Field of Joys by M. Morand (poem), **Gr. 1,** T224

Hop! Chirp! Moo! Oh, Happy Springtime Day!, **Gr. 1,** T372

Hourtide by E. H. Potthast (fine art), **Gr. 1,** T374

I Have a Friend by Anonymous (poem), **Gr. 1,** T225

I Like by M. A. Hoberman (poem), **Gr. 1,** T110

Ice by D. Aldis (poem), **Gr. 1,** T346

It's So Nice on the Ice, **Gr. 1,** T346

Making Music at a Harpsichord by F. Renaldi (fine art), **Gr. K,** T89

Mama, Bake the Johnnycake, Christmas Comin', **Gr. K,** T318

March of the Toys from Babes in Toyland by V. Herbert (listening), **Gr. K,** T317

María Blanca, **Gr. K,** T99

My Kite by B. Brown and B. Brown (poem), **Gr. 1,** T371

O Tannenbaum! (Oh, Christmas Tree!), **Gr. K,** T320

Peanut Butter, **Gr. 1,** T218

Popalong hopcorn! by J. Nicholls (poem), **Gr. K,** T160

Popping Corn, **Gr. K,** T161

School of Ballet by E. Degas (fine art), **Gr. K,** T166

Seesaw (song), **Gr. 1,** T242; (accompaniment), **Gr. 1,** T248

Summertime from Porgy and Bess by G. Gershwin (listening), **Gr. 1,** T375

You're a Grand Old Flag, **Gr. K,** T4

Freedom and Justice. *Throughout history people around the world have worked to achieve freedom for themselves and others.*

America by S. Ward and A. Richardson (listening), **Gr. 8,** 31

America, **Gr. 6,** 388

America, the Beautiful, **Gr. 5,** 388

American Salute by M. Gould (listening), **Gr. 7,** 170

Battle Hymn of the Republic by W. Steffe and J.W. Howe (listening), **Gr. 6,** 389

Concord Hymn by R. W. Emerson (poem), **Gr. 7,** 66

Dreamers, **Gr. 5,** 430

¡El pueblo unido jamás será vencido! by S. Ortega (listening), **Gr. 8,** 90

Elijah Rock (African American spiritual) (song and listening), **Gr. 6,** 52

Emergency by E. M. Harris (listening), **Gr. 7,** 174

Empty Chairs at Empty Tables from Les Misérables by H. Kretzmer and C.-M. Schönberg (listening), **Gr. 8,** 197

Finlandia, Op. 26, No. 7 by J. Sibelius (listening), **Gr. 5,** 257

Follow the Drinkin' Gourd, **Gr. 5,** 142

Freedom by M. W. Smith (listening), **Gr. 7,** 195

Freedom Is a Constant Struggle, **Gr. 7,** 211

Gift, The, by M. Unobsky and A. Scott (listening), **Gr. 7,** 205

God Bless the U.S.A., **Gr. 7,** 136

Hallelujah, Get On Board, **Gr. 5,** 345

Haneirot Halalu (These Lights), **Gr. 5,** 414

Heartbeat of Democracy by V. Brasier (poem), **Gr. 5,** 389

I Have a Dream (speech piece) by M. L. King, Jr. (listening), **Gr. 6,** 416

I'm Gonna Sit at the Welcome Table, **Gr. 6,** 416

Jordan's Angels, **Gr. 6,** 365

Liberty Fanfare (excerpt) by J. Williams (listening), **Gr. 7,** 187

Lift Every Voice and Sing by J. W. and J. R. Johnson (song), **Gr. 5,** 86, (gospel version) (listening), **Gr. 5,** 87,

Lift Every Voice and Sing by J. W. and J. R. Johnson, arr. by J. W. Johnson (listening), **Gr. 5,** 117

Light One Candle, **Gr. 5,** 416

Like a Mighty Stream, **Gr. 5,** 320

Lincoln Gives the Gettysburg Address by Anonymous (fine art), **Gr. 7,** 173

Lion Sleeps Tonight, The, **Gr. 7,** 214

N'kosi sikelel' iAfrika (Lord Bless Africa), **Gr. 6,** 339

National Emblem by E. E. Bagley (listening), **Gr. 7,** 76

New Colossus, The (excerpt) by E. Lazarus (poem), **Gr. 5,** 42

New Colossus, The, by E. Lazarus (poem), **Gr. 7,** 187

People United Will Never Be Defeated!, The, by F. Rzewski (listening), **Gr. 8,** 93

Singabahambayo (An Army Is Marching) (unison), **Gr. 5,** 56, (parts), **Gr. 5,** 76

Smilin' by A. Mayo, W. Luther, C. Lindsey, and M. Green, **Gr. 8,** 80

Stars and Stripes Forever, The, **Gr. 6,** 390

Stars and Stripes Forever, The, by J. P. Sousa (listening), **Gr. 7,** 197

Star-Spangled Banner, The, **Gr. 6,** 386; **Gr. 7,** 194

Star-Spangled Banner, The, music attributed to J. Smith, words by F. S. Key, arr. by M. Hogan (song), **Gr. 5,** 386, (listening), **Gr. 5,** 86

Stonehaven Sunset by J. Denver (listening), **Gr. 7,** 221

Thula Sizwe (South African freedom song) (listening), **Gr. 6,** 73

Times They Are A-Changin', The, **Gr. 5,** 204

Untitled (British Attack on Washington, D.C., in August 1814) by Unknown (fine art), **Gr. 7,** 193

We Shall Overcome by Z. Horton et al (song), **Gr. 7,** 212, (Howard University Gospel Choir) (listening), **Gr. 7,** 213

Friendship and Family Life. *There are many ways to care about the important people in our lives.*

Alchíní Yázhí by S. Burch (listening), **Gr. 5,** 225

Angelina, **Gr. 6,** 8

Banjo Lesson, The, by H. O. Tanner (fine art), **Gr. 3,** 151

Barbacoa para cumpleaños (Summer Family Barbeque) by C. Lomas Garza (fine art), **Gr. 5,** 399

Cedar Swamp, **Gr. 4,** 50

Chorus of Villagers from *The Bartered Bride* by B. Smetana (song), **Gr. 5,** 275, (listening), **Gr. 5,** 274

Cindy, **Gr. 5,** 265

Circle of Friends, **Gr. 5,** 196

Consider Yourself from *Oliver!* by L. Bart (song), **Gr. 3,** 335, (listening), **Gr. 3,** 334

Cotton-Eye Joe (song), **Gr. 4,** 52, (countermelody), **Gr. 4,** 53

Cripple Creek (American folk song) (song), **Gr. 6,** 372, (listening), **Gr. 6,** 375

Cum-ma-la Be-stay, **Gr. 6,** 370

Dere Geliyor (River Overflowing), **Gr. 6,** 232

Doney Gal, **Gr. 6,** 115

Down by the Riverside, **Gr. 6,** 22

Early Light by C. Bremer (listening), **Gr. 6,** 201

El florón (The Flower), **Gr. 3,** 46

El tambor (The Drum), **Gr. 6,** 222

Frog Went A-Courtin', **Gr. 4,** 46

Gee, Mom, I Want to Go Home, **Gr. 6,** 148

Girl I Left Behind Me, The, **Gr. 4,** 249

Goodbye Brother, **Gr. 4,** 273

Great Big House, **Gr. 3,** 14

Hala lala layya, **Gr. 4,** 222

Her kommer vennen min (Norwegian folk song) (listening), **Gr. 3,** 142

Hullaballoo Balay, **Gr. 6,** 10

I Got Rhythm, **Gr. 5,** 187

I Will Be Your Friend, **Gr. 4,** 388

Joban Tanko Bushi (Joban Miners' Song), **Gr. 6,** 142

Just One Planet, **Gr. 4,** 164

Katyusha, **Gr. 4,** 188

Lean on Me, **Gr. 6,** 150

Leila, **Gr. 6,** 376

Let It Roll, **Gr. 6,** 124

Li'l 'Liza Jane, **Gr. 4,** 20

Life by S. DeShetler (poem), **Gr. 5,** 205

Love Somebody, **Gr. 4,** 94

Loving Embrace by K. Mallet (fine art), **Gr. 4,** 35

Mama Don't 'Low, **Gr. 6,** 126

Mi caballo blanco (My White Horse), **Gr. 6,** 60

Mountain Music, **Gr. 6,** 20

Movin' Right Along, **Gr. 3,** 124

My Friend by M. Kibble and J. Kibble (listening), **Gr. 4,** 389

My Friend Tom, **Gr. 3,** 364

Nach Nach Nach (Punjabi song) (listening), **Gr. 6,** 224

Neviděli jste tu mé panenky? (Have You Not Seen My Daughters?), **Gr. 6,** 228

No despiertes a mi niño (Do Not Wake My Little Son), **Gr. 5,** 217

No One Is Alone from *Into the Woods* by S. Sondheim (listening), **Gr. 8,** 86

O, Desayo, **Gr. 6,** 50

Octopus's Garden, **Gr. 4,** 30

Ogguere (Afro-Cuban lullaby) (song), **Gr. 4,** 327, (listening), **Gr. 4,** 329

Old Barn Dance, The, **Gr. 6,** 94

Old Joe Clark, **Gr. 4,** 74

Orange Blossom Special, **Gr. 6,** 33

Please, Mr. Postman, **Gr. 4,** 44

Rage and Roar, **Gr. 6,** 48

River of My People, **Gr. 6,** 176

Room in the House of Mr. Kong, a Peking Merchant, A, by Anonymous (fine art), **Gr. 6,** 26

Scraping Up Sand, **Gr. 6,** 248

Season of Hope, The, **Gr. 5,** 410

Shady Grove, **Gr. 6,** 286

Shady Grove (traditional) (listening), **Gr. 8,** 59

Shepherd's Hey by P. Grainger (listening), **Gr. 6,** 201

Ship in Distress, The, **Gr. 6,** 211

Shoo Fly Pie and Apple Pan Dowdy, **Gr. 3,** 227

Suliram, **Gr. 6,** 58

Summertime from *Porgy and Bess* by G. and I. Gershwin (listening), **Gr. 6,** 120

Sweet and Low, **Gr. 6,** 184

Sweet Potatoes, **Gr. 3,** 16

Symphony No. 9 in D Minor ("Choral") Fourth Movement (excerpt) by L. van Beethoven (listening), **Gr. 5,** 102

This a Way and That a Way, **Gr. 3,** 386

To a Friend Who Sent Me Some Roses by J. Keats (poem), **Gr. 8,** 115

Ua txiab (The Village), **Gr. 6,** 394

Vem Kan Segla (Who Can Sail?), **Gr. 6,** 419

Vive l'amour, **Gr. 5,** 262

Walk by the River (song), **Gr. 3,** 74, (harmony parts), **Gr. 3,** 76

Walk by the River (unison), **Gr. 6,** 74, (parts), **Gr. 6,** 76

Water Is Wide, The, **Gr. 6,** 46

Wayfaring Stranger, **Gr. 6,** 283

Wéané (Menadonese lullaby), **Gr. 3,** 184

Wedding Ball of the Duc de Joyeuse, The, by Anonymous (fine art), **Gr. 6,** 100

What the World Needs Now, **Gr. 5,** 230

Yakety Yak, **Gr. 5,** 308

Yerakina, **Gr. 6,** 216

You Sing for Me, **Gr. 6,** 106

You've Got a Friend by C. King (listening), **Gr. 6,** 418

Fun. *Humor and surprise bring special delight.*

Acitrón (Mexican stone-passing song) (listening), **Gr. 6,** 93

Addams Family Theme, The, **Gr. 3,** 307

Allegretto by X. Montsalvatge (listening), **Gr. 6,** 193

Alley-Oop by D. Frazier (listening), **Gr. 8,** 64

Alphabet Song, **Gr. K,** T54

Anything Goes by C. Porter (listening), **Gr. 8,** 186

Apple Tree by Anonymous (poem), **Gr. 3,** 24

Ball of the Duke of Joyeuse by Anonymous (fine art), **Gr. 8,** 130

Ballad of the Bedbugs and the Beetles, The, **Gr. 3,** 206

Ban Dal by Yoon Kyekyoung (listening), **Gr. 4,** 184

Barber of Seville, The (Overture) by G. Rossini (arr. by The King Singers) (listening), **Gr. 6,** 153

Barber of Seville, The (Overture) by G. Rossini (listening), **Gr. 6,** 152

Belhadawa walla belshaawa by H. Ramzy (listening), **Gr. 6,** 35

Billy, **Gr. 3,** 7

Bim Bom, **Gr. 3,** 218

Blue Suede Shoes, **Gr. 6,** 236

Blue Suede Shoes by C. Perkins (listening), **Gr. 7,** 8

Bo Hai Huan Ten (Chinese folk music) (listening), **Gr. 7,** 56

Boating Party, The, by M. Cassatt (fine art), **Gr. 6,** 47

Body Talk, **Gr. 6,** 88

Boo, **Gr. 3,** 362

Bop 'til You Drop, **Gr. 6,** 87

Bourrée from *Music for the Royal Fireworks* by G. F. Handel (listening), **Gr. 1,** T263

Brinca la tablita (Hop, Hop!), **Gr. 1,** T71

Built My Lady a Fine Brick House, **Gr. 4,** 252

Bulbes ('Taters), **Gr. 6,** 280

Butterfly Come Play with Me, **Gr. 3,** 112

Cape Cod Chantey, **Gr. 6,** 258

Captain Jinks, **Gr. 6,** 266

Carnival of Venice, The, by J. B. Arban (listening), **Gr. 6,** 40

Carousel Waltz, The, from *Carousel* by R. Rodgers and O. Hammerstein II (listening), **Gr. 7,** 69

Chairs to Mend, **Gr. 4,** 272

Chan mali chan (Singaporean folk song), **Gr. 3,** 10

Charleston, **Gr. 6,** 112

Chicken Dance, The (traditional), (listening), **Gr. 7,** 60

Chicken on the Fence Post, **Gr. 3,** 265

Chinese Lion Dance (Chinese folk music) (listening), **Gr. 1,** T363

Chiribim, **Gr. 6,** 57

Chumbara, **Gr. 4,** 172

Circus Music from *The Red Pony Suite* by A. Copland (listening), **Gr. 3,** 285

City Music by T. Mitton (poem), **Gr. 3,** 74

Clapping Music by S. Reich (listening), **Gr. 7,** 130

Clocks, **Gr. 3,** 266

Coffee Break, **Gr. 8,** 241

Come On-A My House by W. Sarovan and R. Bagdasarian (listening), **Gr. 7,** 138

Comedy Tonight, **Gr. 6,** 204

Concert, A, by L. Leonard (fine art), **Gr. 6,** 100

Concerto Grosso No. 9 in F Major, Gavotta (Allegro) by A. Corelli (listening), **Gr. 1,** T175

Conga, **Gr. 6,** 34

Crawdad Song, **Gr. 3,** 107

Dance by M. Chagall (fine art), **Gr. 4,** 68

Dance Myself to Sleep, **Gr. 1,** T314

Dance of the Haymakers by W. S. Mount (fine art), **Gr. 6,** 96

Dance of Youth by P. Picasso (fine art), **Gr. 5,** 207

Dance Together, **Gr. 2,** 264

Dance, Dance, Dance!, **Gr. 2,** 5

Dancing in the Street, **Gr. 6,** 84

Deck the Hall, **Gr. 3,** 374

Deedle, Deedle Dumpling (poem), **Gr. K,** T87

Derry Ding Dong Dason, **Gr. 6,** 249

Diana, **Gr. 1,** T334

Dima, **Gr. 4,** 265

Dinah, **Gr. 3,** 150

Ding Dong Diggy Diggy Dong, **Gr. 3,** 269

Djurdjevka Kolo (Yugoslavian folk song) (listening), **Gr. 6,** 105

Doctor Jazz, **Gr. 6,** 378

Doing the Latest Rag, **Gr. 6,** 314

Doll Song, The, from *Tales of Hoffman* by J. Offenbach (listening), **Gr. K,** T179

Down at the Twist and Shout by M. C. Carpenter (listening), **Gr. 7,** 96

Dreidel Song by E. Rosenzweig (poem), **Gr. 1,** T349

Dry Bones, **Gr. 5,** 406

Eka Muda (Comanche hand-game song) (song), **Gr. 5,** 28, (listening), **Gr. 5,** 27

El barquito (The Tiny Boat), **Gr. 4,** 214

El jarabe (Mexican Hat Dance), **Gr. 5,** 396

Encore by Stomp (listening), **Gr. 8,** 13

Entertainer, The (orchestra version) by S. Joplin (listening), **Gr. 7,** 23

Thematic Index (continued)

Entertainer, The (piano version) by S. Joplin (listening), **Gr. 7**, 22

Evening Party by H. Luting (listening), **Gr. 2**, 99

Famous TV Show Themes (montage) (listening), **Gr. 8**, 140

Ferdinando de' Medici with His Musicians by A. D. Gabbiani (fine art), **Gr. 8**, 5

Festival in the Country by D. Teniers II (fine art), **Gr. 6**, 98

Five Little Pumpkins (traditional poem), **Gr. 1**, T337

Foggy Mountain Breakdown by E. Scruggs (listening), **Gr. 6**, 140

Follow Me, **Gr. K**, T133

Fountain Dance from *Wand of Youth Suite No. 2* by E. Elgar (listening), **Gr. 1**, T233

Frog in the Meadow, **Gr. 3**, 243

Frog Went A-Courtin', **Gr. 4**, 46

Funeral March of a Marionette (excerpt) by C. Gounod (listening), **Gr. 1**, T337

Funny Road, The, by D. Dvorin (listening), **Gr. 3**, 40

Get a Car/Polka Dot from *Dreaming Blue* by L. Larsen (listening), **Gr. 6**, 221

Gi'Me Elbow Room, **Gr. 3**, 88

Girls and Boys, Come Out to Play (excerpt) (poem), **Gr. K**, T98

Git on Board, **Gr. K**, T145

Go A Tin (Lantern Song), **Gr. 1**, T363

Golden Ring Around the Susan Girl, **Gr. 3**, 264

Goober Peas (Civil War marching song) (song and listening), **Gr. 6**, 269

Greatest Show on Earth, The, **Gr. 3**, 308

Guitar Man, The, **Gr. 6**, 138

Gus: The Theatre Cat (excerpt) by T. S. Eliot (poem), **Gr. 8**, 195

Halloween by I. Crichton Smith (poem), **Gr. 1**, T338

Halloween, **Gr. 1**, T340

Hang on Sloopy (The McCoys) by W. Farrell and B. Russell (listening), **Gr. 7**, 29

Hang on Sloopy (The Ohio State Glee Club and Marching Band) by W. Farrell and B. Russell (listening), **Gr. 7**, 32

Hang on Sloopy, **Gr. 7**, 30

Happiness, **Gr. 4**, 124

Here Comes Sally, **Gr. 2**, 220

Here Comes the Band by W. Cole (poem), **Gr. 1**, T80

Here We Come A-Wassailing, **Gr. 1**, T355

Herring, The, **Gr. 3**, 316

Hey, Motswala, **Gr. 3**, 34

Hoedown (American folk song) (listening), **Gr. 6**, 116

Hojas de té (Tea Leaves), **Gr. 4**, 256

I Am Slowly Going Crazy, **Gr. 1**, T127

I Know an Old Lady, **Gr. K**, T26

I Love a Piano, **Gr. 6**, 130

I Made a Valentine, **Gr. K**, T333

I Will Survive by F. Perren and D. Ferakis (listening), **Gr. 8**, 208

I'm Getting Sick of Peanut Butter by K. Nesbitt (poem), **Gr. 1**, T219

I's the B'y, **Gr. 3**, 13

In Good Old Colony Times, **Gr. 3**, 326

In My Little Motor Boat, **Gr. 1**, T159

It Don't Mean a Thing by D. Ellington (song), **Gr. 6**, 164, (listening), **Gr. 6**, 165

It's So Nice on the Ice, **Gr. 1**, T346

It's Time to Get Ready for Christmas, **Gr. 3**, 372

Já do lesa nepojedu (To the Woods I Will Not Go), **Gr. 6**, 227

Jack-in-the-Box, **Gr. K**, T250

Jack-in-the-Box by L. Birkenshaw-Fleming (poem), **Gr. K**, T251

Jede, jede, poštovský panáček (Riding, Riding, Is Mr. Postman), **Gr. 6**, 226

Jewish Musicians in Jerusalem by V. Mnev (fine art), **Gr. 6**, 425

Jim Along, Josie, **Gr. 2**, 194

Jingle Bells, **Gr. 1**, T354

John Jacob Jingleheimer Schmidt, **Gr. 3**, 68

Johnson Boys, **Gr. 4**, 233

Juan Pirulero (Mexican children's song) (listening), **Gr. 1**, T153

Jump in the Line by J. T. Taylor (listening), **Gr. 7**, 199

Keeping the Baby Happy… by Rube Goldberg (fine art), **Gr. 3**, 183

Kreely Kranky, **Gr. 3**, 258

Kuna Indian Textile (fine art), **Gr. 6**, 223

La bamba (Mexican folk song), **Gr. 3**, 236

La Bamba, **Gr. 6**, 381

La camilla (Hispanic fiesta dance song) (listening), **Gr. 1**, T196

La cumparsita by G. M. Rodríguez (listening), **Gr. 6**, 113

La Vie (Life) by M. Chagal (fine art), **Gr. 4**, 374

Land of a Thousand Dances, **Gr. 7**, 12

Land of a Thousand Dances (garage band version) by C. Kenner (listening), **Gr. 7**, 14

Land of a Thousand Dances (Wilson Pickett version) by C. Kenner (listening), **Gr. 7**, 10

Las horas (The Hours), **Gr. K**, T70

Le cirque (The Circus) by G. Seurat (fine art), **Gr. 3**, 285

Let Us Chase the Squirrel, **Gr. 3**, 248

Let's Go Dancing, **Gr. 3**, 196

Let's Go Driving, **Gr. 1**, T52

Let's Twist Again by D. Appell and K. Mann (listening), **Gr. 7**, 11

Limbo Rock, **Gr. 3**, 232

Locomotion by J. Coltrane (listening), **Gr. 6**, 157

London Bridge, **Gr. K**, T99

Long-Legged Sailor, **Gr. 4**, 243

Lullaby of Broadway, **Gr. 6**, 182

Luncheon of the Boating Party by P.-A. Renoir (fine art), **Gr. 7**, 121

Making Music at a Harpsichord by F. Renaldi (fine art), **Gr. K**, T89

Mama Don't 'Low, **Gr. 6**, 126

Mama, Bake the Johnnycake, Christmas Comin', **Gr. K**, T318

Man and a Woman Inside the Palace with Two Musicians, A, by Anonymous (fine art), **Gr. 6**, 100

Mango Walk (song), **Gr. 5**, 90, (countermelody), **Gr. 5**, 92

Marco Polo (speech piece), **Gr. 1**, T90

Mardi Gras Mambo, **Gr. 7**, 88

Marvin's Music's Midnight Music Sale Jingle by B. Hardesty (listening), **Gr. 8**, 223

Medley Polleritas by M. J. Castilla, J. Espinoza, G. Leguizamón, and R. S. Moreno (listening), **Gr. 3**, 111

Thematic Index (continued)

Mein Hut (My Hat), **Gr. 2**, 142

Merecumbé, **Gr. 6**, 276

Merry-Go-Round by R. Field (poem), **Gr. K**, T346

Mississippi Mud (American folk song) (listening), **Gr. 6**, 65

Modern Major General, A, from *The Pirates of Penzance* by W. S. Gilbert and A. Sullivan (listening), **Gr. 6**, 56

Monkees, The (Theme from) (listening), **Gr. 8**, 110

Mrs. Murphy's Chowder, **Gr. 3**, 390

Musicians and Guests at a Festival (art), **Gr. 6**, 224

Must Be Santa, **Gr. K**, T316

My Kite by B. Brown and B. Brown (poem), **Gr. 1**, T371

My Thumbs Are Starting to Wiggle, **Gr. K**, T35

Naming Things by A. Davidson (poem), **Gr. 1**, T221

New Ashmolean Marching Society and Students Conservatory Band, The, **Gr. 6**, 308

O Tannenbaum! (Oh, Christmas Tree!), **Gr. K**, T320

O, Desayo, **Gr. 6**, 50

O, La Le!, **Gr. 6**, 6

O-Bon Festival by K. Eitaku (fine art), **Gr. K**, T31

Octopus's Garden, **Gr. 4**, 30

Oh, Susanna, **Gr. 3**, 153

Oh, the Thinks You Can Think!, **Gr. 2**, 276

Old Abram Brown, **Gr. 4**, 32

Old Barn Dance, The, **Gr. 6**, 94

Old Mister Rabbit, **Gr. 3**, 254

Old Time Rock and Roll by G. Jackson and T. Jones (listening), **Gr. 7**, 98

Ole La'u Papa e, **Gr. 6**, 91

One Potato, Two Potato, **Gr. 3**, 267

One-Eyed Ford, **Gr. 7**, 200

Our Goodman, **Gr. 6**, 245

Ourchestra by S. Silverstein (poem), **Gr. 8**, 34

Papa-oom-mow-mow by A. Frazier et al (listening), **Gr. 7**, 177

Park Rap 1 by C. Judah-Lauder (listening), **Gr. 7**, 70

Park Rap 2 by C. Judah-Lauder (listening), **Gr. 7**, 72

Pat Pat Patty Pat, **Gr. 1**, T308

Pat-a-Pan, **Gr. 3**, 375

Paw Paw Patch, The, **Gr. 3**, 195

Pezinho (Brazilian cantiga) (listening), **Gr. 3**, 230

Playful Pizzicato from *Simple Symphony* by B. Britten (listening), **Gr. 3**, 263

Polly Wolly Doodle, **Gr. 3**, 132

Pop! Goes the Weasel (English ring game) (song), **Gr. 5**, 94, (expanded dance version) (listening), **Gr. 5**, 112

Puddle Hopping, **Gr. 1**, T60

Pumpkin Song, **Gr. 1**, T342

Put On a Costume, **Gr. 1**, T336

Put Your Finger in the Air, **Gr. K**, T230

Red River Valley (traditional American cowboy song) (listening), **Gr. 6**, 96

Reel á bouche (French Canadian song) (listening), **Gr. 6**, 56

Requiebros by G. Cassadó (listening), **Gr. 6**, 80

Riddle Song, **Gr. 2**, 251

Ridin' of a Goat, Leadin' of a Sheep, **Gr. 4**, 251

Ring Around the Rosy (Mother Goose) (song), **Gr. K**, T246, (poem), **Gr. K**, T247

Risseldy, Rosseldy, **Gr. 6**, 264

Rock Around the Clock, **Gr. 6**, 234

Rock Island from *The Music Man* by M. Willson (listening), **Gr. 8**, 74

Running Song (excerpt) by M. Ridlon (poem), **Gr. K**, T98

S'vivon Sov (Dreidel Spin), **Gr. 1**, T348

Sandy McNab, **Gr. 4**, 142

Sansa kroma, **Gr. 4**, 166

School of Ballet by E. Degas (fine art), **Gr. K**, T166

See the Rabbit Running, **Gr. 3**, 255

Seesaw (song), **Gr. 1**, T242; (accompaniment), **Gr. 1**, T248

Sellinger's Round (English Renaissance dance) (listening), **Gr. 6**, 98

Seneca Stomp Dance (listening), **Gr. K**, T345

Serra, serra serrador (Saw, Saw Lumberjack), **Gr. 1**, T133

Seventy-Six Trombones from *The Music Man* by M. Willson (listening), **Gr. 8**, 76

She'll Be Comin' 'Round the Mountain, **Gr. 2**, 33

Short Ride in a Fast Machine by J. Adams (listening), **Gr. 5**, 125

Simon Says, **Gr. 3**, 4

Simple Pleasures by B. McFerrin (listening), **Gr. 8**, 191

Sing a Song of Sixpence, **Gr. K**, T111

Sing After Me, **Gr. 1**, T34

Singing-Time by R. Fyleman (poem), **Gr. K**, T15

Sitting in the Sand by K. Kushkin (poem), **Gr. 1**, T374

Skating in Central Park by A. Tait (fine art), **Gr. K**, T310

Skin and Bones, **Gr. 1**, T340

Skip to My Lou, **Gr. 1**, T102

Slap that Bass, **Gr. 6**, 146

Sleight of Feet from *Cakewalk Suite* by H. Kay (listening), **Gr. 1**, T239

Somebody Come and Play, **Gr. 1**, T92

Somebody Has To by S. Silverstein (poem), **Gr. 1**, T258

Something Funny Outside, **Gr. 1**, T338

Sonata X by J. Cage (listening), **Gr. 6**, 32

Spinning Song by A. Ellmenreich (listening), **Gr. 3**, 128

Step in Time from *Mary Poppins* by R. and R. Sherman (listening), **Gr. K**, T159

String of Pearls, A, by G. Miller (listening), **Gr. 3**, 12

Swing, The, **Gr. 4**, 320

Swing, The, by R. L. Stevenson (poem), **Gr. 1**, T109

Symphony No. 1 in D Major, Op. 25 ("Classical"), Third Movement (Gavotte) by S. Prokofiev (listening), **Gr. 1**, T92

Symphony No. 101 in D Major ("Clock") by F. J. Haydn (listening), **Gr. 8**, 128

Tak for Maden (Thanks for Food), **Gr. 1**, T343

Tako No Uta (The Kite Song), **Gr. 1**, T370

Ten in a Bed, **Gr. K**, T256

Ten Little Frogs, **Gr. K**, T240

Ten Tom-Toms by Anonymous (poem), **Gr. 6**, 57

There Was a Young Lady by E. Lear (poem), **Gr. 7**, 83

This Is My City, **Gr. K**, T120

Till Eulenspiegel's Merry Pranks by R. Strauss (listening), **Gr. 5**, 81

Tina Singu, **Gr. 6**, 36

Tititorea (Maori Stick Game) (New Zealand folk song), **Gr. 3**, 174

Toodala, **Gr. K**, T39

Town Hall Halloween Ball, **Gr. K**, T276

Thematic Index

Triple Play, **Gr. 5,** 355

Troika from *Lieutenant Kijé Suite* (excerpt) by S. Prokofiev (listening), **Gr. 3,** 225

Trumpet and Drum from *Children's Games* by G. Bizet (listening), **Gr. 1,** T231

Tubby the Tuba by K. Lleinsinger (listening), **Gr. 1,** T80

Twist and Shout, **Gr. 7,** 160

Tzakonikos (Greek circle dance) (listening), **Gr. 6,** 214

Tzena, Tzena, **Gr. 5,** 171

Untitled (Chinese wood-block print) (fine art), **Gr. 6,** 27

Untitled (Group of Musicians, Dancers, and Servants) (fine art), **Gr. 6,** 27

Untitled (Haydn Playing with an Ensemble) by Anonymous (fine art), **Gr. 8,** 120

Untitled (Musicians) by R. Bearden (fine art), **Gr. 7,** 16

Untitled haiku by M. Basho, **Gr. 8,** 57

Untitled Sculpture by P. Picasso (fine art), **Gr. 7,** 232

Vinqo (Zulu song) (listening), **Gr. 4,** 24

Wabash Cannonball, The, **Gr. 6,** 30

Waltz of the Flowers from *The Nutcracker* (excerpt) by P. Tchaikovsky (listening), **Gr. 1,** T353

Watching the Dancing Partners by A. Houser (fine art), **Gr. 5,** 26

We Go Together, **Gr. 7,** 158

When I Sing, **Gr. 6,** 44

Who's Got a Fishpole?, **Gr. 4,** 261

Whoop and a Holler on Independence Day, A, by J. W. Scott (fine art), **Gr. K,** T302

Willoughby Wallaby Woo, **Gr. K,** T241

Woodchuck, **Gr. 3,** 246

Yakety Yak, **Gr. 5,** 308

Zudio, **Gr. 7,** 164

Games and Play. *Games and play help us enjoy life.*

A la rueda de San Miguel (To the Wheel of San Miguel), **Gr. 2,** 60

A la rueda rueda ('Round and 'Round), **Gr. 1,** T240

Acka Backa, **Gr. 1,** T256

Afrakakraba (Ghanaian game song) (listening), **Gr. 3,** 102

Apples and Bananas, **Gr. 1,** T151

At the Hop, **Gr. 4,** 306

Augie's Great Municipal Band from *Star Wars Episode 1: The Phantom Menace* (excerpt) by J. Williams (listening), **Gr. 4,** 56

Ball, The, from *Children's Games* by G. Bizet (listening), **Gr. K,** T133

Ballad of the Bedbugs and the Beetles, The, **Gr. 3,** 206

Ban Dal by Yoon Kyekyoung (listening), **Gr. 4,** 184

Bee, Bee, Bumblebee, **Gr. 1,** T250

Bell Doth Toll, The, **Gr. 4,** 276

Big Bunch, a Little Bunch, **Gr. 4,** 267

Billy, **Gr. 3,** 7

Bluebells, **Gr. 1,** T209

Bounce High, Bounce Low, **Gr. K,** T13

Brinca la tablita (Hop, Hop!), **Gr. 1,** T71

Brother, Come and Dance With Me from *Hansel and Gretel* by E. Humperdinck (listening), **Gr. K,** T180

C-A-G by B. Taylor (listening), **Gr. 1,** T241

Carnaval by H. Mendizabal (fine art), **Gr. 3,** 33

Categories, **Gr. 1,** T146

Charlie Over the Ocean, **Gr. 1,** T75

Chase the Squirrel, **Gr. 1,** T88

Children's Dance from *Merry Mount* by H. Hanson (listening), **Gr. 2,** 246

Children's Games by P. Brueghel (fine art), **Gr. 2,** 247

Circle 'Round the Zero, **Gr. 3,** 267

Clap Your Hands (song), **Gr. 1,** T246, (rhythmic pattern), **Gr. 1,** T247

Colors by H. Palmer (listening), **Gr. K,** T58

Come Back, My Little Chicks, **Gr. 1,** T134

¡Dale, dale, dale!, **Gr. 3,** 378

Diou Shou Juan'er, **Gr. 1,** T212

Doggie, Doggie, **Gr. 2,** 59

Double This (game), **Gr. 1,** T94

Down at the Twist and Shout, **Gr. 4,** 308

Early in the Morning at Eight O'Clock, **Gr. 4,** 59

Egy üveg alma (One Jar of Apples), **Gr. 3,** 22

El juego chirimbolo (The Chirimbolo Game), **Gr. 1,** T103

En roulant ma boule (As I Roll My Ball), **Gr. 3,** 100

Farmer in the Dell, The, **Gr. K,** T100

Fiddler and Boy Doing Jig by C. Krieghoff (fine art), **Gr. 3,** 92

Follow the Leader by K. Fraser (poem), **Gr. K,** T132

Garden Hoedown, The, **Gr. K,** T290

Girl I Left Behind Me, The, **Gr. 4,** 249

Go, Go, Go, **Gr. K,** T276

Gogo, **Gr. K,** T188

Head and Shoulders, Baby, **Gr. 1,** T40

Head and Shoulders, **Gr. K,** T238

Heigh Ho, Here We Go, **Gr. 2,** 252

Here We Sit, **Gr. 1,** T251

Hokey Pokey, **Gr. K,** T68

Hop, Hop, Hop, **Gr. K,** T197

Hop Up and Jump Up, **Gr. 4,** 271

I Had a Little Hen (nursery rhyme), **Gr. 1,** T136

I Like Spinach, **Gr. 1,** T163

I See, **Gr. 2,** 266

I Wanna Be a Friend of Yours, **Gr. 1,** T84

In the Mood by J. Garland (listening), **Gr. 4,** 143

Instrument Game, **Gr. K,** T36

Jack, Be Nimble, **Gr. K,** T88

John the Rabbit, **Gr. 1,** T74

Jump, Jim Joe, **Gr. 1,** T89

Kangaroo, The, **Gr. K,** T196

Kreely Kranky, **Gr. 3,** 258

Kuma San (Honorable Bear), **Gr. 3,** 244

La vida es un carnaval (Life Is a Carnival) by V. Daniel (listening), **Gr. 4,** 228

La Zandunga by D. Rivera (fine art), **Gr. 3,** 213

Las mañanitas (The Morning Song) (song), **Gr. 4,** 194, (listening), **Gr. 4,** 197

Lemonade, **Gr. 2,** 19

Let's Go Fly a Kite, **Gr. 2,** 134

Li'l 'Liza Jane, **Gr. 4,** 20

Limbo Rock, **Gr. 3,** 232

Little Ducky Duddle, **Gr. K,** T289

Little Sally Walker, **Gr. 3,** 105

Loco-Motion, The, **Gr. 4,** 312

Looby Loo, **Gr. 1,** T262

Macnamara's Band, **Gr. 4,** 88

Thematic Index (continued)

Marco Polo (speech piece), **Gr. 1,** T90

Matarile, **Gr. 2,** 261

Me Stone, **Gr. 2,** 48

Merry-Go-Round, **Gr. 2,** 267

Merry-Go-Round from *Children's Games* by G. Bizet (listening), **Gr. 2,** 266

Miss Mary Mack, **Gr. 1,** T15

Mizuguruma (The Water Wheel), **Gr. 1,** T260

Molinillo de café (Little Coffee Mill), **Gr. 4,** 250

Mos', Mos'! (Cat, Cat!), **Gr. 1,** T53

My Mama's Calling Me, **Gr. 1,** T54

Name Game, **Gr. K,** T58

New Day, The, **Gr. 4,** 316

Nigun Atik (Israeli folk dance) (listening), **Gr. 3,** 47

Oats, Peas, Beans, and Barley Grow, **Gr. K,** T287

Old Abram Brown, **Gr. 4,** 32

Old Barn Dance, The, **Gr. 3,** 94

Old Joe Clark, **Gr. 4,** 74

Oliver Twist, **Gr. 2,** 268

One Little Elephant, **Gr. 1,** T194

One Potato, Two Potato, **Gr. 3,** 267

One, Two, Three, Four (traditional rhyme), **Gr. 1,** T123

One, Two, Three, Four, Five, **Gr. 1,** T265

Pantomime from *The Comedians* by D. Kabalevsky (listening), **Gr. 1,** T256

Pat Pat Patty Pat, **Gr. 1,** T308

Paw Paw Patch, The, **Gr. 3,** 195

Peasant's Dancing Day, **Gr. 4,** 132

Piñata Song (Mexican traditional poem), **Gr. 1,** T153

Pizza, Pizza, Daddy-O, **Gr. 2,** 62

Plainsies, Clapsies, **Gr. 2,** 248

Poun to, Poun to (Where Is It? Where Is It?) (Greek and Cypriot song) (listening), **Gr. 2,** 175

Punchinella, **Gr. 1,** T216

Rise, Sally, Rise (game), **Gr. 1,** T162

Sailor Went to Sea, Sea, Sea, A (song), **Gr. 1,** T38, (game), **Gr. 1,** T39

Sammy Sackett, **Gr. 2,** 146

Sansa kroma, **Gr. 4,** 166

Sara Watashi (Plate Passing), **Gr. 1,** T67

Sarasponda, **Gr. 4,** 210

Sheep in the Meadow (speech piece), **Gr. 2,** 8

Shoo, Turkey, **Gr. 1,** T76

Simon Says, **Gr. 3,** 4

Simple Simon, **Gr. 1,** T175

Six Little Ducks, **Gr. 1,** T64

Snail, Snail, **Gr. 1,** T252

Soup, Soup!, **Gr. 1,** T358

Spinning Wheel by D. Clayton-Thomas (listening), **Gr. 4,** 211

Tailor, Tailor (traditional poem), **Gr. 1,** T132

Take Me Out to the Ball Game, **Gr. 2,** 56

There's a Hole in the Middle of the Sea, **Gr. 1,** T178

This Is What I Can Do, **Gr. K,** T124

This Old Man, **Gr. 1,** T306

Tinker, Tailor, **Gr. 1,** T131

Tititorea (Maori Stick Game) (New Zealand folk song), **Gr. 3,** 174

Touch Your Shoulders, **Gr. K,** T254

Tug of War from *Outdoor Games* by G. Tailleferre (listening), **Gr. K,** T339

Twenty-four Robbers, **Gr. 1,** 173

Twist and Shout, **Gr. 4,** 314

Two, Four, Six, Eight (song), **Gr. 1,** T246, (rhythmic pattern), **Gr. 1,** T247

Una adivinanza (A Riddle), **Gr. 1,** T138

Vhaya Kadhimba (Zimbabwean children's song) (song and game), **Gr. 1,** T23

Vinqo (Zulu song) (listening), **Gr. 4,** 24

What Did Delaware?, **Gr. 2,** 190

What Did You Do Today at Jeffrey's House? by P. Schickele (listening), **Gr. 4,** 80

Who's Afraid of the Big Bad Wolf? (nursery rhyme), **Gr. 1,** T137

Who's That Tapping at the Window?, **Gr. 2,** 261

Whoop and a Holler on Independence Day, A, by J. W. Scott (fine art), **Gr. K,** T302

Winter Landscape with a Bird Trap by P. Brueghel (fine art), **Gr. 2,** 351

Yankee Doodle, **Gr. 3,** 357

Zui Zui Zukkorbashi (song), **Gr. 1,** T98, (game), **Gr. 1,** T99

Growing Up. *As we grow, we are able to do many new things.*

A be ce, **Gr. 1,** T213

Everything Grows, **Gr. 2,** 204

Going Over the Sea, **Gr. 2,** 216

Head and Shoulders, Baby, **Gr. 1,** T40

Little Dancer of Fourteen by E. Degas (fine art), **Gr. 2,** 25

Loose Tooth (speech piece), **Gr. 2,** 28

Moon Boat by C. Pomerantz (poem), **Gr. 2,** 218

My Feet by L. B. Jacobs (poem), **Gr. 1,** T264

Peter Cottontail, **Gr. K,** T338

Puff, the Magic Dragon, **Gr. 2,** 54

Qué bonita es (How Wonderful It Is), **Gr. K,** T234

They Were Tall, **Gr. K,** T53

Healthy Living. *Good habits, food, and exercise keep our bodies strong and healthy.*

Apple a Day, An (traditional poem), **Gr. 1,** T152

Apples and Bananas, **Gr. 1,** T151

Artichokes, **Gr. 2,** 314

Brush Your Teeth (song and speech piece), **Gr. 1,** T66

Child Falling Asleep from *Scenes from Childhood,* Op. 15 by R. Schumann (listening), **Gr. 2,** 77

Corner Grocery Store, **Gr. 2,** 311

Doing the Weekly Walk, **Gr. K,** T78

Dumplin's, **Gr. 2,** 172

Elbows off the Table by B. McGrath and K. Rex (listening), **Gr. K,** T106

Food, Glorious Food from *Oliver!* by L. Bart (listening), **Gr. 2,** 310

Food Song, The, **Gr. 2,** 318

Good Night, Sleep Tight, **Gr. 2,** 76

Green Eggs and Ham, **Gr. 2,** 284

Hot Cross Buns, **Gr. 2,** 258

I Like Spinach, **Gr. 1,** T163

Ja posejah lubenice (I Planted Watermelons), **Gr. 2,** 316

La bella hortelana (The Beautiful Gardener), **Gr. 2,** 208

Me gase boho (Orange Tree), **Gr. 2,** 317

Nabe, Nabe, Soku, Nuke (Stewpot, Stewpot, Bottomless Pot), **Gr. 2,** 259

On Top of Spaghetti, **Gr. 2,** 312
Oranges and Lemons (English traditional poem), **Gr. 1,** T150
Pairs or Pears, **Gr. 2,** 265
Pease Porridge Hot, **Gr. 1,** T255
Peter Cottontail, **Gr. K,** T338
Piggy by W. Cole (poem), **Gr. 2,** 315
Sleep, Bonnie Bairnie, **Gr. 1,** T26
Table Manners by G. Burgess (poem), **Gr. K,** T107

Heroes and Leaders. *We learn important lessons and develop values from people we admire.*

America, the Beautiful, **Gr. 5,** 388
American Salute by M. Gould (listening), **Gr. 5,** 36
Augie's Great Municipal Band from *Star Wars Episode 1: The Phantom Menace* (excerpt) by J. Williams (listening), **Gr. 4,** 56
Ballad of the Underground Railroad, The, **Gr. 5,** 145, (partner song), **Gr. 5,** 154
Brandenburg Concerto No. 5, Third Movement by J. S. Bach, (listening), **Gr. 6,** 128
Concord Hymn by R. W. Emerson (poem), **Gr. 7,** 66
Cumberland Gap, **Gr. 3,** 99
Daniel Boone Leading Settlers Through the Cumberland Gap by G. C. Bingham (fine art), **Gr. 3,** 98
Dreamers, **Gr. 5,** 430
El Capitán by J. P. Sousa (listening), **Gr. 8,** 6
¡El pueblo unido jamás será vencido! by S. Ortega (listening), **Gr. 8,** 90
Follow the Drinkin' Gourd, **Gr. 5,** 142
Follow Your Dream, **Gr. 7,** 207
Fortune Favors the Brave, **Gr. 6,** 316
Gift, The, by M. Unobsky and A. Scott (listening), **Gr. 7,** 205
Guadalcanal March from *Victory at Sea* by R. Rodgers (listening), **Gr. 4,** 108
Haneirot Halalu (These Lights), **Gr. 5,** 414
Henry Ford, **Gr. 7,** 244
Hero, **Gr. 5,** 312
John Henry, **Gr. 5,** 146
Joshua Fit the Battle of Jericho (African American spiritual) (song), **Gr. 5,** 126, (listening), **Gr. 5,** 127
Lincoln by M. Cohn Livingston (poem), **Gr. 3,** 389
Lincoln Gives the Gettysburg Address by Anonymous (fine art), **Gr. 7,** 173
Macnamara's Band, **Gr. 4,** 88
Night That Goldman Spoke, The, **Gr. 7,** 246
People United Will Never Be Defeated!, The, by F. Rzewski (listening), **Gr. 8,** 93
Poets to Come by W. Whitman (poem), **Gr. 7,** 231
Sankta Lucia (Saint Lucia), **Gr. 5,** 413
Success, **Gr. 7,** 241
We Shall Overcome, **Gr. 4,** 387
What Can One Little Person Do?, **Gr. 4,** 204
When Johnny Comes Marching Home, **Gr. 5,** 34
Who's That Yonder?, **Gr. 3,** 245
William Tell (Overture) (excerpt) by G. Rossini (listening), **Gr. 3,** 64

History. *Throughout time people have met many challenges and made valuable contributions.*

1812 Overture by P. I. Tchaikovsky (listening), **Gr. 8,** 72
Ballad of the Underground Railroad, The, **Gr. 5,** 145, (partner song), **Gr. 5,** 154
Battle Hymn of the Republic by J. W. Howe and W. Steffe (song), **Gr. 5,** 391, (listening), **Gr. 5,** 390
Brandenburg Concerto No. 5, Third Movement by J. S. Bach, (listening), **Gr. 6,** 128
Camelot, **Gr. 6,** 310
Chi Rho from *The Book of Kells* (fine art), **Gr. 5,** 48
Chicka Hanka, **Gr. 4,** 138
Common Step (military traditional) (listening), **Gr. 8,** 39
Concord Hymn by R. W. Emerson (poem), **Gr. 7,** 66
Cumberland Gap, **Gr. 3,** 99
Daniel Boone Leading Settlers Through the Cumberland Gap by G. C. Bingham (fine art), **Gr. 3,** 98
Dreamers, **Gr. 5,** 430
¡El pueblo unido jamás será vencido! by S. Ortega (listening), **Gr. 8,** 90
Elijah Rock (African American spiritual) (song and listening), **Gr. 6,** 52
Empress of the Blues by R. Bearden (fine art), **Gr. 5,** 174
Empty Chairs at Empty Tables from *Les Misérables* by H. Kretzmer and C.-M. Schönberg (listening), **Gr. 8,** 197
Erie Canal, **Gr. 5,** 132
Erie Canal at Little Falls, New York by W. Rickarby Miller (fine art), **Gr. 5,** 133
Follow the Drinkin' Gourd, **Gr. 5,** 142
Fugitives Arriving at Levi Coffin's Indiana Farm by C. Webber (fine art), **Gr. 5,** 11
Get on Board, Children (African American freedom song) (listening), **Gr. 5,** 347
Gift, The, by M. Unobsky and A. Scott (listening), **Gr. 7,** 205
Guadalcanal March from *Victory at Sea* by R. Rodgers (listening), **Gr. 4,** 108
Hallelujah, Get On Board, **Gr. 5,** 345
Haneirot Halalu (These Lights), **Gr. 5,** 414
Haydn Montage (listening), **Gr. 8,** 123
Heartbeat of Democracy by V. Brasier (poem), **Gr. 5,** 389
I'm Gonna Sit at the Welcome Table, **Gr. 6,** 416
I've Got a Robe, **Gr. 7,** 162
Joshua Fit the Battle of Jericho (African American spiritual) (song), **Gr. 5,** 126, (listening), **Gr. 5,** 127
La otra España (The Other Spain) by J. C. Calderon (song), **Gr. 4,** 62, (listening), **Gr. 4,** 64
Lead Man Holler by I. Burgie, **Gr. 7,** 148
Liberty Bell, The, by J. P. Sousa (listening), **Gr. 5,** 395
Library of Congress (architecture), **Gr. 8,** 176
Like a Mighty Stream, **Gr. 5,** 320
Lincoln by M. Cohn` Livingston (poem), **Gr. 3,** 389
Lincoln Gives the Gettysburg Address by Anonymous (fine art), **Gr. 7,** 173
March for Military Band, Op. 99 by S. Prokofiev (listening), **Gr. 8,** 37

Minuteman Minute Song, The, **Gr. 3,** 322

Mr. Scott Joplin's Ragtime Rag!, **Gr. 6,** 110

Music of the Generations (montage) (listening), **Gr. 7,** 3

Música indígena from *Instantaneas Mexicanas* by M. M. Ponce (listening), **Gr. 8,** 126

New Colossus, The (excerpt) by E. Lazarus (poem), **Gr. 5,** 42

New Colossus, The, by E. Lazarus (poem), **Gr. 7,** 187

Oliver Cromwell, **Gr. 4,** 269

Out from the Wilderness, **Gr. 3,** 388

Pat Works on the Railway, **Gr. 4,** 86

People United Will Never Be Defeated!, The, by F. Rzewski (listening), **Gr. 8,** 93

Pop! Goes the Weasel (English Ring Game), **Gr. 5,** 94

Portrait of Dolores Olmeda by D. Rivera (fine art), **Gr. 5,** 101

Preamble, The, **Gr. 3,** 293

Princess Baryatinskaya's Ball by G. Grigorevich Gagarin (fine art), **Gr. 5,** 113

Ride Like the Wind, **Gr. 5,** 130

Romantic Period Music (montage) (listening), **Gr. 8,** 119

Shakers Near Lebanon by N. Currier and J. Ives (fine art), **Gr. 5,** 137

Sounds of Swing by T. Igus (poem), **Gr. 5,** 32

Star-Spangled Banner, The, music attributed to J. Smith, words by F. S. Key, arr. by M. Hogan (song), **Gr. 5,** 386, (listening), **Gr. 5,** 86

Taps (traditional) (listening), **Gr. 7,** 144

Tower of London (architecture), **Gr. 6,** 287

Turkish table (fine art), **Gr. 4,** 222

Untitled (British Attack on Washington, D.C. in August 1814) by Unknown (fine art), **Gr. 7,** 193

Untitled (Cattle Drive) by F. Remington (fine art), **Gr. 3,** 114, **Gr. 6,** 114

Untitled (Engraving of St. Stephen's Cathedral, Vienna, 1825) (architecture), **Gr. 8,** 121

We Shall Overcome, **Gr. 4,** 387

Wells Fargo Wagon, The, from *The Music Man* by M. Willson (listening), **Gr. 8,** 78

What Can One Little Person Do?, **Gr. 4,** 204

Words of Wisdom, **Gr. 5,** 244

Yankee Doodle, **Gr. 4,** 154

Imagination and Fantasy. *Our imaginations can take us to new places and help us develop our creative spirits.*

Atlantic City, **Gr. 7,** 248

Ballad of the Bedbugs and the Beetles, The, **Gr. 3,** 206

Ballerina's Dance from *Petrushka* (excerpt) by I. Stravinsky (listening), **Gr. 6,** 161

Ban Dal by Yoon Kyekyoung (listening), **Gr. 4,** 184

Buckeye Jim, **Gr. 4,** 136

Camelot, **Gr. 6,** 310

Castle on a Cloud, **Gr. 7,** 82

Drops of Jupiter (Tell Me) by P. Monahan, J. Stafford, R. Hotchkiss, C. Colin, and S. Underwood (listening), **Gr. 8,** 103

Famous TV Show Themes (montage) (listening), **Gr. 8,** 140

Gus: The Theatre Cat (excerpt) by T. S. Eliot (poem), **Gr. 8,** 195

Halloween Montage (listening), **Gr. 5,** 404

Hope by E. Dickinson (poem), **Gr. 3,** 166

I Wandered Lonely as a Cloud by W. Wordsworth (poem), **Gr. 7,** 125, **Gr. 8,** 18

Interplanet Janet, **Gr. 3,** 298

Isabela and the Troll (Spanish folk tale), **Gr. 3,** 349

It Dropped So Low by E. Dickinson (poem), **Gr. 7,** 20

John Williams Montage 1 (listening), **Gr. 8,** 134

John Williams Montage 2 (listening), **Gr. 8,** 136

Magic Flute, The (Overture) by W. A. Mozart (listening), **Gr. 4,** 252

Mississippi Mud (American folk song) (listening), **Gr. 6,** 65

Modern Dragon, A (speech piece), **Gr. 4,** 98

New Colossus, The, by E. Lazarus (poem), **Gr. 7,** 187

Nottamun Town, **Gr. 5,** 405

Ourchestra by S. Silverstein (poem), **Gr. 8,** 34

Over the Rainbow, **Gr. 4,** 126

Power of the Dream, The, **Gr. 5,** 44

Rattlesnake, **Gr. 3,** 72

Row, Row, Row Your Boat, **Gr. 4,** 268

Scheherazade (excerpt) by N. Rimsky-Korsakov (listening), **Gr. 4,** 161

Schwanenlied by F. Mendelssohn Hensel (listening), **Gr. 7,** 124

Seventy-Six Trombones from *The Music Man* by M. Willson (listening), **Gr. 8,** 76

Song of Peace by R. Riviere (fine art), **Gr. 7,** 155

Sorcerer's Apprentice, The (excerpt) by P. Dukas (listening), **Gr. 4,** 116

Star Canon, **Gr. 5,** 367

String Instruments in the Orchestra (montage) (listening), **Gr. 7,** 48

String of Pearls, A, by G. Miller (listening), **Gr. 3,** 12

Strings in the Media (montage) (listening), **Gr. 7,** 49

Sweep, Sweep Away, **Gr. 3,** 276

There Was a Young Lady by E. Lear (poem), **Gr. 7,** 83

This Pretty Planet, **Gr. 6,** 194

Trepak from *The Nutcracker* by P. Tchaikovsky (listening), **Gr. 6,** 408

Untitled sculpture by P. Picasso (fine art), **Gr. 7,** 232

Wabash Cannonball, The, **Gr. 6,** 30

Walking in the Air by H. Blake (song), 317, (listening), **Gr. 4,** 319

Way Down South by Anonymous (poem), **Gr. 3,** 8

Wondering, **Gr. 6,** 282

X-5 by R. Indiana (fine art), **Gr. 5,** 212

Yellow Submarine, **Gr. 3,** 320

Individuality. *We are each special in our own way.*

Bronco Buster by F. Remington (fine art), **Gr. 2,** 67

Elephant Carries a Great Big Trunk, The, by Anonymous (poem), **Gr. 2,** 169

Everybody Has Music Inside, **Gr. 2,** 164

Garden Song, **Gr. 2,** 236

George Washington, **Gr. 1,** T368

Green Eggs and Ham, **Gr. 2,** 284

He's Got the Whole World in His Hands (traditional spiritual) (song and listening), **Gr. 2,** 116

Thematic Index

Thematic Index (continued)

Hello, There!, **Gr. 1,** T230

Hen wlad fy nhadau (The Land of My Fathers) by E. James and J. James (listening), **Gr. 2,** 141

Hey, Children, Who's In Town?, **Gr. 1,** T14

Hey, Hey, Look at Me, **Gr. 2,** 245

Hinges by A. Fisher (poem), **Gr. K,** T23

Horton Hears a Who!, **Gr. 2,** 279

I Can't Spell Hippopotamus, **Gr. K,** T199

I Got Shoes, **Gr. K,** T33

I See, **Gr. 2,** 266

I'm Gonna Sing, **Gr. 2,** 9

Johnny Works with One Hammer, **Gr. 1,** T96

Jolly Old Saint Nicholas, **Gr. 1,** T352

Joy, **Gr. 2,** 46

Leatherwing Bat, **Gr. 2,** 304

Legend of George Washington and the Cherry Tree, The (story), **Gr. 1,** T369

Little Dancer of Fourteen by E. Degas (fine art), **Gr. 2,** 25

Martin Luther King, **Gr. 2,** 364

Me I Am! by J. Prelutsky (poem), **Gr. K,** T346

Mein Hut (My Hat), **Gr. 2,** 142

Mi cuerpo (My Body), **Gr. 1,** T32

My Legs and I by L. Jacobs (poem), **Gr. K,** T19

Neat Feet (excerpt) by B. Schmidt (poem), **Gr. K,** T30

No One Like You, **Gr. 1,** T300

Oh, the Thinks You Can Think!, **Gr. 2,** 276

Old Woman and the Pig, **Gr. 2,** 130

Oliver Twist, **Gr. 2,** 268

Only My Opinion by M. Shannon (poem), **Gr. K,** T29

Place in the Choir, A, **Gr. 2,** 308

Say Your Name, **Gr. 2,** 243

Seesaw, Margery Daw, **Gr. K,** T264

Señor Coyote (Mexican folktale), **Gr. 2,** 330

Shake My Sillies Out, **Gr. K,** T175

Shoo, Fly, **Gr. 2,** 222

Sing! Sing! Sing!, **Gr. 2,** 196

Skating, **Gr. 2,** 350

So Glad I'm Here arr. by B. Johnson Reagon (listening), **Gr. 2,** 47

Something About Me (poem), **Gr. K,** T13

Somos Boricuas (We Are Puerto Rican) by J. Gutiérrez (listening), **Gr. 2,** 138

Things I'm Thankful For, **Gr. K,** T308

Wee Falorie Man, The, **Gr. 2,** 375

What's Your Name?, **Gr. 1,** T125

Why the Beetle Has a Gold Coat (Brazilian folktale), **Gr. 1,** T321

Wings by A. Fisher (poem), **Gr. 1,** T250

Memories. *Our memories help us link our past and present, and shape our future.*

Assembly Memories (montage), **Gr. 7,** 42

Banjo Lesson, The, by H. O. Tanner (fine art), **Gr. 3,** 151

Barbacoa para cumpleaños (Summer Family Barbeque) by C. Lomas Garza (fine art), **Gr. 5,** 399

Billy, **Gr. 3,** 7

Camelot, **Gr. 6,** 310

Concord Hymn by R. W. Emerson (poem), **Gr. 7,** 66

Cuando salí de Cuba (I Went Away from Cuba), **Gr. 5,** 168

Daniel Boone Leading Settlers Through the Cumberland Gap by G. C. Bingham (fine art), **Gr. 3,** 98

Girl I Left Behind Me, The, **Gr. 4,** 249

Good Mornin', Blues by H. Ledbetter (song), **Gr. 5,** 177, (listening), **Gr. 5,** 176

Haere Ra (Now Is the Hour), **Gr. 5,** 151

Hitori, **Gr. 4,** 345

Jamaica Farewell by I. Burgie (listening), **Gr. 4,** 73

Kojo No Tsuki (Moon at the Ruined Castle), **Gr. 5,** 149

Let It Roll, **Gr. 6,** 124

Lincoln Gives the Gettysburg Address by Anonymous (fine art), **Gr. 7,** 173

Marvelous Toy, The, **Gr. 3,** 182

Mississippi Mud (American folk song) (listening), **Gr. 6,** 65

Mountain Music, **Gr. 6,** 20

Old Barn Dance, The, **Gr. 6,** 94

Oleanna, **Gr. 3,** 144

One of Those Songs, **Gr. 6,** 54

Processional Medley (montage) (listening), **Gr. 7,** 75

Rocky Top, **Gr. 5,** 352

Tears in Heaven by E. Clapton and W. Jennings (song), **Gr. 7,** 141, (choral arrangement) (listening), **Gr. 7,** 140

Tekanionton'néha' (Mohawk social song and dance) (song), **Gr. 5,** 223, (listening), **Gr. 5,** 222

Untitled (British Attack on Washington, D.C. in August 1814) by Unknown (fine art), **Gr. 7,** 193

Water Come a Me Eye, **Gr. 4,** 90

We Remember, **Gr. 4,** 360

When I First Came to This Land, **Gr. 3,** 28

Yankee Doodle, **Gr. 4,** 154

Nature. *We enjoy the beauty of our world.*

Al lado de mi cabaña (Beside My Cottage), **Gr. 3,** 141

All Around the Buttercup, **Gr. 2,** 210

Ame fure (Rain), **Gr. 4,** 26

Appalachian Spring (excerpt) by A. Copland (listening), **Gr. 2,** 37

Apple Tree by Anonymous (poem), **Gr. 3,** 24

Ara River at Akabane, 1929 by K. Hasui (fine art), **Gr. 2,** 77

Arroyito serrano (Mountain Stream) by C. Guastavino (song), **Gr. 4,** 340, (listening), **Gr. 4,** 341

Autumn Fires by R. L. Stevenson (poem), **Gr. 7,** 26

Autumn Leaves, **Gr. 1,** T331

Autumn Leaves by G. O'Keeffe (fine art), **Gr. K,** T304

Autumn Leaves Are Falling, **Gr. 1,** T330

Beryoza (The Birch Tree), **Gr. 4,** 286

Big Beautiful Planet, **Gr. 2,** 376

Birches from Alberta, Canada by S. Renkes (fine art), **Gr. 2,** 89

Bohm Dong Sahn, Gohd Dong Sahn (Spring Valley, Flower Valley), **Gr. K,** T337

Boll Weevil, **Gr. 3,** 171

Call of the Wild, A (excerpt) by R. W. Service (poem), **Gr. 1,** T139

Carol (excerpt) by K. Grahame (poem), **Gr. 6,** 407

Carol from an Irish Cabin, **Gr. 6,** 408

Cat and Dog, **Gr. 3,** 259

Chiu, Chiu, Chiu, **Gr. 6,** 172

Cip cip cücələrim by G. Huseynli and T. Mutallibov (listening), **Gr. 3,** 215

Thematic Index (continued)

Cliffs of Doneen, The, **Gr. 5,** 46

Clouds by Anonymous (poem), **Gr. 1,** T331

Coasts of High Barbary, The, **Gr. 6,** 329

Colores de caracol (Colors of the Snail) by E. Galarza (poem), **Gr. 5,** 101

Colors of the Wind, **Gr. 3,** 84

Coral, **Gr. 3,** 249

Corre el río (The River Flows By) by P. Vasquez (poem), **Gr. 4,** 183

Country Gardens by P. Grainger (listening), **Gr. 2,** 16

Crossing the Brook by J. M. W. Turner (fine art), **Gr. 8,** 114

Daybreak in Alabama (excerpt) by L. Hughes (poem), **Gr. 6,** 162

De aquel cerro (On the Darkened Hillside), **Gr. 3,** 32

De colores (Many Colors) (unison), **Gr. 5,** 88, (part), **Gr. 5,** 98

Deep Snow by Grandma Moses (fine art), **Gr. 3,** 130

Dere Geliyor (River Overflowing), **Gr. 6,** 232

Deta, Deta (The Moon), **Gr. 5,** 246

Doney Gal, **Gr. 6,** 115

E nānā kākou i nā manu (Look at the Birds in the Sky), **Gr. 4,** 338

Eagle, **Gr. 4,** 337

Earth Child, **Gr. 6,** 426

Earth Folk by W. de la Mare (poem), **Gr. 7,** 174

Echo by W. de la Mare (poem), **Gr. K,** T104

Eency Weency Spider, **Gr. K,** T8

Ēinīnī (Little Birds Sleep), **Gr. 5,** 340

El arroyo que murmura (The Murmuring Brook), **Gr. 3,** 318

El coquí (The Frog), **Gr. 4,** 178

El florón (The Flower), **Gr. 1,** T117

El tecolote (The Owlet), **Gr. 6,** 392

En nuestra Tierra tan linda (On Our Beautiful Planet Earth), **Gr. 2,** 114

Estrella brillante (Shining Star), **Gr. 5,** 373

Étude Op. 25, No. 11 ("The Winter Wind") by F. Chopin (listening), **Gr. 2,** 136

Everything Grows, **Gr. 2,** 204

Exhausted Bird by M. Hewson (fine art), **Gr. 4,** 48

Fallingwater by F. L. Wright (architecture), **Gr. 8,** 226

Farfallina (Butterfly), **Gr. 4,** 244

Fehér liliomszál (Little Water Lily), **Gr. K,** T139

Field of Tulips in Holland, A, by C. Monet (fine art), **Gr. 3,** 134

Finis by H. Newbolt (poem), **Gr. 2,** 76

Flight of the Bumblebee, The, by N. Rimsky-Korsakov (listening), **Gr. K,** T259, **Gr. 2,** 40

Four Trees by E. Shiele (fine art), **Gr. 8,** 92

From Bohemia's Forests and Meadows from *Má Vlast* by B. Smetana (listening), **Gr. 6,** 229

From My Window by D. Bailey (poem), **Gr. 8,** 19

Ga Eul (Fall), **Gr. 5,** 401

Garden Song, **Gr. 2,** 236

Gardens in the Rain from *Estampes* by C. Debussy (listening), **Gr. K,** T337

Gloria from *Mass for the Earth* by L. Larsen (listening), **Gr. 7,** 222

Great Big Sea, A, **Gr. 5,** 334

Great Outdoors, The, **Gr. 2,** 290

Green Grass Grows All Around, The, **Gr. 1,** T148

Green Gravel, **Gr. 4,** 247

Hae Wa Be (Sun and Rain), **Gr. 6,** 273

Hop! Chirp! Moo! Oh, Happy Springtime Day!, **Gr. 1,** T372

Hornpipe from *Water Music Suite* (excerpt) by G. F. Handel (listening), **Gr. 3,** 26

Horse with No Name, A, by D. Bunnell (listening), **Gr. 8,** 161

Hotaru Koi (Come, Firefly), **Gr. 6,** 255

Hummingbird, A, by A. Beach (listening), **Gr. K,** T140

I Heard a Mockingbird, **Gr. 4,** 150

I Walk in Beauty, **Gr. 3,** 29

I Wandered Lonely as a Cloud by W. Wordsworth (poem), **Gr. 7,** 125, **Gr. 8,** 18

Ice, **Gr. 1,** T347

If Things Grew Down by R. Hoeft (poem), **Gr. K,** T292

Im Krapfenwaldl (In Krapfen Woods) Op. 336 by J. Strauss, Jr. (listening), **Gr. 2,** 244

Introduction from *The Rite of Spring* (excerpt) by I. Stravinsky (listening), **Gr. 6,** 423

Irises by V. van Gogh (fine art), **Gr. 2,** 236

It Rained a Mist, **Gr. 4,** 262

It's Raining! It's Pouring!, **Gr. 2,** 233

It's So Nice on the Ice, **Gr. 1,** T346

J'entends le moulin (I Hear the Windmill), **Gr. 3,** 135

Jasmine Flower, **Gr. 3,** 146

Joyful, Joyful from *Sister Act 2* (excerpt) arr. by M. Warren (song), **Gr. 5,** 105, (listening), **Gr. 5,** 104

Joyful, Joyful, We Adore Thee, **Gr. 5,** 103

Kum Bachur (The Rooster), **Gr. 3,** 75

La lluvia by S. Hatfield (listening), **Gr. 2,** 232

La pájara pinta (The Speckled Bird), **Gr. 6,** 268

La sanjuanerita (The Girl from San Juan), **Gr. 4,** 100

Lady, Lady, **Gr. K,** T184

Land of the Silver Birch, **Gr. 2,** 88

Le Mar (The Sea), **Gr. 3,** 110

Lion by L. Eto (listening), **Gr. 6,** 16

Little Seeds (except) by E. Holmelund Minarik (poem), **Gr. 2,** 207

Loch Lomond, **Gr. 5,** 138

Lonesome Dove, **Gr. 6,** 249

Los maizales (The Cornfields), **Gr. 5,** 268

Mama Will Provide, **Gr. 6,** 296

Mars from *The Planets* by G. Holst (listening), **Gr. 6,** 196

Mighty River (speech piece), **Gr. 4,** 217

Milan (Meeting of the Two Rivers) (excerpt) by K. Kale (listening), **Gr. 4,** 208

Miniwanka (or The Moments of Water) by R. M. Schafer (listening), **Gr. 4,** 28

Minor Bird, A, by R. Frost (poem), **Gr. 6,** 156

Mister Sun, **Gr. K,** T343

Moldau, The, from *Má Vlast (My Country)* (excerpt) by B. Smetana (listening), **Gr. 5,** 271

Moldau, The, from *Má Vlast* by B. Smetana (listening), **Gr. 7,** 219

Morning Has Broken (traditional Gaelic melody) (song) **Gr. 4,** 22, (listening), **Gr. 4,** 23

Motive from the County of Nordland by A. Normann (fine art), **Gr. 3,** 143

My Oak Tree, **Gr. K,** T236

Nani Wale Na Hala (The Swaying Pandanus Trees), **Gr. 5,** 276

Nature Sounds (montage) (listening), **Gr. 8,** 18

Neviděli jste tu mé panenky? (Have You Not Seen My Daughters?), **Gr. 6,** 228

Nevoa (Mist) by B. Nugent (fine art), **Gr. 4,** 216

Ngam sang duan (Shining Moon), **Gr. 5,** 376

Night Comes… by B. Schenk de Regniers (poem), **Gr. 1,** T233

Night of the Mockingbird by J. Huling (listening), **Gr. 4,** 153

Nightingale, The, by F. Liszt (listening), **Gr. 6,** 160

Nochebuena (Christmas Eve), **Gr. K,** T323

North Winds Blow, **Gr. K,** T305

O Wind by C. Rossetti (poem), **Gr. 1,** T235

O, Desayo, **Gr. 6,** 50

Ocean Child by P. Winter (listening), **Gr. 7,** 218

Oh, How Lovely Is the Evening, **Gr. 6,** 252

On a Clear Day, **Gr. 6,** 206

On the Trail, from *Grand Canyon Suite* by F. Grofé (listening). **Gr. 8,** 112

Our World, **Gr. 5,** 381

Over in the Meadow, **Gr. 1,** T78

Owl and the Cuckoo, The, **Gr. 4,** 337

Panda Chant II by M. Monk (listening), **Gr. 6,** 263

Paris Street; Rainy Day by G. Caillebotte (fine art), **Gr. 1,** T31

Path to the Moon, **Gr. 5,** 368

Perfect Winter Day, A, **Gr. 6,** 400

Promise of Living, The, from *The Tender Land* by A. Copland (listening), **Gr. 6,** 77

Raccoon Dance Song, **Gr. 3,** 87

Rage and Roar, **Gr. 6,** 48

Rain (haiku), **Gr. 4,** 27

Rain Poem (poem), **Gr. 1,** T31

Rain, Rain, Go Away, **Gr. 1,** T259

Rain Sizes by J. Ciardi (poem), **Gr. 1,** T33

Rainbow Song, The, **Gr. K,** T61

Rainstorm (listening), **Gr. 1,** T35

Ranunculus by C. Belle (fine art), **Gr. 2,** 210

Rattlesnake, **Gr. 3,** 72

Rite of Spring, The (excerpt) by I. Stravinsky (listening), **Gr. 2,** 201

River of My People, **Gr. 6,** 176

River, The, by C. Zolotow (poem), **Gr. K,** T342

Roll On, Columbia, **Gr. 4,** 182

Round and Round, **Gr. 6,** 104

Sakura (Cherry Blossoms), **Gr. 6,** 14

Scraping Up Sand, **Gr. 6,** 248

Sea Shell, **Gr. 4,** 245

Seeds, **Gr. 1,** T120

Seeds and Seasons, **Gr. 2,** 206

Serra, serra serrador (Saw, Saw Lumberjack), **Gr. 1,** T133

Shady Grove, **Gr. 6,** 286

Sing a Little Song, **Gr. K,** T179

Sing! Sing! Sing!, **Gr. 2,** 196

Singing Woods, The, by B. M. Davids (listening), **Gr. 7,** 201

Sitsiritsit, **Gr. 4,** 102

Skaters' Waltz, The (excerpt) by E. Waldteufel (listening), **Gr. 1,** T345

Skating in Central Park by A. Tait (fine art), **Gr. K,** T310

Sky Dances, **Gr. 4,** 206

Snow Toward Evening by M. Cane (poem), **Gr. K,** T311

Snowman, The, **Gr. K,** T313

Somebody Has To… by S. Silverstein (poem), **Gr. 1,** T258

Song of a Seashore (traditional Inuit) (listening), **Gr. 7,** 176

Song of Peace by R. Riviere (fine art), **Gr. 7,** 155

Spell of the Moon (excerpt) by L. Norris (poem), **Gr. K,** T116

Spiders, **Gr. 3,** 282

Spring, **Gr. 1,** T273

Spring Rain by J. Sloan (fine art), **Gr. K,** T336

Star Canon, **Gr. 5,** 367

Starry Night, The, by V. van Gogh (fine art), **Gr. K,** T66

Stonehaven Sunset by J. Denver (listening), **Gr. 7,** 221

Summer Landscape by E. Shiele (fine art), **Gr. 8,** 92

Summertime from *Porgy and Bess* by G. and I. Gershwin (listening), **Gr. 6,** 120

Sun Is First to Rise, The, by E. Coatsworth (poem), **Gr. 2,** 383

Sun Rises While the Moon Sleeps, The, by P. Davidson (fine art), **Gr. 2,** 218

Suomen Salossa (The Finnish Forest), **Gr. 6,** 422

Sweet and Low, **Gr. 6,** 184

Symphony No. 4, Fourth Movement by P. Tchaikovsky (listening), **Gr. 4,** 287

Symphony No. 6 ("Pastoral") (excerpts) by L. van Beethoven (listening), **Gr. 8,** 20

Symphony: Water Music, Movements 3 and 4 by L. Larsen (listening), **Gr. 8,** 155

Tanabata (Seven Evenings), **Gr. 3,** 62

Tehahontanekenhnêha' (Rabbit Dance song) (listening), **Gr. 3,** 51

Tehahontanekenhnêha' (Rabbit Dance story) (listening), **Gr. 3,** 50

There Was a Blue Flower from *Dreaming Blue* by L. Larsen (song), **Gr. 6,** 219, (listening), **Gr. 6,** 218

They Call the Wind Maria, **Gr. 6,** 312

This Land Is Your Land, **Gr. 4,** 146

This Pretty Planet, **Gr. 6,** 194

To a Friend Who Sent Me Some Roses by J. Keats (poem), **Gr. 8,** 115

Troika, **Gr. 6,** 230

Trout, The, **Gr. 6,** 342

Tsing Chun U Chü (Youth Dance Song), **Gr. 6,** 272

Tuileries from *Pictures at an Exhibition* by M. Mussorgsky (listening), **Gr. 1,** T249

Twinkle, Twinkle, Little Star, **Gr. K,** T90

Unfolding Bud by N. Koriyama (poem), **Gr. 6,** 209

Uno de enero (The First of January), **Gr. 3,** 210

Untitled by Anonymous (poem), **Gr. 6,** 218

Untitled haiku by M. Bashō **Gr. 8,** 57

Up the Tree and Down Again by A. Seear (poem), **Gr. 1,** T65

Valley of the Moon, Eliat by J. Yellin Ginat (fine art), **Gr. 4,** 113

Vamos a la mar (Let's Go to the Sea), **Gr. 3,** 56

Wachet auf (Waken Now), **Gr. 6,** 259

Walk by the River (unison), **Gr. 6,** 74, (parts), **Gr. 6,** 76

Water Cadenza from *Water Passion After St. Matthew* by Tan Dun (listening), **Gr. 7,** 233

Water Lilies by C. Monet (fine art), **Gr. K,** T138

Thematic Index

Thematic Index (continued)

We Return Thanks (Iroquois prayer) (poem), **Gr. 6**, 108

Welcome Is the Month of May, **Gr. 2**, 378

Weymouth Bay by J. Constable (fine art), **Gr. 8**, 154

What a Wonderful World (choral arrangement) by G. D. Weiss and B. Thiele (listening), **Gr. 8**, 8

What a Wonderful World by G. D. Weiss and B. Thiele (Louis Armstrong version) (listening), **Gr. 8**, 9

What a Wonderful World by G. D. Weiss and B. Thiele (song and listening), **Gr. 2**, 84

What the World Needs Now, **Gr. 5**, 230

White Sheep by Anonymous (poem), **Gr. 1**, T234

Who Has Seen the Wind? by C. G. Rossetti (poem), **Gr. 2**, 137

Why We Tell the Story, **Gr. 6**, 303

Wie schön leuchtet der Morgenstern (How Brightly Shines the Morning Star) from *Cantata No. 1*, BWV 1 by J. S. Bach (song), **Gr. 5**, 370, (listening), **Gr. 5**, 371

Wind Blew East, The, **Gr. 1**, T234

Wind Blow, **Gr. 1**, T187

Winter (Allegro non molto) from *The Four Seasons* (Concerto No. 4 in F Minor) by A. Vivaldi (listening), **Gr. 6**, 403

Winter Ade (G Major), **Gr. 6**, 132, (G Minor), **Gr. 6**, 133

Winter Wonderland, **Gr. 5**, 408

Wondering, **Gr. 6**, 282

Woodpecker, The, by E. Madox Roberts (poem), **Gr. 4**, 48

Yellow Bird, **Gr. 6**, 154

Yüe lían wan wan (Crescent Moon), **Gr. 6**, 26

Neighborhood and School. *Visiting familiar places and people brings special joy.*

Ach, du lieber Augustin (The More We Get Together), **Gr. 2**, 35

Bonjour, mes amis (Hello, My Friends), **Gr. 1**, T18

Chiapanecas (Ladies of Chiapas), **Gr. 2**, 128

Children's Games by Pieter Brueghel (fine art), **Gr. 2**, 247

Corner Grocery Store, **Gr. 2**, 311

Ears, Far and Near by M. Campbelle-Holman and S. Snyder (poem), **Gr. 1**, T16

El tren (The Train), **Gr. 2**, 326

El zapatero (The Cobbler), **Gr. 2**, 138

En la feria de San Juan (In the Market of San Juan), **Gr. 2**, 226

Hakyo jong (School Bells), **Gr. 1**, T302

Happiest Street in the World, The, **Gr. 1**, T304

Happy Birthday, Happy Birthday, **Gr. K**, T273

Hello, There!, **Gr. 1**, T230

Muffin Man, The, **Gr. K**, T105

People in Your Neighborhood, The, by J. Moss (listenings) (instrumental verses), **Gr. K**, T171, (sung verses), **Gr. K**, T122

Puff, the Magic Dragon, **Gr. 2**, 54

School Is Over by K. Greenaway (poem), **Gr. K**, T85

She'll Be Comin' 'Round the Mountain, **Gr. 2**, 33

So Glad I'm Here arr. by B. Johnson Reagon (listening), **Gr. 2**, 47

Take Me Out to the Ball Game, **Gr. 2**, 56

Winter Landscape with a Bird Trap by P. Brueghel (fine art), **Gr. 2**, 351

Won't You Be My Neighbor?, **Gr. K**, T268

Personal Growth. *Developing our strengths and learning about our weaknesses is a lifelong challenge.*

Ballad of the Underground Railroad, The, **Gr. 5**, 145 (partner song), **Gr. 5**, 154

Beauty and the Beast, **Gr. 5**, 124

Bug, The, by M. Knopfler, **Gr. 8**, 88

Change Is Good by E. Kaecher, J. Tullio, and R. Danko (song), **Gr. 5**, 84, (listening), **Gr. 5**, 85

Circle of Life (choral arrangement) from *The Lion King* by E. John and T. Rice (listening), **Gr. 7**, 84

Circle of Life (The King's Singers) from *The Lion King* by E. John and T. Rice (listening), **Gr. 7**, 84

Circle of Life, **Gr. 7**, 40

Daydreams on a Subway Train by P. M. Fagan (poem), **Gr. 8**, 84

Down by the Riverside, **Gr. 6**, 22

Follow Your Dream, **Gr. 4**, 234

Gonna Build a Mountain from *Stop the World—I Want to Get Off* by A. Newley and L. Bricusse (song), **Gr. 6**, 4, (listening), **Gr. 6**, 5

Good Morning America by T. Melendez (listening), **Gr. 8**, 181

Happiness, **Gr. 4**, 124

Heart, **Gr. 6**, 166

Hero, **Gr. 5**, 312

How Long the Train Been Gone?, **Gr. 4**, 264

I Think I'm Gonna Like It Here, **Gr. 4**, 299

I Want to Be Ready, **Gr. 6**, 12

I Will Survive by F. Perren and D. Ferakis (listening), **Gr. 8**, 208

I'll Rise When the Rooster Crows, **Gr. 4**, 36

It Dropped So Low by E. Dickinson (poem), **Gr. 7**, 20

Lean on Me, **Gr. 6**, 150

Life by S. DeShetler (poem), **Gr. 5**, 205

Lincoln Gives the Gettysburg Address by Anonymous (fine art), **Gr. 7**, 173

Little David Play on Your Harp, **Gr. 4**, 323

N. Y. C., **Gr. 4**, 302

No One Is Alone from *Into the Woods* by S. Sondheim (listening), **Gr. 8**, 86

Old Aunt Dinah, **Gr. 4**, 245

On a Clear Day, **Gr. 6**, 206

Over the Rainbow, **Gr. 4**, 126

Power of the Dream, The, **Gr. 5**, 44

Reach, **Gr. 5**, 14

Respect (two versions) by O. Redding (listening), **Gr. 7**, 5

River of My People, **Gr. 6**, 176

Simple Gifts, **Gr. 5**, 136

Smilin', **Gr. 8**, 80

Tain't What You Do, **Gr. 6**, 18

Take Time in Life, **Gr. 4**, 156

This Train (African American spiritual) (song and listening), **Gr. 4**, 343

Three Little Birds (traditional) (listening), **Gr. 8**, 84

When I Was Young, **Gr. 4**, 187

You're Never Fully Dressed Without a Smile, **Gr. 4**, 304

Thematic Index

Pretending. *Our imaginations can take us to new places.*

¡Adivina lo que es! (Guess What It Is!), **Gr. 1**, T170

Ban Dal (Half Moon), **Gr. 2**, 219

Button, You Must Wander, **Gr. 2**, 176

Chickery Chick, **Gr. 1**, T292

Concerto for Trombone ("Motorbike Concerto"), Fifth Movement by J. Sandström (listening), **Gr. 2**, 193

Dance of the Sugar Plum Fairy from *The Nutcracker Suite* by P. Tchaikovsky (listening), **Gr. 2**, 354

Grasshopper's Wedding by B. Bartók (listening), **Gr. 1**, T245

I Am Slowly Going Crazy, **Gr. 1**, T127

I'd Like to Be a Lighthouse by R Field (poem), **Gr. 1**, T238

If All the World Were Paper, **Gr. 1**, T296

It's Possible, **Gr. 2**, 281

Jugaremos en el bosque (We'll Be Playing in the Forest), **Gr. 2**, 188

Las horas (The Hours), **Gr. K**, T70

Lavender's Blue, **Gr. 1**, T174

Motorcycle Ride by B. Haack and E. Nelson (listening), **Gr. 2**, 192

Papagena! Papagena! Papagena! from *The Magic Flute* by W. A. Mozart (listening), **Gr. 2**, 152

Peter and the Wolf (excerpt) by S. Prokofiev (listening), **Gr. 2**, 160

Peter Cottontail, **Gr. K**, T338

Puff, the Magic Dragon, **Gr. 2**, 54

Rabbit, The, by M. Stelmach (poem), **Gr. 1**, T186

Rattlesnake, **Gr. 1**, T185

Sing Ho! For the Life of a Bear! by A. A. Milne (poem), **Gr. 1**, T114

Somebody Has To… by S. Silverstein (poem), **Gr. 1**, T258

Thoughts of a Rattlesnake by K. Sexton (poem), **Gr. 1**, T185

Up on the Housetop, **Gr. 2**, 356

Wait and See, **Gr. K**, T335

Waltz of the Flowers (excerpt) from *The Nutcracker Suite* by P. Tchaikovsky (listening), **Gr. 2**, 354

Resourcefulness and Problem Solving. *Trying hard and looking at problems in new ways help us find answers.*

Ballad of the Underground Railroad, The, (song), **Gr. 5**, 145, (partner song), **Gr. 5**, 154

Bamboo Flute, **Gr. 4**, 134

Big and Small, **Gr. 1**, T200

Blow, Ye Winds, Blow, **Gr. 3**, 192

Bound No'th Blues by L. Hughes (poem), **Gr. 5**, 181

Bug, The, by M. Knopfler, **Gr. 8**, 88

Cobbler, Cobbler, Mend My Shoe, **Gr. K**, T169

Cobbler, The, by E. Chafee (poem), **Gr. K**, T255

Company Way, The, **Gr. 8**, 244

Digga Digga Dog, **Gr. 3**, 164

Drumming Spider, The (West African folktale), **Gr. 2**, 333

El manisero (Peanut Vendor), **Gr. 4**, 106

Everybody Oughta Know (African American song) arr. by Y. M. Barnwell (song and listening), **Gr. 1**, T361

Exhausted Bird by M. Hewson (fine art), **Gr. 4**, 48

Follow the Drinkin' Gourd, **Gr. 5**, 142

Fugitives Arriving at Levi Coffin's Indiana Farm by C. Webber (fine art), **Gr. 5**, 11

Gebeta Board, The (Ethiopian folk tale), **Gr. 3**, 346

Happy Face by B. Knowles et al (listening), **Gr. 7**, 134

Heart, **Gr. 6**, 166

Hero, **Gr. 5**, 312

I Hear America Singing, **Gr. 5**, 327

I Lost the Farmer's Dairy Key, **Gr. 3**, 273

If I Had a Hammer, **Gr. 6**, 174

In That Great Git'n Up Morning, **Gr. 5**, 10

John Henry, **Gr. 5**, 146

Just Keep Goin' On by D. Smith (song), **Gr. 7**, 18, (listening), **Gr. 7**, 16

Lemonade, **Gr. 2**, 19

Let's Think of Something to Do, **Gr. K**, T270

Life by S. DeShetler (poem), **Gr. 5**, 205

Lincoln Gives the Gettysburg Address by Anonymous (fine art), **Gr. 7**, 173

Little David Play on Your Harp, **Gr. 4**, 323

Martin Luther King, **Gr. 1**, T360

Mayim, Mayim (Water, Water), **Gr. 6**, 102

Movin' Right Along, **Gr. 3**, 124

My Government Claim (unison), **Gr. 5**, 95, (part), **Gr. 5**, 110

Night Herding Song, **Gr. 4**, 110

No One Is Alone from *Into the Woods* by S. Sondheim (listening), **Gr. 8**, 86

On Hearing a Symphony of Beethoven by E. S. V. Millay (poem), **Gr. 8**, 226

Ourchestra by S. Silverstein (poem), **Gr. 8**, 34

Peace in this House, **Gr. 7**, 152

Peter Cottontail, **Gr. K**, T338

Pop! Goes the Weasel (English ring game) (song), **Gr. 5**, 94, (expanded dance version) (listening), **Gr. 5**, 112

Ride Like the Wind, **Gr. 5**, 130

Roll On, Columbia, **Gr. 4**, 182

Señor Coyote (Mexican folktale), **Gr. 2**, 330

Shake the Papaya Down, **Gr. 2**, 90

Sheep Shearing, **Gr. 2**, 102

Shoes of John, **Gr. 6**, 246

Smoke Goes Up the Chimney, **Gr. 3**, 272

Speedy Delivery, **Gr. K**, T279

Symphony No. 45 ("Farewell"), First Movement by F. J. Haydn (listening), **Gr. 8**, 124

Tain't What You Do, **Gr. 6**, 18

Take Time in Life, **Gr. 4**, 156

There Was a Young Lady by E. Lear (poem), **Gr. 7**, 83

There's a Hole in the Bucket, **Gr. 2**, 132

Wade in the Water (African American spiritual) arr. by M. Hogan (listening), **Gr. 5**, 144

Walk by the River (song), **Gr. 3**, 74, (harmony parts), **Gr. 3**, 76

Water Is Wide, The, **Gr. 6**, 46

We All Sing With the Same Voice, **Gr. 1**, T156

We Are the Children of Tomorrow, **Gr. 5**, 114

We Shall Overcome by Z. Horton et al (song), **Gr. 7**, 212, (Howard University Gospel Choir) (listening), **Gr. 7**, 213

We Shall Overcome, **Gr. 4**, 387

Thematic Index

Thematic Index (continued)

Seasons, Weather, Night and Day. *Learning about the ways of nature helps us understand our world.*

All Through the Night (Welsh folk song), **Gr. 4,** 277
Autumn Leaves by G. O'Keeffe (fine art), **Gr. K,** T304
Autumn Music, First Movement (excerpt) by J. Higdon (listening), **Gr. 4,** 121
Bohm (Spring Has Come!), **Gr. 3,** 392
Boogie-Woogie Ghost, The, **Gr. 4,** 368
Clock at Night, A, by S. Miloslavskiy (listening), **Gr. 3,** 66
Days of the Week, **Gr. K,** T81
December Nights, December Lights, **Gr. 4,** 372
Deep Snow by Grandma Moses (fine art), **Gr. 3,** 130
Dok Djampa (The White Jasmine Flower), **Gr. 4,** 392
Eine kleine Nachtmusik (Serenade No. 13 in G, K. 525), Minuet by W. A. Mozart (listening), **Gr. 3,** 168
Entren, santos peregrinos (Enter, Holy Pilgrims), **Gr. 4,** 379
Fall (Allegro) from *The Four Seasons* (Concerto No. 3 in F Major) (excerpt) by A. Vivaldi (listening), **Gr. K,** T305
Frère Jacques (Are You Sleeping?), **Gr. 4,** 260
Frosty Weather, **Gr. 3,** 250
I'll Rise When the Rooster Crows, **Gr. 4,** 36
In the Good Old Summertime by G. Evans (listening), **Gr. K,** T343
Jolly Old St. Nicholas, **Gr. 4,** 382
Joy to the World, **Gr. 4,** 383
L'inverno è già passato (Winter Is Over), **Gr. 4,** 390
La cloche (The Clock), **Gr. 3,** 67
La sanjuanerita (The Girl from San Juan), **Gr. 4,** 100
Las mañanitas (The Morning Song) (song), **Gr. 4,** 194, (listening), **Gr. 4,** 197
Marken er mejet (Out in the Meadow), **Gr. 4,** 364
May Day Carol, **Gr. 3,** 393
Morning Bells, **Gr. 3,** 270
Morning Mood from *Peer Gynt Suite No. 1,* Op. 46 by E. Grieg (listening), **Gr. 3,** 251
New Day, The, **Gr. 4,** 316
Nia (Purpose), **Gr. 4,** 384
Night Herding Song, **Gr. 4,** 110
Night of the Mockingbird by J. Huling (listening), **Gr. 4,** 153
Night Song, **Gr. 3,** 186
Once Upon a Christmastime, **Gr. 4,** 380
Over the River and Through the Wood, **Gr. 4,** 370
Para pedir posada (Looking for Shelter), **Gr. 4,** 377
Qua Cầ Gió Bay (Vietnamese folk song) (listening), **Gr. 4,** 367
Que Llueva (It's Raining), **Gr. 3,** 274
Rain Is Falling Down, **Gr. 3,** 242
S'vivon Sov (Dreidel Spin), **Gr. 4,** 374
Sitsiritsit, **Gr. 4,** 102
Song of Thanksgiving, **Gr. 4,** 371
Spring (Allegro) from *The Four Seasons* (Concerto No. 1 in E Major) (excerpt) by A. Vivaldi (listening), **Gr. 4,** 391
Spring Rain by J. Sloan (fine art), **Gr. K,** T336
Starry Night, The, by V. van Gogh (fine art), **Gr. K,** T66
Summer (Allegro Non Molto) from *The Four Seasons* (Concerto No. 2 in G Minor) (excerpt) by A. Vivaldi (listening), **Gr. 4,** 161
Summer Serenade by E. Jackson (fine art), **Gr. K,** T342
Summertime from *Porgy and Bess* by G. and I. Gershwin (listening), **Gr. 4,** 160
Sun Don't Set in the Mornin', **Gr. 3,** 48, 60
Taps, **Gr. 3,** 281
Tết Trung (Children's Festival), **Gr. 4,** 366
Twinkle, Twinkle, Little Star, **Gr. K,** T90
'Ulili E (The Sandpiper), **Gr. 4,** 396
Uno de enero (The First of January), **Gr. 3,** 210
Wake Up Canon, **Gr. 4,** 326
Waltz of the Snowflakes from *The Nutcracker* (excerpt) by P. Tchaikovsky (listening), **Gr. K,** T311
We Are Here, **Gr. 4,** 394
We Shall Overcome, **Gr. 4,** 387

Stories and Tales. *People have always enjoyed sharing stories.*

1812 Overture by P. I. Tchaikovsky (listening), **Gr. 8,** 72
Adukbe (Adenkum traditional) (listening), **Gr. 8,** 177
Anansi (Ashanti folk tale), **Gr. 3,** 104
Anitra's Dance from *Peer Gynt Suite No. 1,* Op. 46 by E. Grieg (listening), **Gr. 5,** 193
Arianna by C. Monteverdi and P. Schwartz (listening), **Gr. 7,** 94
Ballad of the Underground Railroad, The, **Gr. 5,** 145, (partner song), **Gr. 5,** 154
Barbry Ellen, **Gr. 6,** 208
Beauty and the Beast, **Gr. 5,** 124
Bella Bimba (Pretty Girl), **Gr. 3,** 172
Blow, Ye Winds, Blow, **Gr. 3,** 192
Boll Weevil, **Gr. 3,** 171
Boris, the Singing Bear, **Gr. 1,** T312
Chan mali chan (Singaporean folk song), **Gr. 3,** 10
Chicka-ma, Chicka-ma, Craney Crow, **Gr. 3,** 263
Columbus Sailed with Three Ships, **Gr. 2,** 344
Company Way, The, **Gr. 8,** 244
Concord Hymn by R. W. Emerson (poem), **Gr. 7,** 66
Corner Grocery Store, **Gr. 2,** 311
Cornstalk Fiddle and a Shoestring Bow, **Gr. 3,** 284
Crawdad Song, **Gr. 3,** 107
Daniel Boone Leading Settlers Through the Cumberland Gap by G. C. Bingham (fine art), **Gr. 3,** 98
Daniel in the Lion's Den (excerpt) by F. McBeth (listening), **Gr. 3,** 161
Daydreams on a Subway Train by P. M. Fagan (poem), **Gr. 8,** 84
Death Scene Themes (from *La Bohème* and *Rent*) by G. Puccini and J. Larson (listening), **Gr. 7,** 182
Derby Ram, The, **Gr. 4,** 259
Didn't It Rain, **Gr. 6,** 345
Draw a Bucket of Water, **Gr. 3,** 222
Dreamers, **Gr. 5,** 430
Empty Chairs at Empty Tables from *Les Misérables* by H. Kretzmer and C.-M. Schönberg (listening), **Gr. 8,** 197
Frosty, the Snowman, **Gr. 3,** 366
Gebeta Board, The (Ethiopian folk tale), **Gr. 3,** 346
George Washington, **Gr. 1,** T368
Ghost Ship, The, **Gr. 6,** 323
Giant's Shoes, The, by E. Fallis (poem), **Gr. K,** T32
Greenland Whale Fishery, The, **Gr. 6,** 212
Halloween Montage (listening), **Gr. 5,** 404

Have Pity, Lord, On Me from *St. Matthew Passion* by J. S. Bach (listening), **Gr. 7,** 232

Henry Ford, **Gr. 7,** 244

Hi! My Name Is Joe (rhythmic pattern), **Gr. 1,** T220

Huainito, **Gr. 6,** 351

I Saw Three Ships, **Gr. 2,** 359

I Will Survive by F. Perren and D. Ferakis (listening), **Gr. 8,** 208

Infernal Dance of King Kashchei from *The Firebird Suite* (excerpt) by I. Stravinsky (listening), **Gr. 4,** 191

Interjections, **Gr. 3,** 303

Interplanet Janet, **Gr. 3,** 298

Isabela and the Troll (Spanish folk tale), **Gr. 3,** 349

Jack Was Ev'ry Bit a Sailor, **Gr. 6,** 170

Jamaica Farewell, **Gr. 3,** 156

John Henry, **Gr. 5,** 146

Joshua Fit the Battle of Jericho (African American spiritual) (song), **Gr. 5,** 126, (listening), **Gr. 5,** 127

Kalinka (Little Snowball Bush), **Gr. 3,** 224

Kojo No Tsuki (Moon at the Ruined Castle), **Gr. 5,** 149

Laideronette, Empress of the Pagodas from *Mother Goose Suite* by M. Ravel (listening), **Gr. 1,** T237

Legend of George Washington and the Cherry Tree, The (story), **Gr. 1,** T369

Lincoln Gives the Gettysburg Address by Anonymous (fine art), **Gr. 7,** 173

Little Boy of the Sheep, **Gr. 3,** 188

Little David Play on Your Harp, **Gr. 4,** 323

Little Tommy Tinker, **Gr. 3,** 277

Look High, Look Low, **Gr. 3,** 338

Lukey's Boat, **Gr. 3,** 114

Mai Nozipo by D. Maraire (listening), **Gr. 7,** 228

Mary Had a Baby, **Gr. 2,** 360

Mississippi Mud (American folk song) (listening), **Gr. 6,** 65

Moon Mirrored in a Pool, The, by H. Yanjun (listening), **Gr. K,** T115

Mother, Mother, **Gr. 2,** 254

Nessun dorma from *Turandot* by G. Puccini (listening), **Gr. 5,** 64

Night That Goldman Spoke, The, **Gr. 7,** 246

Noble Duke of York, The, **Gr. K,** T232

Och Jungfrun Hon Går I Ringen (Swedish dance song) (song), **Gr. 5,** 190, (listening), **Gr. 5,** 191

Oh, Susanna, **Gr. 3,** 153

Old Barn Dance, The, **Gr. 3,** 94

Old Carrion Crow, The, **Gr. 4,** 192

Old Jim John, **Gr. 6,** 253

Old Mother Goose (traditional rhyme), **Gr. 1,** T181

Old Roger, **Gr. 3,** 280

On Top of Spaghetti, **Gr. 2,** 312

One More River, **Gr. 3,** 216

Over the Sea to Skye, **Gr. 4,** 344

Pairs or Pears, **Gr. 2,** 265

Pat Works on the Railway (Orff version) (listening), **Gr. 1,** T144

Pay Me My Money Down, **Gr. 3,** 149

Peter and the Wolf (Introduction and excerpt) by S. Prokofiev (listening), **Gr. 1,** T140

Peter Cottontail, **Gr. K,** T338

Pile of Stuff, A (story), **Gr. 1,** T188

Polly Wolly Doodle, **Gr. 3,** 132

Presidents, **Gr. K,** T330

Rabbit in the Moon, The (story to perform), **Gr. 1,** T318

Raccoon Dance Song, **Gr. 3,** 87

Ragtime, **Gr. 7,** 237

Ragtime Epilogue and Finale, **Gr. 7,** 250

Red Iron Ore, **Gr. 6,** 134

Ride Like the Wind, **Gr. 5,** 130

Russian Sailor's Dance from *The Red Poppy* by R. Glière (listening), **Gr. 4,** 266

Sankta Lucia (Saint Lucia), **Gr. 5,** 413

Scheherazade (excerpt) by N. Rimsky-Korsakov (listening), **Gr. 4,** 161

Seasons of Love from *Rent* (choral arrangement) by J. Larson (listening), **Gr. 7,** 86

Seventy-Six Trombones from *The Music Man* by M. Willson (listening), **Gr. 8,** 76

Shady Grove (traditional) (listening), **Gr. 8,** 59

Shepherd, Shepherd, **Gr. 3,** 56

Ship in Distress, The, **Gr. 6,** 211

Shope, Shope (Oh, Shope, Shope), **Gr. 5,** 220

Signature Themes (from *La Bohème* and *Rent*) (listening), **Gr. 7,** 180

Sittin' Down to Eat, **Gr. 1,** T182

Solveig's Song from *Peer Gynt Suite No. 2,* Op. 55 by E. Grieg (listening), **Gr. 5,** 192

Sounds of Africa, The, by Wandile (poem), **Gr. 5,** 74

Spring (Allegro) from *The Four Seasons* (Concerto No. 1 in E Major) (excerpt) by A. Vivaldi (listening), **Gr. 7,** 112

Spring Round Dances from *The Rite of Spring* by I. Stravinsky (listening), **Gr. 7,** 232

Stamping Land, **Gr. K,** T24

Streets of Laredo, **Gr. 5,** 260

Sugar in the Gourd, **Gr. 6,** 251

Swapping Song, **Gr. 4,** 253

Sweet and Low, **Gr. 6,** 184

Tehahontanekenhêha' (Rabbit Dance song) (listening), **Gr. 3,** 51

Tehahontanekenhêha' (Rabbit Dance story) (listening), **Gr. 3,** 50

There Was a Jolly Miller, **Gr. 6,** 250

There Was a Young Lady by E. Lear (poem), **Gr. 7,** 83

There Was an Old Lady by D. Lee (poem), **Gr. 3,** 344

There's a Hole in the Middle of the Sea, **Gr. 1,** T178

Three Little Muffins (speech piece), **Gr. K,** T146

Throw It Out the Window, **Gr. 3,** 94

Tragic Story, A, by B. Britten (listening), **Gr. 4,** 190

Tzakonikos (Greek circle dance) (listening), **Gr. 6,** 214

U.S.S. Constitution by M. Clark (fine art), **Gr. 2,** 171

Ucha Tirvarch (Little Bear Song), **Gr. 3,** 53

Uncle Jessie (African American folk song) (listening), **Gr. 3,** 327

Uncle Pen, **Gr. 5,** 24

Üsküdar, **Gr. 5,** 128

Wabash Cannonball, The, **Gr. 6,** 30

Way Down South by Anonymous (poem), **Gr. 3,** 8

Wéané (Menadonese lullaby), **Gr. 3,** 184

Why the Beetle Has a Gold Coat (Brazilian folk tale), **Gr. 1,** T321

Thematic Index (continued)

Why We Tell the Story, **Gr. 6,** 303
Yankee Doodle, **Gr. 2,** 340
Year-Naming Race, The (Chinese folk tale) (listening), **Gr. 3,** 385

Traditions. *Traditions enrich special celebrations as well as our daily lives.* See Classified Index: Folk and Traditional Music; Holiday and Seasonal Music; Multicultural Materials; Patriotic Music.

Travel. *Trips to places old and new can bring adventure.*
Achshav (Now), **Gr. 4,** 112
Adobe Buildings in Taos Pueblo, New Mexico (architecture), **Gr. 2,** 155
American Salute by M. Gould, **Gr. 5,** 36
Angelina, **Gr. 6,** 8
Antarctica by P. Winter (listening), **Gr. 2,** 110
Arirang (Korean folk song) (song), **Gr. 5,** 50, (listening), **Gr. 5,** 53
Arre, mi burrito (Gid'yup, Little Burro), **Gr. 1,** T257
Away for Rio, **Gr. 2,** 170
Ballad of the Underground Railroad, The, **Gr. 5,** 145, (partner song), **Gr. 5,** 154
Bamboo, **Gr. 4,** 218
Boll Weevil, **Gr. 3,** 171
Bound No'th Blues by L. Hughes (poem), **Gr. 5,** 181
Bus, The, **Gr. K,** T137
Button, You Must Wander, **Gr. 2,** 176
Car Song by W. Guthrie (listening), **Gr. K,** T135
Caribbean Amphibian, **Gr. 1,** T294
Carnegie Hall (architecture), **Gr. 7,** 100
Cathedral and Government Palace in Guadalajara (architecture), **Gr. 5,** 189
Charlie, **Gr. 3,** 208
Choo, Choo, Ch'Boogie, **Gr. 6,** 180
City Blues, **Gr. 5,** 278
City Life, **Gr. 3,** 341
City Traffic by B. Franco (poem), **Gr. 2,** 328
Cliffs of Doneen, The, **Gr. 5,** 46
Coasts of High Barbary, The, **Gr. 6,** 329
Columbus Sailed with Three Ships, **Gr. 2,** 344
Cumberland Gap, **Gr. 3,** 99
Damdama Sahib Temple (architecture), **Gr. 6,** 225
Dandansoy, **Gr. 6,** 356
Debka Kurdit (Yemeni folk dance) (listening), **Gr. 4,** 236
December: Sleighride from *Calendar Collection* by J. Lang Zaimont (listening), **Gr. 1,** T128
Derby Ram, The, **Gr. 4,** 259
Doing the Latest Rag, **Gr. 6,** 314
Down at the Twist and Shout, **Gr. 4,** 308
Dreamers, **Gr. 5,** 430
Eight Bells, **Gr. 4,** 281
El barquito (The Tiny Boat), **Gr. 4,** 214
El quelite (The Village), **Gr. 4,** 362
El tren (The Train), **Gr. 2,** 326
En roulant ma boule (As I Roll My Ball), **Gr. 3,** 100
Engine, Engine Number Nine, **Gr. 2,** 13

Erie Canal, **Gr. 5,** 132
Erie Canal at Little Falls, New York by W. Rickarby Miller (fine art), **Gr. 5,** 133
Follow Your Dream, **Gr. 7,** 207
Galop from *The Comedians* by D. Kabalevsky (listening), **Gr. 4,** 254
Ghost Ship, The, **Gr. 6,** 323
Git Along, Little Dogies, **Gr. 6,** 284
Goin' Home, **Gr. 5,** 108
Going Over the Sea, **Gr. 2,** 216
Haere Ra (Now Is the Hour), **Gr. 5,** 151
Hallelujah, Get On Board, **Gr. 5,** 345
Happy Wanderer, The, **Gr. 3,** 18
Harlech Castle in Wales, Great Britain (architecture), **Gr. 2,** 141
Hill an' Gully, **Gr. 5,** 250
Hitori, **Gr. 4,** 345
I Am a Little Tugboat by C. Huffman (poem), **Gr. K,** T144
I Have a Car, **Gr. 3,** 252
I Wandered Lonely as a Cloud by W. Wordsworth (poem), **Gr. 7,** 125
I'm Going to Georgia, **Gr. 6,** 244
Jamaica Farewell, **Gr. 3,** 156
Jamaica Farewell by I. Burgie (listening), **Gr. 4,** 73
Japanese country house (architecture), **Gr. 6,** 145
Jingle at the Window, **Gr. 3,** 268
Jó Ashílá (Traveling Together) (Navajo song) (song and listening), **Gr. 5,** 224
John Kanaka, **Gr. 5,** 249
Journey, A (speech piece), **Gr. 4,** 14
Kettle Valley Line, The, **Gr. 4,** 348
King's Land, **Gr. 2,** 257
LA Concert Hall (architecture), **Gr. 7,** 100
Little Blue Truck, **Gr. K,** T136
Little Red Caboose, **Gr. 1,** T97
Little Train of the Caipira, The, from *Bachianas Brasileiras No. 2* by H. Villa-Lobos (listening), **Gr. K,** T142
Loch Lomond, **Gr. 5,** 138
Mississippi Mud (American folk song) (listening), **Gr. 6,** 65
Modern Dragon, A (speech piece), **Gr. 4,** 98
Moldau, The, from *Má Vlast* by B. Smetana (listening), **Gr. 7,** 219
Movin' Right Along, **Gr. 3,** 124
Music from Bali (gamelan ensemble) (listening), **Gr. 1,** T142
My Horses Ain't Hungry, **Gr. 3,** 278
Myerson Hall (architecture), **Gr. 7,** 100
New Colossus, The, by E. Lazarus (poem), **Gr. 7,** 187
Noah's Ark by E. Hicks (fine art), **Gr. 4,** 131
O, Desayo, **Gr. 6,** 50
O, The Train's Off the Track, **Gr. 3,** 176
Oh, Susanna, **Gr. 3,** 153
Old Ark's A-Moverin', **Gr. 4,** 130
Oleanna, **Gr. 3,** 144
Orange Blossom Special, **Gr. 6,** 33
Oro, My Bodeen, **Gr. 4,** 279
Over the Sea to Skye, **Gr. 4,** 344
Page's Train, **Gr. 4,** 246
Path to the Moon, **Gr. 5,** 368
Puff, the Magic Dragon, **Gr. 2,** 54
Push Boat Song, **Gr. 4,** 266

Thematic Index (continued)

Railroad Blues by F. Stowers (listening), **Gr. 2,** 327
Red Iron Ore, **Gr. 6,** 134
Ride Like the Wind, **Gr. 5,** 130
Ride on the Wind, **Gr. 6,** 326
Ride the Train, **Gr. K,** T144
Riding in the Buggy, **Gr. 3,** 131
Route 66 by B. Troup (listening), **Gr. 7,** 191
Salamanca Market, **Gr. 6,** 247
Sammy Sackett, **Gr. 2,** 146
Sesame Street Theme, **Gr. 1,** T298
Ship Ahoy, **Gr. 3,** 314
Ship in Distress, The, **Gr. 6,** 211
Shope, Shope (Oh, Shope, Shope), **Gr. 5,** 220
Sounds of Africa, The, by Wandile (poem), **Gr. 5,** 74
Stevedore's Song, **Gr. 3,** 127
Sydney Opera House (architecture), **Gr. 7,** 100
Take Me Out to the Ball Game, **Gr. 2,** 56
Taking Off by M. Green (poem), **Gr. K,** T134
Taos July by J. A. Fleck (fine art), **Gr. 2,** 155
Temple of Neptune and Basilica of Paestum (architecture),
    Gr. 7, 114
This Land Is Your Land, **Gr. 4,** 146
This Train (African American spiritual) (song and listening),
    Gr. 4, 343
Tower of London (architecture), **Gr. 6,** 287
Train in Coal Town by J. Savitsky (fine art), **Gr. 2,** 13
Train Is A-Coming, **Gr. 4,** 270
Trains at Night by F. M. Frost (poem), **Gr. 4,** 246
Travel by E. St. Vincent Millay (poem), **Gr. K,** T144
Troika, **Gr. 6,** 230
Turn the Glasses Over, **Gr. 3,** 260
Two in a Boat (American folk song) (listening), **Gr. 3,** 316
Wabash Cannonball, The, **Gr. 6,** 30
Waiting for Life, **Gr. 6,** 292
Wayfaring Stranger, **Gr. 6,** 283
We're Sailing Down the River, **Gr. 2,** 166
Wells Fargo Wagon, The, **Gr. 5,** 303
Wheels, Wheels, Wheels by N. White Carlstrom (poem),
    Gr. 1, T106
When I First Came to This Land, **Gr. 3,** 28
When Johnny Comes Marching Home (song), **Gr. 5,** 34,
    (traditional) (listening), **Gr. 7,** 168
Whup! Jamboree (English sea chantey) (listening), **Gr. 6,** 318

Water. *Watery places are a special world of wonder.*

Baby Beluga, **Gr. 2,** 26
Birth and Dance of the Mayfly, The, from *The Spider's Feast*
    by A. Roussel (listening), **Gr. K,** T76
Bobby Shafto, **Gr. K,** T265
Caranguejo (The Crab), **Gr. 2,** 306
Colorful Dragon Boat, **Gr. K,** T328
Down by the Bay, **Gr. 1,** T48
Four White Horses, **Gr. 2,** 300
Horses of the Sea, The, by C. Rossetti (poem), **Gr. 1,** T179
Hourtide by E. H. Potthast (fine art), **Gr. 1,** T374
I Chih ha Ma (Frogs), **Gr. 2,** 186
I'd Like to Be a Lighthouse by R. Field (poem), **Gr. 1,** T238
It's Possible, **Gr. 2,** 281
Merrily, We Roll Along, **Gr. K,** T110

Part of Your World, **Gr. 2,** 294
Propel, Propel, Propel, **Gr. K,** T275
Rain, Rain, Go Away, **Gr. 1,** T259
Romper, Stomper, and Boo (traditional story), **Gr. 1,** T36
Row, Row, Row, **Gr. K,** T274
There's a Hole in the Middle of the Sea, **Gr. 1,** T178
Water Lilies by C. Monet (fine art), **Gr. K,** T138

Wishes. *Hopes and dreams for ourselves, our loved ones, and our world can come true at unexpected times.*

All Night, All Day, **Gr. 1,** T232
How Does Your Garden Grow?, **Gr. 1,** T144
I'd Like to Be a Lighthouse by R. Field (poem), **Gr. 1,** T238
Love Grows One by One, **Gr. 1,** T202
Part of Your World, **Gr. 2,** 294
Puff, the Magic Dragon, **Gr. 2,** 54
Shrimp Boats (excerpt) by P. Howard and P. Weston (song),
    Gr. 2, 179, (listening), **Gr. 2,** 178
Star Light, Star Bright, **Gr. 1,** T258
This Little Light of Mine, **Gr. 1,** T238

Work. *Music can help us work together.*

African Postal Workers (listening), **Gr. 7,** 147
All Work Together, **Gr. K,** T12
Allá en el rancho grande (My Ranch), **Gr. 5,** 66
Apple Picker's Reel, **Gr. 2,** 343
Assembly Required by G. Kozak (listening), **Gr. 2,** 36
Bambini Giocando by C. Portunari (fine art), **Gr. 3,** 231
Barcas de Pesca by G. Wells-Hess (fine art), **Gr. 5,** 167
Best That I Can Be!, The, **Gr. K,** T48
By the Singing Water, **Gr. 5,** 270
Chag Asif (Harvest Time), **Gr. 3,** 360
Chairs to Mend, **Gr. 4,** 272
Cobbler, Cobbler, Mend My Shoe, **Gr. K,** T169
Cobbler, The, by E. Chafee (poem), **Gr. K,** T255
Coffee Break, **Gr. 8,** 241
Company Way, The, **Gr. 8,** 244
Cotton-Eye Joe (song), **Gr. 4,** 52, (countermelody),
    Gr. 4, 53
Daydreams on a Subway Train by P. M. Fagan (poem),
    Gr. 8, 84
Doney Gal, **Gr. 6,** 115
El zapatero (The Cobbler), **Gr. 2,** 138
Erie Canal, **Gr. 5,** 132
Garden Song, **Gr. 2,** 236
Gathering Apples by L. Karcsay (fine art), **Gr. 3,** 25
Guitar Man, The, **Gr. 3,** 138
Happy Farmer, The, from *Album for the Young* by
    R. Schumann (listening), **Gr. K,** T209
Harvest, **Gr. 2,** 342
Harvesters, The, by P. Brueghel (fine art), **Gr. 4,** 365
Heave-Ho, Me Laddies, **Gr. 4,** 258
Henry Ford, **Gr. 7,** 244
How to Succeed, **Gr. 8,** 237
I Am a Little Tugboat by C. Huffman (poem), **Gr. K,** T144
I Made a Valentine, **Gr. K,** T333
I's the B'y, **Gr. 3,** 13
Individual Career Mosaic (montage) (listening), **Gr. 8,** 190
It's Only Monday by C. Judah-Lauder (listening), **Gr. 8,** 14

Thematic Index (continued)

It's the Hard-Knock Life, **Gr. 4,** 293

Ja posejah lubenice (I Planted Watermelons), **Gr. 2,** 316

Jack Was Ev'ry Bit a Sailor, **Gr. 6,** 170

Jede, jede, poštovský panáček (Riding, Riding, Is Mr. Postman), **Gr. 6,** 226

John Henry, **Gr. 5,** 146

John Kanaka, **Gr. 5,** 249

Johnny Works with One Hammer, **Gr. 1,** T96

Largo al factotum from *Il Barbiere di Siviglia* by G. Rossini (listening), **Gr. 2,** 217

Lead Man Holler by I. Burgie, **Gr. 7,** 148

Let's Think of Something to Do, **Gr. K,** T270

Los trabajadores agricolas (The Farmers) from *Estancia* by A. Ginastera (listening), **Gr. 6,** 116

Machine from Symphony No. 5 by W. Bolcom (listening), **Gr. 8,** 51

Main Lighthouse (architecture), **Gr. 5,** 5

Mama, Bake the Johnnycake, Christmas Comin', **Gr. K,** T318

March Past of the Kitchen Utensils from *The Wasps* by R. Vaughan Williams (listening), **Gr. 3,** 247

Marvin's Music's Midnight Music Sale Jingle by B. Hardesty (listening), **Gr. 8,** 223

Mill Song, The, **Gr. 2,** 52

Mill, The, by R. van Rijn (fine art), **Gr. 2,** 53

Modern Major General, A, from *The Pirates of Penzance* by W. S. Gilbert and A. Sullivan (listening), **Gr. 6,** 56

Moulinet (Polka) Op. 57 by J. Strauss (listening), **Gr. 2,** 53

Night Herding Song, **Gr. 4,** 110

Oh, A-Hunting We Will Go, **Gr. K,** T62

Palace of Finance, The, Santiago, Chile (architecture), **Gr. 8,** 90

Pat Works on the Railway (song) **Gr. 4,** 86, (Orff version) (listening), **Gr. 1,** T144

Pick a Bale of Cotton, **Gr. 6,** 254

Pitty Patty Polt (nursery rhyme) (rhythmic pattern), **Gr. 1,** T180

Poets to Come by W. Whitman (poem), **Gr. 7,** 231

Promise of Living, The, from *The Tender Land* by A. Copland (listening), **Gr. 3,** 77

Railroad Blues by F. Stowers (listening), **Gr. 2,** 327

Return of the Hunters by P. Brueghel (fine art), **Gr. 6,** 133

Riqui Ran (Sawing Song), **Gr. 2,** 21

Row, Row, Row, **Gr. K,** T274

Sailor, Sailor on the Sea, **Gr. 2,** 262

Sheep Shearing, **Gr. 2,** 102

Shepherd, Shepherd, **Gr. 3,** 56

Shibolet Basadeh (Wheat in the Field), **Gr. 6,** 424

Shrimp Boats (excerpt) by P. Howard and P. Weston (song), **Gr. 2,** 179, (listening), **Gr. 2,** 178

Sixteen Tons by M. Travis (song), **Gr. 7,** 151, (Tennessee Ernie Ford) (listening), **Gr. 7,** 150

Sorcerer's Apprentice, The (excerpt) by P. Dukas (listening), **Gr. 4,** 116

Speedy Delivery, **Gr. K,** T279

Spinning Song by A. Ellmenreich (listening), **Gr. 3,** 128

Stevedore's Song, **Gr. 3,** 127

Success, **Gr. 7,** 241

Tailor, Tailor (traditional poem), **Gr. 1,** T132

Tejedoras by J. Coché Mendoza (fine art), **Gr. 4,** 101

There Was a Jolly Miller, **Gr. 6,** 250

Tinker, Tailor, **Gr. 1,** T131

Turkish Carpet (art), **Gr. 5,** 135

Twee emmertjes (traditional spinning song) (listening), **Gr. 4,** 212

Ujima (Collective Work and Responsibility), **Gr. 5,** 427

Untitled (California Vaquero) by F. Remington, **Gr. 5,** 68

Untitled (Cattle Drive) by F. Remington (fine art), **Gr. 3,** 114, **Gr. 6,** 114

Untitled (Haydn Playing with an Ensemble) by Anonymous (fine art), **Gr. 8,** 120

Untitled (Two Fisherman and a Boy Gossiping) by Anonymous (fine art), **Gr. 6,** 171

Wang Ü Ger (Chinese fishing song), **Gr. 3,** 190

Watermill in Christiania, A, by L. Gurlitt (fine art), **Gr. 4,** 169

Willum, **Gr. 1,** T19

A

ACTION SONGS. *See also* Movement

A la rueda rueda ('Round and 'Round), **Gr. 1,** T240
Acka Backa, **Gr. 1,** T256
A-Rovin', **Gr. 6,** 319
Billy, **Gr. 3,** 7
Bop 'til You Drop, **Gr. 6,** 87
Buffalo Dance Entrance Song, **Gr. 3,** 325
Charlie Over the Ocean, **Gr. 1,** T75
Cheers, **Gr. 7,** 34
Circle 'Round the Zero, **Gr. 3,** 267
Circle of Life (Listening), **Gr. 7,** 85
Come and Sing Together, **Gr. 6,** 281
Come On-A My House (Listening), **Gr. 7,** 139
Conga, **Gr. 6,** 34
Dance, Dance, Dance!, **Gr. 2,** 5
Dancing in the Street, **Gr. 6,** 84
Diou Shou Juan'er (Hide the Handkerchief), **Gr. 1,** T212
Doing the Latest Rag, **Gr. 6,** 314
Down by the Bay, **Gr. 1,** T48
Dreidel Spin, **Gr. 1,** T348
Eency Weency Spider, **Gr. K,** T8; (La pequeñita araña), **Gr. K,** T9
El florón, **Gr. 3,** 46
El jarabe tapatío (Listening), **Gr. 7,** 59
Go, Go, Go, **Gr. K,** T276
Gogo, **Gr. K,** T188
Golden Ring Around the Susan Girl, **Gr. 3,** 264
Gonna Build a Mountain from *Stop the World—I Want to Get Off* by A. Newley and L. Bricusse (song and listening), **Gr. 6,** 4–5
Happy Birthday, **Gr. K,** T347
Head and Shoulders, **Gr. K,** T238
Hi! My Name Is Joe!, **Gr. 1,** T220
Hokey Pokey, **Gr. K,** T68
Hop, Hop, Hop, **Gr. K,** T197
I Like Spinach, **Gr. 1,** T163
I'm Gonna Sit at the Welcome Table, **Gr. 6,** 416
If I Had a Hammer, **Gr. 6,** 174
If You're Happy, **Gr. K,** T6
It's So Good to See You, **Gr. K,** T86
It's Such a Good Feeling, **Gr. K,** T282
It's You I Like, **Gr. K,** T280
Jede, jede poštovský panáček (Riding, Riding, Is Mr. Postman), **Gr. 6,** 226
Jikel' Emaweni (Throw It Down the Slope), **Gr. 6,** 70
Johnny's Flea, **Gr. 1,** T158
Juan Pirulero (Listening), **Gr. 1,** T152
Jump, Jim Joe, **Gr. 1,** T89
Kobuta, **Gr. 1,** T167
Kuma San, **Gr. 3,** 244
La bamba, **Gr. 3,** 236
Lead Man Holler, **Gr. 7,** 148
Let It Roll, **Gr. 6,** 124
Let's Go Dancing, **Gr. 3,** 196

Let's Think of Something to Do, **Gr. K,** T270
Limbo Rock, **Gr. 3,** 232
Listen to the Music, **Gr. 6,** 62
Little Black Bug, **Gr. 1,** T166
Little Sally Walker, **Gr. 3,** 105
Looby Loo, **Gr. 1,** T262
Lucy Locket, **Gr. 1,** T253
Mardi Gras Mambo, **Gr. 7,** 88–89
Miss Mary Mack, **Gr. 1,** T15
Mizuguruma (Water Wheel), **Gr. 1,** T260
My Mama's Calling Me, **Gr. 1,** T55
My Thumbs Are Starting to Wiggle, **Gr. K,** T35
Ɔboɔ Asi Me Nsa, **Gr. K,** T159
Old King Glory, **Gr. 1,** T217
Ole La'u Papa e, **Gr. 6,** 91
One Finger, One Thumb, **Gr. K,** T38
One Little Elephant, **Gr. 1,** T194
One Potato, Two Potato, **Gr. 3,** 267
One, Two, Three, Four, Five, **Gr. 1,** T265
One, Two, Three, Four, **Gr. 1,** T124
One, Two, Tie My Shoe, **Gr. K,** T151
Only Time (Listening), **Gr. 7,** 142
Peace and Quiet, **Gr. K,** T278
Peanut Butter, **Gr. 1,** T218
Pick a Bale of Cotton, **Gr. 6,** 254
Propel, Propel, Propel, **Gr. K,** T275
Punchinella, **Gr. 1,** T215
Put Your Finger in the Air, **Gr. K,** T230
Respect (Listening), **Gr. 7,** 6
Ride on the Wind, **Gr. 6,** 326
Ring Around the Rosy, **Gr. K,** T246
Rise, Sally, Rise, **Gr. 1,** T162
Rock Around the Clock, **Gr. 6,** 234
Roll de Ole Chariot Along, **Gr. 6,** 243
Rondo all'Ongarese (Listening), **Gr. 7,** 115
Round and Round, **Gr. 6,** 104
Row, Row, Row, **Gr. K,** T274
Sara Watashi (Plate Passing), **Gr. 1,** T68
Scraping Up Sand, **Gr. 6,** 248
Sesame Street, **Gr. 1,** T299
Shake My Sillies Out, **Gr. K,** T175
Simon Says, **Gr. 3,** 4
Sing Hosanna, **Gr. 6,** 362
Slap That Bass, **Gr. 6,** 146
Soup, Soup!, **Gr. 1,** T359
Speedy Delivery, **Gr. K,** T279
Stamping Land, **Gr. K,** T24
Stars and Stripes Forever, The (Listening), **Gr. 7,** 196
Time to Sing, **Gr. K,** T16
Tinker, Tailor, **Gr. 1,** T130
Tititorea, **Gr. 3,** 174
Touch Your Shoulders, **Gr. K,** T254
Uga Uga Uga (Cake, Cake, Cake!), **Gr. 1,** T313
Wachet auf (Waken Now), **Gr. 6,** 259
Walk by the River, **Gr. 6,** 74

We Go Together, **Gr. 7**, 158–59
When I Sing, **Gr. 6**, 44
Won't You Be My Neighbor?, **Gr. K**, T268
You Sing for Me, **Gr. 6**, 106
Zudio, **Gr. 7**, 165

B

BIOGRAPHIES

activist
Parks, Rosa, **Gr. 3**, E

amateurs
Truman, Harry S., **Gr. 8**, 40

arrangers
Carter, Roland, **Gr. 5**, 117
Hogan, Moses, **Gr. 5**, 144
Rex, Kristian, **Gr. K**, T107

artist manager
Canning, Kathy, **Gr. 2**, 41

artists
Brueghel, Pieter, **Gr. 4**, 365; **Gr. 6**, 133
Cassatt, Mary, **Gr. 6**, 47
Chagall, Marc, **Gr. 4**, 68, 375
de Caullery, Louis, **Gr. 6**, 100
Degas, Edgar, **Gr. 2**, 25
Dürer, Albrecht, **Gr. 4**, 177
Eitaku, Kobayashi, **Gr. K**, T31
Fabergé, Peter Carl, **Gr. 4**, 153
Ginat, Judith Yellin, **Gr. 4**, 112
Goldberg, Rube, **Gr. 3**, 182
Gray, Harold, **Gr. 4**, 305
Gurlitt, Louis, **Gr. 4**, 169
Hasui, Kawase, **Gr. 2**, 77
Hewson, Marg, **Gr. 4**, 48
Hicks, Edward, **Gr. 4**, 131
Hiroshige, Ando, **Gr. 2**, 101
Leonard, Limosin, **Gr. 6**, 100
Lu, Zhen-Huan, **Gr. K**, T302
Mallett, Keith, **Gr. 4**, 35
Mendoza, Julian Coché, **Gr. 4**, 101
Michelangelo, **Gr. 6**, 100
Mnev, Vladimir, **Gr. 6**, 425
Monet, Claude, **Gr. K**, T139; **Gr. 2**, 271
Mount, William Sidney, **Gr. 6**, 96
Picasso, Pablo, **Gr. 4**, 8
Remington, Frederic, **Gr. 2**, 67; **Gr. 6**, 115
Renkes, Saelon, **Gr. 2**, 89
Rijn, Rembrandt van, **Gr. 2**, 53
Savitsky, Jack, **Gr. 2**, 13
Tait, Agnes, **Gr. K**, T310
Tanner, Henry O., **Gr. 3**, 150
Teniers II, David, **Gr. 6**, 98
Tiepolo, Giovanni Domenico, **Gr. 2**, 144
Van Gogh, Vincent, **Gr. K**, T66, T82
Warhol, Andy, **Gr. 8**, 227

authors
Milne, A.A., **Gr. K**, T204
Tolkien, J.R.R., **Gr. K**, T217

composers
Adler, Richard, **Gr. 6**, 166
Ahrens, Lynn, **Gr. 6**, 305
Anderson, Leroy, **Gr. K**, T223; **Gr. 2**, 132
Anderson, R. Alex, **Gr. 6**, 411
Arbeau, Thoinot, **Gr. 6**, 100
Arlen, Harold, **Gr. K**, T61
Ashman, Howard, **Gr. 5**, 125
Bach, Johann Sebastian, **Gr. 3**, 178; **Gr. 4**, 61; **Gr. 6**, 64, 128
Bacharach, Burt, **Gr. 5**, 230
Barris, Harry, **Gr. 6**, 65
Bart, Lionel, **Gr. 3**, 335
Bartók, Béla, **Gr. 1**, T245; **Gr. 5**, 221
Beach, Amy, **Gr. K**, T140; **Gr. 2**, 26
Beethoven, Ludwig van, **Gr. 2**, 225; **Gr. 4**, 242; **Gr. 5**, 102; **Gr. 8**, 20
Belafonte, Harry, **Gr. 5**, 208
Berlin, Irving, **Gr. 6**, 130
Berlioz, Hector, **Gr. 6**, 121
Bernstein, Leonard, **Gr. 6**, 81
Berry, Chuck, **Gr. 6**, 124
Bizet, Georges, **Gr. 1**, T231; **Gr. 7**, 122
Boulanger, Lili, **Gr. 6**, 253
Bremer, Carolyn, **Gr. 6**, 201
Bricusse, Leslie, **Gr. 6**, 4–5
Britten, Benjamin, **Gr. 3**, 262; **Gr. 4**, 32; **Gr. 5**, 228
Burch, Sharon, **Gr. 4**, 395
Burgie, Irving, **Gr. 6**, 9
Cage, John, **Gr. 6**, 32
Caillet, Lucien, **Gr. 5**, 97
Calderón, Juan Carlos, **Gr. 4**, 64
Cavanaugh, James, **Gr. 6**, 65
Chaminade, Cécile, **Gr. 2**, 262
Chapin, Tom, **Gr. 6**, 194
Charnin, Martin, **Gr. 4**, 305
Chávez, Carlos, **Gr. 2**, 61
Cherubini, Luigi, **Gr. 6**, 256
Chopin, Frédéric, **Gr. 2**, 136
Coleman, Cy, **Gr. 4**, 115
Coltrane, John, **Gr. 6**, 157
Copland, Aaron, **Gr. 2**, 14, 378; **Gr. 5**, 152; **Gr. 6**, 77
Cortázar, Ernesto, **Gr. 5**, 189
Debussy, Claude, **Gr. K**, T337
Denver, John, **Gr. 6**, 21
Desmond, Paul, **Gr. 5**, 212
di Lasso, Orlando, **Gr. K**, T103
Dukas, Paul, **Gr. 4**, 116
Dun, Tan, **Gr. 6**, 28
Dvořák, Antonín, **Gr. K**, T109; **Gr. 5**, 106
Dylan, Bob, **Gr. 5**, 204
Elgar, Edward, **Gr. K**, T53; **Gr. 1**, T233
Ellington, Edward "Duke," **Gr. 4**, 232; **Gr. 6**, 164
Emerson, Roger, **Gr. 5**, 410
Esperón, Manuel, **Gr. 5**, 189
Estefan, Gloria, **Gr. 5**, 15
Eto, Leonard, **Gr. 6**, 16
Eyck, Jacob van, **Gr. 4**, 224
Fauré, Gabriel, **Gr. K**, T149
Feliciano, José, **Gr. 5**, 420

Classified Index

Fernández, Oscar Lorenzo, **Gr. 3**, 265; **Gr. 7**, 203
Flaherty, Stephen, **Gr. 6**, 305
Flores del Campo, Francisco, **Gr. 6**, 61
Forster, John, **Gr. 6**, 194
Foster, Stephen, **Gr. 3**, 153
Freedman, Robert, **Gr. 5**, 208
Gabrieli, Giovanni, **Gr. 6**, 121
Gershwin, George, **Gr. 1**, T168; **Gr. 5**, 187; **Gr. 6**, 146
Gillespie, Avon, **Gr. 6**, 275
Gilmore, Patrick, S., **Gr. 5**, 34
Ginastera, Alberto, **Gr. 6**, 81, 116
Glass, Philip, **Gr. 4**, 144
Gluck, Christoph, **Gr. 2**, 25
Gould, Morton, **Gr. 5**, 36; **Gr. 7**, 170
Grainger, Percy, **Gr. 2**, 17; **Gr. 6**, 201
Grieg, Edvard, **Gr. 2**, 105; **Gr. 3**, 144; **Gr. 5**, 192
Gruber, Franz, **Gr. 6**, 413
Guthrie, Woody, **Gr. K**, T135; **Gr. 4**, 147
Handel, George Frideric, **Gr. 1**, T263; **Gr. 3**, 26; **Gr. 6**, 81, 247
Handy, W.C., **Gr. 3**, 337
Hayden, Franz Joseph, **Gr. 3**, 155; **Gr. 5**, 247
Hays, Lee, **Gr. 6**, 174
Henderson, Bill, **Gr. 6**, 44
Hensel, Fanny Mendelssohn, **Gr. 7**, 125
Herbert, Victor, **Gr. K**, T317
Holly, Buddy, **Gr. 6**, 124
Holst, Gustav, **Gr. 6**, 196
Humperdinck, Engelbert, **Gr. K**, T180
Ibert, Jacques, **Gr. K**, T183
Ives, Charles, **Gr. 5**, 282
Jobim, Antonio Carlos, **Gr. 4**, 92
Joplin, Scott, **Gr. 6**, 110
Kabalevsky, Dimitri, **Gr. 4**, 254
Kay, Hershy, **Gr. 1**, T239
Keetman, Gunild, **Gr. 1**, T234
Khachaturian, Aram, **Gr. 1**, T259
Kidjo, Angelique, **Gr. 4**, 209
King, Carole, **Gr. 6**, 418
Kozak, Gregory, **Gr. 2**, 36
Lane, Burton, **Gr. 6**, 207
Larsen, Libby, **Gr. 6**, 218, 220; **Gr. 8**, 113, 154
Lecuona, Margarita, **Gr. 2**, 20
Ledbetter, Huddie, **Gr. 5**, 176
Luting, He, **Gr. 2**, 99
Marley, Bob, **Gr. 3**, 204
Marx, Aaron, **Gr. 6**, 189
Mayo, Aimee, **Gr. 8**, 81
McCartney, Paul, **Gr. K**, T153
McChesney, Kevin, **Gr. 6**, 121
Menken, Alan, **Gr. 5**, 125
Miller, Glenn, **Gr. 3**, 12
Mills, Alan, **Gr. K**, T27
Mizzy, Vic, **Gr. 8**, 145
Monk, Meredith, **Gr. 6**, 263
Monroe, Bill, **Gr. 5**, 23
Mozart, Wolfgang Amadeus, **Gr. K**, T176; **Gr. 2**, 153; **Gr. 3**, 168; **Gr. 6**, 186; **Gr. 8**, 219
Mussorgsky, Modest, **Gr. 1**, T150
Newley, Anthony, **Gr. 6**, 4

Offenbach, Jacques, **Gr. K**, T179; **Gr. 6**, 265
Orff, Carl, **Gr. 2**, 30
Orozco, José-Luis, **Gr. K**, T341
Otis, Johnny, **Gr. 6**, 87
Pachelbel, Johann, **Gr. 4**, 16
Perkins, Carl, **Gr. 6**, 236
Pixinguinha (Alfredo da Rocha Vianna, Jr.), **Gr. 4**, 129
Ponce, Manuel Maria, **Gr. 8**, 127
Praetorius, Michael, **Gr. 4**, 177, 283
Prokofiev, Sergei, **Gr. 1**, T91; **Gr. 3**, 224, 225; **Gr. 4**, 181; **Gr. 6**, 160
Puccini, Giacomo, **Gr. 5**, 64; **Gr. 6**, 257
Puente, Tito, **Gr. 5**, 68
Purcell, Henry, **Gr. 1**, T176; **Gr. 2**, 145; **Gr. 6**, 121; **Gr. 8**, 5
Ramzy, Hossam, **Gr. 6**, 35
Ravel, Maurice, **Gr. 1**, T236
Reale, Robert, **Gr. 1**, T283
Rimsky-Korsakov, Nicolai, **Gr. K**, T259
Rodgers, Richard, **Gr. 4**, 108
Rodrigo, Joaquín, **Gr. 4**, 13
Roland, Edward, **Gr. 6**, 287
Rose, David, **Gr. 3**, 228
Ross, Jerry, **Gr. 6**, 166
Rossini, Gioacchino, **Gr. 3**, 64; **Gr. 6**, 152
Rouse, Steve, **Gr. 8**, 235
Rzewski, Frederic, **Gr. 8**, 93
Saint-Saëns, Camille, **Gr. K**, T194; **Gr. 2**, 253
Schafer, R. Murray, **Gr. 4**, 29
Schubert, Franz, **Gr. 6**, 344
Schumann, Robert, **Gr. K**, T209; **Gr. 2**, 76; **Gr. 6**, 81; **Gr. 8**, 117
Scruggs. Earl, **Gr. 6**, 140, 375
Seeger, Pete, **Gr. 5**, 287; **Gr. 6**, 174
Siegmeister, Elie, **Gr. 2**, 67
Smetana, Bedřich, **Gr. 5**, 271; **Gr. 6**, 229
Sondheim, Stephen, **Gr. 6**, 204
Sontonga, Enoch Mankayi, **Gr. 6**, 341
Sousa, John Philip, **Gr. 2**, 339; **Gr. 3**, 281; **Gr. 7**, 37
Sowande, Fela, **Gr. 2**, 97
Stevens, Cat, **Gr. 4**, 22
Strauss, Johann, Sr., **Gr. K**, T177
Stravinsky, Igor, **Gr. 4**, 191
Strouse, Charles, **Gr. 4**, 305
Sullivan, Arthur S., **Gr. 6**, 56
Taylor, Billy, **Gr. 1**, T241
Tchaikovsky, Piotr Ilyich, **Gr. K**, T311; **Gr. 4**, 173, 287; **Gr. 5**, 281; **Gr. 6**, 81, 409
Thomson, Virgil, **Gr. K**, T27; **Gr. 4**, 274
Valdes, Gilberto, **Gr. 4**, 327
Verdi, Giuseppe, **Gr. 5**, 148; **Gr. 6**, 169
Villa-Lobos, Heitor, **Gr. K**, T143
Vivaldi, Antonio, **Gr. 2**, 73; **Gr. 6**, 402
Wagner, Richard, **Gr. 2**, 55
Waldteufel, Emil, **Gr. 1**, T344
Walton, William, **Gr. 5**, 280
Warren, Diane, **Gr. 5**, 14
Warren, Harry, **Gr. 6**, 182
Weavers, The, **Gr. 6**, 175
Williams, John, **Gr. 4**, 56

Williams, Ralph Vaughan, **Gr. 3**, 247; **Gr. 7**, 103
Willson, Meredith, **Gr. 5**, 295
Withers, Bill, **Gr. 6**, 151
Wyatt, Lorre, **Gr. 4**, 11
Yarrow, Peter, **Gr. 5**, 417
Yupanqui, Atahualpa, **Gr. 3**, 109
Zaimont, Judith Lang, **Gr. 1**, T128

conductors
Ginwala, Cyrus, **Gr. 8**, 170
Handel, George Frideric, **Gr. 3**, 26

disc jockeys
Freed, Alan, **Gr. 8**, 208

entertainment lawyer
Boyd, Gail, **Gr. 3**, 201

instrument inventor
Franklin, Benjamin, **Gr. 5**, 244

instrument maker
Smith, Paul Reed, **Gr. 8**, 98

instrument salesperson/repairperson
Kane, Jimmy, **Gr. 3**, 41

librettists
Meehan, Thomas, **Gr. 4**, 305

lyricists
Bart, Lionel, **Gr. 3**, 335
Bricusse, Leslie, **Gr. 6**, 4
Burgess, Lord (Irving Burgie), **Gr. 6**, 9, 154
Burgie, Irving (Lord Burgess), **Gr. 6**, 9, 154
Dubin, Al, **Gr. 6**, 182
Gallop, Sammy, **Gr. 3**, 226
Gershwin, Ira, **Gr. 5**, 187; **Gr. 6**, 146
Gilbert, William S., **Gr. 6**, 56
Grieg, Edvard, **Gr. 3**, 144
Howe, Julia Ward, **Gr. 6**, 389
Lerner, Alan Jay, **Gr. 6**, 207
Mohr, Josef, **Gr. 6**, 413
Newley, Anthony, **Gr. 6**, 4
Newton, John, **Gr. 5**, 18
Reale, Willie, **Gr. 1**, T283

master drummer
Ladzekpo, Kobla, **Gr. 5**, 72

music journalist
Zupko, Sarah, **Gr. 7**, 25

painters
Saint James, Synthia, **Gr. 5**, 429
Tsirah, Awa, **Gr. 5**, 445

patrons
Louis XIV, **Gr. 8**, 167

performers
Alabama, **Gr. 6**, 20
Anderson, Marion, **Gr. 5**, 330
Anderson, R. Alex, **Gr. 6**, 411
Armstrong, Louis, **Gr. 2**, 84; **Gr. 8**, 9
Beach Boys, The, **Gr. 5**, 307
Beatles, The, **Gr. 4**, 31
Belafonte, Harry, **Gr. 4**, 73
Bibb, Eric, **Gr. 7**, 17

Boni Puesi Choir, **Gr. 6**, 65
Brazeal Dennard Chorale, The, **Gr. 5**, 117
Britten, Benjamin, **Gr. 3**, 262
Brubeck, Dave, **Gr. 5**, 213
Chang, Sebastian, **Gr. 7**, 127
Chieftains, The, **Gr. 5**, 49
Clapton, Eric, **Gr. 7**, 140
Clooney, Rosemary, **Gr. 7**, 139
Cougat, Xavier, **Gr. 6**, 113
Criddle, Lauren, **Gr. 6**, 121
Cruz, Celia, **Gr. 4**, 228
da Vila, Martinho, **Gr. 8**, 45
Dalglish, Malcolm, **Gr. 4**, 55
Danko, Rick, **Gr. 5**, 84
Denver, John, **Gr. 7**, 221
Donehew, Karla, **Gr. 7**, 52
Dubac, Mark, **Gr. 6**, 81
Estefan, Gloria, **Gr. 6**, 34
Feliciano, José, **Gr. 5**, 420
Fitzgerald, Ella, **Gr. 6**, 165
Flatt, Lester, **Gr. 6**, 375
Ford, Tennessee Ernie, **Gr. 7**, 150
Frost, Lauren, **Gr. 3**, 354
Garcia, Pala, **Gr. 8**, 156
Handy, W.C., **Gr. 3**, 337
Help, Marilyn, **Gr. 1**, T70
Henderson, Bill, **Gr. 6**, 44
Hoey, John, **Gr. 6**, 41
Hurlburt, Sean, **Gr. 7**, 161
Ives, Burl, **Gr. 6**, 269
Jackson, Mahalia, **Gr. 8**, 31
Jackson, Patrick, **Gr. 6**, 81
Jenkins, Ella, **Gr. K**, T214
Johnson, Samuel, **Gr. 8**, 171
Joplin, Scott, **Gr. 6**, 110–112
Jordheim, Alisa, **Gr. 8**, 187
Kidjo, Angélique, **Gr. 7**, 226
King's Singers, The **Gr. 6**, 153
Kissin, Evgeny, **Gr. 2**, 224
Kleiton and Kledir, **Gr. 3**, 231
Kodo (Taiko ensemble), **Gr. 6**, 16
Larrocha, Alicia de, **Gr. 6**, 192
Ledbetter, Huddie, **Gr. 5**, 176
Lentz, Jarrod, **Gr. 7**, 78
Luces, Sir Cedrick, **Gr. 8**, 12
Ma, Yo-Yo, **Gr. 4**, 8
MacMorran, William, **Gr. 6**, 200
Makeba, Miriam, **Gr. 2**, 94; **Gr. 3**, 35
Marley, Bob, **Gr. 3**, 204
Masters of Harmony, The, **Gr. 6**, 65
McCartney, Paul, **Gr. K**, T153
McDonald, Jerry Thundercloud, **Gr. 3**, 52
McGrath, Bob, **Gr. K**, T107
Meyer, Edgar, **Gr. 6**, 149
Miller, Glenn, **Gr. 3**, 12
Milne, Bob, **Gr. 7**, 23
Miranda, Carmen, **Gr. 2**, 91
Mocedades, **Gr. 4**, 64
Monroe, Bill, **Gr. 6**, 375
Monroe, Bill, **Gr. 8**, 71

Moses Hogan Chorale, **Gr. 6**, 52
Mozart, Wolfgang Amadeus, **Gr. 3**, 168
Muckey, Matthew, **Gr. 6**, 40
Nakai, R. Carlos, **Gr. 5**, 26
Neely, Nathan, **Gr. 8**, 59
Nickel Creek, **Gr. 5**, 25
Nissman, Barbara, **Gr. 4**, 181
Ong, Lin, **Gr. 8**, 41
Perlman, Itzhak, **Gr. 8**, 137
Peter, Paul & Mary, **Gr. 6**, 24
Pila, Ben, **Gr. 7**, 216
Premo, Evan (From the Top), **Gr. 6**, 120
Price, Leontyne, **Gr. 2**, 117
Red Leaf Girls Choir, **Gr. 6**, 65
Robert Shaw Chorale, 3 **Gr. 6**, 18
Robeson, Paul, **Gr. 6**, 271
Rodgers, Eileen, **Gr. 8**, 186
Santana, Carlos, **Gr. 5**, 69
Scrap Arts Music, **Gr. 2**, 36
Seeger, Pete, **Gr. 5**, 287
Slawson, Brian, **Gr. 4**, 17
Sosa, Mercedes, **Gr. 3**, 108
Souliere, Jason, **Gr. 8**, 19
Sweet Honey in The Rock, **Gr. 2**, 47
Talens, Deanna, **Gr. 6**, 80
Tan, Lucy, **Gr. 6**, 160
Valens, Ritchie, **Gr. 6**, 382
Williams, Arlene Nofchissey, **Gr. 3**, 329
Withers, Bill, **Gr. 6**, 151
Yanjun, Hua, **Gr. K**, T114
Yarrow, Peter, **Gr. 2**, 54; **Gr. 5**, 417; **Gr. 7**, 92
York, Andrew, **Gr. 8**, 214
Yupanqui, Atahualpa, **Gr. 3**, 109

piano technician
Palmer, Judith, **Gr. 5**, 41

playwright
Ibsen, Henrik Johan, **Gr. 5**, 192

poets
Bennet, Rowena Bastin, **Gr. 4**, 99
Brothers Grimm, **Gr. 2**, 6
de la Mare, Walter, **Gr. K**, T104
Dickinson, Emily, **Gr. 3**, 166
Durham, Jimmie, **Gr. 4**, 206
Freire de Matos, Isabel, **Gr. 5**, 443
Frost, Robert, **Gr. 6**, 156
Harper, Francis Ellen Watkins, **Gr. 6**, 63
Hughes, Langston, **Gr. 4**, 234; **Gr. 6**, 162
Livingston, Myra Cohn, **Gr. 4**, 95
Merriam, Eve, **Gr. K**, T312
Norris, Leslie, **Gr. K**, T116
O'Neill, Mary, **Gr. 5**, 124
Prelutsky, Jack, **Gr. K**, T72, T183
Rosetti, Christina Georgina, **Gr. 2**, 137

priests
Succat, Maewyn (St. Patrick), **Gr. 3**, 390

record producer
Vandross, Luther, **Gr. 5**, 226

scholar
Lomax, Alan, **Gr. 7**, 55

teachers
Help, Marilyn, **Gr. 1**, T70, T72
Ritterling, Soojin Kim, **Gr. 5**, 51

writers
Lobel, Arnold, **Gr. 1**, T283
Reale, Willie, **Gr. 1**, T283

other
Chávez, César, **Gr. 5**, 431
Earhart, Amelia, **Gr. 5**, 431
King, Dr. Martin Luther, Jr., **Gr. 4**, 387; **Gr. 5**, 430
Tubman, Harriet, **Gr. 4**, 204

BROADWAY FOR KIDS. *See also* Performance
A Year With Frog and Toad Junior
Cookies, **Gr. 1**, T 277
Down the Hill, **Gr. 1**, T281
Snail With the Mail, **Gr. 1**, T275
Spring, **Gr. 1**, T273
Year With Frog and Toad, A, **Gr. 1**, T270; (reprise), **Gr. 1**, T282

Annie Junior
I Think I'm Gonna Like It Here, **Gr. 4**, 299
It's the Hard-Knock Life, **Gr. 4**, 293
N.Y.C., **Gr. 4**, 302
Tomorrow, **Gr. 4**, 295
You're Never Fully Dressed Without a Smile, **Gr. 4**, 304

How to Succeed in Business Without Really Trying
Brotherhood of Man, **Gr. 8**, 248
Coffee Break, **Gr. 8**, 245
Company Way, The, **Gr. 8**, 244
How to Succeed, **Gr. 8**, 237

Music Man Junior, The
Iowa Stubborn, **Gr. 5**, 293
Pick-a-Little/Goodnight Ladies, **Gr. 5**, 299
Rock Island, **Gr. 5**, 291
Seventy-Six Trombones, **Gr. 5**, 296
Wells Fargo Wagon, The, **Gr. 5**, 303

Once On This Island Junior, songs
Mama Will Provide, **Gr. 6**, 296
Waiting for Life, **Gr. 6**, 292
Why We Tell the Story, **Gr. 6**, 303

Ragtime
Atlantic City, **Gr. 7**, 248
Henry Ford, **Gr. 7**, 244
Night That Goldman Spoke, The, **Gr. 7**, 246
Ragtime, **Gr. 7**, 237
Ragtime Epilogue and Finale, **Gr. 7**, 250
Success, **Gr. 7**, 241

School House Rock Live! Junior
Interjections, **Gr. 3**, 303
Interplanet Janet, **Gr. 3**, 298
Preamble, The, **Gr. 3**, 293
Three Is a Magic Number, **Gr. 3**, 296

Seussical Junior
Green Eggs and Ham, **Gr. 2**, 284
Horton Hears a Who!, **Gr. 2**, 279
Horton Hears a Who! Two, **Gr. 2**, 280

Classified Index

Classified Index of Songs, Selected Concepts, Skills, and Activities (continued)

It's Possible, **Gr. 2,** 281
Oh, the Thinks You Can Think!, **Gr. 2,** 276
Seussical Mega-Mix, **Gr. 2,** 287

C

CANONS. *See* Form and Genre, canon

CAREERS. *See also* Biographies
agent, **Gr. 8,** 25, 194
arranger, **Gr. 5,** 104, **Gr. 7,** 153
choreographer, **Gr. 3,** 113
composer, **Gr. 7,** 52
conductor, **Gr. 3,** 106, 179; **Gr. 8,** 220
diction coach, **Gr. 7,** 120
director, **Gr. 7,** 182
entertainment lawyer, **Gr. 3,** 201; **Gr. 8,** 211
event planner, **Gr. 8,** 47
instrument maker, **Gr. 4,** 61; **Gr. 8,** 95
instrument salesperson/repairperson, **Gr. 3,** 41
lawyer, **Gr. 8,** 211
lyricist, **Gr. 7,** 192
manager, **Gr. 8,** 194
music company agent, **Gr. 8,** 25
music director of station (deejay), **Gr. 5,** 201
music librarian, **Gr. 4,** 41
music producer for children's programs, **Gr. 4,** 201
music teacher, **Gr. 8,** 164
music technician, **Gr. 8,** 107
musical careers, **Gr. 4,** 335
musical director, **Gr. 8,** 75
musicologist, **Gr. 7,** 78
opera singer, **Gr. 5,** 65
performers, **Gr. 7,** 23, 102; **Gr. 8,** 184–209
piano technician, **Gr. 5,** 41
record producer, **Gr. 4,** 44; **Gr. 5,** 226
recording engineer, **Gr. 8,** 202
sound designer, **Gr. 8,** 135
sound effects engineer, **Gr. 8,** 20
symphony orchestra musician, **Gr. 7,** 102
teacher, **Gr. 7,** 235; **Gr. 8,** 164

CHARACTER DEVELOPMENT. *See Thematic Index*
respect, **Gr. K,** T12, T15, T41, T116, T137; **Gr. 1,** T20, T25, T47, T155, T224, T237; **Gr. 2,** 10-11, 22-23, 309, 325; **Gr. 3,** 33, 34, 40, 59, 393; **Gr. 5,** 59, 81, 107, 235, 269; **Gr. 6,** 20, 65, 71, 73; **Gr. 7,** 3, 14, 29, 46, 71; **Gr. 8,** 3, 27, 126

CHOREOGRAPHY. *For choreography notes, see* Piano Accompaniments *under separate cover; see also* Grade-Level DVD
Broadway for Kids Choreography
76 Trombones, **Gr. 5,** 296 (Grade-Level DVD)
Atlantic City, **Gr. 7,** 248
Brotherhood of Man, **Gr. 8,** 248 (Grade-Level DVD)
Coffee Break, **Gr. 8,** 245
Company Way, The, **Gr. 8,** 244
Cookies, **Gr. 1,** T277 (Grade-Level DVD)
Down the Hill, **Gr. 1,** T281
Green Eggs and Ham, **Gr. 2,** 284
Henry Ford, **Gr. 7,** 244 (Grade-Level DVD)

Horton Hears a Who!, **Gr. 2,** 279
Horton Hears a Who! Two, **Gr. 2,** 280
How to Succeed in Business Without Really Trying, **Gr. 8,** 236
How to Succeed, **Gr. 8,** 237
I Think I'm Gonna Like It here, **Gr. 4,** 299
Interjections, **Gr. 3,** 303
Interplanet Janet, **Gr. 3,** 298 (Grade-Level DVD)
Iowa Stubborn, **Gr. 5,** 293
It's Possible, **Gr. 2,** 281
It's the Hard-Knock Life, **Gr. 4,** 293 (Grade-Level DVD)
Oh, the Thinks You Can Think!, **Gr. 2,** 276
Mama Will Provide, **Gr. 6,** 296 (Grade-Level DVD)
Night that Goldman Spoke, The, **Gr. 7,** 246
N.Y.C., **Gr. 4,** 302
Pick-a-Little/Goodnight Ladies, **Gr. 5,** 299
Preamble, The, **Gr. 3,** 293
Ragtime, **Gr. 7,** 237
Ragtime Epilogue and Finale, **Gr. 7,** 250
Rock Island, **Gr. 5,** 291
Seussical Mega-Mix, **Gr. 2,** 287 (Grade-Level DVD)
Snail With the Mail, **Gr. 1,** T275
Spring, **Gr. 1,** T273
Success, **Gr. 7,** 241
Three is a Magic Number, **Gr. 3,** 296
Tomorrow, **Gr. 4,** 295
Waiting for Life, **Gr. 6,** 292
Wells Fargo Wagon, The, **Gr. 5,** 303
Why We Tell the Story, **Gr. 6,** 303
Year With Frog and Toad, A, **Gr. 1,** T270 (Grade-Level DVD)
Year With Frog and Toad, A (reprise), **Gr. 1,** T282
You're Never Fully Dressed Without a Smile, **Gr. 4,** 304
John Jacobson Choreography
Addams Family Theme, The, **Gr. 3,** 304
All Work Together, **Gr. K,** T12
Ame fure, **Gr. 4,** 26 (Grade-Level DVD)
America, **Gr. K,** T303; **Gr. 1,** T236 (Grade-Level DVD); **Gr. 2,** 338; **Gr. 4,** 354
America, My Homeland, **Gr. 4,** 358 (Grade-Level DVD)
America, the Beautiful, **Gr. 3,** 354 (Grade-Level DVD); **Gr. 5,** 388
Angelina, **Gr. 6,** 8
Animales, **Gr. K,** T192
Animal Fair, **Gr. 2,** 214
At the Hop, **Gr. 4,** 306
Baby Beluga, **Gr. 2,** 26
Ballad of the Underground Railroad, **Gr. 5,** 154
Beauty and the Beast, **Gr. 5,** 124
Best Friends, **Gr. 1,** T222
Best That I Can Be, The, **Gr. K,** T48
Blow, Ye Winds, Blow, **Gr. 3,** 192
Blue Suede Shoes, **Gr. 6,** 236
Bop 'til You Drop, **Gr. 6,** 87
Bus, The, **Gr. K,** T137
Caribbean Amphibian, **Gr. 1,** T294
Change the World, **Gr. 5,** 314
Charleston, **Gr. 6,** 112
Check It Out (It's About Respect)!, **Gr. 2,** 10 (Grade-Level DVD)

Chicken on the Fence Post, **Gr. 3,** 265
Choo Choo Ch' Boogie, **Gr. 6,** 180
Cindy, **Gr. 5,** 265
Conga, **Gr. 6,** 34
Cripple Creek, **Gr. 6,** 372 (Grade-Level DVD)
Dance! Dance! Dance!, **Gr. 2,** 5 (Grade-Level DVD)
Dance Myself to Sleep, **Gr. 1,** T314
Dancing in the Street, **Gr. 6,** 84
Deck the Hall, **Gr. 3,** 374 (Grade-Level DVD)
Digga Digga Dog, **Gr. 3,** 164
Doctor Jazz, **Gr. 6,** 378 (Grade-Level DVD)
Down at the Twist and Shout, **Gr. 4,** 308
Down by the Bay, **Gr. 1,** T48 (Grade-Level DVD)
Dry Bones, **Gr. 5,** 406
Everybody Has Music Inside, **Gr. 2,** 164
Everybody Rejoice, **Gr. 5,** 226
Everything Grows, **Gr. 2,** 204
Ev'ry Time I Feel the Spirit, **Gr. 6,** C
Feliz Navidad, **Gr. 5,** 420
Flip, Flop and Fly, **Gr. 3,** 336
Garden Hoedown, The, **Gr. K,** T276
Garden Song, **Gr. 2,** 236
Gee, Mom, I Want to Go Home, **Gr. 6,** 148 (Grade-Level DVD)
Gilly, Gilly, Gilly Good Morning, **Gr. 1,** T12 (Grade-Level DVD)
God Bless America, **Gr. 5,** 4
God Bless the U.S.A, **Gr. 7,** 136
Goin' to the Zoo, **Gr. 1,** T192
Gonna Build a Mountain, **Gr. 6,** 4
Grandma's Feathered Bed, **Gr. 4,** E (Nat)
Greatest Show on Earth, The, **Gr. 3,** 308
Happiest Street in the World, The, **Gr. 1,** T304
Happiness, **Gr. 4,** 124
Happy Birthday, **Gr. K,** T347
Happy Talk, **Gr. 4,** 84
Hava Nagila, **Gr. 5,** 54
Hello Song, **Gr. K,** T2
Hero, **Gr. 5,** 312
Hey, Look Me Over, **Gr. 4,** 114
He's Got the Whole World in His Hands, **Gr. 2,** 116 (Grade-Level DVD)
Hop! Chirp! Moo! Oh, Happy Springtime Day!, **Gr. 1,** T372 (Grade-Level DVD)
I Got Rhythm, **Gr. 5,** 187
I Love a Piano, **Gr. 6,** 130
I Wanna Be A Friend of Yours, **Gr. 1,** T84
I Will Sing Hello, **Gr. K,** T156
If You're Gonna Play in Texas, **Gr. 5,** K (TX)
It Don't Mean a Thing, **Gr. 6,** 164
Jingle-Bell Rock, **Gr. 5,** 424
Jingle Bells, **Gr. 1,** T354 (Grade-Level DVD)
Jolly Old Saint Nicholas, **Gr. 1,** T353; **Gr. 4,** 382 (Grade-Level DVD)
Joyful, Joyful, **Gr. 5,** 105
Just Like Me, **Gr. K,** T242
Just One Planet, **Gr. 4,** 164
La bamba, **Gr. 3,** 236
Ladybugs' Picnic, **Gr. 1,** T290
Land of a Thousand Dances, **Gr. 7,** 12

Let's Go Driving, **Gr. 1,** T52
Light the Candles, **Gr. 1,** T351
Lion Sleeps Tonight, The, **Gr. 5,** 172
Little Blue Truck, **Gr. K,** T136
Little Tommy Tinker, **Gr. 3,** 277
Little White Duck, **Gr. K,** T192
Loco-Motion, The, **Gr. 4,** 312
Long-Legged Sailor, **Gr. 4,** 243
Look Who's Here!, **Gr. K,** T84
Lullaby of Broadway, **Gr. 6,** 182
Mister Sun, **Gr. K,** T343
Morena de mi Corazon, **Gr. 6,** O
Mountain Music, **Gr. 6,** 20
Movin' Right Along, **Gr. 3,** 124
Mr. Scott Joplin's Ragtime Rag!, **Gr. 6,** 110 (Grade-Level DVD)
Must Be Santa, **Gr. K,** T316
My Friend Tom, **Gr. 3,** 364
O Hanukkah, **Gr. 3,** 368
Oh, Susanna, **Gr. 3,** 153
Old Barn Dance, The, **Gr. 6,** 94
Old Dan Tucker, **Gr. 5,** 253
One of Those Songs, **Gr. 6,** 54
Over My Head, **Gr. 3,** 286
Over the River and Through the Wood, **Gr. 4,** 370 (Grade-Level DVD)
Pat Pat Patty Pat, **Gr. 1,** T308
Peasant's Dancing Day, **Gr. 4,** 132 (Grade-Level DVD)
Planting Seeds, **Gr. K,** T284
Polly Wolly Doodle, **Gr. 3,** 132 (Grade-Level DVD)
Power of the Dream, The, **Gr. 5,** 44
Rock Around the Clock, **Gr. 6,** 234
Seeds, **Gr. 1,** T120
Sesame Street, **Gr. 1,** T298
Shoo Fly Pie and Apple Pan Dowdy, **Gr. 3,** 227
Simon Says, **Gr. 3,** 4
Sing After Me, **Gr. 1,** T34
Sing, America, Sing!, **Gr. 5,** 6 (Grade-Level DVD)
Sing, Sing, Sing, **Gr. 5,** 30
Somebody Come and Play, **Gr. 1,** T92
Something for Me, Something for You, **Gr. 4,** 4
Southern Nights, **Gr. 5,** 310
Stars and Stripes Forever, **Gr. 6,** 390 (Grade-Level DVD)
Surfin' U.S.A, **Gr. 5,** 306
There's a Little Wheel A-Turnin' in My Heart, **Gr. 3,** 129, 137
There's a Song in Me, **Gr. 5,** 183 (Grade-Level DVD)
They Were Tall, **Gr. K,** T52
This a Way and That a Way, **Gr. 3,** 386 (Grade-Level DVD)
This is America, **Gr. 3,** 356
This Is My City, **Gr. K,** T120
This Is My Country, **Gr. 2,** 87
This Land is Your Land, **Gr. 4,** 146
This Little Light of Mine, **Gr. 1,** T238; **Gr. 2,** F
Three Little Birds, **Gr. 3,** 204
Times They Are A-Changin', The, **Gr. 5,** 204
Tinga Layo, **Gr. 2,** 50 (Grade-Level DVD)
Trampin', **Gr. 3,** 287

Classified Index *(vertical tab)*

Twist and Shout, **Gr. 4**, 314; **Gr. 7**, 160
Up on the Housetop, **Gr. 2**, 356
Vive l'amour, **Gr. 5**, 262 (Grade-Level DVD)
Wabash Cannonball, **Gr. 6**, 30
Wake Up the Sun, **Gr. 2**, 124 (Grade-Level DVD)
We All Sing with the Same Voice, **Gr. 1**, T156
We Got the Beat, **Gr. 4**, 310
Welcome to Our Neighborhood Choreography
   Go, Go, Go, **Gr. K**, T276
   Happy Birthday, Happy Birthday, **Gr. K**, T273
   It's Such a Good Feeling, **Gr. K**, T282
   It's You I Like, **Gr. K**, T280
   Let's Think of Something to Do, **Gr. K**, T270
   Peace and Quiet, **Gr. K**, T278
   Propel, Propel, Propel, **Gr. K**, T275
   Row, Row, Row, **Gr. K**, T274
   Speedy Delivery, **Gr. K**, T279
   Won't You Be My Neighbor?, **Gr. K**, T268
We Remember, **Gr. 4**, 360
What a Wonderful World, **Gr. 2**, 84
When I Sing, **Gr. 6**, 44
When the Flag Goes By, **Gr. 1**, T327
When the Saints Go Marching In, **Gr. 5**, 256
Whistle While You Work, **Gr. 2**, 6
Yakety Yak, **Gr. 5**, 308
Yankee Doodle Boy, **Gr. 3**, 357
Yellow Bird, **Gr. 6**, 154
You're a Grand Old Flag, **Gr. K**, T4; **Gr. 3**, 355
   (Grade-Level DVD)
You've Got a Friend in Me, **Gr. 2**, 44

CUMULATIVE SONGS

Ants Go Marching, The, **Gr. 1**, T22
Dinosaurs Dancing (listening), **Gr. K**, T72
I Bought Me a Cat (arr. by A. Copland), **Gr. 2**, 14–15
I Know an Old Lady, **Gr. K**, T26
La bella hortelana (The Beautiful Gardener), **Gr. 2**, 208
Little White Duck, **Gr. K**, T208
Must Be Santa, **Gr. K**, T316
Old MacDonald Had a Farm, **Gr. K**, T211; (arr by
   L. Anderson) (listening), **Gr. 2**, 133
One Finger, One Thumb, **Gr. K**, T38
Pat Pat Patty Pat, **Gr. 1**, T308
She'll Be Comin' 'Round the Mountain, **Gr. 2**, 33
There's a Hole in the Middle of the Sea, **Gr. 1**, T178
This Old Man, **Gr. 1**, T306

CURRICULUM CONNECTION

art. *See also* Fine Art Reproductions
Art Gallery:
   Creative Art Project: animals, **Gr. K**, T219
   Creative Art Project: boats, **Gr. K**, T95
   Creative Art Project: collages, **Gr. 5**, 175
   Creative Art Project: contrasting colors, **Gr. K**, T167
   Creative Art Project: create a mural, **Gr. 1**, T197;
     Gr. 2, 209
   Creative Art Project: create art on "The Water Is
     Wide," **Gr. 6**, 47
   Creative Art Project: create art on occupation,
     Gr. 6, 171
   Creative Art Project: create art with paint and clay,
     Gr. 6, 115

Creative Art Project: create cartoons, **Gr. 3**, 183
Creative Art Project: create expressive art using
   multimedia **Gr. 7**, 193
Creative Art Project: create pointillist paintings,
   Gr. 7, 121
Creative Art Project: create posters on artists of the
   Classical Period, **Gr. 8**, 121
Creative Art Project: create visual art piece to
   represent elements of culture, **Gr. 8**, 127
Creative Art Project: creating a portrait, **Gr. 5**, 100
Creative Art Project: dance murals, **Gr. 3**, 213
Creative Art Project: depict a grand event, **Gr. 1**,
   T175
Creative Art Project: depict a journey, **Gr. 3**, 99
Creative Art Project: depict music performers and
   instruments, **Gr. 7**, 17
Creative Art Project: designs made from initials,
   Gr. 5, 48
Creative Art Project: draw, **Gr. 2**, 151
Creative Art Project: draw dancing, **Gr. 3**, 93
Creative Art Project: draw present-day string
   ensemble, **Gr. 8**, 5
Creative Art Project: experimental drawing, **Gr. 5**, 207
Creative Art Project: glue lines, **Gr. K**, T31
Creative Art Project: illustrating music, **Gr. 4**, 68
Creative Art Project: Japanese woodblock prints,
   Gr. 2, 101
Creative Art Project: light and dark, **Gr. 2**, 52
Creative Art Project: making arks, **Gr. 4**, 131
Creative Art Project: mixed media pictures,
   Gr. 4, 216
Creative Art Project: moods, **Gr. K**, T139
Creative Art Project: musician portraits, **Gr. 4**, 176
Creative Art Project: night sky, **Gr. K**, T67
Creative Art Project: paint a task, **Gr. 3**, 130
Creative Art Project: painting people at work,
   Gr. 4, 100
Creative Art project: prepare mural, **Gr. 6**, 139
Creative Art Project: show emotions with
   brushstrokes, **Gr. 6**, 27
Creative Art Project: sketch designs for a musical
   show, **Gr. 7**, 232
Creative Art Project: sketching or painting historical
   event, **Gr. 5**, 11
Creative Art Project: song collage, **Gr. 3**, 24
Creative Art Project: spirit dolls, **Gr. 4**, 19
Creative Art Project: "The Woodpecker", **Gr. 4**, 48
Creative Art Project: Turkish carpets, **Gr. 5**, 135
Creative Art Project: use the technique of theme and
   variation, **Gr. 8**, 92
Creative Art Project: winter scene, **Gr. 2**, 351
Tropical Themes and Bright Colors: Amos Ferguson,
   Gr. 3, 381
Art Gallery:
   Art Connects to Music: A Balance, **Gr. 6**, 27
   Art Connects to Music: A Room in the House of
     Mr. Kong (anon), **Gr. 6**, 27
   Art Connects to Music: artists and musicians living at
     court, **Gr. 8**, 121

Art Connects to Music: Awa Tsirah (Alfonso Roybal), **Gr. 5,** 445

Art Connects to Music: Baroque Period, **Gr. 2,** 52

Art Connects to Music: Boating Party, The, by Mary Cassatt, **Gr. 6,** 47

Art Connects to Music: Bob Nugent, **Gr. 4,** 216

Art Connects to Music: Brueghel, Pieter (Details), **Gr. 2,** 350

Art Connects to Music: Brueghel, Pieter (Games), **Gr. 2,** 247

Art Connects to Music: collages, **Gr. 5,** 175

Art Connects to Music: Color and Tone, **Gr. 6,** 47

Art Connects to Music: comparative portrayals, **Gr. K,** T218

Art Connects to Music: compare a painting with the national anthem, **Gr. 7,** 193

Art Connects to Music: Composing **Gr. 2,** 100

Art Connects to Music: contrasts, **Gr. K,** T167

Art Connects to Music: Cornelius Krieghoff, **Gr. 3,** 93

Art Connects to Music: Cumberland Gap, **Gr. 3,** 99

Art Connects to Music: Degas, Edgar (Ballet), **Gr. 2,** 25

Art Connects to Music: depicting animals and studying nature, **Gr. 7,** 154

Art Connects to Music: Dürer, Albrecht (Graphic Works), **Gr. 2,** 151

Art Connects to Music: Edward Hicks, **Gr. 4,** 131

Art Connects to Music: embellishments, **Gr. 5,** 48

Art Connects to Music: expression in fine art and music, **Gr. 7,** 173

Art Connects to Music: feelings in music and paintings, **Gr. 1,** T196

Art Connects to Music: Festival in the Country by David Teniers II, **Gr. 6,** 98

Art Connects to Music: foreground and background, **Gr. 5,** 10

Art Connects to Music: *Gathering Apples,* **Gr. 3,** 24

Art Connects to Music: Grandma Moses, **Gr. 3,** 131

Art Connects to Music: higher and lower, **Gr. K,** T67

Art Connects to Music: identification, **Gr. 4,** 176

Art Connects to Music: India: Bhangra music and its roots, **Gr. 6,** 224

Art Connects to Music: Jewish Musicians in Jerusalem by Vladimir Mnev, **Gr. 6,** 425

Art Connects to Music: Katsina Dolls, **Gr. 4,** 19

Art Connects to Music: "La raspa", **Gr. 3,** 213

Art Connects to Music: line and value drawings, **Gr. 5,** 207

Art Connects to Music: line, **Gr. K,** T31

Art Connects to Music: making music from "bits of junk", **Gr. 4,** 48

Art Connects to Music: Marc Chagall, **Gr. 4,** 68, 375

Art Connects to Music: Mexican nationalistic music and art, **Gr. 8,** 127

Art Connects to Music: moods, **Gr. K,** T139

Art Connects to Music: music performers and instruments in works of art, **Gr. 7,** 16

Art Connects to Music: Nineteenth-century painting of fisherman, **Gr. 6,** 171

Art Connects to Music: painters of the Romanic era, **Gr. 7,** 121

Art Connects to Music: painting of seventeenth century string ensemble, **Gr. 8,** 5

Art Connects to Music: photography portrait, **Gr. 6,** 139

Art Connects to Music: Picasso and the music world, **Gr. 7,** 232

Art Connects to Music: Pieter Brueghel, **Gr. 4,** 365

Art Connects to Music: play instruments to react to a painting, **Gr. 1,** T174

Art Connects to Music: portrait of the American West, **Gr. 6,** 115

Art Connects to Music: portraits, **Gr. 5,** 100

Art Connects to Music: rhythm, **Gr. 4,** 8

Art Connects to Music: Rube Goldberg, **Gr. 3,** 182

Art Connects to Music: Savitsky, Jack (Movement), **Gr. 2,** 13

Art Connects to Music: Scenes from the Life of the Prodigal Son by Louis de Caullery, **Gr. 6,** 100

Art Connects to Music: song lyrics and pictures, **Gr. K,** T95

Art Connects to Music: Synthia Saint James, **Gr. 5,** 429

Art Connects to Music: Tiepolo, Giovanni Domenico (Subjects), **Gr. 2,** 144

Art Connects to Music: Turkish carpets, **Gr. 5,** 135

Art Connects to Music: Untitled by Frederic Remington, **Gr. 6,** 114

Art Connects to Music: Wedding Ball of the Duc de Joyeuse, The, (anon), **Gr. 6,** 100

create

    abstract art, **Gr. 7,** 207

    CD cover, **Gr. 8,** 203

    collages, **Gr. 7,** 141

    costume design, **Gr. 7,** 232

    drawing of musical ensemble, **Gr. 8,** 5

    expressing social issues, **Gr. 7,** 42

    inspiration from music, **Gr. 8,** 101, 127

    mosaic, **Gr. 8,** 69

    patriotism, **Gr. 7,** 193

    performance art, **Gr. 8,** 23

    picture diaries, **Gr. K,** T79

    pointillism, **Gr. 7,** 121

    pop art, **Gr. 8,** 227

    portraits of musicians, **Gr. 7,** 17

    poster, **Gr. 8,** 121

    representing sound, **Gr. 7,** 158

    symbols, **Gr. 7,** 60

    texture, **Gr. 7,** 135

    theme and variation, **Gr. 8,** 92

Curriculum Link: Art

    Addams Family Cartoon, **Gr. 8,** 141

    Andy Warhol, **Gr. 8,** 227

    Animal Collages, **Gr. K,** T298

    Animals, **Gr. 1,** T80

    Boats, **Gr. 4,** 11

    Chiapas Crafts, **Gr. 2,** 129

    Classical Architecture, **Gr. 7,** 115

    Collages, **Gr. 7,** 141

Classified Index of Songs, Selected Concepts, Skills, and Activities (continued)

Colors and shapes, **Gr. 1,** T115
colors, **Gr. 5,** 200
costumes, **Gr. 3,** 363
Cover Design, **Gr. 8,** 203
Create a Family Book, **Gr. 1,** T93
Create a Personal Stone, **Gr. 2,** 48
create, **Gr. 3,** 371, 387
decorate, **Gr. 3,** 28
Draw Shapes in Sound, **Gr. 7,** 176
Draw Your Dreams, **Gr. 7,** 207
draw, **Gr. 3,** 103, 349; **Gr. 5,** 27, 29, 207
Eka Muda Game, **Gr. 5,** 28
experiment with colors, **Gr. 3,** 28, 73, 115
Farm Animal Props, **Gr. K,** T211
Flower Drum, **Gr. 5,** 61
Green Eggs, **Gr. 2,** 279
Hold Onto Your Hat, **Gr. 5,** 298
How Are You Feeling? **Gr. K,** T282
I Am Special Book, **Gr. K,** T280
Illustrate the Poem, **Gr. 1,** T316
illustrate, **Gr. 3,** 69
It's Possible, **Gr. 2,** 278
Jack-o'-Lanterns, **Gr. K,** T307
Line in Music and Art, **Gr. 2,** 24
Make "Skeleton" Instruments, **Gr. 5,** 407
Make a Classroom Dragon, **Gr. 2,** 367
Make a Handprint Butterfly, **Gr. 1,** T333
Make an Instrument, **Gr. K,** T35
make, **Gr. 3,** 73, 340
Making a "Song Book," **Gr. 1,** T306
Making an AB Picture, **Gr. 1,** T304
Maracas, **Gr. 1,** T103
Minimalism, **Gr. 7,** 130
Mosaics, **Gr. 8,** 69
Mural, **Gr. 1,** T148; **Gr. 7,** 142
Music as Inspiration, **Gr. 8,** 101
Music for the Eyes, **Gr. 1,** T210
Musician Displays, **Gr. 5,** 395
Paint a Poem, **Gr. K,** T104
Paint a Rainbow, **Gr. K,** T59
Performer's Portrait, A, **Gr. 4,** 224
Props, **Gr. 2,** 330
Pumpkin Patch, **Gr. 1,** T342
Quiet Please, **Gr. K,** T278
Rain Drawings, **Gr. 1,** T60
Rainbows, **Gr. 1,** T33
Retell "Hansel and Gretel," **Gr. K,** T180
Santa Claus, **Gr. K,** T316
self-portraits, **Gr. 1,** T300; **Gr. 3,** B
Shapes and Designs, **Gr. 2,** 149
Shining Stars, **Gr. K,** T91
Song Interpretations, **Gr. 5,** 196
Symbols, **Gr. 7,** 60
Texture, **Gr. 7,** 135
Theme, **Gr. 7,** 42
Winter Scenes, **Gr. 5,** 411
draw, **Gr. 8,** 5
make instruments, **Gr. K,** T35
mosaic, **Gr. 8,** 69
pop art, **Gr. 8,** 227

poster, **Gr. 8,** 121
puppets, **Gr. K,** T23

dance. *See also* Movement
ballet, **Gr. K,** T166, T311
choreography, **Gr. K,** T12, T48, T84, T120, T156, T192, T283
dramatization, **Gr. K,** T77
folk, **Gr. K,** T168
improvised, **Gr. K,** T166
Land of a Thousand Dances, **Gr. 7,** 10, 12–13
line dancing, **Gr. 7,** 165
patterned movement, **Gr. K,** T63
twist, The, **Gr. 7,** 11
waltz, **Gr. K,** T109, T223
Watusi, The, **Gr. 7,** 11
We Go Together, **Gr. 7,** 158

drama. *See* Broadway for Kids; Creative Activities, dramatizing; Curriculum Connection: theater; Performance

health
Curriculum Link: Health
Artichokes, **Gr. 2,** 315
Bananas, **Gr. 1,** T153
Brushing Your Teeth, **Gr. 1,** T69
Chinese Food, **Gr. 3,** 191
Desserts, **Gr. 3,** 227
Document Lifestyles, **Gr. 7,** 191
Emotional Awareness, **Gr. 1,** T254
Hearing Impairment, **Gr. 5,** 102
Hiking for Fitness, **Gr. 3,** 20
Importance of Friends, The, **Gr. 5,** 186
Importance of Sleep, The, **Gr. 1,** T26
Music Therapy, **Gr. 8,** 178
Musician's Lifestyle, **Gr. 8,** 190
Peanuts, **Gr. 1,** T219
Peanuts, **Gr. 4,** 107
Physical Activity, **Gr. K,** T254
Pollution and Health, **Gr. 7,** 220
Posture and Singing, **Gr. 5,** 57
Protecting the Voice, **Gr. 5,** 228
Safety First, **Gr. K,** T73
Sauces, **Gr. 4,** 228
Shellfish Safety, **Gr. 4,** 142
Spinach, **Gr. 1,** T164
Table Manners **Gr. K,** T106
Tuberculosis, **Gr. 7,** 86
Warming, **Gr. 7,** 160

mathematics
Curriculum Link: Mathematics
Add Fractions, **Gr. 7,** 188
Add on One, **Gr. 2,** 132
Addition and Subtraction, **Gr. 1,** T9
Beats Per Minute, **Gr. 7,** 119
Bigger and Smaller, **Gr. 1,** T199
Bunch, The **Gr. 3,** 222
Calculate a Budget, **Gr. 7,** 14
Calculate Running Times, **Gr. 8,** 73
Calendar Math, **Gr. 2,** 7
Calendar, **Gr. K,** T79

Classifying Geometric Shapes, **Gr. 5**, 212
Convert a recipe, **Gr. 6**, 193
Convert Snow to Rain, **Gr. 5**, 408
Count Backward, **Gr. K**, T126, T257
Counting Beats, **Gr. 1**, T108; **Gr. 3**, 156
Counting candles, **Gr. 6**, 405
Counting the Days, **Gr. 2**, 345
Diagram a Dance, **Gr. 7**, 164
Diagram, **Gr. 7**, 223
Estimation, **Gr. 8**, 135
Favorite Pets Graph, **Gr. K**, T215
Find the Ratio, **Gr. 5**, 400
Flow Chart, **Gr. 7**, 93
Fractions, **Gr. 8**, 37
Fractions and Meter, **Gr. 4**, 348
Graphing Statistics, **Gr. 4**, 62
Graphing, **Gr. 8**, 66
Graphs and Charts, **Gr. 7**, 25
How Many Paper Clips?, **Gr. 1**, T92
How Many? **Gr. K**, T319
In a Flash, **Gr. 3**, 296
Line Graph, **Gr. 4**, 297; **Gr. 7**, 150
Make an Organized List, **Gr. 5**, 69
Mayan Math, **Gr. 2**, 61
Meter Arithmetic, **Gr. 3**, 97
Musical Math, **Gr. 5**, 354; **Gr. 6**, 324
Musical Number Nouns, **Gr. 2**, 152
New Shape for the Poem, A, **Gr. K**, T37
Note Values, **Gr. 4**, 15; **Gr. 5**, 8
Number Combinations, **Gr. 7**, 44
Numbers of Musicians, **Gr. 2**, 148
Numbers to Ten. **Gr. K**, T92
Numbers, **Gr. 1**, T132
One Fish Two Fish Red Fish Blue Fish, **Gr. 2**, 278
Ordinal numbers, **Gr. 1**, T215
Parade Patterns, **Gr. 7**, 76
Patterns and sequences, **Gr. 6**, 224
Patterns, **Gr. 2**, 320; **Gr. 8**, 33
Permutations, **Gr. 6**, 37
Pitch and Vibration, **Gr. 8**, 163
Plane Shapes, **Gr. K**, T36
Pricing, **Gr. 8**, 200
Roman Numerals, **Gr. 5**, 167
Salaries, **Gr. 8**, 122
Sampling Theorem, **Gr. 8**, 96
Send a Letter, **Gr. K**, T277–T278
Set Theory, **Gr. 8**, 221
Shape Patterns, **Gr. K**, T153
Shapes, **Gr. K**, T268–T269
Skip-Counting, **Gr. 1**, T291
Soloist's Share, A, **Gr. 5**, 423
Standard Units, **Gr. 5**, 131
Subtraction, **Gr. K**, T309
Taking a Train, **Gr. 5**, 298
Tell Time, **Gr. K**, T14
Tempered tuning, **Gr. 6**, 128
Ticket Sales Math, **Gr. 4**, 297
Time and Distance, **Gr. 7**, 50
Time to the Hour, **Gr. K**, T71
Time, **Gr. 3**, 67
Tone Color Categories, **Gr. K**, T173

Units of Length, **Gr. K**, T112
Visual Symbols, **Gr. 1**, T96
Word Problem, A, **Gr. 1**, T151
mathematics activities
add note values, **Gr. 7**, 44
calculate a budget, **Gr. 7**, 14
calculate beats, **Gr. 7**, 119
calculate frequencies of specific pitches, **Gr. 8**, 163
calculate income based on rate and volume of work,
Gr. 8, 122
calculate sales statistics, **Gr. 8**, 200
calculate time and distance, **Gr. 7**, 50
compare mathematical patterns with musical
patterns, **Gr. 8**, 33
compare running times of themes in an overture,
Gr. 8, 73
convert monetary amounts to adjust for inflation,
Gr. 8, 135
create a flowchart, **Gr. 7**, 93
create a line graph, **Gr. 7**, 150
create graphs and charts, **Gr. 7**, 25
diagram a dance, **Gr. 7**, 164
diagram a parade, **Gr. 7**, 76
diagram a song, **Gr. 7**, 223
graph and compare note values from several
melodies, **Gr. 8**, 66
interpret mathematical statements, **Gr. 8**, 221
represent notes as fractions, **Gr. 7**, 188
research Canchy's sampling theorem, **Gr. 8**, 96
use fractional note values to solve math problems,
Gr. 8, 37

physical education. *See also* Movement
Curriculum Link: Physical Education
Cheerleading, **Gr. 7**, 227
Conducting Exercises, **Gr. 3**, 179
Contra dances, **Gr. 6**, 374
Crazy Cookie Counting, **Gr. 1**, T274
Dance and Physical Activity, **Gr. 5**, 152
Dancing, Benefits of, **Gr. 2**, 94
Evaluate movement, **Gr. 6**, 230
Fad Dances, **Gr. 5**, 424
Gymnastics/Figure Skating, **Gr. 8**, 4
Italian Tempo Markings, **Gr. 4**, 191
jogging, **Gr. K**, T87, T111
Jump Rope, **Gr. 1**, T15; **Gr. 7**, 180; **Gr. 4**, 58
Keep Motivated, **Gr. 7**, 149
Keeping Fit, **Gr. 7**, 134
Mabarung, **Gr. 7**, 101
Music and Exercise, **Gr. 8**, 149
Polyrhythms, **Gr. 7**, 202
Rugby, **Gr. 2**, 140
Sequenced Movement, **Gr. 7**, 65
Teamwork, **Gr. 1**, T111
Walk, Skip, and Gallop, **Gr. K**, T40
reading/language arts
Curriculum Link: Reading
Adaptation, **Gr. 8**, 195
Additional Verses, **Gr. K**, T51
Adjectives That Compare, **Gr. K**, T44
Alliteration, **Gr. 8**, 45

Classified Index of Songs, Selected Concepts, Skills, and Activities (continued)

Alliterative Sounds, **Gr. K**, T148
Analyze Lyrics, **Gr. 8**, 75
Analyze Song Lyrics, **Gr. K**, T27
Ban Dal, **Gr. 4**, 184
Beginning Sounds, **Gr. K**, T57
"Bingo" Book, **Gr. K**, T64
British Terms, **Gr. K**, T265
Building Literacy Readiness, **Gr. 1**, T24
Building Vocabulary, **Gr. 3**, 357
Calendar, **Gr. K**, T79
Ceremonial Poetry, **Gr. 7**, 66
Class Booklet, **Gr. K**, T203
Compare Animal Groups, **Gr. K**, T213
Cumulative Form, **Gr. K**, T28
Cumulative Tales, **Gr. 1**, T180
Dancing Dinosaurs, **Gr. K**, T73
Dragon Myths, **Gr. 2**, 55
Ending Sounds, **Gr. K**, T18
Faster and Slower, **Gr. K**, T19
Finding Opposites, **Gr. K**, T292
Folklore, **Gr. K**, T249
Friends, **Gr. K**, T282–T283
Gullah, **Gr. K**, T327
"Hope", **Gr. 3**, 167
Initial Consonants, **Gr. K**, T187
Intellectual Property, **Gr. 8**, 101
Interpret a Poem, **Gr. 6**, 156; **Gr. 7**, 205
Interview a Delivery Person, **Gr. K**, T278
Letter "D," The, **Gr. K**, T87
Letter "H," The, **Gr. K**, T140
Letter "M," The, **Gr. K**, T115
Mary Poppins, **Gr. 2**, 6
Metaphors, **Gr. 7**, 152
Monster Stories, **Gr. 3**, 307
Mood, **Gr. 8**, 197
Movement Vocabulary, **Gr. K**, T174
New Shape for the Poem, A, **Gr. K**, T37
New Verses, **Gr. K**, T175
Nursery Rhymes, **Gr. 1**, T130
OO Sound, The, **Gr. K**, T196
Paint a Poem, **Gr. K**, T104
Persuasion, **Gr. 8**, 212
Phonemic Awareness, **Gr. K**, T143
Phrases and Sight Words, **Gr. K**, T134
Poem About Manners, **Gr. K**, T107
Poem Accompaniment, **Gr. 8**, 18
Poem, **Gr. K**, T199, T208
Poetic Form, **Gr. 7**, 20
Poetry and Creative Siblings, **Gr. 7**, 125
Poetry and Feelings, **Gr. 7**, 174
Poetry and Freedom, **Gr. 7**, 187
Poetry and Lyrics, **Gr. 7**, 157
Poetry and Rhyme Scheme, **Gr. 7**, 83
Poetry Describes Music, **Gr. 8**, 226
Poetry, 34, **Gr. 8**, 84
Portraying Emotions, **Gr. 8**, 179
Read a Poem, **Gr. 7**, 231, 45, 174, 231
Read excerpts, **Gr. 7**, 211
Read Stories, **Gr. 7**, 180
Reading Free Verse, **Gr. 6**, 209

Reading Theme of "The Treasure of Lemon Brown,"
   Gr. 6, 179
Rhyming Words, **Gr. K**, T183
"Ring Around the Rosy," **Gr. K**, T247
Romantic Poetry, **Gr. 8**, 115
Shakespearean Stories, **Gr. 7**, 84
Sight Words, **Gr. K**, T160
Sing a Song of Sixpence, **Gr. K**, T111
Snow White Variations, **Gr. 2**, 6
Sound/Symbol Correspondence, **Gr. K**, T55
Sound-Symbol, **Gr. 1**, T72
Stories About Ceremonies, **Gr. 7**, 62
Story Time, **Gr. K**, T26
Sweet and Low, **Gr. 6**, 184
Ways to Say, **Gr. K**, T277
"Whispers", **Gr. 4**, 94
Word Play, **Gr. 8**, 142
Words Beginning with "P," **Gr. K**, T96
Write New Verses, **Gr. K**, T62
Curriculum Link: Language Arts
Adjectives, **Gr. 8**, 214
American Sign Language, **Gr. K**, T80
Analogies, **Gr. 7**, 69
Apple Folk Saying, An, **Gr. 2**, 343
Artistic Terms, **Gr. 8**, 11
Australian Terms, **Gr. 2**, 106
Best Friends, **Gr. 1**, T223
Blues lyrics, **Gr. 6**, 180
Call and Response, **Gr. 2**, 19
Categories, **Gr. 1**, T146
Class Song, A, **Gr. 4**, 172
Classifying, **Gr. 8**, 225
Comparing lullabies, **Gr. 6**, 59
Completing a Sentence, **Gr. 1**, T54
Compound Words, **Gr. 4**, 76
Consonants and Rhythm, **Gr. 1**, T96
Context Clues, **Gr. 5**, 139
Create New Words, **Gr. 1**, T292
Creating a Verse, **Gr. 2**, 318
Creative Writing, **Gr. 3**, 380, 383; **Gr. 8**, 112
Dancing, **Gr. 3**, 196
Descriptive Essay, **Gr. 5**, 108
Descriptive Writing, **Gr. 3**, 367
Don't Count Your Chickens, **Gr. 3**, 75
Essay Writing, **Gr. 8**, 129
Essay, **Gr. 7**, 233
Etymology, **Gr. 7**, 108
Fairy Tales, **Gr. 1**, T285
Favorite color poem, **Gr. 6**, 218
Film Collaborations, **Gr. 8**, 137
Finnish Forest, **Gr. 6**, 423
Five Senses, The, **Gr. 8**, 180
Found poems, **Gr. 6**, 32
Guiding principles of Kwanzaa, **Gr. 6**, 415
Haiku, **Gr. 8**, 57
Halloween words, **Gr. 1**, T338
Hearing, **Gr. 4**, 13
Homophones, **Gr. 2**, D
Humor in a song, **Gr. 6**, 56
Humorous lyrics, **Gr. 6**, 148
If I Were President, **Gr. 1**, T368

"In My Little Motor Boat," **Gr. 1,** T159
Inspiration, **Gr. 7,** 150
Inspiring Lyrics, **Gr. 7,** 51
Interview, **Gr. 8,** 111
Irish Cabin, **Gr. 6,** 408
Journalism, **Gr. 8,** 4
Latin, **Gr. 4,** 174
Learning Names, **Gr. 3,** 4
Legendary Hero, **Gr. 3,** 65
Letter to Libby Larsen, **Gr. 8,** 154
Letter to Señor Vargas, A, **Gr. 4,** 196
Letter to the Editor, **Gr. 4,** 7
Living Comic Strip, **Gr. 4,** 297
Lyrics, **Gr. 7,** 97
Metaphors, **Gr. 3,** 57
Meter, **Gr. 7,** 70
"Moon and Me", **Gr. 3,** 220
Music Glossary, **Gr. 8,** 162
Music Terms, **Gr. 5,** 97
Musical Story, A, **Gr. 3,** 88
My Trip to Seussland, **Gr. 2,** 279
Narrator, **Gr. 1,** T140
Nonsense Words, **Gr. 3,** 132; **Gr. 4,** 210
Nonstandard Spelling, **Gr. 5,** 127
Onomatopoeia, **Gr. 4,** 220; **Gr. 7,** 104; **Gr. 8,** 146
Oratorio, **Gr. 8,** 120
Persuasive Letters, **Gr. 4,** 297
Poetry and Meter, **Gr. 7,** 18
Poetry and Rhyme Scheme, **Gr. 7,** 83
Poetry and Rhyme, **Gr. 7,** 13
Poetry Slam, **Gr. 8,** 48
Prefix *Octo-*, The, **Gr. 4,** 128
Prefixes, **Gr. 5,** 20
Questions and Answers, **Gr. 3,** 151
Read a Poem, **Gr. 7,** 231
Read Stories, **Gr. 7,** 180
Reading Instructions, **Gr. 8,** 231
Rebus, **Gr. 1,** T179
Research, **Gr. 5,** 124
Researching the Moon, **Gr. 5,** 368
Reviews, **Gr. 8,** 117
Rhythm in Poetry, **Gr. 7,** 45
Root Word *phone*, **Gr. 1,** T144
Season Poems, **Gr. 1,** T274
Sentence Completion, **Gr. 3,** 236
Similes in song lyrics, **Gr. 6,** 21
Slang and Regional Idioms, **Gr. 8,** 64
Slang, **Gr. 4,** 55
"Somebody Has To," **Gr. 1,** T258
"Something Told the Wild Geese", **Gr. 1,** T261
Song About Dreams, A, **Gr. 4,** 235
Song and Fantasy, **Gr. 4,** 318
Sounds Around the World, **Gr. 2,** 131
Speak Phrases with Expression, **Gr. 7,** 211
Speech Competitions, **Gr. 8,** 50
Story Time, **Gr. 2,** 279
Story with Rhythm, A, **Gr. 4,** 88
Storytelling Grab Bag, **Gr. 5,** 298
Storytelling, **Gr. 6,** 95, 210, 294
Stressed Syllables, **Gr. 1,** T123
Summer Poem, A, **Gr. 2,** 383

Summing Up, **Gr. 5,** 236
Syllables in Words, **Gr. 1,** T87
Syllables, **Gr. 3,** 15
Taking Notes, **Gr. 7,** 74
Taking Turns, **Gr. 2,** 156
Thanksgiving words, **Gr. 6,** 108
Thee and You, **Gr. 1,** T100
Tongue Twisters, **Gr. 3,** 68
Tooth Fairy Folktale, The **Gr. 2,** 28
Trickster Tales, **Gr. 2,** 332
Unfamiliar Words, **Gr. K,** T303; **Gr. 5,** 35, 63
Use of the Apostrophe, **Gr. 5,** 243
Using a prefix, **Gr. 6,** 12
Valentine's Expression, A, **Gr. 2,** 368
Visual Symbols, **Gr. 1,** T96
Vocables, **Gr. 7,** 200
Vocabulary, **Gr. 8,** 76
Word Play, **Gr. 8,** 188
Write a definition, **Gr. 6,** 4
Write a Dialogue, **Gr. 7,** 159
Write a New Refrain, **Gr. 5,** 231
Write a New Verse, **Gr. 5,** 180
Write a poem, **Gr. 6,** 63
Write a review, **Gr. 6,** 197
Write a Review, **Gr. 7,** 233
Write a speech piece, **Gr. 6,** 216
Write a synopsis for a musical, **Gr. 6,** 183
Write About a Song, **Gr. 7,** 33
Write Directions, **Gr. 7,** 164
Write Lyrics, **Gr. 5,** 92, 173, 367
Write Narration, **Gr. 7,** 170
Write new lyrics, **Gr. 6,** 53
Write Poetry, **Gr. 7,** 196
Write with Rhythm, **Gr. 7,** 188
Writing, **Gr. 4,** 358, 380
Writing Lyrics, **Gr. 4,** 334; **Gr. 7,** 46, 221
Writing Stories vs. Writing Music, **Gr. 8,** 175
Writing Verses, **Gr. 3,** 242
Your Heroes, **Gr. 5,** 312

poetry. *See Alphabetical Index of Literature*
poetry analysis
    analyze a poem, **Gr. 7,** 187, 205; **Gr. 8,** 34, 179
    compare meter and rhythm, **Gr. 7,** 20, 70
    compare music and poetry, **Gr. 7,** 157
    compare prose and poetry, **Gr. 7,** 125
    compose a haiku, **Gr. 8,** 57
    create an instrumental accompaniment, **Gr. 8,** 18
    identify characteristic themes, **Gr. 8,** 115
    portray a poetic character, **Gr. 8,** 195
    reading poetry, **Gr. 8,** 84
    select musical accompaniment for a poem, **Gr. 7,** 66
reading/language arts skills
    Build Background, **Gr. 7,** 17, 23, 26, 56, 60, 63, 69, 81, 89, 96, 109, 115, 130, 133, 142, 147, 153, 164, 168, 206, 212, 214, 233
    cause and effect, **Gr. 1,** T76, T201, T204; **Gr. 2,** 28, 65; **Gr. 3,** 189; **Gr. 5,** 155, 235; **Gr. 6,** 20, 36, 195, 209, 215, 220, 411; **Gr. 7,** 37
    classify and categorize, **Gr. 1,** T16, T33, T59, T60,

T63, T64, T65, T72, T75, T79, T81, T91, T99, T137, T148, T159, T167, T168, T171, T173, T176, T185, T215, T219, T224; **Gr. 2**, 12, 24, 25, 55, 88, 92, 127, 133, 135; **Gr. 3**, 16, 20, 23, 29, 32, 36, 53, 59, 63, 77, 115, 139, 172, 175, 213, 215, 229; **Gr. 4**, 8, 49, 56, 64, 69, 71, 91, 93, 95, 113, 139, 143, 147, 151, 155, 172, 173, 184, 187, 188, 189, 195, 219, 229, 236; **Gr. 5**, 12, 24, 59, 63, 129, 131, 169, 171, 181, 184, 228; **Gr. 6**, 27, 35, 48, 59, 68, 75, 95, 127, 131, 139, 141, 175, 212, 219

compare and contrast, **Gr. 1**, T68, T91, T96, T100, T107, T109, T111, T123, T124, T127, T129, T144, T151, T160, T161, T188, T195, T200, T201; **Gr. 2**, 11, 13, 24, 32, 61, 72, 116, 131, 151, 153; **Gr. 3**, 12, 23, 35, 49, 52, 69, 71, 76, 89, 91, 95, 96, 97, 99, 103, 105, 111, 112, 127, 128, 129, 137, 143, 144, 145, 147, 148, 151, 153, 156, 169, 183, 193, 195, 196, 209, 211, 217, 220, 221, 228, 237; **Gr. 4**, 7, 9, 11, 13, 20, 24, 25, 27, 28, 29, 31, 60, 64, 65, 68, 69, 71, 89, 91, 92, 95, 96, 100, 101, 103, 105, 107, 108, 116, 127, 149, 152, 167, 172, 189, 191, 197, 207, 208, 209, 211, 213, 215, 216, 225, 227, 228, 231, 232, 235; **Gr. 5**, 7, 20, 32, 48, 52, 60, 71, 87, 95, 117, 132, 139, 147, 148, 149, 150, 152, 155, 168, 172, 179, 180, 187, 188, 192, 193, 208, 209, 213, 221, 224, 225, 227, 231, 236, 237; **Gr. 6**, 7, 11, 12, 17, 20, 33, 47, 51, 52, 59, 65, 73, 76, 88, 97, 99, 100, 108, 111, 112, 117, 132, 143, 151, 156, 167, 168, 169, 172, 180, 181, 184, 187, 188, 191, 207, 215, 219, 223, 225, 227, 228, 235, 236; **Gr. 7**, 4, 11, 19, 113, 124, 173, 179

connect, **Gr. 5**, 69
consonant digraphs, **Gr. 1**, T67
context, **Gr. 5**, 55
define, **Gr. 5**, 29, 35
describe, **Gr. 5**, 92, 100, 5, 7, 9, 16, 25, 27, 28, 36, 37, 43, 45, 55, 63, 85, 97, 104, 108, 116, 117, 125, 143, 144, 148, 153, 165, 224, 349
   musical elements, **Gr. 8**, 214
   writing process, **Gr. 8**, 175
discuss, **Gr. 5**, 3, 4, 9, 33, 43, 71, 84, 85, 89, 123, 163, 165, 204, 364, 366, 373
distinguish, **Gr. 5**, 23; **Gr. 6**, 52, 53, 71, 152
draw conclusions, **Gr. 1**, T28, T64, T69, T143, T181, T184, T212, T217, T223, T224; **Gr. 2**, 67, 72, 111, 112, 132, 133, 136, 141; **Gr. 3**, 51, 75, 105, 108, 109, 131, 133, 136, 171, 176, 180, 185, 189, 191, 192, 223, 227; **Gr. 4**, 51, 56, 223; **Gr. 5**, 15, 104, 133, 175, 183, 197; **Gr. 6**, 16, 24, 108, 116, 131, 176, 183, 211, 231; **Gr. 7**, 31, 83, 103, 110, 150, 181, 220, 234
evaluate, **Gr. 4**, 77; **Gr. 5**, 19, 191
Follow Directions, **Gr. 7**, 65
form generalizations, **Gr. 3**, 211; **Gr. 5**, 151; **Gr. 6**, 15
identify, **Gr. 2**, 59, 52, 75; **Gr. 5**, 12, 67; **Gr. 7**, 134

Identify Main Idea and Supporting Details, **Gr. 7**, 35, 211
infer, **Gr. 1**, T31, T44, T140, T151; **Gr. 2**, 11, 13, 99; **Gr. 3**, 28, 168, 179, 183, 188; **Gr. 5**, 35, 89, 96, 127, 143, 151, 167, 171, 185, 189, 193, 196, 207, 212; **Gr. 6**, 15, 23, 29, 63, 71, 115, 171, 185, 192; **Gr. 7**, 29, 55, 67, 70, 76, 156, 174, 176, 185, 186, 196, 199, 222, 228
initial and final consonants, **Gr. 1**, T15, T43, T87, T133
interpret, **Gr. 5**, 73, 112, 115
interpret pictures, **Gr. 1**, T180
long vowels, **Gr. 1**, T27, T51, T52, T55
main idea, **Gr. 1**, T21, T73, T109, T135, T185; **Gr. 2**, 87, 91, 103, 108, 129; **Gr. 3**, 15, 27, 47, 55, 57, 61, 65, 69, 77, 168, 169, 171, 179, 185, 209; **Gr. 6**, 13, 61, 68, 135, 147
main ideas and details, **Gr. 5**, 52, 135, 145, 176, 197
make decisions, **Gr. 1**, T148, T200; **Gr. 2**, 60
make generalizations, **Gr. 2**, 92; **Gr. 7**, 97
make judgments, **Gr. 1**, T32, T164, T172, T175, T179, T187, T189, T195, T199, T213, T216, T221; **Gr. 3**, 51, 67, 73, 87, 92, 93, 95, 101, 107, 109, 117, 129, 167, 217, 219, 220, 224, 227, 231; **Gr. 4**, 8, 19, 21, 25, 37, 143, 189, 207, 209, 213, 217, 220, 228, 229, 231, 236, 237; **Gr. 5**, 108, 136, 144; **Gr. 6**, 9, 67, 92, 131, 171, 207, 208, 213, 217; **Gr. 7**, 226
main idea, **Gr. 4**, 12, 53, 99, 156
make predictions, **Gr. 1**, T204; **Gr. 2**, 15, 143; **Gr. 3**, 107; **Gr. 4**, 13, 16; **Gr. 6**, 11, 19, 95, 187, 188, 196
multisyllabic words, **Gr. 1**, T71, T88, T96, T103, T105, T131; **Gr. 2**, 23, 89, 108
other
   identify musical figures based on clues, **Gr. 8**, 225
   dramatize scene for film, **Gr. 8**, 137
   plan elements to create mood, **Gr. 8**, 197
paraphrase, **Gr. 4**, 145, 224, 225; **Gr. 6**, 55; **Gr. 7**, 9
poetry
   analyze poetry, **Gr. 8**, 34, 84, 115, 179, 226
   plan instrumentation for accompaniment to poem, **Gr. 8**, 18
predict, **Gr. 2**, 53, 67; **Gr. 5**, 75, 228, 231; **Gr. 7**, 3, 43, 70, 141, 170, 177, 180, 195
r-controlled vowels, **Gr. 1**, T16, T19, T24, T51
read
   lyrics for character clues, **Gr. 8**, 75
   lyrics for word pay, **Gr. 8**, 142
reality vs. fantasy, **Gr. 4**, 47
recall details, **Gr. 2**, 107, 128, 133; **Gr. 3**, 219; **Gr. 4**, 137, 149; **Gr. 7**, 14, 27, 44, 69, 193, 202
recall story details, **Gr. 1**, T79, T88, T163, T171, T183, T187, T203, T207, T209, T213; **Gr. 3**, 59, 115, 207, 215; **Gr. 4**, 19, 31, 33, 36, 223, 233; **Gr. 5**, 127, 140; **Gr. 6**, 177
recognize steps, **Gr. 2**, 95, 112; **Gr. 3**, 56, 107, 237; **Gr. 4**, 59; **Gr. 5**, 156; **Gr. 6**, 32; **Gr. 7**, 164

Classified Index

rhyme and rhythm, **Gr. 2,** 8
sequence, **Gr. 1,** T28, T35, T40, T163; **Gr. 3,** 7, 113, 117, 157; **Gr. 4,** 29, 31, 48, 112, 117; **Gr. 5,** 215, 217, 219, 220; **Gr. 6,** 76, 104, 133; **Gr. 7,** 37, 205
short vowels, **Gr. 2,** 7
speak, **Gr. 5,** 7, 8, 11, 49, 61, 88, 108, 124, 125, 127, 163, 298
    discuss intellectual property rights, **Gr. 8,** 101
    discuss persuasive language, **Gr. 8,** 212
    discuss slang and idiom, **Gr. 8,** 64
structural analysis: syllables, **Gr. 2,** 17
summarize, **Gr. 1,** T41, T45, T129, T161, T165, T169, T219, T223; **Gr. 2,** 9, 109, 117; **Gr. 3,** 25, 61, 64, 67, 72, 92, 97, 101, 117, 132, 135, 140, 145, 152, 155, 181, 184, 187, 209, 213, 231, 232, 235; **Gr. 4,** 12, 17, 21, 32, 57, 77, 109, 117, 141, 169, 221; **Gr. 5,** 5, 9, 32, 64, 137, 143, 147, 169, 175, 217; **Gr. 6,** 9, 21, 24, 29, 37, 109, 155, 177, 216, 221, 223, 231, 235; **Gr. 7,** 45, 52, 93, 99, 121
supporting details, **Gr. 1,** T141
Synthesize, **Gr. 7,** 52
variant vowels, **Gr. 1,** T36, T39; **Gr. 2,** 16, 29
Vocabulary, **Gr. 7,** 6, 12, 50, 57, 70, 84, 92, 95, 102, 109, 116, 118, 121, 127, 135, 147, 159
    create a glossary, **Gr. 8,** 162
    from The Music Man Jr., **Gr. 5,** 296
    instruments, **Gr. 8,** 76
    onomatopoeia, **Gr. 7,** 104
    origins of baroque, **Gr. 7,** 108
    study meaning and use of refrain, **Gr. 8,** 11
Word Parts, **Gr. 7,** 110
write. *See also* Portfolio Opportunity, **Gr. 5,** 32, 40, 74, 80, 92, 108, 120, 180, 231, 236, 312, 352, 367
    analogies, **Gr. 7,** 69
    critical review, **Gr. 7,** 233
    dialogue based on music, **Gr. 7,** 159
    directions, **Gr. 7,** 164
    essay, **Gr. 7,** 33, 233
    fictional narration, **Gr. 7,** 170
    lyrics, **Gr. 7,** 18, 51, 221
    limericks, **Gr. 7,** 83
    notes from visual observation, **Gr. 7,** 74
    poetry to fit rhythm patterns, **Gr. 7,** 188, 196
    poetry using rhymes, **Gr. 7,** 13
    poetry using vocables, **Gr. 7,** 200
    using sayings, **Gr. 7,** 150
    compare and contrast essay, **Gr. 8,** 129
    critical review, **Gr. 8,** 24, 117
    haiku, **Gr. 8,** 57
    instructions, **Gr. 8,** 231
    interview questions, **Gr. 8,** 111
    letter, **Gr. 8,** 154
    using music for inspiration, **Gr. 8,** 112
    using onomatopoeia, **Gr. 8,** 146

science
  Curriculum Link: Science
    Acting Out a Rain Storm, **Gr. K,** T336
    An Instrument's Sound, **Gr. 5,** 52
    Anatomy of Dance, **Gr. 6,** 111

Animal Research, **Gr. 1,** T295
Animal Sounds, **Gr. 7,** 167
Ants, **Gr. 1,** T22
Australian Animals, **Gr. 2,** 107
Bamboo, **Gr. 4,** 219
Bear, The, **Gr. K,** T202
Bees, **Gr. K,** T258
Beetles, **Gr. 3,** 206
Big Dipper, The, **Gr. 5,** 142
Brass Instruments, **Gr. K,** T55
Broadband, **Gr. 8,** 219
Bugs, **Gr. 1,** T169
Build Instruments, **Gr. 7,** 199
Butterflies, **Gr. 3,** 112
Camel, The, **Gr. K,** T200
Changing Colors, **Gr. 1,** T331
Charting the Weather, **Gr. 1,** T274
Christmas Weather, **Gr. 5,** 409
Classifying Sounds, **Gr. 1,** T5
Colorful Sunsets, **Gr. 3,** 60
Compare Trees, **Gr. K,** T320
Conduct Research, **Gr. 3,** 164
Crawdads, **Gr. 3,** 107
Crickets, **Gr. 3,** 187
Crows, **Gr. 4,** 192
Curiosity, **Gr. K,** T274–T275
Diamonds, **Gr. 4,** 52
Dok Djampa Flower, The, **Gr. 4,** 393
Ducks, **Gr. 1,** T63
Earth Day, **Gr. 1,** T373; **Gr. 5,** 438
Earth Model, **Gr. 6,** 195
Echoes, **Gr. K,** T102; **Gr. 1,** T56
Effect of Distance on a Sound's Volume, The, **Gr. K,** T185
Elephants, **Gr. 1,** T36, T195
Environment and Earth Day, **Gr. 6,** 427
Environmental Update, **Gr. 5,** 439
Explore Acoustics, **Gr. 4,** 310
Fireflies, **Gr. 6,** 255
Frogs, **Gr. 1,** T44
Gray Wolves, **Gr. 1,** T142
Great Lakes, **Gr. 6,** 135
Green Eggs, **Gr. 2,** 279
Grizzly Bears, **Gr. K,** T252
Growing Pumpkins, **Gr. 2,** 347
Hibernation, **Gr. 1,** T127
How Animals Move, **Gr. 1,** T308
How the Larynx Produces Sound, **Gr. 6,** 67
How Woodwind Instruments Work, **Gr. 5,** 219
Hummingbird, The, **Gr. K,** T141
Instruments, **Gr. 7,** 145
Internet Radio, **Gr. 8,** 147
It's Possible, **Gr. 2,** 278
Jasmine, **Gr. 3,** 148
Keyboard Instruments, **Gr. 6,** 131
Korea's King of Animals, **Gr. 1,** T188
Latin Names of Bones, **Gr. 5,** 406
Learning About Bears, **Gr. 1,** T312
Learning About Hands, **Gr. K,** T338
Life of a Flea, **Gr. 1,** T159

Classified Index

Classified Index of Songs, Selected Concepts, Skills, and Activities (continued)

Locomotion, **Gr. 4,** 312
Loud and Soft, **Gr. 1,** T134
Make a Model of a Forest, **Gr. 1,** T149
Mayfly, The, **Gr. K,** T76
MIDI, **Gr. 8,** 206
Midnight Sun, **Gr. 3,** 142
Mockingbirds, **Gr. 4,** 151
Moon, The, **Gr. 3,** 220
Nature, **Gr. 5,** 366
New Island, A, **Gr. 6,** 296
Ocean Mammal, **Gr. 5,** 334
Octopus, **Gr. 4,** 31
Patterns of Change, **Gr. 4,** 149
Percussion Experiment, **Gr. 5,** 141
Pitch, Frequency, and Vibration, **Gr. 7,** 70
Pitch, **Gr. 5,** 23
Plants and Trees, **Gr. K,** T237
Pond World, A, **Gr. 1,** T274
Popular Pets, **Gr. 1,** T172
Prisms, **Grade 2,** A
Producing Pitches, **Gr. 7,** 21
Rain, **Gr. 1,** T32
Rainbows, **Gr. 4,** 127
Rattlesnakes, **Gr. 1,** T182
Record Nature Sounds, **Gr. 7,** 222
Recording Sound Waves, **Gr. 8,** 97
Research Rainbows, **Gr. 3,** 311
Robins, **Gr. 1,** T207
Roosters, **Gr. 4,** 36
Seasons, **Gr. 6,** 397
Seeing the Seasons, **Gr. 1,** T274
Shamrock Surprise, **Gr. 5,** 435
Size and Range, **Gr. 7,** 39
Solar System Sales, **Gr. 3,** 296
Sound of Rain, The, **Gr. 4,** 27
Sound Waves, **Gr. 1,** T5; **Gr. 6,** 24
Sound Waves, **Gr. 7,** 8, 95
Spanish Colors, **Gr. 5,** 99
Sprouting Plants, **Gr. 3,** 393
Sputnik, **Gr. 8,** 227
Storing Root Vegetables, **Gr. 2,** 342
Tone Color Categories, **Gr. K,** T173
Tree Frogs, **Gr. 4,** 179
Turtles, **Gr. 1,** T79
Volcanoes, **Gr. 6,** 411
Warthog and Meerkat, **Gr. K,** T223
Water and Land, **Gr. 2,** 295
Whale Songs, **Gr. 8,** 17
Whale, The, **Gr. 6,** 212
When Does the Sun Set?, **Gr. 3,** 48
Wind and Energy, **Gr. 6,** 328
Wind and Weather, **Gr. 1,** T186
Wind Power, **Gr. 3,** 136
Woodpeckers, **Gr. 4,** 49
Yuletide Plants, **Gr. 5,** 418
social studies. *See also* History and Culture
activities
conduct a poll, **Gr. 7,** 30
create a time line, **Gr. 7,** 7, 195, 234
create time line, **Gr. 8,** 118
describe a map route, **Gr. 7,** 190
research cultural influences, **Gr. 7,** 56, 64, 129, 202
research historical periods, **Gr. 7,** 4
research holiday origins, **Gr. 7,** 204
research music from historical periods, **Gr. 7,** 169
research protest songs, **Gr. 8,** 90
research public parks, **Gr. 7,** 68
use maps, **Gr. 8,** 152
countries and cultures
Afro-Cuban, **Gr. 4,** 327
Akan Culture, The, **Gr. 4,** 166
Appalachia, **Gr. 4,** 74; **Gr. 8,** 58
Brazil, **Gr. 7,** 202
Caribbean Islands, **Gr. 8,** 11
Carnaval, **Gr. 8,** 44
China, **Gr. 7,** 56
Germany, **Gr. 7,** 56
Harlem Renaissance, **Gr. 8,** 33
Hispanic Heritage, **Gr. 5,** 396–399
Hopi, **Gr. 4,** 19
India, **Gr. 5,** 402
Indonesia, **Gr. 7,** 101
Ireland, **Gr. 4,** 187; **Gr. 5,** 435
Israel, **Gr. 5,** 414
Japan, **Gr. 8,** 207
Korea, **Gr. 5,** 400
Laos, **Gr. 5,** 436
Lebanon, **Gr. 4,** 223
Mexico, **Gr. 5,** 440; **Gr. 7,** 56
Native American, **Gr. 5,** 223, 444
Netherlands, The, **Gr. 4,** 212
Newfoundland, **Gr. 5,** 334
Nigeria, **Gr. 4,** 35
North Carolina, **Gr. 4,** 226
Norway, **Gr. 4,** 168
Panama, **Gr. 4,** 215
Peru, **Gr. 4,** 350
Philippines, The, **Gr. 4,** 104
Puerto Rico, **Gr. 5,** 442
South Africa, **Gr. 4,** 24; **Gr. 7,** 214
Sweden, **Gr. 5,** 412
United States, **Gr. 7,** 4, 68, 169
Uruguay, **Gr. 4,** 93
Curriculum Link: Social Studies
Åland Islands, **Gr. 6,** 419
Age of Enlightenment, **Gr. 7,** 118
Akan Culture, The, **Gr. 4,** 166
American Revolution, The, **Gr. 4,** 155
Andes, The, **Gr. 3,** 32
Anthems, **Gr. 5,** 87
Appalachian National Scenic Trail, **Gr. 4,** 137; **Gr. 6,** 74
Appalachians, The, **Gr. 4,** 74; **Gr. 8,** 58
Argentina, **Gr. 3,** 109
Ashanti Kingdom, **Gr. 3,** 104
Aspects of Navajo Culture, **Gr. 5,** 224
Bali, **Gr. 1,** T145
Banana Boats, **Gr. 4,** 72
Beast of Burden, **Gr. 1,** T152
Boats in the British Isles, **Gr. 4,** 279

Classified Index of Songs, Selected Concepts, Skills, and Activities (continued)

Boll Weevil, **Gr. 3**, 170
Brazil, **Gr. 3**, 230; **Gr. 7**, 202
Brazilian Folk Songs, **Gr. 1**, T204
Building Railroads, **Gr. 4**, 86
Cajun Culture, **Gr. 1**, T19
Careers, **Gr. K**, T122
Caribbean Islands, **Gr. 8**, 11
Carnaval, **Gr. 8**, 44
Caucasus Mountains, The, **Gr. 3**, 215
Chavez, Cesar, **Gr. 6**, 295
Cherokee, **Gr. 4**, 207
Cherry Blossoms in Japan, **Gr. 6**, 14
China, **Gr. 1**, T129
Chisholm Trail, The, **Gr. 4**, 111
Civil War, **Gr. 8**, 39
Collaborative Skills, **Gr. 1**, T113
Coming Full Circle, **Gr. 4**, 333
Conduct a Poll, **Gr. 7**, 30
Copyright Law, **Gr. 8**, 234
Create a Time Line, **Gr. 7**, 195
Create an Imaginary City, **Gr. 2**, 328
Daniel Boone, **Gr. 3**, 98
Earth Day, **Gr. 2**, 376
Earth's Seasons, **Gr. 1**, T148
Ecosystems, **Gr. 1**, T109
Editorals, **Gr. 8**, 213
Family Interview, **Gr. 6**, 294
Festival Songs, **Gr. 4**, 350
Fireside Chat, A, **Gr. 4**, 297
Flood Stories, **Gr. 4**, 130
Gamelan in Bali, **Gr. 7**, 101
George Washington, **Gr. 2**, 370
Georgia Sea Islands, **Gr. 3**, 149
Group Discussion, **Gr. 3**, 377
Harlem Renaissance, **Gr. 8**, 33
Harvest, **Gr. 3**, 365
Hebrides Islands, **Gr. 3**, 188
Hispanic Community, **Gr. 5**, 399
Hispanic Countries, **Gr. 6**, 393
Historic Event, **Gr. 6**, 175
Historical and Fictionalized Tales, **Gr. 3**, 84
Historical Events, **Gr. 7**, 4, 82
History in Song, **Gr. 7**, 169
History of Chile, **Gr. 6**, 60
History of Parks, **Gr. 7**, 68
History of the Muscogee, **Gr. 6**, 188
History, **Gr. 3**, 44
Homestead Laws, **Gr. 5**, 110
Humpty Dumpty, **Gr. 3**, 95
Immigrant Chart, **Gr. 5**, 46
Interpret a Map, **Gr. 7**, 190
Ireland, **Gr. 4**, 187
Iroquois Confederacy, The, **Gr. 3**, 50
Israel, **Gr. 3**, 70
It's Right!, **Gr. 3**, 296
Jewish Holidays and History, **Gr. 5**, 416
Karaoke and Japanese Culture, **Gr. 8**, 207
King, Jr., Martin Luther, **Gr. 2**, 364; **Gr. 4**, 4, 386;
    Gr. 6, 295, 416
Klezmer, **Gr. 3**, 141

Korea, **Gr. 5**, 51
Kwanzaa, **Gr. 4**, 385
Language Chart, **Gr. 3**, 22
Learning About Coins, **Gr. K**, T330
Lebanon, **Gr. 4**, 223
Liberty Bell, The, **Gr. 2**, 338
Library of Congress, **Gr. 8**, 176
Lincoln, Abraham, **Gr. 2**, 371
London Bridge, **Gr. K**, T100
Louis XIV of France, **Gr. 8**, 167
Make a Resource Map of Russia, **Gr. 6**, 68
Making a Map, **Gr. 5**, 298
Maori, The **Gr. 3**, 175
Map a Journey, **Gr. 6**, 134
Map Skills, **Gr. 4**, 146
Map the Blues, **Gr. 5**, 183
Maps, **Gr. 8**, 152
Marian Anderson, **Gr. 5**, 330
Mass Media, **Gr. 8**, 111
Merchant Marine, **Gr. 1**, T39
Mexican Animals, **Gr. 2**, 331
Military Funeral Customs, **Gr. 7**, 144
Minutemen, The, **Gr. 2**, 340
Motorboats, **Gr. 1**, T160
Multicultural Histories, **Gr. 7**, 56
Music of the Civil Rights Movement, **Gr. 5**, 321
Musical Immigrants, **Gr. 7**, 129
Napoleon's March on Moscow, **Gr. 8**, 72
Nation Remembers, A, **Gr. 4**, 164
Native American Nations, **Gr. 6**, 429
Native Americans, **Gr. 1**, T73
Netherlands, The, **Gr. 4**, 212
New Holidays, **Gr. 7**, 204
Newfoundland, **Gr. 3**, 115
Newfoundland and Labrador, **Gr. 3**, 13
Nigeria, **Gr. 4**, 35
North Carolina, **Gr. 4**, 226
Origin of State Names, **Gr. 5**, 392
Outdoor Concerts, **Gr. K**, T343
Panama, **Gr. 4**, 215
Parks, Rosa, **Gr. 6**, 295
Perfect World, A, **Gr. 1**, T224
Philippines, The, **Gr. 4**, 103
Plan a Trip to Cuba, **Gr. 5**, 215
Plan a Trip to Japan, **Gr. 6**, 144
Potawatomi Nation, **Gr. 5**, 444
Present-day Monarchs, **Gr. 1**, T175
Protest Songs, **Gr. 8**, 90
Puerto Rico, **Gr. 5**, 421
Quebec, **Gr. 3**, 135
Railroads, Past and Present, **Gr. 4**, 139
Renaissance, The, **Gr. 6**, 100
Report on Serbia, **Gr. 6**, 105
Rosa Parks, **Gr. 3**, E
Rules, **Gr. K**, T272–T273
Same and Different, **Gr. K**, T280–T281
San Fermín Festival, **Gr. 3**, 211
Santa Clara Pueblo, **Gr. K**, T164
September 11, 2001, **Gr. 4**, 360
Silk Road, The, **Gr. 8**, 82

Classified Index of Songs, Selected Concepts, Skills, and Activities (continued)

Songs for Soldiers, **Gr. K,** T331
South Africa Today, **Gr. 7,** 214
South Africa, **Gr. 1,** T77; **Gr. 4,** 25
South African Change, **Gr. 3,** 36
South African Mines, **Gr. 6,** 72
Stars and Stripes, The, **Gr. 1,** T3
State Skits, **Gr. 5,** 394
Stevedores, **Gr. 3,** 126
Sulawesi, **Gr. 3,** 184
Swahili, **Gr. 5,** 428
Time Lines, **Gr. 7,** 7, 234; **Gr. 8,** 118
Timeline of the 1940s, **Gr. 3,** 229
Timeline of World Events, **Gr. 6,** 55
Traditional Instruments Around the World, **Gr. 7,** 64
Traditional Irish Symbols, **Gr. 3,** 391
Train Routes, **Gr. 6,** 31
U.S. Flag, **Gr. 6,** 387
Underground Railroad, The, **Gr. 5,** 155
Uruguay, **Gr. 4,** 93
Using a Map, **Gr. 1,** T298
Voting, **Gr. 3,** 389
Way Up North, **Gr. 3,** 8
topics
   American history, **Gr. 7,** 4, 68, 129, 169; **Gr. 8,** 39, 58, 176, 234
   Carnaval, **Gr. 5,** 338, 364, 432
   Chusok, **Gr. 5,** 400
   Cinco de Mayo, **Gr. 5,** 440
   Civil War, **Gr. 5,** 390
   Diwali, **Gr. 5,** 402
   European history, **Gr. 7,** 118; **Gr. 8,** 72, 167
   freedom marches, **Gr. 5,** 320
   Hanukkah, **Gr. 4,** 374; **Gr. 5,** 414
   Hispanic Heritage Month, **Gr. 4,** 362
   historical dramatizations, **Gr. 7,** 82
   immigration, **Gr. 7,** 56, 129
   King, Jr., Dr. Martin Luther, **Gr. 4,** 387
   Kwanzaa, **Gr. 4,** 384; **Gr. 5,** 426
   Laotian New Year, **Gr. 4,** 392
   Las Posadas, **Gr. 4,** 376
   Liberty Bell, **Gr. 5,** 395
   maps, **Gr. 7,** 190
   military customs, **Gr. 7,** 144
   multicultural influences, **Gr. 7,** 202
   national anthem, **Gr. 4,** 357; **Gr. 5,** 386
   Pike's Peak, **Gr. 5,** 388
   Pony Express, **Gr. 5,** 147
   Powwow, **Gr. 5,** 444
   St. Patrick's Day, **Gr. 5,** 434
   Têt Trung, **Gr. 4,** 366
   time lines, **Gr. 7,** 7, 195, 234
   Underground Railroad, **Gr. 5,** 145
   visual aids, **Gr. 8,** 118, 152
   world history, **Gr. 8,** 82, 207

theater
   Curriculum Link: Theater
      Act Out a Song, **Gr. K,** T42
      Act Out the Opera: *The Barber of Seville,* **Gr. 6,** 152
      Act Out the Story, **Gr. 2,** 355
      Acting Free, **Gr. 3,** 181

Animal Guessing Game, **Gr.1,** T204
Comedy/Tragedy Masks, **Gr. 7,** 141
Dramatic Reading, **Gr. 1,** T339; **Gr. 7,** 26
Dramatization, **Gr. K,** T52
Dramatize Fiction, **Gr. 7,** 181
Dramatize Lyrics, **Gr. K,** T147
Dramatize the Aria, **Gr. K,** T179
Dramatizing a Story, **Gr. 1,** T52
Dramatizing "Romper, Stomper, and Boo," **Gr. 1,** T37
Environmental Update, **Gr. 5,** 439
Expression, **Gr. 5,** 115
Folkloric Drama, **Gr. 5,** 193
Haji Firuz Performance, **Gr. 6,** 421
Improvise a Scene, **Gr. 5,** 15
Into the Woods, **Gr. 8,** 86
Land of the Elephants, **Gr. 1,** T208
Major and Minor, **Gr. 4,** 231
Mardi Gras Costumes, **Gr. 7,** 89
Message for the World, **Gr. 5,** 235
Mimicry, **Gr. 4,** 152
Music and Story, **Gr. 4,** 56
Music Man, The, **Gr. 7,** 36
Pantomime Feelings, **Gr. K,** T282–T283
Pantomime, **Gr. K,** T313, **Gr. 1,** T110
Perform a Play, **Gr. 4,** 189
Perform a Skit, **Gr. 3,** 61
Performance, **Gr. 1,** T135
Performance Art, **Gr. 8,** 23
Plan Party Music, **Gr. 3,** 27
Play About Immigrants, **Gr. 2,** 147
Posada Celebration, **Gr. 4,** 378
Retell "Hansel and Gretel," **Gr. K,** T180
Silent Films, **Gr. 7,** 109
Stage the Song "Heart," **Gr. 6,** 168
State Skits, **Gr. 5,** 394
Stomp, **Gr. 7,** 147
Tableau, The, **Gr. 6,** 296
Thanksgiving Pageant, **Gr. 4,** 370
Write a synopsis for a musical, **Gr. 6,** 183
Writing a Script, **Gr. 5,** 147
theater activities
   adapt fiction for theater, **Gr. 7,** 181
   create performance art, **Gr. 8,** 23
   design a mask, **Gr. 7,** 89
   dramatize a poem, **Gr. K,** T77
   perform dramatic readings, **Gr. 7,** 26
   perform percussion piece, **Gr. 7,** 147
   summarize a play, **Gr. 7,** 36
   write lyrics, **Gr. 8,** 86

D

DESCANT
instrumental
   Jugaremos en el bosque, **Gr. 2,** 189
   When the Saints Go Marching In, **Gr. 5,** 256
vocal
   Cindy, **Gr. 5,** 256
   Elijah Rock, **Gr. 6,** 52
   Gentle River Runs, A, **Gr. 5,** 342

Hallelujah Get on Board, **Gr. 5,** 345

I Hear America Singing, **Gr. 5,** 327

Joban Tanko Bushi, **Gr. 6,** 142

Lion Sleeps Tonight, The, **Gr. 5,** 172; **Gr. 7,** 214–215

Red Iron Ore, **Gr. 6,** 134

Singabahambayo, **Gr. 5,** 75

Uyai Mose, **Gr. 7,** 66–67

Wachet auf, **Gr.6,** 259

We Shall Overcome (Listening), **Gr. 7,** 213

F

FINE ART REPRODUCTIONS AND ARCHITECTURE

architecture

adobe buildings in Taos Pueblo, New Mexico, **Gr. 2,** 155

cathedral and government palace in Guadalajara, **Gr. 5,** 189

Damdama Sahib Temple, **Gr. 6,** 225

Falling Water, **Gr. 8,** 226

Harlech Castle in Wales, Great Britain, **Gr. 2,** 141

Japanese Country House, **Gr. 6,** 145

lighthouse, **Gr. 5,** 5

New York City late 1800s, **Gr. 5,** 106

prairie house, **Gr. 5,** 95

Space Needle, **Gr. 5,** 5

Statue of Liberty, **Gr. 5,** 42–43

subway, **Gr. 5,** 278

Tower of London, **Gr. 6,** 287

Üsküdar train station, **Gr. 5,** 129

fine art reproductions

African crafts

Congo: Kuba cloth, **Gr. 5,** 73

Zulu: beadwork, **Gr. 5,** 56, 57

Zulu: Imbenge basket, **Gr. 5,** 75

American flag, **Gr. 5,** 387

Anonymous: Abraham Lincoln, **Gr. 7,** 173

Anonymous: *"Blind" Lemon Jefferson,* **Gr. 6,** 179

Anonymous: Chariot, **Gr. 6,** 242

Anonymous: Chinese Wood-block print, **Gr. 6,** 27

Anonymous: Cod fishing, **Gr. 6,** 171

Anonymous: Group of musicians, dancers, and servants, **Gr. 6,** 27

Anonymous: Kuna Indian textile, Panama, **Gr. 6,** 223

Anonymous: *Madama Butterfly* illustration, **Gr. 6,** 257

Anonymous: *Man and a Woman Inside the Palace with Two Musicians, A,* **Gr. 6,** 100

Anonymous: Musicians and guests at a festival, **Gr. 6,** 224

Anonymous: Oceanus mosaic, **Gr. 6,** 196

Anonymous: Rangolis, **Gr. 6,** 397

Anonymous: *Room in the House of Mr. Kong, a Peking Merchant,* **Gr. 6,** 26

Anonymous: Three Musicians, **Gr. 4,** 175

Anonymous: Two fishermen and boy, **Gr. 6,** 171

Anonymous: War of 1812, **Gr. 7,** 193

Anonymous: *Wedding Ball of the Duc de Joyeuse,* **Gr. 6,** 100

Audubon, John James: *Bison,* **Gr. K,** T218

Bearden, Romare: *Empress of the Blues,* **Gr. 5,** 174

Bearden, Romare: Untitled mixed media, **Gr. 7,** 16

Belle, Charles: *Ranunculus,* **Gr. 2,** 210

Bingham, George Caleb: *Through the Cumberland Gap,* **Gr. 3,** 98

Brueghel, Pieter: *Children's Games,* **Gr. 2,** 247

Brueghel, Pieter: *Return of the Hunters,* **Gr. 6,** 133

Brueghel, Pieter: *The Harvesters,* **Gr. 4,** 365

Brueghel, Pieter: *Winter Landscape with a Bird Trap,* **Gr. 2,** 351

Caillebotte, Gustave: *Paris Street, Rainy Day,* **Gr. 1,** T31

Cassatt, Mary: *Boating Party, The,* **Gr. 6,** 47

Cassatt, Mary: *Mother and Child,* **Gr. 2,** 185

Chagall, Marc: *Dance,* **Gr. 4,** 68

Chagall, Marc: *The Fiddler,* **Gr. 4,** 375

Clark, Myron: *U.S.S. Constitution,* **Gr. 2,** 171

Constable, John: *Weymouth Bay,* **Gr. 8,** 154

Currier and Ives: *Shakers Near Lebanon,* **Gr. 5,** 137

David: *Coronation of Emperor Napoleon I Bonaparte and Empress Josephine,* **Gr. 1,** T176

Davidson, Peter: *The Sun Rises While the Moon Sleeps,* **Gr. 2,** 218

De Caullery, Louis: *Scenes from the Life of the Prodigal Son,* **Gr. 6,** 100

Degas, Edgar: *Little Dancer of Fourteen,* **Gr. 2,** 25

Dürer, Albrecht: *The Festival of the Rosary,* **Gr. 4,** 174

Dürer, Albrecht: *Two Musicians,* **Gr. 4,** 177

Dürer, Albrecht: *Young Hare,* **Gr. 2,** 151

Fabergé, Peter Carl: *The Fabergé Mosaic Egg of the Royal Collection,* **Gr. 4,** 153

Fleck, Joseph Amadeus: *Taos July,* **Gr. 2,** 155

Gabbiani, Antonio Domenico: *Ferdinando de'Medici with his musicians,* **Gr. 8,** 5

Gagarin, Grigori Grigorevich: *Princess Baryatinskaya's Ball,* **Gr. 5,** 113

Garza, Carmen Lomas: *Barbacoa para cumpeaños,* **Gr. 5,** 399

Ginat, Judith Yellin: *Valley of the Moon, Eilat,* **Gr. 4,** 113

Grandma Moses: *Deep Snow,* **Gr. 3,** 130

Greek statues, **Gr. 5,** 284

Gurlitt, Louis: *A Watermill in Christiania,* **Gr. 4,** 169

Hasui, Kawase: *Ara River at Akabane,* **Gr. 2,** 77

Hewson, Marg: *Exhausted Bird,* **Gr. 4,** 48

Hicks, Edward: *Noah's Ark,* **Gr. 4,** 131

Hicks, Edward: *Peaceable Kingdom,* **Gr. 1,** T17

Hiroshige, Ando: *Two Mandarin Ducks,* **Gr. 2,** 101

Houser, Allan: *Waiting for Dancing Partners,* **Gr. 5,** 26

Indiana, Robert: *X–5,* **Gr. 5,** 212

Karcsay, Lajos: *Gathering Apples,* **Gr. 3,** 25

Krieghoff, Cornelius: *Fiddler and Boy Doing Jig,* **Gr. 3,** 92

Leonard, Limosin: *Concert, A,* **Gr. 6,** 100

Mallett, Keith: *Loving Embrace,* **Gr. 4,** 35

Maori carving, **Gr. 5,** 150

Mendizabal, Haydee: *Carnaval,* **Gr. 3,** 33

Mendoza, Antonio Coché: *Tejedoras,* **Gr. 4,** 101

Miller, William Rickarby: *Erie Canal at Little Falls, New York,* **Gr. 5,** 133

Mnev, Vladmir: *Jewish Musicians in Jerusalem,* **Gr. 6,** 425

Monet, Claude: *A Field of Tulips in Holland,* **Gr. 3,** 134

Monet, Claude: *The Magpie,* **Gr. 2,** 271

Monet, Claude: *Water Lilies,* **Gr. K,** T138

Classified Index

Classified Index of Songs, Selected Concepts, Skills, and Activities (continued)

Mount, William Sidney: *Dance of the Haymakers*, **Gr. 6**, 96

Native American crafts
  Athabascan birch bark baskets, **Gr. 5**, 27
  Comanche beaded bag from Oklahoma (beadwork), **Gr. 5**, 27

Normann, Adelsteen: *Motive from the County of Nordland*, **Gr. 3**, 143

Nugent, Bob: *Nevoa (Mist)*, **Gr. 4**, 216

Picasso, Pablo: *Child with a Dove*, **Gr. 4**, 8

Picasso, Pablo: *Dance of Youth*, **Gr. 5**, 207

Picasso, Pablo: Unnamed sculpture, **Gr. 7**, 232

Portinari, Cándido: *Bambini Giocando*, **Gr. 3**, 231

Potthast, Edward Henry: *Hourtide*, **Gr. 1**, T374

Remington, Frederic: *Bronco Buster*, **Gr. 2**, 67

Remington, Frederic: *Untitled*, **Gr. 6**, 114

Renkes, Saelon: *Birches from Alberta Canada*, **Gr. 2**, 89

Renoir, Pierre-August: *Luncheon of the Boating Party*, **Gr. 7**, 121

Rivera, Diego: *Making Tortillas*, **Gr. 8**, 126

Rivera, Diego: *La Zandunga*, **Gr. 3**, 213

Rivera, Diego: *Portrait of Dolores Olmeda*, **Gr. 5**, 101

Rivera, Diego: *The Well of Toledo*, **Gr. 1**, T197

Riviere, Briton: *Song of Peace*, **Gr. 7**, 155

Rockwell, Norman: *A Boy and His Dog*, **Gr. 2**, 212

Saint James, Synthia: *Kwanzaa Stamp*, **Gr. 5**, 429

Savitsky, Jack: *Train in Coal Town*, **Gr. 2**, 13

Schiele, Egon: *Four Trees Summer Landscape*, **Gr. 8**, 92

Seurat, George: *Le Cirque*, **Gr. 3**, 285

Shaker table, **Gr. 5**, 137

Tanner, Henry Ossawa: *The Banjo Lesson*, **Gr. 3**, 151

Teniers, David II: *Festival in the Country*, **Gr. 6**, 98

Tsireh, Awa: *Basket Dance*, **Gr. 5**, 445

Turkish rug (weaving), **Gr. 5**, 135

Turkish table, **Gr. 4**, 222

Turner, Joseph Mallard William: *Crossing the Brook*, **Gr. 8**, 114

Turtle carving, **Gr. 3**, 52

Unknown: Benjamin Franklin, **Gr. 5**, 244

Unknown: California vaquero (woodcut), **Gr. 5**, 68

Unknown: Chi Rho from The Book of Kells (painting), **Gr. 5**, 48

Unknown: Francis Scott Key (painting), **Gr. 5**, 397

Unknown: Franz Joseph Haydn, **Gr. 5**, 247

Unknown: Franz Joseph Haydn, **Gr. 8**, 120

Van Gogh, Vincent: *Irises*, **Gr. 2**, 236

Van Gogh, Vincent: *Starry Night*, **Gr. K**, T66

Van Rijn, Rembrandt: *The Mill*, **Gr. 2**, 53

Warhol, Andy: *Soup Cans*, **Gr. 8**, 226

Webber, Charles: *Fugitives Arriving at Levi Coffin's Indiana Farm*, **Gr. 5**, 11

Wells-Hess, Gail: *Barcas de pesca*, **Gr. 5**, 167

FOLK AND TRADITIONAL MUSIC

Africa (Sub-Saharan). *See also* Angola, Benin, Cameroon, Congo, Eritrea, Ethiopia, Ghana, Kenya, Liberia, Mozambique, Nigeria, Senegal, Sierra Leone, South Africa, Uganda, Zimbabwe

Adukbe (traditional) (listening), **Gr. 8**, 177

Afirika (listening), **Gr. 7**, 226

African Postal Workers (listening), **Gr. 7**, 147

Agahu Suite from *Dance Suites from West Africa* (listening), **Gr. 7**, 75

Drumming Spider, The (story), **Gr. 2**, 333

Kum Ba Yah, **Gr. K**, T327

Kye Kye Kule, **Gr. 7**, 225

Lion Sleeps Tonight, The, **Gr. 7**, 214

Mɔ-fia mo-ni, **Gr. 5**, 277

Oh, Come Sing a Song, **Gr. 7**, 65

Pata Pata (listening), **Gr. 2**, 94

Uyai Mose, **Gr. 7**, 66

African American. *See also* American

All Night, All Day, **Gr. 1**, T232

Amen, **Gr. 3**, 376

Big Bunch, a Little Bunch, **Gr. 4**, 267

Bye 'n' Bye, **Gr. K**, T67

Charlie Over the Ocean, **Gr. 1**, T75

Circle 'Round the Zero, **Gr. 3**, 267

Crawdad Song, **Gr. 3**, 107

Didn't He Ramble (listening), **Gr. 7**, 143

Didn't It Rain, **Gr. 6**, 345

Do Lord, **Gr. 6**, 260

Down by the Riverside, **Gr. 6**, 22; (listening), **Gr. 3**, 382

Draw a Bucket of Water, **Gr. 3**, 222

Dry Bones, **Gr. 5**, 406

Elijah Rock (song and listening), **Gr. 6**, 52

Ev'ry Time I Feel the Spirit, **Gr. 6**, C

Everybody Oughta Know (song and listening), **Gr. 1**, T361

Follow the Drinkin' Gourd, **Gr. 5**, 142

Freedom Is a Constant Struggle, **Gr. 7**, 211

Get On Board, Children (listening), **Gr. 5**, 347

Git on Board, **Gr. K**, T145

Go Tell It on the Mountain, **Gr. 3**, 377

Good News, **Gr. 6**, 242

Goodbye, My Riley O, **Gr. 4**, 257

He's Got the Whole World in His Hands (listening and song), **Gr. 2**, 116

Head and Shoulders, Baby, **Gr. 1**, T40

Here Comes Sally, **Gr. 2**, 220

How Long the Train Been Gone?, **Gr. 4**, 264

I Got Shoes (song and listening), **Gr. K**, T33

I Lost the Farmer's Dairy Key, **Gr. 3**, 273

I Saw the Light, **Gr. 5**, 252

I Want to Be Ready, **Gr. 6**, 12

I'm Gonna Sing, **Gr. 2**, 9

I'm Gonna Sit at the Welcome Table, **Gr. 6**, 416

I'm On My Way, **Gr. 3**, 382

I've Got a Robe, **Gr. 7**, 162

In That Great Git'n Up Mornin', **Gr. 5**, 10

In the Sweet By and By (listening), **Gr. 7**, 143

Jamaica Farewell, **Gr. 3**, 156

Jordan's Angels, **Gr. 6**, 365

Joshua Fit the Battle of Jericho (song and listening), **Gr. 5**, 126, 127

Just a Closer Walk with Thee (listening), **Gr. 7**, 143

Little David Play on Your Harp, **Gr. 4**, 323

Little David, Play On Your Harp (listening), **Gr. 2**, 9

Little Sally Walker, **Gr. 3**, 105

Little Sally Water, **Gr. 2**, 249

Mary Had a Baby, **Gr. 2**, 360

Miss Mary Mack, **Gr. 1**, T15

'Most Done Ling'rin' Here, **Gr. 4,** 65
My Mama's Calling Me, **Gr. 1,** T54
O, I'm Gonna Sing, **Gr. 5,** 245
Oh, Won't You Sit Down?, **Gr. 4,** 70
Old Ark's A-Moverin', **Gr. 4,** 130
Old Aunt Dinah, **Gr. 4,** 245
Old House, **Gr. 4,** 282
Old Mister Rabbit, **Gr. 3,** 254
Open the Window, Noah, **Gr. 3,** 324
Over My Head, **Gr. 3,** 286
Pay Me My Money Down, **Gr. 3,** 149
Pick a Bale of Cotton, **Gr. 6,** 254
Pizza, Pizza, Daddy-O, **Gr. 2,** 62
Punchinella, **Gr. 1,** T216
Rise Up, Shepherd, and Follow, **Gr. 5,** 422
Rise, Sally, Rise, **Gr. 1,** T162
Roll de Ole Chariot Along, **Gr. 6,** 243
Shepherd, Shepherd, **Gr. 3,** 56
So Glad I'm Here (listening), **Gr. 2,** 47
Somebody's Knocking at Your Door, **Gr. 5,** 254
Sometimes I Feel Like a Motherless Child
    (song and listening), **Gr. 6,** 271
Sweep, Sweep Away, **Gr. 3,** 276
Sweet Potatoes, **Gr. 3,** 16
There's a Little Wheel A-Turnin' in My Heart, **Gr. 3,** 129
This Little Light of Mine, **Gr. 1,** T238; **Gr. 2,** F
This Train (song and listening), **Gr. 4,** 343
Train Is A-Coming, **Gr. 4,** 270
Trampin', **Gr. 3,** 287
Twenty-four Robbers, **Gr. 1,** T173
Ujima, **Gr. 5,** 427
Uncle Jessie (song and listening), **Gr. 3,** 327
Wade in the Water (listening), **Gr. 5,** 144
We Shall Overcome, **Gr. 4,** 387; **Gr. 7,** 212;
    (listening), **Gr. 7,** 213
What You Gonna Call Your Pretty Little Baby?,
    Gr. K, T319
When the Saints Go Marching In, **Gr. 5,** 256
Who's That Yonder?, **Gr. 3,** 245
Woke Up This Morning, **Gr. 3,** 180

American. *See also* African American; Appalachian;
    Hispanic American; Native American; Puerto Rico
Alison's Camel, **Gr. K,** T201
All Around the Buttercup, **Gr. 2,** 210
Alphabet Song, **Gr. K,** T54
Amazing Grace, **Gr. 5,** 19; (bagpipe version)
    (listening), **Gr. 7,** 144
Animal Fair, **Gr. 2,** 214
Animal Song, **Gr. 1,** T288
Away for Rio, **Gr. 2,** 170
Babylon's Fallin', **Gr. 5,** 243
Ballad of the Bedbugs and the Beetles, The, **Gr. 3,** 206
Bear Went Over the Mountain, The, **Gr. K,** T204;
    Gr. 1, T115
Bee, Bee, Bumblebee, **Gr. 1,** T250
Billy, **Gr. 3,** 7
Bingo, **Gr. K,** T64
Blow, Ye Winds, Blow, **Gr. 3,** 192
Bluebells, **Gr. 1,** T209
Bobby Shafto, **Gr. K,** T265

Boll Weevil, **Gr. 3,** 171
Bonjour, mes amis (Hello, My Friends), **Gr. 1,** T18
Born to Be with You (listening), **Gr. 3,** 387
Bounce High, Bounce Low, **Gr. K,** T131
Bow, Wow, Wow, **Gr. 2,** 264
Built My Lady a Fine Brick House, **Gr. 4,** 252
Bus, The, **Gr. K,** T137
Button, You Must Wander, **Gr. 2,** 176
Cape Cod Chantey, **Gr. 6,** 258
Captain Jinks, **Gr. 6,** 266
Cat and Dog, **Gr. 3,** 259
Charlotte Town, **Gr. 6,** 261
Chase the Squirrel, **Gr. 1,** T88
Chicka-hanka, **Gr. 4,** 138
Chicken on the Fence Post, **Gr. 3,** 265
City Blues, The, **Gr. 5,** 278
Clap Your Hands, **Gr. 1,** T246
Clocks, **Gr. 3,** 266
Clog (listening), **Gr. 2,** 68
Cobbler, Cobbler, Mend My Shoe, **Gr. K,** T169
Common Step (traditional) (listening), **Gr. 8,** 39
Coral, **Gr. 3,** 249
Corner Grocery Store, **Gr. 2,** 311
Cornstalk Fiddle and a Shoestring Bow, **Gr. 3,** 284
Cotton-Eye Joe, **Gr. 4,** 52
Cripple Creek, **Gr. 6,** 372
Cuckoo, Where Are You?, **Gr. 2,** 244
Cut the Cake, **Gr. 1,** T232
Daisy Chain, **Gr. 2,** 255
Dance Together, **Gr. 2,** 264
Derby Ram, The, **Gr. 4,** 259
Dinah, **Gr. 3,** 150
Doggie, Doggie, **Gr. 2,** 59
Doney Gal, **Gr. 6,** 115
Down by the Bay, **Gr. 1,** T48
Early in the Morning at Eight O'Clock, **Gr. 4,** 59
Eency Weency Spider, **Gr. K,** T8
Eight Bells, **Gr. 4,** 281
Engine, Engine Number Nine, **Gr. 2,** 13
Erie Canal, **Gr. 5,** 132
Eyes of Texas, The, (listening), **Gr. 7,** 42, 45
Farmer in the Dell, The, **Gr. K,** T100
Five Fat Turkeys, **Gr. K,** T309
Frog in the Meadow, **Gr. 3,** 243
Frog Went A-Courtin', **Gr. 4,** 46
Frosty Weather, **Gr. 3,** 250
Gee, Mom, I Want to Go Home, **Gr. 6,** 148
Gilly, Gilly, Gilly Good Morning, **Gr. 1,** T12
Girl I Left Behind Me, The, **Gr. 4,** 249
Git Along, Little Dogies, **Gr. 6,** 284
Golden Ring Around the Susan Girl, **Gr. 3,** 264
Goober Peas (song and listening), **Gr. 6,** 269
Good Night, Sleep Tight, **Gr. 2,** 76
Goodbye Brother, **Gr. 4,** 273
Granny (speech piece), **Gr. 1,** T104
Grasshoppers Three, **Gr. 1,** T284
Great Big House, **Gr. 3,** 14
Green Grass Grew All Around, The, **Gr. 1,** T148
Green Gravel, **Gr. 4,** 247
Harvest, **Gr. 2,** 342

Classified Index

Heave-Ho Me Laddies, **Gr. 4,** 258
Heigh Ho, Here We Go, **Gr. 2,** 252
Hello Song, **Gr. K,** T2
Hello!, **Gr. 3,** 283
Hello, There! **Gr. 1,** T230
Here Comes a Bluebird, **Gr. 2,** 263
Here Is the Beehive, **Gr. K,** T258
Here We Sit, **Gr. 1,** T251
Hey, Hey, Look at Me, **Gr. 2,** 245
Hi! My Name Is Joe! (speech piece), **Gr. 1,** T220
Hickory, Dickory, Dock (speech piece), **Gr. K,** T49
Hoedown (listening), **Gr. 6,** 116
Hokey Pokey, **Gr. K,** T68
Hold My Mule, **Gr. 4,** 248
Hop Up and Jump Up, **Gr. 4,** 271
Hop, Hop, Hop, **Gr. K,** T197
Hop, Old Squirrel, **Gr. 2,** 258
Hot Dog, **Gr. K,** T69
Hush, Little Baby (listening), **Gr. 4,** 9
I Am Slowly Going Crazy, **Gr. 1,** T127
I Bought Me a Cat (listening and song), **Gr. 2,** 14
I Got a Letter, **Gr. 6,** 270
I Have a Car, **Gr. 3,** 252
I Like Spinach, **Gr. 1,** T163
I See, **Gr. 2,** 266
I Wanna Be a Friend of Yours, **Gr. 1,** T84
If You're Happy, **Gr. K,** T6
I'm Going to Georgia, **Gr. 6,** 244
In and Out, **Gr. 2,** 245
In Good Old Colony Times, **Gr. 3,** 326
It Rained a Mist, **Gr. 4,** 262
Jack, Be Nimble, **Gr. K,** T88
Jig Jog, Jig Jog, **Gr. K,** T260
Jim Along, Josie, **Gr. 2,** 194
Jingle at the Window, **Gr. 3,** 268
John Henry, **Gr. 5,** 146
John Jacob Jingleheimer Schmidt, **Gr. 3,** 68
John Kanaka, **Gr. 5,** 249
John the Rabbit, **Gr. 1,** T74
Johnny Works with One Hammer, **Gr. 1,** T96
Johnny's Flea, **Gr. 1,** T158
Jolly Old Saint Nicholas, **Gr. 1,** T352; **Gr. 4,** 382
Jump, Jim Joe, **Gr. 1,** T89
Just a Closer Walk with Thee (listening), **Gr. 7,** 75
King's Land, **Gr. 2,** 257
Kreely Kranky, **Gr. 3,** 258
Leila, **Gr. 6,** 376
Lemonade, **Gr. 2,** 19
Let Us Chase the Squirrel, **Gr. 3,** 248
Li'l 'Liza Jane, **Gr. 4,** 20
Little Ducky Duddle, **Gr. K,** T289
Little Red Caboose, **Gr. 1,** T97
Little Tommy Tinker, **Gr. 3,** 277
London Bridge, **Gr. K,** T99
Lonesome Dove, **Gr. 6,** 249
Long-Legged Sailor, **Gr. 4,** 243
Love Somebody, **Gr. 4,** 94
Lucy Lockett, **Gr. 1,** T253
Mama Don't 'Low, **Gr. 6,** 126
Mardi Gras Mambo, **Gr. 7,** 88–89
Merrily, We Roll Along, **Gr. K,** T110

Mill Song, The, **Gr. 2,** 52
Mississippi Mud (listening), **Gr. 6,** 65
Mister Rabbit, Mister Rabbit, **Gr. 2,** 150
Mister Sun, **Gr. K,** T343
Morning Bells, **Gr. 3,** 270
Mother, Mother, **Gr. 2,** 254
Mr. Frog, **Gr. 2,** 257
Mulberry Bush, The, **Gr. K,** T112
My Government Claim, **Gr. 5,** 95, 110
My Home's in Montana, **Gr. 4,** 274
My Horses Ain't Hungry, **Gr. 3,** 278
My Thumbs are Starting to Wiggle, **Gr. K,** T35
Never Sleep Late Anymore, **Gr. 6,** 274
Night Herding Song, **Gr. 4,** 110
O, the Train's Off the Track, **Gr. 3,** 176
Oats, Peas, Beans, and Barley Grow, **Gr. K,** T287
Old Blue, **Gr. 2,** 213
Old Dan Tucker, **Gr. 5,** 253
Old Gray Cat, The, **Gr. K,** T43
Old Jim John, **Gr. 6,** 253
Old Joe Clark, **Gr. 4,** 74
Old King Glory, **Gr. 1,** T217
Old MacDonald Had a Farm, **Gr. K,** T211; (listening),
   Gr. 2, 133
Old Paint, **Gr. 4,** 275
Old Turkey Buzzard, **Gr. 5,** 264
Old Woman and the Pig, **Gr. 2,** 130
Oliver Twist, **Gr. 2,** 268
On Top of Spaghetti, **Gr. 2,** 312
One Finger, One Thumb, **Gr. K,** T38
One Little Elephant, **Gr. 1,** T194
One More River, **Gr. 3,** 216
One Potato, Two Potato, **Gr. 3,** 267
One, Two, Three, Four, **Gr. 1,** T123
One, Two, Three, Four, Five, **Gr. 1,** T265
One, Two, Tie My Shoe, **Gr. K,** T151
Our Goodman, **Gr. 6,** 245
Over in the Meadow, **Gr. 1,** T78
Over the River and Through the Wood, **Gr. 4,** 370
Page's Train, **Gr. 4,** 246
Parade in the Parlor (listening), **Gr. 4,** 229
Pat on the Back, A, **Gr. 2,** 74
Pat Works on the Railway, **Gr. 4,** 86; (Orff version)
   (listening), **Gr. 1,** T144
Patriotic Medley, **Gr. 1,** T8
Paw Paw Patch, The, **Gr. 3,** 195
Peanut Butter, **Gr. 1,** T218
Pitty Patty Polt (speech piece), **Gr. 1,** T180
Plainsies, Clapsies, **Gr. 2,** 248
Polly Wolly Doodle, **Gr. 3,** 132
Push Boat Song, **Gr. 4,** 266
Quaker, Quaker, **Gr. 1,** T100
Rain, Rain, Go Away, **Gr. 1,** T259
Rattlesnake, **Gr. 1,** T185
Red Iron Ore (boat song), **Gr. 6,** 134
Red River Valley (listening), **Gr. 6,** 96
Red Rover, **Gr. 2,** 249
Ridin' of a Goat, Leadin' of a Sheep, **Gr. 4,** 251
Riding in the Buggy, **Gr. 3,** 131
Risseldy, Rosseldy, **Gr. 6,** 264

Classified Index of Songs, Selected Concepts, Skills, and Activities (continued)

Route 66 (listening), **Gr. 7,** 191
Row, Row, Row Your Boat, **Gr. 4,** 268
Row, Row, Row, **Gr. K,** T274
Sail Away (song and listening), **Gr. 4,** 54, 55
Sally Go 'Round the Sun, **Gr. 2,** 268
Salsa in the Parlor (listening), **Gr. 4,** 229
Sammy Sackett, **Gr. 2,** 146
Scraping Up Sand, **Gr. 6,** 248
See the Pony Galloping, **Gr. K,** T44
Seesaw, **Gr. 1,** T242
Seesaw, Margery Daw, **Gr. K,** T265
Shady Grove (listening), **Gr. 8,** 59
Shady Grove, **Gr. 6,** 286
She'll Be Comin' 'Round the Mountain, **Gr. 2,** 33
Ship Ahoy, **Gr. 3,** 314
Shoo, Fly, **Gr. 2,** 222
Simple Simon, **Gr. 1,** T175
Sing a Song of Sixpence, **Gr. K,** T111
Six Little Ducks, **Gr. 1,** T64
Sixteen Tons, **Gr. 7,** 151; (listening), **Gr. 7,** 150
Skin and Bones, **Gr. 1,** T340
Skinnamarink, **Gr. 2,** 368
Skip to My Lou, **Gr. 1,** T102
Smoke Goes Up the Chimney, **Gr. 3,** 272
Snail, Snail, **Gr. 1,** T252
Star Light, Star Bright, **Gr. 1,** T258
Star-Spangled Banner, The, **Gr. 7,** 42, 185, 194
Strawberry Roan (listening and song), **Gr. 2,** 66
Streets of Laredo, **Gr. 5,** 260
Sugar in the Gourd, **Gr. 6,** 251
Sun Don't Set in the Mornin', **Gr. 3,** 48, 60
Swapping Song, **Gr. 4,** 253
Sweetly Sings the Donkey, **Gr. K,** T244
Taps (listening), **Gr. 7,** 144
Taps, **Gr. 3,** 281
Ten in a Bed, **Gr. K,** T256
There Was a Jolly Miller, **Gr. 6,** 250
There's a Hole in the Bucket, **Gr. 2,** 132
There's a Hole in the Middle of the Sea, **Gr. 1,** T178
This Is What I Can Do, **Gr. K,** T124
Three Little Muffins (speech piece), **Gr. K,** T127
Throw It Out the Window, **Gr. 3,** 94
Toodala, **Gr. K,** T39
Touch Your Shoulders, **Gr. K,** T254
Turkey in the Straw (listening), **Gr. 2,** 348
Turn the Glasses Over, **Gr. 3,** 260
Twinkle, Twinkle, Little Star, **Gr. K,** T90
Two in a Boat (listening), **Gr. 3,** 316
Vive l'amour, **Gr. 5,** 262
Wake Me, Shake Me, **Gr. 1,** T198
Wake Up Canon, **Gr. 4,** 326
Walk in the Parlor, **Gr. 4,** 226
Walk to School, **Gr. K,** T18
Waltz in the Parlor (listening), **Gr. 4,** 229
'Way Down Yonder in the Brickyard, **Gr. 5,** 255
Wayfaring Stranger, **Gr. 6,** 283
We Are Playing in the Forest, **Gr. K,** T248
We're Sailing Down the River, **Gr. 2,** 166
What Did Delaware?, **Gr. 2,** 190
What's Your Name?, **Gr. 1,** T125
When Johnny Comes Marching Home (listening), **Gr. 7,** 168
Who Has the Penny?, **Gr. 2,** 252
Who's Got a Fishpole?, **Gr. 4,** 261
Who's That Tapping at the Window?, **Gr. 2,** 261
Willowbee, **Gr. 2,** 69
Willum, **Gr. 1,** T19
Woodchuck, **Gr. 3,** 246
Yankee Doodle, **Gr. 2,** 340; **Gr. 4,** 154
You Sing for Me, **Gr. 6,** 106

American Indian. *See* Native American

Appalachia. *See also* American
Buckeye Jim, **Gr. 4,** 136
Cedar Swamp, **Gr. 4,** 50
Cindy, **Gr. 5,** 265
Cumberland Gap, **Gr. 3,** 99
Death of the Robin, **Gr. 3,** 275
I'll Rise When the Rooster Crows, **Gr. 4,** 36
Johnson Boys, **Gr. 4,** 233
Leatherwing Bat, **Gr. 2,** 304

Argentina. *See also* Latin America
Arroyito serrano (Little Mountain Stream), **Gr. 4,** 340
De allacito carnavalito (The Carnival Is Coming), **Gr. 5,** 269
El nido (The Nest), **Gr. 3,** 214
El picaflor (The Humming Bird), **Gr. K,** T141
Huainito, **Gr. 6,** 351
Mi chacra (My Farm), **Gr. K,** T207
¿Quién es ese pajarito? (Who Is That Little Bird?), **Gr. 4,** 284
Tengo, Tengo, Tengo (I Have, I Have, I Have), **Gr. K,** T212

Australia and Pacific Islands
Ake Tonu (listening), **Gr. 5,** 150
Australia's on the Wallaby, **Gr. 2,** 106
Haere Ra (Now Is the Hour), **Gr. 5,** 151
Nani Wale Na Hala (The Swaying Pandanus Trees), **Gr. 5,** 276
Po Atarau (listening), **Gr. 5,** 150
`Ulili E (The Sandpiper), **Gr. 4,** 396

Austria
Lift Up Your Voices, **Gr. 5,** 319
Moulinet (listening), **Gr. 2,** 57
Orchestra Song, **Gr. 5,** 332

Azerbaijan
Bəri Bax! (listening), **Gr. 5,** 233

Bahamas
Wind Blew East, The, **Gr. 1,** T234

Bali
Music from Bali (gamelan ensemble) (listening), **Gr. 1,** T143

Benin. *See also* Africa
Kye Kye Kule, **Gr. 7,** 225

Bolivia. *See also* Latin America
Carnavalito (listening), **Gr. 2,** 251

Brazil. *See also* Latin America
A Zing-a Za, **Gr. 5,** 338

Classified Index

Classified Index of Songs, Selected Concepts, Skills, and Activities (continued)

Afoxé (listening), **Gr. 8,** 34
Aideu (listening), **Gr. 7,** 223
Batucada Brasileira (listening), **Gr. 5,** 433
Caranguejo (The Crab), **Gr. 2,** 306
Cidade Maravilhosa (Wonderful City), **Gr. 5,** 432
Mama eu quero (listening), **Gr. 2,** 92
Mama Paquita, **Gr. 2,** 92
Medley Polleritas (listening), **Gr. 3,** 111
Na Bahia Tem (In Bahia Town), **Gr. K,** T163;
   Gr. 1, T297
Pezinho (listening), **Gr. 3,** 230
Ride the Train, **Gr. K,** T144
Sambalelê (listening), **Gr. 1,** T202
Serra, Serra Serrador (Saw, Saw, Lumberjack),
   Gr. 1, T133
Why the Beetle Has a Gold Coat (folktale), **Gr. 1,** T321

Bulgaria
Bulgarian Folk Melody (listening), **Gr. 5,** 219
Shope, Shope (Oh, Shope, Shope), **Gr. 5,** 220

Cameroon. *See also* Africa
Oh, Come Sing a Song, **Gr. 7,** 65

Canada
America, My Homeland, **Gr. 4,** 358
Chumbara, **Gr. 4,** 172
En roulant ma boule (As I Roll My Ball), **Gr. 3,** 100
Going Over the Sea, **Gr. 2,** 216
Great Big Sea, A, **Gr. 5,** 334
Herring, The, **Gr. 3,** 316
I's the B'y, **Gr. 3,** 13
J'entends le moulin (I Hear the Windmill), **Gr. 3,** 135
Jack Was Ev'ry Bit a Sailor, **Gr. 6,** 170
Kettle Valley Line, The, **Gr. 4,** 348
Land of the Silver Birch, **Gr. 2,** 88
Les saluts (listening), **Gr. 3,** 92
Lots o' Fish in Bonavist' Harbor, **Gr. 5,** 263
Lukey's Boat, **Gr. 3,** 114
Lumber Camp Song, The, **Gr. 6,** 136
Monté sur un éléphant (Riding on an Elephant),
   Gr. K, T218
Old Carrion Crow, **Gr. 4,** 192

Caribbean. *See also* Cuba; Dominica; Jamaica;
   Puerto Rico; Trinidad and Tobago; West Indies
Day-O (listening), **Gr. 4,** 72
Four White Horses, **Gr. 2,** 301
Jamaica Farewell (listening), **Gr. 4,** 73
Jump in the Line (listening), **Gr. 7,** 199
Lead Man Holler, **Gr. 7,** 148
River Come Down, **Gr. 8,** 10
Shake the Papaya Down, **Gr. 2,** 90
Steel Drums Jam (listening), **Gr. 2,** 90
Stevedore's Song, **Gr. 3,** 127
Tinga Layo, **Gr. 2,** 50

China
Antiphonal Singing Song (listening), **Gr. 6,** 65
Bamboo Flute, **Gr. 4,** 134
Bei Fang Chre (North Wind Blows), **Gr. 2,** 367
Bo Hai Huan Ten (listening), **Gr. 7,** 55
Chinese Lion Dance (listening), **Gr. 1,** T363

Colorful Dragon Boat, **Gr. K,** T328
Diou Shou Juan'er (Hide the Handkerchief), **Gr. 1,** T212
Dragon Dance (listening), **Gr. 2,** 366
Evening Party (listening), **Gr. 2,** 99
Fung Yang Song, **Gr. 5,** 58
Gong xi fa cai (Chinese New Year Song), **Gr. 3,** 384
I Chih Ching Wa (Frogs), **Gr. 2,** 186
Jasmine Flower, **Gr. 3,** 146
Magnificent Horses (listening), **Gr. 7,** 104
Singing on the Fisherboats at Dusk (listening), **Gr. 1,** T129
Tsing Chun U Chü (Youth Dance Song), **Gr. 6,** 272
Wan Ü Ger, **Gr. 3,** 190
Year-Naming Race, The (listening), **Gr. 3,** 385
Yüe líang wan wan (Crescent Moon), **Gr. 6,** 26

Colombia. *See also* Latin America
Cumbia del sol (Cumbia of the Sun), **Gr. 5,** 16
Santa Marta, **Gr. 5,** 398

Congo
Dima, **Gr. 4,** 265

Croatia
Ja posejah lubenice (I Planted Watermelons), **Gr. 2,** 316

Cuba. *See also* Caribbean; Latin America
El arroyo que murmura (The Murmuring Brook),
   Gr. 3, 318
El manisero (Peanut Vendor), **Gr. 4,** 106
Guantanamera, **Gr. 5,** 86
Ogguere (song and listening), **Gr. 4,** 327, 329
Son de Camaguey, by L. Dubinsky (listening), **Gr. 8,** 51
Tabu (listening), **Gr. 2,** 20

Cyprus. *See* Greece

Czech Republic
By the Singing Water, **Gr. 5,** 270
Crazy Songs (listening), **Gr. 6,** 65
Ja do lesa ne pasedu (To the Woods I Will Not Go),
   Gr. 6, 227
Jede, jede poštovský panáček (Riding, Riding, Is
   Mr. Postman), **Gr. 6,** 226
Neviděli jste tu mé panenky? (Have You Not Seen My
   Dear Daughters?), **Gr. 6,** 228
Where Is John?, **Gr. 5,** 274

Denmark
Marken er mejet (Out in the Meadow), **Gr. 4,** 365
Tak for Maden (Thanks for Food), **Gr. 1,** T343
Stamping Land, **Gr. K,** T24

Dominica
Plenty Fishes in the Sea, **Gr. 1,** T310

Ecuador. *See also* Latin America
Los pollitos (Little Chickens), **Gr. K,** T288

England
Amazing Grace, **Gr. 5,** 19
A-Rovin', **Gr. 6,** 319
Autumn Leaves, **Gr. 1,** T331
Barbry Ellen, **Gr. 6,** 208
Bell Horses, **Gr. K,** T262
Bobby Shafto, **Gr. K,** T265
Chairs to Mend, **Gr. 4,** 272
Charlie, **Gr. 3,** 208

Chicka-ma, Chicka-ma, Craney Crow, **Gr. 3,** 263

Coasts of High Barbary, The, **Gr. 6,** 329

Derby Ram, The, **Gr. 4,** 259

Derry Ding Dong Dason, **Gr. 6,** 249

Donkey, Donkey, **Gr. 2,** 256

Follow Me, **Gr. K,** T133

Good Day Song, **Gr. K,** T50

Greenland Whale Fishery, **Gr. 6,** 212

Here We Come A-Wassailing, **Gr. 1,** T355

Holly and the Ivy, The, **Gr. 5,** 418

Hot Cross Buns, **Gr. 2,** 258

Hullaballoo Balay, **Gr. 6,** 10

I Saw Three Ships, **Gr. 2,** 359

If All the World Were Paper, **Gr. 1,** T296

Lavender's Blue, **Gr. 1,** T174

Little Robin Redbreast, **Gr. 1,** T208

Looby Loo, **Gr. 1,** T262

May Day Carol, **Gr. 3,** 393

Muffin Man, The, **Gr. K,** T105

My Government Claim, **Gr. 5,** 95, 110

Noble Duke of York, The, **Gr. K,** T232

Nottamun Town, **Gr. 5,** 405

Oh, A-Hunting We Will Go, **Gr. K,** T62

Oh, How Lovely Is the Evening, **Gr. 6,** 252

Old Roger, **Gr. 3,** 280

Oliver Cromwell, **Gr. 4,** 269

Oranges and Lemons (poem), **Gr. 1,** T150

Pairs or Pears, **Gr. 2,** 265

Pease Porridge Hot, **Gr. 1,** T255

Pop! Goes the Weasel, **Gr. 5,** 94

Rain is Falling Down, **Gr. 3,** 242

Rig a Jig Jig, **Gr. 1,** T116

Ring Around the Rosy, **Gr. K,** T246

Rover, **Gr. 2,** 260

Sellinger's Round (listening), **Gr. 6,** 98

Ship in Distress, The, **Gr. 6,** 211

Suite on English Folk Tunes, **Gr. 1,** T136

Sweet and Low, **Gr. 6,** 184

This Old Man, **Gr. 1,** T306

Three Little Kittens, **Gr. K,** T148

Tinker, Tailor, **Gr. 1,** T130

Two, Four, Six, Eight, **Gr. 1,** T246

Water Is Wide, The, **Gr. 6,** 46

We Wish You a Merry Christmas, **Gr. 2,** 358

Eritrea. *See also* Africa

Hashewie (Going Round), **Gr. 2,** 362

Ethiopia. *See also* Africa

Gebeta Board, The (story), **Gr. 3,** 346

Fiji

Na belo (Little Heron), **Gr. 2,** 322

Finland

Suomen Salossa (The Finnish Forest), **Gr. 6,** 422

Vem Kan Segla (Who Can Sail?), **Gr. 6,** 419

France

Belle qui tiens ma vie (My Love, You Hold My Life) (song and listening), **Gr. 6,** 99

Bransle de Champaigne (listening), **Gr. 3,** 96

Frère Jacques (Are You Sleeping?), **Gr. 4,** 260

La cloche (The Clock), **Gr. 3,** 67

Les Anges dans nos campagnes (Angels We Have Heard on High) (trad. carol), **Gr. 6,** 406

Pat-a-Pan, **Gr. 3,** 375

Germany

Ach, du lieber Augustin (The More We Get Together), **Gr. 2,** 35

Ding Dong Diggy Diggy Dong, **Gr. 3,** 269

Himmel und Erde (Music Alone Shall Live), **Gr. 4,** 280

Jack-o'-Lantern, **Gr. K,** T307

Mein Hut (My Hat), **Gr. 2,** 142

Night Song, **Gr. 3,** 186

O Tannenbaum! (O Christmas Tree!), **Gr. K,** T320

Spinning Song (listening), **Gr. 3,** 128

Wachet auf (Waken Now), **Gr. 6,** 259

Winter Ade, **Gr. 6,** 132, 133

Ghana. *See also* Africa

Adukbe (traditional) (listening), **Gr. 8,** 177

African Postal Workers (listening), **Gr. 7,** 147

Afrakakraba (listening), **Gr. 3,** 102

Agahu (song and listening), **Gr. 5,** 72, 73; **Gr. 7,** 75

Dide, **Gr. 3,** 279

Ɔbɔɔ Asi Me Nsa, **Gr. K,** T159

Sansa kroma, **Gr. 4,** 166

Tue Tue (listening), **Gr. 2,** 234

Greece

Poun to, Poun to (listening), **Gr. 2,** 175

Samiotissa, **Gr. 5,** 285

Tzakonikos (listening), **Gr. 6,** 214

Yerakina, **Gr. 6,** 216

Guatemala. *See also* Latin America

La sanjuanerita (The Girl from San Juan), **Gr. 4,** 100

Un lorito de Verapaz (A Parrot from Verapaz), **Gr. 5,** 349

Vamos a la mar (Let's Go to the Sea), **Gr. 3,** 256

Haiti

Azouke Legba (listening), **Gr. 5,** 426

Hispanic American

Afoxé (listening), **Gr. 8,** 34

Aideu (listening), **Gr. 7,** 223

Arre, mi burrito (Gid'yup, Little Burrito), **Gr. 1,** T257

El cóndor pasa (listening), **Gr. 7,** 69

El jarabe tapatío (listening), **Gr. 7,** 55, 58

La camilla (listening), **Gr. 1,** T196

La pequeñita araña (Eency Weency Spider), **Gr. K,** T9

Las horas (The Hours), **Gr. K,** T70

Los mariachis (listening), **Gr. 7,** 90

Macoklis Mango, by Un Solo Pueblo (listening), **Gr. 8,** 46

Mi cuerpo (My Body), **Gr. 1,** T32

Son de Camaguey (listening), **Gr. 8,** 51

Y ahora vamos a cantar (Now We Are Going to Sing), **Gr. K,** T340

Hungary

Come and Sing Together (unison), **Gr. 5,** 270; **Gr. 6,** 281

Come Back, My Little Chicks, **Gr. 1,** T134

Egy üveg alma (One Jar of Apples), **Gr. 3,** 22

Fehér liliomszál (Little Water Lily), **Gr. K,** T139

Mouse, Mousie, **Gr. 2,** 254

Naughty Kitty Cat, **Gr. 1,** T171

Classified Index

Classified Index of Songs, Selected Concepts, Skills, and Activities (continued)

India
Aeyaya balano sakkad (Come, Children), **Gr. 5,** 402
Diwali Song, **Gr. 6,** 396
Fox, the Hen, and the Drum, The (fable), **Gr. K,** T294
Milan (Meeting of the Two Rivers) (excerpt) (listening),
   Gr. 4, 208
Nach Nach Nach (listening), **Gr. 6,** 224
Raga Malika (listening), **Gr. 5,** 403
Yanai (The Elephant), **Gr. 2,** 305

Indonesia
Gêndhing KÊMBANG MARA (listening), **Gr. 7,** 101
Itik Besenda Gurau (The Ducks), **Gr. 2,** 100
Suliram, **Gr. 6,** 58
Wéané, **Gr. 3,** 184

Inuit. *See also* Native American
Song of a Seashore (listening), **Gr. 7,** 176

Iranian
Haji Firuz, **Gr. 6,** 421

Ireland
Brafferton Village/Walsh's Hornpipe (listening),
   Gr. 3, 391
Cliffs of Doneen, The, **Gr. 5,** 46
Ēinīnī, **Gr. 5,** 340
Gold Ring, The (listening), **Gr. 3,** 160
Macnamara's Band, **Gr. 4,** 88
Maggie in the Wood (listening), **Gr. 5,** 49
My Government Claim, **Gr. 5,** 95, 110
Nead na lachan sa mhúta (listening), **Gr. 5,** 48
Oro My Bodeen, **Gr. 4,** 279
Saint Patrick's Day, **Gr. 5,** 434
St. Patrick's Day (listening), **Gr. 2,** 374
Wee Falorie Man, The, **Gr. 2,** 375
When I Was Young, **Gr. 4,** 187

Isle of Man
Morning Has Broken (song and listening), **Gr. 4,** 22, 23

Israel/Hebrew/Jewish/Yiddish
Achshav (Now), **Gr. 4,** 112
Ani Purim, **Gr. 2,** 372
Aquaqua, **Gr. 5,** 258
Bim Bom, **Gr. 3,** 218
Bulbes ('Taters), **Gr. 6,** 280
Chag Asif (Harvest Time), **Gr. 3,** 360
Cherkassiya (listening), **Gr. 2,** 373
Chiribim, **Gr. 6,** 57
Chirri Bim, **Gr. 2,** 70
Eight Days of Hanukkah!, The, **Gr. 3,** 370
Erev Shel Shoshanim (listening), **Gr. 4,** 68
Haneirot Halalu (These Lights), **Gr. 5,** 414
Hashkivenu (listening), **Gr. 7,** 190
Hashual (listening), **Gr. 6,** 404
Hava Nagila, **Gr. 5,** 54
I've a Pair of Fishes, **Gr. 1,** T124
In the Window, **Gr. 2,** 352
Kum bahur (The Rooster), **Gr. 3,** 75
Let's Go Dancing, **Gr. 3,** 196
Ma'oz Tsur (Rock of Ages), **Gr. 6,** 405
My Dreidel, **Gr. 2,** 353
Nigun Atik (listening), **Gr. 3,** 47

Oy Chanuke, **Gr. 3,** 368
S'vivon Sov (Dreidel Spin), **Gr. 1,** T348; **Gr. 4,** 374
Shalom Chaveyrim (Shalom, My Friends), **Gr. 3,** 141
Simi Yadech (Give Me your Hand), **Gr. K,** T168
Tumbai, **Gr. 5,** 194
Uga, Uga, Uga (Cake, Cake, Cake), **Gr. 1,** T313
Zum Gali Gali, **Gr. 4,** 255

Italy
Bella Bimba, **Gr. 3,** 172
Farfallina (Butterfly), **Gr. 4,** 244
Funiculi, Funicula, **Gr. 5,** 62
Sankta Lucia (Saint Lucia) (Swedish Version), **Gr. 5,** 412

Ivory Coast
Sansa kroma, **Gr. 4,** 244

Jamaica. *See also* Caribbean
Banyan Tree, **Gr. 2,** 321
Hill an' Gully, **Gr. 5,** 250
Mango Walk, **Gr. 5,** 90, 92
Three Little Birds (listening), **Gr. 8,** 84
Water Come a Me Eye, **Gr. 4,** 90

Japan
Ame fure (Rain), **Gr. 4,** 26
Bird Island (listening), **Gr. 8,** 56
Chichipapa (The Sparrow's Singing School), **Gr. 2,** 22
Deta, Deta (The Moon), **Gr. 5,** 246
Hitori, **Gr. 4,** 345
Hotaru Koi (Come, Firefly), **Gr. 6,** 255
Joban Tanko Bushi (Joban Miners' Song), **Gr. 6,** 142
Kaeru no Uta (Frog's Song), **Gr. 1,** T112
Kari (Wild Geese), **Gr. 1,** T261
Kobuta (Piglet), **Gr. 1,** T167
Kojo No Tsuki (Moon at the Ruined Castle), **Gr. 5,** 149
Kokiriko (listening), **Gr. 6,** 145
Kuma San (Honorable Bear), **Gr. 3,** 244
Mizuguruma (The Water Wheel), **Gr. 1,** T260
Nabe, Nabe, Soku, Nuke (Stew Pot, Stew Pot,
   Bottomless Pot), **Gr. 2,** 259
Rabbit in the Moon, The (folktale), **Gr. 1,** T318
Sakura (Cherry Blossoms), **Gr. 6,** 14
Sara Watashi, **Gr. 1,** T67
Tako No Uta (The Kite Song), **Gr. 1,** T370
Tanabata, **Gr. 3,** 62
Zui Zui Zukkorbashi (song), **Gr. 1,** T98; (game), **Gr. 1,** T99

Kenya. *See also* Africa
Gogo, **Gr. K,** T188

Korea
Arirang (song and listening), **Gr. 5,** 50, 53
Ban Dal (Half Moon), **Gr. 2,** 219; (listening), **Gr. 4,** 184
Bohm (Spring Has Come!), **Gr. 3,** 392
Dal taro kacha (Come, Pick the Moon), **Gr. 2,** 98
Ga Eul (Fall), **Gr. 5,** 401
Hae Wa Be (Sun and Rain), **Gr. 6,** 273
Juhtgarak (Chopsticks), **Gr. K,** T108
Santoki (Mountain Rabbit) (singing game) (listening),
   Gr. 1, T187
Yongnam Nongak (listening), **Gr. 5,** 70

Laos
Dok Djampa (The White Jasmine Flower), **Gr. 4,** 392

Suk san wan pi mai (New Year's Song), **Gr. 5,** 437
Ua txiab (The Village), **Gr. 6,** 394

Latin

Dona Nobis Pacem, **Gr. 6,** 335
Pauper sum ego (I am Poor), **Gr. 6,** 254

Latin America. *See also* Argentina, Bolivia, Brazil, Colombia, Cuba, Ecuador, Guatemala, Haiti, Mexico, Panama, Peru, Puerto Rico, Uruguay, Venezuela
A be ce (A B C), **Gr. 1,** T213
A la rueda rueda ('Round and 'Round), **Gr. 1,** T240
¡Adivina lo que es! (Guess What It Is), **Gr. 1,** T170
De aquel cerro (On the Darkened Hillside), **Gr. 3,** 32
El burrito enfermo (The Sick Little Donkey), **Gr. 2,** 180
El juego chirimbolo (The Chirimbolo Game), **Gr. 1,** T103
En nuestra Tierra tan linda (On Our Beautiful Planet Earth), **Gr. 2,** 114
Guadalquivir (listening), **Gr. 3,** 30
Mi gallo (My Rooster), **Gr. 5,** 272
Naranja dulce (Sweet Orange), **Gr. 1,** T303
Riqui Ran (Sawing Song), **Gr. 2,** 21
San Sereni, **Gr. 2,** 323
Son de la negra (listening), **Gr. 5,** 397

Lebanon

Hala lala layya, **Gr. 4,** 222

Liberia

Take Time in Life, **Gr. 4,** 156

Maori

Kia Ora (listening), **Gr. 2,** 65
Oma Rapeti (Run Rabbit), **Gr. 2,** 108
Pukaea (listening), **Gr. 2,** 109
Tutira Mai Nga Iwi (listening), **Gr. K,** T17

Mexico. *See also* Latin America
A la rueda de San Miguel (To the Wheel of San Miguel), **Gr. 2,** 60
Acitrón (Mexican stone-passing song) (listening), **Gr. 6,** 93
Allá en el rancho grande (My Ranch), **Gr. 5,** 66
¡Ay, Jalisco no te rajes! (Ay, Jalisco, Never Fail Her!), **Gr. 5,** 188
Bate, bate (Stir, Stir), **Gr. 2,** 242
Caballito blanco (Little White Pony), **Gr. 4,** 278
Chiapanecas (Ladies of Chiapas), **Gr. 2,** 128
Cielito Lindo, **Gr. 3,** 166
Counting Song, **Gr. 1,** T195
¡Dale, dale, dale!, **Gr. 3,** 378
De colores (Many Colors), **Gr. 5,** 88, 98
Diana (Play the Bugle), **Gr. 1,** T334
El atole (The Atole), **Gr. 3,** 396
El charro (The Cowboy), **Gr. 6,** 278
El colación (The Christmas Candies), **Gr. 1,** T357
El florón (The Flower), **Gr. 3,** 46
El jarabe (Mexican Hat Dance), **Gr. 5,** 396
El jarabe tapatío (listening), **Gr. 7,** 55, 58
El palomo y la paloma (The Doves), **Gr. 2,** 381
El quelite (The Village), **Gr. 4,** 362
El rorro (The Babe), **Gr. 1,** T386
El tecolote (The Owl), **Gr. 6,** 392; (listening), **Gr. 4,** 361
El vaquerito (The Little Cowboy) (excerpt) (listening), **Gr. 1,** T335

Entren santos peregrinos (Enter, Holy Pilgrims), **Gr. 4,** 379
Ésta sí que es Nochebuena (This Is Really Christmas Eve), **Gr. 2,** 361
Estrella brillante (Shining Star), **Gr. 5,** 273
Flor de huevo (listening), **Gr. 3,** 359
Hojas de té (Tea Leaves) (speech piece), **Gr. 4,** 256
Juan Pirulero, **Gr. 2,** 270; (listening), **Gr. 1,** T153
Jugaremos en el bosque (We Will Play in the Forest), **Gr. 2,** 188
La bamba, **Gr. 3,** 236; **Gr. 6,** 381
La bella hortelana (The Beautiful Gardener), **Gr. 2,** 208
La mar (The Sea), **Gr. 3,** 110
La pájara pinta (The Speckled Bird), **Gr. 6,** 268
La raspa (listening), **Gr. 3,** 211
La víbora de la mar (The Serpent from the Sea), **Gr. 5,** 441
Las mañanitas (The Morning Song) (song and listening), **Gr. 4,** 194, 197
Los mariachis (listening), **Gr. 3,** 397; **Gr. 7,** 90
María Blanca, **Gr. K,** T99
Matarile, **Gr. 2,** 261
Molinillo de café (Little Coffee Mill) (speech piece), **Gr. 4,** 250
Nochebuena (Christmas Eve), **Gr. K,** T323
Pajarillo barranqueño (Little Bird), **Gr. 3,** 358
Para pedir posada (Looking for Shelter), **Gr. 4,** 376
Pimpón, **Gr. K,** T22
Piñata Song (poem), **Gr. 1,** T153
Piñón, Pirulín, **Gr. 1,** T311
Que llueva (It's Raining), **Gr. 3,** 274
Señor Coyote (story), **Gr. 2,** 330
Sensemayá (excerpt) (listening), **Gr. 3,** 161
Sones de mariachi (listening), **Gr. 2,** 380
Una adivinanza (A Riddle), **Gr. 1,** T138
Uno de enero (The First of January), **Gr. 3,** 210

Mongolia. *See also* China
Magnificent Horses (listening), **Gr. 7,** 104

Mozambique

Yo, Mamana, Yo (Oh, Mama, Oh), **Gr. 1,** T307

Native American

Athabascan
Athabascan Song (listening), **Gr. 5,** 26
Cahuilla
Powama, **Gr. 7,** 63
Comanche
Eka Muda (listening and song), **Gr. 5,** 27, 28
Haliwa-Saponi
Bear Dance (dance song and listening), **Gr. 1,** T103
Hopi
Buffalo Dance Entrance Song, **Gr. 3,** 325
Bu-Vah (Sleep) (song and listening), **Gr. 4,** 18, 19
Coyote and the Bluebirds, The (listening; includes "Nikosi"), **Gr. 2,** 231
Mos', Mos'! (Cat, Cat!), **Gr. 1,** T53
Nikosi, **Gr. 2,** 230
Intertribal
Fancy Dance Song (listening), **Gr. 5,** 444
Grand Entry (Powwow) (listening), **Gr. K,** T344

Honor the Earth Powwow—Grand Entry (listening),
  Gr. 7, 75
One-Eyed Ford, **Gr. 7**, 200

Inuit
  Song of a Seashore (Inuit) (listening), **Gr. 7**, 176

Iroquois
  Tehahontanekenhêha' (story and listening),
    Gr. 3, 50; (song and listening), **Gr. 3**, 51
  Tsiothwatasè:tha, **Gr. 6**, 109

Kiowa
  Prairie Dog Song (listening), **Gr. K**, T220

Mohawk
  Tekanionton'néha' (Alligator Dance) (listening and
    song), **Gr. 5**, 222, 223

Muscogee
  Baby Nodja, **Gr. 2**, 154
  Heleluyan, **Gr. 6**, 188

Nanticoke
  O Hal'lwe, **Gr. 6**, 428

Navajo
  Jó Ashílá (Traveling Together) (listening and song),
    Gr. 5, 224
  Shí Naashá (I Am Going) (listening), **Gr. 1**, T73
  We Are Here, **Gr. 4**, 394

Ottawa
  Raccoon Dance Song, **Gr. 3**, 87

Santa Clara Pueblo
  Santa Clara Corn Grinding Song, **Gr. K**, T164

Seneca
  Seneca Stomp Dance (listening), **Gr. K**, T345

Serrano
  Uch Tirvarch, **Gr. 3**, 53
  Ushkana (listening), **Gr. K**, T75; **Gr. 1**, T44

Taos
  Taos Round Dance, **Gr. 2**, 155

Zuñi
  Locust, The (poem), **Gr. 1**, T285

Netherlands, The
  Sarasponda, **Gr. 4**, 210
  Twee emmertjes (listening), **Gr. 4**, 212

New Zealand
  Tititorea, **Gr. 3**, 174

Nigeria. *See also* Africa
  Allundé, Alluia, **Gr. 4**, 34
  Eh Soom Boo Kawaya, **Gr. 3**, 58
  Fun wa ni alaafia (Send Us Your Peace), **Gr. 5**, 248

Norway
  Her kommer vennen min (listening), **Gr. 3**, 142
  In the Hall of the Mountain King from *Peer Gynt Suite*
    (listening), **Gr. 2**, 346
  Nokken Danser (listening), **Gr. 4**, 168
  Norwegian Dance (listening), **Gr. 3**, 145
  Oleanna, **Gr. 3**, 144
  Såg du noko?, **Gr. 2**, 104

Panama
  El barquito (The Tiny Boat), **Gr. 4**, 214
  El tambor (The Drum), **Gr. K**, T129; **Gr. 6**, 222

Peru
  El cóndor pasa (listening), **Gr. 7**, 69

Festival Dance (listening), **Gr. 4**, 140
La Yunsita, **Gr. 4**, 350
Los maizales (The Cornfields), **Gr. 5**, 268

Philippines, The
  Bahay Kubo (My Nipa Hut), **Gr. 2**, 382
  Dandansoy, **Gr. 6**, 356
  Pusa't daga (Cat and Rat), **Gr. 1**, T289
  Sitsiritsit, **Gr. 4**, 102
  Tinikling (listening), **Gr. 4**, 105

Poland
  But the Critter Got Away (speech piece), **Gr. 1**, T88

Puerto Rico. *See also* American; Caribbean
  A la nanita nana (A Little Lullaby), **Gr. 4**, 230
  Brinca la tablita (Hop, Hop!), **Gr. 1**, T71
  Duérmete mi niño (Go to Sleep, My Baby), **Gr. 1**, T61
  El coquí (The Frog), **Gr. 4**, 178
  El florón (The Flower), **Gr. 1**, T117
  El nacimiento (The Nativity), **Gr. K**, T322
  El zapatero (The Cobbler), **Gr. 2**, 138
  En la feria de San Juan (In the Market of San Juan),
    Gr. 2, 226
  La paloma se fue (The Dove That Flew Away),
    Gr. 5, 259
  Merecumbé, **Gr. 6**, 276
  Qué bonita bandera (What a Beautiful Flag),
    Gr. 5, 442
  Somos Boricuas (We Are Puerto Rican) (listening),
    Gr. 2, 138

Russia
  Ballet of the Unhatched Chicks from *Pictures at an
    Exhibition* (listening), **Gr. 3**, 76
  Beryoza (The Birch Tree), **Gr. 4**, 286
  Kalinka (Little Snowball Bush), **Gr. 3**, 224
  Katyusha, **Gr. 4**, 188
  Korobushka, **Gr. 4**, 285
  Nutcracker Suite, The (listening), **Gr. 2**, 354
  Porushka-Paranya (listening), **Gr. 4**, 208
  Troika, **Gr. 6**, 230
  Tum Balalaika, **Gr. 6**, 68

Scotland
  Gi'Me Elbow Room, **Gr. 3**, 88
  Little Boy of the Sheep, **Gr. 3**, 188
  Loch Lomond, **Gr. 5**, 138
  Over the Sea to Skye, **Gr. 4**, 344
  Scotland's Burning, **Gr. 3**, 257

Senegal. *See also* Africa
  New Africa (listening), **Gr. 4**, 209
  Sing Lo-Lo (listening), **Gr. 4**, 385

Sierra Leone. *See also* Africa
  Mɔfia moni (Ev'rybody Loves Saturday Night),
    Gr. 5, 277

Singapore
  Chan mali chan, **Gr. 3**, 10

South Africa. *See also* Africa
  Hey, Motswala, **Gr. 3**, 34
  Jikel' Emaweni (Throw It Down the Slope), **Gr. 6**, 70
  Lion Sleeps Tonight, The, **Gr. 7**, 214
  Ngikhumbula (listening), **Gr. 5**, 195

Pata Pata (listening), **Gr. 3,** 35
Singabahambayo (An Army Is Marching), **Gr. 5,** 56, 76
Thula Sizwe (listening), **Gr. 6,** 73
Tshotsholoza (listening), **Gr. 1,** T76
Vinqo (listening), **Gr. 4,** 24

Spain
A la puerta del cielo (At the Gates of Heaven), **Gr. 4,** 12
Al lado de mi cabaña (Beside My Cottage), **Gr. 6,** 141
El vito, **Gr. 5,** 210
Isabela and the Troll (story), **Gr. 3,** 349
La otra España (The Other Spain) (song and listening), **Gr. 4,** 62, 64
No despiertes a mi niño (Do Not Wake My Little Son), **Gr. 5,** 217

Sri Lanka
Me gase boho (The Orange Tree), **Gr. 2,** 317

Sweden
Och Jungfrun Hon Går I Ringen (A Girl with a Shiny Ribbon) (song and listening), 190, 192
Sankta Lucia (Saint Lucia) (Swedish Version), **Gr. 5,** 413
Sheep Shearing, **Gr. 2,** 102
Vem Kan Segla (Who Can Sail?) (folk song from Aland, a Swedish-speaking island of Finland), **Gr. 6,** 419

Switzerland
L'inverno è già passato (Winter is Over), **Gr. 4,** 390

Taiwan
Go A Tin (Lantern Song), **Gr. 1,** T363
Tsing Chun U Chü (Youth Dance Song), **Gr. 6,** 272

Thailand
Chang (Elephant), **Gr. 1,** T199
Ngam Sang Duan (Shining Moon), **Gr. 5,** 376
Pleeng Loy Krathong (Full Moon Song), **Gr. 6,** 399

Tongan
Ole La'u Papa e (Tongan stick game song), **Gr. 6,** 91

Trinidad and Tobago. *See also* Caribbean
Me Stone, **Gr. 2,** 48

Turkey
Dere Geliyor (River Overflowing), **Gr. 6,** 232
Üsküdar, **Gr. 5,** 128

Uganda. *See also* Africa
Mwiji Mwena (listening), **Gr. 2,** 235
Wavvuuvuumira (Mister Bamboo Bug), **Gr. K,** T165

Uruguay. *See also* Latin America
Chíu, chíu, chíu (Chirp, Chirp, Chirp), **Gr. 2,** 302; **Gr. 6,** 172
Repicados sobre Madera (excerpt) (listening), **Gr. 4,** 93

Venezuela. *See also* Latin America
El tren (The Train), **Gr. 2,** 326
Macoklis Mango (listening), **Gr. 8,** 46

Vietnam
Qua Cầu Gió Bay (listening), **Gr. 4,** 367
Tết Trung (Children's Festival), **Gr. 4,** 366

Virgin Islands
A Tisket A Tasket, **Gr. 1,** T107

Wales
All Through the Night (song and listening), **Gr. 4,** 277
Deck the Hall, **Gr. 3,** 374
Hen wlad fy nhadau (The Land of My Fathers) (listening), **Gr. 2,** 141
Shoheen Sho, **Gr. 2,** 140

West Indies. *See also* Caribbean
Dumplin's, **Gr. 2,** 172
Mary Ann, **Gr. 5,** 166
Shake the Papaya Down, **Gr. 2,** 90
Steel Drums Jam (listening), **Gr. 2,** 90
Tinga Layo, **Gr. 2,** 50

Yemen
Debka Kurdit (listening), **Gr. 4,** 236

Yugoslavia
Djurdjevka Kolo (listening), **Gr. 6,** 105

Zimbabwe
Sorida, **Gr. 2,** 96
Uyai Mose (Come All You People), **Gr. 7,** 66
Vhaya Kadhimba (listening), **Gr. 1,** T24; (game), **Gr. 1,** T23

Zulu. *See also* Africa
Mbombela (The Train Comes), **Gr. K,** T152
Nampaya omame (Mothers), **Gr. K,** T128

FORM AND GENRE

A
Ballad of the Bedbugs and the Beetles, The, **Gr. 3,** 206
Billy, **Gr. 3,** 7
Blow, Ye Winds, Blow, **Gr. 3,** 192
Chang, **Gr. 1,** T223
Crawdad Song, **Gr. 3,** 107
De aquel cerro, **Gr. 3,** 32
Dinah, **Gr. 3,** 150
Egy üveg alma, **Gr. 3,** 22
Eh Soom Boo Kawaya, **Gr. 3,** 58
El florón, **Gr. 3,** 46
Great Big House, **Gr. 3,** 46
I'll Rise When the Rooster Crows, **Gr. 4,** 36
Jasmine Flower, **Gr. 3,** 146
La cloche, **Gr. 3,** 67
Night Song, **Gr. 3,** 188
O, The Train's Off the Track, **Gr. 3,** 176
One Little Elephant, **Gr. 1,** T195
Paw Paw Patch, The, **Gr. 3,** 195
Rise Up Singin', **Gr. 3,** 138
Stevedore's Song, **Gr. 3,** 127
Sweet Potatoes, **Gr. 3,** 16
Tanabata, **Gr. 3,** 62
Throw It Out the Window, **Gr. 3,** 94
Wang Ü Ger, **Gr. 3,** 190

AA
Bus, The, **Gr. K,** T137
Happy Birthday, Happy Birthday, **Gr. K,** T273
Popping Corn, **Gr. K,** T161
Toodala, **Gr. K,** T39

AAA
Little Sally Walker, **Gr. 3,** 105
There's No Hidin' Place, **Gr. 5,** 266

AAAAAABB

Vinqo, **Gr. 4**, 25

AABA

A la puerta del cielo, **Gr. 4**, 12
Ballet of the Unhatched Chicks, **Gr. 3**, 76
Castle on a Cloud, **Gr. 7**, 82
Comedy Tonight, **Gr. 6**, 204
Digga Digga Dog, **Gr. 3**, 164
Heart, **Gr. 6**, 166
I Got Rhythm, **Gr. 5**, 187
It Don't Mean a Thing by D. Ellington (song and
   listening), **Gr. 6**, 164
J'entends le moulin, **Gr. 3**, 135
Já do lese nepojedu, **Gr. 6**, 227
Jede, jede poštovský panáček, **Gr. 6**, 226
Neviděli jste tu mé panenky?, **Gr. 6**, 228
Over My Head, **Gr. 3**, 286
Samba de Orfeu, **Gr. 6**, 190
Ship in Distress, The, **Gr. 6**, 211
Shoo Fly Pie and Apple Pan Dowdy, **Gr. 3**, 227
Sing, Sing, Sing, **Gr. 5**, 30
Slap That Bass, **Gr. 6**, 146
There's a Little Wheel A-Turning in my Heart,
   Gr. 3, 129, 137
Winter Wonderland, **Gr. 5**, 408
Wondering, **Gr. 6**, 282

AABAA

Blue Little Flower (listening), **Gr. 8**, 83
Norwegian Dance, Op. 35, No. 2 (listening),
   Gr. 3, 145

AABAABB

There's a Song in Me, **Gr. 5**, 183

AABABA

Symphony No. 35 (Haydn), Fourth Movement
   (excerpt), **Gr. 5**, 247

AABB

Bourrée, from *Music for the Royal Fireworks* (listening),
   Gr. 1, T263
Erev Shel Shoshanim, **Gr. 4**, 68
Gi' Me Elbow Room, **Gr. 3**, 88
La paloma se fue, **Gr. 5**, 259
Sonata X by J. Cage (listening), **Gr. 6**, 32

AABBA

Bransle de Champagne, **Gr. 3**, 96
En roulant ma boule, **Gr. 3**, 100
O, la le!, **Gr. 6**, 6

AABBCCDD

Chiribim, **Gr. 6**, 57

AABC

Frosty Weather, **Gr. 3**, 250
Rain Is Falling Down, **Gr. 3**, 242

AB

Al lado de mi cabaña, **Gr. 6**, 141
All Work Together, **Gr. K**, T12
Allá en el rancho grande, **Gr. 5**, 66
America, **Gr. K**, T303
Ani Purim, **Gr. 2**, 373
¡Ay, Jalisco no te rajes!, **Gr. 5**, 189

Ballet of the Unhatched Chicks, **Gr. 3**, 76
Bear Went Over the Mountain, The, **Gr. K**, T204; **Gr. 1**,
   T115
Belle qui tiens ma vie (listening), **Gr. 6**, 99
Best That I Can Be!, The, **Gr. K**, T48
Boris, the Singing Bear, **Gr. 1**, T312
Butterfly, Come Play with Me, **Gr. 3**, 112
Cedar Swamp, **Gr. 4**, 50
Chicken Dance, **Gr. 7**, 61
Chirri Bim, **Gr. 2**, 72
Choo, Choo, Ch'Boogie, **Gr. 6**, 180
Clog (listening), **Gr. 2**, 68
Counting Song, **Gr. 1**, T199
Doing the Weekly Walk, **Gr. K**, T78
Doney Gal, **Gr. 6**, 115
Down by the Riverside, **Gr. 6**, 22
Ēinīnī, **Gr. 5**, 341
El tambor (The Drum), **Gr. K**, T129
Follow Your Dream, **Gr. 4**, 234
Food Song, The, **Gr. 2**, 318–319
Funiculi, Funicula, **Gr. 5**, 62
Garden Hoedown, The, **Gr. K**, T290
Garden Song, **Gr. 2**, 237
Git on Board, **Gr. K**, T145
Go, Go, Go, **Gr. K**, T276
Gogo, **Gr. K**, T188
Good Day Song, **Gr. K**, T50
Great Outdoors, The, **Gr. 2**, 290–291
Guitar Man, The, **Gr. 6**, 138
Happiest Street in the World, The, **Gr. 1**, T304
Hello, Hello, There, **Gr. 2**, 126–127
Hey, Motswala, **Gr. 3**, 34
Hickory, Dickory, Dock, **Gr. K**, T49
Hine Ma Tov, **Gr. 4**, 66
Hop, Chirp! Moo! Oh Happy Springtime Day,
   Gr. 1, T373
I Will Sing Hello, **Gr. K**, T156
Instrument Game, **Gr. K**, T36
It's So Good to See You, **Gr. K**, T86
Jikel' emaweni, **Gr. 6**, 70
Jack, Be Nimble, **Gr. K**, T88
John Jacob Jingleheimer Schmidt, **Gr. 3**, 68
La camilla (listening), **Gr. 1**, T196
La mar, **Gr. 3**, 110
Las horas (The Hours), **Gr. K**, T70
Let's Think of Something to Do, **Gr. K**, T270
Limbo Rock, **Gr. 3**, 232
Little Spotted Puppy, **Gr. K**, T146
Look Who's Here!, **Gr. K**, T84
Love Somebody, **Gr. 4**, 94
Lullaby of Broadway, **Gr. 6**, 182
Mama, Bake the Johnnycake, **Gr. K**, T318
Mi caballo blanco, **Gr. 6**, 60
Mi chacra (My Farm), **Gr. K**, T207
Minuet from *Abdelazar*, **Gr. 1**, T175
Mister Rabbit, Mister Rabbit, **Gr. 2**, 150
Must Be Santa, **Gr. K**, T316
My Grandfather, **Gr. K**, T23
Nampaya omame (Mothers), **Gr. K**, T128
National Emblem, **Gr. 7**, 76
Old Ark's A-Moverin', **Gr. 4**, 130

Classified Index of Songs, Selected Concepts, Skills, and Activities (continued)

Old MacDonald Had a Farm, **Gr. K**, T211
Old Mister Woodpecker, **Gr. K**, T172
One Little Elephant plus poem, Big and Small,
   Gr. 1, T201
People in Your Neighborhood, **Gr. K**, T122
Planting Seeds, **Gr. K**, T284
Pop! Goes the Weasel, **Gr. 5**, 94, 112
Presidents, **Gr. K**, T330
Qué bonito es (How Wonderful It Is), **Gr. K**, T234
Sarasponda, **Gr. 4**, 210
See the Pony Galloping, **Gr. K**, T44
Seeds and Seasons, **Gr. 2**, 207
Simple Gifts, **Gr. 5**, 136
Sing a Little Song, **Gr. K**, T179
Stamping Land, **Gr. K**, T24
They Were Tall, **Gr. K**, T52
Things I'm Thankful For, **Gr. K**, T308
Twee emmertjes, **Gr. 4**, 212
Uncle Pen, **Gr. 5**, 24
Vive L'Amour, **Gr. 5**, 262
Wavvuuvuumira (Mister Bamboo Bug), **Gr. K**, T165
What You Gonna Call Your Pretty Little Baby?,
   Gr. K, T319

ABA

A la nanita nana, **Gr. 4**, 230
Aeyaya balano sakkad, **Gr.5**, 402
Andante (listening), **Gr. 1**, T128
Animales (Animals), **Gr. K**, T192
Best Friends, **Gr. 1**, T224
Circus Music, **Gr. 3**, 285
Conga, **Gr. 6**, 34
Dance, Dance, Dance!, **Gr. 2**, 5
Elephant, The, from *Carnival of the Animals* (listening),
   Gr. 1, T204–T205
Elijah Rock, **Gr. 6**, 152
Gavotte (listening), **Gr. 1**, T113
Gavotte fantastique, **Gr. 2**, 27
Hey, Look Me Over, **Gr. 4**, 114
I Can't Spell Hippopotamus, **Gr. K**, T199
I Want to Be Ready, **Gr. 6**, 12
Im Krapfenwaldl (In Krapfen Woods), Op. 336
   (listening), **Gr. 2**, 244
In That Great Git'n Up Mornin', **Gr. 5**, 10
Jig Jog, Jig Jog, **Gr. K**, T260
Kaeru no Uta, **Gr. 1**, T112
Lady, Lady, **Gr. K**, T184
Little White Duck, **Gr. K**, T208
London Bridge , **Gr. K**, T99
Love Grows One by One, **Gr. 1**, T203
March Past of the Kitchen Utensils, **Gr. 3**, 247
Mi-a-ou from *Dolly Suite* (listening), **Gr. K**, T149
Minuet from Eine Kleine Nachtmusik, **Gr. 3**, 169
Mister Sun, **Gr. K**, T343
Mr. Scott Joplin's Ragtime Rag!, **Gr. 6**, 110
North Winds Blow, **Gr. K**, T305
O Tannenbaum! (O Christmas Tree!), **Gr. K**, T320
Pat on the Back, A, **Gr. 2**, 74–75, 77
Peter Cottontail, **Gr. K**, T338
Radetzky March (listening), **Gr. K**, T177
Rondo "alla turca" from Sonata in A Major, **Gr. 7**, 116

'Round the Corner, Sally, **Gr. 5**, 251
Shepherd, Shepherd, **Gr. 3**, 56
Shoo, Fly, **Gr. 2**, 222–223
Simi Yadech (Give Me Your Hand), **Gr. K**, T168
Sing a Little Song, **Gr. K**, T179
Spinning Song, **Gr. 3**, 128
Sun Don't Set in the Mornin', **Gr. 3**, 48
Tugboat, **Gr. K**, T95
Twinkle, Twinkle, Little Star, **Gr. K**, T90
Wait and See, **Gr. K**, T334
Walking the Dog, **Gr. 1**, T169
Woke Up This Morning, **Gr. 3**, 180

ABAB

Down by the Riverside, **Gr. 6**, 22
Guitar Man, The, **Gr. 6**, 138
Jikel' Emaweni, **Gr. 6**, 70
Land of a Thousand Dances, **Gr. 7**, 12
Movin' Right Along, **Gr. 3**, 124

ABA'B'

Mary Ann, **Gr. 5**, 186

ABABA

Chan mali chan, **Gr. 3**, 10
Country Gardens, **Gr. 2**, 17–18
Nigun Atik, **Gr. 3**, 70

ABA'BA'

Anitra's Dance from *Peer Gynt Suite No. 1*, Op. 46,
   Gr. 5, 193

ABABC

Mayim, Mayim, **Gr. 6**, 102

ABABCBCB

Lean on Me, **Gr. 6**, 150

ABAC

Great Big House, **Gr. 3**, 14
Sun Don Set in the Mornin', **Gr. 3**, 60

ABACA

Trio No. 39, Finale (listening), **Gr. 3**, 155; **Gr. 7**, 115

ABA Coda

I Love a Piano, **Gr. 6**, 130

ABB

Raccoon Dance Song, **Gr. 3**, 87

ABBA

Bransle de Champaigne, **Gr. 3**, 96

ABBAB

Minuet (listening), **Gr. 2**, 145

ABBC

Chicka-ma, Chicka-ma, Craney Crow, **Gr. 3**, 263

ABC

Dry Bones, **Gr. 5**, 407
Hello Song, **Gr. K**, T2
Holiday for Strings, **Gr. 3**, 229
It's Such a Good Feeling, **Gr. K**, T282
It's You I Like, **Gr. K**, T280
Kum bachur, **Gr. 3**, 75
Little Sir Echo, **Gr. K**, T103
Rattlesnake, **Gr. 3**, 72
Ujima, **Gr. 5**, 427
Won't You Be My Neighbor, **Gr. K**, T268

Classified Index

Classified Index of Songs, Selected Concepts, Skills, and Activities (continued)

ABCBCC
Yellow Bird, **Gr. 6,** 154

ABCDEF
Tsiothwatasè:tha, **Gr. 6,** 109

antiphonal
Funiculi, Funicula, **Gr. 5,** 62

aria
Nessun dorma from *Turandot*, **Gr. 5,** 64

ballad
Ballad of the Bedbugs and the Beetles, **Gr. 3,** 206

binary, Gr. 8, 130, 261

bridge
Anitra's Dance from *Peer Gynt Suite No. 1*, Op. 46
   Gr. 5, 193
Guadalcanal March, **Gr. 4,** 109

call and response
Chants de Burgam, **Gr. 3,** 381
Charlie Over the Ocean, **Gr. 1,** T75
Day-O, **Gr. 4,** 72
Dima, **Gr. 4,** 265
El tambor, **Gr. 6,** 222
Everybody Oughta Know, **Gr. 1,** T361
Gift, The, **Gr. 7,** 205
Go, Go, Go, **Gr. K,** T276
Hill an' Gully, **Gr. 5,** 250
Hullaballoo Balay, **Gr. 6,** 10
In That Great Git'n Up Mornin', **Gr. 5,** 10
John the Rabbit, **Gr. 1,** T74
Little Sir Echo, **Gr. K,** T103
Music, **Gr. K,** T157
My Mama's Calling Me, **Gr. 1,** T54
Oh, Won't You Sit Down, **Gr. 4,** 70
Old House, **Gr. 4,** 282
Pay Me My Money Down, **Gr. 3,** 149
Pizza, Pizza, Daddy-O, **Gr. 2,** 62–63
Que Llueva, **Gr. 3,** 274
Rise Up, Shepherd, and Follow, **Gr. 5,** 422
Shoo, Turkey, **Gr. 1,** T76
Tina singu, **Gr. 6,** 36
Train is A-Coming, **Gr. 4,** 270
Trampin', **Gr. 3,** 287
Ujima, **Gr. 5,** 427
'Way Down Yonder in the Brickyard, **Gr. 5,** 255

canon
Alleluia, **Gr. 6,** 186
Allundé Alluia, **Gr. 4,** 34
By the Singing Water (2 part), **Gr. 5,** 270
Canon (Pachelbel), **Gr. 8,** 67
Canon (Purcell), **Gr. 8,** 4
Canon in D, **Gr. 4,** 17
Chairs to Mend, **Gr. 4,** 272
Dance for the Nations (3 part), **Gr. 5,** 206
definition, **Gr. 8,** 66, 262
Dona Nobis Pacem, **Gr. 6,** 335
Eagle, **Gr. 4,** 337
Frère Jacques, **Gr. 4,** 260
Hava Nashira, **Gr. 6,** 67

Heleluyan, **Gr. 6,** 188
Himmel und Erde, **Gr. 4,** 280
Hop Up and Jump Up, **Gr. 4,** 271
Lift Up Your Voices (3 part), **Gr. 5,** 319
Little Tommy Tinker, **Gr. 3,** 277
Mi gallo (3 part), **Gr. 5,** 272
New Day, The, **Gr. 4,** 316
Old Abram Brown, **Gr. 4,** 32
Orchestra Song (5 part), **Gr. 5,** 332
Owl and the Cuckoo, The, **Gr. 4,** 337
Peace Round, **Gr. 4,** 17
Rage and Roar, **Gr. 6,** 48
Round and Round, **Gr. 6,** 104
Row, Row, Row Your Boat, **Gr. 4,** 268
Sandy McNab, **Gr. 4,** 142
scale (2 part), **Gr. 5,** 100
Shalom Chaveryrim, **Gr. 3,** 141
Song of Thanksgiving, **Gr. 4,** 371
Spiders, **Gr. 3,** 282
Star Canon (3 part), **Gr. 5,** 367
Sweet Music (3 part), **Gr. 5,** 319
Tumbai (3 part), **Gr. 5,** 194
Tzena (3 part), **Gr. 5,** 171
Viva la musica, **Gr. 4,** 174
Wake Up Canon, **Gr. 4,** 326
Water Is Wide, The, **Gr. 6,** 46
Where Is John? (3 part), **Gr. 5,** 274

coda, Gr. 8, 15, 169, 261
Allundé Alluia, **Gr. 4,** 34
Anitra's Dance from *Peer Gynt Suite No. 1*, Op. 46,
   Gr. 5, 193
Arirang, **Gr. 5,** 53
Ballad of the Underground Railroad, The, **Gr. 5,** 156
Dancing in the Street, **Gr. 6,** 84
Don't Laugh at Me, **Gr. 7,** 92
Everybody Rejoice, **Gr. 5,** 227
Flip, Flop, and Fly, **Gr. 3,** 337
Frosty the Snowman, **Gr. 3,** 366
Hakuna Matata, **Gr. 2,** 292–293
Hang On Sloopy, **Gr. 7,** 31
Hine Ma Tov, **Gr. 4,** 66
I Love a Piano, **Gr. 6,** 130
I Will Sing Hello, **Gr. K,** T156
Im Krapfenwaldl (In Krapfen Woods), Op. 336
   (listening), **Gr. 2,** 244
Interplanet Janet, **Gr. 3,** 302
Just One Planet, **Gr. 4,** 164
Little Red Caboose, **Gr. 1,** T109
Mi-a-ou from *Dolly Suite* (listening), **Gr. K,** T149
Old Barn Dance, The, **Gr. 6,** 94
Over the Rainbow, **Gr. 4,** 126
Peter Cottontail, **Gr. K,** T338
Pop! Goes the Weasel, **Gr. 5,** 97
Season of Hope, The, **Gr. 5,** 411
Somos el barco, **Gr. 4,** 11
Spinning Wheel, **Gr. 4,** 211
They Were Tall, **Gr. K,** T52
Trio No. 39, Finale, **Gr. 3,** 155
Wake Up the Sun, **Gr. 2,** 124–125

Classified Index of Songs, Selected Concepts, Skills, and Activities (continued)

concertino

Concertino for Marimba, Op. 21, First Movement ("Vigorous"), **Gr. 4,** 120

concerto

Concerto No. 2 for Double Bass, First Movement (excerpt), **Gr. 5,** 161

Concerto No. 3 in B Flat, First Movement (Allegro Moderato), **Gr. 5,** 40

Concerto for Flute, First Movement (excerpt), **Gr. 2,** 120

Concerto for Harp, Op. 4, No. 6, First Movement (excerpt) by G. F. Handel, **Gr. 6,** 81

Winter (Allegro non molto) from *The Four Seasons* (Concerto No. 4 in F Minor) by A. Vivaldi, **Gr. 6,** 403

Concerto for Piano No. 1, Allegro, **Gr. 8,** 179

Concerto for Piano No. 2, Third Movement (excerpt) (listening), **Gr. 2,** 41

Concerto for Trombone ("Motorbike Concerto"), Fifth Movement (listening), **Gr. 2,** 193

Concerto for Two Trumpets, Allegro (listening), **Gr. 2,** 73

Concerto for Violin and Oboe, Adagio (excerpt) (listening), **Gr. 2,** 127

Concerto in B minor, **Gr. 3,** 120

Concierto de Aranjuez, First Movement (excerpt), **Gr. 3,** 41

Spring (Allegro) from *The Four Seasons*, **Gr. 4,** 391; **Gr. 7,** 112

contrasting sections

Goin' to the Zoo, **Gr. 1,** T195

How Does Your Garden Grow? **Gr. 1,** T145

Rig a Jig Jig, **Gr. 1,** T115

cumulative songs

Alison's Camel, **Gr. K,** T201

All Work Together, **Gr. K,** T12

Dinosaurs Dancing (listening), **Gr. K,** T72

Farmer in the Dell, The, **Gr. K,** T100

I Bought Me a Cat, **Gr. 2,** 14-15

La bella hortelana, **Gr. 2,** 208

Las horas, **Gr. K,** T70

Old MacDonald Had a Farm, **Gr. K,** T211; (listening), **Gr. 2,** 133

Pat Pat Patty Pat, **Gr. 1,** T308

She'll Be Comin' 'Round the Mountain, **Gr. 2,** 33

There's a Hole in the Middle of the Sea, **Gr. 1,** T178

When I First Came to This Land, **Gr. 3,** 28

Willoughby Wallaby Woo, **Gr. K,** T241

d.c. al coda

Don't Laugh at Me, **Gr. 7,** 9

defining, Gr. 3, 46, 47

d.s. al coda

Don't Laugh at Me, **Gr. 7,** 9

duet

Hush, Little Baby, **Gr. 4,** 9

echo song

Eight Days of Hanukkah!, The, **Gr. 3,** 371

Funiculi, Funicula, **Gr. 5,** 62

Hoo, Hoo!, **Gr. 1,** T55

I Will Sing Hello, **Gr. K,** T156

Little Sir Echo, **Gr. K,** T103

Look High, Look Low, **Gr. 3,** 338

Rainbow Connection, The, **Gr. 3,** 311

Viva Valentine!, **Gr. 1,** T365

étude

Étude Op. 25, No. 11 ("The Winter Wind"), **Gr. 2,** 136

fanfare

Entrance Fanfare, **Gr. 2,** 86

fugue

Fourth Movement (Allegro Molto) (experpt) from String Quartet in C Major, Op. 59, No. 3, **Gr. 5,** 228

Hallelujah Chorus from *Messiah*, **Gr. 5,** 419

Toccata and Fugue in D Minor, **Gr. 7,** 108

identical, similar, or different

Cidade Maravilhosa, **Gr. 5,** 432

Hallelujah, Get on Board, **Gr. 5,** 347

Lots O' Fish in Bonavist' Harbor, **Gr. 5,** 263

Sweet Music, **Gr. 5,** 319

identifying

Charlie Over the Ocean, **Gr. 1,** T74

Pat on the Back, A, **Gr. 2,** 74–75

Peter and the Wolf (listening), **Gr. 1,** T142

Strawberry Roan, **Gr. 2,** 66–67

We All Sing with the Same Voice, **Gr. 1,** T156

El floron, **Gr. 3,** 46

Kum Bachur, **Gr. 3,** 75

Ballet of the Unhatched Chicks from *Pictures at an Exhibition*, **Gr. 3,** 76

Circus Music from *The Red Pony Suite*, **Gr. 3,** 285

interlude

Arirang, **Gr. 5,** 53

Comedy Tonight, **Gr. 6,** 204

Galop (excerpt) from *The Comedians*, **Gr. 4,** 254

Hang on Sloopy, **Gr. 7,** 31

Hey, Look Me Over, **Gr. 4,** 115

Interjections, **Gr. 3,** 303

Let's Run Across the Hill, **Gr. 5,** 268

Old Barn Dance, The, **Gr. 6,** 94

Orange Blossom Special, **Gr. 6,** 33

Preamble, The, **Gr. 3,** 293

Spinning Wheel, **Gr. 4,** 211

Theme from *The Monkees* (listening), **Gr. 8,** 110

Three Is a Magic Number, **Gr. 3,** 296

Words of Wisdom, **Gr. 5,** 244

introduction, Gr. 8, 15, 261

Addams Family Theme, The, **Gr. 3,** 307

Anitra's Dance from *Peer Gynt Suite No. 1*, Op. 46, **Gr. 5,** 193

Arirang, **Gr. 5,** 53

Bird Island, **Gr. 8,** 57

Fascinating Rhythm, **Gr. 5,** 186

Greatest Show on Earth, The, **Gr. 3,** 308

Guadalcanal March, **Gr. 4,** 109

Hang on Sloopy, **Gr. 7,** 30

Interjections, **Gr. 3,** 303

Interplanet Janet, **Gr. 3,** 298

Little Red Caboose, **Gr. 1**, T109
Let's Run Across the Hill, **Gr. 5**, 268
Mayim, Mayim, **Gr. 6**, 102
Rainbow Connection, The, **Gr. 3**, 310
Rock Around the Clock, **Gr. 6**, 234
Spinning Wheel, **Gr. 4**, 211
Symphony No. 7, Second Movement, **Gr. 7**, 119
Three Is a Magic Number, **Gr. 3**, 296
Three Little Birds, **Gr. 8**, 84

groups
I Love My Country, **Gr. 1**, T328

march, Gr. 7, 37, 261
Children's March (listening), **Gr. K**, T113
Liberty Bell, **Gr. 5**, 394
Look High, Look Low, **Gr. 3**, 338
March from *Children's Games*, **Gr. 1**, T31
March from *Love for Three Oranges*, **Gr. 3**, 201
March of the Toys from *Babes in Toyland* (listening), **Gr. K**, T317
Parade from *Divertissement* from *Un Chapeau de paille d'Italie* (listening), **Gr. K**, T183
Radetzky March (listening), **Gr. K**, T177
Royal March of the Lions, The, from *The Carnival of the Animals*, **Gr. 1**, T25

motive, Gr. 8, 138, 261

notation, Gr. 3, 49

overture, Gr. 8, 73
King Stephen, **Gr. 5**, 255
Magic Flute, The, **Gr. 4**, 252
Overture from *William Tell*, **Gr. 3**, 64

phrases, Gr. 3, 59, 91, 92, 107, 109, 128, 129, 152, 153, 231
analyze, **Gr. 3**, 232
create, **Gr. 3**, 233
defining, **Gr. 3**, 233
Deta, Deta, **Gr. 5**, 246
Fascinating Rhythm, **Gr. 5**, 186
If I Had a Hammer, **Gr. 6**, 174
It Don't Mean a Thing, **Gr. 6**, 164
Mary Ann, **Gr. 5**, 186
Morning Has Broken, **Gr. 4**, 22
Plenty Fishes in the Sea, **Gr. 1**, T310
repeated, **Gr. 3**, 389
River of My People, **Gr. 6**, 170
Tako No Uta, **Gr. 1**, T371
There Are Many Flags in Many Lands, **Gr. 1**, T328
There's a Song in Me, **Gr. 5**, 184
Vive L'amour, **Gr. 5**, 262

refrain, Gr. 8, 262
River Come Down, **Gr. 8**, 10

rondo
create a rondo, **Gr. 2**, 223
Dance for Clarinet and Piano, **Gr. 6**, 189
Jamaica Farewell, **Gr. 3**, 156
"Le Moulinet", **Gr. 2**, 53
Los mariachis, **Gr. 3**, 397
Rondeau, **Gr. 6**, 121

School Band Rondo, **Gr. 7**, 36
Trio for Piano, Violin and Cello No. 39, Finale ("Gypsy Rondo"), **Gr. 3**, 155
Va Pensiero from *Nabucco*, **Gr. 6**, 169

round, Gr. 8, 262
Canon in D (transposed to C Major), **Gr. 8**, 67

sections
Contredanse from *Les Indes galantes*, **Gr. 4**, 97
Erev Shel Shoshanim, **Gr. 4**, 68
Hine Ma Tov, **Gr. 4**, 66
I am But a Small Voice, **Gr. 5**, 325
La colación, **Gr. 1**, T357
One Note Samba, **Gr. 4**, 92
Pizza, Pizza, Daddy-O, **Gr. 2**, 62–63
Sing, Sing, Sing, **Gr. 5**, 30, 33
Spinning Wheel, **Gr. 4**, 211
Sun Don't Set in the Mornin', **Gr. 3**, 48

sequence
De colores, **Gr. 5**, 98
Alleluia, **Gr. 6**, 186
Charleston, **Gr. 6**, 112
Comedy Tonight, **Gr. 6**, 204
Conga, **Gr. 6**, 34
Gee Mom, I Want to Go Home, **Gr. 6**, 148
Lullaby of Broadway, **Gr. 6**, 182
Mi caballo blanco, **Gr. 6**, 60
Neviděli jste tu mé panenky?, **Gr. 6**, 228
One of Those Songs, **Gr. 6**, 55
Suliram, **Gr. 6**, 58
Tum Balalaika, **Gr. 6**, 68
Winter Ade, **Gr. 6**, 132, 133

sixteen-bar blues
One Dime Blues, **Gr. 6**, 178

sonata
Sonata for Bass Trombone, Andantino, **Gr. 5**, 160
Sonata for Cello and Piano, Op. 40, Second Movement, **Gr. 4**, 40
Sonata for Flute and Piano, Third Movement – Presto giocoso, **Gr. 4**, 200
Sonata for Piano No. 2 in D Minor, Vivace (excerpt), **Gr. 4**, 181
Sonata for Piano No. 48 in C, First Movement, **Gr. 8**, 122

sonatina
Sonatina for Three Timpani and Piano, First Movement, **Gr. 4**, 81

strophic, Gr. 7, 124, 262
Barbry Ellen, **Gr. 6**, 208
Blue Suede Shoes, **Gr. 6**, 238
Greenland Whale Fishery, The, **Gr. 6**, 212
If I Had a Hammer, **Gr. 6**, 174
Listen to the Music, **Gr. 6**, 63
Lumber Camp Song, The, **Gr. 6**, 136
Mama Don't 'Low, **Gr. 6**, 126
One of Those Songs, **Gr. 6**, 54
River of My People, **Gr. 6**, 176
Rock Around the Clock, **Gr. 6**, 234
Ship in Distress, The, **Gr. 6**, 211

Classified Index

Classified Index of Songs, Selected Concepts, Skills, and Activities (continued)

Wabash Cannonball, The, **Gr. 6**, 30
Water Is Wide, The, **Gr. 6**, 46

suite, Gr. 7, 102, 262
Anitra's Dance from *Peer Gynt Suite No. 1*, Op. 46,
  Gr. 5, 193
Badinerie from Suite No. 2 for Orchestra, **Gr. 5**, 41
Badinerie from Suite for Orchestra No. 2 in B Minor,
  Gr. 4, 61
Seventeen Come Sunday, **Gr. 7**, 102
Solveig's Song from *Peer Gynt Suite No. 2*, Op. 55,
  Gr. 5, 192
Vivo from Pulcinella Suite, **Gr. 4**, 201
Mars from *The Planets*, **Gr. 6**, 196

symphony
Symphony No. 1 ("Titan"), Third Movement (excerpt),
  Gr. 5, 161
Symphony No. 4, Fourth Movement, **Gr. 4**, 287
Symphony No. 5 in C Minor, Third and Fourth
  Movements, **Gr. 8**, 114
Symphony No. 6 ("Pathetique"), Second Movement,
  Gr. 5, 281
Symphony No. 7, Second Movement, **Gr. 7**, 118
Symphony No. 9 ("Choral"), Fourth Movement
  (excerpt), **Gr. 5**, 102; **Gr. 7**, 156
Symphony No. 40 in G Minor, First Movement, **Gr. 8**,
  218
Symphony No. 45 ("Farewell"), First Movement, **Gr. 8**,
  124
Symphony No. 73 ("La Chasse") ("The Hunt"), Fourth
  Movement, **Gr. 4**, 263
Symphony No. 101 in D Major ("Clock"), **Gr. 8**, 129

tag
Fascinating Rhythm, **Gr. 5**, 186

ternary form, Gr. 7, 262; **Gr. 8**, 262
Castle on a Cloud, **Gr. 7**, 82
Música indígena, **Gr. 8**, 127

theme and variations, Gr. 8, 92, 174, 262
12-bar blues, **Gr. 8**, 270
American Salute, **Gr. 5**, 36
Carnival of Venice, The, **Gr. 6**, 4
Debka Kurdit, **Gr. 4**, 236
Follow Your Dream, **Gr. 4**, 236
People United Will Never Be Defeated!, **Gr. 8**, 93
Pop! Goes the Weasel, **Gr. 5**, 97
Serenade No. 10 in B Flat Major, K.361 ("Gran Partita"),
  Theme and Variations (excerpt), **Gr. 4**, 235
Simple Gifts, **Gr. 5**, 152, 153
Symphony No. 7, Second Movement, **Gr. 7**, 119
Turandot from *Symphonic Metamorphosis on Themes of
  Carl Maria von Weber* (excerpt), **Gr. 4**, 81

tone poem, Gr. 7, 262
Moldau from *Má Vlast*, **Gr. 7**, 219

twelve-bar blues, Gr. 8, 270
Backwater Blues, **Gr. 5**, 174, 175, 180
City Blues, **Gr. 5**, 278
Every Day I Have the Blues, **Gr. 5**, 179, 180
Good Mornin' Blues, **Gr. 5**, 176, 177, 180

variations on a theme, Gr. 7, 170; **Gr. 8**, 92
verse
Skip to My Lou, **Gr. 1**, T111

verse and refrain, Gr. 8, 84
All Work Together, **Gr. K**, T12
Allundé Alluia, **Gr. 4**, 34
Angelina, **Gr. 6**, 9
¡Ay, Jalisco no te rajes!, **Gr. 5**, 188
Baby Beluga, **Gr. 2**, 26–27
Bamboo, **Gr. 4**, 211
Bella bimba, **Gr. 3**, 172
Best That I Can Be!, The, **Gr. K**, T48
Big Big World, **Gr. 5**, 438
Boll Weevil, **Gr. 3**, 171
Boogie-Woogie Ghost, The, **Gr. 4**, 368
Buckeye Jim, **Gr. 4**, 136
Cedar Swamp, **Gr. 4**, 50
Chag Asif, **Gr. 3**, 360
Charlie, **Gr. 3**, 208
Chicken Dance, **Gr. 7**, 61
Chíu, chíu, chíu, **Gr. 6**, 172
Cielito Lindo, **Gr. 3**, 166
Colors (listening), **Gr. K**, T58
Cornstalk Fiddle and a Shoestring Bow, **Gr. 3**, 284
Cumberland Gap, **Gr. 3**, 99
¡Dale, dale, dale!, **Gr. 3**, 378
December Nights, December Lights, **Gr. 4**, 372
Derby Ram, The, **Gr. 4**, 259
Dere Geliyor, **Gr. 6**, 232
Dreamers, **Gr. 5**, 430
Eight Bells, **Gr. 4**, 281
Eight Days of Hanukkah, The, **Gr. 3**, 370
El coquí, **Gr. 4**, 178
El tambor, **Gr. K**, T129; **Gr. 6**, 222
El vaquerito, **Gr. 1**, T334
Everything Grows, **Gr. 2**, 204–205
Follow Your Dream, **Gr. 4**, 234
Frog Went A-Courtin', **Gr. 4**, 46
Gee Mom, I Want to Go Home, **Gr. 6**, 148
Git on Board, **Gr. K**, T145
Goin' to the Zoo, **Gr. 1**, T195
Hang On Sloopy, **Gr. 7**, 30
Happy Talk, **Gr. 4**, 84
Happy Wanderer, The, **Gr. 3**, 18
Hine Ma Tov, **Gr. 4**, 66
I's the B'y, **Gr. 3**, 13
It's a Small World, **Gr. 2**, 298–299
It's Time to Get Ready for Christmas, **Gr. 3**, 372
Jack Was Ev'ry Bit a Sailor, **Gr. 6**, 170
Jamaica Farewell, **Gr. 3**, 156
Just One Planet, **Gr. 4**, 164
Kalinka, **Gr. 3**, 224
Katyusha, **Gr. 4**, 188
L'il 'Liza Jane, **Gr. 4**, 20
La otra España, **Gr. 4**, 62
Las horas, **Gr. K**, T70
Let It Roll, **Gr. 6**, 124
Let's Go Fly a Kite, **Gr. 2**, 134–135
Little Spotted Puppy, **Gr. K**, T147
Look Who's Here!, **Gr. K**, T85

Classified Index of Songs, Selected Concepts, Skills, and Activities (continued)

Macnamara's Band, **Gr. 4**, 88
Marvelous Toy, The, **Gr. 3**, 182
Mi chacra (My Farm), **Gr. K**, T207
Moon and Me, **Gr. 3**, 220
Mountain Music, **Gr. 6**, 21
Mrs. Murphy's Chowder, **Gr. 3**, 390
Music of the World A-Turnin', **Gr. 3**, 44
Must Be Santa, **Gr. K**, T316
My Mom, **Gr. 1**, T373
Nampaya omame, **Gr. K**, T128
Nead na lachan sa mhúta, **Gr. 5**, 48
O, Desayo, **Gr. 6**, 50
Oh, Susanna, **Gr. 3**, 153
Oh, Won't You Sit Down, **Gr. 4**, 70
Old Ark's A-Moverin', **Gr. 4**, 130
Old Carrion Crow, The, **Gr. 4**, 192
Old Joe Clark, **Gr. 4**, 74
Oleanna, **Gr. 3**, 144
One More River, **Gr. 3**, 216
Oro, My Bodeen, **Gr. 4**, 279
Over the Rainbow, **Gr. 4**, 126
Pat Works on the Railway, **Gr. 4**, 86
Polly Wolly Doodle, **Gr. 3**, 132
Presidents, **Gr. K**, T330
Puff, the Magic Dragon, **Gr. 2**, 54–55
Red Iron Ore, **Gr. 6**, 134
Riding in the Buggy, **Gr. 3**, 131
Rig a Jig Jig, **Gr. 1**, T115
Roll On, Columbia, **Gr. 4**, 182
Sail Away, Ladies, **Gr. 4**, 54
Sheep Shearing, **Gr. 2**, 102–103
Simon Says, **Gr. 3**, 4
Sing Alleluia, Allelu, **Gr. 4**, 220
Sky Dances, **Gr. 4**, 206
Something for Me, Something for You, **Gr. 4**, 4
Somos el barco, **Gr. 4**, 10
Spinning Wheel, **Gr. 4**, 211
Stamping Land, **Gr. K**, T24
Step into the Spotlight, **Gr. 2**, A
Strawberry Roan (listening), **Gr. 2**, 66–67
Swapping Song, **Gr. 4**, 253
They Were Tall, **Gr. K**, T52
This A Way and That A Way, **Gr. 3**, 386
This Land is Your Land, **Gr. 4**, 146
Three Little Birds, **Gr. 3**, 204; **Gr. 7**, 84
Tinga Layo, **Gr. 2**, 50–51
Treasure Chests, **Gr. 3**, 90
Troika, **Gr. 6**, 230
Tum Balalaika, **Gr. 6**, 68
Turn the Glasses Over, **Gr. 3**, 260
Ucha Tirvarch, **Gr. 3**, 53
Uncle Pen, **Gr. 5**, 24
Vinqo, **Gr. 4**, 25
Wake Up the Sun, **Gr. 2**, 124–125
Walk by the River, **Gr. 6**, 74
Water Come a Me Eye, **Gr. 4**, 90
Wéané, **Gr. 3**, 184
What Can One Little Person Do?, **Gr. 4**, 204
What You Gonna Call Your Pretty Little Baby?,
    Gr. K, T319
Willowbee, **Gr. 2**, 69
Yankee Doodle, **Gr. 4**, 154
You Sing for Me, **Gr. 6**, 106

FROM THE TOP. *See also* Careers; Music News, Instrument
    Spotlights
performers
Ark, Ariana and Rexton (piano), **Gr. 3**, 40
Bremer, Louis (bass trombone), **Gr. 5**, 160
Brown, Randall (saxophone), **Gr. 3**, 80
Brown, Rebecca (guitar), **Gr. 2**, 200
Chang, Sebastian (piano), **Gr. 7**, 127
Conway, Eoghan (tin whistle), **Gr. 3**, 160
Cope, Todd (clarinet), **Gr. 5**, 40
Criddle, Lauren (voice), **Gr. 4**, 160
Donehew, Karla (violin), **Gr. 7**, 52
Feder, Abraham (cello), **Gr. 4**, 40
Fortenberry, Jewell "Tre" (piano), **Gr. 5**, 80
Garcia, Bianca (flute), **Gr. 2**, 120
Garcia, Pala (violin), **Gr. 8**, 156
Gorton, Heidi (harp), **Gr. 3**, 200
Hurlburt, Sean (saxophone), **Gr. 7**, 161
Jantsch, Carol (tuba), **Gr. 2**, 40
Johnson, Samuel (cello), **Gr. 8**, 171
Jordheim, Alisa (voice), **Gr. 8**, 187
Lentz, Jarrod (voice), **Gr. 7**, 78
MacMoran, William (bagpipes), **Gr. 6**, 200
Marchioni, Toni (oboe), **Gr. 5**, 120
Mucky, Mathew (trumpet), **Gr. 6**, 40
Neely, Nathan (French horn), **Gr. 8**, 59
Ochieng, Trevor (violin), **Gr. 2**, 160
Ong, Lin (percussion), **Gr. 8**, 41
Park, Ariana and Rexton (piano), **Gr. 3**, 40
Pila, Ben (guitar), **Gr. 7**, 216
Premo, Evan (string bass), **Gr. 6**, 120
Ross, David (flute), **Gr. 4**, 200
Souliere, Jason (bassoon), **Gr. 8**, 19
Stewart, Amanda (trombone), **Gr. 7**, 155
Talens, Deanna (cello), **Gr. 6**, 80
Tan, Lucy (piano), **Gr. 6**, 160
Turner, Catherine (French horn), **Gr. 4**, 80
Urioste, Elena (violin), **Gr. 5**, 200
Vante, Barbara (viola), **Gr. 3**, 120
Vasan, Neil (marimba), **Gr. 4**, 120
Yu, Vincent (piano), **Gr. 2**, 80

Web Tips, Gr. 2, 41, 81, 121, 161, 201; **Gr. 3**, 41, 81, 121,
    161, 201; **Gr. 4**, 41, 81, 121, 161, 201; **Gr. 5**, 41, 81,
    121, 161, 201; **Gr. 6**, 41, 81, 121, 161, 201; **Gr. 7**, 52,
    78, 127, 155, 160, 216; **Gr. 8**, 19, 41, 59, 156, 171, 187

G

GAME SONGS
A la rueda de San Miguel (To the Wheel of San Miguel),
    Gr. 2, 60
A la rueda rueda ('Round and 'Round), **Gr. 1**, T240
Acitrón (Mexican stone-passing game) (listening),
    Gr. 6, 92
Acka Backa, **Gr. 1**, T256

Classified Index of Songs, Selected Concepts, Skills, and Activities (continued)

Afrakakraba, **Gr. 3,** 103
Alison's Camel, **Gr. K,** T201
All Around the Buttercup, **Gr. 2,** 210
Apples and Bananas, **Gr. 1,** T151
Bate, Bate (Stir, Stir), **Gr. 2,** 242
Bee, Bee, Bumblebee, **Gr. 1,** T250
Bickle, Bockle, **Gr. K,** T187
Billy, **Gr. 3,** 7
Bus, The, **Gr. K,** T137
Button, You Must Wander, **Gr. 2,** 176
Categories, **Gr. 1,** T146
Charlie Over the Ocean, **Gr. 1,** T75
Chase the Squirrel, **Gr. 1,** T88
Chicka-ma, Chicka-ma, Craney Crow, **Gr. 3,** 263
Circle 'Round the Zero, **Gr. 3,** 267
Circle Game, **Gr. 1,** T289
Cuckoo, Where Are You?, **Gr. 2,** 244
Cut the Cake, **Gr. 1,** T232
Daisy Chain, **Gr. 2,** 255
Deta, Deta, **Gr. 5,** 246
Diou Shjou Juan'er (Hide the Handkerchief), **Gr. 1,** T212
Doggie, Doggie, **Gr. 2,** 59
Draw a Bucket of Water, **Gr. 3,** 223
Dreidel Song (poem), **Gr. 1,** T348
Early in the Morning at Eight O'Clock, **Gr. 4,** 59
Eka Muda, **Gr. 5,** 29
El florón (The Flower), **Gr. 1,** T117; **Gr. 3,** 55
El juego chirimbolo (The Chirimbolo Game), **Gr. 1,** T105
En roulant ma boule, **Gr. 3,** 100
Farmer in the Dell, The, **Gr. K,** T100
Gogo, **Gr. K,** T188
Hello Song, **Gr. K,** T2
Here Comes a Bluebird, **Gr. 2,** 263
Here Is the Beehive, **Gr. K,** T258
Here We Sit, **Gr. 1,** T251
Hey, Hey, Look at Me, **Gr. 2,** 245
Hokey Pokey, **Gr. K,** T68
Hoo, Hoo!, **Gr. 1,** T57
Hop, Hop, Hop, **Gr. K,** T197
Hop, Old Squirrel, **Gr. 2,** 258
Hunt the Cows, **Gr. 1,** T236
I Like Spinach, **Gr. 1,** T163
I See, **Gr. 2,** 266
I Wanna Be a Friend of Yours, **Gr. 1,** T84
If You're Happy, **Gr. K,** T6
In and Out, **Gr. 2,** 245
In My Little Motor Boat, **Gr. 1,** T161
Jingle at the Window, **Gr. 3,** 268
Johnny's Flea, **Gr. 1,** T158
Juan Pirulero, **Gr. 2,** 270
Jugaremos en el bosque (We'll Be Playing in the Forest), **Gr. 2,** 188
Jump, Jim Joe, **Gr. 1,** T88, T99
Knock the Cymbals, **Gr. 2,** 265
Kuma San, **Gr. 3,** 244
L'il 'Liza Jane, **Gr. 4,** 20
Lemonade, **Gr. 2,** 20
Let Us Chase the Squirrel, **Gr. 3,** 248
Little Sally Walker, **Gr. 3,** 105

Looby Loo, **Gr. 1,** T262
Lucy Locket, **Gr. 1,** T253
Me Stone, **Gr. 2,** 48–49
Merecumbé (Puerto Rican children's game song), **Gr. 6,** 276
Miss Mary Mack, **Gr. 1,** T15, T17
Mizuguruma, **Gr. 1,** T260
Mother, Mother, **Gr. 2,** 254
Mouse, Mousie, **Gr. 2,** 254
Mr. Frog, **Gr. 2,** 257
Mulberry Bush, The, **Gr. K,** T112
My Mama's Calling Me, **Gr. 1,** T54, T55
Nabe, Nabe, Soku, Nuke (Stew Pot, Stew Pot, Bottomless Pot), **Gr. 2,** 259
Name Game, **Gr. K,** T57
Nampaya omame (Mothers), **Gr. K,** T128
Oats, Peas, Beans and Barley Grow, **Gr. K,** T287
Ɔbɔɔ Asi Me Nsa, **Gr. K,** T159
Old Turkey Buzzard, **Gr. 5,** 264
Ole La'u Papa e (Tongan stick game song), **Gr. 6,** 91
Oliver Twist, **Gr. 2,** 268
One, Two, Three, Four, **Gr. 1,** T124
One, Two, Three, Four, Five, **Gr. 1,** T265
Orff Instruments, **Gr. 2,** 183
Pat Pat Patty Pat, **Gr. 1,** T308–T309
Pizza, Pizza, Daddy-O, **Gr. 2,** 63
Poun to, Poun to (Where Is It? Where Is It?) (Greek and Cypriot song) (listening), **Gr. 2,** 175
Pumpkin Song, **Gr. 1,** T342
Punchinella, **Gr. 1,** T216
Pusa't daga (Cat and Rat), **Gr. 1,** T289
Que llueva, **Gr. 3,** 274
Red Rover, **Gr. 2,** 249
Ring Around the Rosy, **Gr. K,** T246
Rise, Sally, Rise, **Gr. 1,** T162
Sally Go 'Round the Sun, **Gr. 2,** 268
Sammy Sackett, **Gr. 2,** 147
Sara Watashi (Plate Passing), **Gr. 1,** T67
Say Your Name, **Gr. 2,** 243
See the Pony Galloping, **Gr. K,** T44
Sheep In the Meadow (speech piece), **Gr. 2,** 8
Simon Says, **Gr. 3,** 4
Simple Simon, **Gr. 1,** T175
Singabahambayo, **Gr. 5,** 75
Skip to My Lou, **Gr. 1,** T102
Snail, Snail, **Gr. 1,** T252
Somebody Come and Play, **Gr. 1,** T92
Soup, Soup!, **Gr. 1,** T359
There's a Hole in the Middle of the Sea, **Gr. 1,** T178
This Is What I Can Do, **Gr. K,** T124
Tinker, Tailor, **Gr. 1,** T132
Tisket A Tasket A, **Gr. 1,** T107
Tititorea, **Gr. 3,** 175
Toodala, **Gr. K,** T39
Touch Your Shoulders, **Gr. K,** T254
Tue Tue (Ghanaian song) (listening), **Gr. 2,** 234
Turn the Glasses Over, **Gr. 3,** 261
Vhaya Kadhimba Game, **Gr. 1,** T15, T17
'Way Down Yonder in the Brickyard, **Gr. 5,** 155

Classified Index of Songs, Selected Concepts, Skills, and Activities (continued)

What's Your Name, **Gr. 1**, T125
Who Has the Penny?, **Gr. 2**, 252
Who's That Tapping at the Window?, **Gr. 2**, 261
Who's That Yonder, **Gr. 3**, 245
Zui Zui Zukkorbashi (Mouse in the Rice Sack), **Gr. 1**, T99

GLOBAL VOICES. *See also* Multicultural Materials
  Global Voices Resources, Gr. 1, T382; **Gr. 2**, 393;
    Gr. 3, 409; **Gr. 4**, 424; **Gr. 5**, 457; **Gr. 6**, 441
    Acitrón (Mexico), **Gr. 6**, 92
    Afrakakraba (Ghana), **Gr. 3**, 102
    Ake Tonu (New Zealand), **Gr. 5**, 150
    Ban dal (Korea), **Gr. 4**, 184
    Bəri Bax! (Azerbaijan), **Gr. 5**, 233
    Cip cip cücələrim (Azerbaijan) by G. Huseynli and
      T. Mutallibov, **Gr. 3**, 215
    Her kommer vennen min (Norway), **Gr. 3**, 142
    Juan Pirulero (Mexico), **Gr. 1**, T152, T153
    Kia Ora (New Zealand), **Gr. 2**, 65
    Kokiriko (Japan), **Gr. 6**, 145
    Nach Nach Nach (India), **Gr. 6**, 224
    Nead na lachan sa mhúta (Ireland), **Gr. 5**, 48
    Ngikhumbuli Langa (Swaziland), **Gr. 5**, 195
    Pezinho (Brazil), **Gr. 3**, 230
    Poun to, Poun to (Greek/Cyprus), **Gr. 2**, 175
    Såg du noko (Norway), **Gr. 2**, 104
    Sambalelê (Brazil), **Gr. 1**, T202
    Santoki (Korea), **Gr. 1**, T187
    Thula Sizwe (South Africa), **Gr. 6**, 73
    Tinikling (Philippines), **Gr. 4**, 104
    Tue Tue (Ghana), **Gr. 2**, 234
    Twee emmertjes (Holland), **Gr. 4**, 212
    Vhaya Kadhimba (Zimbabwe), **Gr. 1**, T25
    Vinqo (South Africa), **Gr. 4**, 24

H

HISTORY AND CULTURE. *See also* Biographies
  Accordion in America, The, **Gr. 6**, 135
  Acitrón, **Gr. 6**, 92
  African American Music, **Gr. 1**, T55
  African American Spirituals, **Gr. K**, T318; **Gr. 6**, 22
  African Anthem (N'kosi sikelel' iAfrika), **Gr. 6**, 341
  African Instruments, **Gr. 1**, T211
  African Languages, **Gr. 5**, 426
  Alps, The, **Gr. 3**, 19
  Amazing Grace, **Gr. 7**, 144
  America, **Gr. K**, T303
  American Bandstand, **Gr. 7**, 10
  American Cities, **Gr. 1**, T3
  American Flag, The, **Gr. 1**, T329
  Angolan Folk Song, **Gr. 6**, 51
  Appalachian Folk Songs, **Gr. 4**, 50
  Appalachian Spring, **Gr. 5**, 153
  Arirang, **Gr. 5**, 51
  "Asian" Intervals, **Gr. 3**, 196
  Baby Rhymes, **Gr. 1**, T180
  Background of Our Anthem, **Gr. 5**, 386
  Balkan Folk Songs, **Gr. 4**, 132
  Ball, The, from *Children's Games*, **Gr. K**, T132
  Ballad, The, **Gr. 6**, 208

Ballet of the Unhatched Chicks, **Gr. 3**, 76
Barber of Seville, The, **Gr. 6**, 152
Bəri Bax!, **Gr. 5**, 233
Bartered Bride, The, **Gr. 5**, 274
Bartók, Béla, **Gr. 1**, T245
Bassoon, The, **Gr. 4**, 117
Battle of Jericho, **Gr. 5**, 126
Beginnings of Rock, **Gr. 5**, 425
Bells, **Gr. 7**, 123
Big Bands, **Gr. 5**, 32
Bim Bom, **Gr. 3**, 219
Bird Songs, **Gr. 4**, 152
Birthday History, **Gr. K**, T347
Bizet, Georges, **Gr. 1**, T231
Blue Suede Shoes, **Gr. 6**, 236
Bluegrass Music, **Gr. 6**, 75
Blues, The, **Gr. 5**, 179
Bombo, **Gr. 3**, 33
Bonjour, mes amis (Hello, My Friends), **Gr. 1**, T19
Boy Bands, **Gr. 4**, 315
Branslet, The, **Gr. 3**, 96
Broadway, **Gr. 6**, 309; **Gr. 7**, 81
Buckwheat Zydeco, **Gr. 7**, 89
Buffalo Prairie, **Gr. K**, T219
Bydlo, **Gr. 1**, T151
Caissons Go Rolling Along, The, **Gr. 5**, 37
Call and Response, **Gr. 2**, 360; **Gr. 4**, 70; **Gr. 5**, 422
Calypso Music, **Gr. 3**, 127
Calypso, **Gr. 5**, 91
Career: Arranger, **Gr. 7**, 153
Career: Classical Music Artist Manager, **Gr. 6**, 201
Career: Composer, **Gr. 6**, 23; **Gr. 7**, 52
Career: Conductor, **Gr. 8**, 220
Career: Dancers, **Gr. 1**, T314
Career: Diction Coach, **Gr. 7**, 120
Career: Directors, **Gr. 7**, 182
Career: Entertainment Lawyer, **Gr. 8**, 211
Career: Event Planner, **Gr. 8**, 47
Career: Guitar Maker, **Gr. 6**, 138
Career: Instrument Maker, **Gr. 8**, 95
Career: Lyricist, **Gr. 7**, 192
Career: Music Company Agent, **Gr. 8**, 25
Career: Music Journalist, **Gr. 6**, 237
Career: Music Teacher, **Gr. 8**, 164
Career: Music Technician, **Gr. 8**, 107
Career: Musical Director, **Gr. 8**, 75
Career: Musicologist, **Gr. 7**, 78
Career: Performers, **Gr. 7**, 23, 102
Career: Piano Tuner-Technician, **Gr. 6**, 131
Career: Recording Engineer, **Gr. 8**, 202
Career: Sound Designer, **Gr. 8**, 135
Career: Sound Effects Engineer, **Gr. 8**, 20
Career: Symphony Orchestra Musician, **Gr. 7**, 102
Career: Teacher, **Gr. 7**, 235
Caribbean Music, **Gr. 6**, 155
Caribbean, The, **Gr. 2**, 301
Carillon Technology, **Gr. 7**, 123
Carnival of the Animals, The, **Gr. K**, T195
Carols and Caroling, **Gr. 5**, 419
Carols, **Gr. 6**, 407
Celebrating Hispanic Heritage, **Gr. 3**, 359

Classified Index of Songs, Selected Concepts, Skills, and Activities (continued)

Celebrations around the World, **Gr. 4**, 389
Celtic People, The, **Gr. 5**, 340
Central Asian Lute, **Gr. 6**, 68
Changing Flag, The, **Gr. 5**, 387
Children's Dance, **Gr. 2**, 246
Chinese Lion Dance, **Gr. 1**, T362
Chinese Music, **Gr. 6**, 28
Chinese New Year, **Gr. K**, T329; **Gr. 3**, 385
Chorale Music, **Gr. 6**, 64
Christmas, **Gr. 3**, 372
Christmas Carols, **Gr. 2**, 359
Christmas Desserts, **Gr. 2**, 358
Christmas in France, **Gr. 3**, 374
Cinco de Mayo, **Gr. K**, T340; **Gr. 2**, 381; **Gr. 3**, 397;
　Gr. 5, W, 441
Circus, The, **Gr. 3**, 308
Civil Rights Movement, **Gr. 3**, 181
Classical Period, **Gr. 8**, 124
Classical Pop Music, **Gr. 7**, 49
Classifying Music, **Gr. 5**, 108
"Clicks" in African Languages, **Gr. 4**, 24
Clocks, **Gr. 3**, 66
College Songs, **Gr. 4**, 172
Community Bands, **Gr. 7**, 37
Concerto, The, **Gr. 6**, 403
Conductors, **Gr. 3**, 108
Cotton-Eye Joe, **Gr. 4**, 52
Counting Games, **Gr. 1**, T124
Cowboy Songs, **Gr. 4**, 111
Creole and Cajun Cultures, **Gr. 3**, 16
Creole Music, **Gr. 3**, 276
Cripple Creek, **Gr. 6**, 373
Damn Yankees, **Gr. 6**, 166
Dance in Colonial America, **Gr. 2**, 349
Dancing Master, The, **Gr. 6**, 101
De Colores, **Gr. 5**, 88
Down by the Riverside, **Gr. 6**, 24
Dragon Boats, **Gr. K**, T328
Dreaming Blue, **Gr. 6**, 219
Dreidel Traditions, **Gr. 2**, 353
Dreidels, **Gr. 1**, T349
Drums of Ghana, **Gr. 3**, 102
Dynamic Duo, **Gr. 7**, 126
Early African American Music, **Gr. 4**, 323
Early Cars, **Gr. 3**, 252
Earth Day, **Gr. 3**, 394; **Gr. 5**, 438
Easter, **Gr. K**, T339
El Nacimiento, **Gr. 1**, T356
El tambor, **Gr. 6**, 223
El vito, **Gr. 5**, 211
Elgar, Edward, **Gr. 1**, T233
Erie Canal, The, **Gr. 5**, 132
Fables of Bidpai, **Gr. K**, T294
Farm Aid, **Gr. 7**, 219
Fiddle, **Gr. 3**, 91
First Recorded Words, **Gr. 1**, T287
Fisk Jubilee Singers, **Gr. 3**, 324
Flag Day, **Gr. 3**, 356
Folk Dance on Stage, **Gr. 7**, 225
Folk Tune, **Gr. 5**, 111
Follow the Drinkin' Gourd, **Gr. 5**, 143

Form, **Gr. 3**, 48
Frog Myths, **Gr. 1**, T44
From Spirituals to Hip-Hop, **Gr. 5**, 174
Fung Yang Song, **Gr. 5**, 59
Funiculi, Funicula, **Gr. 5**, 62
Fusion Music, **Gr. 4**, 208
Game Songs, **Gr. 4**, 59
Gamelan Ensemble, **Gr. 1**, T144
Gebeta Game Board, **Gr. 3**, 346
Gershwin, George, **Gr. 1**, T168
Ghanian Music, **Gr. 8**, 85
Giving Thanks, **Gr. 1**, T343
God Bless America, **Gr. 5**, 4
Gonna Build a Mountain, **Gr. 6**, 4
Gospel Music, **Gr. 5**, 87
Grasshoppers (poem), **Gr. 1**, T244
Great American Brass Band Festival, **Gr. 8**, 49
Ground Hog Day, **Gr. 3**, 246
Guadalquivir, **Gr. 3**, 30
Guantanamera, **Gr. 5**, 214
Haere Ra, **Gr. 5**, 151
Halloween Montage, **Gr. 5**, 404
Hammered Dulcimer, The, **Gr. 4**, 55
Handel, George Frideric, **Gr. 1**, T263
Hand-Jive, **Gr. 6**, 87
Hanukkah, **Gr. K**, T314; **Gr. 3**, 369; **Gr. 5**, 415
Hanukkah Traditions, **Gr. 3**, 370
Harmony, **Gr. 3**, 192
Hawaiian Vocal Music, **Gr. 4**, 339
Hey, Motswala, **Gr. 3**, 34
High Lonesome, The, **Gr. 8**, 71
Hispanic Heritage Month, **Gr. 5**, 397
Hopi People, The, **Gr. 3**, 325
How a Piano Works, **Gr. 8**, 160
How Hanukkah Began, **Gr. 2**, 352
How Kwanzaa Began, **Gr. 2**, 363
Hunt the Squirrel, **Gr. 1**, T136
Ice Skating, **Gr. 1**, T347
Improvisation, **Gr. 5**, 184
India's Diwali Festival, **Gr. 5**, 403
Indonesia, **Gr. 6**, 59
Influence of Spirituals, **Gr. 6**, 417
Instrument Families, **Gr. 1**, T141
Instrument: Harpsichord, **Gr. 3**, 154
Instruments in Song, **Gr. 4**, 89
Instruments of the Alps, **Gr. 3**, 21
Instruments of the Orchestra, **Gr. 2**, 77
Irish Folk Music, **Gr. 4**, 186
Irish Traditional Music, **Gr. 2**, 375
Iroquois Music and Dance, **Gr. 3**, 51
Italian Terminology, **Gr. 7**, 112
Italian Terms, **Gr. 5**, 107
Ives, Burl, **Gr. 6**, 269
Jack O' Lantern, **Gr. 1**, T341
Jackson, Mahalia, **Gr. 8**, 31
Japanese Bamboo Flutes, **Gr. 8**, 56
Japanese Folk Tale, A, **Gr. 1**, T319
Japanese Music, **Gr. 1**, T68
Jasmine Flower, **Gr. 3**, 147
Jazz, **Gr. 6**, 380
Jean-Baptiste Lully's Death, **Gr. 8**, 166

Classified Index

Pony Named Macaroni, A, **Gr. 2,** 341
Pop! Goes the Weasel, **Gr. 5,** 94
Powwows, **Gr. K,** T344
Prairie and the Buffalo, **Gr. K,** T220
President's Own United States Marine Band, The, **Gr. 7,** 194
Presidents' Day, **Gr. 1,** T369; **Gr. 3,** 388
Prokofiev, Sergei, **Gr. 1,** T91, T138
Punjab, The, **Gr. 6,** 224
Purcell, Henry, **Gr. 1,** T176
Purim, **Gr. 2,** 373
Ragtime, **Gr. 6,** 315
Railroad Workers' Songs, **Gr. 4,** 139
Rattles, **Gr. 3,** 51
Ravel, Maurice, **Gr. 1,** T236
Reason to Give Thanks, A, **Gr. 2,** 348
Recording Technology, **Gr. 7,** 8
Red River Valley, **Gr. 6,** 96
Renaissance Chanson, The, **Gr. 6,** 336
Re-using Melodies, **Gr. 4,** 182
Ritornello, The, **Gr. 4,** 391
Rock and Roll Ancestors, **Gr. 4,** 311
Rock and Roll, **Gr. 7,** 98
Roll de Ole Chariot Along, **Gr. 6,** 243
Romper, Stomper, and Boo, **Gr. 1,** T36
Rondalla Orchestra, The, **Gr. 4,** 105
Rouse, Steve, **Gr. 8,** 235
Royal Pair: Games We Play, **Gr. 3,** 4
Sailing West to Go East, **Gr. 2,** 344
Saint Patrick's Day, **Gr. 2,** 374
Saint-Saëns, Camille, **Gr. 1,** T23, T203
Samiotissa, **Gr. 5,** 285
Santa Claus, **Gr. 3,** 373
Santa's Many Names, **Gr. 2,** 356
Santa's Reindeer, **Gr. 2,** 357
Santa's Roots, **Gr. 4,** 381
Scat Singing, **Gr. 7,** 173
School Performance History, **Gr. 7,** 28
Scotland's National Instrument, **Gr. 3,** 89
Sea Chanteys, **Gr. 6,** 320
Shakers, The, **Gr. 5,** 136
Sheet Music Publishing, **Gr. 7,** 44
Shenandoah, **Gr. 4,** D
Shiloh, **Gr. K,** T130
Shope, Shope, **Gr. 5,** 220
Showing Pride, **Gr. 1,** T328
Silbar and Henley, **Gr. 6,** E
Silent Night, **Gr. 6,** 413
Simple Gifts, **Gr. 5,** 152
Singing and Clapping Games, **Gr. 3,** 6
Slavery in the Americas, **Gr. 5,** 156
Sleep, Bonnie Bairnie, **Gr. 1,** T27
Smetana, Bedřich, **Gr. 6,** 229
Solveig's Song, **Gr. 5,** 192
Songs and Poems of Peace, **Gr. 4,** 67
Songwriting Duos, **Gr. 4,** 313
Sound of Music, The, **Gr. K,** T189
Sound the Trumpet, **Gr. 5,** 279
South Pacific, **Gr. 4,** 84
Spiritual Heritage, The, **Gr. 6,** 346
Spirituals, **Gr. 3,** 56, 376; **Gr. 6,** C, 22, 367, 417
Square Dancing, **Gr. 4,** 249

St. Louis Music, **Gr. 4,** 233
St. Valentine's Day, **Gr. 4,** 388
Star-Spangled Banner, The, **Gr. 4,** 357
Statue of Liberty, The, **Gr. 5,** 44
Steel Drums, **Gr. 6,** 8
Stravinsky's *Firebird*, **Gr. 4,** 190
Streets of Laredo, **Gr. 5,** 260
String Quartets, **Gr. 1,** T212
Sukkot, **Gr. 3,** 361
Sun Records, **Gr. 8,** 201
Swahili People, **Gr. 2,** 293
Swahili, **Gr. 4,** 384
Sweet Honey in the Rock, **Gr. K,** T33
Swing Music, **Gr. 6,** 18
Symbols of Kwanzaa, **Gr. 6,** 414
Symphony, **Gr. 5,** 103
Synthesizers, **Gr. 7,** 130
Tanabata Festival, **Gr. 3,** 63
Taylor, Billy, **Gr. 1,** T241
Tempo, **Gr. 1,** T108
Tender Land, The, **Gr. 6,** 77
Thai Instruments, **Gr. 1,** T200
Thai Music, **Gr. 5,** 379
Thanksgiving, **Gr. 3,** 364
There's No Hidin' Place, **Gr. 5,** 267
Theseus and the Minotaur, **Gr. 6,** 214
This Pretty Planet, **Gr. 6,** 194
"Toodala" Square Dances, **Gr. K,** T40
Traditional Arabic Rhythms, **Gr. 6,** 35
Train Songs, **Gr. 3,** 176
Train Whistle Signals, **Gr. 1,** T106
Transcontinental Railroad, The, **Gr. 3,** D
Treble and Bass Clefs, The, **Gr. 6,** 132
Trick or Treat, **Gr. 3,** 362
Truman, Harry S, **Gr. 8,** 40
Tshotsholoza, **Gr. 1,** T76
Tubby the Tuba, **Gr. 1,** T80
Tutira Mai Nga Iwi, **Gr. K,** T17
Tzena, Tzena, **Gr. 5,** 170
Ukulele, The, **Gr. 6,** 410
Underground Railroad, The, **Gr. 4,** 342; **Gr. 6,** 242
United Nations, **Gr. 1,** T222
Unpitched Instruments, **Gr. 1,** T92
Uruguayan Music, **Gr. 6,** 172
Using Computers to Make Music, **Gr. 6,** 127
Üsküdar, **Gr. 5,** 128
Valentine's Day, **Gr. 3,** 386
Valentine's Day Cards, **Gr. 2,** 369
Venezuelan Scenery, **Gr. 2,** 326
Victory at Sea, **Gr. 4,** 108
Villancicos, **Gr. 5,** 373
Waldteufel, Emil, **Gr. 1,** T344
Water Music, **Gr. 3,** 26
Water-Related Compositions, **Gr. 8,** 155
Welsh Vocal Music, **Gr. 4,** 277
What is a *Posada?*, **Gr. 4,** 377
William the Hippo, **Gr. K,** T198
Who was John Brown?, **Gr. 5,** 391
Who was Lucia?, **Gr. 5,** 412
Who was St. Patrick?, **Gr. 5,** 434
Winter in the United States, **Gr. 3,** 366

Classified Index

Woodwinds, **Gr. 5**, 218
Work Songs, **Gr. 6**, 10
Writing and Improvisation, **Gr. 1**, T207
Yankee Doodle, **Gr. 4**, 154
You're a Good Man, Charlie Brown, **Gr. 4**, 124
Zaimont, Judith Lang, **Gr. 1**, T128

HOLIDAY AND SEASONAL MUSIC. *See also* Patriotic Music
Autumn
Chusok
Ga Eul, **Gr. 5**, 401
Columbus Day
Columbus Sailed with Three Ships, **Gr. 2**, 344
Diwali
Aeyaya balano sakkad (Come, Children),
Gr. 5, 402
Diwali Song, **Gr. 6**, 396
Raga Malika (listening), **Gr. 5**, 403
Fall (Allegro) from *The Four Seasons* (Concerto No. 3 in
F Major) (excerpt), **Gr. K**, T305
Full Moon Festival
Pleeng Loy Krathong (Full Moon Song) (Thai festival
song), **Gr. 6**, 399
Halloween
Addams Family Theme, The, **Gr. 8**, 142
Boo, **Gr. 3**, 362–363
Boogie-Woogie Ghost, The, **Gr. 4**, 368
Dry Bones, **Gr. 5**, 406
Funeral March of a Marionette (excerpt) (listening),
Gr. 1, T336
Halloween Montage (listening), **Gr. 5**, 404
Halloween, **Gr. 1**, T340
Jack-o'-Lantern, **Gr. K**, T307
Nottamun Town, **Gr. 5**, 405
Pick a Pumpkin, **Gr. 2**, 347
Put On a Costume, **Gr. 1**, T336
Skin and Bones, **Gr. 1**, T340
Something Funny Outside, **Gr. 1**, T338
Thing, The (listening), **Gr. K**, T307
This Is Halloween, **Gr. 2**, 346
Town Hall Halloween Ball, **Gr. K**, T306
Harvest
Apple Picker's Reel, **Gr. 2**, 343
Chag Asif, **Gr. 3**, 360–361
Dide, **Gr. 3**, 279
Harvest, **Gr. 2**, 342
Hispanic Heritage Month
A la nanita nana (A Little Lullaby), **Gr. 4**, 230
Diana (Play the Bugle), **Gr. 1**, T334
El jarabe (Mexican Hat Dance), **Gr. 5**, 396
El quelite (The Village), **Gr. 4**, 362
El tecolote (The Owlet), **Gr. 6**, 392; (listening),
Gr. 4, 363
El vaquerito (listening), **Gr. 1**, T335
Este son by J. C. Ureña (listening), **Gr. 6**, 393
Pajarillo barranqueño, **Gr. 3**, 358–359
Santa Marta, **Gr. 5**, 398
Son de la negra (listening), **Gr. 5**, 397
Hmong New Year
Va txiab, **Gr. 6**, 394

Loy Krathong
Pleeng Loy Krathong, **Gr. 6**, 398
Seasonal, Autumn
Autumn Leaves, **Gr. 1**, T331
Butterfly, Flutter By, **Gr. 1**, T333
Clouds (poem), **Gr. 1**, T330
Ga Eul (Fall), **Gr. 5**, 401
Haiku (Butterflies), **Gr. 1**, T332
Marken er mejet (Out in the Meadow), **Gr. 4**, 364
Qua Cầ Gió Bay (listening), **Gr. 4**, 367
Raga Malika (listening), **Gr. 5**, 403
Thanksgiving
Five Fat Turkeys, **Gr. K**, T309
My Friend Tom, **Gr. 3**, 364–365
Over the River and Through the Wood, **Gr. 4**, 370
Pumpkin Song, **Gr. 1**, T342
Song of Thanksgiving, **Gr. 4**, 371
Tak for Maden (Thanks for Food), **Gr. 1**, T342
(*See also* Autumn)
Thank You, **Gr. 2**, 349
Things I'm Thankful For, **Gr. K**, T308
Turkey in the Straw (listening), **Gr. 2**, 348
Vietnamese Mid-Autumn Festival
Tết Trung (Children's Festival), **Gr. 4**, 366

Winter
Carnaval
Batacuda Brasileira (listening), **Gr. 5**, 433
Cidade Maravilhosa, **Gr. 5**, 432
Chinese New Year
Bei Fang Chre, **Gr. 2**, 367
Bo Hai Huan Ten (listening), **Gr. 7**, 56
Dragon Dance (listening), **Gr. 2**, 366
Go A Tin (Lantern Song), **Gr. 1**, T363
North Wind Blows, **Gr. 2**, 367
Christmas
Amen, **Gr. 3**, 376
Carol from an Irish Cabin, **Gr. 6**, 408
Christmas Tree (poem), **Gr. 1**, T352, T353
Deck the Hall, **Gr. 3**, 374–375
El colación (The Christmas Candies), **Gr. 1**, T357
El nacimiento (The Nativity), **Gr. K**, T322
El rorro (The Babe), **Gr. 1**, T356
Entren, santos peregrinos (Enter, Holy Pilgrims),
Gr. 4, 379
Ésta sí que es Nochebuena (This Is Christmas Eve),
Gr. 2, 361
Feliz Navidad (Merry Christmas), **Gr. 5**, 420
Go Tell It on the Mountain, **Gr. 3**, 377
Hallelujah Chorus from Messiah (listening),
Gr. 5, 419
Here We Come A-Wassailing, **Gr. 1**, T355
Holly and the Ivy, The, **Gr. 5**, 418
I Saw Three Ships, **Gr. 2**, 359
It's Time to Get Ready for Christmas, **Gr. 3**, 372–373
Jingle Bells, **Gr. 1**, T354
Jingle-Bell Rock, **Gr. 5**, 424
Jolly Old Saint Nicholas, **Gr. 1**, T352; **Gr. 4**, 382
Joy to the World, **Gr. 4**, 383
Le Serpent (listening), **Gr. 1**, T358

Les Anges dan nos Campagnes (Angels We Have Heard on High), **Gr. 6,** 406

Mama, Bake the Johnnycake, **Gr. K,** T318

Mary Had a Baby, **Gr. 2,** 360

Mele Kalikimaka (Merry Christmas), **Gr. 6,** 410

Must Be Santa, **Gr. K,** T316

Night of Stars/Silent Night, **Gr. 6,** 412

Nochebuena (Christmas Eve), **Gr. K,** T323

Nutcracker Suite, The (excerpts) (listening), **Gr. 2,** 354

O Tannenbaum! (O Christmas Tree!), **Gr. K,** T320

Once Upon a Christmastime, **Gr. 4,** 380

Para pedir posada (Looking for Shelter), **Gr. 4,** 377

Pat-a-Pan, **Gr. 3,** 375

Rise Up, Shepherd, and Follow, **Gr. 5,** 422

Rudolph, the Red-Nosed Reindeer, **Gr. 1,** T354

Sankta Lucia (Saint Lucia), **Gr. 5,** 413

Trepak from *The Nutcracker* by P. Tchaikovsky (listening), **Gr. 6,** 408

Up on the Housetop, **Gr. 2,** 356

Waltz of the Flowers from *The Nutcracker* (excerpt) (listening), **Gr. 1,** T352, T353

We Wish You a Merry Christmas, **Gr. 2,** 358

What You Gonna Call Your Pretty Little Baby?, **Gr. K,** T319

Hanukkah

Dreidel Song, (poem), **Gr. 1,** T349

Eight Days of Hanukkah!, **Gr. 3,** 370–371

Haneirot Halalu (These Lights), **Gr. 5,** 414

Hanukkah, **Gr. 3,** 368–371

Hanukkah Chag Yafeh, **Gr. 1,** T350

Hanukkah Is Here, **Gr. K,** T314

Hashual (Israeli folk dance) (listening), **Gr. 6,** 404

In the Window, **Gr. 2,** 352

Light One Candle, **Gr. 5,** 416

Light the Candles, **Gr. 1,** T351

Ma'oz Tsur (Rock of Ages) (Jewish folk song), **Gr. 6,** 405

My Dreidel, **Gr. 2,** 353

On This Night, **Gr. K,** T315

S'vivon Sov (Dreidel Spin), **Gr. 1,** T348; **Gr. 4,** 374

Kwanzaa

Azouke Legba (listening), **Gr. 5,** 426

Hashewie, **Gr. 2,** 362

Kwanzaa Time (listening), **Gr. K,** T324

Le Serpent (excerpt) (listening), **Gr. 1,** T358

Nia, **Gr. 4,** 384

Seven Principles of Kwanzaa, The, (listening), **Gr. 6,** 415

Sing Lo Lo (listening), **Gr. 4,** 385

Soup! Soup!, **Gr. 1,** T358

Ujamaa, **Gr. 3,** 380–381

Ujima, **Gr. 5,** 427

Martin Luther King, Jr., Day

Dreamers, **Gr. 5,** 430

Everybody Ought to Know (listening), **Gr. 1,** T361

Freedom is a Constant Struggle, **Gr. 7,** 211

I'm Gonna Sit at the Welcome Table, **Gr. 6,** 416

I'm on My Way, **Gr. 3,** 382–383

Martin Luther King, **Gr. 2,** 364; (song), **Gr. 1,** T360; (speech piece), **Gr. K,** T326

We Shall Overcome, **Gr. 4,** 387; **Gr. 7,** 212, 213

What Can One Little Person Do?, **Gr. 4,** 204

New Year

Go A Tin (Lantern Song), **Gr. 1,** T363

Gong xi fa cai, **Gr. 3,** 384–385

Hmong New Year (Laos)

Ua txiab (The Village), **Gr. 6,** 394

Noruz (Iranian New Year)

Haji Firuz, **Gr. 6,** 421

Presidents' Day

George Washington, **Gr. 1,** T368

Out from the Wilderness, **Gr. 3,** 388–389

Washington's Birthday (listening), **Gr. 2,** 370

Who Chopped the Cherry Tree Down?, **Gr. 2,** 371

Purim

Ani Purim, **Gr. 2,** 372

Cherkassiya (listening), **Gr. 2,** 373

Seasonal Winter

¡Dale, dale, dale!, **Gr. 3,** 378–379

December Nights, December Lights, **Gr. 4,** 372

Frosty, the Snowman, **Gr. 3,** 366–367

Frosty Weather, **Gr. 3,** 250

It's So Nice on the Ice, **Gr. 1,** T346

Perfect Winter Day, A, **Gr. 6,** 400–403

Season of Hope, The, **Gr. 5,** 410

Skaters' Waltz, The (excerpt) (listening), **Gr. 1,** T344

Skating, **Gr. 2,** 350

Snowman, The, **Gr. K,** T313

Time for Love, **Gr. 1,** T347

Winter (Allegro non molto) from *The Four Seasons* (Concerto No. 4 in F Minor) by A. Vivaldi (listening), **Gr. 6,** 403

Winter Wonderland, **Gr. 5,** 408

St. Patrick's Day

Macnamara's Band, **Gr. 4,** 88

Mrs. Murphy's Chowder, **Gr. 3,** 390–391

Saint Patrick's Day, **Gr. 5,** 434; (listening), **Gr. 2,** 374

Wee Falorie Man, The, **Gr. 2,** 375

Wait and See, **Gr. K,** T334

Valentine's Day

I Will Be Your Friend, **Gr. 4,** 388

Love Is the Magic Word, **Gr. 1,** T366

Love Somebody, **Gr. 4,** 94

Mail Myself to You, **Gr. 1,** T366

My Friend (listening), **Gr. 4,** 389

My Valentine (poem), **Gr. 1,** T364

Skinnamarink, **Gr. 2,** 368

This a Way and That a Way, **Gr. 3,** 386–387

Vem Kan Segla, **Gr. 6,** 419

Viva Valentine!, **Gr. 1,** T365

You Are My Sunshine, **Gr. 2,** 369

You've Got a Friend by C. King (listening), **Gr. 6,** 418

Spring

Cinco de Mayo

El atole, **Gr. 3,** 396–397

El palomo y la paloma (The Doves), **Gr. 2,** 380

La víbora de la mar (The Sea Snake), **Gr. 5,** 440

Earth Day

Big Beautiful Planet, **Gr. 2,** 376

Classified Index

Big, Big World, **Gr. 5**, 438
Circle of Life, **Gr. 7**, 40, 84
Earth Child, **Gr. 6**, 426
Earth is Our Mother, The, **Gr. 7**, 220
Just Like the Sun, **Gr. 3**, 394–395
Peaceful World, **Gr. 7**, 154
Stonehaven Sunset, **Gr. 7**, 221
We are Here, **Gr. 4**, 394

Laotian New Year
  Champa Muang Lao (listening), **Gr. 5**, 436
  Dok Djampa (The White Jasmine Flower), **Gr. 4**, 392
  Suk San Wan Pi Mai (New Year's Song), **Gr. 5**, 437

Seasonal Spring
  Appalachian Spring (listening), **Gr. 2**, 378
  Bohm Dong Sahn, Gohd Dong Sahn (Spring Valley, Flower Valley), **Gr. K**, T337
  Bohm, **Gr. 3**, 392
  Hop! Chirp!, Moo! Oh, Happy Springtime Day!, **Gr. 1**, T372
  Introduction from The Rite of Spring (listening), **Gr. 6**, 423
  L'inverno è già passato (Winter is Over), **Gr. 4**, 390
  May Day Carol, **Gr. 3**, 393
  My Kite (poem), **Gr. 1**, T371
  My Mom, **Gr. 1**, T372
  Peter Cottontail, **Gr. K**, T338
  Qua Cà Gió Bay (listening), **Gr. 4**, 367
  Shibolet Basadeh (Wheat in the Field), **Gr. 6**, 424
  Spring (Allegro) from The Four Seasons (listening), **Gr. 4**, 391
  Suomen Salossa (The Finnish Forest), **Gr. 6**, 422
  Tako No Uta, **Gr. 1**, T146
  Welcome Is the Month of May, **Gr. 2**, 378

Yunza Festival (Peru)
  La Yunsita, **Gr. 4**, 350

Summer
Heritage Festival Music (montage) (listening), **Gr. 7**, 55
Patriotic
  America, **Gr. 8**, 31
  El Capitán, **Gr. 8**, 6
Powwow
  Fancy Dance Song (listening), **Gr. 5**, 444
  Grand Entry (Powwow) (listening), **Gr. K**, T344
  Lakota Flute Song (listening), **Gr. 6**, 429
  O Hal'lwe (Nanticoke women's honoring song), **Gr. 6**, 428
  Tsidii-Bird (listening), **Gr. 6**, 429
Puerto Rican Day
  Qué bonita bandera, **Gr. 5**, 442
Seasonal Summer
  Bahay Kubo (My Nip Hut), **Gr. 2**, 382
  Sitting in the Sand (poem), **Gr. 1**, T374
  Summer (Allegro Non Molto) from The Four Seasons (listening), **Gr. 4**, 161
  Summertime from Porgy and Bess (listening), **Gr. 1**, T375
  Sun Is First to Rise, The, **Gr. 2**, 383
  'Ulili E (The Sandpiper), **Gr. 4**, 396

general
Celebration Mosaic, **Gr. 8**, 69
  How Blue Can You Get?, by L. Feather

I'm Scared of You, by N. Cannon, R. Lawrence, K. Holland, C. Hutchison, S. Sweet
Fiddler's Two-Step (traditional fiddler's tune)
Foggy Mountain Breakdown, by E. Scruggs
On Your Toes (traditional polka)
Wind River, by A. Vasquez
I Heard It Through the Grapevine, by N. Whitfield, B. Strong

I

INSTRUMENTAL/VOCAL ENSEMBLES

Instrumental
band, **Gr. K**, T113; **Gr. 2**, 149, 191; **Gr. 3**, 14, 285, 397; **Gr. 4**, 76, 197; **Gr. 5**, 22, 32, 290, 305, 395; **Gr. 7**, 36; **Gr. 8**, 5–6, 36–41
bluegrass band, **Gr. 8**, 71
brass, **Gr. 7**, 37
brass ensemble, **Gr. 2**, 177; **Gr. K**, T103
brass quintet, **Gr. 3**, 121; **Gr. 5**, 228
chamber music ensemble, **Gr. 5**, 219; **Gr. 8**, 215
Chinese orchestra, **Gr. 7**, 56
concert band, **Gr. 7**, 36, 196
drum and bugle corps, **Gr. 8**, 40
drum circle, **Gr. 6**, 37
garage bands, **Gr. 7**, 14
instrumental solo, **Gr. K**, T89, T20
Japanese drumming ensemble, **Gr. 8**, 54
jazz band, **Gr. 6**, 156; **Gr. 8**, 52
jazz orchestra, **Gr. 8**, 32–33
jug band, **Gr. 6**, 30
klezmer band, **Gr. 2**, 70
marching band, **Gr. 7**, 32, 76, 196–197; **Gr. 8**, 36
mariachi band, **Gr. 2**, 61; **Gr. 7**, 58
military band, **Gr. 8**, 37
multicultural ensemble, **Gr. 8**, 82–83, 152–53
orchestra, **Gr. K**, T19, T52, T55, T76, T133, T142, T146, T167, T176, T177, T183, T195, T196, T203, T223; **Gr. 1**, T112, T140, T141, T263; **Gr. 2**, 97, 228; **Gr. 3**, 27, 65, 76, 81, 161, 251, 263, 285; **Gr. 4**, 105; **Gr. 5**, 102, 117; **Gr. 6**, 121; **Gr. 7**, 36; **Gr. 8**, 4–5, 66–67, 112, 128, 131, 167, 170–71
percussion, **Gr. 7**, 39
percussion ensemble, **Gr. 2**, 36; **Gr. 5**, 228; **Gr. 7**, 44; **Gr. 8**, 13, 34–35, 55
piano trio, **Gr. 5**, 121
pop/rock band, **Gr. 8**, 100, 110–11, 148–51
recorder consort, **Gr. 4**, 96–97
steel drum band, **Gr. 6**, 9
steel ensemble, **Gr. 7**, 199
string quartet, **Gr. K**, T109; **Gr. 1**, T251; **Gr. 2**, 121; **Gr. 3**, 228; **Gr. 5**, 228; **Gr. 7**, 228
strings, **Gr. 7**, 48
symphonic bands, **Gr. 6**, 201
taiko drum band, **Gr. 6**, 16
town band, **Gr. 8**, 38–39
woodwind quintet, **Gr. 4**, 121; **Gr. 5**, 228
woodwinds, **Gr. 7**, 38

vocal
a capella ensemble, **Gr. 2**, 47
choir, **Gr. 2**, 141, 235; **Gr. 3**, 52, 312, 317,

320, 324, 328; **Gr. 4,** 340; **Gr. 5,** 87, 117, 326, 371, 419; **Gr. 6,** 46, 52, 65, 257, 318; **Gr. 7,** 36; **Gr. 8,** 30–31
chorus, **Gr. 8,** 8
duet, **Gr. 5,** 80
gospel choir, **Gr. 7,** 213; **Gr. 8,** 30–31
musical vocal ensemble, **Gr. 5,** 302
opera chorus, **Gr. 5,** 274
other, **Gr. 6,** 153, 235
vocal ensemble, **Gr. K,** T33, T153, T159, T163, T222
vocal range, **Gr. 7,** 40

other
African drum circle, **Gr. 6,** 37

INSTRUMENTS, PLAYING. *See also* Music Skills; Ostinatos; Playalongs; the booklets *Spotlight on Orff Orchestrations, Spotlight on Recorder, Spotlight on Guitar* under separate cover
aerophones, **Gr. 7,** 169
agogo bells, **Gr. 1,** T297; **Gr. 5,** 73, 433
alternate sound sources, **Gr. 3,** 332; **Gr. 6,** 6
autoharp, **Gr. 2,** 66, 69; **Gr. 4,** 278, 354, 363, 369; **Gr. 5,** 208, 274, 277
barred instruments, **Gr. 5,** 63
bass, **Gr. 7,** 72
bass drum, **Gr. 5,** 17, 433; **Gr. 7,** 76
bass instruments, **Gr. 5,** 13, 20, 90, 180, 191, 207, 211
bass xylophone, **Gr. 5,** 207, 211
bells, **Gr. 5,** 256; **Gr. 7,** 29, 95, 123, 141, 142; **Gr. 8,** 127
body percussion, **Gr. K,** T16, T24, T39, T63, T64, T72, T73, T79, T80, T81, T86, T87, T89, T116, T117, T171, T305; **Gr. 3,** 7, 8, 9, 11, 13, 15, 17, 28, 35, 36, 59, 70, 94, 125, 131, 132, 133, 152, 153, 157, 167, 169, 171, 172, 176, 180, 181, 184, 191, 195, 212, 213, 217, 224, 234, 235, 236, 237, 272, 273, 274, 276, 279, 306, 321, 326, 357, 365, 385, 389, 391; **Gr. 4,** 9, 17, 27, 36, 47, 48–49, 51, 55, 64, 67, 68, 69, 92, 99, 100–101, 103, 104, 111, 131, 132–133, 136, 145, 147, 158, 167, 168, 169, 175, 176, 180, 183, 184–185, 192, 196, 197, 199, 216, 227, 228, 239, 250, 251, 254, 256, 258, 261, 264, 265, 272, 273, 279, 284, 355, 356–357, 368, 370–371, 377, 381, 389, 395; **Gr. 5,** 9, 15, 16, 28, 29, 71, 73, 89, 96, 128, 207, 213, 219; **Gr. 6,** 19, 34, 88, 165, 264, 267; **Gr. 7,** 66; **Gr. 8,** 62
bongo, **Gr. 5,** 53, 71, 73, 75, 95
brass instruments, **Gr. 8,** 33, 52, 84
castanets, **Gr. 5,** 211
cello, **Gr. 7,** 94
chording instruments, **Gr. 5,** 274, 276, 279
chromatic instruments, **Gr. 8,** 39, 67
clap, **Gr. 7,** 31, 33, 34, 61, 101, 207
clarinet, **Gr. 8,** 138
classroom, **Gr. 8,** 5, 153
claves, **Gr. 1,** T211, T297, T316, T364; **Gr. 5,** 187, 399, 433, 443
compositions, **Gr. 7,** 46
conga drum, **Gr. 1,** T211, T316; **Gr. 5,** 17, 73, 75, 95, 187, 364
cowbell, **Gr. 1,** T211; **Gr. 5,** 17, 73; **Gr. 6,** 284
cymbals, **Gr. 1,** T199, T259; **Gr. 2,** 86; **Gr. 5,** 60; **Gr. 7,** 57
drum, **Gr. K,** T19, T21, T34, T35, T36, T37, T40, T43, T44, T51, T56, T57, T65, T80, T87, T111, T129, T144, T153, T162, T201, T216, T219; **Gr. 1,** T12, T38, T92, T93, T103, T111, T179, T180, T251, T259, T292, T297, T308, T316, T346, T350, T360, T361, T364; **Gr. 2,** 14, 16–17, 23; **Gr. 4,** 157, 195, 242, 284, 395; **Gr. 5,** 28, 29, 49, 96, 129, 136, 207, 389; **Gr. 6,** 37, 173, 213, 274, 429; **Gr. 7,** 168; **Gr. 8,** 7, 37, 56, 84
environmental sounds, **Gr. K,** T170; **Gr. 1,** T56
finger cymbals, **Gr. 1,** T156, T258, T352; **Gr. 2,** 28–29, 71, 135; **Gr. 5,** 20, 187, 403, 437; **Gr. 6,** 233
flute, **Gr. 5,** 184; **Gr. 7,** 94; **Gr. 8,** 138
found sounds, **Gr. K,** T172, T173; **Gr. 2,** 34, 36–37; **Gr. 3,** 332; **Gr. 5,** 338; **Gr. 6,** 6, 32, 93; **Gr. 8,** 12, 14–15, 34, 35
frame drum, **Gr. 5,** 49
glockenspiel, **Gr. 7,** 94
gong, **Gr. 1,** T302, T318, T321
güiro, **Gr. 1,** T156, T284, T294, T308, T316, T361; **Gr. 5,** 17, 187; **Gr. 6,** 277
guitar, **Gr. 4,** 133, 225; **Gr. 5,** 208, 274; **Gr. 6,** 31, 33, 35, 71, 84, 96, 115, 126, 135, 140, 150, 155, 180, 242, 247, 252, 273, 275; **Gr. 7,** 14–15, 18, 31, 59, 93, 129, 137, 141, 148, 156, 161, 214–216, 252; **Gr. 8,** 71, 84, 102, 123, 127, 252
hand bells, **Gr. 7,** 94
hand drum, **Gr. 2,** 16–17, 28–29, 185, 258; **Gr. 5,** 49, 75, 90, 95, 187, 391, 393, 401, 429, 443; **Gr. 7,** 57
harmonic accompaniment, **Gr. 7,** 59, 83
idiophones, **Gr. 7,** 168
instruments, pitched, **Gr. 7,** 238
jingle bells, **Gr. 1,** T316
jug band, **Gr. 4,** 76; **Gr. 6,** 33
keyboard, **Gr. K,** T125; **Gr. 1,** T74, T237; **Gr. 2,** 32; **Gr. 3,** 219, 228, 286; **Gr. 4,** 133, 148, 151, 235, 287; **Gr. 5,** 12, 63, 103, 149, 169, 181, 184, 277; **Gr. 6,** 23, 143, 150, 211, 259, 273; **Gr. 7,** 21, 29, 47, 59, 72, 95, 123, 129, 141, 142, 145, 156, 186, 214, 253; **Gr. 8,** 160, 161, 163, 253
large drum, **Gr. 5,** 53
large gong, **Gr. 5,** 53
mallet instrument, **Gr. 5,** 184
mandolin, **Gr. 8,** 71
maracas, **Gr. 1,** T38, T92, T93, T105, T111, T156, T211, T251, T292, T294, T297, T308, T316, T364; **Gr. 5,** 73, 364, 399, 421, 429, 433; **Gr. 6,** 173
melodic accompaniment, **Gr. 7,** 46; **Gr. 8,** 231
membranophones, **Gr. 7,** 169
MIDI. *See* Technology
Orff instruments, **Gr. K,** T53, T59, T117, T141, T165, T172, T173, T184, T197, T218, T222; **Gr. 1,** T143, T144, T145, T170, T173, T177, T184, T185, T188, T208, T209, T216, T217, T220, T233, T234, T237, T240, T250, T251, T255, T256, T260, T311, T318, T321; **Gr. 2,** 11, 30–33, 92, 115, 117, 135–137, 182–183, 211, 328–329, 333–335; **Gr. 3,** 14, 101, 113, 207, 249, 256, 265, 269, 278; **Gr. 4,** 93, 103, 128–129, 133, 137, 138, 141, 168, 175, 176, 177, 187, 208, 219, 227, 229, 232–233, 371, 373; **Gr. 5,** 12, 13, 20, 51, 61, 90, 111, 143, 169, 180,

181, 191, 207, 211, 254, 277; **Gr. 6,** 15, 196, 213, 258, 284, 388, 395

percussion, **Gr. 5,** 209; **Gr. 7,** 135, 223, 225; **Gr. 8,** 138

percussion, mallet, **Gr. 2,** 20, 54, 92, 181, 246; **Gr. 3,** 266; **Gr. 4,** 71, 73, 93, 103, 105, 128–129, 136–137, 148, 149, 168, 175, 176, 177, 187, 208, 219, 227, 229, 232–233, 244, 265, 269, 371, 373; **Gr. 5,** 51, 111, 143, 167, 168, 169, 170, 177; **Gr. 6,** 93

percussion, pitched, **Gr. K,** T50, T52, T59, T61, T69, T83, T90, T91, T92, T96, T97, T104, T184, T197, T205, T210, T211; **Gr. 1,** T74, T107, T143, T144, T145, T170, T173, T177, T184, T185, T188, T208, T209, T216, T217, T220, T233, T234, T237, T250, T251, T252, T255, T256, T260, T316, T318; **Gr. 2,** 36, 58, 75, 92, 133, 137, 139; **Gr. 3,** 18, 78, 101, 113, 133, 147, 177, 187, 192, 193, 207, 216, 217, 219, 250, 266, 268, 269, 270, 278, 286, 287, 344, 346, 347, 349, 374, 375, 376, 377; **Gr. 4,** 71, 73, 93, 110, 128–129, 136–137, 141, 148, 149, 151, 168, 176, 177, 187, 208, 219, 227, 229, 232–233, 244, 265, 269; **Gr. 5,** 257, 258; **Gr. 6,** 425

percussion, unpitched, **Gr. K,** T12, T34, T35, T36, T37, T51, T54, T65, T78, T79, T80, T81, T86, T87, T90, T101, T108, T111, T116, T117, T119, T129, T133, T144, T145, T152, T153, T162, T165, T171, T187, T201, T215, T221; **Gr. 1,** T91, T99, T101, T105, T111, T116, T117, T119, T143, T168, T179, T180, T188, T193, T199, T200, T216, T217, T220, T240, T251, T256, T341, T342, T358; **Gr. 2,** 20, 24, 34, 87, 107, 111, 270; **Gr. 3,** 17, 22, 29, 37, 57, 71, 73, 134, 147, 156, 169, 175, 177, 181, 183, 185, 189, 197, 201, 208, 242, 243, 244, 246, 250, 252, 253, 256, 262, 263, 269, 276, 279, 280, 318, 327, 328, 332, 336, 344, 347, 348, 349, 350, 351, 355, 359, 360, 362, 363, 364, 365, 370, 371, 374, 375, 378, 379, 385; **Gr. 4,** 15, 27, 46, 49, 64, 68, 77, 88, 92–93, 99, 100–101, 103, 110, 117, 157, 159, 175, 177, 187, 192, 195, 196, 197, 199, 208, 217, 219, 227, 229, 250, 253, 271, 272, 278, 281, 282, 284, 311, 349, 357, 363, 369, 371, 375, 385, 393, 395; **Gr. 5,** 30, 68, 69, 136; **Gr. 6,** 6, 262, 264, 267, 284, 387, 392; **Gr. 7,** 2, 33, 34, 44, 45, 46, 57, 71, 72, 199, 200; **Gr. 8,** 7, 14, 33, 34, 35, 37, 63, 110, 111, 145, 148, 149, 190, 231

piano, **Gr. 5,** 208; **Gr. 7,** 37, 38, 142; **Gr. 8,** 122, 123, 161, 163

rattles/shakers, **Gr. 5,** 28, 29, 75, 95; **Gr. 7,** 63

recorder, **Gr. 3,** 186, 229, 398; **Gr. 4,** 96, 187, 335; **Gr. 5,** 149, 180, 184; **Gr. 6,** 115, 159, 196, 209, 228, 270; **Gr. 7,** 20, 47, 59, 82, 94, 95, 137, 141, 145, 156, 168, 169, 254; **Gr. 8,** 254

resonator bells, **Gr. K,** 69; **Gr. 1,** T260, T302; **Gr. 2,** 11, 53, 116; **Gr. 3,** 173, 207, 209; **Gr. 4,** 112–113, 129, 145, 148, 180, 233, 261, 282, 359, 365, 369, 379; **Gr. 5,** 12, 20, 53, 169, 181, 277; **Gr. 6,** 248

rhythm sticks, **Gr. 1,** T169, T289, T313, T366; **Gr. 2,** 16–17, 20, 25, 108–109, 215, 264

rhythmic accompaniment, **Gr. 7,** 77, 78, 203

ride cymbals, **Gr. 7,** 76

saxophone, **Gr. 8,** 138

scraper, **Gr. 1,** T38, T92, T93, T105, T111

shaker/rattles, **Gr. 2,** 24, 270, 330–332

slap stick, **Gr. 1,** T316, T321

sleigh bells, **Gr. 1,** T352, T354; **Gr. 5,** 425

small drum, **Gr. 5,** 60

small gong, **Gr. 5,** 53

suspended cymbal, **Gr. 5,** 30

tambourine, **Gr. 1,** T12, T292, T308, T360, T361; **Gr. 2,** 29, 71, 328–329; **Gr. 5,** 207, 211, 401, 407, 429, 433; **Gr. 6,** 94, 233; **Gr. 7,** 72

tapping, **Gr. 7,** 58, 83, 101

tone bells, **Gr. 1,** T302; **Gr. 6,** 15; **Gr. 7,** 94

Tonga sticks, **Gr. 6,** 90

triangle, **Gr. 1,** T12, T38, T92, T111, T238, T258, T289, T302, T308, T316, T318, T352; **Gr. 2,** 16–17, 19, 24, 29, 113, 128–129, 333–335; **Gr. 5,** 187, 190, 443; **Gr. 6,** 284

vibraslap, **Gr. 1,** T316, T318

voice, **Gr. 7,** 63, 71, 177, 223, 228

woodblock, **Gr. 1,** T12, T38, T92, T93, T105, T111, T156, T251, T260, T292, T302, T308, T316, T321, T352, T354, T361; **Gr. 2,** 16–17, 19, 24, 52; **Gr. 5,** 407; **Gr. 6,** 245

wood percussion instruments, **Gr. 2,** 24; **Gr. 5,** 267

xylophone, **Gr. 5,** 180; **Gr. 7,** 94; **Gr. 8,** 138

L

LIMITED TONE SONGS

two-tone songs

do mi

Eka Muda, **Gr. 5,** 28

mi so

Bee, Bee, Bumblebee, **Gr. 1,** T250

Categories, **Gr. 1,** T146

Cobbler, Cobbler, Mend My Shoe, **Gr. K,** T169

Come Back My Little Chicks, **Gr. 1,** T134

Cuckoo, Where Are You?, **Gr. 2,** 244

Engine, Engine Number Nine, **Gr. 2,** 13

Head and Shoulders, **Gr. K,** T238

Here We Sit, **Gr. 1,** T251

Hey, Hey, Look at Me, **Gr. 2,** 245

I See, **Gr. 2,** 266

In and Out, **Gr. 2,** 245

Instrument Game, **Gr. K,** T36

Lemonade, **Gr. 2,** 19

Old Mister Woodpecker, **Gr. K,** T172

One, Two, Tie My Shoe, **Gr. K,** T151

Pease Porridge Hot, **Gr. 1,** T255

Quaker, Quaker, **Gr. 1,** T100

Say Your Name, **Gr. 2,** 243

Seesaw, **Gr. 1,** T242, T243, T248

Serra, serra serrador, **Gr. 1,** T131, T133

Tinker, Tailor, **Gr. 1,** T130

Touch Your Shoulders, **Gr. K,** T254

Two, Four, Six, Eight, **Gr. 1,** T246, T247

Una adivinanza, **Gr. 1,** T138

three-tone songs

do re mi

Babylon's Fallin', **Gr. 5,** 243
countermelody to In that Great Git'n Up Mornin', **Gr. 5,** 242
Farfallina, **Gr. 4,** 244
Frog in the Meadow, **Gr. 3,** 243
Good News, **Gr. 6,** 242
Hop, Old Squirrel, **Gr. 2,** 258
Hot Cross Buns, **Gr. 2,** 258
Kuma San, **Gr. 3,** 244
Las horas, **Gr. K,** T70
Long-Legged Sailor, **Gr. 4,** 243
Nabe, Nabe, Soku, Nuke, **Gr. 2,** 259
Night Song, **Gr. 3,** 186
Over My Head, **Gr. 3,** 286
Rain is Falling Down, **Gr. 3,** 242
Roll de Ole Chariot Along, **Gr. 6,** 243
Sailor, Sailor on the Sea, **Gr. 2,** 262
Shoheen Sho, **Gr. 2,** 140
Symphony No. 35, Fourth Movement (excerpt) (listening), **Gr. 5,** 247
Who's That Yonder?, **Gr. 3,** 245
Woodchuck, **Gr. 3,** 246
Words of Wisdom, **Gr. 5,** 244

do mi so
El picaflor, **Gr. K,** T141
Heigh Ho, Here We Go, **Gr. 2,** 252
Mother, Mother, **Gr. 2,** 254
Mouse, Mousie, **Gr. 2,** 254
Sorida, **Gr. 2,** 96
Ten in a Bed, **Gr. K,** T256
Who Has the Penny?, **Gr. 2,** 252

mi so la
Acka Backa, **Gr. 1,** T256
¡Adivina lo que es!, **Gr. 1,** T170
Arre, mi burrito, **Gr. 1,** T257
Bell Horses, **Gr. K,** T262
Bluebells, **Gr. 1,** T209
Bobby Shafto, **Gr. K,** T265
Bounce High, Bounce Low, **Gr. K,** T131
Doggie, Doggie, **Gr. 2,** 59
Eating Lizards, **Gr. 2,** 250
Fehér liliomszál, **Gr. K,** T139
Go A Tin, **Gr. 1,** T363
Good Night, Sleep Tight, **Gr. 2,** 76
Hop, Hop, Hop, **Gr. K,** T197
I Like Spinach, **Gr. 1,** T163
It's Raining! It's Pouring!, **Gr. 2,** 233
Jack Be Nimble, **Gr. K,** T88
Kari, **Gr. 1,** T261
Little Robin Red Breast, **Gr. 1,** T206, T208
Little Sally Water, **Gr. 2,** 249
Lucky Locket, **Gr. 1,** T253
Mill Song, The, **Gr. 2,** 52
Oliver Twist, **Gr. 2,** 268
One, Two, Three, Four, Five, **Gr. 1,** T265
Pizza, Pizza, Daddy-O, **Gr. 2,** 62
Plainsies, Clapsies, **Gr. 2,** 248
Rain, Rain, Go Away, **Gr. 1,** T259
Red Rover, **Gr. 2,** 249
Riddle Song, **Gr. 2,** 251

Seesaw, Margery Daw, **Gr. K,** T265
Snail, Snail, **Gr. 1,** T252
Star Light, Star Bright, **Gr. 1,** T258
Tekanionton'néha', **Gr. 5,** 223
This Is What I Can Do, **Gr. K,** T124
Twenty-four Robbers, **Gr. 1,** T173
We Are Playing in the Forest, **Gr. K,** T248

so₁ la₁ do
Peanut Butter, **Gr. 1,** T218

four-tone songs
do re mi so
All Around the Buttercup, **Gr. 2,** 210
Derry Ding Dong Dason, **Gr. 6,** 249
El zapatero, **Gr. 2,** 138
Follow Me, **Gr. K,** T133
Goodbye Brother, **Gr. 4,** 273
Ifetayo, **Gr. K,** T325
Johnny Works with One Hammer, **Gr. 1,** T96
Matarile, **Gr. 2,** 261
Merrily, We Roll Along, **Gr. K,** T110
Mountain Music, **Gr. 6,** 20
Old Aunt Dinah, **Gr. 4,** 245
Old Blue, **Gr. 2,** 213
Rover, **Gr. 2,** 260
Sammy Sackett, **Gr. 2,** 146
Sea Shell, **Gr. 4,** 245
Who's That Tapping at the Window?, **Gr. 2,** 261

do re mi la
A la rueda rueda, **Gr. 1,** T240
Hello, There!, **Gr. 1,** T230
Old House, **Gr. 4,** 282

do re mi fa
Noble Duke of York, The, **Gr. K,** T232
Oh, A-Hunting We Will Go, **Gr. K,** T62

do mi so la
Bickle, Bockle, **Gr. K,** T187
Billy, **Gr. 3,** 7
Clocks, **Gr. 3,** 266
Daisy Chain, **Gr. 2,** 255
Death of the Robin, **Gr. 3,** 275
Dide, **Gr. 3,** 279
Donkey, Donkey, **Gr. 2,** 256
Egy üveg alma, **Gr. 3,** 22
Every Mornin' When I Wake Up, **Gr. 6,** 275
Hop Up and Jump Up, **Gr. 4,** 271
Johnny's Flea, **Gr. 1,** T158
Juhtgarak, **Gr. K,** T108
King's Land, **Gr. 2,** 257
Let Us Chase the Squirrel, **Gr. 3,** 248
Mr. Frog, **Gr. 2,** 257
O, I'm Gonna Sing, **Gr. 5,** 245
O, The Train's Off the Track, **Gr. 3,** 176
Old Mr. Rabbit, **Gr. 3,** 254
Que llueva, **Gr. 3,** 274
Ring Around the Rosy, **Gr. K,** T246
Scotland's Burning, **Gr. 3,** 257
See the Rabbit Running, **Gr. 3,** 255
Taps, **Gr. 3,** 281
Vamos a la mar, **Gr. 3,** 256

do mi fa so
Ushkana, **Gr. K,** T75

Classified Index

Classified Index of Songs, Selected Concepts, Skills, and Activities (continued)

re mi so la
Rise, Sally Rise, **Gr. 1**, T162

mi so la ti
Hotaru Koi, **Gr. 6**, 255

mi₁ so₁ la₁ do
A la rueda rueda, **Gr. 1**, T240

mi fa so la
Ésta sí que es Nochebuena, **Gr. 2**, 361

so la ti do'
Merecumbé, **Gr. 6**, 276

so₁ la₁ do re so
'Round the Corner, Sally, **Gr. 5**, 251

so₁ la₁ do mi
Shoo, Turkey, **Gr. 1**, T76

so₁ la₁ do mi so la
Brush Your Teeth, **Gr. 1**, T66

so do re mi
Punchinella, **Gr. 1**, T216

so₁ do re mi
A la rueda de San Miguel, **Gr. 2**, 60
Baby Nodja, **Gr. 2**, 154
Jugaremos en el bosque, **Gr. 2**, 188

so₁ do re mi so
Chichipapa, **Gr. 2**, 22

la₁ do re mi
I Got a Letter, **Gr. 6**, 270
Skin and Bones, **Gr. 1**, T340

la₁ do re mi so la
Jambo, **Gr. 1**, T230

ti₁ do re mi
Singabahambayo, **Gr. 5**, 56

five-tone songs

do re mi fa so
Let It Roll, **Gr. 6**, 124
Times They Are A-Changing, The, **Gr. 5**, 204
When the Saints Go Marching In, **Gr. 5**, 256
Winter Ade, **Gr. 6**, 132

so₁ do re mi fa so
Lion Sleeps Tonight, The, **Gr. 5**, 172

la₁ ti₁ do re mi
Dere Geliyor, **Gr. 6**, 232

ti₁ do re mi fa
Kokoleoko, **Gr. 6**, 279

pentatonic songs

do re mi so la
Allundé Alluia, **Gr. 4**, 34–35
Ame fure, **Gr. 4**, 26
Arirang, **Gr. 5**, 50
Ballad of the Bedbugs and the Beetles, The, **Gr. 3**, 206
Bamboo Flute, **Gr. 4**, 134
Best That I Can Be!, The, **Gr. K**, T48
Blow, Ye Winds, Blow, **Gr. 3**, 192
Bohm, **Gr. 3**, 392
Boll Weevil, **Gr. 3**, 171
Bow, Wow, Wow, **Gr. 2**, 264
Buckeye Jim, **Gr. 4**, 136
Built My Lady a Fine Brick House, **Gr. 4**, 252
Button, You Must Wander, **Gr. 2**, 176
Cat and Dog, **Gr. 3**, 259

Charlie, **Gr. 3**, 208
Chicka Hanka, **Gr. 4**, 138
Chicken on the Fence Post, **Gr. 3**, 265
Cindy (melody), **Gr. 5**, 265
Circle 'Round the Zero, **Gr. 3**, 267
Coral, **Gr. 3**, 249
Cornstalk Fiddle and a Shoestring Bow, **Gr. 3**, 284
Crawdad Song, **Gr. 3**, 107
Cumberland Gap, **Gr. 3**, 99
Dal Taro Kacha, **Gr. 2**, 98
Dance Together, **Gr. 2**, 264
Day-O, **Gr. 4**, 73
Derby Ram, The, **Gr. 4**, 259
Deta, Deta, **Gr. 5**, 246
Dinah, **Gr. 3**, 150
Ding Dong Diggy Diggy Dong, **Gr. 3**, 269
Do, Lord, **Gr. 6**, 260
Draw a Bucket of Water, **Gr. 3**, 222
Dumplin's, **Gr. 2**, 172
El florón, **Gr. 3**, 46
En roulant ma boule, **Gr. 3**, 100
Farmer in the Dell, The, **Gr. K**, T100
Frosty Weather, **Gr. 3**, 250
Fun wa ni alaafia, **Gr. 5**, 248
Fung Yang Song, **Gr. 5**, 58
Git on Board, **Gr. K**, T145
Go Tell It on the Mountain, **Gr. 3**, 377
Golden Ring Around the Susan Girl, **Gr. 3**, 264
Goodbye, My Riley O, **Gr. 4**, 257
Great Big House, **Gr. 3**, 14
Heave-Ho, Me Laddies, **Gr. 4**, 258
Heleluyan, **Gr. 6**, 188
Hello!, **Gr. 3**, 283
Here Comes a Bluebird, **Gr. 2**, 263
Here Comes Sally, **Gr. 2**, 220
Hill an' Gully, **Gr. 5**, 250
How Can I Keep from Singing?, **Gr. 5**, 287
How Long the Train Been Gone?, **Gr. 4**, 264
I Bought Me a Cat, **Gr. 2**, 14
I Have a Car, **Gr. 3**, 252
I Heard a Mockingbird, **Gr. 4**, 150
I Lost the Farmer's Dairy Key, **Gr. 3**, 273
I Saw the Light, **Gr. 5**, 252
I'll Rise When the Rooster Crows, **Gr. 4**, 36
I'm Going to Georgia, **Gr. 6**, 244
I'm Gonna Sit at the Welcome Table, **Gr. 6**, 417
In That Great Git'n Up Mornin', **Gr. 5**, 11
Jingle at the Window, **Gr. 3**, 268
Jó ashílá, **Gr. 5**, 224
John Kanaka, **Gr. 5**, 249
Johnson Boys, **Gr. 4**, 233
Juan Pirulero, **Gr. 2**, 270
Knock the Cymbals, **Gr. 2**, 265
Kreely Kranky, **Gr. 3**, 258
Li'l 'Liza Jane, **Gr. 4**, 20
Little Spotted Puppy, **Gr. K**, T147
Little Tommy Tinker, **Gr. 3**, 277
Lonesome Dove, **Gr. 6**, 249
Look Who's Here!, **Gr. K**, T84
Los maizales, **Gr. 5**, 268
Mbombela, **Gr. K**, T152

Classified Index

Classified Index of Songs, Selected Concepts, Skills, and Activities (continued)

Merry-Go-Round, **Gr. 2,** 267
'Most Done Ling'rin' Here, **Gr. 4,** 65
Music of the World A-Turnin', **Gr. 3,** 44
My Horses Ain't Hungry, **Gr. 3,** 278
Never Sleep Late Anymore, **Gr. 6,** 274
Night Herding Song, **Gr. 4,** 110
North Winds Blow, **Gr. K,** T305
Oh, Won't You Sit Down?, **Gr. 4,** 70
Old Ark's A-Moverin', **Gr. 4,** 130
Old Dan Tucker, **Gr. 5,** 253
Old Paint, **Gr. 4,** 275
Old Roger, **Gr. 3,** 280
Old Turkey Buzzard, **Gr. 5,** 264
One More River, **Gr. 3,** 216
One Potato, Two Potato, **Gr. 3,** 267
Pairs or Pears, **Gr. 2,** 265
Push Boat Song, **Gr. 4,** 266
¿Quién es ese pajarito?, **Gr. 4,** 284
Rattlesnake, **Gr. 3,** 72
Ridin' of a Goat, Leadin' of a Sheep, **Gr. 4,** 251
Riding in the Buggy, **Gr. 3,** 131
Rise Up Singin', **Gr. 3,** 138
Salamanca Market, **Gr. 6,** 247
Sally Go 'Round the Sun, **Gr. 2,** 268
Scraping Up Sand, **Gr. 6,** 248
Shady Grove, *(re),* **Gr. 6,** 286
Shoes of John, **Gr. 6,** 246
Somebody's Knockin' at Your Door, **Gr. 5,** 254
Something for Me, Something for You, **Gr. 4,** 4
Spiders, **Gr. 3,** 282
Sugar in the Gourd, **Gr. 6,** 251
Sun Don't Set in the Mornin', **Gr. 3,** 48, 60
Swapping Song, **Gr. 4,** 253
Sweep, Sweep Away, **Gr. 3,** 276
There Was a Jolly Miller, **Gr. 6,** 250
There's A Little Wheel A-Turnin' in My Heart, **Gr. 3,** 129, 137
There's No Hidin' Place, **Gr. 5,** 266
This Is What I Can Do, **Gr. K,** T124
Toodala, **Gr. K,** T39
Train is A-Coming, **Gr. 4,** 270
Trampin', **Gr. 3,** 287
Turn the Glasses Over, **Gr. 3,** 260
Ucha Tirvarch, **Gr. 3,** 53
Wait and See, **Gr. K,** T334
Walk in the Parlor, **Gr. 4,** 226
Wang Ü Ger, **Gr. 3,** 190
'Way Down Yonder in the Brickyard, **Gr. 5,** 255
Wayfaring Stranger *(la),* **Gr. 6,** 283
What Can One Little Person Do?, **Gr. 4,** 204
When I Sing, **Gr. 6,** 44
Willowbee, **Gr. 2,** 69

do re mi so la do¹
Martin Luther King, **Gr. 2,** 364
My Mama's Calling Me, **Gr. 1,** T54
Old Woman and the Pig, **Gr. 2,** 130
When the Flag Goes By, **Gr. 1,** T327
You'll Sing a Song and I'll Sing a Song, **Gr. 2,** 156

so₁ do re mi so la
Columbus Sailed with Three Ships, **Gr. 2,** 344
Mister Rabbit, Mister Rabbit, **Gr. 2,** 150

so₁ la₁ do re mi
Charlie Over the Ocean, **Gr. 1,** T75
Chase the Squirrel, **Gr. 1,** T88
El burrito enfermo, **Gr. 2,** 180
Hashewie, **Gr. 2,** 362
Mizuguruma (The Water Wheel), **Gr. 1,** T260
Soup, Soup!, **Gr. 1,** T358
There's a Hole in the Bucket, **Gr. 2,** 132
Wake Me, Shake Me, **Gr. 1,** T198
What Did Delaware?, **Gr. 2,** 190

so₁ la₁ do re mi so
I Chih Ching Wa, **Gr. 2,** 186
I Wanna Be a Friend of Yours, **Gr. 1,** T84
Old King Glory, **Gr. 1,** T217
Time for Love, **Gr. 1,** T347
We're Sailing Down the River, **Gr. 2,** 166

la₁ do re mi so la
De allacito carnavalito, **Gr. 5,** 269
Diou Shou Juan'er, **Gr. 1,** T212
Land of the Silver Birch, **Gr. 2,** 88
Nottamun Town, **Gr. 5,** 405

so₁ la₁ do re mi so la
Australia's on the Wallaby, **Gr. 2,** 106
Ban Dal, **Gr. 2,** 219
Harvest, **Gr. 2,** 342
Mary Had a Baby, **Gr. 2,** 360
Shrimp Boats, **Gr. 2,** 179
Sing! Sing! Sing!, **Gr. 2,** 196

LISTENING MAPS. See Interactive Listening Maps main category p. 351. *See also* Listening Map Transparencies in *Teacher's Resource Masters* under separate cover

in pupil book

1812 Overture, **Gr. 8,** 73
ILM *American Salute,* **Gr. 5,** 36
ILM Anitra's Dance from *Peer Gynt Suite No. 1,* **Gr. 5,** 193
ILM Augie's Great Municipal Band from *Star Wars Episode 1: The Phantom Menace* (excerpt), **Gr. 4,** 57
ILM Ballet of the Unhatched Chicks from *Pictures at an Exhibition,* **Gr. 3,** 76
Battle Hymn of the Republic, **Gr. 5,** 390
Birth and Dance of the Mayfly from *The Spider's Feast,* **Gr. K,** T76
ILM Blue Little Flower, **Gr. 8,** 83
Bourée from *Music for the Royal Fireworks,* **Gr. 1,** T263
Cherkassiya, **Gr. 2,** 373
ILM Children's March, **Gr. K,** T113
Chinese Dance from *The Nutcracker Suite,* **Gr. 2,** 354
ILM Circus Music, **Gr. 3,** 285
ILM Concerto for Trombone ("Motorbike Concerto"), Fifth Movement, **Gr. 2,** 193
ILM Concerto for Two Trumpets, Allegro, **Gr. 2,** 73
Contredanse from *Les Indes galantes* (excerpt), **Gr. 4,** 97
ILM Crazy Songs by M. Kopelent, **Gr. 6,** 65
Csárdás from *Ritter Pásmán,* **Gr. K,** T28
Cuckoo in the Heart of the Woods from *The Carnival of the Animals,* **Gr. 2,** 253
Dance for Clarinet and Piano, **Gr. 6,** 189
Dance for Piccolo, Oboe, Bassoon, and Side Drum, **Gr. 5,** 219

Classified Index

Classified Index of Songs, Selected Concepts, Skills, and Activities (continued)

ILM Dance of the Mirlitons from *The Nutcracker*, **Gr. 4,** 173

Dance, No. 4 (excerpt), **Gr. 4,** 145

ILM *Danse Macabre,* **Gr. 3,** 363

December: Sleighride from *Calendar Collection*, **Gr. 1,** T128

East St. Louis Toodle-Oo, **Gr. 4,** 232

ILM *Eine kleine Nachtmusik* (Serenade No. 13 in G), Minuet, **Gr. 3,** 169

ILM Elephant, The, from *Carnival of the Animals*, **Gr. 1,** T205

ILM Faeries and Giants from *Wand of Youth Suite No. 1*, **Gr. K,** T52

Festival Prelude, A, **Gr. 8,** 65

ILM Finale from *The Carnival of the Animals*, **Gr. K,** T195

From Bohemia's Forests and Meadows from *Má Vlast*, **Gr. 6,** 229

Funeral March of a Marionette, **Gr. 1,** T337

ILM Galop (excerpt) from *The Comedians*, **Gr. 4,** 254

ILM Gigue from Suite for Orchestra No. 3, **Gr. 2,** 269

Guadalcanal March from *Victory at Sea*, **Gr. 4,** 109

Hang on Sloopy, **Gr. 7,** 32

Holiday for Strings, **Gr. 3,** 229

Hornpipe from *Water Music Suite* (excerpt), **Gr. 3,** 27

Infernal Dance of King Kashchei from *The Firebird Suite* (excerpt), **Gr. 4,** 191

ILM Introduction from *The Rite of Spring*, **Gr. 6,** 423

Jamaican Rumba, **Gr. 5,** 93

Jupiter, the Bringer of Jollity, **Gr. 8,** 40

ILM Liberty Fanfare, **Gr. 7,** 187

Lion, **Gr. 6,** 17

ILM Little Train of the Caipira, The, from *Bachianas Brasileiras No. 2*, **Gr. K,** T142

Little White Donkey, The, **Gr. K,** T245

ILM Los mariachis, **Gr. 7,** 91

ILM Los trabajadores agricolas (The Farmers) from *Estancia*, **Gr. 6,** 117

Mai Nozipo, **Gr. 7,** 229

ILM March from *Children's Games*, **Gr. 1,** T30

ILM March Past of the Kitchen Utensils from *The Wasps*, **Gr. 3,** 247

ILM Marche, **Gr. 8,** 168

ILM Mars from *The Planets*, **Gr. 6,** 197

Medley Polleritas, **Gr. 3,** 111

Miniwanka (or The Moments of Water), **Gr. 4,** 29

ILM Minuet from *Abdelazar*, **Gr. 2,** 145

ILM Moldau, The, from *Má Vlast (My Country)*, **Gr. 5,** 271

Moulinet, **Gr. 2,** 53

ILM Nessun dorma from *Turandot*, **Gr. 5,** 65

ILM On the Trail, **Gr. 8,** 112

ILM Parade from *Divertissement*, **Gr. K,** T183

Partita No 2, **Gr. 8,** 95

ILM Pomp and Circumstance, **Gr. 7,** 50–51

Promise of Living, The, from *The Tender Land* (listening), **Gr. 6,** 77

ILM Rondo "alla turca," **Gr. 7,** 117

ILM Rondo a capriccio Op. 129 ("Rage over a Lost Penny") (excerpt), **Gr. 2,** 225

ILM Seventeen Come Sunday, **Gr. 7,** 103

ILM Skater's Waltz, The (excerpt), **Gr. 1,** T344

ILM Spinning Song, **Gr. 3,** 128

ILM Spinning Wheel, **Gr. 4,** 211

ILM Spring (Allegro) from *The Four Seasons*, **Gr. 4,** 391

St. Patrick's Day, **Gr. 2,** 374

ILM Stars and Stripes Forever, The, **Gr. 4,** 355

ILM String of Pearls, A, **Gr. 3,** 12

String Quartet Op. 76 No. 2 in D Minor, Op. 76, Andante (excerpt), **Gr. 1,** T129

Strings in the Media, **Gr. 7,** 49

Symphony No. 101, **Gr. 8,** 129

Symphony No. 4 (Tchaikovsky), Fourth Movement, **Gr. 4,** 287

ILM Symphony No. 7, Second Movement **Gr. 7,** 119

ILM Symphony No. 9 in E Minor, Op. 95 ("From the New World"), Largo (excerpt), **Gr. 5,** 107

Theme and Percussion Variation from *Young Person's Guide to the Orchestra*, **Gr. 5,** 229

Toccata and Fugue in D Minor, **Gr. 7,** 109

ILM Trepak from *The Nutcracker Suite* by P. Tchaikovsky (listening), **Gr. 6,** 409

ILM Variations on "Simple Gifts" from *Appalachian Spring*, **Gr. 5,** 153

ILM Variations on the Theme "Pop! Goes the Weasel," **Gr. 5,** 97

ILM Walking Song from *Acadian Songs and Dances*, **Gr. K,** T20

ILM *William Tell* (Overture) (excerpt), **Gr. 3,** 65

ILM Wind Blew East, The, **Gr. 1,** T235

in *Teacher's Resource Masters* under separate cover

ILM Akinla from *African Suite*, **Gr. 2,** 97

ILM American Salute, **Gr. 7,** 170

ILM Anvil Chorus from *Il Trovatore*, **Gr. 5,** 170

Anything Goes, **Gr. 8,** 135

ILM Badinerie from Suite for Orchestra No. 2 in B Minor, **Gr. 4,** 60

Ballet Music from *Iphigénie en Aulide*, **Gr. 2,** 25

ILM Belhadawa walla belshaawa, **Gr. 6,** 35

Blue Moon of Kentucky, **Gr. 5,** 165

ILM Brafferton Village/Walsh's Hornpipe, **Gr. 3,** 391

Brandenberg Concerto No. 5, **Gr. 6,** 128

ILM Clock at Night, A, **Gr. 3,** 66

Concerto for Violin and Oboe, Adagio, **Gr. 2,** 127

ILM Crazy Songs (traditional Czech song), **Gr. 6,** 65

Effie Goes Folk Dancing, **Gr. 2,** 168

ILM Entertainer, The, **Gr. 7,** 22

Firecracker, **Gr. 8,** 134

Get a Car/Polka Dot from *Dreaming Blue*, **Gr. 6,** 220

Gift, The, **Gr. 7,** 205

ILM Gigue from Suite No. 1 for Cello, **Gr. 3,** 178

Goin' to the Zoo, **Gr. 1,** T192

Guadalquivir, **Gr. 3,** 30

Hoo, Hoo!, **Gr. 1,** T55

ILM In the Hall of the Mountain King from *Peer Gynt Suite No. 1*, **Gr. 2,** 346

Jetsons, The, **Gr. 8,** 132

John the Rabbit, **Gr. 1,** T74

Jump, Jim Joe, **Gr. 1,** T89

ILM La cumparsita, **Gr. 6,** 112

La raspa, **Gr. 3,** 211

Las mañanitas, **Gr. 4,** 197

Lavender's Blue, **Gr. 1,** T174

Les saluts, **Gr. 3,** 92

ILM Locomotion, **Gr. 6,** 157

Maggie in the Wood, **Gr. 5,** 167

March of the Toys from *Babes in Toyland*, **Gr. K,** 12

Mission Impossible, **Gr. 8,** 133

ILM Música indígena, **Gr. 8,** 131

ILM Night Fight from *Crouching Tiger, Hidden Dragon*, **Gr. 6,** 29

Och Jungfrun Han Går I Ringen, **Gr. 5,** 171

ILM Ode to a Butterfly, **Gr. 5,** 166

ILM Only Time, **Gr. 7,** 142

Over in the Meadow, **Gr. 1,** T78

ILM Pata Pata, **Gr. 3,** 35

Processional Medley, **Gr. 7,** 75

Qua Cầu Gió Bay, **Gr. 4,** 367

Reel á bouche, **Gr. 6,** 56

ILM Seasons of Love, **Gr. 7,** 86

Skip to My Lou, **Gr. 1,** T102

ILM Sonata for Piano No. 2 in D Minor, Vivace (excerpt), **Gr. 4,** 181

Sweet Sound, **Gr. 8,** 136

Symphonic Dances Op. 64, No. 4 (excerpt), **Gr. 2,** 105

ILM Symphony No. 9 ("Choral") (Beethoven), Fourth Movement (excerpt), **Gr. 5,** 168

Symphony No. 9 ("Choral"), Fourth Movement, **Gr. 7,** 156

Take Five, **Gr. 5,** 172

There's a Hole in the Middle of the Sea, **Gr. 1,** T178

Thing, The (listening), **Gr. K,** T307

Tinker Tailor, **Gr. 1,** T130

ILM Trio for Piano, Violin and Cello No. 39, Finale ("Gypsy Rondo"), **Gr. 3,** 155

ILM Wade in the Water, **Gr. 5,** 169

Waltz of the Snowflakes from *The Nutcracker*, **Gr. K,** 11

ILM Washington Post, **Gr. 2,** 339

Water Cadenza, **Gr. 7,** 223

ILM What a Wonderful World, **Gr. 8,** 130

ILM *Young Person's Guide to the Orchestra* (excerpt), **Gr. 2,** 229

LULLABIES

A la nanita nana (A Little Lullaby), **Gr. 4,** 230

Baby Nodja, **Gr. 2,** 154

Berceuse (listening), **Gr. 2,** 183

Bu-Vah (Sleep), **Gr. 4,** 18

Duerme Negrito, **Gr. 3,** 108

Night Song, **Gr. 3,** 186

No despiertes a mi niño (Do Not Wake My Little Son), **Gr. 5,** 217

Ogguere, **Gr. 4,** 327

Shoheen Sho, **Gr. 2,** 140

Sleep, Bonnie Bairnie, **Gr. 1,** T26

Too-ra-loo-ra-loo-ral (That's an Irish Lullaby), **Gr. K,** T335

Ucha Tirvarch, **Gr. 3,** 53

Wéané, **Gr. 3,** 184

Yo Mamana, Yo, **Gr. 1,** T307

M

MINOR/MODAL SONGS

minor

A la nanita nana, **Gr. 4,** 230

Agahu, **Gr. 5,** 72

Al lado de mi cabaño, **Gr. 6,** 141

Animales, **Gr. K,** T192

Arianna (listening), **Gr. 7,** 94

Autumn Leaves Are Falling, **Gr. 1,** T330

Ballad of the Underground Railroad, **Gr. 5,** 145

Bella bimba, **Gr. 3,** 172

Belle qui tiens ma vie (song and listening), **Gr. 6,** 99

Beryoza, **Gr. 4,** 286

Boo, **Gr. 3,** 362

By the Singing Water, **Gr. 5,** 270

Castle on a Cloud, **Gr. 7,** 82

Chag Asif, **Gr. 3,** 360

Chiribim, **Gr. 6,** 57

Chirri Bim, **Gr. 2,** 70

Conga, **Gr. 6,** 34

Dance for the Nations, **Gr. 5,** 206

De allacito carnavalito, **Gr. 5,** 269

Eight Days of Hanukkah, The, **Gr. 3,** 370

El nacimiento, **Gr. K,** T322

El vito, **Gr. 5,** 210

Elijah Rock (song and listening), **Gr. 6,** 52

Erie Canal (verse), **Gr. 5,** 132

Follow the Drinkin' Gourd, **Gr. 5,** 142

Freedom Is a Constant Struggle, **Gr. 7,** 211

Gong xi fa cai, **Gr. 3,** 384

Halloween, **Gr. 1,** T341

Haneirot Halalu, **Gr. 5,** 414

Hanukkah Is Here, **Gr. K,** T314

Hava Nagila, **Gr. 5,** 54

In the Window, **Gr. 2,** 352

J'entend le moulin, **Gr. 3,** 135

Jack-in-the-Box, **Gr. K,** T250

John the Rabbit, **Gr. 1,** T74

Joshua Fit the Battle of Jericho, **Gr. 5,** 126

Katyusha, **Gr. 4,** 188

Kojo No Tsuki, **Gr. 5,** 149

Korobushka, **Gr. 4,** 285

Let's Go Dancing, **Gr. 3,** 196

Light the Candles, **Gr. 1,** T351

Mayim, Mayim, **Gr. 6,** 102

Mi caballo blanco, **Gr. 6,** 60

'Most Done Ling'rin' Here, **Gr. 4,** 65

Nottamun Town, **Gr. 5,** 405

Old House, **Gr. 4,** 282

Old Mister Woodpecker, **Gr. K,** T172

Only Time (listening), **Gr. 7,** 142

Over the Sea to Skye, **Gr. 4,** 344

Oy Chanuke, **Gr. 3,** 368

Pat-a-Pan, **Gr. 3,** 375

Put On a Costume, **Gr. 1,** T336

Qué bonita bandera, **Gr. 5,** 443

¿Quièn es ese pajarito?, **Gr. 4,** 284

Red Iron Ore, **Gr. 6,** 134

Ride Like the Wind, **Gr. 5,** 130

Rise up, O Flame, **Gr. 4,** 283

S'vivon Sov, **Gr. 1,** T348

Shalom Chaveyrim, **Gr. 3,** 141

Sixteen Tons, **Gr. 7,** 151

Tame Bear from *Wand of Youth Suite No. 2*, **Gr. K,** T203

This is Halloween, **Gr. 2,** 346

Toccata and Fugue in D Minor (listening), **Gr. 7**, 108

Tum Balalaika, **Gr. 6**, 68

Tumbai, **Gr. 5**, 194

Üsküdar, **Gr. 5**, 128

What You Gonna Call Your Pretty Little Baby?, **Gr. K**, T319

When Johnny Comes Marching Home, **Gr. 5**, 34

Winter Ade, **Gr. 6**, 133

Zum gali, gali, **Gr. 4**, 255

modal

Aeyaya balano sakkad (B♭ mixolydian), **Gr. 5**, 402

Butterfly, Come Play with Me (E mixolydian), **Gr. 3**, 112

Cumbia del sol (A mixolydian), **Gr. 5**, 16

Digga Digga Dog (F mixolydian), **Gr. 3**, 164

Frog Went A-Courtin' (G mixolydian), **Gr. 4**, 46

Git Along, Little Dogies (C mixolydian), **Gr. 6**, 284

Greenland Whale Fishery, The (G mixolydian), **Gr. 6**, 212

Kalinka (D mixolydian), **Gr. 3**, 224

Let Music Surround You (G mixolydian), **Gr. 6**, 285

Lumber Camp Song, The (D dorian), **Gr. 6**, 136

Old Carrion Crow (D dorian), **Gr. 4**, 192

Old Joe Clark (F mixolydian), **Gr. 4**, 74

Oye como va (D dorian), **Gr. 5**, 69

Rise Up, Shepherd, and Follow (C mixolydian), **Gr. 5**, 422

Round and Round (D dorian), **Gr. 6**, 104

Ship in Distress (D dorian), **Gr. 6**, 211

Tanabata (G mixolydian), **Gr. 3**, 62

MOVEMENT. *See also* Choreography, Broadway for Kids *and* John Jacobson Choreography *on* Grade-Level DVD *under separate cover,* Creative Activities, Movement Glossary; *and* Signing.

Background

Vinqo, **Gr. 4**, 25

Body Percussion

Stamp, Pat, Clap, Snap, The, **Gr. 1**, T41

Choreography. See Choreography main category. *For choreography notes, see* Piano Accompaniments *under separate cover; see also* Grade-Level DVD.

Creative Movement, Gr. 4, 23, 28, 47, 65, 97, 213, 228, 250, 266, 336; **Gr. 5**, 16, 93, 146, 185, 189, 221, 259, 272; **Gr. 6**, E, 32, 72, 84, 86, 89, 107, 114, 145, 189, 223, 233, 251, 283, 308

"Rondo all'Ongarese," **Gr. 7**, 115

adding verses, **Gr. 1**, T309

All Work Together (swinging, swaying, jumping), **Gr. K**, T15, T17

Alphabet Song (move with the steady beat), **Gr. K**, T54; (move to show melodic shape), T91

Autumn Leaves, **Gr. 1**, T331

Ballet Music, **Gr. 2**, 24

Bell Horses (pantomime horses), **Gr. K**, T262

Bella bimba, **Gr. 3**, 172

Bobby Shafto (move to show melodic direction; create movements), **Gr. K**, T265

Car Song (listening) (pantomime actions; movement in pairs), **Gr. K**, T135

Children's Dance, **Gr. 2**, 246

Children's March (listening) (dramatize each song; circle, march to the beat), **Gr. K**, T113

City, The, **Gr. 2**, 329

Colorful Dragon Boat (listening) (pantomime rowing), **Gr. K**, T395

Counting Song (move to show melodic direction), **Gr. K**, T92, T93

Csárdás from *Ritter Pásmán* (listening) (circle, various actions), **Gr. K**, T28

Dance (listening) (hand dancing, moving in shared space), **Gr. K**, T167

Dinah, **Gr. 3**, 150

Dinosaurs Dancing (listening) (dance), **Gr. K**, T72

Dipidu (pantomime paddling canoes), **Gr. K**, T165

Doll Song, The, from *Tales of Hoffman* (listening) (pantomime actions), **Gr. K**, T179

Elbows Off the Table (listening) (move to show beat), **Gr. K**, T106

Engine, Engine Number Nine, **Gr. 2**, 12

Faeries and Giants (listening) (improvise movements to show higher/lower), **Gr. K**, T52

Flight of the Bumblebee, The (listening) (pantomime swarm of bees), **Gr. K**, T259

Garden Hoedown, The, (pantomime garden movements), **Gr. K**, T290

Gardens in the Rain (create movements), **Gr. K**, T403

Gavotte fantastique, **Gr. 2**, 27

Git on Board (pantomime train), **Gr. K**, T145

Gogo (create movements), **Gr. K**, T188

Grizzly Bear (respond to lyrics), **Gr. K**, T252

Hinges (poem) (move as poem suggests), **Gr. K**, T23

Humming Birds (poem) (pantomime humming birds), **Gr. K**, T140

I Got Shoes (listening) (improvise movement), **Gr. K**, T33

improvising movement, **Gr. 7**, 142

It's Such a Good Feeling (move to show melodic direction), **Gr. K**, T282

Jack-in-the-Box (move to show loud/soft), **Gr. K**, T250

Jig Jog, Jig Jog (straight line movement; circle movement), **Gr. K**, T260

Just Like Me (pantomime actions), **Gr. K**, T242

Kreely Kranky, **Gr. 3**, 258

Little Blue Truck (pantomime actions; movement in pairs), **Gr. K**, T136

Little Spotted Puppy (pantomime actions in pairs), **Gr. K**, T147

Mail Myself to You, **Gr. 1**, T367

Major and Minor, **Gr. 3**, 350

Marvelous Toy, The, **Gr. 3**, 183

Merrily, We Roll Along (line formation; pantomime ships; walk to the beat), **Gr. K**, T110

Mi-a-ou (listening) (pantomime cat; move to show same and different), **Gr. K**, T149

Minuet, **Gr. 3**, 168

Moon Mirrored in a Pool, The (listening), (pantomime sailboats; follow the leader), **Gr. K**, T115

moving to "Respect," **Gr. 7**, 6

Mulberry Bush, The (move freely in place to the beat; skip; improvise fantasy activities), **Gr. K**, T112

Classified Index of Songs, Selected Concepts, Skills, and Activities (continued)

My Legs and I (poem) (pat to the tempos; pantomime poem), **Gr. K,** T19

My Thumbs are Starting to Wiggle (pantomime actions), **Gr. K,** T35

Noble Duke of York, The (create movements), **Gr. K,** T232

Norwegian Dance, **Gr. 3,** 144

Old Gray Cat, The, (pantomime actions), **Gr. K,** T43

One Finger, One Thumb (create movements), **Gr. K,** T38

One Small Voice, **Gr. 3,** E

Only My Opinion (poem) (caterpillar movements), **Gr. K,** T17 (move at different tempos), T21, T29

Ourchestra (poem) (move to illustrate lyrics), **Gr. K,** T171

Over the Rainbow (listening) (mirroring; move to show high/low), **Gr. K,** T60

pantomiming work movements, **Gr. 7,** 148

Parade from *Divertissement* from *Un Chapeau de paille d'Italie* (listening) (march, single file), **Gr. K,** T183, T185

Pimpón (move to the beat like marionettes), **Gr. K,** T22

Pizza, Pizza, Daddy-O, **Gr. 2,** 63

Planting Seeds (create movements), **Gr. K,** T284

Polly Wolly Doodle, **Gr. 3,** 133

Popping Corn (pantomime pop-corn), **Gr. K,** T161

Qué bonito es (create movements to show steady beat), **Gr. K,** T234

Row, Row, Row (pantomime actions), **Gr. K,** T274

Royal March of the Lions, The, **Gr. 1,** T25

Scotland's Burning, **Gr. 3,** 257

Seesaw, Margery Daw (pantomime seesaw), **Gr. K,** T265

Snail's Pace (poem) (snail movements), **Gr. K,** T17; (move at different tempos), T21, T29

So Long, Farewell (gesture to show beats of silence), **Gr. K,** T189

Spiders, **Gr. 3,** 282

Spinning Song (poem) (star hands), **Gr. K,** T67

Stamping Land (pantomime text), **Gr. K,** T24, T25

Step into the Spotlight, **Gr. 3,** B

Sweetly Sings the Donkey (trot, gallop), **Gr. K,** T244

Taking Off (poem) (pantomime airplane), **Gr. K,** T136

Thing, The (listening) (choose movement appropriate to meter), **Gr. K,** T307

This Is My City (sway to the strong beat), **Gr. K,** T153

This Is What I Can Do (circle, follow the leader, upper body movement), **Gr. K,** T124

Three Little Kittens (pantomime actions), **Gr. K,** T148

Time to Sing (mirroring; move to the beat), **Gr. K,** T16, T17

Toodala (step, sway, twist, jump, rock; walk to the beat), **Gr. K,** T39

Tugboat (pantomime actions), **Gr. K,** T95, T96

Twinkle, Twinkle, Little Star (move to show sections), **Gr. K,** T91, T95

Uga, Uga, Uga, **Gr. 1,** T313

Walking Song from *Acadian Songs and Dances* (from the movie *Louisiana Story*) (listening) (move to different tempos), **Gr. K,** T21

Waltz in A Major, Op. 54, No. 1 (listening) (move to show same and different), **Gr. K,** T109

Y ahora vamos a cantar (pantomime actions), **Gr. K,** T407

You Never Hear the Garden Grow, **Gr. 2,** 236

Dance
Agahu, **Gr. 5,** 73

Hop Up and Jump Up, **Gr. 4,** 271

Samba, The, **Gr. 8,** 44

Zum gali gali, **Gr. 4,** 255

Expressive Movement, **Gr. 7,** 159

Finger Play
Here Is the Beehive (pantomime actions), **Gr. K,** T258

Noble Duke of York, The (walking fingers), **Gr. K,** T232

Three Little Muffins (game, respond to lyrics), **Gr. K,** T127

Folk Dances. *See* Patterned Movement

Formation, **Gr. 5,** 73, 171

Game, **Gr. 4,** 167, 185, 219, 252; **Gr. 5,** 28, 56, 75, 112, 246, 255, 264; **Gr. 6,** 90, 92
Bounce High, Bounce Low (circle, game involving bouncing a ball), **Gr. K,** T131

Farmer in the Dell, The (circle, game, walk, skip), **Gr. K,** T100, T101

Follow Me (game, follow the leader; improvise locomotion, pose), **Gr. K,** T133

Grizzly Bear (freeze on cue), **Gr. K,** T252

Head and Shoulders (game involving body percussion), **Gr. K,** T238

Jack-in-the-Box (circle game), **Gr. K,** T250

London Bridge (passing through arch, game), **Gr. K,** T99

María Blanca (circle game), **Gr. K,** T98

Mbombela (circle, passing game), **Gr. K,** T152

Muffin Man, The (question and answer game), **Gr. K,** T105

Red Light, Green Light (freeze on cue), **Gr. K,** T272

Ring Around the Rosy (circle game), **Gr. K,** T246

Ten Little Frogs (locomotor game), **Gr. K,** T240

Three Little Muffins (game, respond to lyrics), **Gr. K,** T127

Who Is the Valentine? (Guessing game), **Gr. K,** T398

Improvise
Best Friends, **Gr. 1,** T224

Willum, **Gr. 1,** T20

Limited Movement, **Gr. 4,** 135, 151, 157, 181, 183, 231; **Gr. 6,** 86; **Gr. 8,** 182

Locomotor Movement, **Gr. 4,** 167, 280; **Gr. 5,** 33, 88, 112, 189, 248, 256, 262, 268; **Gr. 6,** 52, 100
Ball, The, from *Children's Games* (listening) (move to the beat; circle, follow the leader), **Gr. K,** T13

create new verses, **Gr. 2,** 195

Csárdás from *Ritter Pázmán* (listening) (move to show fast/slow), **Gr. K,** T28

December: Sleighride (gallop), **Gr. 1,** T128

Deedle, Deedle Dumpling (poem) (jog to a rhyme), **Gr. K,** T87

El juego chirmibolo, **Gr. 1,** T104

Farmer in the Dell, The (circle, game, walk, skip), **Gr. K,** T100, T101

Classified Index

Classified Index of Songs, Selected Concepts, Skills, and Activities (continued)

Follow Me (game, follow the leader; improvise locomotion, pose), **Gr. K,** T133

gallop/skip, **Gr. 2,** 214

Gigue, **Gr. 2,** 269

Girls and Boys, Come Out to Play (poem) (skip), **Gr. K,** T98

Go, Go, Go (circle, walk to the beat), **Gr. K,** T276

Hidden Talents Rare, **Gr. 1,** T322

I Got Shoes (walk), **Gr. K,** T33

It's So Good to See You (walk to show sections; respond to lyrics), **Gr. K,** T86

Jack, Be Nimble (gallop), **Gr. K,** T88

Jasmine Flower, **Gr. 3,** 147

Knock the Cymbals, **Gr. 2,** 265

Let's Think of Something to Do (circle; walk to the beat), **Gr. K,** T270

Little White Donkey, The (trot), **Gr. K,** T245

Locust, The (gallop/skip), **Gr. 1,** T284

Merrily, We Roll Along (line formation; pantomime ships; walk to the beat), **Gr. K,** T110

Merry-Go-Round, **Gr. 2,** 267

My Grandfather (walk to the steady beat), **Gr. K,** T23

Noble Duke of York, The (march to the beat), **Gr. K,** T232

One Finger, One Thumb (skip, gallop), **Gr. K,** T41

Parade (listening) (march, single file), **Gr. K,** T183

Pumpkin Song, **Gr. 1,** T343

Running Song (jog), **Gr. K,** T99

See the Pony Galloping (gallop or walk to show fast/slow), **Gr. K,** T44

Shi Wu (listening) (line formation; pantomime dragon), **Gr. K,** T395

Sidewalks (walk), **Gr. K,** T99

Sing a Song of Sixpence (jog), **Gr. K,** T111

Sonata in C Major (listening) (gallop), **Gr. K,** T89

SoundCheck: Learning About Walking/Skipping/Galloping (listening) (walk, skip, gallop), **Gr. K,** T41

Sweetly Sings the Donkey (trot, gallop), **Gr. K,** T244

They Were Tall (walk to show high/low), **Gr. K,** T53

Time to Sing (circle dance; free locomotor movement), **Gr. K,** T16

Walk on a Happy Street, **Gr. 1,** T305

Walk to School (pat to different tempos; walk to different tempos), **Gr. K,** T19, T20, T21

Movement in Small Spaces

Colors (listening) (respond to lyrics), **Gr. K,** T58

Faeries and Giants (listening) (move to show higher/lower), **Gr. K,** T52

Mister Sun (hand movements), **Gr. K,** T409

Noble Duke of York, The (walking fingers), **Gr. K,** T232

O Tannenbaum! (rock), **Gr. K,** T389

Ten in a Bed (roll one hand over the other), **Gr. K,** T256

Three Little Muffins (game, respond to lyrics), **Gr. K,** T127

Nonlocomotor Movement, Gr. 6, 107

Berceuse (shadow movement), **Gr. 2,** 184

Bye 'n' Bye (mirror hand movements to show higher/lower), **Gr. K,** T67

Clap-Circle-Circle Pattern, **Gr. 2,** 127

Colors (listening) (respond to lyrics), **Gr. K,** T58

Gavotta (sway), **Gr. 1,** T176

Giant's Shoes, The (poem) (pantomime actions), **Gr. K,** T32

Hokey Pokey (move in response to lyrics), **Gr. K,** T68

I Made a Valentine (sway on the strong beats), **Gr. K,** T399

It's So Nice on the Ice, **Gr. 1,** T347

Las horas (The Hours) (pantomime a clock), **Gr. K,** T70

Lavender's Blue (sway), **Gr. 1,** T175

Love Grows One by One, **Gr. 1,** T203

Marco Polo, **Gr. 1,** T90

Mister Sun (hand movements), **Gr. K,** T409

My Oak Tree (move to show melodic direction), **Gr. K,** T236

Nampaya omame (mirroring; move in place to the beat), **Gr. K,** T128

Noble Duke of York, The (move to the beat), **Gr. K,** T232

O Tannenbaum! (rock), **Gr. K,** T389

One Finger, One Thumb (pantomime actions), **Gr. K,** T38

Seneca Stomp Dance (stomp step), **Gr. K,** T411

Sitting in the Sand (poem), **Gr. 1,** T374

Stamping Land (pantomime text), **Gr. K,** T24

Ten in a Bed (roll one hand over the other), **Gr. K,** T256

This Is What I Can Do (circle, follow the leader, upper body movement), **Gr. K,** T124

Wang Ü Ger, **Gr. 3,** 191

We All Stand Together (listening) (sway to the strong beat), **Gr. K,** T153

Patterned Movement, Gr. 4, F, G, 9, 16, 20, 25, 51, 69, 87, 91, 97, 104, 133, 156, 169, 171, 175, 211, 236; Gr. 5, L, S, 7, 31, 55, 90, 104, 150, 171, 191, 206, 234, 263, 265, 277; Gr. 6, C, 32, 96, 97, 99, 103, 105, 108, 109, 111, 112, 191, 215, 217, 231, 244, 267, 280

A la rueda de San Miguel, **Gr. 2,** 60

All Work Together (mirroring; move to the beat), **Gr. K,** T12

Animal Rhythms (speech piece) (move to the beat), **Gr. K,** T56

Apple Tree, **Gr. 3,** 25

Ballet of the Unhatched Chicks, **Gr. 3,** 77

Bingo (walk in a circle; body percussion with partner), **Gr. K,** T64

Bow, Wow, Wow, **Gr. 2,** 264

Brafferton Village/Walsh's Hornpipe, **Gr. 3,** 391

Brother, Come and Dance with Me (listening) (partner dance), **Gr. K,** T180

Bus, The (pantomime actions), **Gr. K,** T137

Butterfly Come Play With Me, **Gr. 3,** 112

Carnavalito, **Gr. 2,** 251

Charlie, **Gr. 3,** 208

Chiapanecas, **Gr. 2,** 128

Clog Dancing, **Gr. 2,** 68

Country Gardens, **Gr. 2,** 16

Dance Together, **Gr. 2,** 264

Double This, **Gr. 1,** T95

El Capitán, **Gr. 8,** 7

Classified Index of Songs, Selected Concepts, Skills, and Activities (continued)

En nuestra Tierra tan linda, **Gr. 2**, 115
Farm, The, **Gr. 2**, 211
Garden Hoedown, The (move to the beat), **Gr. K**, T290
Guadalquivir, **Gr. 3**, 31
hand jive, **Gr. 2**, 223
Hanukkah Is Here (various activities), **Gr. K**, T383
Head and Shoulders (mirroring; responding to lyrics), **Gr. K**, T238
Her kommer vennen min, **Gr. 3**, 143
Here Comes Sallly, **Gr. 2**, 221
Hokey Pokey (move in response to lyrics), **Gr. K**, T68
It's So Good to See You (walk to show sections; respond to lyrics), **Gr. K**, T86
It's You I Like (various activities), **Gr. K**, T280
Jim Along, Josie, **Gr. 2**, 195
La Camilla, **Gr. 1**, T196
La raspa, **Gr. 3**, 212
Les saluts, **Gr. 3**, 92
Let's Go Driving, **Gr. 1**, T51
Light the Candles, **Gr. 1**, T351
Little Tommy Tinker, **Gr. 3**, 277
march, **Gr. 7**, 50
mirrored dance patterns, **Gr. 7**, 139
Must Be Santa (move to show beats of silence), **Gr. K**, T385
Nigun Atik, **Gr. 3**, 47, 71
Oats, Peas, Beans, and Barley Grow (various activities), **Gr. K**, T287
Oh, A-Hunting We Will Go (partner dance), **Gr. K**, T62
One Finger, One Thumb (pantomime actions), **Gr. K**, T38
Patriotic Medley, **Gr. 3**, G
patterned movement, **Gr. 7**, 165
Paw Paw Patch, The, **Gr. 3**, 195
Pezinho, **Gr. 3**, 231
Pizza, Pizza, Daddy-O, **Gr. 2**, 63
Put Your Finger in the Air (pantomime text), **Gr. K**, T230, T231
Raccoon Dance Song, **Gr. 3**, 87
Rainstorm, **Gr. 1**, T35
Rise Up Singin', **Gr. 3**, 139
Sailor Went to Sea, Sea, Sea, A, **Gr. 1**, T39
Samba, The, **Gr. 8**, 44
Shake the Papaya Down, **Gr. 2**, 91
Shoo, Fly, **Gr. 2**, 223
Simi Yadech (partner dance), **Gr. K**, T168
Smoke Goes Up the Chimney, **Gr. 3**, 272
Sorida, **Gr. 2**, 96
Spider King, The, **Gr. 2**, 335
Spinning Song, **Gr. 3**, 128, 155
Staging, **Gr. 8**, 79
Step in Time (listening) (step with the beat; do what words indicate), **Gr. K**, T159
Taos Round Dance, **Gr. 2**, 155
Tehahontanekenhnêha', **Gr. 3**, 52
Ten Little Frogs (pantomime actions), **Gr. K**, T240
Three Little Penguins, **Gr. 2**, 113
Time to Sing (circle dance; free locomotor movement), **Gr. K**, T16
Touch Your Shoulders (respond to lyrics), **Gr. K**, T254
Tschotsholoza, **Gr. 1**, T76
Tugboat (pantomime actions), **Gr. K**, T95
Umoja! (poem) (move with text), **Gr. K**, T390
Wait and See (move to show contrasting sections), **Gr. K**, T334
We Are Playing in the Forest (partner dance), **Gr. K**, T248
We're Sailing Down the River, **Gr. 2**, 167
Willowbee, **Gr. 2**, 69
Woke Up This Morning, **Gr. 3**, 180
Won't You Be My Neighbor? (touch body parts in order), **Gr. K**, T283
Wringing the Dishrag, **Gr. 3**, 260

Shadow Movement
Bamboo Flute, **Gr. 4**, 135

Showing Pitches
Low so, Low la, **Gr. 3**, 116

Signing. *See* Signing *main category.*

MULTICULTURAL MATERIALS. *See also Fiesta de canciones, Festival of Caribbean Music, Festival of World Music, and World Instruments CD-ROM under separate cover*

Professional Article
Including Multicultural Music in Your Teaching, **Gr. K**, T398; **Gr. 1**, T398; **Gr. 2**, 410; **Gr. 3**, 426; **Gr. 4**, 426; **Gr. 6**, 458–459; **Gr. 7**, 288; **Gr. 8**, 284

Key for multicultural materials:
CM Festival of Caribbean Music
WM Festival of World Music
FC-Int ¡Fiesta de canciones! Intermediate
FC-Pri ¡Fiesta de canciones! Primary

Africa (Sub-Saharan)
Adukbe (traditional) (listening), **Gr. 8**, 177
Afirika, **Gr. 7**, 226
Afrakakraba (listening), **Gr. 3**, 102
African Postal Workers (listening), **Gr. 7**, 147
Agahu (song and listening), **Gr. 5**, 72, 73
Agahu Suite from *Dance Suites from West Africa* (listening), **Gr. 7**, 75
Aideu (listening), **Gr. 7**, 223
Akinla from *African Suite* (listening), **Gr. 2**, 97
Allundé, Alluia, **Gr. 4**, 34
Anansi (story), **Gr. 3**, 104
Chants du Burgam (listening), **Gr. 3**, 381
Dide, **Gr. 3**, 279
Dima, **Gr. 4**, 265
Drumming Spider, The (story), **Gr. 2**, 333
Eh Soom Boo Kawaya (Nigerian Boat Song), **Gr. 3**, 58
Fun wa ni alaafia (Send Us Your Peace), **Gr. 5**, 248
Gebeta Board, The (story), **Gr. 3**, 346
Gogo, **Gr. K**, T188
Hashewie (Going Round), **Gr. 2**, 362
Hey, Motswala, **Gr. 3**, 34
I'm On My Way, **Gr. 3**, 382
Jambo (Hello), **Gr. 1**, T230
Jikel' Emaweni (Throw It Down the Slope), **Gr. 6**, 70
Kakokolo, **Gr. 6**, 262
Kokoleoko, **Gr. 6**, 279
Kye Kye Kule, **Gr. 7**, 225

Le Serpent (excerpt) (listening), **Gr. 1,** T359
Lion Sleeps Tonight, The, **Gr. 5,** 172; **Gr. 7,** 214
Mai Nozipo (listening), **Gr. 1,** T211; **Gr. 7,** 228
Mbombela, **Gr. K,** T152
Mɔ-fia mo-ni (Ev'rybody Loves Saturday Night),
    Gr. 5, 277
Mwiji Mwena (listening), **Gr. 2,** 235
N'kosi sikelel' iAfrika (Lord Bless Africa), **Gr. 6,** 339
Nampaya omame (Mothers), **Gr. K,** T128
Ngikhumbula (listening), **Gr. 5,** 195
O, Desayo, **Gr. 6,** 50
Ɔbɔɔ Asi Me Nsa, **Gr. K,** T159
O Mama Bakudala, **Gr. 3,** 328
Oh, Come Sing a Song, **Gr. 7,** 65
Pata, Pata (listening), **Gr. 2,** 94; **Gr. 3,** 35
Sansa kroma, **Gr. 4,** 166
Sing Lo-Lo (listening), **Gr. 4,** 385
Singabahambayo (An Army Is Marching) (unison and
    parts), **Gr. 5,** 56, 76
Snake and the Frog, The (story), **Gr. K,** T297
Sorida (greeting song), **Gr. 2,** 96
Sounds of Africa, The, (poem), **Gr. 5,** 74
Take Time in Life, **Gr. 4,** 156
Thula Sizwe (listening), **Gr. 6,** 73
Tina singu, **Gr. 6,** 36
Tshotsholoza (listening), **Gr. 1,** T76
Tue Tue (listening), **Gr. 2,** 234
Uyai Mose (Come All You People), **Gr. 7,** 66
Vhaya Kadhimba (listening), **Gr. 1,** T24; (game),
    Gr. 1, T23
Vinqo (listening), **Gr. 4,** 24
Wavvuuvvuumira (Mister Bamboo Bug), **Gr. K,** T165
Yo, Mamana, Yo (Oh, Mama, Oh), **Gr. 1,** T307

African American
Aideu (listening), **Gr. 7,** 223
All Night, All Day, **Gr. 1,** T232
Amen, **Gr. 3,** 376
Angelina, **Gr. 6,** 8
Backwater Blues (song and listening), **Gr. 5,** 174, 175
Ballad of the Underground Railroad, The, **Gr. 5,** 145, 154
Big Bunch, a Little Bunch, **Gr. 4,** 267
Big Bunch of Roses (listening), **Gr. 4,** 267
Bon Chien (listening), **Gr. 2,** 178
Bound No'th Blues (poem), **Gr. 5,** 181
Bye 'n' Bye, **Gr. K,** T68
C-A-G (listening), **Gr. 1,** T241
Charlie Over the Ocean, **Gr. 1,** T75
Circle 'Round the Zero, **Gr. 3,** 267
City (poem), **Gr. K,** T134
Crawdad Song, **Gr. 3,** 107
Dancing in the Street, **Gr. 6,** 84
Daydreams on a Subway Train (poem), **Gr. 8,** 85
Didn't He Ramble (listening), **Gr. 7,** 143
Didn't It Rain, **Gr. 6,** 345
Do Lord, **Gr. 6,** 260
Double This (speech piece), **Gr. 1,** T95
Down by the Riverside (listening), **Gr. 3,** 382; (song),
    Gr. 6, 22
Draw a Bucket of Water, **Gr. 3,** 222
Dry Bones, **Gr. 5,** 406

Ears, Far and Near (poem), **Gr. 1,** T16
Elijah Rock (song and listening), **Gr. 6,** 52
Emergency (listening), **Gr. 7,** 174
Entertainer, The (orchestral version) (listening),
    Gr. 7, 23
Entertainer, The (piano version) (listening), **Gr. 7,** 22
Ev'ry Time I Feel the Spirit, **Gr. 6,** C
Every Day I Have the Blues, **Gr. 5,** 179
Everybody Oughta Know (song and listening),
    Gr. 1, T361
Everybody Rejoice, **Gr. 5,** 226
Feel Good, **Gr. 5,** 358
Fifty Nifty United States, **Gr. 5,** 392
Five-Step Waltz (listening), **Gr. 6,** 287
Follow the Drinkin' Gourd, **Gr. 5,** 142
Freedom Is a Constant Struggle, **Gr. 7,** 211
Get on Board, Children (listening), **Gr. 5,** 347
Gift, The (listening), **Gr. 7,** 205
Git on Board, **Gr. K,** T145
Glad About It (listening), **Gr. 8,** 63
Go Tell It on the Mountain, **Gr. 3,** 377
Good Mornin', Blues (song and listening),
    Gr. 5, 176, 177
Good News, **Gr. 6,** 242
Goodbye, My Riley O, **Gr. 4,** 257
Hallelujah Get on Board, **Gr. 5,** 345
Happy Face (listening), **Gr. 7,** 134
He's Got the Whole World in His Hands (listening and
    song), **Gr. 2,** 116
Head and Shoulders, Baby, **Gr. 1,** T40
Here Comes Sally, **Gr. 2,** 220
Hero, **Gr. 5,** 312
How Long the Train Been Gone?, **Gr. 4,** 264
I Got Shoes (listening), **Gr. K,** T33
I Got Shoes, **Gr. K,** T33
I Have a Dream (speech piece) (listening), **Gr. 6,**
    416
I Hear America Singing, **Gr. 5,** 327
I Lost the Farmer's Dairy Key, **Gr. 3,** 273
I Saw the Light, **Gr. 5,** 252
I Want to Be Ready, **Gr. 6,** 12
I Will Survive (listening), **Gr. 8,** 208
I'm Going to Georgia, **Gr. 6,** 244
I'm Gonna Sing, **Gr. 2,** 9
I'm Gonna Sit at the Welcome Table, **Gr. 6,** 416
I've Got a Robe, **Gr. 7,** 162
Ifetayo (Love Brings Happiness), **Gr. K,** T325
In That Great Git'n Up Mornin', **Gr. 5,** 10
In the Sweet By and By (listening), **Gr. 7,** 143
It Don't Mean a Thing (song and listening),
    Gr. 6, 164, 165
Jamaica Farewell, **Gr. 3,** 156
Jersey Bounce (listening), **Gr. 5,** 363
Jordan's Angels, **Gr. 6,** 365
Joshua Fit the Battle of Jericho (song and listening),
    Gr. 5, 126, 127
Joyful, Joyful (excerpt) (song), **Gr. 5,** 104, 105
Just Give Me the Beat (speech piece), **Gr. 5,** 9
Just Keep Goin' On (listening), **Gr. 7,** 16

Classified Index

Classified Index of Songs, Selected Concepts, Skills, and Activities (continued)

Just Keep Goin' On (listening), **Gr. 7,** 16
Just Keep Goin' On, **Gr. 7,** 18
Kum Ba Yah, **Gr. K,** T327
Kwanzaa is... (poem), **Gr. 6,** 414
Kwanzaa Time (listening), **Gr. K,** T324
Land of a Thousand Dances, **Gr. 7,** 12
Land of a Thousand Dances (Garage Band version)
    (listening), **Gr. 7,** 14
Land of a Thousand Dances (performed by Wilson
    Pickett) (listening), **Gr. 7,** 10
Lean On Me, **Gr. 6,** 150
Let's Twist Again (listening), **Gr. 7,** 11
Lift Every Voice and Sing (song and listening), **Gr. 5,**
    86, 87, 117
Like a Mighty Stream, **Gr. 5,** 320
Little David Play on Your Harp, **Gr. 4,** 323
Little David, Play On Your Harp (listening), **Gr. 2,** 9
Little Sally Walker, **Gr. 3,** 105
Little Sally Water, **Gr. 2,** 249
Locomotion (listening), **Gr. 6,** 157
Mai Nozipo (listening), **Gr. 7,** 228
Mama, Bake the Johnnycake, **Gr. K,** T318
Mardi Gras Mamba, **Gr. 7,** 88
Martin Luther King (speech piece), **Gr. K,** T326;
    Gr. 1, T360; **Gr. 2,** 364
Mary Had a Baby, **Gr. 2,** 360
Miss Mary Mack, **Gr. 1,** T15
Mister Rabbit, Mister Rabbit, **Gr. 2,** 150
'Most Done Ling'rin' Here, **Gr. 4,** 65
Mr. Scott Joplin's Ragtime Rag!, **Gr. 6,** 110
My Friend (listening), **Gr. 4,** 389
My Grandfather, **Gr. K,** T23
My Mama's Calling Me, **Gr. 1,** T54
O, I'm Gonna Sing, **Gr. 5,** 245
Oh, Come Sing a Song, **Gr. 7,** 65
Oh, Won't You Sit Down?, **Gr. 4,** 70
Old Ark's A-Moverin', **Gr. 4,** 130
Old Aunt Dinah, **Gr. 4,** 245
Old House, **Gr. 4,** 282
Old Mister Rabbit, **Gr. 3,** 254
One Dime Blues, **Gr. 6,** 178
Open the Window, Noah, **Gr. 3,** 324
Ourchestra (poem), **Gr. 8,** 34
Over in the Meadow, **Gr. 1,** T78
Over My Head, **Gr. 3,** 286
Pay Me My Money Down, **Gr. 3,** 149
Pick a Bale of Cotton, **Gr. 6,** 254
Pizza, Pizza, Daddy-O, **Gr. 2,** 62
Pole, Pole (listening), **Gr. K,** T215
Power of the Dream, The, **Gr. 5,** 44
Punchinella, **Gr. 1,** T216
Respect, **Gr. 7,** 5
Rise Up, Shepherd, and Follow, **Gr. 5,** 422
Rise, Sally, Rise, **Gr. 1,** T162
Roll de Ole Chariot Along, **Gr. 6,** 243
Rumpus in Richmond (listening), **Gr. 8,** 32
Seven Principles of Kwanzaa, The, (listening), **Gr. 6,** 415
She'll Be Comin' 'Round the Mountain, **Gr. 2,** 33
Shepherd, Shepherd, **Gr. 3,** 56
Shoo, Turkey, **Gr. 1,** T76
Simple Pleasures (listening), **Gr. 8,** 191

Sing! Sing! Sing!, **Gr. 2,** 196
Sleight of Feet from *Cakewalk Suite* (listening),
    Gr. 1, T239
So Glad I'm Here (listening), **Gr. 2,** 47
Somebody's Knockin' at Your Door, **Gr. 5,** 254
Sometimes I Feel Like a Motherless Child (song and
    listening), **Gr. 6,** 271
Sounds of Swing (poem), **Gr. 5,** 32
Soup, Soup!, **Gr. 1,** T358
Southern Nights, **Gr. 5,** 310
Sweep, Sweep Away, **Gr. 3,** 276
Sweet Potatoes, **Gr. 3,** 16
There's a Little Wheel A-Turnin' in My Heart,
    Gr. 3, 129, 137
There's No Hidin' Place, **Gr. 5,** 266
This Little Light of Mine, **Gr. 1,** T238; **Gr. 2,** F
This Train (song and listening), **Gr. 4,** 343
Train Is A-Coming, **Gr. 4,** 270
Trampin', **Gr. 3,** 287
Twenty-four Robbers, **Gr. 1,** T173
Ujamaa, **Gr. 3,** 380
Ujima, **Gr. 5,** 427
Umoja! (poem), **Gr. K,** T325
Uncle Jessie (song and listening), **Gr. 3,** 327
Wade in the Water (listening), **Gr. 5,** 144
'Way Down Yonder in the Brickyard, **Gr. 5,** 255
We Shall Overcome, **Gr. 4,** 387; **Gr. 7,** 212; (listening),
    Gr. 7, 213
What a Wonderful World (listening), **Gr. 2,** 84
What You Gonna Call Your Pretty Baby?, **Gr. K,** T319
When I Sing, **Gr. 6,** 44
When I'm Walking (Let Me Walk) (listening), **Gr. 8,** 70
When the Saints Go Marching In, **Gr. 5,** 256
Who's That Yonder?, **Gr. 3,** 245
Woke Up This Morning, **Gr. 3,** 180
Yakety Yak, **Gr. 5,** 308
Yellow Bird, **Gr. 6,** 154
You'll Sing a Song and I'll Sing a Song, **Gr. 2,** 156
Zudio, **Gr. 7,** 164

Asia: Central and South

Aeyaya balano sakkad (Come, Children), **Gr. 5,** 402
Bəri Bax! (listening), **Gr. 5,** 233
Cip cip cücəlärim (listening), **Gr. 3,** 215
Diwali Song, **Gr. 6,** 396, WM 67
Holi Song, WM 112
Me gase boho (The Orange Tree), **Gr. 2,** 317
Milan (Meeting of the Two Rivers) (excerpt) (listening),
    Gr. 4, 208
Nach Nach Nach (Punjabi song) (listening), **Gr. 6,** 224
Raga Malika (listening), **Gr. 5,** 403
Star Canon, **Gr. 5,** 367
Yanai (The Elephant), **Gr. 2,** 305

Asia: East and Southeast

Adongko Dongko a Gakit (Philippine Kulintang
    Wedding Processional), WM 112
Ame fure (Rain), **Gr. 4,** 26
Antiphonal Singing Song (listening), **Gr. 6,** 65
Arirang (song and listening), **Gr. 5,** 50, 53
Arirang, WM 51
Bahay Kubo (My Nipa Hut), **Gr. 2,** 382

Bamboo Flute, **Gr. 4,** 134

Ban Dal (Half Moon), **Gr. 2,** 219; (listening), **Gr. 4,** 184

Bei Fang Chre (North Wind Blows), **Gr. 2,** 367

Bird Island (listening), **Gr. 8,** 56

Bo Hai Huan Ten (Jubilation All Around), WM 113; (listening), **Gr. 7,** 55

Bohm (Spring Has Come!), **Gr. 3,** 392

Bohm Dong Sahn, Gohd Dong Sahn (Spring Valley, Flower Valley), **Gr. K,** T337

Champa Muang Lao (listening), **Gr. 5,** 436

Chan mali chan, **Gr. 3,** 10

Chang (Elephant), WM 3; **Gr. 1,** T199

Chichipapa (The Sparrow's Singing School), **Gr. 2,** 22

Chinese Lion Dance (Chinese Folk Music), WM 112; (listening), **Gr. 1,** T363

Chuột Cấp Trú'ng (The Mouse and the Egg), WM 23

Colorful Dragon Boat, **Gr. K,** T328

Concertino for Xylophone (excerpt) (listening), **Gr. 5,** 201

Concerto for Xylophone and Orchestra (listening), **Gr. 8,** 41

Dal taro kacha (Come, Pick the Moon), **Gr. 2,** 98

Dandansoy, **Gr. 6,** 356

Deta, Deta (The Moon), WM 27; **Gr. 5,** 246

Diou Shou Juan'er (Hide the Handkerchief), **Gr. 1,** T212

Dok Djampa (The White Jasmine Flower), **Gr. 4,** 392

Dragon Dance (listening), **Gr. 2,** 366

Evening Party (listening), **Gr. 2,** 99

Fung Yang Song, **Gr. 5,** 58; WM 61

Ga Eul (Fall), **Gr. 5,** 401

Gêndhing KÊMBANG MARA (listening), **Gr. 7,** 101

Go A Tin (Lantern Song), **Gr. 1,** T363

Gong xi fa cai (Chinese New Year Song), **Gr. 3,** 384

Hae Wa Be (Sun and Rain), **Gr. 6,** 273

Hakyo Jong (School Bells), **Gr. 1,** T302

Hitori, **Gr. 4,** 345

Hong Tsai Me Me (Rainbow Sister), WM 57

Hotaru Koi (Come, Firefly), **Gr. 6,** 255

I Chih Ching Wa (Frogs), **Gr. 2,** 186

Itik Besenda Gurau (The Ducks), **Gr. 2,** 100

Jasmine Flower, **Gr. 3,** 146

Joban Tanko Bushi, **Gr. 6,** 142

Juhtgarak (Chopsticks), **Gr. K,** T108

Kaeru No Uta (Frog's Song), WM 9; **Gr. 1,** T112

Kari (Wild Geese), **Gr. 1,** T261

Kobuta (Piglet), **Gr. 1,** T167

Kojo No Tsuki (Moon at the Ruined Castle), **Gr. 5,** 149

Kokiriko (traditional Japanese folk song) (listening), **Gr. 6,** 145

Kuma San (Honorable Bear), **Gr. 3,** 244

Lek Kansaing (Hiding the Towel), WM 15

Lion (listening), **Gr. 6,** 16

Magnificent Horses (listening), **Gr. 7,** 104

Maliit Na Gagamba (Little Spider), WM 5

Mizuguruma (The Water Wheel), **Gr. 1,** T260

Moon Mirrored in a Pool, The, (listening), **Gr. K,** T115

Music from Bali (gamelan ensemble) (listening), **Gr. 1,** T143

Nabe, Nabe, Soko, Nuke (Stewpot, Stewpot, Bottomless Pot), WM 17; **Gr. 2,** 259

Ngam sang duan (Shining Moon), **Gr. 5,** 376

Niam Es, WM 69

Night Fight from *Crouching Tiger, Hidden Dragon* (listening), **Gr. 6,** 28

Nim Yog Xyoo Nuav (In This Year), WM 59

Pat on the Back, A, **Gr. 2,** 74

Pile of Stuff, A (story), **Gr. 1,** T188

Pleeng Lo Krathong (Full Moon Song), **Gr. 6,** 399

Pung Noy Loy Kratong (Full Moon Float), WM 55

Pusa't daga (Cat and Rat), **Gr. 1,** T289

Qua Cầu Gió Bay (listening), **Gr. 4,** 367

Rabbit in the Moon, The (folk tale), **Gr. 1,** T318

Sakura (Cherry Blossoms), WM 35; **Gr. 6,** 14

San Lun Tsa (Three-Wheeled Taxi), WM 45

Santoki (Mountain Rabbit) (singing game) (listening), **Gr. 1,** T187

Sara Watashi (Plate Passing), **Gr. 1,** T66, (game, T68)

Sarika Kaio (Myna Birds), WM 11

Sasara Ang Bulaklak (The Flower Fades), WM 13

Shi wu (Lion Dance) (listening), **Gr. K,** T329

Shiau Ya (Little Duck), WM 7

Singing on the Fisherboats at Dusk (listening), **Gr. 1,** T129

Sitsiritsit, **Gr. 4,** 102

Suk San Wan Pi Mai (New Year's Song), WM 43; **Gr. 5,** 437

Suliram, **Gr. 6,** 58

Tai Yau Tsai (Herding the Cows), WM 37

Tako No Uta (The Kite Song), **Gr. 1,** T370

Tanabata, **Gr. 3,** 62

Tang Tang Juen (Round, Round, Turn), WM 19

Tết Trung (Children's Festival), WM 53; **Gr. 4,** 366

Ti Ayat (Filipino folk song) (listening), **Gr. 6,** 359

Tinikling (listening), **Gr. 4,** 105

Tsing Chun U Chü (Youth Dance Song), WM 113; **Gr. 6,** 272

Ua Txiab (The Village), WM 49; **Gr. 6,** 394

Untitled haiku (poem), **Gr. 8,** 57

Wang Ü Ger (Chinese Fishing Song), WM 29; **Gr. 3,** 190

Water Cadenza from Water Passion After St. Matthew (listening), **Gr. 7,** 232

Wéané, **Gr. 3,** 184

Year-Naming Race, The (listening), **Gr. 3,** 385

Yongnam Nongak (listening), **Gr. 5,** 70

Yüe líang wan wan (Crescent Moon), **Gr. 6,** 26

Zui Zui Zukkorbashi (song), **Gr. 1,** T98; (game), **Gr. 1,** T99

Asian American

Moonlight Masquerade for Violin and Piano (listening), **Gr. 7,** 127

Australia and Pacific Islands

Ake Tonu (listening), **Gr. 5,** 150

Australia's on the Wallaby, **Gr. 2,** 106

Banyan Tree, **Gr. 2,** 321

Country Gardens (listening), **Gr. 2,** 16

Dance for Piccolo, Oboe, Bassoon, and Side Drum
(listening), **Gr. 5,** 218

E nānā kākou i nā manu (Look at the Birds in the Sky),
Gr. 4, 338

Haere Ra (Now Is the Hour), **Gr. 5,** 151

Hoe Ana Te Vaka (Paddle the Canoe), WM 41

Into the Fog from *Master and Commander* (excerpt)
(listening), **Gr. 3,** 201

Kia Ora (listening), **Gr. 2,** 65

Maori carving (carving), **Gr. 5,** 150

Na belo (Little Heron), **Gr. 2,** 322

Nani Wale Na Hala (The Swaying Pandanus Trees),
Gr. 5, 276

Ole La'u Papa e, **Gr. 6,** 91

Oma Rapeti (Run Rabbit), **Gr. 2,** 108

Po Atarau (listening), **Gr. 5,** 150

Pukaea (listening), **Gr. 2,** 109

Shepherd's Hey (listening), **Gr. 6,** 201

Tititorea (Maori Stick Game), **Gr. 3,** 174, WM 31

Tutira Mai Nga Iwi (listening), **Gr. K,** T17

`Ulili E (The Sandpiper), **Gr. 4,** 396

Canada

America, My Homeland, **Gr. 4,** 358

Assembly Required (listening), **Gr. 2,** 36

Baby Beluga, **Gr. 2,** 26

Big Beautiful Planet, **Gr. 2,** 376

Chumbara, **Gr. 4,** 172

Dragonfly (poem), **Gr. 1,** T44

En roulant ma boule (As I Roll My Ball), **Gr. 3,** 100

Evergreen, Everblue, **Gr. 3,** 330

Everything Grows, **Gr. 2,** 204

Going Over the Sea, **Gr. 2,** 216

Great Big Sea, A, **Gr. 5,** 334

Herring, The, **Gr. 3,** 316

I Know an Old Lady, **Gr. K,** T26

I's the B'y, **Gr. 3,** 13

J'entends le moulin (I Hear the Windmill), **Gr. 3,** 135

Jack Was Ev'ry Bit a Sailor, **Gr. 6,** 170

Just Like the Sun, **Gr. 3,** 394

Kettle Valley Line, The, **Gr. 4,** 348

La lluvia (listening), **Gr. 2,** 232

Land of the Silver Birch, **Gr. 2,** 88

Les saluts (listening), **Gr. 3,** 92

Lots o' Fish in Bonavist' Harbor, **Gr. 5,** 263

Lukey's Boat, **Gr. 3,** 114

Lumber Camp Song, The, **Gr. 6,** 136

Miniwanka (or The Moments of Water) (listening),
Gr. 4, 28

Monté sur un éléphant (Riding on an Elephant),
Gr. K, T217

Motorcycle Ride (listening), **Gr. 2,** 192

Mrs. Murphy's Chowder, **Gr. 3,** 390

Old Carrion Crow, **Gr. 4,** 192

Reel á bouche (French Canadian song) (listening),
Gr. 6, 56

There Was An Old Lady (story), **Gr. 3,** 344

When I First Came to This Land, **Gr. 3,** 28

Willoughby Wallaby Woo, **Gr. K,** T241

Caribbean

A la nanita nana (A Little Lullaby), **Gr. 4,** 230

Angelina, CM 13

Azouke Legba (listening), **Gr. 5,** 426

Banyan Tree, **Gr. 2,** 321

Borinquen (poem), **Gr. 5,** 443

Brinca la tablita (Hop, Hop!), **Gr. 1,** T71

Caribbean Amphibian, **Gr. 1,** T294

Day-O, CM 3; (listening), **Gr. 4,** 72

Duérmete mi niño (Go to Sleep, My Baby), **Gr. 1,**
T61

Dumplin's, **Gr. 2,** 172

El arroyo que murmura (The Murmuring Brook),
Gr. 3, 318

El coquí (The Frog), **Gr. 4,** 178

El florón (The Flower), **Gr. 1,** T117

El manisero (Peanut Vendor), **Gr. 4,** 106

El zapatero (The Cobbler), **Gr. 2,** 138

En la feria de San Juan (In the Market of San Juan),
Gr. 2, 226

Four White Horses, **Gr. 2,** 301

Hill an' Gully, **Gr. 5,** 250

Island in the Sun, CM 33

Jamaica Farewell, CM 17; (listening), **Gr. 4,** 73

Jamaican Rumba (listening), **Gr. 5,** 92

Jump in the Line (listening), **Gr. 7,** 199

Kingston Market, CM 9

La paloma se fue (The Dove That Flew Away),
Gr. 5, 259

Lead Man Holler, CM 21; **Gr. 7,** 148

Mango Walk, **Gr. 5,** 90; (with countermelody) (partner
songs), **Gr. 5,** 92

Mary Ann, **Gr. 5,** 166

Me Stone, **Gr. 2,** 48

Merecumbé, **Gr. 6,** 276

Ogguere (song and listening), **Gr. 4,** 327, 329

Plenty Fishes in the Sea, **Gr. 1,** T310

Qué bonita bandera (What a Beautiful Flag), **Gr. 5,** 442

River Come Down, CM 29; **Gr. 8,** 10

Shake the Papaya Down, **Gr. 2,** 90

Somos Boricuas (We Are Puerto Rican) (listening),
Gr. 2, 138

Steel Drums Jam (listening), **Gr. 2,** 90

Stevedore's Song, **Gr. 3,** 127

Tabu (listening), **Gr. 2,** 20

Three Little Birds, **Gr. 3,** 204; (listening) **Gr. 8,** 84

Tinga Layo, **Gr. 2,** 50

Tisket A Tasket, A, **Gr. 1,** T107

Turn the World Around, **Gr. 5,** 208

Water Come a Me Eye, **Gr. 4,** 90

Wind Blew East, The, **Gr. 1,** T234

Yellow Bird, CM 25

Central and South America (including Mexico)

A be ce (A B C), **Gr. 1,** T213

A la nanita nana, FC-Int 45

A la rueda de San Miguel (To the Wheel of San Miguel),
Gr. 2, 60

A la rueda rueda ('Round and 'Round), **Gr. 1,** T240

A Zing-A Za, **Gr. 5,** 338

Acitrón (Mexican stone-passing song) (listening),
Gr. 6, 93

¡Adivina lo que es! (Guess What It Is), **Gr. 1,** T170

Classified Index

Allá en el rancho grande (My Ranch), **Gr. 5,** 66

Animales (Animals), **Gr. K,** T192

Apple a Day, An (poem), **Gr. 1,** T152

Arroyito Serrano (song and listening), **Gr. 4,** 340, 341

Aserejé, FC-Int 62

¡Ay, Jalisco no te rajes! (Ay, Jalisco, Never Fail Her), **Gr. 5,** 188

Baila esta cumbia (Dance This Cumbia), FC-Int 49

Baile del pescadito (Dance of the Little Fish), FC-Pri 7

Bate, bate (Stir, Stir), **Gr. 2,** 242

Batucada Brasileira (listening), **Gr. 5,** 433

Batuque (listening), **Gr. 3,** 265; **Gr. 7,** 202

Batuque na cozinha (Samba kitchen band) (listening), **Gr. 2,** 307

Caballito blanco (Little White Pony), **Gr. 4,** 278

Caminito de la escuela (Little Road to School), FC-Pri 35

Canción de Amapola (Amapola's Song), FC-Pri 39

Canción de la cafetera (Song of the Coffeemaker), FC-Pri 54

Canción del pie (Foot Song), FC-Pri 73

Canta, Canta, Minha Gente (listening), **Gr. 8,** 45

Cantaré, cantarás (I Will Sing, You Will Sing), FC-Int 53

Caranguejo (The Crab), **Gr. 2,** 306

Carnavalito (listening), **Gr. 2,** 251

Casa de chocolate (House Made of Chocolate), FC-Int 15

Chango Guango (listening), **Gr. 2,** 60

Chiapanecas (Ladies of Chiapas), **Gr. 2,** 128

Chíu, chíu, chíu (Chirp, Chirp, Chirp), **Gr. 2,** 302; **Gr. 6,** 172

Cidade Maravilhosa (Wonderful City), **Gr. 5,** 432

Cielito Lindo, **Gr. 3,** 166

Colores de caracol (poem), **Gr. 5,** 101

Concert for Harp, Op. 25, Third Movement (excerpt) (listening), **Gr. 6,** 81

Conga, **Gr. 6,** 34

Counting Song, **Gr. 1,** T195

Cuando salí de Cuba (I Went Away from Cuba), **Gr. 5,** 168

Cumbia del sol (Cumbia of the Sun), **Gr. 5,** 16

¡Dale, dale, dale!, **Gr. 3,** 378

De allacito carnavalito (The Carnival Is Coming), **Gr. 5,** 269

De aquel cerro (On the Darkened Hillside), **Gr. 3,** 32

Di por qué (Answer Why), FC-Int 32

Diana (Play the Bugle), **Gr. 1,** T334

Duerme Negrito (listening), **Gr. 3,** 108

El atole (The Atole), **Gr. 3,** 396

El barquito (The Tiny Boat), **Gr. 4,** 214

El burrito enfermo (The Sick Little Donkey), **Gr. 2,** 180

El charro (The Cowboy), **Gr. 6,** 278

El chorrito (The Little Squirt of Water), FC-Pri 22

El colación (The Christmas Candies), **Gr. 1,** T357

El cóndor pasa (listening), **Gr. 7,** 69

El florón (The Flower), **Gr. 3,** 46

El jarabe (Mexican Hat Dance), **Gr. 5,** 396

El jarabe tapatío (listening), **Gr. 7,** 55, 58

El juego chirimbolo (The Chirimbolo Game), **Gr. 1,** T103

El nacimiento (The Nativity), **Gr. K,** T322

El nido (The Nest), **Gr. 3,** 214

El palomo y la paloma (The Doves), **Gr. 2,** 381

El picaflor (The Hummingbird), **Gr. K,** T141

El quelite (The Village), **Gr. 4,** 362

El rorro (The Babe), **Gr. 1,** T356

El tambor (The Drum), **Gr. K,** T129; **Gr. 6,** 222

El tecolote (The Owl), **Gr. 6,** 392; (listening), **Gr. 4,** 361

El tren (The Train), **Gr. 2,** 326

El vaquerito (The Little Cowboy) (excerpt) (listening), **Gr. 1,** T335

En la Pulga de San José (San Jose's Flea Market), FC-Pri 61

En nuestra Tierra tan linda (On Our Beautiful Planet Earth), **Gr. 2,** 114

Entren santos peregrinos (Enter, Holy Pilgrims), **Gr. 4,** 379

Ésta sí que es Nochebuena (This Is Christmas Eve), **Gr. 2,** 361

Este son (listening), **Gr. 6,** 393

Estrella brillante (Shining Star), **Gr. 5,** 373

Feliz Navidad (Merry Christmas), **Gr. 5,** 420

Festival Dance (listening), **Gr. 4,** 140

Fiesta en América, FC-Int 28

Flor de huevo (listening), **Gr. 3,** 359

Fotografía (Photograph), FC-Int 24

Guadalquivir (listening), **Gr. 3,** 30

Guantanamera, **Gr. 5,** 215

Hasta mañana (See You In the Morning), FC-Int 11

Hojas de té (Tea Leaves) (speech piece), **Gr. 4,** 256

Hoy tengo que decirte papá (Dad, I Have to Tell You Today), FC-Int 57

Huainito, **Gr. 6,** 351

Juan Pirulero, **Gr. 2,** 270; (listening), **Gr. 1,** T153

Juanito, FC-Pri 15

Jugaremos en el bosque (We'll Be Playing in the Forest), **Gr. 2,** 188

La bamba, **Gr. 3,** 236; **Gr. 6,** 381

La bella hortelana (The Beautiful Gardener), **Gr. 2,** 208

La carcacha (The Old Car), FC-Int 7

La cigarra (The Cicada), **Gr. 6,** 268

La cumparsita (listening), **Gr. 6,** 113

La Gallina Turuleca (The Turuleca Hen), FC-Pri 27

La mar (The Sea), **Gr. 3,** 110

La marcha de las letras (The Letters' Parade), FC-Pri 57

La pájara pinta (The Speckled Bird), **Gr. 6,** 268

La patita (The Little Lady Duck), FC-Pri 64

La pequeñita araña (Eency Weency Spider), **Gr. K,** T9

La ranita cri (The Little Frog Croaks), **Gr. 1,** T27

La raspa (listening), **Gr. 3,** 211

La risa de las vocales (The Vowels Laugh), FC-Pri 50

La sanjuanerita (The Girl from San Juan), **Gr. 4,** 100

La víbora de la mar (The Serpent from the Sea), **Gr. 5,** 440

La Yunsita, **Gr. 4,** 350

Las horas (The Hours), **Gr. K,** T70

Las mañanitas (The Morning Song), **Gr. 4,** 194; (listening), **Gr. 4,** 197

Let's Run Across the Hill (listening), **Gr. 5,** 268

Little Train of the Caipira, The, from *Bachianas Brasileiras No. 2* (listening), **Gr. K,** T142

Los cochinitos (The Three Little Pigs), FC-Pri 11

Los maizales (The Cornfields), **Gr. 5,** 268

Classified Index of Songs, Selected Concepts, Skills, and Activities (continued)

Los mariachis (listening), **Gr. 3,** 397; **Gr. 7,** 90

Los pollitos (Little Chickens), **Gr. K,** T288

Los trabajadores agricolas (The Farmers) from *Estancia* by A. Ginastera (listening), **Gr. 6,** 116

Macoklis Mango (listening), **Gr. 8,** 46

Mama eu quero (listening), **Gr. 2,** 92

Mama Paquita, **Gr. 2,** 92

Mamá, FC-Int 75

Mamacita, ¿Dónde Está Santa Claus? (Mom, Where is Santa Claus?), FC-Int 41

María Blanca, **Gr. K,** T99

Matarile, **Gr. 2,** 261

Medley Polleritas (listening), **Gr. 3,** 111

México lindo (Beautiful and Beloved Mexico), FC-Int 20

Mi caballo blanco (My White Horse), **Gr. 6,** 60

Mi chacra (My Farm), **Gr. K,** T207

Mi gallo (My Rooster), **Gr. 5,** 272

Mi tierra (My Homeland), FC-Int 36

Mil juguetes y un amigo (A Thousand Toys and a Friend), FC-Pri 68

Molinillo de café (Little Coffee Mill) (speech piece), **Gr. 4,** 250

Na Bahia Tem (In Bahia Town), **Gr. K,** T163; **Gr. 1,** T297

Naranja dulce (Sweet Orange), **Gr. 1,** T303

Navidad campesina (Country Christmas), FC-Pri 46

Nochebuena (Christmas Eve), **Gr. K,** T323

Oito Batutas (listening), **Gr. 4,** 128

One Note Samba (listening), **Gr. 4,** 92

Oye como va (song and listening), **Gr. 5,** 69

Pajarillo barranqueño (Little Bird), **Gr. 3,** 358

Pajaritos a volar (Dance Little Bird), FC-Pri 31

Panda Chant II (listening), **Gr. 6,** 263

Para dormir a un elefante (To Put an Elephant to Sleep), FC-Pri 19

Para pedir posada (Looking for Shelter), **Gr. 4,** 376

Patito color de café (Little Brown Duck), FC-Pri 43

Pezinho (listening), **Gr. 3,** 230

Pimpón, **Gr. K,** T22

Piñata Song (poem), **Gr. 1,** T153

Piñón, Pirulín, **Gr. 1,** T311

Que llueva (It's Raining), **Gr. 3,** 274

¿Quién es ese pajarito? (Who Is That Little Bird?), **Gr. 4,** 284

Raza de mil colores (Race of a Thousand Colors), FC-Int 3

Repicados sobre Madera (excerpt) (listening), **Gr. 4,** 93

Ride the Train, **Gr. K,** T144

Riqui Ran (Sawing Song), **Gr. 2,** 21

Samba de Orfeu (Dance of Orpheus), **Gr. 6,** 190

Sambalelê (listening), **Gr. 1,** T202

San Sereni, **Gr. 2,** 323

Santa Marta, **Gr. 5,** 398

Señor Coyote (story), **Gr. 2,** 330

Sensemayá (excerpt) (listening), **Gr. 3,** 161

Serra, Serra Serrador (Saw, Saw, Lumberjack), **Gr. 1,** T133

Sinfonía india (listening), **Gr. 2,** 61

Son de Camaguey (listening), **Gr. 8,** 51

Son de la negra, **Gr. 5,** 397

Sones de mariachi (listening), **Gr. 2,** 380

Soy así (This is the Way I Am), FC-Int 66

Susanita tiene un ratón (Suzy Has a Hamster), FC-Pri 3

Tengo, Tengo, Tengo (I Have, I Have, I Have), **Gr. K,** T212

Tim McCoy, FC-Int 79

Un lorito de Verapaz (A Parrot from Verapaz), **Gr. 5,** 349

Un, dos, tres, FC-Int 70

Una Adivinanza (A Riddle), **Gr. 1,** T138

Uno de enero (The First of January), **Gr. 3,** 210

Uno, dos y tres (One, Two, and Three), **Gr. 5,** 364

Vamos a contar (Let's Count), FC-Int 83

Vamos a jugar (Let's Play), FC-Pri 77

Vamos a la mar (Let's Go to the Sea), **Gr. 3,** 256

Why the Beetle Has a Gold Coat (folktale), **Gr. 1,** T321

Y ahora vamos a cantar (Now We Are Going to Sing), **Gr. K,** T340

Europe

1812 Overture, The (listening), **Gr. 7,** 72

A la puerta del cielo (At the Gate of Heaven), **Gr. 4,** 12

Ach, du lieber Augustin (The More We Get Together), **Gr. 2,** 35

Adagio from *Concierto de Aranjuez* (excerpt) (listening), **Gr. 4,** 13

Al Hebben de Princen haren (listening), **Gr. 4,** 225

Al lado de mi cabaña (Beside My Cottage), **Gr. 6,** 141

All Through the Night (song and listening), **Gr. 4,** 277

All Ye Who Music Love, **Gr. 6,** 336

Allegretto by X. Montsalvatge (listening), **Gr. 6,** 193

Alleluia, **Gr. 6,** 186

Alphabet Song, **Gr. K,** T54

Amazing Grace (song and listening), **Gr. 5,** 19, 21; (bagpipe version) (listening), **Gr. 7,** 144

Anitra's Dance from *Peer Gynt Suite No. 1* (listening), **Gr. 5,** 193

Anvil Chorus from *Il Trovatore* (listening), **Gr. 5,** 148

A-Rovin', **Gr. 6,** 319

Aserejé, FC-Int 62

Autumn Fires (poem), **Gr. 7,** 26

Autumn Leaves, **Gr. 1,** T331

Badinerie from Suite for Orchestra No. 2 in B Minor (listening), **Gr. 4,** 61; **Gr. 5,** 41

Ball, The, from *Children's Games* (listening), **Gr. K,** T133

Ballerina's Dance from *Petrushka* (excerpt) by I. Stravinsky (listening), **Gr. 6,** 161

Ballet Music from *Iphigénie en Aulide* (listening), **Gr. 2,** 25

Barber of Seville, The (Overture) by G. Rossini (arr. by The King's Singers) (listening), **Gr. 6,** 153

Barber of Seville, The (Overture) by G. Rossini (listening), **Gr. 6,** 152

Barbry Ellen, **Gr. 6,** 208

Barcarolle (Belle nuit) from *Tales of Hoffman* by J. Offenbach (listening), **Gr. 6,** 265

Bear Went Over the Mountain, The, **Gr. K,** T204

Bell Horses, **Gr. K,** T262

Bella bimba, **Gr. 3,** 172

Belle qui tiens ma vie (My Love, You Have My Heart) by T. Arbeau (song and listening), **Gr. 6,** 99, 100

Benevenuto Cellini (Overture) (excerpt) by H. Berlioz (listening), **Gr. 6,** 121

Berceuse by G. Keetman (listening), **Gr. 2,** 184

Beryoza (The Birch Tree), **Gr. 4,** 286

Big Turtle–Fanfare from *The South China Sea* (listening), **Gr. 4,** 201

Bingo, **Gr. K,** T64

Birth and Dance of the Mayfly, The, from *The Spider's Feast* (listening), **Gr. K,** T76

Boléro (excerpt) (listening), **Gr. 4,** 41

Bounce High, Bounce Low, **Gr. K,** T131

Bourrée from *Music for the Royal Fireworks* (listening), **Gr. 1,** T263

Bow-Wow (poem), **Gr. 1,** T81

Brafferton Village/Walsh's Hornpipe (listening), **Gr. 3,** 391

Brandenburg Concerto No. 5, Third Movement by J. S. Bach (listening), **Gr. 6,** 128

Bransle de Champaigne (listening), **Gr. 3,** 96

Brother, Come and Dance With Me from *Hansel and Gretel* (listening), **Gr. K,** T180

Bulgarian Folk Melody (listening), **Gr. 5,** 219

But the Critter Got Away (speech piece), **Gr. 1,** T88

By the Singing Water, **Gr. 5,** 270

Bydlo from *Pictures at an Exhibition* (listening), **Gr. 1,** T152

Canon in D (Pachelbel) (listening), **Gr. 4,** 17; **Gr. 8,** 67

Canon, **Gr. 6,** 256

Canon (Purcell) (listening), **Gr. 8,** 4

Carillon from *L'Arlésienne Suite No. 1* (listening), **Gr. 4,** 244; **Gr. 7,** 123

Carmen Fantasy for Violin and Piano (listening), **Gr. 5,** 200

Carnival of Venice, The, by J. B. Arban (listening), **Gr. 6,** 40

Carol from an Irish Cabin, **Gr. 6,** 408

Castle on a Cloud from Les Misérables, **Gr. 7,** 82

Categories, **Gr. 1,** T146

Chairs to Mend, **Gr. 4,** 272

Chamber Ensembles (montage) (listening), **Gr. 5,** 228

Charlie, **Gr. 3,** 208

Chicka-ma, Chicka-ma, Craney Crow, **Gr. 3,** 263

Chicken Dance, The (traditional) (listening), **Gr. 7,** 60

Child Falling Asleep from *Scenes from Childhood,* **Gr. 2,** 77

Children's Chorus from *Hansel and Gretel* (listening), **Gr. 4,** 280

Chinese Dance from *The Nutcracker Suite* (excerpt) (listening), **Gr. 2,** 354

Choo, Choo, Ch'Boogie, **Gr. 6,** 180

Chorus of Villagers from *The Bartered Bride* (listening and song), **Gr. 5,** 274, 275

Cliffs of Doneen, The, **Gr. 5,** 46

Clock at Night, A, (listening), **Gr. 3,** 66

Coasts of High Barbary, The, **Gr. 6,** 329

Come and Sing Together, **Gr. 6,** 281

Come Back, My Little Chicks, **Gr. 1,** T134

Concertino da Camera, First Movement (listening), **Gr. 7,** 161

Concertino for Trombone, Third Movement (Allegro giocoso) (listening), **Gr. 7,** 155

Concerto for Cello in C Major, Third Movement (listening), **Gr. 8,** 171

Concerto for Flute and Orchestra, Allegro (listening), **Gr. 2,** 120

Concerto for Harp, Op. 25, Third Movement (excerpt) by A. Ginastera (listening), **Gr. 6,** 81

Concerto for Harp, Op. 4, No. 6, First Movement (excerpt) by G. F. Handel (listening), **Gr. 6,** 81

Concerto for Orchestra, Second Movement (excerpt) (listening), **Gr. 6,** 41

Concerto for piano No. 1, in D Major, K. 107 (listening), **Gr. 8,** 179

Concerto for Piano No. 2, Third Movement (excerpt) (listening), **Gr. 2,** 41

Concerto for Piano, Violin, and Cello ("Triple Concerto"), Third Movement (excerpt) (listening), **Gr. 5,** 121

Concerto for Trombone ("Motorbike Concerto"), Fifth Movement (listening), **Gr. 2,** 193

Concerto for Two Trumpets (listening), **Gr. 2,** 73

Concerto for Violin and Oboe, Adagio (excerpt) (listening), **Gr. 2,** 127

Concerto Grosso No. 9 in F Major, Gavotta (listening), **Gr. 1,** T175

Concerto Grosso, Op. 6, No. 11, First Movement by G. F. Handel (listening), **Gr. 6,** 247

Concerto in B Minor, Second Movement (listening), **Gr. 3,** 120

Concerto in C Minor, Adagio (listening), **Gr. 5,** 120

Concerto No. 2 for Double Bass, First Movement (excerpt) (listening), **Gr. 5,** 161

Concerto No. 3 in B-Flat, Allegro moderato (listening), **Gr. 5,** 40

Concierto de Aranjuez, First Movement (excerpt) (listening), **Gr. 3,** 41

Consider Yourself from *Oliver!* (listening and song), **Gr. 3,** 334, 335

Contredanse from *Les Indes galantes* (excerpt) (listening), **Gr. 4,** 97

Cortège by L. Boulanger (listening), **Gr. 6,** 253

Counting Song, **Gr. K,** T92

Courante from *Terpsichore* (listening), **Gr. 8,** 130

Cow, The (poem), **Gr. 1,** T236

Crazy Songs (traditional Czech song) (listening), **Gr. 6,** 65

Csárdás from *Ritter Pásmán* (listening), **Gr. K,** T28

Cuckoo in the Heart of the Woods from *The Carnival of the Animals* (listening), **Gr. 2,** 253

Da pacem Domine (Give Us Peace), **Gr. 5,** 261

Dance from *Ballet Suite No. 1* (listening), **Gr. K,** T167

Dance No. 2 from *Six Dances in Bulgarian Rhythm* from Mikrokosmos (listening), **Gr. 5,** 221

Dance of the Mirlitons from *The Nutcracker Suite* (listening), **Gr. 4,** 173

Dance of the Sugar Plum Fairy from *The Nutcracker Suite* (excerpt) (listening), **Gr. 2,** 354

Dance Preludes for Clarinet and Piano, No. 3 (listening), **Gr. 2,** 161

Danse Macabre (excerpt) (listening), **Gr. 3,** 363

Dance Profane (listening), **Gr. 3,** 200

Das Wandern from *Die schöne Müllerin* by F. Schubert (listening), **Gr. 6,** 251

De colores (Many Colors) (unison and 2-part), **Gr. 5,** 88, 98

Deck the Hall, **Gr. 3,** 374

Derby Ram, The, **Gr. 4,** 259
Derry Ding Dong Dason, **Gr. 6,** 249
Ding Dong Diggy Diggy Dong, **Gr. 3,** 269
Djurdjevka kolo (Yugoslavian folk song) (listening),
   Gr. 6, 105
Doing the Weekly Walk, **Gr. K,** T78
Doll Song, The, from *Tales of Hoffman* (listening),
   Gr. K, T178
Donkey, Donkey, **Gr. 2,** 256
Do-Re-Mi, **Gr. 2,** C
Down in the Belgorod (listening), **Gr. 8,** 153
Earth Folk (poem), **Gr. 7,** 174
Echo (poem), **Gr. K,** T104
Echo Song (listening), **Gr. K,** T103
Egy üveg alma (One Jar of Apples), **Gr. 3,** 22
Eine kleine Nachtmusik (Serenade No. 13 in G, K. 525),
   Romance (Andante) (listening), **Gr. K,** T176
Eine kleine Nachtmusik, Minuet (listening), **Gr. 3,** 168
Ēinīnī, **Gr. 5,** 340
El vito, **Gr. 5,** 210
Elephant, The, from *The Carnival of the Animals*
   (listening), **Gr. 1,** T204
Entrada from *The Indian Queen* (listening), **Gr. 7,** 113
Étude in C Sharp Minor (listening), **Gr. 5,** 80
Étude Op. 25 No. 11, "The Winter Wind" (listening),
   Gr. 2, 136
Excuse Us, Animals in the Zoo (poem), **Gr. K,** T195
Exsultate, jubilate, Third Movement by W.A. Mozart
   (listening), **Gr. 6,** 187
Faeries and Giants from *Wand of Youth Suite No. 1*
   (listening), **Gr. K,** T52
Fall (Allegro) from *The Four Seasons* (listening),
   Gr. K, T305
Farfallina (Butterfly), **Gr. 4,** 244
Farm, The, from *Children's Symphony* (listening),
   Gr. 2, 211
Farmer in the Dell, The, **Gr. K,** T100
Fehér liliomszál (Little Water Lily), **Gr. K,** T139
Finale from *The Carnival of the Animals* (listening),
   Gr. K, T195
Finis (poem), **Gr. 2,** 76
Finlandia (listening), **Gr. 5,** 257
First Suite in E Flat for Military Band (listening),
   Gr. 8, 51
Flight of the Bumblebee, The (listening), **Gr. K,** T258;
   Gr. 2, 40
Flute and Drum from *Gunild Keetman Collection*
   (listening), **Gr. 1,** T235
Follow Me, **Gr. K,** T133
Follow the Leader (poem), **Gr. K,** T132
Food, Glorious Food from *Oliver!* (listening),
   Gr. 2, 310
Fortune Favors the Brave, **Gr. 6,** 316
Fountain Dance from *Wand of Youth Suite No. 2*
   (listening), **Gr. 1,** T233
Frère Jacques (Are You Sleeping?), **Gr. 4,** 260
From Bohemia's Forests and Meadows from *Má Vlast*
   (listening), **Gr. 6,** 229
Funeral March of a Marionette (excerpt) (listening),
   Gr. 1, T337
Funiculi, Funicula, **Gr. 5,** 62

Galop from *Masquerade Suite* (listening), **Gr. 1,** T259
Galop from *The Comedians* (excerpt) (listening),
   Gr. 4, 254
Galop from *Suite No. 2 for Small Orchestra* (listening),
   Gr. 7, 126
Galop of Sancho's Donkey from *Don Quixote* (listening),
   Gr. 3, 271
Gardens in the Rain from *Estampes* (listening),
   Gr. K, T337
Gavotte from Suite No. 5 for Cello (listening),
   Gr. 2, 41
Gigue from *Suite for Orchestra No. 3* (listening),
   Gr. 2, 269
Gigue from Suite No. 1 for Cello (listening),
   Gr. 3, 178
Gi'Me Elbow Room, **Gr. 3,** 88
Girls and Boys, Come Out to Play (poem), **Gr. K,** T98
Goin' Home, **Gr. 5,** 108
Gold Ring, The (listening), **Gr. 3,** 160
Gonna Build a Mountain from *Stop the World—I Want to*
   Get Off (song and listening), **Gr. 6,** 4, 5
Good Day Song, **Gr. K,** T50
Grasshopper's Wedding (listening), **Gr. 1,** T245
Greenland Whale Fishery, **Gr. 6,** 212
Hairy Dog, The (poem), **Gr. 2,** 58
Hakuna Matata, **Gr. 2,** 292
Hallelujah Chorus from *Messiah* (listening), **Gr. 5,** 419;
   Gr. 7, 110
Halloween (poem), **Gr. 1,** T338
Happiness (listening), **Gr. 1,** T254
Happy Farmer, The from *Album for the Young* (listening),
   Gr. K, T209
Happy Wanderer, The, **Gr. 3,** 18
Haydn Montage (listening), **Gr. 8,** 123
Head and Shoulders, **Gr. K,** T238
Hello Song, **Gr. K,** T2
Hen wlad fy nhadau (The Land of My Fathers)
   (listening), **Gr. 2,** 141
Her kommer vennen min (listening), **Gr. 3,** 142
Here Is the Beehive, **Gr. K,** T258
Here We Come A-Wassailing, **Gr. 1,** T355
Hickory, Dickory, Dock (poem), **Gr. K,** T49
Himmel und Erde (Music Alone Shall Live), **Gr. 4,** 280
Holiday for Strings (listening), **Gr. 3,** 229
Holly and the Ivy, The, **Gr. 5,** 418
Hopping Frog (poem), **Gr. 1,** T113
Hornpipe from *Water Music Suite* (excerpt) (listening),
   Gr. 3, 26
Horses of the Sea, The (poem), **Gr. 1,** T179
Hot Cross Buns, **Gr. 2,** 258
Hullaballoo Balay, **Gr. 6,** 10
Humming Chorus from *Madama Butterfly* by G. Puccini
   (listening), **Gr. 6,** 257
Hunt the Cows, **Gr. 1,** T236
Hunt the Squirrel from *Suite on English Folk Tunes*
   (listening), **Gr. 1,** T136
I Am a Little Tugboat (poem), **Gr. K,** T95
I Had a Little Hen (nursery rhyme), **Gr. 1,** T136
I Know Not Why (poem), **Gr. 8,** 179
I Saw Three Ships, **Gr. 2,** 359
I've a Pair of Fishes, **Gr. 1,** T124

Classified Index

I Wandered Lonely as a Cloud (poem), **Gr. 8,** 18
If All the World Were Paper, **Gr. 1,** T296
If You're Happy, **Gr. K,** T6
Im Krapfenwaldl (In Krapfen Woods) (listening),
 Gr. 2, 244
In the Hall of the Mountain King from *Peer Gynt Suite
 No. 1* (listening), **Gr. 2,** 346
Infernal Dance of King Kashchei from *The Firebird Suite*
 (listening), **Gr. 4,** 191
Instrument Game, **Gr. K,** T36
Introduction and excerpt from *Peter and the Wolf*
 (listening), **Gr. 1,** T140
Introduction from *The Rite of Spring* by I. Stravinsky
 (listening), **Gr. 6,** 423
Isabela and the Troll (story), **Gr. 3,** 349
It's So Good to See You, **Gr. K,** T86
Já do lesa nepojedu (To the Woods I Will Not Go),
 Gr. 6, 227
Ja posejah lubenice (I Planted Watermelons),
 Gr. 2, 316
Jack, Be Nimble, **Gr. K,** T88
Jack-in-the-Box, **Gr. K,** T250; (poem), **Gr. K,** T251
Jack-o'-Lantern, **Gr. K,** T307
Jede, jede poštovský panáček (Riding, Riding, Is
 Mr. Postman), **Gr. 6,** 226
Jesu, Joy of Man's Desiring (listening), **Gr. 3,** 41
Jig Jog, Jig Jog, **Gr. K,** T260
Joyful, Joyful, We Adore Thee, **Gr. 5,** 103
Jupiter, the Bringer of Jollity (listening), **Gr. 8,** 40
Just Like Me, **Gr. K,** T242
Kalinka (Little Snowball Bush), **Gr. 3,** T224
Kangaroos from *The Carnival of the Animals* (listening),
 Gr. K, T196
Katyusha, **Gr. 4,** 188
King Stephen (Overture) (listening), **Gr. 5,** 255
Korobushka, **Gr. 4,** 285, WM 47
Kurski Funk (listening), **Gr. 8,** 153
La bamba, **Gr. 6,** 381
La canarie from *Dances from Terpsichore* (listening),
 Gr. 4, 176
La choisy by M. Corrette (listening), **Gr. 2,** 177
La cloche (The Clock), **Gr. 3,** 67
Laideronette, Empress of the Pagodas from *Mother
 Goose Suite* (listening), **Gr. 1,** T237
Larenjeiras (listening) from *Saudades do Brasil*
 (listening), **Gr. K,** T55
Largo al factotum from *The Barber of Seville* (listening),
 Gr. 2, 217
Lavender's Blue, **Gr. 1,** T174
Leggiero (Hopscotch) from *Music for Children* (listening),
 Gr. 5, 281
Les Anges dans nos Campagnes (Angels We Have Heard
 on High), **Gr. 6,** 406
Lift Up Your Voices, **Gr. 5,** 319
L'inverno è già passato (Winter is Over), **Gr. 4,** 390
Little Boy of the Sheep, **Gr. 3,** 188
Little Robin Redbreast, **Gr. 1,** T208
Little Sir Echo, **Gr. K,** T103
Little White Donkey, The (listening), **Gr. K,** T244
Loch Lomond, **Gr. 5,** 138
London Bridge, **Gr. K,** T99

Long Gone (poem), **Gr. K,** T72
Looby Loo, **Gr. 1,** T262
Lullaby of Broadway, **Gr. 6,** 182
Luncheon of the Boating Party (painting), **Gr. 7,** 121
Macnamara's Band, **Gr. 4,** 88
Maggie in the Wood (listening), **Gr. 5,** 49
Magic Flute, The (Overture) (listening), **Gr. 4,** 252
Mama Will Provide, **Gr. 6,** 296
March for Military Band, Op. 99 (listening), **Gr. 8,** 37
March from *Children's Games* (listening), **Gr. 1,** T31
March from *Love for Three Oranges* (excerpt) (listening),
 Gr. 3, 201
March from *The Nutcracker Suite* (excerpt) (listening),
 Gr. 2, 354
March Past of the Kitchen Utensils from *The Wasps*
 (listening), **Gr. 3,** 247
Marche (listening), **Gr. 8,** 167
Marken er mejet (Out in the Meadow), **Gr. 4,** 365
Mars from *The Planets* by G. Holst (listening),
 Gr. 6, 196
May Day Carol, **Gr. 3,** 393
Me I Am! (poem), **Gr. K,** T346
Mein Hut (My Hat), **Gr. 2,** 142
Mele Kalikimaka (Merry Christmas), **Gr. 6,** 410
Merrily, We Roll Along, **Gr. K,** T110
Merry-Go-Round from *Children's Games* (listening),
 Gr. 2, 266
Mi-a-ou from *Dolly Suite* (listening), **Gr. K,** T146
Minuet from *Abdelazar* (listening), **Gr. 1,** T175;
 Gr. 2, 145
Mister Sun, **Gr. K,** T343
Modern Major General, A, from *The Pirates of Penzance,*
 by W. S. Gilbert and A. Sullivan (listening), **Gr. 6,** 56
Moldau, The, from *Má Vlast (My Country)* (excerpt)
 (listening), **Gr. 5,** 271; **Gr. 7,** 219
Morceau de concert, First Movement (listening),
 Gr. 8, 59
Morning Has Broken, **Gr. 4,** 22; (listening), **Gr. 4,** 23
Morning Mood from *Peer Gynt Suite No. 1,* Op. 46
 by E. Grieg, **Gr. 3,** 251
Moulinet (listening), **Gr. 2,** 57
Mouse, Mousie, **Gr. 2,** 254
Muffin Man, The, **Gr. K,** T105
Mulberry Bush, The, **Gr. K,** T112
Musette from *Notebook for Anna Magdalena Bach*
 (listening), **Gr. 4,** 261
Music for Strings, Percussion, and Celesta (excerpt)
 (listening), **Gr. 5,** 201
My Oak Tree, **Gr. K,** T236
Name Game, **Gr. K,** T57
Naughty Kitty Cat, **Gr. 1,** T171
Nead na lachan sa mhúta (listening), **Gr. 5,** 48
Nessun dorma (No One Sleeps) from *Turandot*
 (listening), **Gr. 5,** 64
Neviděli jste tu mé panenky? (Have You Not Seen My
 Dear Daughters?), **Gr. 6,** 228
Night Song, **Gr. 3,** 186
Nightingale, The, by F. Liszt (listening), **Gr. 6,** 160
No despiertes a mi niño (Do Not Wake My Little Son),
 Gr. 5, 217
Noble Duke of York, The, **Gr. K,** T232

Classified Index

Nokken Danser (listening), **Gr. 4,** 168

Norwegian Dance (listening), **Gr. 3,** 145

Nottamun Town, **Gr. 5,** 405

O Tannenbaum! (O Christmas Tree!), **Gr. K,** T320

O Wind (poem), **Gr. 1,** T235

Och Jungfrun Hon Går I Ringen (A Girl with a Shiny Ribbon) (song and listening), **Gr. 5,** 190, 191

Octopus's Garden, **Gr. 4,** 30

Ode to Joy (poem), **Gr. 7,** 187

Oh, A-Hunting We Will Go, **Gr. K,** T62

Oh, How Lovely Is the Evening, **Gr. 6,** 252

Old Abram Brown, **Gr. 4,** 32

Old Aunt Dinah, **Gr. 4,** 245

Old Mister Woodpecker, **Gr. K,** T172

Old Mother Goose (poem), **Gr. 1,** T181

Old Roger, **Gr. 3,** 280

Oleanna, **Gr. 3,** 144

Oliphaunt (poem), **Gr. K,** T216

Oliver Cromwell, **Gr. 4,** 269

Only My Opinion (poem), **Gr. K,** T29

Only Time (listening), **Gr. 7,** 142

Oranges and Lemons (poem), **Gr. 1,** T150

Orchestra Song, **Gr. 5,** 332

Oro My Bodeen, **Gr. 4,** 279

Over the Sea to Skye, **Gr. 4,** 344

Overture from *La forza del destino* (listening), **Gr. 3,** 201

Overture from *The Nutcracker Suite* (excerpt) (listening), **Gr. 2,** 354

Pairs or Pears, **Gr. 2,** 265

Pantomime from *The Comedians* (listening), **Gr. 1,** T256

Papagena! Papagena! Papagena! from *The Magic Flute* (listening), **Gr. 2,** 152

Parade from *Divertissement* from *Un Chapeau de paille d'Italic* (listening), **Gr. K,** T183

Parade from *Un Chapeau de paille d'Italie* (listening), **Gr. K,** T183

Parade in the Parlor (listening), **Gr. 4,** 229

Partita No. 2 in D Minor (listening), **Gr. 8,** 95

Pat-a-Pan, **Gr. 3,** 375

Pease Porridge Hot, **Gr. 1,** T255

Peter and the Wolf (excerpt) (listening), **Gr. 2,** 160

Peter Cottontail, **Gr. K,** T338

Playful Pizzicato from *Simple Symphony* (listening), **Gr. 3,** 263

Polegnala e Todora (listening), **Gr. K,** T163

Polovtsian Dances from *Prince Igor* (excerpt) (listening), **Gr. 3,** 81

Pomp and Circumstance March No. 1, Trio (listening), **Gr. 7,** 50

Pop! Goes the Weasel (song and listening), **Gr. 5,** 94

Porushka-Paranya (listening), **Gr. 4,** 208

Poun to, Poun to (listening), **Gr. 2,** 175

Prelude to Act II from *Siegfried* (listening), **Gr. 2,** 54

Prince of Denmark's March (listening), **Gr. 2,** 81

Pulcinella Suite (excerpt) (listening), **Gr. 4,** 201

Quintet for Piano and Strings in A Major ("Trout"), Op. 114, Second Movement by F. Schubert (listening), **Gr. 6,** 344; (excerpt), **Gr. 8,** 189

Quintet, Op. 43, Menuet (excerpt) (listening), **Gr. 4,** 121

Rabbit, The (poem), **Gr. 1,** T186

Radetsky March (listening), **Gr. K,** T177

Rain Is Falling Down, **Gr. 3,** 242

Rainbow Song, The, **Gr. K,** T61

Requiebros by G. Cassado (listening), **Gr. 6,** 80

Rig a Jig Jig, **Gr. 1,** T116

Ring Around the Rosy, **Gr. K,** T246; (poem), **Gr. K,** T247

Rite of Spring, The, (excerpt) (listening), **Gr. 2,** 201

Ritter Pazman: Csardas (listening), **Gr. K,** T28

Romantic Period Music (montage) (listening), **Gr. 8,** 119

Rondeau from *Abdelazar* by H. Purcell (listening), **Gr. 6,** 121

Rondo a capriccio ("Rage over a Lost Penny") (excerpt) (listening), **Gr. 2,** 225

Rondo "alla turea" from Piano Sonata No. 11 in A Major, Third Movement (listening), **Gr. 7,** 116

Rondo all 'Ongarese (Trio for Piano, Violin, and Cello No. 39, Finale) (listening), **Gr. 7,** 115

'Round the Corner, Sally, **Gr. 5,** 251

Rover, **Gr. 2,** 260

Royal March of the Lions, The, from *The Carnival of the Animals* (listening), **Gr. 1,** T25

Russian Sailor's Dance from *The Red Poppy* (listening), **Gr. 4,** 266

Såg du nøko (listening), **Gr. 2,** 104

Samiotissa, **Gr. 5,** 284

Sankta Lucia (Saint Lucia), **Gr. 5,** 412

Sarasponda, **Gr. 4,** 210

Scheherazade (excerpt) (listening), **Gr. 4,** 161

Scherzo and Tarantella (listening), **Gr. 2,** 160

School Is Over (poem), **Gr. K,** T84

Schwanenlied (listening), **Gr. 7,** 124

Scotland's Burning, **Gr. 3,** 257

See the Rabbit Running, **Gr. 3,** 255

Seesaw, Margery Daw, **Gr. K,** T265

Sellinger's Round (English Renaissance dance) (listening), **Gr. 6,** 98

Sérénade (listening), **Gr. 2,** 262

Serenade No. 10 in B Flat Major ("Gran Partita"), Theme and Variations (excerpt) (listening), **Gr. 4,** 235

Seventeen Come Sunday from English Folk Song Suite (listening), **Gr. 7,** 102

Sheep Shearing, **Gr. 2,** 102

Shimmering Air (listening), **Gr. K,** T138

Ship in Distress, The, **Gr. 6,** 211

Shoheen Sho, **Gr. 2,** 140

Shoo Fly Pie and Apple Pan Dowdy, **Gr. 3,** 227

Shope, Shope (Oh, Shope, Shope), **Gr. 5,** 220

Sidewalks (poem), **Gr. K,** T98

Sigh of the Soul for Alyscamp from *Tableaux de Provence* (listening), **Gr. 3,** 80

Sing a Song of Sixpence, **Gr. K,** T111

Sing Ho! For the Life of a Bear! (poem), **Gr. 1,** T114

Singing-Time (poem), **Gr. K,** T15

Skaters' Waltz, The (excerpt) (listening), **Gr. 1,** T345

Slap That Bass, **Gr. 6,** 146

Sleep, Bonnie Bairnie, **Gr. 1,** T27

Classified Index of Songs, Selected Concepts, Skills, and Activities (continued)

Snail's Pace (poem), **Gr. K,** T29

Solveig's Song from *Peer Gynt Suite No. 2* (listening), **Gr. 5,** 192

Sonata for Cello and Piano, Op. 40, Second Movement (listening), **Gr. 4,** 40

Sonata for Flute and Piano, Third Movement (listening), **Gr. 4,** 200

Sonata for Piano and Bassoon, First Movement (listening), **Gr. 8,** 19

Sonata for Piano No. 2 in D Minor, Vivace (excerpt) (listening), **Gr. 4,** 181

Sonata for Piano No. 48 in C, First Movement (listening), **Gr. 8,** 122

Sonata for Violin No. 4, First Movement (listening), **Gr. 8,** 156

Sonata in C Major, Longo 104 (listening), **Gr. K,** T89

Sonatina for Three Timpani and Piano, First Movement (excerpt) (listening), **Gr. 4,** 81

Sonatine for Brass Quintet, First Movement (excerpt) (listening), **Gr. 3,** 121

Song of Peace, **Gr. 5,** 257; (painting), **Gr. 7,** 155

Sorcerer's Apprentice, The (excerpt) (listening), **Gr. 4,** 116

Sound the Trumpet from *I Puritani,* **Gr. 5,** 279; (listening), **Gr. 5,** 279

Spell of the Moon (poem), **Gr. K,** T116

Spinning Song (listening), **Gr. 3,** 128

Spinning Wheel (listening), **Gr. 4,** 211

Spring (Allegro) from *The Four Seasons* (listening), **Gr. 4,** 391; **Gr. 7,** 112

St. Patrick's Day (listening), **Gr. 2,** 374; **Gr. 5,** 434

Stamping Land, **Gr. K,** T24

Step into the Spotlight, **Gr. 2,** A

String Quartet in D Minor (Haydn) (excerpt) (listening), **Gr. 2,** 121

String Quartet No. 2 (Bartók) (excerpt) (listening), **Gr. 2,** 121

String Quartet No. 2 in D Minor, Andante (excerpt) (listening), **Gr. 1,** T129

String Quartet No. 3, Fourth Movement ("The Bird") (listening), **Gr. 1,** T251

Summer (Allegro non molto) from *The Four Seasons* (excerpt) (listening), **Gr. 4,** 161

Suomen Salossa (The Finnish Forest), **Gr. 6,** 422

Susanita tiene un ratón (Suzy Has a Hamster), FC-Pri 3

Sweet and Low, **Gr. 6,** 184

Sweet Music, **Gr. 5,** 319

Sweetly Sings the Donkey, **Gr. K,** T244

Symphonic Dances, Op. 64 No. 4 (excerpt) (listening), **Gr. 2,** 105

Symphony No. 1 ("Titan"), Third Movement (excerpt) (listening), **Gr. 5,** 161

Symphony No. 1 in D Major ("Classical"), Third Movement (Gavotte) (listening), **Gr. 1,** T92

Symphony No. 4, First Movement (excerpt) and Second Movement (excerpt) by P. Tchaikovsky (listening), **Gr. 6,** 41

Symphony No. 4, Fourth Movement by P. Tchaikovsky (listening), **Gr. 4,** 287

Symphony No. 5, First Movement (excerpt) by D. Shostakovich (listening), **Gr. 6,** 161

Symphony No. 5, in C Minor, Third and Fourth Movements (listening), **Gr. 8,** 115

Symphony No. 5, Second Movement by P. Tchaikovsky (excerpt) (listening), **Gr. 5,** 81

Symphony No. 6, ("Pastoral") (listening), **Gr. 8,** 20

Symphony No. 6 ("Pathetique"), Second Movement (listening), **Gr. 5,** 281

Symphony No. 7 in A Major, Second Movement by L. van Beethoven (excerpt) (listening), **Gr. 4,** 242; **Gr. 7,** 118

Symphony No. 8, Second Movement (excerpt) (listening) by L. van Beethoven, **Gr. K,** T234

Symphony No. 9, Fourth Movement (excerpt) (listening), **Gr. 7,** 156

Symphony No. 9 in D Minor ("Choral") Fourth Movement by L. van Beethoven (excerpt) (listening), **Gr. 5,** 102

Symphony No. 9 in E Minor ("From the New World"), Largo by A. Dvořák (excerpt) (listening), **Gr. 3,** 81; **Gr. 5,** 106

Symphony No. 35, Fourth Movement by J. Haydn (excerpt) (listening), **Gr. 5,** 247

Symphony No. 40, in G Minor, K. 550, First Movement (listening), **Gr. 8,** 218

Symphony No. 45 ("Farewell"), First Movement (listening), **Gr. 8,** 124

Symphony No. 73 ("La Chasse") ("The Hunt"), Fourth Movement by J. Haydn (listening), **Gr. 4,** 263

Symphony No. 101, in D Major, ("Clock") (listening), **Gr. 8,** 128

Symphony: Water Music, Movements 3 and 4 (listening), **Gr. 8,** 155

Tak for Maden (Thanks for Food), **Gr. 1,** T343

Tame Bear from *Wand of Youth Suite No. 2* (listening), **Gr. K,** T203

Ten Little Frogs, **Gr. K,** T240

Thank You, **Gr. 2,** 349

Theme and Percussion Variation from *Young Person's Guide to the Orchestra* (listening), **Gr. 5,** 229

They Were Tall, **Gr. K,** T53

This Is My City, **Gr. K,** T120

This Is What I Can Do, **Gr. K,** T124

This Old Man, **Gr. 1,** T306

Three Little Kittens, **Gr. K,** T148

Three Little Muffins (speech piece), **Gr. K,** T127

Till Eulenspiegel's Merry Pranks (listening), **Gr. 5,** 81

Tinker, Tailor, **Gr. 1,** T130

To a Friend Who Sent Me Some Roses (poem), **Gr. 8,** 115

Toccata and Fugue in D Minor (listening), **Gr. 7,** 108

Too-ra-loo-ra-loo-ral (listening), **Gr. K,** T335

Town Hall Halloween Ball, **Gr. K,** T306

Tragic Story, A, (listening), **Gr. 4,** 190

Tree of Peace (speech piece), **Gr. K,** T321

Trepak from *The Nutcracker* by P. Tchaikovsky (listening), **Gr. 6,** 408

Trio for Piano, Violin and Cello, Finale ("Gypsy Rondo") (listening), **Gr. 3,** 155

Trio for Piano, Violin, and Cello, Third Movement (listening), **Gr. 5,** 121

Classified Index of Songs, Selected Concepts, Skills, and Activities (continued)

Troika from *Lieutenant Kijé Suite* (excerpt) (listening),
Gr. 3, 225
Troika, **Gr. 6,** 230
Trumpet and Drum from *Children's Games* (listening),
Gr. 1, T231
Tug of War from *Outdoor Games* (listening), **Gr. K,** T339
Tugboat, **Gr. K,** T95
Tuileries from *Pictures at an Exhibition* (listening),
Gr. 1, T249
Tulloch Castle/Flowers of Red Hill (traditional Celtic
songs) (listening), **Gr. 6,** 200
Tum Balalaika, **Gr. 6,** 68
Turandot from *Symphonic Metamorphosis on Themes of
Carl Maria von Weber* (excerpt) (listening), **Gr. 4,** 81
Twee emmertjes (listening), **Gr. 4,** 212
Twinkle, Twinkle, Little Star, **Gr. K,** T90
Two in a Boat (listening), **Gr. 3,** 316
Two, Four, Six, Eight, **Gr. 1,** T246
Tzakonikos (Greek circle dance) (listening), **Gr. 6,** 215
Una donna a quindici anni from *Così fan tutte*
(listening), **Gr. 8,** 187
Vagabond, The (listening), **Gr. 7,** 78
Va Pensiero from *Nabucco* by G. Verdi (listening),
Gr. 6, 169
Vem Kan Segla (Who Can Sail?), **Gr. 6,** 419
Violin Concerto, First Movement (listening), **Gr. 7,** 52
Vivo from Pulcinella Suite (listening), **Gr. 4,** 201
Vocal Expressions (montage) (listening), **Gr. 5,** 165
Volta from *Dances from Terpsichore* (listening), **Gr. 3,** 121
Wachet auf (Waken Now), **Gr. 6,** 259
Wagon Passes, The, from *Nursery Suite* (listening),
Gr. 1, T243
Wait and See, **Gr. K,** T334
Waiting for Life, **Gr. 6,** 292
Walk by the River, **Gr. 6,** 74, 76
Walking in the Air (song and listening), **Gr. 4,** 317, 319
Waltz in A Major, Op. 54, No. 1 (listening), **Gr. K,** T109
Waltz of the Flowers from *The Nutcracker Suite* (excerpt)
(listening), **Gr. 1,** T353; **Gr. 2,** 354
Waltz of the Snowflakes from *The Nutcracker Suite*
(listening), **Gr. K,** T311
Water Is Wide, The, **Gr. 6,** 46
We Wish You a Merry Christmas, **Gr. 2,** 358
Wee Falorie Man, The, **Gr. 2,** 375
When I Was Young, **Gr. 4,** 187
Where Is John?, **Gr. 5,** 274
Who Has Seen the Wind? (poem), **Gr. 2,** 137
Whup! Jamboree (listening), **Gr. 6,** 318
Why We Tell the Story, **Gr. 6,** 303
Wie schön leuchtet der Morgenstern (How Brightly
Shines the Morning Star) (listening), **Gr. 5,** 371
William Tell (Overture) (excerpt) (listening), **Gr. 3,** 64
Wind Blow, **Gr. 1,** T187
Winter (Allegro non molto) from *The Four Seasons*
(Concerto No. 4 in F Minor) by A. Vivaldi (listening),
Gr. 6, 403
Winter Ade, **Gr. 6,** 132, 133
Wondering, **Gr. 6,** 282
Worms, **Gr. K,** T286
Yellow Submarine, **Gr. 3,** 320

Yerakina, **Gr. 6,** 216
Young Person's Guide to the Orchestra (excerpt)
(listening), **Gr. 2,** 229

European American

76 Trombones, **Gr. 5,** 296
Acka Backa, **Gr. 1,** T256
Addams Family Theme, The, **Gr. 3,** 307; **Gr. 8,** 142
Alison's Camel, **Gr. K,** T201
All Around the Buttercup, **Gr. 2,** 210
All Work Together, **Gr. K,** T12
Alley-Oop (listening), **Gr. 8,** 64
Amazing Grace, (song and listening), **Gr. 5,** 19, 21
America, **Gr. K,** T303; **Gr. 1,** T326; **Gr. 2,** 338;
Gr. 4, 354; **Gr. 6,** 388; (listening), **Gr. 8,** 31
America, the Beautiful, **Gr. 3,** 354; **Gr. 5,** 388
American Salute (listening), **Gr. 5,** 36; **Gr. 7,** 170
Animal Fair, **Gr. 2,** 214
Animal Song, **Gr. 1,** T288
Another Busy Day, **Gr. 1,** T41
Antarctica (listening), **Gr. 2,** 110
Ants Go Marching, The, **Gr. 1,** T22
Anything Goes (listening), **Gr. 8,** 186
Appalachian Spring (listening), **Gr. 2,** 378
Apple Picker's Reel, **Gr. 2,** 343
Apples and Bananas, **Gr. 1,** T151
Arianna (listening), **Gr. 7,** 94
A-Rovin', **Gr. 6,** 319
Artichokes, **Gr. 2,** 314
Atlantic City from *Ragtime*, **Gr. 7,** 248
Augie's Great Municipal Band from *Star Wars Episode 1:
The Phantom Menace* (excerpt) (listening), **Gr. 4,** 56
Autumn Leaves Are Falling, **Gr. 1,** T330
Autumn Music, First Movement (excerpt) (listening),
Gr. 4, 121
Away for Rio, **Gr. 2,** 170
Babylon's Fallin', **Gr. 5,** 243
Ballad of the Bedbugs and the Beetles, The, **Gr. 3,** 206
Ballet of the Unhatched Chicks from *Pictures at an
Exhibition* (listening), **Gr. 3,** 76
Band (listening), 1 **Gr. 7,** 43
Batik (listening), **Gr. 2,** 201
Battle Hymn of the Republic (listening and song),
Gr. K, T331; **Gr. 5,** 390, 391; **Gr. 6,** 389
Be Yours, **Gr. 7,** 189
Bear Hunt (speech piece), **Gr. 1,** T126
Bear Went Over the Mountain, The, **Gr. 1,** T115
Beauty and the Beast, **Gr. 5,** 124
Bee, Bee, Bumblebee, **Gr. 1,** T250
Best Friends, **Gr. 1,** T222
Best That I Can Be!, The, **Gr. K,** T48
Bickle, Bockle, **Gr. K,** 187
Big and Small (speech piece), **Gr. 1,** T200
Big Big World, **Gr. 5,** 438
Billy, **Gr. 3,** 7
Bliss (poem), **Gr. 2,** 212
Blow, Ye Winds, Blow, **Gr. 3,** 192
Blue Bayou (listening), **Gr. 8,** 71
Blue Moon of Kentucky (listening), **Gr. 5,** 23
Blue Suede Shoes, **Gr. 6,** 236; (excerpt) (listening),
Gr. 7, 8

Classified Index of Songs, Selected Concepts, Skills, and Activities **151**

Bluebells, **Gr. 1,** T209

Bobby Shafto, **Gr. K,** T265

Boll Weevil, **Gr. 3,** 171

Bonjour, mes amis (Hello, My Friends), **Gr. 1,** T18

Boo, **Gr. 3,** 362

Bop 'til You Drop, **Gr. 6,** 87

Boris, the Singing Bear, **Gr. 1,** T312

Born to Be with You (listening), **Gr. 3,** 387

Bow, Wow, Wow, **Gr. 2,** 264

Brooklyn Jugs (listening), **Gr. 4,** 77

Brotherhood of Man, **Gr. 8,** 248

Brush Your Teeth. **Gr. 1,** (song), T66, (speech piece), T67

Buckeye Jim, **Gr. 4,** 136

Buffalo Dusk (poem), **Gr. K,** T219

Buffalo Prairie from *Prayer for the Wild Things* (listening), **Gr. K,** T219

Bug, The, **Gr. 8,** 88

Built My Lady a Fine Brick House, **Gr. 4,** 252

Bullfrogs, Bullfrogs on Parade (poem), **Gr. K,** T183

Bus, The, **Gr. K,** T137

Butterfly Come Play With Me, **Gr. 3,** 112

Butterfly, Flutter By, **Gr. 1,** T333

Button, You Must Wander, **Gr. 2,** 176

Caissons Go Rolling Along, The, **Gr. 5,** 37

Call of the Wild, A (excerpt) (poem), **Gr. 1,** T139

Camelot, **Gr. 6,** 310

Candle on the Water, **Gr. 2,** 296

Cape Cod Chantey, **Gr. 6,** 258

Captain Jinks, **Gr. 6,** 266

Car Song (listening), **Gr. K,** T135

Carousel Waltz, The, from *Carousel* (listening), **Gr. 7,** 69

Cat and Dog, **Gr. 3,** 259

Cat and the Mouse, The (listening), **Gr. 2,** 80

Cattle from *The Plow That Broke the Plains* (listening), **Gr. 4,** 274

Cedar Swamp, **Gr. 4,** 50

Celestial Express (listening), **Gr. 8,** 52

Chamber Ensembles (montage) (listening), **Gr. 5,** 228

Change Is Good (song and listening), **Gr. 5,** 84, 85

Change the World, **Gr. 5,** 314

Charleston, **Gr. 6,** 112

Charlotte Town, **Gr. 6,** 261

Chase the Squirrel, **Gr. 1,** T88

Check It Out! (It's About Respect), **Gr. 2,** 10

Cheers, **Gr. 7,** 34

Chicka Hanka, **Gr. 4,** 138

Chicken on the Fence Post, **Gr. 3,** 265

Chickery Chick, **Gr. 1,** T292

Children's Dance from *Merry Mount* (listening), **Gr. 2,** 246

Children's March (listening), **Gr. K,** T113

Christmas Tree (poem), **Gr. 1,** T352

Cindy, **Gr. 5,** 265

Circle of Friends, **Gr. 5,** 196

Circle of Life from *The Lion King* (choral arrangement) (listening), **Gr. 7,** 84; (performed) (listening), **Gr. 7,** 84

Circle of Life, **Gr. 7,** 40

Circle of Song, **Gr. 4,** 330

Circus Music from *The Red Pony Suite* (listening), **Gr. 3,** 285

City Blues, **Gr. 5,** 278

City Life, **Gr. 3,** 341

City Traffic (story), **Gr. 2,** 328

Clap Your Hands, **Gr. 1,** T246

Clocks, **Gr. 3,** 266

Clog (listening), **Gr. 2,** 68

Cobbler, Cobbler, Mend My Shoe, **Gr. K,** T169

Cobbler, The (poem), **Gr. K,** T169

Coffee Break, **Gr. 8,** 241

Colors (listening), **Gr. K,** T58

Colors of the Wind, **Gr. 3,** 84

Columbus Sailed with Three Ships, **Gr. 2,** 344

Come On-A My House (listening), **Gr. 7,** 138

Comedy Tonight, **Gr. 6,** 204

Common Step (traditional) (listening), **Gr. 8,** 39

Company Way, The, **Gr. 8,** 244

Concertino for Marimba Op. 21, First Movement ("Vigorous") (listening), **Gr. 4,** 120

Concord Hymn (poem), **Gr. 7,** 66

Conducting Mirror (listening), **Gr. 8,** 220

Cookies, **Gr. 1,** T277

Coral, **Gr. 3,** 249

Corner Grocery Store, **Gr. 2,** 311

Cornstalk Fiddle and a Shoestring Bow, **Gr. 3,** 284

Cotton-Eye Joe, **Gr. 4,** 52

Cripple Creek (song and listening), **Gr. 6,** 372, 375

Cuckoo, Where Are You?, **Gr. 2,** 244

Cumberland Gap, **Gr. 3,** 99

Cut the Cake, **Gr. 1,** T232

Daisy Chain, **Gr. 2,** 255

Dance for the Nations, **Gr. 5,** 206

Dance Myself to Sleep, **Gr. 1,** T314

Dance No. 4 (excerpt) (listening), **Gr. 4,** 144

Dance Together, **Gr. 2,** 264

Daniel in the Lion's Den (listening), **Gr. 3,** 161

Death of the Robin, **Gr. 3,** 275

December: Sleighride from *Calendar Collection* (listening), **Gr. 1,** T128

Derby Ram, The, **Gr. 4,** 259

Digga Digga Dog, **Gr. 3,** 164

Dinah, **Gr. 3,** 150

Doctor Jazz, **Gr. 6,** 378

Doggie, Doggie, **Gr. 2,** 59

Doing the Latest Rag, **Gr. 6,** 314

Don't Laugh at Me, **Gr. 7,** 93

Doney Gal, **Gr. 6,** 115

Down by the Bay, **Gr. 1,** T48

Down the Hill, **Gr. 1,** T281

Dreamers, **Gr. 5,** 430

Drops of Jupiter (Tell Me) (listening), **Gr. 8,** 103

Eagle, **Gr. 4,** 337

Early in the Morning at Eight O'Clock, **Gr. 4,** 59

Early Light by C. Bremer (listening), **Gr. 6,** 201

Ears, Far and Near (poem), **Gr. 1,** T16

East St. Louis Toodle-Oo (listening), **Gr. 4,** 232

Eating Lizards, **Gr. 2,** 250

Eency Weency Spider, **Gr. K,** T8

Effie Goes Folk Dancing (listening), **Gr. 2**, 168

Eight Bells, **Gr. 4**, 281

El Capitán (listening), **Gr. 8**, 6

Elbows Off the Table (listening), **Gr. K**, T106

Empty Chairs at Empty Tables (listening), **Gr. 8**, 197

Encore (listening), **Gr. 8**, 13

Engine, Engine Number Nine, **Gr. 2**, 13

Entrance Fanfare (listening), **Gr. 2**, 86

Erie Canal, **Gr. 5**, 132

Everyone Has Music Inside, **Gr. 2**, 164

Eyes of Texas, The, (listening), **Gr. 7**, 42, 45

Faire, **Gr. 8**, 215

Falling Water (building), **Gr. 8**, 226

Famous TV Show Themes (montage) (listening),
Gr. 8, 140

Fascinating Rhythm from *Lady, Be Good* (listening),
Gr. 5, 186

Festival Prelude, A (listening), **Gr. 8**, 65

Field of Joys, **Gr. 1**, T224

Firecracker (listening), **Gr. 8**, 182

Five Fat Turkeys, **Gr. K**, T309

Five Little Pumpkins (poem), **Gr. 1**, T337

Flag Goes By, The (poem) **Gr. 7**, 45

Foggy Mountain Breakdown (listening), **Gr. 6**, 140

Food Song, The, **Gr. 2**, 318

Four Trees (painting), **Gr. 8**, 92

Freedom (listening), **Gr. 7**, 195

Frog in the Meadow, **Gr. 3**, 243

Frog Went A-Courtin', **Gr. 4**, 46

Frosty the Snowman, **Gr. 3**, 366

Frosty Weather, **Gr. 3**, 250

Funny Road, The, (listening), **Gr. 3**, 40

Furry Bear (poem), **Gr. K**, T205

Garden Hoedown, The, **Gr. K**, T290

Garden Song, **Gr. 2**, 236

Gavotte fantastique (listening), **Gr. 2**, 26

Gee, Ma, I Want to Go Home, **Gr. 6**, 148

Gentle River Runs, A, **Gr. 5**, 342

George Washington, **Gr. 1**, T368

Get a Car/Polka Dot from *Dreaming Blue* by L. Larsen
(listening), **Gr. 6**, 221

Ghost Ship, The, **Gr. 6**, 323

Gilly, Gilly, Gilly Good Morning, **Gr. 1**, T12

Girl I Left Behind Me, The, **Gr. 4**, 249

Git Along, Little Dogies, **Gr. 6**, 284

Give a Little Love, **Gr. 7**, 128

Give Me Your Tired, Your Poor from *Miss Liberty*
(listening), **Gr. 5**, 42

Glad About It by Joe Pace and the Colorado Mass Choir,
Gr. 8, 63

Go, Go, Go, **Gr. K**, T276

God Bless America (song and listening), **Gr. 5**, 4, 5

God Bless the U.S.A., **Gr. 7**, 136

Goin' Home, **Gr. 5**, 108

Goin' to the Zoo, **Gr. 1**, T192

Golden Ring Around the Susan Girl, **Gr. 3**, 264

Goober Peas (Civil War marching song) (song and
listening), **Gr. 6**, 269

Good Night, Sleep Tight, **Gr. 2**, 76

Goodbye Brother, **Gr. 4**, 273

Grandma's Feather Bed, **Gr. 4**, E

Granny (speech piece), **Gr. 1**, T104

Grasshoppers from *Joyful Noise: Poems for Two Voices*
(listening), **Gr. 1**, T244

Grasshoppers Three, **Gr. 1**, T284

Great Big House, **Gr. 3**, 14

Great Outdoors, The, **Gr. 2**, 290

Greatest Show on Earth, The, **Gr. 3**, 308

Green Eggs and Ham, **Gr. 2**, 284

Green Grass Grew All Around, The, **Gr. 1**, T148

Green Gravel, **Gr. 4**, 247

Grizzly Bear, **Gr. K**, T252

Guadalcanal March from *Victory at Sea* (listening),
Gr. 4, 108

Gus: The Theatre Cat (poem), **Gr. 8**, 195

Hakuna Matata from *The Lion King* (listening),
Gr. K, T222

Halloween, **Gr. 1**, T340

Hang on Sloopy, **Gr. 7**, 30; performed by the McCoys
(listening), **Gr. 7**, 29; performed by Ohio State Glee
Club and Marching Band (listening), **Gr. 7**, 32

Happiest Street in the World, The, **Gr. 1**, T304

Happy Birthday, **Gr. K**, T273, T347

Harvest, **Gr. 2**, 342

Hashkivenu (listening), **Gr. 7**, 190

Have to Have a Habitat (listening), **Gr. 3**, 331

Heart, **Gr. 6**, 166

Heartbeat of Democracy (poem), **Gr. 5**, 389

Heave-Ho Me Laddies, **Gr. 4**, 258

Heigh Ho, Here We Go, **Gr. 2**, 252

Hello!, **Gr. 3**, 283

Hello, Hello, There, **Gr. 2**, 126

Hello, There!, **Gr. 1**, T230

Henry Ford, **Gr. 7**, 244

Here Comes a Bluebird, **Gr. 2**, 263

Here Comes the Band (poem), **Gr. 1**, T80

Here We Sit, **Gr. 1**, T251

Hey, Children, Who's in Town?, **Gr. 1**, T14

Hey, Hey, Look at Me, **Gr. 2**, 245

Hi! My Name Is Joe!, **Gr. 1**, (speech piece), T220

Hinges (poem), **Gr. K**, T23

Hippopotamus, The (poem), **Gr. K**, T199

Hoedown (listening), **Gr. 6**, 116

Hokey Pokey, **Gr. K**, T68

Hold My Mule, **Gr. 4**, 248

Hoo, Hoo!, **Gr. 1**, T55

Hop Up and Jump Up, **Gr. 4**, 271

Hop! Chirp! Moo! Oh, Happy Springtime Day!,
Gr. 1, T372

Hop, Hop, Hop, **Gr. K**, T197

Hop, Old Squirrel, **Gr. 2**, 258

Horse with No Name, A (listening), **Gr. 8**, 161

Horton Hears a Who!, **Gr. 2**, 279

Horton Hears a Who! Two, **Gr. 2**, 280

Hot Dog, **Gr. K**, T69

How Can I Keep From Singing? (song and listening),
Gr. 5, 287

How Does Your Garden Grow?, **Gr. 1**, T144

How to Succeed, **Gr. 8**, 237

Humming Birds (poem), **Gr. K**, T140

Classified Index

Classified Index of Songs, Selected Concepts, Skills, and Activities (continued)

Hummingbird, A (listening), **Gr. K,** T140

Hush, Little Baby (listening), **Gr. 4,** 9

I Am But a Small Voice, **Gr. 5,** 323

I Am Slowly Going Crazy, **Gr. 1,** T127

I Bought Me a Cat, **Gr. 2,** 14; (listening) **Gr. 2,** 14

I Can't Spell Hippopotamus, **Gr. K,** T199

I Got a Letter, **Gr. 6,** 270

I Got Rhythm, **Gr. 5,** 187

I Have a Car, **Gr. 3,** 252

I Have a Friend (poem), **Gr. 1,** T225

I Like (poem), **Gr. 1,** T110

I Like Spinach, **Gr. 1,** T163

I Love a Piano, **Gr. 6,** 130

I Love My Country, **Gr. 1,** T328

I Made a Valentine, **Gr. K,** T333

I See, **Gr. 2,** 266

I Think I'm Going to Like It Here, **Gr. 4,** 299

I Walk the Line (listening), **Gr. 6,** 97

I Wanna Be a Friend of Yours, **Gr. 1,** T84

I Will Sing Hello, **Gr. K,** T156

I'd Like to Be a Lighthouse (poem), **Gr. 1,** T238

I'll Rise When the Rooster Crows, **Gr. 4,** 36

I'm a Believer, **Gr. 3,** 312

I'm Getting Sick of Peanut Butter (poem), **Gr. 1,** T219

I'm Going to Georgia, **Gr. 6,** 244

Ice (poem), **Gr. 1,** T346

If I Had a Hammer, **Gr. 6,** 174

If Things Grew Down (poem), **Gr. K,** T48G, T293

In and Out, **Gr. 2,** 245

In Good Old Colony Times, **Gr. 3,** 326

In My Little Motor Boat, **Gr. 1,** T159

In the Barnyard (poem), **Gr. K,** T207

In the Good Old Summertime (listening), **Gr. K,** T343

In the Mood (listening), **Gr. 4,** 143

Interjections, **Gr. 3,** 303

Interplanet Janet, **Gr. 3,** 298

Iowa Stubborn, **Gr. 5,** 293

Is That Mister Reilly?, **Gr. 5,** 282

It Fell in the City (poem), **Gr. K,** T312

It Rained a Mist, **Gr. 4,** 262

It's a Small World, **Gr. 2,** 298

It's Possible, **Gr. 2,** 281

It's Raining! It's Pouring!, **Gr. 2,** 233

It's So Nice on the Ice, **Gr. 1,** T346

It's Such a Good Feeling, **Gr. K,** T282

It's the Hard-Knock Life, **Gr. 4,** 293

It's Time to Get Ready for Christmas, **Gr. 3,** 372

It's You I Like, **Gr. K,** T280

Jetsons, The, **Gr. 8,** 141

Jim Along, Josie, **Gr. 2,** 194

Jingle at the Window, **Gr. 3,** 268

Jingle Bell Rock, **Gr. 5,** 424

Jingle Bells, **Gr. 1,** T354

John Henry, **Gr. 5,** 146

John Jacob Jingleheimer Schmidt, **Gr. 3,** 68

John Kanaka, **Gr. 5,** 249

John the Rabbit, **Gr. 1,** T74

John Williams Montage 1 (listening), **Gr. 8,** 134

John Williams Montage 2 (listening), **Gr. 8,** 136

Johnny Works with One Hammer, **Gr. 1,** T96

Johnny's Flea, **Gr. 1,** T158

Johnson Boys, **Gr. 4,** 233

Jolly Old Saint Nicholas, **Gr. 1,** T352

Jolly Old St. Nicholas, **Gr. 4,** 382

Joy, **Gr. 2,** 46

Joyful, Joyful from *Sister Act 2* (excerpt) (song), **Gr. 5,** 105

Joyful, Joyful, We Adore Thee, **Gr. 5,** 103

Jump or Jiggle (poem), **Gr. K,** T193; **Gr. 1,** T316

Jump, Jim Joe, **Gr. 1,** T89

Kangaroo, The (poem), **Gr. K,** T196

Kangaroo, The, **Gr. K,** T197

King's Land, **Gr. 2,** 257

Knock the Cymbals, **Gr. 2,** 265

Kreely Kranky, **Gr. 3,** 258

Lady, Lady, **Gr. K,** T184

Ladybugs' Picnic, **Gr. 1,** T290

Leatherwing Bat, **Gr. 2,** 304

Leila, **Gr. 6,** 376

Lemonade, **Gr. 2,** 19

Let Us Chase the Squirrel, **Gr. 3,** 248

Let's Go Driving, **Gr. 1,** T52

Let's Go Fly a Kite, **Gr. 2,** 134

Let's Think of Something To Do, **Gr. K,** T270

Li'l 'Liza Jane, **Gr. 4,** 20

Liberty Bell, The (listening), **Gr. 5,** 395

Library Song, **Gr. 1,** T42

Limbo Rock, **Gr. 3,** 232

Lincoln (poem), **Gr. 3,** 389

Little Black Bug, **Gr. 1,** T166

Little Blue Truck, **Gr. K,** T136

Little Ducky Duddle, **Gr. K,** T289

Little Red Caboose, **Gr. 1,** T97

Little Spotted Puppy, **Gr. K,** T146

Little Tommy Tinker, **Gr. 3,** 277

Little White Duck, **Gr. K,** T208

Lonesome Dove, **Gr. 6,** 249

Long-Legged Sailor, **Gr. 4,** 243

Look High, Look Low, **Gr. 3,** 338

Look Who's Here!, **Gr. K,** T84

Loose Tooth (speech piece), **Gr. 2,** 28

Love Grows, **Gr. 1,** T202

Love Is the Magic Word, **Gr. 1,** T366

Love Somebody, **Gr. 4,** 94

Lucy Lockett, **Gr. 1,** T253

Lullaby of Broadway, **Gr. 6,** 182

Machine from Symphony No. 5 (listening), **Gr. 8,** 51

Mail Myself to You, **Gr. 1,** T366

Major Bowes' Original Amateur Hour (listening),
    Gr. 8, 108

Mama Don't 'Low, **Gr. 6,** 126

Mama Will Provide, **Gr. 6,** 296

March of the Toys from *Babes in Toyland* (listening),
    Gr. K, T317

Marco Polo (speech piece), **Gr. 1,** T90

Marvelous Toy, The, **Gr. 3,** 182

Marvin's Music's Midnight Music Sale Jingle (listening),
    Gr. 8, 223

Mary's Coal Black Lamb, **Gr. 1,** T286

Mass for Earth (listening), **Gr. 7,** 222

Mele Kalikimaka (Merry Christmas), **Gr. 6,** 410

Merry-Go-Round, **Gr. 2**, 267; (poem), **K**, T225
Merry-Go-Round, The, **Gr. K**, T224
Milan (Meeting of the Two Rivers) (excerpt) (listening),
    Gr. 4, 208
Mill Song, The, **Gr. 2**, 52
Minuteman Minute Song, The, **Gr. 3**, 322
Mission: Impossible, **Gr. 8**, 141
Mississippi Mud (listening), **Gr. 6**, 65
Monkees, The, (Theme From) (listening), **Gr. 8**, 110
Monkey, Monkey (speech piece), **Gr. K**, T215
Moon and Me, **Gr. 3**, 220
Morning Bells, **Gr. 3**, 270
Mother, Mother, **Gr. 2**, 254
Mountain Music, **Gr. 6**, 20
Movin' Right Along, **Gr. 3**, 124
Mr. Frog, **Gr. 2**, 257
Music (poem), **Gr. K**, T157; **Gr. 5**, 122
Music of the World A-Turnin', **Gr. 3**, 44
Must Be Santa, **Gr. K**, T316
My Favorite Things from *The Sound of Music* (listening),
    Gr. 3, 313
My Feet (poem), **Gr. 1**, T264
My Friend Tom, **Gr. 3**, 364
My Government Claim (unison and 3-part),
    Gr. 5, 95, 110
My Home's in Montana, **Gr. 4**, 274
My Horses Ain't Hungry, **Gr. 3**, 278
My Kite (poem), **Gr. 1**, T371
My Mom, **Gr. 1**, T372
My Thumbs Are Starting to Wiggle, **Gr. K**, T35
My Valentine (poem), **Gr. 1**, T364
N.Y.C., **Gr. 4**, 302
Naming Things (poem), **Gr. 1**, T221
National Emblem (listening), **Gr. 7**, 76
Never Sleep Late Anymore, **Gr. 6**, 274
New Ashmolean Marching Society and Students
    Conservatory Band, The, **Gr. 6**, 308
New Colossus, The (excerpt) (poem), **Gr. 5**, 42
New Colossus, The (poem), **Gr. 7**, 187
Night Comes... (poem), **Gr. 1**, T233
Night Herding Song, **Gr. 4**, 110
Night That Goldman Spoke, The, **Gr. 7**, 246
No One Is Alone, from *Into the Woods* (listening),
    Gr. 8, 86
No One Like You, **Gr. 1**, T300
O, the Train's Off the Track, **Gr. 3**, 176
Oats, Peas, Beans and Barley Grow, **Gr. K**, T287
Ocean Child (listening), **Gr. 7**, 218
Ode to a Butterfly (listening), **Gr. 5**, 25
Oh, Susanna, **Gr. 3**, 153
Oh, the Thinks You Can Think!, **Gr. 2**, 276
Old Barn Dance, The, **Gr. 6**, 94
Old Blue, **Gr. 2**, 213
Old Dan Tucker, **Gr. 5**, 253
Old Gray Cat, The, **Gr. K**, T43
Old Jim John, **Gr. 6**, 253
Old Joe Clark, **Gr. 4**, 74
Old King Glory, **Gr. 1**, T217
Old MacDonald Had a Farm, **Gr. K**, T211; (listening),
    Gr. 2, 133

Old Paint, **Gr. 4**, 275
Old Time Rock 'n' Roll, **Gr. 7**, 98
Old Turkey Buzzard, **Gr. 5**, 264
Old Woman and the Pig, **Gr. 2**, 130
Oliver Twist, **Gr. 2**, 268
On a Clear Day, **Gr. 6**, 206
On Hearing a Symphony of Beethoven (poem),
    Gr. 8, 196
On the Sunny Side of the Street, **Gr. 5**, 361
On the Trail, from the Grand Canyon Suite (listening),
    Gr. 8, 112
On Top of Spaghetti, **Gr. 2**, 312
One Finger, One Thumb, **Gr. K**, T38
One Little Elephant, **Gr. 1**, T194
One More River, **Gr. 3**, 216
One Potato, Two Potato, **Gr. 3**, 267
One Voice (listening), **Gr. 5**, 326
One, Two, Three, Four, **Gr. 1**, T123
One, Two, Three, Four, Five, **Gr. 1**, T265
One, Two, Tie My Shoe, **Gr. K**, T151
Orange Blossom Special, **Gr. 6**, 33
Our Goodman, **Gr. 6**, 245
Our World, **Gr. 5**, 381
Ourchestra (poem), **Gr. K**, T171
Out from the Wilderness, **Gr. 3**, 388
Over in the Meadow, **Gr. 1**, T78
Over the Rainbow (listening), **Gr. K**, T60
Over the River and Through the Wood, **Gr. 4**, 370
Page's Train, **Gr. 4**, 246
Pairs or Pears, **Gr. 2**, 265
Papa-oom-mow-mow (listening), **Gr. 7**, 177
Park Rap 1 (listening), **Gr. 7**, 70
Park Rap 2 (listening), **Gr. 7**, 72
Part of Your World, **Gr. 2**, 294
Pat on the Back, A, **Gr. 2**, 74
Pat Pat Patty Pat, **Gr. 1**, T308
Pat Works on the Railway (Orff version) (listening),
    Gr. 1, T144; (song) **Gr. 4**, 86
Path to the Moon, **Gr. 5**, 368
Patriotic Medley, **Gr. 1**, T8; **Gr. 2**, H; **Gr. 4**, H
Paw Paw Patch, The, **Gr. 3**, 195
Peace and Quiet, **Gr. K**, T278
Peace in this House, **Gr. 7**, 152
Peaceful World (listening), **Gr. 7**, 154
Peanut Butter, **Gr. 1**, T218
Pegasus Suite, First Movement (excerpt) (listening),
    Gr. 5, 41
People in Your Neighborhood, The, (listening), **Gr. K**,
    T122; (instrumental version) (listening), **Gr. K**, T171
Perfect Winter Day, **Gr. 6**, 400
Pick a Pumpkin, **Gr. 2**, 347
Pick-a-Little/Goodnight Ladies, **Gr. 5**, 300
Pitty Patty Polt (speech piece), **Gr. 1**, T180
Place in the Choir, A, **Gr. 2**, 308
Plainsies, Clapsies, **Gr. 2**, 248
Planting Seeds, **Gr. K**, T284
Poets to Come (poem), **Gr. 7**, 231
Polly Wolly Doodle, **Gr. 3**, 132
Popalong Hopcorn! (poem), **Gr. K**, T160
Popping Corn, **Gr. K**, T161

Classified Index of Songs, Selected Concepts, Skills, and Activities (continued)

Preamble, The, **Gr. 3**, 293

Presidents, **Gr. K**, T330

Promenade from *Golden Goose* (listening), **Gr. 1**, T177

Promise of Living, The, from *The Tender Land* (listening), **Gr. 6**, 77

Propel, Propel, Propel, **Gr. K**, T275

Puddle Hopping, **Gr. 1**, T60

Pumpkin Song, **Gr. 1**, T342

Push Boat Song, **Gr. 4**, 266

Put on a Costume, **Gr. 1**, T336

Put Your Finger in the Air, **Gr. K**, T230

Quaker, Quaker, **Gr. 1**, T100

Rage and Roar, **Gr. 6**, 48

Ragtime, **Gr. 7**, 237

Ragtime Epilogue and Finale, **Gr. 7**, 250

Railroad Blues (listening), **Gr. 2**, 327

Rain, Rain, Go Away, **Gr. 1**, T259

Rain Sizes (poem), **Gr. 1**, T33

Rainbow Connection, The, **Gr. 3**, 310

Rattlesnake, **Gr. 1**, T185; **Gr. 3**, 72

Recycle Rap, **Gr. 3**, 332

Red Iron Ore, **Gr. 6**, 134

Red River Valley (listening), **Gr. 6**, 96

Red Rover, **Gr. 2**, 249

Riddle Song, **Gr. 2**, 251

Ride Like the Wind, **Gr. 5**, 130

Ridin' of a Goat, Leadin' of a Sheep, **Gr. 4**, 251

Riding in the Buggy, **Gr. 3**, 131

Rise Up Singin', **Gr. 3**, 138

Risseldy, Rosseldy, **Gr. 6**, 264

River of My People, **Gr. 6**, 176

River, The, (poem), **Gr. K**, T342

Rock and Roll Is Here to Stay, **Gr. 5**, 316

Rock Around the Clock, **Gr. 6**, 324

Rock Island, **Gr. 5**, 291; (listening), **Gr. 8**, 74

Rocky Top, **Gr. 5**, 352

Romper, Stomper, and Boo (story), **Gr. 1**, T36

Rondo for Lifey (listening), **Gr. 2**, 81

Round-up, from *Western Suite* (listening), **Gr. 2**, 67

Route 66 (listening), **Gr. 7**, 191

Row, Row, Row Your Boat, **Gr. 4**, 268

Row, Row, Row, **Gr. K**, T274

Rudolph, the Red-Nosed Reindeer, **Gr. 1**, T354

Sail Away (song and listening), **Gr. 4**, 54, 55

Sailor Went to Sea, Sea, Sea, A (song), **Gr. 1**, T38; (game), **Gr. 1**, T39

Sailor, Sailor, on the Sea, **Gr. 2**, 262

Salamanca Market, **Gr. 6**, 247

Sally Go 'Round the Sun, **Gr. 2**, 268

Salsa in the Parlor (listening), **Gr. 4**, 229

Sammy Sackett, **Gr. 2**, 146

Say Your Name, **Gr. 2**, 243

Scraping Up Sand, **Gr. 6**, 248

Sea Shell, **Gr. 4**, 245

Season of Hope, The, **Gr. 5**, 410

Seasons of Love from *Rent* (choral arrangement) (listening), **Gr. 7**, 86

See the Pony Galloping, **Gr. K**, T44

Seeds (vocal and instrumental), **Gr. 1**, T120

Seeds and Seasons, **Gr. 2**, 206

Seesaw, **Gr. 1**, T242

Semper Fidelis (listening), **Gr. 3**, 281; **Gr. 6**, 391

Seussical Mega-Mix, **Gr. 2**, 287

Seventy-Six Trombones (listening), **Gr. 5**, 296; **Gr. 8**, 76

Shady Grove, **Gr. 6**, 286; (traditional) (listening), **Gr. 8**, 59

Shake My Sillies Out, **Gr. K**, T175

Shapes (poem), **Gr. K**, T37

She'll Be Comin' 'Round the Mountain, **Gr. 2**, 33

Sheep in the Meadow (speech piece), **Gr. 2**, 8

Ship Ahoy, **Gr. 3**, 314

Shoes of John, **Gr. 6**, 246

Shoo Fly Pie and Apple Pan Dowdy, **Gr. 3**, 227

Shoo, Fly, **Gr. 2**, 222

Short Ride in a Fast Machine (listening), **Gr. 5**, 125

Shrimp Boats (listening and song), **Gr. 2**, 178, 179

Side Show, The (song and listening), **Gr. 5**, 283

Simon Says, **Gr. 3**, 4

Simple Gifts, **Gr. 5**, 136

Simple Simon, **Gr. 1**, T175

Sing a Little Song, **Gr. K**, T179

Sing After Me, **Gr. 1**, T34

Sing Hosanna, **Gr. 6**, 362

Sing, America Sing!, **Gr. 5**, 6

Sing, Sing, Sing (with a Swing) (song and listening), **Gr. 5**, 30, 32

Sittin' Down to Eat, **Gr. 1**, T182

Sitting in the Sand (poem), **Gr. 1**, T374

Six Little Ducks, **Gr. 1**, T64

Sixteen Tons (listening), **Gr. 7**, 150; (song), **Gr. 7**, 151

Skating, **Gr. 2**, 350

Skeleton (listening), **Gr. 8**, 215

Skin and Bones, **Gr. 1**, T340

Skinnamarink, **Gr. 2**, 368

Skip to My Lou, **Gr. 1**, T102

Slap That Bass, **Gr. 6**, 146

Smilin', **Gr. 8**, 80

Smoke Goes Up the Chimney, **Gr. 3**, 272

Snail, Snail, **Gr. 1**, T252

Snail With the Mail, **Gr. 1**, T275

Snow Toward Evening (poem), **Gr. K**, T311

Snowman, The, **Gr. K**, T313

So Long, Farewell from *The Sound of Music* (listening), **Gr. K**, T189

Somebody Come and Play, **Gr. 1**, T92

Somebody Has To… (poem), **Gr. 1**, T258

Something for Me, Something for You, **Gr. 4**, 4

Something Funny Outside, **Gr. 1**, T338

Something Told the Wild Geese (poem), **Gr. 1**, T261

Sonata for Bass Trombone, Andantino (listening), **Gr. 5**, 160

Sonata X by J. Cage (listening), **Gr. 6**, 32

Soup Cans (painting), **Gr. 8**, 226

Speed the Plow Medley (listening), **Gr. 6**, 149

Speedy Delivery, **Gr. K**, T279

Spiders, **Gr. 3**, 282

Spring, **Gr. 1**, T273

Star Canon, **Gr. 5**, 367

Star Light, Star Bright, **Gr. 1**, T258

Classified Index of Songs, Selected Concepts, Skills, and Activities (continued)

Stars and Stripes Forever, The, **Gr. 6,** 390; (listening), **Gr. 4,** 355; (listening) **Gr. 7,** 197

Star-Spangled Banner, The, **Gr. 4,** 356; **Gr. 6,** 386; **Gr. 7,** 42, 185, 194; (listening and song), **Gr. 5,** 86, 386

Step in Time from *Mary Poppins* (listening), **Gr. K,** T159; **Gr. 2,** 6

Step into the Spotlight, **Gr. 1,** T7; **Gr. 4,** A

Strawberry Roan (listening and song), **Gr. 2,** 66

Streets of Laredo, **Gr. 5,** 260

String of Pearls, A, (listening), **Gr. 3,** 12

Success from *Ragtime*, **Gr. 7,** 241

Sugar in the Gourd, **Gr. 6,** 251

Summer Landscape (painting), **Gr. 8,** 92

Summertime from *Porgy and Bess* (listening), **Gr. 1,** T375; **Gr. 4,** 160; **Gr. 6,** 120

Sun Don't Set in the Mornin', **Gr. 3,** 48, 60

Sun Is First to Rise, The (poem), **Gr. 2,** 383

Sunburst (listening), **Gr. 7,** 216

Surfin' U.S.A., **Gr. 5,** 306

Swapping Song, **Gr. 4,** 253

Sweet Sound (listening), **Gr. 8,** 233

Swing, The (poem), **Gr. 1,** T109

Symphony No. 101, in D Major, The Clock (listening), **Gr. 8,** 128

Symphony No. 40, in G Minor, K. 550, First Movement (listening), **Gr. 8,** 218

Symphony No. 5, in C Minor, Third and Fourth Movements (listening), **Gr. 8,** 115

Symphony No. 6, The Pastoral (listening), **Gr. 8,** 20

Symphony No. 7, Second Movement (listening), **Gr. 7,** 118

Symphony No. 9 Fourth Movement (listening), **Gr. 7,** 156

Symphony: Water Music, Movements 3 and 4 (listening), **Gr. 8,** 155

Table Manners (poem), **Gr. K,** T107

Tailor, Tailor (poem), **Gr. 1,** T132

Tain't What You Do, **Gr. 6,** 18

Take Five (listening), **Gr. 5,** 213; (excerpt) (listening), **Gr. 4,** 41

Take Me Out to the Ball Game, **Gr. 2,** 56

Taking Off (poem), **Gr. K,** T134

Taps, **Gr. 3,** 281; (listening), **Gr. 7,** 144

Ten in a Bed, **Gr. K,** T256

That Great Come and Get It Day, **Gr. 6,** 306

Theme from *Sesame Street*, **Gr. 1,** T298

There Are Many Flags in Many Lands, **Gr. 1,** T329; **Gr. 2,** 341

There Was a Blue Flower from *Dreaming Blue* (listening and song), **Gr. 6,** 218, 219

There Was a Jolly Miller, **Gr. 6,** 250

There Was a Young Lady (poem), **Gr. 7,** 83

There's a Hole in the Bucket, **Gr. 2,** 132

There's a Hole in the Middle of the Sea, **Gr. 1,** T178

There's a Song in Me, (melody and 2-part) **Gr. 5,** 164, 183

They Call the Wind Maria, **Gr. 6,** 312

Thing, The (listening), **Gr. K,** T307

Things I'm Thankful For, **Gr. K,** T308

This a Way and That a Way, **Gr. 3,** 386

This Is America, **Gr. 3,** 356

This Is Halloween, **Gr. 2,** 346

This Is My Country, **Gr. 2,** 87

This Pretty Planet, **Gr. 6,** 194

Thoughts of a Rattlesnake (poem), **Gr. 1,** T185

Three is a Magic Number, **Gr. 3,** 296

Three Little Penguins (speech piece), **Gr. 2,** 112

Throw It Out the Window, **Gr. 3,** 94

Tiki Tiki Tiki Room, The, **Gr. 2,** 324

Time for Love, A, **Gr. 1,** T347

Time to Sing, **Gr. K,** T16

Times They Are A-Changin', The, **Gr. 5,** 204

Together (poem), **Gr. 2,** 34

Tomorrow, **Gr. 4,** 295

Toodala, **Gr. K,** T39

Touch Your Shoulders, **Gr. K,** T254

Travel (poem), **Gr. K,** T144

Triple Play, **Gr. 5,** 355

Tubby the Tuba (listening), **Gr. 1,** T80

Turkey in the Straw (listening), **Gr. 2,** 348

Turn the Glasses Over, **Gr. 3,** 260

Turn the World Around, **Gr. 5,** 208

Twist and Shout, **Gr. 7,** 160

Uncle Pen, **Gr. 5,** 24

Up on the Housetop, 3 **Gr. 2,** 56

Up the Hill (poem), **Gr. 1,** T45

Up the Tree and Down Again (poem), **Gr. 1,** T65

Variations on "Simple Gifts" from *Appalachian Spring* (listening), **Gr. 5,** 152

Variations on the Theme "Pop! Goes the Weasel" (listening), **Gr. 5,** 96

Viva Valentine!, **Gr. 1,** T365

Vive l'amour, **Gr. 5,** 262

Wabash Cannonball, The, **Gr. 6,** 30

Waiting for Life, **Gr. 6,** 292

Wake Me, Shake Me, **Gr. 1,** T198

Wake Up Canon, **Gr. 4,** 326

Wake Up the Sun, **Gr. 2,** 124

Walk by the River, **Gr. 6,** 74, 76

Walk in the Parlor, **Gr. 4,** 226

Walk to School, **Gr. K,** T18

Walking (listening), **Gr. 8,** 214

Walking Song (listening), **Gr. K,** T19

Walking the Dog from *Shall We Dance* (listening), **Gr. 1,** T169

Waltz in the Parlor (listening), **Gr. 4,** 229

Waltzing Cat (listening), **Gr. K,** T223

Washington Post (listening), **Gr. 2,** 339

Washington's Birthday (listening), **Gr. 2,** 370

Wayfaring Stranger, **Gr. 6,** 283

We All Sing With the Same Voice, **Gr. 1,** T156

We All Stand Together (listening), **Gr. K,** T153

We Are Playing in the Forest, **Gr. K,** T248

We Are the Children of Tomorrow, **Gr. 5,** 114

We Go Together from *Grease*, **Gr. 7,** 158

We Want to Sing, **Gr. 5,** 235

We're Lookin' Good (listening), **Gr. 2,** 149

We're Sailing Down the River, **Gr. 2,** 166

Welcome Is the Month of May, **Gr. 2,** 378

Wells Fargo Wagon, The, **Gr. 5,** 303; (listening), **Gr. 8,** 78

Classified Index of Songs, Selected Concepts, Skills, and Activities (continued)

What a Wonderful World (listening and song),
Gr. 2, 84; (listening), **Gr. 8,** 8, 9
What Did Delaware?, **Gr. 2,** 190
What Did You Do Today at Jeffrey's House?
(listening), **Gr. 4,** 80
What the World Needs Now, **Gr. 5,** 230
What's Your Name?, **Gr. 1,** T125
Wheels, Wheels, Wheels (poem), **Gr. 1,** T106
When Johnny Comes Marching Home, **Gr. 5,** 34;
(traditional) (listening), **Gr. 7,** 168
When the Flag Goes By, **Gr. 1,** T327
When You Send a Valentine, **Gr. K,** T332
Who Chopped the Cherry Tree Down? **Gr. 2,** 371
Who Has the Penny?, **Gr. 2,** 252
Who's Afraid of the Big Bad Wolf? (nursery rhyme),
Gr. 1, T137
Who's Got the Fishpole?, **Gr. 4,** 261
Who's That Tapping at the Window?, **Gr. 2,** 261
Why We Tell the Story, **Gr. 6,** 303
Wide Open Spaces (listening), **Gr. 7,** 208
Willowbee, **Gr. 2,** 69
Willum, **Gr. 1,** T19
Wings (poem), **Gr. 1,** T250
Winter Wonderland, **Gr. 5,** 408
Won't You Be My Neighbor?, **Gr. K,** T268
Woodchuck, **Gr. 3,** 246
Woodpecker, The (poem), **Gr. K,** T172
Words of Wisdom, **Gr. 5,** 244
Yankee Doodle Boy, **Gr. 3,** 357
Yankee Doodle, **Gr. 2,** 340; **Gr. 4,** 154
Year With Frog and Toad, A, **Gr. 1,** T270; (Reprise),
Gr. 1, T283
You Are My Sunshine, **Gr. 2,** 369
You Sing for Me, **Gr. 6,** 106
You're a Grand Old Flag, **Gr. K,** T4; **Gr. 3,** 355
You're Never Fully Dressed Without a Smile,
Gr. 4, 304
You've Got a Friend by C. King (listening), **Gr. 6,** 418
You've Got a Friend in Me from *Toy Story* (listening
and song), **Gr. 2,** 44

Hispanic American
A la rueda de San Miguel (To the Wheel of San Miguel),
Gr. 2, 60
Afoxé (listening), **Gr. 8,** 34
Arre, mi burrito (Gid'yup, Little Burrito), **Gr. 1,** T257
Good Morning America (listening), **Gr. 8,** 181
La camilla (fiesta dance song) (listening), **Gr. 1,** T196
La carcacha (The Old Car), FC-Int 7
Listening for Walking/Skipping/Galloping (listening),
Gr. K, T41
Mi cuerpo (My Body), **Gr. 1,** T32
Mi tierra (My Homeland), FC-Int 36
Qué bonito es (How Wonderful It Is), **Gr. K,** T234
Reach, **Gr. 5,** 14
Riqui Ran (Sawing Song), **Gr. 2,** 21

Jewish/Israeli
Achshav (Now), **Gr. 4,** 112
Ani Purim (I Am Purim), **Gr. 2,** 372
Aquaqua, **Gr. 5,** 258

Bashana Haba'ah (In the Year to Come), **Gr. 6,** 360
Bim Bom, **Gr. 3,** 218
Bulbes ('Taters), **Gr. 6,** 280
Chag Asif (Harvest Time), **Gr. 3,** 360
Cherkassiya (listening), **Gr. 2,** 373
Chiribim, **Gr. 6,** 57
Chirri Bim, **Gr. 2,** 70
Dance for Clarinet and Piano by A. Marx (listening),
Gr. 6, 189
Dreidel Song (poem), **Gr. 1,** T349
Eight Days of Hanukkah!, The, **Gr. 3,** 370
Erev Shel Shoshanim (listening), **Gr. 4,** 68
Hag Shavuot (Festival of First Fruits), WM 33
Hanerot Halalu (These Lights), **Gr. 5,** 414
Hanukkah Chag Yafeh (Hanukkah Joyous Holiday),
Gr. 1, T350
Hanukkah Is Here, **Gr. K,** T314
Hashual (Israeli folk dance) (listening), **Gr. 6,** 404
Hava Nagila, **Gr. 5,** 54
Hava Nashira (Sing Alleluia), **Gr. 6,** 67
I've a Pair of Fishes, **Gr. 1,** T124
In the Window, **Gr. 2,** 352
Kum bahur (The Rooster), **Gr. 3,** 75
Let's Go Dancing, **Gr. 3,** 196
Light One Candle, **Gr. 5,** 416
Light the Candles, **Gr. 1,** T351
Ma'oz Tsur (Rock of Ages), **Gr. 6,** 405
Mayim, Mayim (Water, Water), **Gr. 6,** 102
My Dreidel, **Gr. 2,** 353
Nigun Atik (listening), **Gr. 3,** 47
On This Night, **Gr. K,** T315
Oy Chanuke, **Gr. 3,** 368
S'vivon Sov (Dreidel Spin), **Gr. 1,** T348; **Gr. 4,** 374
Shalom Chaveyrim (Shalom, My Friends), **Gr. 3,** 141
Shibolet Basadeh (Wheat in the Field), **Gr. 6,** 424
Simi Yadech (Give Me Your Hand), **Gr. K,** T168
Tum Balalaika, **Gr. 6,** 68
Tumbai, **Gr. 5,** 194
Tzena, Tzena, **Gr. 5,** 171
Uga, Uga, Uga (Cake, Cake, Cake), **Gr. 1,** T313
Zum Gali Gali, **Gr. 4,** 255

Middle East and North Africa
Belhadawa walla belshaawa (listening), **Gr. 6,** 35
Dere Geliyor (River Overflowing), **Gr. 6,** 232
Haji Firuz, **Gr. 6,** 421, WM 113
Hala lala layya, **Gr. 4,** 222
Üsküdar, **Gr. 5,** 128, WM 65

Native American (North and South America)
December Snow (listening), **Gr. K,** T313
Earth is Our Mother, The, **Gr. 7,** 220; (listening),
Gr. 7, 220
Night of the Mockingbird (listening), **Gr. 4,** 153
Athabascan
Athabascan Song (listening), **Gr. 5,** 26
Cahuilla
Powama, **Gr. 7,** 63
Ushkana (listening), **Gr. 1,** T44
Comanche
Eka Muda (Red Mule) (listening and song),
Gr. 5, 27, 28

Classified Index of Songs, Selected Concepts, Skills, and Activities (continued)

Haliwa-Saponi
Bear Dance (dance song) (listening), **Gr. 1,** T103

Intertribal
Fancy Dance Song (listening), **Gr. 5,** 444
Grand Entry (Powwow) (listening), **Gr. K,** T344
Honor the Earth Powwow—Grand Entry (listening), **Gr. 7,** 75
One-Eyed Ford, **Gr. 7,** 200

Inuit
Song of a Seashore (listening), **Gr. 7,** 176

Iroquois
Tehahontanekenhnêha' (story and listening), **Gr. 3,** 50; (song and listening), **Gr. 3,** 51
Tsiothwatasè:tha (Round Dance), **Gr. 6,** 109

Kiowa
Prairie Dog Song (Children's Song), **Gr. K,** T220

Mohawk
Singing Woods, The, (listening), **Gr. 7,** 201
Tekanionton'néha' (Alligator Dance) (listening and song), **Gr. 5,** 222, 223

Muscogee (Creek)
Baby Nodja, **Gr. 2,** 154
Heleluyan, **Gr. 6,** 188

Hopi Nation
Buffalo Dance Entrance Song, **Gr. 3,** 325
Bu-Vah (Sleep) (song and listening), **Gr. 4,** 18, 19
Coyote and the Bluebirds, The (listening), **Gr. 2,** 231
Mos' Mos'! (Cat, Cat!), **Gr. 1,** T53
Nikosi, **Gr. 2,** 230

Nanticoke
O Hal'lwe (Nanticoke Women's Honoring Song), **Gr. 6,** 428

Navajo
Ałchíní Yázhí (listening), **Gr. 5,** 225
Earth Child, **Gr. 6,** 426
I Walk in Beauty, **Gr. 3,** 329
Jó Ashílá (Traveling Together) (listening and song), **Gr. 5,** 224
Shí Naashá (I am Going) (listening), **Gr. 1,** T73
Tsidii–Bird by G. Barney (listening), **Gr. 6,** 429
We Are Here, **Gr. 4,** 394

Ottawan
Raccoon Dance Song, **Gr. 3,** 87

Santa Clara Pueblo
Santa Clara Corn Grinding Song, **Gr. K,** T164

Seneca
Seneca Stomp Dance (listening), **Gr. K,** T345

Serrano (Maringa')
Ucha Tirvarch, **Gr. 3,** 53
Ushkana, **Gr. K,** T75; (listening), **Gr. 1,** T44

Sioux
Lakota Flute Song (listening), **Gr. 6,** 429

Taos
Taos Round Dance (listening), **Gr. 2,** 155

Zuni
Locust, The (poem), **Gr. 1,** T285

MUSIC NEWS. *See also* Careers; From the Top
Instrument Spotlights, **Gr. 2,** 40, 80, 120, 160, 200; **Gr. 3,** 41, 81, 121, 161, 201; **Gr. 4,** 41, 81, 121, 161, 201; **Gr. 5,** 41, 81, 121, 161, 201; **Gr. 6,** 41, 81, 121, 161, 201

MUSIC SKILLS (in Footlights at the bottom of Teacher's Edition pages)
Analyze, **Gr. K,** T21, T35, T71, T103, T167, T169, T175, T179, T181, T182, T188, T189, T197, T200, T208, T215, T225; **Gr. 1,** T31, T35, T262; **Gr. 2,** 13, 62, 74; **Gr. 3,** 33, 90, 225, 233, 255, 285; **Gr. 4,** 23, 113, 144, 207, 232, 329, 356, 372; **Gr. 5,** 20, 64, 113, 252, 261; **Gr. 6,** 15, 73, 126, 136, 176, 181, 228, 317; **Gr. 7,** 32, 37, 48, 77, 91, 118, 134, 162, 218, 228; **Gr. 8,** 8, 17, 43, 51, 98, 102, 108, 116, 133, 136, 150, 159, 160, 210
Analyze/Arrange, **Gr. 7,** 38; **Gr. 8,** 30
Analyze/Notate, **Gr. 8,** 14
Autoharp, **Gr. 5,** 169
Compose, **Gr. K,** T96, T112, T171; **Gr. 1,** T187, T214, T247; **Gr. 2,** 18, 46, 139, 146, 189, 195; **Gr. 3,** 192, 249, 254, 283; **Gr. 4,** 28, 60, 71, 96, 144, 192, 217, 248, 259, 269, 270; **Gr. 5,** V, 9, 12, 103, 107, 129, 137; **Gr. 6,** 13, 15, 176, 234, 250, 282, 285, 348; **Gr. 7,** 46, 72, 82, 110, 117, 182, 212, 228; **Gr. 8,** 38, 148, 196
Compose/Notate, **Gr. 8,** 160
Compose/Play, **Gr. 7,** 15; **Gr. 8,** 65
Conduct, **Gr. K,** T227; **Gr. 1,** T78; **Gr. 3,** 117, 171; **Gr. 4,** 6, 75, 117, 183, 251, 262, 359; **Gr. 5,** 215, 309; **Gr. 6,** 126, 129, 174, 227, 250, 401; **Gr. 7,** 40, 94; **Gr. 8,** 154, 168
Create, **Gr. K,** T39, T83, T119, T154, T155, T227; **Gr. 1,** T29, T34, T42, T62, T202, T250; **Gr. 2,** 168, 260; **Gr. 3,** 64, 88, 127, 185, 235; **Gr. 4,** 36, 140, 147, 220, 225, 363; **Gr. 5,** P, 35, 76, 131, 250, 251, 257, 258; **Gr. 6,** 264; **Gr. 7,** 112, 168, 189, 206; **Gr. 8,** 108, 128, 169, 173, 199, 204, 212
Create/Compose, **Gr. 8,** 26
Guitar, **Gr. K,** T74, T78, T89; **Gr. 5,** 68; **Gr. 6,** 33, 71, 76, 126, 140, 150, 174, 176, 249, 260, 266, 270, 274, 276, 285, 352; **Gr. 7,** 18, 31, 156, 161, 215; **Gr. 8,** 110
Guitar/Keyboard, **Gr. 7,** 214
Harmony, **Gr. 4,** 220
Improvise, **Gr. K,** T24, T36, T90, T112, T125, T185, T215, T218; **Gr. 1,** T20, T70, T220, T224, T235, T340; **Gr. 2,** E, 34, 53, 62, 133, 136, 179, 225; **Gr. 3,** 96, 192, 243, 259, 269, 280; **Gr. 4,** E, 33, 46, 245, 253, 267, 272, 273, 282, 395; **Gr. 5,** 17, 113, 180, 270, 319, 338, 362; **Gr. 6,** 34, 143, 168, 192, 245, 250, 262, 270, 284, 286, 314, 331; **Gr. 7,** 63, 84, 122, 148; **Gr. 8,** 12, 60, 86
Inner Hearing, **Gr. 5,** 164
Keyboard, **Gr. K,** T89; **Gr. 2,** 197; **Gr. 3,** 219, 228; **Gr. 4,** 132; **Gr. 5,** 63, 127, 132, 169, 215; **Gr. 6,** 23, 150, 211, 259
Keyboard/Notate, **Gr. 7,** 186
Listen, **Gr. K,** T12, T16, T20, T31, T32, T41, T45, T49, T52, T56, T57, T59, T60, T69, T76, T82, T83, T85, T89, T105, T107, T108, T113, T117, T118, T119, T123, T127, T132, T135, T136, T140, T143, T144, T147, T148, T149, T151, T153, T154, T155, T157, T160, T162, T164, T167, T168, T171, T172, T175, T176, T177, T180, T183, T189, T190, T193, T195, T196, T203, T209, T212, T219, T220, T223, T224; **Gr. 1,** T58, T74, T164, T176; **Gr. 2,** G, 17, 34, 193, 307, 311; **Gr. 3,** 218, 221, 313, 316, 326, 331,

Classified Index

334, 342; **Gr. 4,** 46, 109, 143, 180, 319, 329, 340, 343; **Gr. 5,** 19, 22, 27, 76, 98, 114, 127, 140, 164, 235, 323, 326, 346, 361, 370; **Gr. 6,** 167, 174, 196, 211, 318, 344, 375; **Gr. 7,** 22; **Gr. 8,** 214

Listen/Analyze, **Gr. 7,** 30; **Gr. 8,** 46

Listen/Identify, **Gr. 7,** 12

Listen/Improvise, **Gr. 8,** 110

Locomotor Movement, **Gr. 5,** 256

Music Styles and Functions, **Gr. 7,** 26

Notate, **Gr. K,** T141, T201; **Gr. 1,** T41, T94, T104, T178, T246, T264; **Gr. 2,** 197, 224; **Gr. 3,** 15, 54, 72, 106, 145, 180, 188, 194, 207, 270; **Gr. 4,** 109, 217, 246, 275, 363; **Gr. 5,** 47, 68, 103, 114, 144, 251, 253; **Gr. 6,** 184, 227, 260, 335; **Gr. 7,** 46; **Gr. 8,** 142

Orff Instruments, **Gr. K,** T16, T59, T90, T114, T117, T125, T141, T161, T165, T169, T172, T184, T197, T214, T218, T225; **Gr. 2,** 183, 219; **Gr. 3,** 14, 207, 217, 284; **Gr. 4,** 54, 138, 227, 232, 371, 373; **Gr. 5,** 12, 60, 127, 132; **Gr. 6,** 71, 388

Pitch Syllables/Hand Signs, **Gr. 2,** C, 133; **Gr. 3,** 18, 54, 101, 139, 171; **Gr. 4,** 54; **Gr. 5,** 12, 19; **Gr. 6,** 48, 150

Pitch (Pitch Syllables), **Gr. K,** T91, T97, T103, T117, T124, T162, T184, T195, T205, T225; **Gr. 1,** T147, T206; **Gr. 3,** 18, 101, 111, 139, 171, 219; **Gr. 4,** 21, 71, 367; **Gr. 6,** F; **Gr. 7,** 148, 161, 186, 220; **Gr. 8,** 122

Play, **Gr. K,** T13, T32, T35, T50, T51, T59, T69, T86, T95, T104, T108, T111, T116, T124, T125, T129, T133, T139, T144, T145, T160, T162, T168, T173, T184, T187, T201, T205, T210, T213, T215, T218; **Gr. 1,** T24, T29, T35, T38, T58, T62, T74, T88, T91, T104, T105, T107, T111, T116, T122, T172, T183, T199, T200, T202, T238, T248, T284, T286, T297, T311, T318; **Gr. 2,** 9, 15, 23, 69, 72, 76, 143, 219, 233, 250; **Gr. 3,** A, 156, 193, 216, 235, 253, 256, 266, 278; **Gr. 4,** 92, 128, 227, 247, 278, 281, 354; **Gr. 5,** C, 17, 20, 24, 30, 60, 63, 98, 109, 156, 167, 177, 184, 190, 208, 236, 254, 269; **Gr. 6,** B, 7, 13, 17, 34, 58, 93, 94, 180, 249; **Gr. 7,** 13, 37, 38, 46, 94, 114, 168, 214; **Gr. 8,** 15, 81, 184

Play/Notate, **Gr. 8,** 162

Read, **Gr. K,** T20, T72, T82, T83, T118, T119, T154, T155, T189, T190, T208; **Gr. 1,** T243; **Gr. 2,** 217, 248; **Gr. 3,** 23, 101, 148, 186, 188, 193, 264, 275, 286; **Gr. 4,** 60, 243, 276, 368; **Gr. 5,** G, 35, 63, 109, 127, 131, 132, 140, 144, 178, 195, 215, 217, 223, 283, 286; **Gr. 6,** 25, 136, 143, 146, 184, 276

Read and Notate, **Gr. 7,** 58

Recorder, **Gr. K,** T104, T139, T144; **Gr. 3,** 96, 186; **Gr. 4,** 96; **Gr. 5,** 17, 103, 129; **Gr. 7,** 82, 168

Rhythm, **Gr. 3,** C, 8, 15, 37, 133, 138; **Gr. 6,** G, 260, 261, 266; **Gr. 8,** 55, 62, 81

Rhythm/Compose, **Gr. 8,** 58

Rhythm (Rhythm Syllables), **Gr. K,** T54, T88, T89, T90, T91, T92, T124, T130, T138, T161, T165, T186, T189, T198, T210, T218; **Gr. 1,** T86, T87, T99, T198, T294; **Gr. 2,** 29, 46, 87, 127, 139, 256; **Gr. 4,** A, 6, 14, 60, 64, 88, 128, 132, 138, 140, 147, 150, 197, 257, 264, 268, 354; **Gr. 5,** K, 9, 47, 316; **Gr. 7,** 77, 162; **Gr. 8,** 55, 62, 81

Sing, **Gr. K,** T170, T184; **Gr. 1,** T170, T184; **Gr. 2,** 33, 74, 133, 146; **Gr. 3,** 269, 277, 287; **Gr. 4,** 88, 113, 128, 132; **Gr. 7,** 37; **Gr. 8,** 38

singing from memory, **Gr. K,** T39, T43, T69, T112, T131, T137, T184, T204; **Gr. 1,** T37, T232, T238, T287, T303, T307, T359; **Gr. 2,** 57, 63, 65, 96, 191, 245; **Gr. 3,** 59, 75, 87, 141, 255, 256, 278, 393; **Gr. 5,** 209, 213, 217; **Gr. 6,** 73, 126, 184, 260

Singing On Pitch Syllables, **Gr. 7,** 30

Vocal Development, **Gr. K,** T15, T32, T41, T43, T75, T93, T94, T212; **Gr. 1,** T30, T40, T69, T70; **Gr. 2,** 18, 84, 103, 115, 124, 139, 294, 298, 302, 304, 313, 319; **Gr. 3,** F, 306, 310, 315, 317, 322, 338; **Gr. 4,** C, 23, 113, 207, 218, 306, 308, 314, 317, 321, 322, 330, 347, 349; **Gr. 5,** T, 6, 27, 103, 131, 144, 156, 184, 195, 197, 208, 217, 223, 232, 235, 270, 311, 314, 318, 320, 324, 327, 332, 335, 347, 353, 358, 366, 369, 378, 382; **Gr. 6,** D, 33, 55, 59, 62, 67, 76, 146, 167, 174, 207, 220, 306, 313, 321, 326, 332, 335, 339, 342, 350, 353, 356, 358, 361, 362, 364, 365, 366, 370, 372, 376; **Gr. 7,** 104, 128, 137, 162, 175, 194, 200, 212; **Gr. 8,** 76, 77, 86

N

NON-ENGLISH LANGUAGE SONGS. *See also Fiesta de canciones* and *Festival of World Music* under separate cover

A be ce (A B C) (Spanish), **Gr. 1,** T213

A la nanita nana (Spanish), **Gr. 4,** 230

A la puerta de cielo (Spanish), **Gr. 4,** 12

A la rueda de San Miguel (Spanish), **Gr. 2,** 60

A la rueda rueda ('Round and 'Round) (Spanish), **Gr. 1,** T240

Ach, du lieber Augustin (German), **Gr. 2,** 35

Acitrón (listening) (Spanish), **Gr. 6,** 92

¡Adivina lo que es! (Guess What It Is) (Spanish), **Gr. 1,** T170

Adukbe (listening) (Akan), **Gr. 8,** 177

Aeyaya balano sakkad (Konkani), **Gr. 5,** 402

Agahu (Ewe), **Gr. 5,** 72

Aideu (Yoruban), **Gr. 7,** 223

Al lado de mi cabaña (Spanish), **Gr. 6,** 141

Allá en el rancho grande (Spanish), **Gr. 5,** 66

Allundé Alluia (Nigerian), **Gr. 4,** 34

Ame fure (Japanese), **Gr. 4,** 26

Ani Purim (Hebrew), **Gr. 2,** 372

Animales (Spanish), **Gr. K,** T192

Aquaqua (Vocables), **Gr. 5,** 258

Arianna (Italian), **Gr. 7,** 94

Arirang (Korean), **Gr. 5,** 50

Arre, mi burrito (Spanish), **Gr. 1,** T257

Arroyito serrano (Spanish), **Gr. 4,** 340

Aschav (Hebrew), **Gr. 4,** 112

¡Ay, Jalisco no te rajes! (Spanish), **Gr. 5,** 188

Baby Nodja (Creek), **Gr. 2,** 154

Bahay Kubo (Tagalog), **Gr. 2,** 382

Ban Dal (Korean), **Gr. 2,** 219; **Gr. 4,** 184

Bashana Haba'ah (Hebrew), **Gr. 6,** 360

Bate, Bate (Spanish), **Gr. 2,** 242

Bei Fang Chre (Chinese), **Gr. 2,** 367

Bella bimba (Italian), **Gr. 3,** 172

Classified Index of Songs, Selected Concepts, Skills, and Activities (continued)

Belle qui tiens ma vie (French), **Gr. 6**, 99
Beryoza (Russian), **Gr. 4**, 286
Bim Bom (Hebrew), **Gr. 3**, 218
Bohm (Korean), **Gr. 3**, 392
Bohm Dong Sahn, Gohd Dong Sahn (Korean), **Gr. K**, T337
Brinca la tablita (Hop, Hop!) (Spanish), **Gr. 1**, T71
Buffalo Dance Entrance Song (Hopi), **Gr. 3**, 325
Bulbes (Yiddish), **Gr. 6**, 280
Bu-Vah (Hopi), **Gr. 4**, 18
Caballito blanco (Spanish), **Gr. 4**, 278
Canta, Canta, Minha Gente (listening) (Portuguese),
   Gr. 8, 45
Caranguejo (Portuguese), **Gr. 2**, 306
Chag Asif (Hebrew), **Gr. 3**, 360
Chan mali chan (Malay), **Gr. 3**, 10
Chang (Elephant) (Thai), **Gr. 1**, T199
Che avvien? (Italian), **Gr. 7**, 182
Chiapanecas (Spanish), **Gr. 2**, 128
Chichipapa (Japanese), **Gr. 2**, 22
Chíu, chíu, chíu (Spanish), **Gr. 2**, 302; **Gr. 6**, 172
Chorus of Villagers from *The Bartered Bride* (Czech),
   Gr. 5, 275
Cidade Maravilhosa (Portuguese), **Gr. 5**, 432
Cielito lindo (Spanish), **Gr. 3**, 166
Counting Song (Spanish), **Gr. 1**, T195
Cuando salí de Cuba (Spanish), **Gr. 5**, 168
Cumbia del sol (Spanish), **Gr. 5**, 16
Da pacem Domine (Latin), **Gr. 5**, 261
Dal Taro Kacha (Korean), **Gr. 2**, 98
!Dale, dale, dale! (Spanish), **Gr. 3**, 378
Dandansoy (Visayan), **Gr. 6**, 356
De allacito carnavalito (Spanish), **Gr. 5**, 269
De aquel cerro (Spanish), **Gr. 3**, 32
De colores (Spanish) (unison), **Gr. 5**, 88; (2-part),
   Gr. 5, 98
Dere Geliyor (Turkish), **Gr. 6**, 232
Deta, Deta (Japanese), **Gr. 5**, 246
Diana (Play the Bugle) (Spanish), **Gr. 1**, T334
Dide (Lobi), **Gr. 3**, 279
Dima (Tshiluba), **Gr. 4**, 265
Diou Shou Juan'er (Chinese), **Gr. 1**, T212
Diwali Song (Hindi), **Gr. 6**, 396
Dok Djampa (Laotian), **Gr. 4**, 392
Dona nobis pacem (Latin), **Gr. 6**, 385
Duérmete mi niño (Spanish), **Gr. 1**, T61
E nānā, kākou i nā manu (Hawaiian), **Gr. 4**, 338
Egy üveg alma (Hungarian), **Gr. 3**, 23
Ēinīnī (Gaelic), **Gr. 5**, 340
Eka Muda (Comanche), **Gr. 5**, 28
El arroyo que murmura (Spanish), **Gr. 3**, 318
El atole (Spanish), **Gr. 3**, 396
El barquito (Spanish), **Gr. 4**, 214
El burrito enfermo (Spanish), **Gr. 2**, 180
El charro (Spanish), **Gr. 6**, 278
El colación (Spanish), **Gr. 1**, T357
El coquí (Spanish), **Gr. 4**, 178
El florón (Spanish), **Gr. 1**, T117; **Gr. 3**, 46
El jarabe (Spanish), **Gr. 5**, 396
El juego chirimbolo (The Chirimbolo Game) (Spanish),
   Gr. 1, T103

El manisero (Spanish), **Gr. 4**, 106
El nacimiento (Spanish), **Gr. K**, T322
El Nido (Spanish), **Gr. 3**, 214
El palomo y la paloma (Spanish), **Gr. 2**, 380
El picaflor (Spanish), **Gr. K**, T141
¡El pueblo unido jamás será vencido! (Spanish), **Gr. 8**, 91
El quelite (Spanish), **Gr. 4**, 362
El rorro (The Babe) (Spanish), **Gr. 1**, T356
El tambor (Spanish). **Gr. K**, T129; **Gr. 6**, 222
El tecolote (Spanish), **Gr. 6**, 392
El tren (Spanish), **Gr. 2**, 326
El vito (Spanish), **Gr. 5**, 210
El zapatero (Spanish), **Gr. 2**, 138
En la feria de San Juan (Spanish), **Gr. 2**, 226
En nuestra Tierra tan linda (Spanish), **Gr. 2**, 114
En roulant ma boule (French), **Gr. 3**, 100
Entren, santos peregrinos (Spanish), **Gr. 4**, 379
Ésta sí que es Nochebuena (Spanish), **Gr. 2**, 361
Estrella brillante (Spanish), **Gr. 5**, 373
Farfallina (Italian), **Gr. 4**, 244
Fehér liliomszál (Hungarian), **Gr. K**, T139
Feliz Navidad (Spanish and English), **Gr. 5**, 420
Frère Jacques (French), **Gr. 4**, 260
Fun wa ni alaafia (Yoruba), **Gr. 5**, 248
Fung Yang Song (Chinese), **Gr. 5**, 58
Ga Eul (Korean), **Gr. 5**, 401
Go A Tin (Lantern Song) (Taiwanese), **Gr. 1**, T363
Gong xi fa cai (Chinese), **Gr. 3**, 384
Guantanamera (Spanish), **Gr. 5**, 215
Hae Wa Be (Korean), **Gr. 6**, 273
Haere Ra (Maori), **Gr. 5**, 151
Haji Firuz (Farsi), **Gr. 6**, 421
Hakyo Jong (Korean), **Gr. 1**, T302
Hala lala layya (Arabic), **Gr. 4**, 222
Haneirot Halalu (Hebrew), **Gr. 5**, 414
Hanukkah Chag Yafeh (Hebrew), **Gr. 1**, T350
Hashewie (Tigrinya), **Gr. 2**, 362
Hashkivenu (Hebrew), **Gr. 7**, 190
Hava Nagila (Hebrew), **Gr. 5**, 54
Hava Nashira (Hebrew), **Gr. 6**, 67
Heleluyan (Muscogee), **Gr. 6**, 188
Himmel und Erde (German), **Gr. 4**, 280
Hine Ma Tov (Hebrew), **Gr. 4**, 66
Hitori (Japanese), **Gr. 4**, 345
Hojas de té (Spanish), **Gr. 4**, 256
Hotaru Koi (Japanese), **Gr. 6**, 255
How Brightly Shines the Morning Star (German), **Gr. 5**, 370
Huainito (Spanish), **Gr. 6**, 351
I Chih Ching Wa (Chinese), **Gr. 2**, 186
Ifetayo (Yoruba), **Gr. K**, T325
Itik Besenda Gurau (Bahasa Indonesian), **Gr. 2**, 100
J'entends le Moulin (French), **Gr. 3**, 135
Já do lesa nepojedu (Czech), **Gr. 6**, 227
Ja posejah lubenice (Croatian), **Gr. 2**, 316
Jambo (Swahili), **Gr. 1**, T230
Jasmine Flower (Chinese), **Gr. 3**, 146
Jede, jede poštovský panáček (Czech), **Gr. 6**, 226
Jikel' emaweni (Xhosa), **Gr. 6**, 70
Jó ashílá (Navajo), **Gr. 5**, 224
Johan Tanko Bushi (Japanese), **Gr. 6**, 142

Juan Pirulero (Spanish), **Gr. 2,** 270

Jugaremos en el bosque (Spanish), **Gr. 2,** 188

Juhtgarak (Korean), **Gr. K,** T108

Kaeru no Uta (Japanese), **Gr. 1,** T112

Kakokolo (Lugandan), **Gr. 6,** 262

Kalinka (Russian), **Gr. 3,** 224

Kari (Wild Geese) (Japanese), **Gr. 1,** T261

Katyusha (Russian), **Gr. 4,** 188

Kobuta (Japanese), **Gr. 1,** T167

Kojo No Tsuki (Japanese), **Gr. 5,** 149

Kokiriko (Japanese) (listening), **Gr. 6,** 145

Kokoleoko (Liberian), **Gr. 6,** 279

Korobushka (Russian), **Gr. 4,** 285

Kuma San (Japanese), **Gr. 3,** 244

L'inverno è già passato (Italian), **Gr. 4,** 390

La bamba (Spanish), **Gr. 3,** 236; **Gr. 6,** 381

La bella hortelana (Spanish), **Gr. 2,** 208

La cloche (French), **Gr. 3,** 67

La otra España (Spanish), **Gr. 4,** 62

La pájara pinta (Spanish), **Gr. 6,** 268

La paloma se fue (Spanish), **Gr. 5,** 259

La pequeñita araña (Spanish), **Gr. K,** T9

La ranita cri (Spanish), **Gr. 1,** T27

La sanjuanerita (Spanish), **Gr. 4,** 100

La víbora de la mar (Spanish), **Gr. 5,** 441

La Yunsita (Spanish), **Gr. 4,** 350

Las horas (Spanish), **Gr. K,** T70

Las mañanitas (Spanish), **Gr. 4,** 194

Les anges dans nos campagnes (French), **Gr. 6,** 406

Los maizales (Spanish), **Gr. 5,** 268

Los pollitos (Spanish), **Gr. K,** T288

Lion Sleeps Tonight, The (Zulu), **Gr. 7,** 214

Ma'oz Tsur (Hebrew), **Gr. 6,** 405

Macoklis Mango (Spanish) (listening), **Gr. 8,** 46

María Blanca (Spanish), **Gr. K,** T99

Marken er mejet (Danish), **Gr. 4,** 364

Matarile (Spanish), **Gr. 2,** 261

Mayim, Mayim (Hebrew), **Gr. 6,** 102

Mbombela (Zulu), **Gr. K,** T152

Me gase boho (Sinhalese), **Gr. 2,** 317

Mein Hut (German), **Gr. 2,** 142

Mele Kalikimaka (Hawaiian), **Gr. 6,** 410

Merecumbé (Spanish), **Gr. 6,** 276

Mɔfia moni s'mo ho gbeke (Ga), **Gr. 5,** 277

Mi caballo blanco (Spanish), **Gr. 6,** 60

Mi chacra (Spanish), **Gr. K,** T207

Mi cuerpo (Spanish), **Gr. 1,** T32

Mi gallo (Spanish), **Gr. 5,** 272

Mizuguruma (Japanese), **Gr. 1,** T260

Molinillo de café (Spanish), **Gr. 4,** 250

Monté sur un éléphant (French), **Gr. K,** T217

Mos', Mos'! (Hopi), **Gr. 1,** T53

Na Bahia Tem (Portuguese), **Gr. K,** T163; **Gr. 1,** T297

Na belo (Fijian), **Gr. 2,** 322

Nabe, Nabe, Soku, Nuke (Japanese), **Gr. 2,** 259

Nach Nach Nach (Hindi), **Gr. 6,** 224

Nampaya omame (Zulu), **Gr. K,** T128

Nani Wale Na Hala (Hawaiian), **Gr. 5,** 276

Naranja dulce (Spanish), **Gr. 1,** T303

Neviděli jste tu mé panenky? (Czech), **Gr. 6,** 228

Ngam sang duan (Thai), **Gr. 5,** 376

Nikosi (Hopi), **Gr. 2,** 230

No despiertes a mi niño (Spanish), **Gr. 5,** 217

Nochebuena (Spanish), **Gr. K,** T323

N'kosi Sikelel' i Afrika (Zulu), **Gr. 6,** 339

O Canto da Cidade (Portuguese), **Gr. 7,** 3

O Mama Bakudala (Xhosa), **Gr. 3,** 328

O Tannenbaum! (German), **Gr. K,** T320

O, Desayo (Portuguese), **Gr. 6,** 50

Ɔbɔɔ Asi Me Nsa (Akan), **Gr. K,** T159

Och Jungfrun Hon Går I Ringen (Swedish), **Gr. 5,** 190

Ogguere (Afro-Cuban Spanish), **Gr. 4,** 327

Ole La'u Papa e (Tongan); **Gr. 6,** 91

Oma Rapeti (Maori), **Gr. 2,** 108

Oy Chanuke (Yiddish), **Gr. 3,** 368

Oye como va (Spanish), **Gr. 5,** 69

Pajarillo barranqueño (Spanish), **Gr. 3,** 358

Para pedir posada (Spanish), **Gr. 4,** 377

Pauper sum ego (Latin), **Gr. 6,** 254

Pimpón (Spanish), **Gr. K,** T22

Piñón, Pirulín (Spanish), **Gr. 1,** T311

Pleeng Loy Krathong (Thai), **Gr. 6,** 394

Powama (Cahuilla), **Gr. 7,** 63

Prairie Dog Song (Kiowa), **Gr. K,** T220

Pusa't daga (Tagalog), **Gr. 1,** T289

Quando men vo (Italian), **Gr. 7,** 180

Qué bonita bandera (Spanish), **Gr. 5,** 442

Qué bonito es (Spanish), **Gr. K,** T234

Que llueva (Spanish), **Gr. 3,** 274

¿Quién es ese pajarito? (Spanish), **Gr. 4,** 284

Raccoon Dance Song (Ottawan), **Gr. 3,** 87

Riqui Ran (Spanish), **Gr. 2,** 21

S'vivon Sov (Hebrew), **Gr. 1,** T348; **Gr. 4,** 374

Sakura (Japanese), **Gr. 6,** 14

Samiotissa (Greek), **Gr. 5,** 284

San Sereni (Spanish), **Gr. 2,** 323

Sankta Lucia (Swedish), **Gr. 5,** 412

Sansa kroma (Akan), **Gr. 4,** 167

Santa Marta (Spanish), **Gr. 5,** 398

Santoki (Korean), **Gr. 1,** T187

Sara Watashi (Japanese), **Gr. 1,** T67

Schwanenlied (German), **Gr. 7,** 124

Seneca Stomp Dance (Seneca), **Gr. K,** T345

Serra, Serra Serrador (Portuguese), **Gr. 1,** T133

Shabat Shalom (Hebrew), **Gr. 4,** 170

Shibolet Basadeh (Hebrew), **Gr. 6,** 424

Shope Shope (Bulgarian), **Gr. 5,** 220

Simi Yadech (Hebrew), **Gr. K,** 168

Singabahambayo (Zulu) (unison), **Gr. 5,** 56; (parts), **Gr. 5,** 75

Sitsiritsit (Tagalog), **Gr. 4,** 102

Somos el barco (Spanish), **Gr. 4,** 10

Son de Camaguey (listening) (Spanish), **Gr. 8,** 51

Sorida (Shona), **Gr. 2,** 96

Suk san wan pi mai (Laotian), **Gr. 5,** 437

Suliram (Indonesian), **Gr. 6,** 58

Suomen Salossa (Finnish), **Gr. 6,** 422

Symphony No. 9, Fourth Movement (German), **Gr. 7,** 156

Tako No Uta (Japanese), **Gr. 1,** T370

Tanabata (Japanese), **Gr. 3,** 62

Tekanionton'néha' (Mohawk), **Gr. 5,** 223
Tengo, Tengo, Tengo (Spanish), **Gr. K,** T212
Tết Trung (Vietnamese), **Gr. 4,** 366
Thula Sizwe (Zulu), **Gr. 6,** 73
Tina Singu (Sotho), **Gr. 6,** 36
Tinga Layo (Spanish), **Gr. 2,** 50
Tinikling (Tagalog), **Gr. 4,** 104
Tititorea (Maori), **Gr. 3,** 174
Tsing Chun Li Chü (Chinese), **Gr. 6,** 272
Tumbai (Hebrew), **Gr. 5,** 194
Twee emmertjes (Dutch), **Gr. 4,** 212
Tzena, Tzena (Hebrew), **Gr. 5,** 171
Ua txiab (Hmong), **Gr. 6,** 394
Ucha Tirvarch (Serrano), **Gr. 3,** 53
Uga, Uga, Uga (Hebrew), **Gr. 1,** T313
'Ulili E (Hawaiian), **Gr. 4,** 396
Un lorito de Verapaz (Spanish), **Gr. 5,** 349
Una Adivinanza (Spanish), **Gr. 1,** T138
Uno de enero (Spanish), **Gr. 3,** 210
Uno, dos y tres (Spanish), **Gr. 5,** 364
Ushkana (Cahuilla), **Gr. K,** T75
Üsküdar (Turkish), **Gr. 5,** 128
Uyai Mose (Shona), **Gr. 7,** 66
Vamos a la mar (Spanish), **Gr. 3,** 256
Vem Kan Segla (Swedish), **Gr. 6,** 419
Vinqo (Zulu), **Gr. 4,** 24
Viva la musica (Latin), **Gr. 4,** 174
Wachet auf (German), **Gr. 6,** 259
Wang Ü Ger (Chinese), **Gr. 3,** 190
Wavvuuvuumira (Luganda), **Gr. K,** T165
We Are Here (Navajo), **Gr. 4,** 394
Wéané (Menadonese), **Gr. 3,** 184
Winter Ade (German) **Gr. 6,** 132, 133
Y ahora vamos a cantar (Spanish), **Gr. K,** T340
Yerakina (Greek), **Gr. 6,** 216
Yo, Mamana, Yo (Shangaan), **Gr. 1,** T307
Yüe líang wan wan (Mandarin), **Gr. 6,** 26
Zui Zui Zukkorbashi (song) (Japanese), **Gr. 1,** T98,
Zum gali gali (Hebrew), **Gr. 4,** 255

O

ORFF. *See* Instruments, Playing; Playalongs, Orff
accompaniments; *Spotlight on Orff Orchestrations* under
separate cover

OSTINATOS. *See also* Creative Activities; Playalongs; Texture
body percussion, **Gr. 1,** T35, T38, T39, T40, T41, T90;
  Gr. 2, 209; **Gr. 3,** 34, 131, 185, 217, 243, 256, 272;
  Gr. 4, 51, 64, 103, 115, 131, 175, 196, 242, 254, 263,
  273, 310; **Gr. 5,** 36, 49, 52, 53, 129, 205, 209, 211,
  212, 213, 219, 242, 262, 265, 409; **Gr. 6,** 5, 12, 92;
  Gr. 7, 5, 17, 22, 29, 57, 66, 135, 203, 209, 226
definition, **Gr. 1,** T198;
instrumental, pitched, **Gr. K,** T205; **Gr. 3,** 207, 267, 270,
  286, 377; **Gr. 4,** 36, 37, 59, 64, 75, 103, 129, 137,
  149, 151, 175, 180, 219, 227, 269, 278, 371, 373;
  Gr. 5, 51, 90, 143, 170, 207, 211; **Gr. 6,** 15; **Gr. 7,** 15,
  21, 29, 31, 83, 123, 215, 228
instrumental, unpitched, **Gr. K,** T81, T319; **Gr. 1,** T92,
  T259; **Gr. 2,** 89, 215; **Gr. 3,** 207, 243, 256; **Gr. 4,** 37,
  59, 68, 75, 92, 99, 103, 137, 151, 175, 196, 219, 227,

242, 250, 265, 271, 281, 282, 375; **Gr. 5,** 17, 49, 52,
  53, 68, 73, 75, 84, 90, 129, 135, 205, 207, 209, 211,
  212, 250, 265, 267, 269, 391, 399, 403, 407, 425,
  429, 437; **Gr. 6,** 7, 8, 11, 13, 15, 111, 125, 251;
  Gr. 7, 5, 7, 67, 101, 116, 118, 119, 123, 135, 148,
  201, 209, 225, 228; **Gr. 8,** 7, 14, 34, 37, 56, 63, 110,
  111, 145, 149, 190
movement, **Gr. 3,** 205; **Gr. 5,** 219; **Gr. 7,** 11, 65, 114, 119
music with chairs, **Gr. 8,** 15
perform, **Gr. 3,** 131, 217, 270, 377
spoken, **Gr. 1,** T259; **Gr. 2,** 207, 209, 263; **Gr. 3,** 185,
  207, 217, 243; **Gr. 4,** 263, 271; **Gr. 5,** 52, 219, 265,
  267; **Gr. 7,** 22, 116
sung, **Gr. 1,** T120, T182; **Gr. 3,** 136, 207, 250, 267,
  286; **Gr. 4,** 111, 133, 248, 255, 269; **Gr. 5,** 273, 274;
  Gr. 6, 249, 253

P

PART SONGS. *See also* Form and Genre, canon; Partner Songs
  two-part
    A Rovin', **Gr. 6,** 319
    A Zing-A Za, **Gr. 5,** 338
    All Ye Who Music Love, **Gr. 6,** 336
    Ballad of the Underground Railroad, The, **Gr. 5,** 154
    Bashana Haba'ah, **Gr. 6,** 360
    Battle Hymn of the Republic, **Gr. 5,** 391
    Camelot, **Gr. 6,** 310
    Cheers, **Gr. 7,** 34
    Circle of Friends, **Gr. 5,** 196
    Circle of Song, **Gr. 4,** 330
    City Life (with "I Love the Mountains"), **Gr. 3,** 341
    Cornstalk Fiddle and a Shoestring Bow, **Gr. 3,** 284
    Cripple Creek, **Gr. 6,** 372
    Cum-ma-la Be-stay, **Gr. 6,** 370
    Da pacem Domine, **Gr. 5,** 261
    Dandansoy, **Gr. 6,** 356
    De colores, **Gr. 5,** 98
    Didn't It Rain, **Gr. 6,** 345
    Doctor Jazz, **Gr. 6,** 378
    Doing the Latest Rag, **Gr. 6,** 314
    Don't Let the Music Stop, **Gr. 4,** 334
    Down by the Riverside, **Gr. 6,** 22
    Earth Is Our Mother, The, **Gr. 7,** 220
    Ēinīnī (Gaelic), **Gr. 5,** 340
    Elijah Rock, **Gr. 6,** 53
    Ev'ry Time I Feel the Spirit, **Gr. 6,** C
    Feel Good, **Gr. 5,** 358
    Fortune Favors the Brave, **Gr. 6,** 316
    Fung Yang Song, **Gr. 5,** 58
    Ghost Ship, The, **Gr. 6,** 323
    Great Outdoors, The, **Gr. 2,** 290
    Haere Ra, **Gr. 5,** 151
    Hitori, **Gr. 4,** 345
    Holly and the Ivy, The, **Gr. 5,** 418
    Huainito, **Gr. 6,** 351
    I Am But a Small Voice, **Gr. 5,** 323
    I Hear America Singing, **Gr. 5,** 327
    I Think I'm Gonna Like It Here, **Gr. 4,** 299
    In that Great Git'n Up Mornin', **Gr. 5,** 10, 242
    Jikel' Emaweni, **Gr. 6,** 70

Classified Index of Songs, Selected Concepts, Skills, and Activities (continued)

Joban Tanko Bushi, **Gr. 6,** 142
Jordan's Angels, **Gr. 6,** 365
Kettle Valley Line, The, **Gr. 4,** 348
La Yunsita, **Gr. 4,** 350
Like a Mighty Stream, **Gr. 5,** 320
Little David Play on Your Harp, **Gr. 4,** 323
Look High, Look Low, **Gr. 3,** 338
Magnificent Horses, **Gr. 7,** 104
Mango Walk, **Gr. 5,** 92
Mi caballo blanco, **Gr. 6,** 60
Ngam sang duan, **Gr. 5,** 376
Night of Stars/Silent Night, **Gr. 6,** 412
O, Desayo, **Gr. 6,** 50
O, La Le!, **Gr. 6,** 6
Old Barn Dance, The, **Gr. 6,** 94
On the Sunny Side of the Street, **Gr. 5,** 361
One-Eyed Ford, **Gr. 7,** 200
Our World, **Gr. 5,** 381
Perfect Winter Day, A, **Gr. 6,** 400
Powama, **Gr. 7,** 63
Ride Like the Wind, **Gr. 5,** 130
Ride on the Wind, **Gr. 6,** 325
Rocky Top, **Gr. 5,** 352
Roll On, Columbia, **Gr. 4,** 182
Shope Shope, **Gr. 5,** 220
Sing Hosanna, **Gr. 6,** 364
Sing, America Sing!, **Gr. 5,** 6
Success, **Gr. 7,** 241-43
Suliram, **Gr. 6,** 58
Sun Don't Set in the Mornin', **Gr. 3,** 60
Surfin' U.S.A., **Gr. 5,** 306
That Great Come and Get It day, **Gr. 6,** 306
There's a Song in Me, **Gr. 5,** 183
They Call the Wind Maria, **Gr. 6,** 312
Tina Singu, **Gr. 6,** 36
Trout, The, **Gr. 6,** 342
Tum Balalaika, **Gr. 6,** 69
Turn the World Around, **Gr. 5,** 208
Twist and Shout, **Gr. 7,** 160
'Ulili E, **Gr. 4,** 396
Un lorito de Verapaz, **Gr. 5,** 349
Uncle Pen, **Gr. 5,** 24
Uno, dos y tres, **Gr. 5,** 364
Uyai Mose, **Gr. 7,** 66
Waiting for Life, **Gr. 6,** 292
Walking in the Air, **Gr. 4,** 317
Water Is Wide, The, **Gr. 6,** 46
We Are the Children of Tomorrow, **Gr. 5,** 114
We Remember, **Gr. 4,** 360
We Want to Sing, **Gr. 5,** 235
What the World Needs Now, **Gr. 5,** 230
Why We Tell the Story, **Gr. 6,** 303
Winter Wonderland, **Gr. 5,** 408
Yankee Doodle, **Gr. 4,** 155
You Sing for Me, **Gr. 6,** 106

three-part
Aideu (listening), **Gr. 7,** 223
Atlantic City, **Gr. 7,** 248
Bamboo, **Gr. 4,** 218
Cindy, **Gr. 5,** 265

Coast of High Barbary, The, **Gr. 6,** 329
Estrella brillante, **Gr. 5,** 373
Follow Your Dream, **Gr. 7,** 207
Gentle River Runs, A, **Gr. 5,** 342
Henry Ford, **Gr. 7,** 244–45
I've Got a Robe, **Gr. 7,** 162
Jikel' Emaweni, **Gr. 6,** 70
La Bamba, **Gr. 6,** 381
Leila, **Gr. 6,** 376
Listen to the Music, **Gr. 6,** 63
My Government Claim, **Gr. 5,** 110
N'kosi sikelel' i Afrika, **Gr. 6,** 339
Park Rap **Gr. 7,** 1, 70
Ragtime, **Gr. 7,** 237–40; (Epilogue and Finale),
   Gr. 7, 250–51
Sing Alleluia, Allelu, **Gr. 4,** 220
Twist and Shout, **Gr. 4,** 314

four-part
Lion Sleeps Tonight, The, **Gr. 7,** 214–15
Mama Will Provide, **Gr. 6,** 296
National Emblem by E. E. Bagley (listening), **Gr. 7,** 76
Oh, Come Sing a Song, **Gr. 7,** 65
Singabahambayo, **Gr. 5,** 75
Walk by the River, **Gr. 6,** 74

five-part
Lion Sleeps Tonight, The, **Gr. 5,** 172
Park Rap **Gr. 7,** 2, 73
This Pretty Planet, **Gr. 6,** 194

PARTNER SONGS. *See also* Part Songs
Ballad of the Underground Railroad, The (portion),
   Gr. 5, 154
Chicka Hanka, **Gr. 4,** 138
Hallelujah Get on Board, **Gr. 5,** 345
Já do lesa nepojedu, **Gr. 6,** 227
Jede, jede poštovský panáček, **Gr. 6,** 226
L'il 'Liza Jane, **Gr. 4,** 20
Mango Walk, **Gr. 5,** 93
Neviděli jste tu mé panenky?, **Gr. 6,** 228
Oh, Won't You Sit Down?, **Gr. 4,** 70
Old House, **Gr. 4,** 282
Pay Me My Money Down, **Gr. 3,** 149
Pick-A-Little/Goodnight, Ladies, **Gr. 5,** 299
Triple Play, **Gr. 5,** 355
Twist and Shout, **Gr. 4,** 314

PATRIOTIC MUSIC. *See also* Holiday and Seasonal Music
America, **Gr. 2,** 338; **Gr. 4,** 364; **Gr. 6,** 388; **Gr. 8,** 31
America, My Homeland, **Gr. 4,** 358
America, the Beautiful, **Gr. 3,** 354; **Gr. 5,** 388
American Salute, **Gr. 7,** 170
Battle Hymn of the Republic by W. Steffe and J.W. Howe,
   Gr. K, T331, **Gr. 5,** 390; (listening), **Gr. 6,** 389
Celebration Medley (montage), **Gr. 7,** 185
Dreamers, **Gr. 5,** 430
El Capitán, **Gr. 8,** 6
Fifty Nifty United States, **Gr. 5,** 392
God Bless the U.S.A., **Gr. 7,** 136
Heartbeat of Democracy (poem), **Gr. 5,** 389
Hop, Chirp! Moo! Oh Happy Springtime Day, **Gr. 1,** T372
Liberty Bell March, The (listening), **Gr. 5,** 395

Classified Index of Songs, Selected Concepts, Skills, and Activities (continued)

Liberty Fanfare, **Gr. 7,** 187
My Mom, **Gr. 1,** T372
Patriotic Medley, **Gr. 1,** T8; **Gr. 2,** H; **Gr. 3,** H; **Gr. 4,** H; **Gr. 6,** H
Presidents, **Gr. K,** T330
Semper Fidelis by J. P. Sousa (listening), **Gr. 6,** 391
Sing of America, **Gr. 4,** 359
Spotlight on America, **Gr. 1,** T9
Spring, **Gr. 1,** T273
Stars and Stripes Forever, The, **Gr. 6,** 390; **Gr. 7,** 197
Star-Spangled Banner, The, **Gr. 4,** 356, **Gr. 6,** 386, **Gr. 7,** 194; (listening and song) **Gr. 5,** 86, 386
Step Into the Spotlight, **Gr. 6,** A
Tako No Uta, **Gr. 1,** T370
Taps, **Gr. 7,** 144
There are Many Flags in Many Lands, **Gr. 2,** 341
This Is America, **Gr. 3,** 356
This Land is Your Land, **Gr. 4,** 146
Washington Post (listening), **Gr. 2,** 339
We Remember, **Gr. 4,** 360
When Johnny Comes Marching Home, **Gr. 7,** 168
Yankee Doodle Boy, **Gr. 3,** 357
Yankee Doodle, **Gr. 2,** 340; **Gr. 4,** 154
You're a Grand Old Flag, **Gr. K,** T4; **Gr. 3,** 355

PENTATONIC SONGS. See Limited Tone Songs

PERFORMANCE. See also Broadway for Kids; Spotlight on Performance, **Gr. K,** T268–T299; **Gr. 1,** T268–T323; **Gr. 2,** 273–335; **Gr. 3,** 289–351; **Gr. 4,** 289–351; **Gr. 5,** 289–383; **Gr. 6,** 289–383; **Gr. 7,** 236–251
about the musical (Broadway for Kids), **Gr. 2,** 287–289; **Gr. 3,** 305; **Gr. 4,** 305; **Gr. 5,** 305; **Gr. 7,** 250–251; **Gr. 8,** 250–251
assessment, **Gr. 5,** 39, 79, 119, 159, 199, 239
audience participation, **Gr. 4,** 65; **Gr. 5,** 355
blocking, **Gr. 6,** 291
Broadway for Kids, **Gr. 6,** 290–305
cast, **Gr. 6,** 297, 298
choral songs to perform, **Gr. 1,** T284–T315; **Gr. 3,** 306–351; **Gr. 4,** 306–351; **Gr. 5,** 306–383
choreography (Broadway for Kids), **Gr. 4,** 300, 302, 305; **Gr. 5,** 291, 292, 293, 305
choreography notes. See also Piano Accompaniment Book, **Gr. 1,** T274; **Gr. 3,** 2, 42, 82, 122, 162, 202; **Gr. 4,** 2, 42, 82, 122, 162, 202; **Gr. 5,** 2, 42, 82, 122, 162, 202; **Gr. 6,** 2, 42, 82, 122, 162, 202, 296, 297, 300, 302, 303; **Gr. 7,** 237
copyright law, **Gr. 1,** T280; **Gr. 2,** 280–282; **Gr. 3,** 300–302; **Gr. 4,** 302–304; **Gr. 5,** 301–304; **Gr. 7,** 247–250; **Gr. 8,** 246–247
    collaboration, **Gr. 6,** 301
    Intellectual Property Right, **Gr. 6,** 300, 302
    performance license, **Gr. 6,** 300–301
    printed programs, **Gr. 6,** 299, 303
    royalties, **Gr. 6,** 300–301
costumes (Broadway for Kids), **Gr. 1,** T271; **Gr. 2,** 277; **Gr. 3,** 293, 294; **Gr. 4,** 292, 294–295; **Gr. 5,** 294, 297; **Gr. 6,** 293, 295; **Gr. 7,** 240; **Gr. 8,** 239
curtain call, **Gr. 6,** 291
director's notes, **Gr. 6,** 292, 293, 294, 295, 297, 300, 301, 304

lighting (Broadway for Kids), **Gr. 1,** T270; **Gr. 2,** 276; **Gr. 3,** 293, 300; **Gr. 4,** 292, 293, 294, 296, 297; **Gr. 5,** 293, 295, 299, 302, 304; **Gr. 6,** 292–293; **Gr. 7,** 239; **Gr. 8,** 238, 239
music cue, **Gr. 6,** 292, 296, 303
musical theater vocabulary, **Gr. 1,** T275; **Gr. 2,** 283; **Gr. 3,** 291; **Gr. 4,** 291; **Gr. 5,** 296, 297; **Gr. 6,** 291; **Gr. 7,** 237, 242; **Gr. 8,** 242
performance license, **Gr. 1,** T281; **Gr. 2,** 274; **Gr. 3,** 300, 301; **Gr. 4,** 302, 303; **Gr. 5,** 302; **Gr. 7,** 247–248
performance suggestions (Broadway for Kids), **Gr. 1,** T269; **Gr. 2,** 275–277, 284–286; **Gr. 3,** 292–303; **Gr. 4,** 292–301; **Gr. 5,** 292–300; **Gr. 7,** 237–240; **Gr. 8,** 243–245
pre-performance, **Gr. 5,** 328
printed programs, **Gr. 1,** T278; **Gr. 2,** 275–277, 284–286; **Gr. 3,** 299, 303; **Gr. 4,** 301, 304; **Gr. 5,** 301, 304; **Gr. 7,** 246; **Gr. 8,** 249
program ideas, **Gr. 6,** 82, 122, 162, 202, 369; **Gr. 8,** 2, 29, 54, 81, 107
props (Broadway for Kids), **Gr. 1,** T273; **Gr. 2,** 277; **Gr. 3,** 292, 295, 298, 299, 303; **Gr. 4,** 292, 293, 296, 297; **Gr. 5,** 296, 298, 305; **Gr. 6,** 291, 292; **Gr. 7,** 241; **Gr. 8,** 239
rehearsals, **Gr. 6,** 291, 297, 298
scenery. See Performance, Sets
sets (Broadway for Kids), **Gr. 1,** T269; **Gr. 2,** 275; **Gr. 3,** 292, 293, 304; **Gr. 4,** 292–293; **Gr. 5,** 292; **Gr. 6,** 292; **Gr. 7,** 238; **Gr. 8,** 238
stage, **Gr. 6,** 291
stage crew, **Gr. 6,** 291, 297
stage manager, **Gr. 6,** 297
stories to perform
    City Traffic, **Gr. 2,** 328–329
    Drumming Spider, The, **Gr. 2,** 333–335
    Isabela and the Troll, **Gr. 3,** 349
    Jump or Jiggle, **Gr. 1,** 114–115
    Rabbit in the Moon, The, **Gr. 1,** 116–118
    Señor Coyote, **Gr. 2,** 330–332
    The Gebeta Board, **Gr. 3,** 346
    There Was an Old Lady, **Gr. 3,** 344
    Why the Beetle Has a Gold Coat, **Gr. 1,** 119–121
tableau, **Gr. 6,** 296
theater games, **Gr. 1,** T277; **Gr. 3,** 298; **Gr. 4,** 300; **Gr. 5,** 300; **Gr. 7,** 245
timeline, **Gr. 6,** 297
using dynamics, **Gr. 5,** 313

PLAYALONGS. See also Instruments, Playing
harmonic
    Achshav, **Gr. 4,** 113
    Blow, Ye Winds, Blow, **Gr. 3,** 192
    Caballito Blanco, **Gr. 4,** 278
    Canon, **Gr. 8,** 67
    City Blues, **Gr. 5,** 278
    Cuando salí de Cuba, **Gr. 5,** 169
    Drops of jupiter, **Gr. 8,** 102
    El coquí, **Gr. 4,** 180
    El jarabe tapatío, **Gr. 7,** 58

Classified Index

Every Day I Have the Blues, **Gr. 5**, 181
Good Mornin', Blues, **Gr. 5**, 177
Just Keep Goin' On, **Gr. 7**, 21
Mary Ann, **Gr. 5**, 167
Sound the Trumpet, **Gr. 5**, 279
This Land is Your Land, **Gr. 4**, 148
Tzena, Tzena, **Gr. 5**, 170
instrumental
  Arianna, **Gr. 7**, 94–95
  Buckeye Jim, **Gr. 4**, 137
  Butterfly Come Play with Me, **Gr. 3**, 113
  Caribbean Amphibian, **Gr. 1**, T295
  City Traffic (poem), **Gr. 2**, 328–329
  Drumming Spider, The (poem), **Gr. 2**, 333–335
  Eka Muda, **Gr. 5**, 28
  El jarabe tapatío, **Gr. 7**, 58
  Entertainer, The, **Gr. 7**, 23
  Granny, **Gr. 1**, T104
  Grasshoppers Three, **Gr. 1**, T284
  Hashewie, **Gr. 2**, 363
  Hi! My Name is Joe! (speech piece), **Gr. 1**, T220
  In the Window, **Gr. 2**, 353
  Love Grows, **Gr. 1**, T205
  Moon Boat (poem), **Gr. 2**, 218, 219
  Na Bahia Tem, **Gr. 1**, T297
  Nigun Atik, **Gr. 3**, 71
  Oliver Cromwell, **Gr. 4**, 269
  Polly Wolly Doodle, **Gr. 3**, 133
  Rattlesnake, **Gr. 3**, 73
  Royal March of the Lions, The, **Gr. 1**, T24
  Rumpus in Richmond, **Gr. 8**, 33
  Sailor Went to Sea, A, **Gr. 1**, T38
  Señor Coyote (poem), **Gr. 2**, 330–332
  Shepherd, Shepherd, **Gr. 3**, 57
  Skin and Bones, **Gr. 1**, T340
  Sones de mariachi (listening), **Gr. 2**, 381
  This is Halloween, **Gr. 2**, 347
  This Little Light of Mine, **Gr. 1**, T238
  Tisket, A Tasket, A, **Gr. 1**, T107
  Tzakonikos, **Gr. 6**, 214
  Uga Uga Uga, **Gr. 1**, T313
  Wake Me, Shake Me, **Gr. 1**, T199
  When I First Came to This Land, **Gr. 3**, 29
melodic
  Canon, **Gr. 8**, 67
  Cliffs of Doneen, The, **Gr. 5**, 47
  Common Step, **Gr. 8**, 39
  Gee, Mom, I Want to Go Home, **Gr. 6**, 148
  Happy Wanderer, The, **Gr. 3**, 21
  Heart, **Gr. 6**, 168
  Jack was Ev'ry Bit a Sailor, **Gr. 6**, 170
  Joyful, Joyful, We Adore Thee, **Gr. 5**, 103
  Just Keep Goin' On, **Gr. 7**, 21
  Kojo No Tsuki, **Gr. 5**, 149
  Mi caballo blanco, **Gr. 6**, 61
  One Dime Blues, **Gr. 6**, 179
  Piñón, Pirulín, **Gr. 1**, T311
  Sakura, **Gr. 6**, 15
  Shoheen Sho, **Gr. 2**, 140
  Sun Don't Set in the Mornin', **Gr. 3**, 61

Symphony No. 9, Fourth Movement, **Gr. 7**, 156
This Pretty Planet, **Gr. 6**, 196
Twenty-four Robbers, **Gr. 1**, T173
orff accompaniments
  A la rueda de San Miguel, **Gr. 2**, 60
  All Around the Buttercup, **Gr. 2**, 211
  Amazing Grace, **Gr. 5**, 20
  Arirang, **Gr. 5**, 51, 61
  Bamboo, **Gr. 4**, 219
  Ban Dal, **Gr. 2**, 219
  Chichipapa, **Gr. 2**, 23
  City Traffic (poem), **Gr. 2**, 328–329
  Dance for the Nations, **Gr. 5**, 207
  Drumming Spider, The (poem), **Gr. 2**, 333
  Early in the Morning at Eight O'Clock, **Gr. 4**, 59
  Eating Lizards, **Gr. 2**, 250
  El burrito enfermo, **Gr. 2**, 181
  El vito, **Gr. 5**, 211
  Follow the Drinkin' Gourd, **Gr. 5**, 143
  Good Mornin', Blues/Backwater Blues, **Gr. 5**, 180
  Great Big House, **Gr. 3**, 14
  Hullaballoo Balay, **Gr. 6**, 11
  I Heard a Mockingbird, **Gr. 4**, 151
  I'll Rise When the Rooster Crows, **Gr. 4**, 37
  If You Find You're In a Bind, **Gr. 2**, 332
  In That Great Git'n Up Mornin', **Gr. 5**, 13
  It's Raining! It's Pouring!, **Gr. 2**, 233
  Jikel' Emaweni, **Gr. 6**, 72
  Jugaremos en el bosque, **Gr. 2**, 189
  Lemonade, **Gr. 2**, 32
  Mango Walk, **Gr. 5**, 90
  Mary's Coal Black Lamb, **Gr. 1**, T286
  Mein Hut, **Gr. 2**, 143
  My Government Claim, **Gr. 5**, 111
  Och Jungfrun Hon Går I Ringen, **Gr. 5**, 191
  Old Joe Clark, **Gr. 4**, 75
  Old King Glory (improvised), **Gr. 1**, T217
  Pat Works on the Railway, **Gr. 1**, T144
  Piñón, Pirulín, **Gr. 1**, T311
  Rabbit in the Moon, The (story), **Gr. 1**, T318
  Seesaw, **Gr. 1**, T248
  Señor Coyote (poem), **Gr. 2**, 330
  Sitsiritsit, **Gr. 4**, 103
  Tisket, A Tasket, A, **Gr. 1**, T107
  Twenty-four Robbers, **Gr. 1**, T173
  Village Music, **Gr. 2**, 334
  Viva la musica, **Gr. 4**, 175
  Walk in the Parlor, **Gr. 4**, 227
  When the Saints Go Marching In, **Gr. 5**, 256
  Who Has Seen the Wind? (poem), **Gr. 2**, 137
  Why the Beetle has a Gold Coat, **Gr. 1**, T321
  Winter Wind, The (listening), **Gr. 2**, 136
  You'll Sing a Song and I'll Sing a Song, **Gr. 2**, 157
ostinato, **Gr. 1**, T24, T91, T313; **Gr. 5**, 17, 49, 51, 53, 73, 75, 90, 129, 135, 143, 207, 211, 212
  Angelina, **Gr. 6**, 8
  Brandenburg Concerto No. 5, Third Movement, **Gr. 6**, 128
  Effie Goes Folk Dancing, **Gr. 2**, 169
  Elijah Rock, **Gr. 6**, 53

Classified Index

Greenland Whale Fishery, **Gr. 6,** 212
Here Comes a Bluebird, **Gr. 2,** 263
I Want to Be Ready, **Gr. 6,** 13
If You Find You're In a Bind, **Gr. 2,** 332
Kololeoko, **Gr. 6,** 279
Mars from *The Planets* by G. Holst (listening), **Gr. 6,** 197
Na belo, **Gr. 2,** 322
O, La, Le!, **Gr. 6,** 6
Sakura, **Gr. 6,** 14
Tain't What You Do, **Gr. 6,** 19
Village Music, **Gr. 2,** 334
Yankee Doodle, **Gr. 2,** 341
rhythmic
Achshav, **Gr. 4,** 113
Addams Family Theme, The, **Gr. 8,** 145
Afoxé, **Gr. 8,** 34
Agahu, **Gr. 5,** 73
Allá en el rancho grande, **Gr. 5,** 68
Ame fure, **Gr. 4,** 27
Animal Fair, **Gr. 2,** 215, 216
Arirang, **Gr. 5,** 53
Australia's on the Wallaby, **Gr. 2,** 107
Ballet Music from *Iphigénie en Aulide* (listening), **Gr. 2,** 25
Beatles Medley, **Gr. 8,** 149
Berceuse (listening), **Gr. 2,** 185
Big Beautiful Planet, **Gr. 2,** 377
Bird Island, **Gr. 8,** 56
Bulgarian folk melody, **Gr. 5,** 219
Career Mosaic, **Gr. 8,** 190
Chichipapa (The Sparrow's Singing School), **Gr. 2,** 22
City Traffic (poem), **Gr. 2,** 328–329
Corner Grocery Store, **Gr. 2,** 310
Country Gardens (listening), **Gr. 2,** 16–17
Cumbia del sol, **Gr. 5,** 17
De allacito carnavalito, **Gr. 5,** 269
Dima, **Gr. 4,** 265
Drumming Spider, The (poem), **Gr. 2,** 333
El Capitán, **Gr. 8,** 7
Entertainer, The, **Gr. 7,** 23
Erev Shel Shoshanim, **Gr. 4,** 68
Four White Horses, **Gr. 2,** 300, 301
Frog in the Meadow, **Gr. 3,** 243
Glad About It, **Gr. 8,** 63
Going Over the Sea, **Gr. 2,** 216
Hakuna Matata, **Gr. 2,** 293
Hop Up and Jump Up, **Gr. 4,** 271
"in the store" [rhythm], **Gr. 2,** 310
It's Only Monday, **Gr. 8,** 14
Journey, A, **Gr. 4,** 15
Juan Pirulero, **Gr. 2,** 270
Kye Kye Kule, **Gr. 7,** 225
La otra España, **Gr. 4,** 64
Las mañanitas, **Gr. 4,** 196
Let's Go Fly a Kite, **Gr. 2,** 135
Maggie in the Wood, **Gr. 5,** 49
March for Military Band, **Gr. 8,** 37
Martin Luther King, **Gr. 2,** 365
Me Stone, **Gr. 2,** 49

Mill Song, The, **Gr. 2,** 52
Minuet from *Abdelazar*, **Gr. 2,** 144
Modern Dragon, A, **Gr. 4,** 99
National Emblem, **Gr. 7,** 76–77
Old Abram Brown, **Gr. 4,** 33
Old House, **Gr. 4,** 282
One Note Samba, **Gr. 4,** 92
Rumpus in Richmond, **Gr. 8,** 33
S'vivon Sov, **Gr. 4,** 375
San Serení, **Gr. 2,** 323
Señor Coyote (poem), **Gr. 2,** 330–332
Shepherd, Shepherd, **Gr. 3,** 57
Singabahambayo, **Gr. 5,** 95
Spirit Medley Rondo, **Gr. 7,** 45
Tabu (listening), **Gr. 2,** 20
Take Five, **Gr. 5,** 213
Tehahontanekenhnêha', **Gr. 3,** 51
Theme from The Monkees, **Gr. 8,** 110, 111
Three Little Penguins (speech piece), **Gr. 2,** 112, 113
Tiki Tiki Tiki Room, The, **Gr. 2,** 325
Turn the World Around, **Gr. 5,** 209
Up on the Housetop, **Gr. 2,** 357
Üsküdar, **Gr. 5,** 129, 135
We're Sailing Down the River, **Gr. 2,** 167
Wéané, **Gr. 3,** 185
Yongnam Nongak, **Gr. 5,** 71

R

REACHING ALL LEARNERS

English Language Learners

adjectives for high and low, **Gr. 2,** 31
advertising, **Gr. 8,** 222
arenas, amphitheaters, natural amphitheaters, **Gr. 7,** 95
background for lyrics, **Gr. 8,** 78
Bizet, Georges, **Gr. 7,** 122
blues, **Gr. 7,** 19
brass, woodwinds, percussion, **Gr. 7,** 39
Broadway and off-Broadway, **Gr. 7,** 87
Carmen, **Gr. 7,** 122
charades and alternative ways to communicate, **Gr. 7,** 230
cognates and false cognates, **Gr. 4,** 129, 231
colloquialisms, **Gr. 4,** 4, 47; **Gr. 5,** 11, 24; **Gr. 6,** 164, 183
community events, **Gr. 8,** 206
comparative adjectives, **Gr. 2,** 12
comparative language, **Gr. K,** T216; **Gr. 1,** T59, T63, T123, T173, T201
compare/contrast, **Gr. 1,** T143; **Gr. 6,** 183, 386
compound words, **Gr. 2,** 57; **Gr. 3,** 135, 171; **Gr. 4,** 95, 124
conductor's responsibilities, **Gr. 8,** 167
contractions, **Gr. 1,** T135; **Gr. 2,** E, 11
cultural activities, **Gr. 6,** 113
cultural explanations, **Gr. 1,** T177; **Gr. 3,** 17, 87, 145, 153, 189, 227, 233, 355; **Gr. 4,** 21, 204, 361; **Gr. 5,** 44, 55, 133, 145, 181, 227; **Gr. 6,** 21, 31, 106, 117, 137, 141, 212
dances, **Gr. 5,** 171, 223; **Gr. 6,** 106

days of the week, **Gr. K,** T80

defining freedom and liberty, **Gr. 7,** 186

double meaning, **Gr. 8,** 194

English dialects, **Gr. 3,** 204; **Gr. 4,** 91; **Gr. 6,** 127

figurative speech, **Gr. 3,** 129; **Gr. 4,** 53; **Gr. 5,** 4, 44, 176

First Amendment of the Constitution, **Gr. 7,** 195

folk songs, **Gr. 2,** 105

found instruments, **Gr. 8,** 35

games, explanation of, **Gr. 5,** 29

gestures and visuals to portray meaning, **Gr. K,** T151, T160, T169, T185, T196, T203; **Gr. 3,** 12

Halloween, **Gr. 2,** 346

hello, **Gr. 2,** 95

heroes, **Gr. 2,** 365

holidays and cultures, **Gr. 7,** 60

homonyms, **Gr. 2,** 75

homophones, **Gr. 2,** C

idioms, **Gr. K,** T144; **Gr. 3,** 124

Jefferson, Thomas, and The Declaration of Independence, **Gr. 7,** 211

instruments, **Gr. 1,** T211; **Gr. 5,** 53, 93, 219; **Gr. 6,** 7, 141; **Gr. 8,** 70

long/short sounds, **Gr. 2,** 207

lyrics, explanation of, **Gr. 1,** T4, T161, T201; **Gr. 2,** 4, 67, 112, 153, 170, 191, 207, 222; **Gr. 3,** 44, 84, 164, 189, 233; **Gr. 4,** 53; **Gr. 5,** 11, 25, 44, 84, 86, 95, 133, 145, 168, 388; **Gr. 6,** 44, 84

manager's responsibilities, **Gr. 8,** 229

Martin Luther King, Jr., **Gr. 2,** 365

mood and different expressions, meanings, **Gr. 7,** 133

morphemes, **Gr. 1,** T21; **Gr. 3,** 171; **Gr. 4,** 124

multicultural society and Western music, **Gr. 7,** 107

music in funeral services and memorial ceremonies, **Gr. 7,** 143

music in graduation ceremonies, **Gr. 7,** 51

music in political demonstrations, **Gr. 7,** 153

music in the workplace, **Gr. 7,** 151

music in various events, **Gr. 7,** 43

music therapy, **Gr. 8,** 181

musical terms, **Gr. 1,** T17, T31, T195; **Gr. 3,** 95; **Gr. 4,** 17, 61, 143; **Gr. 6,** 46, 219

musical timeline, **Gr. 7,** 9

musicians, **Gr. 6,** 113, 391

names of geographical locations, **Gr. 4,** 164, 183

national anthem, the and the American flag, **Gr. 7,** 195

national conventions, **Gr. 7,** 77

New Orleans, the mambo and zydeco, **Gr. 7,** 88

non-English words, **Gr. K,** T75; **Gr. 2,** 93, 95; **Gr. 3,** 95, 211; **Gr. 4,** 21, 129, 168, 179, 229; **Gr. 5,** 49, 55, 109, 139, 168; **Gr. 6,** 117

numbers, **Gr. K,** T72, T308; **Gr. 1,** T123

orchestral families, **Gr. 2,** 73

parades, **Gr. 7,** 65

patriotic songs, **Gr. 1,** T6; **Gr. 2,** G; **Gr. 3,** 355; **Gr. 5,** 86, 388, 390; **Gr. 6,** 386

penguins, **Gr. 2,** 112

pep rallies, **Gr. 7,** 35

phonemic awareness, **Gr. K,** T196; **Gr. 1,** T95; **Gr. 3,** 56

plural "s", **Gr. K,** T308

pop music, non-American, **Gr. 7,** 225

possessive "s", **Gr. 1,** T161

prayer/"grace," **Gr. 2,** 349

prefixes, **Gr. 2,** 143; **Gr. 4,** 221

pronunciation, **Gr. K,** T38, T43, T58, T72, T75, T80, T96, T144, T151, T160, T169, T185, T196, T203, T216, T224; **Gr. 1,** T63; **Gr. 5,** 393; **Gr. 6,** 54

ragtime music, Scott Joplin, **Gr. 7,** 23

rap songs and musicals, **Gr. 7,** 73

rhyming words, **Gr. 5,** 117

Romantic period and meaning, **Gr. 7,** 122

spelling, **Gr. 1,** T95; **Gr. 3,** 56

spotlight, **Gr. 2,** A

symbols, **Gr. 1,** T31

synonyms, **Gr. 1,** T89; **Gr. 4,** 9, 143

talent shows, **Gr. 8,** 108

television, **Gr. 8,** 140

Total Physical Response, **Gr. K,** T58, **Gr. 1,** T29, T63, T123

triangles, **Gr. 2,** 143

Twist and Shout, **Gr. 7,** 161

Universal Exposition and Paris, **Gr. 7,** 128

vocabulary, **Gr. K,** T38, T43, T75, T96, T216, T224; **Gr. 1,** T21, T89, T100, T301; **Gr. 3,** 44, 87, 107, 171, 195, 234; **Gr. 4,** 9, 17, 47, 143, 155, 209, 355; **Gr. 5,** 49, 53, 95, 390; **Gr. 6,** 52; **Gr. 8,** 4, 14, 20, 25, 45, 49, 89, 119, 129, 151, 153, 176, 201, 216

When Johnny Comes Marching Home and Lyrics, **Gr. 7,** 171

working with English-proficient students, **Gr. 7,** 172

Gifted and Talented

12-bar blues form, **Gr. 8,** 69

accompaniment, **Gr. 2,** 157, 166, 173, 178; **Gr. 7,** 19

act, **Gr. K,** T65; **Gr. 6,** 208

American spirit, **Gr. 6,** 312

analyze form, **Gr. 7,** 19

analyze harmony, **Gr. 5,** 101

articulation, **Gr. 3,** 229

augmentation and diminution, **Gr. 4,** 193; **Gr. 6,** 187

blues singing style, **Gr. 5,** 179

breath control, **Gr. 2,** 197, 216

chords and arpeggios, **Gr. 4,** 235; **Gr. 6,** 195

compare and contrast, **Gr. 7,** 179

compose 2-measure melody in $\frac{2}{4}$, **Gr. 8,** 221

compose 2-measure melody in $\frac{3}{4}$, **Gr. 8,** 221

compose 2-measure melody in $\frac{4}{4}$, **Gr. 8,** 221

compose 3-pitch melody, **Gr. 1,** T167

compose 4-measure melody, **Gr. 3,** 229

compose 8–16 measure composition, **Gr. 8,** 175

compose 8-measure melody in $\frac{4}{4}$, **Gr. 6,** 377

compose accompaniment, **Gr. 4,** 235; **Gr. 6,** 104, 149

compose countermelody, **Gr. 4,** 7, 115; **Gr. 5,** 344; **Gr. 6,** 49

compose courante, **Gr. 8,** 130

compose encouraging song, **Gr. 8,** 89

compose left-hand accompaniment, **Gr. 8,** 123

compose melodic fragments, **Gr. 4,** 12

compose ostinato, **Gr. 3,** 318; **Gr. 4,** 115; **Gr. 5,** 67

compose rhythm accompaniments, **Gr. 3,** 69, 73; **Gr. 4,** 89

Classified Index

compose rhythm in ⅝, **Gr. 5**, 213

compose rhythm patterns, **Gr. 2**, 333; **Gr. 5**, 15

compose song using existing chord progression, **Gr. 8**, 52

compose using C-pentatonic scale, **Gr. 3**, 9

compose, **Gr. 2**, 29, 37, 124, 129; **Gr. 4**, 49, 113, 133, 237; **Gr. 5**, 105; **Gr. 6**, 337

conduct, **Gr. K**, T28, T92; **Gr. 2**, 149, 216; **Gr. 3**, 36, 177; **Gr. 4**, 133; **Gr. 6**, 347; **Gr. 8**, 32

create arrangement for poem, **Gr. 5**, 71

create arrangement, **Gr. 7**, 19, 32; **Gr. 8**, 71, 138, 143

create composition, **Gr. 7**, 19, 135, 221

create dance movements, **Gr. 3**, 231

create mosaic of songs, **Gr. 7**, 96

create rhythm patterns, **Gr. 7**, 57

create vocal exercise, **Gr. 7**, 191

creating art work, **Gr. 6**, 229; **Gr. 8**, 232

creating montage using movie themes, **Gr. 8**, 136

dance, **Gr. K**, T15

diction, **Gr. 2**, 216

discussing taking private music lessons, **Gr. 8**, 191

drawing graphic representation, **Gr. 8**, 32

drumming pattern, **Gr. 2**, 333

encouragement to pursue music, **Gr. K**, T148

experiment with different guitar strumming patterns, **Gr. 7**, 129

favorite songs, list, **Gr. 5**, 188

hand signs, **Gr. 1**, T165; **Gr. 2**, 44, 149, 290; **Gr. 3**, 29

higher level thinking skills, **Gr. K**, T131

improvise accompaniment, chords, **Gr. 4**, 187

improvise accompaniment, **Gr. K**, T181; **Gr. 4**, 7; **Gr. 6**, 195

improvise accompaniment to Good Morning America, **Gr. 8**, 181

improvise dramatic scenes, **Gr. 1**, T223

improvise harmony, **Gr. 4**, 316

improvise ideas for a Karaoke song, **Gr. 8**, 207

improvise lyrics, **Gr. K**, T181

improvise melody, **Gr. K**, T181; **Gr. 5**, 13, 204

improvise movement, **Gr. K**, T181; **Gr. 4**, 105

improvise music to selected scenes on TV, **Gr. 8**, 103

improvise ornamentation, **Gr. 4**, 225

improvise ostinato, **Gr. 3**, 157

improvise rhythm patterns, **Gr. 4**, 15

instruments, **Gr. 4**, 77

instruments, list, **Gr. 8**, 32

intervals, **Gr. 2**, 290

inversions, **Gr. 6**, 77

key changes, **Gr. 5**, 336

leading tones, **Gr. 4**, 181; **Gr. 5**, 336

listening maps to illustrate A and B sections, **Gr. 1**, T117

listening maps to illustrate melodic direction, **Gr. 1**, T43

lullabies, **Gr. 1**, T81; **Gr. 6**, 185

melodic contour, **Gr. 4**, 12

movement, interpretive, **Gr. 2**, 185, 216

musical elements that work, list, **Gr. 8**, 222

natural ability, understanding, **Gr. K**, T208

notate, **Gr. 2**, 37

notate chords, **Gr. 4**, 149

notate pitch, **Gr. 1**, T137

notate rhythm patterns, **Gr. 1**, T137, T217; **Gr. 6**, 225

octaves, **Gr. 4**, 151

orff instruments, play, **Gr. 3**, 117

ostinato, **Gr. 3**, 217, 318

part sing, **Gr. 2**, 157

phrases, **Gr. 2**, 197

pitch syllables, **Gr. 2**, 44, 149, 213; **Gr. 1**, T165; **Gr. 3**, 29

pitch, making "pipes", **Gr. 4**, 145

pitched instruments, play, **Gr. K**, T65, T92; **Gr. 4**, 7, 32, 141, 151, 187, 225, 235

play keyboard, **Gr. 7**, 129

play rondos, **Gr. 7**, 57

playing complex rhythms, **Gr. 8**, 6

poetry, recite, **Gr. K**, T65

prepare for performance, **Gr. 3**, 137

represent with instruments, **Gr. 1**, T141, T149

research famous jazz musician, **Gr. 5**, 360

rhythm accompaniment, **Gr. K**, T56, T65; **Gr. 1**, T97; **Gr. 4**, 89

rhythm, **Gr. 1**, T125; **Gr. 3**, 36, 61, 177; **Gr. 4**, 195; **Gr. 6**, 13, 93

rondo, **Gr. 2**, 237

round, **Gr. 2**, 33

sing (canon), **Gr. 5**, 195

sing (three-part), **Gr. 4**, 115; **Gr. 5**, 76; **Gr. 6**, 187

sing (two-part), **Gr. 3**, 193; **Gr. 5**, 237; **Gr. 6**, 60

sing (unison), **Gr. K**, T110, **Gr. 4**, 25, 32; **Gr. 6**, 151

sing using pitch syllables, **Gr. 6**, 151, 185

sing with chord roots, **Gr. 5**, 209

steady beat, **Gr. 2**, 8, 185

strong/weak beat, **Gr. 2**, 49

student "music expert", **Gr. K**, T200

tempo, **Gr. 1**, T127

time management, **Gr. 1**, T145

tone color, **Gr. K**, T172; **Gr. 2**, 71, 229; **Gr. 4**, 141

unpitched instruments, play, **Gr. K**, T56, T65; **Gr. 1**, T125; **Gr. 3**, 36; **Gr. 4**, 25, 89, 93, 187; **Gr. 6**, 93

vocal solo, **Gr. 5**, 21

whole and half steps, **Gr. 6**, 104

word rhythm, **Gr. 2**, 8

write exercises and games for rhythm, **Gr. 6**, 37

write lyrics, **Gr. 3**, 73

write one-act play, **Gr. 4**, 32

write poem with rhythm accompaniment, **Gr. 6**, 323

Inclusion

abstract and/or critical thinking, **Gr. 8**, 51, 116

acquire a new skill, **Gr. 1**, T185; **Gr. 3**, 131

add and adjust verses, **Gr. 1**, T40

alternative ways to demonstrate understanding, **Gr. 7**, 61, 217

alternative ways to respond to Music Journal questions, **Gr. 7**, 75, 201

arrange groups, **Gr. 8**, 165, 223

assign responsibilities, **Gr. 8**, 174, 231

Attention Deficit Hyperactivity Disorder, **Gr. 1**, T209

aurally distinguish verse and refrain, **Gr. 6**, 173

autism and music games, **Gr. 1**, T163; **Gr. 3**, 197

basic eighth ¼ beat, **Gr. 6**, 19

behavior, **Gr. K**, T335; **Gr. 2**, 354; **Gr. 3**, 221; **Gr. 5**, 266

Classified Index

behavior rules, **Gr. 8,** 23, 109

break down tasks (Creative Unit Project), **Gr. 7,** 138

children with disabilities, **Gr. 2,** 117, 137, 145, 175, 209, 220, 354, 377

choosing game players, **Gr. 2,** 59

class participation, **Gr. 5,** 245

color coding, **Gr. 2,** 220

combine different verbal concepts, **Gr. K,** T68

complex tasks, instructions for, **Gr. 2,** 169, 377

conduct in two, **Gr. 3,** 273

create a dance, **Gr. 6,** 233

dance steps, **Gr. 5,** 31

deal with anger, **Gr. K,** T271

delayed learning, **Gr. K,** T306; **Gr. 3,** 225

develop controls, **Gr. K,** T270

disruptive behavior, **Gr. 3,** 65

distinguish different sections, **Gr. 1,** T115

distinguish left and right, **Gr. K,** T30

distinguish long and short sounds, **Gr. 1,** T51

draw, **Gr. 4,** 109

educational goals, **Gr. 8,** 6

eye contact, **Gr. 1,** T189; **Gr. 3,** 375; **Gr. 4,** 137

finger play, **Gr. K,** T127

focus attention, **Gr. 3,** 140; **Gr. 5,** 231; **Gr. 6,** 254, 403, 412

gallop with hobby horse, **Gr. K,** T88

hand signs for *so* and *mi,* **Gr. 1,** T255

hand-jive, **Gr. 6,** 89

hearing-impaired/deaf children, **Gr. 2,** 117

identify beat, **Gr. 1,** T139

improvise a rhythmic ostinato, **Gr. 6,** 246

improvise on mallet instruments, **Gr. K,** T220

improvise, **Gr. 5,** 140, 182

inappropriate behavior, **Gr. 7,** 47

Individualized Education Plan (IEP), **Gr. 7,** 5, 103

instructions, **Gr. 8,** 88, 148

involve special learners in song, **Gr. K,** T211

irregular meters, **Gr. 6,** 217

language/speech deficits, children with, **Gr. 2,** 175

learn beats with visual impairment, **Gr. 1,** T131, T242

learn dotted rhythmic values, **Gr. 4,** 175

lip buzzing, **Gr. K,** T135

listening map, **Gr. 5,** 193

move to beat, **Gr. 5,** 89

move to melodic contour, **Gr. 3,** 19; **Gr. 4,** 127

move to steady beat, **Gr. 4,** 258; **Gr. 5,** 8

move to tempo, **Gr. K,** T21

movement and dance, **Gr. 4,** 57

movement with physical impairment, **Gr. 3,** 111

multicultural collaboration, **Gr. 8,** 83

musical phrase with hearing impairment, **Gr. 3,** 91

organizational skills, **Gr. 4,** 173

organizational strategies, **Gr. 8,** 64, 194

ostinato in § meter, **Gr. 5,** 96

pair able students with special learners (Creative Unit Project), **Gr. 7,** 113, 165

participation with health-impairment, **Gr. 1,** T225; **Gr. 3,** 395

partner with "music friend", **Gr. 1,** T171

pentatonic scale, **Gr. 2,** 220

physical adaptations, **Gr. 8,** 103, 134

play an ostinato, **Gr. 6,** 11

play glockenspiel, **Gr. K,** T51

play percussion instruments, **Gr. 5,** 47

present complex tasks, **Gr. 7,** 207

process sensory input, **Gr. 1,** T181

read aloud, **Gr. 5,** 65

read and multiple tasks, **Gr. 6,** 220

read beat icons, **Gr. K,** T25

read music with visual impairment, **Gr. 3,** 169

reading notation, **Gr. 6,** 143

reduce distractions, **Gr. 8,** 43, 55, 205

remember names of instruments, **Gr. K,** T37

repeat signs and alternating parts, **Gr. 6,** 51

self esteem, **Gr. 1,** T221; **Gr. 4,** 73

sensitivity to sound, **Gr. 4,** 29

short attention spans, **Gr. K,** T116

sing pitch syllables and make hand signs, **Gr. 4,** 96

sit through entire concert, **Gr. K,** T177

skip and gallop, **Gr. K,** T100

solfège, **Gr. 4,** 244

steady beat, **Gr. 2,** 8

strong/weak beat, **Gr. 2,** 49

structured learning environment, **Gr. 6,** 155

students acquiring new skills, **Gr. 7,** 35, 228

students lacking in social skills, **Gr. 7,** 11, 97

students with behavioral difficulties, **Gr. 7,** 124, 149, 181

tone color, **Gr. 5,** 229

Tongan stick game, **Gr. 6,** 91

trace melodic contour, **Gr. 4,** 90

treble clef, **Gr. 5,** 166

understanding concepts in class, **Gr. K,** T333; **Gr. 1,** T147

visually impaired children, **Gr. 2,** 145

Professional Article

Reaching Your Special Learners, **Gr. K,** T364; **Gr. 1,** T396; **Gr. 2,** 408–409; **Gr. 3,** 424; **Gr. 4,** 424; **Gr. 5,** 472; **Gr. 6,** 456–457; **Gr. 7,** 286; **Gr. 8,** 286

Reaching Your English Language Learners, **Gr. K,** T362; **Gr. 1,** T394; **Gr.2,** 406–407; **Gr. 3,** 422; **Gr. 4,** 422; **Gr. 5,** 470; **Gr. 6,** 454–455; **Gr. 7,** 284; **Gr. 8,** 284

RECORDED INTERVIEWS

Blair, Richard Scott, **Gr. 7,** 145

Bremer, Louis (From the Top), **Gr. 5,** 160

Brooklyn Jugs, **Gr. 4,** 77

Brown, Randall (From the Top), **Gr. 3,** 80

Brown, Rebecca, **Gr. 2,** 200

Chang, Sebastian/piano, **Gr. 7,** 127

Composer Forum, **Gr. 7,** 107

Conway, Eoghan (From the Top), **Gr. 3,** 160

Cope, Todd (From the Top), **Gr. 5,** 40

Criddle, Lauren (From the Top), **Gr. 4,** 160

Davids, Brent Michael, **Gr. 7,** 201

Donehew, Karla/violin, **Gr. 7,** 52

Feder, Abraham (From the Top), **Gr. 4,** 40

Fortenberry, Jewel "Tre" (From the Top), **Gr. 5,** 80

Garcia, Bianca, **Gr. 2,** 120

Garcia, Pala (From the Top), **Gr. 8,** 156

Classified Index

Classified Index of Songs, Selected Concepts, Skills, and Activities (continued)

Ginwala, Cyrus, **Gr. 8,** 170
Glass, Philip, **Gr. 4,** 144
Gorton, Heidi (From the Top), **Gr. 3,** 200
Help, Marilyn, **Gr. 1,** T73
Hurlburt, Sean, **Gr. 7,** 161
Jacobson, John, **Gr. 7,** 158
Jantsch, Carol, **Gr. 2,** 40
Jenkins, Ella, **Gr. 2,** 157
Johnson, Samuel (From the Top), **Gr. 8,** 171
Jordheim, Alisa (From the Top), **Gr. 8,** 187
Kern, Kevin, **Gr. 8,** 193, 195
Kidjo, Angelique, **Gr. 4,** 209
Kissin, Evgeny, **Gr. 2,** 224
Kozak, Gregory, **Gr. 2,** 36
Ladzekpo, Kobla, **Gr. 5,** 72
Larsen, Libby, **Gr. 8,** 112
Lentz, Jarrod/voice, **Gr. 7,** 78
MacMoran, William, **Gr. 6,** 200
Makeba, Miriam, **Gr. 3,** 35
Marchioni, Toni (From the Top), **Gr. 5,** 120
McDonald, Jerry Thundercloud, **Gr. 3,** 52
Mizzy, Vic, **Gr. 8,** 145
Mucky, Matthew, **Gr. 6,** 40
Neely, Nathan (From the Top), **Gr. 8,** 59
Nissman, Barbara, **Gr. 4,** 181
Ochieng, Trevor, **Gr. 2,** 160
Ong, Lin (From the Top), **Gr. 8,** 41
Park, Ariana and Rexton (From the Top), **Gr. 3,** 40
Pila, Ben /guitar, **Gr. 7,** 216
Premo, Evan, **Gr. 6,** 120
Ritterling, Soojin Kim, **Gr. 5,** 51
Ross, David (From the Top), **Gr. 4,** 200
Rouse, Steve, **Gr. 8,** 234
Smith, Paul Reed, **Gr. 8,** 98
Sosa, Mercedes, **Gr. 3,** 108
Souliere, Jason (From the Top), **Gr. 8,** 19
Stewart, Amanda/trombone, **Gr. 7,** 155
Talens, Deanna, **Gr. 6,** 80
Tan, Lucy, **Gr. 6,** 160
Turner, Catherine (From the Top), **Gr. 4,** 80
Urioste, Elena (From the Top), **Gr. 5,** 200
Vante, Barbara (From the Top), **Gr. 3,** 120
Vasan, Neil (From the Top), **Gr. 4,** 120
Yu, Vincent, **Gr. 2,** 80
Zupko, Sarah, **Gr. 7,** 25

S

SIGNING. *See also* Spotlight on Signing *in* Teacher's Resource Masters (TRM), *under separate cover. See also* Grade-Level DVD *under separate cover.*
All Night, All Day, **Gr. 1,** T232 (Grade-Level DVD)
Alphabet and Numbers, **Gr. K,** (TRM)
Amazing Grace, **Gr. 5,** 19 (Grade-Level DVD)
America, **Gr. 2,** 338 (TRM and Grade-Level DVD)
American Sign Language, **Gr. K,** T80
Battle Hymn of the Republic, **Gr. 6,** 389 (TRM)
Bear Went Over the Mountain, **Gr. K,** T204 (TRM)
Best Friends, **Gr. 1,** T222 (TRM)

Bonjour, mes amis, **Gr. 1,** T18 (TRM)
Colors of the Winds, **Gr. 3,** 84 (TRM)
Consider Yourself, **Gr. 3,** 335 (TRM)
Days of the Week, **Gr. K,** T81
Do Lord, **Gr. 6,** 260 (Grade-Level DVD)
Down by the Riverside, **Gr. 6,** 22 (TRM)
Eight Days of Hanukkah, The, **Gr. 3,** 370 (TRM)
Evergreen, Everblue, **Gr. 3,** 330 (TRM)
God Bless America, **Gr. 5,** 4 (TRM)
Gonna Build a Mountain, **Gr. 6,** 4 (TRM)
Good Day Song, **Gr. K,** T50 (TRM)
Hand Shape Song, **Gr. 6,** (TRM)
Happiest Street in the World, The, **Gr. 1,** T304 (TRM)
Hello, **Gr. 3,** 283 (Grade-Level DVD)
I Got Rhythm, **Gr. 5,** 187 (TRM)
I Saw Three Ships, **Gr. 2,** 359 (TRM)
I Will Be Your Friend, **Gr. 4,** 388 (TRM)
Joy to the World, **Gr. 4,** 383 (TRM and Grade-Level DVD)
Kum Ba Yah, **Gr. K,** T327 (TRM)
Let Music Surround You, **Gr. 6,** 285 (TRM)
Library Song, **Gr. 1,** T42 (TRM)
Lift Every Voice and Sing, **Gr. 5,** 86 (TRM)
Lift Up Your Voices, **Gr. 5,** 319 (Grade-Level DVD)
Little Blue Truck, **Gr. K,** T136 (TRM)
Little Robin Red Breast, **Gr. 1,** T208 (TRM)
Merrily, We Roll Along, **Gr. K,** T110 (TRM)
Must Be Santa, **Gr. K,** T316 (TRM)
Naughty Kitty Cat, **Gr. 1,** T171 (TRM and Grade-Level DVD)
Night of Stars/Silent Night, **Gr. 6,** 412 (TRM)
No One Like You, **Gr. 1,** T300 (TRM)
Oh How Lovely Is the Evening, **Gr. 6,** 252 (Grade-Level DVD)
Old MacDonald Had a Farm, **Gr. K,** T211 (TRM)
Over in the Meadow, **Gr. 1,** T78 (TRM)
Peace Round, **Gr. 4,** 16 (TRM)
Peasant's Dancing Day, **Gr. 4,** 132 (TRM and Grade-Level DVD)
Plenty Fishes in the Sea, **Gr. 1,** T310 (TRM)
Rattlesnake, **Gr. 1,** T185 (TRM)
Rise Up Singin', **Gr. 3,** 138 (TRM
Seeds, **Gr. 1,** T120 (TRM)
Shalom My Friends (Shalom Chaveyrim), **Gr. 3,** 141 (TRM)
Sometimes I Feel Like a Motherless Child, **Gr. 6,** 271 (TRM)
Song of Thanksgiving, **Gr. 4,** 371 (TRM)
Star Light, Star Bright, **Gr. 1,** T258 (Grade-Level DVD)
Sweet Music, **Gr. 5,** 319 (TRM)
Take Me Out to the Ballgame, **Gr. 2,** 56 (Grade-Level DVD)
Taps, **Gr. 3,** 281 (Grade-Level DVD)
Thank You, **Gr. 2,** 349 (Grade-Level DVD)
This Is America, **Gr. 3,** 356 (TRM)
This Is My Country, **Gr. 2,** 87 (TRM)
This Train, **Gr. 4,** 343 (TRM)
Umoja! (poem) (move with text), **Gr. K,** T324
Wake Up Canon, **Gr. 4,** 326 (TRM and Grade-Level DVD)
Wayfaring Stranger, **Gr. 6,** 283 (TRM)
We Are the Children of Tomorrow, **Gr. 5,** 114 (Grade-Level DVD)

Classified Index of Songs, Selected Concepts, Skills, and Activities (continued)

We Shall Overcome, **Gr. 4,** 387 (TRM)
We Want to Sing, **Gr. 5,** 235 (TRM)
We Wish You a Merry Christmas, **Gr. 2,** 358 (TRM)
What the World Needs Now, **Gr. 5,** 230 (TRM)
Willum, **Gr. 1,** T19 (TRM)
Woke Up This Morning, **Gr. 3,** 180 (Grade-Level DVD)
Yellow Submarine, **Gr. 3,** 320 (TRM)
You Are My Sunshine, **Gr. 2,** 369 (TRM)
You'll Sing a Song, **Gr. 2,** 156 (TRM)

SOLO/GROUP SONGS
Aideu, **Gr. 7,** 223
Away for Rio, **Gr. 2,** 170
Circle of Life, **Gr. 7,** 40
Cuckoo, Where Are You?, **Gr. 2,** 244
Dumplin's, **Gr. 2,** 172
Earth Is Our Mother, The, **Gr. 7,** 220
El tambor, **Gr. 6,** 222
El zapatero, **Gr. 2,** 138
Emergency, **Gr. 7,** 175
Give a Little Love, **Gr. 7,** 129
Green Eggs and Ham, **Gr. 2,** 284
Hang On Sloopy, **Gr. 7,** 30
Hashewie, **Gr. 2,** 362
Hello, Hello, There, **Gr. 2,** 126
Henry Ford, **Gr. 7,** 244-245
Hitori, **Gr. 4,** 345
Horton Hears a Who! Two, **Gr. 2,** 280
Horton Hears a Who!, **Gr. 2,** 279
Hullaballoo Balay, **Gr. 6,** 10
I See, **Gr. 2,** 266
In That Great Git'n Up Mornin', **Gr. 5,** 11
Interjections, **Gr. 3,** 303
Interplanet Janet, **Gr. 3,** 298
It's Possible, **Gr. 2,** 281
It's Time to Get Ready for Christmas, **Gr. 3,** 372
Just Keep Goin' On, **Gr. 7,** 19
Kye Kye Kule, **Gr. 7,** 225
L'il 'Liza Jane, **Gr. 4,** 20
Lemonade, **Gr. 2,** 19
Lion Sleeps Tonight, The, **Gr. 7,** 215
Mister Rabbit, Mister Rabbit, **Gr. 2,** 150
Oh, the Thinks You Can Think!, **Gr. 2,** 276
Oh, Won't You Sit Down?, **Gr. 4,** 70
Old House, **Gr. 4,** 282
One-Eyed Ford, **Gr. 7,** 200
Pay Me My Money Down, **Gr. 3,** 149
Pizza, Pizza, Daddy-O, **Gr. 2,** 62
Preamble, The, **Gr. 3,** 293
Rise Up, Shepherd, and Follow, **Gr. 5,** 422
Seussical Mega-Mix, **Gr. 2,** 287
Success, **Gr. 7,** 241-243
Tekanionton'néha', **Gr. 5,** 223
Three is a Magic Number, **Gr. 3,** 296
Train is A-Coming, **Gr. 4,** 270
Ua txiab, **Gr. 6,** 394
Ujima, **Gr. 5,** 427
We Shall Overcome, **Gr. 7,** 212, 217
Who Chopped the Cherry Tree Down?, **Gr. 2,** 371

SOUNDCHECK. *See also* Recorded Interviews
Agahu Dance, **Gr. 5,** 72

Andean Instruments, **Gr. 3,** 32
Animal Sounds: Higher and Lower, **Gr. 1,** T81
Changko Part for "Yongnam Nongak," **Gr. 5,** 71
Echoing Four Kinds of Voices, **Gr. K,** T31
Echoing G Pentatonic, **Gr. 5,** 51
High and Lower Sounds Around Us, **Gr. 1,** T56
Higher and Lower Sounds, **Gr. K,** T51
Learning about Walking and Galloping/Skipping,
    Gr. K, T41
Learning Sorida, **Gr. 2,** 96
Long and Short Sounds Around Us, **Gr. 1,** T53
Major or Minor, **Gr. 5,** 131
Orff Instruments, **Gr. 2,** 183
Recorder Consort, The, **Gr. 4,** 97
Rhythm Practice, **Gr. 5,** 52
Rhythm Scramble, **Gr. 4,** 141
Semachi Rhythm, **Gr. 5,** 52
Sounds Around Us, **Gr. 3,** 45
Verbal Notation, **Gr. 5,** 52
West African Drumming, **Gr. 4,** 44

STYLE, **Gr. 5,** 22
a cappella, **Gr. 4,** 389
Akan, **Gr. 4,** 166
anthem, **Gr. 4,** 356
bailecito, **Gr. 3,** 214
ballad, **Gr. 5,** 146
ballet, **Gr. 2,** 24; **Gr. 4,** 173, 191, 266; **Gr. 5,** 152
baroque, **Gr. K,** T89; **Gr. 1,** T175, T263; **Gr. 7,** 108, 110,
    112, 113, 232
    England, **Gr. 2,** 145; **Gr. 6,** 247; **Gr. 8,** 4
    France, **Gr. 2,** 269; **Gr. 8,** 167
    Germany, **Gr. 5,** 41, 228, 371; **Gr. 6,** 128;
        Gr. 8, 67, 95
    Italy, **Gr. 5,** 120; **Gr. 6,** 402–403
batucada, **Gr. 5,** 433
batuque, **Gr. 3,** 265
bead-chant song, **Gr. 5,** 26
berceuse, **Gr. 2,** 184
big band, **Gr. 4,** 143
bluegrass, **Gr. 2,** 68; **Gr. 3,** 387; **Gr. 5,** 22, 23, 24, 25;
    Gr. 6, 75, 106, 108–109, 140, 375; **Gr. 8,** 59
blues, **Gr. 3,** 337; **Gr. 4,** 389; **Gr. 5,** 174–182, 278;
    Gr. 6, 178, 180; **Gr. 7,** 16, 17, 18
bossa nova, **Gr. 4,** 92
Brazilian, **Gr. 7,** 202
Brazilian Bahian, **Gr. 7,** 226
Brazilian Gaucho, **Gr. 3,** 231
calypso, **Gr. 2,** 50, 90, 172; **Gr. 3,** 126–127; **Gr. 4,** 72,
    73, 90; **Gr. 5,** 90; **Gr. 6,** 6, 8–9, 154–155
camp song, **Gr. 3,** 68, 252, 272, 283
candombe, **Gr. 4,** 93
carnavalitos, **Gr. 3,** 30
carnival song, **Gr. 2,** 92
carol, **Gr. 2,** 358–359; **Gr. 3,** 374; **Gr. 4,** 230, 382, 383
Caribbean, **Gr. 7,** 148; **Gr. 8,** 10
chamber music, **Gr. 5,** 121, 218
chant, **Gr. 4,** 243
chorale, **Gr. 5,** 370
classical, **Gr. K,** T176; **Gr. 1,** T129, T251; **Gr. 3,** 26, 41,
    64, 80, 81, 120, 121, 128, 145, 155, 168, 178, 200,

201, 225, 251, 271, 363; **Gr. 4,** Q, 13, 17, 40, 41, 61, 97, 120, 121, 161, 181, 200, 201, 225, 235, 242, 244, 254, 261, 263, 287, 391; **Gr. 5,** 21; **Gr. 7,** 115
  Austria, **Gr. 5,** 247; **Gr. 6,** 186–187; **Gr. 8,** 122, 124, 128, 171, 179, 187, 218
  Germany, **Gr. 5,** 40, 419; **Gr. 8,** 20, 115, 123
  Italy, **Gr. 5,** 279
classical Indian, **Gr. 5,** 403
compare arrangements, **Gr. 5,** 87, 103, 104
compare styles, **Gr. 5,** 44; **Gr. 6,** 100
comparing, **Gr. 4,** 229
conga, **Gr. 5,** 364
contemporary, **Gr. 7,** 5
country music, **Gr. 6,** 20, 94–97; **Gr. 7,** 96, 208; **Gr. 8,** 71, 80, 88
cowboy, **Gr. 2,** 66, **Gr. 4,** J, 110, 274; **Gr. 6,** 114–116
Cuban son, **Gr. 8,** 51
cumbia, **Gr. 5,** 16
definition of, **Gr. 5,** 22
Dixieland, **Gr. 2,** 191; **Gr. 5,** 21
el son, **Gr. 5,** 397
electronic music, **Gr. 6,** 127
fanfare, **Gr. 2,** 86
film scores, **Gr. K,** T60, T159, T222; **Gr. 4,** 56, 274
flower drum song, **Gr. 5,** 58
folk. *See* Folk and Traditional Music; Multicultural Materials
freedom songs, **Gr. 3,** 180–181
fusion, **Gr. 4,** 208, 209
game song, **Gr. 2,** 59, 62, 175, 176
gospel, **Gr. 5,** 21, 87, 104, 320, 358; **Gr. 8,** 28, 31, 63, 261
gusto, **Gr. 4,** 363
hand-game song, **Gr. 5,** 27
hymn, **Gr. 5,** 19, 21
identify, **Gr. 5,** 85
jazz, **Gr. 1,** T241; **Gr. 4,** A, 41, 92, 232; **Gr. 5,** 31, 186, 213, 361, 363, 390, 391; **Gr. 6,** 146–147, 156–157, 164–165, 378–380; **Gr. 7,** 143; **Gr. 8,** 28, 32, 52, 70, 182, 186, 191
jig, **Gr. 5,** 48
jug band, **Gr. 4,** 76
Katadjait, **Gr. 7,** 176
Klezmer, **Gr. 2,** 70; **Gr. 5,** 54
lullaby, **Gr. 3,** 53, 108, 184, 186; **Gr. 4,** 18, 34, 327; **Gr. 5,** 216
march, **Gr. K,** T113, T177; **Gr. 1,** T25, T31, T230, T235; **Gr. 2,** 339; **Gr. 4,** 355; **Gr. 5,** 395; **Gr. 6,** 388–389, 391; **Gr. 7,** 76, 168, 169, 171, 197; **Gr. 8,** 6, 37, 39
Mariachi, **Gr. 2,** 60; **Gr. 3,** 397; **Gr. 4,** N, 197
medieval, **Gr. 7,** 94, 95
minimalism, **Gr. 7,** 130
movie songs, **Gr. 3,** 124, 307, 308, 310, 312, 313, 334, 336
musical, **Gr. K,** T189, T222; **Gr. 1,** T169, T375; **Gr. 2,** C, 126, 310–311; **Gr. 3,** 84–85, 124–125, 164–165, 313, 335; **Gr. 4,** 84, 114, 160; **Gr. 5,** 42, 226; **Gr. 6,** 4, 56, 147, 166, 168, 182, 204–205, 207, 290–305, 306–317; **Gr. 7,** 40, 69, 82, 84, 86, 158, 236–251; **Gr. 8,** 74, 76, 78, 86, 197, 236–251
national anthem, **Gr. 5,** 86
nationalism, **Gr. 4,** 340; **Gr. 5,** 106
Native American flute, **Gr. 4,** 153
Native American vocables, **Gr. 7,** 200
new age, **Gr. 7,** 142
nongak, **Gr. 5,** 70
opera, **Gr. K,** T178, T180; **Gr. 1,** T375; **Gr. 2,** 152, 217; **Gr. 4,** 252, 280; **Gr. 5,** 64, 148, 165, 274, 279; **Gr. 6,** 152, 219, 257, 265, **Gr. 7,** 94, 95, 180, 182
orchestral. *See* Instrumental/Vocal Ensembles
parade, **Gr. 4,** 229
patriotic, **Gr. 2,** A, H, 338, 340; **Gr. 7,** 136, 137, 187, 194, 195, 197; **Gr. 8,** 31
pop
  American, **Gr. K,** T60, T106, T135; **Gr. 2,** 54; **Gr. 3,** 320; **Gr. 5,** 45, 225, 326; **Gr. 6,** 34, 84, 87–88, 124, 148, 150–151, 174, 180, 234–236, 381, 418; **Gr. 7,** 5, 8, 10, 11, 12, 13, 14, 29, 30, 31, 32, 40, 41, 70–73, 84, 85, 98, 99, 134, 135, 138, 139, 140, 141, 150, 151, 154, 160, 161, 177, 208, 214, 215; **Gr. 8,** 8, 9, 64, 103, 140, 142, 161, 181, 191, 208, 223
  British, **Gr. K,** T153; **Gr. 8,** 110, 149
popular
  American, **Gr. 3,** 227, 228, 232, 236–237; **Gr. 4,** 44, 211, 306, 308, 311, 312, 314
  Brazilian, **Gr. 4,** 128
  Italian, **Gr. 5,** 62
  Korean, **Gr. 4,** 184
  Latino, **Gr. 3,** 236–237
  Mexican, **Gr. 4,** 194
processional music, **Gr. 7,** 50, 65, 66, 67, 75
program music, **Gr. 1,** T25, T31, T140, T152, T204, T231, T233, T237, T242, T256, T259, T337; **Gr. 4,** 116; **Gr. 5,** 125; **Gr. 8,** 20
ragtime, **Gr. 6,** 110–112, 314; **Gr. 7,** 22, 23, 237, 250, 251
railroad song, **Gr. 2,** 32
rap, **Gr. 3,** 332; **Gr. 4,** 4; **Gr. 5,** 9, 428, 429; **Gr. 7,** 70–72
reggae, **Gr. 3,** 204–205; **Gr. 8,** 84
Renaissance, **Gr. K,** T103; **Gr. 3,** 121; **Gr. 4,** 174, 176, 283; **Gr. 6,** 100–101, 336
  German, **Gr. 8,** 130
rock, **Gr. 5,** 85
rock and roll, **Gr. 5,** 306, 308, 316
Romantic, **Gr. K,** T28, T109, T133, T146, T177, T178, T180, T195, T196, T209; **Gr. 1,** T31, T231, T233, T249, T259, T337, T345, T353; **Gr. 7,** 120–125; **Gr. 8,** 40
  Austrian, **Gr. 5,** 161; **Gr. 6,** 342–344; **Gr. 8,** 189
  Belgian, **Gr. 8,** 156
  Czech, **Gr. 5,** 106, 271, 274
  Finnish, **Gr. 5,** 257
  French (late romantic), **Gr. 5,** 121; **Gr. 8,** 19, 59
  German, **Gr. 5,** 81, 102, 121, 228, 255
  Italian, **Gr. 5,** 64, 161
  Norwegian, **Gr. 5,** 192–193
  Polish, **Gr. 5,** 80
  Russian, **Gr. 5,** 81, 281; **Gr. 8,** 72
round dance, **Gr. 2,** 155
salsa, **Gr. 4,** 228, 229
samba, **Gr. 3,** 111; **Gr. 5,** 338, 433; **Gr. 8,** 45, 46
sea/river chantey, **Gr. 3,** 192; **Gr. 4,** D, 258, 266, 281
Senegalese, **Gr. 4,** 385
Shaker, **Gr. 4,** 271

Classified Index

slip jig, **Gr. 5,** 48
South African, **Gr. 7,** 214
spiritual, **Gr. K,** T33, T67, T145, T319; **Gr. 2,** F, 9, 116, 235, 360; **Gr. 3,** 52, 56, 245, 286, 287, 324, 376, 377, 382; **Gr. 4,** 65, 70, 130, 264, 270, 323, 343, 387; **Gr. 5,** 11, 117, 126, 127, 144, 254, 328, 345, 347, 422, 423; **Gr. 6,** C, 12, 22–24, 52, 242, 243, 260, 271, 345, 365, 367, 416; **Gr. 7,** 162, 163, 213
squaw dance, **Gr. 5,** 224
summarize styles, **Gr. 5,** 105
swing, **Gr. 3,** 12; **Gr. 5,** 31, 32; **Gr. 6,** 18
television themes, **Gr. 8,** 140, 142
waltz, **Gr. 4,** 229
western, **Gr. 6,** 116
work songs, **Gr. 3,** 149; **Gr. 4,** 86, 138, 255, 282, 348; **Gr. 6,** 70, 134, 136–137, 319; **Gr. 7,** 148, 150
zydeco, **Gr. 2,** 178–179; **Gr. 7,** 88, 89

T

TECHNOLOGY. *See also* DVD components, under separate cover
DVD Resource Library
  Blending Musical Styles, **Gr. 7,** 17, 89, 203; **Gr. 8,** 35, 71
  Canadian Brass's Inside Brass, **Gr. 7,** 37
  Composers' Specials: Bach, **Gr. 7,** 108, 232; **Gr. 8,** 95
  Composers' Specials: Bizet, **Gr. 7,** 123
  Composers' Specials: Handel, **Gr. 7,** 110
  Mariachi Tradition, The, **Gr. 7,** 58, 90
  Play Alto Saxophone Today, **Gr. 7,** 161, 218; **Gr. 8,** 152
  Play Clarinet Today, **Gr. 8,** 138
  Play Drums Today, **Gr. 7,** 44, 167; **Gr. 8,** 103, 148
  Play Flute Today, **Gr. 8,** 170
  Play Guitar Today, **Gr. 7,** 15, 97, 216; **Gr. 8,** 102, 190, 215
  Play Piano Today, **Gr. 7,** 21; **Gr. 8,** 160
  Play Trumpet Today, **Gr. 8,** 9
  Sounds of Percussion, **Gr. 7,** 39, 148, 198; **Gr. 8,** 13, 44, 54
  Turntable Technique, **Gr. 7,** 73; **Gr. 8,** 198
Global Voices DVD, **Gr. 1,** T24, T211, T153, T187; **Gr. 2,** 62, 102, 174, 234; **Gr. 3,** 102, 142, 215, 230; **Gr. 4,** 22, 102, 182, 210; **Gr. 6,** 70, 90, 142, 222
Grade-Level DVD. *See also* Broadway for Kids, Choreography, From the Top, *and* Signing
  ASL Signing
    All Night All Day, **Gr. 1,** T232
    Amazing Grace, **Gr. 5,** 19
    America, **Gr. 2,** 338
    Do Lord, **Gr. 6,** 260
    Joy to the World, **Gr. 4,** 383
    Lift Up Your Voices, **Gr. 5,** 319
    Naughty Kitty Cat, **Gr. 1,** T303
    Oh, How Lovely Is the Evening, **Gr. 6,** 252
    Peasant's Dancing Day, **Gr. 4,** 132
    Star Light Star Bright, **Gr. 1,** T258
    Step Into the Spotlight, **Gr. 6,** A
    Take Me Out to the Ball Game, **Gr. 2,** 56
    Thank You, **Gr. 2,** 349
    Wake Up Canon, **Gr. 4,** 326 (TRM and Grade-Level DVD)

    We Are the Children of Tomorrow, **Gr. 5,** 114
  John Jacobson Choreography
    Ame fure, **Gr. 4,** 26
    America, **Gr. 1,** T326
    America, My Homeland, **Gr. 4,** 358
    Check It Out! (It's About Respect), **Gr. 2,** 10
    Cripple Creek, **Gr. 6,** 372
    Dance! Dance! Dance!, **Gr. 2,** 5
    Doctor Jazz, **Gr. 6,** 378
    Down by the Bay, **Gr. 1,** T48
    Gee, Mom, I Want to Go Home, **Gr. 6,** 148
    Gilly, Gilly, Gilly Good Morning, **Gr. 1,** T12
    He's Got the Whole World in His Hands, **Gr. 2,** 116
    Hop! Chirp! Moo! Oh, Happy Springtime Day!, **Gr. 1,** T372
    Jingle Bells, **Gr. 1,** T354
    Jolly Old St. Nicholas, **Gr. 4,** 382
    Joy to the World, **Gr. 4,** 383
    Mr. Scott Joplin's Ragtime Rag!, **Gr. 6,** 110
    Over the River and Through the Wood, **Gr. 4,** 370
    Peasant's Dancing Day, **Gr. 4,** 132
    Sing, America, Sing, **Gr. 5,** 6
    Stars and Stripes Forever, The, **Gr. 6,** 390
    Step into the Spotlight, **Gr. 5,** A
    There's a Song in Me, **Gr 5,** 183
    Tinga Layo, **Gr. 2,** 50
    Viva l'amour, **Gr. 5,** 262
    Wake Up the Sun, **Gr. 2,** 124
    When Johnny Comes Marching Home, **Gr. 5,** 34
  Music Theatre International
    76 Trombones, **Gr. 5,** 296
    It's the Hard-Knock Life, **Gr. 4,** 292
    Mama Will Provide, **Gr. 6,** 296
    Seussical Mega-Mix, **Gr. 2,** 287
    Year with Frog and Toad, A, **Gr. 1,** T270
MiDisaurus CD-ROM, **Gr. 2,** 10, 26; **Gr. 3,** 138
music.mmhschool.com, **Gr. 1,** T14, T18, T26, T42, T54, T58, T70, T74, T78, T86, T90, T98, T106, T110, T122, T130, T134, T138, T158, T166, T198, T210, T218, T222; **Gr. 2,** 6, 18, 46, 54, 66, 70, 74, 90, 98, 106, 134, 138, 146, 150, 154, 170, 182, 194, 206, 210, 218, 230, 381; **Gr. 3,** 6, 18, 22, 26, 34, 54, 66, 74, 94, 98, 114, 132, 135, 155, 166, 174, 190, 194, 206, 210, 214, 218, 222, 234; **Gr. 4,** 26, 30, 46, 50, 54, 62, 70, 74, 90, 98, 110, 130, 134, 142, 146, 166, 170, 186, 194, 218, 222, 226, 230, 234; **Gr. 5,** 14, 30, 50, 58, 62, 66, 70, 86, 94, 102, 106, 110, 126, 130, 138, 142, 154, 170, 174, 178, 214, 222, 234; **Gr. 6,** 6, 10, 26, 30, 34, 50, 54, 62, 66, 74, 86, 94, 98, 102, 114, 126, 146, 150, 154, 170, 174, 178, 182, 194, 206, 210, 214, 218, 226, 234
African American spirituals, **Gr. K,** T30, T66; **Gr. 7,** 210
American bluegrass, **Gr. 8,** 54
American blues music, **Gr. 7,** 16
American gospel music, **Gr. 8,** 28
American musicals, **Gr. 7,** 82; **Gr. 8,** 192
American Rock and Roll, **Gr. 8,** 146
Anglo-American folk music and game songs, **Gr. K,** T38, T42, T70, T122, T134, T194, T198, T202, T210
Bach, Johann Sebastian, **Gr. 7,** 232

Classified Index of Songs, Selected Concepts, Skills, and Activities (continued)

Baroque music, **Gr. 7**, 106
Beethoven, Ludwig van, **Gr. 8**, 16, 224
Brass instruments, **Gr. K**, T102; **Gr. 8**, 48
Brazilian folk music, **Gr. K**, T142, T162
Classical period, **Gr. 8**, 126
Composing, **Gr. 8**, 172
Copyright, **Gr. 8**, 100
Davids, Brent Michael, **Gr. 7**, 201
Famous arenas, **Gr. 7**, 94
Flute, oboe, bassoon, **Gr. 8**, 22
Folk and traditional styles, **Gr. K**, T62, T90, T214
French folk music, **Gr. K**, T130
Garage bands, **Gr. 7**, 14
Gospel music, **Gr. 7**, 158
Gould, Morton, **Gr. 8**, 166
Haydn, Franz Joseph, **Gr. 8**, 120
Holiday, patriotic, and seasonal articles and activities,
    Gr. 8, 42
Hungarian folk music, **Gr. K**, T138
Israeli, Hebrew, Jewish, and Yiddish folk music,
    Gr. K, T166
Jazz music, **Gr. 8**, 178
Karaoke, **Gr. 8**, 204
King, Martin Luther, Jr., **Gr. 7**, 205
Korean folk music, **Gr. K**, T106
Larsen, Libby, **Gr. 8**, 154
Larson, Jonathan, **Gr. 7**, 178
Maori folk music, **Gr. K**, T14
March music, **Gr. 7**, 74
Mexican folk music, **Gr. K**, T22, T98
Milne, Bob, and ragged time, **Gr. 7**, 23
Mizzy, Vic, **Gr. 8**, 140
Mozart, Wolfgang Amadeus, **Gr. K**, T174; **Gr. 8**, 178,
    184, 230
Music reviews, **Gr. 7**, 25
Native American folk music, **Gr. K**, T74, T218
Orchestral instruments, **Gr. K**, T110, T146, T178, T182;
    Gr. 8, 166
Pachelbel, Johann, **Gr. 8**, 62
Piano, **Gr. K**, T206
Prokoviev, Sergei, **Gr. 8**, 36
Purcell, Henry, **Gr. 8**, 2
Recording technology, **Gr. 8**, 198
River Come Down, **Gr. 8**, 10
Rock and Roll, **Gr. 7**, 2; **Gr. 8**, 146
Route, **Gr. 7**, 66, 190
Scat music, **Gr. 7**, 172
Schumann, Robert, **Gr. 8**, 114
Sousa, John Philip, **Gr. 7**, 196
South African folk music, **Gr. K**, T126, T150
Star-Spangled Banner, The, **Gr. 7**, 193
Statue of Liberty centennial, **Gr. 7**, 186
Stravinsky, Igor, **Gr. 7**, 126
String instruments, **Gr. K**, T222
Themes and Variations, **Gr. 8**, 88
Train, **Gr. 8**, 100
Violin, **Gr. 8**, 94
West African folk music, **Gr. K**, T158, T186; **Gr. 7**, 224
Williams, John, **Gr. 7**, 187
Willson, Meredith, **Gr. 8**, 74

Winter, Paul, **Gr. 7**, 219
Work songs, **Gr. 7**, 146, 148-49, 150, 151
York, Andrew, **Gr. 8**, 210
Orchestral Instruments CD-ROM, **Gr. 1**, T30, T62, T94,
    T142, T146, T162, T170, T178, T182, T206; **Gr. 2**, 14,
    34, 40, 54, 80, 86, 110, 120, 126, 142, 160, 166, 190,
    226, 354; **Gr. 3**, 27, 40, 62, 70, 80, 90, 120, 126, 160,
    178, 200, 226, 363; **Gr. 4**, 6, 10, 14, 40, 80, 106, 114,
    120, 160, 178, 200; **Gr. 5**, 10, 22, 40, 80, 120, 160,
    182, 190, 200, 206, 218, 226, 394, 412; **Gr. 6**, 18, 40,
    46, 80, 120, 130, 160, 166, 200, 230
  bassoon, **Gr. 7**, 36; **Gr. 8**, 19
  brass instruments, **Gr. 8**, 48
  cello, **Gr. 8**, 171
  clarinet, **Gr. K**, T18
  cymbals, **Gr. 7**, 55
  drums, **Gr. K**, T34, T170
  flutes, **Gr. K**, T18, T50
  French horn, **Gr. 8**, 59
  glockenspiel, **Gr. K**, T94
  guitar, **Gr. 7**, 216
  harpsichord, **Gr. K**, T86
  oboe, **Gr. K**, T18; **Gr. 7**, 36
  percussion instruments, **Gr. 8**, 41, 106
  percussion, **Gr. 7**, 132
  piano, **Gr. K**, T170; **Gr. 7**, 127; **Gr. 8**, 158
  saxophone, **Gr. K**, T170; **Gr. 7**, 36, 161
  strings, **Gr. K**, T58; **Gr. 7**, 48
  trombone, **Gr. K**, T50, T54, T170; **Gr. 7**, 28
  trumpet, **Gr. K**, T170; **Gr. 7**, 28
  tuba, **Gr. K**, T170; **Gr. 7**, 28
  unpitched percussion, **Gr. K**, T34
  violin, **Gr. K**, T18, T26, T58; **Gr. 7**, 52
other
  About Music Theatre International, **Gr. 5**, 290
  About the Broadway Junior Collection, **Gr. 5**, 290
  broadband, **Gr. 8**, 219
  carillon, **Gr. 7**, 123
  CDs, **Gr. 8**, 96-97
  electrophones, **Gr. 7**, 166
  examine music technology, **Gr. 5**, 203
  karaoke, **Gr. 8**, 206-207
  MIDI, **Gr. 8**, 206
  synthesizers, **Gr. 7**, 130
  use audio or video tape recorder, **Gr. 5**, 116
  use notation software, **Gr. 5**, 114, 155, 157
Spotlight on MIDI
  Add Rhythm Parts, **Gr. 2**, 18
  All Night, All Day, **Gr. 1**, T232
  Alleluia, **Gr. 6**, 186
  Amazing Grace, **Gr. 5**, 18
  America, the Beautiful, **Gr. 5**, 388
  Animal Fair, **Gr. 2**, 214
  Ants Go Marching, The, **Gr. 1**, T22
  Be a Studio Engineer, **Gr. 8**, 203
  Bending Pitch on a Latin Groove, **Gr. 1**, T162
  Bim Bom, **Gr. 3**, 218
  Bizet's L'Arlésienne, Suite No. 2, **Gr. 7**, 120
  Bluebells, **Gr. 1**, T209
  Boll Weevil, **Gr. 3**, 171

Classified Index of Songs, Selected Concepts, Skills, and Activities (continued)

Branch of the Blues, A, **Gr. 6,** 178
Button, You Must Wander, **Gr. 2,** 174
Changing Tempo to Add Expression, **Gr. 5,** 114
Charlie, **Gr. 3,** 208
Chíu, Chíu, Chíu, **Gr. 6,** 172
Choose and Play Rhythms, **Gr. 2,** 22
Classic Dose of Reality, A, **Gr. 6,** 218
Classic Journey Through Tempo, A, **Gr. 3,** 66
Composing with Sixteenths, **Gr. 3,** 134
Crawdad Song, **Gr. 3,** 107
Create a Pop Song, **Gr. 7,** 15
Create a Rap Track, **Gr. 7,** 71
Create a Rap, **Gr. 6,** 296, 370
Create Music for a Film Scene, **Gr. 8,** 139
Create Music for an Action Movie, **Gr. 4,** 56
Create Music with an Afro-Cuban beat, **Gr. 7,** 15
Create Polyphonic Texture, **Gr. 6,** 29, 226
Create Program Music with Notes That Tell a Story,
    Gr. 4, 114
Create Slow and Fast, **Gr. 1,** T106
Create Using Elements of 12-Tone and Chance Music,
    Gr. 6, 162, 220
Create with Bluegrass, Slow or Fast, **Gr. 8,** 71
Discover Loud and Soft, **Gr. 1,** T30
Doggie, Doggie, **Gr. 2,** 58
Doney Gal, **Gr. 6,** 115
Dorian Waltz, A, **Gr. 6,** 104
Down By the Bay, **Gr. 1,** T48, T50
Down by the Riverside, **Gr. 6,** 22
Driving Fast and Slow to New Orleans, **Gr. 1,** T126
Early Bird Rise and Shine Melodies, **Gr. 2,** 234
Early in the Morning at Eight O'Clock, **Gr. 4,** 58
El barquito (The Tiny Boat), **Gr. 4,** 214
El tambor (The Drum), **Gr. 6,** 220
El vito, **Gr. 5,** 210
Erie Canal, **Gr. 5,** 132
Excitement of Rhythm, The, **Gr. 6,** 6
Exploring Sounds from Japan, **Gr. 6,** 142
Frog Went A-Courtin', **Gr. 4,** 46
Fugue Activity, **Gr. 8,** 95
Fusing Rock to Sounds, **Gr. 4,** 206
Gallop Into Swing, **Gr. 3,** 12
Hava Nagila, **Gr. 5,** 54
He's Got the Whole World in His Hands, **Gr. 2,** 114
Hip Swung Sixteenths Add Hop to Hip Hop, **Gr. 5,** 126
How About Some Ragtime, **Gr. 2,** 42
I Have a Car, **Gr. 3,** 252
Improvise in Dorian, **Gr. 6,** 136, 211
Inspirational Songs, **Gr. 7,** 204
I's the B'y, **Gr. 3,** 13
Jazz Activity, **Gr. 8,** 33
Jazzy Loudness, A Jazzy Softness, A, **Gr. 1,** T34
Jingle at the Window, **Gr. 3,** 268
John Henry, **Gr. 5,** 146
John Jacob Jingleheimer Schmidt, **Gr. 3,** 68
Lavender's Blue, **Gr. 1,** T174
Li'l Liza Jane, **Gr. 4,** 20
Little Red Caboose, **Gr. 1,** T97
Long-Legged Sailor, **Gr. 4,** 243
Magic Carpet Ride, **Gr. 1,** T70; **Gr. 2,** 98

Making Melodies, **Gr. 4,** 150
Mama Don't 'Low, **Gr. 6,** 126
Mango Walk, **Gr. 5,** 90
Many Shades of Tone Colors, **Gr. 2,** 70
Mary Ann, **Gr. 5,** 166
Meet a Waltz, **Gr. 3,** 166
Melody of Morning News, **Gr. 3,** 270
Mixed Styles, **Gr. 4,** 228
Mood Seesaws and Mi, So, and La, **Gr. 1,** T206
Mozart's Rondo "alla turca," **Gr. 7,** 114
Musette from Notebook for Anna Magdalena Bach,
    Gr. 4, 261
Musical Conversation, **Gr. 7,** 170
Musical Moods, **Gr. 7,** 140
M_-fia mo-ni (Ev'rybody Loves Saturday Night),
    Gr. 5, 277
Oh, Susanna, **Gr. 3,** 153
Old Carrion Crow, The, **Gr. 4,** 190
Old King Glory, **Gr. 1,** T214, T217
Our Musical World, **Gr. 2,** 82
Pat Works on the Railway, **Gr. 4,** 86
Percussion Jamming, **Gr. 5,** 52
Perform and Improvise in Mixolydian, **Gr. 6,** 212
Perform and Improvise with the 12-Bar Blues,
    Gr. 6, 178
Perform/Improvise in Five-Four Meter, **Gr. 6,** 211
Play a Modern 12-Bar Blues, **Gr. 5,** 178
Playing Timpani in a Symphony, **Gr. 5,** 35
Power of Rhythm, The, **Gr. 4,** 130
Program Music for a Train Ride, **Gr. 4,** 114
Radiating the 88s with 12-Bar Blues, **Gr. 5,** 174
Rain, Rain, Go Away, **Gr. 1,** T259
Rhythm Times Two, **Gr. 3,** 194
Rhythms of Africa, **Gr. 6,** 71
Sarasponda, **Gr. 4,** 210
She'll Be Comin' Round the Mountain, **Gr. 2,** 30
Shoo, Fly, **Gr. 2,** 222
Singing Synthesizers, **Gr. 2,** 329
Spicy Latin Rhythms, **Gr. 5,** 14
Steel Bands, **Gr. 7,** 198
Steel Drums Activity, **Gr. 8,** 10
Story that Waltzes, A, **Gr. 2,** 126
Suliram, **Gr. 6,** 58
Sun Don't Set in the Mornin', **Gr. 3,** 48
Sweet Potatoes, **Gr. 3,** 16
Swing That Tempo, **Gr. 4,** 190
Swung 16ths and Crazy Synths, **Gr. 3,** 320
Take Me Out to the Ball Game, **Gr. 2,** 54
Take Time in Life, **Gr. 4,** 156
Talking Telephones, **Gr. 1,** T98
That Tricky Dixieland Sound, **Gr. 2,** 190
Theme and Variations, **Gr. 5,** 35
There's a Hole in the Bucket, **Gr. 2,** 130
This Old Man, **Gr. 1,** T306
Time to Rest, **Gr. 1,** T158
Timely Ragtime, **Gr. 3,** 74
Tinker, Tailor, **Gr. 1,** T130
To Rock or Not to Rock, **Gr. 5,** 226
Turn Stubborn Ostinatos into Grooves, **Gr. 4,** 34

Turn the Glasses Over, **Gr. 3,** 260
Using Rhythm in Turnip Tunes, **Gr. 1,** T178
Water Come a Me Eye, **Gr. 4,** 90
Web of Rhythm, **Gr. 5,** 74
When I Was Young, **Gr. 4,** 187
When the Saints Go Marching In, **Gr. 5,** 256
Who's That Tapping at the Window?, **Gr. 2,** 261
Yankee Doodle, **Gr. 2,** 340; **Gr. 4,** 154
Web Tips
   From the Top, **Gr. 2,** 41, 81, 121, 161, 201; **Gr. 3,** 41,
      81, 121, 161, 201; **Gr. 4,** 41, 81, 121, 161, 201;
      Gr. 5, 41, 81, 121, 161, 201; **Gr. 6,** 41, 81, 121,
      161, 201; **Gr. 7,** 52, 78, 127, 155, 160, 216;
      Gr. 8, 41, 59, 156, 171, 187
World Instruments CD-ROM, **Gr. 1,** T34, T66, T98, T114,
   T126, T194; **Gr. 2,** 22, 94, 186, 200, 360, 362, 366,
   370, 374, 380; **Gr. 3,** 86, 110, 146, 182, 186, 358,
   360, 363, 378, 381; **Gr. 4,** 26, 34, 66, 94, 126, 138,
   150, 206; **Gr. 5,** 26, 74, 98, 134, 186, 396, 398, 400,
   402, 432, 436, 440, 442, 444; **Gr. 6,** 14, 30, 106, 138,
   190, 394, 396, 398, 406, 418, 420, 422, 426, 428
   erhu, **Gr. K,** T114; **Gr. 8,** 80
   guitar, **Gr. K,** T78; **Gr. 7,** 10, 14; **Gr. 8,** 68
   mandolins, **Gr. 8,** 68
   maracas, **Gr. 7,** 62
   pipa, **Gr. 8,** 80
   sheng, **Gr. 8,** 80
   tabla, **Gr. 8,** 80

TONE COLOR. *See also* Instruments, Identifying;
   Instruments, Playing; SoundCheck
arco, **Gr. 5,** 193
banjo, **Gr. 1,** T139
bass, **Gr. 1,** T139
bluegrass, **Gr. 5,** 23, 24
bodhrán, **Gr. 5,** 49
body percussion, **Gr. 1,** T35, T39; **Gr. 2,** 369; **Gr. 3,** 28;
   Gr. 4, 27, 28, 167; **Gr. 5,** 191; **Gr. 6,** 129; **Gr. 7,** 5,
   17, 33, 135, 147
brass, **Gr. 5,** 228; **Gr. 7,** 5, 37, 38, 58, 167, 171
Chinese *erhu,* **Gr. 1,** T212
choral balance and blend, **Gr. 6,** 67
clapping, **Gr. 1,** T17, T19, T32, T39, T40, T85, T86, T87,
   T88, T89, T175, T233, T244, T246, T251, T253, T259,
   T285, T288, T292, T310, T319; **Gr. 3,** 28; **Gr. 4,** 27;
   Gr. 7, 5, 130, 135
clarinet, **Gr. 6,** 69
contrasting, **Gr. 5,** 191
defining, **Gr. 3,** 26, 27
drum set, **Gr. 6,** 20, 124
drums, **Gr. K,** T87, T115, T129; **Gr. 1,** T73; **Gr. 2,** 201;
   Gr. 3, 29, 31, 32, 33; **Gr. 4,** 92; **Gr. 7,** 38, 75, 167, 171
drums and voices, **Gr. 5,** 445
electronic, **Gr. 4,** 23, 92; **Gr. 7,** 75, 167, 233
flute, **Gr. 1,** T64
gamelan, **Gr. 1,** T144
guitar, **Gr. 1,** T139
harp, **Gr. 7,** 48
instrumental, **Gr. K,** T76, T90, T104, T115, T117, T294,
   T295, T268; **Gr. 1,** T140, T210; **Gr. 2,** 70, 72–73,
   133, 182, 188, 228, 371; **Gr. 3,** 27, 29, 31, 32, 51;

Gr. 4, 12, 23, 36, 76, 108, 116, 144, 152, 227;
   Gr. 6, 120, 123, 127, 151, 153, 192, 193, 423, 427,
   429; **Gr. 7,** 5, 23, 48, 56, 69, 75, 135, 166, 167, 171,
   182, 208, 213, 219, 232, 233
keyboard, **Gr. 7,** 69, 75, 166, 167
organ, **Gr. 7,** 69
percussion, **Gr. K,** T61, T64, T80; **Gr. 1,** T92, T99, T143,
   T144, T200, T227, T294; **Gr. 2,** 24, 229; **Gr. 3,** 23,
   28, 29, 31, 32, 33; **Gr. 4,** 28; **Gr. 5,** 191, 228, 229;
   Gr. 6, 129; **Gr. 7,** 5, 38, 56, 64, 75, 166, 167, 171,
   232, 233, 228
piano, **Gr. 6,** 124
pizzicato, **Gr. 5,** 193
range, **Gr. 5,** 160
Renaissance instruments, **Gr. 6,** 101
steel drums, **Gr. 5,** 91
strings, **Gr. K,** T274; **Gr. 1,** T129, T211, T212;
   Gr. 2, 229; **Gr. 3,** 31, 32, 179; **Gr. 5,** 193, 228;
   Gr. 6, 151, 153; **Gr. 7,** 5, 48, 56, 58, 166, 171,
   228, 232, 233
synthesizer, **Gr. 6,** 127
tambourine, **Gr. 6,** 124
Thai instruments, **Gr. 1,** T200
triangle, **Gr. 5,** 191
tuba, **Gr. 1,** T64
violin, **Gr. 6,** 124
vocal, **Gr. 1,** T68, T69; **Gr. 2,** 84, 110, 217, 375;
   Gr. 3, 24, 29; **Gr. 4,** 28, 29; **Gr. 5,** 227; **Gr. 6,** 65,
   75, 362, 364, 415, 419, 423
   adult male, adult female, student, **Gr. 5,** 226, 227
   adult soprano and young person, **Gr. 5,** 192, 193
   changing voices, **Gr. 6,** 360
   chest voice versus head voice, **Gr. 6,** 362, 364, 365, 367
   soprano, alto, tenor, bass, **Gr. 5,** 192
   three different voices, **Gr. 5,** 431
   unique tone colors, **Gr. 5,** 291
vocal and orchestral, **Gr. 1,** T140, T218; **Gr. 6,** 76, 153;
   Gr. 7, 5, 40, 41, 51, 172, 173, 176, 177, 182, 213,
   219, 228
woodwind, **Gr. 5,** 27, 228; **Gr. 6,** 69, 151; **Gr. 7,** 38, 56,
   167, 171, 232
Zimbabwean instruments, **Gr. 1,** T211

U

UNIVERSAL ACCESS. *See* Reaching All Learners

V

VOCAL DEVELOPMENT

a cappella singing, **Gr. 7,** 13, 18, 63, 85, 212
articulation and pronunciation, **Gr. 2,** 139, 216, 298,
   302, 319; **Gr. 3,** 101, 111, 306, 334; **Gr. 4,** 10, 12,
   18, 23, 26, 34, 63, 66, 88, 101, 102, 106, 112, 113,
   167, 178, 188, 194, 214, 222, 230, 256, 260, 265,
   284, 285, 286, 317, 322, 326, 330, 338, 341, 345,
   351, 362, 364, 366, 374, 376, 379, 390, 392, 396;
   Gr. 5, 217, 311, 327; **Gr. 6,** 55, 58, 76, 146, 151, 207,
   306, 350, 353, 358, 370, 372, 376; **Gr. 7,** 111, 128,
   162, 191; **Gr. 8,** 86

Classified Index of Songs, Selected Concepts, Skills, and Activities (continued)

breath control, **Gr. 4,** 113; **Gr. 5,** 184; **Gr. 8,** 76

breath support, **Gr. 5,** 232, 314, 320; **Gr. 8,** 86

breathing, **Gr. K,** T43; **Gr. 1,** T40; **Gr. 2,** 124, 216, 304, 313; **Gr. 3,** 310, 314, 315; **Gr. 4,** 23, 113, 306, 308, 314, 322, 324, 347; **Gr. 5,** 314; **Gr. 6,** 151, 306, 326, 356

changing voices, **Gr. 6,** 250, 261, 321, 332, 335, 358–359, 364, 366, 370; **Gr. 7,** 40–41

chest voice/head voice, **Gr. 6,** 262, 276, 339, 365

chorus, **Gr. 3,** 306; **Gr. 8,** 181

diction, **Gr. 5,** 184; **Gr. 8,** 86

dynamics, **Gr. 2,** 103, 124, 293, **Gr. 4,** 322; **Gr. 5,** 242, 324, 366; **Gr. 6,** 362; **Gr. 7,** 38, 39, 51

enunciation, **Gr. 5,** 156

expression, **Gr. 4,** 207; **Gr. 5,** 311; **Gr. 6,** 167; **Gr. 7,** 41, 149, 157, 175, 182, 211; **Gr. 8,** 81, 87, 89, 151

face-relaxing exercises, **Gr. 4,** 321

four voices: speaking, singing, calling, whispering, **Gr. K,** T41; **Gr. 1,** T69, T70

harmony, **Gr. 5,** 131, 208; **Gr. 7,** 215, 220; **Gr. 8,** 125

head tones, **Gr. 1,** 68, 134, 238, 287; **Gr. 2,** 294, 307, 341

identify verse and refrain, **Gr. 5,** 6; **Gr. 7,** 98

identify theme, **Gr. 7,** 103

imitate, **Gr. 7,** 39, 49, 51, 104, 128

inner hearing, **Gr. 5,** 242, 249; **Gr. 7,** 37

legato, **Gr. 2,** 296–297, 307; **Gr. 6,** 342

maintain healthy voice, **Gr. 5,** 378

melisma, **Gr. 5,** 372, 373, 374

melody, **Gr. 8,** 141, 153, 191

memorization, *See* Singing from Memory *under Music Skills main category*

mouth shape, **Gr. 5,** 314, 366, 368, 376

other, **Gr. K,** T41; **Gr. 1,** T69; **Gr. 3,** E, 64, 101, 127, 133, 253, 269, 277, 306; **Gr. 4,** 207, 321

phrases/phrasing, **Gr. 2,** 297, 319; **Gr. 5,** 103, 197, 369, 378, 383; **Gr. 6,** 326; **Gr. 7,** 30, 137

pitch, **Gr. K,** T50, T75, T212; **Gr. 1,** T30; **Gr. 2,** 18, 115; **Gr. 3,** E, 18, 23, 101, 111, 139, 171, 193, 218, 219, 221, 254, 266, 269, 317, 322; **Gr. 4,** 11, 21, 71, 115, 128, 245, 267, 347, 367; **Gr. 5,** 223, 318, 335, 353, 382; **Gr. 6,** 313; **Gr. 7,** 37; **Gr. 8,** 122

pitch syllables, **Gr. 7,** 30, 148, 161, 186

posture, **Gr. 1,** 238; **Gr. 2,** 300, 304, 308, 341; **Gr. 3,** 306; **Gr. 4,** 306, 308, 314, 317, 321; **Gr. 5,** 197, 314, 347; **Gr. 6,** 151, 207, 306

projection, **Gr. 6,** 306

range and register, **Gr. K,** T15; **Gr. 2,** 294, 307; **Gr. 4,** 330, 347; **Gr. 5,** 335; **Gr. 6,** 362; **Gr. 7,** 40, 111, 194; **Gr. 8,** 8

rhythm, **Gr. 8,** 11

sight reading, **Gr. 7,** 102

sing parts, **Gr. 4,** 218, 349; **Gr. 5,** 195, **Gr. 6,** 62, 174; **Gr. 7,** 129, 175, 212, 200, 223; **Gr. 8,** 75, 91

sing solo, **Gr. 7,** 200

singing parts and solos, **Gr. 1,** T70; **Gr. 2,** 325; **Gr. 3,** 287, 338, 342; **Gr. 6,** 62, 174

staccato, **Gr. 5,** 332

tone color, **Gr. 2,** 84

vocal independence, **Gr. 5,** 235

vocal quality, **Gr. 5,** 27

warm-up exercises, **Gr. 4,** 330; **Gr. 5,** 369

Classified Index

The Pitch and Rhythm Index provides a listing of songs for teaching specific rhythms or pitches. Songs that use only the rhythms or pitches under the heading are labeled *entire*. Specific measure numbers are indicated in parentheses when the rhythms or pitches apply to part of a song. The letter *a* indicates that the anacrusis to the measure is included.

Pitch Index: The pitch index is organized by teaching sequence Within each category, the pitch sets are arranged alphabetically.

Rhythm Index: Rhythms in this section are indexed in the approximate order in which they are introduced in *Spotlight on Music*. The Grades and Units in which they are first introduced are indicated. The other song and listening selections entries are included for use as supplementary reading materials or as review of the indicated rhythm feature.

PITCH

MI SO

Grade K
Best That I Can Be!, The (1–7), T48
Bickle, Bockle (1–3, 5–7), T187
Cobbler, Cobbler, Mend My Shoe (entire), T169
El picaflor (The Hummingbird) (entire), T141
Head and Shoulders (entire), T238
Hello Song (8, 10), T2
Instrument Game (entire), T36
Jig Jog, Jig Jog (1–3, 4–6, 13–15), T260
Lady, Lady (1–4, 9–12), T184
My Grandfather (1, 5, 7, 14), T23
Name Game (1, 3), T58
Old Mister Woodpecker (entire), T172
One, Two, Tie My Shoe (entire), T150
Put Your Finger in the Air (6–7), T230
Qué bonito es (How Wonderful It Is) (1–3, 9–11), T234
Ride the Train (1–2,4–5), T144
Ring Around the Rosy (1–6), T246
See the Pony Galloping (2, 7, 11), T44
Shake My Sillies Out (a1–2), T175
Touch Your Shoulders (entire), T254

Grade 1
A be ce (a1–2, a9–10), T213
A la rueda rueda ('Round and 'Round) (17–20), T240
Categories (entire), T146
Chickery Chick (9), T292
El juego chirimbolo (The Chirimbolo Game) (a5–13), T103
Hanukkah Chag Yafeh (1–2, 9–10), T350
Hoo, Hoo! (a5–8), T55
Hello There! (a1–2, a7–10), T230
Little Red Caboose (1–2), T97
Quaker, Quaker (entire), T100
See Saw (entire), T242
Serra, serra, serrador (Saw, Saw, Lumberjack) (entire), T133
Two, Four, Six, Eight (entire),T246
Una adivinanza (A Riddle) (entire), T138
What's Your Name? (entire), T125

Grade 2
Columbus Sailed with Three Ships (a9–12), 344
Cuckoo, Where Are You? (entire), 244
Engine, Engine Number Nine (entire), 13
Hey, Hey, Look at Me (entire), 245

In and Out (entire), 245
I See (entire), 266
Lemonade (entire), 32
Mill Song, The (2, 6), 52
Mother, Mother (1–3), 254
Oliver Twist (1–2, 4–5), 268
Riqui Ran (Sawing Song) (a1–2, 6, 8, 10), 21
Say Your Name (entire), 243
Who Has the Penny? (1–3), 252

Grade 4
Big Bunch, a Little Bunch (3, 5), 267
El manisero (Peanut Vendor) (1–4, 25–26), 106
How Long the Train Been Gone? (3), 264
Macnamara's Band (a1–2, a9–10, a 17–18, a25–26), 88
Page's Train (1), 246

LA

mi so la

Grade K
Bell Horses (entire), T262
Bickle, Bockle (3), T187
Bobby Shafto (entire), T265
Farmer in the Dell, The (5–6), T100
Fehér liliomszál (Little Water Lily) (entire), T139
Hop, Hop, Hop (3–6), T197
Seesaw, Margery Daw (entire), T264
This Is What I Can Do (entire), T124
We Are Playing in the Forest (entire), T248

Grade 1
¡A divina lo que es! (Guess What It Is!) (entire), T170
A la rueda rueda ('Round and 'Round) (1–8), T240
Bear Went Over the Mountain, The (a9–12), T115
Bluebells (1–6), T209
Boris, the Singing Bear (3–4), T312
Diou Shou Juan'er (Hide the Hankerchief) (5–6), T212
Hakyo jong (The School Bell is Ringing) (1–3, 5–6), T302
Go A Tin (Lantern Song) (entire), T363
I Like Spinach (entire), T163
Little Robin Redbreast (entire), T206
Mi cuerpo (My Body) (a1–2, a5–6), T32
Plenty of Fishes in the Sea (1–2), T310
Rig a Jig Jig (a1–2), T116
Rise, Sally, Rise (1–2), T162
Twenty-four Robbers (entire), T173

Pitch and Rhythm Index (continued)

Grade 2
Columbus Sailed with Three Ships (a9–16), 344
Doggie, Doggie (entire), 59
Eating Lizards (entire), 250
Good Night, Sleep Tight (entire), 76
Here Comes a Bluebird (1–4, 9–12), 263
King's Land (1–7), 257
Little Sally Water (entire), 249
Mill Song, The (entire), 52
Mister Rabbit, Mister Rabbit (5–8), 150
Mr. Frog (1–4), 257
Oliver Twist (entire), 268
Plainsies, Clapsies (entire), 248
Pizza, Pizza, Daddy-O (entire), 62
Red Rover (entire), 249
Riddle Song, A (entire), 251
Tinga Layo (a1, 4), 50

Grade 3
Circle 'Round the Zero (1–2), 267
Coral (1–2), 249
Frosty Weather (5–7), 250
Great Big House (1–3, 5–6), 14
I Have a Car (1–3, a5–7), 252
Jingle at the Window (1–3, 5–6), 268

Grade 4
Please, Mr. Postman (1–2, 5–6, 19–21, 35–37), 44

Grade 5
Caissons Go Rolling Along, The (a1–4), 37
I Hear America Singing (a13–14, 17–18, 21–22), 327
Somebody's Knockin' at Your Door (21–22), 254

Grade 6
Ole La'u Papa e (1–2), 91

DO
do mi
Grade 1
Let's Go Driving (1–2, 9–10), T52
Six Little Ducks (8), T64
Shoo, Turkey (2, 4, 6, 8, 10, 12), T76
Two, Four, Six, Eight (entire), T246

Grade 3
Clocks (1–4), 266
Old Mister Rabbit (1–5), 254
Who's That Yonder? (1–3), 245

Grade 4
Oh, Won't You Sit Down? (9–10, 13–14), 70

do mi so
Grade 1
Brinca la tablita (Hop! Hop!) (2), T71
Hunt the Cows (1–3, 5–6), T236
Johnny Works with One Hammer (1–2, 5–6), T96
Ladybug's Picnic (1–4, 33–35), T290
Sara Watashi (Plate Passing) (9–10), T67
Skip to My Lou (1–2, 5–6), T102

Grade 2
Daisy Chain (1–2, 5–8), 255
Donkey, Donkey (2, 4, 8), 256
He's Got the Whole World in His Hands (1, 5), 116

Itik Besenda Gurau (The Ducks) (1, 3, 18, 20, 22), 100
Knock the Cymbals (1–3, 5–6), 265
Mama Paquita (a1–3, 16–19), 92
Mother, Mother (entire), 254
Mousie, Mousie (entire), 254
Old Blue (1–2, 5–6), 213
Shake the Papaya Down (1, 5), 91
Sheep Shearing (1–2, 5–6), 102
Sorida (entire), 96
Who Has the Penny? (entire), 252

Grade 3
Limbo Rock (a1–2), 232
Turn the Glasses Over (3–5, 7), 260
Vamos a la mar (a5–7, a11–12), 256

do mi so la
Grade 1
I've a Pair of Fishes (1–6), T124
Johnny's Flea (entire), T158
Naranja dulce (Sweet Orange) (a1, a5), T303

Grade 2
Australia's on the Wallaby (a1–2, 11–12), 106
Bow, Wow, Wow (1–6), 264
Daisy Chain (entire), 255
Dal taro kacha (Come, Pick the Moon) (1–6, 9–14), 98
Dance Together (1–3), 264
Donkey, Donkey (entire), 256
He's Got the Whole World in His Hands (a1–3), 116
Juan Pirulero (1–2), 270
King's Land (entire), 257
Knock the Cymbals (1–3, 5–8), 265
Mr. Frog (entire), 257
Sally Go 'Round the Sun (1–6), 268
Willowbee (1–6), 69
You'll Sing a Song and I'll Sing a Song (a3–4), 156

Grade 3
Que llueva (entire), 274
Smoke Goes up the Chimney (3–5, 11–13), 272
When I First Came to This Land (a1–3), 28

Grade 4
Hop Up and Jump Up (entire), 271

do so
Grade 1
Hunt the Cows (9–16), T236
Ladybug's Picnic (9–12), T290
Wind Blew East, The (a1–6), T234

Grade 4
My Town, My World (18–21, 26–29, 43–47), 7
Sea Shell (1–2, 5–6), 245

RE
do re mi
Grade 2
Bow, Wow, Wow (7–8), 264
Here Comes a Bluebird (5–8, 13–16), 263
Hop, Old Squirrel (entire), 258
Hot Cross Buns (entire), 258
Juan Pirulero (3–4), 270
Matarile (1–2, 5–6), 261

Pitch and Rhythm Index

Pitch and Rhythm Index (continued)

Mister Rabbit, Mister Rabbit (1–4), 150
Nabe, Nabe, Soku, Nuke (Stewpot, Stewpot, Bottomless Pot)
    (entire), 259
Old Blue (3–4, 7–8), 213
Rover (1–3, 5–8), 260
Sailor, Sailor on the Sea (entire), 262
Sally Go 'Round the Sun (7–8), 268
Sammy Sackett (1–3), 146
Shoheen Sho (entire), 140
Who's That Tapping at the Window (3–4, 7–8), 261

Grade 3
Cielito Lindo (1–6), 166
Frog in the Meadow (entire), 243
Kuma San (Honorable Bear) (entire), 244
Kum bahur (1–8), 75
Night Song (entire), 186
Over My Head (entire), 286
Preamble, The (1–4), 293
Rain Is Falling Down (entire), 242
See the Rabbit Running (1–3), 255
Smoke Goes up the Chimney (a1–4), 272
Who's That Yonder? (6–8), 245
Woodchuck (entire), 246

Grade 4
Farfallina (Butterfly) (entire), 244
Long-legged Sailor (entire), 243
Oh, Won't You Sit Down? (5–16), 70

Grade 5
Dry Bones (a1–8), 406
Hallelujah, Get on Board (a18–20), 345
Jó ashílá (7–9, 14–19), 224
Mɔfia moni, (1–8), 277
Pick-a-Little/Goodnight Ladies (voice 2, 3–4), 300
Rocky Top (part 1, 3–4, 7–8, 11–12, 15–16, 23–26), 352
Singabahambayo (part 3, a1–5), 75
Ujima (9–10), 427
'Way Down Yonder in the Brickyard (3–4, 7–8, 11–12,
    15–16, 19–20, 23–24), 255
Where Is John? (1–4), 274

Grade 6
Down By the Riverside (3–4, 7–8, 11–12, a19–23), 22
Good News (entire), 242
Haji Firuz (1–4, 17–20), 421
Mi caballo blanco (1–2, lower voice), 60
Roll de Ole Chariot Along (entire), 243
Tina singu (3–4, 7–8), 36

do re mi la
Grade 5
By the Singing Water (1–2), 270

do re mi so
Grade 2
All Around the Buttercup (entire), 210
Dance Together (1–2, 4–8), 264
El zapatero (The Cobbler) (entire), 138
Knock the Cymbals (1–6), 265
Matarile (entire), 261
Old Blue (entire), 213
Old Woman and the Pig (a1–4, a7–10), 130

Pairs or Pears (1–2, 5–6), 265
Rover (entire), 260
Sammy Sackett (entire), 146
Who's That Tapping at the Window (entire), 261
Willowbee (7–14), 69
You'll Sing a Song and I'll Sing a Song (a7–8), 156

Grade 3
Let Us Chase the Squirrel (entire), 248
Dide (entire), 279
Egy üveg alma (entire), 22
One Potato, Two Potato (1–3), 267

Grade 4
Goodbye Brother (7), 273
Old Aunt Dinah (entire), 245
Sea Shell (entire), 245

Grade 5
Goin' Home (1–4, 9–10), 108
How Can I Keep from Singing? (a9–12), 287
John Kanaka (1–16), 249
Los maizales (3–6), 268
Pick-a-Little/Goodnight Ladies (voice 2, 6–10), 300
O, I'm Gonna Sing (entire), 245
Ujima (1–8), 427
'Way Down Yonder in the Brickyard (1–4), 255

Grade 6
Mountain Music (entire), 20
Old Barn Dance, The (a1–8, upper voice), 94

do re mi so la
Grade 2
Bow, Wow, Wow (entire), 264
Button, You Must Wander (entire), 176
Columbus Sailed with Three Ships (a9–18), 344
Dance Together (entire), 264
Harvest (1–5), 342
Here Comes a Bluebird (entire), 263
Here Comes Sally (entire), 220
I Bought Me a Cat (entire), 14
Jim Along, Josie (1–10), 194
Juan Pirulero (entire), 270
Knock the Cymbals (entire), 265
Mary Had a Baby (5–8), 360
Merry-Go-Round (entire), 267
Mister Rabbit, Mister Rabbit (1–16), 150
Pairs or Pears (entire), 265
Sally Go 'Round the Sun (entire), 268
Willowbee (entire), 69
You'll Sing a Song and I'll Sing a Song (a2–4, a6–8), 156

Grade 3
Blow, Ye Winds (entire), 192
Coral (entire), 249
El florón (entire), 46
Frosty Weather (entire), 250
Great Big House (entire), 14
I Have a Car (entire), 252
I'm a Believer (19–32), 312
I'm On My Way (8–13), 382
Trampin' (entire), 287

Pitch and Rhythm Index (continued)

Grade 4
Built My Lady a Fine Brick House (4–8), 252
Countermelody for Cotton-Eye Joe (entire), 53
Green Gravel (a1–4), 247
Page's Train (entire), 246

Grade 5
Deta, Deta (The Moon) (entire), 246
We Want to Sing (entire), 235

Grade 6
I'm Going to Georgia (entire), 244
Kakokolo (1–8), 262
Lonesome Dove (entire), 249

re mi so la
Grade 3
El arroyo que murmura (17–18), 318

SO₁
so₁ do
Grade 3
Scotland's Burning (1–2, 7–8), 257
Ucha Tirvarch (1–6), 53

Grade 5
La víbora de la mar (1–2, 38–43), 440
Lift Up Your Voices (9–12), 319
Mi gallo (17–24), 272

Grade 6
A-Rovin' (a7–10, lower voice), 319
Bulbes (1–2), 280
Derry Ding Dong Dason (9–11), 249

so₁ do mi so
Grade 2
Going Over The Sea (a1–12, a4–6), 216

Grade 3
Sweep, Sweep Away (6–10), 276
Taps (entire), 281

so₁ do re mi
Grade 2
Ach, du lieber Augustin (The More We Get Together)
    (a9–12), 35
A la rueda de San Miguel (To the Wheel of San Miguel)
    (entire), 60
El burrito enfermo (The Sick Little Donkey) (a1–8), 180
I'm Gonna Sing (a1–5), 9
Jugaremos en el bosque (We Will Play in the Forest)
    (entire), 188
Mister Rabbit, Mister Rabbit (a1–4), 150

Grade 3
Rainbow Connection (47–50), 310
Scotland's Burning (1–4), 257
Tanabata (1–4), 62
Yankee Doodle Boy (25–28), 357

Grade 5
Amazing Grace (a13–16), 19
La víbora de la mar (1–13), 440
Old Dan Tucker (3–4), 253

Grade 6
La pájara pinta (a1–3), 268
Water Is Wide, The (1–4), 46

so₁ do re mi so
Grade 2
Chichipapa (Sparrow's Singing School, The) (entire), 22
Grade 3
O Hanukkah (a1–4, a9–18), 368
Little Boy of the Sheep (5–8), 188
Scotland's Burning (entire), 257
Vamos a la mar (Let's Go to the Sea) (entire), 256

Grade 6
Derry Ding Dong Dason (entire), 249

so₁ do re mi so la
Grade 3
Sweep, Sweep Away (entire), 276

Grade 4
Old Paint (7), 275
Walk in the Parlor (entire), 226

Grade 5
Pop! Goes the Weasel (a1–8), 94

so₁ do re mi fa so la
Grade 4
Chairs to Mend (a5–6), 272
Frère Jacques (Are You Sleeping?) (7–8), 260

so₁ la₁ do re mi
Grade 5
Amazing Grace (a1–4), 19
Arirang (1–8, 13–16), 50
Ballad of the Underground Railroad, The, (melody 11–18),
    154
Hill an' Gully (a5–12), 250
Old Dan Tucker (9–12), 253

so₁ la₁ do re mi so
Grade 5
Amazing Grace (entire), 19
Arirang (entire), 50
How Can I Keep from Singing? (entire), 287
Ngam sang duan (a11–18, a27–42), 376
Old Dan Tucker (entire), 253

so₁ la₁ do re mi so la
Grade 4
Girl I Left Behind Me, The (entire), 249
Hold My Mule (1–2), 248

Grade 5
Cindy (entire), 265
I Saw the Light (entire), 252

LA₁
la₁ do mi
Grade 5
Rock and Roll Is Here to Stay (13–16, 29–33), 316
Somebody's Knockin' at Your Door (17–18), 254

Pitch and Rhythm Index

Pitch and Rhythm Index (continued)

la₁ do re mi

Grade 2
This Is Halloween (7–8), 346
Shrimp Boats (a1–3, 5–7), 179

Grade 3
Bim Bom (1, 8–10), 218
Cielito Lindo (17–24), 166
Death of the Robin (1–4, 6–9), 275
Old Mister Rabbit (entire), 254
See the Rabbit Running (entire), 255

Grade 4
Chicka-hanka (entire), 138
'Most Done Ling'rin' Here (entire), 65
Old House (entire), 282

Grade 6
I Got a Letter (entire), 270
Sakura (1–4), 14

la₁ do re mi la

Grade 3
Sun Don't Set in the Mornin' (entire), 60

la₁ do re mi so

Grade 5
Southern Nights (9–12, 16–20), 310

la₁ do re mi so la

Grade 2
Land of the Silver Birch (entire), 88

Grade 3
Rattlesnake (entire), 72

Grade 5
Ballad of the Underground Railroad, The,
    (bottom part 19–26), 154
Los maizales (entire), 268
Southern Nights (entire), 310
There's No Hidin' Place (entire), 266

so₁ la₁ do

Grade 3
Chickama, Chickama, Craney Crow (entire), 263
Kreely Kranky (7–8), 258
My Friend Tom (a1–3, 5–6, 13–14, 17–18), 364
Turn the Glasses Over (1–2), 260
Golden Ring Around the Susan Girl (1–6), 264

Grade 6
Lean on Me (a25–26, a29–30), 150
Merecumbé (a1–3), 276
Pleeng Loy Krathong (10–12), 399
Tain't What You Do (1–2), 18

so₁ la₁ do mi so

Grade 3
Turn the Glasses Over (1–6), 260

so₁ la₁ do re

Grade 3
Kreely Kranky (1–4), 258

so₁ la₁ do re mi

Grade 2
El burrito enfermo (The Sick Little Donkey) (entire), 180
I'm Gonna Sing (a1–6), 9

Shrimp Boats (1–7, 13–16), 179
There's a Hole in the Bucket (entire), 132
What Did Delaware? (entire), 190

Grade 3
Boll Weevil (3–15), 171
Cat and Dog (entire), 259
En roulant ma boule (As I Roll My Ball) (entire), 100
Evergreen, Everblue (24–27), 330
Go Tell it on the Mountain (entire), 377
Kreely Kranky (entire), 258
Old Roger (entire), 280
Simon Says (entire), 4
Tititorea (12–16), 174
Treasure Chests (1–6), 90
Turn the Glasses over (1–8, 13–16), 260
Ucha Tirvarch (1–13), 53
Woke Up This Morning (1–16), 180

Grade 4
Cotton-Eye Joe (entire), 52
Ridin' of a Goat, Leadin' of a Sheep (entire), 251
Something for Me, Something for You (entire), 4
Swapping Song (entire), 253

Grade 5
Somebody's Knockin' at Your Door (1–4, 13–16), 254

Grade 6
Do Lord (entire), 260
Down by the Riverside (a1–12, a19–23), 22
It Don't Mean a Thing (entire), 164
Never Sleep Late Anymore (entire), 274
Our Goodman (entire), 245
There Was a Jolly Miller (entire), 250

so₁ la₁ do re mi so

Grade 2
I Chih ha Ma (Frogs) (entire), 186

Grade 3
Ballad of the Bedbugs and the Beetles, The (entire), 206
Charlie (1–3, 5–11, 13–16), 208
Chicken on the Fence Post (1–6), 265
De aquel cerro (entire), 33
Evergreen, Everblue (28–37), 330
Golden Ring Around the Susan Girl (1–6), 265
Minuteman Minute Song, The (9–14, 23–28, 35–40), 322
Music of the World a-Turnin' (entire), 44
My Horses Ain't Hungry (a1, 3–5, a7–8), 278
Raccoon Dance Song (entire), 87
Tanabata (entire), 62
You're a Grand Old Flag (a1–4, a17–20), 355

Grade 4
Johnson Boys (entire), 223
Night Herding Song (entire), 110

Grade 6
I'm Gonna Sit at the Welcome Table (entire), 417
You Sing for Me (a17–8), 106

so₁ la₁ do re mi so la

Grade 2
Australia's on the Wallaby (a3–4, a7–8, a15–16), 106
Ban Dal (Half Moon) (entire), 219

Pitch and Rhythm Index (continued)

Shrimp Boats (entire), 179
Sing! Sing! Sing! (entire), 196

Grade 3
Crawdad Hole (entire), 107
Spiders (entire), 282
Turn the Glasses Over (entire), 260
Uncle Jessie (entire), 327

Grade 4
Girl I Left Behind Me, The (entire), 249
Goodbye, My Riley O (1, 5), 257
Hold My Mule (entire), 248
What Can One Little Person Do? (entire), 204

Grade 6
Heleluyan (entire), 188
Wayfaring Stranger (entire), 283

so₁ la₁ do re mi fa so
Grade 3
Little Sally Walker (entire), 105

DOᴵ

do mi so doᴵ
Grade 3
Clocks (entire), 266
¡Dale, dale, dale! (a1–6), 378
Morning Bells (entire), 270

do mi so la doᴵ
Grade 2
This I My Country (1–8), 87

Grade 4
Hop Up and Jump Up (entire), 271

do re mi fa so
Grade 4
Love Somebody (1–8), 94

do re mi fa so doᴵ
Grade 4
Early in the Morning at Eight O'Clock (entire), 59
Row, Row, Row Your Boat (5), 268

do re mi fa so la
Grade 4
Happiness (1–7), 124
It Rained a Mist (3, 5), 262

do re mi fa so la doᴵ
Grade 4
Octopus's Garden (entire), 30
Sarasponda (entire), 210
Sing Alleluia, Allelu (entire), 220
Water Come a Me Eye (entire), 90

Grade 5
Joyful, Joyful (13–17), 105
Suk san wan pi mai (New Year's Song) (entire), 437
Where Is John? (entire), 274

do re mi so doᴵ
Grade 3
Little Tommy Tucker (entire), 277
Hello (entire), 283

do re mi so la doᴵ
Grade 2
I Bought Me a Cat (entire), 14
Seeds and Seasons (entire), 206
Take Me Out to the Ball Game (1–8, a17–23), 56
You'll Sing a Song and I'll Sing a Song (entire), 156

Grade 3
Buffalo Dance Entrance Song (entire), 325
Cornstalk Fiddle and a Shoestring Bow (entire), 284
Ding Dong Diggy Diggy Dong (entire), 269
I Lost the Farmer's Dairy Key (entire), 273
One Potato, Two Potato (entire), 267
Riding in the Buggy (entire), 131
Rise Up Singin' (entire), 138
Wang Üger (Chinese Fishing Song) (entire), 190

Grade 4
Ame fure (Rain) (entire), 26
Bamboo Flute (1–18), 134
Buckeye Jim (entire), 136
I Heard a Mockingbird (entire), 150
I'll Rise When the Rooster Crows (entire), 36
Li'l 'Liza Jane (entire), 20
Old Ark's A-Moverin' (entire), 130

Grade 5
Fun wa ni alaafia (entire), 65
Ēinīnī (entire), 340
In That Great Gitn' Up Morning (entire), 10
John Kanaka (entire), 249
Jó ashílá (entire), 224
Old Turkey Buzzard (entire), 264
Triple Play (part 3, 9–15, 25–28), 355
'Way Down Yonder in the Brickyard (entire), 255

Grade 6
Salamanca Market (entire), 247
Scraping Sand (1–14), 248
Shady Grove (entire), 286

la₁ do mi so la doᴵ
Grade 5
John Henry (1–10), 146

Grade 6
Every Mornin' When I Wake Up (entire), 275

la₁ do re mi so la doᴵ
Grade 3
Circle Round the Zero (entire), 267
Colors of the Wind (a1–10, 16–20), 85
Sun Don't Set in the Mornin' (entire), 48
There's a Little Wheel a-Turnin' in My Heart (entire), 129, 137

Grade 4
¿Quién es ese pajarito? (1–6), 284
Train Is A-Coming (3–5), 270

Grade 5
De allacito carnavalito (entire), 269
Fung Yang Song (entire), 58
Somebody's Knockin' at Your Door (entire), 254

mi so la doᴵ
Grade 5
Southern Nights (5–7, 13–15, 22–25, 31–33), 310

Pitch and Rhythm Index

Pitch and Rhythm Index (continued)

so do|
Grade 5
Where Is John? (a9–12), 274

so| do re mi fa so
Grade 4
Achshav (Now) (entire), 112
Sandy McNab (entire), 142

so| do re mi fa so la
Grade 4
A la puerta del cielo (entire), 12
Frère Jacques (Are You Sleeping?) (3–6), 260
La otra Espana (The Other Spain) (entire), 62

so| la| do re mi fa so
Grade 4
Happy Talk (9–12), 84
Who's Got a Fishpole? (4), 261

so| la| do re mi so la do|
Grade 4
Allundé, Alluia (entire), 34
Cedar Swamp (entire), 50
Sail Away, Ladies (entire), 54

Grade 5
Ngam sang duan (entire), 376

Grade 6
Sugar in the Gourd (entire), 251

MI|

mi| so| la| do
Grade 5
Lift Every Voice and Sing (16–19), 86

mi| so| la| do re mi
Grade 6
Sakura (4–7), 14
When I Sing (entire), 44

FA

do mi fa so
Grade 3
O, The Train's Off the Track (entire), 176

Grade 5
Change the World (5–6), 314
When the Saints Go Marching In (a1–2), 127

do mi fa so do|
Grade 3
Shoo Fly Pie and Apple Pan Dowdy (7–8), 227

Grade 4
Oliver Cromwell (entire), 269

do mi fa so la
Grade 3
One More River (entire), 216
Shepherd, Shepherd (17–20), 56

do re mi fa
Grade 3
Consider Yourself (a49–51), 335
La Bamba (1–4, 7–8, 11–12), 236
O Mama Bakudala (1–3, 4–7), 328

Grade 5
Chorus of Villagers from *The Bartered Bride* (1–4), 275
Estrella brillante (part 1, 30–36), 373
Song of Peace, (1–8, a13–16, a21–24), 257
Suk san wan pi mai (New Year's Song) (a9–10), 437
Wie schön leuchtet der Morgenstern (How Brightly Shines the Morning Star) (19–22), 370

do re mi fa so
Grade 3
Deck the Hall (1–2, 5–6, 13–14), 374
Greatest Show on Earth (28–32), 308
May Day Carol (a1–4), 393
Moon and Me (1, 3–5, 7–8, 14–16), 220
Pat-a-Pan (a1–4), 375
Polly Wolly Doodle (a1–3, a7–11m a15–16), 132
Throw It Out the Window (1–3, a7–10, a14–15), 95

Grade 5
Circle of Friends (part 2, 1–11), 196
Da pacem Domine (Give Us Peace) (part 1, entire), 261
De colores (2-part) (13–22), 98
Hallelujah Get on Board (32–55), 345
I Am But a Small Voice (part 2, 17–24), 323
Is That Mister Reilly? (a13–16), 282
Joyful, Joyful (1–4), 105
Joyful, Joyful, We Adore Thee (1–8, 13–16), 103
Lift Up Your Voices (1–4), 319
Like a Mighty Stream (9–16), 320
Mɔfia moni, 277
Rocky Top (part 2, 1–16), 352
There's a Song in Me (2-part) (part 1, a20–27), 183
Times They Are A-Changin', The (entire), 204
Tzena, Tzena (1–5), 171
Un lorito de Verapaz (part 1, 26–28), 349
We Want to Sing (part 2, 1–17), 235
When the Saints Go Marching In (entire), 127

Grade 6
Angelina (a1–5), 8
Dere Geliyor (entire), 232
El tambor (a5–9, a14–17), 222
O, Desayo (1–4), 50
Round and Round (1–2), 104
Winter Ade (entire), 132
Wondering (5–6), 282
Yerakina (5–16), 216

do re mi fa so do|
Grade 3
Frosty, the Snowman (a6–10), 336

do re mi fa so la
Grade 3
Bella Bimba (a1–8, 13–16), 172
Deck the Hall (15–16), 374
Gi'Me Elbow Room (entire), 88
Kum bahur (entire), 75
Oh, Susanna (entire), 153
Pay Me Money Down (entire), 149
Ship Ahoy (4–14), 315
When I First Came to this Land (1–6, 8–13, 15–25), 28

Pitch and Rhythm Index (continued)

Grade 5
A Zing-A Za (part 2, 9–17), 338
Caissons Go Rolling Along, The (a1–8), 37
Estrella brillante (part 2, 7–14), 373
Fifty Nifty United States (13–16), 392
God Bless America (13–22), 4
I Am But a Small Voice (a7–8), 323
La víbora de la mar (14–37), 440
Reach (a19–31), 14
Santa Marta (6–10), 398
Song of Peace (entire), 257
Ujima (1–17), 427
Uno, dos y tres (part 1, entire), 364
We Want to Sing (descant, 18–34), (part 2, 18–34), 235
Wie schön leuchtet der Morgenstern (How Brightly Shines the Morning Star) (a9–10, a15–16), 370

Grade 6
Alleluia (1–8), 186
America (7–14), 388
Dona Nobis Pacem (9–16), 335
Earth Child (1–21), 426
Mayim, Mayim (1–4), 102
Neviděli jste tu mé panenky? (entire), 228
Oh, How Lovely is the Evening (entire), 252
Suliram (a1–7), 59
Troika (7–16), 230
Yerakina (entire), 216

do re mi fa so la do¹
Grade 3
Chan Mali Chan (entire), 10
La cloche (The Clock) (entire), 67
Open the Window, Noah (entire), 324
Smoke Goes Up the Chimney (entire), 272
The Marvelous Toy (a1–22), 182
Three Little Birds (a1–5, 8–13, 16–32), 204
Uno de enero (entire), 210

Grade 6
Cripple Creek (5–18, Part 1), 372

do re mi fa so la do¹ re¹
Grade 5
Funiculi, Funicula (35–52), 62

la₁ do re mi fa so
Grade 3
Yellow Submarine (entire), 320

la₁ do re mi fa so la
Grade 3
Interjections (11–22), 303
Oleana (1–3, 5–7), 144

mi fa so
Grade 5
Change the World (7–12, 17–18), 314
Cuando salí de Cuba (1–4), 168
De colores (unison) (1–6), 88
Orchestra Song (part 2, entire), 332

Grade 6
Oh, How Lovely is the Evening (7–8), 252
Sometimes I Feel Like a Motherless Child (1–2), 271

mi fa so la ti do¹
Grade 6
Walk by the River (1–8), 74

mi fa so la ti do¹ re¹
Grade 6
Sweet and Low (entire), 184

re mi fa so la do¹
Grade 3
Ujamaa (1– 3), 380

so₁ do re mi fa
Grade 3
J'entends le moulin (entire), 135
Mrs. Murphy's Chowder (a1–3), 390
This Is America (1–8), 356

Grade 5
Sound the Trumpet (1–4), 279

Grade 6
Let It Roll (entire), 124

so₁ do re mi fa so
Grade 3
Herring, The (a17–20), 316
Sweet Potatoes (entire), 16
It's Time to Get Ready for Christmas (a1–2), 372

Grade 5
Joyful, Joyful, We Adore Thee (entire), 103
Lion Sleeps Tonight, The (melody) (entire), 172
Our World (a3–6, a10–13, a29–32), 381
Pick-a-Little/Goodnight Ladies (voice 1, 8–16), 300
Simple Gifts (9–16) (entire), 139
Sound the Trumpet (5–8, 17–20), 279
We Are the Children of Tomorrow (1–20), 114

Grade 6
Star–Spangled Banner, The (a29–32), 386
Tina singu (entire, Part 1), 36

so₁ do re mi fa so la
Grade 3
It's Time to Get Ready for Christmas (coda), 372
Look High, Look Low (entire), 338
Paw Paw Patch, The (1–2, 5–8), 195

Grade 5
La víbora de la mar (entire), 440
Like a Mighty Stream (part 1, 25–30), 320
Mango Walk (a1–2, a5–6), 90
My Government Claim (unison) (entire), 95
Santa Marta (entire), 398

Grade 6
Chiribim (entire), 57
El tecolote (entire), 392
Les Anges dans nos Compagnes (entire), 406
Old Jim John (entire), 253
Rock Around the Clock (entire), 234

so₁ la₁ do re mi fa
Grade 3
Eh Soom Boo Kawaya (Nigerian Boat Song) (a1–8), 58

Grade 5
I Got Rhythm (1–16), 187

so₁ la₁ do re mi fa so

Grade 3
I Walk in Beauty (1–4, 7–9, 11–12, 14–18), 329
I's the B'y (entire), 13
Simon Says (entire), 4
Stevedore's Song (1–5), 127
This a Way and That a Way (1–15), 386
Treasure Chests (entire), 91

Grade 5
I Got Rhythm (25–34) (entire), 187

Grade 6
You Sing For Me (Part 1) (a17–32), 106

so₁ la₁ do re mi fa so la

Grade 3
John Jacob Jingleheimer Schmidt (3–9), 68
Limbo Rock (entire, high do in B secton), 232

Grade 5
Loch Lomond (entire), 138
Uncle Pen (entire), 24

Grade 6
O Hal'lwe (entire), 428

so₁ la₁ do re mi fa so la do¹

Grade 3
Amen (entire), 476
Preamble, The (36–60), 293

so₁ la₁ do re mi so la

Grade 3
Cumberland Gap (entire), 99
Draw a Bucket of Water (entire), 222
Wéané (9–16, 27–20, 25–31), 184

so₁ la₁ do re mi so la do¹

Grade 3
Jasmine Flower (entire), 146

so₁ la₁ do re mi

Grade 3
Lukey's Boat (a1–6, 8–10), 114

so₁ la ti do

Grade 3
Billy (entire), 7

TI

do mi fa so la ti do¹ re¹

Grade 4
Morning Has Broken (entire), 22

do re mi fa so la ti do¹

Grade 4
Chumbara (entire), 172
El barquito (The Tiny Boat) (entire), 214
El coquí (The Frog) (entire), 178
Joy to the World (1–10), 383
Sansa kroma (entire), 166

Grade 5
A Zing-A Za (part 1, entire), 338
Caissons Go Rolling Along, The (entire), 37
Chorus of Villagers from The Bartered Bride (entire), 275
Feel Good (8–15), 358

Funiculi, Funicula (a1–17), 62
Lots o' Fish in Bonavist' Harbor (entire), 263
Tzena, Tzena (1–13), 171
Wie schön leuchtet der Morgenstern (How Brightly Shines the Morning Star) (a22–24), 370

Grade 6
Angelina (entire), 8
Mayim, Mayim (entire), 102
Ship in Distress, The (a6–12), 211
Suliram (entire, upper voice), 59

do re mi fa so la ti do¹ re¹

Grade 4
Oro, My Bodeen (entire), 279

Grade 5
Cuando salí de Cuba (entire), 168
Turn the World Around (entire, part 1 descant), 208
Tzena, Tzena (entire), 171
We Want to Sing (entire), 235

do re mi fa so la ti do¹ re¹ mi¹

Grade 5
Goin' Home (entire), 108

Grade 6
Rage and Roar (entire), 48
Samba de Orfeu (entire), 190
Wachet auf (entire), 259

do re mi fa so la ti do¹ re¹ mi¹ fa¹

Grade 6
Hava Nashira (entire), 67
Night of Stars/Silent Night (entire), 412

fa₁ so₁ la₁ ti₁ do re mi fa so

Grade 4
Viva la musica (entire), 174

Grade 6
Tina singu (entire), 36

la₁ ti₁ do

Grade 5
Mɔfia moni (14–16), 277

la₁ ti₁ do re

Grade 5
Estrella brillante (part 2, 30–36), 373
Light One Candle (a9–12), 416
Vive l'amour (13–16), 262

la₁ ti₁ do re mi

Grade 5
Erie Canal (a1–8), 132
Feliz Navidad (13–17, 21–24), 420
Lift Every Voice and Sing (16–19), 86
Light One Candle (a13–16), 416
Wells Fargo Wagon, The (18–20), 303

Grade 6
Goober Peas (21–22), 269

la₁ ti₁ do re mi fa

Grade 4
Peasant's Dancing Day (entire), 132
Take Time in Life (entire), 156

Pitch and Rhythm Index (continued)

Grade 5
Haneirot Halalu (a9–12), 414
Kojo No Tsuki (5–8), 149

la₁ ti₁ do re mi fa so
Grade 5
Mɔfia moni (entire), 277
Turn the World Around (entire), 208

Grade 6
All Ye Who Music Love (a3–16, Part 1), 336
Wondering (entire), 282

la₁ ti₁ do re mi fa so la
Grade 4
A la nanita nana (A Little Lullaby) (1–8), 230
Old Abram Brown (entire), 32
Shabat Shalom (entire), 170
Korobushka (10), 285

Grade 5
Haneirot Halalu (Part 1) (a9–20), 341
Sing, Sing, Sing (entire), 30

Grade 6
Listen to the Music (entire), 63
Old Barn Dance, The (entire), 94

la₁ ti₁ do re mi fa so la ti do¹
Grade 4
Over the Rainbow (1–12, 16–20), 126

Grade 6
Kakokolo (entire), 262

la₁ ti₁ do re mi la
Grade 5
By the Singing Water (entire), 270

la₁ ti₁ do re mi so la ti do¹
Grade 6
Tum Balalaika (entire), 68

la₁ ti₁ do re mi do¹
Grade 4
Rise Up, O Flame (entire), 283

mi₁ fa₁ so₁ la₁ do re mi
Grade 6
Battle Hymn of the Republic (entire), 389

mi₁ fa₁ so₁ la₁ ti₁ do
Grade 5
Agahu (entire), 72

mi fa so la ti do¹ re¹
Grade 5
Estrella brillante (part 1, 15–22), 373
Feliz Navidad (1–8), 420

mi fa so la ti do¹ re¹ mi
Grade 4
Follow Your Dream (entire), 234

mi₁ fa₁ so₁ la₁ ti₁ do re
Grade 4
Pat Works on the Railway (entire), 86

Grade 5
Feliz Navidad (1–8), 420

mi₁ fa₁ so₁ la₁ ti₁ do re mi
Grade 5
Dreamers (entire), 430

mi₁ fa₁ so₁ la₁ ti₁ do re mi fa
Grade 4
Sky Dances (entire), 206

Grade 5
Light One Candle (entire), 416

mi₁ la₁ ti₁ do re mi
Grade 5
Haneirot Halalu (a17–26), 414

mi₁ la₁ ti₁ do re mi so la
Grade 4
Katyusha (entire), 188

mi so la ti
Grade 6
Hotaru Koi (entire), 255

mi₁ so₁ la₁ ti₁ do re
Grade 5
Nani wale na hala, (entire), 276
When Johnny Comes Marching Home (entire), 34

mi₁ so₁ la₁ ti₁ do re mi
Grade 4
Peace Round (entire), 16

Grade 6
Carol from an Irish Cabin (entire), 408

mi₁ so₁ la₁ ti₁ do re mi fa
Grade 5
Vive l'amour (entire), 262

mi₁ so₁ la₁ ti₁ do re mi fa so la
Grade 6
Vem Kan Segla (entire), 419

mi₁ so₁ la₁ ti₁ do re mi so
Grade 6
Doney Gal (entire), 115

re mi fa so la ti
Grade 5
America, the Beautiful (a1–4), 388

re mi fa so la ti do¹
Grade 4
Caballito blanco (3), 278

re₁ mi₁ fa₁ so₁ la₁ ti₁ do re mi
Grade 6
Goober Peas (entire), 269
Jikel' Emaweni (entire), 70

so₁ do re mi fa so la ti do¹
Grade 6
Ma'oz Tsur (entire), 405

so la ti do¹ re¹ mi¹

Grade 5
America, the Beautiful (a9–16), 388

so la ti do¹ re¹ mi¹ fa¹ so¹

Grade 5
Star-Spangled Banner, The (a25–32), 38

so₁ la₁ ti₁ do re

Grade 5
Da pacem Domine (part 2, entire), 261
Good Mornin', Blues (a9–11), 177
Wells Fargo Wagon, The (12–18), 303

so₁ la₁ ti₁ do re mi

Grade 4
Jolly Old St. Nicholas (5, 13), 382

Grade 5
Season of Hope, The (1–16), 410
What the World Needs Now (13–31), 230

Grade 6
Captain Jinks (a4–6), 266
Risseldy, Rosseldy (a1–8), 264

so₁ la₁ ti₁ do re mi fa

Grade 5
Wells Fargo Wagon, The (entire), 303

Grade 6
Down by the Riverside (entire), 22
Lean On Me (entire), 150
One of Those Songs (entire), 54

so₁ la₁ ti₁ do re mi fa do¹

Grade 6
Tsing Chun U Chü (Youth Dance Song) (entire), 272

so₁ la₁ ti₁ do re mi fa so

Grade 4
Roll On, Columbia (entire), 182
Star-Spangled Banner, The (a25–32), 356
Yankee Doodle (entire), 154

Grade 5
Da pacem Domine (entire), 261
Is That Mister Reilly? (entire), 282
Och Jungfun Hon Går I Ringen (entire), 190
Sound the Trumpet (entire), 279
Star Canon (entire), 367
There's a Song in Me, (2-part) (part 1, a20–34), 183
Un lorito de Verapaz (8–16), 349

Grade 6
Al lado de mi cabaña (entire), 141
Belle qui tiens ma vie (entire), 100
Captain Jinks (entire), 266
El charro (entire), 278
El tambor (entire), 222
Gonna Build a Mountain (entire), 5
Greenland Whale Fishery, The (entire), 212
Star-Spangled Banner, The (a25–32), 386
This Pretty Planet (entire), 194

Wabash Cannonball, The (entire), 30
Water is Wide, The (entire), 46

so₁ la₁ ti₁ do re mi fa so la

Grade 4
Eight Bells (a1–6, a11), 281

Grade 5
God Bless America (entire), 4
Guantanamera (entire), 215
Holly and the Ivy, The (entire), 418

Grade 6
Troika (entire), 230
Yellow Bird (entire), 154

so₁ la₁ ti₁ do re mi fa so la ti do¹

Grade 5
Power of the Dream, The (entire), 44

so₁ la₁ ti₁ do re mi so

Grade 5
Erie Canal (1–16), 132
Hero (13–18), 312

Grade 6
Mama Don't 'Low (entire), 126

so₁ la₁ ti₁ do re mi so la ti do¹

Grade 4
Just One Planet (entire), 164

so₁ ti₁ do re mi

Grade 6
Conga (entire), 34

so₁ ti₁ do re mi fa

Grade 4
This Land Is Your Land (entire), 146

Grade 5
Uno, dos y tres (part 2, 13–40), 364

Grade 6
La pájara pinta (entire), 268

so₁ ti₁ do re mi fa so

Grade 4
Las mañanitas (entire), 194

Grade 5
Lift Up Your Voices (entire), 319
Simple Gifts (entire), 136
Streets of Laredo (entire), 260

Grade 6
Charlotte Town (entire), 261
Let Music Surround You (entire), 285
O, Desayo (entire), 50
Sometimes I Feel Like a Motherless Child (entire), 271
Water is Wide, The (5–12), 46

so₁ ti₁ do re mi fa so la

Grade 4
Bell Doth Toll, The (a7), 276

Grade 5
Mango Walk (entire), 90
Mi gallo (entire), 272

Pitch and Rhythm Index (continued)

Grade 6
Cripple Creek (entire), 372
Dona Nobis Pacem (entire), 335
River of My People (entire), 176
Suomen Salossa (entire), 422

so₁ ti₁ do re mi fa so la ti
Grade 6
Canon (entire), 256
Troika (entire), 230

so₁ ti₁ do re mi so la
Grade 5
Hero (17–21), 312

ti₁ do re mi fa
Grade 6
Hae Wa Be (1–4), 273
Kokoleoko (entire), 279
Ship in Distress, The (a1–2), 211

ti₁ do re mi fa so
Grade 5
De colores (2-part) (13–24), 98
Is That Mister Reilly? (a5–8), 282
Like a Mighty Stream (part 1, 31–34, 45–50), 320
Mary Ann (entire), 166

Grade 6
Belle qui tiens ma vie (1–8), 100

ti₁ do re mi fa so la
Grade 5
Lift Every Voice and Sing (a1–12, a25–28), 86

Grade 6
America (entire), 388
Earth Child (entire), 426
Haji Firuz (entire), 421
Mi caballo blanco (entire), 60
Trout, The (a7–14, upper voice), 342

ti₁ do re mi fa so la ti
Grade 5
Winter Wonderland (Parts 1 and 2) (a1–9, a18–26), 408

Grade 6
Guitar Man, The (entire), 138
Jack Was Ev'ry Bit a Sailor (entire), 170
Lumber Camp Song, The (entire), 136
Red Iron Ore (entire), 134
Shibolet Basade (entire), 424

ti₁ do re mi fa so la ti do¹
Grade 4
When I Was Young (entire), 187

RHYTHM

♩♫

(Introduced in Grade 1, Unit 3; In Grade K, Unit 4:
   Aural and Iconic Preparation Only)

Grade K
Bobby Shafto $\frac{4}{4}$, T265
Bounce High, Bounce Low $\frac{2}{4}$, T131
Cobbler, Cobbler, Mend My Shoe $\frac{2}{4}$, T169
El picaflor (The Hummingbird) $\frac{2}{4}$, T141
Head and Shoulders $\frac{2}{4}$, T238
Los pollitos (Little Chickens) $\frac{2}{4}$, T288
Music (poem) $\frac{2}{4}$, T157
This Is What I Can Do $\frac{2}{4}$, T124
Touch Your Shoulders $\frac{2}{4}$, T254
Twinkle, Twinkle, Little Star $\frac{2}{4}$, T90
Walk to School $\frac{2}{4}$, T18
We Are Playing in the Forest $\frac{2}{4}$, T248

Grade 1
¡A divina lo que est! (Guess What It Is!) $\frac{4}{4}$, T170
Bee, Bee, Bumblebee $\frac{2}{4}$, T250
Bluebells $\frac{2}{4}$, T209
Clap Your Hands $\frac{2}{4}$ (rhythm only), T246
Come Back Home, My Little Chicks $\frac{2}{4}$, T134
Double This (poem) $\frac{4}{4}$, T95
Granny (poem) $\frac{4}{4}$, T104
Here We Sit $\frac{4}{4}$, T251
I Am Slowly Going Crazy $\frac{4}{4}$, T127
I've A Pair of Fishes $\frac{2}{4}$, T124
Lucy Locket $\frac{2}{4}$, T253
One, Two, Three Four $\frac{2}{4}$, T123
Quaker, Quaker $\frac{2}{4}$, T100
See-Saw $\frac{2}{4}$, T242
Snail, Snail $\frac{2}{4}$, T252
Two, Four, Six, Eight $\frac{2}{4}$, T246
Una adivinanza (A Riddle) $\frac{4}{4}$, T138

Grade 2
Bate, Bate (speech piece) $\frac{2}{4}$, 242
Cuckoo, Where Are You? $\frac{2}{4}$, 244
Daisy Chain $\frac{2}{4}$, 255
Dance Together $\frac{2}{4}$, 264
Doggie, Doggie $\frac{2}{4}$, 59
Engine, Engine Number Nine $\frac{2}{4}$, 13
Good Night, Sleep Tight $\frac{2}{4}$, 76
Hey, Hey, Look at Me $\frac{2}{4}$, 245
Lemonade $\frac{2}{4}$, 19
Little Sally Water $\frac{2}{4}$, 249
Mouse, Mousie $\frac{2}{4}$, 254
Plainsies, Clapsies $\frac{2}{4}$, 248
Red Rover $\frac{2}{4}$, 249
Say Your Name $\frac{2}{4}$, 243
Three Little Penguins (poem) $\frac{2}{4}$, 112

Grade 3
Apple Tree (poem) $\frac{2}{4}$, 24
Billy $\frac{4}{4}$ (highlighted measures only), 7
De aquel cerro $\frac{2}{2}$, (ostinato pattern only), 32
Egy uveg alma (One Jar of Apples) $\frac{2}{4}$, 22
Frosty Weather $\frac{2}{4}$, 250

Great Big House $\frac{2}{4}$ (Verse 1 only), 14
Keely Kranky $\frac{2}{4}$, 258
La cloche (The Clock) $\frac{2}{4}$, 67
See the Rabbit Running $\frac{2}{4}$, 255
Scotland's Burning $\frac{2}{4}$, 257
Way Down South $\frac{2}{4}$ (iconic rhythm notation only), 9

Listening: Tehahontanekenhnêha' (Rabbit Dance Story) $\frac{4}{4}$ (ostinato patterns only), 50
Listening: Bransle de Champaigne, (rhythm of composition), 96

Grade 4
Long-Legged Sailor $\frac{2}{4}$, 243

Grade 6
Pauper sum ego (I am Poor) $\frac{3}{4}$, 254

♩ ♫ ♩

(Introduced in Grade 1, Unit 5; In K, Unit 5 – Aural and
    Iconic Preparation Only)

Grade K
Animal Rhythms (poem) $\frac{4}{4}$, T56
Bell Horses $\frac{2}{4}$ (rhythm only), T262
Bickle, Bockle $\frac{2}{4}$, T187
Deedle, Deedle Dumpling (poem) $\frac{2}{4}$, T87
Fehér liliolszál (Little Water Lily) $\frac{2}{4}$, T139
Grizzly Bear $\frac{2}{4}$ T252
Hanukkah Is Here $\frac{4}{4}$, T314
Hop, Hop, Hop $\frac{2}{4}$, T197
Monkey, Monkey (poem) $\frac{4}{4}$, T215
Name Game $\frac{4}{4}$, T57
North Winds Blow $\frac{2}{4}$, T305
Old Mister Woodpecker $\frac{4}{4}$, T172
Ring Around the Rosy $\frac{2}{4}$, T246
When You Send A Valentine $\frac{2}{4}$, T332

Grade 1
A la rueda rueda ('Round and 'Round) $\frac{6}{8}$, T240
Acka Backa $\frac{2}{4}$, T256
Animal Song $\frac{4}{4}$, T288
Arre mi burrito (Gid'yup, Little Burro) $\frac{2}{4}$, T256
Autumn Leaves $\frac{4}{4}$ (iconic rhythm only), T254
Johnny's Flea $\frac{4}{4}$ (iconic rhythm only), T158
Jolly Old Saint Nicholas $\frac{2}{4}$, T352
Kari $\frac{4}{4}$, T261
Kaeru no Uta $\frac{4}{4}$, T112
Little Black Bug $\frac{2}{4}$ (rhythm only), T166
Little Robin Red Breast $\frac{4}{4}$, T206, T208
Naughty Kitty Cat $\frac{4}{4}$, T171
Pease Porridge Hot $\frac{2}{4}$, T255
Pitty Patty Polt (poem) $\frac{4}{4}$, T180
Punchinella $\frac{4}{4}$ (rhythm ostinati only), T214
Rain, Rain, Go Away $\frac{2}{4}$, T259
Simple Simon (poem) $\frac{2}{4}$, T175
Star Light, Star Bright $\frac{2}{4}$, T258, P99
Tinker, Tailor $\frac{2}{4}$, T130
Twenty-Four Robbers $\frac{4}{4}$, T173
What's Your Name? $\frac{2}{4}$, T125
Wind Blow $\frac{4}{4}$, T187

Grade 2
All Around the Buttercup $\frac{2}{4}$, 210
Bow, Wow, Wow $\frac{2}{4}$, 264

Chichipapa (The Sparrows' Singing School) $\frac{4}{4}$, 22
Eating Lizards $\frac{2}{4}$, 250
Heigh Ho, Here We Go $\frac{2}{4}$, 252
Hop, Old Squirrel $\frac{2}{4}$, 258
Hot Cross Buns $\frac{2}{4}$, 258
In and Out $\frac{2}{4}$, 245
Jim Along, Josie $\frac{4}{4}$, 194
King's Land $\frac{2}{4}$, 257
Loose Tooth (poem) $\frac{2}{4}$, 28
Matarile $\frac{2}{4}$, 261
Mill Song, The $\frac{2}{4}$, 52
Mother, Mother $\frac{4}{4}$, 254
Mr. Frog $\frac{2}{4}$, 257
Nabe, Nabee, Soku, Nuke $\frac{2}{4}$, 259
Pairs or Pairs $\frac{2}{4}$, 265
Rain on the Green Grass $\frac{2}{4}$, 233
Riddle Song $\frac{4}{4}$, 251
Sammy Sackett $\frac{4}{4}$, 146
Sheep Shearing $\frac{3}{4}$, T102
Who Has the Penny? $\frac{2}{4}$, 252

Listening: "Children's Dance" from Merry Mount (patterns), 246

Grade 3
Circle 'Round the Zero $\frac{4}{4}$, 267
Frog in the Meadow $\frac{2}{4}$, 243
I Have a Car $\frac{2}{2}$, 252
Kuma San $\frac{2}{4}$, 244
Let Us Chase the Squirrel $\frac{2}{4}$, 248
Old Mister Rabbit $\frac{2}{4}$, 254
Patterns for Composing $\frac{2}{4}$, 36
Rain Is Falling Down $\frac{2}{4}$, 242
Tanabata (Seven Evenings) $\frac{2}{4}$, 62
Vamos a la mar (Let's Go to the Sea) $\frac{2}{4}$, 256
Weané $\frac{2}{4}$ (ostinato only), 185
Who's That Yonder? $\frac{2}{4}$, 245
Woodchuck $\frac{2}{4}$, 246

Grade 4
A la puerta del cielo (At the Gate of Heaven) $\frac{2}{4}$, 12
I'll Rise When the Rooster Crows $\frac{2}{4}$, 36
Journey, A $\frac{4}{4}$, 14
Marken er mejet $\frac{2}{4}$, 364
Old Aunt Dinah $\frac{4}{4}$, 245
Rhythm Patterns 1, 2 and 3 $\frac{4}{4}$, 242
Sea Shell $\frac{2}{4}$, 245
T t Trung (Children's Festival) $\frac{4}{4}$, 366

Listening: Erev Shel Shoshanim (playalong patterns), 68
Listening: One Note Samba (playalong patterns), 92
Listening: Symphony No. 7, 2nd Mvt. (playalong patterns), 242
Listening: Carillon, from "L'Arlesienne Suite, No. 1," 244

Grade 5
Deta, Deta (The Moon) $\frac{2}{4}$, 246
Great Good Morning (Countermelody for song on page 10) $\frac{4}{4}$, 242
Just Give Me the Beat $\frac{4}{4}$, 9
Rhythm Patterns for "Cumbia del sol ("Cumbia of the Sun") $\frac{4}{4}$, 17
Words of Wisdom $\frac{4}{4}$, 244

Pitch and Rhythm Index

Pitch and Rhythm Index (continued)

Grade 6
Kakokolo $\frac{4}{4}$ (Refrain), 262
O, La Le! $\frac{4}{4}$ (rhythm pattern), 7

$\downarrow$

(Introduced in Grade 2, Unit 3)

Grade 2
Apple Picker's Reel $\frac{4}{4}$, 343
Baby Nodja $\frac{4}{4}$, 154
Bahay Kubo (My Nipa Hut) $\frac{3}{4}$, 382
Banyan Tree $\frac{3}{4}$, 321
Button You Must Wander $\frac{2}{4}$, 176
Caballito Blanco $\frac{3}{4}$, 278
Corner Grocery Store $\frac{4}{4}$, 311
Donkey, Donkey $\frac{4}{4}$, 256
El Zapatero (The Cobbler) $\frac{4}{4}$, 138
Here Comes A Bluebird $\frac{2}{4}$, 263
Hik Besenda Gurau (the Ducks) $\frac{4}{4}$, 100
In the Window $\frac{3}{4}$, 352
Knock the Cymbals $\frac{2}{4}$, 265
Land of the Silver Birch $\frac{4}{4}$, 88
La paloma se fue (The Dove That Flew Away) $\frac{4}{4}$, 259
Little Heron $\frac{2}{4}$, 322
Mary Had a Baby $\frac{4}{4}$, 360
Mein Hut (My Hat) $\frac{3}{4}$, 142
Old Blue $\frac{4}{4}$, 213
Oro, My Bodeen $\frac{4}{4}$, 279
Rain Before Seven $\frac{2}{4}$, 233
Rover $\frac{2}{4}$, 260
Sailor, Sailor on the Sea $\frac{3}{4}$, 262
Shoheen Sho $\frac{2}{4}$, 140
Shrimp Boats $\frac{3}{4}$, 179
Take Me Out to the Ball Game $\frac{3}{4}$, 56
Thank You $\frac{4}{4}$, 349
Up on the Housetop $\frac{4}{4}$, 356
What Did Delaware? $\frac{4}{4}$, 190
Who's That Tapping at the Window? $\frac{2}{4}$, 261
You'll Sing a Song and I'll Sing a Song $\frac{4}{4}$, 156

Listening: Minuet $\frac{3}{4}$ (rhythm patterns), 144
Listening: Theme from "We're Looking Good," 149

Grade 3
Ballad of the Bedbugs and the Beetles $\frac{2}{4}$ (pattern only), 207
Bim Bom $\frac{4}{4}$, 218
Bohm (Spring Has Come!) $\frac{3}{4}$, 392
Blow, Ye Winds, Blow $\frac{4}{4}$, 192
Cat and Dog $\frac{4}{4}$, 259
Chag Asif (Harvest Time) $\frac{2}{4}$, 360
Coral $\frac{2}{4}$, 249
Cornstalk Fiddle and a Shoestring Bow, $\frac{4}{4}$ (countermelody), 284
Cumberland Gap $\frac{2}{4}$, 99
Es Soom Boo Kawaya (Nigerian Boat Song) $\frac{4}{4}$, 58
Frosty Weather $\frac{2}{4}$ (ostinato), 250
Go Tell It on the Mountain $\frac{4}{4}$, 377
I've Been Working on the Railroad $\frac{4}{4}$, C
Jasmine Flower $\frac{4}{4}$, 146

Kum bachur (The Rooster) $\frac{2}{4}$, 75
Little Tommy Tinker $\frac{4}{4}$, 277
Morning Bells $\frac{4}{4}$, 270
Night Song, $\frac{4}{4}$ (ostinatos only), 187
Oguerre $\frac{4}{4}$, 327
Rattlesnake $\frac{2}{4}$, 72
Sun Don't Set in the Morning $\frac{2}{4}$, 48
Sun Don't Set in the Morning $\frac{2}{4}$ (countermelody), 60
Sweep, Sweep Away $\frac{4}{4}$, 276
Tititorea (Maori Stick Game) $\frac{3}{4}$, 174
Turn the Glasses Over $\frac{4}{4}$, 258
Uve Tirvarch (Little Bear Song) $\frac{2}{4}$ (Verse only), 53
Wake Up Canon $\frac{4}{4}$, 326
Weané $\frac{2}{4}$ (ostinato only), 185
When I First Came to This Land $\frac{2}{4}$, 28
Who Killed Cock Robin? $\frac{4}{4}$, 275

Listening: Nigun Atik $\frac{4}{4}$, 47
Listening: Theme from "March Past of the Kitchen Utensils" from *The Wasps* $\frac{4}{4}$, 246

Grade 4
A la nanita nana (A Little Lullaby) $\frac{3}{4}$, 230
Bamboo $\frac{4}{4}$, 218
Bamboo Flute $\frac{2}{4}$, 134
Bell Doth Toll, The $\frac{4}{4}$, 276
Cotton-Eye Joe $\frac{2}{4}$, 52
Countermelody for Cotton-Eye Joe $\frac{2}{4}$, 53
Eagle $\frac{4}{4}$, 337
Farfallina (Butterfly) $\frac{4}{4}$, 244
Frère Jacques $\frac{4}{4}$, 260
Green Gravel $\frac{3}{4}$, 247
Hine Ma Tov $\frac{4}{4}$, 66
Hold My Mule $\frac{4}{4}$, 248
How Long the Train Been Gone? $\frac{4}{4}$, 264
Jolly Old St. Nicholas $\frac{4}{4}$, 382
New Day $\frac{3}{4}$, 316
Old Abram Brown $\frac{4}{4}$, 32
Old Paint $\frac{3}{4}$, 275
Page's Train $\frac{4}{4}$, 246
¿Quién en ese pajarito? (Who Is that Little Bird?) $\frac{3}{4}$, 284
Rhythm Pattern 4 $\frac{4}{4}$, 242
Sandy McNab $\frac{3}{4}$, 142
Sing Alleluia, Allelu $\frac{4}{4}$, 220
Somewhere Over the Rainbow $\frac{4}{4}$, 126

Listening: "Canon," $\frac{4}{4}$ (percussion patterns), 17

Grade 5
Amazing Grace $\frac{3}{4}$, 19
Babylon's Fallin' $\frac{2}{4}$, 243
Fung Yang Song $\frac{4}{4}$, 58
God Bless America $\frac{4}{4}$, 4
Kojo No Tsuki (Moon at the Ruined Castle) $\frac{4}{4}$, 149
Mi Gallo $\frac{2}{4}$, 272
Och Jungfrun Hon Går I Ringen (A Girl With a Shiny Ribbon) $\frac{3}{4}$, 190
Oh, How Lovely is the Evening $\frac{3}{4}$, 252
O, I'm Gonna Sing $\frac{4}{4}$, 245
Star Canon $\frac{4}{4}$, 367

Wie schön leuchtet der Morgenstern (How Brightly Shines the Morning Star) $\frac{4}{4}$, 370

Listening: Wie schön leuchtet der Morgenstern (How Brightly Shines the Morning Star), 371

Grade 6
Alleluia $\frac{2}{2}$, 186
All Ye Who Music Love $\frac{4}{4}$; $\frac{3}{4}$, 336
Belle Qui Tiens Ma Vie $\frac{4}{4}$, 99
Canon $\frac{2}{2}$, 256
Cripple Creek $\frac{2}{2}$, 372
Derry Ding Dong Dason $\frac{3}{4}$, 249
Dona Nobis Pacem $\frac{3}{4}$, 334
Doney Gal $\frac{3}{4}$, 115
Good News $\frac{4}{4}$, 242
Have Nashira $\frac{4}{4}$, 67
I'm Going to Georgia $\frac{4}{4}$, 244
Já do lesa nepojedu $\frac{3}{4}$, 227
Jede, jede, poštovský panácek (Riding, Riding, Is Mr. Postman) $\frac{3}{4}$, 226
Lonesome Dove $\frac{3}{4}$, 249
N'kosi sikelel' iAfrika $\frac{4}{4}$, 339
Our Goodman $\frac{2}{2}$, 245
Roll de Ole Chariot Along $\frac{4}{4}$, 243
Round and Round $\frac{4}{4}$, 104
Sakura (Cherry Blossoms) $\frac{4}{4}$, 14
Sing Hosanna $\frac{4}{4}$, 362
Stars and Stripes Forever, The $\frac{4}{4}$, 390
Suliram $\frac{4}{4}$, 58
Trout, The $\frac{2}{2}$, 342
Tum Balalaika $\frac{3}{4}$, 68
Wachet auf $\frac{3}{4}$, 259
Wondering $\frac{4}{4}$, 282

♩.

(Introduced in Grade 2, Unit 4)

Grade 2
America, the Beautiful $\frac{4}{4}$, 354
Banyan Tree $\frac{3}{4}$, 321
Chiapanecas (Ladies of Chiapas) $\frac{3}{4}$, 128
Corner Grocery Store $\frac{4}{4}$, 311
Dandansoy $\frac{3}{4}$, 356
Dumplin's $\frac{4}{4}$, 172
El Zapatero (The Cobbler) $\frac{4}{4}$, 138
Hello, Hello There $\frac{3}{4}$, 126
On Top of Spaghetti $\frac{3}{4}$, 312
Let's Go Fly a Kite $\frac{3}{4}$, 134
Me gasa boho (Orange Tree) $\frac{3}{4}$, 317
Mein Hut (My Hat) $\frac{3}{4}$, 142
Sailor, Sailor on the Sea $\frac{3}{4}$, 262
Take Me Out to the Ball Game $\frac{3}{4}$, 56
There Are Many Flags in Many Lands $\frac{4}{4}$, 341
This Is My Country $\frac{4}{4}$, 87

Listening: Minuet $\frac{3}{4}$ (rhythm patterns), 144

Grade 3
Amen $\frac{4}{4}$, 376
Dide $\frac{4}{4}$, 279

Happy Wanderer $\frac{4}{4}$, 18
Hey, Motswala $\frac{3}{4}$, 34
In Good Old Colony Times $\frac{2}{2}$, 326
Little Tommy Tinker $\frac{4}{4}$, 277
Lukey's Boat $\frac{4}{4}$, 114
My Horses Ain't Hungry $\frac{3}{4}$, 278
Night Song $\frac{4}{4}$, 186
O, The Train's Off the Track $\frac{4}{4}$, 176
Oy Chanuke $\frac{4}{4}$, 368
Sweep, Sweep Away $\frac{4}{4}$, 276
Tititorea (Maori Stick Game) $\frac{3}{4}$, 174

Grade 4
America $\frac{3}{4}$, 354
America, My Homeland $\frac{4}{4}$, 358
Bamboo $\frac{4}{4}$, 218
Bell Doth Toll, The $\frac{4}{4}$, 276
Eagle $\frac{4}{4}$, 337
Entren, santos peregrinos (Enter Holy Pilgrims) $\frac{4}{4}$, 379
Himmel und Erde (Music Alone Shall Live) $\frac{3}{4}$, 280
Hine Ma Tov $\frac{4}{4}$, 66
Joy to the World $\frac{2}{4}$, 381
Morning Has Broken $\frac{3}{4}$, 22
Oguerre $\frac{4}{4}$, 327
Old Paint $\frac{3}{4}$, 275
¿Quién en ese pajarito? (Who Is that Little Bird?) $\frac{3}{4}$, 284
Rise Up, O Flame $\frac{3}{4}$, 283
Sing Alleluia, Allelu $\frac{4}{4}$, 220

Grade 5
Amazing Grace $\frac{3}{4}$, 19
Arirang $\frac{2}{4}$ (Including accompanying pattern), 50
Cliffs of Doneen, The $\frac{3}{4}$, 46
God Bless America $\frac{4}{4}$, 4
Haere Ra (Now Is the Hour) $\frac{3}{4}$, 151
Home on the Range $\frac{3}{4}$, D
Kojo No Tsuki (Moon at the Ruined Castle) $\frac{4}{4}$, 149
La paloma se fue (The Dove That Flew Away) $\frac{4}{4}$, 259
Song of Peace $\frac{4}{4}$, 257
Star Canon $\frac{4}{4}$, 367
'Way Down Yonder in the Brickyard $\frac{4}{4}$, 255

Grade 6
Cape Cod Chantey $\frac{4}{4}$, 258
Derry Ding Dong Dason $\frac{3}{4}$, 249
Dona Nobis Pacem $\frac{3}{4}$, 334
Greenland Whale Fishery, the $\frac{4}{4}$, 212
Hae Wa Be (Sun and Rain) $\frac{3}{4}$, 273
I'm Going to Georgia, $\frac{4}{4}$, 244
Listen to the Music $\frac{4}{4}$, 63
Lonesome Dove $\frac{3}{4}$, 249
Oh, How Lovely is the Evening $\frac{3}{4}$, 252
Ole la'u Papa e $\frac{4}{4}$, 91
Our Goodman $\frac{2}{2}$, 245
Rage and Roar $\frac{4}{4}$, 48
River of My People $\frac{3}{4}$, 176
Shoes of John $\frac{4}{4}$, 246
Stars and Stripes Forever, The $\frac{4}{4}$, 390
Suliram $\frac{4}{4}$, 58
Tum Balalaika $\frac{3}{4}$, 68
Wayfaring Stranger $\frac{3}{2}$, 283

Pitch and Rhythm Index (continued)

Winter Ade (Winter, Farewell) $\frac{3}{4}$, 132
Yellow Bird $\frac{4}{4}$, 154

♫♫♫ (four sixteenth notes)

(Introduced in Grade 3, Unit 4)

Grade 2
En la feria de San Juan $\frac{2}{4}$, 225
I Chih Ching Wa (Frogs) $\frac{2}{4}$, 186

Grade 3
Boll Weevil $\frac{2}{4}$, 171
Chicken on the Fence Post $\frac{2}{4}$, 265
Clocks $\frac{2}{4}$, 266
Digga Digga Dog $\frac{4}{4}$, 164 (Introduction)
Dinah $\frac{2}{4}$, 150
Ding Dong Diggy Diggy Dong $\frac{2}{4}$, 269
Draw a Bucket of Water $\frac{2}{4}$, 222
Golden Ring Around the Susan Girl $\frac{2}{4}$, 264
J'entends le Moulin (I Hear the Windmill) $\frac{2}{4}$, 135
  (aural preparation only)
Jingle at the Window $\frac{2}{4}$, 268
Molinillo (Little Coffee Mill) (Speech Game) $\frac{2}{4}$, 251
Mrs. Murphy's Chowder $\frac{2}{4}$, 390
One Potato, Two Potato $\frac{2}{4}$, 267
Ostinato for There's a Little Wheel A-Turnin' in My Heart $\frac{4}{4}$, 137
Paw Paw Patch, The $\frac{2}{4}$ (also patterns, 194), 195
Polly Wolly Doodle $\frac{2}{2}$ (aural identification of four
  sounds to a beat), 132
Riding in the Buggy, $\frac{2}{4}$ (aural identification of four sounds to
  a beat), 131
Rise Up Singin' $\frac{2}{4}$, 138

Grade 4
Cedar Swamp $\frac{2}{4}$, 50
Chicka Hanka $\frac{2}{4}$, 138
Cotton-Eye Joe $\frac{2}{4}$, 52
Countermelody for Cotton-Eye Joe $\frac{2}{4}$, 53
Early in the Morning at Eight O'Clock $\frac{2}{4}$, 59
El barquito (The Tiny Boat) $\frac{2}{4}$, 214
Frog Went A-Courtin' $\frac{2}{4}$, 46
Girl I Left Behind Me, The $\frac{2}{4}$, 249
Hop Up and Jump Up $\frac{2}{4}$, 271
Johnson Boys $\frac{2}{4}$, 233
Love Somebody $\frac{2}{4}$, 94
Old Carrion Crow, The $\frac{2}{4}$, 192
Old Joe Clark $\frac{3}{4}$, 74
Ridin' of a Goat, Leadin' of a Sheep $\frac{2}{4}$, 251
S'vivon Sov (Dreidel Spin) $\frac{2}{4}$, 374
Swapping Song $\frac{2}{4}$, 253
Walk in the Parlor $\frac{2}{4}$, 226
When I Was Young $\frac{2}{4}$, 187
Zum gali gali $\frac{2}{4}$, 255

Listening: *Badinerie* (play rhythm pattern, then listen), 61
Listening: *Overture* from *The Magic Flute*, 252
Listening: *Galop,* from *The Comedians*, 254
Listening: *Minuette* from *Notebook for Anna Magdalena Bach*, 261

Grade 5
Aeyaya balano sakkad (Come, Children) $\frac{4}{4}$, 402
A Zing-A Za $\frac{2}{4}$, 338

By the Singing Water $\frac{2}{4}$, 270
Estrella brillante (Shining Star) $\frac{2}{4}$, 373
Great Big Sea, The $\frac{2}{4}$, 334
In That Great Git'n Up Mornin' $\frac{4}{4}$, 10
Joshua Fit the Battle of Jericho $\frac{2}{4}$, 126
Los maizales (The Cornfields) $\frac{2}{4}$, 268
Simple Gifts $\frac{2}{4}$, 136
Tumbai $\frac{4}{4}$, 194
Üsküdar $\frac{3}{4}$, 128

Grade 6
Bulbes ('Taters) $\frac{2}{4}$, 280
Chiribim $\frac{4}{4}$, 57
Come and Sing together $\frac{2}{4}$, 281
Kokoleoko $\frac{2}{4}$, 279
Never Sleep Late Anymore $\frac{2}{4}$, 274
Old Barn Dance $\frac{4}{4}$, 94
Pick a Bale of Cotton $\frac{3}{4}$, 254
Salamanca Market $\frac{2}{4}$, 247
There Was a Jolly Miller $\frac{2}{4}$, 250
Tsing Chun U Chü (Youth Dance Song) $\frac{2}{4}$, 272
Ye liang wan wan (Crescent Moon) $\frac{2}{4}$, 26

Listening: *Concerto Grosso, Opus 6, No. 11*, 247

♫♩ (eighth-two sixteenths / dotted rhythm)

(Introduced in Grade 4, Unit 2)

Grade 2
A la rueda de San Miguel (To the Wheel of San Miguel) $\frac{2}{4}$, 60
I Chih Ching Wa (Frogs) $\frac{2}{4}$, 186
Ja posejah lubenice (I Planted Waterlmelons) $\frac{2}{4}$, 316
Jugaremos en el bosque (We Will Play in the Forest) $\frac{2}{4}$, 188
Leatherwing Bat, $\frac{2}{4}$, 304
Me Stone $\frac{2}{4}$, 48
Shoo, Fly $\frac{2}{4}$, 222
We're Sailing Down the River (Verse) $\frac{2}{4}$, 166

Grade 3
Boll Weevil $\frac{2}{4}$,
Crawdad Song $\frac{2}{4}$, 107
Digga Digga Dog $\frac{4}{4}$ (Introduction), 164
El florón (The Flower) $\frac{2}{4}$, 46
Kalinka $\frac{2}{4}$, 224
La Bamba $\frac{2}{4}$, 236
Paw Paw Patch, The $\frac{2}{4}$, 195
Rattlesnake $\frac{2}{4}$, 72
Sun Don't Set in the Morning $\frac{2}{4}$, 48
Treasure Chests $\frac{2}{4}$, 90

Grade 4
Buckeye Jim $\frac{2}{4}$, 136-137
Cedar Swamp $\frac{2}{4}$, 50
Cotton-Eye Joe $\frac{2}{4}$, 52 (Countermelody on 53)
Early in the Morning at Eight O'Clock $\frac{2}{4}$, 59
El barquito (The Tiny Boat) $\frac{2}{4}$, 214
Frog Went A-Courtin' $\frac{2}{4}$, 46
Hala lala layya $\frac{4}{4}$, 222
Hop Up and Jump Up $\frac{2}{4}$, 271
I'll Rise When the Rooster Crows $\frac{2}{4}$, 36
Johnson Boys $\frac{2}{4}$, 233
Joy to the World $\frac{2}{4}$, 381

Pitch and Rhythm Index *(vertical tab, left margin)*

Pitch and Rhythm Index (continued)

Kettle Valley Line $\frac{2}{4}$, 248
La Yunsita $\frac{2}{4}$ 350
Little David, Play on Your Harp $\frac{4}{4}$, 323
Love Somebody $\frac{2}{4}$, 94
Molinillo (Little Coffee Mill) (Speech Game) $\frac{2}{4}$, 251
'Most Done Ling'rin' Here $\frac{2}{4}$, 65
Old Carrion Crow,The $\frac{2}{4}$, 192
Ridin' of a Goat, Leadin' of a Sheep $\frac{2}{4}$, 251
Sail Away, Ladies $\frac{2}{4}$, 54
Swapping Song $\frac{2}{4}$, 253
Walk in the Parlor $\frac{2}{4}$, 226
When I Was Young $\frac{2}{4}$, 187
Who's Got a Fishpole? $\frac{4}{4}$, 261
Zum gali gali $\frac{2}{4}$, 255

Listening: Play rhythm pattern, then listen for
    it in *Badinerie*, by J. S. Bach, 61
Listening: Rhythm of Melody of *Galop*, from
    <u>The Comedians</u>, by Kabalevsky, 254
Listening: Melody of A Section of "Contredanse,"
    from *Les Indes galantes*, by Rameau, 97
Listening: Melody of *Spring*, from <u>The Seasons</u>, by Vivaldi, 391

Grade 5
Aeyaya balano sakkad (Come, Children) $\frac{4}{4}$, 402
De allacito carnavalito (The Carnival Is Coming) $\frac{2}{4}$, 269
Estrella brillante (Shining Star) $\frac{2}{4}$, 373
Get On Board $\frac{2}{4}$, 345
Great Big Sea, The $\frac{2}{4}$, 334
Joshua Fit the Battle of Jericho $\frac{2}{4}$, 126
La vibora de la mar (The Sea Snake) $\frac{2}{4}$ and $\frac{3}{4}$, 440
Orchestra Song $\frac{3}{4}$, 332–333
Simple Gifts $\frac{2}{4}$, 136
Sugar in the Gourd $\frac{2}{4}$, 251
There's No Hidin' Place $\frac{4}{4}$, 266
Tumbai $\frac{4}{4}$, 194
Üsküdar $\frac{3}{4}$, 128

Grade 6
Bulbes ('Taters) $\frac{2}{4}$, 280
Chiribim $\frac{4}{4}$, 57
Didn't It Rain $\frac{4}{4}$, $\frac{5}{4}$, $\frac{2}{4}$, 345
Kokoleoko $\frac{2}{4}$, 279
Mama Don't 'Low $\frac{2}{4}$, 126
Never Sleep Late Anymore $\frac{2}{4}$, 274
Old Barn Dance $\frac{4}{4}$, 94
Pleeng Loy Krathong (Full Moon Song) $\frac{4}{4}$, 399
Shady Grove $\frac{2}{4}$, 286
There Was a Jolly Miller $\frac{2}{4}$, 250
Tsing Chun U Chü (Youth Dance Song) $\frac{2}{4}$, 272
Yüe liang wan wan (Crescent Moon) $\frac{2}{4}$, 26

♫♫

(Introduced in Grade 4, Unit 2)

Grade 2
I Chih Ching Wa (Frogs) $\frac{2}{4}$, 186
It's Raining, It's Pouring $\frac{2}{4}$, 233
Ja posejah lubenice (I Planted Waterlmelons) $\frac{2}{4}$, 316
Leatherwing Bat, $\frac{2}{4}$, 304
Yanai, (The Elephant) $\frac{2}{4}$, 305

Grade 3
Boll Weevil $\frac{2}{4}$
Draw a Bucket of Water $\frac{2}{4}$, 222
J'entends le Moulin (I Hear the Windmill) $\frac{2}{4}$, 135
Mrs. Murphy's Chowder $\frac{2}{4}$, 390
My Friend Tom $\frac{4}{4}$, 364
Rattlesnake $\frac{2}{4}$, 72
Riding in the Buggy, $\frac{2}{4}$, 131

Grade 4
Built My Lady a Fine Brick House $\frac{2}{4}$, 252
Buckeye Jim $\frac{2}{4}$, 136
Cedar Swamp $\frac{2}{4}$, 50
Circle of Song $\frac{4}{4}$, 330
Cotton-Eye Joe $\frac{2}{4}$, 52 (Countermelody on 53)
Early in the Morning at Eight O'Clock $\frac{2}{4}$, 59
El barquito (The Tiny Boat) $\frac{2}{4}$, 214
Frog Went A-Courtin' $\frac{2}{4}$, 46
Hop Up and Jump Up $\frac{2}{4}$, 271
I'll Rise When the Rooster Crows $\frac{2}{4}$, 36
Old Carrion Crow, The $\frac{2}{4}$, 192
Sail Away, Ladies $\frac{2}{4}$, 54
S'vivon Sov (Dreidel Spin) $\frac{2}{4}$, 374
Swapping Song $\frac{2}{4}$, 253
This Train $\frac{4}{4}$, 343
Walk in the Parlor $\frac{2}{4}$, 226
Zum gali gali $\frac{2}{4}$, 255

Listening: "Contredanse" from *Les Indes galantes*, 97

Grade 5
Aeyaya balano sakkad (Come, Children) $\frac{4}{4}$, 402
Estrella brillante (Shining Star) $\frac{2}{4}$, 373
Get On Board $\frac{2}{4}$, 345
Great Big Sea, The $\frac{2}{4}$, 334
Hava Nagila $\frac{4}{4}$, 54
In That Great Git'n Up Mornin' $\frac{4}{4}$, 10
Joshua Fit the Battle of Jericho $\frac{2}{4}$, 126
Üsküdar $\frac{3}{4}$, 128
There's No Hidin' Place $\frac{4}{4}$, 266

Grade 6
Bulbes ('Taters) $\frac{2}{4}$, 280
Come and Sing together $\frac{2}{4}$, 281
Didn't It Rain $\frac{4}{4}$, $\frac{5}{4}$, $\frac{2}{4}$, 345
Mama Don't 'Low $\frac{2}{4}$, 126
Mayim, Mayim $\frac{2}{4}$, 102
Never Sleep Late Anymore $\frac{2}{4}$, 274
Old Barn Dance $\frac{4}{4}$, 94
Pick a Bale of Cotton $\frac{3}{4}$, 254
Pleeng Loy Krathong (Full Moon Song) $\frac{4}{4}$, 399

♪♪♪

(Introduced in Grade 4, Unit 4)

Grade 2
Apple Picker's Reel $\frac{4}{4}$, 343
Dumplin's $\frac{4}{4}$, 172
Little Heron $\frac{2}{4}$, 322
Shake the Papaya Down $\frac{4}{4}$, 90
Shoo, Fly $\frac{2}{4}$, 222
This Is My Country $\frac{4}{4}$, 87

Grade 3
Amen $\frac{4}{4}$, 376
Ballad of the Bedbugs and the Beetles $\frac{2}{4}$, 206
Es Soom Boo Kawaya (Nigerian Boat Song) $\frac{4}{4}$, 58
Go Tell It on the Mountain $\frac{4}{4}$, 377
John Jacob Jingleheimer Schmidt $\frac{4}{4}$, 68
Kum Bachur (The Rooster) $\frac{2}{4}$, 75
Limbo Rock $\frac{4}{4}$, 232
Oh, Susanna $\frac{2}{4}$, 153
Out from the Wilderness (Old Abe Lincoln) $\frac{4}{4}$, 388
Open the Window, Noah $\frac{4}{4}$, 324
Riding in the Buggy, $\frac{2}{4}$, 131
Sun Don't Set in the Morning $\frac{2}{4}$, 48
Woke Up This Morning $\frac{4}{4}$, 180
Yankee Doodle Boy $\frac{2}{4}$ 357
You're a Grand Old Flag, $\frac{2}{4}$, 355

Grade 4
Achshav $\frac{2}{4}$, 112
Bamboo $\frac{4}{4}$, 218
Big Bunch, a Little Bunch $\frac{2}{4}$ 267
Buckeye Jim $\frac{2}{4}$, 136-137
Dima $\frac{4}{4}$, 265
Chicka Hanka $\frac{4}{4}$, 138-139
Good-bye, Brother $\frac{4}{4}$, 273
Hine Ma Tov $\frac{4}{4}$, 66
How Long the Train Been Gone? $\frac{4}{4}$, 264
I Heard a Mockingbird $\frac{4}{4}$, 150
Katyusha $\frac{2}{4}$, 188
Lil 'Liza Jane $\frac{2}{4}$, 20
Little David, Play on Your Harp $\frac{4}{4}$, 323
Old Ark's A-Moverin' $\frac{2}{4}$, 130
Peasant's Dancing Day $\frac{4}{4}$, 132
Push Boat Song $\frac{2}{4}$, 266
Shabat Shalom $\frac{4}{4}$, 170
Sing Alleluia, Allelu $\frac{4}{4}$, 220
Take Time in Life $\frac{4}{4}$, 156
This Train $\frac{4}{4}$, 343
Yankee Doodle $\frac{2}{4}$ (descant), 154

Listening: "Festival Dance" $\frac{4}{4}$ (rhythm patterns), 140
Listening: "Russian Sailor's Dance" from *The Red Poppy*, 266
Listening: Big Bunch of Roses, 267

Grade 5
Allá en el rancho grande (My Ranch) $\frac{2}{4}$, 66
¡Ay, Jalisco ne te rajes! (Ay, Jalisco, Never Fail Her!) $\frac{2}{4}$, 188
Caissons Go Rolling Along, The $\frac{2}{4}$, 37
Follow the Drinkin' Gourd, $\frac{2}{2}$, 142
Fung Yang Song $\frac{4}{4}$, 58
Fun wa ni alaafia (Send Us Your Peace) $\frac{4}{4}$, 248
Get On Board $\frac{2}{4}$, 345
Hava Nagila $\frac{4}{4}$, 54
Hill an' Gully $\frac{2}{4}$, 250
I Saw the Light $\frac{4}{4}$, 252
John Kanaka $\frac{2}{4}$, 249
Mango Walk $\frac{4}{4}$, 90
Mary Ann (Instrumental Accompaniment Pattern) $\frac{4}{4}$, 167
Ngam sang duan (Shining Moon) $\frac{4}{4}$, 376
Old Dan Tucker $\frac{4}{4}$, 253
Patterns for Improvisation, 141

Que bonita bandera (What a Beautiful Flag) $\frac{4}{4}$, 442
Rhythm Patterns with Syncopation $\frac{4}{4}$, 251
'Round the Corner, Sally $\frac{4}{4}$, 251
Singahambayo (An Army Is Marching) $\frac{4}{4}$, 56
Singahambayo (An Army Is Marching) (Accompaniment Patterns) $\frac{4}{4}$, 75
Somebody's Knockin' at Your Door $\frac{2}{4}$, 254
There's No Hidin' Place $\frac{4}{4}$, 266
Uncle Pen $\frac{4}{4}$; $\frac{2}{4}$, 24
When the Saints Go Marching In (Bell Pattern) $\frac{4}{4}$, 256

Listening: *Allá en el rancho grande* (My Ranch) (accompaniment patterns), 68
Listening: *Oye como va* (Listen How It Goes) (accompaniment patterns), 69

Grade 6
Cripple Creek $\frac{2}{2}$, 372
Do Lord $\frac{4}{4}$, 260
Ev'ry Time I Feel the Spirit $\frac{4}{4}$, C
Elijah Rock $\frac{2}{2}$, 52
Gee, Mom, I Want to Go Home $\frac{3}{4}$, 148
Ghost Ship, The $\frac{2}{4}$, 323
I Got a Letter $\frac{4}{4}$, 270
I'm Gonna Sit at the Welcome Table $\frac{2}{2}$, 426
It Don't Mean a Thing (cut time), 164
Kakokolo $\frac{4}{4}$, 262
Kokoleoko $\frac{2}{4}$, 279
Leila $\frac{2}{4}$, 376
Mayim, Mayim $\frac{2}{4}$, 102
Mele Kalikimaka (Merry Christmas) $\frac{2}{2}$, 410
Old Barn Dance $\frac{4}{4}$, 94
Ole la'u Papa e $\frac{4}{4}$, 91
Shibolet Basadeh (Wheat in the Fields) $\frac{4}{4}$, 424
Sing Hosanna $\frac{4}{4}$ 362
Sometimes I Feel Like a Motherless Child $\frac{4}{4}$, 271
Yellow Bird $\frac{4}{4}$, 154

Listening: Belhadawa walla belshaawa (Arabic drumming) (rhythm patterns) $\frac{4}{4}$, 35

°
Grade 2
Caranguejo (The Crab) $\frac{2}{4}$, 306
Dumplin's $\frac{4}{4}$, 172
Land of the Silver Birch $\frac{4}{4}$, 88
This Is My Country $\frac{4}{4}$, 87
Who Chopped the Cherry Tree Down? $\frac{4}{4}$, 371

Grade 3
I've Been Working on the Railroad $\frac{4}{4}$, C
Jasmine Flower $\frac{4}{4}$, 146
Over My Head $\frac{4}{4}$ (ostinato), 286
Sweep, Sweep Away $\frac{4}{4}$, 276
Who Killed Cock Robin? $\frac{4}{4}$, 275
Woke Up This Morning $\frac{4}{4}$, 18

Grade 4
Amo fure (Rain) $\frac{4}{4}$ (Playalong patterns only), 27
Bamboo $\frac{4}{4}$, 218
Dok Djampa (The White Jasmine Flower) $\frac{4}{4}$, 392
Dok Djampa $\frac{4}{4}$, 392
Hine Ma Tov $\frac{4}{4}$, 66

How Long the Train Been Gone? 4/4, 264
Jolly Old St. Nicholas 4/4, 382
Oguerre 4/4, 327
Somewhere Over the Rainbow 4/4, 126
We Shall Overcome 4/4, 387

Grade 5
Beauty and the Beast 4/4, 124
Follow the Drinkin' Gourd, 2/2, 142
God Bless America 4/4, 4
Rocky Top 4/4, 352
Uncle Pen 4/4 and 2/4, 24
Star Canon 4/4, 367

Grade 6
Do Lord 4/4, 260
Down by the Riverside 4/4, 22
I Got a Letter 4/4, 270
Listen to the Music 4/4, 63
Lullaby of Broadway 4/4, 182
Samba de Orfeu (Dance of Orpheus) 2/2, 190
Stars and Stripes Forever, The 4/4, 390
Suliram 4/4, 58
Chiribim 4/4, 57
Water Is Wide, The 4/4 46

♩ ♪

(Introduced in Grade 4, Unit 5)

Grade 2
Ach, du lieber Augustin (The More We Get Together) 3/4, 35
America 3/4, 338
Australia's on the Wallaby 4/4, 106
En nuestra Tierra tan Linda (On Our Beautiful Planet Earth) 3/4, 114
Leatherwing Bat, 2/4, 304
Caranguejo (The Crab) 2/4, 306
El palomo y la paloma (The Doves) 2/4, 380
Little Heron 2/4, 322
Mister Rabbit, Mister Rabbit 2/4, 150
My Dreidel 4/4, 352
Old Blue 4/4, 213
San Sereni 2/4, 333
Strawberry Roan 3/4, 66
This Is My Country 4/4, 87
Tititorea (Maori Stick Game) 3/4, 174

Grade 3
America, the Beautiful 4/4, 354
Ballad of the Bedbugs and the Beetles 2/4, 206
Chag Asif (Harvest Time) 2/4, 360
¡Dale, dale, dale! 4/4, 378
Deck the Halls 4/4, 374
Happy Wanderer 4/4, 18
Hey, Motswala 3/4, 34
Jasmine Flower 4/4, 146
John Jacob Jingleheimer Schmidt 4/4, 68
Just Like the Sun 4/4, 394
Marvelous Toy, The 4/4, 182
Sea, The 3/4, 110
Stevedore's Song 4/4, 127
Sweet Potatoes 4/4, 16

There's a Little Wheel A-Turnin' in My Heart 4/4, 129
Treasure Chests 2/4, 90
Weané 2/4, 184
Yankee Doodle Boy 2/4, 357
You're a Grand Old Flag 2/4, 355

Grade 4
Achshav 2/4, 112
All Through the Night 4/4, 277
America 3/4, 354
America, My Homeland 4/4, 358
Bamboo 4/4 (instrument pattern), 219
Bell Doth Toll, The 4/4, 276
Beryoza (The Birch Tree) 2/4, 286
Chairs to Mend 4/4, 272
Eagle 4/4, 337
El barquito (The Tiny Boat) 2/4, 214
Entren, santos peregrinos (Enter Holy Pilgrims) 4/4, 379
Hitori 4/4, 345
Himmel und Erde (Music Alone Shall Live) 3/4, 280
Hine Ma Tov 4/4, 66
Korobushka 2/4, 285
Katyusha 2/4, 188
Las manañitas 3/4, 194
Lil 'Liza Jane 4/4, 20
My Home's in Montana 3/4, 274
Oh, Won't You Sit Down? 4/4, 70
Old Abram Brown 4/4, 32
Old Paint 3/4, 275
Rise Up, O Flame 3/4, 283
Roll On, Columbia 3/4, 182
Sarasponda 4/4, 210-211
Shenandoah 4/4, D
Take Time in Life 4/4, 156
Viva la musica 4/4, 174
Water, Come a Me Eye 4/4, 90
We Shall Overcome 4/4, 387

Listening: "Cattle" from *The Plow that Broke the Plains*, 274
Listening: *Symphony No. 4, 4th Mvt.*, 287

Grade 5
Allá en el rancho grande (My Ranch) 2/4, 66
Amazing Grace 3/4, 19
America, the Beautiful 4/4, 388
Arirang 2/4, 50
Battle Hymn of the Republic 4/4, 391
Cliffs of Doneen, The 3/4, 46
Dance for the Nations 2/4 (instrument pattern), 207
Da pacem Domini 4/4, 261
Dry Bones 4/4, 406
Gentle River Runs, A 4/4, 342
Going Home 4/4, 108
Haneirot Halalu (These Lights) 4/4, 415
Home on the Range 3/4, D
John Kanaka 2/4, 249
Kojo No Tsuki (Moon at the Ruined Castle) 4/4, 149
Lift Up Your Voices 3/4, 319
Ngam sang duan (Shining Moon) 4/4, 376
Old Dan Tucker 4/4, 253
Sankta Lucia (Saint Lucia) 3/4, 413

Somebody's Knockin' at Your Door $\frac{2}{4}$, 254
Streets of Laredo $\frac{3}{4}$, 260
Tzena, Tzena $\frac{4}{4}$, 171
Uncle Pen $\frac{4}{4}$: $\frac{2}{4}$, 24
Uno, dos y tres (One, Two and Three) $\frac{2}{4}$, 364
When the Saints Go Marching In $\frac{4}{4}$, 256

Listening: *Allá en el rancho grande* (My Ranch), 68
Listening: "Maggie in the Wood," 49
Listening: *Oye como va* (Listen How It Goes), 69
Listening: *Agahu*, 73
Listening: *Symphony No. 9 in E minor, Op. 95 ("From the New World") (Excerpt)*, 106
Listening: *Chorus of Villagers* from *The Bartered Bride*, 274

Grade 6
Alleluia $\frac{2}{4}$, 186
America $\frac{3}{4}$, 388
A-Rovin' $\frac{2}{2}$, 319
Bashana Haba'ah (In the Year to Come) $\frac{2}{4}$, 360
Cape Cod Chantey $\frac{4}{4}$, 258
Chiu, Chio, Chiu $\frac{4}{4}$, 172
Do Lord $\frac{4}{4}$, 260
Dona Nobis Pacem $\frac{3}{4}$, 334
Down by the Riverside $\frac{4}{4}$, 22
Ghost Ship, The $\frac{2}{4}$, 323
Greenland Whale Fishery, the $\frac{4}{4}$, 212
Jack Was Ev'ry Bit a Sailor $\frac{4}{4}$, 179
Les Anges dans nos Campagnes (Angels We Have Heard on High) $\frac{4}{4}$, 406
Ma'oz Tsur (Rock of Ages) $\frac{4}{4}$, 405
Stars and Stripes Forever, The $\frac{4}{4}$, 390
Star-Spangled Banner, The $\frac{3}{4}$, 386
They Call the Wind Maria $\frac{4}{4}$, 312
Tina Singu $\frac{4}{4}$, 36
Trout, The $\frac{2}{2}$, 342
Tum Balalaika $\frac{3}{4}$, 68
Wachet auf $\frac{3}{4}$, 259

Listening: Panda Chant II, 263

♪ ♩

(Introduced in Grade 4, Unit 5)

Grade 4
Buckeye Jim $\frac{2}{4}$, 136
Goodbye Brother $\frac{4}{4}$, 273

Grade 5
Erie Canal $\frac{4}{4}$, 176
Feliz Navidad $\frac{4}{4}$, 352
Mango Walk $\frac{4}{4}$, 70
When the Saints Go Marching In $\frac{4}{4}$, 127

Grade 6
Charlotte Town $\frac{2}{4}$, 261
Chíu, chíu, chíu $\frac{4}{4}$, 172
Tina Singu $\frac{4}{4}$, 36

♫♩

(Introduced in Grade 5, Unit 4)

Grade 2
A Pat on the Back $\frac{2}{4}$, 74

Apple Picker's Reel $\frac{4}{4}$, 343
Artichokes $\frac{4}{4}$, 314
Corner Grocery Store $\frac{4}{4}$, 311
Dal Taro Kacha (Come, Pick the Moon) $\frac{2}{4}$, 98
I Chih Ching Wa (Frogs) $\frac{2}{4}$, 186
Leatherwing Bat, $\frac{2}{4}$, 304
Mama Paquita $\frac{2}{4}$, 92
Mary Had a Baby $\frac{4}{4}$, 360
This Is My Country $\frac{4}{4}$, 87
Tinga Layo $\frac{4}{4}$, 50
Yankee Doodle $\frac{2}{4}$, 340

Grade 3
¡Dale, dale, dale! $\frac{4}{4}$, 378
Draw a Bucket of Water $\frac{2}{4}$, 222
El atole (The Atole) $\frac{3}{4}$, 396
Gon xi fa cai (Chinese New Year Song) $\frac{4}{4}$, 384
I Love the Mountains (With "City Life") $\frac{4}{4}$, 341
I've Been Working on the Railroad $\frac{4}{4}$, C
Happy Wanderer $\frac{4}{4}$, 18
John Jacob Jingleheimer Schmidt $\frac{4}{4}$, 68
Kalinka $\frac{2}{4}$, 224
Mrs. Murphy's Chowder $\frac{2}{4}$, 390
Oh, Susanna $\frac{2}{4}$, 153
Oleanna $\frac{4}{4}$, 144
Sun Don't Set in the Morning $\frac{2}{4}$, 48
Wang U Ger $\frac{2}{4}$, 190
Yankee Doodle Boy $\frac{2}{4}$, 357
Yellow Submarine $\frac{4}{4}$, 321
You're a Grand Old Flag, $\frac{2}{4}$, 355

Grade 4
Amo fure (Rain) $\frac{4}{4}$, 26
Boogie-Woogie Ghost $\frac{4}{4}$, 368
Buckeye Jim $\frac{2}{4}$, 136
Frog Went A-Courtin' $\frac{2}{4}$, 46
Going Home, $\frac{4}{4}$, 108
Joyful, Joyful, We Adore Thee $\frac{4}{4}$, 103
Joy to the World $\frac{2}{4}$, 381
La Yunsita $\frac{2}{4}$, 350
Old Carrion Crow, The $\frac{2}{4}$, 192
Old Joe Clark $\frac{3}{4}$, 74
Sail Away, Ladies $\frac{2}{4}$, 54
Star-Spangled Banner, The $\frac{3}{4}$, 356
When I Was Young $\frac{2}{4}$, 187
Yankee Doodle $\frac{2}{4}$, 154

Grade 5
A Zing-A Za $\frac{2}{4}$, 338
Battle Hymn of the Republic $\frac{4}{4}$, 391
Caissons Go Rolling Along, The $\frac{2}{4}$, 37
City Blues $\frac{4}{4}$, 278
De allacito carnavalito (The Carnival Is Coming) $\frac{2}{4}$ (accompaniment pattern), 269
Dry Bones $\frac{4}{4}$, 406
Erie Canal (Refrain) $\frac{4}{4}$, 132
God Bless America $\frac{4}{4}$, 4
Estrella brillante (Shining Star) $\frac{2}{4}$, 373
Every Day I Have the Blues $\frac{4}{4}$, 179
Get On Board $\frac{2}{4}$, 345
Haneirot Halalu (These Lights) $\frac{4}{4}$, 415
Hava Nagila $\frac{4}{4}$, 54

Pitch and Rhythm Index

La vibora de la mar (The Sea Snake) $\frac{2}{4}$; $\frac{3}{4}$, 440
Loch Lomond $\frac{4}{4}$, 138
Simple Gifts $\frac{2}{4}$, 136
Sound the Trumpet $\frac{4}{4}$, 279
Star-Spangled Banner, The $\frac{3}{4}$, 386
There's No Hidin' Place $\frac{4}{4}$, 266
Tzena, Tzena $\frac{4}{4}$, 171
Üsküdar $\frac{3}{4}$, 128
Winter Wonderland $\frac{2}{2}$, 408

Listening: *Arirang,* 53
Listening: *SoundCheck: Yongnam Nongak (Korean Agricultural Music),* 70
Listening: Sound the Trumpet, 279
Listening: *Symphony No. 9, Op. 125 ("Choral") Fourth Mvt. (Excerpt),* 102
Listening: *Symphony No. 9 in E minor, Op. 95 ("From the New World") (Excerpt),* 102
Listening: *Yongnam Nongak (Korean Agricultural Music),* 70

Grade 6
Charlotte Town $\frac{2}{4}$, 261
Choo, Choo, Ch'Boogie $\frac{4}{4}$, 180
El Tambor $\frac{2}{4}$, 222
Heart $\frac{4}{4}$, 166
Kokoleoko $\frac{2}{4}$ (instrument patterns), 279
Old Jim John $\frac{4}{4}$, 253
Ole La'u Pupa e $\frac{4}{4}$, 90
Pleeng Loy Krathong (Full Moon Song) $\frac{4}{4}$, 399
Shady Grove $\frac{2}{4}$, 286
Suomen Salossa (The Finnish Forest) $\frac{2}{4}$, 422
Star-Spangled Banner, The $\frac{3}{4}$, 386
Sugar in the Gourd $\frac{2}{4}$, 251
Tsing Chun U Chü (Youth Dance Song) $\frac{2}{4}$, 272

Listening: Cortege, by L. Boulanger, 253

♫

Grade 2
He's Got the Whole World in His Hands $\frac{4}{4}$, 117
Let's Go Fly a Kite $\frac{3}{4}$, 134
Mister Rabbit, Mister Rabbit $\frac{2}{4}$, 150
Old Blue $\frac{4}{4}$, 213
There Are Many Flags in Many Lands $\frac{4}{4}$, 341
This Is My Country $\frac{4}{4}$, 87
Yanai (The Elephant) $\frac{2}{4}$, 305

Grade 3
I'm on My Way $\frac{4}{4}$, 382
Shoo Fly Pie and Apply Pan Dowdy $\frac{2}{2}$, 227

Grade 4
Buckeye Jim $\frac{2}{4}$, 136
Chicka Hanka $\frac{2}{4}$, 138
El barquito (The Tiny Boat) $\frac{2}{4}$, 214
Shenandoah $\frac{4}{4}$, D
Kettle Valley Line $\frac{2}{4}$, 248
Love Somebody $\frac{2}{4}$, 94

Grade 5
Get On Board $\frac{2}{4}$, 345
In That Great Git'n Up Mornin' $\frac{4}{4}$, 10

Loch Lomond $\frac{4}{4}$, 138
Patterns for Improvisation, 141
Santa Marta $\frac{4}{4}$, 398

Grade 6
Carol from an Irish Cabin $\frac{6}{8}$, 408
Let Music Surround You $\frac{4}{4}$, 285
Pick a Bale of Cotton $\frac{3}{4}$, 254
Walk by the River $\frac{2}{4}$, 74

$\frac{6}{8}$ ♩♪, ♫♩, ♩·
(Introduced in Grade 2, Units 5 and 6)

Grade 2
I See $\frac{6}{8}$, 266
Oliver Twist $\frac{6}{8}$, 268
Skating $\frac{6}{8}$, 350
Wee Falorie Man, The $\frac{6}{8}$, 375
Welcome Is the Month of May $\frac{6}{8}$, 378

Grade 3
Butterfly Come Play With Me $\frac{6}{8}$ (A Section only), 110
Charlie $\frac{6}{8}$, 208
Chicke-ma, Chicka-ma, Craney Crow $\frac{6}{8}$, 261
El arroyo que murmura (The Murmuring Brook) $\frac{6}{8}$, 318
El nido (The Next) $\frac{6}{8}$ (patterns only), 214
En roulant ma boule (As I Roll My Ball) $\frac{6}{8}$, 100
Gi' Me Elbow Room $\frac{6}{8}$, 88
I Raised A Great Hullabaloo (poem) $\frac{6}{8}$, (read, create with patterns), 234
Little Boy of the Sheep $\frac{6}{8}$, (patterns only), 189
Spiders $\frac{6}{8}$, 282
Threw It Out the Window, $\frac{6}{8}$ (patterns only), 95
Uno de enero (The First of January) $\frac{6}{8}$, 210

Listening: "Playful Pizzicato" from *Simple Symphony* $\frac{6}{8}$ (Identify ♫♩♫♩), 261

Grade 4
El quelite $\frac{6}{8}$, 362
Goodbye, My Riley O $\frac{6}{8}$, 257
Heave Ho, Me Laddies $\frac{6}{8}$, 258
Hojas de te (Speech Game) $\frac{6}{8}$, 257
Modern Dragon, A (poem) $\frac{6}{8}$ (instrument pattern), 99
Oliver Cromwell $\frac{6}{8}$, 269
Over the River and Through the Woods $\frac{6}{8}$, 370
Row, Row, Row Your Boat $\frac{6}{8}$, 268
Sing of America $\frac{6}{8}$, 359

Grade 5
De colores $\frac{6}{8}$, 88
Lift Every Voice and Sing $\frac{6}{8}$, 86
Lots o' Fish in Bonavist' Harbor $\frac{6}{8}$, 263
Pop! Goes the Weasel $\frac{6}{8}$, 94
Where Is John? $\frac{6}{8}$, 274

Listening: Variations on the Theme "Pop! Goes the Weasel," 96
Listening: "Chorus of Villagers" from *The Bartered Bride,* 274

Grade 6
Diwali Song $\frac{6}{8}$, 396
Goober Peas $\frac{6}{8}$, 269
Haji Firuz $\frac{6}{8}$, 421

Pitch and Rhythm Index

Pitch and Rhythm Index (continued)

Hullaballoo Balay 6/8, (accompaniment patterns), 11
Joban Tanko Bushi (Joban Miners' Song) 6/8, 142

Listening: *Barcarolle* from Tales of Hoffman, 6/8 (read rhythm patterns for sections A, B, C; then, follow in music), 265

6/8 ♩ ♪, ♫, ♩ ♪
(Introduced in Grade 4, Unit 3)

Grade 2
Merry-Go-Round 6/8, 267
Sally Go 'Round the Sun 6/8, 268

Grade 3
Look High, Look Low 6/8, 338

Grade 4
Hey, Look Me Over 6/8, 114

6/8 ♫♩
(Introduced in Grade 6, Unit 3)

Grade 2
A Bella Hortelana (The Beautiful Gardener) 6/8, 208
Seeds and Seasons 6/8, 206

Grade 4
Night Herding Song 6/8, 110
Arroyito Serrano (Little Mountain Stream) 6/8, 341
Over the Sea to Skye 6/8, 344

Grade 5
St. Patrick's Day 6/8, 434
Un lerito de Verepaz (The Parrot of Verapaz) 6/8, 349

Grade 6
Carol from an Irish Cabin 6/8, 408
El tecolote (The Owlet) 6/8, 392
Git Along, Little Dogies 6/8, 284
Hotaru Koi (Come, Firefly) 2/4, 255
Red Iron Ore 6/8, 134
Silent Night 6/8, 412
Sweet and Low 6/8, 184
Vem Kan Segla (Who Can Sail?) 6/8, 419

6/8 ♫♫
(Introduced in Grade 6, Unit 3)

Grade 6
Red Iron Ore 6/8, 134
Sugar in the Gourd 2/4, 251
This Pretty Planet 6/8, 194

6/8 ♩ ♫
(Introduced in Grade 6, Unit 3)

Grade 6
This Pretty Planet 6/8, 194

♫♩
(Introduced in Grade 4, Unit 4)

Grade 2
Tingalayo 4/4, 50

Grade 3
Draw a Bucket of Water 2/4, 222

Grade 4
When I Was Young 2/4, 187
El barquito (The Tiny Boat) 2/4, 214

Grade 5
A Zing-A Za 2/4, 338
Get On Board 2/4, 345
La vibora de la mar (The Sea Snake) 2/4 and 3/4, 440
Los maizales (The Cornfields) 2/4, 268
Mawfia moni (Ev'rybody Loves Saturday Night) 2/4, 277
Patterns Using Sixteenths, 134
Southern Nights 4/4, 310

Grade 6
El Tambor 2/4, 222
Merecumbe 2/4, 276
Never Sleep Late Anymore 2/4, 274

♫ (triplet)
Grade 2
A Pat on the Back 2/4, 74
Skinnamarink 4/4, 368
Pizza, Pizza, Daddy-O 4/4, 62

Grade 3
I've Been Working on the Railroad 4/4, C
Minuteman Minute Song, The 2/4 (Introduction), 322

Grade 5
Arirang 2/4, 50
Every Day I Have the Blues 4/4, 179

Grade 6
Let Music Surround You 4/4, 285
Rock Around the Clock 4/4, 234

♫♩ (triplet)
Grade 3
City Life (with "I Love the Mountains") 4/4, 341

Grade 4
La otra España (The Other Spain) 4/4, 62
We Shall Overcome 4/4, 387

Grade 5
¡Ay, Jalisco ne te rajes! (Ay, Jalisco, Never Fail Her!) 2/4, 188
Follow the Drinkin' Gourd, 2/2, 142
Nottamun Town, 3/2; 2/2, 405

Grade 6
Blue Suede Shoes 2/2, 236
Choo, Choo, Ch'Boogie 4/4, 180
La bamba 4/4; 2/2, 381
Ride on the Wind 4/4, 326
Sing Hosanna 4/4, 362

Spotlight on Music's resources for teaching recorder include three-, four-, and five-note songs that are simple for students to play, songs from *Spotlight on Recorder* (under separate cover) that can be integrated into the sequenced lessons you teach, and additional teaching opportunities to support and extend both your teaching of recorder and specific concepts and skills.

Spotlight on Music Songs for Recorder

The keys of each selection are indicated in parentheses. Selections in keys other than G can be easily transposed for inclusion in a recorder curriculum.

do re mi

Carillon from *L'Arlesienne Suite No. 1*, (E), **Gr. 4,** 244
Farfallina (Butterfly), (G), **Gr. 4,** 244
Frog in the Meadow, (G), **Gr. 3,** 243
Good News, (G), **Gr. 6,** 242
Hop, Old Squirrel, (G), **Gr. 2,** 258
Horse with No Name, A, (G), **Gr. 8,** 161
Hot Cross Buns, (G), **Gr. 2,** 258
Kuma San (Honorable Bear), (G), **Gr. 3,** 244
Las horas (The Hours), (E), **Gr. K,** T70
Long-Legged Sailor, (F), **Gr. 4,** 243
Mary's Coal Black Lamb, (C), **Gr. 1,** T286
Nabe, Nabe, Soku, Nuke (Stewpot, Stewpot, Bottomless Pot), (G), **Gr. 2,** 259
Night Song, (G), **Gr. 3,** 186
Over My Head, (G), **Gr. 3,** 286
Pitch Review Warm-Up, **Gr. 7,** 47
Rain Is Falling Down, (G), **Gr. 3,** 242
Shoheen Sho, (G), **Gr. 2,** 140
Who's That Yonder?, (F), **Gr. 3,** 245
Woodchuck, (G), **Gr. 3,** 246
Words of Wisdom, (G), **Gr. 5,** 244

do re mi fa

Head and Shoulders, (F), **Gr. K,** T238
Merecumbé, (C), **Gr. 6,** 276
Spirit Medley Rondo (Notre Dame Victory March), (G), **Gr. 7,** 46
Spirit Medley Rondo (Fight On (USC)), (G), **Gr. 7,** 46
Tinker, Tailor, (F), **Gr. 1,** T130

do re mi fa so

Da pacem Domine (Give Us Peace), (G), **Gr. 5,** 261 (Part 1)
Heigh Ho, Here We Go, (G) **Gr. 2,** 252
Joyful, Joyful, We Adore Thee, (G), **Gr. 5,** 103 (Includes low D)
Lemonade, (G), **Gr. 2,** 32
Lion Sleeps Tonight, The, (G), **Gr. 5,** 173 (Verse)
Nikosi (Bluebirds), (G), **Gr. 2,** 230
Oh, Won't You Sit Down?, (G), **Gr. 4,** 70 (Verse)
Old Aunt Dinah, (G), **Gr. 4,** 245
Spirit Medley Rondo (The Eyes of Texas), (G), **Gr. 7,** 46
Turn the World Around, (G), **Gr. 5,** 209 (Refrain)
When the Saints Go Marching In, (G), **Gr. 5,** 256
Winter ade (G Major), (G), **Gr. 6,** 132
Yankee Doodle, (G), **Gr. 4,** 155 (Refrain descant)

Spotlight on Recorder Songs for Recorder

A la nanita nana (A Little Lullaby), **Gr. 4,** 230, **SOR 3–4,** 61
Amazing Grace, **Gr. 5,** 19, **SOR 5–6,** 7–8
America, **Gr. 6,** 388, **SOR 5–6,** 69
Angels We Have Heard on High, **Gr. 6,** 406, **SOR 5–6,** 71
Arirang, **Gr. 5,** 50, **SOR 5–6,** 11
Au clair de la lune, **SOR 3–4,** 17
Bamboo Flute, **Gr. 4,** 134, **SOR 3–4,** 51
Bella bimba (Pretty Girl), **Gr. 3,** 172, **SOR 3–4,** 7
Belle Qui Tiens Ma Vie, **Gr. 6,** 99, **SOR 5–6,** 47
Beryoza (The Birch Tree), **Gr. 4,** 286, **SOR 3–4,** 67
Butterly Come Play with Me, **Gr. 3,** 112, **SOR 3–4,** 5
Charlie, **Gr. 3,** 208, **SOR 3–4,** 11
Chicka-ma, Chicka-ma, Craney Crow, **Gr. 3,** 263, **SOR 3–4,** 9
Circle Round the Zero, **Gr. 3,** 267, **SOR 3–4,** 11
Clementine, **SOR 5–6,** 24
City Blues, **Gr. 5,** 278, **SOR 5–6,** 33
Coral, **Gr. 3,** 249, **SOR 3–4,** 7
Cuando salí de Cuba, **Gr. 5,** 168, **SOR 5–6,** 27
De colores, **Gr. 5,** 88, **SOR 5–6,** 13
Doney Gal, **Gr. 6,** 115, **SOR 5–6,** 51
Entren, santos peregrinos (Enter, Holy Pilgrims), **Gr. 4,** 379, **SOR 3–4,** 69
Frère Jacques (Are You Sleeping?), **Gr. 4,** 260, **SOR 3–4,** 17; **SOR 5–6,** 37
From G to B and Back Again, **SOR 3–4,** 19
Fun wa ni alaafia, **Gr. 5,** 248, **SOR 5–6,** 9–10
Go Tell Aunt Rhody, **SOR 3–4,** 59
Golden Ring Around the Susan Girl, **Gr. 3,** 264, **SOR 3–4,** 5
Greenland Whale Fishery, The, **Gr. 6,** 212, **SOR 5–6,** 63
Guantanamera, **Gr. 5,** 215, **SOR 5–6,** 31
Happy Wanderer, The, **Gr. 3,** 18, **SOR 3–4,** 13
Hey, Motswala, **Gr. 3,** 34, **SOR 3–4,** 11
Hot Cross Buns, **Gr. 2,** 258, **SOR 3–4,** 1, 17, 29; **SOR 5–6,** 1, 53
Hullaballoo Balay, **Gr. 6,** 10, **SOR 5–6,** 39
In That Great Git'n Up Mornin', **Gr. 5,** 10, **SOR 5–6,** 5–6
Jamaica Farewell, **Gr. 3,** 156, **SOR 3–4,** 31
Joshua Fit the Battle of Jericho, **Gr. 5,** 126, **SOR 5–6,** 17
Joy to the World, **Gr. 4,** 383, **SOR 3–4,** 69
Kojo No Tsuki, **Gr. 5,** 149, **SOR 5–6,** 21
L'inverno è già passato (Winter is Over), **Gr. 4,** 390, **SOR 3–4,** 71
Las mañanitas (The Morning Song), **Gr. 4,** 194, **SOR 3–4,** 57
Lukey's Boat, **Gr. 3,** 114, **SOR 3–4,** 33
Lumber Camp Song, The, **Gr. 6,** 136, **SOR 5–6,** 55
Marvelous Toy, The, **Gr. 3,** 182, **SOR 3–4,** 31
Mary Ann, **Gr. 5,** 166, **SOR 5–6,** 23
'Most Done Ling'rin' Here, **Gr. 4,** 65, **SOR 3–4,** 39

Index of Songs for Recorder

Index of Songs for Recorder (continued)

My Horses Ain't Hungry, **Gr. 3**, 278, **SOR 3–4**, 15

Nani Wala Na Hala, **Gr. 5**, 276, **SOR 5–6**, 9–10

Night Song, **Gr. 3**, 186, **SOR 3–4**, 19

No despiertes a mi niño, **Gr. 5**, 217, **SOR 5–6**, 35

Och Jungfrau Hon Går I Ringen, **Gr. 5**, 190, **SOR 5–6**, 29

Ode to Joy, **Gr. 5**, 103 (Joyful, Joyful, We Adore Thee), **SOR 5–6**, 15

Oh, Won't You Sit Down?, **Gr. 4**, 70, **SOR 3–4**, 41

Old Ark's A-Moverin', **Gr. 4**, 130, **SOR 3–4**, 49

Old Carrion Crow, **Gr. 4**, 192, **SOR 3–4**, 55

Old Roger, **Gr. 3**, 280, **SOR 3–4**, 15

Old Song, An, **SOR 3–4**, 33

Over My Head, **Gr. 3**, 286, **SOR**, 23

Pat Works on the Railway, **Gr. 4**, 86, **SOR 3–4**, 45

Paw Paw Patch, The, **Gr. 3**, 195, **SOR 3–4**, 9

¿Quién es ese pajarito? (Who Is That Little Bird?), **Gr. 4**, 284, **SOR 3–4**, 65

Rock Around the Clock, **Gr. 6**, 234, **SOR 5–6**, 67

Round and Round, **Gr. 6**, 104, **SOR 5–6**, 49

Sakura, **Gr. 6**, 247, **SOR 5–6**, 41

Shalom Chaveyrim (Shalom, My Friends), **Gr. 3**, 141, **SOR 3–4**, 9

Simple Gifts, **Gr. 5**, 136, **SOR 5–6**, 19

Sun Don't Set in the Mornin', **Gr. 3**, 48, 60, **SOR 3–4**, 23

Sweet and Low, **Gr. 6**, 184, **SOR 5–6**, 61

Tanabata (Seven Evenings), **Gr. 3**, 62, **SOR 3–4**, 3

This Land is Your Land, **Gr. 4**, 146, **SOR 3–4**, 53

Tzakonikos (listening), **Gr. 6**, 215, **SOR 5–6**, 65

Tzena Tzena, **Gr. 5**, 171, **SOR 5–6**, 27

Water Come a Me Eye, **Gr. 4**, 90, **SOR 3–4**, 47

Water Is Wide, The, **Gr. 6**, 46, **SOR 5–6**, 45

What's in your Bag?, **SOR 3–4**, 19

Winter Ade, **Gr. 6**, 132, **SOR 5–6**, 53

Woke Up this Morning, **Gr. 3**, 180, **SOR 3–4**, 21

Yellow Bird, **Gr. 6**, 154, **SOR 5–6**, 57

Yerakina, **Gr. 6**, 216, **SOR 5–6**, 65

Yüe líang wan wan, **Gr. 6**, 26, **SOR 5–6**, 43

Zum gali gali, **Gr. 4**, 255, **SOR 3–4**, 63

Additional Teaching Opportunities for Recorder

Accompaniment. *See also* Compose, accompaniment; Improvise, accompaniment

  chord root

    Joyful, Joyful, We Adore Thee, **Gr. 5**, 103

    Üsküdar, **Gr. 5**, 129

  playalong

    Arianna, **Gr. 7**, 94–95

    Castle on a Cloud, **Gr. 7**, 82–83

    Kojo Jo Tsuki, **Gr. 5**, 148, 149

    Spirit Medley Rondo, **Gr. 7**, 46

    Symphony No. 9, Fourth Movement, **Gr. 7**, 156

    Tears in Heaven, **Gr. 7**, 141

    When Johnny Comes Marching Home, **Gr. 7**, 168–169

Articulation, Gr. 3, 229

Compose

  accompaniment

    Castle on a Cloud, **Gr. 7**, 82–83

  countermelody

    Contredanse, **Gr. 4**, 96–97

  melody, **Gr. 3**, 229; **Gr. 6**, 159; **Gr. 7**, 47

Gifted and Talented, Gr. 3, 229; **Gr. 4**, 187

Improvise

  accompaniment

    Good Mornin' Blues, **Gr. 5**, 180

    When I Was Young, **Gr. 4**, 187

  interlude

    I Got a Letter, **Gr. 6**, 270

  melody

    Üsküdar, **Gr. 5**, 129

Perform/Play

  Barbry Ellen, **Gr. 6**, 209

  Contredanse, **Gr. 4**, 96–97

  Cumbia del sol, **Gr. 5**, 17

  Doney Gal, **Gr. 6**, 115

  God Bless America, **Gr. 7**, 137

  I Got a Letter, **Gr. 6**, 270

  Joyful, Joyful, We Adore Thee, **Gr. 5**, 103

  Night Song, **Gr. 3**, 186

  Taps, **Gr. 7**, 144–145

  There's a Song in Me, **Gr. 5**, 184

  When I Was Young, **Gr. 4**, 187

Pictures of, Gr. 3, 31; **Gr. 4**, 42–43, 96–97; **Gr. 5**, 83

Playing the recorder

  fingering, **Gr. 3**, 393; **Gr. 4**, 398; **Gr. 5**, 446; **Gr. 6**, 430; **Gr. 7**, 20, 254; **Gr. 8**, 25

  reading/playing, **Gr. 7**, 20, 47

Recorder Consort, Gr. 3, 96–97

Index of Songs for Recorder

Index of Curriculum Links and Activities

Curriculum Links connect music content to other disciplines and offer opportunities to extend the content of each lesson. Links that are activities will engage students in cross-curricular learning and allow for effortless integration of music into any type of classroom setting.

ART

Art Gallery:

Agrarian Leader Zapata by Diego Rivera
  Art Connects to Music: compare indigenous and nationalistic elements in Mexican music and art, **Gr. 8,** 127
  Creative Art Project: create a visual art piece that highlights elements of a culture, **Gr. 8,** 127 **(Activity)**

Bagpipe Player by Giambologna
  Art Connects to Music: musicians in art, **Gr. 4,** 176
  Creative Art Project: draw or paint a musician, **Gr. 4,** 176 **(Activity)**

Basket Dance by Awa Tsireh
  Art Connects to Music: dancers in art and music, **Gr. 5,** 445

Bison by John James Audobon
  Art Connects to Music: animals in art, **Gr. K,** T218
  Creative Art Project: create an animal portrait, **Gr. K,** T219 **(Activity)**

Boating Party, The by Mary Cassatt
  Art Connects to Music: the combination of elements that create a unified whole in music and art, **Gr. 6,** 47
  Creative Art Project: depict the theme "the water is wide," **Gr. 6,** 47

Chi Rho from *The Book of Kells*
  Art Connects to Music: embellishment in music and art, **Gr. 5,** 48
  Creative Art Project: create an intricate design with initials, **Gr. 5,** 48 **(Activity)**

Chinese wood-block print from about 1500
  Art Connects to Music: balance of elements in music and art, **Gr. 6,** 27
  Creative Art Project: use brushstrokes and color to create balance, **Gr. 6,** 27 **(Activity)**

Coronation of Emperor Napolieon I Bonaparte and empress Josephine, The (detail) by Jacques Louis David
  Art Connects to Music: expression in music and art, **Gr. 1,** T174
  Creative Art Project: depict a grand event, **Gr. 1,** T175 **(Activity)**

Dance by Marc Chagall
  Art Connects to Music: form and structure in music and art, **Gr. 4,** 68
  Creative Art Project: create drawings to illustrate the form, structure and rhythm of a piece of music, **Gr. 4,** 68 **(Activity)**

Dance of Youth by Pablo Picasso
  Art Connects to Music: line in art and musical arrangements, **Gr. 5,** 207
  Creative Art Project: create line drawings, **Gr. 5,** 207 **(Activity)**

Daniel Boone Leading Settlers Through the Cumberland Gap by Caleb Bingham
  Art Connects to Music: feelings expressed in music and art, **Gr. 3,** 99
  Creative Art Project: create art works that depict journeys, **Gr. 3,** 99 **(Activity)**

Deep Snow by Grandma Moses
  Art Connects to Music: motion in music and art, **Gr. 3,** 130
  Creative Art Project: paint a picture of a daily task with sensory details, **Gr. 3,** 131 **(Activity)**

Empress of the Blues by Romare Bearden
  Art Connects to Music: music and art with "found" elements, **Gr. 5,** 175
  Creative Art Project: create a collage with found elements, **Gr. 5,** 175 **(Activity)**

Exhausted Bird by Marg Hewson
  Art Connects to Music: choice and organization of sounds and media, **Gr. 4,** 48
  Creative Art Project: create sculptures from found objects, **Gr. 4,** 48 **(Activity)**

Ferdinando de'Medici with his musicians by Antonio Domenico Gabbiani
  Art Connects to Music: art and music of the seventeenth century, **Gr. 8,** 5
  Creative Art Project: draw a present-day musical ensemble, **Gr. 8,** 5 **(Activity)**

Fiddler, The by Marc Chagall
  Art Connects to Music: musicians in art, **Gr. 4,** 375

Fiddler and Boy Doing Jig by Cornelius Krieghoff
  Art Connects to Music: dance in music and art, **Gr. 3,** 93
  Creative Art Project: draw a dancer, **Gr. 3,** 93 **(Activity)**

Fishermen in the nineteenth century
  Art Connects to Music: mood in music and art, **Gr. 6,** 170
  Creative Art Project: illustrate an occupation **Gr. 6,** 171 **(Activity)**

Fugitives Arriving at Levi Coffin's Indiana Farm by Charles Webber
  Art Connects to Music: "foreground and background" in music and art, **Gr. 5,** 10
  Creative Art Project: create a historical scene with foreground and background, **Gr. 5,** 11 **(Activity)**

Gathering Apples by Lajos Karcsay
  Art Connects to Music: dynamics in music and art, **Gr. 3,** 24
  Creative Art Project: create collages with light and dark images, **Gr. 3,** 24 **(Activity)**

Harvesters, The by Pieter Brueghel
  Art Connects to Music: nature in music and art, **Gr. 4,** 375

Curriculum Links and Activities (continued)

Hourtide by Edward Henry Potthast
Art Connects to Music: imagination in music and art, **Gr. 1**, T375

Jewish Musicians in Jerusalem by Vladimir Mnev
Art Connects to Music: musicians in music and art, **Gr. 6**, 425

Katsinthu art created by the Hopi people
Art Connects to Music: care and comfort in music and art, **Gr. 4**, 19
Creative Art Project: create art that represents care and comfort, **Gr. 4**, 19 **(Activity)**

Keeping the Baby Happy by Rube Goldberg
Art Connects to Music: humor in music and art, **Gr. 3**, 182
Creative Art Project: create cartoons, **Gr. 3**, 183 **(Activity)**

Kwanzaa Stamp by Synthia Saint James
Art Connects to Music: celebrations in music and art, **Gr. 5**, 429

La Zandunga by Diego Rivera
Art Connects to Music: dance in music and art, **Gr. 3**, 213
Creative Art Project: create dance murals, **Gr. 3**, 213 **(Activity)**

Lincoln delivering the Gettysburg Address
Art Connects to Music: the voice as a means of expression, **Gr. 7**, 173

Little Dancer of Fourteen by Edgar Degas
Art Connects to Music: line in music and art, **Gr. 2**, 24
Creative Art Project: draw pictures to show two sections of music, **Gr. 2**, 25 **(Activity)**

Luncheon of the Boating Party by Pierre-August Renoir
Art Connects to Music: music and art of the Romantic Period, **Gr. 7**, 121
Creative Art Project: create pointillist paintings **Gr. 7**, 121 **(Activity)**

Mill, The by Rembrandt van Rijn
Art Connects to Music: contrast of light and dark in music and art **Gr. 2**, 52
Creative Art Project: draw pictures to show light and dark, **Gr. 2**, 52 **(Activity)**

Minuet by Giovanni Domenico Tiepolo
Art Connects to Music: imagination and realism in music and art, **Gr. 2**, 144
Creative Art Project: make masks, **Gr. 2**, 144 **(Activity)**

Nevoa by Bob Nugent
Art Connects to Music: nature in music and art, **Gr. 4**, 216
Creative Art Project: create a nature picture with mixed media, **Gr. 4**, 216 **(Activity)**

Noah's Ark by Edward Hicks
Art Connects to Music: stories in music and art, **Gr. 4**, 131
Creative Art Project: create an ark, **Gr. 4**, 131 **(Activity)**

O-Bon Festival by Kobayashi Eitaku
Art Connects to Music: line in art and music, **Gr. K**, T31
Creative Art Project: glue line art, **Gr. K**, T31 **(Activity)**

Painting by unknown artist
Art Connects to Music: art and music of the eighteenth century, **Gr. 8**, 121
Creative Art Project: research artists from the Classical Period, **Gr. 8**, 121 **(Activity)**

Peasants by Diego Rivera
Art Connects to Music: art that shows music, **Gr. 2**, 208
Creative Art Project: create a mural, **Gr. 2**, 209 **(Activity)**

Portrait of Dolores Olmeda by Diego Rivera
Art Connects to Music: music and art about people, **Gr. 5**, 100
Creative Art Project: create a portrait of a friend, **Gr. 5**, 100 **(Activity)**

School of Ballet by Edgar Degas
Art Connects to Music: contrast in music and art, **Gr. K**, T167
Creative Art Project: paint pictures with two contrasting colors, **Gr. K**, T167 **(Activity)**

Song of Peace by Briton Riviere
Art Connects to Music: nature in music and art, **Gr. 7**, 154

Starry Night by Vincent van Gogh
Art Connects to Music: compare and contrast music and art, **Gr. K**, T66

Summer Landscape and *Four Trees* by Egon Schiele
Art Connects to Music: theme and variations, **Gr. 8**, 92
Creative Art Project: create a piece or art with theme and variation, **Gr. 8**, 92 **(Activity)**

Tejedoras by Julian Coché Mendoza
Art Connects to Music: vibrance and intensity in music and art, **Gr. 4**, 100
Creative Art Project: paint a watercolor with vivid colors, **Gr. 4**, 100 **(Activity)**

Train in Coal Town by Jack Savitsky
Art Connects to Music: movement in music and art, **Gr. 2**, 13

Turkish Carpet
Art Connects to Music: pattern in music and art **Gr. 5**, 134
Creative Art Project: create a patterned design, **Gr. 5**, 135 **(Activity)**

Two Mandarin Ducks by Ando Hiroshige
Art Connects to Music: composing in music and art, **Gr. 2**, 100
Creative Art Project: make potato-block prints, **Gr. 2**, 101 **(Activity)**

Unnamed sculpture by Pablo Picasso (stands in the Daley Plaza in downtown Chicago, IL)
Art Connects to Music: an artist's connection to music, **Gr. 7**, 232
Creative Art Project: sketch set and costume designs for a musical show, **Gr. 7**, 232 **(Activity)**

Untitled by Romare Bearden
Art Connects to Music: musicians in music and art, **Gr. 7**, 16
Creative Art Project: create a portrait of a musician **Gr. 7**, 17 **(Activity)**

Untitled by Frederic Remington
Art Connects to Music: drama in music and art,
Gr. 6, 115
Creative Art Project: depict a theme "Gotta Dance!"
Gr. 6, 115 **(Activity)**
Untitled by Unknown (The British attackon Washington,
D.C., in August 1814)
Art Connects to Music: comparte elements in music
and art, **Gr. 7**, 193
Creative Art Project: create art that expresses feelings
about our national anthem, **Gr. 7**, 193 **(Activity)**
Water Lillies by Claude Monet
Art Connects to Music: mood of music and art,
Gr. K, T139
Creative Art Project: draw a picture that portrays a
particular mood, **Gr. K**, T139 **(Activity)**
Well of Toledo, The by Diego Rivera
Art Connects to Music: expression in music and art,
Gr. 1, T196
Creative Art Project: create group murals, **Gr. 1**, T197
(Activity)
Winter Landscape with a Bird Trap by Pieter Brueghel
Art Connects to Music: details in music and art,
Gr. 2, 350
Creative Art Project: create a winter scene, **Gr. 2**, 351
(Activity)
Young Hare by Albrecht Dürer
Art Connects to Music: shading in music and art,
Gr. 2, 151
Creative Art Project: use details to shade in a pencil
drawing, **Gr. 2**, 151 **(Activity)**
Curriculum Link: Art
Animals, **Gr. 1**, T80
Artist Representation, **Gr. 3**, 69 **(Activity)**
Big State of Texas, **Gr. 1**, T8
Boats, **Gr. 4**, 11 **(Activity)**
Chiapas Crafts, **Gr. 2**, 129
Colors and shapes, **Gr. 1**, T115 **(Activity)**
Costumes, **Gr. 3**, 363 **(Activity)**
Create a Family Book, **Gr. 1**, T93
Create a Pattern, **Gr. 2**, 215 **(Activity)**
Create a Personal Stone, **Gr. 2**, 48 **(Activity)**
create, **Gr. 3**, 296, 371, 387
decorate, **Gr. 3**, 28 **(Activity)**
draw, **Gr. 3**, 103, 349; **Gr. 5**, 27, 29, 207
Drawing Characters, **Gr. 3**, 349 **(Activity)**
Eka Muda Game, **Gr. 5**, 28 **(Activity)**
experiment with colors, **Gr. 3**, 28, 73, 115
Flower Drum, **Gr. 5**, 61
Ghanaian Art, **Gr. 3**, 103 **(Activity)**
Green Eggs, **Gr. 2**, 279
Hold Onto Your Hat, **Gr. 5**, 298
Illustrate the Poem, **Gr. 1**, T316 **(Activity)**
illustrate, **Gr. 3**, 69
It's Possible, **Gr. 2**, 278
Line in Music and Art, **Gr. 2**, 24 **(Activity)**
Make "Skeleton" Instruments, **Gr. 5**, 407 **(Activity)**
Make a Classroom Dragon, **Gr. 2**, 367 **(Activity)**
Make a Handprint Butterfly, **Gr. 1**, T333 **(Activity)**
make, **Gr. 3**, 73, 340

Making a "Song Book," **Gr. 1**, T306 **(Activity)**
Making a Mural, **Gr. 3**, 340 **(Activity)**
Making an AB Picture, **Gr. 1**, T304 **(Activity)**
Making Instruments, **Gr. 6**, 6
Making Mexican Maracas, **Gr. 2**, X **(Activity)**
Maracas, **Gr. 1**, T103 **(Activity)**
Menorahs, **Gr. 3**, 371 **(Activity)**
Moon Shapes, **Gr. 2**, 219 **(Activity)**
Multimedia Architecture, **Gr. 4**, R
Mural, **Gr. 1**, T148 **(Activity)**; **Gr. 3**, 139 **(Activity)**;
Gr. 6, 139 **(Activity)**
Music for the Eyes, **Gr. 1**, T210 **(Activity)**
Musician Displays, **Gr. 5**, 395 **(Activity)**
Parents and Children, **Gr. 2**, 184 **(Activity)**
Patterns, **Gr. 3**, 73 **(Activity)**, 115 **(Activity)**
Performer's Portrait, A, **Gr. 4**, 224 **(Activity)**
Picturing the Trout, **Gr. 6**, 343 **(Activity)**
Props, **Gr. 2**, 330
Pumpkin Patch, **Gr. 1**, T342 **(Activity)**
Rain Drawings, **Gr. 1**, T60
Rainbows, **Gr. 1**, T33 **(Activity)**
Rondo Patterns, **Gr. 2**, 224 **(Activity)**
Self-Portraits, **Gr. 1**, T300 **(Activity)**
Shapes and Designs, **Gr. 2**, 149 **(Activity)**
Song Interpretations, **Gr. 5**, 196
Sound Pictures, **Gr. 6**, 227
Texture Collage, **Gr. 6**, 157 **(Activity)**
Valentines, **Gr. 3**, 387 **(Activity)**
Winter Scenes, **Gr. 5**, 411 **(Activity)**

HEALTH
Curriculum Link: Health
Artichokes, **Gr. 2**, 315 **(Activity)**
Bananas, **Gr. 1**, T153
Brushing Your Teeth, **Gr. 1**, T69 **(Activity)**
Chinese Food, **Gr. 3**, 191
Desserts, **Gr. 3**, 227
Emotional Awareness, **Gr. 1**, T254
Hearing Impairment, **Gr. 5**, 102 **(Activity)**
Hiking for Fitness, **Gr. 3**, 20 **(Activity)**
Importance of Friends, The, **Gr. 5**, 186
Importance of Sleep, The, **Gr. 1**, T26 **(Activity)**
Peanuts, **Gr. 1**, T219; **Gr. 4**, 107
Posture and Singing, **Gr. 5**, 57
Protecting the Voice, **Gr. 5**, 228
Sauces, **Gr. 4**, 228
Shellfish Safety, **Gr. 4**, 142
Spinach, **Gr. 1**, T164

LANGUAGE ARTS
Curriculum Link: Language Arts
A Musical Story, **Gr. 3**, 88
Alphabetical Order, **Gr. 2**, Q **(Activity)**
Apple Folk Saying, An, **Gr. 2**, 343 **(Activity)**
Australian Terms, **Gr. 2**, 106
Best Friends, **Gr. 1**, T223 **(Activity)**
Blues lyrics, **Gr. 6**, 180
Call and Response, **Gr. 2**, 19 **(Activity)**
Categories, **Gr. 1**, T146
Class Song, A, **Gr. 4**, 172 **(Activity)**
Comparing lullabies, **Gr. 6**, 59

Curriculum Links and Activities (continued)

Completing a Sentence, **Gr. 1,** T54 **(Activity)**
Compound Words, **Gr. 4,** 76
Consonants and Rhythm, **Gr. 1,** T96
Context Clues, **Gr. 5,** 139
Conversations, **Gr. 2,** 172 **(Activity)**
Create New Words, **Gr. 1,** T292 **(Activity)**
Creating a Verse, **Gr. 2,** 318
Creative Writing, **Gr. 3,** 380, 383 **(Activity)**
Dancing, **Gr. 3,** 196 **(Activity)**
Descriptive Essay, **Gr. 5,** 108 **(Activity)**
Descriptive words, **Gr. 2,** L **(Activity)**
Descriptive Writing, **Gr. 3,** 367 **(Activity)**
Don't Count Your Chickens, **Gr. 3,** 75
English Words from Spanish, **Gr. 4,** M
Fairy Tales, **Gr. 1,** T285
Favorite color poem, **Gr. 6,** 218
Finnish Forest, **Gr. 6,** 423 **(Activity)**
Found poems, **Gr. 6,** 32 **(Activity)**
George Washington Celebrations, **Gr. 3,** R
Guiding principles of Kwanzaa, **Gr. 6,** 415 **(Activity)**
Halloween words, **Gr. 1,** T338 **(Activity)**
Hearing, **Gr. 4,** 13 **(Activity)**
Humor in a song, **Gr. 6,** 56
Humorous lyrics, **Gr. 6,** 148 **(Activity)**
Idioms, **Gr. 3,** L
If I Were President, **Gr. 1,** T368 **(Activity)**
"In My Little Motor Boat," **Gr. 1,** T159 **(Activity)**
Irish Cabin, An, **Gr. 6,** 408 **(Activity)**
Javelina, **Gr. 3,** R
Latin, **Gr. 4,** 174
Learning Names, **Gr. 3,** 4 **(Activity)**
Legendary Hero, **Gr. 3,** 65
Letter to Señor Vargas, A, **Gr. 4,** 196 **(Activity)**
Letter to the Editor, **Gr. 4,** 7 **(Activity)**
Letters, **Gr. 3,** 176 **(Activity)**
Living Comic Strip, **Gr. 4,** 297
Metaphors, **Gr. 3,** 57 **(Activity)**
"Moon and Me", **Gr. 3,** 220 **(Activity)**
Music Terms, **Gr. 5,** 97
Musical Story, A, **Gr. 3,** 88 **(Activity)**
My Trip to Seussland, **Gr. 2,** 279
Narrator, **Gr. 1,** T140
Nonsense Words, **Gr. 3,** 132 **(Activity); Gr. 4,** 210 **(Activity)**
Nonstandard Spelling, **Gr. 5,** 127
Onomatopoeia, **Gr. 4,** 220
Persuasive Letters, **Gr. 4,** 297
Pets, **Gr. 2,** 212 **(Activity)**
Prefix *Octo-*, The, **Gr. 4,** 128 **(Activity)**
Prefixes, **Gr. 5,** 20
Questions and Answers, **Gr. 3,** 151
Rebus, **Gr. 1,** T179
Research, **Gr. 5,** 124 **(Activity)**
Researching the Moon, **Gr. 5,** 368 **(Activity)**
Root Word *phone*, **Gr. 1,** T144 **(Activity)**
Season Poems, **Gr. 1,** T274
Sentence Completion, **Gr. 3,** 236 **(Activity)**
Similes in song lyrics, **Gr. 6,** 21
Slang, **Gr. 4,** 55 **(Activity)**
"Somebody Had To...", **Gr. 1,** T258 **(Activity)**

Something Told the Wild Geese", **Gr. 1,** T261 **(Activity)**
Song About Dreams, A, **Gr. 4,** 235 **(Activity)**
Song and Fantasy, **Gr. 4,** 318 **(Activity)**
Sounds Around the World, **Gr. 2,** 131
Spanish Texas, **Gr. 3,** M
Spinning Tales, **Gr. 3,** 129 **(Activity)**
Story Time, **Gr. 2,** 279
Story with Rhythm, A, **Gr. 4,** 88 **(Activity)**
Storytelling Grab Bag, **Gr. 5,** 298
Storytelling, **Gr. 3,** 95 **(Activity); Gr. 6,** 95 **(Activity)**, 210 **(Activity)**, 294
Stressed Syllables, **Gr. 1,** T123 **(Activity)**
Summer Poem, A, **Gr. 2,** 383
Summing Up, **Gr. 5,** 236 **(Activity)**
"Sweet and Low", **Gr. 6,** 184 **(Activity)**
Syllables in Words, **Gr. 1,** T87
Syllables, **Gr. 3,** 15 **(Activity)**
Taking Turns, **Gr. 2,** 156 **(Activity)**
Texas Map Rap, **Gr. 6,** R
Thanksgiving Words, **Gr. 6,** 108 **(Activity)**
Thee and You, **Gr. 1,** T100 **(Activity)**
Tongue Twisters, **Gr. 3,** 68 **(Activity)**
Tooth Fairy Folktale, The **Gr. 2,** 28
Trickster Tales, **Gr. 2,** 332
Unfamiliar Words, **Gr. 5,** 35 **(Activity)**, 63
Use of the Apostrophe, **Gr. 5,** 243
Using a prefix, **Gr. 6,** 12 **(Activity)**
Valentine's Expression, A, **Gr. 2,** 368
Visual Symbols, **Gr. 1,** T96
Write a Ballad, **Gr. 6,** J
Write a Bluegrass Song, **Gr. 3,** 75 **(Activity)**
Write a definition, **Gr. 6,** 4
Write a New Refrain, **Gr. 5,** 231 **(Activity)**
Write a New Verse, **Gr. 5,** 180
Write a poem, **Gr. 6,** 63 **(Activity)**
Write a review, **Gr. 6,** 197 **(Activity)**
Write a speech piece, **Gr. 6,** 216 **(Activity)**
Write a Story, **Gr. 3,** 347 **(Activity)**
Write a synopsis for a musical, **Gr. 6,** 183 **(Activity)**
Write Lyrics, **Gr. 3,** H; **Gr. 4,** G **(Activity); Gr. 5,** 92 **(Activity)**, 173, 367 **(Activity)**
Write new lyrics, **Gr. 6,** 53 **(Activity)**
Writing Lyrics, **Gr. 4,** 334
Writing Verses, **Gr. 3,** 242
Writing, **Gr. 4,** 358, 380 **(Activity)**
Your Heroes, **Gr. 5,** 312 **(Activity)**
poetry
  Gr. 3, 8, 9, 24, 25, 74, 166, 167, 262; **Gr. 4,** 23 **(Activity)**, 27, 84, 209, 320 **(Activity); Gr. 5,** 32 **(Activity)**, 43, 71, 74 **(Activity)**, 123, 141, 173, 205, 237, 312 **(Activity)**, 352 **(Activity)**, 389

MATHEMATICS
Curriculum Link: Mathematics
  A Soloist's Share, **Gr. 5,** 423 **(Activity)**
  Add on One, **Gr. 2,** 132 **(Activity)**
  Addition and Subtraction, **Gr. 1,** T9
  Bigger and Smaller, **Gr. 1,** T199 **(Activity)**
  Bunch, The **Gr. 3,** 222 **(Activity)**
  Calendar Math, **Gr. 2,** 7 **(Activity)**

Curriculum Links and Activities (continued)

Classifying Geometric Shapes, **Gr. 5**, 212 (**Activity**)
Convert a recipe, **Gr. 6**, 193 (**Activity**)
Convert Snow to Rain, **Gr. 5**, 408 (**Activity**)
Counting Beats, **Gr. 1**, T108; **Gr. 3**, 156 (**Activity**)
Counting candles, **Gr. 6**, 405 (**Activity**)
Counting the Days, **Gr. 2**, 345
Find the Ratio, **Gr. 5**, 400 (**Activity**)
Fractions and Meter, **Gr. 4**, 348 (**Activity**)
Graphing Statistics, **Gr. 4**, 62 (**Activity**)
How Many Paper Clips?, **Gr. 1**, T92
In a Flash, **Gr. 3**, 296
Line Graph, **Gr. 4**, 297
Make an Organized List, **Gr. 5**, 69 (**Activity**)
Mayan Math, **Gr. 2**, 61 (**Activity**)
Meter Arithmetic, **Gr. 3**, 97
Musical Math, **Gr. 5**, 354 (**Activity**); **Gr. 6**, 324
Musical Number Nouns, **Gr. 2**, 152
Note Values, **Gr. 4**, 15 (**Activity**); **Gr. 5**, 8 (**Activity**)
Numbers of Musicians, **Gr. 2**, 148 (**Activity**)
Numbers, **Gr. 1**, T132
One Fish Two Fish Red Fish Blue Fish, **Gr. 2**, 278
Ordinal numbers, **Gr. 1**, T215 (**Activity**)
Patterns and sequences, **Gr. 6**, 224 (**Activity**)
Patterns, **Gr. 2**, 320
Permutations, **Gr. 6**, 37 (**Activity**)
Roman Numerals, **Gr. 5**, 167
Skip-Counting, **Gr. 1**, T291 (**Activity**)
Standard Units, **Gr. 5**, 131
Taking a Train, **Gr. 5**, 298
Tempered tuning, **Gr. 6**, 128 (**Activity**)
Ticket Sales Math, **Gr. 4**, 297
Time, **Gr. 3**, 67 (**Activity**)
Visual Symbols, **Gr. 1**, T96
Word Problem, A, **Gr. 1**, T151

PHYSICAL EDUCATION
Curriculum Link: Physical Education
Conducting Exercises, **Gr. 3**, 179 (**Activity**)
Contra dances, **Gr. 6**, 374
Crazy Cookie Counting, **Gr. 1**, T274
Dance and Physical Activity, **Gr. 5**, 152
Dancing, Benefits of, **Gr. 2**, 94
Evaluate movement, **Gr. 6**, 230
Fad Dances, **Gr. 5**, 424 (**Activity**)
Italian Tempo Markings, **Gr. 4**, 191 (**Activity**)
Jump Rope, **Gr. 1**, T15
Jumping Rope, **Gr. 4**, 58
Rugby, **Gr. 2**, 140
Steps, Skips, and Leaps, **Gr. 2**, 231 (**Activity**)
Teamwork, **Gr. 1**, T111 (**Activity**)

READING
Curriculum Link: Reading
Ban Dal, **Gr. 4**, 184 (**Activity**)
Blank Verse, **Gr. 6**, 209
Building Literacy Readiness, **Gr. 1**, T24
Building Vocabulary, **Gr. 3**, 357 (**Activity**)
Cumulative Tales, **Gr. 1**, T180 (**Activity**)
Dragon Myths, **Gr. 2**, 55
"Hope", **Gr. 3**, 167 (**Activity**)
Humor in a Song, **Gr. 6**, 56
Interpreting a poem, **Gr. 6**, 156 (**Activity**)
Monster Stories, **Gr. 3**, 307
Nursery Rhymes, **Gr. 1**, T130 (**Activity**)
Poem, **Gr. 2**, 194 (**Activity**), 237 (**Activity**)
Reading blank verse, **Gr. 6**, 209
Snow White Variations, **Gr. 2**, 6
Sound-Symbol, **Gr. 1**, T72
Theme of The Treasure of Lemon Brown, **Gr. 6**, 179 (**Activity**)
"Whispers", **Gr. 4**, 94

SCIENCE
Curriculum Link: Science
A New Island, **Gr. 6**, 296
An Instrument's Sound, **Gr. 5**, 52 (**Activity**)
Anatomy of dance, **Gr. 6**, 111
Animal Research, **Gr. 1**, T295 (**Activity**)
Ants, **Gr. 1**, T22 (**Activity**)
Armadillo, The, **Gr. 2**, A
Australian Animals, **Gr. 2**, 107
Bamboo, **Gr. 4**, 219 (**Activity**)
Beetles, **Gr. 3**, 206
Big Dipper, The, **Gr. 5**, 142
Bugs, **Gr. 1**, T169
Butterflies, **Gr. 3**, 112 (**Activity**)
Changing Colors, **Gr. 1**, T331
Charting the Weather, **Gr. 1**, T274
Christmas Weather, **Gr. 5**, 409
Classifying, **Gr. 2**, R (**Activity**)
Colorful Sunsets, **Gr. 3**, 60 (**Activity**)
Conduct Research, **Gr. 3**, 164
Crawdads, **Gr. 3**, 107
Crickets, **Gr. 3**, 187
Crows, **Gr. 4**, 192
Diamonds, **Gr. 4**, 52
Dok Djampa Flower, The, **Gr. 4**, 393 (**Activity**)
Ducks, **Gr. 1**, T63
Earth Day, **Gr. 1**, T373 (**Activity**)
Earth model, **Gr. 6**, 195 (**Activity**)
Echoes, **Gr. 1**, T56
Elephants, **Gr. 1**, T36, T195
Environment and Earth Day, **Gr. 6**, 427 (**Activity**)
Environmental Update, **Gr. 5**, 439 (**Activity**)
Explore Acoustics, **Gr. 4**, 310 (**Activity**)
Fireflies, **Gr. 6**, 255
Frogs, **Gr. 1**, T44 (**Activity**)
Geographic Regions, **Gr. 4**, E
Gray Wolves, **Gr. 1**, T142
Great Lakes, **Gr. 6**, 135 (**Activity**)
Green Eggs, **Gr. 2**, 279
Growing Pumpkins, **Gr. 2**, 347
Hibernation, **Gr. 1**, T127
How Animals Move, **Gr. 1**, T308 (**Activity**)
How the Larynx Produces Sound, **Gr. 6**, 67 (**Activity**)
How Woodwind Instruments Work, **Gr. 5**, 219
It's Possible, **Gr. 2**, 278
Jasmine, **Gr. 3**, 148 (**Activity**)
Keyboard instruments, **Gr. 6**, 131 (**Activity**)
Kites, **Gr. 2**, 135 (**Activity**)
Korea's King of Animals, **Gr. 1**, T188

Latin Names of Bones, **Gr. 5**, 406 **(Activity)**
Learning About Bears, **Gr. 1**, T312 **(Activity)**
Life of a Flea, **Gr. 1**, T159
Lightning Whelk, **Gr. 2**, F
Locomotion, **Gr. 4**, 312 **(Activity)**
Loud and Soft, **Gr. 1**, T134
Make a Model of a Forest, **Gr. 1**, T149
Microphones, **Gr. 6**, V
Midnight Sun, **Gr. 3**, 142
Mockingbirds, **Gr. 4**, 151
Monarch Butterflies, **Gr. 3**, F
Moon, The, **Gr. 3**, 220
Ocean Mammal, **Gr. 5**, 334
Octopus, **Gr. 4**, 31
Patterns of Change, **Gr. 4**, 149
Percussion Experiment, **Gr. 5**, 141 **(Activity)**
Pitch, **Gr. 5**, 23
Pond World, A, **Gr. 1**, T274
Popular Pets, **Gr. 1**, T172 **(Activity)**
Prairie as Ecosystem, **Gr. 5**, U **(Activity)**
Rain, **Gr. 1**, T32
Rainbows, **Gr. 4**, 127 **(Activity)**
Rattlesnakes, **Gr. 1**, T182
Research Rainbows, **Gr. 3**, 311 **(Activity)**
Robins, **Gr. 1**, T207
Roosters, **Gr. 4**, 36
San Jacinto, **Gr. 3**, H
Seasons, **Gr. 6**, 397
Seeing the Seasons, **Gr. 1**, T274
Shamrock Surprise, **Gr. 5**, 435 **(Activity)**
Solar System Sales, **Gr. 3**, 296
Sound of Rain, The, **Gr. 4**, 27
Sound waves, **Gr. 6**, 24 **(Activity)**
Spanish Colors, **Gr. 5**, 99 **(Activity)**
Sprouting Plants, **Gr. 3**, 393 **(Activity)**
Storing Root Vegetables, **Gr. 2**, 342
Tree Frogs, **Gr. 4**, 179 **(Activity)**
Turtles, **Gr. 1**, T79
Using Maps, **Gr. 3**, F
Volcanoes, **Gr. 6**, 411 **(Activity)**
Water and Land, **Gr. 2**, 295
Whale, The, **Gr. 6**, 212
When Does the Sun Set?, **Gr. 3**, 48 **(Activity)**
Wind and energy, **Gr. 6**, 328 **(Activity)**
Wind and Weather, **Gr. 1**, T186 **(Activity)**
Wind Power, **Gr. 3**, 136
Woodpeckers, **Gr. 4**, 49 **(Activity)**
Yuletide Plants, **Gr. 5**, 418 **(Activity)**

SOCIAL STUDIES
countries and cultures
Afro-Cuban, **Gr. 4**, 327
Akan Culture, The, **Gr. 4**, 166
Appalachia, **Gr. 4**, 50, 74 **(Activity)**
Hispanic Heritage, **Gr. 5**, 396-399
Hopi, **Gr. 4**, 19
India, **Gr. 5**, 402
Ireland, **Gr. 4**, 187; **Gr. 5**, 435 **(Activity)**
Israel, **Gr. 5**, 414
Korea, **Gr. 5**, 400

Laos, **Gr. 5**, 436
Lebanon, **Gr. 4**, 223
Mexico, **Gr. 5**, 440
Native American, **Gr. 5**, 223, 444 **(Activity)**
Netherlands, The, **Gr. 4**, 212
Newfoundland, **Gr. 5**, 334 **(Activity)**
Nigeria, **Gr. 4**, 35
North Carolina, **Gr. 4**, 226
Norway, **Gr. 4**, 168
Panama, **Gr. 4**, 215
Peru, **Gr. 4**, 350
Philippines, The, **Gr. 4**, 104
Puerto Rico, **Gr. 5**, 442 **(Activity)**
South Africa, **Gr. 4**, 24
Sweden, **Gr. 5**, 412 **(Activity)**
Uruguay, **Gr. 4**, 93
Curriculum Link: Social Studies
Abraham Lincoln, **Gr. 2**, 371
Akan Culture, The, **Gr. 4**, 166
American Revolution, The, **Gr. 4**, 155
Andes, The, **Gr. 3**, 32 **(Activity)**
Anthems, **Gr. 5**, 87 **(Activity)**
Appalachian National Scenic Trail, **Gr. 4**, 137; **Gr. 6**, 74
Appalachians, The, **Gr. 4**, 74 **(Activity)**
Argentina, **Gr. 3**, 109
Ashanti Kingdom, **Gr. 3**, 104
Aspects of Navajo Culture, **Gr. 5**, 224 **(Activity)**
Bali, **Gr. 1**, T145
Banana Boats, **Gr. 4**, 72
Beast of Burden, **Gr. 1**, T152
Biographies, **Gr. 6**, B **(Activity)**
Boats in the British Isles, **Gr. 4**, 279
Boll Weevil, **Gr. 3**, 170 **(Activity)**
Brazil, **Gr. 3**, 230
Brazilian folk songs, **Gr. 1**, T204
Building Railroads, **Gr. 4**, 86
Cajun culture, **Gr. 1**, T19
Cardinal Directions, **Gr. 2**, F **(Activity)**
Caucasus Mountains, the, **Gr. 3**, 215
Chavez, Cesar, **Gr. 6**, 295
Cherokee, **Gr. 4**, 207
Cherry blossoms in Japan, **Gr. 6**, 16
China, **Gr. 1**, T129
Chisholm Trail, The, **Gr. 4**, 111 **(Activity)**
City Songs, **Gr. 6**, U
Collaborative Skills, **Gr. 1**, T113 **(Activity)**
Coming Full Circle, **Gr. 4**, 333 **(Activity)**
Create an Imaginary City, **Gr. 2**, 328
Daniel Boone, **Gr. 3**, 98 **(Activity)**
Dr. Martin Luther King, Jr., **Gr. 2**, 364; **Gr. 4**, 386
Earth Day, **Gr. 2**, 376
Earth's Seasons, **Gr. 1**, T148
Ecosystems, **Gr. 1**, T109
Family Interview, **Gr. 6**, 294
Festival Songs, **Gr. 4**, 350
Fireside Chat, A, **Gr. 4**, 297
Flood Stories, **Gr. 4**, 130
Geographic and Cultural Regions, **Gr. 6**, F **(Activity)**
George Washington, **Gr. 2**, 370
Georgia Sea Islands, **Gr. 3**, 149

Index of Curriculum Links and Activities

Curriculum Links and Activities (continued)

Group Discussion, **Gr. 3,** 377
Harvest, **Gr. 3,** 365 **(Activity)**
Hebrides Islands, **Gr. 3,** 188
Hispanic Community, **Gr. 5,** 399 **(Activity)**
Hispanic countries, **Gr. 6,** 393 **(Activity)**
Historic event (If I Had a Hammer), **Gr. 6,** 175
Historical and Fictionalized Tales, **Gr. 3,** 84
History of Chile, **Gr. 6,** 60 **(Activity)**
History of Dallas, **Gr. 6,** G
History of the Muscogee, **Gr. 6,** 188 **(Activity)**
History, **Gr. 3,** 44
Homestead Laws, **Gr. 5,** 110 **(Activity)**
Humpty Dumpty, **Gr. 3,** 95
Immigrant Chart, **Gr. 5,** 46
Ireland, **Gr. 4,** 187
Iroquois Confederacy, The, **Gr. 3,** 50
Israel, **Gr. 3,** 70
It's Right!, **Gr. 3,** 296
Jewish Holidays and History, **Gr. 5,** 416 **(Activity)**
King, Jr., Martin Luther, **Gr. 6,** 295, 416
Klezmer, **Gr. 3,** 141
Korea, **Gr. 5,** 51
Kwanzaa, **Gr. 4,** 385
Language Chart, **Gr. 3,** 22 **(Activity)**
Lebanon, **Gr. 4,** 223
Liberty Bell, The, **Gr. 2,** 338
Make a resource map of Russia, **Gr. 6,** 68 **(Activity)**
Making a Map, **Gr. 5,** 298
Maori, the **Gr. 3,** 175
Map a journey, **Gr. 6,** 134 **(Activity)**
Map Skills, **Gr. 4,** 146 **(Activity)**
Map the Blues, **Gr. 5,** 183 **(Activity)**
Marian Anderson, **Gr. 5,** 330 **(Activity)**
Merchant Marine, **Gr. 1,** T39
Mexican Animals, **Gr. 2,** 331
Minutemen, The, **Gr. 2,** 340
Motorboats, **Gr. 1,** T160
Music of the Civil Rights Movement, **Gr. 5,** 321 **(Activity)**
Nation Remembers, A, **Gr. 4,** 164
Native American nations, **Gr. 6,** 429 **(Activity)**
Native Americans, **Gr. 1,** T73
Netherlands, The, **Gr. 4,** 212
Newfoundland and Labrador, **Gr. 3,** 13
Newfoundland, **Gr. 3,** 115
Nigeria, **Gr. 4,** 35
North Carolina, **Gr. 4,** 226
Origin of State Names, **Gr. 5,** 392 **(Activity)**
Panama, **Gr. 4,** 215
Parks, Rosa, **Gr. 6,** 295 **(Activity)**
Perfect World, A, **Gr. 1,** T224
Philippines, The, **Gr. 4,** 103
Plan a Trip to Cuba, **Gr. 5,** 215 **(Activity)**
Plan a trip to Japan, **Gr. 6,** 144 **(Activity)**
Potawatomi Nation, **Gr. 5,** 444 **(Activity)**
Present-day Monarchs, **Gr. 1,** T175 **(Activity)**
Puerto Rico, **Gr. 5,** 421 **(Activity)**
Quebec, **Gr. 3,** 135
Railroads, Past and Present, **Gr. 4,** 139
Renaissance, The, **Gr. 6,** 100 **(Activity)**

Report on Serbia, **Gr. 6,** 105 **(Activity)**
San Fermín Festival, **Gr. 3,** 211 **(Activity)**
September 11, 2001, **Gr. 4,** 360 **(Activity)**
Shared Border, A, **Gr. 2,** M
South Africa, **Gr. 1,** T77 **(Activity)**; **Gr. 4,** 25
South African Change, **Gr. 3,** 36 **(Activity)**
South African mines, **Gr. 6,** 72
South Korea, **Gr. 2,** 99 **(Activity)**
State Skits, **Gr. 5,** 394 **(Activity)**
Stevedores, **Gr. 3,** 126
Sulawesi, **Gr. 3,** 184
Swahili, **Gr. 5,** 428
Sweden, **Gr. 6,** 419 **(Activity)**
Texas Independence Day, **Gr. 2,** W
Texas Missions, **Gr. 2,** N
Timeline of the 1940s, **Gr. 3,** 229 **(Activity)**
Timeline of world events, **Gr. 6,** 55 **(Activity)**
Traditional Irish Symbols, **Gr. 3,** 391 **(Activity)**
Train routes, **Gr. 6,** 31 **(Activity)**
U.S. Constitution, **Gr. 2,** 10 **(Activity)**
U.S. flag, **Gr. 6,** 387
Underground Railroad, The, **Gr. 5,** 155 **(Activity)**
Uruguay, **Gr. 4,** 93 **(Activity)**
Using a Map, **Gr. 1,** T298 **(Activity)**
Voting, **Gr. 3,** 389 **(Activity)**
Way Up North, **Gr. 3,** 8 **(Activity)**
topics
  Carnaval, **Gr. 5,** 338, 364, 432
  Chusok, **Gr. 5,** 400 **(Activity)**
  Cinco de Mayo, **Gr. 5,** 441
  Civil War, **Gr. 5,** 390
  Diwali, **Gr. 5,** 402
  freedom marches, **Gr. 5,** 320
  Hanukkah, **Gr. 4,** 374; **Gr. 5,** 414
  Hispanic Heritage Month, **Gr. 4,** 362
  King, Jr., Dr. Martin Luther, **Gr. 4,** 387
  Kwanzaa, **Gr. 4,** 384; **Gr. 5,** 426
  Laotian New Year, **Gr. 4,** 392 **(Activity)**
  Las Posadas, **Gr. 4,** 376
  Liberty Bell, **Gr. 5,** 395 **(Activity)**
  national anthem, **Gr. 4,** 357; **Gr. 5,** 386
  Pike's Peak, **Gr. 5,** 388
  Pony Express, **Gr. 5,** 147 **(Activity)**
  Powwow, **Gr. 5,** 444 **(Activity)**
  St. Patrick's Day, **Gr. 5,** 434 **(Activity)**
  Tết Trung Thu, **Gr. 4,** 366
  Underground Railroad, **Gr. 5,** 145

THEATER
Curriculum Link: Theater
  Act out the opera Barber of Seville, **Gr. 6,** 152 **(Activity)**
  Act Out the Story, **Gr. 2,** 355 **(Activity)**
  Acting Free, **Gr. 3,** 181 **(Activity)**
  Animal Guessing Game, **Gr. 1,** T204 **(Activity)**
  Dramatic Reading, **Gr. 1,** T339 **(Activity)**
  Dramatizing "Romper, Stomper, and Boo", **Gr. 1,** T37
  Dramatizing a Story, **Gr. 1,** T52 **(Activity)**
  Environmental Update, **Gr. 5,** 439 **(Activity)**
  Expression, **Gr. 5,** 115 **(Activity)**
  Folkloric Drama, **Gr. 5,** 193

Curriculum Links and Activities (continued)

Index of Reading and Language Arts Skills

The instructional material of *Spotlight on Music* incorporates reading and language arts skills for reinforcement at all levels of reading and language arts proficiency.

Kindergarten

Analyze Story Structure: Character, T71, T160, T180, T219

Analyze Story Structure: Fantasy/Reality, T32, T56, T67, T96, T109, T165, T171

Analyze Story Structure: Plot, T43, T140, T179

Analyze Story Structure: Problem and Solution, T129, T137, T145

Analyze Story Structure: Setting, T139, T141, T180

Analyze Text Features: Use Illustrations, T21, T76, T95, T113, T127, T167, T195, T200, T204, T215, T224

Analyze Text Features: Use Photographs, T40, T103

Analyze Text Structure: Sequence, T15, T36, T39, T45, T64, T68, T100, T116, T133, T149, T152, T153, T159, T168, T175, T185, T203, T207, T208, T212

Generate Rhyme, T63

Phoneme Categorization (Beginning Sound), T87, T105, T111

Phoneme Categorization (Ending Sound), T15

Phoneme Categorization (Medial Sound), T139, T161

Phoneme Categorization (Rhyme), T29, T72, T92, T151, T196, T199

Phoneme Isolation, T72, T187, T217

Summarize: Retell, T27, T132, T148

Syllable Segmentation, T57, T79, T80, T124, T223

Use Inferences and Imagery: Cause and Effect, T24, T68, T115

Use Inferences and Imagery: Classify and Categorize, T16, T25, T31, T33, T37, T39, T59, T61, T81, T88, T92, T104, T108, T112, T131, T144, T164, T188, T197

Use Inferences and Imagery: Compare and Contrast, T19, T20, T23, T41, T43, T51, T55, T59, T65, T76, T91, T96, T99, T107, T117, T128, T135, T147, T163, T172, T200, T203, T213, T220, T225

Use Inferences and Imagery: Make Inferences, T27, T35, T52, T71, T75, T123, T136, T143, T204, T209, T211, T216

Use Inferences and Imagery: Make Predictions, T28, T52, T143, T176, T183, T220

Grade 1

Cause and Effect, T76, T201, T204

Classify and Categorize, T16, T33, T59, T60, T63, T64, T65, T72, T75, T79, T81, T91, T99, T137, T148, T159, T167, T168, T171, T173, T176, T185, T215, T224

Compare and Contrast, T68, T91, T96, T100, T107, T109, T111, T123, T124, T129, T144, T151, T160, T161, T188, T195, T200

Consonant Digraphs, T67

Controlled Vowels, T16, T19, T24, T51

Draw Conclusions, T28, T64, T69, T143, T181, T184, T211, T217

Infer, T31, T140, T151

Initial and Final Consonants, T16, T43, T87, T133

Interpret Pictures, T180

Long Vowels, T27, T51, T52

Main Idea, T21, T73, T109, T135, T185

Make Decisions, T148

Make Judgments, T32, T164, T172, T175, T179, T187, T189, T205, T215

Multisyllabic Words, T71, T88, T96, T103, T105, T131

Predict, T204

Recall Story Details, T79, T88, T163, T171, T183, T187, T207, T213

Sequence, T28, T35, T40, T163

Summarize, T41, T45, T129, T161, T165, T169, T219, T223

Supporting Details, T141

Variant Vowels, T36, T39

Grade 2

Cause and Effect, 28, 32, 65

Classify and Categorize, 12, 24, 25, 88, 92, 100, 127, 133, 135, 173, 179, 216

Compare and Contrast, 11, 13, 24, 25, 61, 71, 116, 131, 139, 151, 153, 167, 171, 176, 183, 192, 197, 212, 217, 227, 228, 235, 237

Critical Thinking/Draw Conclusions, 36

Draw Conclusions, 48, 67, 72, 111, 112, 132, 133, 136, 141

Identify, 52, 59, 68, 75

Infer, 11, 99, 145, 212, 219

Main Idea, 87, 91, 103, 108, 129

Make Decisions, 60

Make Generalizations, 92

Make Judgments, 104, 148, 184

Multisyllabic Words, 89, 108, 208

Predict, 15, 23, 52, 67, 143

Read Aloud, 35

Recall Details, 133, 213, 229

Recall Story Details, 107, 128

Recognize Steps, 95, 96, 112

Rhyme and Rhythm, 6

Sequence, 20, 181

Short Vowels, 7

Solution, 175

Summarize, 9, 109, 113, 117, 185, 197

Syllables, 8, 17, 23

Variant Vowels, 29

Grade 3

Cause and Effect, 189

Classify and Categorize, 16, 20, 23, 29, 31, 36, 53, 59, 63, 77, 115, 141, 149, 172, 173, 175, 213, 215, 229

Compare and Contrast, 12, 23, 35, 49, 52, 69, 71, 76, 89, 91, 95, 96, 97, 99, 103, 111, 112, 127, 128, 129, 133, 137, 139, 143, 144, 145, 147, 148, 151, 153, 156, 169, 183, 193, 195, 196, 209, 211, 217, 220, 221, 228, 237

Draw Conclusions, 51, 75, 105, 108, 109, 131, 133, 136, 171, 176, 180, 185, 189, 191, 192, 223, 227

Index of Reading and Language Arts Skills

Index of Reading and Language Arts Skills (continued)

Form Generalizations, 211
Infer, 28, 168, 179, 183, 188
Main Idea, 15, 27, 47, 55, 57, 61, 65, 69, 77, 168, 169, 171, 177, 179, 185, 189, 197, 209
Make Judgments, 51, 67, 73, 87, 92, 93, 95, 101, 107, 109, 117, 129, 167, 217, 219, 220, 224, 227, 231
Predict, 107
Recall Details, 207, 215, 219
Recall Story Details, 59, 115, 141, 173
Recognize Steps, 56, 107, 237
Sequence, 7, 113, 117, 157
Summarize, 25, 61, 64, 67, 72, 92, 97, 101, 117, 132, 135, 140, 145, 152, 155, 181, 184, 187, 193, 209, 213, 231, 232, 235

Grade 4
Classify and Categorize, 8, 29, 56, 64, 69, 71, 91, 93, 95, 113, 137, 139, 143, 147, 151, 155, 172, 173, 184, 187, 188, 189, 195, 208, 209, 213, 215, 216, 227, 231, 232, 235
Compare and Contrast, 7, 8, 11, 13, 20, 23, 24, 25, 27, 28, 29, 31, 35, 60, 64, 65, 68, 69, 71, 89, 91, 92, 95, 100, 101, 103, 105, 107, 108, 116, 126, 149, 152, 167, 172, 184, 189, 191, 197, 219, 229
Draw Conclusions, 51, 56, 223
Evaluate, 77
Infer, 52, 60, 76, 87, 179
Main Idea, 12, 53, 73, 99, 129, 156
Make Judgments, 8, 19, 21, 25, 35, 37, 189, 207, 209, 211, 213, 217, 220, 225, 228, 229, 231
Paraphrase, 145, 224, 225
Predict, 13, 16
Reality vs. Fantasy, 47
Recall Details, 149
Recall Story Details, 19, 23, 31, 33, 35, 36, 223, 233
Recognize Steps, 59
Sequence, 29, 37, 48, 112, 177
Summarize, 12, 17, 21, 32, 57, 77, 109, 117, 141, 169, 221

Grade 5
Categorize, 59, 63
Cause and Effect, 155, 235
Classify, 12, 24
Classify and Categorize, 129, 133, 169, 171, 181, 184, 228
Compare and Contrast, 7, 20, 32, 48, 52, 60, 71, 87, 95, 117, 132, 139, 147, 148, 149, 150, 152, 155, 168, 172, 179, 180, 187, 188, 192, 193, 208, 209, 213, 221, 224, 225, 227, 231, 236, 237
Connect, 55, 69
Describe, 92, 100
Distinguish, 23
Draw Conclusions, 15, 104, 133, 175, 183, 197
Evaluate, 19, 191
Form Generalizations, 151
Identify, 12, 67
Infer, 35, 89, 96, 127, 143, 151, 167, 171, 185, 189, 193, 196, 207, 212
Interpret, 112, 115
Interpret Pictures, 73
Main Idea, 135, 145, 176, 197

Main Ideas and Details, 52
Make Judgments, 108, 136, 144
Predict, 75, 228, 231
Recall Story Details, 127, 140
Recognize Steps, 156
Sequence, 215, 217, 219, 220
Summarize, 9, 32, 64, 137, 143, 147, 169, 175, 217

Grade 6
Analyze, 184
Cause and Effect, 20, 36, 195, 209, 215, 220
Classify, 175
Classify and Categorize, 27, 35, 48, 59, 75, 95, 127, 131, 139, 141, 212, 219
Compare and Contrast, 7, 11, 12, 17, 20, 33, 47, 51, 52, 59, 65, 68, 73, 76, 88, 97, 99, 100, 108, 111, 112, 132, 143, 151, 156, 167, 168, 169, 172, 180, 181, 184, 187, 188, 191, 197, 207, 213, 215, 219, 223, 225, 227, 228, 236
Distinguish, 52, 53, 71, 152
Draw Conclusions, 16, 24, 108, 116, 131, 176, 183, 211, 231
Form Generalizations, 15, 31
Infer, 15, 23, 29, 63, 71, 115, 171, 179, 185, 192
Main Idea, 13, 61, 68, 135, 147
Make Judgments, 9, 67, 92, 131, 171, 207, 208, 213, 217
Paraphrase, 55
Predict, 11, 19, 95, 187, 188, 196
Recall Story Details, 177, 197
Recognize Steps, 32
Sequence, 76, 104, 133
Summarize, 9, 21, 24, 29, 37, 109, 155, 177, 216, 221, 223, 231, 235

Grade 7
Build Background, 17, 23, 26, 56, 60, 63, 69, 81, 89, 96, 109, 115, 130, 133, 142, 147, 153, 164, 168, 206, 212, 214, 233
Cause and Effect, 37
Compare and Contrast, 4, 11, 19, 113, 124, 173, 179
Draw Conclusions, 31, 83, 103, 110, 150, 181, 220, 234
Follow Directions, 65
Identify Main Idea and Supporting Details, 35, 211
Identify, 134
Infer, 29, 55, 67, 70, 76, 156, 174, 176, 185, 186, 196, 199, 222, 228
Make Generalizations, 97
Make Judgments, 226
Predict, 43
Paraphrase, 9
Predict, 3, 70, 141, 170, 177, 180, 195
Recall Details, 14, 44, 69, 193, 202
Recall Story Details, 27
Recognize Steps, 164
Sequence, 37, 205
Summarize, 45, 52, 93, 99, 121
Synthesize, 52
Vocabulary, 6, 12, 50, 57, 70, 84, 92, 95, 102, 109, 116, 118, 121, 127, 135, 147, 159
Word Parts, 110

Index of Reading and Language Arts Skills (continued)

Grade 8

Analyze, 78, 81, 89, 159, 170, 181, 196

Build Background, 3, 11, 17, 23, 29, 37, 43, 49, 55, 63, 69, 75, 81, 89, 90, 95, 101, 107, 115, 121, 127, 141, 147, 153, 159, 173, 179, 193, 211, 219, 225, 231

Categorize, 225

Classify and Categorize, 179, 219

Compare and Contrast, 3, 5, 40, 47, 58, 64, 86, 109, 112, 113, 121, 125, 128, 156, 164, 170, 188, 190, 207

Draw Conclusions, 14, 38, 180

Evaluate, 25

Form Generalizations, 55

Identify, 216

Infer, 98, 135

Main Idea, 66, 231

Main Idea and Details, 49, 50, 167, 182

Main Idea and Supporting Details, 92, 104, 145, 154, 197, 223

Make Judgments, 26, 111, 137, 201, 223

Predict, 72

Recall Story Details, 76

Sequence, 101, 177

Speculate, 208

Summarize, 9, 53, 95, 104, 116, 119, 151, 183, 191, 203, 208

Synthesize, 79, 87

Vocabulary, 4, 6, 8, 20, 31, 39, 40, 44, 46, 119, 127, 200, 232

Index of Reading and Language Arts Skills

Macmillan/McGraw-Hill Reading ©2005

The following materials from *Spotlight on Music* may be used with each theme in *Macmillan/McGraw-Hill Reading.*

Grade K

Unit 1: Experience, Subtheme 1: At Home
Alison's Camel, T201
All Work Together, T12
Alphabet Song, T54
America, T303
Animales (Animals), T192
Battle Hymn of the Republic, T331
Bear Went Over the Mountain, The, T204
Bell Horses, T262
Best That I Can Be!, The, T48
Bickle, Bockle, T187
Bingo, T64
Bobby Shafto, T265
Bohm Dong Sahn, Gohd Dong Sahn (Spring Valley, Flower Valley), T337
Bounce High, Bounce Low, T131
Buffalo Dusk (poem), T219
Bullfrogs, Bullfrogs on Parade (poem), T183
Bus, The, T137
Bye 'n' Bye, T67
City (poem), T134
Cobbler, The (poem), T169
Colorful Dragon Boat, T328
Counting Song, T92
Doing the Weekly Walk, T78
Echo (poem), T104
Eency Weency Spider, T8
El picaflor (The Hummingbird), T141
El tambor (The Drum), T129
Excuse Us, Animals in the Zoo (poem), T195
Fall (Allegro) from *The Four Seasons* (Concerto No. 3 in F Major) (excerpt), T305
Farmer in the Dell, The, T100
Fehér liliomszál (Little Water Lily), T139
Follow Me, T133
Follow the Leader (poem), T132
Fox, the Hen, and the Drum, The, T294
Furry Bear (poem), T205
Garden Hoedown, The, T290
Girls and Boys, Come Out to Play (poem), T98
Git on Board, T145
Go, Go, Go, T276
Gogo, T188
Good Day Song, T50
Grizzly Bear, T252
Happy Birthday, T273

Happy Birthday, T347
Head and Shoulders, T238
Hello Song, T2
Here Is the Beehive, T258
Hickory, Dickory, Dock (poem), T49
Hinges (poem), T23
Hippopotamus, The (poem), T199
Hokey Pokey, T68
Hop, Hop, Hop, T197
Hot Dog, T69
Humming Birds (poem), T140
I Am a Little Tugboat (poem), T95
I Am a Little Tugboat by C. Huffman (poem), T144
I Can't Spell Hippopotamus, T199
I Got Shoes, T33
I Know an Old Lady, T26
I Made a Valentine, T333
I Will Sing Hello, T156
If Things Grew Down (poem), T48G, T293
If You're Happy, T6
Ifetayo (Love Brings Happiness), T325
In the Barnyard (poem), T207
Instrument Game, T36
It Fell in the City (poem), T312
It's So Good to See You, T86
It's Such a Good Feeling, T282
It's You I Like, T280
Jack, Be Nimble, T88
Jack-in-the-box (poem), T251
Jack-in-the-Box, T250
Jig Jog, Jig Jog, T260
Juhtgarak (Chopsticks), T108
Jump or Jiggle (poem), T193
Just Like Me, T242
Kangaroo, The (poem), T196
Kangaroo, The, T197
Kum Ba Yah, T327
La pequeñita araña (Eency Weency Spider), T9
Lady, Lady, T184
Las horas (The Hours), T70
Let's Think of Something To Do, T270
Little Blue Truck, T136
Little Ducky Duddle, T289
Little Sir Echo, T103
Little Spotted Puppy, T146
Little White Duck, T208
London Bridge, T99
Long Gone (poem), T72
Look Who's Here!, T84
Los pollitos (Little Chickens), T288

Mama, Bake the Johnnycake, T318
María Blanca, T99
Martin Luther King (speech piece), T326
Mbombela (The Train Comes), T152
Me I Am! (poem), T346
Merrily, We Roll Along, T110
Merry-Go-Round (poem), T225
Mi chacra (My Farm), T207
Mister Sun, T343
Monkey, Monkey, T215
Monté sur un éléphant (Riding on an Elephant), T217
Muffin Man, The, T105
Mulberry Bush, The, T112
Music (poem), T157
My Grandfather, T23
My Oak Tree, T236
My Thumbs are Starting to Wiggle, T35
Na Bahia Tem (In Bahia Town), T163
Name Game, T57
Nampaya omame (Mothers), T128
Noble Duke of York, The, T232
Oats, Peas, Beans and Barley Grow, T287
Ɔbɔɔ Asi Me Nsa, T159
Oh, A-Hunting We Will Go, T62
Old Gray Cat, The, T43
Old MacDonald Had a Farm, T211
Old Mister Woodpecker, T172
Oliphaunt (poem), T216
On This Night, T315
One Finger, One Thumb, T38
One, Two, Tie My Shoe, T151
Only My Opinion (poem), T29
Ourchestra (poem), T171
Peace and Quiet, T278
Pimpón, T22
Planting Seeds, T284
Popalong Hopcorn! (poem), T160
Popping Corn, T161
Prairie Dog Song (Kiowa Children's Song), T220
Presidents, T330
Propel, Propel, Propel, T275
Put Your Finger in the Air, T230
Qué bonito es (How Wonderful It Is), T234
Rainbow Song, The, T61
Ride the Train, T144
Ring Around the Rosy, T246
Ring-a-ring (poem), T247
River, The, (poem), T342
Row, Row, Row, T274
Santa Clara Corn Grinding Song, T164

School Is Over (poem), T84
See the Pony Galloping, T44
Seesaw, Margery Daw, T265
Shake My Sillies Out, T175
Shapes (poem), T37
Sidewalks (poem), T98
Simi Yadech (Give Me Your Hand), T168
Sing a Little Song, T179
Sing a Song of Sixpence, T111
Singing-Time (poem), T15
Snail's Pace (poem), T29
Snake and the Frog, The (story), T297
Snow Toward Evening (poem), T311
Snowman, The, T313
Speedy Delivery, T279
Spell of the Moon (poem), T116
Stamping Land, T24
Sweetly Sings the Donkey, T244
Table Manners (poem), T107
Taking Off (poem), T134
Ten in a Bed, T256
Ten Little Frogs, T240
Tengo, Tengo, Tengo (I Have, I Have, I Have), T212
They Were Tall, T53
Things I'm Thankful For, T308
This Is My City, T120
This Is What I Can Do, T124
Three Little Kittens, T148
Three Little Muffins (speech piece), T127
Time to Sing, T16
Toodala, T39
Touch Your Shoulders, T254
Travel (poem), T144
Tree of Peace (speech piece), T321
Tugboat, T95
Twinkle, Twinkle, Little Star, T90
Umoja! (poem), T325
Ushkana (Damsel Fly Song), T75
Wait and See, T334
Walk to School, T18
Wavvuuvuumira (Mister Bamboo Bug), T165
We Are Playing in the Forest, T248
When You Send a Valentine, T332
Willoughby Wallaby Woo, T241
Won't You Be My Neighbor?, T268
Woodpecker, The (poem), T172
Worms, T286
Y ahora vamos a cantar (Now We Are Going to Sing), T340
You're a Grand Old Flag, T4

Unit 1: Experience, Subtheme 2: School Days

Bus, The, T137
Days of the Week, T81
Happy Birthday, Happy Birthday, T273
I Am a Little Tugboat by C. Huffman (poem), T144
Little Blue Truck, T136

Muffin Man, The, T105
Ride the Train, T144
School Is Over by K. Greenaway (poem), T85
Taking Off by M. Green (poem), T134
Travel by E. St. Vincent Millay (poem), T144
Twinkle, Twinkle, Little Star, T90
Won't You Be My Neighbor?, T268

Unit 2: Connections, Subtheme 1: Working Together

Alison's Camel, T201
All Work Together, T12
Alphabet Song, The, T54
America, T303
Animales (Animals), T192
Battle Hymn of the Republic, T331
Bear Went Over the Mountain, The, T204
Bell Horses, T262
Best That I Can Be!, The, T48
Bickle, Bockle, 187
Bingo, T64
Bobby Shafto, T265
Bohm Dong Sahn Gohd Dong Sahn (Spring Valley, Flower Valley), T337
Bounce High, Bounce Low, T131
Buffalo Dusk (poem), T219
Bullfrogs, Bullfrogs on Parade (poem), T183
Bus, The, T137
Bye 'n' Bye, T68
City (poem), T134
Cobbler, The (poem), T169
Cobbler, The, by E. Chafee (poem), T255
Colorful Dragon Boat, T328
Counting Song, T92
Doing the Weekly Walk, T78
Echo (poem), T104
Eency Weency Spider, T8
El picaflor (The Hummingbird), T141
El tambor (The Drum), T129
Excuse Us, Animals in the Zoo (poem), T195
Farmer in the Dell, The, T100
Fehér liliomszál (Little Water Lily), T139
Follow Me, T133
Follow the Leader (poem), T132
Furry Bear (poem), T205
Garden Hoedown, The, T290
Girls and Boys, Come Out to Play (poem), T98
Git on Board, T145
Go, Go, Go, T276
Gogo, T188
Good Day Song, T50
Grizzly Bear, T252
Happy Birthday, T273
Happy Birthday, T347
Head and Shoulders, T238

Hello Song, T2
Here Is the Beehive, T258
Hickory, Dickory, Dock (poem), T49
Hinges (poem), T23
Hippopotamus, The (poem), T199
Hokey Pokey, T68
Hop, Hop, Hop, T197
Hot Dog, T69
Humming Birds (poem), T140
I Am a Little Tugboat (poem), T95
I Am a Little Tugboat by C. Huffman (poem), T95
I Can't Spell Hippopotamus, T199
I Got Shoes, T33
I Know an Old Lady, T26
I Made a Valentine, T333
I Will Sing Hello, T156
If Things Grew Down (poem), T48G, T293
If You're Happy, T6
Ifetayo (Love Brings Happiness), T325
In the Barnyard (poem), T207
Instrument Game, T36
It Fell in the City (poem), T312
It's So Good to See You, T86
It's Such a Good Feeling, T282
It's You I Like, T280
Jack, Be Nimble, T88
Jack-in-the-box (poem), T251
Jack-in-the-Box, T250
Jig, Jog, Jig, Jog, T260
Juhtgarak (Chopsticks), T108
Jump or Jiggle (poem), T193
Just Like Me, T242
Kangaroo, The (poem), T196
Kangaroo, The, T197
Kum Ba Yah, T327
La pequeñita araña (Eency Weency Spider), T9
Lady, Lady, T184
Las horas (The Hours), T70
Let's Think of Something To Do, T270
Little Blue Truck, T136
Little Ducky Duddle, T289
Little Sir Echo, T103
Little Spotted Puppy, T146
Little White Duck, T208
London Bridge, T99
Long Gone (poem), T72
Look Who's Here!, T84
Los pollitos (Little Chickens), T288
Mama, Bake the Johnnycake, T318
María Blanca, T99
Martin Luther King (speech piece), T326
Mbombela, T152
Me I Am! (poem), T346
Merrily, We Roll Along, T110
Merry-Go-Round (poem), T225
Merry-Go-Round, The, T224
Mi chacra (My Farm), T207
Mister Sun, T343

Monkey, Monkey, T215
Monté sur un éléphant (Riding on an Elephant), T217
Muffin Man, The, T105
Mulberry Bush, The, T112
Music (poem), T157
My Grandfather, T23
My Oak Tree, T236
My Thumbs Are Starting to Wiggle, T35
Na Bahia Tem (In Bahia Town), T163
Name Game, T57
Nampaya omame (Mothers), T128
Noble Duke of York, The, T232
Oats, Peas, Beans and Barley Grow, T287
Ɔbɔɔ Asi Me Nsa, T159
Oh, A-Hunting We Will Go, T62
Old Gray Cat, The, T43
Old MacDonald Had a Farm, T211
Old Mister Woodpecker, T172
Oliphaunt (poem), T216
On This Night, T315
One Finger, One Thumb, T38
One, Two, Tie My Shoe, T151
Only My Opinion (poem), T29
Ourchestra (poem), T171
Peace and Quiet, T278
Pimpón, T22
Planting Seeds, T284
Popalong Hopcorn! (poem), T160
Popping Corn, T161
Prairie Dog Song (Kiowa Children's Song), T220
Presidents, T330
Propel, Propel, Propel, T275
Put Your Finger in the Air, T230
Qué bonito es (How Wonderful It Is), T234
Rainbow Song, The, T61
Ride the Train, T144
Ring Around the Rosy, T246
Ring-a-ring (poem), T247
River, The, (poem), T342
Row, Row, Row, T274
Santa Clara Corn Grinding Song, T164
School Is Over (poem), T84
See the Pony Galloping, T44
Seesaw, Margery Daw, T265
Shake My Sillies Out, T175
Shapes (poem), T37
Sidewalks (poem), T98
Simi Yadech (Give Me Your Hand), T168
Sing a Little Song, T179
Sing a Song of Sixpence, T111
Singing-Time (poem), T15
Snail's Pace (poem), T29
Snake and the Frog, The (story), T297
Snow Toward Evening (poem), T311
Snowman, The, T313
Speedy Delivery, T279

Spell of the Moon (poem), T116
Stamping Land, T24
Sweetly Sings the Donkey, T244
Table Manners (poem), T107
Taking Off (poem), T134
Ten in a Bed, T256
Ten Little Frogs, T240
Tengo, Tengo, Tengo (I Have, I Have, I Have), T212
They Were Tall, T53
Things I'm Thankful For, T308
This Is My City, T120
This Is What I Can Do, T124
Three Little Kittens, T148
Three Little Muffins, T127
Time to Sing, T16
Toodala, T39
Touch Your Shoulders, T254
Travel (poem), T144
Tree of Peace (speech piece), T321
Tugboat, T95
Twinkle, Twinkle, Little Star, T90
Umoja! (poem), T325
Umoja! by M. Evans (poem), T325
Ushkana (Damsel Fly Song), T75
Wait and See, T334
Walk to School, T18
Wavvuuvuumira (Mister Bamboo Bug), T165
We Are Playing in the Forest, T248
What You Gonna Call Your Pretty Baby?, T319
When You Send a Valentine, T332
Willoughby Wallaby Woo, T241
Won't You Be My Neighbor?, T268
Woodpecker, The (poem), T172
Worms, T286
Y ahora vamos a cantar (Now We Are Going to Sing), T340
You're a Grand Old Flag, T4

Unit 2: Connections, Subtheme 2: Playing Together

Alison's Camel, T201
All Work Together, T12
Alphabet Song, T54
America, T303
Animales (Animals), T192
Battle Hymn of the Republic, T331
Bear Went Over the Mountain, The, T204
Bell Horses, T262
Best That I Can Be!, The, T48
Bickle, Bockle, 187
Bingo, T64
Bobby Shafto, T265
Bohm Dong Sahn Gohd Dong Sahn (Spring Valley, Flower Valley), T337
Bounce High, Bounce Low, T131
Buffalo Dusk (poem), T219
Bullfrogs, Bullfrogs on Parade (poem), T183

Bus, The, T137
Bye 'n' Bye, T68
City (poem), T134
Cobbler, Cobbler, Mend My Shoe, T169
Cobbler, The (poem), T169
Colorful Dragon Boat, T328
Counting Song, T92
Doing the Weekly Walk, T78
Echo (poem), T104
Eency Weency Spider, T8
El picaflor (The Hummingbird), T141
El tambor (The Drum), T129
Excuse Us, Animals in the Zoo (poem), T195
Farmer in the Dell, The, T100
Fehér liliomszál (Little Water Lily), T139
Follow Me, T133
Follow the Leader (poem), T132
Furry Bear (poem), T205
Garden Hoedown, The, T290
Girls and Boys, Come Out to Play (poem), T98
Git on Board, T145
Go, Go, Go, T276
Gogo, T188
Good Day Song, T50
Grizzly Bear, T252
Happy Birthday, T273
Happy Birthday, T347
Head and Shoulders, T238
Hello Song, T2
Here Is the Beehive, T258
Hickory, Dickory, Dock (poem), T49
Hinges (poem), T23
Hippopotamus, The (poem), T199
Hokey Pokey, T68
Hop, Hop, Hop, T197
Hot Dog, T69
Humming Birds (poem), T140
I Am a Little Tugboat (poem), T95
I Can't Spell Hippopotamus, T199
I Got Shoes, T33
I Know an Old Lady, T26
I Made a Valentine, T333
I Will Sing Hello, T156
If Things Grew Down (poem), T48G, T293
If You're Happy, T6
Ifetayo (Love Brings Happiness), T325
In the Barnyard (poem), T207
Instrument Game, T36
It Fell in the City (poem), T312
It's So Good to See You, T86
It's Such a Good Feeling, T282
It's You I Like, T280
Jack, Be Nimble, T88
Jack-in-the-box (poem), T251
Jig Jog, Jig Jog, T260
Juhtgarak (Chopsticks), T108
Jump or Jiggle (poem), T193
Just Like Me, T242

Thematic Correlations to Reading Series (continued)

Hickory, Dickory, Dock (poem), T49
Hinges (poem), T23
Hippopotamus, The (poem), T199
Hokey Pokey, T68
Hop, Hop, Hop, T197
Hot Dog, T69
Humming Birds (poem), T140
I Am a Little Tugboat (poem), T95
I Can't Spell Hippopotamus, T199
I Got Shoes, T33
I Know an Old Lady, T26
I Made a Valentine, T333
I Will Sing Hello, T156
If Things Grew Down (poem), T48G, T293
If You're Happy, T6
Ifetayo (Love Brings Happiness), T325
In the Barnyard (poem), T207
Instrument Game, T36
It Fell in the City (poem), T312
It's So Good to See You, T86
It's Such a Good Feeling, T282
It's You I Like, T280
Jack, Be Nimble, T88
Jack-in-the-box (poem), T251
Jack-in-the-Box, T250
Jig Jog, Jig Jog, T260
Juhtgarak (Chopsticks), T108
Jump or Jiggle (poem), T193
Just Like Me, T242
Kangaroo, The (poem), T196
Kangaroo, The, T197
Kum Ba Yah, T327
La pequeñita araña (Eency Weency Spider), T9
Lady, Lady, T184
Las horas (The Hours), T70
Let's Think of Something To Do, T270
Little Blue Truck, T136
Little Ducky Duddle, T289
Little Sir Echo, T103
Little Spotted Puppy, T146
Little White Duck, T208
London Bridge, T99
Long Gone (poem), T72
Look Who's Here!, T84
Los pollitos (Little Chickens), T288
Mama, Bake the Johnnycake, T318
María Blanca, T99
Martin Luther King (speech piece), T326
Mbombela, T152
Me I Am! (poem), T346
Merrily, We Roll Along, T110
Merry-Go-Round (poem), T225
Merry-Go-Round, The, T224
Mi chacra (My Farm), T207
Mister Sun, T343
Monkey, Monkey, T215
Monté sur un éléphant (Riding on an Elephant), T217

Muffin Man, The, T105
Mulberry Bush, The, T112
Music (poem), T157
My Grandfather, T23
My Legs and I by L. Jacobs (poem), T19
My Oak Tree, T236
My Thumbs Are Starting to Wiggle, T35
Na Bahia Tem (In Bahia Town), T163
Name Game, T57
Nampaya omame (Mothers), T128
Neat Feet (excerpt) by B. Schmidt (poem), T30
Noble Duke of York, The, T232
Oats, Peas, Beans and Barley Grow, T287
Ɔbɔɔ Asi Me Nsa, T159
Oh, A-Hunting We Will Go, T62
Old Gray Cat, The, T43
Old MacDonald Had a Farm, T211
Old Mister Woodpecker, T172
Oliphaunt (poem), T216
On This Night, T315
One Finger, One Thumb, T38
One, Two, Tie My Shoe, T151
Only My Opinion (poem), T29
Ourchestra (poem), T171
Peace and Quiet, T278
Pimpón, T22
Planting Seeds, T284
Popalong Hopcorn! (poem), T160
Popping Corn, T161
Prairie Dog Song (Kiowa Children's Song), T220
Presidents, T330
Propel, Propel, Propel, T275
Put Your Finger in the Air, T230
Qué bonito es (How Wonderful It Is), T234
Rainbow Song, The, T61
Ride the Train, T144
Ring Around the Rosy, T246
Ring-a-ring (poem), T247
River, The, (poem), T342
Row, Row, Row, T274
Santa Clara Corn Grinding Song, T164
School Is Over (poem), T84
See the Pony Galloping, T44
Seesaw, Margery Daw, T264
Shake My Sillies Out, T175
Shapes (poem), T37
Sidewalks (poem), T98
Simi Yadech (Give Me Your Hand), T168
Sing a Little Song, T179
Sing a Song of Sixpence, T111
Singing-Time (poem), T15
Snail's Pace (poem), T29
Snake and the Frog, The (story), T297
Snow Toward Evening (poem), T311
Snowman, The, T313
Something About Me (poem), T13

Speedy Delivery, T279
Spell of the Moon (poem), T116
Spinning Song by C. Shields (poem), T67
Stamping Land, T24
Sweetly Sings the Donkey, T244
Table Manners (poem), T107
Taking Off (poem), T134
Ten in a Bed, T256
Ten Little Frogs, T240
Tengo, Tengo, Tengo (I Have, I Have, I Have), T212
They Were Tall, T53
Things I'm Thankful For, T308
This Is My City, T120
This Is What I Can Do, T124
Three Little Kittens, T148
Three Little Muffins (speech piece), T146
Three Little Muffins, T127
Time to Sing, T16
Toodala, T39
Touch Your Shoulders, T254
Travel (poem), T144
Tree of Peace (speech piece), T321
Tugboat, T95
Twinkle, Twinkle, Little Star, T90
Umoja! (poem), T325
Ushkana (Damsel Fly Song), T75
Wait and See, T334
Walk to School, T18
Wavvuuvuumira (Mister Bamboo Bug), T165
We Are Playing in the Forest, T248
Willoughby Wallaby Woo, T241
Won't You Be My Neighbor?, T268
Woodpecker, The (poem), T172
Worms, T286
Y ahora vamos a cantar (Now We Are Going to Sing), T340
You're a Grand Old Flag, T4

Unit 3: Expression, Subtheme 2: Let's Pretend

Alphabet Song, T54
America, T303
Battle Hymn of the Republic, T331
Bounce High, Bounce Low, T13
Deedle, Deedle Dumpling (poem), T87
Farmer in the Dell, The, T100
Follow Me, T133
Follow the Leader by K. Fraser (poem), T132
Garden Hoedown, The, T290
Girls and Boys, Come Out to Play (excerpt) (poem), T98
Git on Board, T145
Go, Go, Go, T276
Gogo, T188
Head and Shoulders, T238
Hokey Pokey, T68
Hop, Hop, Hop, T197

Thematic Correlations to Reading Series (continued)

I Know an Old Lady, T26
I Will Sing Hello, T156
If You're Happy, T6
Instrument Game, T36
It's Such a Good Feeling, T282
It's You I Like, T280
Jack, Be Nimble, T88
Jack-in-the-box by L. Birkenshaw-Fleming (poem), T251
Jack-in-the-Box, T250
Kangaroo, The, T196
Las horas (The Hours), T70
Little Ducky Duddle, T289
London Bridge, T99
Merry-Go-Round by R. Field (poem), T346
My Thumbs Are Starting to Wiggle, T35
Name Game, T58
Oats, Peas, Beans, and Barley Grow, T287
One Finger, One Thumb, T46
Ourchestra by S. Silverstein (poem), T171
Put Your Finger in the Air, T230
Ring Around the Rosy (Mother Goose) (song), T246, (poem), T247
Running Song (excerpt) by M. Ridlon (poem), T98
Sing a Song of Sixpence, T111
Singing-Time by R. Fyleman (poem), T15
Spinning Song by C. Shields (poem), T67
Ten in a Bed, T256
Ten Little Frogs, T240
This Is My City, T120
This Is What I Can Do, T124
Toodala, T39
Touch Your Shoulders, T254
Wait and See, T335
When You Send a Valentine, T332
Willoughby Wallaby Woo, T241

Unit 4: Inquiry, Subtheme 1: In My Backyard

Alison's Camel, T201
Animal Rhythms (poem), T56
Bingo, T64
Bohm Dong Sahn, Gohd Dong Sahn (Spring Valley, Flower Valley), T337
Bullfrogs, Bullfrogs on Parade by J. Prelutsky (poem), T183
Counting Song, T92
Echo by W. de la Mare (poem), T104
Eency Weency Spider, T8
Fehér liliomszál (Little Water Lily), T139
Fox, the Hen, and the Drum, The (Indian fable), T294
Good Day Song, T50
Hickory, Dickory, Dock (poem), T49
Hot Dog, T69

If Things Grew Down by R. Hoeft (poem), T292
In the Barnyard by D. Aldis (poem), T207
Lady, Lady, T184
Little Spotted Puppy, T146
Los pollitos (Little Chickens), T288
Mi chacra (My Farm), T207
Mister Sun, T343
My Oak Tree, T236
North Winds Blow, T305
Old Gray Cat, The, T43
Old MacDonald Had a Farm, T207
Rainbow Song, The, T61
River, The, by C. Zolotow (poem), T342
Santa Clara Corn Grinding Song, T164
See the Pony Galloping, T44
Sing a Little Song, T179
Snow Toward Evening by M. Cane (poem), T311
Snowman, The, T313
Spell of the Moon (excerpt) by L. Norris (poem), T116
Sweetly Sings the Donkey, T244
Tengo, Tengo, Tengo (I Have, I Have, I Have), T212
Three Little Kittens, T146
Twinkle, Twinkle, Little Star, T90

Unit 4: Inquiry, Subtheme 2: Wonders of Nature

Animales (Animals), T192
Bear Went Over the Mountain, The, T204
Bobby Shafto, T265
Bohm Dong Sahn, Gohd Dong Sahn (Spring Valley, Flower Valley), T337
Buffalo Dusk by C. Sandburg (poem), T219
Bye 'n' Bye, T67
City by L. Hughes (poem), T134
Colorful Dragon Boat, T328
Days of the Week, T81
Echo by W. de la Mare (poem), T104
Eency Weency Spider, T8
El picaflor (The Hummingbird), T141
Excuse Us, Animals in the Zoo by A. Wynne (poem), T195
Fehér liliomszál (Little Water Lily), T139
Furry Bear by A. A. Milne (poem), T205
Grizzly Bear, T252
Here Is the Beehive, T258
Hippopotamus, The, by J. Prelutsky (poem), T199
Humming Birds by B. Sage (poem), T140
If Things Grew Down by R. Hoeft (poem), T292
It Fell in the City by E. Merriam (poem), T312
Kangaroo, The, by E. Coatsworth (poem), T196

Kangaroo, The, T196
La pequeñita araña (Eency Weency Spider), T9
Lady, Lady, T184
Little Sir Echo, T103
Little White Duck, T208
Mayflies by P. Fleischmann (poem), T76
Merrily, We Roll Along, T110
Mi chacra (My Farm), T207
Mister Sun, T343
Monkey, Monkey (speech piece), T215
Monté sur un éléphant (Riding on an Elephant), T218
My Oak Tree, T236
North Winds Blow, T305
Oh, A-Hunting We Will Go, T62
Old Mister Woodpecker, T172
Oliphaunt by J. R. R. Tolkien (poem), T216
Prairie Dog Song (Kiowa children's song), T220
Propel, Propel, Propel, T275
Rainbow Song, The, T61
River, The, by C. Zolotow (poem), T342
Row, Row, Row, T274
Sidewalks by P. Hubbell (poem), T98
Sing a Little Song, T179
Snail's Pace by A. Fisher (poem), T29
Snake and the Frog, The (story), T297
Snow Toward Evening by M. Cane (poem), T311
Snowman, The, T313
Spell of the Moon (excerpt) by L. Norris (poem), T116
Twinkle, Twinkle, Little Star, T90
Ushkana (Damselfly Song), T75
Wavvuuvuumira (Mister Bamboo Bug), T165
Woodpecker, The, by E. Roberts (poem), T173
Worms, T286

Unit 5: Problem Solving, Subtheme 1: Try and Try Again

Cobbler, Cobbler, Mend My Shoe, T169
Cobbler, The, by E. Chafee (poem), T255
Let's Think of Something to Do, T270
Qué bonita es (How Wonderful It Is), T234
Speedy Delivery, T279
They Were Tall, T53

Unit 5: Problem Solving, Subtheme 2: Teamwork

All Work Together, T12
Best That I Can Be!, The, T48
Cobbler, Cobbler, Mend My Shoe, T16
Cobbler, The, by E. Chafee (poem), T255

I Am a Little Tugboat by C. Huffman (poem), T144
I Made a Valentine, T333
Let's Think of Something to Do, T270
Oh, A-Hunting We Will Go, T62
Row, Row, Row, T274
Speedy Delivery, T279

Unit 6: Making Decisions, Subtheme 1: Good Choices

Doing the Weekly Walk, T78
Table Manners by G. Burgess (poem), T107

Unit 6: Making Decisions, Subtheme 2: Let's Decide

Cobbler, Cobbler, Mend My Shoe, T169
Cobbler, The, by E. Chafee (poem), T255
Let's Think of Something to Do, T270
Speedy Delivery, T279

Grade1

Unit 1: Experience, Day by Day

A be ce (A B C), T213
A la rueda rueda ('Round and 'Round), T240
Acka Backa, T256
¡Adivina lo que es! (Guess What It Is), T170
All Night, All Day, T232
America, T326
Animal Song, T288
Another Busy Day, T41
Ants Go Marching, The, T22
Apple a Day, An (poem), T152
Apples and Bananas, T151
Arre, mi burrito (Gid'yup, Little Burrito), T257
Autumn Leaves Are Falling, T330
Autumn Leaves, T331
Bear Hunt (poem), T126
Bear Went Over the Mountain, The, T115
Bee, Bee, Bumblebee, T250
Best Friends, T222
Big and Small (speech piece), T200
Bluebells, T209
Bonjour, mes amis (Hello, My Friends), T18
Boris, the Singing Bear, T312
Bow-Wow (poem), T81
Brinca la tablita (Hop, Hop!), T71
Brush Your Teeth (song), T66, (speech piece), T67
Bug (poem), T167
But the Critter Got Away (speech piece), T88
Butterfly, Flutter By, T333

Call of the Wild, A (excerpt) (poem), T139
Caribbean Amphibian, T294
Categories, T146
Chang (Elephant), T199
Charlie Over the Ocean, T75
Chase the Squirrel, T88
Chickery Chick, T292
Clap Your Hands, T246
Come Back, My Little Chicks, T134
Cookies, T277
Counting Song, T195
Cow, The (poem), T236
Cut the Cake, T232
Dance Myself to Sleep, T314
Diana, T334
Diou Shou Juan'er (Hiding a Handkerchief), T212
Double This (speech piece), T95
Down by the Bay, T48
Down the Hill, T281
Dragonfly (poem), T44
Duérmete mi niño (Go to Sleep, My Baby), T61
Ears, Far and Near (poem), T16
El florón (The Flower), T117
El juego chirimbolo (The Chirimbolo Game), T103
Field of Joys, T224
Five Little Pumpkins (poem), T337
George Washington, T368
Gilly, Gilly, Gilly Good Morning, T12
Go A Tin (Lantern Song), T363
Goin' to the Zoo, T192
Granny (speech piece), T104
Grasshoppers Three, T284
Green Grass Grows All Around, The, T148
Hakyo Jong (School Bells), T302
Happiest Street in the World, The, T304
Head and Shoulders, Baby, T40
Hello, There!, T230
Here Comes the Band (poem), T80
Here We Sit, T251
Hey, Children, Who's in Town?, T14
Hi! My Name Is Joe! (speech piece), T220
Hoo, Hoo!, T55
Hop! Chirp! Moo! Oh, Happy Springtime Day!, T372
Hopping Frog (poem), T113
Horses of the Sea, The (poem), T179
How Does Your Garden Grow?, T144
Hunt the Cows, T236
I Am Slowly Going Crazy, T127
I Had a Little Hen (nursery rhyme), T136
I Have a Friend (poem), T225
I Like (poem), T110
I Like Spinach, T163

I Love My Country, T328
I Wanna Be a Friend of Yours, T84
I'd Like to Be a Lighthouse (poem), T238
I'm Getting Sick of Peanut Butter (poem), T219
I've a Pair of Fishes, T124
Ice (poem), T346
If All the World Were Paper, T296
In My Little Motor Boat, T159
It's So Nice on the Ice, T346
Jambo (Hello), T230
John the Rabbit, T74
Johnny Works with One Hammer, T96
Johnny's Flea, T158
Jump or Jiggle (poem), T316
Jump, Jim Joe, T89
Kaeru no Uta (Frog's Song), T112
Kari (Wild Geese), T261
Kobuta, T168
La ranita cri (The Little Frog Croaks), T27
Ladybugs' Picnic, T290
Lavender's Blue, T174
Let's Go Driving, T52
Library Song, T42
Light the Candles, T351
Little Black Bug, T166
Little Red Caboose, T97
Little Robin Redbreast, T208
Locust, The (poem), T285
Looby Loo, T262
Love Grows, T202
Love Is the Magic Word, T366
Lucy Lockett, T253
Mail Myself to You, T366
Marco Polo (speech piece), T90
Martin Luther King, T360
Mary's Coal Black Lamb, T286
Mi cuerpo (My Body), T32
Miss Mary Mack, T15
Mizuguruma (The Water Wheel), T260
Mos', Mos'! (Cat, Cat!), T53
My Feet (poem), T264
My Feet by L. B. Jacobs (poem), T264
My Kite (poem), T371
My Mama's Calling Me, T54
My Mom, T372
Na Bahia Tem (In Bahia Town), T297
Naming Things (poem), T221
Naranja dulce (Sweet Orange), T303
Naughty Kitty Cat, T171
Night Comes… (poem), T233
No One Like You, T300
O Wind (poem), T235
Old King Glory, T217
Old Mother Goose (poem), T181
One Little Elephant, T194
One, Two, Three, Four, Five, T265
One, Two, Three, Four, T123

Oranges and Lemons (poem), T150
Over in the Meadow, T78
Pat Pat Patty Pat, T308
Peanut Butter, T218
Pease Porridge Hot, T255
Pile of Stuff, A (story), T188
Piñata Song (poem), T153
Piñón, Pirulín, T311
Pitty Patty Polt (speech piece), T180
Plenty Fishes in the Sea, T310
Puddle Hopping, T60
Pumpkin Song, T342
Punchinella, T216
Pusa't daga (Cat and Rat), T289
Quaker, Quaker, T100
Rabbit in the Moon, The (folktale), T318
Rabbit, The (poem), T186
Rain Sizes (poem), T33
Rain, Rain, Go Away, T259
Rattlesnake, T185
Rig a Jig Jig, T116
Rise, Sally, Rise, T162
Romper, Stomper, and Boo (story), T36
Sailor Went to Sea, Sea, Sea, A (song), T38, (game), T39
Sara Watashi (Plate Passing), T66
Seeds (vocal and instrumental), T120
Seesaw (song), T242, (accompaniment), T248
Serra, Serra Serrador (Saw, Saw, Lumberjack), T133
Shoo, Turkey, T76
Simple Simon, T175
Sing After Me, T34
Sing Ho! For the Life of a Bear! (poem), T114
Sittin' Down to Eat, T182
Sitting in the Sand (poem), T374
Six Little Ducks, T64
Skip to My Lou, T102
Sleep, Bonnie Bairnie, T27
Snail With the Mail, T275
Snail, Snail, T252
Somebody Come and Play, T92
Somebody Has To... (poem), T258
Something Funny Outside, T338
Something Told the Wild Geese (poem), T261
Soup, Soup!, T358
Spanish Days of the Week by Anonymous (poem), T108
Spotlight on America, T9
Spring, T273
Star Light, Star Bright, T258
Summertime from *Porgy and Bess*, T375
Swing, The (poem), T109
Tailor, Tailor (poem), T132
Tak for Maden (Thanks for Food), T343
Tako No Uta (The Kite Song), T370

Theme from *Sesame Street*, T298
There Are Many Flags in Many Lands, T329
There's a Hole in the Middle of the Sea, T178
This Little Light of Mine, T238
This Old Man, T306
Thoughts of a Rattlesnake (poem), T185
Time for Love, A, T347
Tinker, Tailor, T130
Tisket A Tasket, A, T107
Twenty-four Robbers, T173
Two, Four, Six, Eight, T246
Uga, Uga, Uga (Cake, Cake, Cake), T313
Una Adivinanza (A Riddle), T138
Up the Hill (poem), T45
Up the Tree and Down Again (poem), T65
Wake Me, Shake Me, T198
We All Sing With the Same Voice, T156
What's Your Name?, T125
Wheels, Wheels, Wheels (poem), T106
When the Flag Goes By, T327
Who's Afraid of the Big Bad Wolf? (nursery rhyme), T137
Why the Beetle Has a Gold Coat (folktale), T321
Willum, T19
Wind Blew East, The, T234
Wind Blow, T187
Wings (poem), T250
Year With Frog and Toad, A (Reprise), T283
Year With Frog and Toad, A, T270
Yo, Mamana, Yo (Oh, Mama), T307
Zui Zui Zukkorbashi (song), T98, (game), T99

Unit 2: Connections, Together Is Better

A be ce (A B C), T213
A la rueda rueda ('Round and 'Round), T240
Acka Backa, T256
¡Adivina lo que es! (Guess What It Is), T170
All Night, All Day, T232
America, T326
Animal Song, T288
Another Busy Day, T41
Ants Go Marching, The, T22
Apple a Day, An (poem), T152
Apples and Bananas, T151
Arre, mi burrito (Gid'yup, Little Burrito), T257
Autumn Leaves Are Falling, T330
Autumn Leaves, T331
Bear Hunt (speech piece), T126
Bear Went Over the Mountain, The, T115

Bee, Bee, Bumblebee, T250
Best Friends, T222
Big and Small (speech piece), T200
Bluebells, T209
Bonjour, mes amis (Hello, My Friends), T18
Boris, the Singing Bear, T312
Bow-Wow (poem), T81
Brinca la tablita (Hop, Hop!), T71
Brush Your Teeth (song), T66, (speech piece), T67
Bug (poem), T167
But the Critter Got Away (speech piece), T88
Butterfly, Flutter By, T333
Call of the Wild, A (excerpt) (poem), T139
Caribbean Amphibian, T294
Categories, T146
Chang (Elephant), T199
Charlie Over the Ocean, T75
Chase the Squirrel, T88
Chickery Chick, T292
Clap Your Hands, T246
Come Back, My Little Chicks, T134
Cookies, T277
Counting Song, T195
Cow, The (poem), T236
Cut the Cake, T232
Dance Myself to Sleep, T314
Diana (Play the Bugle), T334
Diou Shou Juan'er (Hiding a Handkerchief), T212
Double This (speech piece), T95
Down by the Bay, T48
Down the Hill, T281
Dragonfly (poem), T44
Duérmete mi niño (Go to Sleep, My Baby), T61
Duérmete mi niño (Go to Sleep, My Baby), T61
Ears, Far and Near (poem), T16
El florón (The Flower), T117
El juego chirimbolo (The Chirimbolo Game), T103
Field of Joys, T224
Five Little Pumpkins (poem), T337
George Washington, T368
Gilly, Gilly, Gilly Good Morning, T12
Go A Tin (Lantern Song), T363
Goin' to the Zoo, T192
Granny (speech piece), T104
Grasshoppers Three, T284
Green Grass Grows All Around, The, T148
Hakyo Jong (School Bells), T302
Happiest Street in the World, The, T304
Head and Shoulders, Baby, T40
Hello, There!, T230
Here Comes the Band (poem), T80

Here We Sit, T251

Hey, Children, Who's in Town?, T14

Hi! My Name Is Joe! (speech piece), T220

Hoo, Hoo!, T55

Hop! Chirp! Moo! Oh, Happy Springtime Day!, T372

Hopping Frog (poem), T113

Horses of the Sea, The (poem), T179

How Does Your Garden Grow?, T144

Hunt the Cows, T236

I Am Slowly Going Crazy, T127

I Had a Little Hen (nursery rhyme), T136

I Have a Friend (poem), T225

I Like (poem), T110

I Like by M. A. Hoberman (poem), T110

I Like Spinach, T163

I Love My Country, T328

I Wanna Be a Friend of Yours, T84

I'd Like to Be a Lighthouse (poem), T238

I'm Getting Sick of Peanut Butter (poem), T219

I've a Pair of Fishes, T124

Ice (poem), T346

If All the World Were Paper, T296

In My Little Motor Boat, T159

It's So Nice on the Ice, T346

Jambo (Hello), T230

John the Rabbit, T74

Johnny Works with One Hammer, T96

Johnny's Flea, T158

Jump or Jiggle (poem), T316

Jump, Jim Joe, T89

Kaeru no Uta, T112

Kari (Wild Geese), T261

Kobuta, T168

La ranita cri (The Little Frog Croaks), T27

Ladybugs' Picnic, T290

Lavender's Blue, T174

Let's Go Driving, T52

Library Song, T42

Light the Candles, T351

Little Black Bug, T166

Little Red Caboose, T97

Little Robin Redbreast, T208

Locust, The (Zuñi poem), T285

Looby Loo, T262

Love Grows, T202

Love Is the Magic Word, T366

Lucy Lockett, T253

Mail Myself to You, T366

Marco Polo (speech piece), T90

Martin Luther King, T360

Mary's Coal Black Lamb, T286

Mi cuerpo (My Body), T32

Miss Mary Mack, T15

Mizuguruma (The Water Wheel), T260

Mos', Mos'! (Cat, Cat!), T53

My Feet (poem), T264

My Kite (poem), T371

My Mama's Calling Me, T54

My Mom, T372

Na Bahia Tem (In Bahia Town), T297

Naming Things (poem), T221

Naranja dulce (Sweet Orange), T303

Naughty Kitty Cat, T171

Night Comes… (poem), T233

No One Like You, T300

O Wind (poem), T235

Old King Glory, T217

Old Mother Goose (poem), T181

One Little Elephant, T194

One, Two, Three, Four, Five, T265

One, Two, Three, Four, T123

Oranges and Lemons (poem), T150

Over in the Meadow, T78

Pat Pat Patty Pat, T308

Peanut Butter, T218

Pease Porridge Hot, T255

Pile of Stuff, A (story), T188

Piñata Song (poem), T153

Piñón, Pirulín, T311

Pitty Patty Polt (speech piece), T180

Plenty Fishes in the Sea, T310

uddle Hopping, T60

Pumpkin Song, T342

Punchinella, T216

Pusa't daga (Cat and Rat), T289

Quaker, Quaker, T100

Rabbit in the Moon, The (folktale), T318

Rabbit, The (poem), T186

Rain Sizes (poem), T33

Rain, Rain, Go Away, T259

Rattlesnake, T185

Rig a Jig Jig, T116

Rise, Sally, Rise, T162

Romper, Stomper, and Boo (story), T36

Sailor Went to Sea, Sea, Sea, A (song), T38, (game), T39

Sara Watashi (Plate Passing), T66

Seeds (vocal and instrumental), T120

Seesaw, T242

Serra, Serra Serrador (Saw, Saw, Lumberjack), T133

Shoo, Turkey, T76

Simple Simon, T175

Sing After Me, T34

Sing Ho! For the Life of a Bear! (poem), T114

Sittin' Down to Eat, T182

Sitting in the Sand (poem), T374

Six Little Ducks, T64

Skip to My Lou, T102

Sleep, Bonnie Bairnie, T27

Snail With the Mail, T275

Snail, Snail, T252

Somebody Come and Play, T92

Somebody Has To… (poem), T258

Something Funny Outside, T338

Something Told the Wild Geese (poem), T261

Soup, Soup!, T358

Spanish Days of the Week by Anonymous (poem), T108

Spring, T273

Star Light, Star Bright, T258

Summertime from *Porgy and Bess*, T375

Swing, The (poem), T109

Tailor, Tailor (poem), T132

Tak for Maden (Thanks for Food), T343

Tako No Uta (The Kite Song), T370

Theme from *Sesame Street*, T298

There Are Many Flags in Many Lands, T329

There's a Hole in the Middle of the Sea, T178

This Little Light of Mine, T238

This Old Man, T306

Thoughts of a Rattlesnake (poem), T185

Time for Love, A, T347

Tinker, Tailor, T130

Tisket A Tasket, A, T107

Twenty-four Robbers, T173

Two, Four, Six, Eight, T246

Uga, Uga, Uga (Cake, Cake, Cake), T313

Una Adivinanza (A Riddle), T138

Untitled (Butterflies) (haiku), T332

Up the Hill (poem), T45

Up the Tree and Down Again (poem), T65

Wake Me, Shake Me, T198

We All Sing With the Same Voice, T156

What's Your Name?, T125

Wheels, Wheels, Wheels (poem), T106

When the Flag Goes By, T327

Who's Afraid of the Big Bad Wolf? (nursery rhyme), T137

Why the Beetle Has a Gold Coat (folktale), T321

Willum, T19

Wind Blew East, The, T234

Wind Blow, T187

Wings (poem), T250

Year With Frog and Toad, A (Reprise), T283

Year With Frog and Toad, A, T270

Yo, Mamana, Yo (Oh, Mama), T307

Zui Zui Zukkorbashi (song), T98, (game), T99

Unit 3: Expression, Stories to Tell

A be ce (A B C), T213

A la rueda rueda ('Round and 'Round), T240

Acka Backa, T256

¡Adivina lo que es! (Guess What It Is), T170

Thematic Correlations to Reading Series

Thematic Correlations to Reading Series (continued)

Thematic Correlations to Reading Series (continued)

Shoo, Turkey, T76
Simple Simon, T175
Sing After Me, T34
Sing Ho! For the Life of a Bear! (poem),
    T114
Sittin' Down to Eat, T182
Sitting in the Sand (poem), T374
Six Little Ducks, T64
Skip to My Lou, T102
Sleep, Bonnie Bairnie, T27
Snail With the Mail, T275
Snail, Snail, T252
Somebody Come and Play, T92
Somebody Has To… (poem), T258
Something Funny Outside, T338
Something Told the Wild Geese
    (poem), T261
Soup, Soup!, T358
Spanish Days of the Week by
    Anonymous (poem), T108
Spotlight on America, T9
Spring, T273
Star Light, Star Bright, T258
Summertime from *Porgy and Bess*, T375
Swing, The (poem), T109
Tailor, Tailor (poem), T132
Tak for Maden (Thanks for Food), T343
Tako No Uta (The Kite Song), T370
Theme from *Sesame Street*, T298
There Are Many Flags in Many Lands,
    T329
There's a Hole in the Middle of the Sea,
    T178
This Little Light of Mine, T238
This Old Man, T306
Thoughts of a Rattlesnake (poem),
    T185
Time for Love, A, T347
Tinker, Tailor, T130
Tisket A Tasket, A, T107
Twenty-four Robbers, T173
Two, Four, Six, Eight, T246
Uga, Uga, Uga (Cake, Cake, Cake), T313
Una Adivinanza (A Riddle), T138
Untitled (Butterflies) (haiku), T332
Up the Hill (poem), T45
Up the Tree and Down Again (poem),
    T65
Wake Me, Shake Me, T198
We All Sing With the Same Voice, T156
What's Your Name?, T125
Wheels, Wheels, Wheels (poem), T106
When the Flag Goes By, T327
Who's Afraid of the Big Bad Wolf?
    (nursery rhyme), T137
Why the Beetle Has a Gold Coat
    (folktale), T321
Willum, T19
Wind Blew East, The, T234
Wind Blow, T187
Wings (poem), T250

Year With Frog and Toad, A (Reprise),
    T283
Year With Frog and Toad, A, T270
Yo, Mamana, Yo (Oh, Mama), T307
Zui Zui Zukkorbashi (song), T98,
    (game), T99

Unit 4: Inquiry, Let's Find Out!

Animal Song, T288
Ants Go Marching, The, T22
Arre, mi burrito (Gid-yup, Little Burro),
    T257
Bear Hunt (poem), T126
Bear Went Over the Mountain, The,
    T115
Big and Small by E. McCullough
    Brabson, T200
Boris, the Singing Bear, T312
Bow-Wow by Mother Goose (poem),
    T81
Bug by L. Simmie (poem), T167
But the Critter Got Away (speech
    piece), T88, (poem), T89
Butterfly, Flutter By, T333
Caribbean Amphibian, T294
Chang (Elephant), T199
Chase the Squirrel, T88
Chickery Chick, T292
Clouds by Anonymous (poem), T331
Come Back, My Little Chicks, T134
Cookies, T278
Cow, The, by R. L. Stevenson (poem),
    T236
Cut the Cake, T232
Down the Hill, T281
Dragonfly by D. M. Violin (poem), T44
Field of Joys by M. Morand (poem),
    T224
Goin' to the Zoo, T192
Granny (traditional poem), T104
Grasshoppers Three, T284
Hop! Chirp! Moo! Oh, Happy
    Springtime Day!, T372
Hopping Frog by C. Rossetti (poem),
    T113
Horses of the Sea, The, by C. Rossetti
    (poem), T179
Hunt the Cows, T236
I Had a Little Hen (nursery rhyme),
    T136
I Have a Friend by Anonymous (poem),
    T225
I Like by M. A. Hoberman (poem),
    T110
I've a Pair of Fishes, T124
Ice by D. Aldis (poem), T346
It's So Nice on the Ice, T346
Johnny's Flea, T158
Jump or Jiggle by E. Beyer (poem),
    T316
Kaeru no Uta, T112

Kari (Wild Geese), 101
La ranita cri (The Little Frog Croaks), T27
Ladybugs' Picnic, T290
Little Black Bug, T166
Little Robin Red Breast (English rhyme)
    (song), T208, (rhythmic pattern),
    T207
Locust, The (Zuñi poem), T285
Mary's Coal Black Lamb, T286
Mizuguruma (The Water Wheel), T260
Mos', Mos'! (Cat, Cat!), T53
My Kite by B. Brown and B. Brown
    (poem), T371
Naughty Kitty Cat, T171
One Little Elephant, T194
Over in the Meadow, T78
Peanut Butter, T218
Pusa't daga (Cat and Rat), T289
Rabbit, The, by M. Stelmach (poem),
    T186
Rattlesnake, T185
Romper, Stomper, and Boo (traditional
    story), T36
Seesaw (song), T242,
    (accompaniment), T248
Simple Simon, T175
Sing Ho! For the Life of a Bear! By A.A.
    Milne (poem), T114
Sittin' Down to Eat, T182
Six Little Ducks, T64
Snail With the Mail, T274
Snail, Snail (song), T252, (three-tone),
    T252
Something Told the Wild Geese by R.
    Field (poem), T261
Thoughts of a Rattlesnake by K. Sexton
    (poem), T185
Untitled (Butterflies) (haiku), T332
Up the Hill by W. J. Smith (poem), T45
White Sheep by Anonymous (poem),
    T234
Who's Afraid of the Big Bad Wolf?
    (nursery rhyme), T137
Year with Frog and Toad, A (reprise),
    T283
Year with Frog and Toad, A, T270

Unit 5: Problem Solving, Think About It!

A la rueda rueda ('Round and 'Round),
    T240
Acka Backa, T256
Apples and Bananas, T151
Bee, Bee, Bumblebee, T250
Bluebells, T209
Brinca la tablita (Hop, Hop!), T71
Categories, T146
Charlie Over the Ocean, T75
Chase the Squirrel, T88
Clap Your Hands (song), T246,
    (rhythmic pattern), T247

Come Back, My Little Chicks, T134
Diou Shou Juan'er, T212
Double This (game), T94
El juego chirimbolo (The Chirimbolo Game), T103
Head and Shoulders, Baby, T40
Here We Sit, T251
I Had a Little Hen (nursery rhyme), T136
I Like Spinach, T163
I Wanna Be a Friend of Yours, T84
John the Rabbit, T74
Jump, Jim Joe, T89
Looby Loo, T262
Marco Polo (speech piece), T90
Miss Mary Mack, T15
Mizuguruma (The Water Wheel), T260
Mos', Mos'! (Cat, Cat!), T53
My Mama's Calling Me, T54
One Little Elephant, T194
One, Two, Three, Four (traditional rhyme), T123
One, Two, Three, Four, Five, T265
Pat Pat Patty Pat, T308
Piñata Song (Mexican traditional poem), T153
Punchinella, T216
Rise, Sally, Rise (game), T162
Sailor Went to Sea, Sea, Sea, A (song), T38, (game), T39
Sara Watashi (Plate Passing), T67
Shoo, Turkey, T76
Simple Simon, T175
Six Little Ducks, T64
Snail, Snail (song), T252, (three-tone), T252
Soup, Soup!, T358
Tailor, Tailor (traditional poem), T132
There's a Hole in the Middle of the Sea, T178
This Old Man, T306
Tinker, Tailor, T131
Twenty-four Robbers, 173
Two, Four, Six, Eight (song), T246, (rhythmic pattern), T247
Una adivinanza (A Riddle), T138
Vhaya Kadhimba (Zimbabwean children's song) (song), T23, (game), T23
Who's Afraid of the Big Bad Wolf? (nursery rhyme), T137
Zui Zui Zukkorbashi (song), T98, (game), T99

Unit 6: Making Decisions, Many Paths

Apple a Day, An (traditional poem), T152
Apples and Bananas, T151
Brush Your Teeth (song), T66, (speech piece), T66
I Like Spinach, T163

Oranges and Lemons (English traditional poem), T150
Pease Porridge Hot, T255
Sleep, Bonnie Bairnie, T26

Grade 2

Unit 1: Experience, What's New?

A la rueda de San Miguel (To the Wheel of San Miguel), 60
Ach, du lieber Augustin (The More We Get Together), 35
All Around the Buttercup, 210
America, 338
Ani Purim, 372
Animal Fair, 214
Apple Picker's Reel, 343
Artichokes, 314
Australia's on the Wallaby, 106
Away for Rio, 170
Baby Beluga, 26
Baby Nodja, 154
Bahay Kubo (My Nipa Hut), 382
Ban Dal (Half Moon), 219
Banyan Tree, 321
Bate, bate (Stir, Stir), 242
Big Beautiful Planet, 376
Bliss (poem), 212
Bow, Wow, Wow, 264
Button, You Must Wander, 176
Candle on the Water, 296
Caranguejo (The Crab), 306
Check It Out! (It's About Respect), 10
Chiapanecas (Ladies of Chiapas), 128
Chichipapa (The Sparrow's Singing School), 22
Child Falling Asleep from Scenes from Childhood, 77
Chirri Bim, 70
Chíu, Chíu, Chíu (Chirp, Chirp, Chirp), 302
City Traffic (poem), 328
Columbus Sailed with Three Ships, 344
Corner Grocery Store, 311
Cuckoo, Where Are You?, 244
Daisy Chain, 255
Dal taro kacha (Come, Pick the Moon), 98
Dance Together, 264
Doggie, Doggie, 59
Donkey, Donkey, 256
Drumming Spider, The (story), 333
Dumplin's, 172
Dumplin's, 172
Eating Lizards, 250
El burrito enfermo (The Sick Little Donkey), 180
El palomo y la paloma (The Doves), 381
El tren (The Train), 326

El zapatero (The Cobbler), 138
En la feria de San Juan (In the Market of San Juan), 226
En nuestra Tierra tan linda (On Our Beautiful Planet Earth), 114
Engine, Engine Number Nine, 13
Everyone Has Music Inside, 164
Everything Grows, 204
Finis (poem), 76
Food Song, The, 318
Four White Horses, 301
Garden Song, 236
Going Over the Sea, 216
Good Night, Sleep Tight, 76
Great Outdoors, The, 290
Green Eggs and Ham, 284
Hairy Dog, The (poem), 58
Hakuna Matata, 292
Harvest, 342
Hashewie (Going Round), 362
Heigh Ho, Here We Go, 252
Hello, Hello, There, T126
Here Comes a Bluebird, 263
Here Comes Sally, 220
Hey, Hey, Look at Me, 245
Hop, Old Squirrel, 258
Horton Hears a Who! Two, 280
Horton Hears a Who!, 279
Hot Cross Buns, 258
I Bought Me a Cat, 14
I Chih ha Ma (Frogs), 186
I Saw Three Ships, 359
I See, 266
In and Out, 245
In the Window, 352
It's a Small World, 298
It's Possible, 281
It's Raining! It's Pouring!, 233
Itik Besenda Gurau (The Ducks), 100
Ja posejah lubenice (I Planted Watermelons), 316
Jim Along, Josie, 194
Joy, 46
Juan Pirulero, 270
Jugaremos en el bosque (We Will Play in the Forest), 188
King's Land, 257
Knock the Cymbals, 265
La bella hortelana (The Beautiful Gardener), 208
Land of the Silver Birch, 88
Leatherwing Bat, 304
Lemonade, 19
Let's Go Fly a Kite, 134
Little Sally Water, 249
Loose Tooth (speech piece), 28
Mama Paquita, 92
Martin Luther King, 364
Mary Had a Baby, 360
Matarile, 261

Unit 2: Connections, Just Between Us

Unit 3: Expression, Express Yourself

Thematic Correlations to Reading Series (continued)

Piggy by W. Cole (poem), 315
Place in the Choir, A, 308
Puff, the Magic Dragon, 54
Rover, 260
Sammy Sackett, 146
Seeds and Seasons, 206
Señor Coyote (Mexican folktale), 330
Sheep in the Meadow (speech piece), 8
Sheep Shearing, 102
Sing! Sing! Sing!, 196
Sun Is First to Rise, The, by E. Coatsworth (poem), 383
Take Me Out to the Ball Game, 56
Three Little Penguins (speech piece), 112
Tiki Tiki Tiki Room, The, 324
Tinga Layo, 50
We're Sailing Down the River, 166
Welcome Is the Month of May, 378
Who Has Seen the Wind? by C. G. Rossetti (poem), 137
Yanai (The Elephant), 305

Unit 5: Problem Solving, Figure It Out

A la rueda de San Miguel (To the Wheel of San Miguel), 60
Ach, du lieber Augustin (The More We Get Together), 35
Check It Out! (It's About Respect), 10
Chíu, chíu, chíu (Chirp, Chirp, Chirp), 302
Doggie, Doggie, 59
Drumming Spider, The (West African folktale), 333
El zapatero (The Cobbler), 138
Heigh Ho, Here We Go, 252
I See, 266
It's a Small World, 298
Lemonade, 19
Let's Go Fly a Kite, 134
Martin Luther King, 364
Matarile, 261
Me Stone, 48
Merry-Go-Round, 267
Mouse, Mousie, 254
Oliver Twist, 268
Pizza, Pizza, Daddy-O, 62
Plainsies, Clapsies, 248
Sammy Sackett, 146
Señor Coyote (Mexican folktale), 330
Shake the Papaya Down, 90
Sheep in the Meadow (speech piece), 8
Sheep Shearing, 102
Step in Time, 6
Take Me Out to the Ball Game, 56
There's a Hole in the Bucket, 132
Together by P. Engle (poem), 34
What Did Delaware?, 190
Who's That Tapping at the Window?, 261

Unit 6: Making Decisions, Starting Now

Apple Picker's Reel, 343
Artichokes, 314
Australia's on the Wallaby, 106
Big Beautiful Planet, 376
Corner Grocery Store, 311
Dal taro kacha (Come, Pick the Moon), 98
Drumming Spider, The (West African folktale), 333
Dumplin's, 172
El zapatero (The Cobbler), 138
En nuestra Tierra tan linda (On Our Beautiful Planet Earth), 114
Everything Grows, 204
Food Song, The, 318
Garden Song, 236
Good Night, Sleep Tight, 76
Great Outdoors, The, 290
Green Eggs and Ham, 284
Harvest, 342
Hot Cross Buns, 258
Ja posejah lubenice (I Planted Watermelons), 316
La bella hortelana (The Beautiful Gardener), 208
Land of the Silver Birch, 88
Lemonade, 19
Little Seeds (except) by E. Holmelund Minarik (poem), 207
Me gase boho (Orange Tree), 317
Mill Song, The, 52
Nabe, Nabe, Soku, Nuke (Stewpot, Stewpot, Bottomless Pot), 259
Oma Rapeti (Run, Rabbit), 108
On Top of Spaghetti, 312
Pairs or Pears, 265
Piggy by W. Cole (poem), 315
Riqui Ran (Sawing Song), 21
Sailor, Sailor on the Sea, 262
Seeds and Seasons, 206
Señor Coyote (Mexican folktale), 330
Shake the Papaya Down, 90
Sheep Shearing, 102
Thank You, 349
There's a Hole in the Bucket, 132
Wake Up the Sun, 124
Who Has Seen the Wind? by C. G. Rossetti (poem), 137

Grade 3

Unit 1: Experience, Great Adventures

Addams Family Theme, The, 307
Amen, 376
America, the Beautiful, 354
Ballad of the Bedbugs and the Beetles, The, 206
Bella Bimba, 172

Billy, 7
Bim Bom, 218
Blow, Ye Winds, Blow, 192
Bohm (Spring Has Come!), 392
Bohm, 392
Boll Weevil, 171
Boo, 362
Buffalo Dance Entrance Song, 325
Butterfly Come Play With Me, 112
Cat and Dog, 259
Chan mali chan, 10
Charlie, 208
Chicka-ma, Chicka-ma, Craney Crow, 263
Chicken on the Fence Post, 265
Cielito Lindo, 166
Circle 'Round the Zero, 267
City Life, 341
Clocks, 266
Colors of the Wind, 84
Coral, 249
Cornstalk Fiddle and a Shoestring Bow, 284
Crawdad Song, 107
Cumberland Gap, 99
¡Dale, dale, dale!, 378
De aquel cerro (On the Darkened Hillside), 32
Death of the Robin, 275
Dide, 279
Digga Digga Dog, 164
Dinah, 150
Ding Dong Diggy Diggy Dong, 269
Draw a Bucket of Water, 222
Egy üveg alma (One Jar of Apples), 22
Eh Soom Boo Kawaya, 58
El arroyo que murmura (The Murmuring Brook), 318
El atole (The Atole), 396
El florón (The Flower), 46
El nido (The Nest), 214
En roulant ma boule (As I Roll My Ball), 100
Evergreen, Everblue, 330
Frog in the Meadow, 243
Frosty Weather, 250
Gebeta Board, The (story), 346
Gi'Me Elbow Room, 88
Go Tell It on the Mountain, 377
Golden Ring Around the Susan Girl, 264
Great Big House, 14
Greatest Show on Earth, The, 308
Hag Asif, 360-361
Happy Wanderer, The, 18
Hello!, 283
Herring, The, 316
Hey, Motswala, 34
Hope by E. Dickinson (poem), 166
I Have a Car, 252
I Lost the Farmer's Dairy Key, 273

I Walk in Beauty, 329
I'm a Believer, 312
I'm On My Way, 382
I's the B'y, 13
In Good Old Colony Times, 326
Interjections, 303
Interplanet Janet, 298
Isabela and the Troll (story), 349
J'entends le moulin (I Hear the Windmill), 135
Jamaica Farewell, 156
Jasmine Flower, 146
John Jacob Jingleheimer Schmidt, 68
Just Like the Sun, 394
Kalinka (Little Snowball Bush), 224
Kreely Kranky, 258
Kum bahur (The Rooster), 75
Kuma San (Honorable Bear), 244
La bamba, 236
La cloche (The Clock), 67
La mar (The Sea), 110
Let Us Chase the Squirrel, 248
Let's Go Dancing, 196
Limbo Rock, 232
Lincoln (poem), 389
Little Boy of the Sheep, 188
Little Sally Walker, 105
Little Tommy Tinker, 277
Look High, Look Low, 338
Lukey's Boat, 114
Marvelous Toy, The, 182
May Day Carol, 393
Minuteman Minute Song, The, 322
Moon and Me, 220
Morning Bells, 270
Morning Mood from Peer Gynt Suite No. 1, Op. 46 by E. Grieg, 251
Movin' Right Along, 124
Mrs. Murphy's Chowder, 390
Music of the World A-Turnin', 44
My Friend Tom, 364
My Horses Ain't Hungry, 278
Night Song, 186
O, the Train's Off the Track, 176
Oh Mama Bakudala, 328
Oh, Susanna, 153
Old Barn Dance, The, 94
Old Mister Rabbit, 254
Old Roger, 280
Oleanna, 144
One More River, 216
One Potato, Two Potato, 267
Open the Window, Noah, 324
Out from the Wilderness, 388
Over My Head, 286
Pajarillo barranqueño (Little Bird), 358
Pat-a-Pan, 375
Paw Paw Patch, The, 195
Pay Me My Money Down, 149
Pit-A-Pan, 375
Polly Wolly Doodle, 132

Preamble, The, 293
Que llueva (It's Raining), 274
Raccoon Dance Song, 87
Rain is Falling Down, 242
Rainbow Connection, The, 310
Rattlesnake, 72
Recycle Rap, 332
Riding in the Buggy, 131
Rise Up Singin', 138
Scotland's Burning, 257
See the Rabbit Running, 255
Shalom Chaveyrim (Shalom, My Friends), 141
Shepherd, Shepherd, 56
Ship Ahoy, 314
Shoo Fly Pie and Apple Pan Dowdy, 227
Simon Says, 4
Smoke Goes Up the Chimney, 272
Spiders, 282
Stevedore's Song, 127
Sun Don't Set in the Mornin', 48, 60
Sweep, Sweep Away, 276
Sweet Potatoes, 16
Tanabata, 62
Taps, 281
There Was An Old Lady (story), 344
There's a Little Wheel A-Turnin' in My Heart, 129, 137
This a Way and That a Way, 386
This Is America, 356
Three is a Magic Number, 296
Three Little Birds, 204
Throw It Out the Window, 94
Tititorea, 174
Trampin', 287
Turn the Glasses Over, 260
Uch Tirvarch, 53
Uno de enero (The First of January), 210
Vamos a la mar (Let's Go to the Sea), 256
Walk by the River (song), 74, (harmony parts), 76
Wan Ü Ger, 190
Wéané, 184
When I First Came to This Land, 28
Who's That Yonder?, 245
Woke Up This Morning, 180
Woodchuck, 246
Yankee Doodle, 357
Yellow Submarine, 320
You're a Grand Old Flag, 355

Unit 2: Connections, Nature Links
Al lado de mi cabaña (Beside My Cottage), 141
Apple Tree by Anonymous (poem), 24
Bohm (Spring Has Come!), 392
Boll Weevil, 171
Cat and Dog, 259
Colors of the Wind, 84
Coral, 249

Crawdad Song, 107
De aquel cerro (On the Darkened Hillside), 32
El arroyo que murmura (The Murmuring Brook), 318
Evergreen, Everblue, 330
Frosty Weather, 250
I Walk in Beauty, 329
J'entends le moulin (I Hear the Windmill), 135
Jasmine Flower, 146
Just Like the Sun, 394
Kum Bachur (The Rooster), 75
La cloche (The Clock), 67
Le Mar (The Sea), 110
May Day Carol, 393
Morning Bells, 270
Night Song, 186
Oh Mama Bakdala (Xhosa folk song), 328
Que Llueva (It's Raining), 274
Raccoon Dance Song, 87
Rain Is Falling Down, 242
Rattlesnake, 72
Recycle Rap, 332
Spiders, 282
Sun Don't Set in the Mornin', 48, 60
Tanabata (Seven Evenings), 62
Taps, 281
Uno de enero (The First of January), 210
Vamos a la mar (Let's Go to the Sea), 256

Unit 3: Expression, Be Creative!
Addams Family Theme, The, 307
Amen, 376
America, the Beautiful, 354
Anansi (Ashanti folk tale), 104
Apple Tree by Anonymous (poem), 24
Ballad of the Bedbugs and the Beetles, The, 206
Bella Bimba, 172
Billy, 7
Bim Bom, 218
Blow, Ye Winds, Blow, 192
Bohm, 392
Boll Weevil, 171
Buffalo Dance Entrance Song, 325
Butterfly Come Play With Me, 112
Cat and Dog, 259
Chan mali chan, 10
Charlie, 208
Chicka-ma, Chicka-ma, Craney Crow, 263
Chicken on the Fence Post, 265
Cielito Lindo, 166
Circle 'Round the Zero, 267
City Life, 341
City Music by T. Mitton (poem), 74
Clocks, 266

Thematic Correlations to Reading Series (continued)

Thematic Correlations to Reading Series (continued)

Way Down South by Anonymous (poem), 8
Woke Up This Morning, 180

Unit 5: Problem Solving, Think It Through

Ballad of the Bedbugs and the Beetles, The, 206
Billy, 7
Blow, Ye Winds, Blow, 192
Chag Asif (Harvest Time), 360
Circle 'Round the Zero, 267
Colors of the Wind, 84
Crawdad Song, 107
¡Dale, dale, dale!, 378
De aquel cerro (On the Darkened Hillside), 32
Digga Digga Dog, 164
Egy üveg alma (One Jar of Apples), 22
Eh Soom Boo Kawaya (Nigerian boat song), 58
En roulant ma boule (As I Roll My Ball), 100
Evergreen, Everblue, 330
Gebeta Board, The (Ethiopian folk tale), 346
Gi'Me Elbow Room, 88
Guitar Man, The, 138
I Lost the Farmer's Dairy Key, 273
I's the B'y, 13
Just Like the Sun, 394
Kreely Kranky, 258
Kuma San (Honorable Bear), 244
Limbo Rock, 232
Little Sally Walker, 105
Movin' Right Along, 124
Oh Mama Bakdala (Xhosa folk song), 328
Old Barn Dance, The, 94
One Potato, Two Potato, 267
Paw Paw Patch, The, 195
Recycle Rap, 332
Scotland's Burning, 257
Shalom Chaveyrim (Shalom, My Friends), 141
Shepherd, Shepherd, 56
Simon Says, 4
Smoke Goes Up the Chimney, 272
Stevedore's Song, 127
Tititorea (Maori Stick Game) (New Zealand folk song), 174
Treasure Chests, 90
Ucha Tirvarch (Little Bear Song), 53
Walk by the River (song), 74, (harmony parts), 76
Wang Ü Ger (Chinese fishing song), 190
William Tell (Overture) (excerpt) by G. Rossini, 64
Yankee Doodle, 357

Unit 6: Making Decisions, Turning Points

Billy, 7
Boll Weevil, 171
Charlie, 208
City Life, 341
Cumberland Gap, 99
Death of the Robin, 275
En roulant ma boule (As I Roll My Ball), 100
Guitar Man, The, 138
Happy Wanderer, The, 18
Hello!, 283
I Have a Car, 252
I'm a Believer, 312
Jamaica Farewell, 156
Jingle at the Window, 268
Lincoln by M. Cohn Livingston (poem), 389
Marvelous Toy, The, 182
Minuteman Minute Song, The, 322
Movin' Right Along, 124
Music of the World A-Turnin', 44
My Horses Ain't Hungry, 278
O, The Train's Off the Track, 176
Oh, Susanna, 153
Oleanna, 144
Out from the Wilderness, 388
Preamble, The, 293
Riding in the Buggy, 131
Ship Ahoy, 314
Stevedore's Song, 127
Three Is a Magic Number, 94
Three Little Birds, 204
Turn the Glasses Over, 260
Way Down South by Anonymous (poem), 8
When I First Came to This Land, 28
Who's That Yonder?, 245
William Tell (Overture) (excerpt) by G.

Grade 4

Unit 1: Experience, Reflections

A la nanita nana (A Little Lullaby), 230
A la puerta del cielo (At the Gates of Heaven), 12
Achshav (Now), 112
Allundé, Alluia, 34
Ame fure (Rain), 26
America, 364
America, My Homeland, 358
Arroyito Serrano (Little Mountain Brook, 340
Bamboo Flute, 134
Bereza (The Birch Tree), 286
Big Bunch, a Little Bunch, 267
Boogie-Woogie Ghost, The, 368
Buckeye Jim, 136
Built My Lady a Fine Brick House, 252

Caballito blanco (Little White Pony), 278
Cedar Swamp, 50
Chairs to Mend, 272
Chicka-hanka, 138
Chumbara, 172
Circle of Song, 330
Cotton-Eye Joe (song), 52, (countermelody), 53
December Nights, December Lights, 372
Derby Ram, The, 259
Dima, 265
Dok Djampa (The White Jasmine Flower), 392
Don't Let the Music Stop, 334
E nānā, kākou i nā manu (Look at the Birds in the Sky), 338
Eagle, 337
Early in the Morning at Eight O'Clock, 59
Eight Bells, 281
El barquito (The Tiny Boat), 214
El coquí (The Frog), 178
El manisero (Peanut Vendor), 106
El quelite (The Village), 362
Farfallina (Butterfly), 244
Follow Your Dream, 234
Frère Jacques (Are You Sleeping?), 260
Frog Went A-Courtin', 46
Girl I Left Behind, 249
Goodbye Brother, 273
Goodbye, My Riley O, 257
Green Gravel, 247
Hala lala layya, 222
Happiness, 124
Happy Talk, 84
Heave-Ho Me Laddies, 258
Hey, Look Me Over, 114
Himmel und Erde (Music Alone Shall Live), 280
Hine Ma Tov (How Good It Is), 66
Hitori, 345
Hojas de té (Tea Leaves) (speech piece), 256
Hold My Mule, 248
Hop Up and Jump Up, 271
How Long the Train Been Gone?, 264
I Think I'm Going to Like It Here, 299
I Will Be Your Friend, 388
I'll Rise When the Rooster Crows, 36
It Rained a Mist, 262
It's the Hard-Knock Life, 293
Johnson Boys, 233
Joy to the World, 383
Just One Planet, 164
Katyusha, 188
Kettle Valley Line, The, 348
Korobushka, 285
L'inverno è già passato (Winter is Over), 390

Thematic Correlat
to Reading Series

Unit 2: Connections, Something in Common

Thematic Correlations to Reading Series *(side tab)*

Bamboo, 218
Bell Doth Toll, The, 276
Beryoza (The Birch Tree), 286
Big Bunch, a Little Bunch, 267
Boogie-Woogie Ghost, The, 368
Buckeye Jim, 136
Built My Lady a Fine Brick House, 252
Cedar Swamp, 50
Chairs to Mend, 272
Chicka Hanka, 138
Chumbara, 172
Circle of Song, 330
Corre el río (The River Flows By) by P. Vasquez (poem), 183
Cotton-Eye Joe (song), 52,
December Nights, December Lights, 372
Derby Ram, The, 259
Dima, 265
Dok Djampa (The White Jasmine Flower), 392
Down at the Twist and Shout, 308
E nānā, kākou i nā manu (Look at the Birds in the Sky), 338
Eagle, 337
Early in the Morning at Eight O'Clock, 59
Eight Bells, 281
El barquito (The Tiny Boat), 214
El coquí (The Frog), 178
El quelite (The Village), 362
Farfallina (Butterfly), 244
Follow Your Dream, 234
Frère Jacques (Are You Sleeping?), 260
Frog Went A-Courtin', 46
Girl I Left Behind Me, The, 249
Green Gravel, 247
Happiness, 124
Hitori, 345
Hojas de té (Tea Leaves), 256
Hold My Mule, 248
Hop Up and Jump Up, 271
How Long the Train Been Gone?, 264
I Heard a Mockingbird, 150
I Think I'm Gonna Like It Here, 299
I Will Be Your Friend, 388
I'll Rise When the Rooster Crows, 36
It Rained a Mist, 262
Johnson Boys, 233
Journey, A (speech piece), 14
Joy to the World, 383
Just One Planet, 164
Kettle Valley Line, The, 348
L'inverno è già passato (Winter Is Over), 390
La sanjuanerita (The Girl from San Juan), 100
La Yunsita, 350
Li'l 'Liza Jane, 20
Little David Play on Your Harp, 323
Loco-Motion, The, 312

Long-Legged Sailor, 243
Macnamara's Band, 88
Marken er mejet (Out in the Meadow), 364
Mighty River (speech piece), 217
Modern Dragon, A (speech piece), 98
Molinillo de café (Little Coffee Mill), 250
'Most Done Ling'rin Here, 65
My Town, My World, 6
N. Y. C., 302
New Day, The, 316
Night Herding Song, 110
Octopus's Garden, 30
Oh, Won't You Sit Down?, 70
Old Abram Brown, 32
Old Ark's A-Moverin', 130
Old Aunt Dinah, 245
Old House, 282
Old Joe Clark, 74
Oro, My Bodeen, 279
Over the Rainbow, 126
Over the Sea to Skye, 344
Owl and the Cuckoo, The, 337
Page's Train, 246
Para pedir posada (Looking for Shelter), 377
Pat Works on the Railway, 86
Peace Round, 16
Peasant's Dancing Day, 132
Please, Mr. Postman, 44
Push Boat Song, 266
Rain (haiku), 27
Ridin' of a Goat, Leadin' of a Sheep, 251
Roll On, Columbia, 182
Row, Row, Row Your Boat, 268
Sail Away, Ladies, 54
Sandy McNab, 142
Sansa kroma, 166
Sarasponda, 210
Sea Shell, 245
Sitsiritsit, 102
Sky Dances, 206
Something for Me, Something for You, 4
Somos el barco (We are the Boat), 10
Swing, The, 320
Take Time in Life, 156
This Land Is Your Land, 146
Train Is A-Coming, 270
Trains at Night by F. M. Frost (poem), 246
Twist and Shout, 314
'Ulili E (The Sandpiper), 396
Wake Up Canon, 326
We Are Here, 394
We Shall Overcome, 387
What Can One Little Person Do?, 204
When I Was Young, 187
Who's Got a Fishpole?, 261
Woodpecker, The, by E. Madox Roberts (poem), 48

You're Never Fully Dressed Without a Smile, 304
Zum gali gali, 255

Unit 5: Problem Solving, Make a Plan
Ame fure (Rain), 26
Bamboo Flute, 134
Cedar Swamp, 50
Cotton-Eye Joe (song), 52, (countermelody), 53
El manisero (Peanut Vendor), 106
Frog Went A-Courtin', 46
Girl I Left Behind Me, The, 249
Goodbye Brother, 273
Hala lala layya, 222
I Will Be Your Friend, 388
Just One Planet, 164
Katyusha, 188
Li'l 'Liza Jane, 20
Little David Play on Your Harp, 323
Love Somebody, 94
Night Herding Song, 110
Octopus's Garden, 30
Old Joe Clark, 74
Please, Mr. Postman, 44
Rain (haiku), 27
Roll On, Columbia, 182
Take Time in Life, 156
This Land Is Your Land, 146
We Are Here, 394
We Shall Overcome, 387
Woodpecker, The, by E. Madox Roberts (poem), 48

Unit 6: Making Decisions, Sorting It Out
Ame fure (Rain), 26
Bamboo Flute, 134
Chicka Hanka, 138
El manisero (Peanut Vendor), 106
Girl I Left Behind Me, The, 249
Goodbye, My Riley O, 257
Heave-Ho, Me Laddies, 258
Hey, Look Me Over, 114
Hitori, 345
It's the Hard-Knock Life, 293
Johnson Boys, 233
Kettle Valley Line, The, 348
Little David Play on Your Harp, 323
Night Herding Song, 110
Oh, Won't You Sit Down?, 70
Old Ark's A-Moverin', 130
Oliver Cromwell, 269
Over the Sea to Skye, 344
Pat Works on the Railway, 86
Rain (haiku), 27
Roll On, Columbia, 182
Take Time in Life, 156
This Land Is Your Land, 146
Water Come a Me Eye, 90

We Are Here, 394
We Remember, 360
We Shall Overcome, 387
What Can One Little Person Do?, 204
Woodpecker, The, by E. Madox Roberts (poem), 48
Yankee Doodle, 154

Grade 5

Unit 1: Experience, Time of My Life

76 Trombones, 296
A Zing-a Za, 338
Aeyaya balano sakkad (Come, Children), 402
Allá en el rancho grande (My Ranch), 66
Amazing Grace, 19
America, the Beautiful, 388
Aquaqua, 258
¡Ay, Jalisco no te rajes! (Ay, Jalisco, Never Fail Her!), 188
Babylon's Fallin', 243
Ballad of the Underground Railroad, The, 145, 154
Beauty and the Beast, 124
Big Big World, 438
Borinquen (poem), 443
Bound No'th Blues (poem), 181
By the Singing Water, 270
Caissons Go Rolling Along, The, 37
Change the World, 314
Cidade Maravilhosa, 432
Cindy, 265
Circle of Friends, 196
City Blues, 278
Cliffs of Doneen, The, 46
Colores de caracol (poem), 101
Come and Sing Together (unison), 270
Cuando salí de Cuba (I Went Away from Cuba), 168
Cumbia del sol (Cumbia of the Sun), 16
Da pacem Domine (Give Us Peace), 261
Dance for the Nations, 206
De allacito carnavalito (The Carnival Is Coming), 269
De colores (Many Colors) (unison and 2-part), 88, 98
Deta, Deta (The Moon), 246
Dreamers, 430
Dry Bones, 406
Ēinīnī, 340
El jarabe (Mexican Hat Dance), 396
El vito, 210
Erie Canal, 132
Estrella brillante (Shining Star), 373
Every Day I Have the Blues, 179
Everybody Rejoice, 226

Feel Good, 358
Fifty Nifty United States, 392
Follow the Drinkin' Gourd, 142
Fun wa ni alaafia (Send Us Your Peace), 248
Fung Yang Song, 58
Funiculi, Funicula, 62
Ga Eul, 401
Gentle River Runs, A, 342
Goin' Home, 108
Great Big Sea, A, 334
Guantanamera, 215
Haere Ra (Now Is the Hour), 151
Hallelujah, Get On Board, 345
Hava Nagila, 54
Heartbeat of Democracy (poem), 389
Hero, 312
Hill an' Gully, 250
I Am But a Small Voice, 323
I Got Rhythm, 187
I Hear America Singing, 327
I Saw the Light, 252
In That Great Git'n Up Mornin', 10
Iowa Stubborn, 293
Is That Mister Reilly?, 282
John Henry, 146
John Kanaka, 249
Joyful, Joyful, We Adore Thee, 103
Just Give Me the Beat (speech piece), 9
Kojo No Tsuki (Moon at the Ruined Castle), 149
Kookaburra, 264
La paloma se fue (The Dove That Flew Away), 259
La víbora de la mar (The Serpent from the Sea), 441
Life by S. DeShetler (poem), 205
Lift Up Your Voices, 319
Light One Candle, 416
Like a Mighty Stream, 320
Lion Sleeps Tonight, The, 172
Loch Lomond, 138
Los maizales (The Cornfields), 268
Lots o' Fish in Bonavist' Harbor, 263
Mango Walk (song), 90, (countermelody), 92
Mary Ann, 166
Mɔfia moni (Ev'rybody Loves Saturday Night), 277
Mi gallo (My Rooster), 272
Music (poem), 122
My Government Claim (unison and 3-part), 95, 110
Nani Wale Na Hala (The Swaying Pandanus Trees), 276
New Colossus, The (excerpt) (poem), 42
Ngam Sang Duan (Shining Moon), 376
No despiertes a mi niño (Do Not Wake My Little Son), 217

Nottamun Town, 405
O, I'm Gonna Sing, 245
Old Dan Tucker, 253
Old Turkey Buzzard, 265
On the Sunny Side of the Street, 361
Orchestra Song, 332
Our World, 381
Path to the Moon, 368
Pick-a-Little/Goodnight Ladies, 300
Qué bonita bandera, 442
Reach, 14
Ride Like the Wind, 130
Rise Up, Shepherd, and Follow, 422
Rock and Roll Is Here to Stay, 316
Rock Island, 291
Rocky Top, 352
'Round the Corner, Sally, 251
Samiotissa, 284
Sankta Lucia (Saint Lucia), 412
Santa Marta, 398
Season of Hope, The, 410
Shope, Shope (Oh, Shope, Shope), 220
Simple Gifts, 136
Sing, America Sing!, 6
Singabahambayo (An Army Is Marching), 56, 76
Somebody's Knockin' at Your Door, 254
Son de la negra, 397
Song of Peace, 257
Sound the Trumpet, 279
Sounds of Africa, The, (poem), 74
Sounds of Swing (poem), 32
Southern Nights, 310
Star Canon, 367
Streets of Laredo, 260
Surfin' U.S.A., 306
Sweet Music, 319
There's a Song in Me, (melody and 2-part) 164, 183
There's No Hidin' Place, 266
Times They Are A-Changin', The, 204
Triple Play, 355
Tumbai, 194
Turn the World Around, 208
Tzena, Tzena, 171
Ujima, 427
Un lorito de Verapaz (A Parrot from Verapaz), 349
Uncle Pen, 24
Uno, dos y tres (One, Two, and Three), 364
Üsküdar, 128
Vive l'amour, 262
'Way Down Yonder in the Brickyard, 255
We Are the Children of Tomorrow, 114
We Want to Sing, 235
Wells Fargo Wagon, The, 303
What the World Needs Now, 230

Thematic Correlations to Reading Series (continued)

Thematic Correlations to Reading Series (continued)

Thematic Correlations to Reading Series (continued)

Bound No'th Blues by L. Hughes (poem), 181
City Blues, 278
Cliffs of Doneen, The, 46
Colores de caracol (Colors of the Snail) by E. Galarza (poem), 101
De colores (Many Colors) (unison), 88, (parts), 98
Deta, Deta (The Moon), 246
Dreamers, 430
Ēinīnī (Little Birds Sleep), 240
Erie Canal, 132
Estrella brillante (Shining Star), 373
Follow the Drinkin' Gourd, 142
Ga Eul (Fall), 401
Goin' Home, 108
Great Big Sea, A, 334
Haere Ra (Now Is the Hour), 151
Hallelujah, Get On Board, 345
Hero, 312
Hill an' Gully, 250
John Henry, 146
John Kanaka, 249
Joyful, Joyful, We Adore Thee, 103
Life by S. DeShetler (poem), 205
Loch Lomond, 138
Los maizales (The Cornfields), 268
Nani Wale Na Hala (The Swaying Pandanus Trees), 276
Ngam sang duan (Shining Moon), 376
Nottamun Town, 405
Our World, 381
Path to the Moon, 368
Reach, 14
Ride Like the Wind, 130
Sankta Lucia (Saint Lucia), 413
Shope, Shope (Oh, Shope, Shope), 220
Simple Gifts, 136
Sounds of Africa, The, by Wandile (poem), 74
Star Canon, 367
Wells Fargo Wagon, The, 303
What the World Needs Now, 230
When Johnny Comes Marching Home, 34
Winter Wonderland, 408

Unit 5: Problem Solving, Bright Ideas
Ballad of the Underground Railroad, The, 145, (partner song), 154
Big Big World, 438
Bound No'th Blues by L. Hughes (poem), 181
Cindy, 265
Circle of Friends, 196
Dreamers, 430
Erie Canal, 132
Follow the Drinkin' Gourd, 142
Hallelujah, Get On Board, 345

Heartbeat of Democracy by V. Brasier (poem), 389
Hero, 312
I Am But a Small Voice, 323
I Got Rhythm, 187
I Hear America Singing, 327
In That Great Git'n Up Morning, 10
John Henry, 146
Life by S. DeShetler (poem), 205
Like a Mighty Stream, 320
My Government Claim (unison), 95, (parts), 110
New Colossus, The (excerpt) by E. Lazarus (poem), 42
No despiertes a mi niño (Do Not Wake My Little Son), 217
Our World, 381
Ride Like the Wind, 130
Season of Hope, The, 410
Sounds of Swing by T. Igus (poem), 32
Star Canon, 367
Vive l'amour, 262
We Are the Children of Tomorrow, 114
What the World Needs Now, 230
Words of Wisdom, 244
Yakety Yak, 308

Unit 6: Making Decisions, Crossroads
America, the Beautiful, 388
Ballad of the Underground Railroad, The, 145, (partner song), 154
Big Big World, 438
Bound No'th Blues by L. Hughes (poem), 181
Caissons Go Rolling Along, The, 37
Change the World, 314
Cuando salí de Cuba (I Went Away from Cuba), 168
Dreamers, 430
Erie Canal, 132
Follow the Drinkin' Gourd, 142
Haere Ra (Now Is the Hour), 151
Hallelujah, Get On Board, 345
Heartbeat of Democracy by V. Brasier (poem), 389
Hero, 312
I Am But a Small Voice, 323
I Hear America Singing, 327
In That Great Git'n Up Morning, 10
John Henry, 146
Kojo No Tsuki (Moon at the Ruined Castle), 149
Life by S. DeShetler (poem), 205
Like a Mighty Stream, 320
My Government Claim (unison), 95, (parts), 110
New Colossus, The (excerpt) by E. Lazarus (poem), 42
Our World, 381
Ride Like the Wind, 130

Rocky Top, 352
Singabahambayo (An Army Is Marching) (unison), 56, (parts), 76
Sounds of Swing by T. Igus (poem), 32
Star Canon, 367
Surfin' U.S.A., 306
Times They Are A-Changin', The, 204
We Are the Children of Tomorrow, 114
Words of Wisdom, 244

GRADE 6

Unit 1: Experience, Pathways
A Perfect Winter Day, 400–403
Al lado de mi cabaña, 141
All Ye Who Music Love, 336
Alleluia, 186
America, 388
Angelina, 8
A-Rovin', 319
Barbry Ellen, 208
Bashana Haba'ah, 360
Blue Suede Shoes, 236
Body Talk, 88
Bop 'til You Drop, 87
Bulbes ('Taters), 280
Camelot, 310
Canon, 256
Cape Cod Chantey, 258
Captain Jinks, 266
Carol (poem), 407
Carol from an Irish Cabin, 408
Charleston, 112
Charlotte Town, 261
Chiribim, 57
Chíu, Chíu, Chíu, 172
Choo, Choo, Ch'Boogie, 180
Coasts of High Barbary, The, 329
Come and Sing Together, 281
Comedy Tonight, 204
Conga, 34
Cripple Creek, 372
Dancing in the Street, 84
Dandansoy, 356
Daybreak in Alabama (excerpt) by L. Hughes (poem), 162
Dere Geliyor (River Overflowing), 232
Derry Ding Dong Dason, 249
Didn't It Rain, 345
Do Lord, 260
Doctor Jazz, 378
Doing the Latest Rag, 314
Doney Gal, 115
Down by the Riverside, 22
El charro (The Cowboy), 278
El tambor (The Drum), 222
El tecolote (The Owl), 392
Fortune Favors the Brave, 316
Gee, Mom, I Want to Go Home, 148
Ghost Ship, The, 323
Git Along, Little Dogies, 284

Thematic Correlations to Reading Series (continued)

Good News, 242
Greenland Whale Fishery, 212
Guitar Man, The, 138
Hae Wa Be (Sun and Rain), 273
Haji Firuz, 421
Hal'lwe (Nanticoke Women's honoring song), 428
Hava Nashira, 67
Heart, 166
Heleluyan, 188
Hmong New Year (Laos)
Hotaru Koi (Come, Firefly), 255
Huainito, 351
Hullaballoo Balay, 10
I Got a Letter, 270
I Love a Piano, 130
I Want to Be Ready, 12
I'm Going to Georgia, 244
I'm Gonna Sit at the Welcome Table, 416
If I Had a Hammer, 174
Já do lesa nepojedu (To the Woods I Will Not Go), 227
Jack Was Ev'ry Bit a Sailor, 170
Jede, jede, poštovský panáček (Riding, Riding, Is Mr. Postman), 226
Jikel' Emaweni (Throw It Down the Slopes), 70
Joban Tanko Bushi, 142
Jordan's Angels, 365
Kakokolo, 262
Kokoleoko, 279
La bamba, 381
La pájara pinta (The Speckled Bird), 268
Lean On Me, 150
Leila, 376
Let It Roll, 124
Lonesome Dove, 249
Lullaby of Broadway, 182
Lumber Camp Song, The, 136
Ma'oz Tsur (Rock of Ages), 405
Mama Don't 'Low, 126
Mama Will Provide, 296
Mayim, Mayim, 102
Merecumbé, 276
Mi caballo blanco, 60
Mountain Music, 20
Mr. Scott Joplin's Ragtime Rag!, 110
N'kosi sikelel' iAfrika (Lord Bless Africa), 339
Never Sleep Late Anymore, 274
Neviděli jste tu mé panenky? (Have You Not Seen My Dear Daughters?), 228
New Ashmolean Marching Society Students Conservatory Band, The, 308
O Hal'lwe (Women's honoring song), 428
O, Desayo, 50
O, La Le!, 6

Oh, How Lovely Is the Evening, 252
Old Barn Dance, The, 94
Old Jim John, 253
Ole La'u Papa e, 91
On a Clear Day, 206
One Dime Blues, 178
One of Those Songs, 54
Orange Blossom Special, 33
Our Goodman, 245
Perfect Winter Day, 400
Pick a Bale of Cotton, 254
Pleeng Loy Krathong, 398
Rage and Roar, 48
Red Iron Ore, 134
Ride on the Wind, 326
Risseldy, Rosseldy, 264
River of My People, 176
Rock Around the Clock, 324
Roll de Ole Chariot Along, 243
Sakura, 14
Salamanca Market, 247
Samba de Orfeu (Dance of Orpheus), 190
Scraping Up Sand, 248
Shady Grove, 286
Shibolet Basadeh (Wheat in the Field), 424
Ship in Distress, The, 211
Shoes of John, 246
Sing Hosanna, 362
Slap that Bass, 146
Songs for the People (excerpt) by F. E. Watkins Harper (poem), 62
Stars and Stripes Forever, The, 390
Star-Spangled Banner, The, 386
Sugar in the Gourd, 251
Suliram, 58
Suomen Salossa (The Finnish Forest), 422
Sweet and Low, 184
Tain't What You Do, 18
Ten Tom-Toms by Anonymous (poem), 57
That Great Come and Get It Day, 306
The Lumber Camp Song, 136
There Was a Jolly Miller, 250
They Call the Wind Maria, 312
This Pretty Planet, 194
Tina Singu, 36
Troika, 230
Trout, The, 342
Tsing Chun U Chü (Youth Dance Song), 272
Tsiothwatasè:tha (Round Dance), 109
Tum Balalaika, 68
Ua txiab (The Village), 394
Vem Kan Segla, 419
Wabash Cannonball, The, 30
Wachet auf (Waken Now), 259
Waiting for Life, 292
Walk by the River, 74, 76

Water Is Wide, The, 46
Wayfaring Stranger, 283
When I Sing, 44
Why We Tell the Story, 303
Winter Ade (folk melody), 132
Winter Ade, 132, 133
Wondering, 282
Yellow Bird, 154
Yerakina, 216
You Sing for Me, 106
Yüe líang wan wan (Crescent Moon), 26

Unit 2: Connections, A Common Thread
Angelina, 8
Barbry Ellen, 208
Carol by K. Grahame (poem), 407
Come and Sing Together, 281
Cum-ma-la Be-stay, 370
Dancing in the Street, 84
Dere Geliyor (River Overflowing), 232
Didn't It Rain, 345
Doney Gal, 115
Down by the Riverside, 22
El Tambor (The Drum), 222
Gee, Mom, I Want to Go Home, 148
Ghost Ship, The, 323
Greenland Whale Fishery, The, 212
Heleluyan (Alleluia), 188
Huainito, 351
Hullaballoo Balay, 10
I'm Gonna Sit at the Welcome Table, 416
Jack Was Ev'ry Bit a Sailor, 170
Jede, jede, poštovský panáček (Riding, Riding, Is Mr. Postman), 226
Joban Tanko Bushi (Joban Miners' Song), 142
Lean on Me, 150
Leila, 376
Let It Roll, 124
Let Music Surround You, 285
Listen to the Music, 63
Lumber Camp Song, The, 136
Mama Don't 'Low, 126
Mi caballo blanco (My White Horse), 60
Mountain Music, 20
N'kosi sikelel' iAfrika (Lord Bless Africa), 339
Neviděli jste tu mé panenky? (Have You Not Seen My Dear Daughters?), 228
O, Desayo, 50
Old Barn Dance, The, 94
Old Jim John, 253
Orange Blossom Special, 33
Pick a Bale of Cotton, 254
Rage and Roar, 48
Red Iron Ore, 134
River of My People, 176

Thematic Correlations to Reading Series (continued)

Thematic Correlations to Reading Series (continued)

Wabash Cannonball, The, 30
Wachet auf (Waken Now), 259
Waiting for Life, 292
Walk by the River, 74, 76
Water Is Wide, The, 46
Wayfaring Stranger, 283
We Return Thanks (Iroquois prayer), 108
When I Sing, 44
Why We Tell the Story, 303
Winter Ade, 132, 133
Wondering, 282
Yellow Bird, 154
Yerakina, 216
You Sing for Me, 106
Yüe líang wan wan (Crescent Moon), 26

Unit 4: Inquiry, Seek and Discover
Angelina, 8
Camelot, 310
Carol (excerpt) by K.Grahame (poem), 407
Carol from an Irish Cabin, 408
Chiu, Chiu, Chiu, 172
Choo, Choo, Ch'Boogie, 180
Coasts of High Barbary, The, 329
Dandansoy, 356
Daybreak in Alabama (excerpt) by L. Hughes (poem), 162
Dere Geliyor (River Overflowing), 232
Doing the Latest Rag, 314
Doney Gal, 115
Down by the Riverside, 22
Earth Child, 426
El tecolote (The Owlet), 392
Ghost Ship, The, 323
Git Along, Little Dogies, 284
Hae Wa Be (Sun and Rain), 273
Heart, 166
Hotaru Koi (Come, Firefly), 255
I Want to Be Ready, 12
I'm Going to Georgia, 244
I'm Gonna Sit at the Welcome Table, 416
If I Had a Hammer, 174
La pájara pinta (The Speckled Bird), 268
Lean on Me, 150
Lonesome Dove, 249
Mama Will Provide, 296
Mayim, Mayim (Water, Water), 102
Minor Bird, A, by R. Frost (poem), 156
Mr. Scott Joplin's Ragtime Rag!, 110
Neviděli jste tu mé panenky? (Have You Not Seen My Dear Daughters?), 228
O, Desayo, 50
Oh, How Lovely Is the Evening, 252
On a Clear Day, 206
Orange Blossom Special, 33
Perfect Winter Day, A, 400

Rage and Roar, 48
Red Iron Ore, 134
Ride on the Wind, 326
River of My People, 176
Round and Round, 104
Sakura (Cherry Blossoms), 14
Salamanca Market, 247
Scraping Up Sand, 248
Shady Grove, 286
Ship in Distress, The, 211
Shoes of John, 246
Suomen Salossa (The Finnish Forest), 422
Sweet and Low, 184
Tain't What You Do, 18
They Call the Wind Maria, 312
This Pretty Planet, 194
Troika, 230
Trout, The, 342
Tsing Chun U Chü (Youth Dance Song), 272
Unfolding Bud by N. Koriyama (poem), 209
Untitled by Anonymous (poem), 218
Wabash Cannonball, The, 30
Wachet auf (Waken Now), 259
Waiting for Life, 292
Walk by the River (unison), 74, (parts), 76
Water Is Wide, The, 46
Wayfaring Stranger, 283
We Return Thanks (Iroquois prayer) (poem), 108
Why We Tell the Story, 303
Winter Ade (G Major), 132, (G Minor), 133
Wondering, 282
Yellow Bird, 154
Yüe lían wan wan (Crescent Moon), 26

Unit 5: Problem Solving, Brainstorms
America, 388
Angelina, 8
A-Rovin', 319
Camelot, 310
Carol by K. Grahame (poem), 407
Choo, Choo, Ch'Boogie, 180
Come and Sing Together, 281
Cum-ma-la Be-stay, 370
Dancing in the Street, 84
Dere Geliyor (River Overflowing), 232
Doney Gal, 115
Down by the Riverside, 22
El Tambor (The Drum), 222
Fortune Favors the Brave, 316
Gee, Mom, I Want to Go Home, 148
Git Along, Little Dogies, 284
Greenland Whale Fishery, The, 212
Heart, 166
Hullaballoo Balay, 10

I Want to Be Ready, 12
I'm Gonna Sit at the Welcome Table, 416
If I Had a Hammer, 174
Joban Tanko Bushi (Joban Miners' Song), 142
Jordan's Angels, 365
Lean on Me, 150
Leila, 376
Let It Roll, 124
Let Music Surround You, 285
Listen to the Music, 63
Lumber Camp Song, The, 136
Ma'oz Tsur (Rock of Ages), 405
Mama Don't 'Low, 126
Mayim, Mayim (Water, Water), 102
Mi caballo blanco (My White Horse), 60
Mountain Music, 20
N'kosi sikelel' iAfrika (Lord Bless Africa), 339
Neviděli jste tu mé panenky? (Have You Not Seen My Dear Daughters?), 228
O, Desayo, 50
Old Barn Dance, The, 94
One Dime Blues, 178
Orange Blossom Special, 33
Rage and Roar, 48
Red Iron Ore, 134
River of My People, 176
Scraping Up Sand, 248
Shady Grove, 286
Ship in Distress, The, 211
Shoes of John, 246
Stars and Stripes Forever, The, 390
Star-Spangled Banner, The, 386
Suliram, 58
Sweet and Low, 184
Tain't What You Do, 18
This Pretty Planet, 194
Ua txiab (The Village), 394
Vem Kan Segla (Who Can Sail?), 419
Wabash Cannonball, The, 30
Walk by the River (unison), 74, (parts), 76
Water Is Wide, The, 46
Wayfaring Stranger, 283
Wondering, 282
Yerakina, 216
You Sing for Me, 106

Unit 6: Making Decisions, All Things Considered
Angelina, 8
Camelot, 310
Choo, Choo, Ch'Boogie, 180
Coasts of High Barbary, The, 329
Dandansoy, 356
Doing the Latest Rag, 314
Gee, Mom, I Want to Go Home, 148
Ghost Ship, The, 323

Thematic Correlations to Reading Series (continued)

Harcourt Trophies ©2003

The following materials from *Spotlight on Music* may be used with each theme in Harcourt's *Harcourt Trophies*.

Grade K

Theme 1: Getting to Know You

Alison's Camel, T201
All Work Together, T12
Alphabet Song, The, T54
Animal Rhythms (poem), T56
Best That I Can Be!, The, T48
Bingo, T64
Bullfrogs, Bullfrogs on Parade by J. Prelutsky (poem), T183
Cobbler, Cobbler, Mend My Shoe, T169
Cobbler, The, by E. Chafee (poem), T255
Counting Song, T92
Fox, the Hen, and the Drum, The (Indian fable), T294
Good Day Song, T50
Happy Birthday, Happy Birthday, T273
Hickory, Dickory, Dock (poem), T49
Hot Dog, T69
I Am a Little Tugboat by C. Huffman (poem), T144
I Am a Little Tugboat by C. Huffman (poem), T95
I Made a Valentine, T333
In the Barnyard by D. Aldis (poem), T207
Jig, Jog, Jig, Jog, T260
Let's Think of Something to Do, T270
Let's Think of Something to Do, T270
Little Spotted Puppy, T146
London Bridge, T99
Los pollitos (Little Chickens), T288
Mama, Bake the Johnnycake, Christmas Comin', T318
Merry-Go-Round by R. Field (poem), T223
Merry-Go-Round, The, T225
Mi chacra (My Farm), T207
Muffin Man, The, T105
Mulberry Bush, The, T112
Na Bahia Tem (In Bahia Town), T163
Oh, A-Hunting We Will Go, T62
Old Gray Cat, The, T43
Old MacDonald Had a Farm, T207
On This Night, T315
One, Two, Tie My Shoe, T150
Peace and Quiet, T278
Pimpón, T22
Row, Row, Row, T274
Santa Clara Corn Grinding Song, T164

School Is Over by K. Greenaway (poem), T85
See the Pony Galloping, T44
Speedy Delivery, T279
Sweetly Sings the Donkey, T244
Tengo, Tengo, Tengo (I Have, I Have, I Have), T212
Three Little Kittens, T146
Time to Sing, T16
Tugboat, T95
Umoja! by M. Evans (poem), T325
We Are Playing in the Forest, T248
Won't You Be My Neighbor?, T268

Theme 2: I Am Special

Alison's Camel, T201
All Work Together, T12
Alphabet Song, T54
America, T303
Animales (Animals), T192
Battle Hymn of the Republic, T331
Bear Went Over the Mountain, The, T204
Bell Horses, T262
Best That I Can Be!, The, T48
Bickle, Bockle, 187
Bingo, T64
Bobby Shafto, T265
Bohm Dong Sahn Gohd Dong Sahn (Spring Valley, Flower Valley), T337
Bounce High, Bounce Low, T131
Buffalo Dusk (poem), T219
Bullfrogs, Bullfrogs on Parade (poem), T183
Bus, The, T137
Bye 'n' Bye, T68
City (poem), T134
Cobbler, Cobbler, Mend My Shoe, T169
Cobbler, The (poem), T169
Colorful Dragon Boat, T328
Counting Song, T92
Doing the Weekly Walk, T78
Echo (poem), T104
Eency Weency Spider, T8
El picaflor (The Hummingbird), T141
El tambor (The Drum), T129
Excuse Us, Animals in the Zoo (poem), T195
Faeries and Giants from *Wand of Youth Suite No. 1* (listening), T52
Farmer in the Dell, The, T100
Fehér liliomszál (Little Water Lily), T139
Follow Me, T133

Follow the Leader (poem), T132
Furry Bear (poem), T205
Garden Hoedown, The, T290
Girls and Boys, Come Out to Play (poem), T98
Git on Board, T145
Go, Go, Go, T276
Gogo, T188
Good Day Song, T50
Grizzly Bear, T252
Happy Birthday, T273
Happy Birthday, T347
Head and Shoulders, T238
Hello Song, T2
Here Is the Beehive, T258
Hickory, Dickory, Dock (poem), T49
Hinges (poem), T23
Hinges by A. Fisher (poem), T23
Hippopotamus, The (poem), T199
Hokey Pokey, T68
Hop, Hop, Hop, T197
Hot Dog, T69
Humming Birds (poem), T140
I Am a Little Tugboat (poem), T95
I Can't Spell Hippopotamus, T199
I Got Shoes, T33
I Know an Old Lady, T26
I Made a Valentine, T333
I Will Sing Hello, T156
If Things Grew Down (poem), T48G, T293
If You're Happy, T6
Ifetayo (Love Brings Happiness), T325
In the Barnyard (poem), T207
Instrument Game, T36
It Fell in the City (poem), T312
It's So Good to See You, T86
It's Such a Good Feeling, T282
It's You I Like, T280
Jack, Be Nimble, T88
Jack-in-the-Box, T250
Jack-o'-Lantern, T307
Jig Jog, Jig Jog, T260
Juhtgarak (Chopsticks), T108
Jump or Jiggle (poem), T193
Just Like Me, T242
Kangaroo, The, T197
Kum Ba Yah, T327
La pequeñita araña (Eency Weency Spider), T9
Lady, Lady, T184
Las horas (The Hours), T70
Let's Think of Something To Do, T270
Little Blue Truck, T136

Thematic Correlations to Reading Series (continued)

Theme 3: Around the Table

Theme 4: Silly Business

Sing a Song of Sixpence, T111
Singing-Time by R. Fyleman (poem), T15
Stamping Land, T24
Taking Off by M. Green (poem), T134
Ten in a Bed, T256
Ten Little Frogs, T240
This Is My City, T120
Three Little Muffins (speech piece), T146
Toodala, T39
Travel by E. St. Vincent Millay (poem), T144
Wait and See, T335
Willoughby Wallaby Woo, T241
You're a Grand Old Flag, T4

Theme 5: Family Ties
Alison's Camel, T201
All Work Together, T12
Alphabet Song, T54
America, T303
Animal Rhythms (poem), T56
Animales (Animals), T192
Battle Hymn of the Republic, T331
Bear Went Over the Mountain, The, T204
Bell Horses, T262
Best That I Can Be!, The, T48
Bickle, Bockle, T187
Bingo, T64
Bobby Shafto, T265
Bohm Dong Sahn Gohd Dong Sahn (Spring Valley, Flower Valley), T337
Bounce High, Bounce Low, T131
Buffalo Dusk (poem), T219
Bullfrogs, Bullfrogs on Parade (poem), T183
Bus, The, T137
Bye 'n' Bye, T67
City (poem), T134
Cobbler, Cobbler, Mend My Shoe, T169
Cobbler, The (poem), T169
Colorful Dragon Boat, T328
Counting Song, T92
Days of the Week, T81
Doing the Weekly Walk, T78
Echo (poem), T104
Eency Weency Spider, T8
El picaflor (The Hummingbird), T141
El tambor (The Drum), T129
Excuse Us, Animals in the Zoo (poem), T195
Fall (Allegro) from The Four Seasons (Concerto No. 3 in F Major) (excerpt), T305
Farmer in the Dell, The, T100
Fehér liliomszál (Little Water Lily), T139
Follow Me, T133
Follow the Leader (poem), T132

Fox, the Hen, and the Drum, The, T294
Furry Bear (poem), T205
Garden Hoedown, The, T290
Girls and Boys, Come Out to Play (poem), T98
Git on Board, T145
Go, Go, Go, T276
Gogo, T188
Good Day Song, T50
Grizzly Bear, T252
Happy Birthday, T273
Happy Birthday, T347
Head and Shoulders, T238
Hello Song, T2
Here Is the Beehive, T258
Hickory, Dickory, Dock (poem), T49
Hinges (poem), T23
Hippopotamus, The (poem), T199
Hokey Pokey, T68
Hop, Hop, Hop, T197
Hot Dog, T69
Humming Birds (poem), T140
I Am a Little Tugboat (poem), T95
I Can't Spell Hippopotamus, T199
I Got Shoes, T33
I Know an Old Lady, T26
I Made a Valentine, T333
I Will Sing Hello, T156
If Things Grew Down (poem), T48G, T293
If You're Happy, T6
Ifetayo (Love Brings Happiness), T325
In the Barnyard (poem), T207
Instrument Game, T36
It Fell in the City (poem), T312
It's So Good to See You, T86
It's Such a Good Feeling, T282
It's You I Like, T280
Jack, Be Nimble, T88
Jack-in-the-box (poem), T251
Jack-in-the-Box, T250
Jig Jog, Jig Jog, T260
Juhtgarak (Chopsticks), T108
Jump or Jiggle (poem), T193
Just Like Me, T242
Kangaroo, The (poem), T196
Kangaroo, The, T197
Kum Ba Yah, T327
La pequeñita araña (Eency Weency Spider), T9
Lady, Lady, T184
Las horas (The Hours), T70
Let's Think of Something To Do, T270
Little Blue Truck, T136
Little Ducky Duddle, T289
Little Sir Echo, T103
Little Spotted Puppy, T146
Little White Duck, T208
London Bridge, T99
Long Gone (poem), T72
Look Who's Here!, T84

Los pollitos (Little Chickens), T288
Mama, Bake the Johnnycake, T318
María Blanca, T99
Martin Luther King (speech piece), T326
Mbombela (The Train Comes), T152
Mbombela, T152
Me I Am! (poem), T346
Merrily, We Roll Along, T110
Merry-Go-Round (poem), T225
Merry-Go-Round, The, T224
Mi chacra (My Farm), T207
Mister Sun, T343
Monkey, Monkey, T215
Monté sur un éléphant (Riding on an Elephant), T217
Muffin Man, The, T105
Mulberry Bush, The, T112
Music (poem), T157
My Grandfather, T23
My Oak Tree, T236
My Thumbs are Starting to Wiggle, T35
Na Bahia Tem (In Bahia Town), T163
Name Game, T57
Nampaya omame (Mothers), T128
Noble Duke of York, The, T232
Oats, Peas, Beans, and Barley Grow, T287
Ɔbɔɔ Asi Me Nsa, T159
Oh, A-Hunting We Will Go, T62
Old Gray Cat, The, T43
Old MacDonald Had a Farm, T211
Old Mister Woodpecker, T172
Oliphaunt (poem), T216
On This Night, T315
One Finger, One Thumb, T38
One, Two, Tie My Shoe, T151
Only My Opinion (poem), T29
Ourchestra (poem), T171
Peace and Quiet, T278
Pimpón, T22
Planting Seeds, T284
Popalong Hopcorn! (poem), T160
Popping Corn, T161
Prairie Dog Song (Kiowa Children's Song), T220
Presidents, T330
Propel, Propel, Propel, T275
Put Your Finger in the Air, T230
Qué bonito es (How Wonderful It Is), T234
Rainbow Song, The, T61
Ride the Train, T144
Ring Around the Rosy, T246
Ring-a-ring (poem), T247
River, The, (poem), T342
Row, Row, Row, T274
Santa Clara Corn Grinding Song, T164
School Is Over (poem), T84
See the Pony Galloping, T44
Seesaw, Margery Daw, T265

Shake My Sillies Out, T175
Shapes (poem), T37
Sidewalks (poem), T98
Simi Yadech (Give Me Your Hand), T168
Sing a Little Song, T179
Sing a Song of Sixpence, T111
Singing-Time (poem), T15
Snail's Pace (poem), T29
Snake and the Frog, The (story), T297
Snow Toward Evening (poem), T311
Snowman, The, T313
Speedy Delivery, T279
Spell of the Moon (poem), T116
Stamping Land, T24
Sweetly Sings the Donkey, T244
Table Manners (poem), T107
Taking Off (poem), T134
Ten in a Bed, T256
Ten Little Frogs, T240
Tengo, Tengo, Tengo (I Have, I Have, I Have), T212
They Were Tall, T53
Things I'm Thankful For, T308
This Is My City, T120
This Is What I Can Do, T124
Three Little Kittens, T146
Three Little Muffins, T127
Time to Sing, T16
Toodala, T39
Touch Your Shoulders, T254
Travel (poem), T144
Tree of Peace (speech piece), T321
Tugboat, T95
Twinkle, Twinkle, Little Star, T90
Umoja! (poem), T325
Ushkana, T75
Wait and See, T334
Walk to School, T18
Wavvuuvuumira (Mister Bamboo Bug), T165
We Are Playing in the Forest, T248
What You Gonna Call Your Pretty Little Baby?, T319
When You Send a Valentine, T332
Willoughby Wallaby Woo, T241
Won't You Be My Neighbor?, T268
Woodpecker, The (poem), T172
Worms, T286
Y ahora vamos a cantar (Now We Are Going to Sing), T340
You're a Grand Old Flag, T4

Theme 6: Animal Families

Animales (Animals), T192
Bear Went Over the Mountain, The, T204
Bounce High, Bounce Low, T13
Buffalo Dusk by C. Sandburg (poem), T219
El picaflor (The Hummingbird), T141

Excuse Us, Animals in the Zoo by A. Wynne (poem), T195
Farmer in the Dell, The, T100
Follow the Leader by K. Fraser (poem), T132
Furry Bear by A. A. Milne (poem), T205
Garden Hoedown, The, T290
Go, Go, Go, T276
Gogo, T188
Grizzly Bear, T252
Head and Shoulders, T238
Hippopotamus, The, by J. Prelutsky (poem), T199
Hokey Pokey, T68
Hop, Hop, Hop, T197
Humming Birds by B. Sage (poem), T140
Instrument Game, T36
Jack, Be Nimble, T88
Kangaroo, The, T196
La pequeñita araña (Eency Weency Spider), T9
Little Ducky Duddle, T289
Little White Duck, T208
Mayflies by P. Fleischmann (poem), T76
Monkey, Monkey (speech piece), T215
Monté sur un éléphant (Riding on an Elephant), T218
Name Game, T58
Oats, Peas, Beans, and Barley Grow, T287
Oh, A-Hunting We Will Go, T62
Old Mister Woodpecker, T172
Oliphaunt by J. R. R. Tolkien (poem), T216
Prairie Dog Song (Kiowa children's song), T220
Snail's Pace by A. Fisher (poem), T29
Snake and the Frog, The (story), T297
This Is What I Can Do, T124
Touch Your Shoulders, T254
Ushkana (Damselfly Song), T75
Wavvuuvuumira (Mister Bamboo Bug), T165
Woodpecker, The, by E. Roberts (poem), T173
Worms, T286

Theme 7: Bug Surprises

Animales (Animals), T192
Bear Went Over the Mountain, The, T204
Bohm Dong Sahn, Gohd Dong Sahn (Spring Valley, Flower Valley), T337
Buffalo Dusk by C. Sandburg (poem), T219
Bye 'n' Bye, T67
City by L. Hughes (poem), T134
Days of the Week, T81
Echo by W. de la Mare (poem), T104
Eency Weency Spider, T8

El picaflor (The Hummingbird), T141
Excuse Us, Animals in the Zoo by A. Wynne (poem), T195
Fehér liliomszál (Little Water Lily), T139
Furry Bear by A. A. Milne (poem), T205
Grizzly Bear, T252
Here Is the Beehive, T258
Hippopotamus, The, by J. Prelutsky (poem), T199
Humming Birds by B. Sage (poem), T140
If Things Grew Down by R. Hoeft (poem), T292
It Fell in the City by E. Merriam (poem), T312
Jack-o'-Lantern, T307
Kangaroo, The, T196
La pequeñita araña (Eency Weency Spider), T9
Lady, Lady, T184
Little Sir Echo, T103
Little White Duck, T208
Mayflies by P. Fleischmann (poem), T76
Mi chacra (My Farm), T207
Mister Sun, T343
Monkey, Monkey (speech piece), T215
Monté sur un éléphant (Riding on an Elephant), T218
My Oak Tree, T236
North Winds Blow, T305
Oh, A-Hunting We Will Go, T62
Old Mister Woodpecker, T172
Oliphaunt by J. R. R. Tolkien (poem), T216
Prairie Dog Song (Kiowa children's song), T220
Rainbow Song, The, T61
River, The, by C. Zolotow (poem), T342
Sidewalks by P. Hubbell (poem), T98
Sing a Little Song, T179
Snail's Pace by A. Fisher (poem), T29
Snake and the Frog, The (story), T297
Snow Toward Evening by M. Cane (poem), T311
Snowman, The, T313
Spell of the Moon (excerpt) by L. Norris (poem), T116
Twinkle, Twinkle, Little Star, T90
Ushkana (Damselfly Song), T75
Wavvuuvuumira (Mister Bamboo Bug), T165
Woodpecker, The, by E. Roberts (poem), T173
Worms, T286

Theme 8: Animal Adventures

Animales (Animals), T192
Bear Went Over the Mountain, The, T204
Bobby Shafto, T265

Buffalo Dusk by C. Sandburg (poem), T219

Bye 'n' Bye, T67

City by L. Hughes (poem), T134

Colorful Dragon Boat, T328

Echo by W. de la Mare (poem), T104

El picaflor (The Hummingbird), T141

Excuse Us, Animals in the Zoo by A. Wynne (poem), T195

Furry Bear by A. A. Milne (poem), T205

Grizzly Bear, T252

Here Is the Beehive, T258

Hippopotamus, The, by J. Prelutsky (poem), T199

Humming Birds by B. Sage (poem), T140

It Fell in the City by E. Merriam (poem), T312

Jack-o'-Lantern, T307

Kangaroo, The, T196

La pequeñita araña (Eency Weency Spider), T9

Little Sir Echo, T103

Little White Duck, T208

Mayflies by P. Fleischmann (poem), T76

Merrily, We Roll Along, T110

Mi chacra (My Farm), T207

Monkey, Monkey (speech piece), T215

Monté sur un éléphant (Riding on an Elephant), T218

Oh, A-Hunting We Will Go, T62

Old Mister Woodpecker, T172

Oliphaunt by J. R. R. Tolkien (poem), T216

Prairie Dog Song (Kiowa children's song), T220

Propel, Propel, Propel, T275

Rainbow Song, The, T61

Row, Row, Row, T274

Sidewalks by P. Hubbell (poem), T98

Snail's Pace by A. Fisher (poem), T29

Snake and the Frog, The (story), T297

Twinkle, Twinkle, Little Star, T90

Ushkana (Damselfly Song), T75

Wavvuuvuumira (Mister Bamboo Bug), T165

Woodpecker, The, by E. Roberts (poem), T173

Worms, T286

Grade 1

Theme 1: I Am Your Friend

El rorro (The Babe), T356

How Does Your Garden Grow?, T144

I Like by M. A. Hoberman (poem), T110

Lucy Locket, T253

Miss Mary Mack, T15

Serra, serra serrador (Saw, Saw Lumberjack), T133

We All Sing With the Same Voice, T156

Theme 2: Just For Fun

Apple a Day, An (traditional poem), T152

Apples and Bananas, T151

Arre, mi burrito (Gid-yup, Little Burro), T257

Brinca la tablita (Hop, Hop!), T71

Brush Your Teeth (song), T66, (speech piece), T66

Bug by L. Simmie (poem), T167

Caribbean Amphibian, T294

Dance Myself to Sleep, T314

Diana, T334

Five Little Pumpkins (traditional poem), T337

Go A Tin (Lantern Song), T363

Here Comes the Band by W. Cole (poem), T80

I Am Slowly Going Crazy, T127

I Like Spinach, T163

I'm Getting Sick of Peanut Butter by K. Nesbitt (poem), T219

In My Little Motor Boat, T159

It's So Nice on the Ice, T346

Let's Go Driving, T52

Little Red Caboose, T97

Marco Polo (speech piece), T90

My Kite by B. Brown and B. Brown (poem), T371

Naming Things by A. Davidson (poem), T221

Oranges and Lemons (English traditional poem), T150

Pat Pat Patty Pat, T308

Pease Porridge Hot, T255

Puddle Hopping, T60

Pumpkin Song, T342

Seesaw (song), T242, (accompaniment), T248

Sing After Me, T34

Sitting in the Sand by K. Kushkin (poem), T374

Skin and Bones, T340

Skip to My Lou, T102

Sleep, Bonnie Bairnie, T26

Somebody Come and Play, T92

Something Funny Outside, T338

Swing, The, by R. L. Stevenson (poem), T109

Tak for Maden (Thanks for Food), T343

Tako No Uta (The Kite Song), T370

Theme from *Sesame Street*, T298

Wheels, Wheels, Wheels by N. White Carlstrom (poem), T106

Theme 3: It's My Turn Now

A be ce, T213

A la rueda rueda ('Round and 'Round), T240

Acka Backa, T256

¡Adivina lo que es! (Guess What It Is!), T170

Animal Song, T288

Ants Go Marching, The, T22

Apples and Bananas, T151

Arre, mi burrito (Gid-yup, Little Burro), T257

Autumn Leaves Are Falling, T330

Autumn Leaves, T331

Bee, Bee, Bumblebee, T250

Big and Small by E. McCullough Brabson, T200

Bluebells, T209

Boris, the Singing Bear, T312

Bow-Wow by Mother Goose (poem), T81

Brinca la tablita (Hop, Hop!), T71

Bug by L. Simmie (poem), T167

But the Critter Got Away (speech piece), T88, (poem), T89

Butterfly, Flutter By, T333

Call of the Wild, A (excerpt) by R. W. Service (poem), T139

Caribbean Amphibian, T294

Categories, T146

Charlie Over the Ocean, T75

Chase the Squirrel, T88

Chickery Chick, T292

Clap Your Hands (song), T246, (rhythmic pattern), T247

Clouds by Anonymous (poem), T331

Come Back, My Little Chicks, T134

Cookies, T278

Cow, The, by R. L. Stevenson (poem), T236

Cut the Cake, T232

Dance Myself to Sleep, T314

Diana, T334

Diou Shou Juan'er, T212

Double This (game), T94

Down by the Bay, T48

Down the Hill, T281

Dragonfly by D. M. Violin (poem), T44

El florón (The Flower), T117

El juego chirimbolo (The Chirimbolo Game), T103

Field of Joys by M. Morand (poem), T224

Five Little Pumpkins (traditional poem), T337

George Washington, T368

Go A Tin (Lantern Song), T363

Goin' to the Zoo, T192

Granny (traditional poem), T104

Grasshoppers Three, T284

Green Grass Grows All Around, The, T148

Head and Shoulders, Baby, T40

Hello, There!, T230

Here Comes the Band by W. Cole (poem), T80

Here We Sit, T251

Hey, Children, Who's In Town?, T14

Hop! Chirp! Moo! Oh, Happy Springtime Day!, T372

Hopping Frog by C. Rossetti (poem), T113

Horses of the Sea, The, by C. Rossetti (poem), T179

Horses of the Sea, The, by C. Rossetti (poem), T179

Hunt the Cows, T236

I Am Slowly Going Crazy, T127

I Had a Little Hen (nursery rhyme), T136

I Have a Friend by Anonymous (poem), T225

I Like by M. A. Hoberman (poem), T110

I Like Spinach, T163

I Wanna Be a Friend of Yours, T84

I'd Like to Be a Lighthouse by R Field (poem), T238

I'm Getting Sick of Peanut Butter by K. Nesbitt (poem), T219

I've a Pair of Fishes, T124

Ice by D. Aldis (poem), T346

Ice, T347

If All the World Were Paper, T296

In My Little Motor Boat, T159

It's So Nice on the Ice, T346

John the Rabbit, T74

Johnny Works with One Hammer, T96

Johnny's Flea, T158

Jump or Jiggle by E. Beyer (poem), T316

Jump, Jim Joe, T89

Kaeru no Uta, T112

La ranita cri (The Little Frog Croaks), T27

Ladybugs' Picnic, T290

Lavender's Blue, T174

Legend of George Washington and the Cherry Tree, The (story), T369

Let's Go Driving, T52

Little Black Bug, T166

Little Robin Red Breast (English rhyme) (song), T208, (rhythmic pattern), T207

Locust, The (Zuñi poem), T285

Looby Loo, T262

Marco Polo (speech piece), T90

Martin Luther King, T360

Mary's Coal Black Lamb, T286

Mi cuerpo (My Body), T32

Miss Mary Mack, T15

Mizuguruma (The Water Wheel), T260

Mos', Mos'! (Cat, Cat!), T53

My Feet by L. B. Jacobs (poem), T264

My Kite by B. Brown and B. Brown (poem), T371

My Mama's Calling Me, T54

Naming Things by A. Davidson (poem), T221

Naughty Kitty Cat, T171

Night Comes... by B. Schenk de Regniers (poem), T233

No One Like You, T300

O Wind by C. Rossetti (poem), T235

One Little Elephant, T194

One, Two, Three, Four (traditional rhyme), T123

One, Two, Three, Four, Five, T265

Over in the Meadow, T78

Pat Pat Patty Pat, T308

Peanut Butter, T218

Piñata Song (Mexican traditional poem), T153

Pitty Patty Polt (nursery rhyme) (rhythmic pattern), T180

Puddle Hopping, T60

Pumpkin Song, T342

Punchinella, T216

Pusa't daga (Cat and Rat), T289

Rabbit, The, by M. Stelmach (poem), T186

Rain Poem (poem), T31

Rain Sizes by J. Ciardi (poem), T33

Rain, Rain, Go Away, T259

Rattlesnake, T185

Rise, Sally, Rise (game), T162

Romper, Stomper, and Boo (traditional story), T36

Sailor Went to Sea, Sea, Sea, A (song), T38, (game), T39

Sara Watashi (Plate Passing), T67

Seeds, T120

Seesaw (song), T242, (accompaniment), T248

Serra, serra serrador (Saw, Saw Lumberjack), T133

Shoo, Turkey, T76

Simple Simon, T175

Sing After Me, T34

Sing Ho! For the Life of a Bear! By A.A. Milne (poem), T114

Sittin' Down to Eat, T182

Sitting in the Sand by K. Kushkin (poem), T374

Six Little Ducks, T64

Skin and Bones, T340

Skip to My Lou, T102

Snail With the Mail, T274

Snail, Snail (song), T252, (three-tone), T252

Somebody Come and Play, T92

Somebody Has To... by S. Silverstein (poem), T258

Something Funny Outside, T338

Soup, Soup!, T358

Spring, T273

Swing, The, by R. L. Stevenson (poem), T109

Tailor, Tailor (traditional poem), T132

Tak for Maden (Thanks for Food), T343

Tako No Uta (The Kite Song), T370

There's a Hole in the Middle of the Sea, T178

This Old Man, T306

Thoughts of a Rattlesnake by K. Sexton (poem), T185

Tinker, Tailor, T131

Twenty-four Robbers, 173

Two, Four, Six, Eight (song), T246, (rhythmic pattern), T247

Una adivinanza (A Riddle), T138

Untitled (Butterflies) (haiku), T332

Up the Hill by W. J. Smith (poem), T45

Up the Tree and Down Again by A. Seear (poem), T65

Vhaya Kadhimba (Zimbabwean children's song) (song), T23, (game), T23

We All Sing With the Same Voice, T156

What's Your Name?, T125

White Sheep by Anonymous (poem), T234

Who's Afraid of the Big Bad Wolf? (nursery rhyme), T137

Why the Beetle Has a Gold Coat (Brazilian folktale), T321

Willum, T19

Wind Blew East, The, T234

Wind Blow, T187

Wings by A. Fisher (poem), T250

Year with Frog and Toad, A (reprise), T283

Year with Frog and Toad, A, T270

Zui Zui Zukkorbashi (song), T98, (game), T99

Theme 4: I Think I Can

A be ce, T213

All Night, All Day, T232

Animal Song, T288

Another Busy Day (speech piece), T41

Ants Go Marching, The, T22

Arre, mi burrito (Gid-yup, Little Burro), T257

Bear Hunt (poem), T126

Best Friends, T222

Big and Small by E. McCullough Brabson, T200

Bonjour, mes amis (Hello, My Friends), T18

Boris, the Singing Bear, T312

Bow-Wow by Mother Goose (poem), T81

Bug by L. Simmie (poem), T167

But the Critter Got Away (speech piece), T88, (poem), T89

Butterfly, Flutter By, T333

Call of the Wild, A (excerpt) by R. W. Service (poem), T139

Thematic Correlations to Reading Series (continued)

Thematic Correlations to Reading Series (continued)

Tisket A Tasket, A, T107
Twenty-four Robbers, T173
Two, Four, Six, Eight, T246
Uga, Uga, Uga (Cake, Cake, Cake), T313
Una adivinanza (A Riddle), T138
Untitled (Butterflies) (haiku), T332
Up the Hill (poem), T45
Up the Tree and Down Again (poem), T65
Wake Me, Shake Me, T198
We All Sing With the Same Voice, T156
What's Your Name?, T125
Wheels, Wheels, Wheels (poem), T106
When the Flag Goes By, T327
White Sheep by Anonymous (poem), T234
Who's Afraid of the Big Bad Wolf? (nursery rhyme), T137
Why the Beetle Has a Gold Coat (folktale), T321
Willum, T19
Wind Blew East, The, T234
Wind Blow, T187
Wings (poem), T250
Year With Frog and Toad, A (Reprise), T283
Year With Frog and Toad, A, T270
Yo, Mamana, Yo (Oh, Mama), T307
Zui Zui Zukkorbashi (song), T98, (game), T99

Theme 6: Going Places

Apple a Day, An (traditional poem), T152
Apples and Bananas, T151
Arre, mi burrito (Gid-yup, Little Burro), T257
Autumn Leaves Are Falling, T330
Autumn Leaves, T331
Bear Hunt (poem), T126
Bear Went Over the Mountain, The, T115
Brinca la tablita (Hop, Hop!), T71
Brush Your Teeth (song), T66, (speech piece), T66
Bug by L. Simmie (poem), T167
Call of the Wild, A (excerpt) by R. W. Service (poem), T139
Caribbean Amphibian, T294
Chang (Elephant), T199
Clouds by Anonymous (poem), T331.0
Dance Myself to Sleep, T314
Diana, T334
Down by the Bay, T48
El florón (The Flower), T117
Five Little Pumpkins (traditional poem), T337
Go A Tin (Lantern Song), T363
Goin' to the Zoo, T192
Green Grass Grows All Around, The, T148

Here Comes the Band by W. Cole (poem), T80
Hoo, Hoo!, T55
Hop! Chirp! Moo! Oh, Happy Springtime Day!, T372
Horses of the Sea, The, by C. Rossetti (poem), T179
I Am Slowly Going Crazy, T127
I Like Spinach, T163
I'd Like to Be a Lighthouse by R Field (poem), T238
I'm Getting Sick of Peanut Butter by K. Nesbitt (poem), T219
Ice, T347
In My Little Motor Boat, T159
It's So Nice on the Ice, T346
Kari (Wild Geese), 101
Let's Go Driving, T52
Library Song, T42
Little Red Caboose, T97
Marco Polo (speech piece), T90
Mizuguruma (The Water Wheel), T260
My Kite by B. Brown and B. Brown (poem), T371
Naming Things by A. Davidson (poem), T221
Night Comes... by B. Schenk de Regniers (poem), T233
O Wind by C. Rossetti (poem), T235
Oranges and Lemons (English traditional poem), T150
Over in the Meadow, T78
Pat Pat Patty Pat, T308
Pease Porridge Hot, T255
Puddle Hopping, T60
Pumpkin Song, T342
Rain Poem (poem), T31
Rain Sizes by J. Ciardi (poem), T33
Rain, Rain, Go Away, T259
Romper, Stomper, and Boo (traditional story), T36
Seeds, T120
Seesaw (song), T242, (accompaniment), T248
Serra, serra serrador (Saw, Saw Lumberjack), T133
Sing After Me, T34
Sitting in the Sand by K. Kushkin (poem), T374
Skin and Bones, T340
Skip to My Lou, T102
Sleep, Bonnie Bairnie, T26
Somebody Come and Play, T92
Somebody Has To... by S. Silverstein (poem), T258
Something Funny Outside, T338
Something Told the Wild Geese by R. Field (poem), T261
Spanish Days of the Week by Anonymous (poem), T108
Spring, T273

Swing, The, by R. L. Stevenson (poem), T109
Tak for Maden (Thanks for Food), T343
Tako No Uta (The Kite Song), T370
Theme from Sesame Street, T298
There's a Hole in the Middle of the Sea, T178
Up the Tree and Down Again by A. Seear (poem), T65
Wheels, Wheels, Wheels by N. White Carlstrom (poem), T106
White Sheep by Anonymous (poem), T234
Who's Afraid of the Big Bad Wolf? (nursery rhyme), T137
Wind Blew East, The, T234
Wind Blow, T187

Grade 2

Theme 1: Being Me

A la rueda de San Miguel (To the Wheel of San Miguel), 60
Ach, du lieber Augustin (The More We Get Together), 35
All Around the Buttercup, 210
America, 338
Animal Fair, 214
Apple Picker's Reel, 343
Artichokes, 314
Australia's on the Wallaby, 106
Australia's on the Wallaby, 106
Away for Rio, 170
Baby Beluga, 26
Baby Nodja, 154
Bahay Kubo (My Nipa Hut), 382
Ban Dal (Half Moon), 219
Banyan Tree, 321
Bate, bate (Stir, Stir), 242
Big Beautiful Planet, 376
Bliss (poem), 212
Bow, Wow, Wow, 264
Button, You Must Wander, 176
Candle on the Water, 296
Caranguejo (The Crab), 306
Check It Out! (It's About Respect), 10
Chiapanecas (Ladies of Chiapas), 128
Chichipapa (The Sparrow's Singing School), 22
Child Falling Asleep from Scenes from Childhood, 77
Chirri Bim, 70
Chíu, Chíu, Chíu (Chirp, Chirp, Chirp), 302
City Traffic (story), 328
Columbus Sailed with Three Ships, 344
Corner Grocery Store, 311
Cuckoo, Where Are You?, 244
Daisy Chain, 255
Dal taro kacha (Come, Pick the Moon), 98

Dance Together, 264
Do You Want My Little Frog? by H. Copeland (poem), 187
Doggie, Doggie, 59
Donkey, Donkey, 256
Drumming Spider, The (story), 333
Dumplin's, 172
Eating Lizards, 250
El burrito enfermo (The Sick Little Donkey), 180
El palomo y la paloma (The Doves), 380
El tren (The Train), 326
El zapatero (The Cobbler), 138
Elephant Carries a Great Big Trunk, The, by Anonymous (poem), 169
En la feria de San Juan (In the Market of San Juan), 226
En nuestra Tierra tan linda (On Our Beautiful Planet Earth), 114
Engine, Engine Number Nine, 13
Everybody Has Music Inside, 164
Everyone Has Music Inside, 164
Everything Grows, 204
Finis (poem), 76
Food Song, The, 318
Four White Horses, 300
Garden Song, 236
Going Over the Sea, 216
Good Night, Sleep Tight, 76
Great Outdoors, The, 290
Green Eggs and Ham, 284
Hairy Dog, The (poem), 58
Hakuna Matata, 292
Harvest, 342
Heigh Ho, Here We Go, 252
Hello, Hello, There, T126
Here Comes a Bluebird, 263
Here Comes Sally, 220
Hey, Hey, Look at Me, 245
Hop, Old Squirrel, 258
Horton Hears a Who! Two, 280
Horton Hears a Who!, 279
Hot Cross Buns, 258
I Bought Me a Cat, 14
I Chih ha Ma (Frogs), 186
I Heard a Bird Sing by O. Herford (poem), 271
I See, 266
I'm Gonna Sing, 9
In and Out, 245
In the Window, 352
It's a Small World, 298
It's Possible, 281
It's Raining! It's Pouring!, 233
Itik Besenda Gurau (The Ducks), 100
Ja posejah lubenice (I Planted Watermelons), 316
Jim Along, Josie, 194
Joy, 46
Juan Pirulero, 270

Jugaremos en el bosque (We Will Play in the Forest), 188
King's Land, 257
Knock the Cymbals, 265
La bella hortelana (The Beautiful Gardener), 208
Land of the Silver Birch, 88
Leatherwing Bat, 304
Lemonade, 19
Let's Go Fly a Kite, 134
Little Sally Water, 249
Loose Tooth (speech piece), 28
Mama Paquita, 92
Martin Luther King, 364
Matarile, 261
Me gase boho (The Orange Tree), 317
Me Stone, 48
Mein Hut (My Hat), 142
Merry-Go-Round, 267
Mill Song, The, 52
Mister Rabbit, Mister Rabbit, 150
Moon Boat by C. Pomerantz (poem), 218
Mother, Mother, 254
Mouse, Mousie, 254
Mr. Frog, 257
Na belo (Little Heron), 322
Nabe, Nabe, Soku, Nuke (Stew Pot, Stew Pot, Bottomless Pot), 259
Nikosi, 230
North Wind Blows, 367
Oh, the Thinks You Can Think!, 276
Old Blue, 213
Old Woman and the Pig, 130
Oliver Twist, 268
Oma Rapeti (Run, Rabbit), 108
On Top of Spaghetti, 312
Pairs or Pears, 265
Part of Your World, 294
Pat on the Back, A, 74
Pick a Pumpkin, 347
Piggy by W. Cole (poem), 315
Pizza, Pizza, Daddy-O, 62
Place in the Choir, A, 308
Plainsies, Clapsies, 248
Puff, the Magic Dragon, 54
Red Rover, 249
Riddle Song, 251
Riqui Ran (Sawing Song), 21
Rover, 260
Sailor, Sailor, on the Sea, 262
Sally Go 'Round the Sun, 268
Sammy Sackett, 146
San Sereni, 323
Say Your Name, 243
Seeds and Seasons, 206
Señor Coyote (story), 330
Seussical Mega-Mix, 287
Shake the Papaya Down, 90
She'll Be Comin' 'Round the Mountain, 33

Sheep in the Meadow (speech piece), 8
Sheep Shearing, 102
Shoheen Sho, 140
Shoo, Fly, 222
Sing! Sing! Sing!, 196
Skating, 350
Sorida (greeting song), 96
Sun Is First to Rise, The (poem), 383
Take Me Out to the Ball Game, 56
Taos Round Dance, 155
Thank You, 349
There Are Many Flags in Many Lands, 341
There's a Hole in the Bucket, 132
This Is My Country, 87
Three Little Penguins (speech piece), 112
Tiki Tiki Tiki Room, The, 324
Tinga Layo, 50
Together (poem), 34
Wake Up the Sun, 124
We're Sailing Down the River, 166
Welcome Is the Month of May, 378
What Did Delaware?, 190
Whistle While You Work, 6
Who Chopped the Cherry Tree Down? 371
Who Has Seen the Wind? (poem), 137
Who Has the Penny?, 252
Who's That Tapping at the Window?, 261
Willowbee, T69
Yanai (The Elephant), 305
Yankee Doodle, 340
You Are My Sunshine, 369
You'll Sing a Song and I'll Sing a Song, 156

Theme 2: Helping Hands
A la rueda de San Miguel (To the Wheel of San Miguel), 60
Ach, du lieber Augustin (The More We Get Together), 35
Apple Picker's Reel, 343
Artichokes, 314
Australia's on the Wallaby, 106
Big Beautiful Planet, 376
Candle on the Water, 296
Check It Out! (It's About Respect), 10
Chíu, chíu, chíu (Chirp, Chirp, Chirp), 302
Corner Grocery Store, 311
Daisy Chain, 255
Dal taro kacha (Come, Pick the Moon), 98
Dal taro kacha (Come, Pick the Moon), 98
Doggie, Doggie, 59
Drumming Spider, The (West African folktale), 333
Dumplin's, 172

Thematic Correlations to Reading Series (continued)

Thematic Correlations to Reading Series (continued)

Thematic Correlations to Reading Series (continued)

Theme 3: Celebrate Our World

Thematic Correlations to Reading Series (continued)

Theme 4: Something Special

Thematic Correlations to Reading Series (continued)

Ding Dong Diggy Diggy Dong, 269
Egy üveg alma (One Jar of Apples), 22
El florón (The Flower), 46
En roulant ma boule (As I Roll My Ball), 100
Frog in the Meadow, 243
Gebeta Board, The (Ethiopian folk tale), 346
Gi'Me Elbow Room, 88
Golden Ring Around the Susan Girl, 264
Greatest Show on Earth, The, 308
Herring, The, 316
Hey, Motswala, 34
Hope by E. Dickinson (poem), 166
I Lost the Farmer's Dairy Key, 273
I'm a Believer, 312
I'm On My Way, 382
I's the B'y, 13
In Good Old Colony Times, 326
John Jacob Jingleheimer Schmidt, 68
Kreely Kranky, 258
Kuma San (Honorable Bear), 244
La bamba (Mexican folk song), 236
Let Us Chase the Squirrel, 248
Let's Go Dancing, 196
Limbo Rock, 232
Lincoln by M. Cohn Livingston (poem), 389
Little Sally Walker, 105
Marvelous Toy, The, 182
Moon and Me, 220
Movin' Right Along, 124
Mrs. Murphy's Chowder, 390
Oh, Susanna, 153
Old Barn Dance, The, 94
Old Mister Rabbit, 254
Oleanna, 144
One Potato, Two Potato, 267
Pat-a-Pan, 375
Paw Paw Patch, The, 195
Paw Paw Patch, The, 195
Polly Wolly Doodle, 132
Rainbow Connection, The, 310
Scotland's Burning, 257
See the Rabbit Running, 255
Simon Says, 4
Smoke Goes Up the Chimney, 272
Sun Don't Set in the Mornin', 48, 60
Tititorea (Maori Stick Game) (New Zealand folk song), 174
Trampin', 287
Walk by the River (song), 74, (harmony parts), 76
Who's That Yonder?, 245
Woodchuck, 246
Yankee Doodle, 357

Theme 5: What a Team!
Colors of the Wind, 84
Crawdad Song, 107

De aquel cerro (On the Darkened Hillside), 32
Eh Soom Boo Kawaya (Nigerian boat song), 58
Evergreen, Everblue, 330
Gebeta Board, The (Ethiopian folk tale), 346
Gi'Me Elbow Room, 88
Just Like the Sun, 394
Oh Mama Bakdala (Xhosa folk song), 328
Recycle Rap, 332
Scotland's Burning, 257
Shalom Chaveyrim (Shalom, My Friends), 141
Treasure Chests, 90
Ucha Tirvarch (Little Bear Song), 53
Wang Ü Ger (Chinese fishing song), 190
William Tell (Overture) (excerpt) by G. Rossini, 64

Theme 6: Friends to Grow With
Anansi (Ashanti folk tale), 104
Ballad of the Bedbugs and the Beetles, The, 206
Bella Bimba (Pretty Girl), 172
Billy, 7
Blow, Ye Winds, Blow, 192
Boll Weevil, 171
Chan mali chan (Singaporean folk song), 10
Chicka-ma, Chicka-ma, Craney Crow, 263
Cielito lindo (Mexican folk song), 166
Circle 'Round the Zero, 267
Cornstalk Fiddle and a Shoestring Bow, 284
Crawdad Song, 107
¡Dale, dale, dale!, 378
Death of the Robin, 275
Draw a Bucket of Water, 222
Egy üveg alma (One Jar of Apples), 22
El florón (The Flower), 46
En roulant ma boule (As I Roll My Ball), 100
Frost, the Snowman, 366
Gebeta Board, The (Ethiopian folk tale), 346
Great Big House, 14
Guitar Man, The, 138
Hello!, 283
Hope by E. Dickinson (poem), 166
I'm a Believer, 312
I'm On My Way, 382
Interjections, 303
Interplanet Janet, 298
Isabela and the Troll (Spanish folk tale), 349
Jamaica Farewell, 156
Kalinka (Little Snowball Bush), 224

Kreely Kranky, 258
Kuma San (Honorable Bear), 244
Limbo Rock, 232
Little Boy of the Sheep, 188
Little Sally Walker, 105
Little Tommy Tinker, 277
Look High, Look Low, 338
Lukey's Boat, 114
Marvelous Toy, The, 182
Moon and Me, 220
Movin' Right Along, 124
Music of the World A-Turnin', 44
My Friend Tom, 364
O, The Train's Off the Track, 176
Oh, Susanna, 153
Old Barn Dance, The, 94
Old Roger, 280
Oleanna, 144
One More River, 216
One Potato, Two Potato, 267
Paw Paw Patch, The, 195
Pay Me My Money Down, 149
Polly Wolly Doodle, 132
Raccoon Dance Song, 87
Rainbow Connection, The, 310
Shepherd, Shepherd, 56
Shoo Fly Pie and Apple Pan Dowdy, 227
Simon Says, 4
Sun Don't Set in the Mornin', 48, 60
Sweet Potatoes, 16
There Was An Old Lady by D. Lee (poem), 344
This a Way and That a Way, 386
Three Is a Magic Number, 94
Three Little Birds, 204
Throw It Out the Window, 94
Tititorea (Maori Stick Game) (New Zealand folk song), 174
Trampin', 287
Ucha Tirvarch (Little Bear Song), 53
Walk by the River (song), 74, (harmony parts), 76
Way Down South by Anonymous (poem), 8
Wéané (Menadonese lullaby), 184
When I First Came to This Land, 28
Yankee Doodle, 357

Grade 4

Theme 1: You Can Do It!
Achshav (Now), 112
All Through the Night (Welsh folk song), 277
Allundé Alluia, 34
Ame fure (Rain), 26
At the Hop, 306
Bamboo Flute, 134
Bamboo, 218
Bell Doth Toll, The, 276

Thematic Correlations to Reading Series

Thematic Correlations to Reading Series (continued)

Achshav (Now), 112
Allundé Alluia, 34
Ame fure (Rain), 26
America, 354
America, My Homeland, 358
Bamboo Flute, 134
Bereza (The Birch Tree), 286
Big Bunch, a Little Bunch, 267
Buckeye Jim, 136
Built My Lady a Fine Brick House, 252
Caballito blanco (Little White Pony), 278
Cedar Swamp, 50
Chairs to Mend, 272
Chicka-hanka, 138
Chumbara, 172
Circle of Song, 330
Cotton-Eye Joe (song), 52, (countermelody), 53
Derby Ram, The, 259
Dima, 265
Dok Djampa (The White Jasmine Flower), 392
E nānā, kākou i nā manu (Look at the Birds in the Sky), 338
Eagle, 337
Early in the Morning at Eight O'Clock, 59
Eight Bells, 281
El barquito (The Tiny Boat), 214
El coquí (The Frog), 178
El manisero (Peanut Vendor), 106
El quelite (The Village), 362
Farfallina (Butterfly), 244
Frère Jacques (Are You Sleeping?), 260
Frog Went A-Courtin', 46
Girl I Left Behind Me, The, 249
Goodbye Brother, 273
Goodbye My Riley O, 257
Green Gravel, 247
Hala lala layya, 222
Heave-Ho Me Laddies, 258
Himmel und Erde (Music Alone Shall Live), 280
Hitori, 345
Hojas de té (Tea Leaves) (speech piece), 256
Hold My Mule, 248
Hop Up and Jump Up, 271
How Long the Train Been Gone?, 264
I Think I'm Going to Like It Here, 299
I Will Be Your Friend, 388
I'll Rise When the Rooster Crows, 36
It Rained a Mist, 262
It's the Hard-Knock Life, 293
Johnson Boys, 233
Just One Planet, 164
Katyusha, 188
Kettle Valley Line, The, 348
Korobushka, 285
La sanjuanerita (The Girl from San Juan), 100

La Yunsita, 350
Li'l 'Liza Jane, 20
L'inverno è già passato (Winter if Over), 390
Little David Play on Your Harp, 323
Long-Legged Sailor, 243
Love Somebody, 94
Macnamara's Band, 88
Marken er mejet (Harvest Song), 365
Molinillo de café (Little Coffee Mill) (speech piece), 250
Morning Has Broken, 22
'Most Done Ling'rin' Here, 65
My Home's in Montana, 274
N.Y.C., 302
Night Herding Song, 110
Octopus's Garden, 30
Oh, Won't You Sit Down?, 70
Old Abram Brown, 32
Old Ark's A-Moverin', 130
Old Aunt Dinah, 245
Old Carrion Crow, 192
Old House, 282
Old Joe Clark, 74
Old Paint, 275
Oliver Cromwell, 269
Oro My Bodeen, 279
Over the River and Through the Wood, 370
Over the Sea to Skye, 344
Page's Train, 246
Pat Works on the Railway, 86
Please, Mr. Postman, 44
Push Boat Song, 266
¿Quién es ese pajarito? (Who Is That Little Bird?), 284
Ridin' of a Goat, Leadin' of a Sheep, 251
Row, Row, Row Your Boat, 268
Sansa kroma, 166
Sarasponda, 210
Sea Shell, 245
Sitsiritsit, 102
Something for Me, Something for You, 4
Star-Spangled Banner, The, 356
Swapping Song, 253
Take Time in Life, 156
Tomorrow, 295
Train Is A-Coming, 270
`Ulili E (The Sandpiper), 396
Wake Up Canon, 326
Walk in the Parlor, 226
Water Come a Me Eye, 90
We Are Here, 394
We Shall Overcome, 387
When I Was Young, 187
Who's Got the Fishpole?, 261
Yankee Doodle, 154
You're Never Fully Dressed Without a Smile, 304
Zum Gali Gali, 255

Theme 4: Creative Minds
A la nanita nana (A Little Lullaby), 230
A la puerta del cielo (At the Gates of Heaven), 12
Allundé Alluia, 34
America, My Homeland, 358
Bamboo Flute, 134
Buckeye Jim, 136
Caballito blanco (Little White Pony), 278
Circle of Song, 330
Derby Ram, The, 259
Don't Let the Music Stop, 334
El manisero (Peanut Vendor), 106
Follow Your Dream, 234
Frog Went A-Courtin', 46
Girl I Left Behind Me, The, 249
Goodbye, My Riley O, 257
Happiness, 124
Happy Talk, 84
Heave-Ho, Me Laddies, 258
Hey, Look Me Over, 114
Himmel und Erde (Music Alone Shall Live), 280
Hine Ma Tov (How Good It Is), 66
Hitori, 345
I'll Rise When the Rooster Crows, 36
It's the Hard-Knock Life, 293
Johnson Boys, 233
Just One Planet, 164
Kettle Valley Line, The, 348
Korobushka, 285
Little David Play on Your Harp, 323
Love Somebody, 94
Modern Dragon, A (speech piece), 98
'Most Done Ling'rin Here, 65
My Home's in Montana, 274
Night Herding Song, 110
Oh, Won't You Sit Down?, 70
Old Ark's A-Moverin', 130
Old Carrion Crow, The, 192
Old Paint, 275
Over the Rainbow, 126
Over the Sea to Skye, 344
Pat Works on the Railway, 86
Please, Mr. Postman, 44
¿Quién es ese pajarito? (Who Is That Little Bird?), 284
Rise Up, O Flame, 283
Roll On, Columbia, 182
Row, Row, Row Your Boat, 268
Sail Away, Ladies, 54
Shabat Shalom, 170
Sing Alleluia, Allelu, 220
Swapping Song, 253
Take Time in Life, 156
Tomorrow, 295
Water Come a Me Eye, 90
We Remember, 360
We Shall Overcome, 387
What Can One Little Person Do?, 204
Yankee Doodle, 154

Thematic Correlations to Reading Series

Thematic Correlations to Reading Series

Grade 5

Theme 1: Look Inside

Thematic Correlations to Reading Series

Thematic Correlations to Reading Series (continued)

Grade 6

Theme 1: Personal Best

Thematic Correlations to Reading Series

Thematic Correlations to Reading Series (continued)

Thematic Correlations to Reading Series

Thematic Correlations to Reading Series (continued)

Thematic Correlations to Reading Series

Houghton Mifflin Reading ©2005

The following materials from *Spotlight on Music* may be used with each theme in *Houghton Mifflin Reading*.

Grade K

Theme 1: Look at Us!

Alison's Camel, T201
All Work Together, T12
Alphabet Song, T54
America, T303
Animales (Animals), T192
Battle Hymn of the Republic, T331
Bear Went Over the Mountain, The, T204
Bell Horses, T262
Best That I Can Be!, The, T48
Bickle, Bockle, 187
Bingo, T64
Bobby Shafto, T265
Bohm Dong Sahn, Gohd Dong Sahn (Spring Valley, Flower Valley), T337
Bounce High, Bounce Low, T131
Buffalo Dusk (poem), T219
Bullfrogs, Bullfrogs on Parade (poem), T183
Bus, The, T137
Bye 'n' Bye, T67
City (poem), T134
Cobbler, Cobbler, Mend My Shoe, T169
Cobbler, The (poem), T169
Colorful Dragon Boat, T328
Counting Song, T92
Doing the Weekly Walk, T78
Echo (poem), T104
Eency Weency Spider, T8
El picaflor (The Hummingbird), T141
El tambor (The Drum), T129
Excuse Us, Animals in the Zoo (poem), T195
Farmer in the Dell, The, T100
Fehér liliomszál (Little Water Lily), T139
Follow Me, T133
Follow the Leader (poem), T132
Fox, the Hen, and the Drum, The, T294
Furry Bear (poem), T205
Garden Hoedown, The, T290
Giant's Shoes, The, by E. Fallis (poem), T32
Girls and Boys, Come Out to Play (poem), T98
Git on Board, T145
Go, Go, Go, T276
Gogo, T188
Good Day Song, T50
Grizzly Bear, T252

Happy Birthday, T273
Happy Birthday, T347
Head and Shoulders, T238
Hello Song, T2
Here Is the Beehive, T258
Hickory, Dickory, Dock (poem), T49
Hinges (poem), T23
Hippopotamus, The (poem), T199
Hokey Pokey, T68
Hop, Hop, Hop, T197
Hot Dog, T69
Humming Birds (poem), T140
I Am a Little Tugboat (poem), T95
I Can't Spell Hippopotamus, T199
I Got Shoes, T33
I Know an Old Lady, T26
I Made a Valentine, T333
I Will Sing Hello, T156
If Things Grew Down (poem), T48G, T293
If You're Happy, T6
Ifetayo (Love Brings Happiness), T325
In the Barnyard (poem), T207
Instrument Game, T36
It Fell in the City (poem), T312
It's So Good to See You, T86
It's Such a Good Feeling, T282
It's You I Like, T280
Jack, Be Nimble, T88
Jack-in-the-box (poem), T251
Jack-in-the-Box, T250
Jig, Jog, Jig, Jog, T260
Juhtgarak (Chopsticks), T108
Jump or Jiggle (poem), T193
Just Like Me, T242
Kum Ba Yah, T327
La pequeñita araña (Eency Weency Spider), T9
Lady, Lady, T184
Las horas (The Hours), T70
Let's Think of Something To Do, T270
Little Blue Truck, T136
Little Ducky Duddle, T289
Little Sir Echo, T103
Little Spotted Puppy, T146
Little White Duck, T208
London Bridge, T99
Long Gone (poem), T72
Look Who's Here!, T84
Los pollitos (Little Chickens), T288
Mama, Bake the Johnnycake, T318
María Blanca, T99
Martin Luther King (speech piece), T326

Martin Luther King (speech piece), T326
Mbombela, T152
Me I Am! (poem), T346
Merrily, We Roll Along, T110
Merry-Go-Round (poem), T225
Mi chacra (My Farm), T207
Mister Sun, T343
Monkey, Monkey, T215
Monté sur un éléphant (Riding on an Elephant), T217
Muffin Man, The, T105
Mulberry Bush, The, T112
Music (poem), T157
My Grandfather, T23
My Legs and I by L. Jacobs (poem), T19
My Oak Tree, T236
My Thumbs Are Starting to Wiggle, T35
Na Bahia Tem (In Bahia Town), T163
Name Game, T57
Nampaya omame (Mothers), T128
Neat Feet (excerpt) by B. Schmidt (poem), T30
Noble Duke of York, The, T232
Oats, Peas, Beans, and Barley Grow, T287
Ɔbɔɔ Asi Me Nsa, T159
Oh, A-Hunting We Will Go, T62
Old Gray Cat, The, T43
Old MacDonald Had a Farm, T211
Old Mister Woodpecker, T172
Oliphaunt (poem), T216
One Finger, One Thumb, T38
One, Two, Tie My Shoe, T151
Only My Opinion (poem), T29
Ourchestra (poem), T171
Peace and Quiet, T278
Pimpón, T22
Planting Seeds, T284
Popalong Hopcorn! (poem), T160
Popping Corn, T161
Presidents, T330
Propel, Propel, Propel, T275
Put Your Finger in the Air, T230
Qué bonito es (How Wonderful It Is), T234
Rainbow Song, The, T61
Ride the Train, T144
Ring Around the Rosy, T246
Ring-a-ring (poem), T247
River, The, (poem), T342
Row, Row, Row, T274
Santa Clara Corn Grinding Song, T164

Thematic Correlations to Reading Series (continued)

School Is Over (poem), T84
See the Pony Galloping, T44
Seesaw, Margery Daw, T264
Shake My Sillies Out, T175
Shapes (poem), T37
Sidewalks (poem), T98
Simi Yadech (Give Me Your Hand), T168
Sing a Little Song, T179
Sing a Song of Sixpence, T111
Singing-Time (poem), T15
Snail's Pace (poem), T29
Snake and the Frog, The (story), T297
Snow Toward Evening (poem), T311
Snowman, The, T313
Something About Me (poem), T13
Speedy Delivery, T279
Spell of the Moon (poem), T116
Stamping Land, T24
Sweetly Sings the Donkey, T244
Table Manners (poem), T107
Taking Off (poem), T134
Ten in a Bed, T256
Ten Little Frogs, T240
Tengo, Tengo, Tengo (I Have, I Have, I Have), T212
They Were Tall, T53
This Is My City, T120
This Is What I Can Do, T124
Three Little Kittens, T148
Three Little Muffins (speech piece), T127
Time to Sing, T16
Toodala, T39
Touch Your Shoulders, T254
Travel (poem), T144
Tree of Peace (speech piece), T321
Tugboat, T95
Twinkle, Twinkle, Little Star, T90
Umoja! (poem), T325
Ushkana, T75
Wait and See, T334
Walk to School, T18
Wavvuuvuumira (Mister Bamboo Bug), T165
We Are Playing in the Forest, T248
Willoughby Wallaby Woo, T241
Won't You Be My Neighbor?, T268
Woodpecker, The (poem), T172
Worms, T286
Y ahora vamos a cantar (Now We Are Going to Sing), T340
You're a Grand Old Flag, T4

Theme 2: Colors All Around

Alison's Camel, T201
All Work Together, T12
Alphabet Song, T54
America, T303
Animales (Animals), T192
Battle Hymn of the Republic, T331

Bear Went Over the Mountain, The, T204
Bell Horses, T262
Best That I Can Be!, The, T48
Bickle, Bockle, 187
Bingo, T64
Bobby Shafto, T265
Bohm Dong Sahn Gohd Dong Sahn (Spring Valley, Flower Valley), T337
Bounce High, Bounce Low, T131
Buffalo Dusk (poem), T219
Bullfrogs, Bullfrogs on Parade (poem), T183
Bus, The, T137
Bye 'n' Bye, T68
City (poem), T134
Cobbler, Cobbler, Mend My Shoe, T169
Cobbler, The (poem), T169
Colorful Dragon Boat, T328
Counting Song, T92
Deedle, Deedle Dumpling (poem), T87
Doing the Weekly Walk, T78
Echo (poem), T104
Eency Weency Spider, T8
El picaflor (The Hummingbird), T141
El tambor (The Drum), T129
Excuse Us, Animals in the Zoo (poem), T195
Farmer in the Dell, The, T100
Fehér liliomszál (Little Water Lily), T139
Follow Me, T133
Follow the Leader (poem), T132
Furry Bear (poem), T205
Garden Hoedown, The, T290
Girls and Boys, Come Out to Play (poem), T98
Git on Board, T145
Go, Go, Go, T276
Gogo, T188
Good Day Song, T50
Grizzly Bear, T252
Happy Birthday, T273
Happy Birthday, T347
Head and Shoulders, T238
Hello Song, T2
Here Is the Beehive, T258
Hickory, Dickory, Dock (poem), T49
Hinges (poem), T23
Hippopotamus, The (poem), T199
Hokey Pokey, T68
Hop, Hop, Hop, T197
Hot Dog, T69
Humming Birds (poem), T140
I Am a Little Tugboat (poem), T95
I Can't Spell Hippopotamus, T199
I Got Shoes, T33
I Know an Old Lady, T26
I Made a Valentine, T333
I Will Sing Hello, T156
If Things Grew Down (poem), T48G, T293

If You're Happy, T6
Ifetayo (Love Brings Happiness), T325
In the Barnyard (poem), T207
Instrument Game, T36
It Fell in the City (poem), T312
It's So Good to See You, T86
It's Such a Good Feeling, T282
It's You I Like, T280
Jack, Be Nimble, T88
Jack-in-the-box (poem), T251
Jack-in-the-Box, T250
Jig Jog, Jig Jog, T260
Juhtgarak (Chopsticks), T108
Jump or Jiggle (poem), T193
Just Like Me, T242
Kum Ba Yah, T327
La pequeñita araña (Eency Weency Spider), T9
Lady, Lady, T184
Las horas (The Hours), T70
Let's Think of Something To Do, T270
Little Blue Truck, T136
Little Ducky Duddle, T289
Little Sir Echo, T103
Little Spotted Puppy, T146
Little White Duck, T208
London Bridge, T99
Long Gone (poem), T72
Look Who's Here!, T84
Los pollitos (Little Chickens), T288
Mama, Bake the Johnnycake, T318
María Blanca, T99
Martin Luther King (speech piece), T326
Mbombela, T152
Me I Am! (poem), T346
Merrily, We Roll Along, T110
Merry-Go-Round (poem), T225
Merry-Go-Round, The, T224
Mi chacra (My Farm), T207
Mister Sun, T343
Monkey, Monkey, T215
Monté sur un éléphant (Riding on an Elephant), T217
Muffin Man, The, T105
Mulberry Bush, The, T112
Music (poem), T157
My Grandfather, T23
My Oak Tree, T236
My Thumbs Are Starting to Wiggle, T35
Na Bahia Tem (In Bahia Town), T163
Name Game, T57
Name Game, T58
Nampaya omame (Mothers), T128
Noble Duke of York, The, T232
Oats, Peas, Beans and Barley Grow, T287
Ɔbɔɔ Asi Me Nsa, T159
Oh, A-Hunting We Will Go, T62
Old Gray Cat, The, T43
Old MacDonald Had a Farm, T211

Thematic Correlations to Reading Series (continued)

Old Mister Woodpecker, T172
Oliphaunt (poem), T216
One Finger, One Thumb, T38
One, Two, Tie My Shoe, T151
Only My Opinion (poem), T29
Ourchestra (poem), T171
Peace and Quiet, T278
Pimpón, T22
Planting Seeds, T284
Popalong Hopcorn! (poem), T160
Popping Corn, T161
Prairie Dog Song (Kiowa Children's Song), T220
Presidents, T330
Propel, Propel, Propel, T275
Put Your Finger in the Air, T230
Qué bonito es (How Wonderful It Is), T234
Rainbow Song, The, T61
Ride the Train, T144
Ring Around the Rosy, T246
Ring-a-ring (poem), T247
River, The, (poem), T342
Row, Row, Row, T274
Running Song (excerpt) by M. Ridlon (poem), T98
Santa Clara Corn Grinding Song, T164
School Is Over (poem), T84
See the Pony Galloping, T44
Seesaw, Margery Daw, T265
Shake My Sillies Out, T175
Shapes (poem), T37
Sidewalks (poem), T98
Simi Yadech (Give Me Your Hand), T168
Sing a Little Song, T179
Sing a Song of Sixpence, T111
Singing-Time (poem), T15
Snail's Pace (poem), T29
Snake and the Frog, The (story), T297
Snow Toward Evening (poem), T311
Snowman, The, T313
Speedy Delivery, T279
Spell of the Moon (poem), T116
Stamping Land, T24
Sweetly Sings the Donkey, T244
Table Manners (poem), T107
Taking Off (poem), T134
Ten in a Bed, T256
Ten Little Frogs, T240
Tengo, Tengo, Tengo (I Have, I Have, I Have), T212
They Were Tall, T53
This Is My City, T120
This Is What I Can Do, T124
Three Little Kittens, T148
Three Little Muffins, T127
Time to Sing, T16
Toodala, T39
Touch Your Shoulders, T254
Travel (poem), T144

Tree of Peace (speech piece), T321
Tugboat, T95
Twinkle, Twinkle, Little Star, T90
Umoja! (poem), T325
Ushkana (Damsel Fly Song), T75
Wait and See, T334
Walk to School, T18
Wavvuuvuumira (Mister Bamboo Bug), T165
We Are Playing in the Forest, T248
What You Gonna Call Your Pretty Baby?, T319
When You Send a Valentine, T332
Willoughby Wallaby Woo, T241
Won't You Be My Neighbor?, T268
Woodpecker, The (poem), T172
Worms, T286
Y ahora vamos a cantar (Now We Are Going to Sing), T340
You're a Grand Old Flag, T4

Theme 3: We're a Family

Alison's Camel, T201
All Work Together, T12
Alphabet Song, T54
America, T303
Animales (Animals), T192
Battle Hymn of the Republic, T331
Bear Went Over the Mountain, The, T204
Bell Horses, T262
Best That I Can Be!, The, T48
Bickle, Bockle, T187
Bingo, T64
Bobby Shafto, T265
Bohm Dong Sahn Gohd Dong Sahn (Spring Valley, Flower Valley), T337
Bounce High, Bounce Low, T131
Buffalo Dusk (poem), T219
Bullfrogs, Bullfrogs on Parade (poem), T183
Bus, The, T137
Bye 'n' Bye, T67
City (poem), T134
Cobbler, Cobbler, Mend My Shoe, T169
Cobbler, The (poem), T169
Colorful Dragon Boat, T328
Counting Song, T92
Doing the Weekly Walk, T78
Echo (poem), T104
Eency Weency Spider, T8
El picaflor (The Hummingbird), T141
El tambor (The Drum), T129
Excuse Us, Animals in the Zoo (poem), T195
Farmer in the Dell, The, T100
Fehér liliomszál (Little Water Lily), T139
Follow Me, T133
Follow the Leader (poem), T132
Fox, the Hen, and the Drum, The, T294

Furry Bear (poem), T205
Garden Hoedown, The, T290
Girls and Boys, Come Out to Play (poem), T98
Git on Board, T145
Go, Go, Go, T276
Gogo, T188
Good Day Song, T50
Grizzly Bear, T252
Happy Birthday, T273
Happy Birthday, T347
Head and Shoulders, T238
Hello Song, T2
Here Is the Beehive, T258
Hickory, Dickory, Dock (poem), T49
Hinges (poem), T23
Hippopotamus, The (poem), T199
Hokey Pokey, T68
Hop, Hop, Hop, T197
Hot Dog, T69
Humming Birds (poem), T140
I Am a Little Tugboat (poem), T95
I Can't Spell Hippopotamus, T199
I Got Shoes, T33
I Know an Old Lady, T26
I Made a Valentine, T333
I Will Sing Hello, T156
If Things Grew Down (poem), T48G, T293
If You're Happy, T6
Ifetayo (Love Brings Happiness), T325
In the Barnyard (poem), T207
Instrument Game, T36
It Fell in the City (poem), T312
It's So Good to See You, T86
It's Such a Good Feeling, T282
It's You I Like, T280
Jack, Be Nimble, T88
Jack-in-the-box (poem), T251
Jack-in-the-Box, T250
Jig Jog, Jig Jog, T260
Juhtgarak (Chopsticks), T108
Jump or Jiggle (poem), T193
Just Like Me, T242
Kum Ba Yah, T327
La pequeñita araña (Eency Weency Spider), T9
Lady, Lady, T184
Las horas (The Hours), T70
Let's Think of Something To Do, T270
Little Blue Truck, T136
Little Ducky Duddle, T289
Little Sir Echo, T103
Little Spotted Puppy, T146
Little White Duck, T208
London Bridge, T99
Long Gone (poem), T72
Look Who's Here!, T84
Los pollitos (Little Chickens), T288
Mama, Bake the Johnnycake, T318
María Blanca, T99

Martin Luther King (speech piece), T326

Mbombela, T152

Me I Am! (poem), T346

Merrily, We Roll Along, T110

Merry-Go-Round (poem), T225

Merry-Go-Round, The, T224

Mi chacra (My Farm), T207

Mister Sun, T343

Mister Sun, T343

Monkey, Monkey, T215

Monté sur un éléphant (Riding on an Elephant), T217

Muffin Man, The, T105

Mulberry Bush, The, T112

Music (poem), T157

My Grandfather, T23

My Oak Tree, T236

My Thumbs are Starting to Wiggle, T35

Na Bahia Tem (In Bahia Town), T163

Name Game, T57

Nampaya omame (Mothers), T128

Noble Duke of York, The, T232

Oats, Peas, Beans, and Barley Grow, T287

Ɔbɔɔ Asi Me Nsa, T159

Oh, A-Hunting We Will Go, T62

Old Gray Cat, The, T43

Old MacDonald Had a Farm, T211

Old Mister Woodpecker, T172

Oliphaunt (poem), T216

One Finger, One Thumb, T38

One, Two, Tie My Shoe, T151

Only My Opinion (poem), T29

Ourchestra (poem), T171

Peace and Quiet, T278

Pimpón, T22

Planting Seeds, T284

Popalong Hopcorn! (poem), T160

Popping Corn, T161

Presidents, T330

Propel, Propel, Propel, T275

Put Your Finger in the Air, T230

Qué bonito es (How Wonderful It Is), T234

Rainbow Song, The, T61

Ride the Train, T144

Ring Around the Rosy, T246

Ring-a-ring (poem), T247

River, The, (poem), T342

Row, Row, Row, T274

Santa Clara Corn Grinding Song, T164

School Is Over (poem), T84

See the Pony Galloping, T44

Seesaw, Margery Daw, T265

Shake My Sillies Out, T175

Shapes (poem), T37

Sidewalks (poem), T98

Simi Yadech (Give Me Your Hand), T168

Sing a Little Song, T179

Sing a Song of Sixpence, T111

Singing-Time (poem), T15

Snail's Pace (poem), T29

Snake and the Frog, The (story), T297

Snow Toward Evening (poem), T311

Snowman, The, T313

Speedy Delivery, T279

Spell of the Moon (poem), T116

Stamping Land, T24

Sweetly Sings the Donkey, T244

Table Manners (poem), T107

Taking Off (poem), T134

Ten in a Bed, T256

Ten Little Frogs, T240

Tengo, Tengo, Tengo (I Have, I Have, I Have), T212

They Were Tall, T53

This Is My City, T120

This Is What I Can Do, T124

Three Little Kittens, T148

Three Little Muffins, T127

Time to Sing, T16

Toodala, T39

Touch Your Shoulders, T254

Travel (poem), T144

Tree of Peace (speech piece), T321

Tugboat, T95

Twinkle, Twinkle, Little Star, T90

Umoja! (poem), T325

Ushkana (Damsel Fly Song), T75

Wait and See, T334

Walk to School, T18

Wavvuuvuumira (Mister Bamboo Bug), T165

We Are Playing in the Forest, T248

Willoughby Wallaby Woo, T241

Won't You Be My Neighbor?, T268

Woodpecker, The (poem), T172

Worms, T286

Y ahora vamos a cantar (Now We Are Going to Sing), T340

You're a Grand Old Flag, T4

Theme 4: Friends Together

All Work Together, T12

Alphabet Song, The, T54

America, T303

Battle Hymn of the Republic, T331

Best That I Can Be!, The, T48

Bickle, Bockle, T187

Go, Go, Go, T276

Happy Birthday, Happy Birthday, T273

Hello Song, T2

I Will Sing Hello, T156

If You're Happy, T6

Ifetayo (Love Brings Happiness), T325

It's So Good to See You, T86

It's Such a Good Feeling, T282

It's You I Like, T280

Just Like Me, T242

London Bridge, T99

Look Who's Here!, T84

Mbombela (The Train Comes), T152

Muffin Man, The, T105

Mulberry Bush, The, T112

My Grandfather, T23

Nampaya omame (Mothers), T128

One Finger, One Thumb, T46

One, Two, Tie My Shoe, T150

Ourchestra by S. Silverstein (poem), T171

Peace and Quiet, T278

Pimpón, T22

School Is Over by K. Greenaway (poem), T85

Simi Yadech (Give Me Your Hand), T168

Spinning Song by C. Shields (poem), T67

They Were Tall, T53

Time to Sing, T16

Umoja! by M. Evans (poem), T325

Walk to School, T18

Won't You Be My Neighbor?, T268

Y ahora vamos a cantar (Now We Are Going to Sing), T340

Theme 5: Let's Count!

America, T303

Battle Hymn of the Republic, T331

Cobbler, Cobbler, Mend My Shoe, T169

Cobbler, The, by E. Chafee (poem), T255

I Will Sing Hello, T156

If You're Happy, T6

It's Such a Good Feeling, T282

It's You I Like, T280

Let's Think of Something to Do, T270

One Finger, One Thumb, T46

Ourchestra by S. Silverstein (poem), T171

Speedy Delivery, T279

Spinning Song by C. Shields (poem), T67

When You Send a Valentine, T332

Theme 6: Sunshine and Raindrops

Bohm Dong Sahn, Gohd Dong Sahn (Spring Valley, Flower Valley), T337

Bye 'n' Bye, T67

City by L. Hughes (poem), T134

Days of the Week, T81

Echo by W. de la Mare (poem), T104

Eency Weency Spider, T8

Fehér liliomszál (Little Water Lily), T139

Here Is the Beehive, T258

If Things Grew Down by R. Hoeft (poem), T292

It Fell in the City by E. Merriam (poem), T312

Lady, Lady, T184

Little Sir Echo, T103
Mi chacra (My Farm), T207
Mister Sun, T343
My Oak Tree, T236
North Winds Blow, T305
Rainbow Song, The, T61
River, The, by C. Zolotow (poem), T342
Sidewalks by P. Hubbell (poem), T98
Sing a Little Song, T179
Snow Toward Evening by M. Cane (poem), T311
Snowman, The, T313
Spell of the Moon (excerpt) by L. Norris (poem), T116
Twinkle, Twinkle, Little Star, T90

Theme 7: Wheels Go Around
Bus, The, T137
Cobbler, Cobbler, Mend My Shoe, T169
Cobbler, The, by E. Chafee (poem), T255
I Am a Little Tugboat by C. Huffman (poem), T144
Jig, Jog, Jig, Jog, T260
Let's Think of Something to Do, T270
Little Blue Truck, T136
Merry-Go-Round by R. Field (poem), T223
Merry-Go-Round, The, T225
Na Bahia Tem (In Bahia Town), T163
Ride the Train, T144
Speedy Delivery, T279
Taking Off by M. Green (poem), T134
Travel by E. St. Vincent Millay (poem), T144
Tugboat, T95
We Are Playing in the Forest, T248

Theme 8: Down on the Farm
Alison's Camel, T201
All Work Together, T12
Alphabet Song, T54
America, T303
Animal Rhythms (poem), T56
Animales (Animals), T192
Battle Hymn of the Republic, T331
Bear Went Over the Mountain, The, T204
Bell Horses, T262
Best That I Can Be!, The, T48
Bickle, Bockle, 187
Bingo, T64
Bobby Shafto, T265
Bohm Dong Sahn, Gohd Dong Sahn (Spring Valley, Flower Valley), T337
Bounce High, Bounce Low, T131
Buffalo Dusk (poem), T219
Bullfrogs, Bullfrogs on Parade (poem), T183
Bus, The, T137
Bye 'n' Bye, T67

City (poem), T134
Cobbler, Cobbler, Mend My Shoe, T169
Cobbler, The (poem), T169
Cobbler, The, by E. Chafee (poem), T255
Colorful Dragon Boat, T328
Counting Song, T92
Doing the Weekly Walk, T78
Echo (poem), T104
Eency Weency Spider, T8
El picaflor (The Hummingbird), T141
El tambor (The Drum), T129
Excuse Us, Animals in the Zoo (poem), T195
Farmer in the Dell, The, T100
Fehér liliomszál (Little Water Lily), T139
Follow Me, T133
Follow the Leader (poem), T132
Fox, the Hen, and the Drum, The, T294
Furry Bear (poem), T205
Garden Hoedown, The, T290
Girls and Boys, Come Out to Play (poem), T98
Git on Board, T145
Go, Go, Go, T276
Gogo, T188
Good Day Song, T50
Grizzly Bear, T252
Happy Birthday, T273
Happy Birthday, T347
Head and Shoulders, T238
Hello Song, T2
Here Is the Beehive, T258
Hickory, Dickory, Dock (poem), T49
Hinges (poem), T23
Hippopotamus, The (poem), T199
Hokey Pokey, T68
Hop, Hop, Hop, T197
Hot Dog, T69
Humming Birds (poem), T140
I Am a Little Tugboat (poem), T95
I Can't Spell Hippopotamus, T199
I Got Shoes, T33
I Know an Old Lady, T26
I Made a Valentine, T333
I Will Sing Hello, T156
If Things Grew Down (poem), T48G, T293
If You're Happy, T6
Ifetayo (Love Brings Happiness), T325
In the Barnyard (poem), T207
Instrument Game, T36
It Fell in the City (poem), T312
It's So Good to See You, T86
It's Such a Good Feeling, T282
It's You I Like, T280
Jack, Be Nimble, T88
Jack-in-the-box (poem), T251
Jack-in-the-Box, T250
Jig Jog, Jig Jog, T260

Juhtgarak (Chopsticks), T108
Jump or Jiggle (poem), T193
Just Like Me, T242
Kangaroo, The (poem), T196
Kangaroo, The, T197
Kum Ba Yah, T327
La pequeñita araña (Eency Weency Spider), T9
Lady, Lady, T184
Las horas (The Hours), T70
Let's Think of Something To Do, T270
Little Blue Truck, T136
Little Ducky Duddle, T289
Little Sir Echo, T103
Little Spotted Puppy, T146
Little White Duck, T208
London Bridge, T99
Long Gone (poem), T72
Look Who's Here!, T84
Los pollitos (Little Chickens), T288
Mama, Bake the Johnnycake, T318
María Blanca, T99
Martin Luther King (speech piece), T326
Mbombela, T152
Me I Am! (poem), T346
Merrily, We Roll Along, T110
Merry-Go-Round (poem), T225
Merry-Go-Round, The, T224
Mi chacra (My Farm), T207
Mister Sun, T343
Mister Sun, T343
Monkey, Monkey, T215
Monté sur un éléphant (Riding on an Elephant), T217
Muffin Man, The, T105
Mulberry Bush, The, T112
Music (poem), T157
My Grandfather, T23
My Oak Tree, T236
My Thumbs Are Starting to Wiggle, T35
Na Bahia Tem (In Bahia Town), T163
Name Game, T57
Nampaya omame (Mothers), T128
Noble Duke of York, The, T232
Oats, Peas, Beans and Barley Grow, T287
Ɔbɔɔ Asi Me Nsa, T159
Oh, A-Hunting We Will Go, T62
Old Gray Cat, The, T43
Old MacDonald Had a Farm, T207
Old Mister Woodpecker, T172
Oliphaunt (poem), T216
One Finger, One Thumb, T38
One, Two, Tie My Shoe, T151
Only My Opinion (poem), T29
Ourchestra (poem), T171
Peace and Quiet, T278
Pimpón, T22
Planting Seeds, T284

Thematic Correlations to Reading Series (continued)

Popalong Hopcorn! (poem), T160
Popping Corn, T161
Prairie Dog Song (Kiowa Children's Song), T220
Presidents, T330
Propel, Propel, Propel, T275
Put Your Finger in the Air, T230
Qué bonito es (How Wonderful It Is), T234
Rainbow Song, The, T61
Ride the Train, T144
Ring Around the Rosy, T246
Ring-a-ring (poem), T247
River, The, (poem), T342
Row, Row, Row, T274
Santa Clara Corn Grinding Song, T164
School Is Over (poem), T84
See the Pony Galloping, T44
Seesaw, Margery Daw, T265
Shake My Sillies Out, T175
Shapes (poem), T37
Sidewalks (poem), T98
Simi Yadech (Give Me Your Hand), T168
Sing a Little Song, T179
Sing a Song of Sixpence, T111
Singing-Time (poem), T15
Snail's Pace (poem), T29
Snake and the Frog, The (story), T297
Snow Toward Evening (poem), T311
Snowman, The, T313
Speedy Delivery, T279
Spell of the Moon (poem), T116
Stamping Land, T24
Sweetly Sings the Donkey, T244
Table Manners (poem), T107
Taking Off (poem), T134
Ten in a Bed, T256
Ten Little Frogs, T240
Tengo, Tengo, Tengo (I Have, I Have, I Have), T212
They Were Tall, T53
This Is My City, T120
This Is What I Can Do, T124
Three Little Kittens, T148
Three Little Muffins, T127
Time to Sing, T16
Toodala, T39
Touch Your Shoulders, T254
Travel (poem), T144
Tree of Peace (speech piece), T321
Tugboat, T95
Twinkle, Twinkle, Little Star, T90
Umoja! (poem), T325
Ushkana, T75
Wait and See, T334
Walk to School, T18
Wavvuuvvuumira (Mister Bamboo Bug), T165
We Are Playing in the Forest, T248
Willoughby Wallaby Woo, T241
Won't You Be My Neighbor?, T268

Woodpecker, The (poem), T172
Worms, T286
Y ahora vamos a cantar (Now We Are Going to Sing), T340
You're a Grand Old Flag, T4

Theme 9: Spring Is Here

Bobby Shafto, T265
Bohm Dong Sahn, Gohd Dong Sahn (Spring Valley, Flower Valley), T337
Colorful Dragon Boat, T328
Days of the Week, T81
Echo by W. de la Mare (poem), T104
Eency Weency Spider, T8
Fehér liliomszál (Little Water Lily), T139
If Things Grew Down by R. Hoeft (poem), T292
Lady, Lady, T184
Merrily, We Roll Along, T110
Mister Sun, T343
My Oak Tree, T236
North Winds Blow, T305
Propel, Propel, Propel, T275
Rainbow Song, The, T61
River, The, by C. Zolotow (poem), T342
Row, Row, Row, T274
Sing a Little Song, T179
Snow Toward Evening by M. Cane (poem), T311
Snowman, The, T313
Spell of the Moon (excerpt) by L. Norris (poem), T116
Twinkle, Twinkle, Little Star, T90

Theme 10: A World of Animals

Alison's Camel, T201
Animal Rhythms (poem), T56
Animales (Animals), T192
Bear Went Over the Mountain, The, T204
Bingo, T64
Buffalo Dusk by C. Sandburg (poem), T219
Bullfrogs, Bullfrogs on Parade by J. Prelutsky (poem), T183
Counting Song, T92
El picaflor (The Hummingbird), T141
Excuse Us, Animals in the Zoo by A. Wynne (poem), T195
Fox, the Hen, and the Drum, The (Indian fable), T294
Furry Bear by A. A. Milne (poem), T205
Good Day Song, T50
Grizzly Bear, T252
Hickory, Dickory, Dock (poem), T49
Hippopotamus, The, by J. Prelutsky (poem), T199
Hot Dog, T69
Humming Birds by B. Sage (poem), T140
In the Barnyard by D. Aldis (poem), T207

Kangaroo, The, by E. Coatsworth (poem), T196
Kangaroo, The, T196
La pequeñita araña (Eency Weency Spider), T9
Little Spotted Puppy, T146
Little White Duck, T208
Los pollitos (Little Chickens), T288
Mayflies by P. Fleischmann (poem), T76
Mi chacra (My Farm), T207
Monkey, Monkey (speech piece), T215
Monté sur un éléphant (Riding on an Elephant), T218
Oh, A-Hunting We Will Go, T62
Old Gray Cat, The, T43
Old MacDonald Had a Farm, T207
Old Mister Woodpecker, T172
Oliphaunt by J. R. R. Tolkien (poem), T216
Prairie Dog Song (Kiowa children's song), T220
Santa Clara Corn Grinding Song, T164
See the Pony Galloping, T44
Snail's Pace by A. Fisher (poem), T29
Snake and the Frog, The (story), T297
Sweetly Sings the Donkey, T244
Tengo, Tengo, Tengo (I Have, I Have, I Have), T212
Three Little Kittens, T146
Ushkana (Damselfly Song), T75
Wavvuuvvuumira (Mister Bamboo Bug), T165
Woodpecker, The, by E. Roberts (poem), T173
Worms, T286

Grade 1

Theme 1: All Together Now

A be ce (A B C), T213
A la rueda rueda ('Round and 'Round), T240
Acka Backa, T256
¡Adivina lo que es! (Guess What It Is), T170
All Night, All Day, T232
America, T326
Animal Song, T288
Another Busy Day, T41
Ants Go Marching, The, T22
Apple a Day, An (poem), T152
Apples and Bananas, T151
Arre, mi burrito (Gid'yup, Little Burrito), T257
Autumn Leaves Are Falling, T330
Autumn Leaves, T331
Bear Hunt (speech piece), T126
Bear Went Over the Mountain, The, T115
Bee, Bee, Bumblebee, T250

Thematic Correlations to Reading Series (continued)

Best Friends, T222

Big and Small (speech piece), T200

Bluebells, T209

Bonjour, mes amis (Hello, My Friends), T18

Bonjour, mes amis (Hello, My Friends), T18

Boris, the Singing Bear, T312

Bow-Wow (poem), T81

Brinca la tablita (Hop, Hop!), T71

Brush Your Teeth (song), T66, (speech piece), T67

Bug (poem), T167

But the Critter Got Away (speech piece), T88

Butterfly, Flutter By, T333

Call of the Wild, A (excerpt) (poem), T139

Caribbean Amphibian, T294

Categories, T146

Chang (Elephant), T199

Charlie Over the Ocean, T75

Chase the Squirrel, T88

Chickery Chick, T292

Clap Your Hands, T246

Come Back, My Little Chicks, T134

Cookies, T277

Counting Song, T195

Cow, The (poem), T236

Cut the Cake, T232

Dance Myself to Sleep, T314

Diana (Play the Bugle), T334

Diou Shou Juan'er (Hiding a Handkerchief), T212

Double This (speech piece), T95

Down by the Bay, T48

Down the Hill, T281

Dragonfly (poem), T44

Duérmete mi niño (Go to Sleep, My Baby), T61

Ears, Far and Near (poem), T16

El florón (The Flower), T117

El juego chirimbolo (The Chirimbolo Game), T103

Field of Joys, T224

Five Little Pumpkins (poem), T337

George Washington, T368

Gilly, Gilly, Gilly Good Morning, T12

Go A Tin (Lantern Song), T363

Goin' to the Zoo, T192

Granny (speech piece), T104

Grasshoppers Three, T284

Green Grass Grows All Around, The, T148

Hakyo jong (School Bells), T302

Happiest Street in the World, The, T304

Head and Shoulders, Baby, T40

Hello, There!, T230

Here Comes the Band (poem), T80

Here We Sit, T251

Hey, Children, Who's in Town?, T14

Hi! My Name Is Joe (rhythmic pattern), T220

Hi! My Name Is Joe! (speech piece), T220

Hoo, Hoo!, T55

Hop! Chirp! Moo! Oh, Happy Springtime Day!, T372

Hopping Frog (poem), T113

Horses of the Sea, The (poem), T179

How Does Your Garden Grow?, T144

Hunt the Cows, T236

I Am Slowly Going Crazy, T127

I Had a Little Hen (nursery rhyme), T136

I Have a Friend (poem), T225

I Like (poem), T110

I Like Spinach, T163

I Love My Country, T328

I Wanna Be a Friend of Yours, T84

I'd Like to Be a Lighthouse (poem), T238

I'm Getting Sick of Peanut Butter (poem), T219

I've a Pair of Fishes, T124

Ice (poem), T346

If All the World Were Paper, T296

In My Little Motor Boat, T159

It's So Nice on the Ice, T346

Jambo (Hello), T230

John the Rabbit, T74

Johnny Works with One Hammer, T96

Johnny's Flea, T158

Jump or Jiggle (poem), T316

Jump, Jim Joe, T89

Kaeru no Uta, T112

Kari (Wild Geese), T261

Kobuta, T168

La ranita cri (The Little Frog Croaks), T27

Ladybugs' Picnic, T290

Lavender's Blue, T174

Legend of George Washington and the Cherry Tree, The (story), T369

Let's Go Driving, T52

Library Song, T42

Little Black Bug, T166

Little Red Caboose, T97

Little Robin Redbreast, T208

Locust, The (poem), T285

Looby Loo, T262

Love Grows, T202

Love Is the Magic Word, T366

Lucy Lockett, T253

Mail Myself to You, T366

Marco Polo (speech piece), T90

Martin Luther King, T360

Mary's Coal Black Lamb, T286

Mi cuerpo (My Body), T32

Miss Mary Mack, T15

Mizuguruma (The Water Wheel), T260

Mos', Mos'! (Cat, Cat!), T53

My Feet (poem), T264

My Kite (poem), T371

My Mama's Calling Me, T54

My Mom, T372

Na Bahia Tem (In Bahia Town), T297

Naming Things (poem), T221

Naranja dulce (Sweet Orange), T303

Naughty Kitty Cat, T171

Night Comes… (poem), T233

No One Like You, T300

O Wind (poem), T235

Old King Glory, T217

Old Mother Goose (poem), T181

One Little Elephant, T194

One, Two, Three, Four, Five, T265

One, Two, Three, Four, T123

Oranges and Lemons (poem), T150

Over in the Meadow, T78

Pat Pat Patty Pat, T308

Peanut Butter, T218

Pease Porridge Hot, T255

Pile of Stuff, A (story), T188

Piñata Song (poem), T153

Piñón, Pirulín, T311

Pitty Patty Polt (speech piece), T180

Plenty Fishes in the Sea, T310

Puddle Hopping, T60

Pumpkin Song, T342

Punchinella, T216

Pusa't daga (Cat and Rat), T289

Quaker, Quaker, T100

Rabbit in the Moon, The (folktale), T318

Rabbit, The (poem), T186

Rain Sizes (poem), T33

Rain, Rain, Go Away, T259

Rattlesnake, T185

Rig a Jig Jig, T116

Rise, Sally, Rise, T162

Romper, Stomper, and Boo (story), T36

Sailor Went to Sea, Sea, Sea, A (song), T38, (game), T39

Sara Watashi (Plate Passing), T66

Seeds (vocal and instrumental), T120

Seesaw, T242

Serra, Serra Serrador (Saw, Saw, Lumberjack), T133

Shoo, Turkey, T76

Simple Simon, T175

Sing After Me, T34

Sing Ho! For the Life of a Bear! (poem), T114

Sittin' Down to Eat, T182

Sitting in the Sand (poem), T374

Six Little Ducks, T64

Skip to My Lou, T102

Sleep, Bonnie Bairnie, T27

Snail With the Mail, T275

Snail, Snail, T252

Somebody Come and Play, T92

Somebody Has To… (poem), T258

Something Funny Outside, T338

Something Told the Wild Geese (poem), T261

Soup, Soup!, T358

Spanish Days of the Week by Anonymous (poem), T108

Spotlight on America, T9

Spring, T273

Star Light, Star Bright, T258

Summertime from *Porgy and Bess*, T375

Swing, The (poem), T109

Tailor, Tailor (poem), T132

Tak for Maden (Thanks for Food), T343

Tako No Uta (The Kite Song), T370

Theme from *Sesame Street*, T298

There Are Many Flags in Many Lands, T329

There's a Hole in the Middle of the Sea, T178

This Little Light of Mine, T238

This Old Man, T306

Thoughts of a Rattlesnake (poem), T185

Time for Love, A, T347

Tinker, Tailor, T130

Tisket A Tasket, A, T107

Twenty-four Robbers, T173

Two, Four, Six, Eight, T246

Uga, Uga, Uga (Cake, Cake, Cake), T313

Una Adivinanza (A Riddle), T138

Untitled (Butterflies) (haiku), T332

Up the Hill (poem), T45

Up the Tree and Down Again (poem), T65

Wake Me, Shake Me, T198

We All Sing With the Same Voice, T156

What's Your Name?, T125

Wheels, Wheels, Wheels (poem), T106

When the Flag Goes By, T327

Who's Afraid of the Big Bad Wolf? (nursery rhyme), T137

Why the Beetle Has a Gold Coat (folktale), T321

Willum, T19

Wind Blew East, The, T234

Wind Blow, T187

Wings (poem), T250

Wings by A. Fisher (poem), T250

Year With Frog and Toad, A (Reprise), T283

Year With Frog and Toad, A, T270

Yo, Mamana, Yo (Oh, Mama), T307

Zui Zui Zukkorbashi (song), T98, (game), T99

Theme 2: Surprise!

¡Adivina lo que es! (Guess What It Is!), T170

Brinca la tablita (Hop, Hop!), T71

Bug by L. Simmie (poem), T167

Chickery Chick, T292

Dance Myself to Sleep, T314

Diana, T334

Five Little Pumpkins (traditional poem), T337

Go A Tin (Lantern Song), T363

Here Comes the Band by W. Cole (poem), T80

I Am Slowly Going Crazy, T127

I'd Like to Be a Lighthouse by R Field (poem), T238

I'm Getting Sick of Peanut Butter by K. Nesbitt (poem), T219

If All the World Were Paper, T296

In My Little Motor Boat, T159

It's So Nice on the Ice, T346

Lavender's Blue, T174

Let's Go Driving, T52

Marco Polo (speech piece), T90

My Kite by B. Brown and B. Brown (poem), T371

Naming Things by A. Davidson (poem), T221

Pat Pat Patty Pat, T308

Puddle Hopping, T60

Pumpkin Song, T342

Rabbit, The, by M. Stelmach (poem), T186

Rattlesnake, T185

Seesaw (song), T242, (accompaniment), T248

Sing After Me, T34

Sing Ho! For the Life of a Bear! By A.A. Milne (poem), T114

Sitting in the Sand by K. Kushkin (poem), T374

Skip to My Lou, T102

Somebody Come and Play, T92

Somebody Has To... by S. Silverstein (poem), T258

Something Funny Outside, T338

Swing, The, by R. L. Stevenson (poem), T109

Tak for Maden (Thanks for Food), T343

Tako No Uta (The Kite Song), T370

Thoughts of a Rattlesnake by K. Sexton (poem), T185

Theme 3: Let's Look Around!

A be ce (A B C), T213

A la rueda rueda ('Round and 'Round), T240

Acka Backa, T256

¡Adivina lo que es! (Guess What It Is), T170

All Night, All Day, T232

America, T326

Animal Song, T288

Another Busy Day, T41

Ants Go Marching, The, T22

Apple a Day, An (poem), T152

Apples and Bananas, T151

Arre, mi burrito (Gid'yup, Little Burrito), T257

Autumn Leaves Are Falling, T330

Autumn Leaves, T331

Bear Hunt (poem), T126

Bear Went Over the Mountain, The, T115

Bee, Bee, Bumblebee, T250

Best Friends, T222

Big and Small (speech piece), T200

Bluebells, T209

Bonjour, mes amis (Hello, My Friends), T18

Boris, the Singing Bear, T312

Bow-Wow (poem), T81

Brinca la tablita (Hop, Hop!), T71

Brush Your Teeth (song), T66, (speech piece), T67

Bug (poem), T167

But the Critter Got Away (speech piece), T88

Butterfly, Flutter By, T333

Call of the Wild, A (excerpt) (poem), T139

Caribbean Amphibian, T294

Categories, T146

Chang (Elephant), T199

Charlie Over the Ocean, T75

Chase the Squirrel, T88

Chickery Chick, T292

Clap Your Hands, T246

Clouds by Anonymous (poem), T331

Come Back, My Little Chicks, T134

Cookies, T277

Cookies, T278

Counting Song, T195

Cow, The (poem), T236

Cut the Cake, T232

Dance Myself to Sleep, T314

Diana (Play the Bugle), T334

Diou Shou Juan'er (Hiding a Handkerchief), T212

Double This (speech piece), T95

Down by the Bay, T48

Down the Hill, T281

Dragonfly (poem), T44

Duérmete mi niño (Go to Sleep, My Baby), T61

Ears, Far and Near (poem), T16

El florón (The Flower), T117

El juego chirimbolo (The Chirimbolo Game), T103

Field of Joys, T224

Five Little Pumpkins (poem), T337

George Washington, T368

Gilly, Gilly, Gilly Good Morning, T12

Go A Tin (Lantern Song), T363

Goin' to the Zoo, T192

Granny (speech piece), T104

Grasshoppers Three, T284

Thematic Correlations to Reading Series

Thematic Correlations to Reading Series (continued)

Thematic Correlations to Reading Series (continued)

Rattlesnake, T185

Romper, Stomper, and Boo (traditional story), T36

Simple Simon, T175

Sing Ho! For the Life of a Bear! By A.A. Milne (poem), T114

Sittin' Down to Eat, T182

Six Little Ducks, T64

Snail With the Mail, T274

Snail, Snail (song), T252, (three-tone), T252

Something Told the Wild Geese by R. Field (poem), T261

Thoughts of a Rattlesnake by K. Sexton (poem), T185

Untitled (Butterflies) (haiku), T332

Up the Hill by W. J. Smith (poem), T45

White Sheep by Anonymous (poem), T234

Who's Afraid of the Big Bad Wolf? (nursery rhyme), T137

Year with Frog and Toad, A (reprise), T283

Year with Frog and Toad, A, T270

Theme 7: We Can Work It Out

A la rueda rueda ('Round and 'Round), T240

Acka Backa, T256

Apples and Bananas, T151

Bee, Bee, Bumblebee, T250

Big and Small by E. McCullough Brabson, T200

Bluebells, T209

Brinca la tablita (Hop, Hop!), T71

Categories, T146

Charlie Over the Ocean, T75

Chase the Squirrel, T88

Clap Your Hands (song), T246, (rhythmic pattern), T247

Come Back, My Little Chicks, T134

Diou Shou Juan'er, T212

Double This (game), T94

El juego chirimbolo (The Chirimbolo Game), T103

Head and Shoulders, Baby, T40

Here We Sit, T251

How Does Your Garden Grow?, T144

I Had a Little Hen (nursery rhyme), T136

I Like by M. A. Hoberman (poem), T110

I Like Spinach, T163

I Wanna Be a Friend of Yours, T84

John the Rabbit, T74

Johnny Works with One Hammer, T96

Jump, Jim Joe, T89

Looby Loo, T262

Lucy Locket, T253

Marco Polo (speech piece), T90

Martin Luther King, T360

Miss Mary Mack, T15

Mizuguruma (The Water Wheel), T260

Mos', Mos'! (Cat, Cat!), T53

My Mama's Calling Me, T54

One Little Elephant, T194

One, Two, Three, Four, Five, T265

Pat Pat Patty Pat, T308

Piñata Song (Mexican traditional poem), T153

Pitty Patty Polt (nursery rhyme) (rhythmic pattern), T180

Punchinella, T216

Rise, Sally, Rise (game), T162

Sailor Went to Sea, Sea, Sea, A (song), T38, (game), T39

Sara Watashi (Plate Passing), T67

Serra, serra serrador (Saw, Saw Lumberjack), T133

Shoo, Turkey, T76

Simple Simon, T175

Six Little Ducks, T64

Snail, Snail (song), T252, (three-tone), T252

Soup, Soup!, T358

Tailor, Tailor (traditional poem), T132

There's a Hole in the Middle of the Sea, T178

This Old Man, T306

Tinker, Tailor, T131

Twenty-four Robbers, 173

Two, Four, Six, Eight (song), T246, (rhythmic pattern), T247

Una adivinanza (A Riddle), T138

Vhaya Kadhimba (Zimbabwean children's song) (song), T23, (game), T23

We All Sing With the Same Voice, T156

Who's Afraid of the Big Bad Wolf? (nursery rhyme), T137

Willum, T19

Zui Zui Zukkorbashi (song), T98, (game), T99

Theme 8: Our Earth

All Night, All Day, T232

Autumn Leaves Are Falling, T330

Autumn Leaves, T331

Call of the Wild, A (excerpt) by R. W. Service (poem), T139

Clouds by Anonymous (poem), T331

Down by the Bay, T48

El florón (The Flower), T117

Green Grass Grows All Around, The, T148

Hop! Chirp! Moo! Oh, Happy Springtime Day!, T372

Horses of the Sea, The, by C. Rossetti (poem), T179

How Does Your Garden Grow?, T144

I'd Like to Be a Lighthouse by R Field (poem), T238

I'd Like to Be a Lighthouse by R Field (poem), T238

Ice, T347

It's So Nice on the Ice, T346

Love Grows, T202

Night Comes… by B. Schenk de Regniers (poem), T233

O Wind by C. Rossetti (poem), T235

Over in the Meadow, T78

Rain Poem (poem), T31

Rain Sizes by J. Ciardi (poem), T33

Rain, Rain, Go Away, T259

Romper, Stomper, and Boo (traditional story), T36

Seeds, T120

Serra, serra serrador (Saw, Saw Lumberjack), T133

Somebody Has To… by S. Silverstein (poem), T258

Spring, T273

Star Light, Star Bright, T258

There's a Hole in the Middle of the Sea, T178

This Little Light of Mine, T238

Up the Tree and Down Again by A. Seear (poem), T65

White Sheep by Anonymous (poem), T234

Wind Blew East, The, T234

Wind Blow, T187

Theme 9: Special Friends

A be ce (A B C), T213

A la rueda rueda ('Round and 'Round), T240

Acka Backa, T256

¡Adivina lo que es! (Guess What It Is), T170

All Night, All Day, T232

America, T326

Animal Song, T288

Another Busy Day, T41

Ants Go Marching, The, T22

Apple a Day, An (poem), T152

Apples and Bananas, T151

Arre, mi burrito (Gid'yup, Little Burrito), T257

Autumn Leaves Are Falling, T330

Autumn Leaves, T331

Bear Hunt (speech piece), T126

Bear Went Over the Mountain, The, T115

Bee, Bee, Bumblebee, T250

Best Friends, T222

Big and Small (speech piece), T200

Bluebells, T209

Bonjour, mes amis (Hello, My Friends), T18

Boris, the Singing Bear, T312

Bow-Wow (poem), T81

Brinca la tablita (Hop, Hop!), T71

Brush Your Teeth (song), T66, (speech piece), T67
Bug (poem), T167
But the Critter Got Away (speech piece), T88
Butterfly, Flutter By, T333
Call of the Wild, A (excerpt) (poem), T139
Caribbean Amphibian, T294
Categories, T146
Chang (Elephant), T199
Charlie Over the Ocean, T75
Chase the Squirrel, T88
Chickery Chick, T292
Clap Your Hands, T246
Clouds (poem), T330
Come Back, My Little Chicks, T134
Cookies, T277
Counting Song, T195
Cow, The (poem), T236
Cut the Cake, T232
Dance Myself to Sleep, T314
Diana (Play the Bugle), T334
Diou Shou Juan'er (Hiding a Handkerchief), T212
Double This (speech piece), T95
Down by the Bay, T48
Down the Hill, T281
Dragonfly (poem), T44
Duérmete mi niño (Go to Sleep, My Baby), T61
Ears, Far and Near (poem), T16
El florón (The Flower), T117
El juego chirimbolo (The Chirimbolo Game), T103
Field of Joys, T224
Five Little Pumpkins (poem), T337
George Washington, T368
Gilly, Gilly, Gilly Good Morning, T12
Go A Tin (Lantern Song), T363
Goin' to the Zoo, T192
Granny (speech piece), T104
Grasshoppers Three, T284
Green Grass Grows All Around, The, T148
Haiku Butterflies (poem), T332
Hakyo Jong (School Bells), T302
Haliwa-Saponi
Happiest Street in the World, The, T304
Head and Shoulders, Baby, T40
Hello, There!, T230
Here Comes the Band (poem), T80
Here We Sit, T251
Hey, Children, Who's in Town?, T14
Hi! My Name Is Joe! (speech piece), T220
Hoo, Hoo!, T55
Hop, Chirp! Moo! Oh Happy Springtime Day, T372
Hopping Frog (poem), T113
Horses of the Sea, The (poem), T179

How Does Your Garden Grow?, T144
Hunt the Cows, T236
I Am Slowly Going Crazy, T127
I Had a Little Hen (nursery rhyme), T136
I Have a Friend (poem), T225
I Like (poem), T110
I Like Spinach, T163
I Love My Country, T328
I Wanna Be a Friend of Yours, T84
I'd Like to Be a Lighthouse (poem), T238
I'm Getting Sick of Peanut Butter (poem), T219
I've a Pair of Fishes, T124
Ice (poem), T346
If All the World Were Paper, T296
In My Little Motor Boat, T159
It's So Nice on the Ice, T346
Jambo (Hello), T230
John the Rabbit, T74
Johnny Works with One Hammer, T96
Johnny's Flea, T158
Jump or Jiggle (poem), T316
Jump, Jim Joe, T89
Kaeru no Uta (Frog's Song), T112
Kari (Wild Geese), T261
Kobuta, T168
La ranita cri (The Little Frog Croaks), T27
Ladybugs' Picnic, T290
Lavender's Blue, T174
Legend of George Washington and the Cherry Tree, The (story), T369
Let's Go Driving, T52
Library Song, T42
Little Black Bug, T166
Little Red Caboose, T97
Little Robin Redbreast, T208
Locust, The (poem), T285
Looby Loo, T262
Love Grows, T202
Love Is the Magic Word, T366
Lucy Lockett, T253
Mail Myself to You, T366
Marco Polo (speech piece), T90
Martin Luther King, T360
Mary's Coal Black Lamb, T286
Mi cuerpo (My Body), T32
Miss Mary Mack, T15
Mizuguruma (The Water Wheel), T260
Mos', Mos'! (Cat, Cat!), T53
My Feet (poem), T264
My Kite (poem), T371
My Mama's Calling Me, T54
My Mom, T372
Na Bahia Tem (In Bahia Town), T297
Naming Things (poem), T221
Naranja dulce (Sweet Orange), T303
Naughty Kitty Cat, T171
Night Comes… (poem), T233

No One Like You, T300
O Wind (poem), T235
Old King Glory, T217
Old Mother Goose (poem), T181
One Little Elephant, T194
One, Two, Three, Four, Five, T265
One, Two, Three, Four, T123
Oranges and Lemons (poem), T150
Over in the Meadow, T78
Pat Pat Patty Pat, T308
Peanut Butter, T218
Pease Porridge Hot, T255
Pile of Stuff, A (story), T188
Piñata Song (poem), T153
Piñón, Pirulín, T311
Pitty Patty Polt (speech piece), T180
Plenty Fishes in the Sea, T310
Puddle Hopping, T60
Pumpkin Song, T342
Punchinella, T216
Pusa't daga (Cat and Rat), T289
Quaker, Quaker, T100
Rabbit in the Moon, The (folktale), T318
Rabbit, The (poem), T186
Rain Sizes (poem), T33
Rain, Rain, Go Away, T259
Rattlesnake, T185
Rig a Jig Jig, T116
Rise, Sally, Rise, T162
Romper, Stomper, and Boo (story), T36
Sailor Went to Sea, Sea, Sea, A (song), T38, (game), T39
Sara Watashi (Plate Passing), T66
Seeds (vocal and instrumental), T120
Seesaw, T242
Serra, Serra Serrador (Saw, Saw, Lumberjack), T133
Shoo, Turkey, T76
Simple Simon, T175
Sing After Me, T34
Sing Ho! For the Life of a Bear! (poem), T114
Sittin' Down to Eat, T182
Sitting in the Sand (poem), T374
Six Little Ducks, T64
Skip to My Lou, T102
Sleep, Bonnie Bairnie, T27
Snail With the Mail, T275
Snail, Snail, T252
Somebody Come and Play, T92
Somebody Has To… (poem), T258
Something Funny Outside, T338
Something Told the Wild Geese (poem), T261
Soup, Soup!, T358
Spotlight on America, T9
Spring, T273
Star Light, Star Bright, T258
Suite on English Folk Tunes, T136
Summertime from *Porgy and Bess*, T375

Thematic Correlations to Reading Series (continued)

Swing, The (poem), T109
Tailor, Tailor (poem), T132
Tak for Maden (Thanks for Food), T343
Tako No Uta, T146
Theme from *Sesame Street*, T298
There Are Many Flags in Many Lands, T329
There's a Hole in the Middle of the Sea, T178
This Little Light of Mine, T238
This Old Man, T306
Thoughts of a Rattlesnake (poem), T185
Time for Love, T347
Tinker, Tailor, T130
Tisket A Tasket, A, T107
Twenty-four Robbers, T173
Two, Four, Six, Eight, T246
Uga, Uga, Uga (Cake, Cake, Cake), T313
Una adivinanza (A Riddle), T138
Up the Hill (poem), T45
Up the Tree and Down Again (poem), T65
Wake Me, Shake Me, T198
We All Sing With the Same Voice, T156
What's Your Name?, T125
Wheels, Wheels, Wheels (poem), T106
When the Flag Goes By, T327
Who's Afraid of the Big Bad Wolf? (nursery rhyme), T137
Why the Beetle Has a Gold Coat (folktale), T321
Willum, T19
Wind Blew East, The, T234
Wind Blow, T187
Wings (poem), T250
Year With Frog and Toad, A (Reprise), T283
Year With Frog and Toad, A, T270
Yo, Mamana, Yo (Oh, Mama), T307
Zui Zui Zukkorbashi (song), T98, (game), T99

Theme 10: We Can Do It!

Apple a Day, An (traditional poem), T152
Apples and Bananas, T151
Arre, mi burrito (Gid-yup, Little Burro), T257
Bear Hunt (poem), T126
Big and Small by E. McCullough Brabson, T200
Brush Your Teeth (song), T66, (speech piece), T66
Call of the Wild, A (excerpt) by R. W. Service (poem), T139
Goin' to the Zoo, T192
Hoo, Hoo!, T55
I Like Spinach, T163
In My Little Motor Boat, T159

Johnny Works with One Hammer, T96
Let's Go Driving, T52
Library Song, T42
Martin Luther King, T360
Oranges and Lemons (English traditional poem), T150
Pease Porridge Hot, T255
Pitty Patty Polt (nursery rhyme) (rhythmic pattern), T180
Romper, Stomper, and Boo (traditional story), T36
Sleep, Bonnie Bairnie, T26
Spanish Days of the Week by Anonymous (poem), T108
Tailor, Tailor (traditional poem), T132
Tinker, Tailor, T131
We All Sing With the Same Voice, T156
Wheels, Wheels, Wheels by N. White Carlstrom (poem), T106
Willum, T19

Grade 2

Theme 1: Silly Stories

Artichokes, 314
Ban Dal (Half Moon), 219
Button, You Must Wander, 176
Chíu, chíu, chíu (Chirp, Chirp, Chirp), 302
Columbus Sailed with Three Ships, 344
Corner Grocery Store, 311
Dance Together, 264
Dance, Dance, Dance!, 5
Everybody Has Music Inside, 164
Green Eggs and Ham, 284
Here Comes Sally, 220
I'm Gonna Sing, 9
It's Possible, 281
Jim Along, Josie, 194
Joy, 46
Jugaremos en el bosque (We Will Play in the Forest), 188
Mein Hut (My Hat), 142
Mother, Mother, 254
Oh, the Thinks You Can Think!, 276
On Top of Spaghetti, 312
Pairs or Pears, 265
Part of Your World, 294
Place in the Choir, A, 308
Puff, the Magic Dragon, 54
Riddle Song, 251
She'll Be Comin' 'Round the Mountain, 33
Skating, 350
Thank You, 349
This is My Country, 87
Yankee Doodle, 340
You Are My Sunshine, 369

Theme 2: Nature Walk

All Around the Buttercup, 210
Artichokes, 314
Australia's on the Wallaby, 106
Away for Rio, 170
Baby Beluga, 26
Bei Fang Chre (North Wind Blows), 367
Big Beautiful Planet, 376
Button, You Must Wander, 176
Caranguejo (The Crab), 306
City Traffic by B. Franco (poem), 328
Columbus Sailed with Three Ships, 344
Corner Grocery Store, 311
Dal taro kacha (Come, Pick the Moon), 98
Dumplin's, 172
El tren (The Train), 326
En nuestra Tierra tan linda (On Our Beautiful Planet Earth), 114
Engine, Engine Number Nine, 13
Everything Grows, 204
Finis by H. Newbolt (poem), 76
Food Song, The, 318
Four White Horses, 300
Garden Song, 236
Going Over the Sea, 216
Good Night, Sleep Tight, 76
Great Outdoors, The, 290
Green Eggs and Ham, 284
Hot Cross Buns, 258
I Chih ha Ma (Frogs), 186
It's Possible, 281
It's Raining! It's Pouring!, 233
Ja posejah lubenice (I Planted Watermelons), 316
King's Land, 257
La bella hortelana (The Beautiful Gardener), 208
Land of the Silver Birch, 88
Little Seeds (except) by E. Holmelund Minarik (poem), 207
Me gase boho (Orange Tree), 317
Nabe, Nabe, Soku, Nuke (Stewpot, Stewpot, Bottomless Pot), 259
Oma Rapeti (Run, Rabbit), 108
On Top of Spaghetti, 312
Pairs or Pears, 265
Part of Your World, 294
Piggy by W. Cole (poem), 315
Puff, the Magic Dragon, 54
Sammy Sackett, 146
Seeds and Seasons, 206
Sing! Sing! Sing!, 196
Sun Is First to Rise, The, by E. Coatsworth (poem), 383
Take Me Out to the Ball Game, 56
Thank You, 349
Wake Up the Sun, 124

Thematic Correlations to Reading Series

Thematic Correlations to Reading Series (continued)

Thematic Correlations
to Reading Series

Who Chopped the Cherry Tree Down?, 371
Who Has Seen the Wind? (poem), 137
Who Has the Penny?, 252
Who's That Tapping at the Window?, 261
Willowbee, T69
Yanai (The Elephant), 305
Yankee Doodle, 340
You Are My Sunshine, 369
You'll Sing a Song and I'll Sing a Song, 156

Theme 4: Amazing Animals
Animal Fair, 214
Artichokes, 314
Australia's on the Wallaby, 106
Baby Beluga, 26
Bliss by E. Farjeon (poem), 212
Bow, Wow, Wow, 264
Candle on the Water, 296
Caranguejo (The Crab), 306
Chichipapa (The Sparrows' Singing School), 22, 31
Corner Grocery Store, 311
Cuckoo, Where Are You?, 244
Daisy Chain, 255
Dal taro kacha (Come, Pick the Moon), 98
Do You Want My Little Frog? by H. Copeland (poem), 187
Doggie, Doggie, 59
Donkey, Donkey, 256
Drumming Spider, The (West African folktale), 333
Dumplin's, 172
Eating Lizards, 250
El burrito enfermo (The Sick Little Donkey), 180
El palomo y la paloma (The Doves), 380
Elephant Carries a Great Big Trunk, The, by Anonymous (poem), 169
Food Song, The, 318
Four White Horses, 300
Good Night, Sleep Tight, 76
Green Eggs and Ham, 284
Hairy Dog, The, by H. Asquith (poem), 58
Hakuna Matata, 292
Hello, Hello There, 126
Here Comes a Bluebird, 263
Hop, Old Squirrel, 258
Horton Hears a Who!, 279
Hot Cross Buns, 258
I Chih ha Ma (Frogs), 186
I Heard a Bird Sing by O. Herford (poem), 271
Itik Besenda Gurau (The Ducks), 100
Ja posejah lubenice (I Planted Watermelons), 316

Jugaremos en el bosque (We Will Play in the Forest), 188
La bella hortelana (The Beautiful Gardener), 208
Leatherwing Bat, 304
Mama eu quero (I Want My Mama) (Brazilian carnival song), 92
Me gase boho (Orange Tree), 317
Mister Rabbit, Mister Rabbit, 150
Mouse, Mousie, 254
Mr. Frog, 257
Na belo (Little Heron), 322
Nabe, Nabe, Soku, Nuke (Stewpot, Stewpot, Bottomless Pot), 259
Old Blue, 213
Old Woman and the Pig, 130
Oma Rapeti (Run, Rabbit), 108
On Top of Spaghetti, 312
Opposite of Two, The, by R. Wilbur (poem), 45
Pairs or Pears, 265
Pat on the Back, A, 74
Piggy by W. Cole (poem), 315
Place in the Choir, A, 308
Rover, 260
Señor Coyote (Mexican folktale), 330
Sheep in the Meadow (speech piece), 8
Sheep Shearing, 102
Shoheen Sho, 140

Theme 5: Family Time
Three Little Penguins (speech piece), 112
Tiki Tiki Tiki Room, The, 324
Tinga Layo, 50
Yanai (The Elephant), 305
You'll Sing a Song and I'll Sing a Song, 156

Theme 6: Talent Show
A la rueda de San Miguel (To the Wheel of San Miguel), 60
Ban Dal (Half Moon), 219
Button, You Must Wander, 176
Doggie, Doggie, 59
Elephant Carries a Great Big Trunk, The, by Anonymous (poem), 169
Everybody Has Music Inside, 164
Everything Grows, 204
Garden Song, 236
Going Over the Sea, 216
Green Eggs and Ham, 284
Heigh Ho, Here We Go, 252
Hey, Hey, Look at Me, 245
Horton Hears a Who!, 279
I See, 266
I'm Gonna Sing, 9
It's Possible, 281
Joy, 46
Jugaremos en el bosque (We Will Play in the Forest), 188

Leatherwing Bat, 304
Lemonade, 19
Let's Go Fly a Kite, 134
Loose Tooth (speech piece), 28
Martin Luther King, 364
Matarile, 261
Me Stone, 48
Mein Hut (My Hat), 142
Merry-Go-Round, 267
Moon Boat by C. Pomerantz (poem), 218
Oh, the Thinks You Can Think!, 276
Old Woman and the Pig, 130
Oliver Twist, 268
Part of Your World, 294
Pizza, Pizza, Daddy-O, 62
Place in the Choir, A, 308
Plainsies, Clapsies, 248
Puff, the Magic Dragon, 54
Sammy Sackett, 146
Say Your Name, 243
Señor Coyote (Mexican folktale), 330
Sheep in the Meadow (speech piece), 8
Shoo, Fly, 222
Sing! Sing! Sing!, 196
Skating, 350
Take Me Out to the Ball Game, 56
What Did Delaware?, 190
Who's That Tapping at the Window?, 261

Grade 3

Theme 1: Off to Adventure!
Cielito lindo (Mexican folk song), 166
El florón (The Flower), 46
Gebeta Board, The (Ethiopian folk tale), 346
Hope by E. Dickinson (poem), 166
I'm a Believer, 312
I'm On My Way, 382
Marvelous Toy, The, 182
Moon and Me, 220
Oleanna, 144
Rainbow Connection, The, 310
Scotland's Burning, 257
Sun Don't Set in the Mornin', 48, 60
Trampin', 287
William Tell (Overture) (excerpt) by G. Rossini, 64

Theme 2: Celebrating Traditions
Addams Family Theme, The, 307
America, the Beautiful, 354
Ballad of the Bedbugs and the Beetles, The, 206
Bella Bimba, 172
Billy, 7
Bim Bom, 218
Blow, Ye Winds, Blow, 192
Bohm, 392

Thematic Correlations to Reading Series (continued)

Theme 3: Incredible Stories

Chicken on the Fence Post, 265
Circle 'Round the Zero, 267
City Music by T. Mitton (poem), 74
Clocks, 266
Colors of the Wind, 84
Coral, 249
Cornstalk Fiddle and a Shoestring Bow, 284
Crawdad Song, 107
De aquel cerro (On the Darkened Hillside), 32
Death of the Robin, 275
Dinah, 150
Ding Dong Diggy Diggy Dong, 269
Draw a Bucket of Water, 222
Egy üveg alma (One Jar of Apples), 22
Eh Soom Boo Kawaya (Nigerian boat song), 58
El arroyo que murmura (The Murmuring Brook), 318
El nido (The Nest), 214
En roulant ma boule (As I Roll My Ball), 100
Evergreen, Everblue, 330
Flip, Flop, and Fly!, 336
Frog in the Meadow, 243
Gebeta Board, The (Ethiopian folk tale), 346
Gi'Me Elbow Room, 88
Golden Ring Around the Susan Girl, 264
Greatest Show on Earth, The, 308
Guitar Man, The, 138
Happy Wanderer, The, 18
Hello!, 283
Herring, The, 316
Hey, Motswala, 34
Hope by E. Dickinson (poem), 166
I Walk in Beauty, 329
I'm a Believer, 312
I's the B'y, 13
In Good Old Colony Times, 326
Interjections, 303
Interplanet Janet, 298
Isabela and the Troll (Spanish folk tale), 349
J'entends le moulin (I Hear the Windmill), 135
Jamaica Farewell, 156
Jasmine Flower, 146
John Jacob Jingleheimer Schmidt, 68
Just Like the Sun, 394
Kalinka (Little Snowball Bush), 224
Kreely Kranky, 258
Kum Bachur (The Rooster), 75
Kuma San (Honorable Bear), 244
La bamba (Mexican folk song), 236
Le Mar (The Sea), 110
Let Us Chase the Squirrel, 248
Let's Go Dancing, 196
Limbo Rock, 232

Little Boy of the Sheep, 188
Little Sally Walker, 105
Little Tommy Tinker, 277
Look High, Look Low, 338
Lukey's Boat, 114
Mrs. Murphy's Chowder, 390
Music of the World A-Turnin', 44
O, The Train's Off the Track, 176
Oh Mama Bakdala (Xhosa folk song), 328
Oh, Susanna, 153
Old Barn Dance, The, 94
Old Mister Rabbit, 254
Old Roger, 280
One More River, 216
One Potato, Two Potato, 267
Over My Head, 286
Pat-a-Pan, 375
Paw Paw Patch, The, 195
Pay Me My Money Down, 149
Polly Wolly Doodle, 132
Raccoon Dance Song, 87
Rattlesnake, 72
Recycle Rap, 332
Riding in the Buggy, 131
Rise Up Singin', 138
See the Rabbit Running, 255
Shalom Chaveyrim (Shalom, My Friends), 141
Shepherd, Shepherd, 56
Simon Says, 4
Spiders, 282
Sweep, Sweep, Away, 276
Tanabata (Seven Evenings), 62

Theme 4: Animal Habitats
There Was An Old Lady by D. Lee (poem), 344
There's a Little Wheel A-Turnin' in My Heart, 129, 137
This a Way and That a Way, 386
Three Is a Magic Number, 94
Three Little Birds, 204
Throw It Out the Window, 94
Tititorea (Maori Stick Game) (New Zealand folk song), 174
Treasure Chests, 90
Ucha Tirvarch (Little Bear Song), 53
Uno de enero (The First of January), 210
Vamos a la mar (Let's Go to the Sea), 256
Walk by the River (song), 74, (harmony parts), 76
Wang Ü Ger (Chinese fishing song), 190
Way Down South by Anonymous (poem), 8
Way Down South by Anonymous (poem), 8
Wéané (Menadonese lullaby), 184

Woke Up This Morning, 180
Woodchuck, 246
Yankee Doodle, 357
Yellow Submarine, 320

Theme 5: Voyagers
Boll Weevil, 171
Charlie, 208
City Life, 341
Cumberland Gap, 99
En roulant ma boule (As I Roll My Ball), 100
Happy Wanderer, The, 18
I Have a Car, 252
Jamaica Farewell, 156
Jingle at the Window, 268
Movin' Right Along, 124
My Horses Ain't Hungry, 278
O, The Train's Off the Track, 176
Oh, Susanna, 153
Oleanna, 144
Riding in the Buggy, 131
Ship Ahoy, 314
Stevedore's Song, 127
Turn the Glasses Over, 260
When I First Came to This Land, 28
Bohm (Spring Has Come!), 392
Frosty Weather, 250
La cloche (The Clock), 67
May Day Carol, 393
Morning Bells, 270
Night Song, 186
Que Llueva (It's Raining), 274
Rain Is Falling Down, 242
Sun Don't Set in the Mornin', 48, 60
Taps, 281
Uno de enero (The First of January), 210
Gebeta Board, The (Ethiopian folk tale), 346
Scotland's Burning, 257
William Tell (Overture) (excerpt) by G. Rossini, 64

Theme 6: Smart Solutions
Blow, Ye Winds, Blow, 192
Chag Asif (Harvest Time), 360
Colors of the Wind, 84
Crawdad Song, 107
De aquel cerro (On the Darkened Hillside), 32
Death of the Robin, 275
Digga Digga Dog, 164
Evergreen, Everblue, 330
Gebeta Board, The (Ethiopian folk tale), 346
Guitar Man, The, 138
Hello!, 283
I Lost the Farmer's Dairy Key, 273
I's the B'y, 13
Just Like the Sun, 394

Thematic Correlations to Reading Series

Thematic Correlations to Reading Series (continued)

Green Gravel, 247
Hala lala layya, 222
Heave-Ho Me Laddies, 258
Himmel und Erde (Music Alone Shall Live), 280
Hitori, 345
Hojas de té (Tea Leaves) (speech piece), 256
Hold My Mule, 248
Hop Up and Jump Up, 271
How Long the Train Been Gone?, 264
I Think I'm Going to Like It Here, 299
I Will Be Your Friend, 388
I'll Rise When the Rooster Crows, 36
It Rained a Mist, 262
It's the Hard-Knock Life, 293
Johnson Boys, 233
Just One Planet, 164
Katyusha, 188
Kettle Valley Line, The, 348
Korobushka, 285
L'inverno è già passato (Winter is Over), 390
La sanjuanerita (The Girl from San Juan), 100
Li'l 'Liza Jane, 20
L'inverno è già passato (Winter if Over), 390
Little David Play on Your Harp, 323
Long-Legged Sailor, 243
Love Somebody, 94
Macnamara's Band, 88
Marken er mejet (Harvest Song), 365
Marken er mejet (Out in the Meadow), 364
Molinillo de café (Little Coffee Mill) (speech piece), 250
'Most Done Ling'rin' Here, 65
My Home's in Montana, 274
N.Y.C., 302
Night Herding Song, 110
Octopus's Garden, 30
Oh, Won't You Sit Down?, 70
Old Abram Brown, 32
Old Ark's A-Moverin', 130
Old Aunt Dinah, 245
Old Carrion Crow, 192
Old House, 282
Old Joe Clark, 74
Old Paint, 275
Oliver Cromwell, 269
Oro My Bodeen, 279
Over the Sea to Skye, 344
Page's Train, 246
Pat Works on the Railway, 86
Push Boat Song, 266
¿Quién es ese pajarito? (Who Is That Little Bird?), 284
Ridin' of a Goat, Leadin' of a Sheep, 251
Row, Row, Row Your Boat, 268

Sansa kroma, 166
Sarasponda, 210
Sea Shell, 245
Sing of America, 359
Sitsiritsit, 102
Something for Me, Something for You, 4
Star-Spangled Banner, The, 356
Swapping Song, 253
Take Time in Life, 156
This Land is Your Land, 146
Tomorrow, 295
Train Is A-Coming, 270
`Ulili E (The Sandpiper), 396
Uruguay
Wake Up Canon, 326
Walk in the Parlor, 226
Water Come a Me Eye, 90
We are Here, 394
We Remember, 360
We Shall Overcome, 387
What Can One Little Person Do?, 204
When I Was Young, 187
Who's Got the Fishpole?, 261
Yankee Doodle, 154
You're Never Fully Dressed Without a Smile, 304
Zum Gali Gali, 255

Theme 6: Nature: Friend and Foe
'Ulili E (The Sandpiper), 396
All Through the Night (Welsh folk song), 277
Ame fure (Rain), 26
Beryoza (The Birch Tree), 286
Corre el río (The River Flows By) by P. Vasquez (poem), 183
December Nights, December Lights, 372
Dok Djampa (The White Jasmine Flower), 392
E nānā, kākou i nā manu (Look at the Birds in the Sky), 338
Eagle, 337
El coquí (The Frog), 178
Farfallina (Butterfly), 244
Frère Jacques (Are You Sleeping?), 260
Green Gravel, 247
I Heard a Mockingbird, 150
I'll Rise When the Rooster Crows, 36
It Rained a Mist, 262
L'inverno è già passato (Winter Is Over), 390
La sanjuanerita (The Girl from San Juan), 100
Marken er mejet (Out in the Meadow), 364
Mighty River (speech piece), 217
New Day, The, 316
Night Herding Song, 110
Owl and the Cuckoo, The, 337
Rain (haiku), 27

Roll On, Columbia, 182
Sea Shell, 245
Sitsiritsit, 102
Sky Dances, 206
This Land Is Your Land, 146
Wake Up Canon, 326
We Are Here, 394
We Shall Overcome, 387
Woodpecker, The, by E. Madox Roberts (poem), 48

Grade 5

Theme 1: Nature's Fury
American Salute by M. Gould, 36
Ballad of the Underground Railroad, The, 145, (partner song), 154
Beauty and the Beast, 124
Big Big World, 438
Bound No'th Blues by L. Hughes (poem), 181
City Blues, 278
Cliffs of Doneen, The, 46
Colores de caracol (Colors of the Snail) by E. Galarza (poem), 101
De colores (Many Colors) (unison), 88, (parts), 98
Deta, Deta (The Moon), 246
Dreamers, 430
Dry Bones, 406
Ēinīnī (Little Birds Sleep), 240
El jarabe (Mexican Hat Dance), 396
Erie Canal, 132
Estrella brillante (Shining Star), 373
Ga Eul (Fall), 401
Goin' Home, 108
Great Big Sea, A, 334
Haere Ra (Now Is the Hour), 151
Hallelujah, Get On Board, 345
Hill an' Gully, 250
I Am But a Small Voice, 323
John Henry, 146
John Kanaka, 249
Joyful, Joyful, We Adore Thee, 103
Kojo No Tsuki (Moon at the Ruined Castle), 149
Loch Lomond, 138
Los maizales (The Cornfields), 268
Mango Walk (song), 90, (countermelody), 92
Nani Wale Na Hala (The Swaying Pandanus Trees), 276
Ngam sang duan (Shining Moon), 376
Nottamun Town, 405
Our World, 381
Path to the Moon, 368
Ride Like the Wind, 130
Sankta Lucia (Saint Lucia), 413
Shope, Shope (Oh, Shope, Shope), 220
Sounds of Africa, The, by Wandile (poem), 74

Thematic Correlations to Reading Series (continued)

Thematic Correlations to Reading Series

Thematic Correlations to Reading Series (continued)

Thematic Correlations to Reading Series (continued)

We Are the Children of Tomorrow, 114
We Want to Sing, 235
Wells Fargo Wagon, The, 303
What the World Needs Now, 230
When Johnny Comes Marching Home, 34
When the Saints Go Marching In, 256
Where Is John?, 274
Winter Wonderland, 408
Words of Wisdom, 244
Yakety Yak, 308

Theme 6: Animal Encounters
Cliffs of Doneen, The, 46
Colores de caracol (Colors of the Snail) by E. Galarza (poem), 101
De colores (Many Colors) (unison), 88, (parts), 98
Deta, Deta (The Moon), 246
Ēinīnī (Little Birds Sleep), 240
Estrella brillante (Shining Star), 373
Ga Eul (Fall), 401
Great Big Sea, A, 334
Joyful, Joyful, We Adore Thee, 103
Loch Lomond, 138
Los maizales (The Cornfields), 268
Nani Wale Na Hala (The Swaying Pandanus Trees), 276
Ngam sang duan (Shining Moon), 376
Our World, 381
Path to the Moon, 368
Star Canon, 367
What the World Needs Now, 230
Winter Wonderland, 408

Grade 6

Theme 1: Courage
Angelina, 8
Carol by K. Grahame (poem), 407
Choo, Choo, Ch'Boogie, 180
Cum-ma-la Be-stay, 370
Dere Geliyor (River Overflowing), 232
Doney Gal, 115
Down by the Riverside, 22
El Tambor (The Drum), 222
Fortune Favors the Brave, 316
Gee, Mom, I Want to Go Home, 148
Greenland Whale Fishery, The, 212
Heart, 166
Hullaballoo Balay, 10
I Want to Be Ready, 12
I'm Gonna Sit at the Welcome Table, 416
Joban Tanko Bushi (Joban Miners' Song), 142
Lean on Me, 150
Leila, 376
Let It Roll, 124
Lumber Camp Song, The, 136
Ma'oz Tsur (Rock of Ages), 405

Mama Don't 'Low, 126
Mi caballo blanco (My White Horse), 60
Mountain Music, 20
Neviděli jste tu mé panenky? (Have You Not Seen My Dear Daughters?), 228
O, Desayo, 50
Old Barn Dance, The, 94
On a Clear Day, 206
One Dime Blues, 178
Orange Blossom Special, 33
Rage and Roar, 48
Red Iron Ore, 134
River of My People, 176
Scraping Up Sand, 248
Shady Grove, 286
Ship in Distress, The, 211
Suliram, 58
Sweet and Low, 184
Tain't What You Do, 18
Ua txiab (The Village), 394
Vem Kan Segla (Who Can Sail?), 419
Walk by the River (unison), 74, (parts), 76
Water Is Wide, The, 46
Wayfaring Stranger, 283
Yerakina, 216
You Sing for Me, 106

Theme 2: What Really Happened?
Barbry Ellen, 208
Blue Suede Shoes, 236
Body Talk, 88
Bop 'til You Drop, 87
Bulbes ('Taters), 280
Cape Cod Chantey, 258
Captain Jinks, 266
Charleston, 112
Chiribim, 57
Comedy Tonight, 204
Conga, 34
Dancing in the Street, 84
Derry Ding Dong Dason, 249
Didn't It Rain, 345
Doctor Jazz, 378
Doing the Latest Rag, 314
Ghost Ship, The, 323
Greenland Whale Fishery, The, 212
Guitar Man, The, 138
Heart, 166
Huainito, 351
I Love a Piano, 130
If I Had a Hammer, 174
Já do lesa nepojedu (To the Woods I Will Not Go), 227
Jack Was Ev'ry Bit a Sailor, 170
Jede, jede, poštovský panáček (Riding, Riding, Is Mr. Postman), 226
La Bamba, 381
Lullaby of Broadway, 182
Mama Don't 'Low, 126

Mayim, Mayim (Water, Water), 102
Merecumbé, 276
New Ashmolean Marching Society and Students Conservatory Band, The, 308
O, Desayo, 50
O, La Le!, 6
Old Barn Dance, The, 94
Old Jim John, 253
Ole La'u Papa e, 91
Our Goodman, 245
Red Iron Ore, 134
Risseldy, Rosseldy, 264
Rock Around the Clock, 234
Ship in Distress, The, 211
Shoes of John, 246
Slap that Bass, 146
Sugar in the Gourd, 251
Sweet and Low, 184
Tain't What You Do, 18
Ten Tom-Toms by Anonymous (poem), 57
There Was a Jolly Miller, 250
Tina Singu, 36
Wabash Cannonball, The, 30
Water Is Wide, The, 46
When I Sing, 44
Why We Tell the Story, 303

Theme 3: Growing Up
Angelina, 8
A-Rovin', 319
Camelot, 310
Carol by K. Grahame (poem), 407
Come and Sing Together, 281
Dancing in the Street, 84
Down by the Riverside, 22
Git Along, Little Dogies, 284
Heart, 166
I Want to Be Ready, 12
I'm Gonna Sit at the Welcome Table, 416
Lean on Me, 150
Let It Roll, 124
Let Music Surround You, 285
Listen to the Music, 63
Lumber Camp Song, The, 136
Mi caballo blanco (My White Horse), 60
Mountain Music, 20
Old Barn Dance, The, 94
On a Clear Day, 206
One of Those Songs, 54
Rage and Roar, 48
River of My People, 176
Tain't What You Do, 18
Walk by the River (unison), 74, (parts), 76
Water Is Wide, The, 46
Yerakina, 216
You Sing for Me, 106

Theme 6: New Frontiers: Oceans and Space

Thematic Correlations to Reading Series (continued)

Scholastic Literacy Place ©2004

The following materials from *Spotlight on Music* may be used with each theme in *Scholastic Literacy Place*.

Grade K

Unit 1: Personal Voice, Stories About Us

Alison's Camel, T201
All Work Together, T12
Alphabet Song, T54
America, T303
Animales (Animals), T192
Battle Hymn of the Republic, T331
Bear Went Over the Mountain, The, T204
Bell Horses, T262
Best That I Can Be!, The, T48
Bickle, Bockle, 187
Bingo, T64
Bobby Shafto, T265
Bohm Dong Sahn Gohd Dong Sahn (Spring Valley, Flower Valley), T337
Bounce High, Bounce Low, T131
Buffalo Dusk (poem), T219
Bullfrogs, Bullfrogs on Parade (poem), T183
Bus, The, T137
Bye 'n' Bye, T67
City (poem), T134
Cobbler, Cobbler, Mend My Shoe, T169
Cobbler, The (poem), T169
Colorful Dragon Boat, T328
Counting Song, T92
Doing the Weekly Walk, T78
Echo (poem), T104
Eency Weency Spider, T8
El picaflor (The Humming Bird), T141
El tambor (The Drum), T129
Excuse Us, Animals in the Zoo (poem), T195
Farmer in the Dell, The, T100
Fehér liliomszál (Little Water Lily), T139
Five Fat Turkeys, T309
Follow Me, T133
Follow the Leader (poem), T132
Fox, the Hen, and the Drum, The, T294
Furry Bear (poem), T205
Garden Hoedown, The, T290
Giant's Shoes, The, by E. Fallis (poem), T32
Girls and Boys, Come Out to Play (poem), T98
Git on Board, T145
Go, Go, Go, T276
Gogo, T188

Good Day Song, T50
Grizzly Bear, T252
Happy Birthday, T273
Happy Birthday, T347
Head and Shoulders, T238
Hello Song, T2
Here Is the Beehive, T258
Hickory, Dickory, Dock (poem), T49
Hinges (poem), T23
Hippopotamus, The (poem), T199
Hokey Pokey, T68
Hop, Hop, Hop, T197
Hot Dog, T69
Humming Birds (poem), T140
I Am a Little Tugboat (poem), T95
I Can't Spell Hippopotamus, T199
I Got Shoes, T33
I Know an Old Lady, T26
I Will Sing Hello, T156
If Things Grew Down (poem), T48G, T293
If You're Happy, T6
Ifetayo (Love Brings Happiness), T325
In the Barnyard (poem), T207
Instrument Game, T36
It Fell in the City (poem), T312
It's So Good to See You, T86
It's Such a Good Feeling, T282
It's You I Like, T280
Jack, Be Nimble, T88
Jack-in-the-box (poem), T251
Jack-in-the-Box, T250
Jack-o'-Lantern, T307
Jig Jog, Jig Jog, T260
Juhtgarak (Chopsticks), T108
Jump or Jiggle (poem), T193
Just Like Me, T242
Kangaroo, The, T197
Kum Ba Yah, T327
La pequeñita araña (Eency Weency Spider), T9
Lady, Lady, T184
Las horas (The Hours), T70
Let's Think of Something To Do, T270
Little Blue Truck, T136
Little Ducky Duddle, T289
Little Sir Echo, T103
Little Spotted Puppy, T146
Little White Duck, T208
London Bridge, T99
Long Gone (poem), T72
Look Who's Here!, T84
Los pollitos (Little Chickens), T288
Mama, Bake the Johnnycake, T318

María Blanca, T99
Martin Luther King (speech piece), T326
Mbombela, T152
Me I Am! (poem), T346
Merrily, We Roll Along, T110
Merry-Go-Round (poem), T225
Merry-Go-Round, The, T224
Mi chacra (My Farm), T207
Mister Sun, T343
Monkey, Monkey, T215
Monté sur un éléphant (Riding on an Elephant), T217
Muffin Man, The, T105
Mulberry Bush, The, T112
Music (poem), T157
My Grandfather, T23
My Legs and I by L. Jacobs (poem), T19
My Oak Tree, T236
My Thumbs are Starting to Wiggle, T35
Na Bahia Tem (In Bahia Town), T163
Name Game, T57
Nampaya omame (Mothers), T128
Neat Feet (excerpt) by B. Schmidt (poem), T30
Noble Duke of York, The, T232
Oats, Peas, Beans, and Barley Grow, T287
Ɔbɔɔ Asi Me Nsa, T159
Oh, A-Hunting We Will Go, T62
Old Gray Cat, The, T43
Old MacDonald Had a Farm, T211
Old Mister Woodpecker, T172
Oliphaunt (poem), T216
On This Night, T315
One Finger, One Thumb, T38
One, Two, Tie My Shoe, T151
Only My Opinion (poem), T29
Ourchestra (poem), T171
Peace and Quiet, T278
Pimpón, T22
Planting Seeds, T284
Popalong Hopcorn! (poem), T160
Popping Corn, T161
Presidents, T330
Propel, Propel, Propel, T275
Put Your Finger in the Air, T230
Qué bonito es (How Wonderful It Is), T234
Rainbow Song, The, T61
Ride the Train, T144
Ring Around the Rosy, T246
Ring-a-ring (poem), T247

Thematic Correlations to Reading Series (continued)

Unit 6: Community Involvement, Join In!

Muffin Man, The, T105

Mulberry Bush, The, T112

Music (poem), T157

My Grandfather, T23

My Oak Tree, T236

My Thumbs Are Starting to Wiggle, T35

Na Bahia Tem (In Bahia Town), T163

Name Game, T57

Nampaya omame (Mothers), T128

Noble Duke of York, The, T232

Oats, Peas, Beans and Barley Grow, T287

Ɔbɔɔ Asi Me Nsa, T159

Oh, A-Hunting We Will Go, T62

Old Gray Cat, The, T43

Old MacDonald Had a Farm, T211

Old Mister Woodpecker, T172

Oliphaunt (poem), T216

On This Night, T315

One Finger, One Thumb, T38

One, Two, Tie My Shoe, T151

Only My Opinion (poem), T29

Ourchestra (poem), T171

Peace and Quiet, T278

Pimpón, T22

Planting Seeds, T284

Popalong Hopcorn! (poem), T160

Popping Corn, T161

Prairie Dog Song (Kiowa Children's Song), T220

Presidents, T330

Propel, Propel, Propel, T275

Put Your Finger in the Air, T230

Qué bonito es (How Wonderful It Is), T234

Rainbow Song, The, T61

Ride the Train, T144

Ring Around the Rosy, T246

Ring-a-ring (poem), T247

River, The, (poem), T342

Row, Row, Row, T274

Santa Clara Corn Grinding Song, T164

School Is Over (poem), T84

See the Pony Galloping, T44

Seesaw, Margery Daw, T265

Shake My Sillies Out, T175

Shapes (poem), T37

Sidewalks (poem), T98

Simi Yadech (Give Me Your Hand), T168

Sing a Little Song, T179

Sing a Song of Sixpence, T111

Singing-Time (poem), T15

Snail's Pace (poem), T29

Snake and the Frog, The (story), T297

Snow Toward Evening (poem), T311

Snowman, The, T313

Speedy Delivery, T279

Spell of the Moon (poem), T116

Stamping Land, T24

Sweetly Sings the Donkey, T244

Table Manners (poem), T107

Taking Off (poem), T134

Ten in a Bed, T256

Ten Little Frogs, T240

Tengo, Tengo, Tengo (I Have, I Have, I Have), T212

They Were Tall, T53

Things I'm Thankful For, T308

This Is My City, T120

This Is What I Can Do, T124

Three Little Kittens, T148

Three Little Muffins, T127

Time to Sing, T16

Toodala, T39

Touch Your Shoulders, T254

Travel (poem), T144

Tree of Peace (speech piece), T321

Tugboat, T95

Twinkle, Twinkle, Little Star, T90

Umoja! (poem), T325

Ushkana (Damsel Fly Song), T75

Wait and See, T334

Walk to School, T18

Wavvuuvuumira (Mister Bamboo Bug), T165

We Are Playing in the Forest, T248

Willoughby Wallaby Woo, T241

Won't You Be My Neighbor?, T268

Woodpecker, The (poem), T172

Worms, T286

Y ahora vamos a cantar (Now We Are Going to Sing), T340

You're a Grand Old Flag, T4

Grade 1

Unit 1: Personal Voice, Hello!

A be ce (A B C), T213

A la rueda rueda ('Round and 'Round), T240

Acka Backa, T256

¡Adivina lo que es! (Guess What It Is), T170

All Night, All Day, T232

America, T326

Animal Song, T288

Another Busy Day, T41

Ants Go Marching, The, T22

Apple a Day, An (poem), T152

Apples and Bananas, T151

Arre, mi burrito (Gid'yup, Little Burrito), T257

Autumn Leaves Are Falling, T330

Autumn Leaves, T331

Bear Hunt (speech piece), T126

Bear Went Over the Mountain, The, T115

Bee, Bee, Bumblebee, T250

Best Friends, T222

Big and Small (speech piece), T200

Bluebells, T209

Bonjour, mes amis (Hello, My Friends), T18

Boris, the Singing Bear, T312

Bow-Wow (poem), T81

Brinca la tablita (Hop, Hop!), T71

Brush Your Teeth (song), T66, (speech piece), T67

Bug (poem), T167

But the Critter Got Away (speech piece), T88

Butterfly, Flutter By, T333

Call of the Wild, A (excerpt) (poem), T139

Caribbean Amphibian, T294

Categories, T146

Chang (Elephant), T199

Charlie over the Ocean, T75

Chase the Squirrel, T88

Chickery Chick, T292

Clap Your Hands, T246

Clouds (poem), T330

Clouds by Anonymous (poem), T331

Come Back, My Little Chicks, T134

Cookies, T277

Counting Song, T195

Cow, The (poem), T236

Cut the Cake, T232

Dance Myself to Sleep, T314

Diana (Play the Bugle), T334

Diou Shou Juan'er (Hiding a Handkerchief), T212

Double This (speech piece), T95

Down by the Bay, T48

Down the Hill, T281

Dragonfly (poem), T44

Dreidel Song (poem), T349

Duérmete mi niño (Go to Sleep, My Baby), T61

Ears, Far and Near (poem), T16

El florón (The Flower), T117

El juego chirimbolo (The Chirimbolo Game), T103

Field of Joys, T224

Five Little Pumpkins (poem), T337

George Washington, T368

Gilly, Gilly, Gilly Good Morning, T12

Go A Tin (Lantern Song), T363

Goin' to the Zoo, T192

Granny (speech piece), T104

Grasshoppers Three, T284

Green Grass Grows All Around, The, T148

Haiku Butterflies (poem), T332

Hakyo jong (School Bells), T302

Haliwa-Saponi

Happiest Street in the World, The, T304

Head and Shoulders, Baby, T40

Hello, There!, T230

Here Comes the Band (poem), T80

Here We Sit, T251

Hey, Children, Who's In Town?, T14
Hi! My Name Is Joe! (speech piece), T220
Hoo, Hoo!, T55
Hop, Chirp! Moo! Oh Happy Springtime Day, T372
Hopping Frog (poem), T113
Horses of the Sea, The (poem), T179
How Does Your Garden Grow?, T144
Hunt the Cows, T236
I Am Slowly Going Crazy, T127
I Had a Little Hen (nursery rhyme), T136
I Have a Friend (poem), T225
I Like (poem), T110
I Like Spinach, T163
I Love My Country, T328
I Wanna Be a Friend of Yours, T84
I'd Like to Be a Lighthouse (poem), T238
I'm Getting Sick of Peanut Butter (poem), T219
I've a Pair of Fishes, T124
Ice (poem), T346
If All the World Were Paper, T296
In My Little Motor Boat, T159
It's So Nice on the Ice, T346
Jambo (Hello), T230
John the Rabbit, T74
Johnny Works with One Hammer, T96
Johnny's Flea, T158
Jump or Jiggle (poem), T316
Jump, Jim Joe, T89
Kaeru no Uta, T112
Kari (Wild Geese), T261
Kobuta, T168
La ranita cri (The Little Frog Croaks), T27
Ladybugs' Picnic, T290
Lavender's Blue, T174
Legend of George Washington and the Cherry Tree, The (story), T369
Let's Go Driving, T52
Library Song, T42
Light the Candles, T351
Little Black Bug, T166
Little Red Caboose, T97
Little Robin Redbreast, T208
Locust, The (poem), T285
Looby Loo, T262
Love Grows, T202
Love Is the Magic Word, T366
Lucy Lockett, T253
Mail Myself to You, T366
Marco Polo (speech piece), T90
Martin Luther King, T360
Mary's Coal Black Lamb, T286
Mi cuerpo (My Body), T32
Miss Mary Mack, T15
Mizuguruma (The Water Wheel), T260
Mos', Mos'! (Cat, Cat!), T53
My Feet (poem), T264
My Kite (poem), T371

My Mama's Calling Me, T54
My Mom, T372
My Valentine (poem), T364
Na Bahia Tem (In Bahia Town), T297
Naming Things (poem), T221
Naranja dulce (Sweet Orange), T303
Naughty Kitty Cat, T171
Night Comes… (poem), T233
No One Like You, T300
O Wind (poem), T235
Old King Glory, T217
Old Mother Goose (poem), T181
One Little Elephant, T194
One, Two, Three, Four, Five, T265
One, Two, Three, Four, T123
Oranges and Lemons (poem), T150
Over in the Meadow, T78
Pat Pat Patty Pat, T308
Peanut Butter, T218
Pease Porridge Hot, T255
Pile of Stuff, A (story), T188
Piñata Song (poem), T153
Piñón, Pirulín, T311
Pitty Patty Polt (speech piece), T180
Plenty Fishes in the Sea, T310
Puddle Hopping, T60
Pumpkin Song, T342
Punchinella, T216
Pusa't daga (Cat and Rat), T289
Quaker, Quaker, T100
Rabbit in the Moon, The (folktale), T318
Rabbit, The (poem), T186
Rain Sizes (poem), T33
Rain, Rain, Go Away, T259
Rattlesnake, T185
Rig a Jig Jig, T116
Rise, Sally, Rise, T162
Romper, Stomper, and Boo (story), T36
Sailor Went to Sea, Sea, Sea, A (song), T38, (game), T39
Sara Watashi (Plate Passing), T66
Seeds (vocal and instrumental), T120
Seesaw, T242
Serra, Serra Serrador (Saw, Saw, Lumberjack), T133
Shoo, Turkey, T76
Simple Simon, T175
Sing After Me, T34
Sing Ho! For the Life of a Bear! (poem), T114
Sittin' Down to Eat, T182
Sitting in the Sand (poem), T374
Six Little Ducks, T64
Skin and Bones, T340
Skip to My Lou, T102
Sleep, Bonnie Bairnie, T27
Snail With the Mail, T275
Snail, Snail, T252
Somebody Come and Play, T92
Somebody Has To… (poem), T258
Something Funny Outside, T338

Something Told the Wild Geese (poem), T261
Soup, Soup!, T358
Spanish Days of the Week by Anonymous (poem), T108
Spotlight on America, T9
Spring, T273
Star Light, Star Bright, T258
Suite on English Folk Tunes, T136
Summertime from *Porgy and Bess*, T375
Swing, The (poem), T109
Tailor, Tailor (poem), T132
Tak for Maden (Thanks for Food), T343
Tako No Uta (The Kite Song), T370
Theme from *Sesame Street*, T298
There Are Many Flags in Many Lands, T329
There's a Hole in the Middle of the Sea, T178
This Little Light of Mine, T238
This Old Man, T306
Thoughts of a Rattlesnake (poem), T185
Time for Love, A, T347
Tinker, Tailor, T130
Tisket A Tasket, A, T107
Twenty-four Robbers, T173
Two, Four, Six, Eight, T246
Uga, Uga, Uga (Cake, Cake, Cake), T313
Una Adivinanza (A Riddle), T138
Untitled (Butterflies) (haiku), T332
Up the Hill (poem), T45
Up the Tree and Down Again (poem), T65
Wake Me, Shake Me, T198
We All Sing With the Same Voice, T156
What's Your Name?, T125
Wheels, Wheels, Wheels (poem), T106
When the Flag Goes By, T327
Who's Afraid of the Big Bad Wolf? (nursery rhyme), T137
Why the Beetle Has a Gold Coat (folktale), T321
Willum, T19
Wind Blew East, The, T234
Wind Blow, T187
Wings (poem), T250
Year With Frog and Toad, A (Reprise), T283
Year With Frog and Toad, A, T270
Yo, Mamana, Yo (Oh, Mama), T307
Zui Zui Zukkorbashi (song), T98, (game), T99

Unit 2: Problem Solving, Problem Patrol

A be ce, T213
Big and Small by E. McCullough Brabson, T200
Everybody Oughta Know (African American song) arr. by Y. M. Barnwell, T361

Head and Shoulders, Baby, T40
Martin Luther King, T360
My Feet by L. B. Jacobs (poem), T264
We All Sing With the Same Voice, T156

Unit 3: Teamwork, Team Spirit

A la rueda rueda ('Round and 'Round), T240
Acka Backa, T256
Another Busy Day (speech piece), T41
Apple a Day, An (traditional poem), T152
Apples and Bananas, T151
Arre, mi burrito (Gid-yup, Little Burro), T257
Bear Hunt (poem), T126
Bee, Bee, Bumblebee, T250
Best Friends, T222
Bluebells, T209
Brinca la tablita (Hop, Hop!), T71
Brush Your Teeth (song), T66, (speech piece), T66
Bug by L. Simmie (poem), T167
Call of the Wild, A (excerpt) by R. W. Service (poem), T139
Categories, T146
Charlie Over the Ocean, T75
Chase the Squirrel, T88
Clap Your Hands (song), T246, (rhythmic pattern), T247
Come Back, My Little Chicks, T134
Dance Myself to Sleep, T314
Diana, T334
Diou Shou Juan'er, T212
Double This (game), T94
Dreidel Song by E. Rosenzweig (poem), T349
Duérmete mi niño (Go to Sleep, My Baby), T61
El juego chirimbolo (The Chirimbolo Game), T103
El rorro (The Babe), T356
Field of Joys by M. Morand (poem), T224
Five Little Pumpkins (traditional poem), T337
Gilly, Gilly, Gilly Good Morning, T12
Go A Tin (Lantern Song), T363
Goin' to the Zoo, T192
Happiest Street in the World, The, T304
Head and Shoulders, Baby, T40
Here Comes the Band by W. Cole (poem), T80
Here We Sit, T251
Hoo, Hoo!, T55
How Does Your Garden Grow?, T144
I Am Slowly Going Crazy, T127
I Had a Little Hen (nursery rhyme), T136
I Have a Friend by Anonymous (poem), T225

I Like by M. A. Hoberman (poem), T110
I Like Spinach, T163
I Wanna Be a Friend of Yours, T84
I'm Getting Sick of Peanut Butter by K. Nesbitt (poem), T219
In My Little Motor Boat, T159
It's So Nice on the Ice, T346
Jambo (Hello), T230
Jingle Bells, T354
John the Rabbit, T74
Johnny Works with One Hammer, T96
Jump, Jim Joe, T89
Let's Go Driving, T52
Library Song, T42
Light the Candles, T351
Looby Loo, T262
Lucy Locket, T253
Marco Polo (speech piece), T90
Miss Mary Mack, T15
Mizuguruma (The Water Wheel), T260
Mos', Mos'! (Cat, Cat!), T53
My Kite by B. Brown and B. Brown (poem), T371
My Mama's Calling Me, T54
My Mom, T372
Naming Things by A. Davidson (poem), T221
One Little Elephant, T194
One, Two, Three, Four, Five, T265
Oranges and Lemons (English traditional poem), T150
Pat Pat Patty Pat, T308
Pease Porridge Hot, T255
Piñata Song (Mexican traditional poem), T153
Pitty Patty Polt (nursery rhyme) (rhythmic pattern), T180
Puddle Hopping, T60
Pumpkin Song, T342
Punchinella, T216
Quaker, Quaker, T100
Rig a Jig Jig, T116
Rise, Sally, Rise (game), T162
Romper, Stomper, and Boo (traditional story), T36
Sailor Went to Sea, Sea, Sea, A (song), T38, (game), T39
Sara Watashi (Plate Passing), T67
Seesaw (song), T242, (accompaniment), T248
Serra, serra serrador (Saw, Saw Lumberjack), T133
Shoo, Turkey, T76
Simple Simon, T175
Sing After Me, T34
Sitting in the Sand by K. Kushkin (poem), T374
Six Little Ducks, T64
Skin and Bones, T340
Skip to My Lou, T102
Sleep, Bonnie Bairnie, T26

Snail, Snail (song), T252, (three-tone), T252
Somebody Come and Play, T92
Something Funny Outside, T338
Soup, Soup!, T358
Spanish Days of the Week by Anonymous (poem), T108
Swing, The, by R. L. Stevenson (poem), T109
Tailor, Tailor (traditional poem), T132
Tak for Maden (Thanks for Food), T343
Tako No Uta (The Kite Song), T370
There's a Hole in the Middle of the Sea, T178
This Old Man, T306
Time for Love, A, T347
Tinker, Tailor, T131
Twenty-four Robbers, 173
Two, Four, Six, Eight (song), T246, (rhythmic pattern), T247
Una adivinanza (A Riddle), T138
Vhaya Kadhimba (Zimbabwean children's song) (song), T23, (game), T23
Wake Me, Shake Me, 198
We All Sing With the Same Voice, T156
What's Your Name?, T125
Wheels, Wheels, Wheels by N. White Carlstrom (poem), T106
Who's Afraid of the Big Bad Wolf? (nursery rhyme), T137
Willum, T19
Yo, Mamana, Yo (Oh, Mama), T307
Zui Zui Zukkorbashi (song), T98, (game), T99

Unit 4: Creative Expression, Imagine That!

¡Adivina lo que es! (Guess What It Is!), T170
All Night, All Day, T232
Best Friends, T222
Chickery Chick, T292
How Does Your Garden Grow?, T144
I Am Slowly Going Crazy, T127
I Love My Country, T328
I'd Like to Be a Lighthouse by R Field (poem), T238
If All the World Were Paper, T296
Lavender's Blue, T174
Love Grows, T202
Love Is the Magic Word, T366
Mail Myself to You, T366
My Mom, T372
My Valentine by M. C. Parsons (poem), T364
Naranja dulce, T303
Night Comes... by B. Schenk de Regniers (poem), T233
Rabbit, The, by M. Stelmach (poem), T186

Rattlesnake, T185

Sing After Me, T34

Sing Ho! For the Life of a Bear! By A.A. Milne (poem), T114

Somebody Has To… by S. Silverstein (poem), T258

Star Light, Star Bright, T258

This Little Light of Mine, T238

Thoughts of a Rattlesnake by K. Sexton (poem), T185

Tisket A Tasket, A, T107

When the Flag Goes By, T327

Wings by A. Fisher (poem), T250

Unit 5: Managing Information, Information Finders

Animal Song, T288

Ants Go Marching, The, T22

Arre, mi burrito (Gid-yup, Little Burro), T257

Autumn Leaves Are Falling, T330

Autumn Leaves, T331

Bear Hunt (poem), T126

Bear Went Over the Mountain, The, T115

Big and Small by E. McCullough Brabson, T200

Boris, the Singing Bear, T312

Bow-Wow by Mother Goose (poem), T81

Bug by L. Simmie (poem), T167

But the Critter Got Away (speech piece), T88, (poem), T89

Butterfly, Flutter By, T333

Call of the Wild, A (excerpt) by R. W. Service (poem), T139

Caribbean Amphibian, T294

Chang (Elephant), T199

Chase the Squirrel, T88

Chickery Chick, T292

Clouds by Anonymous (poem), T331

Come Back, My Little Chicks, T134

Cow, The, by R. L. Stevenson (poem), T236

Down by the Bay, T48

Dragonfly by D. M. Violin (poem), T44

El florón (The Flower), T117

Goin' to the Zoo, T192

Granny (traditional poem), T104

Grasshoppers Three, T284

Green Grass Grows All Around, The, T148

Hop! Chirp! Moo! Oh, Happy Springtime Day!, T372

Hopping Frog by C. Rossetti (poem), T113

Horses of the Sea, The, by C. Rossetti (poem), T179

Hunt the Cows, T236

I Had a Little Hen (nursery rhyme), T136

I'd Like to Be a Lighthouse by R Field (poem), T238

I've a Pair of Fishes, T124

Ice, T347

It's So Nice on the Ice, T346

Johnny's Flea, T158

Jump or Jiggle by E. Beyer (poem), T316

Kaeru no Uta, T112

Kari (Wild Geese), 101

La ranita cri (The Little Frog Croaks), T27

Ladybugs' Picnic, T290

Little Black Bug, T166

Little Robin Red Breast (English rhyme) (song), T208, (rhythmic pattern), T207

Locust, The (Zuñi poem), T285

Mary's Coal Black Lamb, T286

Mizuguruma (The Water Wheel), T260

Mos', Mos'! (Cat, Cat!), T53

Naughty Kitty Cat, T171

Night Comes… by B. Schenk de Regniers (poem), T233

O Wind by C. Rossetti (poem), T235

One Little Elephant, T194

Over in the Meadow, T78

Pusa't daga (Cat and Rat), T289

Rabbit, The, by M. Stelmach (poem), T186

Rain Poem (poem), T31

Rain Sizes by J. Ciardi (poem), T33

Rain, Rain, Go Away, T259

Rattlesnake, T185

Romper, Stomper, and Boo (traditional story), T36

Seeds, T120

Serra, serra serrador (Saw, Saw Lumberjack), T133

Simple Simon, T175

Sing Ho! For the Life of a Bear! By A.A. Milne (poem), T114

Sittin' Down to Eat, T182

Sitting in the Sand (poem), T374

Six Little Ducks, T64

Snail With the Mail, T274

Snail, Snail (song), T252, (three-tone), T252

Somebody Has To… by S. Silverstein (poem), T258

Something Told the Wild Geese by R. Field (poem), T261

Spring, T273

There's a Hole in the Middle of the Sea, T178

Thoughts of a Rattlesnake by K. Sexton (poem), T185

Untitled (Butterflies) (haiku), T332

Up the Hill by W. J. Smith (poem), T45

Up the Tree and Down Again by A. Seear (poem), T65

White Sheep by Anonymous (poem), T234

Who's Afraid of the Big Bad Wolf? (nursery rhyme), T137

Wind Blew East, The, T234

Wind Blow, T187

Year with Frog and Toad, A (reprise), T283

Year with Frog and Toad, A, T270

Unit 6: Community Involvement, Hometowns

A be ce (A B C), T213

A la rueda rueda ('Round and 'Round), T240

Acka Backa, T256

¡Adivina lo que es! (Guess What It Is), T170

All Night, All Day, T232

America, T326

Animal Song, T288

Another Busy Day, T41

Ants Go Marching, The, T22

Apple a Day, An (poem), T152

Apples and Bananas, T151

Arre, mi burrito (Gid'yup, Little Burrito), T257

Autumn Leaves Are Falling, T330

Autumn Leaves, T331

Bear Hunt (poem), T126

Bear Went Over the Mountain, The, T115

Bee, Bee, Bumblebee, T250

Best Friends, T222

Big and Small (speech piece), T200

Bluebells, T209

Bonjour, mes amis (Hello, My Friends), T18

Boris, the Singing Bear, T312

Bow-Wow (poem), T81

Brinca la tablita (Hop, Hop!), T71

Brush Your Teeth (song), T66, (speech piece), T67

Bug (poem), T167

But the Critter Got Away (speech piece), T88

Butterfly, Flutter By, T333

Call of the Wild, A (excerpt) (poem), T139

Caribbean Amphibian, T294

Categories, T146

Chang (Elephant), T199

Charlie over the Ocean, T75

Chase the Squirrel, T88

Chickery Chick, T292

Clap Your Hands, T246

Clouds (poem), T330

Come Back, My Little Chicks, T134

Cookies, T277

Thematic Correlations to Reading Series

Thematic Correlations to Reading Series (continued)

Say Your Name, 243
Seeds and Seasons, 206
Señor Coyote (story), 330
Seussical Mega-Mix, 287
Shake the Papaya Down, 90
She'll Be Comin' 'Round the Mountain, 33
Sheep in the Meadow (speech piece), 8
Sheep Shearing, 102
Shoheen Sho, 140
Shoo, Fly, 222
Sing! Sing! Sing!, 196
Skating, 350
Sorida, 96
Sun Is First to Rise, The, 383
Take Me Out to the Ball Game, 56
Taos Round Dance, 155
Thank You, 349
There Are Many Flags in Many Lands, 341
There's a Hole in the Bucket, 132
This Is Halloween, 346
This Is My Country, 87
Three Little Penguins (speech piece), 112
Tiki Tiki Tiki Room, The, 324
Tinga Layo, 50
Together (poem), 34
Up on the Housetop, 356
Wake Up the Sun, 124
We're Sailing Down the River, 166
Welcome Is the Month of May, 378
What Did Delaware?, 190
Whistle While You Work, 6
Who Chopped the Cherry Tree Down? 371
Who Has Seen the Wind? (poem), 137
Who Has the Penny?, 252
Who's That Tapping at the Window?, 261
Willowbee, 69
Yanai (The Elephant), 305
Yankee Doodle, 340
You Are My Sunshine, 369
You'll Sing a Song and I'll Sing a Song, 156

Unit 2: Problem Solving, Super Solvers

Drumming Spider, The (West African folktale), 333
Lemonade, 19
Señor Coyote (Mexican folktale), 330
Shake the Papaya Down, 90
Sheep Shearing, 102
There's a Hole in the Bucket, 132

Unit 3: Teamwork, Lights! Camera! Action!

A la rueda de San Miguel (To the Wheel of San Miguel), 60

Ach, du lieber Augustin (The More We Get Together), 35
Apple Picker's Reel, 343
Artichokes, 314
Ban Dal (Half Moon), 219
Button, You Must Wander, 176
Check It Out! (It's About Respect), 10
Chíu, chíu, chíu (Chirp, Chirp, Chirp), 302
Dance Together, 264
Dance, Dance, Dance!, 5
Doggie, Doggie, 59
Drumming Spider, The (West African folktale), 333
El zapatero (The Cobbler), 138
Everybody Has Music Inside, 164
Garden Song, 236
Green Eggs and Ham, 284
Harvest, 342
Heigh Ho, Here We Go, 252
Here Comes Sally, 220
I See, 266
I'm Gonna Sing, 9
It's a Small World, 298
It's Possible, 281
Ja posejah lubenice (I Planted Watermelons), 316
Jim Along, Josie, 194
Joy, 46
Jugaremos en el bosque (We Will Play in the Forest), 188
Lemonade, 19
Let's Go Fly a Kite, 134
Martin Luther King, 364
Matarile, 261
Me Stone, 48
Mein Hut (My Hat), 142
Merry-Go-Round, 267
Mill Song, The, 52
Mouse, Mousie, 254
Oh, the Thinks You Can Think!, 276
Oliver Twist, 268
Part of Your World, 294
Pizza, Pizza, Daddy-O, 62
Place in the Choir, A, 308
Plainsies, Clapsies, 248
Puff, the Magic Dragon, 54
Riddle Song, 251
Riqui Ran (Sawing Song), 21
Sailor, Sailor on the Sea, 262
Sammy Sackett, 146
Shake the Papaya Down, 90
She'll Be Comin' 'Round the Mountain, 33
Sheep in the Meadow (speech piece), 8
Sheep Shearing, 102
Skating, 350
Step in Time, 6
Take Me Out to the Ball Game, 56
Thank You, 349

There's a Hole in the Bucket, 132
This is My Country, 87
Together by P. Engle (poem), 34
Up on the Housetop, 356
What Did Delaware?, 190
Who's That Tapping at the Window?, 261
You Are My Sunshine, 369

Unit 4: Creative Expression, Story Studio

A la rueda de San Miguel (To the Wheel of San Miguel), 60
Ach, du lieber Augustin (The More We Get Together), 35
All Around the Buttercup, 210
America, 338
Ani Purim, 372
Animal Fair, 214
Apple Picker's Reel, 343
Artichokes, 314
Australia's on the Wallaby, 106
Away for Rio, 170
Baby Beluga, 26
Baby Nodja, 154
Bahay Kubo (My Nip Hut), 382
Ban Dal (Half Moon), 219
Banyan Tree, 321
Bate, bate (Stir, Stir), 242
Big Beautiful Planet, 376
Bliss (poem), 212
Bow, Wow, Wow, 264
Button, You Must Wander, 176
Candle on the Water, 296
Caranguejo (The Crab), 306
Check It Out! (It's About Respect), 10
Chiapanecas (Ladies of Chiapas), 128
Chichipapa (The Sparrow's Singing School), 22
Child Falling Asleep from Scenes from Childhood, 77
Chirri Bim, 70
Chíu, Chíu, Chíu (Chirp, Chirp, Chirp), 302
City Traffic (story), 328
Columbus Sailed with Three Ships, 344
Corner Grocery Store, 311
Cuckoo, Where Are You?, 244
Daisy Chain, 255
Dal taro kacha (Come, Pick the Moon), 98
Dance Together, 264
Doggie, Doggie, 59
Donkey, Donkey, 256
Drumming Spider, The (story), 333
Dumplin's, 172
Eating Lizards, 250
El burrito enfermo (The Sick Little Donkey), 180
El palomo y la paloma (The Doves), 380

Thematic Correlations to Reading Series (continued)

Unit 5: Managing Information, Animal World

Here Comes a Bluebird, 263
Hop, Old Squirrel, 258
I Chih ha Ma (Frogs), 186
I Heard a Bird Sing by O. Herford (poem), 271
It's Possible, 281
It's Raining! It's Pouring!, 233
Itik Besenda Gurau (The Ducks), 100
Jugaremos en el bosque (We Will Play in the Forest), 188
La bella hortelana (The Beautiful Gardener), 208
Land of the Silver Birch, 88
Leatherwing Bat, 304
Little Seeds (except) by E. Holmelund Minarik (poem), 207
Mister Rabbit, Mister Rabbit, 150
Mouse, Mousie, 254
Mr. Frog, 257
Na belo (Little Heron), 322
Old Blue, 213
Old Woman and the Pig, 130
Oma Rapeti (Run, Rabbit), 108
Part of Your World, 294
Piggy by W. Cole (poem), 315
Place in the Choir, A, 308
Rover, 260
Seeds and Seasons, 206
Señor Coyote (Mexican folktale), 330
Sheep in the Meadow (speech piece), 8
Sheep Shearing, 102
Sing! Sing! Sing!, 196
Sun Is First to Rise, The, by E. Coatsworth (poem), 383
Thank You, 349
Three Little Penguins (speech piece), 112
Tiki Tiki Tiki Room, The, 324
Tinga Layo, 50
Wake Up the Sun, 124
Welcome Is the Month of May, 378
Who Has Seen the Wind? by C. G. Rossetti (poem), 137
Yanai (The Elephant), 305

Unit 6: Community Involvement, Lend a Hand

Ach, du lieber Augustin (The More We Get Together), 35
Candle on the Water, 296
Chiapanecas (Ladies of Chiapas), 128
Corner Grocery Store, 311
Daisy Chain, 255
Dal taro kacha (Come, Pick the Moon), 98
El tren (The Train), 326
El zapatero (The Cobbler), 138
En la feria de San Juan (In the Market of San Juan), 226
Hakuna Matata, 292
Hello, Hello There, 126
Horton Hears a Who!, 279

Mama eu quero (I Want My Mama) (Brazilian carnival song), 92
Mary Had a Baby, 360
Opposite of Two, The, by R. Wilbur (poem), 45
Part of Your World, 294
Pat on the Back, A, 74
Puff, the Magic Dragon, 54
She'll Be Comin' 'Round the Mountain, 33
Shoheen Sho, 140
Take Me Out to the Ball Game, 56
You'll Sing a Song and I'll Sing a Song, 156

Grade 3

Unit 1: Personal Voice, What's New?

Addams Family Theme, The, 307
Amen, 376
America, the Beautiful, 354
Ballad of the Bedbugs and the Beetles, The, 206
Bella Bimba, 172
Billy, 7
Bim Bom, 218
Blow, Ye Winds, Blow, 192
Bohm, 392
Boll Weevil, 171
Buffalo Dance Entrance Song, 325
Butterfly Come Play With Me, 112
Cat and Dog, 259
Chan mali chan, 10
Charlie, 208
Chicka-ma, Chicka-ma, Craney Crow, 263
Chicken on the Fence Post, 265
Cielito Lindo, 166
Circle 'Round the Zero, 267
City Life, 341
Clocks, 266
Colors of the Wind, 84
Coral, 249
Cornstalk Fiddle and a Shoestring Bow, 284
Crawdad Song, 107
Cumberland Gap, 99
¡Dale, dale, dale!, 378-379
De aquel cerro (On the Darkened Hillside), 32
Death of the Robin, 275
Dide, 279
Digga Digga Dog, 164
Dinah, 150
Ding Dong Diggy Diggy Dong, 269
Draw a Bucket of Water, 222
Egy üveg alma (One Jar of Apples), 22
Eh Soom Boo Kawaya, 58
El arroyo que murmura (The Murmuring Brook), 318

El atole, 396-397
El florón (The Flower), 46
El nido (The Nest), 214
En roulant ma boule (As I Roll My Ball), 100
Evergreen, Everblue, 330
Frog in the Meadow, 243
Frosty Weather, 250
Gebeta Board, The (story), 346
Gi'Me Elbow Room, 88
Golden Ring Around the Susan Girl, 264
Great Big House, 14
Greatest Show on Earth, The, 308
Hag Asif, 360-361
Happy Wanderer, The, 18
Hello!, 283
Herring, The, 316
Hey, Motswala, 34
I Have a Car, 252
I Lost the Farmer's Dairy Key, 273
I Walk in Beauty, 329
I'm a Believer, 312
I'm on My Way, 382-383
I's the B'y, 13
In Good Old Colony Times, 326
Interjections, 303
Interplanet Janet, 298
Isabela and the Troll (story), 349
J'entends le moulin (I Hear the Windmill), 135
Jamaica Farewell, 156
Jasmine Flower, 146
John Jacob Jingleheimer Schmidt, 68
Just Like the Sun, 394–395
Kalinka (Little Snowball Bush), 224
Kreely Kranky, 258
Kum bahur (The Rooster), 75
Kuma San (Honorable Bear), 244
La bamba, 236
La cloche (The Clock), 67
La mar (The Sea), 110
Let Us Chase the Squirrel, 248
Let's Go Dancing, 196
Limbo Rock, 232
Lincoln (poem), 389
Little Boy of the Sheep, 188
Little Sally Walker, 105
Little Tommy Tinker, 277
Look High, Look Low, 338
Lukey's Boat, 114
Marvelous Toy, The, 182
May Day Carol, 393
Minuteman Minute Song, The, 322
Moon and Me, 220
Morning Bells, 270
Morning Mood from Peer Gynt Suite No. 1, Op. 46 by E. Grieg, 251
Movin' Right Along, 124
Mrs. Murphy's Chowder, 390-391
Music of the World A-Turnin', 44

Thematic Correlations to Reading Series (continued)

My Friend Tom, 364–365
My Horses Ain't Hungry, 278
Night Song, 186
O, the Train's Off the Track, 176
Oh Mama Bakudala, 328
Oh, Susanna, 153
Old Mister Rabbit, 254
Old Roger, 280
Oleanna, 144
One More River, 216
One Potato, Two Potato, 267
Open the Window, Noah, 324
Out from the Wilderness, 388-389
Over My Head, 286
Pajarillo barranqueño, 358-359
Pat-a-Pan, 375
Paw Paw Patch, The, 195
Pay Me My Money Down, 149
Pit-A-Pan, 375
Polly Wolly Doodle, 132
Preamble, The, 293
Que llueva (It's Raining), 274
Raccoon Dance Song, 87
Rain is Falling Down, 242
Rainbow Connection, The, 310
Rattlesnake, 72
Recycle Rap, 332
Riding in the Buggy, 131
Rise Up Singin', 138
Scotland's Burning, 257
See the Rabbit Running, 255
Shalom Chaveyrim (Shalom, My
    Friends), 141
Shepherd, Shepherd, 56
Ship Ahoy, 314
Shoo Fly Pie and Apple Pan Dowdy, 227
Simon Says, 4
Smoke Goes Up the Chimney, 272
Spiders, 282
Stevedore's Song, 127
Sun Don't Set in the Mornin', 48, 60
Sweep, Sweep Away, 276
Sweet Potatoes, 16
Tanabata, 62
Taps, 281
There Was An Old Lady (story), 344
There's a Little Wheel A-Turnin' in My
    Heart, 129, 137
This a Way and That a Way, 386-387
This Is America, 356
Three is a Magic Number, 296
Three Little Birds, 204
Throw It Out the Window, 94
Tititorea, 174
Trampin', 287
Turn the Glasses Over, 260
Uch Tirvarch, 53
Uno de enero (The First of January),
    210
Vamos a la mar (Let's Go to the Sea),
    256

Wan Ü Ger, 190
Wéané, 184
When I First Came to This Land, 28
Who's That Yonder?, 245
Woke Up This Morning, 180
Woodchuck, 246
Yankee Doodle Boy, 357
Yellow Submarine, 320
You're a Grand Old Flag, 355

Unit 2: Problem Solving, Big Plans
Blow, Ye Winds, Blow, 192
Cumberland Gap, 99
Digga Digga Dog, 164
Gebeta Board, The (Ethiopian folk tale),
    346
I Lost the Farmer's Dairy Key, 273
Lincoln by M. Cohn Livingston (poem),
    389
Movin' Right Along, 124
Smoke Goes Up the Chimney, 272
Walk by the River (song), 74, (harmony
    parts), 76
Who's That Yonder?, 245

Unit 3: Teamwork, On the Job
Blow, Ye Winds, Blow, 192
Chag Asif (Harvest Time), 360
Crawdad Song, 107
Death of the Robin, 275
Digga Digga Dog, 164
Eh Soom Boo Kawaya (Nigerian boat
    song), 58
Gebeta Board, The (Ethiopian folk tale),
    346
Gi'Me Elbow Room, 88
Guitar Man, The, 138
Hello!, 283
I Lost the Farmer's Dairy Key, 273
I's the B'y, 13
Movin' Right Along, 124
Music of the World A-Turnin', 44
Shalom Chaveyrim (Shalom, My
    Friends), 141
Shepherd, Shepherd, 56
Smoke Goes Up the Chimney, 272
Stevedore's Song, 127
Three Is a Magic Number, 94
Three Little Birds, 204
Treasure Chests, 90
Ucha Tirvarch (Little Bear Song), 53
Walk by the River (song), 74, (harmony
    parts), 76
Wang Ü Ger (Chinese fishing song), 190
Way Down South by Anonymous
    (poem), 8

Unit 4: Creative Expression, Hit
Series
Addams Family Theme, The, 307
Anansi (Ashanti folk tale), 104
Apple Tree by Anonymous (poem), 24

Ballad of the Bedbugs and the Beetles,
    The, 206
Bella Bimba (Pretty Girl), 172
Billy, 7
Bim Bom, 218
Blow, Ye Winds, Blow, 192
Boll Weevil, 171
Boo, 362
Butterfly Come Play with Me, 112
Chan mali chan (Singaporean folk
    song), 10
Chicka-ma, Chicka-ma, Craney Crow,
    263
Chicken on the Fence Post, 265
Cielito lindo (Mexican folk song), 166
Circle 'Round the Zero, 267
City Music by T. Mitton (poem), 74
Clocks, 266
Cornstalk Fiddle and a Shoestring Bow,
    284
Crawdad Song, 107
¡Dale, dale, dale!, 378
Deck the Hall, 374
Dinah, 150
Ding Dong Diggy Diggy Dong, 269
Draw a Bucket of Water, 222
Egy üveg alma (One Jar of Apples), 22
El florón (The Flower), 46
El nido (The Nest), 214
En roulant ma boule (As I Roll My Ball),
    100
Flip, Flop, and Fly!, 336
Frog in the Meadow, 243
Frost, the Snowman, 366
Gebeta Board, The (Ethiopian folk tale),
    346
Gi'Me Elbow Room, 88
Go Tell It on the Mountain, 377
Golden Ring Around the Susan Girl,
    264
Greatest Show on Earth, The, 308
Happy Wanderer, The, 18
Herring, The, 316
Hey, Motswala, 34
Hope by E. Dickinson (poem), 166
I'm a Believer, 312
I'm On My Way, 382
I's the B'y, 13
In Good Old Colony Times, 326
Interjections, 303
Interplanet Janet, 298
Isabela and the Troll (Spanish folk tale),
    349
Jamaica Farewell, 156
John Jacob Jingleheimer Schmidt, 68
Kalinka (Little Snowball Bush), 224
Kreely Kranky, 258
Kuma San (Honorable Bear), 244
La bamba (Mexican folk song), 236
Let Us Chase the Squirrel, 248
Let's Go Dancing, 196

Thematic Correlations to Reading Series (continued)

Thematic Correlations to Reading Series (continued)

Grade 4

Unit 1: Personal Voice, Chapter by Chapter

Thematic Correlations to Reading Series (continued)

Take Time in Life, 156
This Land is Your Land, 146
Tomorrow, 295
Train Is A-Coming, 270
`Ulili E (The Sandpiper), 396
Uruguay
Wake Up Canon, 326
Walk in the Parlor, 226
Water Come a Me Eye, 90
We Are Here, 394
We Remember, 360
We Shall Overcome, 387
What Can One Little Person Do?, 204
When I Was Young, 187
Whispers by M. Cohn Livingston (poem), 95
Who's Got the Fishpole?, 261
Yankee Doodle, 154
You're Never Fully Dressed Without a Smile, 304
Zum Gali Gali, 255

Unit 2: Problem Solving, What an Idea!

A la nanita nana (A Little Lullaby), 230
A la puerta del cielo (At the Gates of Heaven), 12
Allundé Alluia, 34
Bamboo Flute, 134
Buckeye Jim, 136
Circle of Song, 330
Don't Let the Music Stop, 334
El manisero (Peanut Vendor), 106
Follow Your Dream, 234
Frog Went A-Courtin', 46
Happy Talk, 84
Hine Ma Tov (How Good It Is), 66
Just One Planet, 164
Little David Play on Your Harp, 323
Modern Dragon, A (speech piece), 98
'Most Done Ling'rin Here, 65
Night Herding Song, 110
Over the Rainbow, 126
Please, Mr. Postman, 44
Rise Up, O Flame, 283
Roll On, Columbia, 182
Row, Row, Row Your Boat, 268
Sail Away, Ladies, 54
Shabat Shalom, 170
Take Time in Life, 156
Tomorrow, 295
We Shall Overcome, 387

Unit 3: Teamwork, Discovery Teams

Achshav (Now), 112
Allundé Alluia, 34
Bamboo, 218
Cedar Swamp, 50
Chicka Hanka, 138
Circle of Song, 330

Cotton-Eye Joe (song), 52, (countermelody), 53
Derby Ram, The, 259
Down at the Twist and Shout, 308
Eight Bells, 281
El barquito (The Tiny Boat), 214
El quelite (The Village), 362
Hitori, 345
Hold My Mule, 248
I Will Be Your Friend, 388
Journey, A (speech piece), 14
Just One Planet, 164
Kettle Valley Line, The, 348
La Yunsita, 350
Macnamara's Band, 88
Modern Dragon, A (speech piece), 98
'Most Done Ling'rin Here, 65
My Town, My World, 6
Oh, Won't You Sit Down?, 70
Old Ark's A-Moverin', 130
Old House, 282
Oliver Cromwell, 269
Oro, My Bodeen, 279
Over the Sea to Skye, 344
Page's Train, 246
Pat Works on the Railway, 86
Peace Round, 16
Please, Mr. Postman, 44
Push Boat Song, 266
Sail Away, Ladies, 54
Something for Me, Something for You, 4
Somos el barco (We are the Boat), 10
This Land Is Your Land, 146
Train Is A-Coming, 270
Trains at Night by F. M. Frost (poem), 246
We Shall Overcome, 387
What Can One Little Person Do?, 204
Yankee Doodle, 154
Zum gali gali, 255

Unit 4: Creative Expression, The Funny Side

America, My Homeland, 358
At the Hop, 306
Bell Doth Toll, The, 276
Big Bunch, a Little Bunch, 267
Built My Lady a Fine Brick House, 252
Caballito blanco (Little White Pony), 278
Cedar Swamp, 50
Chairs to Mend, 272
Chumbara, 172
Cotton-Eye Joe (song), 52, (countermelody), 53
Dima, 265
Down at the Twist and Shout, 308
Early in the Morning at Eight O'Clock, 59
El barquito (The Tiny Boat), 214
Frog Went A-Courtin', 46

Girl I Left Behind Me, The, 249
Goodbye Brother, 273
Hala lala layya, 222
Happiness, 124
Himmel und Erde (Music Alone Shall Live), 280
Hojas de té (Tea Leaves), 256
Hop Up and Jump Up, 271
I Will Be Your Friend, 388
I'll Rise When the Rooster Crows, 36
Johnson Boys, 233
Just One Planet, 164
Katyusha, 188
Korobushka, 285
Li'l 'Liza Jane, 20
Loco-Motion, The, 312
Long-Legged Sailor, 243
Love Somebody, 94
Macnamara's Band, 88
Molinillo de café (Little Coffee Mill), 250
My Home's in Montana, 274
New Day, The, 316
Octopus's Garden, 30
Old Abram Brown, 32
Old Joe Clark, 74
Old Paint, 275
Pat Works on the Railway, 86
Peasant's Dancing Day, 132
Please, Mr. Postman, 44
¿Quién es ese pajarito? (Who Is That Little Bird?), 284
Ridin' of a Goat, Leadin' of a Sheep, 251
Sandy McNab, 142
Sansa kroma, 166
Sarasponda, 210
Sing Alleluia, Allelu, 220
Swing, The, 320
Twist and Shout, 314
We Remember, 360
Who's Got a Fishpole?, 261

Unit 5: Managing Information, Nature Guides

All Through the Night (Welsh folk song), 277
Ame fure (Rain), 26
Beryoza (The Birch Tree), 286
Boogie-Woogie Ghost, The, 368
Corre el río (The River Flows By) by P. Vasquez (poem), 183
December Nights, December Lights, 372
Dok Djampa (The White Jasmine Flower), 392
E nānā kākou i nā manu (Look at the Birds in the Sky), 338
Eagle, 337
El coquí (The Frog), 178

Thematic Correlations to Reading Series (continued)

Thematic Correlations to Reading Series (continued)

Thematic Correlations to Reading Series

Unit 6: Community Involvement, Cityscapes

Thematic Correlations to Reading Series (continued)

Scott Foresman Reading ©2004

The following materials from *Spotlight on Music* may be used with each theme in *Scott Foresman Reading*.

Grade K

Volume 1: Getting to Know Us

Alison's Camel, T201
All Work Together, T12
Alphabet Song, The, T54
America, T303
Animales (Animals), T192
Battle Hymn of the Republic, T331
Bear Went Over the Mountain, The, T204
Bell Horses, T262
Best That I Can Be!, The, T48
Bickle, Bockle, 187
Bingo, T64
Bobby Shafto, T265
Bohm Dong Sahn Gohd Dong Sahn (Spring Valley, Flower Valley), T337
Bounce High, Bounce Low, T131
Buffalo Dusk (poem), T219
Bullfrogs, Bullfrogs on Parade (poem), T183
Bus, The, T137
Bye 'n' Bye, T67
City (poem), T134
Cobbler, Cobbler, Mend My Shoe, T169
Cobbler, The (poem), T169
Colorful Dragon Boat, T328
Counting Song, T92
Deedle, Deedle Dumpling (poem), T87
Doing the Weekly Walk, T78
Echo (poem), T104
Eency Weency Spider, T8
El nacimiento (The Nativity), T322
El picaflor (The Humming Bird), T141
El tambor (The Drum), T129
Excuse Us, Animals in the Zoo (poem), T195
Farmer in the Dell, The, T100
Fehér liliomszál (Little Water Lily), T139
Five Fat Turkeys, T309
Follow Me, T133
Follow the Leader (poem), T132
Fox, the Hen, and the Drum, The, T294
Furry Bear (poem), T205
Garden Hoedown, The, T290
Giant's Shoes, The, by E. Fallis (poem), T32
Girls and Boys, Come Out to Play (excerpt) (poem), T98
Girls and Boys, Come Out to Play (poem), T98

Git on Board, T145
Go, Go, Go, T276
Gogo, T188
Good Day Song, T50
Grizzly Bear, T252
Happy Birthday, T347
Head and Shoulders, T238
Hello Song, T2
Here Is the Beehive, T258
Hickory, Dickory, Dock (poem), T49
Hinges (poem), T23
Hippopotamus, The (poem), T199
Hokey Pokey, T68
Hop, Hop, Hop, T197
Hot Dog, T69
Humming Birds (poem), T140
I Am a Little Tugboat (poem), T95
I Can't Spell Hippopotamus, T199
I Got Shoes, T33
I Know an Old Lady, T26
I Will Sing Hello, T156
If Things Grew Down (poem), T48G, T293
If You're Happy, T6
Ifetayo (Love Brings Happiness), T325
In the Barnyard (poem), T207
Instrument Game, T36
It Fell in the City (poem), T312
It's So Good to See You, T86
It's Such a Good Feeling, T282
It's You I Like, T280
Jack, Be Nimble, T88
Jack-in-the-Box, T250
Jack-o'-Lantern, T307
Jig, Jog, Jig, Jog, T260
Juhtgarak (Chopsticks), T108
Jump or Jiggle (poem), T193
Just Like Me, T242
Kangaroo, The, T197
La pequeñita araña (Eency Weency Spider), T9
Lady, Lady, T184
Las horas (The Hours), T70
Let's Think of Something To Do, T270
Little Blue Truck, T136
Little Ducky Duddle, T289
Little Sir Echo, T103
Little Spotted Puppy, T146
Little White Duck, T208
London Bridge, T99
Long Gone (poem), T72
Look Who's Here!, T84
Los pollitos (Little Chickens), T288

Mama, Bake the Johnnycake, T318
María Blanca, T99
Martin Luther King (speech piece), T326
Mbombela, T152
Me I Am! (poem), T346
Merrily, We Roll Along, T110
Merry-Go-Round (poem), T225
Mi chacra (My Farm), T207
Mister Sun, T343
Monkey, Monkey, T215
Monté sur un éléphant (Riding on an Elephant), T217
Muffin Man, The, T105
Mulberry Bush, The, T112
Music (poem), T157
Must Be Santa, T316
My Grandfather, T23
My Legs and I by L. Jacobs (poem), T19
My Oak Tree, T236
My Thumbs Are Starting to Wiggle, T35
Na Bahia Tem (In Bahia Town), T163
Name Game, T57
Nampaya omame (Mothers), T128
Neat Feet (excerpt) by B. Schmidt (poem), T30
Noble Duke of York, The, T232
Oats, Peas, Beans, and Barley Grow, T287
Ɔbɔɔ Asi Me Nsa, T159
Oh, A-Hunting We Will Go, T62
Old Gray Cat, The, T43
Old MacDonald Had a Farm, T211
Old Mister Woodpecker, T172
Oliphaunt (poem), T216
On This Night, T315
One Finger, One Thumb, T38
One, Two, Tie My Shoe, T150
Only My Opinion (poem), T29
Ourchestra (poem), T171
Peace and Quiet, T278
Peter Cottontail, T338
Pimpón, T22
Planting Seeds, T284
Popalong Hopcorn! (poem), T160
Popping Corn, T161
Presidents, T330
Propel, Propel, Propel, T275
Put Your Finger in the Air, T230
Qué bonito es (How Wonderful It Is), T234
Rainbow Song, The, T61
Ride the Train, T144

Ring Around the Rosy, T246
Ring-a-ring (poem), T247
River, The, (poem), T342
Row, Row, Row, T274
Running Song (excerpt) by M. Ridlon
 (poem), T98
Santa Clara Corn Grinding Song, T164
School Is Over (poem), T84
See the Pony Galloping, T44
Seesaw, Margery Daw, T265
Shake My Sillies Out, T175
Shapes (poem), T37
Sidewalks (poem), T98
Simi Yadech (Give Me Your Hand),
 T168
Sing a Little Song, T179
Sing a Song of Sixpence, T111
Singing-Time (poem), T15
Snail's Pace (poem), T29
Snake and the Frog, The (story), T297
Snow Toward Evening (poem), T311
Snowman, The, T313
Something About Me (poem), T13
Speedy Delivery, T279
Spell of the Moon (poem), T116
Stamping Land, T24
Sweetly Sings the Donkey, T244
Table Manners (poem), T107
Taking Off (poem), T134
Ten in a Bed, T256
Ten Little Frogs, T240
Tengo, Tengo, Tengo (I Have, I Have,
 I Have), T212
They Were Tall, T53
Things I'm Thankful For, T308
This Is My City, T120
This Is What I Can Do, T124
Three Little Kittens, T148
Three Little Muffins, T127
Time to Sing, T16
Toodala, T39
Touch Your Shoulders, T254
Travel (poem), T144
Tree of Peace (speech piece), T321
Tugboat, T95
Twinkle, Twinkle, Little Star, T90
Umoja! (poem), T325
Ushkana, T75
Wait and See, T334
Walk to School, T18
Wavvuuvuumira (Mister Bamboo Bug),
 T165
We Are Playing in the Forest, T248
What You Gonna Call Your Pretty Little
 Baby?, T319
Willoughby Wallaby Woo, T241
Won't You Be My Neighbor?, T268
Woodpecker, The (poem), T172
Worms, T286
Y ahora vamos a cantar (Now We Are
 Going to Sing), T340
You're a Grand Old Flag, T4

Volume 2: A World of Wonders
Alphabet Song, T54
Animales (Animals), T192
Bear Went Over the Mountain, The,
 T204
Bell Horses, T262
Buffalo Dusk by C. Sandburg (poem),
 T219
Bye 'n' Bye, T67
City by L. Hughes (poem), T134
Deedle, Deedle Dumpling (poem), T87
Doing the Weekly Walk, T78
Echo by W. de la Mare (poem), T104
El picaflor (The Hummingbird), T141
El tambor (The Drum), T129
Excuse Us, Animals in the Zoo by A.
 Wynne (poem), T195
Follow Me, T133
Furry Bear by A. A. Milne (poem), T205
Girls and Boys, Come Out to Play
 (excerpt) (poem), T98
Git on Board, T145
Grizzly Bear, T252
Happy Birthday, Happy Birthday, T273
Here Is the Beehive, T258
Hippopotamus, The, by J. Prelutsky
 (poem), T199
Humming Birds by B. Sage (poem),
 T140
I Know an Old Lady, T26
It Fell in the City by E. Merriam (poem),
 T312
Jack-in-the-Box, T250
Jack-o'-Lantern, T307
Kangaroo, The, T196
La pequeñita araña (Eency Weency
 Spider), T9
Las horas (The Hours), T70
Little Sir Echo, T103
Little White Duck, T208
London Bridge, T99
María Blanca, T99
Mayflies by P. Fleischmann (poem), T76
Merry-Go-Round by R. Field (poem),
 T346
Mi chacra (My Farm), T207
Monkey, Monkey (speech piece), T215
Monté sur un éléphant (Riding on an
 Elephant), T218
Muffin Man, The, T105
Must Be Santa, T316
My Thumbs Are Starting to Wiggle,
 T35
Oh, A-Hunting We Will Go, T62
Old Mister Woodpecker, T172
Oliphaunt by J. R. R. Tolkien (poem),
 T216
Peter Cottontail, T338
Popalong hopcorn! by J. Nicholls
 (poem), T160
Popping Corn, T161

Prairie Dog Song (Kiowa children's
 song), T220
Put Your Finger in the Air, T230
Rainbow Song, The, T61
Ring Around the Rosy (Mother Goose)
 (song), T246, (poem), T247
Running Song (excerpt) by M. Ridlon
 (poem), T98
School Is Over by K. Greenaway
 (poem), T85
Sidewalks by P. Hubbell (poem), T98
Sing a Song of Sixpence, T111
Singing-Time by R. Fyleman (poem),
 T15
Snail's Pace by A. Fisher (poem), T29
Snake and the Frog, The (story), T297
Table Manners by G. Burgess (poem),
 T107
Ten in a Bed, T256
Ten Little Frogs, T240
This Is My City, T120
Toodala, T39
Twinkle, Twinkle, Little Star, T90
Ushkana (Damselfly Song), T75
Wavvuuvuumira (Mister Bamboo Bug),
 T165
Willoughby Wallaby Woo, T241
Won't You Be My Neighbor?, T268
Woodpecker, The, by E. Roberts
 (poem), T173
Worms, T286
You're a Grand Old Flag, T4

Volume 3: So Much to Do
Alison's Camel, T201
Animal Rhythms (poem), T56
Bingo, T64
Bullfrogs, Bullfrogs on Parade by J.
 Prelutsky (poem), T183
Bus, The, T137
Bye 'n' Bye, T67
City by L. Hughes (poem), T134
Counting Song, T92
Echo by W. de la Mare (poem), T104
El nacimiento (The Nativity), T388
Five Fat Turkeys, T309
Fox, the Hen, and the Drum, The
 (Indian fable), T294
Good Day Song, T50
Happy Birthday, Happy Birthday, T273
Here Is the Beehive, T258
Hickory, Dickory, Dock (poem), T49
Hot Dog, T69
I Am a Little Tugboat by C. Huffman
 (poem), T144
In the Barnyard by D. Aldis (poem),
 T207
It Fell in the City by E. Merriam (poem),
 T312
Jack-o'-Lantern, T307
Juhtgarak (Chopsticks), T108

Thematic Correlations to Reading Series (continued)

Kum Ba Yah, T327
Las horas (The Hours), T70
Little Blue Truck, T136
Little Sir Echo, T103
Little Spotted Puppy, T146
Los pollitos (Little Chickens), T288
Mi chacra (My Farm), T207
Muffin Man, The, T105
Old Gray Cat, The, T43
Old MacDonald Had a Farm, T207
Peter Cottontail, T338
Rainbow Song, The, T61
Ride the Train, T144
Santa Clara Corn Grinding Song, T164
School Is Over by K. Greenaway (poem), T85
See the Pony Galloping, T44
Shapes by S. Silverstein (poem), T37
Sidewalks by P. Hubbell (poem), T98
Sweetly Sings the Donkey, T244
Taking Off by M. Green (poem), T134
Tengo, Tengo, Tengo (I Have, I Have, I Have), T212
Three Little Kittens, T146
Travel by E. St. Vincent Millay (poem), T144
Tree of Peace (speech piece), T321
Twinkle, Twinkle, Little Star, T90
Wait and See, T335
Won't You Be My Neighbor?, T268

Volume 4: Every Day Is Special

All Work Together, T12
America, T303
Battle Hymn of the Republic, T331
Best That I Can Be!, The, T48
Bickle, Bockle, T187
Bobby Shafto, T265
Cobbler, Cobbler, Mend My Shoe, T169
Cobbler, The, by E. Chafee (poem), T255
Colorful Dragon Boat, T328
Days of the Week, T81
Go, Go, Go, T276
Happy Birthday, Happy Birthday, T273
Hello Song, T2
I Am a Little Tugboat by C. Huffman (poem), T95
I Will Sing Hello, T156
If You're Happy, T6
Ifetayo (Love Brings Happiness), T325
It's So Good to See You, T86
It's Such a Good Feeling, T282
It's You I Like, T280
Jig, Jog, Jig, Jog, T260
Just Like Me, T242
Let's Think of Something to Do, T270
Look Who's Here!, T84
Mbombela (The Train Comes), T152
Merrily, We Roll Along, T110

Merry-Go-Round by R. Field (poem), T223
Merry-Go-Round, The, T225
My Grandfather, T23
Na Bahia Tem (In Bahia Town), T163
Nampaya omame (Mothers), T128
Oh, A-Hunting We Will Go, T62
One Finger, One Thumb, T46
Ourchestra by S. Silverstein (poem), T171
Peter Cottontail, T338
Propel, Propel, Propel, T275
Row, Row, Row, T274
Simi Yadech (Give Me Your Hand), T168
Speedy Delivery, T279
Spinning Song by C. Shields (poem), T67
They Were Tall, T53
Tugboat, T95
Twinkle, Twinkle, Little Star, T90
Walk to School, T18
We Are Playing in the Forest, T248
What You Gonna Call Your Pretty Little Baby?, T319
Y ahora vamos a cantar (Now We Are Going to Sing), T340

Volume 5: Off We Go

America, T303
Animales (Animals), T192
Battle Hymn of the Republic, T331
Bear Went Over the Mountain, The, T204
Bell Horses, T262
Bohm Dong Sahn, Gohd Dong Sahn (Spring Valley, Flower Valley), T337
Bounce High, Bounce Low, T13
Buffalo Dusk by C. Sandburg (poem), T219
Cobbler, Cobbler, Mend My Shoe, T169
Cobbler, The, by E. Chafee (poem), T255
Doing the Weekly Walk, T78
Echo by W. de la Mare (poem), T104
Eency Weency Spider, T8
El picaflor (The Hummingbird), T141
El tambor (The Drum), T129
Excuse Us, Animals in the Zoo by A. Wynne (poem), T195
Farmer in the Dell, The, T100
Fehér liliomszál (Little Water Lily), T139
Follow the Leader by K. Fraser (poem), T132
Furry Bear by A. A. Milne (poem), T205
Garden Hoedown, The, T290
Giant's Shoes, The, by E. Fallis (poem), T32
Go, Go, Go, T276
Gogo, T188
Grizzly Bear, T252

Head and Shoulders, T238
Hinges by A. Fisher (poem), T23
Hippopotamus, The, by J. Prelutsky (poem), T199
Hokey Pokey, T68
Hop, Hop, Hop, T197
Humming Birds by B. Sage (poem), T140
I Can't Spell Hippopotamus, T199
I Got Shoes, T33
I Will Sing Hello, T156
If Things Grew Down by R. Hoeft (poem), T292
If You're Happy, T6
Instrument Game, T36
It's Such a Good Feeling, T282
It's You I Like, T280
Jack, Be Nimble, T88
Kangaroo, The, T196
La pequeñita araña (Eency Weency Spider), T9
Lady, Lady, T184
Las horas (The Hours), T70
Let's Think of Something to Do, T270
Little Ducky Duddle, T289
Little White Duck, T208
María Blanca, T99
Mayflies by P. Fleischmann (poem), T76
Me I Am! by J. Prelutsky (poem), T346
Mister Sun, T343
Monkey, Monkey (speech piece), T215
Monté sur un éléphant (Riding on an Elephant), T218
My Legs and I by L. Jacobs (poem), T19
My Oak Tree, T236
Name Game, T58
Neat Feet (excerpt) by B. Schmidt (poem), T30
Noble Duke of York, The, T232
North Winds Blow, T305
Oats, Peas, Beans, and Barley Grow, T287
Oh, A-Hunting We Will Go, T62
Old Mister Woodpecker, T172
Oliphaunt by J. R. R. Tolkien (poem), T216
One Finger, One Thumb, T46
Only My Opinion by M. Shannon (poem), T29
Ourchestra by S. Silverstein (poem), T171
Peter Cottontail, T338
Popalong hopcorn! by J. Nicholls (poem), T160
Popping Corn, T161
Prairie Dog Song (Kiowa children's song), T220
Presidents, T330
Rainbow Song, The, T61
River, The, by C. Zolotow (poem), T342
Seesaw, Margery Daw, T264

Thematic Correlations to Reading Series (continued)

Shake My Sillies Out, T175
Sing a Little Song, T179
Snail's Pace by A. Fisher (poem), T29
Snake and the Frog, The (story), T297
Snow Toward Evening by M. Cane (poem), T311
Snowman, The, T313
Something About Me (poem), T13
Speedy Delivery, T279
Spell of the Moon (excerpt) by L. Norris (poem), T116
Spinning Song by C. Shields (poem), T67
Stamping Land, T24
Table Manners by G. Burgess (poem), T107
Things I'm Thankful For, T308
This Is What I Can Do, T124
Three Little Muffins (speech piece), T146
Touch Your Shoulders, T254
Twinkle, Twinkle, Little Star, T90
Ushkana (Damselfly Song), T75
Wait and See, T335
Wavvuuvuumira (Mister Bamboo Bug), T165
Woodpecker, The, by E. Roberts (poem), T173
Worms, T286
You're a Grand Old Flag, T4

Volume 6: Open the Doors

All Work Together, T12
Alphabet Song, The, T54
Bell Horses, T262
Best That I Can Be!, The, T48
Bickle, Bockle, T187
Bohm Dong Sahn, Gohd Dong Sahn (Spring Valley, Flower Valley), T337
Bounce High, Bounce Low, T13
Bus, The, T137
Cobbler, Cobbler, Mend My Shoe, T169
Cobbler, The, by E. Chafee (poem), T255
Echo by W. de la Mare (poem), T104
Eency Weency Spider, T8
El tambor (The Drum), T129
Farmer in the Dell, The, T100
Fehér liliomszál (Little Water Lily), T139
Follow the Leader by K. Fraser (poem), T132
Garden Hoedown, The, T290
Go, Go, Go, T276
Gogo, T188
Happy Birthday, Happy Birthday, T273
Head and Shoulders, T238
Hello Song, T2
Hokey Pokey, T68
Hop, Hop, Hop, T197
I Am a Little Tugboat by C. Huffman (poem), T144

If Things Grew Down by R. Hoeft (poem), T292
Ifetayo (Love Brings Happiness), T325
Instrument Game, T36
It's So Good to See You, T86
It's You I Like, T280
Jack, Be Nimble, T88
Just Like Me, T242
Kangaroo, The, T196
Lady, Lady, T184
Let's Think of Something to Do, T270
Little Blue Truck, T136
Little Ducky Duddle, T289
London Bridge, T99
Look Who's Here!, T84
María Blanca, T99
Mbombela (The Train Comes), T152
Mister Sun, T343
Mulberry Bush, The, T112
My Grandfather, T23
My Oak Tree, T236
Name Game, T58
Nampaya omame (Mothers), T128
North Winds Blow, T305
Oats, Peas, Beans, and Barley Grow, T287
Oh, A-Hunting We Will Go, T62
On This Night, T315
One, Two, Tie My Shoe, T150
Peace and Quiet, T278
Peter Cottontail, T338
Pimpón, T22
Popalong hopcorn! by J. Nicholls (poem), T160
Popping Corn, T161
Rainbow Song, The, T61
Ride the Train, T144
River, The, by C. Zolotow (poem), T342
Row, Row, Row, T274
Simi Yadech (Give Me Your Hand), T168
Sing a Little Song, T179
Snowman, The, T313
Speedy Delivery, T279
Spell of the Moon (excerpt) by L. Norris (poem), T116
Taking Off by M. Green (poem), T134
They Were Tall, T53
This Is What I Can Do, T124
Time to Sing, T16
Touch Your Shoulders, T254
Travel by E. St. Vincent Millay (poem), T144
Twinkle, Twinkle, Little Star, T90
Umoja! by M. Evans (poem), T325
Walk to School, T18
What You Gonna Call Your Pretty Little Baby?, T319
Y ahora vamos a cantar (Now We Are Going to Sing), T340
You're a Grand Old Flag, T4

Grade 1

Volume 1: Good Times We Share

A la rueda rueda ('Round and 'Round), T240
America, T326
Another Busy Day (speech piece), T41
Apple a Day, An (traditional poem), T152
Apples and Bananas, T151
Bear Hunt (poem), T126
Best Friends, T222
Bonjour, mes amis (Hello, My Friends), T18
Butterfly, Flutter By, T333
Call of the Wild, A (excerpt) by R. W. Service (poem), T139
Clouds by Anonymous (poem), T331
Cookies, T278
Counting Song, T195
Cut the Cake, T232
Down the Hill, T281
Duérmete mi niño (Go to Sleep, My Baby), T61
El juego chirimbolo (The Chirimbolo Game), T103
El rorro (The Babe), T356
Field of Joys by M. Morand (poem), T224
Gilly, Gilly, Gilly Good Morning, T12
Go A Tin (Lantern Song), T363
Goin' to the Zoo, T192
Hakyo jong (School Bells), T302
Happiest Street in the World, The, T304
Hoo, Hoo!, T55
Hop! Chirp! Moo! Oh, Happy Springtime Day!, T372
How Does Your Garden Grow?, T144
I Have a Friend by Anonymous (poem), T225
I Like by M. A. Hoberman (poem), T110
I Like Spinach, T163
I Wanna Be a Friend of Yours, T84
Ice by D. Aldis (poem), T346
In My Little Motor Boat, T159
It's So Nice on the Ice, T346
Jambo (Hello), T230
Kaeru no Uta, T112
Let's Go Driving, T52
Library Song, T42
Light the Candles, T351
Locust, The (Zuñi poem), T285
Lucy Locket, T253
Martin Luther King, T360
Miss Mary Mack, T15
Mizuguruma (The Water Wheel), T260
My Kite by B. Brown and B. Brown (poem), T371
My Mom, T372
Na Bahia Tem (In Bahia Town), T297

Thematic Correlations to Reading Series (continued)

Peanut Butter, T218
Pease Porridge Hot, T255
Piñon, Pirulín, T311
Plenty Fishes in the Sea, T310
Punchinella, T216
Pusa't daga (Cat and Rat), T289
Quaker, Quaker, T100
Rig a Jig Jig, T116
Romper, Stomper, and Boo (traditional story), T36
Rudolph, the Red-Nosed Reindeer, T354
Seesaw (song), T242, (accompaniment), T248
Serra, serra serrador (Saw, Saw Lumberjack), T133
Sleep, Bonnie Bairnie, T26
Somebody Come and Play, T92
Soup, Soup!, T358
Spanish Days of the Week by Anonymous (poem), T108
Tako No Uta (The Kite Song), T370
There Are Many Flags in Many Lands, T329
Time for Love, A, T347
Uga, Uga, Uga (Cake, Cake, Cake), T313
Untitled (Butterflies) (haiku), T332
Wake Me, Shake Me, T198
We All Sing With the Same Voice, T156
What's Your Name?, T125
Wheels, Wheels, Wheels by N. White Carlstrom (poem), T106
Willum, T19
Yo, Mamana, Yo (Oh, Mama), T307
Zui Zui Zukkorbashi (song), T98, (game), T99

Volume 2: Take a Closer Look
Animal Song, T288
Ants Go Marching, The, T22
Apple a Day, An (traditional poem), T152
Apples and Bananas, T151
Arre, mi burrito (Gid-yup, Little Burro), T257
Autumn Leaves Are Falling, T330
Autumn Leaves, T331
Bear Hunt (poem), T126
Big and Small by E. McCullough Brabson, T200
Boris, the Singing Bear, T312
Bow-Wow by Mother Goose (poem), T81
Bug by L. Simmie (poem), T167
But the Critter Got Away (speech piece), T88, (poem), T89
Butterfly, Flutter By, T333
Call of the Wild, A (excerpt) by R. W. Service (poem), T139
Caribbean Amphibian, T294

Chase the Squirrel, T88
Chickery Chick, T292
Clouds by Anonymous (poem), T331
Come Back, My Little Chicks, T134
Cow, The, by R. L. Stevenson (poem), T236
Dragonfly by D. M. Violin (poem), T44
El florón (The Flower), T117
Goin' to the Zoo, T192
Granny (traditional poem), T104
Grasshoppers Three, T284
Green Grass Grows All Around, The, T148
Hoo, Hoo!, T55
Hop! Chirp! Moo! Oh, Happy Springtime Day!, T372
Hopping Frog by C. Rossetti (poem), T113
Horses of the Sea, The, by C. Rossetti (poem), T179
Hunt the Cows, T236
I Had a Little Hen (nursery rhyme), T136
I Like Spinach, T163
I've a Pair of Fishes, T124
Ice, T347
In My Little Motor Boat, T159
It's So Nice on the Ice, T346
Johnny's Flea, T158
Jump or Jiggle by E. Beyer (poem), T316
Kaeru no Uta, T112
La ranita cri (The Little Frog Croaks), T27
Ladybugs' Picnic, T290
Let's Go Driving, T52
Library Song, T42
Little Black Bug, T166
Locust, The (Zuñi poem), T285
Mary's Coal Black Lamb, T286
Mos', Mos'! (Cat, Cat!), T53
Naughty Kitty Cat, T171
Night Comes... by B. Schenk de Regniers (poem), T233
O Wind by C. Rossetti (poem), T235
One Little Elephant, T194
Oranges and Lemons (English traditional poem), T150
Over in the Meadow, T78
Pease Porridge Hot, T255
Pusa't daga (Cat and Rat), T289
Rabbit, The, by M. Stelmach (poem), T186
Rain Poem (poem), T31
Rain Sizes by J. Ciardi (poem), T33
Rain, Rain, Go Away, T259
Rattlesnake, T185
Romper, Stomper, and Boo (traditional story), T36
Seeds, T120
Serra, serra serrador (Saw, Saw Lumberjack), T133

Simple Simon, T175
Sing Ho! For the Life of a Bear! By A.A. Milne (poem), T114
Sittin' Down to Eat, T182
Six Little Ducks, T64
Sleep, Bonnie Bairnie, T26
Snail With the Mail, T274
Snail, Snail (song), T252, (three-tone), T252
Somebody Has To... by S. Silverstein (poem), T258
Spanish Days of the Week by Anonymous (poem), T108
Spring, T273
Thoughts of a Rattlesnake by K. Sexton (poem), T185
Untitled (Butterflies) (haiku), T332
Up the Hill by W. J. Smith (poem), T45
Wheels, Wheels, Wheels by N. White Carlstrom (poem), T106
White Sheep by Anonymous (poem), T234
Wind Blew East, The, T234
Wind Blow, T187
Year with Frog and Toad, A, T270

Volume 3: Let's Learn Together
Animal Song, T288
Another Busy Day (speech piece), T41
Ants Go Marching, The, T22
Apple a Day, An (traditional poem), T152
Apples and Bananas, T151
Arre, mi burrito (Gid-yup, Little Burro), T257
Best Friends, T222
Big and Small by E. McCullough Brabson, T200
Boris, the Singing Bear, T312
Bow-Wow by Mother Goose (poem), T81
Brush Your Teeth (song), T66, (speech piece), T66
Bug by L. Simmie (poem), T167
But the Critter Got Away (speech piece), T88, (poem), T89
Butterfly, Flutter By, T333
Caribbean Amphibian, T294
Chase the Squirrel, T88
Chickery Chick, T292
Clouds by Anonymous (poem), T331
Come Back, My Little Chicks, T134
Cookies, T278
Cow, The, by R. L. Stevenson (poem), T236
Cut the Cake, T232
Down the Hill, T281
Dragonfly by D. M. Violin (poem), T44
Duérmete mi niño (Go to Sleep, My Baby), T61
El rorro (The Babe), T356

Field of Joys by M. Morand (poem), T224

George Washington, T368

Gilly, Gilly, Gilly Good Morning, T12

Goin' to the Zoo, T192

Granny (traditional poem), T104

Grasshoppers Three, T284

Happiest Street in the World, The, T304

Hi! My Name Is Joe (rhythmic pattern), T220

Hop! Chirp! Moo! Oh, Happy Springtime Day!, T372

Hopping Frog by C. Rossetti (poem), T113

Horses of the Sea, The, by C. Rossetti (poem), T179

How Does Your Garden Grow?, T144

Hunt the Cows, T236

I Had a Little Hen (nursery rhyme), T136

I Have a Friend by Anonymous (poem), T225

I Like by M. A. Hoberman (poem), T110

I Like Spinach, T163

I Love My Country, T328

I Wanna Be a Friend of Yours, T84

I've a Pair of Fishes, T124

Ice by D. Aldis (poem), T346

It's So Nice on the Ice, T346

Jambo (Hello), T230

Johnny Works with One Hammer, T96

Johnny's Flea, T158

Jump or Jiggle by E. Beyer (poem), T316

Kaeru no Uta, T112

La ranita cri (The Little Frog Croaks), T27

Ladybugs' Picnic, T290

Light the Candles, T351

Little Black Bug, T166

Locust, The (Zuñi poem), T285

Love Grows, T202

Love Is the Magic Word, T366

Lucy Locket, T253

Mail Myself to You, T366

Mary's Coal Black Lamb, T286

Miss Mary Mack, T15

Mos', Mos'! (Cat, Cat!), T53

My Kite by B. Brown and B. Brown (poem), T371

My Mom, T372

My Valentine by M. C. Parsons (poem), T364

Naranja dulce, T303

Naughty Kitty Cat, T171

Night Comes... by B. Schenk de Regniers (poem), T233

Old Mother Goose (traditional rhyme), T181

One Little Elephant, T194

Oranges and Lemons (English traditional poem), T150

Over in the Meadow, T78

Peanut Butter, T218

Pease Porridge Hot, T255

Pile of Stuff, A (story), T188

Pusa't daga (Cat and Rat), T289

Quaker, Quaker, T100

Rabbit, The, by M. Stelmach (poem), T186

Rattlesnake, T185

Rig a Jig Jig, T116

Romper, Stomper, and Boo (traditional story), T36

Rudolph, the Red-Nosed Reindeer, T354

Seesaw (song), T242, (accompaniment), T248

Serra, serra serrador (Saw, Saw Lumberjack), T133

Simple Simon, T175

Sing After Me, T34

Sing Ho! For the Life of a Bear! By A.A. Milne (poem), T114

Sittin' Down to Eat, T182

Six Little Ducks, T64

Sleep, Bonnie Bairnie, T26

Snail With the Mail, T274

Snail, Snail (song), T252, (three-tone), T252

Somebody Come and Play, T92

Spanish Days of the Week by Anonymous (poem), T108

Tailor, Tailor (traditional poem), T132

There's a Hole in the Middle of the Sea, T178

Thoughts of a Rattlesnake by K. Sexton (poem), T185

Time for Love, A, T347

Tinker, Tailor, T131

Tisket A Tasket, A, T107

Untitled (Butterflies) (haiku), T332

Up the Hill by W. J. Smith (poem), T45

Viva Valentine!, T365

Wake Me, Shake Me, 198

We All Sing With the Same Voice, T156

What's Your Name?, T125

When the Flag Goes By, T327

White Sheep by Anonymous (poem), T234

Why the Beetle Has a Gold Coat (Brazilian folktale), T321

Willum, T19

Wings by A. Fisher (poem), T250

Year with Frog and Toad, A, T270

Yo, Mamana, Yo (Oh, Mama), T307

Volume 4: Favorite Things Old and New

A be ce (A B C), T213

A la rueda rueda ('Round and 'Round), T240

Acka Backa, T256

¡Adivina lo que es! (Guess What It Is), T170

All Night, All Day, T232

America, T326

Animal Song, T288

Another Busy Day, T41

Ants Go Marching, The, T22

Apple a Day, An (poem), T152

Apples and Bananas, T151

Arre, mi burrito (Gid'yup, Little Burrito), T257

Autumn Leaves Are Falling, T330

Autumn Leaves, T331

Bear Hunt (speech piece), T126

Bear Went Over the Mountain, The, T115

Bee, Bee, Bumblebee, T250

Best Friends, T222

Big and Small (speech piece), T200

Bluebells, T209

Bonjour, mes amis (Hello, My Friends), T18

Boris, the Singing Bear, T312

Bow-Wow (poem), T81

Brinca la tablita (Hop, Hop!), T71

Brush Your Teeth (song), T66, (speech piece), T67

Bug (poem), T167

Bug by L. Simmie (poem), T167

But the Critter Got Away (speech piece), T88

Butterfly, Flutter By, T333

Call of the Wild, A (excerpt) (poem), T139

Caribbean Amphibian, T294

Categories, T146

Chang (Elephant), T199

Charlie over the Ocean, T75

Chase the Squirrel, T88

Chickery Chick, T292

Clap Your Hands, T246

Clouds (poem), T330

Come Back, My Little Chicks, T134

Cookies, T277

Counting Song, T195

Cow, The (poem), T236

Cut the Cake, T232

Dance Myself to Sleep, T314

Diana, T334

Diou Shou Juan'er, T212

Double This (game), T94

Down by the Bay, T48

Down the Hill, T281

Dragonfly (poem), T44

Dreidel Song (poem), T349

Duérmete mi niño (Go to Sleep, My Baby), T61

Ears, Far and Near (poem), T16

El florón (The Flower), T117

El juego chirimbolo (The Chirimbolo Game), T103

El rorro (The Babe), T386
Field of Joys, T224
Five Little Pumpkins (poem), T337
George Washington, T368
Gilly, Gilly, Gilly Good Morning, T12
Go A Tin (Lantern Song), T363
Goin' to the Zoo, T192
Granny (traditional poem), T104
Grasshoppers Three, T284
Green Grass Grows All Around, The, T148
Haiku Butterflies (poem), T332
Hakyo Jong (School Bells), T302
Haliwa-Saponi
Happiest Street in the World, The, T304
Head and Shoulders, Baby, T40
Hello, There!, T230
Here Comes the Band (poem), T80
Here We Sit, T251
Hey, Children, Who's in Town?, T14
Hi! My Name Is Joe! (speech piece), T220
Hoo, Hoo!, T55
Hop, Chirp! Moo! Oh Happy Springtime Day, T372
Hopping Frog (poem), T113
Horses of the Sea, The (poem), T179
How Does Your Garden Grow?, T144
Hunt the Cows, T236
I Am Slowly Going Crazy, T127
I Had a Little Hen (nursery rhyme), T136
I Have a Friend (poem), T225
I Like (poem), T110
I Like by M. A. Hoberman (poem), T110
I Like Spinach, T163
I Love My Country, T328
I Wanna Be a Friend of Yours, T84
I'd Like to Be a Lighthouse (poem), T238
I'm Getting Sick of Peanut Butter (poem), T219
I've a Pair of Fishes, T124
Ice (poem), T346
If All the World Were Paper, T296
In My Little Motor Boat, T159
It's So Nice on the Ice, T346
Jambo (Hello), T230
Jingle Bells, T354
John the Rabbit, T74
Johnny Works with One Hammer, T96
Johnny's Flea, T158
Jolly Old Saint Nicholas, T352
Jump or Jiggle (poem), T316
Jump, Jim Joe, T89
Kaeru no Uta, T112
Kari (Wild Geese), T261
Kobuta, T168
La ranita cri (The Little Frog Croaks), T27
Ladybugs' Picnic, T290

Lavender's Blue, T174
Let's Go Driving, T52
Library Song, T42
Light the Candles, T351
Little Black Bug, T166
Little Red Caboose, T97
Little Robin Redbreast, T208
Locust, The (poem), T285
Looby Loo, T262
Love Grows, T202
Love Is the Magic Word, T366
Lucy Lockett, T253
Mail Myself to You, T366
Marco Polo (speech piece), T90
Martin Luther King, T360
Mary's Coal Black Lamb, T286
Mi cuerpo (My Body), T32
Miss Mary Mack, T15
Mizuguruma (The Water Wheel), T260
Mos', Mos'! (Cat, Cat!), T53
My Feet (poem), T264
My Kite (poem), T371
My Mama's Calling Me, T54
My Mom, T372
My Valentine (poem), T364
Na Bahia Tem (In Bahia Town), T297
Naming Things (poem), T221
Naranja dulce, T303
Naughty Kitty Cat, T171
Night Comes... (poem), T233
No One Like You, T300
O Wind (poem), T235
Old King Glory, T217
Old Mother Goose (poem), T181
One Little Elephant, T194
One, Two, Three, Four, Five, T265
Oranges and Lemons (poem), T150
Over in the Meadow, T78
Pat Pat Patty Pat, T308
Peanut Butter, T218
Pease Porridge Hot, T255
Pile of Stuff, A (story), T188
Piñata Song (poem), T153
Piñón, Pirulín, T311
Pitty Patty Polt (speech piece), T180
Plenty Fishes in the Sea, T310
Puddle Hopping, T60
Pumpkin Song, T342
Punchinella, T216
Pusa't daga (Cat and Rat), T289
Put On a Costume, T336
Quaker, Quaker, T100
Rabbit in the Moon, The (folktale), T318
Rabbit, The (poem), T186
Rain Sizes (poem), T33
Rain, Rain, Go Away, T259
Rattlesnake, T185
Rig a Jig Jig, T116
Rise, Sally, Rise, T162
Romper, Stomper, and Boo (story), T36

Rudolph, the Red-Nosed Reindeer, T354
S'vivon sové (Dreidel Spin), T348
Sailor Went to Sea, Sea, Sea, A (song), T38, (game), T39
Sara Watashi (Plate Passing), T67
Seesaw, T242
Serra, Serra Serrador (Saw, Saw, Lumberjack), T133
Shoo, Turkey, T76
Simple Simon, T175
Sing After Me, T34
Sing Ho! For the Life of a Bear! (poem), T114
Sittin' Down to Eat, T182
Sitting in the Sand (poem), T374
Six Little Ducks, T64
Skin and Bones, T340
Skip to My Lou, T102
Sleep, Bonnie Bairnie, T26
Snail With the Mail, T275
Snail, Snail, T252
Somebody Come and Play, T92
Somebody Has To... (poem), T258
Something Funny Outside, T338
Something Told the Wild Geese (poem), T261
Soup, Soup!, T358
Spanish Days of the Week by Anonymous (poem), T108
Spotlight on America, T9
Spring, T273
Star Light, Star Bright, T258
Suite on English Folk Tunes, T136
Swing, The (poem), T109
Tailor, Tailor (poem), T132
Tak for Maden (Thanks for Food), T343
Tako No Uta, T146
Theme from *Sesame Street*, T298
There Are Many Flags in Many Lands, T329
There's a Hole in the Middle of the Sea, T178
This Little Light of Mine, T238
This Old Man, T306
Thoughts of a Rattlesnake (poem), T185
Time for Love, A, T347
Tinker, Tailor, T130
Tisket A Tasket, A, T107
Twenty-four Robbers, 173
Two, Four, Six, Eight, T246
Uga, Uga, Uga (Cake, Cake, Cake), T313
Una adivinanza (A Riddle), T138
Untitled (Butterflies) (haiku), T332
Up the Hill (poem), T45
Up the Tree and Down Again (poem), T65
Viva Valentine!, T365
Wake Me, Shake Me, T198
We All Sing With the Same Voice, T156

Puddle Hopping, T60
Pumpkin Song, T342
Punchinella, T216
Pusa't daga (Cat and Rat), T289
Put on a Costume, T336
Quaker, Quaker, T100
Rabbit in the Moon, The (folktale), T318
Rabbit, The (poem), T186
Rain Sizes (poem), T33
Rain, Rain, Go Away, T259
Rattlesnake, T185
Rig a Jig Jig, T116
Rise, Sally, Rise, T162
Romper, Stomper, and Boo (story), T36
Rudolph, the Red-Nosed Reindeer, T354
S'vivon Sov (Dreidel Spin), T348
Sailor Went to Sea, Sea, Sea, A (song), T38, (game), T39
Sara Watashi (Plate Passing), T66
Seeds (vocal and instrumental), T120
Seesaw, T242
Serra, Serra Serrador (Saw, Saw, Lumberjack), T133
Shoo, Turkey, T76
Simple Simon, T175
Sing After Me, T34
Sing Ho! For the Life of a Bear! (poem), T114
Sittin' Down to Eat, T182
Sitting in the Sand (poem), T374
Six Little Ducks, T64
Skin and Bones, T340
Skip to My Lou, T102
Sleep, Bonnie Bairnie, T27
Snail With the Mail, T275
Snail, Snail, T252
Somebody Come and Play, T92
Somebody Has To... (poem), T258
Something Funny Outside, T338
Something Told the Wild Geese (poem), T261
Soup, Soup!, T358
Spanish Days of the Week by Anonymous (poem), T108
Spotlight on America, T9
Spring, T273
Star Light, Star Bright, T258
Summertime from Porgy and Bess, T375
Swing, The (poem), T109
Tailor, Tailor (poem), T132
Tako No Uta (The Kite Song), T370
There Are Many Flags in Many Lands, T329
There's a Hole in the Middle of the Sea, T178
This Little Light of Mine, T238
This Old Man, T306
Thoughts of a Rattlesnake (poem), T185
Time for Love, A, T347
Tinker, Tailor, T130
Tisket A Tasket, A, T107

Twenty-four Robbers, T173
Two, Four, Six, Eight, T246
Uga, Uga, Uga (Cake, Cake, Cake), T313
Una Adivinanza (A Riddle), T138
Up the Hill (poem), T45
Up the Tree and Down Again (poem), T65
Viva Valentine!, T365
Wake Me, Shake Me, T198
We All Sing With the Same Voice, T156
What's Your Name?, T125
Wheels, Wheels, Wheels (poem), T106
When the Flag Goes By, T327
White Sheep by Anonymous (poem), T234
Who's Afraid of the Big Bad Wolf? (nursery rhyme), T137
Why the Beetle Has a Gold Coat (folktale), T321
Willum, T19
Wind Blew East, The, T234
Wind Blow, T187
Wings (poem), T250
Year with Frog and Toad, A, T270
Yo, Mamana, Yo (Oh, Mama), T307
Zui Zui Zukkorbashi (song), T98, (game), T99

Volume 6: Surprise Me
¡Adivina lo que es! (Guess What It Is!), T170
All Night, All Day, T232
Another Busy Day (speech piece), T41
Arre, mi burrito (Gid-yup, Little Burro), T257
Autumn Leaves Are Falling, T330
Autumn Leaves, T331
Best Friends, T222
Boris, the Singing Bear, T312
Call of the Wild, A (excerpt) by R. W. Service (poem), T139
Caribbean Amphibian, T294
Chickery Chick, T292
Clouds by Anonymous (poem), T331
Duérmete mi niño (Go to Sleep, My Baby), T61
El florón (The Flower), T117
El rorro (The Babe), T356
Field of Joys by M. Morand (poem), T224
George Washington, T368
Gilly, Gilly, Gilly Good Morning, T12
Green Grass Grows All Around, The, T148
Happiest Street in the World, The, T304
Hop! Chirp! Moo! Oh, Happy Springtime Day!, T372
How Does Your Garden Grow?, T144
I Am Slowly Going Crazy, T127
I Have a Friend by Anonymous (poem), T225

I Wanna Be a Friend of Yours, T84
I'd Like to Be a Lighthouse by R Field (poem), T238
Ice, T347
If All the World Were Paper, T296
It's So Nice on the Ice, T346
Jambo (Hello), T230
Lavender's Blue, T174
Light the Candles, T351
Little Red Caboose, T97
Love Grows, T202
My Mom, T372
Night Comes... by B. Schenk de Regniers (poem), T233
O Wind by C. Rossetti (poem), T235
Old Mother Goose (traditional rhyme), T181
Over in the Meadow, T78
Pile of Stuff, A (story), T188
Quaker, Quaker, T100
Rabbit in the Moon, The (story to perform), T318
Rabbit, The, by M. Stelmach (poem), T186
Rain Poem (poem), T31
Rain Sizes by J. Ciardi (poem), T33
Rain, Rain, Go Away, T259
Rattlesnake, T185
Rig a Jig Jig, T116
Seeds, T120
Serra, serra serrador (Saw, Saw Lumberjack), T133
Sing Ho! For the Life of a Bear! By A.A. Milne (poem), T114
Sittin' Down to Eat, T182
Somebody Come and Play, T92
Somebody Has To . . . by S. Silverstein (poem), T258
Spanish Days of the Week by Anonymous (poem), T108
Spring, T273
Star Light, Star Bright, T258
There's a Hole in the Middle of the Sea, T178
This Little Light of Mine, T238
Thoughts of a Rattlesnake by K. Sexton (poem), T185
Time for Love, A, T347
Wake Me, Shake Me, 198
What's Your Name?, T125
Wheels, Wheels, Wheels by N. White Carlstrom (poem), T106
White Sheep by Anonymous (poem), T234
Why the Beetle Has a Gold Coat (Brazilian folktale), T321
Willum, T19
Wind Blew East, The, T234
Wind Blow, T187
Yo, Mamana, Yo (Oh, Mama), T307

Thematic Correlations to Reading Series

Grade 2

Volume 1: New Beginnings, You + Me = Special

Ach, du lieber Augustin (The More We Get Together), 35
Artichokes, 314
Australia's on the Wallaby, 106
Big Beautiful Planet, 376
Bliss by E. Farjeon (poem), 212
Bow, Wow, Wow, 264
Check It Out! (It's About Respect), 10
Chíu, chíu, chíu (Chirp, Chirp, Chirp), 302
Corner Grocery Store, 311
Dal taro kacha (Come, Pick the Moon), 98
Do You Want My Little Frog? by H. Copeland (poem), 187
Doggie, Doggie, 59
Donkey, Donkey, 256
Drumming Spider, The (West African folktale), 333
Dumplin's, 172
El burrito enfermo (The Sick Little Donkey), 180
El zapatero (The Cobbler), 138
En nuestra Tierra tan linda (On Our Beautiful Planet Earth), 114
Everything Grows, 204
Food Song, The, 318
Four White Horses, 300
Garden Song, 236
Going Over the Sea, 216
Good Night, Sleep Tight, 76
Great Outdoors, The, 290
Green Eggs and Ham, 284
Hairy Dog, The, by H. Asquith (poem), 58
Heigh Ho, Here We Go, 252
Hot Cross Buns, 258
It's a Small World, 298
Itik Besenda Gurau (The Ducks), 100
La bella hortelana (The Beautiful Gardener), 208
Land of the Silver Birch, 88
Lemonade, 19
Loose Tooth (speech piece), 28
Martin Luther King, 364
Me gase boho (Orange Tree), 317
Moon Boat by C. Pomerantz (poem), 218
Mouse, Mousie, 254
Nabe, Nabe, Soku, Nuke (Stewpot, Stewpot, Bottomless Pot), 259
Old Blue, 213
Old Woman and the Pig, 130
Oma Rapeti (Run, Rabbit), 108
On Top of Spaghetti, 312
Pairs or Pears, 265
Piggy by W. Cole (poem), 315
Puff, the Magic Dragon, 54
Rover, 260
Seeds and Seasons, 206
Señor Coyote (Mexican folktale), 330
Shake the Papaya Down, 90
Sheep in the Meadow (speech piece), 8
Sheep Shearing, 102
Step in Time, 6
Thank You, 349
There's a Hole in the Bucket, 132
Tinga Layo, 50
Together by P. Engle (poem), 34
Wake Up the Sun, 124
Who Has Seen the Wind? by C. G. Rossetti (poem), 137

Volume 1: New Beginnings, Zoom In

Ach, du lieber Augustin (The More We Get Together), 35
America, 338
Animal Fair, 214
Australia's on the Wallaby, 106
Baby Beluga, 26
Bliss by E. Farjeon (poem), 212
Bow, Wow, Wow, 264
Caranguejo (The Crab), 306
Check It Out! (It's About Respect), 10
Chichipapa (The Sparrows' Singing School), 22, 31
Columbus Sailed with Three Ships, 344
Corner Grocery Store, 311
Cuckoo, Where Are You?, 244
Do You Want My Little Frog? by H. Copeland (poem), 187
Doggie, Doggie, 59
Donkey, Donkey, 256
Drumming Spider, The (West African folktale), 333
Eating Lizards, 250
El burrito enfermo (The Sick Little Donkey), 180
El palomo y la paloma (The Doves), 380
Elephant Carries a Great Big Trunk, The, by Anonymous (poem), 169
Food Song, The, 318
Four White Horses, 300
Hairy Dog, The, by H. Asquith (poem), 58
Here Comes a Bluebird, 263
Hop, Old Squirrel, 258
I Chih ha Ma (Frogs), 186
I Heard a Bird Sing by O. Herford (poem), 271
I Saw Three Ships, 359
It's a Small World, 298
Itik Besenda Gurau (The Ducks), 100
Jugaremos en el bosque (We Will Play in the Forest), 188
Leatherwing Bat, 304

Martin Luther King, 364
Mary Had a Baby, 360
Mister Rabbit, Mister Rabbit, 150
Mother, Mother, 254
Mouse, Mousie, 254
Mr. Frog, 257
Na belo (Little Heron), 322
Old Blue, 213
Old Woman and the Pig, 130
Oma Rapeti (Run, Rabbit), 108
On Top of Spaghetti, 312
Pairs or Pears, 265
Piggy by W. Cole (poem), 315
Place in the Choir, A, 308
Rover, 260
Señor Coyote (Mexican folktale), 330
Sheep in the Meadow (speech piece), 8
Sheep Shearing, 102
There Are Many Flags in Many Lands, 341
Three Little Penguins (speech piece), 112
Tiki Tiki Tiki Room, The, 324
Tinga Layo, 50
Yanai (The Elephant), 305
Yankee Doodle, 340

Volume 1: New Beginnings, Side by Side

A la rueda de San Miguel (To the Wheel of San Miguel), 60
Ach, du lieber Augustin (The More We Get Together), 35
All Around the Buttercup, 210
America, 338
Ani Purim, 372
Animal Fair, 214
Apple Picker's Reel, 343
Artichokes, 314
Australia's on the Wallaby, 106
Away for Rio, 170
Baby Beluga, 26
Baby Nodja, 154
Bahay Kubo (My Nipa Hut), 382
Ban Dal (Half Moon), 219
Banyan Tree, 321
Bate, bate (Stir, Stir), 242
Big Beautiful Planet, 376
Bliss (poem), 212
Bow, Wow, Wow, 264
Button, You Must Wander, 176
Candle on the Water, 296
Caranguejo (The Crab), 306
Check It Out! (It's About Respect), 10
Chiapanecas (Ladies of Chiapas), 128
Chichipapa (The Sparrow's Singing School), 22
Chirri Bim, 70
Chíu, Chíu, Chíu (Chirp, Chirp, Chirp), 302
City Traffic (story), 328

Thematic Correlations to Reading Series (continued)

Thematic Correlations to Reading Series (continued)

Thematic Correlations to Reading Series (continued)

Thematic Correlations to Reading Series

Volume 2: My Time to Shine, Just Imagine

Ach, du lieber Augustin (The More We Get Together), 35
All Around the Buttercup, 210
America, 338
Apple Picker's Reel, 343
Artichokes, 314
Australia's on the Wallaby, 106
Ban Dal (Half Moon), 219
Bei Fang Chre (North Wind Blows), 367
Big Beautiful Planet, 376
Button, You Must Wander, 176
Check It Out! (It's About Respect), 10
Chiapanecas (Ladies of Chiapas), 128
Corner Grocery Store, 311
Dal taro kacha (Come, Pick the Moon), 98
Dumplin's, 172
El tren (The Train), 326
El zapatero (The Cobbler), 138
Elephant Carries a Great Big Trunk, The, by Anonymous (poem), 169
En la feria de San Juan (In the Market of San Juan), 226
En nuestra Tierra tan linda (On Our Beautiful Planet Earth), 114
Everybody Has Music Inside, 164
Everything Grows, 204
Finis by H. Newbolt (poem), 76
Food Song, The, 318
Garden Song, 236
Good Night, Sleep Tight, 76
Great Outdoors, The, 290
Green Eggs and Ham, 284
Harvest, 342
Hey, Hey, Look at Me, 245
Horton Hears a Who!, 279
Hot Cross Buns, 258
I See, 266
I'm Gonna Sing, 9
It's a Small World, 298
It's Possible, 281
It's Raining! It's Pouring!, 233
Jugaremos en el bosque (We Will Play in the Forest), 188
La bella hortelana (The Beautiful Gardener), 208
Land of the Silver Birch, 88
Little Seeds (except) by E. Holmelund Minarik (poem), 207
Martin Luther King, 364
Me gase boho (Orange Tree), 317
Mein Hut (My Hat), 142
Mill Song, The, 52
Nabe, Nabe, Soku, Nuke (Stewpot, Stewpot, Bottomless Pot), 259
Oh, the Thinks You Can Think!, 276
Old Woman and the Pig, 130
Oliver Twist, 268

Oma Rapeti (Run, Rabbit), 108
On Top of Spaghetti, 312
Pairs or Pears, 265
Part of Your World, 294
Piggy by W. Cole (poem), 315
Place in the Choir, A, 308
Puff, the Magic Dragon, 54
Riqui Ran (Sawing Song), 21
Sailor, Sailor on the Sea, 262
Say Your Name, 243
Seeds and Seasons, 206
Señor Coyote (Mexican folktale), 330
She'll Be Comin' 'Round the Mountain, 33
Sheep Shearing, 102
Shoo, Fly, 222
Sing! Sing! Sing!, 196
Skating, 350
Sun Is First to Rise, The, by E. Coatsworth (poem), 383
Take Me Out to the Ball Game, 56
Thank You, 349
There Are Many Flags in Many Lands, 341
Up on the Housetop, 356
Wake Up the Sun, 124
Wee Falorie Man, The, 375
Welcome Is the Month of May, 378
Who Has Seen the Wind? by C. G. Rossetti (poem), 137

Grade 3

Volume 1: Imagine That, Finding My Place

Ballad of the Bedbugs and the Beetles, The, 206
Billy, 7
Boll Weevil, 171
Charlie, 208
Cielito lindo (Mexican folk song), 166
Circle 'Round the Zero, 267
City Life, 341
Crawdad Song, 107
Cumberland Gap, 99
¡Dale, dale, dale!, 378
Death of the Robin, 275
Egy üveg alma (One Jar of Apples), 22
Eh Soom Boo Kawaya (Nigerian boat song), 58
El florón (The Flower), 46
En roulant ma boule (As I Roll My Ball), 100
Gebeta Board, The (Ethiopian folk tale), 346
Gi'Me Elbow Room, 88
Great Big House, 14
Guitar Man, The, 138
Happy Wanderer, The, 18
Hello!, 283

Hope by E. Dickinson (poem), 166
I Have a Car, 252
I'm a Believer, 312
I'm On My Way, 382
Jamaica Farewell, 156
Jingle at the Window, 268
Kreely Kranky, 258
Kuma San (Honorable Bear), 244
Lincoln by M. Cohn Livingston (poem), 389
Little Sally Walker, 105
Marvelous Toy, The, 182
Moon and Me, 220
Movin' Right Along, 124
Music of the World A-Turnin', 44
My Friend Tom, 364
My Horses Ain't Hungry, 278
O, The Train's Off the Track, 176
Oh, Susanna, 153
Old Barn Dance, The, 94
Oleanna, 144
One Potato, Two Potato, 267
Paw Paw Patch, The, 195
Rainbow Connection, The, 310
Riding in the Buggy, 131
Scotland's Burning, 257
Shalom Chaveyrim (Shalom, My Friends), 141
Ship Ahoy, 314
Shoo Fly Pie and Apple Pan Dowdy, 227
Simon Says, 4
Stevedore's Song, 127
Sun Don't Set in the Mornin', 48, 60
Sweet Potatoes, 16
This a Way and That a Way, 386
Three Is a Magic Number, 94
Three Little Birds, 204
Trampin', 287
Treasure Chests, 90
Turn the Glasses Over, 260
Ucha Tirvarch (Little Bear Song), 53
Wang Ü Ger (Chinese fishing song), 190
Way Down South by Anonymous (poem), 8
Wéané (Menadonese lullaby), 184
When I First Came to This Land, 28
Who's That Yonder?, 245
Yankee Doodle, 357

Volume 1: Imagine That, The Whole Wide World

Al lado de mi cabaña (Beside My Cottage), 141
Apple Tree by Anonymous (poem), 24
Ballad of the Bedbugs and the Beetles, The, 206
Blow, Ye Winds, Blow, 192
Bohm (Spring Has Come!), 392

Thematic Correlations to Reading Series (continued)

Boll Weevil, 171
Cat and Dog, 259
Cielito lindo (Mexican folk song), 166
Colors of the Wind, 84
Coral, 249
Crawdad Song, 107
De aquel cerro (On the Darkened Hillside), 32
Digga Digga Dog, 164
El arroyo que murmura (The Murmuring Brook), 318
El florón (The Flower), 46
Evergreen, Everblue, 330
Frosty Weather, 250
Gebeta Board, The (Ethiopian folk tale), 346
Hope by E. Dickinson (poem), 166
I Lost the Farmer's Dairy Key, 273
I Walk in Beauty, 329
I'm a Believer, 312
I'm On My Way, 382
Interplanet Janet, 298
Isabela and the Troll (Spanish folk tale), 349
J'entends le moulin (I Hear the Windmill), 135
Jasmine Flower, 146
Just Like the Sun, 394
Kum Bachur (The Rooster), 75
La cloche (The Clock), 67
Le Mar (The Sea), 110
Marvelous Toy, The, 182
May Day Carol, 393
Moon and Me, 220
Morning Bells, 270
Movin' Right Along, 124
Night Song, 186
Oh Mama Bakdala (Xhosa folk song), 328
Oleanna, 144
Que Llueva (It's Raining), 274
Raccoon Dance Song, 87
Rain Is Falling Down, 242
Rainbow Connection, The, 310
Rattlesnake, 72
Recycle Rap, 332
Smoke Goes Up the Chimney, 272
Spiders, 282
Sun Don't Set in the Mornin', 48, 60
Sweep, Sweep, Away, 276
Tanabata (Seven Evenings), 62
Taps, 281
Trampin', 287
Uno de enero (The First of January), 210
Vamos a la mar (Let's Go to the Sea), 256
Way Down South by Anonymous (poem), 8
Yellow Submarine, 320

Volume 1: Imagine That, Getting the Job Done

Chag Asif (Harvest Time), 360
Cielito lindo (Mexican folk song), 166
Crawdad Song, 107
Eh Soom Boo Kawaya (Nigerian boat song), 58
El florón (The Flower), 46
Gebeta Board, The (Ethiopian folk tale), 346
Gi'Me Elbow Room, 88
Great Big House, 14
Guitar Man, The, 138
Hope by E. Dickinson (poem), 166
I'm a Believer, 312
I'm On My Way, 382
I's the B'y, 13
Marvelous Toy, The, 182
Moon and Me, 220
Movin' Right Along, 124
My Friend Tom, 364
Oleanna, 144
Rainbow Connection, The, 310
Shalom Chaveyrim (Shalom, My Friends), 141
Shepherd, Shepherd, 56
Shoo Fly Pie and Apple Pan Dowdy, 227
Stevedore's Song, 127
Sun Don't Set in the Mornin', 48, 60
Sweet Potatoes, 16
This a Way and That a Way, 386
Trampin', 287
Treasure Chests, 90
Ucha Tirvarch (Little Bear Song), 53
Wang Ü Ger (Chinese fishing song), 190

Volume 2: Picture This, From Past to Present

Amen, 376
America, the Beautiful, 354
Anansi (Ashanti folk tale), 104
Ballad of the Bedbugs and the Beetles, The, 206
Bella Bimba (Pretty Girl), 172
Billy, 7
Bim Bom, 218
Blow, Ye Winds, Blow, 192
Bohm, 392
Boll Weevil, 171
Boo, 362
Buffalo Dance Entrance Song, 325
Butterfly Come Play With Me, 112
Cat and Dog, 259
Chan mali chan, 10
Charlie, 208
Chicka-ma, Chicka-ma, Craney Crow, 263
Chicken on the Fence Post, 265
Cielito Lindo, 166

Circle 'Round the Zero, 267
City Life, 341
Clocks, 266
Colors of the Wind, 84
Coral, 249
Cornstalk Fiddle and a Shoestring Bow, 284
Crawdad Song, 107
Cumberland Gap, 99
¡Dale, dale, dale!, 378
De aquel cerro (On the Darkened Hillside), 32
Death of the Robin, 275
Deck the Hall, 374
Dide, 279
Digga Digga Dog, 164
Dinah, 150
Ding Dong Diggy Diggy Dong, 269
Draw a Bucket of Water, 222
Egy üveg alma (One Jar of Apples), 22
Eh Soom Boo Kawaya, 58
El atole, 396-397
El florón (The Flower), 46
El nido (The Nest), 214
En roulant ma boule (As I Roll My Ball), 100
Evergreen, Everblue, 330
Frog in the Meadow, 243
Frosty, the Snowman, 366-367
Frosty Weather, 250
Gebeta Board, The (story), 346
Gi'Me Elbow Room, 88
Go Tell It on the Mountain, 377
Golden Ring Around the Susan Girl, 264
Gong xi fa cai (Chinese New Year Song), 384
Great Big House, 14
Greatest Show on Earth, The, 308
Hag Asif (Harvest Time), 360
Happy Wanderer, The, 18
Hello!, 283
Herring, The, 316
Hey, Motswala, 34
I Have a Car, 252
I Lost the Farmer's Dairy Key, 273
I Walk in Beauty, 329
I'm a Believer, 312
I'm On My Way, 382
I's the B'y, 13
In Good Old Colony Times, 326
Interjections, 303
Interplanet Janet, 298
Isabela and the Troll (story), 349
J'entends le moulin (I Hear the Windmill), 135
Jamaica Farewell, 156
Jasmine Flower, 146
John Jacob Jingleheimer Schmidt, 68
Just Like the Sun, 394

Thematic Correlations to Reading Series

Unit 5: Other Times, Other Places

Thematic Correlations to Reading Series (continued)

Sankta Lucia (Saint Lucia), 413
Season of Hope, The, 410
Sounds of Swing by T. Igus (poem), 32
Vive l'amour, 262
What the World Needs Now, 230
When Johnny Comes Marching Home, 34
Words of Wisdom, 244
Yakety Yak, 308

Unit 2: My World and Yours

Allá en el rancho grande (My Ranch), 66
America, the Beautiful, 388
Ballad of the Underground Railroad, The, 145, (partner song) 154
Beauty and the Beast, 124
Bound No'th Blues by L. Hughes (poem), 181
By the Singing Water, 270
Caissons Go Rolling Along, The, 37
Change the World, 314
Circle of Friends, 196
Cliffs of Doneen, The, 46
Colores de caracol (Colors of the Snail) by E. Galarza (poem), 101
Da pacem Domine (Give Us Peace), 261
De colores (Many Colors) (unison), 88, (parts), 98
Deta, Deta (The Moon), 246
Dreamers, 430
Ēinīnī (Little Birds Sleep), 240
Erie Canal, 132
Estrella brillante (Shining Star), 373
Follow the Drinkin' Gourd, 142
Fun wa ni alaafia (Send Us Your Peace), 248
Ga Eul (Fall), 401
Gentle River Runs, A, 342
Great Big Sea, A, 334
Hallelujah, Get On Board, 345
Haneirot Halalu (These Lights), 414
Heartbeat of Democracy by V. Brasier (poem), 389
Hero, 312
I Am but a Small Voice, 323
I Hear America Singing, 327
In That Great Git'n Up Morning, 10
John Henry, 146
John Kanaka, 249
Joyful, Joyful, We Adore Thee, 103
Kwanzaa stamp by S. Saint James (art), 429
Life by S. DeShetler (poem), 205
Light One Candle, 416
Like a Mighty Stream, 320
Loch Lomond, 138
Los maizales (The Cornfields), 268
Main Lighthouse (architecture), 5
My Government Claim (unison), 95, (parts), 110

Nani Wale Na Hala (The Swaying Pandanus Trees), 276
New Colossus, The (excerpt) by E. Lazarus (poem), 42
Ngam sang duan (Shining Moon), 376
Our World, 381
Path to the Moon, 368
Reach, 14
Ride Like the Wind, 130
Simple Gifts, 136
Singabahambayo (An Army Is Marching) (unison), 56, (parts), 76
Song of Peace, 257
Star Canon, 367
Surfin' U.S.A., 306
Times They Are A-Changin', The, 204
Ujima (Collective Work and Responsibility), 427
We Are the Children of Tomorrow, 114
We Want to Sing, 235
What the World Needs Now, 230
Winter Wonderland, 408

Unit 3: A Job Well Done

Ballad of the Underground Railroad, The, 145, (partner song), 154
Beauty and the Beast, 124
Big Big World, 438
Caissons Go Rolling Along, The, 37
Change the World, 314
Cliffs of Doneen, The, 46
Colores de caracol (Colors of the Snail) by E. Galarza (poem), 101
De colores (Many Colors) (unison), 88, (parts), 98
Deta, Deta (The Moon), 246
Dreamers, 430
Ēinīnī (Little Birds Sleep), 240
Estrella brillante (Shining Star), 373
Ga Eul (Fall), 401
Great Big Sea, A, 334
Hero, 312
I Am But a Small Voice, 323
Joyful, Joyful, We Adore Thee, 103
Life by S. DeShetler (poem), 205
Light One Candle, 416
Loch Lomond, 138
Los maizales (The Cornfields), 268
Nani Wale Na Hala (The Swaying Pandanus Trees), 276
Ngam sang duan (Shining Moon), 376
Our World, 381
Path to the Moon, 368
Reach, 14
Ride Like the Wind, 130
Simple Gifts, 136
Star Canon, 367
Surfin' U.S.A., 306
What the World Needs Now, 230
Winter Wonderland, 408

Unit 4: Time and Time Again

76 Trombones, 296
A Zing-A Za, 338
Aeyaya balano sakkad (Come, Children), 402
Allá en el rancho grande (My Ranch), 66
America, the Beautiful, 388
¡Ay, Jalisco no te rajes! (Ay, Jalisco, Never Fail Her), 188
Babylon's Fallin', 243
Ballad of the Underground Railroad, The, 145, 154
Beauty and the Beast, 124
Big, Big World, 438
Borinquen (poem), 443
Bound No'th Blues (poem), 181
By the Singing Water, 270
Caissons Go Rolling Along, The, 37
Change the World, 314
Cidade Maravilhosa, 432
Cindy, 265
Circle of Friends, 196
City Blues, The, 278
Cliffs of Doneen, The, 46
Colores de caracol (poem), 101
Come and Sing Together (unison), 270
Cuando salí de Cuba (I Went Away from Cuba), 168
Cumbia del sol (Cumbia of the Sun), 16
Da pacem Domine (Give Us Peace), 261
Dance for the Nations, 206
De allacito carnavalito (The Carnival Is Coming), 269
De colores (Many Colors) (unison and 2-part), 88, 98
Deta, Deta (The Moon), 246
Dreamers, 430
Dry Bones, 406
El jarabe (Mexican Hat Dance), 396
El vito, 210
Erie Canal, 132
Estrella brillante (Shining Star), 273
Every Day I Have the Blues, 179
Everybody Rejoice, 226
Feel Good, 358
Fifty Nifty United States, 392
Follow the Drinkin' Gourd, 142
Fun wa ni alaafia (Send Us Your Peace), 248
Fung Yang Song, 58
Funiculi, Funicula, 62
Gentle River Runs, A, 342
Goin' Home, 108
Great Big Sea, A, 334
Guantanamera, 215
Haere Ra (Now Is the Hour), 151
Hallelujah Get on Board, 345
Hava Nagila, 54

Alphabetical Index of Interactive Listening Maps

By Composer

African American Spiritual/Hogan: Elijah Rock, **Gr. 6**, 52
African American Spiritual/Hogan: Wade in the Water, **Gr. 5**, 144
African Traditional Adenkum: Adukbe, **Gr. 8**, 177
Anderson: Waltzing Cat, **Gr. K**, T223
Arban: The Carnival of Venice, **Gr. 6**, 40
Bach: Badinerie from *Suite for Orchestra No. 2 in B Minor*, **Gr. 4**, 61
Bach: Gigue from *Suite for Orchestra No. 3*, **Gr. 2**, 269
Bach: Gigue from *Suite No. 1 for Cello*, **Gr. 3**, 178
Bahamian Folk Song: The Wind Blew East, **Gr. 1**, T234
Bart: Food, Glorious Food from *Oliver!*, **Gr. 2**, 310
Beach: A Hummingbird, **Gr. K**, T140
Beethoven: Rondo a capriccio, Op. 129 ("Rage Over a Lost Penny") (excerpt), **Gr. 2**, 225
Beethoven: Symphony No. 5 in C Minor, Third and Fourth Movements, **Gr. 8**, 115
Beethoven: Symphony No. 7, Second Movement, **Gr. 7**, 118
Beethoven: Symphony No. 8, Second Movement (excerpt), **Gr. K**, T235
Beethoven: Symphony No. 9 in D Minor ("Choral"), Fourth Movement (excerpt), **Gr. 5**, 102
Bizet: Carillon from *L'Arlesienne Suite No. 1*, **Gr. 7**, 123
Bizet: March from *Children's Games*, **Gr. 1**, T31
Brazilian Folk Music: Batucada Brasileira, **Gr. 5**, 433
Brazilian Traditional/Dunlap: Afoxé, **Gr. 8**, 34
Bremer: Early Light, **Gr. 6**, 201
Britten: Young Person's Guide to the Orchestra (excerpt), **Gr. 2**, 229
Caillet: Variations on the Theme "Pop! Goes the Weasel", **Gr. 5**, 97
Chaminade: Trio for Piano, Violin, and Cello, Op. 11, Third Movement (Presto Leggiero), **Gr. 5**, 121
Chinese Folk Song: Bo Hai Huan Ten, **Gr. 7**, 56
Chinese Folk Song: Singing on the Fisherboats at Dusk, **Gr. 1**, T129
Chinese Traditional: Blue Little Flower, **Gr. 8**, 82
Chopin: Étude Op. 25, No. 11 ("The Winter Wind"), **Gr. 2**, 136
Clayton-Thomas: Spinning Wheel, **Gr. 4**, 211
Coleman and Mohi: Pukaea (excerpt), **Gr. 2**, 109
Coltrane: Locomotion, **Gr. 6**, 157
Copland: Circus Music from *The Red Pony Suite* (excerpt), **Gr. 3**, 285
Copland: Variations on "Simple Gifts" from *Appalachian Spring*, **Gr. 5**, 153
di Lasso: Echo Song, **Gr. K**, T103
Dun: Night Fight from *Crouching Tiger, Hidden Dragon*, **Gr. 6**, 28
Dvořák: Symphony No. 9 in E Minor, Op. 95 ("From the New World"), Largo (excerpt), **Gr. 5**, 107
Elgar: Faeries and Giants from *Wand of Youth Suite No. 1*, **Gr. K**, T52
Elgar: Pomp and Circumstance March No. 1 (excerpt), **Gr. 7**, 50

Ellington: It Don't Mean a Thing, **Gr. 6**, 165
Ellmenreich: Spinning Song, **Gr. 3**, 128
Enya, Ryan, and Ryan: Only Time, **Gr. 7**, 142
Fernândez: Batuque, **Gr. 7**, 202
Garland: In the Mood, **Gr. 4**, 143
Gershwin: Summertime from *Porgy and Bess*, **Gr. 1**, T375
Gershwin: Walking the Dog from *Shall We Dance*, **Gr. 1**, T169
Gershwin and Gershwin: Fascinating Rhythm from *Lady Be Good*, **Gr. 5**, 186
Ginastera: Los trabajadores agrícolas (The Farmers) from *Estancia*, **Gr. 6**, 116
Glière: Russian Sailor's Dance from *The Red Poppy*, **Gr. 4**, 266
Goldman: Children's March, **Gr. K**, T113
Gould: American Salute, **Gr. 5**, 36
Gray and De Lange: String of Pearls, A, **Gr. 3**, 12
Grieg: Anitra's Dance from *Peer Gynt Suite No. 1*, Op. 46, **Gr. 5**, 193
Grieg: In the Hall of the Mountain King from *Peer Gynt Suite No. 1*, Op. 46, **Gr. 2**, 346
Grofé: On the Trail from *Grand Canyon Suite*, **Gr. 8**, 112
Guem: Le Serpent (excerpt), **Gr. 1**, T359
Guthrie: Car Song, **Gr. K**, T135
Handel: Hallelujah Chorus from *Messiah*, **Gr. 5**, 419
Hatfield: La lluvia (The Rain), **Gr. 2**, 232
Haydn: String Quartet, Opus 76, No. 2 in D Minor, Andante (excerpt), **Gr. 1**, T129
Haydn: Symphony No. 35, Fourth Movement (excerpt), **Gr. 5**, 247
Haydn: Trio for Piano, Violin and Cello No. 39, Finale ("Gypsy Rondo"), **Gr. 3**, 155
Holst: Mars from *The Planets*, **Gr. 6**, 196
Humperdinck: Brother, Come and Dance with Me from *Hansel and Gretel*, **Gr. K**, T180
Ibert: Concertino da Camera, First Movement, **Gr. 7**, 161
Ibert: Parade from Divertissement from *Un Chapeau de paille d'Italie*, **Gr. K**, T183
Indian Classical Music: Raga Malika (excerpt), **Gr. 5**, 402
Irish Folk Music: Brafferton Village/Walsh's Hornpipe, **Gr. 3**, 391
Israeli Folk Dance: Nigun Atik, **Gr. 3**, 47
Ives: Washington's Birthday (excerpt), **Gr. 2**, 370
Joplin: The Entertainer, **Gr. 7**, 23
Kabalevsky: Galop (excerpt) from *The Comedians*, **Gr. 4**, 254
Kale: Milan (Meeting of the Two Rivers) (excerpt), **Gr. 4**, 208
Kaneko: Bird Island, **Gr. 8**, 56
Kay: Sleight of Feet from *Cakewalk Suite*, **Gr. 1**, T239
Keetman: Flute and Drum from *Gunild Keetman Collection*, **Gr. 1**, T235
Khachaturian: Galop from *Masquerade Suite*, **Gr. 1**, T259
Kibble and Kibble: My Friend, **Gr. 4**, 389
Kidjo, Hebrail, and Faragher: Afirika, **Gr. 7**, 226
Knopfler: The Bug, **Gr. 8**, 88
Kopelent: Crazy Songs, **Gr. 6**, 65
Kozak: Assembly Required, **Gr. 2**, 36
Larsen: Gloria from *Mass for the Earth* (excerpt), **Gr. 7**, 222

Alphabetical Index of Interactive Listening Maps (continued)

Larson: Seasons of Love from *Rent*, **Gr. 7**, 86

Liszt: The Nightingale, **Gr. 6**, 160

Lully: Marche, **Gr. 8**, 168

Makeba: Pata Pata (excerpt), **Gr. 3**, 35

Mariachi: Chango Guango, **Gr. 2**, 60

Mariachi: Los mariachis, **Gr. 3**, 397

Marley: Three Little Birds (excerpt), **Gr. 8**, 84

Mellencamp: Peaceful World, **Gr. 7**, 154

Miloslavskiy: A Clock at Night, **Gr. 3**, 66

Monahan, Stafford, Hotchkiss, Colin, and Underwood: Drops of Jupiter (Tell Me), **Gr. 8**, 103

Montsalvatge: Allegretto, **Gr. 6**, 193

Mountain Folk Dance: Sail Away, **Gr. 4**, 55

Mozart: Eine Kleine Nachtmusik (Serenade No. 13 in G, K. 525), Minuet, **Gr. 3**, 169

Mozart: Exsultate, jubilate, Third Movement, **Gr. 6**, 187

Mozart: Papagena! Papagena! Papagena! from *The Magic Flute*, **Gr. 2**, 152

Mozart: Rondo "alla turca" (Third Movement) from *Piano Sonata No. 11 in A Major*, K. 331, **Gr. 7**, 116

Mozart: Serenade No. 10 in B Flat Major, K. 361 ("Gran Partita"), Theme and Variations (excerpt), **Gr. 4**, 235

Mozart: Symphony No. 40 in G Minor, First Movement, **Gr. 8**, 218

Mussorgsky: Tuileries from *Pictures at an Exhibition*, **Gr. 1**, T249

Mussorgsky/Ravel: Ballet of the Unhatched Chicks from *Pictures at an Exhibition*, **Gr. 3**, 76

Mussorgsky/Ravel: Bydlo (The Ox Cart) from *Pictures at an Exhibition*, **Gr. 1**, T152

Nakai: December Snow, **Gr. K**, T313

Newton: Amazing Grace, **Gr. 7**, 144

Norwegian Folk Melody: Nokken Danser, **Gr. 4**, 168

Offenbach: Barcarolle (Belle nuit) from *Tales of Hoffman*, **Gr. 6**, 265

Ponce: Música indígena from *Instantaneous Mexicanas*, **Gr. 8**, 126

Praetorius: Courante from *Terpsichore*, **Gr. 8**, 130

Praetorius: La canarie from *Dances from Terpsichore*, **Gr. 4**, 177

Praetorius: Volta from *Dances from Terpsichore*, **Gr. 3**, 121

Prima: Sing, Sing, Sing (with a Swing), **Gr. 5**, 32

Prokofiev: March for Military Band, Op. 99, **Gr. 8**, 37

Prokofiev: Sonata for Piano No. 2 in D Minor, Vivace (excerpt), **Gr. 4**, 181

Prokofiev: Symphony No. 1 in D Major, Op. 25 ("Classical"), Third Movement (Gavotte), **Gr. 1**, T92

Prokofiev: Troika from *Lieutenant Kijé Suite* (excerpt), **Gr. 3**, 225

Puccini: Nessun dorma from *Turandot*, **Gr. 5**, 64

Puente: Oye como va, **Gr. 5**, 69

Purcell: Minuet from *Abdelazar*, **Gr. 2**, 145

Radetzky: Radetzky March, **Gr. K**, T177

Ramzy: Belhadawa walla belshaawa, **Gr. 6**, 35

Ravel: Laideronette, Empress of the Pagodas from *Mother Goose Suite*, **Gr. 1**, T237

Renaissance/anon.: Packington's Pound, **Gr. 2**, 200

Rimsky-Korsakov: Scheherazade (excerpt), **Gr. 4**, 161

Rimsky-Korsakov: The Flight of the Bumblebee, **Gr. K**, T259

Rodgers and Hammerstein: My Favorite Things from *The Sound of Music*, **Gr. 3**, 313

Rodgers and Hammerstein: So Long, Farewell from *The Sound of Music*, **Gr. K**, T189

Rodrigo: Adagio (excerpt) from *Concierto de Aranjuez*, **Gr. 4**, 13

Rodrigo: Concierto de Aranjuez, First Movement (excerpt), **Gr. 3**, 41

Rodriguez: La cumparsita, **Gr. 6**, 113

Rossini: Largo al factotum from *Il Barbiere di Siviglia*, **Gr. 2**, 217

Rossini: William Tell (Overture) (excerpt), **Gr. 3**, 65

Rzewski: The People United Will Never Be Defeated (Theme and Variations 5, 13, 26), **Gr. 8**, 93

Saint-Denis: Shimmering Air, **Gr. K**, T139

Saint-Saëns: Danse Macabre, **Gr. 3**, 363

Saint-Saëns: The Elephant from *The Carnival of the Animals*, **Gr. 1**, T204

Saint-Saëns: Finale from *The Carnival of the Animals*, **Gr. K**, T195

Sandström: Concerto for Trombone, Fifth Movement ("Motorbike Concerto"), **Gr. 2**, 193

Scruggs: Foggy Mountain Breakdown, **Gr. 6**, 140

Shostakovich: Dance from *Ballet Suite No. 1*, **Gr. K**, T167

Sibelius: Finlandia, Op. 26, No. 7 (excerpt), **Gr. 5**, 257

Smetana: The Moldau from *Má Vlast* (My Country), **Gr. 5**, 271

Sondheim: No One Is Alone from *Into the Woods* (excerpt), **Gr. 8**, 86

Sousa: Semper Fidelis, **Gr. 3**, 281

Sousa: The Stars and Stripes Forever, **Gr. 4**, 355

Sousa: Washington Post March, **Gr. 2**, 339

South African Work Song: Tshotsholoza, **Gr. 1**, T76

Southern Appalachian Folk Song: Shady Grove, **Gr. 8**, 59

Sowande: Akinla from *African Suite*, **Gr. 2**, 97

Stravinsky: Galop from *Suite No. 2 for Small Orchestra*, **Gr. 7**, 126

Stravinsky: Introduction from *The Rite of Spring*, **Gr. 6**, 423

Stravinsky: Vivo from *Pulcinella Suite*, **Gr. 4**, 201

Taylor: C-A-G, **Gr. 1**, T241

Tchaikovsky: Dance of the Mirlitons from *The Nutcracker*, **Gr. 4**, 173

Tchaikovsky: Dance of the Sugar Plum Fairy from *The Nutcracker Suite*, **Gr. 2**, 355

Tchaikovsky: Trepak from *The Nutcracker*, **Gr. 6**, 408

Tchaikovsky: Waltz of the Flowers (excerpt) from *The Nutcracker*, **Gr. 1**, T353

Thile: Ode to a Butterfly, **Gr. 5**, 25

Thomson: Cattle from *The Plow That Broke the Plains*, **Gr. 4**, 274

Thomson: Walking Song from *Acadian Songs and Dances*, **Gr. K**, T20

Travis: Sixteen Tons, **Gr. 7**, 151

Vaughan Williams: March Past of the Kitchen Utensils from *The Wasps*, **Gr. 3**, 247

Vaughan Williams: Seventeen Come Sunday from *English Folk Song Suite*, **Gr. 7**, 102

Verdi: Anvil Chorus from *Il Trovatore*, **Gr. 5**, 148

Verdi: Va Pensiero from *Nabucco*, **Gr. 6**, 169

Villa Lobos: The Little Train of the Caipira from *Bachianas Brasileiras No. 2*, **Gr. K**, T142

Vivaldi: Concerto for Two Trumpets, Allegro, **Gr. 2**, 73

Alphabetical Index of Interactive Listening Maps

Alphabetical Index of Interactive Listening Maps (continued)

Vivaldi: Fall (Allegro) from *The Four Seasons (Concerto No. 3 in F Major)* (excerpt), **Gr. K**, T305

Vivaldi: Spring (Allegro) from *The Four Seasons (Concerto No. 1 in E Major)*, **Gr. 4**, 391

Vivaldi: Winter (Allegro non molto) from *The Four Seasons (Concerto No. 4 in F Minor)*, **Gr. 6**, 403

Waldteufel: The Skaters' Waltz (excerpt), **Gr. 1**, T344

Weiss and Thiele: What a Wonderful World, **Gr. 8**, 9

Williams: Augie's Great Municipal Band from *Star Wars Episode 1: The Phantom Menace* (excerpt), **Gr. 4**, 57

Williams: Liberty Fanfare, **Gr. 7**, 187

Willson: Seventy-Six Trombones from *The Music Man*, **Gr. 8**, 76

Winter: Ocean Child, **Gr. 7**, 218

Worsley: Promenade from *Golden Goose*, **Gr. 1**, T176

Yanjun: The Moon Mirrored in a Pool, **Gr. K**, T115

York: Skeleton, **Gr. 8**, 215

York: Sunburst, **Gr. 7**, 216

By Title

Adagio (excerpt) from *Concierto de Aranjuez* by Rodrigo, **Gr. 4**, 13

Adukbe (African Traditional Adenkum), **Gr. 8**, 177

Afirika by Kidjo, Hebrail, and Faragher, **Gr. 7**, 226

Afoxé (Brazilian Traditional/Dunlap arr.), **Gr. 8**, 34

Akinla from *African Suite* by Sowande, **Gr. 2**, 97

Allegretto by Montsalvatge, **Gr. 6**, 193

Amazing Grace by Newton, **Gr. 7**, 144

American Salute by Gould, **Gr. 5**, 36

Anitra's Dance from *Peer Gynt Suite No. 1, Op. 46* by Grieg, **Gr. 5**, 193

Anvil Chorus from *Il Trovatore* by Verdi, **Gr. 5**, 148

Assembly Required by Kozak, **Gr. 2**, 36

Augie's Great Municipal Band from *Star Wars Episode 1: The Phantom Menace* (excerpt) by Williams, **Gr. 4**, 57

Badinerie from *Suite for Orchestra No. 2 in B Minor* by Bach, **Gr. 4**, 61

Ballet of the Unhatched Chicks from *Pictures at an Exhibition* by Mussorgsky/Ravel, **Gr. 3**, 76

Barcarolle (Belle nuit) from *Tales of Hoffman* by Offenbach, **Gr. 6**, 265

Batucada Brasileira (Brazilian Folk Music), **Gr. 5**, 433

Batuque by Fernândez, **Gr. 7**, 202

Belhadawa walla belshaawa by Ramzy, **Gr. 6**, 35

Bird Island by Kaneko, **Gr. 8**, 56

Blue Little Flower (Chinese Traditional), **Gr. 8**, 82

Bo Hai Huan Ten (Chinese Folk Song), **Gr. 7**, 56

Brafferton Village/Walsh's Hornpipe (Irish Folk Music), **Gr. 3**, 391

Brother, Come and Dance with Me from *Hansel and Gretel* by Humperdinck, **Gr. K**, T180

Bug, The by Knopfler, **Gr. 8**, 88

Bydlo (The Ox Cart) from *Pictures at an Exhibition* by Mussorgsky/Ravel, **Gr. 1**, T152

C-A-G by Taylor, **Gr. 1**, T241

Car Song by Guthrie, **Gr. K**, T135

Carillon from *L'Arlesienne Suite No. 1* by Bizet, **Gr. 7**, 123

Carnival of Venice, The by Arban, **Gr. 6**, 40

Cattle from *The Plow That Broke the Plains* by Thomson, **Gr. 4**, 274

Chango Guango (Mariachi), **Gr. 2**, 60

Children's March by Goldman, **Gr. K**, T113

Circus Music from *The Red Pony Suite* (excerpt) by Copland, **Gr. 3**, 285

Clock at Night, A by Miloslavskiy, **Gr. 3**, 66

Concertino da Camera, First Movement by Ibert, **Gr. 7**, 161

Concerto for Trombone, Fifth Movement ("Motorbike Concerto") by Sandström, **Gr. 2**, 193

Concerto for Two Trumpets, Allegro by Vivaldi, **Gr. 2**, 73

Concierto de Aranjuez, First Movement (excerpt) by Rodrigo, **Gr. 3**, 41

Courante from *Terpsichore* by Praetorius, **Gr. 8**, 130

Crazy Songs by Kopelent, **Gr. 6**, 65

Dance from *Ballet Suite No. 1* by Shostakovich, **Gr. K**, T167

Dance of the Mirlitons from *The Nutcracker* by Tchaikovsky, **Gr. 4**, 173

Dance of the Sugar Plum Fairy from *The Nutcracker Suite* by Tchaikovsky, **Gr. 2**, 355

Danse Macabre by Saint-Saëns, **Gr. 3**, 363

December Snow by Nakai, **Gr. K**, T313

Drops of Jupiter (Tell Me) by Monahan, Stafford, Hotchkiss, Colin, and Underwood, **Gr. 8**, 103

Early Light by Bremer, **Gr. 6**, 201

Echo Song by di Lasso, **Gr. K**, T103

Eine Kleine Nachtmusik (Serenade No. 13 in G, K. 525), Minuet by Mozart, **Gr. 3**, 169

Elephant, The from *The Carnival of the Animals* by Saint-Saëns, **Gr. 1**, T204

Elijah Rock (African American Spiritual/Hogan arr.), **Gr. 6**, 52

Entertainer, The by Joplin, **Gr. 7**, 23

Étude Op. 25, No. 11 ("The Winter Wind") by Chopin, **Gr. 2**, 136

Exsultate, jubilate, Third Movement by Mozart, **Gr. 6**, 187

Faeries and Giants from *Wand of Youth Suite No. 1* by Elgar, **Gr. K**, T52

Fall (Allegro) from *The Four Seasons (Concerto No. 3 in F Major)* (excerpt) by Vivaldi, **Gr. K**, T305

Fascinating Rhythm from *Lady Be Good* by Gershwin and Gershwin, **Gr. 5**, 186

Finale from *The Carnival of the Animals* by Saint-Saëns, **Gr. K**, T195

Finlandia, Op. 26, No. 7 (excerpt) by Sibelius, **Gr. 5**, 257

Flight of the Bumblebee, The by Rimsky-Korsakov, **Gr. K**, T259

Flute and Drum from *Gunild Keetman Collection* by Keetman, **Gr. 1**, T235

Foggy Mountain Breakdown by Scruggs, **Gr. 6**, 140

Food, Glorious Food from *Oliver!* by Bart, **Gr. 2**, 310

Galop (excerpt) from *The Comedians* by Kabalevsky, **Gr. 4**, 254

Galop from *Masquerade Suite* by Khachaturian, **Gr. 1**, T259

Galop from *Suite No. 2 for Small Orchestra* by Stravinsky, **Gr. 7**, 126

Gigue from *Suite for Orchestra No. 3* by Bach, **Gr. 2**, 269

Gigue from *Suite No. 1 for Cello* by Bach, **Gr. 3**, 178

Gloria from *Mass for the Earth* (excerpt) by Larsen, **Gr. 7**, 222

Hallelujah Chorus from *Messiah* by Handel, **Gr. 5**, 419

Hummingbird, A by Beach, **Gr. K**, T140

Alphabetical Index of Interactive Listening Maps (continued)

In the Hall of the Mountain King from *Peer Gynt Suite No. 1, Op. 46* by Grieg, **Gr. 2**, 346

In the Mood by Garland, **Gr. 4**, 143

Introduction from *The Rite of Spring* by Stravinsky, **Gr. 6**, 423

It Don't Mean a Thing by Ellington, **Gr. 6**, 165

La canarie from *Dances from Terpsichore* by Praetorius, **Gr. 4**, 177

La cumparsita by Rodriguez, **Gr. 6**, 113

La lluvia (The Rain) by Hatfield, **Gr. 2**, 232

Laideronette, Empress of the Pagodas from *Mother Goose Suite* by Ravel, **Gr. 1**, T237

Largo al factotum from *Il Barbiere di Siviglia* by Rossini, **Gr. 2**, 217

Le Serpent (excerpt) by Guem, **Gr. 1**, T359

Liberty Fanfare by Williams, **Gr. 7**, 187

Little Train of the Caipira, The from *Bachianas Brasileiras No. 2* by Villa Lobos, **Gr. K**, T142

Locomotion by Coltrane, **Gr. 6**, 157

Los mariachis (Mariachi), **Gr. 3**, 397

Los trabajadores agrícolas (The Farmers) from *Estancia* by Ginastera, **Gr. 6**, 116

March for Military Band, Op. 99 by Prokofiev, **Gr. 8**, 37

March from *Children's Games* by Bizet, **Gr. 1**, T31

March Past of the Kitchen Utensils from *The Wasps* by Vaughan Williams, **Gr. 3**, 247

Marche by Lully, **Gr. 8**, 168

Mars from *The Planets* by Holst, **Gr. 6**, 196

Milan (Meeting of the Two Rivers) (excerpt) by Kale, **Gr. 4**, 208

Minuet from *Abdelazar* by Purcell, **Gr. 2**, 145

Moldau, The from *Má Vlast* (My Country) by Smetana, **Gr. 5**, 271

Moon Mirrored in a Pool, The by Yanjun, **Gr. K**, T115

Música indígena from *Instantaneous Mexicanas* by Ponce, **Gr. 8**, 126

My Favorite Things from *The Sound of Music* by Rodgers and Hammerstein, **Gr. 3**, 313

My Friend by Kibble and Kibble, **Gr. 4**, 389

Nessun dorma from *Turandot* by Puccini, **Gr. 5**, 64

Night Fight from *Crouching Tiger, Hidden Dragon* by Dun, **Gr. 6**, 28

Nightingale, The by Liszt, **Gr. 6**, 160

Nigun Atik (Israeli Folk Dance), **Gr. 3**, 47

No One Is Alone from *Into the Woods* (excerpt) by Sondheim, **Gr. 8**, 86

Nokken Danser (Norwegian Folk Melody), **Gr. 4**, 168

Ocean Child by Winter, **Gr. 7**, 218

Ode to a Butterfly by Thile, **Gr. 5**, 25

On the Trail from *Grand Canyon Suite* by Grofé, **Gr. 8**, 112

Only Time by Enya, Ryan, and Ryan, **Gr. 7**, 142

Oye como va by Puente, **Gr. 5**, 69

Packington's Pound (Renaissance/anon.), **Gr. 2**, 200

Papagena! Papagena! Papagena! from *The Magic Flute* by Mozart, **Gr. 2**, 152

Parade from Divertissement from *Un Chapeau de paille d'Italie* by Ibert, **Gr. K**, T183

Pata Pata (excerpt) by Makeba, **Gr. 3**, 35

Peaceful World by Mellencamp, **Gr. 7**, 154

People United Will Never Be Defeated, The (Theme and Variations 5, 13, 26) by Ortega and Rzewski, **Gr. 8**, 93

Pomp and Circumstance March No. 1 (excerpt) by Elgar, **Gr. 7**, 50

Promenade from *Golden Goose* by Worsley, **Gr. 1**, T176

Pukaea (excerpt) by Coleman and Mohi, **Gr. 2**, 109

Radetzky March by Radetzky, **Gr. K**, T177

Raga Malika (excerpt) (Indian Classical Music), **Gr. 5**, 402

Rondo "alla turca" (Third Movement) from *Piano Sonata No. 11 in A Major*, K. 331 by Mozart, **Gr. 7**, 116

Rondo a capriccio, Op. 129 ("Rage Over a Lost Penny") (excerpt) by Beethoven, **Gr. 2**, 225

Russian Sailor's Dance from *The Red Poppy* by Glière, **Gr. 4**, 266

Sail Away (Mountain Folk Dance), **Gr. 4**, 55

Scheherazade (excerpt) by Rimsky-Korsakov, **Gr. 4**, 161

Seasons of Love from *Rent* by Larson, **Gr. 7**, 86

Semper Fidelis by Sousa, **Gr. 3**, 281

Serenade No. 10 in B Flat Major, K. 361 ("Gran Partita"), Theme and Variations (excerpt) by Mozart, **Gr. 4**, 235

Seventeen Come Sunday from *English Folk Song* Suite by Vaughan Williams, **Gr. 7**, 102

Seventy-Six Trombones from *The Music Man* by Willson, **Gr. 8**, 76

Shady Grove (Southern Appalachian Folk Song), **Gr. 8**, 59

Shimmering Air by Saint-Denis, **Gr. K**, T139

Sing, Sing, Sing (with a Swing) by Prima, **Gr. 5**, 32

Singing on the Fisherboats at Dusk (Chinese Folk Song), **Gr. 1**, T129

Sixteen Tons by Travis, **Gr..7**, 151

Skaters' Waltz, The (excerpt) by Waldteufel, **Gr. 1**, T344

Skeleton by York, **Gr. 8**, 215

Sleight of Feet from *Cakewalk Suite* by Kay, **Gr. 1**, T239

So Long, Farewell from *The Sound of Music* by Rodgers and Hammerstein, **Gr. K**, T189

Sonata for Piano No. 2 in D Minor, Vivace (excerpt) by Prokofiev, **Gr. 4**, 181

Spinning Song by Ellmenreich, **Gr. 3**, 128

Spinning Wheel by Clayton-Thomas, **Gr. 4**, 211

Spring (Allegro) from *The Four Seasons (Concerto No. 1 in E Major)* by Vivaldi, **Gr. 4**, 391

Stars and Stripes Forever, The by Sousa, **Gr. 4**, 355

String of Pearls, A by Gray and De Lange, **Gr. 3**, 12

String Quartet, Opus 76, No. 2 in D Minor, Andante (excerpt) by Haydn, **Gr. 1**, T129

Summertime from *Porgy and Bess* by Gershwin, **Gr. 1**, T375

Sunburst by York, **Gr. 7**, 216

Symphony No. 1 in D Major, Op. 25 ("Classical"), Third Movement (Gavotte) by Prokofiev, **Gr. 1**, T92

Symphony No. 5 in C Minor, Third and Fourth Movements by Beethoven, **Gr. 8**, 115

Symphony No. 7, Second Movement by Beethoven, **Gr. 7**, 118

Symphony No. 8, Second Movement (excerpt) by Beethoven, **Gr. K**, T235

Symphony No. 9 in D Minor ("Choral"), Fourth Movement (excerpt) by Beethoven, **Gr. 5**, 102

Symphony No. 9 in E Minor, Op. 95 ("From the New World"), Largo (excerpt) by Dvořák, **Gr. 5**, 107

Symphony No. 35, Fourth Movement (excerpt) by Haydn, **Gr. 5**, 247

Alphabetical Index of Interactive Listening Maps (continued)

Symphony No. 40 in G Minor, First Movement by Mozart, **Gr. 8**, 218

Three Little Birds (excerpt) by Marley, **Gr. 8**, 84

Trepak from *The Nutcracker* by Tchaikovsky, **Gr. 6**, 408

Trio for Piano, Violin and Cello No. 39, Finale ("Gypsy Rondo") by Haydn, **Gr. 3**, 155

Trio for Piano, Violin, and Cello, Op. 11, Third Movement (Presto Leggiero) by Chaminade, **Gr. 5**, 121

Troika from *Lieutenant Kijé Suite* (excerpt) by Prokofiev, **Gr. 3**, 225

Tshotsholoza (South African Work Song), **Gr. 1**, T76

Tuileries from *Pictures at an Exhibition* by Mussorgsky, **Gr. 1**, T249

Va Pensiero from *Nabucco* by Verdi, **Gr. 6**, 169

Variations on "Simple Gifts" from *Appalachian Spring* by Copland, **Gr. 5**, 153

Variations on the Theme "Pop! Goes the Weasel" by Caillet, **Gr. 5**, 97

Vivo from *Pulcinella Suite* by Stravinsky, **Gr. 4**, 201

Volta from *Dances from Terpsichore* by Praetorius, **Gr. 3**, 121

Wade in the Water (African American Spiritual/Hogan arr.), **Gr. 5**, 144

Walking Song from *Acadian Songs and Dances* by Thomson, **Gr. K**, T20

Walking the Dog from *Shall We Dance* by Gershwin, **Gr. 1**, T169

Waltz of the Flowers (excerpt) from *The Nutcracker* by Tchaikovsky, **Gr. 1**, T353

Waltzing Cat by Anderson, **Gr. K**, T223

Washington Post March by Sousa, **Gr. 2**, 339

Washington's Birthday (excerpt) by Ives, **Gr. 2**, 370

What a Wonderful World by Weiss and Thiele, **Gr. 8**, 9

William Tell (Overture) (excerpt) by Rossini, **Gr. 3**, 65

Wind Blew East, The (Bahamian Folk Song), **Gr. 1**, T234

Winter (Allegro non molto) from *The Four Seasons (Concerto No. 4 in F Minor)* by Vivaldi, **Gr. 6**, 403

Young Person's Guide to the Orchestra (excerpt) by Britten, **Gr. 2**, 229

By Grade

Grade K

Brother, Come and Dance with Me from *Hansel and Gretel* by Humperdinck, T180

Car Song by Guthrie, T135

Children's March by Goldman, T113

Dance from *Ballet Suite No. 1* by Shostakovich, T167

December Snow by Nakai, T313

Echo Song by di Lasso, T103

Faeries and Giants from *Wand of Youth Suite No. 1* by Elgar, T52

Fall (Allegro) from *The Four Seasons (Concerto No. 3 in F Major)* (excerpt) by Vivaldi, T305

Finale from *The Carnival of the Animals* by Saint-Saëns, T195

Flight of the Bumblebee, The by Rimsky-Korsakov, T259

Hummingbird, A by Beach, T140

Little Train of the Caipira, The from *Bachianas Brasileiras No. 2* by Villa Lobos, T142

Moon Mirrored in a Pool, The by Yanjun, T115

Parade from Divertissement from *Un Chapeau de paille d'Italie* by Ibert, T183

Radetzky March by Radetzky, T177

Shimmering Air by Saint-Denis, T139

So Long, Farewell from *The Sound of Music* by Rodgers and Hammerstein, T189

Symphony No. 8, Second Movement (excerpt) by Beethoven, T235

Walking Song from *Acadian Songs and Dances* by Thomson, T20

Waltzing Cat by Anderson, T223

Grade 1

Bydlo (The Ox Cart) from *Pictures at an Exhibition* by Mussorgsky/Ravel, T152

C-A-G by Taylor, T241

Elephant, The from *The Carnival of the Animals* by Saint-Saëns, T204

Flute and Drum from *Gunild Keetman Collection* by Keetman, T235

Galop from *Masquerade Suite* by Khachaturian, T259

Laideronette, Empress of the Pagodas from *Mother Goose Suite* by Ravel, T237

Le Serpent (excerpt) by Guem, T359

March from *Children's Games* by Bizet, T31

Promenade from *Golden Goose* by Worsley, T176

Singing on the Fisherboats at Dusk (Chinese Folk Song), T129

Skaters' Waltz, The (excerpt) by Waldteufel, T344

Sleight of Feet from *Cakewalk Suite* by Kay, T239

String Quartet, Opus 76, No. 2 in D minor, Andante (excerpt) by Haydn, T129

Summertime from *Porgy and Bess* by Gershwin, T375

Symphony No. 1 in D Major, Op. 25 ("Classical"), Third Movement (Gavotte) by Prokofiev, T92

Tshotsholoza (South African Work Song), T76

Tuileries from *Pictures at an Exhibition* by Mussorgsky, T249

Walking the Dog from *Shall We Dance* by Gershwin, T169

Waltz of the Flowers (excerpt) from *The Nutcracker* by Tchaikovsky, T353

Wind Blew East, The (Bahamian Folk Song), T234

Grade 2

Akinla from by Sowande, 97

Assembly Required by Kozak, 36

Chango Guango (Mariachi), 60

Concerto for Trombone, Fifth Movement ("Motorbike Concerto") by Sandström, 193

Concerto for Two Trumpets, Allegro by Vivaldi, 73

Dance of the Sugar Plum Fairy from *The Nutcracker Suite* by Tchaikovsky, 355

Étude Op. 25, No. 11 ("The Winter Wind") by Chopin, 136

Food, Glorious Food from *Oliver!* by Bart, 310

Gigue from *Suite for Orchestra No. 3* by Bach, 269

In the Hall of the Mountain King from *Peer Gynt Suite No. 1*, Op. 46 by Grieg, 346

La lluvia (The Rain) by Hatfield, 232

Largo al factotum from *Il Barbiere di Siviglia* by Rossini, 217

Minuet from *Abdelazar* by Purcell, 145

Packington's Pound (Renaissance/anon.), 200

Alphabetical Index of Interactive Listening Maps

Alphabetical Index of Interactive Listening Maps (continued)

Papagena! Papagena! Papagena! from *The Magic Flute* by Mozart, 152

Pukaea (excerpt) by Coleman and Mohi, 109

Rondo a capriccio, Op. 129 ("Rage Over a Lost Penny") (excerpt) by Beethoven, 225

Washington Post March by Sousa, 339

Washington's Birthday (excerpt) by Ives, 370

Young Person's Guide to the Orchestra (excerpt) by Britten, 229

Grade 3

Ballet of the Unhatched Chicks from *Pictures at an Exhibition* by Mussorgsky/Ravel, 76

Brafferton Village/Walsh's Hornpipe (Irish Folk Music), 391

Circus Music from *The Red Pony Suite* (excerpt) by Copland, 285

Clock at Night, A by Miloslavskiy, 66

Concierto de Aranjuez, First Movement (excerpt) by Rodrigo, 41

Danse Macabre by Saint-Saëns, 363

Eine Kleine Nachtmusik (Serenade No. 13 in G, K. 525), Minuet by Mozart, 169

Gigue from *Suite No. 1 for Cello* by Bach, 178

Los mariachis (Mariachi), 397

March Past of the Kitchen Utensils from *The Wasps* by Vaughan Williams, 247

My Favorite Things from *The Sound of Music* by Rodgers and Hammerstein, 313

Nigun Atik (Israeli Folk Dance), 47

Pata Pata (excerpt) by Makeba, 35

Semper Fidelis by Sousa, 281

Spinning Song by Ellmenreich, 128

String of Pearls, A by Gray and De Lange, 12

Trio for Piano, Violin and Cello No. 39, Finale ("Gypsy Rondo") by Haydn, 155

Troika from *Lieutenant Kijé Suite* (excerpt) by Prokofiev, 225

Volta from *Dances from Terpsichore* by Praetorius, 121

William Tell (Overture) (excerpt) by Rossini, 65

Grade 4

Adagio (excerpt) from *Concierto de Aranjuez* by Rodrigo, 13

Augie's Great Municipal Band from *Star Wars Episode 1: The Phantom Menace* (excerpt) by Williams, 57

Badinerie from *Suite for Orchestra No. 2 in B Minor* by Bach, 61

Cattle from *The Plow That Broke the Plains* by Thomson, 274

Dance of the Mirlitons from *The Nutcracker* by Tchaikovsky, 173

Galop (excerpt) from *The Comedians* by Kabalevsky, 254

In the Mood by Garland, 143

La canarie from *Dances from Terpsichore* by Praetorius, 177

Milan (Meeting of the Two Rivers) (excerpt) by Kale, 208

My Friend by Kibble and Kibble, 389

Nokken Danser (Norwegian Folk Melody), 168

Russian Sailor's Dance from *The Red Poppy* by Glière, 266

Sail Away (Mountain Folk Dance), 55

Scheherazade (excerpt) by Rimsky-Korsakov, 161

Serenade No. 10 in B Flat Major, K. 361 ("Gran Partita"), Theme and Variations (excerpt) by Mozart, 235

Sonata for Piano No. 2 in D Minor, Vivace (excerpt) by Prokofiev, 181

Spinning Wheel by Clayton-Thomas, 211

Spring (Allegro) from *The Four Seasons (Concerto No. 1 in E Major)* by Vivaldi, 391

Stars and Stripes Forever, The by Sousa, 355

Vivo from *Pulcinella Suite* by Stravinsky, 201

Grade 5

American Salute by Gould, 36

Anitra's Dance from *Peer Gynt Suite No. 1, Op. 46* by Grieg, 193

Anvil Chorus from *Il Trovatore* by Verdi, 148

Batucada Brasileira (Brazilian Folk Music), 433

Fascinating Rhythm from *Lady Be Good* by Gershwin and Gershwin, 186

Finlandia, Op. 26, No. 7 (excerpt) by Sibelius, 257

Hallelujah Chorus from *Messiah* by Handel, 419

Moldau, The from *Má Vlast (My Country)* by Smetana, 271

Nessun dorma from *Turandot* by Puccini, 64

Ode to a Butterfly by Thile, 25

Oye como va by Puente, 69

Raga Malika (excerpt) (Indian Classical Music), 402

Sing, Sing, Sing (with a Swing) by Prima, 32

Symphony No. 9 in D Minor ("Choral"), Fourth Movement (excerpt) by Beethoven, 102

Symphony No. 9 in E Minor, Op. 95 ("From the New World"), Largo (excerpt) by Dvořák, 107

Symphony No. 35, Fourth Movement (excerpt) by Haydn, 247

Trio for Piano, Violin, and Cello, Op. 11, Third Movement (Presto Leggiero) by Chaminade, 121

Variations on "Simple Gifts" from *Appalachian Spring* by Copland, 153

Variations on the Theme "Pop! Goes the Weasel" by Caillet, 97

Wade in the Water (African American Spiritual/Hogan arr.), 144

Grade 6

Allegretto by Montsalvatge, 193

Barcarolle (Belle nuit) from *Tales of Hoffman* by Offenbach, 265

Belhadawa walla belshaawa by Ramzy, 35

Carnival of Venice, The by Arban, 40

Crazy Songs by Kopelent, 65

Early Light by Bremer, 201

Elijah Rock (African American Spiritual/Hogan arr.), 52

Exsultate, jubilate, Third Movement by Mozart, 187

Foggy Mountain Breakdown by Scruggs, 140

Introduction from *The Rite of Spring* by Stravinsky, 423

It Don't Mean a Thing by Ellington, 165

La cumparsita by Rodriguez, 113

Locomotion by Coltrane, 157

Los trabajadores agrícolas (The Farmers) from *Estancia* by Ginastera, 116

Mars from *The Planets* by Holst, 196

Night Fight from *Crouching Tiger, Hidden Dragon* by Dun, 28

Nightingale, The by Liszt, 160

Trepak from *The Nutcracker* by Tchaikovsky, 408

Va Pensiero from *Nabucco* by Verdi, 169

Winter (Allegro non molto) from *The Four Seasons (Concerto No. 4 in F Minor)* by Vivaldi, 403

Alphabetical Index of Interactive Listening Maps (continued)

Grade 7

Afirika by Kidjo, Hebrail, and Faragher, 226

Amazing Grace by Newton, 144

Batuque by Fernândez, 202

Bo Hai Huan Ten (Chinese Folk Song), 56

Carillon from *L'Arlesienne Suite No. 1* by Bizet, 123

Concertino da Camera, First Movement by Ibert, 161

Entertainer, The by Joplin, 23

Galop from *Suite No. 2 for Small Orchestra* by Stravinsky, 126

Gloria from *Mass for the Earth* (excerpt) by Larsen, 222

Liberty Fanfare by Williams, 187

Ocean Child by Winter, 218

Only Time by Enya, Ryan, and Ryan, 142

Peaceful World by Mellencamp, 154

Pomp and Circumstance March No. 1 (excerpt) by Elgar, 50

Rondo "alla turca" (Third Movement) from *Piano Sonata No. 11 in A Major,* K. 331 by Mozart, 116

Seasons of Love from *Rent* by Larson, 86

Seventeen Come Sunday from *English Folk Song Suite* by Vaughan Williams, 102

Sixteen Tons by Travis, 151

Sunburst by York, 216

Symphony No. 7, Second Movement by Beethoven, 118

Grade 8

Adukbe (African Traditional Adenkum), 177

Afoxé (Brazilian Traditional/Dunlap arr.), 34

Bird Island by Kaneko, 56

Blue Little Flower (Chinese Traditional), 82

Bug, The by Knopfler, 88

Courante from *Terpsichore* by Praetorius, 130

Drops of Jupiter (Tell Me) by Monahan, Stafford, Hotchkiss, Colin, and Underwood, 103

March for Military Band, Op. 99 by Prokofiev, 37

Marche by Lully, 168

Música indígena from *Instantaneous Mexicanas* by Ponce, 126

No One Is Alone from *Into the Woods* (excerpt) by Sondheim, 86

On the Trail from *Grand Canyon Suite* by Grofé, 112

People United Will Never Be Defeated, The (Theme and Variations 5, 13, 26) by Ortega and Rzewski, 93

Seventy-Six Trombones from *The Music Man* by Willson, 76

Shady Grove (Southern Appalachian Folk Song), 59

Skeleton by York, 215

Symphony No. 5 in C Minor, Third and Fourth Movements by Beethoven, 115

Symphony No. 40 in G Minor, First Movement by Mozart, 218

Three Little Birds (excerpt) by Marley, 84

What a Wonderful World by Weiss and Thiele, 9

Alphabetical Index of Interactive Listening Maps